TRAUMA

ALSO BY MICHAEL PALMER

MICHAEL PALMER

TRAUMA

ST. MARTIN'S PRESS ⧯ NEW YORK

TRAUMA. Copyright © 2015 by Michael Palmer. All rights reserved. Printed in the United States of America. For information address St. Martin's Press, 175 Fifth Avenue, New York, N.Y. 10010.

www.stmartins.com

The Library of Congress Cataloging-in-Publication Data is available upon request.

978-1-250-03089-4 (hardcover)
978-1-250-03087-0 (e-book)

St. Martin's Press books may be purchased for educational, business, or promotional use. For information on bulk purchases, please contact the Macmillan Corporate and Premium Sales Department at 1-800-221-7945, extension 5442, or write to specialmarkets@macmillan.com.

First Edition: May 2015

10 9 8 7 6 5 4 3 2 1

With great respect and admiration, Trauma *is dedicated
to Dr. David Grass of McLean, Virginia. This book would
not have been possible without his dedication to the
medical profession, his skill and experience as a
practitioner, his imagination, and his support and
contributions to this project from start to finish.*

To say I couldn't have gotten here without him is an understatement.

D.P.

TRAUMA

CHAPTER 1

It began, innocently enough, with a fall.

Beth Stillwell, a slight, thirty-five-year-old mother of three with kind eyes and an infectious laugh, was shopping at Thrifty Dollar Store with her kids in tow. She'd been stocking up on school supplies and home staples when she lost her balance and tumbled to the grimy linoleum floor. It was bad enough to have to shop at the dollar store, something new since her separation from her philandering husband of fifteen years. It was downright humiliating to be sprawled out on their floor, her leg bent in a painful angle beneath her.

Beth wasn't hurt, but as her six-year-old daughter Emily tried to help her stand, her left leg felt weak, almost rubbery. Leaning against a shelf stocked with cheap soap, Beth took a tentative step only to have the leg nearly buckle beneath her. She kept her balance, and after another awkward step, decided she could walk on it.

The strength in Beth's left leg mostly returned, but a slight stiffness and a disconcerting drag lingered for weeks. Beth's sister told her to see a doctor. Beth said she would, but it was an empty promise. Running a licensed day care out of her Jamaica Plain home, Beth was in charge of seven kids in addition to her own, and any downtime put tremendous strain on her limited finances. She rarely had time to make a phone call. But the leg was definitely a bother, and the lingering weakness was a constant worry. She occasionally stumbled, but the last straw was losing control of her urine while in charge of toddlers who could

1

hold their bladders better than she could. That drove her to the doctor.

An MRI confirmed a parasagittal tumor originating from the meninges with all the telltale characteristics of a typical meningioma: a brain tumor. The tumor was already big enough to compress brain tissue, interrupting the normal complex communication from neuron to neuron and causing a moderate degree of edema, swelling from the pressure on the brain's blood vessels.

Beth would need surgery to have it removed.

Dr. Carrie Bryant stood in front of the viewbox, examining Beth Stillwell's MRI. A fourth-year neurosurgical resident rotating through Boston Community Hospital (BCH), she would be assisting chief resident Dr. Fred Michelson with Beth's surgery. The tumor pressed upon the top of the brain on the right side. Carrie could see exactly why Beth's left leg had gone into a focal seizure and why she'd lost control of her urine. It was not a particularly large mass, about walnut-sized, but its location was extremely problematic. If it were to grow, Beth would develop progressive spasticity in her leg and eventually lose bladder control completely.

Carrie absently rubbed her sore quadriceps while studying Beth's films. She had set a new personal best at yesterday's sprint distance triathlon, finally breaking the elusive ten-minute-mile pace during the run, and her body was letting her know she had pushed it too hard. Her swim and bike performance were shaky per usual, and all but guaranteed a finish in the bottom quartile for her age group—but at least she was out there, battling, doing her best to get her fitness level back to where it had been.

Carrie's choice to jump right into triathlons was perhaps not the wisest, but she never did anything half measure. She enjoyed pushing her body to new limits. She'd also used the race to raise more than a thousand dollars for BCH: a tiny fraction of what was needed, but every bit helped.

BCH served the poor and uninsured. Carrie felt proud to be a part of that mission, but lack of funding was a constant frustration. In her opinion, the omnipotent budgeting committee relied too heavily on cheap labor to fill the budget gap, which explained why fourth- and fifth-year residents basically ran the show whenever they rotated through BCH. Attending physicians, those docs who had finished residency, were supposed to provide oversight, but they had too much work and too few resources to do the job.

If the constant budget shortfalls had a silver lining, it could be summed up in a single word: experience. With each BCH rotation the hours would be long, the demands exhausting, but Carrie never groaned or complained. She was getting the best opportunity to hone her skills.

Thank goodness Chambers University did its part to fund the storied health-care institution, which had trained some of Boston's most famous doctors, including the feared but revered Dr. Stanley Metcalf, staff neurosurgeon at the iconic White Memorial Hospital. For now, the doors to BCH were open, the lights on, and people like Beth Stillwell could get exceptional medical care even without exceptional insurance.

So far, Beth had been a model patient. She'd spent two days in the hospital, and in that time Carrie had had the pleasure of meeting both her sister and her children. Carrie prepped for Beth's surgery wondering when having a family of her own would fit into her hectic life. At twenty-nine, she had thought it might happen with Ian, her boyfriend of two years, but apparently her dedication to residency did not jibe with his vision of the relationship. She should have known when Ian began referring to his apartment as Carrie's "on-call room" that their union was headed for rocky times.

At half past eleven, Carrie was on her way to scrub when Dr. Michelson stopped her in the hallway.

"Two cases of acute lead poisoning just rolled in," he announced.

Carrie smiled weakly at the dark humor: two gunshot victims needed the OR.

"We can do Miss Stillwell at five o'clock," Michelson said. It was not a request. Working at one of New England's busiest trauma hospitals meant that patients often got bumped for the crisis of the moment, and Dr. Michelson fully expected Carrie to accommodate him.

Carrie would have been fine with his demand regardless. Her social calendar had been a long string of empty boxes ever since Ian called things off. During the relationship vortex, Carrie had evidently neglected her apartment as well as her friends, and it would take time to get everything back to pre-Ian levels. Carrie agreed to move Beth's surgery even though she had no real say in the matter.

The time change gave Carrie an opportunity to finish the rest of her rotations on the neurosurgical floor. She met with several different patients, and concluded her rounds with Leon Dixon, whom Dr. Metcalf had admitted as a private patient that morning. She would be assisting Dr. Metcalf with his surgery the next day.

Carrie entered Leon's hospital room after knocking, and found a handsome black man propped up in his adjustable bed, drinking water through a straw. Leon was watching *Antiques Roadshow* with his wife, who sat in a chair pushed up against the bed. They were holding hands. Leon was in his early fifties, with a kind but weathered face.

"Hi, Leon, I'm Dr. Carrie Bryant. I'll be assisting with your operation tomorrow. How you feeling today?"

"Pre—eh-eh-eh-eh."

"I'm Phyllis, Leon's wife. He's feeling pretty crappy, is what he's trying to say."

Carrie shook hands with the attractive woman who had gone from being a wife to a caregiver in a matter of weeks. The heavy makeup around Phyllis's tired eyes showed just how difficult those weeks had been. Carrie had yet to review Leon's films, but was not surprised about his speech problems; the chart said he'd presented aphasic. She doubted he'd stuttered before, but she was not going to embarrass him by asking.

"Leon, could you close your eyes and open your mouth for me?" Carrie asked.

Leon got his eyes shut, but his mouth stayed closed as well. Carrie sent a text message to Dr. Nugent in radiology. She wanted to look at his films, stat.

"He has a lot of trouble following instructions," Phyllis said as she brushed tears from her eyes. "Memory and temper problems, too."

Something is going on in Leon's left temporal lobe, Carrie thought. *Probably a tumor.*

Carrie observed other symptoms as well. The right side of Leon's face drooped slightly, and his right arm drifted down when he held out his arms in front of him with his eyes closed. His reflexes were heightened in the right arm and leg, and when Carrie scraped the sole of his right foot with the reflex hammer, his great toe extended up toward his face—a Babinski sign, indicating damage to the motor system represented on the left side of Leon's brain.

Carrie took hold of Leon's dry and calloused hand and looked him in the eye.

"Leon, we're going to do everything we can to make you feel better. I'm going to go look at your films now, and I'll see you tomorrow for your surgery." Carrie wrote her cell phone number on a piece of paper. Business cards were for after residency. "If you need anything, this is how to reach me," she said.

Carrie preferred not to cut the examination short, but a text from Dr. Robert Nugent said he'd delay his meeting for Carrie if she came now. Carrie was rushed herself. She needed to get to Beth Stillwell for her final pre-op consultation.

Dr. Nugent, a married father of two, was a competitive triathlete who had finished well ahead of Carrie in the last race they had done together. Over the years, Carrie had learned that it paid to be friends with the radiologists for situations just like this, and nothing fostered camaraderie quite like the race circuit.

The radiology department was located in the bowels of BCH, in a windowless section of the Glantz Wing, but somehow Dr. Nugent appeared perpetually tan, even after the brutal New England winter.

"Thanks for making some time for me, Bob," Carrie said. "Leon just materialized on my OR schedule and I haven't gotten any background on him from Dr. Metcalf yet."

Dr. Nugent shrugged. He knew all about Dr. Metcalf's surprise patients. "Yeah, from what I was told, Dixon's doctor is good friends with Metcalf."

"Let me guess: Leon has no health insurance."

"Bingo."

Carrie chuckled and said, "Why am I not surprised?"

It was unusual to see a private patient at Community. Just about every patient was admitted through the emergency department and assigned to resident staff. Dr. Metcalf was known for his philanthropy, and when he rotated through Community he often took on cases he could not handle at White Memorial because of insurance issues.

All the residents looked forward to working with Dr. Metcalf, and Carrie's peers had expressed jealousy more than once. Assisting Dr. Metcalf was the ultimate test of a resident's skill, grace under the most extreme pressure. Dr. Metcalf had earned a reputation for being exacting and demanding, even a bully at times, but his approach paid off. He taught technique, didn't assume total control, and was supremely patient with the less experienced surgeons. Like many world-class surgeons, Dr. Metcalf was sometimes tempestuous and always demanding, but Carrie was willing to take the bitter with the sweet if it helped with her career.

Dr. Nugent put Leon's MRI films up on the viewbox.

"It's most likely a grade three astrocytoma," he said.

The irregular mass was 1.5 by 2 centimeters in size, located deep in the left temporal lobe and associated with frondlike edema. No doubt this was the cause of Leon's aphasic speech and confused behavior.

"So Dr. Metcalf's scheduled to take this one out tomorrow," Dr. Nugent said.

"As much as he can, anyway."

Dr. Nugent agreed.

Carrie was about to ask Dr. Nugent a question when she noticed the time. She was going to be late for the final pre-op consultation with Beth. *Damn.* There were never enough hours in the day.

Carrie made it to Beth's hospital room at four thirty and found the anesthesiologist already there. By the end of Carrie's consult, Beth looked teary-eyed.

"You'll be holding your children again in no time, trust me," Carrie assured her.

Even with her head newly shaved, Beth was a strikingly beautiful woman, young and vivacious. Despite Carrie's words of comfort, Beth did not look convinced.

"Just make sure I'll be all right, Dr. Bryant," Beth said. "I have to see my kids grow up."

At quarter to five, Beth was taken from the patient holding area to OR 15. Carrie had her mask, gown, and head covering already donned, and was in the scrub room, three minutes into her timed five-minute anatomical scrub, when Dr. Michelson showed up.

"How would you feel about doing the Stillwell case on your own?" he asked. "The attending went home for the day, and I got a guy with a brain hemorrhage who's going to be ART if I don't evacuate the clot and decompress the skull."

Carrie rolled her eyes at Michelson. She was not a big fan of some of the medical slang that was tossed around, and ART, an especially callous term, was an acronym for "approaching room temperature," a.k.a. dead.

"No problem on Stillwell," Carrie said. Her heart jumped a little. She had never done an operation without the oversight of an attending or chief resident before.

Quick as the feeling came, Carrie's nerves settled. She was an excellent surgeon with confidence in her abilities, and, if the hospital grapevine were to be believed, the staff's next chief resident. It would certainly be a nice feather in her surgical cap, and helpful in securing a fellowship at the Cleveland Clinic after residency.

"Unfortunately, I'm going to need OR fifteen. Everything else is already booked," Michelson said.

Carrie nodded. Par for the course at BCH. "Beth can wait," she said.

"I checked the schedule for you. OR six or nine should be open in a couple of hours."

Carrie did some quick calculations to make sure she could handle the Stillwell operation and still be rested enough to assist Dr. Metcalf with Leon's operation in the morning. *Three to four hours, tops,* Carrie thought, *and Beth will be back in recovery.*

"No problem," Carrie said. "I'll let you scrub down and save the day."

"Thanks, Doc Bryant," Michelson said. "But you're the real lifesaver here. I don't think there's another fourth year I'd trust with this operation."

"Your faith in me inspires."

Carrie did not mention the promise she'd made to Beth during her pre-op consultation. Michelson would not have approved. If one thing was certain about surgery, it was that nothing, no matter how routine or simple it seemed, was ever 100 percent guaranteed.

CHAPTER 2

Carrie had met Beth again in the preoperative area, this time accompanied by Rosemary, a certified registered nurse anesthetist. While Carrie had never worked with Rosemary before, watching her insert the IV into Beth's arm made Carrie confident in the CRNA's ability. Rosemary gave Beth a light dose of midazolam, which decreased anxiety and would mercifully bring about amnesia. Some things were best not remembered, brain surgery among them.

Once in the OR, Rosemary got Beth connected to the monitors that tracked vitals. She delivered a dose of propofol to induce general anesthesia, followed by a push of succinylcholine to bring on temporary muscle paralysis. From that moment on, the endotracheal tube would do all the breathing for Beth.

Dr. Saleem Badami, originally from Bangalore, India, and a highly regarded intern, was to assist with the operation. This was really a one-person show, so Dr. Badami was there primarily to monitor Beth's neurological status during surgery.

The circulating nurse had painstakingly prepared the necessary equipment, including the Midas Rex drill, which Carrie would use to penetrate the skull and turn the flap. Last on the team was Valerie, a scrub nurse born in Haiti. A longtime vet of BCH, Valerie was one of the best scrub nurses on staff. As usual, Valerie looked in total command of her craft as she prepped her station for the upcoming operation. It was Valerie who had introduced Carrie to the joys of listening to jazz while operating, and over the years the two had grown close.

If there was one drawback to working with Valerie, it was her unwavering commitment to finding Carrie a date. Beneath her surgical cap and scrubs, Carrie had luxurious brown hair down to her shoulders, almond-shaped brown eyes, enviably high cheekbones, and a body toned and muscled from hours of training. All that, combined with her intellect and outgoing personality, and Dr. Carrie Bryant was somebody's total package. Despite Carrie's repeated assurances that she was happily single, Valerie never failed to bring a list of eligible bachelors to surgery.

"His name is James, and he's some hotshot at a biotech startup in Cambridge. My mother knows his family."

"Thanks for the suggestion," Carrie said, checking over the equipment, "but today the only man I'm interested in is John Coltrane. Let's fire up the music, please."

Carrie waited for the first notes from "Out of this World," the first cut from *Coltrane (Deluxe Edition),* to play before she picked up the scalpel and positioned it for the initial cut. The little stomach jitter that had been kicking around was gone. The first solo flight had to happen to everyone at some point, and today was her day.

You've got this, Doc. You trained hard.

Any and all distractions faded. Lingering thoughts of her ex-boyfriend, Valerie's biotech guy, and tomorrow's surgery with Dr. Metcalf were just ghosts in her consciousness. Her focus was intense. She loved being in the zone; this level of concentration was a rush like no other. Prior to surgery, Carrie had managed sundry pro forma tasks, those checklist items requiring no thought or decision. Following standard procedure, she had used Mayfield pins to secure Beth's head in three fixation points.

It was time to operate.

Carrie made the first scalp incision, expertly cutting the shape of a large semicircle over the crown of Beth's shaved and immobilized skull. She paused to examine her work. It was a fine first cut, and Carrie was pleased with the results. The skin flap was certainly large enough.

The growth was sitting underneath the skull, originating from the meninges, the membrane that covers the brain. It was directly adjacent to the superior sagittal sinus, the major venous channel coursing between the brain's hemispheres. From what Carrie had seen in the MRI, the sinus appeared to be open. This was one of her chief concerns going in. If the tumor were adhering to the sinus, Carrie could do only a partial resection, which would mean Beth would need additional treatment, such as radiation therapy or another surgery.

Why did you make that promise?

It was probably seeing Beth's kids, especially little six-year-old Emily with her sweet toothy smile, that had clouded Carrie's better judgment. If the tumor were free from the sinus, the only treatment Beth would need would be careful follow-up to ensure no recurrence, and perhaps an anticonvulsant medication to reduce the risks of residual seizures.

Surgeons were not, in Carrie's opinion, like normal people. They were more like clutch shooters who took the ball with three seconds left and the basketball game on the line. Difficult times seemed to bring out the best in their cool. Sure, Carrie had sweated for just a bit at the start of the operation, but that was normal. Good, even. She was young, inexperienced, and it was smart for her to be cautious. Things could head south in a flash, but Carrie was not overly concerned. By the fourth year of residency, any surgeon who would cower in a decisive moment had been culled from the herd.

Carrie set to work placing the Raney clips around the margins of the retracted tissue to hold the scalp in place. The slim blue clips were atraumatic, designed to minimize injury and limit both bleeding and tissue damage.

Thirty minutes into surgery.

It took another fifteen minutes for Carrie to set all the clips in place. Now it was time for her to drill. Carrie held the high-speed stylus in her steady right hand and made four expertly placed burr holes on either side of the parasagittal sinus.

"Change the drill, please," Carrie said.

The circulating nurse handed Carrie a different high-speed pneumatic drill, and she used that one to cut through the skull between the burr holes. Carrie took in a breath as she lifted the bone flap over the dura. She carefully handed the bone flap to Valerie for safekeeping until she was ready to reconstitute the skull after removing the tumor.

Valerie, being Valerie, anticipated Carrie wanting bone wax to control bleeding from the exposed skull margins.

You've got a great team here, Carrie thought.

Pausing, Carrie examined the dura, a thick membrane that is the outermost of the three layers of the meninges surrounding the brain, for any signs of damage. Using her gloved fingers, she carefully palpated the hard, solid tumor beneath. She judged the location of the growth to be perfect for resection, and then used cotton pledgets to tamp down the margins of the exposed dura.

Carrie was exceedingly careful with the pledgets, because too much traction on the dura might cause tugging on critical veins over the surface of the brain, which could result in bleeding. When the pledgets were properly positioned, Carrie was ready for her next incision, keeping in mind that she would cut one centimeter away from the tumor.

One centimeter. Exact. Precise.

Done. After her perfect cut, Carrie used the coagulator and Gelfoam sponges judiciously to control hemostasis and limit bleeding. And there it was, the tumor, sitting on the top of the brain, pressing down on the cortex that controlled Beth Stillwell's leg and bladder. It was not too big, but it sure was ugly, and more vascular in appearance than she had expected from the MRI image. Thank goodness it was not adherent to the sinus! Carrie could resect it cleanly. Still, the vascular supply was far more complex than she had predicted.

"James is a heck of a lot better-looking than that nasty thing," Valerie said.

Carrie laughed lightly.

The time was 10:30 P.M. Beth had been in surgery for two and a half hours, a little bit longer than Carrie had anticipated, but not unusually long.

"Vitals?" Carrie asked.

"Looking fine," Rosemary said.

One hour and I'll be done, Carrie estimated.

Working with care, Carrie removed the tumor, along with the adherent patch of excised dura, which would be sent off to pathology for a frozen section. It did not appear malignant by gross inspection. She would want to be sure the margins were clean and there was no evidence of malignancy elsewhere. At this point, Carrie figured she could get to the on-call room by midnight and grab five or so hours of sleep before she needed to be back in the OR by seven o'clock the next morning for surgery with Dr. Metcalf.

Ah, the glorious life of a doctor. Her dad, an internist at Mass General, had warned Carrie about the rigors of residency, but his description paled in comparison with the real thing.

Carrie paused to examine her work once more. Something was beginning to bother her. The margins of the craniotomy looked to be oozing blood, much more than usual.

"More Gelfoam and four-by-fours." Carrie's voice sounded calm, but had a noticeable edge.

Valerie complied with speed. As Carrie dabbed away the bleeding, her whole body heated up beneath her surgical scrubs.

"Vitals?"

"Blood pressure stable at one hundred over seventy, normal sinus at ninety."

What the heck is happening?

Carrie did everything she could to stanch the bleeding, but the ooz-ing persisted. She started to worry.

Why isn't Beth's blood clotting?

Her pre-op labs had showed a normal coagulation profile. She should not be having this problem during surgery. *What is going on? Where is the bleeding coming from?*

From the beginning of her residency, Carrie had been taught to think on her feet, but her mind was drawing blanks.

Think, dammit! Think!

As if Dr. Metcalf were whispering in her ear, Carrie got the germ of an idea. She recalled a case from back in her internship year. A seventy-year-old woman undergoing a craniotomy for an anaplastic meningi-oma lost blood pressure during surgery and at the same time developed significant skin hemorrhages.

The body normally regulates blood flow by clotting to heal breaks on blood vessel walls, and after the bleeding stops it dissolves those clots to allow for regular blood flow. But some conditions cause the same clotting factors to become overactive, leading to excessive bleeding, as in the case of that seventy-year-old woman. Carrie recalled the out-come grimly.

Could it be DIC—disseminated intravascular coagulation—causing Beth's bleeding? A tissue factor associated with the tumor could be trig-gering the cascade of proteins and enzymes that regulate clotting. It was a rare complication of meningiomas, but it did happen, especially if the tumors were highly vascular like Beth's.

"Vitals?" Carrie asked again.

"Stable, Carrie."

Victims of DIC often suffered effects of vascular clotting throughout the body. Once the clotting factors were all used up, patients began to bleed, and bleed profusely—the skin, the GI tract, the kidneys and urinary system. DIC could be sudden and catastrophic.

"Get me a pro time/INR, APTT, CBC with platelet count, and fibrin split products," Carrie ordered. "Saline, please. Rosemary, keep up her fluids."

In a perfect world, Carrie would get a hematology consult pronto, but at such a late hour, nobody would be available. Valerie entered the lab test orders into the OR computer.

"Blood pressure is down a bit to one hundred systolic," Rosemary said.

Carrie continued to control the bleeding at the tumor site as best she could. Now she was in the waiting game. Nobody spoke. Carrie asked Valerie to shut off the music, and the only sounds in the OR were the persistent noises of the monitors and the rhythmic breathing of the ventilator.

Fifteen minutes later Beth's labs came back. Carrie was sponging away a fresh ooze of blood as Valerie read the results off the OR computer.

"Pro time and APTT markedly elevated," Valerie said. "Platelets down to five thousand. Crit down to twenty-two percent—about half normal. Fibrin split products positive."

No doubt about it, Carrie thought, *this is DIC.* Beth had been typed and crossed prior to surgery. Carrie ordered FFP, fresh frozen plasma, and a transfusion of packed red blood cells.

"Carrie," Saleem said, his voice steeped in worry, "I'm seeing hemorrhagic lesions all over Beth's arms."

Carrie stopped sponging to examine Beth's extremities. Sure enough, blood was pooling underneath the skin, forming ugly bruises marred by bumpy raised patches that looked like charcoaled burn marks. Carrie bit her lip as she cleared beads of perspiration from her brow with the back of her hand.

On paper, she had made no missteps. There was no way for her to have predicted this rare complication of a meningioma surgery. It was just the nature of how the tissue itself could react and explode in the tightly regulated, complex coagulation homeostasis process. One small tip of the scale could have been enough to send the entire well-balanced system into complete disarray. The reduced hematocrit meant that Beth was bleeding internally as well—within her GI and urinary tracts, perhaps elsewhere. Sure enough, the indwelling Foley collecting bag was filling with blood-tinged urine.

"Give me two liters of normal saline."

At this point, the FFP and PRBC were ready for transfusion.

"BP down to ninety over sixty. Pulse one twenty," Rosemary announced.

Carrie took in the information, but she remained calm.

I'm not going to let you die.

At one o'clock in the morning, Carrie had another decision to make. Should she treat Beth with heparin, too? The drug could dramatically worsen the bleeding because it was a blood thinner, but on the other hand, Carrie remembered from her rotation on the medical service that heparin could help by preventing the clotting that caused the consumption of coagulation factors. In some DIC cases, a blood thinner could actually promote clotting. It was a crapshoot. Carrie had been right to give Beth a traditional treatment thus far, but her condition was again deteriorating, and rapidly.

"I want a heparin infusion, now."

The words left Carrie's mouth before she realized she'd spoken them. Though her team was masked and gowned, Carrie had no trouble seeing the astonished looks on everyone's faces. Saleem hesitated, but Carrie barked the order again, and this time he jumped. Everyone held a collective breath as the drug was administered intravenously. Carrie kept a careful watch over the wound and continued to sponge away the bleeding. To her eye, the blood flow seemed to have lessened.

Still not out of the woods. Not even close.

All Carrie and her team could do now was contain the bleeding, keep administering fluids, and pray the decision to use heparin was the right course of action.

At four o'clock in the morning, Beth finally seemed to be stabilizing. Her blood pressure had risen to 110/65. By that point, everyone in the OR was utterly exhausted, with Carrie in the worst shape of all. This was her patient—on her watch! Carrie's feet had swollen to the size of water balloons and her back strained against the tug of eight grueling hours spent standing.

Carrie ordered another set of labs. This time, while the FSP was still elevated, the PT and APTT were definitely showing signs of improvement. The bleeding looked better, too.

Valerie appeared stunned, as did Saleem.

"Carrie, whatever in the world inspired you to give this poor darling heparin?" Valerie asked.

Carrie was breathing as though she had just finished a sprint-distance tri. "Just a thought I had, I guess."

At five forty-five in the morning, Beth Stillwell was handed off from surgical to the medical and hematology teams in the ICU. Her DIC was still a problem and she would need much more intensive work to stabilize her, but the major bleeding seemed to be contained. Fifteen minutes later, Valerie and Beth were changing out of their bloodstained surgical scrubs in the women's locker room.

"She's going to make it because of you, because of what you did in there," Valerie said, brushing tears from her eyes.

Carrie had never seen Valerie cry before, and the sight set a lump in her throat. "But what's the quality of her survival going to be?" Carrie answered. "She bled a lot."

"Carrie Bryant, don't be so hard on yourself. If it had been any other doc in there, they wouldn't have ordered the heparin and we'd be having a very different conversation right now."

"Maybe."

Valerie turned fierce. "Don't you maybe me, Dr. Bryant! You diagnosed DIC quick as you did, and correctly at that. Then treating her with heparin? Girl, in my humble opinion, you are a hero here. Real and true, and I want to give you a hug."

Valerie opened her arms and Carrie fell into her embrace. The moment she did, the tears broke and would not stop for more than a minute. It had been such a long night. *I made a promise. . . .*

Carrie broke away from Valerie, but could not get the faces of Beth's young daughters out of her mind. She took a moment to regain her composure, then checked the time on her phone. It was six fifteen in the morning. She was due back in the OR for the astrocytoma surgery with Dr. Metcalf in forty-five minutes.

"I've got to go break the news to Beth's sister," Carrie said, her chest filling with a heavy sadness.

The conversation would be briefer than the family deserved, but she'd page Dr. Michelson and make sure he could be there for follow-up questions. At this point, Carrie only had time to take a quick shower and wolf down a peanut-butter-and-jelly sandwich with a black coffee chaser outside the OR.

That was all the time she ever seemed to have.

CHAPTER 3

Carrie arrived to scrub fifteen minutes late, expecting to see Dr. Stanley Metcalf already gowned and glowering. Next to medical incompetence, Dr. Metcalf despised tardiness most of all. She was surprised and more than a little relieved to discover he had yet to show up for Leon Dixon's brain surgery.

In addition to making sure the circulating and scrub nurses were at their stations and ready to go, it was Carrie's responsibility to get the patient prepped, properly positioned, and draped correctly. The only part of the pre-op routine Carrie did not oversee belonged to Dr. Lucas Fellows, the anesthesiologist, who would take care of getting the patient anesthetized and intubated. Surgeons and anesthesiologists did not always play nicely in the same sandbox, each guarding their turf with vigor.

Still, when it came time to put scalpel to skin, Dr. Metcalf was the general in charge. Most surgeons with a reputation like his came with a plus-sized ego. The man could be bombastic, often arrogant, always meticulous, and so demanding of his assistants that a healthy dose of fear was advisable for any underling assigned to him.

Despite his intimidating reputation, the advantages of working with Dr. Metcalf were undeniable. He offered the best opportunity for growth and learning, and for that alone, Carrie was grateful to be his foot soldier. But having incurred Dr. Metcalf's wrath once before, Carrie was glad to have a few extra minutes to set up the OR.

Still, she'd have to hurry.

Thinking of Beth, Carrie finished scrubbing in a daze. Breaking bad news was a part of the job, but that did not make the task any easier. Beth's sister, Amanda, had been told the surgery should not take longer than three hours, so she knew something had gone terribly wrong before Carrie set foot inside the waiting room.

"I'm sorry, but I have some bad news." Carrie had been taught to use that phrase, but still, there were few words a doctor despised saying more than those.

I'm sorry . . .

Valerie had accompanied Carrie into the cramped conference room where she had taken Amanda to consult with her in private. Because of Carrie's back-to-back surgeries, Valerie offered to hold the conference with Dr. Michelson instead, but Carrie believed the privilege of caring for sick people came with the added burden of being the messenger.

"Is she going to live?" Amanda had asked after Carrie finished.

Amanda was a sweet-faced woman, five years younger than Beth, and the strain in her kind eyes put a lump in Carrie's throat.

"We're doing everything possible to make sure that she does," Carrie said.

Amanda bit at her lower lip, but could not hold back the rush of tears in her eyes. In response, Carrie reached across the table and clutched the young woman's trembling hand.

"I'm so sorry, Amanda, we're doing everything we can. Please know that. I'm deeply sorry for what's happened here."

A single nod sent Valerie off to get Amanda some water. Carrie did her best to answer Amanda's many questions, though she suspected the young woman would retain little of it. Carrie spoke frankly but compassionately, and promised to follow up with the hematology team looking after Beth as soon as she could.

In the OR, prepping for the next patient, Carrie struggled to push

Amanda's tears, Beth's three children, and the complexity of Beth's case out of her mind. A man with a serious brain tumor was waiting for her in the OR, and he deserved her undivided attention.

Margaret, the circulating nurse, was on her first day at BCH, so she was shy and quiet as she assisted Carrie with her surgical gown and gloves. It was just as well. Carrie's guilt and exhaustion left her in no mood for small talk.

Scrubbed and gowned, Carrie entered the OR and headed straight to the viewbox. The films weren't there. She looked around and saw that X-ray had delivered them, but Margaret hadn't put them up, probably because she was new and nervous.

Though the task was the new nurse's, it was easier for Carrie to do it herself. Carrie grumbled under her breath as she removed the MRI image from the protective envelope.

Dammit!

The moment her gloved hand came in contact with the film, Carrie realized her mistake. She had broken scrub by touching a nonsterile object with her sterilized gloved hand. She'd have to go through the sterilization procedures all over again. It would mean being even more rushed during prep than she already was. Dr. Metcalf could arrive at any second, and if he did not see everything in pristine order, ready to drill, there would be serious fireworks.

For now, it was back to Leon's film.

Carrie had given him only a cursory examination previously, but she remembered that Leon had exhibited cognitive and behavioral problems, some muscular control issues, memory problems, and difficulty controlling his temper.

Carrie tossed the film up on the viewbox, a film she had seen only once before, briefly, in Dr. Nugent's office. That felt like a lifetime ago. Based on visual characteristics, the brain tumor was probably an astrocytoma, the most common form of tumor, but pathology would have to confirm. From what Carrie could see, the mass was not characteristic of a systemic cancer, something that had metastasized to the brain. Good news for Leon. Still, she doubted it was a totally unsuspected abscess, something that surgery plus a prolonged course of antibiotics could essentially cure. Dr. Nugent had said something similar during his brief consult.

Regardless, it didn't do any good to speculate. They would sample the tissue, get the pathology report, and go from there.

Carrie saw that the mass was located deep in the temporal lobe. It looked angry, with a good deal of edema. Leon would most likely need additional surgery to debulk the tumor, followed by radiation and chemotherapy treatments. He might get a few more quality years before the tumor came back to take it all away.

Carrie's dry eyes ached from lack of sleep. At least this case would not be difficult for Dr. Metcalf, who had probably done a thousand of these procedures. She'd be home sometime after noon and asleep a few minutes after that. Assuming, of course, that Dr. Metcalf actually made it to surgery. Carrie had never worked a case before where he'd been so late, and she was beginning to wonder if he had the wrong date on his schedule. In an administrative behemoth like BCH, stranger things had happened.

Back at the sink, Carrie followed the proper protocol for the anatomical scrub, and had Margaret help her get gowned and gloved again. Precious minutes lost.

The scrub nurse, Sam Talbot, had done a fine job making sure the operating room was clean and ready for surgery. He had prepared the instruments and equipment and was double-checking his work when Carrie reentered the OR. Carrie was glad Talbot was on the ball so she could concentrate her efforts on Leon.

Leon was on the operating room table, already anesthetized and intubated. Dr. Lucas Fellows monitored vital signs and adjusted the combination of agents used to keep Leon in a state of blissful unconsciousness.

With Margaret's help, Carrie positioned Leon on his back, elevated the head, and turned him toward his left side. Carrie prepped Leon's shaved skull using antiseptic Betadine that turned his dark skin orange. As Carrie finished with her final swab, the OR door swung open and Dr. Metcalf bounded in, fully scrubbed. Margaret, caught by surprise, shrank a little in his presence. A bear of a man with a full beard, broad shoulders, and a barrel chest, Dr. Metcalf struck an imposing figure in the operating room—or anyplace, for that matter. He held up his arms for Margaret to get him gowned and gloved.

"Sorry for the late arrival," Dr. Metcalf said in his deep, rich baritone. "There was a rollover on I-95 and traffic was backed up for miles. I thought we might have to reschedule, but a friendly cop gave me an escort down the breakdown lane. I can't count the number of angry looks I got."

Dr. Metcalf chuckled and Carrie felt at ease. He seemed to have already observed all of the hard work that had gone into surgical preparation and deemed it fit. He approached Leon and looked over his mask at Carrie, who was standing on the other side of the operating room table.

Dr. Metcalf's brown eyes narrowed. "Goodness, you look terrible, Carrie," he said. "Are you feeling all right?"

Carrie nodded. "Tough operation last night, that's all," she said. "I'm fine."

The persistent throbbing behind Carrie's temple suggested otherwise, but she knew her limits. She could handle one more case.

A few more hours . . . you can do it.

Dr. Metcalf scanned the OR and chuckled again. "Forgot I'm not at White Memorial for a second there. I was looking for the NeuroStation."

Carrie smiled behind her mask. A NeuroStation was a state-of-the-art workstation for localizing brain tumors using a frameless stereotactic system that gave surgeons an unprecedented view into the operative field while relaying the location of instruments to the preoperative imaging data. It cost hundreds of thousands of dollars—well over a million when factoring in all the ancillary equipment. The fancy folks over at White Memorial could afford such luxuries, but BCH didn't have enough funding for such an extravagant expense.

"No worries," Dr. Metcalf said. "I remember when we used to do these operations without a Midas Rex drill. Hell, the drill and bit set we used during *my* residency looked like something you'd pick up at Sears."

Everyone laughed politely.

"All right, Dr. Bryant," he said. "We'll be finished here in no time."

CHAPTER 4

Dr. Metcalf had made the semicircular incision in the temporal-parietal craniotomy site. He was so skilled, had so many years of training, he probably could have done the procedure blindfolded. Nothing was remarkable about his deft handling, except that Carrie could not recall him doing it. It had happened, of course. The skin flap was there, and Dr. Metcalf was busy setting the Raney clips in place, but somehow Carrie had no memory of him actually making the cut. It was like highway hypnosis, only in the OR.

Carrie's body burned with exhaustion that did not justify her lack of concentration. She had pulled plenty of long shifts without her performance suffering. Then again, she'd never been primary surgeon on an operation with serious complications.

Beneath her mask, Carrie gritted her teeth against an onslaught of memories—the blood that kept seeping, the blackened subdermal patches of clotted blood. Beth's operation was hours in the past. She needed to stop it from affecting her performance here and now. Adding to her burden, Carrie's back throbbed from fatigue. Her calf muscles were bowstring tight, and every two seconds she had to fight the urge to rub at her bleary eyes.

Carrie wondered if she'd ever be able to emulate Dr. Metcalf's level of discipline and focus. How did he never seem to tire, no matter how difficult the operation? One thing Carrie knew for certain: She would need his Zen-like mastery of that particular skill to achieve all her professional goals.

"How about some Gelfoam here," Dr. Metcalf said.

The command snapped Carrie out of her daze. She went to work on the incision area, using Avitene on a pledget and Gelfoam to stanch the bleeding.

"Drill."

Sam Talbot placed the stainless steel handle of the Midas Rex pneumatic drill in Dr. Metcalf's outstretched hand. The specialized air drill was designed to stop drilling as soon as the skull was penetrated, preventing injury to the brain. With enviable control and precision, Dr. Metcalf whistled a low and indistinct tune as he created the burr holes, each perfectly placed, one behind the standard key point, others located posteriorly in the temporal bone.

"Vitals?" Dr. Metcalf asked.

The anesthesiologist checked his monitors. "All fine," Dr. Fellows said.

Dr. Metcalf switched to the footplate attachment and started at the temporal burr hole, cutting in a curvilinear fashion, until this region of bone could be removed. Carrie helped by stanching the annoying small bleeders that cropped up on occasion. Everything appeared to be going exactly as planned. Because Leon's tumor was situated deep within the brain, and not a part of the meninges, the dura would have to be excised, which Dr. Metcalf did with great care.

Soon it was time to locate the actual source of Leon's troubles. In the absence of the NeuroStation, Dr. Metcalf relied on the MRI film Carrie had put up on the viewbox to show him where to insert the needle probes. The needles were not really necessary, and Carrie knew Dr. Metcalf was using them for teaching purposes.

Carrie had done this procedure many times herself, but always under careful supervision. Because Dr. Metcalf could not see the tumor, he used the probes to feel for subtle texture changes indicative of touching a growth. For guidance, he occasionally glanced at the MRI while advancing the needle. Carrie knew from her read of the film that the tumor site was approximately 3.5 centimeters deep within the temporal lobe, and Dr. Metcalf was probing in that exact spot.

Carrie watched him work, admiring his steady hand, calm concentration, when Beth again entered her thoughts. Seeing someone so close to her in age suffer like that was a stark reminder of her own good fortune. It was shameful that it took an incident in the OR to make her appreciate her many blessings: her career in medicine, the mentors like Dr. Metcalf who had helped bring her to this point, her family— and even Ian, for ending the relationship and giving her a chance to learn more about herself.

Dr. Metcalf advanced the probe a bit further, then paused. Lifting his head, he gave Carrie a curious stare—not a disapproving look, but something in his eyes looked nonplussed. He maneuvered the probe some more, but this time without a second glance at Carrie. The bleeders were typical for the surgery. No alarms for the patient's vitals, either.

It must have been nothing, because Metcalf removed the probes and was getting the bipolar coagulator and aspirator ready to go. It was time to get Leon's tumor out, or as much of it as they could.

Dr. Metcalf adjusted the frequency on the bipolar coagulator, an instrument with two electrical poles used to cauterize and remove tissue. The tissue here was soft and would require a lower frequency than something more fibrous. The disposable forceps with two small electrodes decreased risk of thrombosis formation, caused minimal tissue damage without suturing, and were effective at hemorrhage prevention.

Dr. Metcalf carefully advanced the bipolar coagulator through the inferior temporal gyros, using a surgical aspirator, more crudely known as a "sucker," to remove blood and fluids while taking away as little good brain tissue as possible.

Should be at the tumor site any second now, Carrie thought.

The sounds of machinery thrummed in Carrie's ears as her anticipation grew. As Dr. Metcalf shifted his attention from Leon to the MRI image, a shadow crossed his face, and his furrowed brow put Carrie on edge. Focused again on the work site, Dr. Metcalf advanced the coagulator perhaps a centimeter more, then stopped. Carrie tried to read his expression. He was obviously anxious. Could it be another complication? Goodness, she had no stamina to endure another surgical mishap.

Dr. Metcalf adjusted a power setting on the frequency generator. A second later, the persistent hum of the bipolar coagulator came to an abrupt stop. The absence of sound filled the room.

Dr. Metcalf looked up and his eyes narrowed in a way that made Carrie shrink inside. "Carrie, I can't find any abnormal tissue here, and I'm at the tumor site."

A chill raced up Carrie's spine.

No . . . no . . . everything is fine . . . it's not panic time . . . not yet . . .

"Let's take a closer look at the MRI," Dr. Metcalf suggested.

Carrie followed Dr. Metcalf over to the viewbox and saw up close what she had observed from a distance. The mass was easy to spot in the medial temporal lobe. It was obvious Dr. Metcalf was seeing the same thing.

"What's going on here?" he asked, mostly to himself. "Jesus, could this be the wrong patient?"

Carrie and Dr. Metcalf simultaneously looked down at the name on the film. As soon as Carrie saw the lettering, a jolt of horror ripped through her body and her breathing stopped. The name was correct, but the letters were reversed!

Oh, God, Carrie thought. *Oh my God, no. Please no!*

Grim-faced now, Dr. Metcalf let his arms fall limply to his side as he fixated on the text, disbelieving.

"Carrie, do you see this? The film was put up backward."

Carrie staggered on her feet as the room began to spin. She had reversed the film. Following a backwards image, Carrie had set the patient up for an operation on the wrong side of his brain.

She flashed on her brief meeting with Leon, and it hit her. Not only did he have a droopy face, his reflexes were heightened in the right arm and leg, indicative of a left-side problem. But more telling was his speech. He had trouble saying simple words and had not been able to follow one of her commands; those were left-sided problems. If she had remembered, Carrie would have seen her mistake and clipped the image up properly.

This can't be happening . . . this cannot be happening. . . .

The shattered look in Dr. Metcalf's eyes cleaved Carrie's heart.

Leon, who already had damage to the left temporal lobe because of the mass, would now have additional damage to the right side of the brain where Dr. Metcalf had probed and removed completely viable brain tissue. It was all her fault.

Dr. Metcalf glowered at the new circulating nurse, Margaret, with venom in his eyes.

"What happened here? What the hell happened here? Don't you know how to read?" Dr. Metcalf's wrathful voice sent Margaret scurrying to a corner.

Dr. Fellows and Sam Talbot stared at each other in disbelief. Carrie took in a shaky breath, but could barely get a sip of air into her lungs. Her face felt flushed, burning hot, and soon the rest of her skin prickled with sweat as a sick feeling washed over her from head to toe. She opened her mouth to speak but at first no sound came out. Courage finally came to her.

"I put the MRI on the viewbox, not Margaret," Carrie said. "It was my error."

With that, she lowered her head and began a solemn march to the exit door.

CHAPTER 5

By the time Steve Abington made his decision, the April sun had hit its midpoint for the day. Steve had hated Philadelphia since arriving there almost a year ago. It wasn't really any worse than Bridgeport, or Manhattan, or East Brunswick, or any of the other cities through which he'd passed. Maybe it was the homeless shelters in Philly that had gotten to him, or maybe it was just life itself.

Still, the Philadelphia shelters were an abomination. Steve hated being jammed inside an airless room with a hundred other misbegotten men. The stale stench of cigarette smoke escaping from the ratty fabric of soiled clothes. Rows of metallic bunk beds like those on a submarine topped with thin mattresses squirming with vermin, sometimes even live mice. Corroded showerheads on tiled walls caked with mold revolted him.

It was chaos, a constant chatter that grated on Steve's eardrums so he couldn't ever relax. Not for a second. Of course a shelter does not pretend to be a Holiday Inn, but with the reception area located behind reinforced glass, it felt like a country jail segregating the inmates from the cons. The drunks were the worst. Screaming, belligerent, and always getting hurt—either tripping over nothing or cracking their skulls on the concrete floor after tumbling out of bed. There was food, at least, breakfast and dinner. But tuna fish sandwiches most every day could make a man want to give up eating.

Steve preferred the streets.

Or he did until he was robbed.

They came at him in the middle of the night, four teenagers, while he slept on a heat vent, wrapped inside a threadbare blue blanket he'd fished out of a trash can. They came with pipes, steel rods, and a bat. They smashed the side of his face pretty good and throttled his leg, but the blows were meant to intimidate, not kill. They made off with his life savings—a few hundred dollars he had scraped together from change tossed in his jar and the occasional crinkled bill. The next morning the bruise on his cheek still stung, his leg felt a bit lame, and the vision in his eye where one of them managed to land a solid right hook was blurry. Could have been worse; he had shocked them when he fought back. Some skills get drilled into you so hard they become reflex.

Funny how just a few years ago Steve had a fancy uniform with plenty of eye-catching chest candy. He had a purpose in life. Now he had the streets and not much else. At least the little bastards didn't get his SIG Sauer, a trophy he'd snuck back from Afghanistan that was hidden at the bottom of an oily knapsack.

That gun meant the world to Steve. It was like a time machine. Soon as he gripped the cool steel handle he was right back in his CHU—containerized housing unit—on Forward Operating Base Eagle. In a lot of ways the CHU was a mirror of a Philly shelter. It was a crowded, noisy affair that smelled like a sweaty gym most of the time, but it had been home when he was Staff Sergeant Abington. He had felt at ease inside the chaotic womb, among his friends, his brothers in arms, the soldiers he would have given his life for. Back in the theater they had depended on each other. It was simple, pure, and in a way, beautiful. When he got home, the world stopped making sense.

But now Steve had made a decision. He had a new plan, a little flash of inspiration. He'd had enough of the streets, the shelters, the cold, and the beatings. He used to be somebody—a staff sergeant in the United States Army, a husband to Janine, a father to Olivia. They were phantoms now. Steve did not blame Janine for cutting him out of her life. He had pushed her to it. She feared for their daughter's safety. He had threatened them, been violent at times, sober rarely, and a person could only take so much. No, he blamed the wound in his mind. Not a single drop of his blood had ever spilled in combat, but he was broken all the same. Injured with scars. Haunted.

All he could focus on was survival, and his needs were immediate and simple: Food. Shelter. Money. He had a plan to get those things.

CHAPTER 6

The BCH conference room was nearly full. By quarter to eight in the morning, all but Knox Singer, the gray-haired CEO of Community, had arrived for the meeting. Carrie was sandwiched between Julie Stafford, the head nurse for 4C, the neurosurgical floor where Leon Dixon had stayed before surgery, and Emily Forrester, legal counsel for White Memorial Hospital. As part of her official residency at White Memorial, Carrie rotated through various satellite hospitals, including BCH. Her operating room mistake had dragged the neurosurgical departments of two organizations into this legal morass.

Sitting across from Carrie were Dr. Stanley Metcalf and Brandon Olyfson, the CEO of White Memorial. Olyfson was whippet-thin, with a long and narrow face, and hawkish eyes that made Carrie shrivel inside. There was coffee, of course, but the usual platters of donuts and pastries were absent, probably in deference to the gravity of the situation. No one was chatting; periodic, desultory sips of coffee were all that broke the silence.

Olyfson and Dr. Metcalf exchanged a few quiet words. Carrie was deeply unsettled by the tension on their faces. Her actions had not only injured a patient, but she had damaged the credibility of her hospital and the man whose skill and poise she had worked so tirelessly to emulate. Her failure was egregious. Unconscionable. Soon she'd hear it dissected in all its grotesque detail by the higher-ups at BCH and White Memorial.

Until a few hours ago, Carrie had been in the same scrubs she'd worn to Leon Dixon's surgery. Now she had on her most professional-looking outfit: a dark suit jacket, slacks, and a blue blouse. Carrie had returned home to her empty Brookline apartment; fed her goldfish, Limbic, named after a primitive memory circuit in the brain; and passed out on the futon, getting a fitful couple hours of sleep. She awoke mired in self-loathing and disbelief, and the pang in her heart confirmed it had really happened.

She did a reasonable job pulling herself together. After studying the spectral being she'd become in the bathroom mirror—her skin was moonlight pale, with dark circles ringing each eye, and her tousled hair stuck out in all directions—she'd swept her hair into a ponytail and figured they'd at least see she was suffering.

At two minutes past eight, the door to the conference room swung open. In strode Knox Singer, accompanied by Carla Mason, head of legal for BCH. Singer was all alpha male, tall and broad-shouldered, with a finely coiffed mane of silver hair and the swarthy good looks of a guy who made his living doing Cialis commercials. Mason was pint-sized by comparison, but her severe bangs, ramrod-straight back, and sharply tailored business suit seemed to add a few inches of height.

Emily Forrester grabbed a chair from against the wall and wheeled it over for Mason, while Singer took a seat at the head of the conference table.

"Sorry I'm late," Knox said in a rumbling low voice. His tone suggested this was the worst possible way to start his day. "Let me begin by saying this meeting is privileged. No minutes. The reputation of Community has to trump the glaring negligence from any member of its staff. So, tell me, Stan, what happened in there?"

Mason managed to get Knox Singer's attention, and she gave him a look he understood.

"Wait," Knox said, preempting Dr. Metcalf's response. "Do you want counsel, Stan? You can have it. Just say the word."

Dr. Metcalf sat stone-faced and issued no response. None was necessary. Everyone knew what this meant: There was no defense. As the attending physician, Dr. Metcalf was responsible for everything that happened in the OR, including the negligent actions of his first assistant.

Carrie sat rigid in her chair and felt a tight band pull across her chest. Her throat had gone Sahara dry, but she could not manage even a sip from the glass of ice water in front of her. They might be talking to Dr. Metcalf, but this meeting was about her. She fixed her gaze on her hands, which were clutched together in her lap. She needed to keep it together.

"Got it," Knox said. "So I'll ask again, and pardon my language, but what the fuck happened in there?"

Carrie lifted her head and somehow found the courage to look Knox in the eyes.

"It was my mistake," she said. Her voice came out in a whisper, so she had to repeat herself. Louder. "I'm the one responsible." Carrie pursed her lips against a sob, a few tears leaking down.

Julie Stafford's nursing instincts kicked in, and she put a comforting arm around Carrie's shaking shoulders. Gently, Julie eased the glass of water closer to Carrie and encouraged her to drink. Carrie couldn't; she was nauseated with grief.

Knox appraised Carrie thoughtfully. He bore a sympathetic expression, as did about half of those seated at the table, with Dr. Metcalf being the most notable exception.

"How did this happen, Dr. Bryant?" Knox asked more mildly.

Carrie shook her head slowly, still in shock. On the occasions when Carrie checked her cell phone while driving, she tried to imagine what it would feel like to cause a traffic fatality, as a way of weaning herself from the habit. But now she knew. She knew exactly what it felt like. It was a sickening, horrible feeling she would not wish on anybody.

"I put the film up backward," Carrie said, struggling with her voice.

"I should have known——I should have——Mr. Dixon was aphasic, his right side was weaker, he had a right Babinski. All the signs were there to remind me that the problem was in the left hemisphere, but somehow I just forgot. I guess I was tired from my last surgery, but I know that's not an excuse, I know that. I'm so very sorry to everyone involved."

Carrie braved eye contact with everyone at the table, desperate to convey her sincerity. Dr. Metcalf focused on his notepad as if refusing to look at Carrie somehow separated him from her and her mistake.

"Had you reviewed the film prior?" asked Sam Stern, the sixty-five-year-old chief of neurosurgery at Community. It was obvious he would try to shift the blame to another department, and radiology was as good a target as any.

Carrie swallowed hard. "I reviewed the MRI with Dr. Nugent the day before the surgery," she said. "I'd seen the films, Sam. I have no excuse."

The silence that followed lasted several seconds before Knox spoke up and broke the spell.

"Julie, what's Mr. Dixon's status?"

Julie Stafford had been head nurse on the neurosurgical floor for fifteen years, and a staff nurse at Community for fifteen years before that. She essentially ran the place. Jokes abounded about her supernatural ability to know everything that happened on her floor, even before it seemed to happen. It was a well-established fact that Nurse Stafford could make or break the career of any resident rotating through 4C with just a few choice words. But she'd always been good to Carrie; they shared the same work ethic and commitment.

"Mr. Dixon is stable," Julie said. "But he's mute and won't follow any commands. Right now his wife and his brother are with him. They know what happened. Dr. Metcalf hasn't been in to see him, though." Dr. Metcalf shot Julie a stern look.

Carla Mason had been quietly taking notes and looked up over her glasses. "I've told him not to," Carla said.

"I would like to go on record here and say a few words," Julie said. With a nod Knox gave his consent, and Julie spoke.

"I have worked with Carrie Bryant since the start of her residency, when her responsibilities were limited to doing mostly scut work at all hours of the day. Carrie, more than anyone, took the extra time to get to know her patients and families. I understand that she had been up all night operating on a complicated case. I spoke personally with Beth Stillwell's sister, Amanda, who praised Carrie's kindness and compassion. I've personally seen Dr. Metcalf tear apart residents for any delays that derailed his schedule, so I'm sure that played a role in Carrie rushing to get the OR set up right. Carrie made a terrible mistake. There's no denying that fact, but she's not the only culpable party."

Dr. Metcalf made daggers with his eyes.

"I refuse to be intimidated by any doctor on staff, regardless of their stature here," Julie continued. "In my opinion, I'm tired of the attending physicians using the hospital like a personal garage whenever a physician friend wanted a favor. Look, I sincerely appreciate our close relationship with White Memorial and the excellent doctors from there who otherwise wouldn't be in a position to care for our city's less fortunate. But perhaps if Dr. Metcalf deigned to venture up to 4C to see his patient before operating, or God forbid at least look at the MRI prior, none of this would have happened."

A heavy silence ensued, and Carrie felt somewhat vindicated. Better procedures for double-checking should have been in place, and Carrie believed protocols would change as a result.

"Look, there's really no issue here," Carla Mason interjected.

As chief counsel for Community, Carla was directly responsible for malpractice cases like this one. Unfortunately, they seemed to be happening with greater and greater frequency. The majority of these cases were meritless, but the hospital continued to cough up millions in legal fees defending them, not to mention countless hours of deposition, fact-finding, and copying records. The impact on productivity was now just a cost of doing business. For everyone involved, the expense of a lengthy trial was more than a matter of money; it was years of legal wrangling in terms of time, reputation, and emotional well-being. Carla tried to avoid the courtroom whenever possible, even for the most meritless claims—a strategy Knox Singer fully endorsed.

"The family will sue and the hospital will settle," Carla said. "And the sooner this is done, the better. The last thing BCH and Chambers University need is something like this getting out to the press and the public."

"Carla and I are meeting with the Dixons at eleven," said Emily Forrester, the lawyer for White Memorial. "We will advise them to seek counsel immediately. Knox, I take it you'd agree to our informing the family that the hospital and university will offer a very generous settlement, and will assume responsibility for any upcoming and future medical care that the Dixons might require. I've already discussed this with Brandon, who concurs."

Brandon Olyfson nodded. As CEO of White Memorial Hospital, he wanted out of this meeting, and quick. Olyfson thought of BCH as nothing more than a cesspool. Three-quarters of the patients were drunks or drugged out. No one had insurance. He could give a crap about Leon Dixon, Carrie believed. All that mattered to Olyfson was that Dr. Metcalf, his choice for the next chief of neurosurgery, was now a potential plague on the reputation of White Memorial Hospital.

"So, this Dixon guy. I mean, he was probably going to have problems regardless of any surgery, right?" Olyfson asked.

Dr. Metcalf became indignant. "Brandon, Mr. Dixon has a left temporal lobe tumor, most likely an astrocytoma. But of course, we don't know that for certain now. His tumor may be aggressive, and if so, his prognosis wouldn't be very good. Maybe a few years with radiation and chemotherapy. But just maybe, this could have been an abscess and potentially curable. The MRI isn't definitive. It can't distinguish between

an abscess and a tumor. But we can't operate on the other side until
we know what damage we caused by this error."

"So was Mr. Dixon going to be compromised regardless?" Olyfson
asked.

"The tumor might be less aggressive and potentially more amenable
to adjunctive treatments than usual," Metcalf said. "One never really
knows. Mr. Dixon was losing control of his speech. Now we've only
added to his deficits. He may never speak another word. He may lose all
his memory function. His behavior is likely to be very different. Hell, he
could lose functional control of his sphincters for all we know. Bottom line is he will now be functionally dependent for the rest of his
life, however long that's going to be. Considerably shorter, I suspect.
We can do a simple biopsy of his tumor at some point, but because of
the damage we've done, aggressive care won't be of any benefit."

Carla Mason and Emily Forrester took copious notes, but Carrie
looked only at her lap. She was finished. She sat silent, holding herself
together by remaining as still as possible. But she couldn't stop the tears,
which cascaded down her cheeks, dripping into her lap. Once again,
Julie put an arm around Carrie to comfort her.

"It's going to be okay, sweetie," Julie whispered. "We'll get through
this. I promise."

"Carrie, anything else you want to add?" Knox asked.

"Just that I'm tendering my resignation," Carrie said. "Effective immediately."

CHAPTER 7

The First National Bank of Philadelphia occupied the lower level of a five-story brick building on the corner of Eighth Avenue and Sutcliff. Abington picked it because he was standing near it when inspiration struck.

As he expected, he drew suspicious looks from his first step inside. With his flyaway straw-colored hair, haggard face, baggy eyes, and mountain man–style beard, Abington made Nick Nolte's mug shot look like a high school yearbook picture.

Four customers were inside the bank when Abington entered, and none made direct eye contact with him as he crossed the marble floor to the teller windows. Though the bank was not crowded, Abington still had to wait in line, which made him edgy. He was especially mindful of the man to his right, filling out a deposit slip. That guy seemed to not notice Abington at all, which was unusual. Could this guy's obliviousness be an act? Abington's gut told him it was a cop, either undercover or off duty.

The brunette behind teller window number five motioned Abington forward. For a moment he contemplated walking out. He felt naked without a hat or sunglasses, and the security cameras had already gotten a clear shot of his face. *Oh, what the hell.* He was here. She wouldn't know the gun in his back pocket wasn't loaded. She'd give him the money.

As Abington approached, the brunette recoiled subtly, her brow creasing and the corners of her mouth turning downward. She maintained an air of professionalism, but her demeanor had turned hard-bitten and judgmental.

"Can I help you?" she asked in a tone that implied otherwise. Be it a handout, food, booze—whatever it was, she was not there to assist.

"I would like some money." Abington was surprised at the shakiness of his voice. He had meant to sound forceful, but instead spoke in a raspy near whisper.

The teller rolled her eyes and Abington took a moment to look over his shoulder at the man filling out the deposit slip. *How many checks is that guy cashing?* He had to be a cop.

Walk away . . . head out that door and just walk away. . . .

Abington was about to turn around when he flashed on the faces of those bastards pummeling him with bats and steel rods. He pictured the grate where he'd slept the night before. He thought of the many shelters he had called home, and felt a pang of hunger. A tide of violence rose in his blood as he thought of the VA that had failed him. He drew his weapon.

The color drained from the teller's face. Before she could scream, Abington put his finger to his lip, shielding the piece with his body.

"Don't do anything stupid," Abington said, gratified to hear more authority in his voice this time. "Give me the money." From underneath Abington's grimy shirt he produced an equally soiled paper bag, and handed it to the teller.

The teller's hands shook as she filled the bag with thick wads of banded cash, but twice she glanced up to look over Abington's shoulder at the man to his back.

While the teller filled the bag, Abington counted the seconds in his head. *Five . . . then ten . . .*

How much money had she put in there? Maybe a couple thousand. Maybe a little more. It didn't matter. It wasn't like he'd stop to count. He needed to get out of there.

The teller was reaching for another drawer when Abington realized she was stalling. Her hands were steadier, and she seemed less nervous. Maybe she had tripped the silent alarm.

Reaching over the counter, Abington ripped the bag from the teller's hand, leaving her with a little piece of brown paper. He swung around, gun in one hand, money in the other, and saw that the man with the deposit slip had snuck up behind him.

Midforties with short hair and a square head, the guy trained his weapon—a Glock—on Abington's chest. He shouted, "Freeze! Police!"

Abington did not hesitate. The SIG Sauer may have been useless without bullets, but Abington had trained with the SEALs and Delta Force. Even out of shape and practice, he was a fine weapon on his own. Abington dropped his gun and the bag of money and started to raise his hands.

No trouble. I surrender.

The officer started to relax, thinking the fight was over. In a fluid motion, Abington grabbed hold of the Glock's barrel with his right hand while latching his left hand onto the officer's left wrist. Without hesitating, Abington pulled the left wrist toward him at the same instant he pushed on the barrel of the gun. Thrown off balance, the cop stumbled awkwardly, and a fraction of a second later the Glock had transferred into Abington's hands. Abington swung the gun in a wide arc, clocking the cop on his left temple with the butt of the weapon. Two heavy thuds followed: one after the impact, and the other when the cop's limp body crumpled to the floor.

Reaching down, Abington retrieved the bag of money and his treasured gun. He sprang up waving the cop's loaded weapon, shooing the terrified customers back.

"Just leave me alone and nobody gets hurt!" Abington shouted.

Outside the bank, the sun's glare punished Abington's corneas. He blinked to clear his vision, but his head was buzzing and he felt lost. What had he done? Jesus, he hadn't made a plan. No figuring out how he might escape.

In the distance Abington heard a steady whine of sirens. They were coming for him. *Stupid . . . stupid!* His choices were simple: run and get caught, or stand in front of the bank and get caught. He looked at the cop's gun.

He supposed he had a third choice. Abington put the weapon to his temple, closed his eyes, and conjured up Janine's beautiful face. They had had happy times; he tried to focus on those.

"I'm sorry, baby girl," Abington muttered, thinking of his daughter Olivia. "I let you down, sweetie. I let you down so bad."

Abington pressed the barrel of the Glock hard against his skin and squeezed the trigger ever so slightly. Ironic: with all the bullets flying around him in Afghanistan, this would be the one and only time he'd be shot. Abington took a breath. The squeal of sirens seemed to be coming from all directions.

Can they even identify me? Will they let Mom know I'm dead?

A screech of tires in front of him caused Abington to open his eyes. A windowless cargo van had pulled up, and before it came to a complete stop, a clean-shaven man with short-cropped hair jumped out the passenger-side door. He wore a tailored blue suit and approached with hurried steps. The sirens got louder.

"You don't need to do that, Steve," he said. "You made a bad choice here, but we can help. Just get in the van."

As if on cue, the van's rear double doors swung open, inviting Abington to step inside. Abington hesitated.

"Who are you?" he asked.

"Two seconds, Steve. We've been watching you, and we can help you, but you've got to move, soldier. Now!"

Abington's training kicked in, making it difficult to ignore the command. He dashed to the back of the van, where two arms reached out from the darkness and hauled him inside. At the same instant, the van pulled away from the curb with another screech of tires and made a quick U-turn. The back doors slammed shut, leaving only slivers of dim light. Steve could not get a clear view of the interior, or the person who had helped him aboard.

The van straightened out and drove away from the scene at a measured pace meant to appear inconspicuous. He could still hear sirens, but they were heading in the opposite direction. The interior lights came on, but Abington could not comprehend what he was seeing.

The back of the van was crowded with medical equipment: a stretcher and an IV stand with fluid bags attached, as if this were the rear of an ambulance. The man who had helped him inside wore a surgical mask, head covering, and blue latex gloves. His gray eyes were expressionless.

"Welcome, Steve," the man said from behind his mask. "We've been looking forward to having you."

Steve looked down at the man's gloved hands and saw a needle and syringe. Fast as a cobra strike, the man sank a two-inch needle deep into Steve's neck and depressed the plunger.

A warm feeling swept through Steve's body. He felt light-headed, a bit dizzy, but also at peace. Finally at peace.

CHAPTER 8

The town of Hopkinton, Massachusetts, was known—if at all—as the official starting place of the Boston Marathon, but to Carrie it was simply home. The four-bedroom Victorian house where she grew up, with its many gabled windows, wraparound porch, and verdant gardens, was still lovingly maintained by Carrie's parents, Howard and Irene, who were now in their sixties and showed no signs of slowing down. Howard Bryant continued to work at Mass General Hospital, and Irene had gone back to school to become a speech pathologist, which had led to her current job at a nearby nursing facility.

Carrie's visits were limited mostly to holidays, an occasional birthday dinner, and of course Marathon weekend, which had turned into a homecoming of sorts for many of her childhood friends. Aside from Facebook, Carrie did not see these buddies on a regular basis, though when they did get together the night always ended with a promise to do it more often.

Carrie drove her beat-up Subaru down the long driveway. In a few more weeks the tiger lilies would start to sprout and the rest of her mother's gardens would come alive, but right now the desolate landscape was brown and barren in a way that matched Carrie's mood. She parked in front of the basketball hoop, next to her mother's Volvo, in the pullout to the right of the detached two-car garage, mindful not to block her father in.

She stepped out into a chilly afternoon. Spring might have officially arrived, but winter did not seem ready to let go its icy grasp. One of the garage doors was open, and Led Zeppelin blasted from within the darkness. Adam must be in there working on his car, as always; the music was probably coming from the boom box she'd bought to welcome him home.

Adam, who'd aced AP biology and gravitated toward STEM subjects, was expected to extend the streak of Bryant doctors that included two of Carrie's grandparents, but to everyone's surprise he'd enlisted in the army right after high school. Adam's commitment to the military had ended years ago, but in his mind, the war raged on.

Wearing jeans and a fleece jacket over a blue V-neck sweater from Macy's, Carrie wandered into the doorway of the garage, feeling strange not to be dressed in scrubs or sweats. Her brother was bent over the Camaro's open hood, which looked like it was swallowing him. He wiped engine grime from his hands on his already soiled jeans, and only when Carrie cleared her throat did he pull his head out to look her way.

Adam's face lit up. "Hey, sweetie!" He approached with his arms open wide. "What brings you out here?" Before they hugged, Adam realized he was covered in filth, so he opted for a quick peck on her cheek. "It's good to see you."

Carrie looked at her brother's drawn face and hollow cheeks and tried not to let her worry show. The old Adam was in there somewhere. If she closed her eyes, Carrie could still picture the handsome, sharp-eyed boy she'd looked out for back in high school. He still had his wry smile, but the glint in his eyes and that playful cocky attitude were gone.

Adam had cut his hair short again, a throwback to his army days, and had a whisper of a mustache that was new as well. Carrie did not love the look, but Adam was doing a lot of experimenting, perhaps searching for an outside transformation to make him feel whole inside. The rest of him looked the same. He had a narrow, lean build coupled with a muscular chest, arms, and legs. His pallid complexion called attention to his dark and sunken eyes, reminding Carrie of the drug addicts she used to operate on at BCH.

Used to.

How could it be over? The thought of never operating again stretched a band around her chest so tight Carrie thought she might stop breathing. She was utterly lost, completely bewildered, and had never been closer to understanding how Adam must feel.

"Mom and Dad didn't tell me you were coming," Adam said.

The garage looked exactly as Carrie had expected, a tale of two personalities. Dad's side, with his beloved BMW 325i, was neat and ordered, just like Howard Bryant. Freestanding shelves kept clutter to a minimum; beloved tools were carefully organized on several wood pegboards. Adam's side was like a teenager's bedroom. Tools were scattered everywhere, and the workbench and shelves were covered in oily rags, greasy papers, and indiscriminate mounds of car parts.

"Mom and Dad don't know I'm coming," Carrie said.

Adam gave Carrie a conspiratorial look. "Everything all right?"

Carrie nodded her head vigorously and tightened her lips. "Yeah, it's fine." *Change the subject. Prevent the waterworks.* "Hey, the car is looking really good."

Adam's answer was to stand a little taller. His mouth crested upward as he turned to face the Camaro. He set his hands on his hips and paused to relish his accomplishment. "It's coming along, huh?"

The Camaro had shown up six weeks after Adam left his warrior transition unit, WTC in military parlance, without any definitive cure. He reentered civilian life directionless, with empty, fidgety hands. Fixing up a car that reminded him of his carefree high school days seemed like a good idea, though their parents were not as certain when they saw the mound of scrap towed to their garage. The car sat untouched for a long while, until one day when Adam's inspiration inexplicably kicked in. Now that the body was fixed up and a fresh coat of red paint had been applied, it looked truly special. If only Adam could be fixed up with some elbow grease and determination.

The WTC had begun as an army unit, but a deluge of wounded warriors from two wars had necessitated a rapid expansion. War recovery had become a major cost for the military's budget, and now close to forty of these transition units were fanned out across the country, helping soldiers to heal. Still, they couldn't guarantee Adam would leave his program with a cure. Four years and four different therapists later, Adam had his Camaro and not much else.

"Want to hear it purr?" Adam asked.

Carrie gave Adam two wiggly thumbs up. Anything for her beloved brother. Adam got settled behind the wheel and caressed the dash as if it were a stallion he needed to calm before mounting. He put the key in the ignition and gave it a turn. The engine sputtered, but then it just started to click. A series of loud clicks like the countdown of a bomb.

Click-click-click . . .

He turned the key again.

Click-click-click . . .

Adam's forehead wrinkled in a scowl. Darkness radiated from him as he slammed his fists against the steering wheel and yelled, "FUCK!" so loud Carrie flinched. His inner storm flared and he continued to pound the car with his fists—the seat, the steering wheel, the dashboard. Adam flung open the car door and stumbled out with a look of madness. His face was red with rage.

Adam scrounged on the ground and came up holding a large, rusty wrench.

"No, Adam! No!"

There was no stopping him. Adam brought the wrench down on the side mirror, snapping it clean off with a single strike and sending it to the concrete floor with a clatter. Next he went after the passenger window, shattering it before falling to his knees, breathing hard, spent from his tirade.

Carrie knelt beside him, blanketing him in her arms. She rocked him as he wept, his body shaking.

"I'm sorry, I just—lost it. I'm sorry, Carrie—I don't know why I got so angry. I . . . I just snapped."

"It's okay. It's okay, Adam," Carrie said. "I'm so sorry. I'm so sorry for everything you're going through."

Carrie held her brother while he wept. She did not see or hear her father enter the garage, but when she turned he was there.

For his age, Howard Bryant was exceedingly thin, almost rubbery, with long arms and legs that Carrie was fortunate to have inherited. He wore khakis and his trademark plaid shirt with a sweater vest. Just the sight of him filled Carrie with relief.

"Hi, sweetheart," Howard said from the entrance to the garage. His voice came out raspy, a little aged, but it was soothing in a way only a daddy could speak to a daughter. Carrie held on to Adam; she was not ready to let go, and he still needed her. Howard looked worried, but unsurprised.

"Come on in the house when you're ready," Howard said. "Your mother's made soup. I'll heat you up a bowl."

CHAPTER 9

David Hoffman, eyes still closed, stretched out on his futon and sent the stack of papers at his feet fluttering to the hardwood floor. His orange tabby Bosra perched placidly on his chest, undisturbed by the movement. David waited a few seconds, enjoying the special peace of an afternoon nap. Before he drifted back to sleep, David opened his eyes and checked the time on his phone. It was deadline day, which meant Anneke would be calling. He was fine with blowing her off again, but he could not sound half asleep while doing it.

Something about lying on that futon, especially when the fabric was warm from the sun, was like mainlining melatonin. The report he'd been reading was of no help, either. While the Institute of American Medicine was an upstanding organization, their take on PTSD in the military was all jargon and imperiousness. Forty-eight bucks down the drain; Anneke would not be pleased. David could have written in a paragraph what the IAM took sixty pages to convey. *Good on you, DOD and VA, for trying to fix this mess. Bad on you, because PTSD in the military is getting worse, and you have no ability to track the outcomes.*

David turned his head toward the window and the view, unobstructed by the greenery that would develop with spring. The apartment, though small, felt roomy, and an obtrusive tree branch was a fine tradeoff for cheap rent in Porter Square.

Bosra meowed, and David responded with a gentle scratch between his ears. The cat, a rescue, was named after ancient ruins in Syria. The name reminded David of one of many spectacular sites he had visited as a journalist, and an aspect of his career he missed. Having spent the majority of his professional life chasing political strife, David had become addicted to the rush. Nothing could match the intensity of covering an angry mob, of documenting people's most visceral passion for freedom and security. For someone who'd smoked marijuana only a couple of times and who was rendered tipsy by a single scotch, political upheaval was a different sort of drug, and David missed the high. While some of David's classmates from Columbia embedded with a military unit only to up their profile with a newspaper or network, David honestly enjoyed dangerous assignments, though he preferred politics to platoons.

A knock on the door pushed David to get up. Meowing in protest, Bosra leapt off David's chest and landed noiselessly on the hardwood floor. David ambled over to his front door. "Who is it?" he called, knowing full well.

"David, it's Emma."

David opened the door, grinning. He suspected his bushy brown hair was standing up like a Chia pet, and he was dressed abysmally in gray sweats and a blue T-shirt, but he was uninhibited with Emma. She had started out as his landlord, became his friend, and then briefly his lover, until both decided that friends was where they belonged. Now he loved her in a way that would have been difficult had they still been dating. Emma was holding Gabby, a delightful four-year-old, in her arms. Gabby had cheeks to cause a chipmunk envy and two animated, big brown eyes. Her shoulder-length blond hair was tied into pigtails. Gabby's whole body squirmed excitedly when she saw David.

"Hi, Uncle David!"

David warmed every time she called him that. Emma handed Gabby to him and the little girl squealed and kicked as David tickled under her chin. Whenever Gabby laughed, a sweet high-pitched chuckle, the world stopped turning.

"Who's gotten so much bigger since the last time I saw you?" He could not resist speaking to her in a high-pitched voice.

"David, you ate breakfast with us this morning."

"Kids develop quickly these days."

"Can I play with the toys?" Gabby whirled her legs instead of asking to be put down.

"You know the spot," David said.

Soon as he set her on the floor, Gabby bounded over to a corner featuring a play mat and a bunch of toys—blocks, Thomas trains, and enough plastic animals to re-create the San Diego Zoo in miniature. Emma did not remove her own brown tweed coat and wool hat, which let David know she would not be staying.

"She sure does like coming up here."

"And I like having her here," David said.

Emma got a wistful look as she watched Gabby playing with the toys.

"No offense," she said, in a quiet, almost conspiratorial tone, "but it would be nice if once in a while she got to visit with her father instead of her surrogate dad."

"None taken," David said. "And it would be nice if her father hadn't moved to California for work." David put air quotes around the word "work," in this case a euphemism for "girlfriend"—the real reason Emma's ex had left them.

"He Skypes with her, just so you know," Emma said. Emma could not resist the compulsion to defend the father of her only child.

David squeezed Emma's hand. "I'm sure he loves her," David said.

Emma and The Ex owned a yellow clapboard two-family home within walking distance of some of the best shopping in Cambridge. They lived on the ground floor, and David rented the apartment above. The Ex had moved out three months after David moved in, and Emma turned to her new upstairs tenant as a lifeline.

With long strawberry blond hair, high cheekbones, and a full, sensuous mouth, Emma O'Donnell was by anybody's measure a stunning woman. But David was not all about looks, and they knew after a month of romance that the chemistry was not there.

"Could you watch her for an hour while I run to the market?"

"Nothing in life would bring me more joy," David said.

Emma looked at him with suspicion. "Really, is it inconvenient?"

David's grin only broadened. "Your needs are my needs, darling. Just pick me up something for dinner. Preferably a food item that won't make me gassy."

At thirty-two, David was still tall and lean, close to his high school weight, and could eat just about anything, to the dismay of his many envious friends.

"Too bad," Emma said. "We're having burritos."

David turned Emma around and gave her a playful nudge out. "Gabby and I are going to work on our Middle Eastern geography while you're gone. Prepare to retrieve a genius upon return."

Gabby overheard her name and came running.

"Can we look at the pictures, Uncle David?"

"Look, she's already a genius," Emma said with more than a dash of pride. "She heard you say geography and thought of your pictures."

David had read somewhere that kids, especially the young ones, love repetition. In a world where so much was new and varied, seeing the same things over again must feel comforting. His walls were adorned with framed photos he had taken, and showing them to Gabby gave him pleasure as well. The pleasure of revisiting memories. The themes, however, were decidedly adult, and it took great concentration to explain them to the child without inducing nightmares.

"What's this one?" Gabby asked.

The photograph, taken a month before former president Morsi was forced out of office, showed a sea of people waving Egyptian flags and holding pictures of the Muslim Brotherhood candidate. *The Guardian* had paid David two thousand dollars for the story, but they went with an AP photo instead of his.

"That's in Egypt," David said. "The city of Cairo." David carried Gabby over to the world map tacked to his wall and pointed to the country.

"Why were they waving flags?" Gabby asked.

"They wanted a new leader."

"Did they get one?"

"Oh yes," David said. "They got one, all right."

Gabby wrapped her arms around David's neck with python force and pointed to the picture on the wall behind him. She always went in the same order, though David varied his explanations.

"What's that one?"

It was one of his favorites—a black-and-white image of a riot in Tripoli right after Gaddafi loyalists managed to kill the rebel leader, Abdel Fattah Younes. *The New York Times* had paid five hundred for the photo and three thousand for his story. It had been a good afternoon.

"That's a bunch of people acting very excited," David said.

"Why are they excited? Did they get new toys?"

David loved the way she said "toys"—her enthusiasm was contagious.

"No, not new toys. They just needed to jump around and yell a lot. Sometimes grown-ups do those things."

"What about that one?"

First, David brought her over to the wall map and pointed to Libya, the location of the last image. She touched the same spot as he did, and then rubbed her hands all over Europe.

"Libya," David said.

"Libya," Gabby repeated, then pointed to the image showing thousands of red-shirted populist supporters of Thailand's ousted prime minister, Thaksin Shinawatra. "Are they excited about the same things?"

"Well, not exactly," David said.

"How come they're all wearing the same color shirt?"

"Because they believe in the same things," David said. "They're a group."

"What group do you belong to?"

"I don't," David said. "I work for myself."

David was a stringer. He had built his career working as a freelancer, forgoing a regular salary in exchange for the opportunity to cover stories that actually interested him. Most of the time that interest took him to places the State Department was advising Americans to avoid. Syria. Iraq. Afghanistan. Yemen. A journalistic tumbleweed, he would probably still be in some red-flagged country had he not been kidnapped.

It was not a terrible ordeal, nor was it an experience he would willingly relive. The opposition forces in Syria had decided that David was part of Assad's regime and, without judge or jury, took him prisoner. For three weeks David lived in a windowless concrete room and had no contact with the outside world. Eventually, he befriended a guard who was looking to learn English. With the guard's help, David was able to contact the State Department. A contact at *The Current,* technically David's employer, spoke by satellite phone to the opposition forces holding him hostage. The editor managed to convince those in charge that David was in the country on assignment and that David's reporting could be of help to their cause back in the United States. A few hours later they let David go, and the next day he was on a plane headed home. Somebody else would have to help the rebels' crusade.

Word of David's ordeal spread quickly to all the people who regularly hired him for stringer jobs. In just a few weeks, David's greatest asset—his willingness to put himself in harm's way to get the story— became his biggest liability. Nobody wanted to bail "Cowboy Dave" out of any more international hot water, and suddenly the only work he could drum up was for local newspapers like the *Lowell Observer.*

A reporter buddy hooked David up with Anneke, a respected editor who had dialed down her career in exchange for some of her remaining stomach lining. Though he was grateful for the work, a feel-good piece about a marine conquering his PTSD was not his dream assignment.

"Are you going to join a group?" Gabby asked.

David's cell phone buzzed. *Anneke.*

"Hmmm, I might be asked to leave another group," David said, setting Gabby down on the floor. "Go play for a bit. I have to talk on the phone."

Gabby ran over to the toys.

"Anneke," David answered, sounding chipper and cheery. "I was just going to call you."

"Because your e-mail doesn't work? No worries. I've got a pen. You can dictate it to me."

"Ha, that's actually kind of funny."

"I'm a real gas. Where's the story, David?"

David could picture Anneke's scowl by the tone of her voice. She was fifty-something, fit and slim from running and Pilates, with shoulder-length blond hair. Poor Anneke walked under a black cloud; everywhere she went, it was raining deadlines. And David was only adding to her misery.

He'd make it up to her. A bottle of Chianti and she'd forget this little lapse. She owed him a pass anyway. His first story for her was supposed to be a puff piece about a bright foster kid from Lowell who won some creative writing contest. The fifteen hundred words she asked for turned into a high-impact story that ran over several days and exposed a huge scandal involving the Department of Children and Families. David could always tell where the real story was, and he knew this particular assignment should not be about one triumphant marine.

"The story is in progress," David said.

"Have you interviewed Sergeant Thompson yet?"

Sergeant Jesse Thompson was a Billerica native who'd lost an arm to an IED and was helping other vets overcome their PTSD symptoms with some success.

"Almost."

"How can you almost interview somebody?"

"I've thought about calling him, but I'm working on a different angle right now."

David was more interested in the staggering numbers of vets with PTSD. The problem was approaching epidemic levels, with one out of four servicemen and -women returning from combat significantly *different*.

"This isn't *The New York Times*," Anneke said. "We're a local paper. We've never won a Pulitzer, and I don't think my boss really cares if we do."

"Never say never," David responded.

Anneke sighed. "How much longer do you need?"

Small community paper or not, he and his boss were still cut from the same stock. Both of them wanted to do good work, important journalism. If a story were here, Anneke would want David to find it.

"Give me a couple weeks. Sergeant Thompson isn't going anywhere. We can do a flashy piece on him anytime. But I want to explore this a little bit more."

"You're thinking series."

He pursed his lips. "The phone's not ringing to send me back to Syria."

"What's your plan?"

"I'm going to talk to some vets. The guys who haven't been helped."

"Give me some names." Testing to make sure David was actually working.

Luckily, he had his notes handy. "How about I give you three?" David said. "William Bird, Max Soucey, and Adam Bryant."

Click. Anneke had hung up without a good-bye. It was David's signal to get to work.

CHAPTER 10

The house hadn't changed much since Carrie left for college. The wall-to-wall carpeting had long ago been replaced with hardwood flooring, and Carrie's bedroom had been converted into a guest room, but those were minor adjustments. Everything here, down to the round oak table in the kitchen, was familiar.

The framed pictures on the walls reflected a close-knit family. Usually they filled her with nostalgia, but today they made Carrie think about Leon Dixon. How many memories had Carrie erased with her mistake?

Carrie broke free of such painful, paralyzing thoughts to look at photos of herself and Adam through various life stages. She especially loved the vacation pictures. Some photos recorded ski trips to the mountains of New Hampshire and Maine, others showed their European adventures, a few had been taken in the Caribbean, and one displayed Howard and Adam riding elephants side by side on an African safari. There were probably as many photographs of Puckels, the shaggy and much-beloved family dog who had died a few years back, as there were of the kids. Carrie had encouraged her father to go to the shelter for another animal, but Howard quoted the comedian Louis C.K., who called puppies "a countdown to sorrow."

Carrie noticed Adam's military portraits were missing. In their place Carrie's mom had hung a couple landscapes she painted herself. Carrie was impressed by her mother's latent artistic ability, though Irene credited her teacher for her rapid progress.

After some time, Carrie wandered into the kitchen, where Howard was warming up the soup. Her dad had a full head of hair, but it was more gray than brown, and thinning. Carrie's mom had once bought him a color treatment, but Howard never opened the box. "Vanity is a young's man game," he'd say. Steam from two hot mugs of green tea fogged up the glasses on Howard's round face, magnifying two of the kindest eyes Carrie had ever seen.

"Your mom will be home in a bit, but you and I can catch up."

When the soup was ready, Howard sat at the table. Carrie joined him. The tea was a perfect temperature, and the soup smelled savory and delicious. Carrie had been living off cafeteria food for so long she'd all but forgotten what home cooking tasted like. She took a sip of tea.

"Your hands are shaking," her father said. "I know it's hard to see your brother like this."

Carrie set her tea down. "It's not just Adam, Dad."

Dad.

The word was a safety net. It allowed Carrie to let everything out. Her eyes closed tight, a sob escaping, and tears streamed down her cheeks.

Howard pulled his chair close and put his arms around her. "What's going on, honey?"

Carrie took a few ragged breaths. "Something really awful happened. . . ."

It was not an easy story to tell. For most of it, Carrie struggled to get the words out. At first she cried a lot, breathing hard, short of breath, but eventually she settled and managed to tell it all.

Howard looked impressed as Carrie recounted Beth's surgery and the DIC episode. Details about Leon's surgery were fuzzier, perhaps because Carrie had blocked them out, but she remembered Dr. Metcalf's worried expression as he tried to locate the tumor.

Howard did not flinch when Carrie revealed her mistake. His eyes held no trace of judgment. He was full of compassion when she told him about the meeting that followed and her resignation.

Carrie could not have asked for a better confidant. Her father had spent years honing his listening skills. He had long believed that what a patient said, and how they said it, was sometimes more telling than the actual examination. These were skills that he had imparted to his daughter, and they'd been working well. But even Howard, who always seemed to know just the right thing to say, looked at a loss for words. In the prolonged silence that followed Carrie's story, he poured them both more tea.

"I've let everyone down," Carrie said, an all-too-familiar tightness creeping back into her chest.

"Sweetheart, right now is not the time for advice or instruction. Just know I am here for you. And your mother is, too. And in a way, so is Adam. We love you, and we'll stand by you through all of this."

Carrie embraced her father again, and Howard kissed the top of her head.

"Tell me what you need. Anything."

Carrie laughed because she could not believe what she was about to ask.

"With my student loans and no income, I just don't have the money to afford my apartment. Not without a job."

Howard nodded. "I can lend you whatever you need. Mom and I can cover your rent for a while."

Carrie shook off that idea. "Some doctor I turned out to be. I'm twenty-nine years old and I need my parents to pay my rent. No, thank you."

"Don't let pride get in your way. Think of it as a loan."

Carrie tossed her hands in the air. "It's not pride. It's practicality. How am I going to repay it?" she asked. "I don't know what I'm going to do. I'm completely lost here."

"Then don't repay it."

Carrie shook her head again. "I can't accept that. Not without a plan. It wouldn't feel right to me. I might not even want to stay in town. Maybe I need to go get a research job, something in academia. I don't know."

"Then what do you want to do in the interim?"

Carrie sensed her father already knew. Again her thoughts went to Adam. They had taken two different paths, and yet found themselves at the same destination. It must be discouraging for her father to have worked so hard to raise independent children, only to have them turn out unable to function in the world.

"I spoke to my landlord," Carrie said. "He'll let me break my lease and give me my deposit back."

"That's fine, but where are you going to go?" Howard asked.

Carrie shrugged and tried not to look so crestfallen. "I'd like to move back here for a bit, if that's okay with you and Mom. At least until I figure out my next step."

Howard put his hand over Carrie's. "This is your home, sweetheart," he said. "It'll always be your home."

CHAPTER 11

Carrie glanced out the sidelight window at an unfamiliar car, a Zipcar rental, parked in the driveway. The Bryants hadn't had many visitors in the two weeks since Carrie had moved home. No one had rung the bell, so whoever it was must have come to see Adam.

Good. Carrie was still in her pajamas, and didn't feel like making small talk. Since she had gotten home, she'd done next to nothing except watch old movies with her dad. She wasn't feeling cute, clean, or the least bit congenial—hardly ready to face the outside world.

For all the recent tumult, coming home had been seamless. Adam had helped with the move, such as it was. The U-Haul truck she had rented was far too big for her few possessions. Everything Carrie owned—a futon, two bookcases, three boxes of books (mostly medical texts and some fiction), a flea market coffee table, a small color television and scuffed TV stand, some clothes, a few framed pictures, and a dresser—fit into a small corner of her parents' basement. It was depressing to realize her life's accumulations could take up so little space. For so long, her focus had been on nothing but medicine. Carrie wondered what could possibly take its place.

Carrie had settled in her old bedroom, but it was far from cozy or comforting. Limbic, Carrie's goldfish, swam unfazed in his large bowl, which rested atop the same blue dresser she'd had as a kid. It was still her childhood bedroom, even with all her old memorabilia boxed up, and the twin bed covered in the emerald green Tibetan quilt Carrie had bought on her travels to the Far East. Living here again was dispiriting, though better than living in Boston with her parents paying the rent.

Stress had triggered insomnia, which in turn triggered a new dependence on Ambien that left her perpetually exhausted. Her runs, if they could be called runs, were uninspired and dangerously close to being brisk walks. She was probably clinically depressed, but Carrie wasn't going to get help for it. She didn't deserve to feel better. Carrie's actions had substantially reduced Leon's quality of life. It was unclear whether his symptoms would improve over time. Carrie deserved to feel lousy.

Carrie's mother, Irene, a petite sixty-year-old woman, entered the foyer through the dining room, rubbing lotion on her hands. She was dressed in a blue denim shirt and khaki pants, the uniform of a passionate gardener.

"Who's here?" Carrie asked.

"A reporter from the *Lowell Observer*," Irene said. "Here's here to interview Adam for a story."

Carrie's eyes narrowed. "Adam?" Since his discharge from the WTC, Adam preferred solitude. Friends rarely came over. This guest was a surprise to her.

Irene said, "I got a call from Everett Barnes, the director of veteran outreach for the Home Base Program, asking to see if Adam would tell his story. I told him about it and I guess he agreed."

Carrie understood now.

Home Base had been set up by the Red Sox Foundation to give clinical care and support services to Iraq and Afghanistan service members, veterans, and their families all through New England. It dealt specifically with veterans and their families affected by stress or traumatic brain injuries sustained on deployment or in combat. Sadly, the organization could not grow fast enough.

"I'll go see how it's going," Irene said, pushing her bangs off her forehead and tucking a strand of dark, shoulder-length hair behind her ear. "Oh, and your father is in the kitchen. He wants to speak with you."

Carrie found her dad sitting at the kitchen table, sipping from a mug of steaming coffee. He drank his coffee no-frills; the whole family did. Was this learned or inherited?

Carrie poured herself a cup. "You wanted to speak with me?"

Howard's face tensed.

Carrie ignored a tic of anxiety and sat down, preparing herself for anything.

"I've been thinking about things," Howard began, choosing each word carefully. "And I think you've come too far to quit now."

Carrie folded her arms and looked away, her instinct for self-preservation kicking in. This felt like an ambush. She had made it abundantly clear that reconsideration was not an option. To be a great surgeon required great confidence, and Carrie would be a danger in the OR.

Still, this was her dad, and the soul of kindness. He deserved that she sit still and listen.

"You are a gifted neurosurgeon," he continued, "with only one more year to complete your residency. I know that you had your heart set on that fellowship at the Cleveland Clinic, and then who knows what? I don't want to say something trite like 'everybody makes mistakes,' but I honestly can't think of one successful person, especially not doctors, who hasn't gone through a personal hell of some sort or another. Sleepless nights. A crisis of confidence. Not one." He picked up his coffee cup again and took a long drink.

Carrie's voice caught, and came out a bit shaky. Contradicting her father had never come easily. "Dad, you don't know how badly Leon is hurt. Honestly, just the thought of operating makes me anxious. I was never this way before."

Howard nodded. His eyes brimmed with empathy. "I know," he said. "You've said that many times. But there's something I never told you that I think you should hear." He shifted in his chair. "When I was an intern, I accidentally overdosed a young man suffering from a seizure."

Carrie said nothing. In the silence, the revelation became its own uncomfortable presence.

"I gave him too much phenobarbital. I'll never forget it. He stopped breathing and his blood pressure collapsed. We had to call a code, and the poor guy almost died. Because of me. Because of my mistake. I saw him every day in the ICU for the next week, and each time I was racked with terrible, terrible guilt.

"Even today, I always double-check myself when I administer drugs," her father said. "Especially that drug."

Carrie could relate. The last she heard, Beth Stillwell had recovered and returned to work, but Leon had been transferred to a long-term nursing care facility. Not all of Leon's deficits were attributed to Carrie's mistake, but she'd owned all the guilt regardless.

"Unlike Leon, my patient was going to get entirely better before I made him worse," her father continued. "For weeks I couldn't sleep. Barely could eat. Thankfully he did recover, but I think you get my point. My mistake almost cost this man his life. But that's a part of the job. We're expected to be perfect, but no human being is infallible. Not you. Not me. Not Dr. Metcalf. Mistakes happen. But it's how we deal with the adversity that defines our character. You can make peace with this and find a way to move forward. I did. Now, I've a suggestion."

Carrie could guess where he was going with all this, but—it was too soon. Too soon. She could not pick up another scalpel. Not now, and despite what he said, maybe not ever.

"You're a grown woman, and these are ultimately your decisions. But I have some years and some perspective, so I ask only that you hear me out. A couple of weeks ago I went to a dinner on Parkinson's disease sponsored by a pharmaceutical company. I sat next to a man who was taking their drug, a patient. Turns out he had deep brain stimulation to help his treatment and now, with the combination of DBS and his meds, he's doing better. He was able to attend meetings like this one."

Carrie knew all about DBS, a surgical treatment involving the implantation of a brain pacemaker and wires that delivered electrical impulses to targeted areas of the brain. It was used to treat movement disorders such as Parkinson's, but researchers and clinicians were exploring other applications, including treatments for OCD, major depression, and chronic pain.

"This man was very pleased with his results," Howard said. "He talked at great length about his treatment at the VA under Dr. Alistair Finley, whom I know from way back when I did my internship. I haven't seen him since, but why don't you go talk with him? He's right in town. Use my name. We weren't especially close, but I'm sure he'd remember me."

"Thanks, Dad," Carrie said. "I'll give it some thought." She turned her coffee cup in her hands. "I'm not particularly interested in Parkinson's. I mean, that's not what we really do in neurosurgery."

Howard conceded with a nod. "I understand it may seem less glamorous. But maybe, given your . . . your reluctance to get back in the saddle, it could be just what the doctor ordered."

Carrie smiled. She was about to tease him about dads being doctors when the doorbell rang.

Howard got up to see who was there. A moment later, Carrie heard him exclaim, "Oh my gosh!"

Howard returned to the kitchen with a tall, lanky man who was bleeding profusely from the nose. The oily rag he was using to stanch the flow had smeared a good portion of his face with engine grease.

"Adam apparently took offense to something." Howard spoke without emotion. He'd long since realized it didn't help to get upset about his son's new hair-trigger temper. "Could you please get this gentleman some ice? I'm going to go look for your mother and my boy."

Carrie took the stranger by the arm and led him to a chair at the kitchen table. "Tilt your head back," she said once he was seated. He looked like a boxer ready to concede the fight.

"I'm David. I'm from the *Lowell Observer*." Between the rag and the injury, his voice was especially high and nasal.

Carrie got a clean roll of paper towel from the pantry, then filled a plastic bag with ice from the freezer. Applied to the bridge of the nose, the bag of ice reduced the swelling and the pressure, and the bleeding stopped after a minute or two.

"What the heck happened?"

David smiled sheepishly and shook his head. "It was my fault," he said. "Really. I'm to blame here, not Adam."

Carrie gave David a fresh paper towel and refilled his plastic bag with ice. She studied her patient. Probably around her age, he had attractively messy hair and a kind face. She suspected he was something of a charmer.

"Go on," Carrie said. "I'm all ears."

"I came here to interview Adam for a story I'm writing about PTSD, but your mother showed up and Adam had a change of heart. No longer wanted to talk."

Carrie grimaced. "You didn't take no for an answer, did you?"

David laughed, and Carrie thought the sound was warm and inviting. He was obviously embarrassed, but he had enough humility to see a little humor in it.

"No's not my style," he said. "I didn't think I was being pushy, but I don't back down so easily."

Carrie thought of her conversation with her dad. *Neither do I,* she realized.

CHAPTER 12

After prying his eyes open, Steve Abington could not make sense of what he saw. He knew this place intimately, but for the life of him could not figure out how he had returned. The last thing he remembered was—was what? Nothing came to mind. He felt as if he had been living in absolute darkness, the blackest infinity, until this very moment, until light flooded his eyes and he saw again the desolate farm field where it all began.

Abington tried to stand, but he felt weighed down. It took a moment to realize he was wearing an ILBE pack, one so fully packed he had to hunch over while getting to his feet.

He also held a rifle, an M4 rifle fitted with an M68 red-dot optic. Where had that come from? And what else did he have on? Cautiously, Abington reached up and felt the Kevlar of an advanced combat helmet. He wore a MultiCam pattern uniform, too. How did that get on him? Why was he here? He thought he was through with all this.

"Steve. Steve, can you hear me?"

Abington spun in a tight circle, but saw no one. The voice, one he did not recognize, came out of the ether. He circled once more, and this time noticed foxholes, several of them. Nearby stood a makeshift structure, like a tree stand but on the ground. It was covered in green camo netting, and he thought he remembered putting it together. It was a command operation center, which meant this place must be the security outpost for Forward Operating Base Darwin. Yes, of course it was. There was the tree line, a hundred meters out. Beyond those trees, the snowcapped Hindu Kush mountain range cut a jagged tear across an endless azure horizon. If he walked west about two klicks, Abington was sure he'd find the remote roadway his squad had been patrolling. The Taliban were setting IEDs along the MSR—main supply route—and his unit used that road to make a quick exit.

"Steve!"

That voice again. Bodiless. Everywhere and nowhere. Where was it coming from?

Lightning bolts erupted behind his eyes, making Abington's head throb. He trotted over to the nearest foxhole. The sunglasses tinted the world, but shielded his eyes against a steady wind's peppering of sand and dirt. Inside the spray of dust, thousands of chiggers and sand fleas took flight in search of soft targets.

"Steve."

The voice. Was it in his head? Had he gone crazy? Had he never actually left this godforsaken place?

"Hello!" Abington called. His voice had the grit of sandpaper, and his throat felt as dry as the ground. *So dry. So thirsty.* "Is anybody here?"

The wind swallowed Abington's words. He crouched and dug his hands into the hard earth. It felt real. He managed to rake up a small pile of dirt using the tips of his fingers. This was how he described the country to anyone who asked: dirt, piles of dirt, dirt everywhere you looked. The soil carried fungus that blew deep into blast wounds to fester and take away limbs that otherwise could have been saved. How was he back in this hellhole? Back guarding FOB Darwin. Had he ever even left?

Abington remembered. He remembered everything about living here, including his squad. But where was everybody?

His gaze fell back to the parched earth, and Abington saw a scorpion crawling by his feet. He crushed it beneath the heel of his well-worn military boot with a satisfying crunch. But what he really wanted to crush was the Taliban. A familiar burning hatred boiled up, warming Abington like Kentucky's best bourbon. There was no better feeling than sending coordinates up the satellite link and watching the ground evaporate where the hardware dropped.

This was a backward country: no real infrastructure. No proper roads. Nothing here except for dirt, and caves, and Taliban. The only thing the Taliban respected was battle. They trained their young children to kill, and in their downtime played polo with dead animals. Pure savagery. Neanderthals with guns.

Abington searched the horizon for any signs of life. This was a Tier 1 area, no civilians allowed. Any person with a full beard and loose-fitting robes could be legitimately engaged. But the landscape was as barren as the surface of Mars. He was alone. All alone.

"Do you see it, Steve? Do you see what's happening?"

Abington readied his rifle and trained the weapon in all directions. His eyes narrowed and he bared his teeth like cobra fangs. He could see nothing but dirt, trees, and the mountains in the distance.

"He must be seeing it," the voice said.

"I . . . I don't see it." Abington's voice came out as a whisper.

"It's there, Steve. You can see it. You can see everything."

Abington glanced at the foxholes and caught a flash of movement from inside one of them. Was it just his shadow? How could that be? The sun was in front of him. Could he have imagined it? Abington moved cautiously toward that foxhole, his weapon at the ready.

"Is anybody in there?" Abington called out. "Hello!"

Abington took another step forward, then another. He could see a shape now. The silhouette of a figure, but it shimmered like a mirage. Abington advanced a couple more feet.

From out of nowhere, a tracer whizzed above his head. In an instant the air erupted with the sounds of gunfire snapping all around him. Bursts from a Russian PKM machine gun crackled in Abington's ears, rattling his teeth. Bullets pocked the earth, and shattered rock sprayed in all directions. Abington heard a whistle above him, like a screech from a bird of prey, followed by a loud thud somewhere to his back. An ear-splitting boom came next, causing the ground to shake beneath his feet.

Abington turned and saw two billowing dust clouds no more than twenty yards away. This was Afghanistan. One moment all was quiet, and the next it was chaos.

From the foxhole somebody shouted. "RPGs! RPGs!"

Abington broke into a sprint. The foxhole was safety. As he neared, a different shadowy figure lurched up from another hole, and flashes exploded from his rifle. A second later several mortars landed close by and Abington heard shrapnel bounce off the heavy armor of some parked trucks. Wait, had those trucks been there before? Not now. Questions for another time.

Abington dove headfirst into the closest foxhole. He hit the hard ground and felt the breath leave his body. Shockwaves from gunfire and erupting mortar punctured the air and echoed across the bleak landscape. The foxhole had room for two, and the man Abington had joined returned fire with his M16.

"Steve! Start shooting! Unless you're hit, put that gun to use, *hombre!*"

Hombre. Only one person called him that. Abington squinted and his eyes strained. He could not see the man's face clearly, but he recognized the thin build and knew that reedy voice anywhere. PFC Rich Phillips—Roach—who, like the bug, couldn't seem to be killed. Eventually the man came into clear focus, and the specter with the M16 was his best friend, all right. The same guy whose guts Abington had stuffed back into his blown-open stomach right after an RPG struck their foxhole.

"Steve? What is it? What are you seeing?" The disembodied voice again.

"Look at his face," another voice said. "He's right there."

CHAPTER 13

Carrie could not shake the smile off her face. The occasional glint of sunlight slipping through a persistent cloud cover seemed intended just for her, and buoyed her spirits. Her footsteps on her walk to the VA parking lot came quick and purposeful.

She no longer felt directionless or adrift. After two hours with Dr. Alistair Finley, she could visualize some kind of future. It wasn't a fully realized vision, but a sprig of hope had sprung from her despair. Carrie could not help but think of the final line from *Casablanca,* which she had watched with her dad the previous night. *"Louie, I think this is the beginning of a beautiful friendship."*

It was funny that David Hoffman's bloody nose was partially responsible. His passion for his work, undaunted by a violent subject, had reminded her of herself.

I don't back down so easily.

She'd been in no mood to socialize, but after Carrie cleaned David up, it was easy to say yes to an invitation to have coffee later. She was under no illusions about his motives: He wanted information about Adam and their family for his story. But he'd made her laugh.

"I usually only have coffee with rocket scientists," he said. "I guess I could slum with a brain surgeon."

Adam never came back to make amends, leaving Howard and Irene to do the apologizing.

"Don't even mention it," David had said with a wave of his hand.

His battered nose would heal just fine. "If it's okay with Adam, maybe we can try again sometime. People need to know what's happened to our servicemen and -women. They need to see the war after the war."

For the rest of that night, Carrie thought only of her father's suggestion and David's persistence. She *had* come too far to quit. She called Dr. Finley's office at the VA the next morning.

To Carrie's surprise, Dr. Finley answered his own phone.

"My name is Carrie Bryant," she said. "My father, Howard, suggested I give you a call."

For whatever reason, Carrie felt at ease with Dr. Finley. His voice was intimate, with no discernable accent, and he spoke to her as a colleague. He remembered her father, and was interested in her background and experience.

"Can you come by the hospital this afternoon?" he asked.

Carrie hadn't expected that. It felt fast, but that was good. No chance to get cold feet. A few hours later, she was sitting in Dr. Finley's office anteroom, flipping through an issue of *People* magazine. Five minutes later, she was in front of Dr. Finley himself.

Unlike his fancy headshot on the VA Web site, Dr. Finley looked every bit the harried professor. His long hours showed in the silver that streaked his mop of wavy, light hair, and in his pale cheeks and burrowed eyes. He might have been intimidating, except for his cheerful expression and a slightly disheveled appearance.

Dr. Finley shook Carrie's hand firmly. "Please, come into my office. The executive suite," he said with a smile.

She wouldn't have called the attendings' offices at Community comfortable, but they seemed luxurious compared to the décor here. Two metal folding chairs faced an L-shaped desk that looked like a Walmart special. An overhead fluorescent light fixture gave off a persistent hum. The walls were bare, except for a couple of diplomas and the requisite pictures of the president and the secretary of Veterans Affairs. The VA reeked of institutionalism, like body odor. Still, the man seated at the desk had a warm and inviting smile.

Carrie gazed out a square window that overlooked the parking lot, focusing on an adjacent multistory brick building under construction. The building was covered in rusted scaffolding and tattered blue tarps, but Carrie could still see signage over the front entrance: VA HOSPITAL ANNEX. Most of the windows on the annex were boarded up, but some remained intact.

Dr. Finley noticed her looking. "That was supposed to be our gleaming new facilities," he said, a bit wistful. "But we've been caught up in a bit of a funding crunch, I'm sorry to say. Work stopped almost two years ago."

"The building has been vacant this whole time?"

"Unfortunately, yes," Dr. Finley said. "There were ambitious plans for hospital expansion, but most everything has been put on hold because of ongoing budget constraints. Perhaps one day the fortunes will change. But we're not here to discuss the fiscal woes of the VA."

"No, we're not," Carrie said, taking a seat on one of Dr. Finley's metal chairs. "My father sends his regards."

"He's a good man," Dr. Finley said of Carrie's father. "That was a great time. Great. Internship was without a doubt the hardest year of my life, but it was probably the best, too. I want you to know he's not the reason I invited you down here. Your call may have come at a fortuitous time for us both, and I'd like to know more about you."

For the next thirty minutes Carrie shared her experience, career plans, and ultimately the incident that had derailed her. Dr. Finley listened with rapt attention. His avuncular interest let Carrie tell him all the whys and wherefores without embarrassment.

"And so I resigned," she concluded. "I couldn't see how I could continue a surgical residency. But now that I've had a few weeks to think about it, I realize that doesn't mean I need to be finished with medicine."

Dr. Finley added some final notes to those he'd been keeping during Carrie's story.

"Well, let me tell you a little bit about our work here."

For several minutes, Dr. Finley detailed what sounded to Carrie like a typical neurological practice. The hospital had a fully staffed neurosurgical department with an accredited residency program. Together with Dr. Finley's neurology practice, they treated everything from brain tumors to migraines. But of all the work being done by the Department of Neurology and Neurosurgery at the VA, Dr. Finley was most excited about his deep brain stimulation program.

He talked at length and with great enthusiasm about how DBS uses a neurostimulator placed in the brain to deliver electrical impulses to targeted regions, and the great potential it has for treating a wide range of neurological conditions. Mostly he focused its application for treating movement disorders, and he made several references to the patient Carrie's father met during that sponsored dinner on Parkinson's disease. He hinted at other applications for DBS, but kept those allusions intentionally vague, she believed.

"Look, Carrie," Dr. Finley said after his impromptu lecture on DBS, "I can't offer you an actual residency position here. Our program is fully staffed—and besides, it's mid-year."

Carrie tried not to look deflated. In their brief conversation, her expectations had gone from zero to high.

"But I do think I may be in a position to help," Dr. Finley continued. "And I suspect what I have to offer would help renew your confidence."

"I'm interested," Carrie said.

"A stint with the VA would, in my opinion, increase your chances of getting back into a formal neurosurgery residency program next year, while teaching you an awful lot about brain diseases one normally doesn't deal with in the usual neurosurgery program."

If the residency positions were filled, what could he have in mind? "I could certainly do some research on depth electrode stimulation treatment for Parkinson's disease," Carrie said, anticipating what she assumed Dr. Finley would be able to offer, some sort of research position, nothing that involved actual patients. "It sounds like fascinating medicine."

Again Dr. Finley checked his notes. "I tell you what. Better than that, I've got clinic on Thursday morning, and some follow-up patients will be there. Could you come?"

"You want me to come on rounds with you?"

"If you'd be so inclined."

"I'm just curious," she said. "If there's no residency positions, why was the timing of my call fortuitous for us both? How are you in a position to help me?"

"Come to rounds on Thursday," Dr. Finley said. "I'll explain everything then."

CHAPTER 14

It felt like divine intervention to be going on rounds again. Carrie thrummed with excitement. A few days ago she had been listless on the couch, trolling Facebook and doing what her mother always advised against, comparing her insides to everybody's outsides. But today she was back in a hospital, about to visit with patients, and feeling both curiosity and confidence return.

Carrie had dressed professionally in a blue blouse and dark slacks, but felt a bit naked without a white coat. She reminded herself that she was here to observe, nothing more. So far.

Patience—first things first. Let's see what this DBS is all about.

Carrie introduced herself to the receptionist. A few minutes later, a nurse took her into the neurology clinic. The aromas and sounds were instantly familiar, and she felt like a shipwreck survivor spotting dry land.

Inside exam room eight, Carrie found Dr. Finley and an obviously married couple who appeared to be in their late sixties. The man seated on the examination table was heavyset, with a horseshoe head of hair, a weather-beaten face, and loose skin all around. Petite and well put together in a dress suitable for church, the woman kept her hands interlocked in front of her. Concern for her companion was etched on her face.

Dr. Finley's expression brightened on Carrie's arrival.

"Dr. Bryant," he said. "Let me introduce you. Donald and Nancy

McCall, this is Dr. Carrie Bryant. She's an accomplished neurosurgeon, visiting today to learn more about DBS."

The compliment boosted Carrie's morale considerably. She *was* an accomplished neurosurgeon. Giving up on her career would do nothing to erase the damage she had accidently inflicted on poor Leon. Every day she would try and make penance. Surgery was and always would be her true calling. In the same way Howard Bryant double-checked each injection of phenobarbital, Carrie would take special care with pre-surgery preparations.

Dr. Finley provided a brief patient history. Donald McCall had well-established Parkinson's disease (PD), and had undergone a deep brain stimulation treatment twelve weeks earlier. Carrie observed the parallel scars on Donald's scalp where cuts had been made to implant wires in his brain. A horizontal scar ran along the base of Donald's neck, and a vertical one on his chest marked the pulse generator's location. Those scars were harder to see. In time, they'd be nearly invisible. Carrie was amazed that so much technology could be so effectively concealed. Even a keen observer would have no idea Don McCall was one of the walking wired.

"This is Mr. McCall's eighth visit to us," said Dr. Finley. "We're just fine-tuning the electrical settings." He turned to Nancy. "Mrs. McCall, would you mind telling Dr. Bryant a little about the changes you've observed, before and after the implant?"

Nancy sparked to life. "At first I thought Don was just depressed," she said. "He stopped talking much, and when he spoke it was like there was no feeling, and his voice got soft." Her own voice softened, as if in sympathy. "I can't say he looked sad—more like he wasn't there. And he started to stare at me for long periods, which was odd and made me uncomfortable. He slowed down, too. It was all very gradual, at first.

"But then he started falling, and my Don had always been so balanced. He used to play ice hockey in an adult league, and now he was stooping when he walked. Then his hand started shaking. A doctor put him on some sort of antidepressant, but that didn't do anything. Don was only fifty-five, but he acted like a man in his eighties."

Carrie nodded. Nancy had her complete and undivided attention.

"It was no surprise when he lost his job at Home Depot," Nancy went on. "I saw that coming miles away. Finally, what—ten years ago now?— we started seeing another doctor, and he knew it was Parkinson's just like that." Nancy snapped her fingers. "He started Don on Sinemet and he got a lot better. But I'm sure you know the story. He started to get worse again, even after increasing his medication. He was taking it almost every hour, it seemed, trying a bunch of new stuff. It got very frustrating." Nancy reached out and caressed Don's shoulder, reminding Carrie of her parents. "Then he started developing these wild movements all over, his arms, legs, neck, and torso."

"Peak dose dyskinesia," Dr. Finley said.

Nancy said, "At other times he seemed almost frozen solid, and it got so you couldn't tell when one state would change to another. It was like a switch."

"On-off effect," Dr. Finley elaborated.

"We saw a bunch of neurologists, but no one could do anything new or different. Then Dr. Sawyer learned about Dr. Finley's program, and since Don is a vet—two tours in Vietnam—he thought Don might be a good candidate for the deep brain stimulation." Nancy exhaled a protracted sigh. "I felt like I was Don's nurse for thirty hours a day."

Don sat on the table, his expression vacant.

"Don, I'd like Dr. Bryant to examine you briefly, if that's okay," Dr. Finley said. "Don's machine is off, and we asked him to hold his medication this morning."

Don nodded, his stare still blank. He'd been poked and prodded by plenty of strangers before. Carrie would just be the latest.

Carrie slipped back into the role of caregiver without missing a step. It really was like getting back on a bicycle, even after an ugly fall.

Don had textbook PD, she thought. Pill-rolling rest tremor of right upper limb, dystonic turned-in posturing of the right foot.

Don gazed unblinking out the window and showed little expression. It was easy to empathize with Nancy. The poor woman had to care for a ghost of her husband. Carrie asked Don a few simple questions—his name, birthday, and home address. His voice came out soft and stuttered, barely intelligible.

Carrie helped him down from the exam table and tested his mobility. He followed her movement instructions with all the grace and fluidity of the Tin Man: classic cogwheel rigidity in all limbs. Positive glabellar tap response, classic flexed posture of the trunk. The Parkinsonian shuffle was on full display as he attempted to walk, and it was no surprise when he froze midway while turning to his left.

Carrie recounted all that she had observed, and Dr. Finley looked pleased.

"A lot of neurosurgical residents who rotate through my program don't seem to know a thing about movement disorders or show that they can conduct a decent neuro exam," he said. "You're already two steps ahead."

From a nearby countertop Dr. Finley retrieved a compact device, approximately the size of a deck of cards. It had a plastic case, several buttons, and a small display screen.

"This programming unit will help us fine-tune Don's stimulation settings," Dr. Finley said. "It uses radio communication to adjust the stimulus parameters of the surgically implanted unit. Last time we set the frequency at one hundred and forty cycles per second, and the pulse width at eighty milliseconds. Today, we're going to increase the voltage amplitude just a bit, to two and a half."

Dr. Finley peeled away the paper covers over the sticky pads on the back of a plastic dock and adhered the unit over the scar on Don's chest. He snapped the programming device into place on the dock, then spent some time making sure the programming unit worked properly. When he was satisfied, he said, "I'll be back in a while to take another look at you, Don, and we'll see how you're doing 'plugged in,' as they say. And then we'll put you back on your medication and see how the whole package is working.

"As you know, Nancy, this is going to take some time," he added. "I'll be here checking on other folks for a while. Why don't you get yourself some coffee?" He turned to Carrie. "My job is to make sure the patients receive the proper dosage of medicine and stimulation. It would be up to you to get those wires precisely where they need to be. And believe me, Dr. Bryant, this is no simple feat."

Up to you. Did he mean it? Could she work here?

THE VA'S cafeteria, even down to the food, was about what Carrie had expected. "Institutional" was apparently a flavor, as well as a design aesthetic. Still, so far, she was enjoying every minute of her time with Dr. Finley. They had looked in on several more patients, and Dr. Finley suggested they take a coffee break before concluding with Don McCall.

"So, what did you think?" he asked once they were seated.

"Well, the management of movement disorders is far more nuanced than I appreciated," Carrie said. "It's interesting, and really necessary work."

Dr. Finley looked pleased. "Let me be very candid with you, Carrie," he said. "I've checked your references, and I know even more about the incident we discussed in my office. Believe me, everyone at Community and White is heartsick over what happened. They really like you, and I know you saved a woman's life the night before. I've got to tell you, Metcalf is still pissed—but he's all massive ego anyway."

Carrie shrank at the mention of Metcalf's name. "I hope you didn't ask him for a reference."

Dr. Finley laughed. "I don't think you'll ever get back into his good graces. But I don't need his commendation to know talent when I see it."

"I'm really glad to hear that, but I guess I'm a bit confused," Carrie said.

"Why is that?"

"When we met in your office you said there were no residency openings available, but you also said my timing was fortuitous. Can you explain that now?"

A shadow crossed Dr. Finley's face. He spent a moment stirring the cream in his coffee. When he looked up, his eyes showed strain and more than a hint of sadness.

"A few weeks ago our DBS surgeon, Sam Rockwell, was in a terrible, terrible car accident coming back from his vacation home in Maine. I saw the photos. His car crumpled like a tin can. His condition is too tenuous to MedFlight him to White Memorial, so his family has been keeping vigil at his bedside in a Bangor hospital. He's in a drug-induced coma with multi-organ failure and sepsis. There's a good chance he won't make it. It's a definite blow to our program."

"That's horrible," Carrie said, feeling a stab of sadness for Dr. Finley and for Rockwell's family.

"Sam and I were extremely close, and I'm—I'm just devastated. Anyway, there's no way Sam is coming back here any time soon, and we need someone to take over his responsibilities. I know you would be an excellent replacement. There is some time sensitivity to this offer. I'm afraid we may lose funding for a very special initiative if we don't get someone into the role posthaste, but I can't take just anybody. And, as you know, most of the qualified candidates are currently employed. We can't wait for them to become available to us."

Carrie nodded grimly. "I see now why you said my call was fortuitous." Medicine was a Darwinian world. One doc's misfortune was another doc's golden opportunity. Still, it felt ugly to profit from tragedy.

"Listen, Carrie, I know this seems wrong, given Sam's unfortunate circumstance, but a person with your considerable skill and talent would be a huge asset to us. You'd be able to jump right in without missing a beat. I've got the funds, and while this would not be a formal residency, it might help you get your groove back, so to speak. The surgical schedule is not too demanding, not at all like what you're used to. We try to limit the surgeries to one or two per week. There simply isn't a large staff to conduct proper patient evaluations and handle follow-up care."

"That's a wonderful offer," Carrie began, but Finley stopped her.

"But here are the restrictions," he said. "You're my hire. You work for me on this, not the VA. I'd be able to pay you out of the DARPA funds, and that includes benefits. Those funds give me a tremendous degree of clout with the VA's leadership team, including the acting medical director. You won't be part of the residency program, but that's no issue. I know you're a good surgeon, and your reputation precedes you. I know what you did for Beth Stillwell, and I thought it was remarkable. I truly believe you'd make an incredible addition to our team."

"How do I get credentialed?" she asked. "It's going to take so long to get on board here."

Dr. Finley showed no concern. "Carrie, you have a medical license. You got that when you graduated medical school. Your residency is for training, but legally, if you wanted to go out and start a practice, you could have done that. Some people need five years of residency to get where they need to be, some get it after three, but my inquiries have persuaded me that you got it after one or two. You've got enough talent, enough training to do this job. Even though I run the neurology residency at the VA, I'm hiring you under private funding for this program. It's a very unusual opportunity, and you'll be able to use this experience to enhance your credentials if you wish to get back to formal residency—though my hope is that you'll stay with my special initiative for years to come."

"And what exactly is the special initiative?"

An inscrutable look came to Dr. Finley's face, then it morphed into a grin.

"Come with me," he said.

Carrie followed Dr. Finley back to Don McCall's hospital room, where Nancy McCall greeted them with a bright smile.

"Already much improved," Nancy said.

"Have a look for yourself," Dr. Finley said to Carrie.

Right away, Carrie noticed the rest tremor was significantly decreased.

"How are you feeling, Don?" Carrie asked as she checked the mobility of his limbs. It was not enough to get him back on the ice, but the degree of movement made Carrie think somebody had replaced one Don with another.

"I'm feeling much better, Doc," Don said.

The stutter was gone and his voice was strong and intelligible.

After her brief exam concluded, Carrie followed Dr. Finley back into the hallway.

"Impressive, isn't it?" Dr. Finley said.

"Yes, very much so," Carrie said. "But treating Parkinson's with DBS isn't all that new, at least not according to my research. So I'm still curious about that special initiative you mentioned."

"What if I told you that we could use DBS to cure PTSD—not treat it, but cure it?"

Adam came to Carrie's mind with a flash of wonder. How was it possible? Could it be possible?

"If that were true, Dr. Finley," Carrie said, "I'd say you had yourself a brand-new DBS surgeon."

CHAPTER 15

On Wednesday afternoon, a week after her coffee with Dr. Finley, Carrie followed a crowd of doctors into the cramped VA hospital auditorium for the monthly grand rounds conference, which was usually a welcome break from the grind. This gathering hummed with extra excitement because Dr. Finley was expected to make a big announcement regarding the deep brain stimulation program. The room was packed with neurosurgery, neurology, and psychiatry attending and resident physicians, as well as a number of other parties who were interested in hearing what Dr. Alistair Finley had to say about DBS. Dr. Finley, who'd been working at this VA for years, was considered a pioneer in applying the technique to a variety of brain and mental disorders. Perhaps that was why this GR was so well attended.

Or maybe it was the free pizza.

Carrie settled into one of the cushioned seats in the second row, where she had a good view of the rather small screen used for the PowerPoint projection. Most everyone was dressed in scrubs and white coats, except for two men Carrie had noticed in the back of the hall. One was bald, with close-set eyes and a round face. The other had a square head, broad shoulders, and a football player's neck. His stone-hard gaze held all the joy of a funeral, and Carrie got a shiver when they briefly locked eyes.

For the past week Carrie had been obsessively studying the software that did most of the heavy lifting in the OR. When it came to DBS

procedures, precision, surgical skill, and patience were the chief operational skills required, and she would have to work as part of a team.
It was painstaking, complicated work; a typical procedure could last
five to six hours. That explained why nobody was available to assume
Sam Rockwell's responsibilities.

The entire Department of Neurology and Neurosurgery at the VA
consisted of only three full-time physicians. Three! It was microscopic
even by BCH standards. Dr. Finley was the staff neurologist, and
Dr. Sandra Goodwin and Dr. Evan Navarro comprised the surgical
team. Dr. Goodwin, a severe-looking woman in her late fifties with a
broad forehead and aquiline nose, was the head of the neurosurgery
department and therefore perpetually bogged down with administrative work. As a result, most of the actual surgical responsibilities fell
to the staff attending, Dr. Navarro.

Dr. Navarro, a thin man with a small face, dark hair, and ferret eyes,
was also in charge of the residents who rotated through the VA from
satellite hospitals, much as Carrie had done at Community. Carrie and
Navarro had not quite hit it off. She found him cold and disinterested—a
typical ego on legs. Goodwin was more affable, but harried by the
constant demands on her time. The good news was that Carrie's involvement with Navarro would be limited. For the DBS program to
flourish, Finley needed the dedication of one committed, exclusive neurosurgeon. That role would be Carrie's, her sole responsibility.

At five minutes past the hour Dr. Finley strode to the lectern and
slipped on his half-moon reading glasses. His hair was tousled as usual,
but with his starched long white lab coat, crisply pressed white shirt, and
classic repp tie, he shone with authority. The attendees, largely sleep-
deprived residents, made the effort to stop eating and pay attention.

"Show the video first, please," Dr. Finley called.

Carrie noticed a resident to her right spontaneously close his eyes with
the dimming of the lights. The rigors of a residency program were uni-
versally brutal, and Carrie understood his fatigue. She hoped none of

the VA residents would ever have to endure the nightmare she and, more importantly, Leon Dixon had suffered because of her own exhaustion.

"This gentleman, we'll call him Patient X . . ." With the start of Dr. Finley's lecture, Carrie cleared her troubled thoughts and focused on her new boss's narration.

"Patient X developed signs of Parkinson's disease in his early forties. He had been exposed to Agent Orange while in Vietnam in his late teens."

The video was a series of home movies. A life well lived, but as the film soon revealed, one quickly diminished by the ravages of disease. The symptoms were a mirror of Don McCall's ailment. The footage went on to show the crippling nature of PD—frozen movement, violent tremors, spastic limbs. Dr. Finley reviewed the anatomy of the basal ganglia and its interconnections, structures deep in the brain that were affected in Parkinson's disease. Then he began to discuss the DBS treatments.

"We first stimulated the right ventral lateral nucleus of the thalamus. That benefitted his left arm tremor, but not much more. That electrode has been removed, and six months ago we placed electrodes bilaterally in the globus pallidus interna. This next video shows his current status."

The audience, impartial before, was captivated by Patient X's freedom of movement. Had Carrie not witnessed Don McCall's dramatic improvement for herself, she would have had a hard time believing the footage.

"Deep brain stimulation is a form of stereotactic neurosurgery," Dr. Finley continued. "We insert electrodes guided by a stereotactic frame, as well as CT and MRI imaging, deep into brain nuclear complexes that are involved in complex movement patterns. Lights, please."

As the lights came on, some in the audience began rubbing their eyes. Dr. Finley removed his glasses. "The value of DBS has been proven in

Parkinson's disease. But what's particularly exciting for us at the VA is that we're exploring the use of DBS as a new chapter in psychosurgery. We believe we are at the vanguard of hope in treating conditions that have defied the most comprehensive drug and counseling programs."

Dr. Finley smiled. Everyone was there to find out about the planned DBS program expansion. Sam Rockwell had done a number of procedures, but the pilot program had been operating in stealth mode.

Dr. Finley said, "As many of you are well aware, here at the VA, both outpatient and inpatient psychiatry have become overwhelmed by the number of PTSD cases."

For several minutes Dr. Finley presented a sobering array of statistics. "One-third of veterans from the wars in Iraq and Afghanistan have contemplated suicide." When he compared this to the 3.7 percent of the general adult population who had serious thoughts of suicide, the military stat looked stark. He coupled these statistics with the numbers of actual military suicides: "Twenty-two per day by current estimates, which also far outpaces the rate from fifteen years ago," Finley said.

"Long-term mental health care is perceived by many to be detrimental to military career advancement. Misguided as that is, it remains a fact. Close to fifty percent of servicemen and -women suffering from PTSD will not seek treatment because of this stigma or—and I say this knowing who pays my salary—the challenges of navigating the VA's antiquated bureaucracy."

Dr. Finley paused until the chuckles died down.

"An operation, I believe, would be far more attractive to those afflicted, and thus would dramatically increase the numbers of those willing to be treated."

Dr. Finley fell silent to allow the notion to sink in.

"It has been reported that the economic impact of PTSD, limited to just the military, is anywhere between four to six *billion* dollars. And this does not take into account the spouses and children whose lives are further traumatized. I would argue that four billion grossly under-estimates the economic toll."

Of course Carrie thought of Adam: his lost wages and diminished potential, coupled with the burden on her parents emotionally, financially, and in scaled-back career plans for themselves. Her family was just a tiny fraction of that billion-dollar crisis.

Dr. Finley showed a schematic of the limbic system, a complex network of structures ringing the ventricular system deep in the brain. Its functions were many, including regulation of emotion and basic drives and motivation. It also regulated the initial processing and emotional aspects of memories, and the body's response to stress including blood pressure, pulse, and respiratory rate, as well as sleep patterns. Tiny as it was, the almond-shaped amygdala nucleus, located deep and medially in the temporal lobe, was accountable for a whole host of critical functions.

"We believe the basolateral nucleus of the amygdala represents the most promising target for DBS in treating PTSD. Here is where fear and its memory converge."

Dr. Finley advanced the slide. The amygdala was now circled in red.

"This is the epicenter—where our primitive fight or flight reactions form in response to a threat, where unchecked rage can be unleashed in response to a disturbing memory. Regardless of how much we try to alleviate these terrible memories through therapy or pharmaceuticals, we know that PTSD symptoms are structurally imbedded, literally imprinted, in the brain. And we believe this processing involves the amygdala nucleus significantly."

Dr. Finley came out from behind the lectern. He made eye contact with Carrie, and she smiled.

"We have realized something that you may find counterintuitive. Traditionally the goal of treatment has been focused on the mitigation of disturbing thoughts and memories, analogous to the way we treat many phobias. Think of the man who is afraid of heights, for example. We may subject him to systematic desensitization by gradually introducing him to higher heights. And indeed, such treatment is often effective, at least partially, for phobias, but war zone trauma is something else entirely.

"We are discovering in controlled laboratory experiments that electroshock therapy administered to animals in close proximity to a traumatic event greatly suppresses those animals' behavioral response when immediately re-exposed to the trauma. In other words, they seem to have forgotten their emotional response to the initial trauma."

Dr. Finley went on to discuss a group of human test subjects who were involved in a different memory experiment involving electroshock therapy, more commonly known as ECT. These patients were first shown images of terribly unpleasant events and asked to recall them. Surprisingly, the researchers found that the patients were not able to remember any details of the disturbing event the day following their ECT, even though they had been told explicitly to remember the event in as much detail as possible. The shock treatment seemed to interfere with storing a new memory in the brain. The researchers concluded that there was a period of time when stored memories were accessed, in which they could be vulnerable to manipulation. They could be modified, changed in some way, reconfigured or "reconsolidated."

Dr. Finley continued, "We know the intense connections of memory tied to emotions sends the amygdala into overdrive in PTSD. If we can dampen that hyperactivity in the amygdala, all the social and psychological consequences we see in PTSD—the nightmares, depression and apathy, anxiety and fear, the likely drift into drug and alcohol abuse, the emotional roller coaster, potential flashes of aggression—all this can potentially be negated."

Dr. Finley went on to present a series of slides referring more specifically to the anatomy of the amygdala and its connections to other limbic structures.

"Our goal is not to erase the memory per se, but to erase the emotion associated with the memory. Let me repeat: The goal of our DBS program is emotional erasure. To do this, we first need to reproduce the soldier's trauma, as vividly as possible. And just then, after the memory has been reproduced, we suppress the amygdala by deep brain stimulation of the amygdala's basolateral nucleus, interrupting its emotional and physiological connections to that memory, and in so doing, reconsolidate the memory without the emotional context."

A hand shot up from one of the psychiatric social workers seated directly behind Carrie.

"How would you do that? How do you plan to re-create these memories so vividly?"

Dr. Finley's expression brightened as if this question had been planted and anticipated.

"Glad you asked, Wanda. Today I am officially announcing a very exciting pilot program, initiated with the assistance of DARPA."

Dr. Finley's gaze traveled to the back of the room, where the two men in suits were seated. Carrie guessed they were from the government.

"By a show of hands, how many of you have heard of DARPA?"

Fewer than half the hands in the room went up. One person felt a need to clarify. "The initials, yes, but I'm not sure what it stands for."

Dr. Finley gave a slight nod. "It stands for Defense Advanced Research Projects Agency. Their mission is to create breakthrough technologies for national security. They're the folks who gave us the Internet—sorry, Al Gore."

The reference inspired scattered laughter.

Dr. Finley continued. "PTSD is approaching epidemic levels in the military, so DARPA has been experimenting with exposure therapy using virtual reality simulations."

Carrie felt a jolt. DARPA was remaking the war in pixels.

"We can re-create that IED event when a soldier's buddies were killed or maimed." Dr. Finley spoke to a hushed audience. "And while the brain is forcibly agitated, we have an opportunity to treat that individual with deep brain stimulation with the hope that we will actually erase the emotion associated with those terrible memories forever. I'm not talking suppressed. I'm talking *gone,* forever. Ladies and gentlemen, I am pleased to see Calvin Trent from DARPA has joined us today. Cal, could you please stand up?"

Cal, the man with Atlas shoulders and cold eyes, glanced briefly at his companion and stood up slowly. He acknowledged the audience, then sat right back down. Dr. Finley either did not recognize or did not know the other suit that had accompanied Cal Trent. Either way, the bald guy with a round face and beady eyes got no introduction.

Dr. Finley said, "Cal oversees all aspects of the program, including the virtual reality simulation, which is used prior to the DBS surgery to reconsolidate the negative memory. The virtual reality does leave many patients highly agitated, but that's a temporary state. We need the emotion heightened, the negative memory fresh, as close to surgery as possible. Once the electrical stimulation commences, the emotion gets dampened. It's as simple as that. Cal's pulled together an amazing team of people to run this program, and I know you'll extend him your every courtesy."

Carrie could sense excitement building in the audience. Just about everyone there had had some contact with a returning soldier who was devastated by PTSD, or his or her family. She thought again, always, of Adam.

It had been eye-opening to live with her brother, and see the difficulties he and her parents had been enduring. Sometimes his nightmares were so savage it sounded like he was being murdered. She saw how Adam avoided going out, especially into crowds. Even walks in the woods behind the house were an ordeal. Everywhere he went, he was scouring the ground for IEDs. At least he had started going running with her—well, more like she followed Adam as he sprinted. Poor kid could easily outrun her, but not his demons.

The hope she saw in Dr. Finley's eyes, the enthusiasm in his words, buoyed Carrie's commitment. Dr. Finley had told her about the program after she had accepted the position, but seeing everyone else respond with excitement reinforced her own enthusiasm. She was proud to be on the cutting edge of such critical care. Funny that she'd named her goldfish Limbic, the system the amygdala resided in.

Was fate at work here?

CHAPTER 16

The operating room was Carrie's amphitheater, and she was the violinist about to dazzle. She was back in uniform: green scrubs underneath a white lab coat. Soon she would enter the preoperative holding area to visit a patient, her first at the VA. His would be the first burr holes she would drill in almost two months.

Jealousy from the other resident physicians had been an initial worry. Other residents had competed for their positions, while Carrie had been handed what many would perceive as a post-resident fellowship, working directly with one attending on a single project, without the onerous responsibilities of taking call or being responsible for patient care. It was a plum assignment for sure, but Dr. Finley made it clear to everyone that Carrie would not receive credit toward her residency requirements. No, this was a different trial for her. Would she perform to her ability?

While the DBS procedure she would perform would be relatively simple and straightforward, it was by no means free of complications. Opening the brain involved significant, life-threatening risks, every time. Still, implanting wires was not like sucking out blood clots deep in an already swollen brain where the surgeon had to be both swift and meticulous. DBS required a tremendous amount of patience and an OCD-like attention to detail. Carrie took a few calming breaths. She ought to wait for Dr. Kauffman, the anesthesiologist, but felt she could handle the preoperative consultation just fine.

Five minutes later Carrie entered the preoperative holding area, where she was struck by the sight of a man who could have been her brother's twin. Seated on a beige armchair, reclined ever so slightly, the man looked like Adam not before the war, but after. He had Adam's strong jaw and sharp-featured face, but his shaved head called attention to his concave cheeks, and he appeared frail and skeletal. His arms were spotted with ugly purple bruises that spiraled outward like mini nebulas. But it was the eyes that truly alarmed her. They looked hollow, a stare that seemed to stretch out into space.

Carrie was not sure what to expect from patients after they'd been subjected to the virtual reality therapy, but it certainly was not this. Her patient had the dazed look of a car accident victim. She knew he would be sedated, but it was tough to see his suffering. Carrie usually treated the sorts of injuries and ailments that appeared on an MRI. This man's wounds were just as significant, even if they couldn't be imaged.

She checked her chart. She knew the soldier's name, but wanted to double-check to make sure she got it right. Her father's lesson on the importance of details had taken root.

Abington. Staff Sergeant Steve Abington.

Carrie helped Abington out of the chair and onto the exam table, positioned kitty-corner in one end of the room near a counter with a built-in sink. Above the sink was a steel medical supply cabinet affixed to the wall. At first Carrie thought Abington was too thin, but once he was standing she could see he was rippled with muscle. He had the minimal body fat of an athlete.

"How are you doing today, Steve?"

No response.

Abington had fixed his gaze on the framed print of the Boston Common on the wall before him, but he seemed to be looking through it, not at it. Carrie was close enough to smell detergent and cleanser; he smelled institutionally clean. She checked her chart again. No address listed. No emergency contacts. He could have been homeless, and now in the care of the VA system. What did they use for soap where he lived?

"I'm the surgeon who is going to perform your DBS procedure today. I wanted to meet you before the operation in case you had any questions for me. Do you have any questions, Steve?"

Abington turned his head slowly, dreamlike, as through pushing through molasses. His mouth began to twitch, perhaps to form a word. But all that came out was a guttural noise like the clearing of a throat.

Carrie knew that the DBS had to be done within a window of opportunity immediately following the virtual reality simulation, when the negative memory was most fresh in the mind. She did not know exactly where DARPA conducted the simulations, or who had escorted Abington to the exam room, or where that person had gone. Those questions were well outside her area of responsibility.

"There are lots of bruises on your arms, Steve. Can you tell me how you got them?"

Abington shifted his gaze to one of his battered arms. He lifted the limb slowly, like a marionette whose string was pulled, and studied the arm with detached, vague curiosity. Then his face slipped back into that dead-eyed gaze.

Carrie moved to check his vitals, and he did not resist. Blood pressure: 90/60. Perfectly normal. His temperature was 98.6 degrees, and his reflexes were normal. Heart rate was also in normal range for a resting adult. She put a penlight up to his eyes—five-millimeter pupils, a bit dilated but equal, and briskly reactive to the flashlight. *Good.* All the consent forms had been signed. There was no reason not to proceed with the surgery.

"Steve, do you understand what's going to happen? You're scheduled for a very important operation."

Once again, Abington's mouth began to twitch with words he could not quite form. Then, surprisingly, he started to move his body, bouncing where he sat like an anxious child, and massaging the bruises on his arms. To Carrie it looked as though his drained battery had some-how sparked back to life.

"You don't know—you don't know," Abington mumbled. He peri-odically stopped rubbing to run his fingers over his newly shaved pate.

"What don't I know?" Carrie asked.

"I don't belong here."

"I know you're scared, Steve. But we're here to help."

Abington shook that off. "It's not all right. I don't belong here." His voice rose in pitch and volume. "You don't know."

"Steve, take it easy."

Abington went still. His arms dropped to his lap.

Carrie let out a relieved breath, wishing that she'd waited for Dr. Finley or Dr. Kauffman before starting the consultation. Dr. Finley had warned her that patients could be highly agitated pre-op. They were fragile following the virtual reality treatment.

"Steve, let me explain what—"

Abington reached out and seized her by the throat, pressing on her windpipe. Shocked, Carrie started to panic, her eyes bugging out, able to take only tiny gasps of air. She reeled backward, pulling Abington off the exam table. As he dropped to the floor, Abington let go of her throat, so Carrie whirled around and sprang for the door. But Abington charged her. With speed that belied his earlier torpor, he snatched the back of Carrie's flapping lab coat just as she was within reach of the door handle. He pulled her toward him and she fell back into his arms, then he spun Carrie around to face him.

His mouth formed a fearsome snarl—from lifeless to rabid in a mat-ter of moments. His sedative must have worn off, revealing murder in his eyes.

"I don't belong here," he hissed in her face. "Got to get out!"

His back was to the door she had closed for their interview, and hers was to the counter and medicine cabinet. Carrie wriggled free from Abington's grasp.

"Somebody please help me!" Carrie yelled, though it was doubtful anyone would hear her. The walls were made of thick concrete, and the nurses' station was located way down the hall. Carrie flashed on an idea and turned her back to Abington to focus on the locked supply cabinet.

"Help!" Carrie cried out again. "Somebody help!"

From behind, Carrie heard Abington gibber unintelligibly. Carrie fumbled in her pocket for the keys. Did she dare risk turning her head? She could not resist. Abington paced in front of the door like a caged animal. He took a step toward Carrie and said, "I'm not here. I don't belong here."

He could have left the room, but he wanted something else. He wanted her. Carrie retrieved the keys, but her hands shook so violently it could be impossible to work the lock. *Which key opens the damn cabinet, anyway?*

Carrie fumbled with the keys some more. There were too many attached to the ring. She heard Abington take another step toward her. One. Single. Step. Carrie's throat ached where he had grabbed her. The soldier's labored breaths seemed to come from every corner of the room.

Carrie located a small key among the jumble on her ring and tried to jam it into the lock. No good. Wrong fit. She searched for another. The cabinet was made of metal; otherwise she would have broken the glass.

"Help!" Carrie yelled.

There was another small key on the ring. But was it the same one she had just tried?

Abington muttered, "Listen to me. I don't belong here." Carrie jammed the second key into the lock, and this time it fit. The lock turned easily and Carrie ripped open the door. Mixed in with a number of medical supplies she found various vials of medication and several wrapped syringes.

"I don't belong here," Abington said from someplace behind her.

Carrie fumbled through many vials of medicine, until she found the Valium. She held the Valium in one hand, and used her teeth to rip open a syringe package. Carrie kept her back to Abington as she worked to get the syringe inserted into the top of the vial.

"Steve, it's okay. You're going to be okay. Please believe me. I'm going to give you a shot to calm you down."

Carrie filled the syringe just as Abington charged and struck her in the back. His momentum slammed Carrie against the lip of the counter hard enough to take away her breath. Abington wrapped his arms around her waist and together they tumbled to the floor. Carrie held on to the syringe with her life. She twisted underneath him, intending to claw at his face. But Abington flipped her onto her back and dug his knees into her ribs hard enough she feared he'd snap her sternum.

Once again Abington took hold of Carrie's throat, but this time he did not squeeze. "Where's Smokes? Hunter. Is Hunter here? What about Roach?" His voice was plaintive. "Roach!"

Carrie forced herself to stop struggling.

Just don't squeeze . . . please don't squeeze.

Years of surgery gave Carrie tremendous hand dexterity. She was able to position the syringe for an effective strike without drawing Abington's attention.

"Please, Steve, I'm not here to hurt you."

"That you, Roach?" Abington said. "You got to get me out of here. I don't belong."

Abington tightened his grip around Carrie's throat like a python readying to squeeze. She had one chance. One. It was hard to hit under normal circumstances. But induction time was everything. The drug needed to work and work fast. Abington squeezed some more. Carrie could still get air into her lungs, but it was barely a breath. Gurgling noises bubbled up from her throat, from all the saliva that had no place to go.

One chance . . . one . . .

Abington's jugular vein pulsed like a thick blue target. Carrie swung her arm in a wide arc. Abington leaned away from the strike and his body position shifted. Instead of hitting his neck, Carrie slammed the needle into Abington's shoulder, right into the muscle. It would delay induction, but she depressed the plunger anyway.

Carrie tried to speak, but no words came out. She left the syringe dangling in Abington's arm and used her fingers to try and pry Abington's hands free. Abington acted unfazed. He pressed harder on Carrie's throat. The loss of oxygen started to get to her, and she couldn't control her panic. She kicked and bucked wildly, but could not toss him. Her legs began to spasm and her eyes watered.

This isn't how I'm supposed to die. . . .

Gripped by panic, Carrie thrashed beneath Abington, kicking over a metal stool that clattered noisily to the floor, but it was no use. He would not let go. She felt herself slip into unconsciousness. Her body became heavy, Novocain for blood. Carrie closed her eyes. She did not want the last thing she'd see to be the face of her murderer.

And then she was filled with a sense of profound peace, of weightlessness. She felt her fear fall away as the darkness grew deeper and darker.

In the very next moment Carrie could breathe again, and the room went from dark to bright. The feeling of weightlessness slipped away as she blinked her eyes open. Dr. Finley knelt beside her. He looked as worried as her father might.

"Carrie, are you okay? Can you hear me?"

Through her blurred vision, Carrie saw Dr. Kauffman and a sizable orderly restraining Abington.

CHAPTER 17

David Hoffman carried two drinks over to the table where Adam Bryant sat waiting. The young veteran had called unexpectedly and invited him to coffee in Hopkinton, so David, worried that Adam could easily return to his shell, canceled his plans with Gabby and Emma. David didn't like to disappoint Gabby, but he'd bring her to the children's museum some other day.

"You take it black, right?" David said, setting down a steaming mug.

Adam took a sip in response.

"Usually, I drink tea these days, the chosen beverage of the Afghan people, but for whatever reason I'm in the mood for a good cup of joe."

David had shown up fifteen minutes early and found Adam already there, his jean jacket and faded T-shirt fitting the coffee shop's bohemian vibe. Adam's darting eyes and alert posture told David he'd chosen their seats deliberately, with the best sight lines and quick access to the exit. Adam's training and caution had kept him alive during the war. His body might be thousands of miles from Afghan soil, but certain instincts remained.

David settled in his comfy chair with his espresso. Compared to the stuff they served in the Middle East, this coffee tasted like water.

He'd thought he had a shot at a Reuters job that would send him to Saudi Arabia, but evidently his reputation still preceded him. David knew he would get back in those good graces eventually, so the setback was not overly discouraging. Besides, his story on PTSD was too important to rush. He wanted to tell it right, and Adam's perspective would help.

"I'm glad you called," David said. "I didn't think you would."

"Yeah," Adam replied. "I wasn't sure myself. Figured the least I owed you was an apology."

"You don't owe me anything, Adam. I just want to get your story out there. If you're willing to share."

Adam inspected David's face. "Nose looks pretty good," he said. "Look, I'm really sorry I lost my cool."

"I was pushy. I asked for it."

Adam didn't disagree.

"Do you mind if I take notes?" David asked.

"No, man, you gotta get it right."

David took out his pad and pen. "So how do you want to begin?"

"I'm not sure. Hard to say what got me all screwed up."

"You mean there wasn't a specific incident?"

The corners of Adam's mouth ticked up a couple degrees into the hint of a smile. "It was *all* a specific incident, man."

"Start wherever you'd like, whatever feels natural." David acted as if they had all the time in the world.

If Adam had been privy to the terse conversation David had had with Anneke on his drive to Hopkinton, he would know that was not the case. She continued to hound David for the story, and he continued to come up with appropriate delay tactics. So far he had interviewed the two other vets he'd mentioned to Anneke, spoken with an administrator at Walter Reed, networked with a retired brigadier general, and read several books on PTSD that covered everything from science to sociology. The books were enlightening, but they could not adequately convey the depth of pain David saw in Adam's eyes.

Adam seemed lost for words.

"What was it like for you over there?" David said. "How about describing a typical day."

Adam thought. "Well, I guess on a typical day you'd do PT from zero five thirty, and it could go until the CO wanted to puke. Most of the time it was just an hour, though. PT, that's physical training."

"Got the reference, but thanks."

Adam said, "Then it's SSS—that's shower, shit, shave—before breakfast. Just the normal stuff. A lot of time it was real quiet. You know? Funny, because the quiet was the toughest part. It gave you time and space to think about stuff, home, all the things you missed, but mostly you focused on your friend who got blown up the other day. You had time to think that you were going out on patrol soon enough and maybe you'd get 'blowed up' yourself." Adam put the words "blowed up" inside air quotes.

"Basically, that was the life. It was patrol and post," he continued. "We'd go out four or five hours in the morning, come back and eat something, then back on patrol, and then you'd have dinner and maybe do another patrol after that. Or sometimes you go out on patrol and some T-man is shooting your ass up. Or sometimes you didn't come back."

David guessed "T-man" meant Taliban. He would check later, as he did not want to interrupt Adam's flow.

"You can come back from patrol so racked up," Adam said. "Good luck getting any sleep. And then before you know it, you got PT all over again. And then boom—you're back on patrol, same as the day before. It's Groundhog Day over there."

"Even the firefights?"

"Yeah, well that's the only break in the routine, but on a COP even that becomes routine. You know?"

David nodded as he jotted down the word "COP" in his notebook, something else to look up. "Can you tell me about one of the patrols where things did not go well?"

Watching Adam, David was reminded of friends who had embedded with U.S. forces in Iraq and Afghanistan and got shot at, or navigated an IED (or worse, did not), and who all came back haunted. David did not believe in ghosts, and his religious views bordered on agnostic, but those who came back often seemed burdened by a malevolent spirit that would not let them find peace.

Adam's expression shifted, like a shadow that crossed his face, as he seemed to settle on a particularly unpleasant memory.

"On my last tour we set up a COP in an abandoned school." Adam's voice turned softer. "A COP is combat outpost, in case you were wondering."

David made a note next to the abbreviation in his notebook.

"We were sleeping on cots with our guns and packs tossed around like a bunch of school kids on a camping trip," Adam said. "The air there never circulated. It was so damn hot at night it was like sleeping in a sauna. The only breeze you'd catch is if the guy next to you cut wind. But you know the drill, right?"

"Patrol and post," David said.

Adam looked pleased. "So I'm on patrol. The day before, we had some T-men shooting at us, and some kids from the village said they knew where they were. For ten bucks and a few Twix bars you can get all sorts of good intel from the locals. We took two fire teams out on a hunting expedition. We got an AK, RPK, RPG, lots of firepower with us. Going to get us some T-men."

Adam's leg began to bounce, fast enough to shake the table. David kept his eyes on Adam while he silently moved their drinks to an adjacent table to avoid a spill.

"So we're following these kids on some shitty nothing road." Adam's voice gained energy with the telling. "Moving west to east. The whole time I'm looking for upturned dirt. You see, predeployment training teaches you that upturned dirt could mean an IED. But let me tell you, the dirt's upturned everywhere you look. Everywhere. So any step could be it. Boom! Any single step."

It was cool inside the coffee shop, but a sheen of sweat coated Adam's forehead. His eyes darted in all directions, as though he were scanning the tiled floor in search of upturned dirt.

Adam said, "By the time we reach the village we're all sorts of jacked, and most of the kids we're following go on back to their little mud huts. Of course the villagers come out to greet us, but it's hard to know which are allies and which are Taliban. Now, in addition to IEDs, we're keeping eyes out for guns poking out of robes, because rules of engagement say we can't shoot anybody who's unarmed. But it's a kinetic area— violent, I mean. You just don't know who's there to kill you and who wants help. It's a constant Charlie Foxtrot. That would be 'cluster fuck,' in your vernacular."

Adam reached for his coffee and took a long drink, then returned it to the adjacent table. David could relate distantly to Adam's ordeal, having been in some dicey situations of his own, but what Adam had endured was on a different level. The idea that any step could be one's last was truly terrifying. David could not see how anybody could return from that sort of grinding stress unchanged.

"So we're back moving, with just one guide now, a twelve-year-old kid, maybe fourteen. He's skinny and dirty and waving frantically to us to hurry."

Adam waved his arms, pantomiming the kid's gestures. His breath turned shallow.

"He points to these trees maybe a hundred meters away, just past the outskirts of the village. Hell, even the trees are brown over there. Sometimes when I get stressed I have to look at something green to remind myself where I am." Adam paused to gaze out the window at the green of Hopkinton, but when he looked back, he did not appear convinced he was safe.

"Anyway we follow this kid a bit further down the road, but every step, you know, we're doing our check. That upturned dirt. And then the kid turns around and he just smiles at us. I'll never forget that look on his face. It was pure joy. And then he reaches into his robe, takes out a pistol, and he fires. PFC O'Malley is right there in front, and he takes the bullet in the side. Damn kid gets this lucky shot. Bullet doesn't even nick O'Malley's SAPI plate."

Adam was breathing harder now. His eyes darted about, seeing phantoms everywhere. The sweat on his forehead began to drip down his face, as if he was back in the Afghani heat.

"A couple guys jump on O'Malley right away. But I'm focused on the kid. He fires again, but we're all moving now so he doesn't get a clean shot. Now I've got good lines on him. My AK is up, and I get off a burst. *Rat-tat-tat. Rat-tat-tat.*"

Adam raised his hands as if he was holding his gun. He trained the imaginary weapons on patrons at the coffee shop. A few noticed and flinched in response. Adam's voice choked with raw emotion, and he sucked down air in gulps.

"I ripped him apart. You know?" Tears streamed down Adam's face. He wiped them away with the back of his hand.

"I fucking tore this kid in half. Pink mist everywhere. And we're all scrambling for cover, thinking T-Men are right there and now it's an ambush. But there weren't any T-men—just IEDs all over the side of the road. The kid knew he was going to die. He just wanted us to scamper. To be careless." With the tears, the sweat, the snot, Adam was clearly reliving the moment, as he probably did most every night in his nightmares.

"Sure enough I heard the boom, and then another, and then somebody's arm hit me in the face. There were limbs everywhere, man. Fucking flying everywhere. Bodies aren't supposed to be blown apart like that. Blood and limbs and guts everywhere you looked."

David's heart was racing now as well.

"So we're all over it, you know. *Fix our wounded!* Fix 'em! Four things. Restore the breathing. Stop the bleeding. Protect the wound. Treat for shock. We got this QuikClot shit, and I can see Doc P working on

O'Malley, using it like caulk on a leaky window. But blood's spurting out of him like a whale shoots water out a blowhole. And I'm just looking around. My ears are ringing. It's like I'm underwater. And LT Carlson is coming toward me, doing a commando crawl, but then I can see his legs are blown off and he's dragging his intestines behind him."

Adam fell silent and bowed his head. When he looked up his eyes were ringed in red, but the tears had stopped falling.

"Bodies aren't meant to be broken apart that way."

CHAPTER 18

Steve Abington was breathing comfortably, twelve times each minute, heavily sedated, his oxygen delivered via an endotracheal tube. Just hours ago he had been rabid, but now he looked peaceful thanks to the combo of propofol and fentanyl, which the anesthesiologist, Dr. William Kauffman, titrated expertly. The patient was hooked to a ventilator as well as the usual monitors for ECG, blood pressure, and pulse oximetry. Abington's labs came back within normal limits. Still, he almost hadn't gotten to this operating table.

The whole team had met for a lengthy discussion in the conference room down the hall from where Carrie had been attacked. For the first several minutes Dr. Finley apologized profusely to Carrie for not having been clearer about security and safety measures. He promised a thorough review of all practices and standards, and said he would have new protocols in place by the end of the week.

In the meantime, there was the matter of Abington. This was a medical meeting, but Cal Trent from DARPA was present, along with Dr. Finley, Dr. Kauffman, and Carrie. Trent was dressed nattily in a tailored blue suit that showed off his muscular frame. At the grand rounds, she'd thought him cold and distant, but here he acted warm and conciliatory.

"I'm really sorry for what happened to you," Trent said in his low, gravelly voice. "You must still be very shaken."

"I'm doing all right," Carrie replied, which was only a half-truth.

She was shaken, but perfectly functional. She'd had a brief medical exam, and despite some bruising on her neck, she was unharmed and experiencing no shock. She had recovered her composure rapidly.

"Timing here is everything," Dr. Finley said. "Abington is active right now."

"Active?" Carrie asked.

"He's been subjected to the VR simulation program. This is the time when those re-created memories are being enhanced emotionally by connections through the amygdala. The DBS has to block those emotional connections, and we'll lose our chance if the memory evaporates. It's not like PD, where we have the luxury of making subtle adjustments over weeks and months."

"There's no telling if the virtual reality would be effective again," Trent added. "We don't have any data on this. Essentially it could be a one-shot deal for him. If we don't get a DBS system installed and working, Abington might miss his only opportunity to lead a normal life."

"Carrie, I want you to know that it is up to you," Dr. Finley said. "Medically speaking, I see no reason not to proceed. But obviously we need our head surgeon to be at the top of her game."

All eyes fell on Carrie. She was starting to develop a conference room complex; the last time she'd been in one with all eyes on her like this, the conversation went horribly.

And again, Carrie had an important decision to make. Should she go ahead with the procedure? Though the decision was hers, there was no mistaking what Dr. Finley and the rest of the team wanted her to choose. As for Abington, it was clear that the hyper-realistic virtual reality simulation had triggered his rage. Carrie felt deep empathy for her attacker, and would not hold him accountable for his actions. But she wondered what he had seen during the simulation. Was Smokes there? Roach? What had happened to them over there?

While Carrie had come to the VA to recover from a devastating professional setback of her own, this procedure might be a way to truly help people like Adam and Steve, whose minds and lives had been turned into a daily nightmare. Right now, Carrie was the only surgeon here. It was her job, and the window was fast closing. If DBS could ease Abington's grievous memories, in a Don McCall miracle way, Carrie owed it to him to try.

"I'm fine to proceed. Let's do it."

CARRIE COULD not believe how natural it felt to be back in the OR. This was an environment where she could feel herself in control. The old adage of riding a bike was not lost on her. Unlike the vets whose PTSD she hoped to cure, Carrie had no trouble blocking out the memory of Abington's assault. She was focused on the task, summoning not only her recent training, but her years of residency work as well.

As she prepared to drill the burr holes, Carrie thought back to the time, not long ago, when Beth Stillwell's life had rested in her hands. Today's procedure was technically a breeze by comparison.

Acting as the team's neurophysiologist, Dr. Finley was in the operating room to record the electrical discharge patterns from nerve cells when Carrie worked the electrode, ever so slowly, toward the basolateral nucleus of the amygdala.

Intraoperative neurophysiological monitoring was a demanding discipline, and obtaining certification required years of additional study. Carrie was impressed by Dr. Finley's dedication to his calling. There was no question that the doctor brought world-class medical skill to the VA.

In addition to Dr. Finley and Dr. Kauffman, the team included Dr. R. T. Patel, a first-year neurosurgical resident. Though Patel was primarily there to observe, he was also scrubbed, should Carrie require any unforeseen assistance. Intracranial hemorrhaging remained Carrie's chief concern during the operation, and post-op she would be vigilant about monitoring for signs of infection.

Also present was Donna Robinson, the scrub nurse, who looked of an age to have treated vets from Vietnam, and Louise Phillips, who, as a circulating nurse, was not scrubbed. Carrie doubted she'd find anybody quite like Valerie on the VA staff, but she was optimistic about the skill and diligence of these women, and hoped over time to develop a rapport with her new colleagues.

The real art of DBS work was developing leadership and communication skills in order to bring the team along with her during each operation. Fortunately, though everyone made it clear he was loved and missed, she sensed no lingering resentment over her replacing Sam Rockwell.

For what it was worth, during scrub, Donna expressed her admiration for Carrie's toughness and grit. Hours ago Carrie had been afraid for her life, but instead of retreating, she had brushed off the experience like a kid after a playground tumble. Having spent most of her career working for the VA, Donna measured a person by their ability to endure.

Carrie attached the stereotactic frame to Steve Abington's shaved head with four screws using a local anesthetic, just to be sure, even though he had already been sedated. Then, he was wheeled next door where an MRI dedicated exclusively to OR protocols had been waiting, and a series of ultra-thin-cut T1 and T2 weighted images of his brain were acquired. Abington was wheeled back to the OR while the scans were loaded onto the planning station. Computer images provided exact XYZ coordinates of Abington's amygdala, giving Carrie all the information she would need to guide the stimulating electrodes to her target by the least invasive path. This sort of equipment would have prevented the Leon Dixon disaster, Carrie thought ruefully. It was a supremely expensive setup, and she wondered how much of the bill DARPA was covering. Probably most of it.

Dr. Kauffman kept Abington unconscious with propofol and fentanyl. He would add isoflurane if deeper sedation became required. With Parkinson's and dystonia patients, who had to be awakened intermittently in order to assess their motor function, agents like propofol were ideal. But the last thing anyone needed was another violent outburst during surgery, so it was best to keep this patient insensate.

Carrie made a curvilinear, right precoronal scalp incision and penetrated the underlying skull with the Midas Rex, making a standard fourteen-millimeter burr hole. A Stimloc was screwed in. The electronic drive system was attached to the frame and Carrie sliced open the dura. Next, the long metal cannula, guided by the drive platform, was ever so slowly introduced through the brain. Carrie took her time. She made certain the drive plane avoided any sulcus where some juicy artery or vein might be lurking.

Carrie inched the cannula another millimeter forward. She checked her computer and inched it some more. Long minutes passed as Carrie meticulously worked the cannula toward the target area. By now, Carrie's legs ached, and a glossy sweat coated her brow and had to be dabbed away. The pull on her back left an unpleasant and persistent dull ache. As the hours passed, Carrie began to feel every stitch of Abington's assault. She blocked out the throbbing of her throat and the hurt in her shoulder from when she hit the floor. Her concentration had to be total, and it was.

While this was still neurosurgery, it exercised a different set of muscles, which compounded Carrie's fatigue. She pushed, persevered, and tapped into the kind of mental toughness she'd taken up triathlons to build.

At the start of the operation, Dr. Finley and others did frequent welfare checks with Carrie. Her two-word answer, "I'm fine," never varied, so the last check had come more than an hour ago.

Three hours into the surgery Carrie announced softly, "I'm pretty sure we're at ground zero." She removed the stylus and replaced it with three micro recording electrodes.

"Wow, I'm getting an excellent signal," said Dr. Finley. "I'm getting a typical pattern of neuronal firing from the basolateral amygdaloid nucleus. Great job, Carrie! You're right on target with the first pass. The anatomical and physiological coordinates could not be more perfect."

The microelectrodes were replaced by the stimulating electrode, and its surrounding stylet was removed. Carrie placed on the locking clip. All that was left would be to tunnel the exposed lead component into the chest. Four hours had ticked off the clock. Abington was shifted onto his left side. The right side of his neck and chest were bathed in Beta-dine. Carrie made an incision in the scalp and another five-centimeter cut in the right side of his chest, just under the collarbone.

Carrie inserted her fingers to enlarge a pocket where the subcuta-neous pulse stimulator would fit. Then she inserted a t-tunneler and pushed it under the scalp and through the neck to reach the chest wound. The exposed lead was next introduced through the tunneler and connected to the generator in the chest. The scalp and chest were closed. The system was now in place, and potentially operational.

Five hours of surgery were complete.

Abington would spend the night in neuro recovery. Then it was home, wherever that was, and back in three weeks to follow up with Dr. Finley, who would assume responsibility for adjustments of the stimulus generator signal.

Dr. Finley checked the signal readings once more. "Dr. Bryant, you've just hit a grain of rice in a three-pound mass of Jell-O. Congratula-tions!"

Carrie removed her mask and grinned.

CHAPTER 19

During the day the canteen in the basement of the VA hospital buzzed with activity, but at this late hour it was a ghost town. Food service stopped at three o'clock for everything except K-cup coffee and whatever the vending machines supplied. Food at the VA was partly subsidized by the government, which could explain why there was no dinner service for the staff.

Carrie had slipped on a fresh pair of scrubs and joined Dr. Finley at a long table. Steve Abington was in neuro recovery and, Carrie figured, emerging from the effects of anesthesia about now. She could enjoy a cup of coffee and then go check up on her first, and most eventful, DBS patient.

Dr. Finley was all smiles. "Carrie, that was just splendid. You were like a veteran in the OR, no pun intended."

Carrie's face lit up with a genuine smile and she blew on her coffee to cool it. "Thanks, I appreciate the compliment."

"The microelectrodes are perfectly placed," he continued, "right in the basolateral nucleus of the amygdala. The neuronal firing pattern, the post-op CT, everything's perfect. You were so calm and focused. I knew you could do this work."

"It was a team effort, like you said it would be."

"Ha! A modest neurosurgeon—now that might be a first."

One small step for Carrie Bryant, one hopefully enormous leap for Staff Sergeant Steve Abington.

"Given all that you've been through, and I don't just mean the attack, what you did today was nothing short of astonishing. I really can't say enough good to you, Carrie."

Carrie tried to keep her composure, but blushed at his praise. She'd fought so hard to find her way back to her field, she was amazed to be here. Now, given the extent of her day, Carrie figured she'd be bone weary, but it was the opposite. Maybe she'd crash later, but for the moment Carrie felt electrified.

After about twenty minutes talking about DBS, the surgery, and Abington's prospects for recovery, Dr. Finley glanced at his wristwatch. "Whoa. It's after eight. I mean, I love this place, but I gave up on the idea of using any hospital as a bunkhouse back in my residency years. So will I see you tomorrow?" Dr. Finley winked.

It was his way of asking if Carrie was coming back. Given the threat to her life, it was a reasonable question.

"You couldn't keep me away," Carrie said with a smile.

"Well, no more unaccompanied consultations," Dr. Finley said. "We need our best DBS surgeon safe, if we're going to fix the PTSD problem one patient at a time."

Carrie saluted. "Dr. Bryant will be reporting for duty, sir."

Dr. Finley chuckled as he stood. The crow's-feet marking the corners of his eyes seemed to have deepened. "We're lucky you're both resilient and dedicated. But I suggest you go home and get some rest. It's been an eventful day."

Carrie nodded. "You go on ahead. I'm going to nurse this coffee a while longer and catch up on some e-mails."

Dr. Finley gathered his briefcase and gave Carrie's shoulder a couple of friendly pats before heading for the door. Carrie sipped her drink and watched him go. She took in the quiet; it was one of her favorite times to be at a hospital. At Community, Carrie had been responsible for a whole team of patients, any of whom might turn for the worse at a moment's notice, and too often did. She had always been grateful for any fifteen-minute respite.

Maybe this job would be a stepping-stone back into other types of neurosurgery, but maybe not. Her mother preached mindfulness, living in the moment. Carrie was not opposed to the idea of making a long-term commitment here. Perhaps after she spoke with Abington, once Carrie could see the impact the procedure had made—a Don McCall miracle—it would encourage her transition to becoming a career DBS surgeon.

Carrie laughed at herself as she got up to throw her coffee cup away. Who knew how long Carrie would last at the VA? Hell, she was happy just to be back in the OR. But the same ambition that drove Carrie into neurosurgery had climbed back into the driver's seat of her mind.

From now on, Carrie would focus just on her patients. She'd barely started this job. She needed to be here a while and experience the whole program before making any decisions. Best to get her head on her task. And right now, that was checking up on Steve Abington before checking out for the day. This crazy day.

Even though Carrie functioned as an attending physician, her instinct was to go see her patient post-op. It had been ingrained in her for the past four years. One of an attending's privileges was being able to do the surgery and leave the scut to the residents. But Carrie was still a resident in both her heart and mind, and so a check on Abington was almost like a reflex. Steve Abington might well have taken Carrie's life, but he had also been instrumental in giving back her career.

Inside the elevator Carrie pressed "3" and headed up to the neuro recovery floor.

The hall outside the elevator was dim, quiet, and empty as she walked down to the four-bed unit. Hospitals could be lonely places in the evenings, but the VA seemed especially dormant.

Carrie pushed the intercom and waited for the double doors to buzz open. Inside, three of the four glassed-in rooms were empty. Steve

Abington was in the bed at the far end of the last room, extubated and resting comfortably, reclining with his head up fifteen degrees, IV in place, a bedside gooseneck lamp illuminating his face.

Marianne, the full-figured night nurse, sat behind a wide desk with her face buried in a book. In front of Marianne was a row of monitors, all dark except for the one reporting Abington's heart rate and BP. Taped to a wall in the nurses' station, easy to read from a distance, was a list of phone extensions for ordering various tests. As if Carrie needed another reminder she did not belong on the floor, at the bottom of the list, in bold lettering, was Evan Navarro's ordering number, as well as his user name and password to the system where lab orders and such were entered. This was clearly his domain.

"It's all quiet tonight." Marianne spoke in a reedy voice, alert to her surroundings, despite keeping her eyes on her book, a bodice-ripper romance. Carrie grabbed Abington's chart and walked toward his bed.

"I'm not used to seeing docs up here at this hour," Marianne called out. "Usually, I just call 'em if things go bad, and they usually don't with these DBS folks. Anesthesia extubates them and they breathe just fine. Haven't had a problem yet. Hey, you new here?"

Carrie came back to the desk. With a smile, she extended her hand. "I'm Dr. Carrie Bryant. I work with Dr. Finley. I'm the new DBS surgeon."

ABINGTON'S HOSPITAL room held little warmth. With a crush of high-tech gear and monitors, the place was intimidating at best, and not intended for long-term stays. The electric hum of equipment buzzed, and in the quiet of the floor every beep could be heard in perfect clarity.

Carrie paused at the door and eyed her attacker with compassion. She reminded herself that the man who hours ago had his hands wrapped around Carrie's throat was not the same person who lay on this hospital bed. The image of Abington's crazed-eye look flashed through her mind and sent a chill down her spine. She could recall every detail of the attack: the feeling of pressure on her throat, the coursing terror as her windpipe closed. The smell of his hot breath when he hovered over her, his eyes aglow. But—it wasn't with hate, was it? It had been fear. Yes, Abington was terrified when he attacked. In a way, the assault was more like a drowning person flailing at a would-be rescuer.

She went to Abington's bedside and pulled a penlight from her coat pocket.

"Good evening, Mr. Abington," Carrie said. "I'd like to check your pupils. Would you kindly follow my light?"

Steve Abington opened his eyes ever so slowly and stared vacantly toward his doctor. If he remembered Carrie and what he'd done to her, it did not register on his face.

Carrie quickly checked his pupillary reactivity and then his eye movements. "Now please follow my light. Up . . . good. Left. Right . . . good."

Abington's shaved head was dressed in bandages, but the stereotactic frame had been removed and he looked handsome now that he was free of the elaborate computerized apparatus.

"Well, you've had quite a day. We haven't had a proper introduction. Do you remember anything about meeting me?"

Abington, who appeared quite groggy still, didn't respond. Carrie checked his reflexes, and made sure he was moving all fours pretty much equally.

"You were extremely upset when they brought you in," Carrie said. "Do you remember? You were very confused, telling me you didn't belong here."

Abington mumbled something under his breath. He looked utterly lost and alone. Confusion smoldered in his darting eyes.

"Steve, can you tell me the last thing you remember?"

Like a veil had been lifted, Abington came alive and looked wildly about. His jaw set and a snarl overtook his face. He covered his ears with his hands and began to shake his head as if something was lodged inside his ears. Carrie worried he would rip the IVs out of his arm.

"Enough. Shut up, shut up, shut up," Abington said. His speech came out thickly. His expression was that of a cornered animal.

"Steve, what's wrong? What's going on?"

Abington continued to turn his head frantically from one side to the other, keeping his hands over his ears.

"Where are you? Stop it! Stop saying that! Follow my light, follow my light, follow my light! What light? What light? Stop it!"

"Steve, calm down. You've got to calm down. Everything is all right."

Abington appeared to have heard Carrie, but his expression became even more agitated.

"Why do you keep saying it's all right? Nothing is all right. Nothing is all right! Nothing is all right! Stop saying that!"

Abington flipped onto his stomach and buried his head under the pillow. But Carrie could hear him muttering the same words over and over.

"Follow my light . . . follow my light . . ."

Carrie bolted for the door. It would be easy to get Abington sedated. The question was, could she ever get him cured?

CHAPTER 20

The badge dangling from a red lanyard identified the nurse as Lee Taggart. He wore crisply pressed white scrubs and unblemished matching canvas sneakers that carried him down the long hallway at a brisk pace. He stopped in front of Marianne's workstation and leaned forward, hoping to catch her eye.

"Reading anything good?"

Lee's warm voice drew Marianne's attention. When she looked up, he flashed her a brilliant smile. Marianne smiled back. Lee had an athletic body and smooth ebony skin, and was not unaccustomed to flattering looks. He had never met Marianne before, but that was not so unusual here. Staff seemed to change as often as shifts, and Marianne would need only to see the red lanyard and white uniform to believe he was a staff nurse.

Marianne glanced down at the cover of her book, which featured a bare-chested Adonis riding a stallion with a scantily clad buxom woman clutched in his massive arms. She laughed flirtatiously.

"Oh, just something to pass the time," she said, embarrassed enough to cover the book jacket with a clipboard.

The look in Lee's brown eyes turned conspiratorial. "Another slow night, eh?" he said.

He knew it had not been slow in the least. Everything that could have gone wrong with Abington had gone wrong.

"I prefer that to the alternative," Marianne said as she glanced at one of the dark monitors and caught a glimpse of her reflection within. She noticed her hair was a bit tousled, which she promptly corrected, using her hand as a comb.

"Well, I got assigned to Dr. Goodwin's staff tonight," Lee said. "Just got to go in and check on the patient. He's in four, right?"

"That's right. He's in four."

Marianne was having a heck of a time keeping her eyes off this new nurse. She was also struggling with Tinder, and every other dating site where she'd posted a profile. The VA offered slim pickings when it came to the opposite sex, so she was enjoying this pleasant surprise to the fullest.

Before Lee headed off to room four, Marianne checked Abington's vitals in the only active monitor. His heart and pulse were optimal, but the patient had been in a blissful haloperidol stupor for the past couple of hours, with not a peep since his earlier outburst. She had been told to be extra vigilant for any Q-T prolongation or incidence of arrhythmia, but so far he and the drug were working well together.

Dr. Bryant had ordered ten milligrams of diazepam IV after Abington went crazy, and Marianne had bolted from her chair and gotten the syringe promptly. Within a few minutes, the patient was relaxed again, and his eyes closed.

"Looks like he didn't need too much on top of that residual anesthesia," Dr. Bryant had said.

Having had enough excitement for one night, Marianne had been satisfied with that explanation, but Dr. Bryant still looked perplexed.

"I've never seen anything like that," she had said. "It's like he was hallucinating. Hearing voices, the same phrase over and over again. He repeated what I said, and then he answered my question multiple times. I only said it once, but somehow it never stopped for him."

Marianne was not concerned. "They're all agitated in some way," she said, not sharing Carrie's concern. "It's not unusual for them to get extra sedation. The residents are used to it and they're trained for it, so I can see why it was a shock to you."

Marianne's words did not seem to have much impact on the new DBS surgeon.

Dr. Bryant wrote a prn sedative order, administer as needed. She told Marianne to call if there was a problem, and to give the phone number to her relief at the eleven o'clock shift change. Sam Rockwell used to do the same. Marianne had looked in on Abington twice since then. He seemed a bit restless, his limbs moving involuntarily, shaking, but those were common side effects of the sedative.

"He's been a handful, that's for sure," Marianne said to Nurse Taggart. "Very agitated. Not sure what's going on with him."

"Well, that's why I'm here to check up on things."

"If he starts to give you trouble, you just holler," Marianne said.

"I sure will," Lee replied, "but I'm pretty good at handling most any situation on my own." With a wink, Lee headed to Abington's room.

Marianne focused her gaze on his well-defined backside as he walked away.

I bet you are. She smiled and went back to her book.

———————

Relentless heat bathed the back of Abington's neck, and sandy grit somehow wormed underneath his eyelids to scratch at his corneas. Place? Time? Where was he? What had happened? Somewhere off in the distance, Abington heard the thunderous roll of artillery shells detonating as the ground beneath him rumbled and shook with each massive blast. He felt around for his weapon, but his arms responded spastically like they had a mind of their own.

One of Abington's pawing hands felt something made of steel. He clutched his M16 and pulled the weapon close to him. He managed to get onto his hands and knees, but each breath came at a price. Something was wrong. Something was horribly wrong with him.

The air parted as bullets whizzed overhead. Abington forced open his eyes and blinked in response to the oppressive sunlight. When his vision cleared, he saw he was still in Afghanistan. Again, he was back where it all began, inside the foxhole, and Roach was with him just as before. Only now the indestructible Roach had had his guts ripped open by a peppering of bullets and he was bleeding out.

In lumbering, agonizingly slow motion, Abington flipped onto his belly and crawled over to his wounded comrade. He could not understand why his movements were so labored, dreamlike. But this could not be a dream. It was all too real. He could feel the heat scorching his skin, and a stench of gunpowder mixed with blood was visceral and genuine.

Gasping, Abington made his way toward Roach, who groaned and clutched at his injured stomach. If Abington did not stop the bleeding soon, his friend would die. All over again.

From close by, Abington heard a spit of gunfire. In the same instant, sand and dirt sprayed his face. With a burst of surprising adrenaline, Abington brushed his face clean and lurched forward, landing almost on top of Roach. With nothing to stop the bleeding, Abington placed his hands over the pulsing wound. He cried out in horror as his fingers sank deep inside the bloody cavity. Muscles and tendons pulsed around Abington's probing fingers, but the blood continued to ooze out. Roach moaned deliriously, fading in and out of consciousness.

Abington was about to scream for a medic when he noticed a shadow looming. He looked up just in time to see the figure of a man leap into the foxhole with them. Abington blinked to clear his vision. He had thought the dark-skinned man was wearing white hospital scrubs, but now there were no scrubs. The man was dressed in camouflage, with the combat medic's Red Cross insignia sewn onto his sleeve.

"What's happening here, Steve?" the man asked.

Abington had so much to say, but he could not utter a single word.

Instead, the medic's voice tumbled about his head and Abington heard the words "what's happening . . . what's happening . . . what's happening" like a scratched record.

Abington pulled his hands from the gruesome gut wound and covered his ears to try and block out the sound. His red-stained palms lathered his face with warm blood, but those words kept rolling about his head like an endless echo.

What's happening . . . what's happening . . . what's happening . . .

"Steve, you're going to feel a little funny in a moment."

Steve you're going to feel . . . Steve you're going to feel . . . Steve you're going to feel.

"Stop! Stop saying that! Just fix Roach!"

Now it was Abington's voice providing the echo.

Fix Roach . . . fix Roach . . . fix Roach . . .

The medic moved inches from Abington's face as he produced a syringe full of clear liquid from his pocket. At first the medic appeared to be injecting the syringe into thin air, but Abington's vision altered and he saw the needle had penetrated the tubing of his own intravenous line. How did he get a line in his arm when it was Roach who had been shot?

"It's called potassium chloride, and while it's not fatal, you're going to feel very uncomfortable," the medic whispered benevolently. "I'll see you in a minute, Steve."

The medic climbed out of the foxhole and was gone—but not his voice, which remained and echoed mercilessly in his ears.

I'll see you in a minute . . . see you in a minute . . . in a minute . . .

Seconds later, a new sensation came over Abington, something strange and unnerving. He inhaled sharply and fought against the tightness in his chest, curling into a fetal position and rhythmically rocking. He rubbed Roach's blood all over his head, hair, and neck in an effort to stop the noise in his head. Nearby, Roach lay on his back, mouth open, with a dead-eyed gaze up to the heavens.

The tightness changed into something else. Abington's heartbeat began to flutter, then it morphed into a pounding. Abington could feel the palpitations in his chest, throat, and neck. He turned his head and locked his gaze on his dead friend, certain he would soon be joining him.

Lee Taggart had made it to the elevator bank when Abington's alarm went off. While he was not at all surprised, Lee still made a show of it, and raced back to Marianne, who had a look of panic on her face. Some of the nurses were stoics—they could handle any stressful situation thrown at them—while others were not at all adept at managing crises. They tended to relish the relative calm of the neuro recovery floor.

"Something is wrong," she said. "His heartbeat just went crazy."

"He's on haloperidol, right?" Lee said. "Arrhythmia can be a side effect. I'm here, let me rush him down to the med ICU."

Marianne looked relieved. She was definitely not the good-in-emergencies type.

CHAPTER 21

The house was quiet when Carrie got home. The front porch light was on; it was always on when Carrie stayed out after her parents had gone to sleep. Traffic on the Mass Pike had been mercifully light, but it was still almost midnight when Carrie pulled into her parents' driveway.

She'd spent the drive running Abington's surgical procedure through her mind. It had been an exhilarating, terrifying, and utterly strange first day on the job and she was glad to be home. Carrie had given some thought to moving out now that she had an income stream again, but opted against it. Until she had some permanence she was not going to make any big changes.

When Carrie walked into the kitchen, she was delighted to find a card waiting for her on the table, propped against a small vase of flowers—daisies mostly, her favorite. The handwritten note from her mom and dad congratulated her on what they assumed had been a successful first surgery. She had debated telling them about Abington, but worried they would worry.

Reading her parents' note, Carrie became keenly aware of the soreness around her neck. It was tight, and every time she looked to the left, she felt a sharp, gripping pain that stretched across the back of her head. It was the pain of a muscle spasm, not a fracture. She also had additional pain along the outside of her right knee, but not with every step. In the morning she'd probably wake up with visible signs of the day's violence. Those would need to be explained, or perhaps just covered up.

Carrie heard a floorboard creak behind her and turned to see Adam in the entrance to the kitchen. He was wearing a T-shirt and sweats. For a moment she saw him as her little brother again, but that vision was blown apart by his haunted, hooded eyes. Eyes that resembled Abington's.

"Hey Carrie," Adam said as he trudged over to the fridge. "How'd the first surgery go?"

"Pretty good," Carrie said. "Nobody died."

Adam returned a fractured smile. "Well, I'd call that a big success." He chuckled. "Want some OJ?"

"Love some."

Adam poured two glasses and joined Carrie at the kitchen table. Carrie moved the flowers and card to the side to make room, surreptitiously checking her arms to make sure there were no visible marks or scratches. If her parents found out, they'd certainly be concerned about safety, but Adam could go ballistic.

"Can I ask you something?"

Adam took a swig of OJ. "Anything."

Carrie softened her voice. "What do you think would happen if you saw a virtual reality simulation of something that happened to you over in Afghanistan?"

"What do you mean by that? Like a computer simulation?"

"Along those lines," Carrie said. "But hyper-realistic."

Adam tossed his hands in the air. "I dunno."

Carrie thought not only of Abington's initial assault, but of his second outburst after the surgery, which required a haloperidol drip to calm him. Having experienced Adam's explosive temper, it was not a stretch to envision her brother in Abington's place.

"Could you maybe . . . become violent?" Carrie asked.

This was a sensitive subject for the family. Adam owned several guns, including a pistol and rifle, and threatened to move out before he'd give them up. He was a lawful and responsible gun owner, and nobody disagreed, but nobody wanted him to have those weapons either. The worry was for Adam's safety, since PTSD and gun ownership were often a lethal mix. Adam returned an indifferent shrug.

"I hit a reporter for no real good reason. So I suppose anything is possible."

Carrie laughed. "Did you call to apologize?"

"I did better than that," Adam said. "I met the guy for coffee. Gave him everything he could possibly want to hear, and probably more than he expected."

Carrie made a mental note to call David Hoffman; she'd agreed to a coffee date as well. Seeing sadness in her brother's eyes, Carrie reached across the table and took hold of Adam's hand. "Even I haven't heard those stories."

Adam squeezed her hand. "For a reason."

"If you ever want to talk about it—"

"You're here for me. I know that, Carrie. You've always had my back." He raised his hands in a pantomime of a pneumatic drill. "Hey, what do you think of this work you're doing? Should I have you drill into my head and stick me with wires?" Adam gave a cartoon evil scientist's maniacal laugh.

Based on Abington's reaction to the treatment, Carrie could not say with certainty, but she still believed in the program and its promise. It might be worth the pain of reconsolidating bad memories through virtual reality therapy to get positive results, though Carrie had reason to worry about potential side effects.

Her mind picked at the odd verbal exchange with Abington right before he went off the rails. The man's voice had sounded so distressed as he repeated, "Follow my light, follow my light." *It was like he heard my voice in his head over and over again,* Carrie thought.

"I don't know yet," she said to Adam. "I need more time to see it in action before I can say, though I do think there's tremendous promise."

Adam swallowed his orange juice in a long gulp and pushed back his chair to stand. "I'm beat." He stretched and yawned.

"Hi Beat, I'm Carrie." She held out her hand and Adam shook it, smiling at their long-running joke. "Have a good night. I'll see you in the morning."

"Night, Carrie." At the doorway Adam paused and turned. "Hey, it's good to have you here. It's good for all of us."

Carrie blew him a kiss. "When are you going to take me for a ride in that Camaro of yours?"

"I almost got it running today."

Carrie grimaced as she recalled the last time Adam almost got it running.

Adam noticed her reaction. "Don't worry," he said. "I'm not going to go all *Christine* on it."

Christine, the film adaptation of the Stephen King novel, was Adam's favorite movie these days. He'd seen it on cable after he came home from the war. He was referring to the scene when the high school kids trashed the car named Christine using aluminum bats, only to be killed after the car magically repaired itself and sought revenge. Adam seemed to like the idea of a thing that was indestructible, perhaps because he felt so vulnerable.

"Good night, Adam," Carrie said, crossing the room to give her brother a warm embrace. God, she hoped the DBS treatment worked. She hoped it was the cure for PTSD. She wanted her brother to feel whole again, but he was more like his Camaro he could not get running than Christine, which could magically put itself back together again.

Upstairs in her bedroom, Carrie went to put her phone on the dresser, and saw by the display that she'd missed a call during her drive home.

"Dr. Bryant, this is Marianne from the VA. You asked me to call if there was any problem with Patient Abington. He was rushed down to the medical ICU by a nurse on Dr. Goodwin's staff. Abington developed an arrhythmia and his blood pressure fell. The monitor showed ventricular tach with a wide QRS. I'm sorry to have to leave you this message. I tried you a couple times, but I couldn't reach you."

Carrie felt her own heart start to race. She checked the call log, and sure enough: two missed calls from the VA, including the call where Marianne had left her the voice message.

Carrie muttered to herself, "The haloperidol, dammit."

She probably should have just given Abington more Valium, since it was already in his system from before. Except she had checked his ECG, and the Q-T interval was not prolonged or anything, and it had calmed him down. She felt physically ill. She had made the call, she had ordered the drug, and Steve Abington in the ICU was on her.

Carrie thought of other ways she could have handled the situation, but kept returning to the haloperidol. He had seemed so crazy, beyond agitated. She had never experienced a post-op patient with symptoms resembling anything like Abington's. His repeating the same phrase, and that look in his eyes—that was fear and terror she saw. It was different from the confused agitated state or delirium she'd seen time and time again, whether someone was in the throes of DTs, or suffering the consequences of acute stroke, or sepsis, or, well, a host of other medical and surgical disorders. This was something unique, and she did not know what to make of it.

What else could have caused the arrhythmia?

A hemorrhage?

Goodness, that was always a risk after surgery. And Carrie had seen at least one case where a subarachnoid hemorrhage had resulted in a serious arrhythmia. While negative drug reaction remained the most probable event, other considerations besides a hemorrhage dotted her thoughts. It could be an infection. Fever. Perhaps a seizure, or even a stroke. A CT of the brain would be the logical first step.

However, she could do nothing about it now. Abington's welfare was in the hands of the med ICU team. Before she could do anything, Abington needed to be stabilized. His blood pressure, heart rhythm, vital signs in general had to be under control. To go barging in there at this late hour would be counterproductive. They would take all the necessary precautions. She could picture Abington lying in an ICU bed, intubated again and hooked to a ventilator, IV fluids and antiarrhythmic drugs flowing through his veins. Dopamine and other vasopressors keeping his blood pressure up. The baton had been passed; Abington was not a neurosurgical post-op case any longer.

Still, she would go see him first thing in the morning.

CHAPTER 22

It was dark when the alarm went off. Cocooned in her bed, Carrie thought about hitting the snooze button, but decided to get an early start. Despite the aches in her body and neck—the result of a buildup of lactic acid and inflammation—she managed to arrive at the VA a little after seven thirty. She wanted to check on Abington before her day officially started. Even though the med ICU staff was more than capable, she had done the invasive procedure and felt ultimately responsible for his outcome. It could be that all she did was give them her thanks and a pat on the back, but she had to do something. Either way, she had to know the outcome.

Carrie had just flashed her security badge at the front desk when her phone began to vibrate. To her surprise, it was a text message from Dr. Sandra Goodwin, head of neurosurgery. *Come see me as soon as you arrive. I'm in my office now.* The text came across as a bit edgy. Carrie belonged to Dr. Finley, head of neurology and his DBS program, so even though surgery resided under Dr. Goodwin's purview, the line of responsibility to her was a dotted one at most, and thus far Carrie had had little interaction with the woman. Still, Abington could wait. Carrie stopped by the cafeteria for coffee before making her way to Dr. Goodwin's second-floor office.

Seated behind a metal desk that had probably been manufactured in the 1970s, Dr. Goodwin eyed Carrie with contempt. Carrie had not expected to see Dr. Evan Navarro, who ran the residency program, there as well. Navarro sat on one of two uncushioned folding chairs set in front of Dr. Goodwin's desk. The concrete brick walls were painted a sorry shade of yellow, and the low ceiling covered with cheap acoustic tiles made Carrie feel uncomfortably confined. Other than a couple of struggling plants, Dr. Goodwin's home away from home had all the life of a pathology lab.

Dr. Navarro turned the chair next to him slightly and offered it to Carrie. She sat down gingerly, which had more to do with Navarro's hard stare than with her aching knee. Dr. Navarro was short—Carrie probably had two inches on him—but he had a reputation for being pugnacious and for bringing residents to tears. His dark hair was gelled back, showing off a prominent widow's peak.

Dr. Goodwin looked every bit her fifty-five years. She wore her hair in a bob that called attention to her face's sharp features, and nothing warm or fuzzy showed in her hazel eyes. She was all business and all about maximizing every minute in her day. Wearing a white lab coat over a set of blue scrubs, her clothing implied she would touch a scalpel at some point in the day, which Carrie highly doubted. Dr. Goodwin was an administrator. But maybe she liked looking the part of a surgeon.

Dr. Goodwin spoke bluntly. "I heard you went to see Steve Abington in the neuro recovery floor yesterday."

No "Hello." No "How are you adjusting to the new job." No "I heard you almost got killed." Dr. Goodwin was as efficient with her words as she was with her time.

"I did." Carrie did not know what else to say.

Dr. Goodwin's glowering expression said that the chief of neurosurgery did not approve. "Yes, I see," Dr. Goodwin replied. "I heard about yesterday, and I'm aware of the circumstance. I'm sorry that happened, though I do believe Dr. Finley expressed to you beforehand that the PTSD patients should never be seen without accompaniment."

Carrie felt a bit ashamed by the accusation, but she bristled. It sounded like victim-blaming.

"I guess I didn't fully appreciate the need for the warning," Carrie said.

"That may be," Dr. Goodwin replied coldly, "and because of the extenuating circumstances here, Evan and I thought it would be appropriate to review our department policies with you with respect to post-op care, among other things."

"That's the job of the residents," Navarro said in a sharp tone. "You may think of yourself as one of the gang, but you're not."

Dr. Goodwin shot Navarro an admonishing look, perhaps to call back her attack dog. "What Evan is trying to say, Carrie, is that you are basically an employee of Dr. Finley. Your situation here is highly unique. Unusual, is the word I would choose to describe it. To be blunt, the hospital has a well-organized residency program, and you're not part of it. Surely you understand that we have procedures in place for patient care, and a hierarchy for addressing emergent situations. You show your face and nurses don't know who to call if there's a problem. Do they call you? You're not even insured here if something does go wrong. You expose this program to added risk by this behavior."

Carrie's face felt hot. "I was simply curious to see how my first DBS patient was doing."

"That's understandable," Dr. Goodwin said. "Which is why we're having a friendly chat about it."

Doesn't feel friendly, Carrie thought.

"If the residents think you're undermining them, it will throw my entire program into disarray," Navarro said.

"It was certainly not my intention."

"Yes, well, our best intentions may have unintended consequences."

"Well, how is Abington doing?" Carrie asked. "All I know is that he was moved to medical ICU."

"And that's all you need to know," Navarro answered curtly.

Dr. Goodwin held up her hand again. Navarro apparently needed an even shorter leash.

"I guess I'm a bit confused," Carrie said. "I just wanted to see how my patient was doing after *my* surgery."

Dr. Goodwin's intense expression ticked up a few notches. "Let me take a moment to clarify your role here," she said. "You are the DBS surgeon. Period. You did your surgery just fine. Dr. Finley brought you on board exclusively for that purpose. And I, for one, did not support your appointment."

No kidding.

"I would have preferred we bring in somebody who had gone through a formal residency program *successfully*," Dr. Goodwin continued. "But Dr. Finley is the one who has the funds, and he insisted your skills as a surgeon trumped any concerns we may have had regarding your . . . unfortunate history."

Carrie tensed at the reference, and in doing so caused a stab of pain in her aching knee.

"Your job is to do the DBS installations, and that's it," Dr. Goodwin said.

"And the next link in that chain is me," Navarro added.

Carrie felt like she had just been body-slammed.

"So you see, Carrie, you're here because the DBS surgeries are lengthy and do require a dedicated resource. You're quite simply a hired hand, and it's best if you keep your involvement to that."

Carrie's cheeks flushed. She could feel her anger starting to percolate. Digging deep, she mustered restraint. "I understand." She directed her attention to Navarro. "Would you mind giving me an update on Abington's condition? I understand he's been moved to the medical ICU. I did the procedure. I feel a responsibility for the patient outcome. I think I deserve that professional courtesy."

Dr. Goodwin and Navarro exchanged an inscrutable look.

"Let's make sure we got this clear, Carrie," Dr. Goodwin said. "You do the surgery and you're done. The residents and Dr. Navarro will do the post-op care. If a patient is moved to another unit, that patient becomes the responsibility of others. Not us. We take care of our responsibilities as they apply to neurosurgery, and do not go chasing after patients when they become the province of a different department. This is the way our organization is effectively maintained. Do I make myself clear?"

Carrie was shocked. She could not believe the tone Dr. Goodwin was using with her, the utter disdain. It was as if Carrie, by acting in a thoughtful and caring manner toward a patient, had violated some sacred oath and thereby single-handedly put the entire system in a state of dysfunctional disrepair.

Carrie knew all about "turfing," the idea that a patient who was moved off one floor and brought to another became OPP, other people's problem. But she had never worked in an environment where the hush-hush practice was so openly supported and, in fact, endorsed. The notion made Carrie sick to her stomach. This was not what she had signed up for, and she had every intention of making her feelings known to Dr. Finley.

For now, the best, most politically expedient strategy for this meeting was to appear compliant and retreat. *Never poke an angry bear.*

"You've made yourself clear," Carrie said. "So if I'm not scheduled to do any DBS surgeries, what then?"

"As long as you respect our procedures, that is not my concern. You do what you feel is best for you and your career, Carrie," Dr. Goodwin said.

Dr. Goodwin's smile held all the warmth of a snow cone. Carrie didn't have to be told to stand; this meeting was clearly adjourned.

CHAPTER 23

Carrie spent fifteen minutes in her cramped, windowless office trying to decompress. Her blood pressure had settled, but she was having enormous trouble concentrating on her DBS research. She was halfway through a difficult paper on dysarthria in Parkinson's disease, but the words jumbled on the page.

She was ruminating on that contentious conversation—ambush was more like it—with Drs. Goodwin and Navarro. The insinuations were absolutely infuriating. Carrie had not taken the job just to be a surgical tool. A hammer for a nail, so to speak. Dr. Finley had told her she'd be part of the team, and that was how she'd envisioned her role.

I would have preferred we bring in somebody who had gone through a formal residency program successfully. Dr. Goodwin's words bit hard.

Out of frustration, Carrie balled up the printout she'd been reading and threw it against the wall. That woman had been cutting, disparaging, and downright offensive. Something odd had happened with Steve Abington, something potentially related to his DBS treatment. It was more than the agitated state the duty nurse had described. This was something—but what? She was focused mostly on his strange response. In her mind, she could still hear him muttering the same phrase over again, repeating what she had said.

Follow my light . . . follow my light . . .

Abington seemed to experience some form of auditory hallucination. It was unusual, not the type she had seen in schizophrenics where disturbing voices outside the head seemed to speak directly to victims. She was keen to try and understand. Even if she were prohibited from seeing Abington, her time was her own, and Carrie could still work his case.

Take that, Dr. Goodwin!

Carrie squeezed into the crowded elevator. Her finger hovered over the button to the medical ICU floor before she resisted the temptation. It was one thing to do some research in the library on a "turfed" patient, but she couldn't flagrantly ignore Dr. Goodwin's instructions minutes after they had been issued. It was best for now to keep her investigation academic.

The library at the VA was located on the first floor, just off the lobby, and it did not look like it got much use. The floor was covered with a threadbare carpet, and though it had a few wooden carrels, none had a chair. Unlike the gift shop, which was staffed by volunteers dressed in brightly colored smocks adorned with patriotic pins, the library reception desk was unattended. In place of a human, a sign in an acrylic holder provided instructions on how to obtain a password to access the computer and navigate to the home page. Some of the more recent medical journals—what limited print supply was on hand—were stuffed haphazardly into a standing magazine rack, but the library's shelves were notably barren.

Carrie located a plastic chair and set it facing a terminal. A thought of her dad flashed across her mind. How would he go about this? Her father loved doing research. To him, it was a major part of the challenge of medicine. He and Carrie could not have been more different in this regard. As a surgeon, Carrie preferred her puzzle pieces manifested not as words, but rather lab results, machine readouts, and whatever visual cues she could derive from inside the human body.

She was typical of the field; few surgeons loved doing research. Carrie recalled her third year in medical school, during her clinical clerkship, when she was on hospital rounds with the attending physician and

a host of medical interns and residents. The resident would summarize the previous day's events, what the blood work or imaging studies
revealed, while the rest hovered over the patient's bedside like specta-
tors at a sporting event.

While these bedside rounds may have been a bit intrusive, they were
always interesting and instructive. Until, that is, some suck-up student
or resident would inevitably blurt out something like, "Thompson et al.
in last week's *Lancet* . . . " Then they'd go into detail about some study
that was published and how it might relate to the patient before them.

Inwardly, Carrie would groan her displeasure. To Carrie, rounds on
surgical services were about practical information and hands-on study.
The book learning, though important, was no longer the focus. Instead,
her attention was on the ins and outs of active treatment. She held nothing but respect for internal medicine docs, or "fleas," as the surgeons
called them. Her dad was one, for goodness' sake, and he would always
be her idol. But from day one Carrie felt more comfortable in her skin
as a surgeon.

An old joke came to mind: an internal medicine doc, a pathologist,
and a surgeon are out duck hunting. Suddenly a flock of birds goes by.
The internist says, "They quack like ducks, they fly like ducks, they've
got the coloring of ducks. They're probably ducks." The surgeon glances
over at his friend, raises his shotgun, and shoots the birds out of the sky.
Then he says to the pathologist, "Go see if they're ducks."

Carrie was a surgeon.

After about a minute of aimless clicking and browsing, Carrie called
her dad.

"Hi, sweetie," Howard Bryant said.

Carrie smiled at the sound of his voice. "Hi, Dad. I could use some
help."

After she'd explained what she was after, Carrie's father pinpointed
the problem: She was at the wrong library. It felt liberating to walk out
the front doors of the VA, leaving the building Dr. Goodwin occupied,

for the Orange Line T stop. Carrie could have driven to the Harvard Medical Library, but parking at this time of day would be a hassle. Thirty minutes later, Carrie traded the warm spring day for the cool interior of the Francis A. Countway Library of Medicine.

The Harvard library was a sprawling, multifloor building, with a winding marble staircase and a spacious courtyard gloriously situated beneath a massive atrium ceiling. It took Carrie some time to find the *Index Medicus,* which had stopped publication in 2004, toppled by medical search engines, but respecting her dad's library research attack plan, she'd start with the tried and true.

Two hours into her effort Carrie still had not found anything useful, but she remained dedicated to the task. It was some relief that Carrie could find no cases of DBS-induced arrhythmia, which quieted the voice in her head that wanted to blame her for that part of Abington's condition. As for his delirium, the medical search engines offered up a host of unusual types of hallucinations that took her nowhere: hypnogogic hallucinations associated with sleep stage alterations, peduncular hallucinosis associated with brainstem diseases, musical hallucinations that seemed more benign and could even be pleasurable, but nothing that seemed like Abington's case.

Carrie examined a few old textbooks: *Noyes' Modern Clinical Psychiatry* from the '60s. Useless. She got up to stretch her legs. Another hour slipped by. And then another. Carrie's stomach was rumbling, but she was not ready to stop. She recalled the pure terror on Abington's face as she filled out a reference request card for an obscure medical journal. Her hunger for lunch seemed small next to the needs of the patient.

"I'll be sitting over there," Carrie said to the delicate and bony eighty-year-old woman working the desk, who hefted enormous tomes with seemingly little effort.

"I'll get it for you . . . I'll get it for you," the librarian said, repeating her words in what was probably a lifelong habit.

It reminded Carrie of Abington.

Follow my light . . . follow my light . . .

That was when it struck her. Carrie had been so focused on calling Abington's symptoms hallucinations that she had found articles specific only to that condition. But Abington was not exhibiting hallucinations. These were not totally false perceptions. It was more of a misperception of what Carrie had said. She had asked him a question and he had responded multiple times. He only thought she was saying it over and over again, when in fact she had uttered it only once, a simple single phrase.

As a neurosurgeon, Carrie was well aware of the difference between an illusion and a hallucination. She had focused on the wrong issue. A hallucination is a *false* perception, with no external stimulus involved. Whatever the individual hallucinates is an internal, personal experience. But an illusion is a *misperception* of reality, and in these cases an external stimulation is always present. With Abington, the external stimulation was Carrie's voice.

Carrie raced back to her desk and grabbed a standard textbook, *Principles of Neurology* by Adams and Victor. She had already read up on hallucinations, but this time she aimed elsewhere.

Illusions.

Carrie rifled through the index until she found: illusions, auditory, page 759. There, down toward the bottom of the page, was a reference to auditory illusions associated with lesions of the temporal lobe, where "words may be repeated, a kind of perseveration." Yes! Perseveration, the uncontrolled repetition of a word or phrase that was associated with brain injury. He was not hearing things, but rather he had a misperception of what was heard. It was a subtle twist, but it made all the difference.

Carrie's pulse jumped. She was onto something. She read about palinacousis, a condition first described by Bender in 1965, and elaborated by Jacobs with a number of case studies in 1973. Came from the Greek, *palin* (again) and *akouein* (to hear). All cases were attributed to lesions in the temporal lobe, where sound was processed in the brain. Some cases were due to a form of seizure, like a type of localized epilepsy. Single words or more extensive phrases would be repeated several times—in other words, perseverated.

The sounds could even be louder and more vivid than the original. Many patients became upset and quite disturbed by the event. Carrie read about several patients who were coherent enough to figure out that the sounds seemed to come from one particular side of their head. As it turned out, doctors were able to determine that instances of palinacousis manifest on the side opposite the brain lesion. If that were true, Abington would have heard Carrie's words, "Follow my light," only in one ear—more accurately, the left auditory field, on the opposite side of the lesion.

Palinacousis was extremely rare. Carrie could find only a handful of described cases despite an extensive literature search. She spent some time contemplating possible reasons why Abington had developed the condition. He certainly did not exhibit it prior to his surgery. Then again, he was not in any coherent state during her pre-op exam. Perhaps he was having the illusion then. Maybe that had triggered his rage. Could it have been seizure-related? Or did he have a hemorrhage in the temporal lobe post-op? The amygdala was not in the anatomical area that processed sounds, but could the DBS have done this, in some indirect way?

Carrie's head was spinning. Was this auditory illusion somehow connected to the arrhythmia, or did the haloperidol bring it on? Perhaps it was a combination of factors. At least Carrie had one possible answer, and a name, palinacousis, to account for Abington's strange behavior.

Such a bizarre and unusual disorder; she could imagine how anyone would get agitated, believing someone was yelling the same thing over and over again in your ear. And you could not see the person who was doing the yelling or where it was coming from. It was an illusion. The implications were troubling. The condition indicated a localized disturbance in the brain, specifically the part of the temporal lobe that processed auditory information.

Carrie returned to the idea that the condition could be a side effect of DBS. It would mean Abington's confused agitation was not the commonly encountered post-op delirium, a temporary consequence of anesthesia or other drugs. Carrie needed to see Abington, to examine him further, but obstacles blocked her way, namely Goodwin and Navarro.

She saw another path forward. This one involved a friend, perhaps her only one at the VA.

CHAPTER 24

The timing could not have been better.

Functioning as Dr. Finley's private DBS surgeon, Carrie had no clinic responsibilities, but he had sent her an e-mail to ask her to join him this morning because of a specific case on the schedule, one of his first patients who had undergone DBS for PTSD. The stars appeared to have aligned just for her.

Carrie had replayed her conversation with Abington dozens of times in her head. She had no doubt that he had repeated the phrase "follow my light" numerous times, and seemed to answer her question each time he thought it was asked, but that was not proof of palinacousis. Since Abington was off-limits, the best way to learn more, Carrie concluded, was to see another patient like him. Dr. Finley's e-mail was like manna from heaven.

At this point, Carrie's investigation into palinacousis was nothing more than an intellectual challenge. She simply wanted to know if the behavior ever manifested in others, or if Abington was truly an outlier. She was not in a position yet to broach the subject with Dr. Finley. Her confidence was nowhere near where it should be, and any claims made had to be based on evidence, not conjecture.

She had found nothing that reported auditory illusions in DBS cases treated for Parkinson's or other movement disorders. But with these PTSD patients, electrodes were being placed in a completely different area of the brain, the amygdala nucleus.

Carrie pondered this. The amygdala was not generally associated with hearing perception. She knew that. But this was an experimental program, and the brain was still an organ of profound mysteries.

Carrie was scheduled to meet with Dr. Finley on Wednesday morning, after the general neurology clinic. Dr. Finley was supposed to supervise the neurology clinic, which was otherwise run largely by the residents who rotated on three-month shifts through the VA. But Finley's increasing commitments to the deep brain stimulation program had gradually displaced his direct teaching and supervisory obligations, and on a typical Wednesday he would hold court from his office, making himself available as needed for residents. For the most part, the residents preferred to leave him alone and solve clinical problems by themselves.

Carrie had attended just one clinical round since she joined the VA's rank and file, but the DBS patients she saw that day were being treated for movement disorders, not PTSD. She had no way to correlate those patients to Steve Abington's condition. Traumatic brain injury patients comprised the majority of cases Carrie observed, with cognitive, perceptual, and language deficits usually accompanied by a hemi- or quadriparesis or seizures. Those patients whose foremost symptoms were post-traumatic stress were often referred to the psychiatry clinic, which was bursting through its seams.

Everyone realized these veterans were suffering from a brain disorder, but treatment was limited to antidepressants, antianxiety medication, or ineffective psychotropics. Acceptance into the DBS program was extremely limited during these early clinical stages, and the pent-up demand dwarfed the number of operations performed to date. Unless humanity put an end to war—likely only if humanity put an end to itself—a cure for PTSD seemed the only palliative measure for the VA's mushrooming resource woes.

Carrie arrived at Dr. Finley's office five minutes after the clinical rounds concluded and gently knocked on his door. She worried about interrupting him, but he threw the door open, as if in anticipation. A reassuring smile eased much of her concern, and he was filled with effervescence.

"Really exciting day, Carrie. I've just been reviewing the neuropsych tests on Ramón. We are clearly on track. Look at this."

He handed Carrie a bulging manila folder full of test results and graphics referencing one Ramón Hernandez, a thirty-two-year-old male, and a veteran of war in Afghanistan. Carrie leafed through the studies.

"He was one of our first DBS cases, because he failed all the usual therapies," Dr. Finley said. "I remember that Sam Rockwell had some difficulties with his surgery, and actually had to reposition the stimulating electrodes several times before we got adequate signals from the amygdala, but fortunately there were no obvious complications."

No follow my light, Carrie thought. *No arrhythmia.*

With an expression like a proud papa's, Dr. Finley went on.

"Ramón Hernandez has gone from living on the streets, or in jail, to holding a respectable job as a logistics analyst for a Target distribution center. He's still on sertraline one hundred and fifty milligrams, but the Oxycontin, benzos, and beta blockers are gone, and he regularly attends the weekly counseling sessions with his clinical social worker. Last I heard, he's even got a girlfriend."

Lifting the folder, Dr. Finley said, "This battery of psychometrics documents Ramón's impressive progress. In addition to the MMPI, we concentrated mostly on tests of all aspects of memory function, emotional intelligence, and executive functioning. There's an alexithymia scale."

Carrie was familiar with the Minnesota Multiphasic Personality Inventory, or MMPI, but had not heard of the alexithymia scale and asked Dr. Finley to clarify.

"It's when people have difficulty describing and expressing their own emotions," Dr. Finley said. "Kind of a measure of how much people are in touch with their feelings. It's a useful addition to other tests of emotional intelligence and frustration tolerance. They're far from perfect, but we get a pretty good picture of someone's personality when we analyze the entire test battery results."

Adam didn't seem to have that much difficulty there, Carrie thought. He seemed as caring and understanding as ever. But she could not deny his explosiveness, as seen in David's bloodied nose and the damage Adam had inflicted on his Camaro. Adam was a firework of violence, awaiting only a match.

"You thought Don McCall was impressive," Dr. Finley said. "Wait until you meet Ramón."

CHAPTER 25

The Department of Neurology and Neurosurgery at the VA occupied an H-shaped section of the second floor in the main building. There was some talk that the department would move if they ever finished construction on the annex, but that was a very big "if." While it was a bit cramped, there was a certain convenience to having the surgical suites and the neurology exam rooms all in close proximity.

Dr. Finley led Carrie at a brisk pace to exam room five in the neurology unit. The exam room was like most Carrie had been in over the years; not that different from the one where she'd almost died. It had a waist-high counter, a sink, and various instruments for checking vitals.

Seated in the aluminum chair next to the examination table was a clean-cut, neatly but casually dressed and well-groomed Hispanic gentleman, who stood and shook hands with Dr. Finley. He was powerfully built and quite handsome, Carrie noted.

"Hey, Doc. Good to see you." He spoke with a youthful and vibrant voice, the voice of somebody excited for the future.

Carrie had to look carefully to see the slight asymmetry of the neck where the stimulating wires had been tunneled from the scalp, running down beneath his right clavicle to attach to the battery pack in his upper chest.

"This is Dr. Carrie Bryant, who has taken over for Dr. Rockwell."

"Yeah, I heard about his accident," Ramón said. "Terrible. He was a

terrific guy. Nice to meet you, Dr. Bryant. You've got big shoes to fill."
Ramón's hand, half the size of a baseball mitt, swallowed Carrie's as
he gave her a firm but gentle handshake.

"I've heard only great things about Dr. Rockwell," Carrie said.

"Mind if she examines you, Ramón?"

"Be my guest," Ramón said. "But I can probably examine myself by
now."

Carrie resisted the urge to come right out and ask if he ever heard
the same words spoken over and over again. Her old pal Val would say
Carrie possessed all the subtlety of a jackhammer.

Carrie proceeded through a series of questions pertaining to Ramón's
current lifestyle. It was clear that he was socially appropriate, concentrated well, and attended to questions with insight and flexibility. He
enjoyed his work, and even gave some thought to getting married to
his longtime girlfriend.

"Considering she could have charged me with domestic assault not
that long ago, I'd say I've come a long way." Ramón's smile projected
the kind of cocky confidence required for the battlefield.

"Can you elaborate?" Carrie asked.

How far had Ramón really come, she wanted to know.

"I used to get drunk and jealous. I hit her. More than once. Not
something I'm proud of, obviously. Once I got my anger under control
with the DBS I could actually listen to what the therapists were trying
to tell me."

"And that is?"

"That I was trying to control her because I was really afraid I was
going to lose her."

The insight impressed Carrie, but she was curious to see how he
would react to questions about his war memories. "What happened
during that ambush? Do you mind talking about it?"

Ramón's eyes flashed, but he just shrugged. "Honestly, I don't remember all of it."

"Share what you can," Carrie said.

"I was stationed at Camp Dwyer in the Helmand Province, a place we lovingly referred to as 'Hell, man.' Luxury there was a sandbag that could double as a couch," Ramón said, with the detachment of a newscaster. "We were on a scouting mission, looking for a terrorist named Nasser Umari. He was a big-time anti-Coalition dickhead, pardon my language—hooked up with the Taliban, and other militant groups, too, I suppose. We had just fast-roped from an MH-47 helicopter, did our patrols, and after that, exfiltrated back toward our extraction point. There were about fifteen of us in the fire team." He paused to remember. "Yeah, about fifteen. It was the usual oven hot that day. A few more degrees and the sand would have turned to glass. We had just vaulted a mud wall in what looked like an abandoned town when machine-gun fire seemed to come out of nowhere. Me and three other guys fell back into an alley where I figured we'd get a better read on the enemy position. But the Taliban had machine-gun positions all around and next thing I knew I got shot in the arm. Hurt like a mother, you know what."

Ramón rolled up the sleeve on his white cotton T-shirt to show Carrie a scar on his bulging trapezius a little bigger than a quarter. She was sure his body was riddled with other scars that had nothing to do with DBS surgery.

Ramón continued. "We were returning fire, but I had crawled into a doorway to try and clot the wound. Next thing I knew, an RPG struck our position and two of the guys in the alley with me couldn't have an open casket at their wakes. It was that fast. But, I guess that's war. The bad guys are after us, and we're after them. Kill or be killed, right?"

Carrie was taken by how calm and controlled Ramón seemed. She saw no reticence or protectiveness. He remained focused, his mind targeted in the present, the past trauma mitigated by perspective. She was duly impressed. If emotion was a color, Ramón's ambush had been rendered in simple black and white.

"So, what sort of problems are you having?" Carrie asked.

Ramón gave this some thoughtful consideration. "Well, sometimes I don't seem to care about things all that much," he eventually confessed. "I don't get as worked up about a lot of things that used to bother me, either. Mostly that's good, but I wonder if sometimes I'm too relaxed. If I get behind in work, I don't seem to care or worry as much. That's not me. And I don't remember a lot about my time in Afghanistan. I mean I do, but I don't. There's lots of holes. People have to tell me things, and sometimes it doesn't make sense. But I can live with that."

"What about your hearing? Do you hear voices?" Carrie asked.

"No."

"How about hearing sounds or voices that you know are real, but they seem to go on and on in your head, like an echo that never stops?"

Dr. Finley looked at Carrie, nonplussed. She knew these questions would produce that kind of reaction. They were way off base for this sort of exam, but Dr. Finley did not intervene.

"No," Ramón said.

Carrie went on to complete her examination, standard bedside tests of memory and cognition that she knew he would pass with flying colors. She analyzed his vision and eye movements, his hearing, speech, and swallowing. His motor functioning, gait, sensation, and reflexes were all perfectly normal.

"Thanks," she said. "It was a real pleasure meeting and talking with you. And thank you for your service."

"My pleasure. See you again. And good luck with the program."

She shook hands again and Carrie followed Dr. Finley out of the exam room. Dr. Finley had more to discuss with Ramón, but he said he wanted to speak with Carrie in private first.

"Amazing, right?"

"I'm truly astounded," Carrie said.

Dr. Finley's pride and enthusiasm were infectious, but Carrie could not embrace the moment to his degree. Ramón had reinvigorated her mojo, but her curiosity had not been fully satiated.

"Was Steve Abington ever diagnosed with schizophrenia? Any history of the disease in his family?"

Dr. Finley thought on it and shook his head.

"No, why do you ask?"

"Just curious," Carrie said.

The answer was expected and did nothing to waylay her concerns. Post-op delirium or some strange side effect to DBS? It was impossible for her to say. Carrie contemplated her next move. She was scheduled to be back in the OR on Friday, for a DBS surgery on a marine named Eric Fasciani. Before she could share Dr. Finley's enthusiasm completely, she had to see whether the condition happened again.

If she were careful, Carrie could go see that patient post-op, and Goodwin would never be the wiser.

CHAPTER 26

Carrie had never acquired much of a taste for alcohol. She seldom drank, but on Friday night, two days after meeting Ramón Hernandez, she sat alone in a booth at Bertucci's and sipped from her glass of Sauvignon Blanc. Her thoughts were dim from fatigue. She had spent seven grueling hours on her feet performing another successful DBS surgery on Eric Fasciani.

The operation had gone smoothly enough, and it was easy to see how her job could become routine. Two Parkinson's cases were already on the schedule for next week, and they would be virtually identical procedures. Today it had been Eric Fasciani's turn on the table, and depending on what Carrie found out, it could change everything.

A middle-aged waitress with a kind face and friendly smile scuttled past Carrie's table, but backtracked when she noticed the empty wineglass.

"Do you want another?" She cleared the glass along with the remains of Carrie's salad meal. "Maybe some dessert? The chocolate mousse is amazing."

"Sounds tempting," Carrie said, "but I'll just get a coffee. Black."

The waitress departed and Carrie checked the hour on her smartphone, then frowned. She was eager to get to Fasciani on the neuro recovery floor, but it was too early to see him. Her latest DBS patient represented a possible answer to the Steve Abington mystery, but he would be too heavily sedated for Carrie to properly evaluate. She needed him more alert.

Fasciani's operation had been long, but without incident. At the advice of Dr. Finley, Carrie had skipped pre-op consultation altogether. Better for her nerves, it was thought. Instead of greeting a troubled and nervous patient, Carrie saw only a shaved, bald-headed young man, deeply sedated and intubated with his endotracheal tube tied to a ventilator, and an IV drip open to KVO. It was probably better this way, and it fit right in with Dr. Goodwin's view of her role as hired help. Carrie was a technician, not a doctor. At least Dr. Finley had briefed her on the poor fellow's history.

"Three tours in Afghanistan, but it was the last one that did him in," Dr. Finley had said. "Apparently, the attack was highly organized. A hundred fifty Taliban came running down the hillsides from four directions and riddled his base with gunfire and RPGs."

Carrie wondered if anybody came back from the war unchanged.

"The outpost went up in flames," Dr. Finley continued. "After this, he was a quivering wreck. He couldn't sleep without his dead buddies waking him in a sweat. They MedFlighted him out of there and eventually got him back home to Worcester. But he failed reentry miserably. He suffers from horrible flashbacks and daily panic attacks. We actually found him on the street, living out of an old shopping cart. We've got him in a shelter now, but he's made little progress."

Carrie felt a fleeting sense of gratitude. Adam had a home, loving and helpful parents, and her. She looked over at Fasciani and saw the scars and needle tracks in his arms and neck, and the dozens of skin-raising scars on his limbs and trunk. One of his demons was heroin.

"He hasn't done too well with talk therapy," Dr. Finley added. "And most of the time, his blood work comes back with no evidence that he's even taking the antidepressants we've prescribed. Just Valium, alcohol, Oxycontin, and other opiates. So in this case, Carrie, DBS is not just a treatment, it's his only hope, a prayer."

The surgery was Abington redux. The small burr holes for fixing the stereotactic frame, the CT scan and superimposed computerized mapping with his earlier MRI images. The 14mm burr hole placed just where the images told her to drill, the cannula driven through to the basolateral nucleus of the amygdala, finally the electrodes, only to await Dr. Finley's confident voice coming up from the monitor on the other side of the table: "Great, Carrie. Precise and perfect signals. Lock 'em in."

After, Dr. Finley and Carrie had met outside the OR. Her boss was beaming with pride, overjoyed.

"This is your second case this week, and you are, in a word, terrific," Dr. Finley said. "Trust me, Carrie, you have what it takes to do this. You're a machine. I mean despite all those computerized gizmos, a lot of times Dr. Rockwell had to reposition the cannula, three or more passes at times, and I always worried about an increased risk of infection or hemorrhage. But with you, I'm sure we've got those electrodes placed where they need to be, and I'm just that much more confident in the results."

From the corner of her eye, Carrie could see Eric Fasciani's stretcher being wheeled into the elevator on its way up to the third floor, neuro post-op ICU.

"Thanks for the vote of confidence," she said.

"Rockwell's a fine doc," Dr. Finley said. "And I pray he makes a full recovery. But no matter what happens, I think you've got his job."

Carrie blushed, a little uncomfortable that her good fortune had come at another's misfortune. She politely refused Dr. Finley's invitation to dinner, instead heading off on her own to kill time.

That was three hours ago. Carrie checked her smartphone once more, paid her bill in cash including a hefty tip, and slid out of the booth. As she hurried to her car, she thought: *If Fasciani exhibits the same symptoms as Abington, nobody is going to have Sam Rockwell's job.*

CHAPTER 27

The doctors' parking lot at the VA was virtually deserted when Carrie drove up in her trusty Subaru. She parked some distance from the entrance, out of the way of prying eyes. Only the residents' on-call spaces were occupied, and somebody working for Navarro might recognize Carrie's car. That could lead to questions, and Carrie's workday had technically ended the moment Fasciani got wheeled out of the OR. A little extra precaution was the right prescription for this evening's unsanctioned jaunt.

The VA was not in the best neighborhood, and the quiet of the surrounding streets set Carrie on edge. A biting wind rippled the plastic sheets draped over the long-neglected scaffolding that framed much of the darkened annex. Carrie did not know if the VA's administrators were counting on continued DARPA funds to get construction going again, but she had her suspicions.

Carrie pinned a clipboard to her side with one arm, and shielded her hands from the cold within the thin fabric pockets of her long white lab coat. *Some spring.* Beneath her coat, Carrie wore a clean pair of blue scrubs. She needed to look official, here on hospital business.

The automatic doors of the rear hospital entrance swooshed open as Carrie approached. Once inside, Carrie scuttled past the lone security guard stationed at a wood podium with a quick flash of her hospital ID. To him, she was another doc on the job and nothing more. The VA's empty corridors amplified Carrie's footsteps. At this hour, BCH would have been bustling, and Carrie was reminded of the days when ambulances arrived in steady streams hauling everything from panic attacks to gunshot wounds.

On her way to the elevator, Carrie spied a young woman dressed in green scrubs who approached from the opposite direction. She could have been one of Navarro's, but Carrie did not take a close look to confirm. With the clipboard to her face, Carrie lowered her head and pretended to study something important.

The ruse worked. Not a glance. Not even a hitch in the other woman's stride. The experience made Carrie feel a little bit foolish. She was a surgeon, not some fly-by-night medical detective. It was all a bit absurd, but exhilarating at the same time. Most of her life Carrie had been a rule follower, not breaker, but in this instance she felt justified, and believed her actions were absolutely necessary. Carrie quickened her pace and was a bit breathless when she reached the elevators.

Moments later, Carrie was back on neuro recovery. She pushed the intercom and waited for the duty nurse to unlock the double doors securing access to the unit. Carrie heard a faint click, pulled on the door handle, and headed inside.

Marianne was off tonight, apparently, and a different nurse occupied the nurses' station. Carrie did not recognize the attractive black male in his thirties who was too busy charting to bother to look at whom he buzzed inside.

"Good evening," Carrie said.

The man glanced up from his monitor. He had a handsome face and almond-shaped eyes the color of dark caramel. Carrie's eyes dropped to his ID badge, but it was concealed by shadows and impossible to read.

"Quiet night tonight," Carrie said.

Only one doc was supposed to be doing rounds, and it was certainly not Carrie. For this reason alone, Carrie would have preferred to avoid conversation altogether, but that would have come across as odd. Nurses expected a bit of small talk from the doctors.

"Only got one patient on the floor tonight," the nurse said. His resonant voice sounded neither pleased nor bothered by the lack of activity. Abington had also been the only patient on the floor the night Carrie visited, which pinged her curiosity. Were vets slated for DBS surgery specifically on days when no other major neuro surgeries were scheduled? It would make sense to isolate them, given how agitated and volatile these patients could become. Either way, the scheduling practice worked in Carrie's favor.

"How's our patient doing?"

"He's been pretty quiet. But these vets aren't in the best of shape to begin with."

"I'm just going to pop in and check on him. I'm the surgeon who did his DBS installation."

"Um-hum." The nurse could not have sounded less impressed if he tried. On a whim, Carrie decided to secure a little extra insurance on her clandestine visit.

"What's your name?" she asked.

The nurse returned a wary glance. Docs do not always bother with such pleasantries. "Lee Taggart," he said, holding up his badge for Carrie to see and read.

"Look, Lee," Carrie said, leaning over the nurses' station to deliver her message. "I'd appreciate it if you kept my visit here a secret. I'm really supposed to let the residents handle things, but I guess I'm a bit of a control freak."

Carrie flashed a playful smile that did not appear to soften Lee any. She got the distinct impression that Lee Taggart did not care about hospital politics in any way, shape, or form, so long as his checks cleared.

"You do what you need to do," Taggart said as his focus returned to his charts. "I don't tell people anything they don't ask or need to know."

Carrie gave Taggart an appreciative smile he did not see, and left.

Fifteen steps later, she was inside Fasciani's room. These hospital quarters were nothing but glass cubicles with a freestanding wardrobe closet and a flimsy curtain for privacy. The patients were kept isolated to reduce the spread of infection, and while there were not many rooms to choose from, Carrie observed that Fasciani occupied the same bed as Abington had before his transfer to med ICU.

A gooseneck lamp mounted above Fasciani's hospital bed illuminated his face enough to show Carrie his glassy-eyed stare. He was awake, and Carrie commended herself for getting the timing of the anesthesia right. She closed the door, pulled the curtain shut, and turned on the overhead fluorescent.

Fasciani's eyes were sunken and ringed with dark circles. His hollow cheeks, missing teeth, and shaved head made him look more like a POW than a hospital patient. At least Fasciani did not have that accusatory stare and look of terror she had seen in Steve Abington's eyes. Maybe this was all for naught. She would know soon enough.

Carrie approached Fasciani's bed and spoke in a whisper. "I'm Dr. Bryant, Eric. I did the surgery on you earlier today."

Nothing. If anything, his vacant gaze worked harder to penetrate the wall in front of him.

"I just came to check on you," Carrie said, resting her hands on the bed railing. "I hope you're doing okay. Sometimes, patients feel a little nauseated from the anesthesia right about now, and I suspect you have a bit of a headache."

More silence. Fasciani's only response, if it could be called that, was to turn his head away from Carrie. His movements came in slow motion. Carrie's stomach tightened and her earlier confidence fell away. She thought of only one cause for such languorous motility.

He's still too sedated, dammit!

She was certain she had given him enough recovery time. This many hours post-op, Fasciani should have been coherent enough to play checkers. In his current condition, there would be no way for Carrie to effectively evaluate him. She doubted Fasciani would spend another night in the neuro ICU. If Carrie was going to evaluate him, it needed to be tonight. She had no other option. Carrie would have to retreat and come back later. Her curiosity had become its own gravitational force. She hoped whoever worked the overnight shift would be as accommodating as Lee Taggart.

Carrie came around to the front of the bed and examined his chart. With a quick scan of his meds, she saw the problem right away: Valium, a lot of it. Fasciani must have become agitated at some point and the nurse had wisely put him under. Evidently Lee Taggart thought an infusion of a major sedative was a detail Carrie did not need to know, and certainly she had not thought to ask. Well, at least she could trust the tight-lipped nurse to keep her visit here a secret.

Dammit again!

The situation was essentially hopeless. Fasciani was going to spend the night sedated. Carrie could come back at midnight or two in the morning, and it would not make a difference.

Though daunted, Carrie was not ready to give up. She had inherited her mother's willful determination. Addressing Fasciani from the foot of the bed, Carrie asked, "Eric, can you tell me how you're feeling?"

He gave no response, but Carrie expected none. She went around to the left side of the bed to check Fasciani's pupil reaction to her penlight, and saw that his lips looked dry and chapped. She smoothed an ice chip taken from a plastic cup at his bedside over his cracked lips like a healing balm. Fasciani's empty stare went beyond a thousand yards. After several passes with the ice, Fasciani turned away from Carrie, his movements slowed by the drugs in his system, and came to a rest with his head facing the door. Carrie wondered if he was going to call for the nurse, but Fasciani was so doped up she doubted he even knew where he was.

She decided to make one more attempt, though it was an obvious sucker's bet. She went around to the other side of the bed so she could look him in the eyes.

"Eric, I want to help you," Carrie said. Her voice cracked slightly under the strain of emotion. The pang in her chest felt like heartbreak; her deep compassion went far beyond her duty as a doctor. The rawness of these feelings came from Adam. She heard echoes of her brother in Fasciani's struggles. Abington's, too. And while Adam seemed to be coping, a distinct possibility remained that he could one day fall into the abyss—first to the streets, then to drugs, the shelters, and eventually maybe to some hospital bed at the VA, with or without wires in his brain. In this way, Fasciani was not just another wounded vet. He was like family.

Fasciani's bedsheets rustled as he turned away from Carrie to face the wall opposite the door. This time his movements struck Carrie as a bit strange. *Did he just turn away intentionally?* Carrie waited a moment, perhaps as long as two minutes, purposefully silent. When enough time passed, she repositioned Fasciani's head so he again faced the door. He offered no resistance and stayed with his head in that direction, unmoving, hardly blinking. She took a couple steps toward the door.

"Eric, can you hear me?" she asked.

One second . . . then two . . . then three . . . then . . .

Fasciani turned his head and faced the wall opposite the door.

Twice. That's nothing, Carrie thought. I spoke and he turned his head away from my voice twice. Could just be a coincidence. For a third time Carrie repositioned Fasciani's head to face the door. Again she spoke. "Eric, can you hear me?"

To herself, Carrie counted: *One . . . and two . . . and three . . .*

Fasciani showed Carrie the back of his head as he again faced the wall opposite the door. She repeated the test again with the same result. She spoke to Fasciani from the right side of the bed, and he turned his head to the left.

Carrie said, "Holy crap. It's as though he's hearing my voice from that side of the room!"

Carrie tested him one more time, but in a different way. "Eric, I want you to answer me each time you hear this," she said.

Fasciani repositioned his head to face left and mumbled in a groggy, drug-slurred voice, "I hear you, I hear, I hear you."

Carrie's breath caught. This was classic and just what she had read in the literature. Many patients were able to localize their illusion to the side opposite the pathology in the brain. She felt certain the auditory processing of the right temporal lobe in Fasciani's brain was not working right.

Carrie's training kicked in as she battled to slow her thinking. She did not want to be reactive, but found it hard to control her emotions.

Abington and Fasciani both exhibited symptoms of palinacousis, and the commonality was DBS. But was that the root cause? Carrie could not say with certainty. Again she went back to a hemorrhage, but could there be a stroke from a blocked blood vessel? She wanted a CT scan or MRI, stat. An EEG, too. Could it be a seizure? Something else? Why didn't Ramón experience anything like this? Or had he, and his memory was fogged?

Carrie felt urgency and curiosity, but also anger. She was trapped. She had no business being here, and had no one to call on for help. She couldn't even order these tests without Goodwin torpedoing her career.

She had no authority to intervene, unless she went to Dr. Finley. But what then?

Hi boss, sorry I put your program and the hospital at risk by acting like a resident when I haven't been credentialed.

That could create all sorts of problems. At a minimum, Dr. Finley would have to make some excuse for Carrie examining Fasciani, or he'd simply lie and say that he himself had followed up on the patients. But Dr. Finley was not even a surgeon, and that explanation, Carrie knew, would not wash.

Before Carrie could approach Dr. Finley, she needed more specifics. The worst thing she could do would be nothing at all. The second worst thing would be to make some wild claim about a huge DBS side

effect, one that nobody else had noticed before, without any supporting evidence. Her credibility was still in the repair stages, and Carrie
was already on unstable ground. She thought she was onto something,
but what? She could not do anything about it at nine thirty at night.

Unless . . .

An idea came to Carrie so ingenious her whole body tensed. The
next shift was due to come on at eleven o'clock. Carrie could go home,
call the duty nurse, and order a CAT scan using Dr. Navarro's hospital
ID. It was pinned to the nurses' station for everyone to see.

It was a risky move, but asking for a scan was not like ordering nar-
cotics. She could say that Navarro had personally asked her to call in
the labs. Chances were nobody would question the order. If the nurse
on the next shift was anything like Lee Taggart, it was almost a certainty. The scan could be done overnight or very early in the morning.
Carrie would go by radiology first thing and have a look at the films
herself. No one was likely to see her if she showed up early enough.
Once she checked out the CAT scan and the EEG, she'd decide what
to do from there. Carrie gently touched Fasciani's face. His skin felt
spongy, no give. Her heart ached for him. Something had to be done.

It was not perfect, but at least it was a plan.

CHAPTER 28

A glance at the speedometer showed Carrie was going seventy. Her thoughts raced, and it was no surprise the surge of adrenaline had her driving so fast. Carrie checked the time on the dashboard clock. In thirty minutes she could make the call she had rehearsed into memory.

The radio was off, but Carrie's fingers drummed an erratic rhythm against the steering wheel as she exited the highway. Her thoughts returned to Fasciani, Abington, and this bizarre palinacousis. The implications of the discovery both exhilarated and bewildered her. DBS sat at the epicenter of a renaissance in psychosurgery, a groundswell that Carrie's discovery might disrupt. It was the last outcome Dr. Finley had imagined when he brought her on board.

Carrie kept to the speed limit and arrived home at quarter to eleven, leaving fifteen minutes until shift change and showtime. It was difficult not to project into the future. If DBS proved detrimental in the way she suspected, it would put an immediate halt to Dr. Finley's pilot program, and put her right out of a job. What she was about to do carried a burden of guilt, lots of it. Dr. Finley had given her a second chance, and here she was going behind his back, working covertly to dismantle what might be Nobel Prize—worthy work in the treatment of PTSD.

While the surgical community had embraced DBS as a neurosurgical treatment for a variety of ailments, the public would key in on the brain damage it caused, and would have a hard time not seeing the procedure as a harkening back to the days of rusty implements and drooling, mindless patients. Some side effects to experimental surgery would be tolerable, but palinacousis was not one of them. The extremely rare condition made it impossible for anyone to function, with bodiless voices constantly shouting in one ear. If it was not a fate worse than death, it sure was close.

Irene Bryant was in the living room working on a painting when Carrie arrived. Adam was stretched out on the sofa. Dressed in gray shorts and a loose-fitting T-shirt, he struck a Rubenesque pose as he munched on an apple. If only he were as plump and healthy-looking as those models. After hanging up her coat, Carrie came around to the front of the easel. She fully expected Adam would be part of her mother's creation, but Irene had painted only the bowl of fruit on the coffee table. It was so realistic-looking it tricked Carrie's mind into smelling citrus mixed in with the scent of fresh oil paint.

"It's beautiful, Mom," Carrie said.

Standing beside Carrie, Irene appraised her work thoughtfully, body akimbo. "I'm thinking of calling it *Bowl of Fruit*."

"Very clever title," Carrie said. She pointed to an apple in the fruit bowl. "May I?" Carrie asked. She had eaten only a salad for dinner, and her belly was rumbling. She needed something to settle her stomach before making the call, and her mother's painting had given her a craving for fruit.

"My work here is done, so be my guest."

Adam tossed Carrie an apple. She noticed the tips of her brother's fingers were blackened with engine grease, which he somehow managed to keep off the furniture but not her apple. Carrie tossed the apple back to her brother.

"I'll get my own. Thanks."

"I almost got the beast running today," Adam said.

The distant look in Adam's eyes and his downcast expression caused Irene's bright smile to retreat. It made Carrie sad, thinking how this must be for her mother. Adam's past was stunting his potential, his future, and the mental shackles he wore kept him in a seemingly inescapable limbo. Here was Carrie, at the helm of a major mental health breakthrough, in a position to help Adam and others like him, but she was about to do the exact opposite.

Irene turned her attention to Carrie and fixed her daughter with a worried stare. Irene's ability to see what others missed made her gifted at the canvas as well as a difficult parent to hide from. Carrie had learned that lesson the hard way in her rebellious middle school years, most notably the one and only time she came home a little tipsy from a friend's house. Her mother's powers of observation never failed to amaze. Perhaps Carrie had inherited some of that talent, and it allowed her to see in Abington and Fasciani what others at the VA had not.

"Is something wrong, sweetheart?" Irene asked.

I'm just about to blow my future up again, Carrie thought. *Mine and Adam's.*

"No. I'm fine," was all Carrie managed.

"Good day?"

"Great. But I'm going to turn in. Big day tomorrow." *Maybe the biggest, depending on what those tests show, or don't show.*

"Yeah, me too," Adam said, sounding sarcastic. "I'm going to do nothing, and then in the afternoon I have a big heap of nothing on my plate."

Irene shot Adam a slightly disapproving look, only because the truth in his humor hurt. Adam had nothing to do except work on that car of his. He could not hold a job, see his friends, or concentrate on a task without his frustration and pent-up anger getting the better of him.

Carrie crossed the room, wrapped her arms around her brother, and gave him a kiss on the forehead. "I love you, brother," Carrie said. "And we're going to get through this together."

Adam returned a weak smile that seemed to contradict her conviction. "Maybe in my next life," he said.

The guilt returned. The ache of betrayal, of secrets Carrie would have to keep, weighed heavy and would probably grow more burdensome over time. As she headed for the stairs, Carrie paused to apply a quick peck on her mother's cheek. The look Carrie got in response said her loving gesture hadn't lightened her mother's lingering concern.

Carrie bounded up the stairs and closed her bedroom door behind her. *Home again, home again.* But not home. No, no really. This was transient living; Carrie's life was in flux, much like Adam's.

Carrie sat on her bed with her smartphone in hand. She did not know the VA's phone number by memory, and after looking it up, wrote it down on the same scratch paper where she had earlier jotted Navarro's hospital ID and his user name/password combination. Navarro had posted those numbers as a personal convenience so he would not have to approve and enter every lab order from a resident. It was a bit lazy, but not at all an uncommon practice. Still, Carrie did not want to keep Navarro's login credentials on her smartphone, lest Goodwin employed hackers as spies. She could not be too cautious.

Carrie knew without checking that her pupils were slightly dilated and her heartbeat accelerated, all neurological responses to stress. Intellectually, she understood that her sympathetic nervous system was causing a biochemical imbalance, not that the knowledge reduced her anxiety any.

The phone rang. Her hands turned clammy.

The operator answered. "VA, can I help you?"

"Yes, neuro recovery ICU, please."

"One moment."

A beat of silence preceded the phone ringing once again. Carrie took a breath and exhaled slowly. She studied Navarro's ID number, committing the digits to memory.

You can do this. Just sound confident.

Another ring. Carrie tensed, gripping her phone even tighter. But the phone kept on ringing. No answer. *Where's the duty nurse?* Carrie considered the possibility that Fasciani had suffered a setback. Maybe he was being triaged at that moment, or he could have coded. Naturally, Carrie's mind went to the worst possible outcomes. Was it related to the DBS?

Carrie waited fifteen minutes, then called back. The operator connected her to the unit for a second time. By twelve thirty, after three attempts to reach the duty nurse, Carrie was an emotional wreck. Something horrible was happening to Eric Fasciani, she felt certain of it. She dialed the operator once more.

"This is Dr. Carrie Bryant," she announced. "Could you please page the duty nurse on the neuro recovery ICU and have whoever it is call me back ASAP."

Carrie gave the operator her number and waited anxiously for the call back. When her phone finally rang some seventeen minutes later, she was on the floor trying to stretch out a bit of tightness in her legs and back. Days after Abington's unprovoked assault, Carrie still felt a persistent ache. She should have gone downstairs and grabbed something to eat, but Adam was up watching television and Carrie was in no mood to confront her guilt again.

She staved off a bout of light-headedness from having stood too quickly, and answered the call. "This is Dr. Bryant," Carrie said into the phone.

"Yeah, Dr. Bryant, this is Mandy, the operator here."

"Mandy?" Carrie was confused. *Where's the duty nurse?*

"Um, okay," was all Carrie could think to say.

"There's nobody up on the ICU neuro recovery floor."

The light-headedness Carrie had experienced returned with a vengeance. "What do you mean? That's impossible. I was just visiting a patient there not more than a few hours ago."

Mandy made a bit of an exasperated sigh as if to imply the docs never knew what was really going on.

"That may very well be," Mandy said. "But there ain't no patients up there now. Security checked it for me. The lights are out, the doors are locked, and nobody is home."

CHAPTER 29

Carrie kept a light foot on the gas on her early-morning drive back to the VA. She had espresso for blood. The notion that Fasciani had somehow gotten up and walked away from neuro recovery simply did not compute. Could Fasciani have had a medical emergency like Abington's? Perhaps he coded, maybe an arrhythmia like Abington, and had been transferred to the med ICU—"turfed," as Goodwin would call it. DBS-induced palinacousis and arrhythmia? Carrie could not dream up a more bizarre set of symptoms.

If Carrie could have called Lee Taggart or the duty nurse for the eleven o'clock shift from home, she would have. The problem was, Carrie did not have access to the scheduling application. She was Dr. Finley's employee and had no IT privileges. If she wanted to speak with the nursing staff, her only option was to return to the hospital. Not a problem. Carrie had reheated a burrito in the microwave, and a Red Bull would keep her alert for hours.

Besides, this would give her an excuse to go to the med ICU to look for Fasciani and personally check up on Abington, assuming he was still a patient there. It would be easy enough to walk the floor without raising too many eyebrows. Her goal was modest and obtainable. She would get to work hours before everyone else, find out what she needed to know, and maybe grab a few hours' sleep in a vacant on-call room.

A little past one thirty in the morning, Carrie arrived at the VA and parked in the same spot she had occupied hours ago. Then it was back through the rear entrance with a head nod and a flash of her badge, this time to a different security guard. She raced down the hallway, eager to confirm what she already knew to be true. The hospital, like most of the patients here, seemed fast asleep.

The elevator stopped on the third floor and Carrie hurried out. In no time she was back at the double doors to the neuro ICU. They were locked, but that was standard procedure. More unusual was the view through the windows built into the swinging doors. The hallway lights were off. The glow from various screen savers illuminated the nurses' station enough for Carrie to see it was unoccupied.

Unoccupied, but why? What had happened to her patient? Not her patient, but rather Navarro's and Goodwin's.

If Fasciani was still in the hospital—and where else would he be?— Carrie reasoned she would find him in the med ICU. He'd coded, or something. The arrhythmia. It was the only logical explanation.

Soon Carrie was standing outside the locked doors to the med ICU, looking through the glass into a well-lit, active unit. Carrie buzzed the intercom and announced herself as Dr. Bryant. The doors unlocked and Carrie strode over to the nurses' station. A black woman in her late twenties, hair pulled back, high cheekbones, pretty and slight, looked up from her monitor and gave Carrie a quiet smile.

"Morning, Doctor, what brings you here?"

"I just wanted to see if you had a patient by the name of Eric Fasciani brought here this evening?"

The woman, Dot according to her name badge, clicked at her keyboard and shook her head slightly.

"The name doesn't sound familiar. No, I'm sorry. He's not here."

Carrie's brow furrowed and her eyes narrowed into slits. Where could he have gone? She asked, "Is Steve Abington still here?"

Dot executed more key taps than a ticket broker at an airline counter. That slight frown returned. "We don't have a Steve Abington here, either," she said.

"Well, he was transferred to the floor the day before yesterday."

Dot checked her screen again, thinking she might have missed something. "I'm sorry, we don't have his record, so I can't tell you where he went."

"Can we check the computer?" Carrie asked.

"Sorry, I can't do that," Dot said. "This new electronic medical record system is great in some ways, but we're still in classes for access authorization. I've spent about a hundred hours and all I'm allowed to do now is input vitals and other nursing data."

Carrie was not the least bit surprised. She understood this all too well.

"I can look up labs," Dot offered. "But I still can't see things like patient demographics. Don't ask me why. Most everyone hates it, but I suspect we'll get the hang of it soon enough."

Carrie brightened. "Could you check for any labs you might have done for Steve Abington in the last day or two?"

Dot nodded and her fingers went flying over the keyboard. "There's nothing in the system."

"Nothing? Is that common? I mean, he was a patient here."

"Honey, at the VA we see it all. The only thing common is that nothing is common, if you get my drift. By the way, who are you?"

That was it. The last thing Carrie needed was a leak of her presence getting back to Dr. Goodwin or Navarro. She had to bring her concern to somebody who could really help.

CHAPTER 30

Clutching a cup of coffee, Carrie made her way to Dr. Alistair Finley's office after making sure his midnight blue E-class Mercedes coupe was parked in its assigned space. The parking lot was already half full, and the hallways around the main entrance were starting to bustle with activity. The hospital had yawned and stretched, and was coming to life like a once dormant giant.

Around her the gloom of the early morning gave way to sparkling sunshine and a pleasing warm breeze. By all accounts, it would be a glorious day. Carrie wondered where Fasciani and Abington might be experiencing it.

She walked to Dr. Finley's office in a bleary-eyed daze, having secured just two hours of sleep on a lumpy mattress while baking inside a stuffy on-call room. Dr. Finley always began his day at eight; Carrie rushed to get there without any primping at all. This had to be the first news of his morning.

When she arrived at five minutes to the hour, Carrie found Dr. Finley's office door was closed—the equivalent of a hotel's Do Not Disturb sign—but she knocked anyway.

Typically genial, Dr. Finley came off a bit gruff when he summoned Carrie inside. As she entered, she noticed that he hadn't yet turned his laptop on, and she doubted he'd finished his first cup of Starbucks. The action was happening before he was officially ready to face the day.

Dr. Finley looked surprised to see Carrie. He took a quick glance at the surgical schedule, tacked to a cork bulletin board that hung on the wall over his computer.

"We don't have surgery today, do we?" he asked, picking up his coffee.

"They're gone," Carrie said. "Abington and Fasciani. They've disappeared. I can't find either of them."

Dr. Finley squinted. "What are you talking about?" he said as he gestured toward one of the metal office chairs. "Carrie, sit down, please. You look awful. Have you had any sleep?"

Carrie had not checked her appearance in any mirror, but suspected it bordered on grisly. She'd slept in her lab coat and scrubs, and it showed. Her hair was a tousled mess. By contrast, Dr. Finley was well-groomed and dressed neatly in a striped oxford and sharp red tie.

Realizing she had barreled in like a hurricane, Carrie sat down as directed. She worked to slow her thoughts. Neurologists of his stature at White Memorial would have panoramic views of the Charles River, but here, Dr. Finley had a view of an abandoned construction site. He was uncelebrated and understated, and Carrie wanted to do right by the man who'd brought her under his wing and given her a chance at redemption.

Dr. Finley swiveled his chair to face Carrie. He leaned back and rested his chin on his thumb, his other arm folded across his chest. "Now, just what are you talking about? Can I get you some coffee or something?"

Carrie showed him her coffee. "No, thanks. I've got some."

Carrie's stomach used that particular moment to rumble like approaching thunder. She had not had a decent meal in hours. After her visit to the med ICU, Carrie had spent some time sitting practically alone in the cafeteria, nursing a cup of coffee and staring at a scoopful of powdered scrambled eggs and canned fruit that stared back at her.

"What's on your mind?" Dr. Finley asked.

"I checked up on Steve Abington after his surgery," Carrie said. "I didn't think anything of it. It's something I've always done with my patients. It's something you would do, too. You feel responsible when you order tests or perform a procedure on someone to follow up on their status, right?"

"Of course. I think I know where this conversation is headed."

"Evidently that's frowned upon here. Dr. Goodwin and Dr. Navarro both told me—no, make it *insisted*—that I not follow up on my patients. But I only heard that after I went to see Steve Abington."

"You went to the ICU post-op?"

Carrie nodded. "I've got to tell you, Abington was not doing well at all. He was still confused and agitated when I saw him, but that's probably because he was just coming out of anesthesia. But then it got worse. The nurse and I ended up having to give him a drip of haloperidol in addition to Valium."

Dr. Finley grimaced. A line had been crossed. "Yeah, Goodwin accosted me in the hall and spoke at length about your conversation," he said. "But I didn't know you had done any post-op care. Now I know why she was so pissy with me."

"What did she say?"

Dr. Finley chuckled. "Nothing I need to repeat. I promised her I was going to speak to you, but as a point of protest I decided to not bring it up all. You're an adult and I trust you to follow department protocols. That said, I think Goodwin possesses all the tact of a wrecking ball."

Carrie deflated in her seat. She had more to share, but Dr. Finley's look of sympathy was a sharp stab of guilt to the chest. Instead of being a team player, taking her probationary period seriously by following the departmental rules, Carrie insisted on creating chaos.

"Well, I didn't set out to violate hospital policy," Carrie said in her own defense. "After I got home, that's when I learned Abington had been moved to the med ICU because of a cardiac problem, but before

I could go in to see him the next morning, Dr. Goodwin confronted me and told me I should stay away, that he was somebody else's concern now."

"As much as I hate to admit it, she's right, Carrie," Dr. Finley said, trying to not sound overly reproachful. "The day-to-day care of patients has to be maintained by a coherent and well-organized staff, and that has to be under the direction of those two. Even though you're kind of my private hire, you technically fall under her department's responsibility. The truth is, I stay away from them as much as possible, and I suggest you do the same. It would just be too confusing otherwise. Besides, Goodwin can make a mess of things if she decides she doesn't want you on the staff."

Carrie looked alarmed. "She could do that?"

Dr. Finley did not appear overly concerned. "Your salary may come out of my private funds, but ultimately it's all the government's money. So technically it's Goodwin's show to run," he said. "That said, if we're successful here, you and I will share all the accolades and honors and Goodwin will have to take a backseat."

Carrie could not quite grasp the logic. But, if Dr. Finley agreed to the policy, it made a little more sense for her to retreat. However, two patients were missing. Surely Dr. Goodwin would not be satisfied by that outcome.

Dr. Finley chuckled. "Trouble seems to find you wherever you go, doesn't it? So how much damage control do I need to do here? And what's this talk about missing patients? I thought you said you only went to see Steve Abington."

Carrie shrank further in her seat. "Well, I have to confess I couldn't keep myself from at least following up on Eric. I know, I know—I shouldn't have done it. But I had only done his surgery a few hours before and I was worried he was going to have the same post-op reaction as Abington. Wouldn't you do that, too?"

"Maybe."

Carrie cringed at his disapproving tone. To violate protocol inadvertently with Abington was one thing, but to blatantly disregard Goodwin to check up on Fasciani pushed the boundaries of what Dr. Finley could condone. But Carrie couldn't do anything about that now. She had to press her case.

"When I went to see Fasciani, he wasn't there. The unit was empty and closed," she said with measured composure. Carrie left out the part about going home to order the labs. Now was not the time to bring up her larger concern. "Since I was at the hospital, I decided to pop down to the med ICU to see Steve Abington."

Dr. Finley slapped his hand to his forehead. "Good gracious, Carrie! You're trampling all over Goodwin here."

"But Abington wasn't there," Carrie said, ignoring the rebuke. "And Dot, the nurse in the med ICU, had no record of him *ever* being there."

"What time did all this start?" Dr. Finley asked.

"It was probably after ten," she said. "I grabbed a bite to eat after the surgery, and then I came back to get something I left in my office. That's when I decided to check up on Fasciani."

"Carrie." Dr. Finley was obviously displeased.

"I know I shouldn't have done it," Carrie said. "But I was curious. I'm just not used to letting go of my patients. It's hard for me."

At last, something Carrie said seemed to sit well with Dr. Finley. A trace of a smile put her slightly at ease.

"I get it," he agreed. "You have a unique job in the VA's unique culture. There's a lot of bureaucracy to navigate, and your position here doesn't make it any easier. So after you couldn't find our patient in neuro recovery, you went to see Abington in the med ICU—do I have that right?"

"That's right," Carrie said. She had knowingly bent the truth, but did not break it. "Call it professional curiosity."

"I'd call it very, very strange," Dr. Finley said, rubbing his chin. "Not what you did, but these patients going missing. Honestly, I don't know what to tell you at this moment, but I promise you that I will look into this right away. Let's meet again this afternoon. I'm booked all day, but I'll make room for you at four. That will give me time to get to the bottom of this. But you, my dear, should take advantage of your day off and go home and get some sleep." He rose from his chair. The solicitude reminded her of her father. "Let me do the work. And take my advice and stay away from Goodwin. She has fangs."

"Navarro too, I suppose."

"That one also bites."

"In that case, I'll see you at four."

Carrie walked out of Dr. Finley's office, glad she had not shared her worry about palinacousis. She'd thought about it, but resisted the temptation. Her concern about the cause behind the condition—a stroke or hemorrhage, a seizure or some unrecognized complication of the DBS procedure itself, or who knows what—remained unchanged. All of medical literature held only a handful of palinacousis case reports, and seeing it in two patients back-to-back was more than coincidence. For this reason she would need evidence before calling Dr. Finley's entire program into question. She would need to see the cold, hard facts. She needed the CAT scan and EEG to help exclude a more common explanation for what she observed.

Instead of driving home and driving back, Carrie decided to grab a few more hours of sleep in the on-call room, and spend the afternoon doing research before her four o'clock meeting with Dr. Finley. After downing a protein bar purchased at the cafeteria, Carrie had no trouble finding a vacant on-call room this early in the morning. She fell down on the mattress and closed her eyes.

Her thoughts kept her from falling asleep right away. She had so many possibilities to consider. What if the condition no longer presented in Abington and Fasciani once they were found? It might suggest the palinacousis was temporary. In that case, Carrie could push for a neurological post-op exam as a component of the DARPA program to see if it manifested in others. The plan was not optimal, because Carrie hesitated to do any more surgeries until she could rule out the potential side effect. A lot would depend on her meeting at four.

Unable to focus, Carrie closed her eyes. She took a couple of calming breaths and tried to clear her mind. Exhaustion made her wired, and she could not let it go. Again she focused on the idea of the condition being temporary. The more she thought about it, the more it made the most sense. Otherwise, Dr. Finley would have come across it by now and said something to Carrie. Perhaps Goodwin knew about the side effect and was keeping it a secret. But why would she do that? Carrie could not come up with anything.

A thought occurred to her and she bolted upright in bed. Her stomach lurched. What if nobody had seen the condition because it had never happened before? What if Carrie had caused it during surgery? What if *she* was the problem, and not DBS?

CHAPTER 31

The Humvee hit a ditch at a high rate of speed and almost bounced Steve Abington to the floor. He scrambled back into his seat and peered out the square window on the left side of the vehicle. The horizon seemed a million miles away and the parched landscape zooming by stretched out like an endless blanket of brown. The unrelenting sun stood high in the sky and roasted the cracked earth like the inside of an oven. Where was this place? What province? Paktika? Khost? Hell, it all looked the same.

Outside the vehicle Abington heard the pop of small-arms gunfire blended with the familiar *rat-tat-tat* of automatic weapons. The bullets seemed to come from all directions, impossible to pin down a source. Abington had fired an M2 Browning from the open roof of a Humvee more times than he could count. But now he looked up and saw this vehicle was not equipped with a canopy. They would have to drive through the firestorm. Maybe catch up with a convoy if they were out on their own. One thing for certain: Whoever was doing the driving did not appear to be in any real hurry.

"Hey, put some zip in this pig," Abington shouted.

Somebody chortled to Abington's right. Only now did Abington become aware of the other passenger sitting beside him. He was a muscular white male, with a square, chiseled face, and prominent nose. The man's mouth broke into a crooked smile and beneath his shades Abington imagined a playful glint in his eyes. Abington had never seen this man before. Or had he? He was confused. Disoriented.

Where had he been before riding in this Humvee? Abington searched his memory, but came up blank. In fact, he could not come up with anything at all. His brain felt like a sieve trying to collect water. He knew only that this was Afghanistan, though he could not recall how long he'd been there, or when he'd arrived. It felt like the whole shit mess had blended into one endless day. Maybe that was why he could not remember how he got here. The sameness of it all made it easy to forget one moment from the next.

Abington blinked to clear his vision. For a second, the man to his right looked to be wearing civilian clothes—black shirt and pants under a dark zip-up jacket. A second later that changed, and Abington saw the man wore camo and Kevlar like everyone else. But why was he wearing a boonie hat. He should have had on a Kevlar helmet.

Steady gunfire ripped up the air and pockmarked the ground on the side of the road. Spires of red clay and dust sprayed skyward like earthy geysers. Abington could not believe this vehicle was not riddled with bullet holes, nor could he understand why the driver seemed so unconcerned.

"Hey, the speed limit here is get the fuck out. Let's step on it!"

The driver nonchalantly craned his head and cocked a quizzical eyebrow in Abington's direction. The driver was a black man with short hair and almond-shaped eyes. He had a pleasant face, showing no grit, grime, or even traces of fatigue. He looked soft, like someone who did work other than the business of war. He showed no particular concern about the bullets, either. If anything, Abington detected an officious air about him. Maybe this man was someone important, an LTC or even a full-bird colonel. Whoever he was, Abington withered slightly under the man's hard stare.

"We're going fast enough," the driver said. His tone served to placate Abington and end the discussion at the same time.

The man seated to Abington's right—Boonie Hat—started to laugh.

Abington heard, "We're going fast enough . . . we're going fast enough . . ." repeating in his left ear. But the voice, like the bullets, seemed to come from nowhere and everywhere.

"This guy might be the most gone of the whole bunch."

"Yeah, he's struggling for sure," the driver said.

It was difficult for Abington to follow the conversation, because everything they said kept repeating.

Boonie Hat said, "Well, at least some of them come out all right. For a while anyway."

Driver chuckled. "Yeah, it'd be a pretty messed-up gig if they were all like him."

Abington squinted, straining to make sense of the odd exchange.

"What do you mean?" Abington asked. "Did Roach make it? Is he alive? Where's Roach? Where are the others?"

Abington heard, "Where are the others . . . where are the others . . ."

Boonie Hat laughed even harder this time. A stab of pain focused Abington's attention. He looked down at his leg in time to see the man extract a needle from his thigh, the contents of the syringe evidently emptied into his bloodstream intramuscularly.

"Hey, what's that all about?" Abington cried out.

Boonie Hat smirked and tapped the driver's shoulder. The driver looked back at Boonie Hat and the empty syringe.

"I can't listen to this nut job for the next five hours," Boonie Hat said. "I just can't do it."

Nut job? Why would he say that?

Abington asked, "What did you give me?" Already his speech sounded thick and slurred as his tongue swelled inside his mouth. A bitter taste soured the back of his throat.

"Just a push of adrenaline," Boonie Hat said in a semi-mocking tone. "Um . . . all the Special Ops guys are using it."

"Special Ops? What are we doing? Where's Roach? I was with Roach when we took fire."

Took fire . . . took fire . . . took fire . . .

"Yeah, you were with Roach," Boonie Hat said, sounding unconvinced and uninterested. "Whatever you say."

Abington blinked in rapid succession, trying to keep alert, but his eyes grew heavy just the same. He wanted to sleep. Soon enough, the sound of gunfire receded into the background until, like Abington's other senses, it all just faded away.

WHEN HE came to, Abington was lying on the ground. He recognized this place right away. This was where he and Roach had done battle with the Taliban, the same place where his best buddy got his stomach shredded by bullets. The Humvee was parked nearby and the sound of gunfire still filled the air, but Abington could not see any tracers. Boonie Hat and Driver sure did not act like two guys about to get shot.

"We got heat coming in!" Abington shouted. His voice came out thick and garbled. His body felt flulike, achy joints and all. He still heard the echo, but it was fainter, easier to ignore.

Abington looked around for a place to take cover and saw a hole dug in the earth, but it looked different than what he was used to seeing. This hole was longer, more rectangular, more like a coffin.

Boonie Hat approached, his face hidden in shadows. "Climb in," he said, pointing to the hole. The driver leaned against the Humvee, feet out in front of him, arms folded across his chest, looking as unhurried as a Sunday morning.

Abington hesitated. Something was wrong here. Something was horribly wrong. But his thoughts were scattered. He was seeing something between the slivers of his recollections. For a moment, he seemed to be experiencing a different reality. There were trees, tall pines encircling an open enclosure. Sure, Afghanistan had large forest trees, but this terrain had been more desert. Or was it? The strange image Abington saw fell away, and the desert returned. Then the trees came back. It was like a light switch being turned on and off, and each time it happened the scenery would change. Could it be from that adrenaline shot?

Boonie Hat rolled his eyes. He looked frustrated about something.

"Enemy fire," Boonie said without a hint of anxiety or enthusiasm. "Get in the foxhole, asshole."

Abington held his ground. The man's appearance changed with his surroundings. It kept shifting between tactical gear and black-colored civilian clothing.

What the hell is happening to me?

"Maybe it's wearing off," the driver said. "Talk him up, Curtis. Play it real. I don't want to have to chuck him in there by force. I'm beat from all that driving."

Curtis. Boonie Hat's name is Curtis.

Abington had the distinct impression he had seen this man before. The name was familiar and it had triggered some memory. The memory felt real, not like the shifting scenery, but it was not from this place. No, it had happened elsewhere. A dark place. A cubby, almost. No, more like a cell. Why would he have been in a cell? Who was Curtis? He was feeling for something that was lost within an impenetrable fog. For a second he thought he had latched on to it. The name Curtis came at Abington like a speeding train, but the clarity lasted only a moment, and soon it tumbled off into the dark corners of his mind.

Curtis . . . Boonie Hat is Curtis . . . who is the driver?

"Get in the hole!" Curtis shouted.

No, Abington was not going to budge. Not without answers. Like where was Roach? Why did these two not care about getting shot?

The driver and Curtis exchanged looks.

A sly smile creased the corners of Curtis's mouth just before a pan-icked look overtook his expression. "Enemy fire!" Curtis shouted, in true terror. "Get in the foxhole, Stevie! Hurry!"

The ground around Abington's feet erupted with bullets. Nothing made sense to him anymore, but he jumped into the hole anyway.

"Stay there! Stay there!" Curtis yelled. "Help is coming."

Then Curtis laughed. Inside the hole Abington clutched his legs to his chest, taking an almost fetal position. This was a womb of sorts, a safe place. Above him he heard footsteps whenever the spatter of gun-fire died down enough.

Something liquid poured down on him. Was it a chemical strike? It smelled like gasoline and it got into Abington's eyes and stung. His vi-sion went white and the horrible burning sensation continued no mat-ter how hard he rubbed.

"You're a sick freak, you know that?" the driver said. "We can do this the humane way. Like shoot him first."

Abington yowled in agony. The gas stung his eyes and singed his mouth as if he had dove headfirst into a pool of man-o'-wars.

Curtis said, "I've been thinking about it. I just want to know what happens."

"I repeat, you're a sick freak," the driver said. "I'm going to wait in the car. I don't want to see this. Make sure to pulverize the bone into ash before you finish burying him."

Through a film of tears, Abington saw Curtis toss a metal lighter into the hole. The top was open and the flame was lit. The lighter touched gas and bright orange flames erupted all around. Abington screamed as his skin began to bubble. It peeled first down to muscle and then to bone. His cries turned into something animal-like, savage, primal. Curtis watched from the lip of the hole.

At some point the driver reappeared. Abington saw him, but his brain could only process the pain. He saw the driver take out a gun and point his weapon into the hole, but didn't understand it. Abington could smell his own burning flesh and hair—an awful, abhorrent odor. His bubbling, iron-rich blood gave off a coppery, metallic smell.

"Man, you are really messed in the head, Curtis."

The driver fired a single bullet that ended Steve Abington's misery.

CHAPTER 32

"That just doesn't make any sense," Carrie said. She studied the papers clutched in her hand, head shaking slightly, incredulous.

Dr. Finley's deeply troubled expression mirrored Carrie's growing dismay. He bit the tip of his reading glasses, and rotated his chair to face Carrie.

She looked up from the medical discharge forms to see his puzzled expression. "Goodwin signed off on this?" she asked.

"She did," Dr. Finley answered.

Carrie lowered her gaze and rested her chin on her knuckles, striking a pose reminiscent of Rodin's *The Thinker*. She recalled a lecture from medical school that included the fact that 1 to 2 percent of all hospitalizations resulted in the patient leaving AMA—against medical advice. The percentage was skewed to those with alcohol and substance abuse problems, which applied to both Abington and Fasciani. It was not an entirely surprising statistic, given how powerfully some patients needed to get back to whatever substance they abused. But her two DBS patients had exhibited no notable withdrawal symptoms. Something else was going on with them—confusion and agitation for sure, but she did not believe they left AMA to go get high.

Carrie leaned across Dr. Finley's desk and pointed to the box on the AMA form indicating the date for a follow-up visit. "Do you think they'll show?"

Dr. Finley looked sad. "This is a large program," he said. "Cal Trent has a number of different specialists involved. I do my part, but that's certainly not the whole. We're a part of a much larger effort involving VR technicians, accident reconstruction specialists, psychiatrists, psychologists, and even biochemists. Each patient knows they're going to receive monitoring and study over the course of many months. But not everybody is diligent about coming to the VA or DARPA's other facilities for the follow-up appointments. In this case, I'm afraid we might have lost two of our participants. And it's not going to reflect well on us. Cal will be most displeased, I'm sure of it."

Carrie thought back to the presentation Dr. Finley had given in the grand rounds during her first week on the job. She remembered the bald man with close-set eyes and a round face who'd sat next to Trent. At the time she'd found it interesting Dr. Finley did not introduce him, but it made more sense to her now. The scope of this effort extended far beyond the confines of the VA, and Dr. Finley probably did not even know Trent's companion. The insight did nothing to assuage her concern for these missing patients.

"Why would they leave? Where would they even go?"

"I'm as troubled as you are. We've got two guys out there with wires stuck in their heads who are technically our responsibility. I want to find them as much as you do. Goodwin had no choice but to let them walk. This isn't a prison. But the behavior is highly anomalous. We've treated dozens of vets in the DBS program, and these are the first two who have done anything like this. Sure we have to coddle and remind them to come in for follow-up appointments from time to time, but to leave like this? To just walk out? It hasn't happened. Not ever."

Carrie shrank in her seat, but Dr. Finley did not appear to take notice. It was his word choice that had really struck her. *Anomalous.* The palinacousis was beyond strange, but now each patient had exhibited what appeared to be extremely poor judgment. If it had never been observed before, then the only common factor, the only real link, was

Carrie. She had done both surgeries only to discover each patient had presented with the same bizarre set of symptoms.

"Well, I don't have any idea what Abington was like when he requested to be discharged," Carrie said. "But I had just seen Fasciani last night, and I don't think he was coherent enough to do something like that."

"I know what you say you saw, Carrie," Dr. Finley said. He took the papers from Carrie's hands to look them over again. "But here are the forms. Signed by Abington and Fasciani. Look. Their signatures match with the pre-op releases." Dr. Finley turned the pages so that Carrie could see where his finger was pointed. "Both have been countersigned by Dr. Goodwin. She told me she tried to convince them to stay and admitted they both seemed a bit wifty, but she made the judgment call that they were sufficiently compos mentis to leave AMA. Evidently, after you left, the overnight night nurse called Navarro and he went to Goodwin because Fasciani was demanding to be discharged."

Carrie stiffened.

"Don't worry," Dr. Finley said. "I didn't get the sense Goodwin knew about your after-hours visit. And from what I'm reading here, Abington had signed himself out earlier in the day. His cardiac condition had stabilized. In fact, she said he had no more arrhythmia and his mental status had cleared dramatically. They sent him to the neuro unit and he demanded to be discharged, just like Fasciani."

"Well then, why wasn't there any record of Abington in the med ICU?"

"That's a good point. I forgot you told me that. Let's have a look, shall we?" Dr. Finley logged into his computer. Moments later he was able to access Abington's electronic medical record. Carrie stood and looked over Dr. Finley's shoulder as he navigated a series of menus and forms displayed inside various gray-colored boxes.

Right away Carrie could see a long list of medical treatments and corresponding chargemaster codes pertaining to his care. Toward the bottom of the ledger was an entry for Abington's transfer to med ICU.

It was all there. Everything the med ICU nurse could not find, including treatments, nursing notes, physician notes, and lab tests ordered. The last entry was the AMA request and signatures. Abington had not gone missing after all. He had simply wanted out.

A fresh spike of anxiety put a tight band around Carrie's chest. Could the DBS be affecting their judgment, too? The electrodes had been placed in the amygdala, that almond-shaped nucleus deep in the anterior medial temporal lobe. That section was at the heart of the brain's processing of fear and its memory. This type of DBS work was uncharted territory, and Carrie's concerns about having caused post-op complications had doubled. The need to locate the missing vets and gather the pertinent data felt even more pressing than before. She had to rule out all other possibilities before she'd willingly shoulder the blame.

"What now?" Carrie asked.

"Now we have a new vet scheduled for surgery later this week. I guess we'll have to proceed as planned, and hope these two missing guys turn up."

Another person for me to injure? Carrie thought. *No, thanks.*

On the spot, Carrie made herself a promise. If she could not locate Abington and Fasciani in time, there would be no more surgeries. Simple as that. She would resign and the whole program would be cast into limbo. Her deadline was set, and would not move.

"Are you worried about infection?" Carrie asked. "What about trouble with the DBS system itself?"

"Well, of course, I'm worried," Dr. Finley said. "On both those counts. But what do you suggest?"

"Looks like I have some days off before our next surgery. Let me see if I can find them."

Dr. Finley gave no apparent objection. He mulled over the idea a moment, humming softly with a tip of the glasses back in his mouth. "I do think the situation warrants a bit of extreme measures, if you're willing to put in the effort."

"What about Goodwin? Should I go speak with her?" Carrie asked. "Maybe she has some thoughts on where they might have gone."

Dr. Finley scratched at his head. "To be honest, I'm not sure that's such a great idea," he said. "She doesn't know you went looking after her patients."

"What if I told her?"

"If you speak with her, what would you say?"

"I'd ask what the patients were like when they requested the AMA," Carrie said.

Dr. Finley raised his eyebrows. "And how do you think she'll respond?"

Carrie thought a beat. "She'll want to know why I care. It's not my problem. It's none of my business."

"And then?" Dr. Finley was goading Carrie, encouraging her to play out the scenario to its inevitable conclusion.

"She'll wonder why I haven't understood my job here."

"And that will put us right back to square one, that being Goodwin doing her very best to get you ousted. So I'll have two missing patients and no DBS surgeon, and that might just put an end to my involvement with DARPA. I think I liked your other plan better."

"Go looking for them?"

Dr. Finley smiled and returned a playful wink. "I know it's outside your job description."

"I'm highly motivated," Carrie said. *For reasons you don't even know,* she thought.

Carrie's phone buzzed inside her lab coat pocket. The sound startled her. She retrieved the device and saw a text message from David Hoffman.

I'm at the VA for an interview. Can I buy you a cup of coffee?

"Well, it's our lucky day," Carrie said with a slight smile.

Sure. Java du Jour, 15 minutes?

She sheathed the phone back in the pocket of her lab coat.

Dr. Finley returned a curious look.

"And why's that?"

"Well, I may not be a detective, but I just got invited out to coffee by an investigative reporter."

"Will he help you?"

"I can be pretty persuasive," she said. "I'm going to find them, Alistair. It's a promise." *And with luck, I'll prove it wasn't me who did anything wrong.*

Leon Dixon seemed destined to loom over Carrie like a shadow she could never discharge. Her thoughts went from Dixon to Abington, and her mind flashed on Abington's terror-filled eyes during the attack. She saw him hovering over her, and felt his strong hands around her throat applying exquisite pressure.

She paused at the door, thinking. What had triggered Abington's insane outburst? She knew prior to surgery Abington had been subjected to his most traumatic war memory via virtual reality. At that moment, Carrie wanted to know as much about these vets and the DBS program as she could. Goodwin could think what she wanted, but Carrie would never willingly put herself into a silo.

"Dr. Finley?"

He turned to face her.

"I'd like to try out that virtual reality device."

CHAPTER 33

Java du Jour, the quaint and cozy coffee shop a block away from the VA, was surprisingly only half full. The place was usually jumping with activity, so perhaps four thirty was a slow time. Carrie stepped inside and saw David sitting alone at one of the few wooden tables adjacent to the stone fireplace, tucked invitingly beneath the large bow window. Their eyes met. He got to his feet and held out a chair.

Nice touch, Carrie thought. Her ex hadn't been given to such chivalrous behavior—nor were most of her contemporaries, for that matter.

"Thanks for meeting me," he said. "Cappuccino?"

Carrie took notice of David's style of dress. He had on a blue oxford shirt, dark jeans, and polished black shoes. He was taller than she remembered, and his outfit revealed a pleasing fit and trim frame. Not a gym rat, but clearly somebody who liked to keep his body in shape. As for the coffee, Carrie usually went for the black gold, but the way David said "cappuccino" somehow made it seem like the perfect choice.

"Yeah, a cappuccino sounds great."

Carrie took a seat and was already starting to doubt her plan when David went to place the order. Maybe it was foolish to go looking for these men, but she didn't know what else to do. She could not shake the thought that somehow the DBS, and more specifically her technique, might be behind the singularly rare complications of palinacousis and poor judgment. These conditions would surely have presented before in other PTSD patients. Since it had never been reported, Carrie could look only at the mirror for a culprit. She struggled to fit all the pieces together.

Carrie glanced up and saw David already seated, looking soothingly at her with two cups of cappuccino in front of him.

"Twenty seconds," David said with a glint in his eyes.

"What?"

"That's how long it took for you to realize I'd come back."

Carrie gave an embarrassed little laugh. "Sorry. I was just thinking. Excuse me."

"No worries," David said. "I've been accused of doing that from time to time."

Carrie laughed again as David pushed her cappuccino across the table. She picked up the cup and the aroma came at her with force. She savored it before taking a sip. Maybe she was a cappuccino girl after all.

"I'm glad we could meet up," David said. "To tell you the truth, I'd been meaning to give you a call. I thought we could talk about Adam, but I'd first like to find out what's going on with you."

Carrie found something very comforting about David. The way he'd handled her brother's assault was impressive enough. But more was going on here than that. He radiated confidence, and perhaps that was what intrigued her. He seemed so comfortable in his journalistic skin that she held no reservations about confiding in him. It did not hurt that he was damn good-looking, too.

Carrie knew her work at the VA would be of great interest to David and his story, but she had a different agenda. The conversation hit a lengthy lull as Carrie contemplated how to proceed.

"Are you always silent as a lamb?" David asked playfully.

Carrie laughed a little.

"Sorry. Lost in thought again. And that was an utterly terrifying movie, by the way. Couldn't watch it."

David pretended to look offended. "It's only one of the best."

"What about *Titanic?*"

"Knew the ending going in. Kind of spoiled it for me," David said with a wink and a smile. "What about *The Killing Fields?*" he asked.

"Never saw it," Carrie admitted. "And my father and I watch old movies all the time."

"*New York Times* journalist covering the civil war in Cambodia?" David said. "No? Doesn't register? Now that's a film after my own heart."

"Have you always worked for—" Carrie looked somewhat embarrassed. "What's the paper again?"

"That would be the *Lowell Observer,*" David said. "And no. I'm a stringer, what you might call a freelancer. I go to places like Cambodia and Thailand, and pretty much anywhere the government would warn us against visiting."

David went on to talk at some length about his adventures overseas and his kidnapping episode in Syria that led to his taking a job with the *Lowell Observer.* Carrie found this facet of David's personality quite intriguing. In medical school, she had done a research paper on why some people were drawn to intense, often fear-inducing thrills while others shunned the thought.

Evidence exists to suggest that dopamine stimulates the insular cortex, a portion of the cerebral cortex deep within the temporal lobe. The trait was thought to be a carryover from the earliest humans who'd risked everything to feed and shelter their families. Carrie had often caught herself analyzing her ex Ian's behavior based solely on what she imagined was going on in his brain. She was doing the same now with David, after only minutes alone together. Carrie had wished she and Ian had more adventures together, and David's active insula fascinated her.

"So enough about me," David said. "Tell me more about your work at the VA."

"I don't know quite where to begin," Carrie said. She slowly circled the rock sugar swizzle stick in her cappuccino, and looked up directly into his hazel eyes. "This is pretty confidential stuff and you're a reporter."

"Meaning you don't trust me."

"But I'm desperate for some investigative expertise. My career may depend on it."

"Oh, a conundrum. I love it. Do you know the term 'deep background'?"

"No, but if you hum a few bars I can fake it."

It took David a minute before he smiled.

"Cute," he said.

"Old family joke."

"Deep background means you can't be quoted in any story I might write. You're just enhancing my view of a topic."

"This might turn into a story, but for now, I'd like to talk friend-to-friend—or maybe as colleagues on the issue of PTSD."

David was cautious. "All right, I'm not taking notes. But if you tell me something I think I can use, I'm going to be pushy about asking for permission to use it. That's my job."

"I understand that," Carrie said. "And I wouldn't tell you any of this if I didn't think it might eventually turn into a story for you."

"Go on, then," David said.

"DARPA and the VA have launched a joint pilot program to try and cure PTSD. Not treat it, cure it."

David's expression brightened as if a movie star had walked into the coffee shop. He leaned forward with an ardent air. "You might be my new hero," he said. "Although my editor will think otherwise."

Carrie pulled back. "Why is that?" she asked.

"Because if you have something really interesting here, I'll have to push out my deadline again, until you give me permission to use this. Anneke will be none too pleased."

"Until I get permission from my boss, this is off the record," she repeated.

"Deal," he said.

"No, I'm being serious, David. I need your help with something and I'll trade information for assistance, but we have to do everything aboveboard. If word leaks about the program, it could jeopardize funding. A lot of vets are counting on this, my brother included."

"Helpful is my middle name. Well, actually it's Charles."

"We're off the record," Carrie reminded him. "Because I need your help."

David held up two fingers and said, "Scout's honor."

Carrie appeared dubious. "Adam was a Boy Scout," she said. "I think it's three fingers, and your hand is supposed to go the other way."

David took his hand down and gave Carrie a sheepish look. "You get the point," he said.

Carrie smiled. For whatever reason, she trusted him. "Well, I'm the surgeon responsible for inserting electrodes into the brains of vets with PTSD. We're using DBS—that's electrical deep brain stimulation—to try and eliminate the emotion from memory of what's causing the PTSD."

David looked incredulous. "Um, you can do that?" he asked.

"It's very experimental, leading-edge stuff. For it to work, we have to reconsolidate the fears and horrible memories these soldiers have suffered."

"Reconsolidate how?"

"With virtual reality," Carrie said. "Those memories, and especially the fear and other emotions associated with a traumatic event, are processed to a great extent in a nucleus of cells deep in our brains called the amygdala."

"Is it cheesy to say I like it when you talk science?"

"A little," Carrie said, not bothered at all. "Anyway, we reconsolidate the memories by subjecting the patients to a virtual reality program that is supposed to vividly reproduce that bad memory, and right after that we stick an electrode into the amygdala. In theory, when we then stimulate the amygdala, we hope to erase any fear associated with that memory, and perhaps the memory itself."

"And it works?"

"Four major successes so far, and one who I examined personally could be called a total cure without much of a stretch."

"Who qualifies for the surgery?"

"The program is only for vets who have failed all other forms of conventional drug and psychotherapy. Some of the participants are homeless, but I understand that they've got living support from this program. I think they're housed somewhere on the VA campus. I'm sorry I can't give you more specifics."

She stared at David, but no need to worry. He hadn't taken his eyes from her, nor sipped his coffee. Carrie felt bad about being a tease, but she would reward him with the scoop by getting Dr. Finley and the folks at DARPA to agree to let David cover the story. *After.*

"Carrie, are you telling me that you may be curing these folks?"

Everyone was familiar with post-traumatic stress—called shell shock in World War I—at least to a degree of having sympathy for these vets, and although the problem was probably bigger than anyone wanted to admit, the idea of having a possible targeted and effective treatment was beyond exciting.

"Well, that's the idea. But some things don't seem right, David, and that's why I really wanted to talk to you."

"And I thought it was my infectious personality that got you to go out with me for coffee," he said.

"Honestly? It was the bloody nose."

"Oh, that."

"And my problem," Carrie added.

"What's going on?"

"I've operated on two patients so far," Carrie said. "I thought the surgery went well, and so did Dr. Finley."

"I'm guessing it didn't," David said.

Carrie spent some time going over the cases of Abington and Fasciani, and in the telling gave a detailed accounting of Goodwin and Navarro's ambush. In doing so, she felt compelled to vaguely explain her unorthodox hiring, while omitting all details about Leon Dixon and her decision to leave residency. She did not know this man well enough to share such a painful experience. After three coffee dates maybe, but certainly not on the first.

"A persisting echo? That sounds like a nightmare," David said when Carrie described palinacousis.

"There are only a handful of case reports in the literature," Carrie said. "I have no idea what could be causing it. In the cases I've read about, some patients had a stroke. In others it was attributed to a seizure or a hemorrhage in the part of the brain where auditory information is processed. Some may have had an unusual encephalitis, or even a rare form of migraine. The point is, I doubt whether a neurologist or a neurosurgeon would ever see a single case, let alone two in a row. So I can't help but think this is something I've done. Did I put the electrodes in right? I can't say for sure. But they're not placed anywhere near where the brain deals with acoustic processing. Did I cause a bleed? Could it be the first sign of a brain infection? These are things I have to wrestle with. But there's more."

Both cappuccinos were getting cold. David wiggled his chair a bit closer.

"Both of these patients have disappeared," Carrie said. "They signed out against medical advice, and I have no idea how to find them."

David's expression became slightly strained—evidence of deep thought. The compassion and steely determination in his eyes set Carrie further at ease. She felt right to have confided in him.

"So what can I do to help?" David asked.

"I need to find these guys—Steve Abington and Eric Fasciani. I don't even know where to begin to look."

David leaned back in his chair with a confident air. "You need help finding people? Well, I'm your man for that gig. . . . I'm guessing my getting the scoop on this DBS program is contingent on patient location?"

Carrie held up her hands to show him that was her plan, straight-forward and simple.

"This is even more up my alley than you know," he said. "I've been working on this story for a lot longer than my editor wants. I know the shelters, the different services they might go to. And by 'services,' I mean flophouses and crack dens. It's lovely how we let some of the people who fought for our freedom waste away—but we're not here to fix the system, right?"

Carrie bristled a little. "I am," she said.

David finally took a sip of his too-cold cappuccino. "I get your worry about these guys," he said. "The only things I can hurt are people's reputations and feelings."

"The pen is mightier than the sword."

"But perhaps less potent than the electrode."

Carrie's smile was genuine. "Are you always this clever?" she asked.

"Only when I'm having coffee with an intellectual dynamo I'm trying to impress."

"You only want the scoop," Carrie said. "I know your type."

"I want to help," David said in a serious tone. "You're telling me no-body has ever seen this condition before?"

"I'm telling you that the DBS surgeons aren't supposed to check up on the patients post-op, per Herr Doktors Goodwin and Navarro. We are persona non grata outside the OR."

"*You* are," David corrected. "You told me Goodwin's beef was with you. She wanted a more traditional hire, right? And you've kept your concern about the palina-whatever-it's-called a secret from your boss because you think you might have caused it."

"Palinacousis," Carrie corrected. "And sort of. It's not a secret. It's a theory. I need more data before I start making unsubstantiated claims that could put an end to this whole program. It's a quandary, and I'm not doing another DBS surgery on a vet until we find these guys. If we can't find them, I'll come forward about my concerns and resign from the program. Essentially, I'll hammer the last nail in the coffin of my career."

"These two are important to find. I got it."

"And you're right about Goodwin having it out for me. But why is that important?"

Things were clicking for him; Carrie could see that in David's eyes. At that moment, Carrie suspected David Hoffman was a supremely competent reporter, which only enhanced his attractiveness.

"Maybe somebody else has seen the same symptoms, but didn't even know what was happening. You're a bright doctor; I'm guessing more observant than most."

Carrie blushed a little. "I don't know about that," she said, and felt forced to look away. "But I've thought the same."

"Who was the surgeon before you?" David asked.

"Sam Rockwell. He was in a car accident, and he's still in the hospital in a medically induced coma."

David took the information in. "I'd put in a call to that hospital of his if I were you," he suggested. "Doc Rockwell wakes up for some reason, maybe he has answers. In the meantime, get your best walking shoes out of the closet. Tomorrow you and I are going on a hunting expedition."

CHAPTER 34

After six hours of driving around and hunting for parking spaces, Carrie and David had acquired two sizable parking tickets and no leads. They had already been to the Motel 6 where Dr. Finley thought the vets were staying. DARPA covered the bill, but the manager said that Abington and Fasciani had not returned to their rooms all week. Carrie and David would have to keep looking.

Their current stop, the Pine Street Inn, was located in a multistory redbrick building tucked away on a quiet section of Harrison Avenue in downtown Boston. Two words on the placard mounted beside the front entrance communicated the nonprofit's singular mission: END-ING HOMELESSNESS.

The day had been as eye-opening as it was frustrating. At BCH, Carrie had treated many of the city's poor, but the shelters were an entirely different world. They housed hope and despair in equal measure. Having dealt with the bureaucracy of BCH, Carrie could only imagine the budget battles taking place at these shelters to keep the lights on and the people fed. After things settled down, she vowed, she'd donate her time and her funds, when possible, to do more to help. She had no doubt David would join her effort if she asked.

Carrie had seen some run-down, grungy-looking shelters through-out the day. The inside of the Pine Street Inn was, by contrast, a breath of fresh air. The building was clean, and the rooms she could see from the lobby looked airy, well lit, and filled with people of all colors, from all walks of life.

Carrie and David went straight to the reception area. From a plastic bag, Carrie removed colored printouts of the two missing men, taken from their veteran ID cards, which were on file with the VA. The photos were small and bore only a vague resemblance to the haunted men Carrie had operated on. She presented the printouts to the fresh-faced, mocha-skinned woman at the reception desk.

"Hi there," Carrie said. "I'm searching for these two men. I was wondering if they've been here recently."

Furrowing her brow, the receptionist gave each image a careful look. She handed the printouts back to Carrie with a pursed lip and a shake of the head.

"I don't think so," she said. "But we see a lot of folks coming and going. I suggest you keep checking back."

David removed a small stack of printouts from his canvas carry bag and stepped forward.

"Could you take these and circulate them among the staff?" he asked.

"These fellows aren't in any trouble, are they?" the receptionist asked. A wary look crossed her face.

David smiled as he produced his press ID. "No, not in the least," he said. "I'm working on a story for my paper and I could use their help. That's all."

The receptionist accepted the explanation without question. Perhaps it was David's charming smile, or the way he was dressed in a tailored blazer, crisp slacks and shirt, and blue patterned tie. Conducting the search under the guise of a reporter's story, and not Carrie's medical concerns, proved to be a winning idea. If confronted, Fasciani and Abington might be leery about anything having to do with leaving the VA against medical advice. But it had been strikeout after strikeout, everywhere they went. The Pine Street Inn was the last place on their list of Boston-area shelters.

Carrie and David ambled back to her Subaru in grim silence. By now, her legs had begun to tire, and after settling in behind the wheel Carrie massaged a bothersome knot out of her right quad. Another casualty of her troubles at the VA had been her commitment to her tri training. Her ligaments seemed to have shortened, and her joints were achy and stiff. Adding to the discomfort, the humid day had turned the car uncomfortably warm, and Carrie rolled down the windows without firing up the engine. No reason to waste gas, because she had no idea where they might be headed next.

David set his blazer down neatly on the backseat and picked up his clipboard of maps and notes. Looking over his shoulder, Carrie watched David draw a thick line with his Sharpie through the Pine Street Inn. The sheet of paper was full of thick lines—lots of places they had looked, dozens in all.

"What now?" Carrie asked. The dashboard clock said it was close to three o'clock. They had been out searching for seven hours without so much as a lunch break.

"We can drive to Worcester or Fall River," David suggested as his eyes scanned the map.

Carrie was about to suggest they go get something to eat when David's cell phone went off. His ringtone was a series of wind chimes, very new-agey, and not at all what Carrie imagined he would have set as the default.

David noticed Carrie's look. "My downstairs neighbor has a four-year-old. She liked that ringtone best," he said.

Carrie accepted the explanation with a smile as David glanced at the number. His expression changed. He clearly knew the caller and liked whoever it was. "Speak of the neighbor," he said.

David put the caller on speakerphone. "Emma, light of my life, tell me you've got something."

"Hey, you," answered a female voice. "Listen, if I get fired for this, you have to find me a newspaper gig. Deal?"

"Deal," David said. "As soon as I find one for myself."

Carrie did not know who Emma was, but the woman, and more specifically her relationship to David, had her intrigued. Perhaps it was David's reaction to her that piqued Carrie's curiosity. She sounded young, and if a voice could make somebody attractive, it was Emma's. The twinge of jealousy surprised Carrie. She did not know the first thing about David or Emma, or their relationship, but the feeling was undeniable.

"Now, what did you get for me?" David asked.

"Are you with that cute doctor you told me about?"

David's face turned a shade of red. "Whoa, whoa, whoa," he said. "I'm with Carrie right now, and *you* happen to be on speakerphone."

Emma laughed. Carrie felt relaxed with this woman, as if they could be friends.

Carrie raised an eyebrow and gave David an amused grin. "Hi Emma, I'm Carrie."

"Delighted," Emma said. "And yes, I have some useful intel."

David's reddened face returned to its normal pallor as he reached for a pen on the seat beside him.

"Go on," he said.

"Steve Abington's mother lives in Bangor, Maine. She has an unlisted phone number, I'm afraid; I checked. But I can text you the address."

"Oh, Emma, you're a lifesaver."

"You can thank the DMV and the fact that I know my supervisor's passwords."

Carrie thought of her own bit of subterfuge with Navarro's pass code, and her opinion of this Emma person spiked.

"Text what you got," David said. "You're a treasure."

"That's dear of you to say. But it was easy. You knew her name."

"How did you know Steve's mother's name?" Carrie asked David.

"I'm a journalist," David said with a shrug. "It's my business to find stuff out."

"And he's good at it," Emma said. "Careful with this one, Carrie. If he gets out of line, you call me."

Carrie laughed. "I will."

"Oh, Gabby wants to say hello," Emma said. "Hang on a moment."

Seconds later, a small, high-pitched voice squealed through the phone. "Hi, Uncle David!"

David's whole face went supernova. Carrie's heart swelled at seeing his reaction to the little girl's voice. At this point she assumed Emma was David's sister, and oddly, it felt like a relief.

"How are you, sweetheart?" David said.

"Good."

"Are you being helpful to Mommy?"

"Yes."

"Okay, I'll see you soon."

"Bye."

The call went dead.

"All our calls are like that," David said.

"So Emma is your sister?" Carrie asked.

"My landlord," David said, and added, "It's a long story."

"And just who was that cute doctor your landlord was talking about?"

"What say we skip Worcester altogether and take a drive to see Steve's mother in Bangor, Maine? She might know where he's gone." The redness in his face had come back.

"What time would we get there?" Carrie asked.

"If we leave now, we'd arrive around seven," David said. "We could swing by her home, get a hotel, and come back in the morning."

Carrie said, "Sure," before she realized she'd spoken the word.

CHAPTER 35

Squatting with his palms on a thin mat in the center of his Spartan living room, Braxton Price pressed his knees into his arms and slipped into a crow pose, getting both feet off the ground. He was nearing the end of what had been an invigorating ninety-minute yoga workout.

Braxton had the build of an elite athlete, though it was difficult to see under his nurse's uniform. Before he became a nurse, Braxton had worn a different uniform, that of a Green Beret in the United States Army. After twenty-one continuous months of combat in Afghanistan, Braxton joined a small combat team tasked with training and arming Afghan fighters who wished to rebel against the Taliban.

It was good work. Honest work. Bloody work.

He was part of a somewhat loosely organized counterinsurgency effort promoted by General David Petraeus to win the locals' hearts and minds. As a weapons sergeant, Braxton served a key role in the Green Berets' twelve-member Alpha Team, the A-team. Before his deployment to the Middle East, Braxton had attended forty-three weeks of Weapons Sergeant School, where he learned how to adapt to any situation and improvise on the field. He could speak Pashto better than Dari, but was conversant in both.

Braxton came to appreciate his interaction with the locals, but it was nothing compared to the high he got as part of a hunter-killer team, smashing down doors and putting bullets into targets. Killing was just a part of the job, and he did it without remorse.

Braxton's time in Afghanistan might have come to an end, but he was not lacking for work. His new role required a dozen weeks of training, during which he learned all about charting, taking vitals, administering drugs intravenously; rudimentary knowledge, at best. He could hardly be considered a registered nurse, but one day, just like that, he had a badge with the name "Lee Taggart" and was on staff at the VA. No questions asked.

Even though he did no real nursing, he knew it was good work. Honest work. Bloody work.

Braxton got into a plank position on his mat. Thirty seconds into the hold, he could feel every muscle fiber start to twitch. Closing his eyes, Braxton let his mind replay Steve Abington's final screams.

Fucking Gantry, he thought.

Curtis Gantry was a thug, prone to violence and lacking professionalism, but he was also Braxton's best friend, former A-team member, and the guy who had saved his life more times than he had fingers. But this part of the operation was Braxton's to run as he saw fit, and not Gantry's. In hindsight, he should have made Gantry put a bullet in Abington's head. The screams did not bother Braxton in the least, but Abington was a brother in arms and he deserved to go quick.

Braxton knew all about the long suffer. Some of his interrogations in Afghanistan had lasted for weeks. The job description was "information extraction," not torture, but the line was a blurry one at best. Braxton kept his enjoyment of the work a secret, thinking he otherwise might not get it.

A minute and a half holding the plank and Braxton looked like a bronzed statue. His core was on fire, but there was no noticeable shake in his arms or legs. Fitness was always a passion. He could be sent back to war tomorrow and do just fine over there. In a way he was still at war, doing battle of a different sort.

At the two-minute mark one of Braxton's cell phones rang, the important one. Braxton cursed; he had two more minutes to go in his hold. But only one person had that phone number, and the call needed to be answered.

Braxton sprang to his feet and padded across the two-bedroom condo's gleaming hardwood floor. Light spilled in through a bank of bay windows that framed a glorious view of the Charles River. It would be impossible to afford this place on a soldier's salary, but his current employers were more than happy to pay the bill. In return, he was more than happy to answer their phone call.

"Speak," Braxton said.

"The girl."

"I figured."

Braxton recognized the baritone voice with a distinctive rasp. He saw no reason not to speak freely. Besides, these were stealth phones that used a machine-generated international mobile equipment identifier to make calls more secure and virtually untraceable. A warning system would alert Braxton if somebody were trying to intercept the call. In that case, he would turn his phone off and on to reset the IMEI number. Dive back into the shadows.

"She's proving to be a problem."

"I'm not surprised," Braxton said. "She's tenacious. Is there an order, sir?"

A pause. Braxton made no inference. He waited for his next instruction as he had been trained.

"Can Gantry be trusted?"

"To not hurt her?"

"We're not there just yet."

"Yeah, I think Gantry can be trusted." Braxton's mind flashed on Gantry's twisted grin as he stood at the lip of the pit, lighter in hand, Abington moments from immolation. "He can be trusted, for sure."

"I'll call back when we know what we want him to do."

"Very good," Braxton said. "What about the next one?"

"We still need him."

Fine with Braxton as well. He got paid regardless.

"You know, I'm scheduled for a shift. But there's no removals pending."

"We can take care of that. You're sick until further notice."

"I'm sick, all right," Braxton said with a laugh.

"Just make sure Gantry does what we want."

"You know you can count on me, sir," Braxton said.

Braxton called him "sir" because anybody over him in the food chain was a "sir." It was not meant as a show of respect.

"Very well. I'll be in touch."

Braxton ended the call and returned to his mat. He got back into the plank position and began his hold once more.

Thirty seconds into it and Braxton was questioning his endorsement of Gantry. While he considered Gantry a friend, Braxton knew he *would* do something to Carrie Bryant before he killed her, and he doubted it would have anything to do with fire.

CHAPTER 36

Rita Abington lived on a busy street in a ramshackle ranch home with a sagging roof and paint-chipped front stairs. The yard was just a small square, a bit more brown than green with nothing to spruce it up, no landscaping of any kind. Shrubs grew as they wished and a few of the taller trees might have been bent by ice storms, never straightening.

Carrie followed David up the narrow front walk. She noticed that all of the curtains were drawn. The only indication someone might be home was the Chevy Cobalt parked in the narrow driveway, battered-looking as the house.

David pushed the doorbell, but nothing happened. No rings. No chimes. He knocked. Carrie heard footsteps from within, and a moment later the door came open just a crack to reveal part of a woman's hard-bitten face.

The woman said, "I don't want to buy nothing, save a whale, or go to heaven, so I figure you've got no business being here."

David laughed.

The woman spoke with a notable Downeast accent. She also had a throaty voice, and Carrie suspected an X-ray of her lungs would reveal at least a pack-a-day habit.

"Are you Rita Abington?" David asked.

"Depends if you're looking for money."

"I'm looking for your son, Steve."

With that, the door came fully open to reveal a tiny woman, thin up top and below, wearing a sleeveless white blouse that showed off moles like archipelagos dotting her arms. Her skin was brown and wrinkled, but it appeared to be from hard living rather than too much sun. She had sunken cheeks and a neck thin enough to give Carrie a good look at the tendons. Rita's hair came down to her shoulders and was thin like the rest of her, with all the color and luster of what might be found in one of her ashtrays.

Rita said, "You seen Stevie?"

"We were hoping you had," Carrie said.

Rita stepped aside. Carrie figured this was her way of inviting them in and she went, with David following.

The living room was not much more than a few pieces of Goodwill furniture spread out over a well-worn rug. The stale smell of smoke hovered in the air and taxed Carrie's breathing some, but she managed to ignore it after a few minutes. Plenty of pictures hung on the walls and stood on tables; apparently Steve was not Rita Abington's only child.

Carrie and David waited on the plaid sofa while Rita got a pitcher of iced tea from the kitchen. She poured three glasses and took a seat on an armchair covered by a patchwork quilt. She lit up—Benson and Hedges—and took a puff. This was her home, and she saw no reason to ask anybody's permission.

"Forgive me," Rita said. "I haven't had a lot of visitors come around. It's been quiet here since Winston died."

"Was Winston your husband?" David asked.

"My dog," Rita said. "I got more love from that little dog than I ever did my ex, rest his soul."

With that, Rita rose from her chair, the cigarette dangling in a practiced way between two long fingers, went to the hallway, and removed a picture from the wall. She handed the framed photograph to Carrie and used her hand to fan away the smoke.

"He's so cute," Carrie said of the tiny, silky-haired dog with ears reminiscent of furry satellite dishes. "What kind of dog was Winston?"

"I don't know," Rita said, as she took a puff. "A good one, that's enough."

Carrie showed the picture to David, who acknowledged Winston's cuteness with a smile. Carrie hung the picture back on the wall and noticed another framed photographed, long and rectangular—this one of a group of soldiers, some wearing shirts and others without. Not all the guys had beards, but everyone had guns.

Carrie pointed at this photo. "Is this Steve?" she asked.

Rita came over, squinting, to take a look. She took the rectangular photo off the wall. "Eyes aren't so good these days," she said, almost apologizing. Her expression brightened. "That's Stevie, right there." She pointed. "How do you know my Stevie, anyway?"

"I'm his doctor," Carrie said. "I was treating him and, well, he sort of took off."

Rita carried the photograph back to her seat. "He's always taking off," she said.

"Have you heard from him?" Carrie asked.

Rita spit out a laugh. "That's a good one. No. No, I haven't," she said. "My two other boys haven't, either. Ben lives over to Orono. Comes to visit from time to time with the grandkids. Ian, well, let's just say he likes fishing more than he likes people."

Tough life, hard living, Carrie thought of the Abington clan. Rita would have no idea about Steve's DBS operation, or his involvement with the DARPA program, and Carrie was not about to violate his privacy by sharing those details. Her vague answer about being Abington's doctor had seemed to satisfy Rita's equally vague curiosity. Carrie got the sense all Rita really cared about was hearing Steve's voice one more time.

"Would you have any idea where he might have gone?" Carrie asked.

Rita let her gaze travel to the floor. "I haven't seen him in years. I couldn't tell you."

"So he had no contact with his family?"

"None," Rita said. "He came back from that war broken. No other way to put it. Stevie used to be my sweetie pie. Light of my life. He was the example for his brothers. But when he came back, it was just a ghost of that boy. Not the kid I raised. He took to the drink and the drugs, for sure, but there was more. He left something back in that desert."

"What's that?" Carrie asked.

A shadow crossed Rita's face. "His soul," she said.

Carrie stood, crossed the room, and put her hand on Rita's shoulder. The woman gazed up, clutched Carrie's hand, and batted back some tears.

"He was a good boy," Rita said, looking at the framed picture in her lap. "The sweetest."

Carrie stooped and pointed to the thin, muscular man in the photograph who had his arm around Steve. "Who is that?" she asked.

A sad smile of some memory deepened the wrinkles on Rita's face.

"Why, that's Roach," Rita said. "Stevie's best buddy. They called him Roach on account that nothing ever could kill him. Nothing. Then he died in Stevie's arms. Honestly, I think that's when it all began to go bad for him."

Roach.

The name meant a lot to Carrie, but she kept quiet about the terrifying ordeal during which Steve had asked for his departed friend. Carrie's eyes fell on another man in the photograph, this one taller than most, with broad shoulders and a handsome face. He had the neck of a football player, but without the asymmetry of the stimulating wires she had observed during her examination. Ramón Hernandez's dazzling smile contradicted the photograph's harsh setting.

Carrie's thoughts reeled. How was it two people who'd had contact with each other over in Afghanistan ended up in the same DARPA DBS program? Did Hernandez refer Abington, or was their involvement coincidental?

"Did Steve know this man?" Carrie said, pointing to Hernandez.

Rita shook her head. "If he did, he didn't mention it to me."

As Carrie studied the photograph one more time she noticed a figure in the background, tall and lean, shirtless and rippling with muscles, his face partly obscured by shadows. She could not make out the visage, but the man called to mind Lee Taggart, the nurse working the neuro recovery floor the night Eric Fasciani disappeared.

THE GREEN Garden Inn was just off the highway, and was the kind of roadside motel Carrie's father seemed always drawn to on long family drives. It was nothing special: green vinyl siding, black shutters, and landscaping that looked like a PGA golf course compared to Rita's place. Night had fallen and Carrie was ready to let go of the day, the endless, fruitless search—put on some bad television and drift off into oblivion. David brought in the plastic bag with two toothbrushes, some sweatpants, and T-shirts they had bought at Walmart, and the paper bag with takeout Chinese food.

Though she was ravenous, Carrie took a fifteen-minute shower. She thought about Ramón Hernandez. She'd told David about seeing him in the photo and he thought it could be a coincidence. If she'd been sure the other man was Lee Taggart, she wouldn't have let David convince her.

Out of the shower, Carrie put on her new sweats. Her hair was tangled and stringy, and a quick check in the bathroom mirror confirmed she looked as exhausted as she felt. Not the impression she had wanted to make. Not even close. When she emerged from the bathroom, David was slurping noodles from a paper carton and drinking Heineken from a glass bottle, lying on one of the two twin beds and watching ESPN.

"Your dinner is on the table," he said. "Happy to change the channel if you want."

Carrie scooped up a bowl of chicken and broccoli, grabbed a Heineken

David had opened and set on ice, and climbed onto the empty bed, feeling better than she had all day.

"Do you want me to change it?" David asked.

Carrie looked up at the television and shrugged. "It's fine," she said. "I've been watching a lot of ESPN with Adam since I moved back home."

"You know, I was going to ask you about that."

"About why I'm twenty-nine and living with my parents?"

"You forgot brain surgeon."

"You really want the whole story?"

David gave Carrie a sidelong glance. "I'm a reporter. I may write the CliffsNotes version, but I don't ever ask for it." He shut off the TV.

For the next twenty minutes Carrie provided a detailed accounting of everything that had happened at BCH, starting with Beth Stillwell and ending with her resignation. She could not fathom why it felt so comfortable, so natural to share with him, but it did. Once she started to open up, she could not stop.

David sat on the bed facing Carrie, with his feet on the floor and his food going cold. On occasion, he'd sip from his beer, but mostly his eyes were on her the entire time, and Carrie thought that was just fine. When she finished, Carrie gave a little shrug because she had nothing more to say.

David took a final swig of his beer. "You didn't have to quit," he said. "Dr. Metcalf was in charge. You were just a resident."

"It was my fault," Carrie said.

"But you're a damn good doc."

"You can't say that for sure. I've never operated on your brain."

"But if I needed brain surgery, I would totally want you to do it. I have a really good gut instinct for this sort of thing."

Carrie chuckled. "Yeah, well, talent isn't everything. You were good at your job and look where that got you."

"What's that supposed to mean?"

"It means you were a great stringer, if that's the right term, putting

yourself at risk, doing more than the others, always pushing the boundaries. And because of that, you were taken captive, held hostage, and
suddenly your maverick ways turned you from an asset to a liability.
Our stories aren't so dissimilar, if you think about it."

David gave this some serious thought. "We both pushed ourselves
out of the jobs we loved."

"And now here we are in a motel room in the middle of Maine."

"Yeah, here we are," David said.

A lengthy silence followed. David swung his feet back on the bed
and turned up the volume on the TV a couple clicks to hear a report
on how the Pacers had outlasted the Celtics in a grueling overtime
match. The scrollbar along the bottom of the screen was nothing but
a string of abstract letters and numbers. Carrie had no focus, and her
thoughts became fuzzy as her arms and legs seemed to melt into the
bed. Her eyelids were shutting, voluntarily or not. They snapped back
open when David spoke up.

"Goodwin," he said.

"What?"

"Why doesn't she want you to see the patients post-op?"

Carrie shook her head and dislodged a few of the cobwebs.

"I don't know," she said. "It's her policy. She's a control freak, I guess."

"What if she's not," David suggested.

"What do you mean?"

David returned to his earlier position, feet on the floor, eyes on
Carrie.

"I guess what I'm getting at is what if the palino—you know."

"Palinacousis," Carrie said.

"Yeah, that. What if it only happens in a few patients, not all of them?
And that's why Goodwin doesn't want you or Dr. Finley to look after
her charges. She doesn't want you to know."

Carrie mulled this over. "But there's been a lot of patients, David.
Somebody would have found out by now."

"Not if it's temporary," he said. "She makes sure nobody knows about it. Or if they do, it gets reported to her or Navarro, and that information doesn't get back to you."

"But why?" Carrie asked.

Here David shrugged. "That's the big question, isn't it?"

"So why did Abington and Fasciani check out AMA?"

"Maybe something was different with those two, and Abington and Fasciani had to disappear. Something about their symptoms wasn't going to be temporary."

"Then explain to me how she got them to leave?" Carrie asked.

"She could have paid them off. Or maybe she took them."

"Kidnapping?"

"It's a possibility."

"Goodness, you're a conspiracy theorist, David. Who knew?"

David held up his hands, evidently pleased to embrace the label.

"I think there's a reason Goodwin wants to keep you from looking at those patients, and that it goes beyond protocol. That's all I'm saying."

"We would need a motive. Why would Goodwin want to hide a potential side effect, and then purposefully work to remove patients not only from the program, but the hospital?"

"I know a way we could find out," David said.

"How? By asking her?"

"As a reporter I've had to learn things about people they wouldn't say directly to my face," David said almost apologetically. "So, let's just say I have access to some devices that could aid our effort."

"Elaborate, please."

"If you want to know Goodwin's private conversations, you've got to listen to them."

"You want to bug Goodwin's office?"

"Think about everything you've experienced so far. It all points back to Goodwin. She's up to something, Carrie. The question is, what?"

"I'll think about it," Carrie said.

"You can help get me inside, and I can set it up. The offer is on the table."

"I appreciate it," Carrie said, and she meant it.

David went back to watching television. Carrie turned her gaze to the ceiling. She was not thinking about bugging Goodwin, or any possible motive for hiding the patients. She was thinking about David. Part of it, she knew, was driven by loneliness. While Carrie did not regret putting her career first and foremost in her life priorities, she was also a woman with needs. But she was not ready to act on the impulse—not yet, anyway. The focus had to be on Abington and Fasciani. It had to be on saving her career.

Mind reading, Carrie knew, was nothing but a parlor trick; even so she caught David looking at her and sensed he was having similar thoughts. Carrie held his gaze a moment, then said, "Well, it's late and I'm pretty tired. I'll see you in the morning. Thanks for being there for me, David. It means a lot."

Carrie shut off her bedside lamp and turned her back to David.

David said, "You know, I would have helped you even without getting the story."

In the darkness, Carrie smiled.

CHAPTER 37

Carrie used the VA locker room to change into her running clothes. Her sneakers, size nine Newton's the color of watermelon with electric blue piping, felt stiff from nonuse. Soon enough, she imagined, her legs would be aching from nonuse as well. She had no particular destination in mind, just a desire to get out there and slap some pavement. Her body ached from a bad night's sleep on a crummy mattress, plus all those hours of driving, and a good run would hopefully loosen her up.

She and David had returned from Maine late morning, and Carrie had gone straight to the VA to visit with Gerald Wright for his pre-op consultation.

Wright, a sixty-five-year-old grandfather of eleven and a fighter pilot during the Vietnam War, had been on the surgical schedule for months. His advanced-stage Parkinson's disease couldn't have cared less about two missing vets and Carrie's growing concern about DBS therapy. She had contemplated backing out of the surgery altogether, but worried that might make Goodwin overly suspicious, more careful of what she was willing to say behind closed doors.

On the drive south, Carrie had given David the green light to get whatever equipment was necessary to conduct the surveillance. She trusted his instincts about Goodwin, among other things, including his belief that the Wright operation would go without a hitch.

"It's not Parkinson's that's the problem," David had said. "There are too many DBS procedures involving patients with that condition. Something would have surfaced by now. It's got to be related to PTSD."

It was strange to be back at the VA. Everything felt so normal. Dr. Finley had joined Carrie for the pre-op consultation and he seemed to be in a jovial mood. Immediately following her meeting with Wright, Carrie gave Dr. Finley a briefing on her search, and expressed regret at not having made more progress.

"I appreciate your efforts," Dr. Finley said. "But as I told you back in my office, not everybody who has had the procedure returns for follow-up appointments. We are dealing with very fragmented individuals here."

When Carrie mentioned seeing Ramón Hernandez in a photograph with Abington, he did not seem at all fazed by the discovery.

"It could be that's how Steve got involved. I can check with Ramón, or Cal Trent, but there is a referral component to the DARPA program, so it's not entirely surprising to find a connection between them."

Something that was probably nothing.

All this did was get Carrie's thoughts churning even faster. Maybe what she had observed in Abington and Fasciani was an aberration, and her theory about palinacousis was entirely groundless. After all, Fasciani never actually articulated what she assumed was the condition. It was his behavior that had made her suspect it. Perhaps she was projecting symptoms on these two men to fit a puzzle she'd created.

Her doubts were not enough to call off David's plan to bug Goodwin's office. She was willing to accept Ramón's connection to Abington as potentially coincidental, but there were too many other unusual happenings for Carrie to discount. In any event, a good run might pound some clarity into an increasingly murky situation.

After some light stretching in the parking lot, Carrie tightened the laces of her shoes and set off at what she thought was a ten-minute-mile pace. The cityscape provided the perfect backdrop. She had enough to look at to keep her interested, but not so many cars and pedestrians to make it dangerous or distracting.

She turned right on Brynmar Street, thinking it might be nice to run through Healey Park. Evidently, she was not the only one with this idea. It was not the starting line in Hopkinton on Marathon Monday by any stretch, but plenty of joggers, bikers, and walkers were catching the final rays of sunshine on what had turned into a pleasantly cool afternoon.

Carrie's mind was beginning to let go and she remembered why she had fallen in love with running. Twenty minutes into her jog, her lungs felt great. Concern about her out-of-shape legs became an unfounded worry. The pitch was mostly level, but a few hills challenged her breathing and form.

Out of the corner of her eye Carrie caught a flash of movement. In the next few seconds a couple, fit and trim and dressed in fancy athletic gear, zipped past her on the right. Carrie quickened her pace to keep up until her lungs begged her to retreat. She slipped back to her natural gait, slowed her speed considerably, and laughed at her competiveness.

Always trying to be the best. Always pushing the limits.

It reminded Carrie of her conversation with David in the motel room, about the symmetry of their circumstances. She had almost succumbed to impulse and climbed into bed with him. It probably would not have been something she'd have regretted. Part of her wondered if that had been on David's mind as well.

Carrie was not sure what drew her attention to the jogger behind her. She glanced over her shoulder at the muscular man, who wore blue Nike training pants and a dark running jacket. A Red Sox baseball hat and sunglasses concealed most of his head and face. Carrie ran on, but she could hear the man behind her, his footfalls landing like soft taps against the pavement.

Curious if he was going to pass her, Carrie looked again. He had not gained a step. He also did not appear to be breathing very hard. This guy with tree trunks for legs must have another gear, but for whatever reason he'd opted not to use it. He evidently preferred to run behind Carrie, in that dead space where he was not a stalker, but not invisible either. There was plenty of room for all runners, and after a hundred yards with him on her tail it got irritating. She decided to put some pep in her step and lose this guy.

Her muscles responded, and soon she was running at what felt like a nine-minute-mile pace. Carrie's heart rate jacked and her lungs felt squeezed, but it was a manageable pace, at least for a while.

After about a minute Carrie took a peek behind and saw the same man running the exact same distance away from her. He had not fallen back, not even a few feet, which meant he had increased his speed to match Carrie's. It did not look like he was breathing any harder, either. Once again he maintained the exact distance that allowed him to be a presence, but not a threat.

Carrie switched sides of the road and picked up her pace a little bit more. She was probably running a sub-nine-minute mile now, well outside her comfort zone. Whatever her exact speed, Carrie's form suffered as a result, and she no longer landed with the mid-foot strike that helped prevent injury. The bad form caused joint strain, and made her breathing even more labored. But she pushed on, refusing to look behind her, not wanting to give in to curiosity or fuel her growing unease.

Her resolve lasted all of ten strides. As she passed a tall oak tree, Carrie craned her neck to look over her left shoulder and immediately spotted the same man running behind her. He had crossed the road with her and picked up speed to keep pace.

His arms pumped effortlessly, and his legs looked as if they could go on moving that way forever. This run was nothing to him, she could tell. He acted completely nonchalant. To anybody else, it would look like two runners working out. Maybe he was using her as a pace car, or for motivation. Since other joggers were around, Carrie was not too panicked. But she had moved beyond just being annoyed.

It's your mind playing tricks, Carrie assured herself. *Nothing more.*

She ran another fifty yards with the man in the dark hat and sunglasses behind her before she decided to turn around. She slowed and made a wide, arching turn, and a few moments later she passed Hat Man on her left. He kept his head forward and his running rhythm steady with no change in direction. She took one glance behind her and saw Hat Man was still running away from her, just a guy out doing his own thing.

Carrie laughed at her paranoia and kept her gaze forward as she ran. The urge to look back once more felt almost oppressive, but she refused to cave in to her paranoia again. The incident was innocuous, she decided. She continued at a pace still above her norm, but the urge to look back would not let go.

Just take one look—one quick check—one . . . little . . . glance . . .

Carrie turned her head and her body followed. As her gaze traveled back, a feeling of relief came over her. Nobody was there.

Once again, Carrie laughed at her perceived ridiculousness. Fear was easy to catch. This made her think of Adam, and how he lived with that sinking feeling almost every second of the day. Like Abington and Fasciani, Adam was caught in terror's unrelenting grasp.

Ahead, she spied a turnoff to a cut-through that bisected the park. The path was narrow and paved with dirt, less demanding on the joints, and Carrie went that way. The sides of the path were lined with tall grasses and trees with budding leaves. Carrie absorbed the scenic beauty, appreciating every bush, cloud, and birdsong.

Behind her, a new sound entered her ears: the soft crunching of dirt. Somebody running. The tall grasses became a long green blur in Carrie's peripheral vision.

It's nothing, Carrie said to herself.

Five yards became ten, but Carrie still did not look back. Fifteen. Then twenty. The impulse to check was irresistible. She turned her body and gave a look. A sinking feeling swallowed her gut and Carrie's pulse took off. He was there, running behind her, hat on his head, sunglasses in place, keeping the same distance as before. Carrie had no idea how he'd snuck up on her, but she believed he wanted her to notice him.

Fear uncoiled as a surge of adrenaline hastened her strides. Carrie's heart hammered in her throat. She looked ahead, but the dirt path was vacant, no other joggers or bikers in sight.

She broke into a sprint, panting. Her eyes started to tear, and her thoughts turned black with terror. Her burning lungs needed more air. She opened her mouth wider, but that did little to help.

Straining her ears, Carrie heard the persistent patter of footsteps. Panic set in. She looked left, then right; would the tall grasses give her an escape route, or would they just slow her down? She decided to keep to the path. Run as hard as she possibly could.

Her only chance was to get to the main road and find someone to help. Carrie staggered sideways, unable to keep a straight line. Her eyes stayed fixed to the ground as she navigated around roots and rocks. Despite the intense exertion on her legs and lungs, Carrie managed to find still another gear. Her arms were pumping wildly to keep up the pace.

Ahead, she saw an opening where the cut-through path intersected the main road. People would be there, and safety.

Carrie risked another check behind her. He was still there, running at a brisk pace, but as before, he did not appear to be gaining. Why? Was he toying with her? Did he get off on her fear?

She saw a smile on his face, and a flash of something in his hand—a knife, or perhaps even a gun. The tall grasses that she'd thought might aid her escape would be the perfect place to hide her rape or murder.

A fresh blast of terror filled her. She wanted to scream, but her battered lungs needed every bit of air and left nothing for her voice.

The path ended maybe a hundred yards ahead. He could still catch her. She sprinted in a blind panic. How could she have been so stupid, to take this cut-through?

The road was about seventy-five yards away.

Her focus wavered. In the next instant Carrie's ankle twisted, sending her sprawling. She landed on the hard, packed ground and skidded several feet on her knees. Momentum carried her forward and she got back to her feet, almost without breaking stride. Her only recourse was to keep running, and she refused to waste a second to see if he was gaining. Of course he was—he had to be. The ankle burned, as did her knees where she skidded, and every other stride hurt like running barefoot across shards of glass.

Don't look, don't look! Just run!

But Carrie could not resist. Her back and head turned and the man was there, five feet away, sporting a broad grin on his face. A scream of sorts escaped from her lips, more like a low moan that grew increasingly louder. Sweat glossed her skin and her thoughts became gummed with terror. Her legs kicked furiously, arms swinging in wild arcs. The numbness in the legs turned intense, beyond unpleasant. Her lungs screamed for her to stop, but Carrie blocked out the pain and she urged herself on.

Faster! Faster!

She wondered if it was the man's breath that made her neck so hot. She could almost feel his fingers gripping at her clothes.

Five more steps . . . five more.

As Carrie stumbled from the path, she collided with a female jogger who had no time to react. The impact was not too much, but Carrie's weakened ankle sent her tumbling to the ground. The other jogger let out a gasp, and once she figured out what had just happened, turned back to Carrie.

"Are you all right?" she asked, without offering to help her to her feet.

Carrie was down on her stomach, unable to see the path, but she still managed to get out a warning.

"Behind you, behind you!" she yelled. "He's behind you!"

The woman turned to look as Carrie scrambled to her feet. A moment later, the man in the baseball cap emerged from the cut-through with a worried look on his face. He came over to Carrie and she saw now a scar like a jagged lightning bolt on his cheek, and a shamrock tattoo that decorated the side of his neck.

"Nasty tumble you took there," he said.

Carrie skirted back several feet.

"Get away from me," she snapped.

The man looked only slightly aggrieved.

"Hey, I was just trying to help," he said with a shrug and a what-can-I-do kind of smile. He turned on his heels, and started back down the same dirt path.

"Do you need me to call the cops?" the woman jogger asked.

"No," Carrie said. "I'm fine. Thanks for asking. Sorry to run into you."

The jogger waved and went on her way.

Favoring her good ankle, Carrie watched Hat Man run away from her. Soon enough he was a pinprick on the horizon, and then he was gone. All she saw were the tall grasses swaying in concert with the gentle breeze.

CHAPTER 38

Adam was shooting hoops when Carrie got home. She parked her car in the pullout and ambled over to him, trying to not favor her swelling left ankle. Worried about alarming everyone, especially Adam, Carrie had decided to keep the incident at the park a secret.

Adam took a shot, swished it from fifteen feet out, got his rebound, and bounced the ball with a display of his substantial dribbling skills. He appraised Carrie warily.

"What happened to you?" he asked.

Carrie was taken aback. She thought she'd done a good job concealing the minor sprain, and glanced down to make sure her pants hid the scrapes from her fall. "I'm fine. Why do you ask?"

"You're limping," Adam said.

Irene had passed her keen observation genes to her son as well as to her daughter.

"It's nothing," Carrie said.

Adam tossed Carrie the basketball, with a little heat on the pass. He never held back when it came to playing sports. He loved competition, as did Carrie, but he took it to a whole different level. It was one aspect of his personality that had driven him into the military.

Carrie took a shot, but her balance was off on account of her ankle, and the ball clanged off the rim. Adam snagged the rebound, and in a fluid, dancerlike motion, turned and fired a jump shot that sent the ball in a high arc before it eventually found the center of the hoop.

Everything about Adam's body was in perfect working order, Carrie observed. He was lithe, agile, and quick on his feet. It was a bit surreal to see how able he appeared when Carrie knew he was anything but.

"You seem a little shaken," Adam said, dribbling once more. "Everything all right?"

On a whim, she decided to tell the truth. The experience had been truly frightening. Who better to share it with than someone who understood fear so well? "Oh, I just had a really creepy, scary incident at the park, while I was running. It's nothing."

Adam's stern expression indicated otherwise. "What happened?"

Carrie had not spaced on Adam's overly protective tendencies. The dark expression that overtook Adam's face after she had finished was more than a little unsettling.

"You sure he was just using you to set the pace?" Adam said.

"I don't know. I think so," Carrie said, not sounding at all convinced. "He came up to me after and seemed to feel badly about it."

Adam said, "Yeah, well, don't trust anybody, and run with somebody else, will you please? I told you that like a thousand times. People do terrible things to each other, Carrie. Really terrible things."

Carrie was not sure whether Adam was talking about the jogger in the park, or himself. She set her hands on Adam's shoulders. "Look, it's nothing," she said. "I'm fine. And I'll be more careful next time."

Adam took a couple dribbles to get centered, and looked at Carrie the way she might examine a patient during a pre-op exam. She could tell he was looking for any hint of deceit. Adam said nothing, but it seemed he had picked up on Carrie's lingering apprehension.

"It really was harmless," Carrie said.

In the back of her mind, though, she wondered about the timing. The incident with the jogger came on the heels of her plot to bug Goodwin and in the middle of her search for two missing vets.

Still unconvinced, Adam said, "Just remember, I'm your brother. I'm always going to look out for you. Always."

Adam slugged Carrie playfully in the arm, and she slugged him back with an even lighter tap. During this exchange, the garage door came open and Carrie snatched the ball from Adam's grasp while he was distracted. She launched a solid ten-footer that found the net, no problem.

Howard Bryant emerged from the garage, carrying a tray of gardening tools, dressed for that sort of work. He set down the tools and sauntered over to his kids.

"Who's up for a game of Horse?" Howard asked with a star-bright smile on his face. Like their mother, Howard wanted his two children living on their own, but the sparkle in his eyes said he would cherish every moment spent together as a family under any circumstance.

Adam passed the ball to his father with maybe a little less zip than his delivery to Carrie. Not missing a beat, Howard caught the ball with two hands, took a couple of dribbles, and fired off a shot that could have been a mirror of Adam's earlier jumper. It hit nothing but net.

The game commenced as the sun beat a final retreat and birdsong filled the sweet-smelling air with joyful chatter. Howard started off the game with a layup, made it, and passed the ball to Adam, who also made the shot. Carrie, still favoring her left ankle, dribbled awkwardly to the hoop and clanged the ball off the rim.

"Carrie's a bit lame," Adam said.

Carrie acted indignant. "We're *playing* Horse," she said. "I'm not one."

"Just keep the move-and-shoot to a minimum, Dad. I'd hate for us to have to put her down."

Howard made a face, but the truth was that he'd been encouraging Adam to lighten up, to relax. Any show of levity was a minor victory in an otherwise endless war. Howard saved his expression of concern for Carrie.

"Did you hurt yourself, sweetheart?" he asked.

Carrie shot Adam a nervous glance, fearing he might say something about the incident in the park. Her dad might not think it was so innocuous, either. The world was full of predators, and Carrie was not interested in a lecture on safety. Adam gave Carrie a look that said she could trust him.

"I'm fine," Carrie said. "It's just a slight sprain, that's all. I fell while jogging. I can still take you boys on."

The winner of the game was basically predetermined. The real contest was between Howard and Carrie for second place. Adam seemed to relish his expected victory, and a fraction of a grin overtook his face, until his gaze settled on the dysfunctional Camaro visible in the garage. Adam stomped over to the garage, pushed the button to shut the door, and returned to the basketball game with a look of disgust.

"Come morning, I'm turning that pile of metal into scrap," he said.

The glower on Adam's face remained until he buried three free throws in a row. Neither Carrie nor Howard reacted. They had heard the same threat many times before.

Carrie tried another shot and missed. *H-O*. Not wanting to earn the final three letters, Carrie decided her ankle needed a more supportive sneaker. She excused herself to go inside and change footwear.

Carrie could not locate the sneakers she wanted in her closet at first, but eventually saw them to the left of her black riding boots. It was a bit odd; Carrie was normally fastidious about her closet, and those sneakers were always to the right of her boots, kept in order of size. She sat on the bed and put on her sneakers, then got up to feed Limbic.

While Limbic gobbled every flake of food offered, Carrie opened her dresser to change into a different T-shirt. Right away she could tell someone had rifled through her clothing. Her shirts were folded, but not exactly as she would have done it. Close, but not perfect. Not her stamp.

Carrie was on high alert, every muscle tense. She scanned her bedroom for other anomalies. They were not especially difficult to spot. The sheet on her bed had not been pulled as tight as she would have done, and a stack of papers on her desk seemed closer to the window by about six inches. All these details were minor, but Carrie cut her teeth obsessing over the minor details. She noticed everything. Somebody had been in her room. Not just in her room, but looking through her things.

Carrie tried to make sense of it and arrived at one disturbing conclusion—Adam had spied on her. Who else could have done it? As much as she tried, Carrie could not come up with another logical explanation. His mental state was obviously fragile, but he had never done anything this strange, this out of character. Carrie's pulse accelerated as she descended the stairs, but at the bottom step she paused.

Deep breaths . . . deep breaths . . .

The surge of anger subsided like the tide rolling out to sea. There was an answer, Carrie assured herself. It would just take a conversation with Adam to clear things up.

Outside, Carrie found her father and brother shooting around. She approached tentatively, hands on her hips.

Howard stopped dribbling and said, "What happened to you? You look pale."

Carrie's heart fluttered as the anger returned. "Was somebody in my room?" She looked right at Adam, and her composure vanished.

"What are you talking about?" Howard asked.

"Somebody went through all my things. My clothes, under the bed. Somebody was in my room."

Adam's eyes narrowed and his face reddened like a boiled lobster. "Why are you looking at me?" he asked.

"I'm just asking," Carrie snapped. "I'm trying to figure it out."

Howard said, "No. No. Of course not. Nobody went into your room."

Adam took a step forward. "Are you accusing me of something?" His voice held violence. His eyes were like pools of lava bubbling just below the surface and about to go volcanic.

Carrie changed her approach. One slight push might be enough to send Adam over the edge. "I'm trying to figure out if somebody went into my room, or not, that's all."

The answer, of course, was that *somebody* had been in there. The question was who.

Adam was not about to beat a retreat. He had been accused of wrongdoing and felt victimized. "Maybe you're getting paranoid," he said. "First you think a guy is chasing you in the park, and now they're rummaging through your stuff?"

"What guy?" Howard asked, turning to Carrie.

"It's nothing, Dad."

Adam let the basketball roll into the woods and approached Carrie in a menacing, threatening manner. His shoulders were forward, his arms out in front of his body, palms facing up. "Maybe the jogger is the guy who went into your room," he said.

Maybe, Carrie thought.

But that seemed incredible. It was too bizarre to reconcile. Why would somebody go into her room? What could they be looking for?

"Were you here all day?" Carrie asked, not yet ready to back down.

Easy, Carrie . . . Easy . . .

"Yeah, I've been here all day. Going through your crap."

"Adam, that's not necessary," Carrie said in a softer tone. "I'm just trying to understand what happened."

"Understand this," Adam said. He held up two hands with his two middle fingers fully extended, then turned and marched his indignation all the way down the driveway.

Carrie felt sick to her stomach, but it had been the most logical conclusion. While her father and mother were out and about, Adam had free rein around the house.

Howard appeared crestfallen. "You have to be careful with him, Carrie," he admonished.

Now she felt even worse. Disappointing her father, her hero, even a smidge, put a crimp on her heart.

"I'm sorry, Dad, but somebody was in my room."

"Well, obviously it wasn't your mother or me, and I'm willing to believe Adam. You're under a lot of strain, Carrie."

Carrie took a sharper tone. "Are you suggesting I'm making it up? I know what I saw, Dad."

Howard did not take the bait, and he was not going to get into it with her. "Just go easy on your brother," he said. "You two need each other. And I need to know that you're there for him in case we're not."

Carrie understood the subtext. She nodded glumly at the thought of her parents' demise. It would be many years away, she prayed, but one day they would be gone, and her dad was right: She would be Adam's lifeline.

"You can count on me, Dad," Carrie said. "I won't ever let him go."

Howard leaned forward and kissed his daughter gently on the cheek. "Good," he said. And with that, Howard headed down the driveway to go looking for his son.

CHAPTER 39

At five thirty the next morning Carrie was back at the VA for Gerald Wright's DBS surgery. Parkinson's disease had crept into and enveloped the retired lieutenant colonel's life over the previous fifteen years, and as with all the other PD candidates for DBS, medication management had become unreliable. The surgical team, including Carrie, Dr. Finley, and the anesthesiologist, Dr. Kauffman, met to review Wright's MRI from the day before and the CT scan from that morning to determine where best to insert the leads.

To Carrie's surprise, Dr. Evan Navarro showed up for the meeting. The images had just been brought up on the computer when Navarro entered the conference room without knocking, as though he belonged there. He gave Carrie a cool smile as he walked through the door.

"What are you doing here, Evan?" Carrie asked.

"Sandra wanted me to observe this morning," Navarro said. He fell silent, feeling no compulsion to further elaborate.

Carrie's heart began to thunder. In the aftermath of yesterday's tumult in the park, she gave serious consideration to the possibility that the missing vets, the encounter with the jogger, and the ransacking of her room were all somehow connected. Now that Navarro had shown up unexpectedly, this notion took deeper roots.

Navarro looked snappy in his white lab coat, red-and-white-striped tie, and dark trousers. His hair looked extra oily, slicked back as if in homage to Eddie Munster, widow's peak and all. Carrie bristled at the thought of him joining her. A glance told her that Dr. Finley was equally displeased.

"Why would Dr. Goodwin want that?" Carrie asked.

"Surgery is her department, Carrie," Navarro answered coolly. "I don't ask how she runs it. I just do my job." His tone was condescending, implying Carrie would benefit from doing the same.

Dr. Finley stepped forward. "This is entirely inappropriate, Evan." His face was a shade of crimson Carrie had never seen on him before. "Nobody cleared this with me."

Navarro just shrugged. "You'll have to take that up with Sandra, too, I guess."

"And I damn well will do just that," Dr. Finley said. "We both know what this is about, don't we, Evan? And it's total bullcrap."

Navarro's smarmy expression set Carrie's blood on fire. "Well, Alistair, last I checked, this is surgery that you're doing here. And that would be my boss's area of responsibility. So I can only offer the same reply to you that I just gave to Carrie, which is if you don't want me here, you'll need to take that up with Sandra. Otherwise, I'm not interested in pissing her off today—or any day, for that matter."

Navarro set his beady little eyes on Carrie. She glanced over at Dr. Finley, who glowered at Navarro until he softened. No value in wasting energy, his expression conveyed. He pulled Carrie aside.

"I suspect this is a bit of payback for questioning her AMA orders," Dr. Finley said in a whispered voice. "I know her style. She's letting you know you're on notice. Don't worry about it, and try to ignore Navarro if you can. I'll speak to Sandra after and see if I can smooth things over. Nobody wants to work under a microscope."

Carrie gave a nod. She had her own payback in mind for Goodwin, and after the surgery she would help David make that plan a reality. For now, Carrie would dedicate all her attention to her patient and ignore Navarro as Dr. Finley advised.

The question now was where to place the electrodes.

Wright's facial inexpressiveness, unblinking vacant stare, and almost inaudible whisper of a voice belied a reasonably intact intellect, but significant personality and behavioral problems had influenced Dr. Finley's decision. The apathy and depression, for example. Were these behaviors a direct consequence of his disease, or an understandable psychiatric reaction to the devastations of a failing motor system?

Wright had had enough problems for Dr. Finley to decide on the right globus pallidus interna for the stimulating electrode target. This would seem to afford the best opportunity to reduce the left arm tremor and improve Gerald Wright's overall motor status. Dr. Finley and Carrie considered other target placements, but the risk of psychiatric complications favored the GPi as the better choice.

"He may be a bilateral case," Dr. Finley told Carrie as she went in to scrub for the surgery, "but let's see how he does with this side first. He's pretty intact cognitively, but I'm concerned about his behaviors and the neuropsych testing reports we've gotten back."

Carrie was still schooling herself in the subtleties of Parkinson's disease and the options of DBS surgeries. Like everything else in medicine, this was a rapidly evolving discipline, meaning patient and doctor alike were on steeply ascending learning curves. Carrie reprimanded herself for not spending more time studying about PD, even though she was still new to the program. She'd had too many distractions.

Like missing vets.

The familiar harsh smell of Betadine scrub and the lather up above her elbows brought her mind back to the problem at hand, retired LTC Gerald Wright. She smiled slightly beneath her mask. Despite all that was going on, she was still a surgeon at heart, and she could focus all her attention on her profession and the task at hand.

Funny how at the most unpredictable of times, she became aware of the transformational effects of training. No one had ever taught her to feel like a competent doctor, a leader. But that was how she felt as she did her second scrub midway up the forearms, and then the third, just the hands.

She entered the OR not feeling as comfortably in the zone as she was accustomed.

The procedure was becoming commonplace, which played in her favor: affix the stereotactic frame with four screws under local anesthesia first thing in the morning, then down to MRI for ultra-thin slices, with the images sent over to the planning station in the OR. Carrie selected the optimum XYZ coordinates to minimize risk of brain injury or hemorrhage as the needle advanced its way to Gerald Wright's globus pallidus interna.

He was awake for this procedure, kept comfortable with just the right amount of propofol. That way, Dr. Finley could monitor the patient's motor status directly and also use the electrode recording techniques that signaled their specific placement. They were a team now, Dr. Alistair Finley and Dr. Carrie Bryant. They were able to carry out the extended, time-consuming procedure with little back-and-forth dialogue, as if they were reading each other's thoughts, despite the fact that they had worked together on only a handful of cases.

Evan Navarro's presence was as innocuous as the familiar sounds of the operating room machinery. Maybe the choice of music helped Carrie block out the unpleasant distraction. Gerald Wright was also a jazz fan, and he had requested Bill Evans's *Portrait in Jazz* for his big day in the OR. The melodies reminded Carrie of her life at BCH, and friends like Valerie, with whom she was no longer in touch. Even in the Facebook era, friendships forged at work faded quickly once that bond was broken. But now she had a new community, a new team she counted on and who counted on her.

"Are you doing all right, Carrie?"

Carrie's focus had been so total that Dr. Finley repeated himself.

"Yeah, I'm fine. Why?"

"You're about to go off your line by about three micrometers. Do you need a rest?"

"I'm sorry," Carrie said. "Maybe just a minute and some water."

Navarro's black eyes seemed to be smiling.

Carrie was not 100 percent, and Dr. Finley seemed to know it. A thin film of grit blanketed her eyes, left behind from a bad night's sleep plagued by nightmares of men chasing her in the dark. Adam had crashed on the couch watching TV, and Carrie woke him by accident getting ready for work.

Yesterday's fight was in the past. He had smiled warmly at her and wished her a good day without having read the long note of apology Carrie had left on the kitchen table. Seeing Navarro's wicked look made Carrie more willing to believe her brother. Could Evan Navarro have been in her bedroom? Could Goodwin have put him up to it? And if so, why? Carrie had a gut feeling that bugging Goodwin's office would get her some answers.

After a short break, Carrie resumed her work. Dr. Finley recorded the electrical discharge patterns as Carrie sank the electrodes on the sweet spot. Navarro did not stay for the entire show. Evidently, he had made his point and was off to other things. Soon enough he, or one of his residents, would be looking in on Gerald Wright, and Carrie would probably never see this patient again. Even if everything that had been happening lately had a logical explanation, Carrie doubted she could continue to work under such rigid constraints.

In total, it took seven hours to drill the holes and close up the skull, and in that time Carrie developed knots in her shoulders the size of walnuts.

"You seemed a little off today," Dr. Finley said back in the scrub room. "You sure everything is okay?"

"Navarro had me a bit rattled," Carrie replied.

"Well, leave that to me. I'm going to speak with Sandra right now. That won't happen again, I assure you."

Carrie went to the locker room to take a shower and get changed. After that, she stopped by the hospital cafeteria for her second coffee of the day. Next, it was on to the front desk where Carrie would arrange a temporary ID for David Hoffman. They had settled on the ruse that he was a medical student coming to the VA tonight to help with some research. To keep their activities as covert as possible, David asked Carrie to use an alias, and she picked "Michael Stephen," which were the first two names that had popped into her head.

She texted David her chosen moniker and headed to an on-call room to grab a few hours of shut-eye on the narrow, industrial bed before Mission Possible commenced.

Carrie's cell phone buzzed in her lab coat pocket, which she assumed was David responding. She checked the number, but did not recognize the caller.

"Hello, Dr. Carrie Bryant speaking."

"Dr. Bryant, I'm Dr. Abbey Smerling from Seacoast Memorial Hospital in Maine."

Carrie's entire body came alive. "Yes, Dr. Smerling. What can I do for you?"

"You placed a call regarding a patient, Dr. Sam Rockwell, and asked to be notified if there were any developments."

Carrie braced for the news to come. A potential link to the mystery of what might have happened to Abington and Fasciani had probably just died.

"Yes, that's correct," Carrie said.

"Well, I have some good news to share."

This was what Carrie had hoped for. It was common practice for doctors to share patient information with other doctors irrespective of the new privacy laws. Some habits were harder to break than others.

Dr. Smerling said, "The brain swelling had begun to recede, so we lightened up the coma to see if he could come back."

"And?"

"And we got something," Dr. Smerling said. "A lot more than we expected."

CHAPTER 40

At precisely seven o'clock that evening, David arrived at the VA ready to get to work. As far as he knew, Carrie was already on the road, headed back to Maine. She had called with the exciting news about Sam Rockwell and suggested they reschedule tonight's activities, but David saw no need. He could get the job done as long as Carrie did her part to help.

At the front desk David almost forgot to use the alias "Michael Stephen," but remembered at the last possible second, before the conversation with the receptionist turned decidedly awkward. Carrie had assured him nobody would ask for ID, and she was right. Even so, for backup, David had printed a bogus one using a template procured off the Internet, and had it laminated for authenticity. It proved an unnecessary precaution, but David seldom left anything to chance.

"Here you go, dear," the kind-faced receptionist said as she handed David his temporary badge.

One obstacle cleared, thought David.

He headed to the third floor, following a rudimentary map drawn from Carrie's brief description of the hospital layout. Walking these institutionalized halls, David felt suffocated at the thought of having to work in such an antiseptic environment. Journalistic stringers were free spirits, and David relished the uncertainty of his chosen profession. He was all about new possibilities, and shied away from anything that could anchor him—a permanent job, a mortgage, a car, material possessions, and yes, even love. He often wondered if the issues between him and Emma were a product of mismatched pheromones or his wandering spirit. Guarded as he was, something told David one kiss from Carrie Bryant might be enough to tame his wanderlust permanently.

Carrie's office was third to the last down a long hallway lined with ordinary wooden doors without any markings on them. She had left the door unlocked, as she said she would, and David went inside.

His first impression was that Carrie essentially worked in a closet. His prison cell in Syria had been only slightly bigger. She had enough room for a chair and a metal desk, which Carrie wisely kept uncluttered. A small, square window offered a narrow view of a gritty construction effort under way. All in all, David found it a depressing place. He much preferred the dangers of the field.

Carrie had left a pair of scrubs on the door hook, and they fit David fine. He turned the lock on the doorknob before he closed the door, and checked the hallway to make sure nobody was coming. Carrie had rightly said most everyone would be gone by now, and the halls were museum-quiet.

From the pocket of his pants David retrieved a leather case that contained a tension wrench and set of picks. He tested his picking chops on Carrie's door. It was open in less than a minute. Having worked in dangerous locales over the years, David had acquired a unique set of unsavory skills. In addition to picking locks, forging documents, and planting bugs, David was competent with a gun and could also hot-wire some cars.

Returning to the main hallway, David passed a few people on his way to Goodwin's office, but nobody gave him a second glance. The modest disguise more than sufficed.

Following Carrie's directions, David took a right turn at the first hallway branch, and stopped at a door with a mounted placard that read: DR. SANDRA L. GOODWIN, CHIEF OF NEUROSURGERY, M.D.

David put his ear to the door and gave a listen. Not a sound. He gave the knob a gentle turn. Locked. *Good.* David had the door open in less time than it had taken him to manipulate the pins on Carrie's lock. He entered quickly, closed and locked the door behind him, and flicked on the light.

The office within was larger than Carrie's by a good amount, with nicer furniture, and a bigger window, too, but the intuitional stamp was just the same. David fished the Sonit-21 mini voice recorder from his pocket. The device had cost five hundred dollars, a fortune for David at the time, but the investment had paid back ten-fold in the information covertly obtained. The voice-activated rectangular device was a bit larger than a Bic lighter, weighed just eight grams, and could record for 120 hours on a single charge.

David searched the office for the best place to hide the recorder. The Sonit's black case blended well with the dirt of one of Goodwin's ailing plants. After he turned on the voice activation mode, David covered the recorder with a thin layer of soil to better conceal it, and took a seat in Goodwin's chair.

"Testing one, two, three," David said in a normal speaking voice. "Testing. Testing."

He retrieved the device, cleared away the dirt, and pressed the playback button. His voice echoed loud and clear. David returned the recorder to the pot and flicked enough dirt to make it disappear.

He got halfway to the door when he heard footsteps coming down the hall. He moved behind the desk, feeling sweat bead up on his brow. The doorknob to Goodwin's office turned from the outside.

David looked around for anyplace to hide. The ceiling tiles could be removed, but the chance of him climbing up there before the door came open was slim to none. Keys rattled. Color drained from his face. David had to act quickly, rationally. The only place he could think to hide was under the desk.

He moved the chair back a foot to squeeze his body into the small crawl space underneath the desk. The desk's metal front would partly shield him from anybody walking in, but half a foot of space between the legs and the metal sides left him horribly exposed. All somebody had to do was look down, and they'd see David huddled in a little ball on the floor.

To get his body off the ground, David pressed his back against one side of the desk and put his feet up against the other side. Next, he engaged his core, arched his hips, and raised his body off the floor. The strain on his stomach muscles was instant and intense. It took all of a few seconds for the spasms to begin, his midsection shaking like an earthquake.

David swallowed a breath and concentrated on relaxing. He heard the key go into the lock and a slight noise as the doorknob engaged. David worried his bottom might be sagging a bit, and he lifted it up higher. The burn intensified. He heard two sets of footsteps enter, and then a man's voice.

"I just need to grab a file for Sandra and then we'll be out of here."

A female voice said, "Maybe we should stay a while longer."

David's heart pounded in his ears. Every muscle in his core was fully engaged, and his joints ached from the oppressive strain. The crawl space under the desk was unpleasantly cramped, but David elevated his hips some more without making a sound. Closing his eyes, he breathed through his nose and began to count in his head.

One . . . two . . . three . . .

"Got it," the man said.

"I got it, too, Evan," the woman said.

David heard a groan of pleasure escape Evan's lips. This had to be Evan Navarro, Goodwin's minion Carrie had told him about.

"Residents are not supposed to fraternize with their boss," Evan said in a breathy voice.

"Is squeezing and rubbing the same as fraternizing?" asked the woman.

David snapped his eyes closed and fought against the growing fatigue. Sweat poured out of his body and began to drip on the floor. Evan groaned again and David heard the sounds of sloppy kissing. David's mind began to quit on him.

Just give it up . . . drop to the floor . . .

He felt his grip slipping, and the desperate urge to let go intensified. His violent body shakes persisted and threatened to dislodge him.

Sixteen . . . seventeen . . . eighteen . . .

"Maybe we should skip dinner tonight," Evan said.

"I know what I want for dessert," the woman cooed.

The kissing resumed while tears of pain streaked down David's cheeks. Both legs burned equally, and it felt like sharp needles were being jammed into his stomach. He kept his eyes closed tight and kept counting.

Thirty-five . . . thirty-six . . . thirty-seven . . .

David feared he might black out. He had to let go. There was no way to hold on. His body was screaming as the agony turned exquisite.

The kissing sounds abruptly stopped.

"Let's take this to a more comfortable location," Evan suggested.

Please . . . please . . .

A consuming blackness came over him. David's back was slipping. His legs were giving out on him. His whole body was drenched in sweat. The traction simply was not there. He slid down an inch.

"Maybe we should do it here?" the woman suggested.

A beat. David slid some more. His legs had turned to Jell-O.

"If you want to do it in an office, let's use mine," Evan said. "I'll have visions of Sandra in my head, and that's just not a turn-on."

David dropped another inch. His back began to sag, and if somebody glanced at the floor they would have no trouble seeing him. His lower back and hips were clearly visible.

"Let's just go to your place," the woman said. "A bed would be far more comfortable than a desk."

David heard a thunderclap sound when somebody slapped the top of the desk. The vibration nearly dislodged him, and his body dipped even more. He kept his gaze fixed upward. A biting on his tongue helped him regain focus.

Hold on.

His muscles went into full spasm. David was going to drop.

I can do this . . . just hold on a few more seconds . . .

"Couldn't agree more," Evan said.

In the back of his mind, through a fog of pain, David heard footsteps and the sound of a door opening. The office lights went out as David's body let go. He crashed to the floor at the same instant the office door slammed shut.

CHAPTER 41

Seacoast Memorial Hospital was south of Bangor, overlooking beautiful Elkhorn Lake. According to Carrie's navigation app, it was a four-and-a-half-hour drive from Boston, mostly a straight shot up I-95 North. The sameness of the route had lulled Carrie into a trance, and the classic rock station she found did a marginal job at keeping her awake and alert. She rolled down her window and took in a refreshing blast of fresh air. Sunset was approaching, and off in the distance Carrie spotted a helicopter making lazy circles against a sky brushed with hues of pink and yellow. She figured it was a news chopper, but traffic on this stretch of highway was light and it would have to fly elsewhere to find any congestion.

On a whim, Carrie exited the highway at Brunswick, and merged onto Route 1 headed north. The detour would add only twenty minutes or so to her drive, but would take her along the gorgeous scenic coastline.

A few miles down the road, Carrie's phone rang and gave her a start. She checked the number, thinking it might be David with news, but the ID came up as Dr. Abbey Smerling.

"Hi there, Dr. Smerling," Carrie said, fumbling with the phone's settings to activate her Bluetooth and make the call hands-free.

"Hi, Carrie, you had asked for an update on Sam Rockwell's condition."

There was no small talk. Abbey Smerling, like most every doc Carrie knew, squeezed phone calls in the way they did meals. Carrie again braced herself for a disappointing report.

"We just did his Glasgow score and it came out a six."

Carrie's mouth fell open. *A six!* She could hardly believe her ears. This was up two points from when she had last spoken to Smerling.

The Glasgow score provided neurologists with a way to gauge the severity of an acute brain injury. By measuring various functions, including eye opening, verbal response, and motor response, a patient's prognosis could be predicted with surprising accuracy. Anything eight and above had a good chance for recovery, while a score between three and five was most likely fatal. A six was the nether world—not great, not dismal. Perfectly in between.

Sam Rockwell had suffered a massive hemorrhage that went below the arachnoid membrane and into the cerebrospinal fluid, according to what Dr. Smerling had told her. The hemorrhage had grown, too, in part because of a course of anticoagulant medication. The increased swelling from fluid collection around the hemorrhage site caused further pressure on the brain structure and additional neurological injury.

For Rockwell to have emerged from his coma and get a six on the Glasgow score was about as likely as Goodwin inviting Carrie on a girls' weekend.

"So what's driving the number?" Carrie asked.

"We've got a little more verbal response than before, but his speech is still incomprehensible. He's a two there. His eyes have opened in response to pain, and he's got the same decerebrate posture as before."

Based on that alone, Carrie pictured Rockwell in his hospital bed, arms and legs held straight out, his toes pointed downward, and his head and neck arched back. The abnormal posture was a sign of severe brain damage and earned him a two on the widely used scale. The eye movement was the new development, having gone from a plus one to a plus two in under a day. It was encouraging progress.

While there was no real reason for Carrie to rush up to Maine,

Rockwell's scores were not low enough to keep her from making the drive. As Dr. Smerling confirmed, his scores could improve at any time, and perhaps the verbal could get up to a four. The conversation in that case might be confused, but he might be able to answer some simple questions.

Did you ever see palinacousis in the vets before?

Did you notice any side effects from the DBS surgery?

Did any of your patients ever go missing?

As long as there was hope for Rockwell's further improvement, Carrie could stay a day or two before her next scheduled surgery.

"Well, I appreciate you keeping me in the loop," Carrie said. "I'll be up there in a few hours."

Carrie ended the call and her foot got a little bit heavy on the gas. She noticed the helicopter high up in the sky, hovering like a dragonfly as it made several passes over the highway. *You're not going to find any traffic here either,* she thought.

Twenty minutes later, Carrie made a pit stop at a roadside gas station, an oasis on a lonely stretch of road. She filled the tank and took a much-needed stretch. She got a chicken salad at an attached restaurant, and was back in her Subaru thirty minutes later, enjoying a glorious sunset.

Up ahead, Carrie noticed a red Ford F-150 truck pulled over to the side of the road. She checked for oncoming traffic, wanting to give the truck a wide berth as she passed. She was maybe fifteen feet away when the Ford's engine revved, its taillights flashed, and the pickup spun out into the road in front of her.

Carrie shrieked and slammed on the brakes, burning rubber that left long black trails behind her. She had been going forty-five, and avoided a rear-bumper collision by inches. Carrie leaned hard on her car horn to let the pickup driver know exactly what she thought of that maneuver. The F-150 sped on ahead, and Carrie released her white-knuckled grip on the steering wheel. Her hands trembled slightly as the adrenaline rush lingered.

"What an asshole," Carrie muttered under her breath.

The F-150's brake lights lit up as if the driver had heard her and wanted to escalate the confrontation. Carrie tapped on her brakes to keep distance, but the truck had slowed to a crawl and the gap between them closed in a blink. Clenching her jaw tight enough to hurt, Carrie braked some more, but the truck had come to a near standstill; before she knew it, the bumpers were almost touching.

Carrie hit her horn again, but with a little less force. The beeps were meant to urge the driver to pick up speed, not show her anger. She noticed the license plate was from Maine. Probably some local kids who did not take kindly to tourists who dared use the horn on them.

The truck picked up speed, and Carrie did as well, but inexplicably the driver braked again. The next time it accelerated, Carrie kept some distance that she would use to try and pass on the left. She had no desire to play this obnoxious game for the remainder of her drive.

She checked the traffic, moved over a lane, and gunned the accelerator to pass. All four of the Subaru's engine cylinders worked overdrive to build up some speed. Carrie glanced to her right as she passed the truck, but the driver was just a shadow. She drove on ahead and felt her blood pressure spike when a check in her rearview showed the truck gaining. The truck was flashing its lights and slamming the horn. Carrie had one chilling thought.

Road rage.

She accelerated, but the more powerful pickup easily kept pace. The truck's horn blared and its headlights flashed. Carrie rolled down her window and waved her arm to encourage the pickup to pass. The truck gained speed, but did not change lanes. The driver got so close to her Subaru the bumpers nearly kissed. Carrie's heartbeat accelerated. She brought her arm back inside her vehicle. If the driver was not

going to pass, she might have to get to the side of the road and let
him go by.

A flash of fear came over her. What if she stopped and he did as well?
There were no other cars on this stretch of highway. She checked her
phone: no signal. Carrie could not imagine being in a more vulnerable
position.

She put her arm out the window and gave another urging wave. This
time the truck veered left into the oncoming lane, and then right, then
left again, weaving down the road. Before Carrie could make sense of
it, the pickup switched lanes and accelerated again. Carrie punched the
gas, but the F-150 easily kept pace. They were driving alongside each
other, but only the Ford was at risk for a head-on collision. Carrie dared
a glance to her left and saw a single broad-shouldered driver in the cab.
His face was an empty shadow, or so she believed. For a second, Carrie
thought he had on a black mask. She did not get a chance for a better
look.

Panic gripped her. Carrie floored the accelerator around a sharp bend
and her car shot forward like a rocket. Her tires skidded, but never lost
grip of the road. The Ford stayed in the left lane and kept pace as it
inched closer to her car. She would have to leave the road to get any
distance. Ahead was a long, straight stretch of highway with no oncoming traffic. Again Carrie leaned on her horn, giving it a long and angry
blast, and then intentionally let up on the accelerator, hoping the Ford
would decide to pass. The pickup's driver anticipated her plan somehow, and slowed as well.

The truck kept parallel to Carrie's car as it maneuvered yet another
inch closer. The distance between them was no greater than a hair's
width. Carrie heard a sudden and tremendous crack as the truck snapped
off her side mirror. The piercing scrape of metal on metal followed.

Instinctively, Carrie turned the wheel hard right as the pickup swerved
away. She straightened out her course just as the pickup came back again.
This time, the truck slammed into the side of her car. Carrie gave a

yell and swung the wheel right. Her only thought was to get away from danger. She did not contemplate the consequences of making such a violent and sudden turn. Once the skid started, it was not going to stop.

Carrie screamed as her car veered off the highway going forty and headed for a dense copse of trees. Everything was a blur of green. She heard tree branches snap violently and metal and glass shatter. There was a huge crash, and a crack of splitting wood louder than thunder. Carrie's head snapped back and she heard another sickening crunch of metal and plinking glass as the car stopped abruptly. A gunshot sound followed as the airbag deployed. It happened so fast, Carrie could not even register what hit her, but it felt as if somebody had slapped her face as hard as they could. Chalky dust went into her eyes and up her nose as she choked on a pungent stench.

For a moment, Carrie could see nothing but the white of the air-bag. But then the pain came and the whiteness of the bag gave way to black.

CHAPTER 42

Braxton Price and Curtis Gantry used the police scanner in the pickup to listen in on the aftermath of Carrie's accident. The accident drew two fire trucks, two police cruisers, and an ambulance to the scene. The driver was conscious and reported that a red Ford F-150 with Maine plates had driven her off the road.

The APB included no plate number, so Carrie had not seen, or could not recall it. Either way, Braxton was not worried about the police pulling them over. They were driving Gantry's blue Chevy pickup with Massachusetts plates. Braxton had ditched the Ford on a prearranged side street off Route 1 about ten miles from where the accident occurred. Gantry had picked him up there, per the plan, and together they resumed the drive north. The whole operation had been improvised when they got word Carrie was headed to Maine.

Braxton took the chopper north, secured a car to use, and got behind Carrie's Subaru with help of the chopper and Gantry, who had tailed Carrie all the way from Massachusetts. Braxton figured on taking her down near Bangor when she left the highway, but Carrie had opted for a scenic detour, so he and Gantry had arranged a different meeting place. It helped that Carrie had stopped for something to eat. Braxton was able to pull ahead and wait for her while Gantry got even farther down the road. The transition from one truck to the other took no time at all.

Gantry was acting like a boy at the skate park—all smiles and pumped full of adrenaline. He loved missions, any missions, but especially successful ones.

"So she didn't die," he said. "Does that mean we get a bonus?"

"No, it means we didn't screw up," Braxton said.

"What's the worst thing that could have happened?"

"We're about to permanently take out Rockwell. We don't need two docs going dark on the same day from the same hospital who happen to work for the same program. It's not the sort of coincidence our employers are interested in explaining away. What we did wasn't optimal, but we had to do something. Besides, she's still considered an asset to the program—at least, that's the word from up high. I figured if Rockwell didn't die after we ran him off a cliff, Carrie could survive a little action in the trees. Maybe we got lucky here, but we did all right."

Gantry went silent. He seemed almost reflective, though Braxton knew his friend's thoughts seldom strayed far from guns, sex, and money.

"Good thing we had the bird in the sky," Gantry said. "I had lost her for a while there."

"There are no helicopters where we're headed next. No backup, either. We get caught, we've got to go dark ourselves. You carrying?"

From the pocket of his denim jacket Gantry fished out a white pill the size of a Tic Tac and popped it into his mouth.

"Hey, don't screw around with that!" Braxton snapped.

Gantry hid his teeth and pressed the cyanide capsule between his lips. He flashed Braxton a toothless smile. "I t'ank you're purty, Braxton. You like me?"

"Get that out of your mouth before you bite it and die."

Gantry spit the pill into his hand and tucked it back inside his jacket pocket. "Who did you give the money to?" he asked.

"None of your damn business."

"I'm guessing it's Jesse."

"Guess all you want."

"How long since you've seen him?"

Braxton thought a beat. "Maybe five years. Maybe more."

"So he's what, fifteen now?"

"Something like that."

Gantry gave a long, low whistle. "Imagine being that young and getting, what is it, half a million dollars? Just like that? Shit, if I had that kind of money at that age I'd have screwed myself into a coma deeper than Rockwell's."

"He's not going to get the money, because we're not going to get caught."

"Maybe I won't take the pill," Gantry said.

"Who did you give the money to?"

"My mom," Gantry said.

"So we get caught, you're dead regardless, and instead of your mom winning the lottery, somebody other than you will be planning her funeral. Look, Gantry, the poor woman had it hard enough raising your sorry ass. Give her the peace of mind she deserves, man."

Gantry nodded. He saw the logic in Braxton's thinking. Always did.

"Speaking of piece, Carrie's got a great ass," Gantry said.

"That's a different kind of piece," Braxton said.

"Whatever. I'm just saying I followed her on a jog in Healey Park, and she has tremendous assets. I'd love to tag that."

"That's how you conduct surveillance?"

"Hey man, I'm just doing my job. Checked out her room, too. Nothing there, but I did have a nice time lying down on her bed and thinking dirty thoughts."

"Nobody saw you?" Braxton asked.

"Nah, man. Her brother is a drone. He was watching TV and didn't hear me come in. I think that guy could use the wires, if you get my drift."

Braxton shook his head dismissively, turned on the radio, and eventually found the local NPR station.

Gantry listened for all of three minutes before he tired of hearing about the struggles of life in Libya and switched to a pop station. "You and your freakin' NPR. I don't know how you listen to that crap. We're like the Odd Couple, man," Gantry said.

Braxton shot Gantry an annoyed look. "Have you ever even seen that show? I know for sure you didn't read the play. Do you even know what you're talking about?"

To Braxton's surprise Gantry returned a broad, sloppy grin and hummed in perfect tune the opening bars to the show starring Tony Randall and Jack Klugman.

"The Internet has everything, asshole," Gantry said, and he resumed humming. On they drove, speeding into the twilight on their way to Seacoast Memorial Hospital, with Gantry humming *The Odd Couple* theme as if it was his favorite show of all time.

GANTRY PULLED into the hospital parking lot a little after nine o'clock. The two-story, mostly brick structure appeared to be undergoing a major renovation, and Gantry drove around until he found a parking space out of the way, near a loading zone. He cut the engine only after making sure that no surveillance cameras were around to record them.

Meanwhile, Braxton maneuvered inside the cramped cab and pulled off his loose-fitting sweats and T-shirt to reveal the green custodial uniform he wore underneath. He had in his possession an employee badge from Seacoast Memorial with his picture on it, but Lee Taggart's name. The uniform and badge were precautions taken a while back, as soon as they'd known Rockwell would be a patient at Seacoast Memorial for a while. In the shadows of some scaffolding he checked his supplies: a syringe and a vial of clear liquid.

"I'll be out in ten minutes," Braxton said as he filled the syringe with liquid to the last marked line.

Gantry winked and blew Braxton a kiss. "Careful, sweetheart. I'll be thinking of you."

Braxton ignored him and headed for the main entrance. Inside the hospital, he flashed security his ID and continued on his way. No problems there. Braxton's badge opened all the doors, a modern miracle courtesy of some supremely competent computer types who worked for his employers. Deep pockets bought a lot more than aerial surveillance.

Braxton walked the halls until he found a janitor's cart—complete with a broom, cleaning supplies, and a twenty-gallon vinyl bag for trash—tucked away in an unobtrusive nook. He wheeled the cart over to the long-term-care wing on the first floor. The diffused fluorescent lighting, powerful stench of cleansers, beeps of various machines, and unpleasant stale air reminded Braxton of the VA. All hospitals were essentially the same, and the people who came to them were the same as well: They got better, got worse, or got dead.

Braxton went in and out of several rooms, emptying the trash and wiping down furniture. The two duty nurses did not give him a second look. He was the help, one of the invisibles who worked behind the scenes to keep the place clean enough to cure.

"Good evening," Braxton said to a stout nurse who sat behind a desk covered with monitors.

Same shit, different location.

"Evening," the nurse said. She gave Braxton only a cursory glance before her focus returned to those monitors.

Braxton wheeled his cart into Sam Rockwell's room. For a guy who had been in a coma for so long, Rockwell actually looked pretty good. The bruises and cuts had mostly healed, and he appeared to be sleeping peacefully.

With practiced skill, Braxton injected succinylcholine intravenously and titrated the flow to speed up induction. Beneath the skin, invisible to the eye, Rockwell's muscles had begun to twitch and spasm. Almost immediately Rockwell's heart rate accelerated to help get oxygen to the brain. But the neuromuscular blocker, widely used by anesthesiologists and easy for Braxton to procure, would stop that heart in short order.

A patient as injured as Rockwell would not be subjected to an autopsy, Braxton had been told, and there was little chance of discovering the breakdown product, succinic acid.

Braxton counted to thirty before he wheeled his cart out of Rockwell's room and over to the nurses' station. "I'm no doc," he said, "but that guy in there looks like he's having a real hard time breathing."

As if on cue, an alarm sounded. The nurse leapt up from her chair as though it were on fire, and rushed into action. Braxton heard the code call come over the loudspeaker. A moment later, a crush of doctors and nurses headed for Rockwell's room like galloping racehorses.

Braxton became invisible again as he wheeled the janitor's cart nonchalantly down the hallway, whistling the tune from *The Odd Couple* as he went.

CHAPTER 43

"It looks a lot worse than it feels," Carrie said.

Using the tips of his fingers, gentle as possible, David touched the large bruised area that marred much of Carrie's right cheek. His face expressed sympathy and heartfelt concern.

The Starbucks was packed at the bustling strip mall near the VA where the two had met. In less than an hour, Carrie was scheduled to see a demonstration of the virtual reality program that had sent Steven Abington off the rails. David had plans of his own at the hospital.

Carrie removed her sunglasses to show David the full extent of her injuries, but bright sunshine stabbed her eyes, and she quickly slipped the shades back into place. The ER doc who had treated Carrie in Maine warned that her sensitivity to light might last a few weeks. After she showed the doc a picture of her crumpled Subaru he added, "Be grateful that's your biggest concern."

Carrie had spent a few days resting at home after the accident, but her body still ached in every conceivable way—stiff joints, throbbing pain in her knees and wrists, tight muscles, pounding headache. David's touch, at least, made her forget the discomfort for a moment.

"I wish you'd called me from Maine," David said. "I would have come to get you."

Carrie had actually given the idea some measured consideration, but opted for her brother instead, in part because of vanity. Days after the accident, Carrie's left eye was still swollen, her split lip had not fully healed, and her nose, though not broken, looked like a doorknob squished on her face. Most of the damage was the result of airbag deployment, but without it Carrie knew her injuries could have been fatal.

As for Adam, her brother had been incredibly supportive throughout the ordeal. He had dished out all the expected brotherly jabs: "You look hot," he'd said, and, "It might be an improvement." But those had come later, on the drive home. The first thing he did was to give Carrie a long embrace, and the first words he spoke were, "I'm so grateful you're all right." Carrie managed to hold back the waterworks until Adam kissed her bruised forehead and told her how much he loved her.

Howard's treasured BMW was off-limits to all, so Adam drove Carrie home in their mother's Volvo.

"If I had that stupid Camaro running, I could have picked you up in style," he had said.

"I'm just glad you came," Carrie said.

"Anything for my favorite sister."

"Um—I'm your only sister."

"Yeah, semantics, whatever," Adam said.

During the drive home, Adam pulled alongside any red pickup truck so that Carrie could get a good look at the driver. She was almost glad it never was the guy who ran her off the road because her brother had a murderous look in his eyes.

The Subaru was a total loss so Carrie had co-opted her mom's Volvo to get to the VA. Arrangements to see the virtual reality demo were made with Cal Trent before the accident, and Dr. Finley had suggested they reschedule. Carrie convinced him otherwise. All DBS surgeries were on hold until Carrie was medically cleared to operate, and she felt useless just sitting around at home. More than anything, Carrie wanted to keep this appointment. Her suspicions were in full bloom, and she needed to learn more about the DARPA program posthaste. The best place to begin, she believed, was at the point in the process where those negative memories got reconsolidated.

Carrie checked the time to make sure she was not running late for the demo.

David saw her preparing to go and gave her a concerned look. "Are you sure you shouldn't just be in bed?" he asked.

Carrie brushed aside the suggestion. "I'm fine. Really."

David read something in Carrie's eyes. "You don't think it was road rage, do you?" he asked.

"A lot of things have happened since Abington and Fasciani went missing. The timing is more than a little unusual, don't you think?"

"But you told me Rockwell died of heart failure," David said.

The call with the sad news had come while Carrie was at the hospital waiting for Adam to show. Though she had never met Sam Rockwell in person, Carrie's emotions vacillated between stunned and heartbroken. The intensity of her feelings came as a surprise, but Carrie understood their origin. She and Rockwell were connected in ways that went beyond the operating room at the VA. Ways Carrie believed she was on the cusp of discovering.

"His body was incredibly damaged, and for the heart to stop was not a shock to anybody. Normally I would agree—but again, the timing makes me highly suspicious. I get run off the road, and suddenly he dies. Think about it."

"What about an autopsy?"

"There's not going to be one, according to Dr. Smerling. The family doesn't want it, and I can't start spouting conspiracy theories. The best way to find out what really happened to Sam is to keep the pressure on Goodwin."

"You really think there's a connection to Rockwell?" David asked.

"I don't think," Carrie said. "I know."

"You're sure Goodwin's not around?"

"I checked her schedule. She's in an all-day meeting. Are you sure you can get inside her office?"

David fished out the lock-pick kit from his pocket and showed it to Carrie with a smile. "Of course," he said. "I have the key."

CARRIE WORE her lab coat, and for that reason alone garnered plenty of curious looks while navigating the halls of the VA. It was one thing to see an injured person in a hospital, but something else entirely when that individual also happened to be a doctor. It set people on edge.

Dr. Finley, who had only spoken with Carrie by phone and had not seen her injuries, grimaced at the sight. "My goodness," he said, rising from his chair. He gave Carrie a warm embrace that conveyed utter relief.

"It looks worse than it feels," Carrie said, repeating what she'd told David. It was the same lie she told everyone.

"Well, I just hope they catch whoever did this to you."

Carrie thanked him, and he sat back down.

Dr. Finley glanced at the letter on his desk, written on his personal stationery. "I've spent the last hour trying to figure out what to say to Sam's wife," he said. "I'm just devastated. Nothing I write expresses how I really feel. I let my hopes get up when he came out of the coma, but now—" Dr. Finley slipped off his glasses and rubbed at his reddened eyes. Carrie got the feeling he had been crying. "Now, I just have memories."

"I'm so sorry for your loss. I wish I had gotten to know him."

"We were pioneers in this together from the start," Dr. Finley said. "We owe a lot to Sam. I owe a lot to him."

"He sounded like a wonderful man," Carrie said, and then fell silent. If anything, her eyes were even wider, her expression more empathetic. "Listen, Alistair, there's something I'd like to talk with you about."

Dr. Finley noticed Carrie's apprehension. "You look upset, Carrie. Please take a seat. I'll let Cal know we're running a few minutes late."

Carrie's anxiety bubbled like uncorked champagne while Dr. Finley texted his message to Trent. He put his smartphone away and locked his gaze on Carrie. "Go on," he urged.

Although Carrie had planned what to say, the reality of the moment felt weighty and more difficult than anticipated. "My car accident happened in Maine," she began.

"Yes, you said you were there following up on an Abington lead."

"Yes and no," Carrie said. "I was headed to the hospital to see Sam."

Dr. Finley looked confused. "Sam? Heavens, why?"

Carrie said, "I wanted to know if he'd ever seen palinacousis in a DBS patient before. Specifically one of the PTSD patients."

Dr. Finley seemed mystified. Carrie watched him mull over the word "palinacousis," as if it was something he had heard before but could not put into any context. When it finally came to him, a surprised look came over his face. "Palinacousis? Good gracious, what on earth would make you want to ask him that?"

Carrie explained her encounter with Abington and later with Fasciani, and noted how both patients had disappeared. She also revealed her own self-doubt about causing the auditory hallucination in addition to the impaired judgment issues exhibited by both patients in their choice to leave the hospital AMA.

When she finished, Dr. Finley said, "And you thought you caused all this?" in a way that absolved Carrie of any responsibility.

"I admit my confidence was shaken when I started working here. And when they both presented with palinacousis, well, I naturally questioned my technique."

"To be honest here, Carrie," Dr. Finley said in an even tone, "I think you're reading symptoms that simply aren't there. Palinacousis? I've treated dozens of vets here and haven't seen a single case reported. And you watched me examine Ramón Hernandez. Did he seem off to you?"

"No," Carrie said. "Not at all."

Dr. Finley's puzzlement remained. "I've never seen a case of that in my whole career, and it's been a long career. But I have seen your work, and it's exemplary. There's no way you caused anything like that in these men. Impossible."

Carrie was not ready to back off. "What about the connection between Ramón Hernandez and Steve Abington," she said. "The two had met. I told you about the picture at Rita Abington's home."

Dr. Finley was unmoved. "I spoke to Cal about that and he did some digging. Steve was referred to the DARPA program through other channels, so their knowing each other is just a coincidence, that's all. But you can speak to Cal on that if you'd like."

Carrie agreed. For a moment she contemplated sharing her belief that Lee Taggart, the VA nurse, was also in the same photograph. But the evidence was not conclusive enough for her to stake that claim.

Dr. Finley leaned forward in his chair and set his hand over Carrie's in an avuncular gesture. In that moment, her convictions fell away and she felt foolish for confiding in Dr. Finley without first obtaining proof to support her claims.

If only she had found those men . . .

"But what about both Abington and Fasciani leaving AMA?" Carrie asked.

Dr. Finley shrugged it off. "Carrie, these men were unstable to begin with. And we exacerbate that problem by agitating them with the virtual reality."

Carrie saw the logic, but was not quite ready to back away. "And my getting run off the road and Sam dying on the same day? You don't see any connections there?"

Dr. Finley leaned back in his chair and cast Carrie a look of shock and disgust. His expression conveyed his belief that her insinuations bordered on the absurd.

"You said yourself it was road rage. Honestly, Carrie, I'm more worried I hired a conspiracy theorist than anything else. To be candid, I see you drawing a lot of lines between events that have no logical connections."

Carrie decided it was time to beat a hasty retreat. Dr. Finley was visibly bothered by her theory, his head shaking in disbelief. Several psychological causes explained conspiracy theorists, including anxiety disorders, paranoia, and psychosis. None of those labels would do her or her career any good.

While Carrie was not willing to abandon her search for the missing link that would connect these strange happenings in some logical manner, she would have to wait for the answers. Other questions of hers would have to wait as well. Was the jogger in the park really as harmless as he professed? Had someone other than Adam been in her room? Perhaps Dr. Finley was right, and those were unrelated events as well, but Carrie was not ready to concede. Surely the Goodwin recordings would reveal something—something that would convince Dr. Finley she was not a theorist at all.

Dr. Finley gathered his composure and stood. "So, can we put this behind us for the moment and concentrate on getting you better and getting us back to work?" he asked. "I want us to finish what Sam and I started. We're on the verge of something important here, Carrie, and I'd rather focus our energies on the patients who want our help and not those who walked away."

"Yes," Carrie said. "I feel better just talking it out."

"Good," Dr. Finley said, clapping his hands together. "Now then, let's send you to war."

CHAPTER 44

Carrie's stomach knotted when Dr. Finley pushed open the conference room door. What would she see through the looking glass? Would it help her better understand Adam, give her a glimpse into his world of constant fear? She could hardly imagine how horrible the simulation must have been, how real, how visceral, to elicit such a violent and disturbed reaction in Abington.

It was ironic, Carrie thought, that before she'd joined this endeavor to cure PTSD, she'd had no profoundly disturbing memories. Nothing of real substance she could draw upon as fodder for simulation. Now she had a whole host of experiences to use.

On the long table inside the windowless conference room, Carrie saw a laptop computer and some futuristic eyewear, a cross between ski goggles and wraparound sunglasses. The eyewear was connected to the laptop via a USB port. Calvin Trent stood to greet Carrie and Dr. Finley, wearing a blue suit that fit snugly against his broad shoulders. With Trent was the bald man Carrie had seen at grand rounds.

Trent extended a hand to Carrie, warmth entering his gray eyes. "Nice to see you again," he said. It was then he noticed Carrie's face. "Goodness, what happened to you?"

Carrie said, "Car accident."

Trent grimaced in solidarity. "Well, I'll make sure there are no car crashes in your simulation. I can imagine you have a little PTSD already from that experience. Wouldn't want to make things worse."

Carrie gave a little laugh. "Yeah, let's do that," she said.

Trent turned to his companion. "This is Bob Richardson," he said. "He's been helping with operations. Bob, this is Dr. Alistair Finley and Dr. Carrie Bryant with the VA."

Carrie watched Dr. Finley shake hands with Richardson for what appeared to be the first time, confirming her earlier belief that he had not been introduced to her at the grand rounds simply because the two had never met before.

A related question popped into Carrie's mind. "How many people are involved with this program?" she asked.

Trent said, "I'd say with all the technicians, and medical staff and such, we're probably close to a hundred."

"Close to a hundred," Carrie repeated. "Where is everybody?"

"Spread out," Trent said. "We don't have an official base of operations just yet. Believe it or not, the government is always looking to save a buck or two, so to minimize costs we utilize the workspace of our experts and consultants whenever possible."

"I explained to Carrie that there's a lot more going on here than just neurology and neurosurgery," Dr. Finley said.

Trent nodded in agreement. "That's correct. We have psychologists, physiologists, simulation technicians, a wide variety of specialists involved. There are even plans in the works for building a dormitory or semi-permanent housing, but for now vets in the program who come to us without a permanent residence have to settle for Motel Six, which is a lot nicer than the streets where most of them had been living. We have contracts in place with a car service to shuttle our program participants to all their various appointments."

Richardson said, "Having everything decentralized does create some operational challenges."

"I can't imagine driving Abington anywhere without an armed guard," Carrie said. The memory of Abington's assault replayed in her mind.

"I heard you had a terrible experience there," Richardson said in a sincerely apologetic tone.

Carrie said, "That's for sure."

Trent said, "We intentionally run the simulation on the premises here at the VA to minimize travel time. Once the DBS system is installed, most of the vets are a lot more docile, I can assure you. But I'm sorry about what happened to you."

"I'm assuming you know that he's gone," Carrie said to Trent. "Fasciani too. Both vanished."

Trent grimaced. "Yes, I'm aware. We're looking for both of them. Many in our program have issues with alcohol and drugs, which can lead to all sorts of erratic behavior."

"They left AMA," Carrie said. "We signed them out."

Trent looked at Dr. Finley. "Yes, Alistair told me. In fact, we have a meeting scheduled with Dr. Goodwin to come up with better protocols moving forward. We don't want this to become a trend. We're too close to finishing phase three."

"What's the next phase?" Carrie asked.

"Full deployment of the solution. Tested, validated, and FDA sanctioned. It's the game changer," Trent said.

Bob Richardson manipulated the laptop and did something to make the screen turn black.

"We're ready whenever you are, Cal," he said. Richardson spoke in a hard, dry voice. It was the voice of someone accustomed to commanding a crowd. He did not strike Carrie as a subordinate. Who was this guy, really?

"Are you ready, Carrie?" Trent asked.

Carrie had that funny feeling in the pit-in-her-stomach that preceded any roller coaster ride. "Sure thing," she said.

"We're using a simulation from one of our program participants," Richardson said. "But for privacy reasons, I'm not at liberty to tell you which one."

Carrie smiled politely. "Of course. I understand."

Carrie took a seat at the conference table with Richardson on her right, Trent on her left, and Dr. Finley across from her. The goggles were lightweight and fit over Carrie's head with minimum adjustments required. The earbuds slipped right into place. Through the lens Carrie could see only black.

"Are you ready?" Trent's voice was slightly muffled, but clear enough for Carrie to give him a thumbs-up sign.

Blackness gave way to light, and a desert scene unfolded in Carrie's view. A digitally rendered lone figure stood on a bridge that crossed over a sand-covered road. What appeared to be palm trees stood in the background, with a few scattered tufts of vegetation. In front of the bridge were two heavily armed and armored Humvees, and behind those vehicles were two kneeling soldiers, each holding automatic weapons.

While shadows and lighting enhanced the reality of the 3-D graphics, the scene itself still looked like something out of a video game. Adam could no longer play "Call of Duty," but Carrie had seen him shooting up the enemy enough times to be reminded of a lightweight version of that game.

The sound of Humvee engines rumbled in Carrie's ear, and the graphics began to move. First, the kneeling soldiers stood, and then the Humvees inched ahead. Carrie turned her head from side to side, but her field of view remained unchanged. This was more like watching a computer-generated movie than the total-immersion experience she had expected.

The Humvees rolled under the bridge with the two soldiers bringing up the rear. There was movement from the figure on the bridge, and Carrie saw him using what appeared to be a cell phone. The animation was close to the natural arcs and curves of the human body, but not quite there.

In her headphones, Carrie heard the sound of an explosion, and in the next instant the ground in front of the lead Humvee became a debris field. The now-mangled Humvee lifted several feet above the virtual ground before it crash-landed hard on four tires. The graphics showed the vehicle's shock absorbers doing their job as the wheels bounced several times before they finally settled. Dust and sand kicked skyward, but it was still video game dust and sand. While the whole sequence was surprising, Carrie did not find it overly frightening or hyper-realistic.

The gunmen on foot returned fire and shot at the man on the bridge, while three burned and bleeding soldiers crawled out from the wrecked Humvee. The graphics here were well done, and Carrie could see that two of the men had lost limbs, one an arm, and the other a leg. The third solider to climb out bled profusely from a head wound.

A second explosion followed. This one swallowed one of the two soldiers on foot. When that virtual dust cleared, the sand beneath the soldier's body was colored red, and he was without limbs. The surviving soldier fired at the man on the bridge, this time striking him somewhere—torso, head, it was difficult for Carrie to tell. The dead insurgent tumbled off the bridge and landed on the desert sand with a thud.

The scene faded to black and Carrie removed her headset.

Richardson appraised Carrie as if she might need to be sedated like Abington.

"Well, I hope that wasn't too traumatic for you," he said.

Carrie removed the earbuds and stared down at her lap for several seconds. When she looked up, Carrie's face showed signs of strain, and her composure was compromised.

"If you re-created my car accident, I'd be in tears right now," Carrie said. "I can only imagine what the soldiers go through after seeing their own worst nightmares replayed on screen."

Carrie glanced around the room and felt confident everyone believed her lie. She had expected so much more from the simulation, based on Abington's violent reaction.

Dr. Finley said, "The reconsolidation of the negative memory is a necessary albeit unfortunate step in the process. With the memory fresh in the mind, we can use electric stimulation to remove the emotion associated with the event. Ramón Hernandez can watch his virtual reality simulation now like it's the movie of the week, when before it would have sent him into a violent rage."

Carrie believed Adam could see a similar demo of his traumatic experience in Afghanistan, and while it might add a few notches to his blood pressure, that would be it. It was simply not believable enough, in her estimation, to incite such a strong emotional reaction. Carrie recalled the crazed look in Abington's eyes just before the attack, as well as the mysterious words he had uttered.

I don't belong here . . . I don't belong . . .

What had Trent really done to him prior to surgery?

By now, David had probably retrieved the recording device. Carrie could hardly wait to see him, to share what she had learned during the demo, and to listen in on Goodwin's private conversations. She had a strong feeling they would reveal something significant.

"Amazing, I'm really impressed," Carrie said. "Cal and Bob, I want to thank you for taking the time to arrange this demo for me. It really did open my eyes."

"You're very welcome," Trent said. "We view you as a vital part of this team, Carrie. I speak for Bob and the rest of the DARPA organization when I say how grateful we are to have you on board. And, not to be glib here, but I'm also hopeful you'll be able to operate with your injuries. If you asked Alistair, he'd say you're one of the best surgeons he's ever worked with. Everyone is simply devastated about what happened to Sam, but if we had to replace him, we're glad it's you at the helm."

Carrie returned a slight smile, no teeth showing. "I'm glad to be a part," she said. "And thank you for your endorsement. I really do appreciate it."

Carrie took out her phone and pretended to type a message. In reality, she had snapped a photo of Bob Richardson. With David's help, she hoped they could figure out who he really was.

CHAPTER 45

Gabby, the little girl with pigtails, gave Carrie a delightful, gap-toothed smile and hugged her knees only because she was not tall enough to reach higher. Gabby's surprise embrace tugged at Carrie's heart. This complete sweetie pie paid no attention to Carrie's injuries. To her innocent eyes, Carrie was just a friend of her "Uncle David," as she called him, nothing more. There was no judgment, no pretense, nothing but total acceptance.

Carrie's heart warmed more when Gabby turned to David and gazed up at him with wide-eyed reverence.

"Can you play with me?" Gabby asked.

"In a little bit, sweetheart," David said. "I have some grown-up talk to do first."

Emma and Gabby had come up to David's apartment a minute or so after Carrie had arrived. At first Carrie felt a spark of jealousy when she saw how pretty Emma was, how put-together she seemed in her hip-hugging jeans and cute turquoise top, but the feeling passed quickly. Emma and David had an undeniable intimacy, but Carrie got the vibe it was not based on any romantic love. Try as she might, Carrie could not quite figure out what David did not see in Emma, or Emma in David, but she was not going to question it. She knew what she felt for David, and suspected he felt the same. Something was going to happen between them. She could see it in the way he looked at her, and feel it in the way his look made her skin tingle.

David took Carrie's phone and sent Emma the picture she'd taken.

Emma glanced at her phone's display and showed the photo to David and Carrie for confirmation. "This is the guy?"

The picture Carrie had taken included part of Cal Trent, but Bob Richardson was front and center.

"That's him," David said. "How good is the facial recognition software at the DMV?"

"Very good," Emma said. "We're required to run a one-to-many comparison before issuing a driver's license, permit, or ID."

"What's a one-to-many comparison?" Carrie asked.

Emma said, "One-to-many compares photos of an applicant with all the other customers on file at DMV. We get alerted if there are possible matches between customers under different names. We examine the possible matches to determine whether it's simply very similar-looking individuals, or possibly the same individual under different names."

"Sounds good to me," David said.

"Me too," Carrie said. "But what if he's not a licensed Massachusetts driver?"

Emma shrugged. "We have a new data-sharing initiative to give law enforcement agencies more access to our data. I've helped with the roll-out, so I have contacts who could do a search for me if I don't get any local hits. I used it before to locate Rita Abington's address. Give me a few days on this," Emma said.

"Thanks," David said. "I really appreciate it."

Emma collected Gabby from the toy corner, and together they left David's apartment with some substantial protests that could be heard while the pair descended the stairs.

"She's such a cutie pie," Carrie said.

"She's the best," David said. "Her dad doesn't know what he's missing."

Carrie suspected David would make a terrific father, someone who would be patient, kind, and capable. The thought made him more attractive to her. David's cozy apartment was similar to her old place in Brookline. It was bright, airy, and sparsely furnished. She wanted to take a closer look at the many photographs lining his wall, but that would have to wait. They had business to discuss.

"Tell me about the VR before we listen to the recording," David said.

Carrie recounted her experience in the neurology unit conference room in considerable detail.

David seemed troubled by what he heard. "There was no position tracking?" he asked after she had finished.

"No, it was more like watching a movie. The view didn't change when I moved my head."

"This is DARPA," David said, sounding incredulous. "You'd think they would have the most sophisticated technology available. A completely immersive experience."

"That's what I thought, too. Something didn't seem right about it."

"Let's have a listen to those recordings," David said.

He set up the two portable speakers on a scuffed coffee table and plugged in a connecting cable. While this was going on, an orange tabby cat padded out from the bedroom, gracefully leapt from the floor onto the sofa, and immediately began to knead the cushion with its claws.

"That's Bosra," David said. "This is his favorite spot. Well, mine too. We nap here a lot."

Within a few seconds the cat had condensed into a tight ball, so that no part of its body existed outside the beam of sunlight that streamed through the tall bay window. Bosra purred delightedly when Carrie scratched behind the ears.

"How long have you had him?" Carrie asked.

"Her," David corrected. "About a year. She's a rescue."

Carrie imagined David and Bosra taking long naps together on this very couch, and believed it had enough room for all three to partake.

As if reading her thoughts, David sat down on the other side of Carrie so Bosra would not be disturbed. He pressed Play on the recording device and a burst of static gave way to the sound of a phone ringing.

"It's noise-activated," David explained. "So there may be a lot of ringing phones before we hear any actual dialogue. Hopefully we won't have to listen to your colleague, Evan, having sex."

Carrie knew all about Evan's sexcapades in Goodwin's office, as well as David's gravity-defying stint underneath the desk. It was a glimpse into the lengths he would go for the story, and gave Carrie a keener understanding of how David had ended up a prisoner of the Syrian opposition forces.

The recorded phone rang once more. Somebody answered on the second ring, and Carrie knew the woman's voice immediately—Goodwin. Though Carrie was privy to only half of the conversation, she could tell it was a vendor calling about an intracranial pressure monitoring device. Goodwin sounded uninterested from the start. She ended the call with the terse parting words, "Let me get back to you when I have time."

A number of unrelated conversations had been recorded over several days, and Carrie and David listened to each without learning anything especially interesting about Goodwin. She chatted with Evan pleasantly enough, always about the VA. It was utterly unrevealing. Goodwin gave a resident some thoughtful advice, which Carrie thought a bit out of character for the ice queen. Twice Goodwin spoke by phone with her mother, and Carrie got the distinct impression a vendor call would have been more welcome.

It was not until the third day of recordings that Carrie heard a new voice, an older voice she recognized: Cal Trent. It took Carrie just a few seconds to realize Goodwin had an edge to her voice.

"Hello, Cal," Goodwin said. "Have a seat."

According to the time stamp on the recording device, the conversation took place two days after Carrie's accident.

"Thanks, Sandra. How are you?"

"I'm fine. Need anything to drink?"

"No, I'm fine. What's up? Why the urgency?"

"I'm worried," Goodwin said. "I think we need to scale back. Even go dark."

Cal's laugh expressed his utter contempt for the idea. "Good one," he said. "What's next on your agenda, Sandra?"

"Please, Cal."

"The pipeline is full. We're moving forward. That's the plan."

Carrie glanced at David's notepad, where he jotted the word "pipeline" and put a question mark after it.

"I don't think that's a good idea," Goodwin said on the recording.

"And how will the board take it when we pull funding for your movable prosthetics initiative?" Trent asked. "How many of the millions we've committed to the VA have already been spent? That's not something your bosses are going to give up on easily. A lot of questions will be raised. A lot of fingers will be pointed at you. And then I think you'll point them back at me. And we can't have that, can we? I'm not trying to be subtle or coy here, Sandy. I think you get my meaning. I've got a pipeline of patients to send your way and we're going to send them. You get that DBS surgery done. That's your job. And you let me do the rest."

Silence.

"Are we all set here?" Trent asked.

"We're all set," Goodwin said, her voice going soft.

Carrie and David heard background noise as Trent got up from his chair, opened the office door, and closed it. The recording picked up Goodwin's labored breathing and other sounds: a desk drawer opening up, a squeaking chair, and the click of Goodwin's keyboard as she furiously typed a message.

David shut off the recorder and turned to face Carrie. "What exactly is a movable prosthetic?" He glanced at his notes. "I'm assuming it's not what's commonly out there."

David's eyes had gone wild. Bosra perked up her head, yawned, stretched, climbed down off the sofa, and padded away. Evidently the energy in the room had become too much for her to handle.

"I'm sure he's talking about reliable neural-interface technology, RE-NET," Carrie said. "I've attended a few lectures about it at different neurosurgery conferences over the years. One lecture showed a video demonstration of a man using targeted muscle re-innervation to pick up a coffee cup."

"Re-innervation?" David repeated for confirmation. "Is that like the re-animation of nerves?"

"Very much so," Carrie said, nodding. "There are still nerves firing even after a limb is severed. It's just that the signal doesn't go anywhere. With computers, robotics, and a whole lot of sophistication, a prosthetic can learn to recognize these signals and contract the muscles like a working limb. TRM-controlled prosthetics is very cutting-edge stuff."

"And there's nothing like it at the VA currently?"

She shook her head. "Not that I know of, but I'm just a technician, remember." Carrie said "technician" with exaggerated contempt.

"Is it possible that Trent is getting his DBS patients from outside the system?"

"That's what it sounded like to me," Carrie said. "Patients come to the VA through a very bureaucratic process. If someone is bypassing that system, there's got to be a good reason for it."

"Maybe Goodwin wanted to minimize your role at the VA to keep you from finding out what that circumvention was all about?"

Carrie processed David's words. "Maybe the last DBS surgeon got too close to that answer," she said.

Now it was David's turn to process. "What have you gotten yourself into here, Carrie?" he asked.

"I don't know," Carrie said. "I really don't know."

They listened to hours of Sandra being Sandra, and found nothing of further interest on those recordings—nothing incriminating, nothing to explain what she and Cal were doing.

David put his hands behind his head, stretched, and looked to the ceiling.

"Anneke is going to be pretty ticked off at me," David said.

"Yeah? Why's that?" Carrie asked.

"Because I got a feeling this story is going to take a hell of a long time for me to write."

CHAPTER 46

Carrie returned to the VA the following morning, unsure what the next step should be. She had hoped David's plan would provide further clarity, but instead it created more seemingly unconnected threads. How did Abington's and Fasciani's disappearances relate to Goodwin's ambitions with regards to reliable neural-interface technology? How did Abington come to join the DBS program? How many vets had been treated? Where were they all living?

These were questions that extended far beyond her purview. She was at the VA to drill and to insert wires, and nothing more. Sandra Goodwin had erected a wall between her and the patients' postoperative care for a very specific reason. But what was it? And who exactly was Bob Richardson? Carrie felt confident he was more than a bit player in Cal Trent's world. In this way, Dr. Finley appeared marginalized as well. Trent's operation included a cast of unknowns, of people who played pivotal roles and were introduced only on a need-to-know basis.

In the intervening hours from when she heard the recording to her return to the hospital, Carrie did some digging on Cal Trent and sent an e-mail to David with a fairly exhaustive dossier. Admittedly, it gave them no real insights. Trent got his BS in mechanical engineering from the University of Miami, and went on to receive an MBA from Northwestern. He was an associate with the consulting firm McKinsey & Company, and worked for BEA Systems before he found employment with DARPA. Trent had been married for eighteen years, with two kids and a permanent residence in Bethesda. He seemed like a regular guy, though graft and corruption stained the noblest professions.

Carrie and David agreed not to play the recording for anybody— not Dr. Finley, and certainly not the police. They had nothing criminal to investigate, just a lot of innuendo. As for Dr. Finley, if he knew Carrie had secretly recorded Sandra Goodwin, she'd be fired in a heartbeat, and any hope of closure would be lost. So long as Dr. Finley employed her, Carrie could investigate Goodwin and Trent from the shadows.

Until Carrie was officially cleared to operate, all DBS procedures were on hold, and waiting patients would need to be rescheduled. During this downtime, Dr. Finley informed Carrie of his plans to conduct neurological exams on both DBS and regular VA patients, and get caught up on some backlogged paperwork. Carrie could not stay at home and do nothing all day, so she came to the VA to get caught up on her journal reading—or so she said to Dr. Finley. In reality, Carrie was there to keep her eyes and ears open.

When Dr. Finley invited Carrie to join him in examining another vet from the DBS program, Carrie jumped at the chance. It was Ramón Hernandez redux. This vet's name was Terry Bushman, an über-fit male in his early thirties with short-cropped blond hair, his arms covered with tattoos and scars. Carrie asked the same questions of Bushman as she had of Hernandez. The answers were decidedly similar. No experience with voice illusion, no issues with his DBS, and while he expressed lingering PTSD symptoms, they were not nearly as debilitating as before. Same as Hernandez, there was some asymmetry of Bushman's neck where the stimulating wires had been tunneled from the scalp, and he had small scars on the chest where the generator was placed.

Near the end of the exam, Carrie asked Bushman to tell her how he got involved in the program.

"I was living at a halfway house," Bushman said. He had a youthful voice, like a California surfer. "So, these guys from DARPA show up, give me all sorts of psych testing, and next I know I'm living at a different halfway house outside of Boston with wires in my head. Simple as that."

Carrie had wondered if Ramón had recruited Bushman, or if he had ever met Abington or Fasciani. The answers were no to all. Carrie got some background on Bushman, and it seemed he had a decent relationship with his family, nothing like Abington. Carrie was willing to accept a dead end when she hit one. But still something did not make sense. Why would two vets seem perfectly fine and two others exhibit strange neurological behaviors?

Carrie joined Dr. Finley in the cafeteria for a post-exam coffee. It was approaching dinnertime, and Bushman was Dr. Finley's last patient of the day.

He was exuberant as ever. "I think in another week you should be recovered enough to get back to the OR," he said. "When I first met Terry, he suffered from debilitating uncomplicated PTSD with persistent reexperiencing of the traumatic event, had trouble with crowds because he associated the stimuli with the trauma, and there was a lot of self-medicating going on. Now look at him."

"It is impressive," Carrie admitted.

"We have four cases like Terry Bushman and Ramón Hernandez. Four. Once we get to ten, I think we'll be able to trumpet success."

"What about the others?" Carrie asked.

Dr. Finley's glow dimmed. "Not everyone gets better, Carrie. Not every drug, not every therapy works a miracle. But these four represent the possibilities. We need to stay positive."

"Do you mind if I look over your patient records?"

Dr. Finley's prominent eyebrows rose an inch or so. "Um, I guess. Sure. Mind if I ask why?"

"Call it professional curiosity. I just really want to know these men."

Carrie got a quick nod of approval.

"Yes, of course," he said. "I'll pull them together for you and you can look at them in the morning."

Those files, Carrie believed, would show her whether other vets left the neuro recovery unit under special circumstances like Abington and Fasciani.

"Thanks, that would be great," she said.

Dr. Finley stood. "Time for me to go home," he said. "You should do the same. I'm worried you're going to push yourself too hard."

Carrie thanked him for his concern, and returned to her office to gather her things. She was there only a few minutes before someone knocked on her door. Carrie's heart nearly stopped at the sight of Sandra Goodwin lurking in the open doorway, as if she'd been there watching for some time.

Without an invitation, Goodwin entered Carrie's incommodious office, sporting a chilly smile. She wore her hair up in a tight bun, and the harsh glare of the fluorescents highlighted the severe angles of her face. Goodwin's sharp eyes bore down on Carrie in a way that turned her blood to ice.

"Carrie, I'm glad I caught you," Goodwin said in a honey-dripped voice. "Do you have a minute?"

"I was just heading out," Carrie said.

"This won't take long," Goodwin said coolly.

"Sure," Carrie said. "What can I do for you?"

"I think you and I got off on the wrong foot," Goodwin said. "And I'd like for us to be friends."

Because you know I'm on to you, Carrie thought.

"Sandra, I really don't know what you're talking about. I've kept a clear line between my job and what Evan does ever since our little chat. If you want to be professionally cordial, then perhaps you'll explain to me why you signed Abington and Fasciani out AMA." Carrie almost let slip something about reliable neural-interface technology, which could have been disastrous if Goodwin found out she'd been bugged.

"I told Dr. Finley I had little choice. They were both extremely insistent."

"I saw Fasciani after his surgery. He was so doped up on Valium I don't see how he could have done that."

Something flashed in Goodwin's expression that gave Carrie shivers. "You saw him?" Goodwin asked. "Could you explain yourself, please?"

Carrie's chest tightened. Goodwin had her trapped. *Dammit!*

"Yes, I went up to see him after my surgery," Carrie admitted. "I honestly think this policy of yours is ludicrous."

"Think what you will," Goodwin said in a sharp-edged voice. "It's my law, and I'm surprised and more than a little disappointed you decided to ignore the directive."

"Well, I apologize," Carrie said, rather insincerely. "But you need to see this from my point of view."

"You weren't credentialed by us, Carrie, and for that reason alone you have no business interacting with the patients outside the OR. I thought this was clear."

Goodwin leaned against a wall and let her white lab coat fall open to show off the scrubs she wore underneath, as if Carrie needed the reminder they both were surgeons.

"Eric could not have possibly given his consent," Carrie said. "He was too drugged."

"But he did," Goodwin retorted. "I was called to the floor and I signed the papers after he issued his demands. I spent time trying to talk him out of it. I'm sorry I don't have any of those conversations recorded so you could believe me." She gave Carrie a foxy grin.

Carrie held her breath, paralyzed, expecting any moment to be accused of spying.

"What do you want me to say, Sandra? I'm not at all comfortable with how you've handled this. I did an invasive procedure on two men who checked out AMA and subsequently vanished. Something isn't right."

Goodwin took a step into Carrie's office and gave a look meant to incite fear. "I'll tell you what isn't right," Goodwin said. "I have a presentation due in a couple days for an upcoming meeting with the top brass here. I have to go through every surgical procedure from the past year and catalogue every complication. That's going to take me hours. If you so want to be a part of this team, I think you should do the work."

"Me?" Carrie could not contain her incredulousness.

"It would be a shame to inform the VA of your unwillingness to follow my rules. I could get you suspended in about five minutes, and fired in a day. You'll be out of here quicker than it takes me to fill out an AMA form."

Carrie eyed Goodwin with disgust. "That's blackmail," she said.

"No, Carrie darling, it's called being a team player. Stay right here. I'll come down with the files. You don't have access to the electronic system, so I'm afraid paper will have to do. And I'm afraid you can't remove anything from the premises. But that's okay. You're used to working late nights, aren't you?"

The glimmer in Goodwin's eyes dimmed, along with her phony smile.

CHAPTER 47

"Drained" did not capture Carrie's whole-body exhaustion. The stacks of medical records took up most of her desk space. The work was decidedly tedious and excruciatingly time-consuming. Many of the files Carrie reviewed were several inches thick and offered no means by which to conduct a keyword search for complications. Carrie had to painstakingly review each case down to the last period. She could have punted on the whole thing, done a half-baked job, but that was not in her nature. If she were going to do something, even scut work, she'd do it right.

That was just her wiring.

The complications Carrie recorded on her impressive spreadsheet were commonplace and did not denote a pattern of incompetence, or at least nothing Carrie could derive from the data. The VA might not have state-of-the-art equipment like White Memorial, but it appeared to be a first-class facility with top-notch surgeons. Even though Carrie thought Navarro was an ass, and Goodwin a shrew, they each performed their respective roles admirably and even, at times, in exemplary form.

Carrie's grueling residency had trained her for endurance work, and she probably could have gone another hour before giving in to fatigue. Thankfully, that was unnecessary. Carrie closed the last manila folder and fired off a tersely worded e-mail to Goodwin with her Excel spreadsheet attached. Her findings corresponded with well-established industry standards. Stereotactic radiosurgery, more commonly known as "gamma knife" surgery, had the lowest rate of complications. By contrast, transsphenoidal surgery, a relatively safe procedure, had a statistically significant number of issues. The other surgical complications Carrie came across ran the gamut and included hematomas, infection, and leakage of cerebrospinal fluid. There were a number of non-neurosurgical complications like deep venous thrombosis, and a few cases of pulmonary emboli, cardiac arrhythmias, blood sugar and electrolyte imbalances, but all in all, the VA seemed to be well within the norm of surgical maladies.

Carrie massaged her eyes and took a long drink of the Diet Coke that had kept her alert these many hours. While Goodwin may have won the battle, the victor in the larger war had yet to be determined. Carrie was going to blow the lid off Goodwin's dealings with Trent. It was just a matter of time.

Carrie shut down her computer, collected her purse, and turned out the lights. Her depleted resolve sparked back to life as she closed and locked her office door. But the feeling was fleeting. Her limbs were heavy with fatigue, and the idea of making the long drive home seemed intolerable, perhaps even dangerous. Studies proved drowsy driving was equivalent to drunk driving, and her eyes were already closing. The on-call room beckoned her, and Carrie gave in. Four or five hours or so of sleep and she could be back at her desk, looking through the files Dr. Finley had promised to provide by morning.

Carrie headed to the on-call room through hospital halls that were deathly quiet, eerily so. She reached the stairwell without encountering a single person, unusual for any time, day or night. The harsh glare of the white vinyl floor was like needles in her eyes. Carrie made an unusually quick ascent to the third floor. A creeping fear tickled at the back of her neck that hastened her strides. Maybe it was the jogger in the park, or the car crash, but the quiet made her jittery.

All three on-call rooms were vacant, and Carrie opted for the one at the far end of the hall. She locked the door behind her and glanced at the time on the analog clock mounted to the concrete wall.

Three o'clock in the morning.

What a brutal day.

Carrie plumped down on the thin, unforgiving mattress and heard every click in her stiff and achy joints. At least she had on scrubs, which were just as good as pajamas, if not better.

For a moment she felt incredibly alone and lonely and wished David was with her. But the feeling faded as Carrie closed her eyes. Even her resentment and anger toward Goodwin could not keep her from drifting off. Exhaustion took over, and thoughts of David and Goodwin receded into the back of Carrie's consciousness. Her body melted into the bed, legs and arms became heavy as her breathing turned shallow.

The minute hand on the clock ticked off seconds like a hypnotic metronome. Then the noise was gone. All noise was gone.

Then sleep.

At last sleep, finally sleep.

Until something woke her.

Carrie's eyes fluttered open. She had no idea how long she'd been out. A few minutes? A few hours? The darkness was impenetrable, and she could not see the clock on the wall. Her body felt queasy, off-kilter from having woken up so suddenly. Her eyes would adjust to the dark, but right now Carrie could not make out any shapes at all. She might as well have been blindfolded. But her ears worked just fine and they picked up a faint noise, the slight sound of a metallic click. That noise must have awoken her. Carrie listened, but the only sound now was her heart slamming against her ribs.

The noise came again, and this time it was distinct and distinguishable. It was the sound of a doorknob turning ever so slightly. The soft jiggle of the handle boomed in Carrie's ears, and the click of the cylinder as it turned thundered loud as a crashing wave. She was about to call out that the room was occupied when a terrifying thought came to her. She had locked the door! The knob should not be turning at all, and yet it was. David had shown her how easily he manipulated those antiquated lock tumblers with a pick and a tension wrench. This was not just a resident looking for a place to crash. Somebody specifically wanted to get into her room.

Carrie's heart lodged in her throat, beating like a hummingbird's wings. Terror turned her skin clammy. She heard the noise again, a steady creak like the winding of a spring. Her thoughts raced. This corridor was empty. She could call out for help, but whoever was beyond that door would be on her in a flash. If he had a knife, a gun, her time in this life would be over.

The door opened a crack. Carrie held her breath and somehow managed to keep perfectly still. Her eyes remained open, but only as slits. She wanted to appear to be sleeping, the equivalent of playing dead.

Light from the hallway illuminated the silhouette of an imposing figure entering her room. He was at least six feet tall, and solidly built. Carrie's breathing turned ragged and every effort she made to slow it faltered. The intruder had to think she was sound asleep, unaware. Her body heated as fear took hold.

This can't be happening . . . this is a dream . . . a nightmare . . . Wake up, Carrie! Wake up!

But she was awake, and it was a battle not to scream.

The man closed the door behind him, but left it open so a bit of light seeped in. He needed to see to attack. It was enough light for Carrie to track his approach. Breathing through her nose, Carrie could not seem to take in enough air. If she hyperventilated, he would know she was awake.

The man took another silent step toward her. Carrie dug her fingers into the bedsheets as if she were dangling from a cliff. She saw the pillow in his hands, presumably one taken from an adjacent on-call room.

He had not come here to sleep. She was certain this man had entered her room with the intention of smothering her to death.

As her mind clicked over, Carrie understood the plan's sickening simplicity. No blood. No screams. No loud noise of any sort. She could be disposed of in a relatively clean manner; her body could be removed from the building in a laundry bin.

The assassin remained absolutely calm. Carrie's panic induced feelings of paralysis she prayed to overcome. There would be a moment, a precise opportunity, when surprise would be her singular advantage.

He reached the edge of her bed and looked down at her. He watched her sleep. She could hear his soft breathing and feel his smothering presence. She kept her body rigid and still as the dead. Through her peripheral vision she watched the man lift up the pillow.

Wait, Carrie . . . wait . . . not yet . . .

The anticipation became agony. Carrie held her breath and tried to keep her face muscles from twitching.

The man took his time. She was asleep, after all. He maneuvered the pillow over her face like a bombardier setting his sights on a building below.

At the last possible second, Carrie lashed out with a punch that connected solidly with the man's unguarded testicles. She heard him make an agonized sound, one that gurgled up from his gut and came out as a hiss of air. The man dropped to his knees, disabled.

Wasting no time, Carrie scrambled off the bed and darted for the door.

CHAPTER 48

From behind, Carrie heard the man call, "You bitch," and felt his strong hand grab her ankle. With her free leg, Carrie kicked blindly backward and connected hard with something—his face, his chest, something.

The blow was enough to knock him off balance. The man let out a yowl, more angry than hurt. His grip weakened and Carrie wiggled her ankle free from his grasp. Any hesitation could be fatal. Carrie bolted for the door, reaching it in one long stride. She spilled into the empty hallway at the same instant a scream, like a low, moaning train whistle, tumbled from her lips.

"Help me," Carrie wailed, breaking into a frantic sprint. "Please! Somebody!"

The VA was already like a crypt, and the on-call rooms were purposely out of the way, to maximize quiet. A cardiac care unit was on the other side of the floor, Carrie remembered, but she would never outrun her attacker.

The stairwell entrance was in front of her, about thirty feet away. On the wall adjacent to that door a red fire alarm caught Carrie's eye. Surviving meant reaching one of the lower levels. She slowed to keep from ramming the door full speed. Her feet skidded on the vinyl floor as if it were made of ice. With her left hand, Carrie ripped the stairwell door open, and with her right hand she reached out and pulled the alarm. The strobe mounted above the stairwell started to flash and a series of loud beeps sounded like a fleet of trucks backing up.

Carrie took only two steps and jumped the remaining stairs. Her momentum carried her into the concrete wall of the landing below. She bounced off the wall, but managed to stay on her feet. The piercing alarm drowned out most of her screams.

Above her, the man appeared in the doorway like some nightmare incarnate. He made the same leap Carrie did, just as she reached the bottom of the next set of stairs. Her pursuer ping-ponged off the concrete wall, but quickly regained his footing, and was soon on the move again.

Carrie knew police were nearby. The VA Police were well-armed officials with full police powers to enforce all federal laws. At least one VA Police officer would be stationed at the front entrance—with luck, more. Descending rapidly, Carrie heard her footfalls reverberate in the stairwell as she crossed the landing to the next flight of stairs. Behind her the man's wretched, rage-filled grunts intensified, and grew closer. His pace had quickened.

Carrie stumbled down the next flight of stairs and used her wrists to absorb most of the shock as her body careened off an unforgiving cement wall. One more flight to go.

She screamed as loud as her lungs permitted, "Help me!" Impossible to know if anyone heard her. The crack of a gunshot roared from somewhere above, followed by the sound of concrete splintering as a bullet struck the wall. Carrie made another long jumper's leap with a cat's grace. She reached the bottom landing just as another shot rang out and hit the wall near her head. The bullet sent shards of concrete in every direction. Carrie launched herself against the steel panic bar and used her body weight to throw the door open.

She tumbled out into the first-floor hallway. The fire alarm was loud, and strobe lights blinked everywhere. She would have to make a long run down an empty corridor to get help and would be an easy target even for a poor shot. Her eyes went to the wheelchair pushed up against the wall.

Wasting no time, Carrie gathered the folded wheelchair and took up position against the wall. A second later the hulking monster burst through the door with his weapon drawn.

With an explosive motion, Carrie shoved the wheelchair out in front of her, catching her attacker completely unaware. The strike connected at the lower part of the man's legs, and he went toppling forward, over the wheelchair, arms outstretched to brace his fall. He landed hard, and the force of his fall dislodged the gun from his hand. The weapon skated down the hall, maybe ten feet from Carrie. She was already headed in that direction, but so was her pursuer. His athleticism was nothing short of extraordinary as he got back to his feet in a blink.

Her focus was on the gun. It seemed counterintuitive, but going for the weapon would get her killed. He was fast as a puma and would be on her the second she picked up the gun. But there was another solution: keep *him* from getting the gun. Without breaking stride, Carrie gave the pistol a solid kick with her right foot, and it slid like a shuffleboard piece a good distance.

Carrie bellowed at the top of her lungs: "Somebody help me!"

"Bitch!" The man's harsh voice felt like claws raking her back.

Carrie gave the gun another solid kick. She made it halfway down the hall and prayed help was nearby. Up ahead, Carrie saw movement. Her focus sharpened on a police officer with his gun drawn. He came charging forward, and close on his heels were two sizable orderlies. Carrie kept up her sprint, but something told her the man behind her had slowed. She glanced over her shoulder and saw him turn to go the other direction. But from that end of the hall another armed police officer appeared, accompanied by two additional security guards. The VA might not have all the best medical equipment, but budget constraints did not extend to security. The hospital was a military target and therefore heavily guarded.

"Freeze!" one of the policemen shouted. "Hands in the air."

Carrie ran into the arms of an orderly. Soon, she was barricaded behind a wall of people. The man who had chased her was trapped between two groups of security personnel, and they were closing in fast.

Their sharp voices, audible over the piercing alarm, commanded him to get down on the ground. He wore hospital scrubs like an orderly, and filled them out like a football player, but she had never seen him at the VA before. But she had seen him, hadn't she? The jawline, perhaps that was most familiar. His face was handsome and covered with hard guy's stubble. His gray, wolflike eyes held a devilish glint as he slowly raised his hands. Carrie stayed locked on his every movement. He paused to bite his wrist as his hands came over his head. The curious smile on his face was directed right at Carrie.

Police approached with caution, and again ordered the man to get facedown on the floor. He obliged. Carrie stood back and watched the surreal events unfold from a safe distance. A second wave of security moved in, and quickly had the man's hands bound with steel handcuffs. He lifted his head slightly off the floor, still keeping his menacing gaze locked on Carrie. His hateful eyes held a secret; Carrie could feel it.

The police swarmed the area, speaking to each other and to their captive. Just then, the man started to grunt, not once but several times, as if he had something lodged in his throat. He began to writhe and froth at the mouth. His legs went completely spasmodic. He wiggled like a distressed worm. Carrie thought she knew what had happened. When he put his mouth to his wrist, he'd ingested something—sodium cyanide perhaps, the more lethal of the two cyanide salts.

The police realized their captive was in distress and flipped him on his back. "We need a doctor!" one police officer shouted.

Carrie rushed to help. The instinct to triage trumped what this monster had done to her, and what he almost did. She was a doctor, but this was a hopeless case. She knew the highly toxic chemical interferes with the body's ability to use oxygen, and the brain dies within minutes of ingestion. It took four men to lift the convulsing detainee off the ground and onto a stretcher.

The man frothed at the mouth, gurgled and choked, until he went still and fell silent. Carrie knew he had expired, but they would try to revive him. Cyanokit and sodium thiosulfate were both cyanide antidotes administered intravenously.

At that point he was in full respiratory distress, and Carrie ran alongside his stretcher, administering chest compressions over the middle of the chest. It was at this moment Carrie noticed a mark on the man's neck. She looked closely.

A tattoo of a shamrock.

CHAPTER 49

Detective Kowalski from the Boston PD would be showing up soon. Carrie tried to calm her crackling nerves, but was gripped by an icy terror. Six hours after the attack she could feel the man's powerful hand wrapped around her ankle. The VA Police arranged transport, since she was too rattled to drive, and they also set up the meeting with the Boston PD.

David drove up to the Bryants' home in a Zipcar rental and followed Carrie to her bedroom for a private conversation. The police would want to know why somebody had tried to kill her, and she wanted David's help with her answer. For a while, neither could speak. Carrie's body shook as though suffering a chill. She was exhausted physically and mentally and it was David's news that pulled her from the fog of fear.

"I know who Bob Richardson is," he announced. "Emma finally accessed the database the DMV shared with law enforcement and came up with a hundred percent facial match."

Bob Richardson, according to the bio David printed off the corporate Web site, was a senior vice president at CerebroMed, a Virginia-based biopharmaceutical company focused primarily on discovering drugs affecting cerebral function.

"What the heck is Bob Richardson doing giving me a virtual reality demo?"

"Are there any drug trials involved with what you're doing?" David asked.

Carrie felt her senses sharpening. Having something to focus on helped her to settle.

"No," Carrie said. "Unless Goodwin and Trent are doing something Dr. Finley and I don't know about."

"Which we know she is."

"But what?" Carrie asked.

"What if Goodwin is letting Trent experiment on these patients with a drug of some sort—maybe related to PTSD, maybe not—and in exchange she receives money for her advanced neurological procedures?"

Carrie mulled this over. "I thought the virtual reality was insufficient," she said. "But a drug? Now *that* could explain the palinacousis, some sort of side effect."

"Yeah, a side effect," David said. "One that Goodwin hid by getting those patients off the floor."

Carrie nodded. "She wanted them gone. They weren't exhibiting poor judgment after all. She *made* them sign out AMA."

"Not every patient has the side effect," David said. "That was always one of our working assumptions. You just happened to investigate two who did."

"It would explain why Goodwin didn't want me to check in on any of my patients post-op. She didn't want me to discover the side effect and alert somebody. It would have thrown the program into disarray. The vets would be subjected to a battery of tests and maybe the drug would be discovered. Game over."

David thought. "You've got some success stories, though, right?"

"So far I've met Ramón Hernandez and Terry Bushman. But Dr. Finley mentioned two others."

"Maybe the side effects are temporary in some cases, so they just need time to clear."

"It's possible," Carrie said.

"Can you get access to the patient records of the vets who have been treated with DBS?"

"I had asked Dr. Finley if I could see them before I was attacked," Carrie said. "Why?"

"It would be interesting to see if any other vets left the neuro recovery unit like Abington and Fasciani. And speaking of your boss, what about him?"

Carrie looked incredulous. "Who? Alistair? No," she said. Alistair was Carrie's confidant, her mentor, the man who had given her career new life—but she could discount his involvement for other reasons, too.

"He didn't even know Richardson," Carrie said, "and he had plenty of opportunities to introduce him to me. I think I have a pretty good read on people, and Alistair's commitment is to the patients, to this program. He didn't care that I went looking for Abington and Fasciani. He encouraged it. The problem was Goodwin—who, by the way, signed those AMA forms. She's the last link in the chain. Alistair has had my back with Goodwin since day one. There's a reason Goodwin has had it out for me from the get-go. She didn't want me on staff, and was very vocal about it."

David looked intrigued. "Goodwin runs the surgical staff, right?"

"That's right," Carrie said.

"So what about Rockwell?"

Carrie said, "I was a special hire by Dr. Finley, but Sam Rockwell was on Goodwin's staff from the start, and a fully accredited VA neurosurgeon."

"So Goodwin didn't want you hired."

"Another reason I think the buck stops with her."

"She gave you that bogus assignment, knowing you would be at the hospital late," David said.

Carrie went pale. "You think Goodwin set me up to be killed?"

"It's possible," David said. "And perhaps she did the same to Rockwell."

"What do you mean?"

"What if Dr. Finley didn't know what Goodwin was up to, but Rockwell did?" David said.

Carrie considered this. "Rockwell knew," she said in a soft voice. "He had to. Maybe he wanted out, or was going to blow the whistle, or something. That's why they tried to kill him."

"And he was as good as dead, too," David said. "At least until he started to wake up."

A sour, acidic taste burned the back of Carrie's throat. "Goodwin must have known I was on my way to see him," she said.

"It's possible Rockwell's doc called Goodwin to report a change in his condition. He was her employee, after all, so they probably had some kind of relationship. The other doctor might have mentioned you were coming up to see him."

"And Goodwin told Trent," Carrie said. "So what do we tell the police?" Carrie stopped pacing and sat on the edge of the bed beside David.

"We don't have much evidence," David said. "We have a recording that really doesn't validate anything we just discussed. Everything here is conjecture, not proof. We go to the police with what we have, and the whole operation could go dark. Evidence could be destroyed, or worse, those missing vets might be permanently silenced—like Rockwell."

Carrie sat back on the bed and leaned against the wall to keep from tipping over. Fatigue seeped into her bones, leaving her completely enervated. A feeling of dread had wormed into her gut and Carrie clamped a hand over her mouth to stifle a sob.

"What have I gotten myself into?" she muttered, just barely holding it together.

David took hold of Carrie's hand. He held her gaze until the fear swirling inside calmed like a windless sea. In that moment, the only sound Carrie could hear was her own racing heart. She felt strangely hypnotized by the flecks of gold that ringed David's penetrating eyes.

For the first time, Carrie noticed the scar across David's cheek and wondered if he got that in Syria, or some other dangerous place he called the office. For a moment his touch completely possessed her, and blocked out all other sensations.

"Whatever you decide," David said, still holding her hand, "I'll be with you every step of the way."

Carrie's mother called from downstairs, "Sweetheart, Detective Kowalski is here."

DETECTIVE KOWALSKI sipped from the mug of tea Howard Bryant had replenished. After greetings and introductions, it was time to get down to business.

Everyone gathered around the kitchen table: Carrie, Irene, Howard, Adam, and David. Adam hung back, leaning against a wall, and made no effort to shield his glowering expression. His anger appeared reserved for—and directed solely at—David, for reasons Carrie could not fathom.

Everyone was dressed casually, but the proceedings carried an air of formality. To his credit, Detective Kowalski, a trim man in his fifties with a salt-and-pepper crew cut, a snub nose, and kind brown eyes, took his time getting started. His patience helped Carrie to relax, though her hand shook with a persistent tremor every time she sipped her tea. David's touch had quieted Carrie's nerves, but the horror of what she'd endured persisted. Irene stood behind her daughter, her hands perched protectively on Carrie's shoulders.

"So you've seen this guy before? That's what I heard." Kowalski spoke with a heavy South Boston accent.

It was an effort to focus, but she looked at the color picture of the dead man Kowalski put in front of her. The photograph did not show where he had taped the cyanide capsule to the inside of his wrist.

"At the park," Carrie said. "I thought he was following me. I guess he was." She glanced at Adam, who looked distraught.

"Any reason?" Kowalski asked. "I mean, I can't say I've ever come across a stalker who carried cyanide capsules on him before."

"Can you order those online?" Howard asked.

Kowalski pondered the question. "Yeah, I think so," he said. "I remember some guy took a pill in court after he was convicted of arson. Couldn't do the time, I guess. Maybe our guy had a 'get caught' plan as well."

"Maybe," Irene said.

Carrie and David exchanged glances. This was the moment of truth—should they share what limited information they had? She gazed down at the photograph of the man with the shamrock tattoo, taken post-life, and felt five sets of eyes boring down on her.

"We've got no ID," Kowalski said. "Serial numbers are wiped clean from the gun. DNA testing will take some time, same as a dental match. For now he's a John Doe. I don't know why this guy was after you, where your paths might have crossed other than the park, but there's something here. A patient of yours, somebody you saw at the VA, one of your other jobs, during medical school, at a party? I don't know you. You tell me." Detective Kowalski took a long, unhurried drink and eyed Carrie over the rim of his mug.

Carrie shot David a sidelong glance and picked up the photograph. She studied it silently for half a minute, then set it back down on the table.

"I don't know why he attacked me," she finally said.

CHAPTER 50

Everyone crammed into the compact foyer of the Bryants' home to say good-bye to Detective Kowalski.

At the door Kowalski paused and focused on Carrie once more. "You have my card," he said. "Anything changes, you let me know."

"I will," Carrie said. "And thank you, Detective, for everything you've done."

"Wish I could do more," Kowalski said. "I'm sorry this happened to you, I really am. Just know we're going to do everything possible to figure out who this guy was and what he wanted."

Carrie felt a stab of guilt, knowing it would be wasted effort. If the police even sniffed around DARPA, she firmly believed the whole operation would be shuttered, evidence purged, and everything Carrie had endured would be for naught. She owed it to Steve Abington and Eric Fasciani to hand the federal district attorneys an airtight case against Goodwin, Richardson, and Trent. Perhaps they would find the missing vets, or maybe evidence that Goodwin and Trent had plotted her murder, or that of Sam Rockwell.

Carrie had already formulated the next steps in her mind. What she needed now was time alone with David to finalize those plans. With Kowalski gone, Howard and Irene returned to the kitchen to clean up, and Carrie went outside for a breath of fresh air. David followed.

Carrie ambled down the walkway and David caught up with her just before she reached the driveway. He took her hand again and pulled her in close to him.

"You made the right call," David said.

"Right call about what?"

Carrie and David whirled at the sound of Adam's voice. He wore the same saturnine look Carrie had observed in the kitchen, something truly unsettled.

Adam folded his arms across his chest in a hostile manner, but kept his distance. "Right about what?" he repeated.

"Nothing, Adam," Carrie said. "Just something David and I were discussing. It's private."

Adam closed the gap between them until only a few feet remained.

"Here's what I think," Adam said, his voice directed solely at David. A shadow crossed Adam's face, a darkness Carrie found deeply troublesome. "I think since you two have been hanging out, a lot of bad things have happened to my sister."

David took a single step toward Adam. He remained calm and composed, nonthreatening, nonconfrontational. Of course, Adam did not see it that way. His eyes dared David to throw the first punch.

"Adam, no," David said. "This has nothing to do with me."

"Yeah? Well, I don't see it that way," Adam said. "Carrie's been followed, somebody broke into her bedroom, somebody ran her off the road, and now someone tried to kill her. All that happened when? When, David?"

Carrie came forward. She knew how close Adam was to exploding. "Adam, this isn't David's doing," Carrie said.

Adam maneuvered so close to David the two could almost touch noses. To his credit, David did not back away. But to Carrie's eyes, David was nervous, and rightly so.

"Let's be level-headed about this, Adam," David said.

"Yeah, let's," Adam said in David's face. "This is my sister and I love her, and I'd do anything to protect her. *Anything.* So I think the level-headed thing to do is stay away from her. Whatever you're doing is dangerous, and if something happens to my sister, something happens to you. How's that sound?"

Adam did not give an inch. His stare made Carrie hold her breath.

"Are you going to hit me again?" David asked in a calm voice.

By this point, Howard and Irene had noticed something going on, and they came outside to investigate.

Irene rushed down the walkway. "What's happening?" she called.

The spell seemed to break. *Not a second too soon,* Carrie thought.

Adam turned around. "Nothing, Mom," he said. He locked eyes with David once more. "David was just leaving, and I came out to say goodbye."

———

Braxton Price stood on the bank of the Charles River and watched the sailboats carve graceful lines across the rippling water. Any minute now the call would come with his directive. *Fifty-fifty,* he thought. He knew which direction he wanted it to go. Gantry was a brother and a friend, and Carrie Bryant needed to die.

How a brain surgeon had taken down Gantry, a well-trained, hardcore soldier, was difficult for Price to fathom, but his friend was dead and that was that. The plan all along had been to take Carrie out in the parking lot early that morning, silent-like—certainly not in the hospital, which had a larger police presence. Gantry had evidently improvised, and somehow she got the better of him.

Pity.

Something like this was bound to happen, and Price had warned his employers on several occasions about the risk of continuing after Rockwell's decommissioning. But once a grunt, always a grunt, and Price knew the suits were not about to take that kind of strategic direction from a low-level operator. *Whatever.* At least the group within DARPA who got this program off the ground had listened to him when it mattered most.

Nothing about Price's motivations was especially patriotic. It was all about the money, and he'd balked at the notion of getting his muscle from a ragtag group of mercenaries whose loyalties could easily be compromised. Employing members from Price's former squad, like Gantry, assured him that even under extreme duress his team would not falter. As individuals, each one of them had been tested, and while bones and bodies broke over in Afghanistan, allegiances never did. Price did not fight for his country; he fought solely for his brothers. When Gantry took that pill, he'd metaphorically leapt on a grenade to save his comrades. So Price would avenge him. It was not a matter of if, but when.

The air was still and warm, not unusual for this time of year. Price wanted to remove his jacket, but it hid the wires that would scramble the expected call. It also concealed his favorite pistol, a Beretta 92FS with a fifteen-round magazine and impeccable long-range accuracy.

At four thirty the call came in. Price wore an earpiece, but that was commonplace these days, so nobody took notice of him talking to himself on the bank of the Charles River. Price reached into his jacket pocket and pushed the Talk button without needing to check the phone's display.

"Speak," Price said.

"It's a no-go," a man's voice said in his ear.

"Fine."

"Too much scrutiny right now. There's another way to get her removed."

"Are we going dark?"

"No."

"Bad idea. We should go dark."

"Not my call," the man said.

Price could not help but smile. "Yeah," he said with a chuckle. "We're all just players here."

CHAPTER 51

Carrie woke to the sound of persistent knocking on her bedroom door. She panicked, thinking she was back in the on-call room, and whoever was knocking had come to do her harm.

"Carrie, are you awake?" Adam asked. "Can we talk?"

She shook her head to clear the cobwebs from her mind. "Yeah, come in," she said, her voice raspy with sleep.

Adam entered, looking distraught.

Dressed in the same clothes she had worn to her interview with Detective Kowalski, Carrie sat up in bed and spun around to put her feet on the floor. She eyed her brother with concern. "What's wrong?" she asked.

She knew what was wrong, of course. Adam was coming unhinged. It was obvious in the way he had threatened David. The encounter had left Carrie rattled and unnerved. David, to his credit, took it all in stride, but Carrie wished Adam had apologized to him in some way. Perhaps Adam had experienced a change of heart.

Adam eyed Limbic before plopping down on Carrie's desk chair. He slouched forward, and Carrie waited for him to speak.

"What's going on, Adam?" she asked at last.

"David," Adam said in a hushed voice.

"I have his number. I'm sure he'd love to hear your apology."

"That's not why I came to talk to you." Adam's expression was grave, his haunted eyes encircled by dark rings.

Carrie felt the weight of his gaze. "What, then?" she asked.

"Outside, when I was toe to toe with him, I had thoughts that scared me."

"Thoughts?"

Adam bounced his legs up and down. Evidently, it was not enough to settle him, because he took a ballpoint pen from Carrie's desk and twirled it about his fingers like a miniature baton. He had learned the trick in high school and tried to teach Carrie the method, but she never quite caught on.

"I wanted to kill him," Adam said.

Carrie gasped. "Adam, what are you saying?"

The pen tumbled from Adam's hand and dropped to the floor. His gaze never left Carrie, and his cold stare sent a chill down her spine.

Adam's eyes turned red, and he looked on the verge of tears. "I'm saying I didn't just want to hurt him, I wanted to kill him." His hushed voice was almost hypnotic. "It took everything in me not to grab his head and break his neck. I could have done it, too. I don't know how I held back. If you hadn't been there, I don't think I would have."

Carrie was stunned. A hollow pit in her gut allowed all sorts of feelings to roll in: fear, disgust, sadness, hopelessness. It was a cocktail of emotions she could not process.

"Why are you telling me this?" she asked.

"I'm telling you because I need your help," Adam said.

Carrie's guard fell immediately. She could look past Adam's confession to focus instead on the guilt and fear that seemed to consume him. She reached for Adam's hand, but he jerked away from her touch and rose to his feet.

"What can I do to help?" Carrie asked, rising as well. "We'll talk to Mom and Dad. Maybe find you a new therapist."

"I don't need a therapist," Adam said through clenched teeth. "I need the wires."

Carrie blanched. "What did you say?"

"You heard me," Adam said. "I want those wires in my brain. Scramble this shit up so I stop thinking the way I do."

Carrie sank down onto her bed. "I can't do that," she said.

"What do you mean you can't? You're in charge of the thing."

"No, no. I'm just a surgeon." This was an odd bit of irony, to embrace the role Goodwin had tried to thrust upon her. But she did not know what else to say.

"You still have pull, don't you? You're the brain surgeon. You can get me in and get me cured."

"It's not that simple," Carrie said.

"Why?"

"Because it might not work." Carrie cringed inwardly, knowing her argument had holes.

"I was at dinner when you told Mom and Dad all about that Ramón guy. And who was the other one? Bushman or something. It worked for them. You said it worked for two others, too."

"But they're the exception, not the rule."

"So? What's the worst thing that can happen to me?" Adam asked. "I get some surgery that doesn't do anything. Then I go back to being a walking time bomb, but this time with actual wires in my body."

Carrie imagined Adam lying in a hospital bed, his head bandaged, muttering "Follow my light . . . follow my light . . . follow my light" the way Steve Abington had.

"No, it's not that simple," said Carrie. "I'm not entirely sure it's safe."

Adam looked flustered. "Have you done the surgery before?"

"Yes."

"And?"

"And two of my patients are missing."

"Because of the surgery?"

"No," Carrie said, but corrected herself. "I just don't know. I'm still trying to figure it all out."

Carrie did not know how much to say. Yes, the DBS procedure could produce a specific side effect, but that was almost secondary to what Sandra Goodwin and Cal Trent were cooking up. And she still did not know how Bob Richardson from CerebroMed fit in this equation. Until she had some answers, she would never put Adam forward as a candidate for the surgery. Never.

"There's a reason I've been followed and twice nearly killed," Carrie said.

Adam glowered. "Yeah. And I think that reason is David. Who knows who he's pissed off? Believe me, I've seen those embedded reporters in action. They can be like jackals. Maybe he dug up the wrong details on the wrong people and now that he's hanging out with you, you're a target, too."

"I don't think so," Carrie said.

Adam fell to his knees and clutched Carrie's hands with force. "Please," he said. "I need to feel better." He panted to catch his breath. His emotions choked back his voice, and his eyes brimmed with desperation.

"Until I know it's completely safe, I just can't do it. I'm sorry."

"I don't care about any damn side effects!" Adam shouted. His ferocity took Carrie by surprise and frightened her. "I'll take any side effect right now." Adam sprang to his feet and began to pace. "What I'm afraid of is that next time I feel like I did with David, I won't be able to hold back."

"I'm sorry, Adam," Carrie said. "But I just can't. And I don't want you to get your hopes up for this treatment, either. We need to focus on therapy. You need therapy."

Adam nodded glumly, several times in quick succession. Without another word, he marched out of Carrie's bedroom but left the door open. She had expected him to slam it shut.

Carrie exhaled loudly and took a moment to collect her thoughts. Part of her believed Adam would be fine if he did get the operation. That he'd be like Ramón or Terry Bushman, one of the fab four for whom DBS had been a life-saving procedure. Another part of her worried he'd vanish without a trace, like Abington and Fasciani. Until she had answers, there could be no wires.

A few minutes later, Carrie heard a loud crash followed by the shattering of glass. She raced downstairs, arriving in the foyer at the same instant as her worried parents.

Without words, Carrie followed her parents into the living room, where Adam perched upon the couch so he could reach the photographs on the wall. His face had a wicked look, a darkness she had never seen. In his hand, Adam wielded a massive hammer that Carrie recognized from his toolbox. He had already shattered one photo, and now Adam swung the hammer at a second, this one a picture of the siblings dressed in ski gear, taken at Sunday River in Maine. The hammer struck dead center, and the glass shattered into thousands of jagged pieces.

Adam was not selecting photos at random. Each picture was of him and Carrie. He swung again, and this time shattered the glass on a picture of brother and sister taken in front of Big Ben when they were in their teens. The face of the hammer put a large hole where Carrie's head had been.

"Adam!" Irene screamed. "What are you doing?" She sank to the floor, her hands covering her mouth but not silencing her sobs.

Howard Bryant held Carrie back. Adam was in a blind rage; who knew what he would do if she approached?

Adam cocked his arm back once more, and aimed the hammer at another photograph, but paused to shoot his mother an annoyed look.

"I'm just showing my sister the same kind of love she showed me," Adam said. He brought the hammer forward again, and the sound of breaking glass filled the room once more.

CHAPTER 52

The next morning, Carrie was back in her mom's Volvo, making what had become a routine drive from Hopkinton to the VA. Adam had stormed out after his terrifying tirade and never returned. Where he'd gone, Carrie could not say. Part of her worried he'd never come back home, another part worried that he would. Carrie's distraught parents had left the house before she did, to continue to look for their son.

However, Adam was not Howard and Irene's only concern. Her parents had thought her return to work was too much, too soon, but Carrie had insisted. After all, the man the police believed to be an emotionally unstable, well-armed stalker was dead.

While Carrie sounded convincing, the reality was a far cry from her assurances. The drive to the VA proved tense, as Carrie remained on high alert. Until Goodwin and Trent were decommissioned, she remained a target, and certainly DARPA had more deadly resources to throw at her. So long as she kept with the crowds, on the roads, or in the halls of the VA, however, Carrie felt moderately safe.

What she would not do, misguided or not, was cower, go into hiding, or hire an armed detail to guard her 24/7. She had to live her life, terror be damned.

Bottom line: she was on a mission.

Her voice mail and e-mail were flooded with messages from concerned friends and former colleagues, many of whom had heard about Carrie's ordeal on the local news. Dr. Finley had called, but she let it go to voice mail too. He'd side with her mother and insist Carrie rest at home for the day. Among those checking in was Carrie's old pal Valerie from BCH, who called during the morning commute. Their conversation was brief, but Val's worry touched Carrie's heart. The former colleagues made plans to get together for drinks and dinner in the coming weeks.

"You have no idea who that man was?" Val asked.

"Police are still looking. They think they'll get an ID soon enough."

"Well, I'm just grateful you're all right. And I want you to know, Carrie, that you're deeply missed around here. I mean that."

Carrie's eyes welled, but she did not cry. No need to make Val feel worse. "I'm doing okay," she said. "I mean it."

Val, being Val, said, "You got somebody to talk to?"

"Like a therapist?" Carrie asked.

"Well, not exactly," Val said.

"Oh, that," Carrie said.

"Just saying, it would help."

Carrie laughed. "Yeah, I've got someone to talk to."

"Well, I want to hear all about him."

"Who said it's a he?"

Val scoffed. "It could be a woman. Don't matter to me. But I am pretty sure we're not talking about a stuffed animal here, darling. You can give me all the four-one-one when I see you. And take care of yourself, Carrie. I mean it."

"I will."

As she hung up with Val, the car in front, no signal given, abruptly changed lanes. Carrie had to hit the brakes hard to avoid a collision. She hit her horn, and muttered a string of expletives that would have made her mother blush first and cringe second.

The other driver's maneuver was not unusual during rush hour, and Carrie's outburst surprised her. *Stress-induced,* she figured, and in that moment she forgave Adam for everything. Her brother's anger, directed toward her and at David, was triggered by constant duress. In the aftermath of her own extreme stress, Carrie could better relate to Adam's persistent volatility. She called her parents to check on the search and was told they had been unable to locate Adam. They would resume the effort later, after they returned home from work. Carrie had her doubts they would have any success. Something about Adam's last tirade made Carrie believe she would never see her brother again.

Carrie remained extra vigilant as she navigated through the crush of morning traffic. At one point, she glanced in her rearview mirror and noticed a red Camaro a few cars back that looked a lot like Adam's. Of course that was impossible. If Adam had gotten that car fired up, they'd have seen a celebration worthy of Mardi Gras on his side of the garage. Curious, though, Carrie tried to get a look at the driver, but the car was too far back for her to see much of anything.

Frustrated with the pace of her commute, Carrie took the next exit, not her usual. A short time later the Camaro reappeared in her rearview. Carrie relived the sinking feeling she'd had in the park, when her future would-be murderer became something to fear. A block later, though, the Camaro turned down a side street; just like that, it was gone.

The uneasy feelings—the fear and paranoia, a sense that something horrible could happen any minute, a terror that pawed at the back of her neck—those feelings lasted all the way to the VA and followed her into the building.

CARRIE BRACED herself for an onslaught of attention that did not come. Even in the busy main foyer, nobody took notice of her. In a way, the silence was a stark reminder of her low profile at the hospital. While her face had been splashed all over the TV, she was not a well-known figure here. Her role fit in that netherworld between employee and contractor. At the main entrance, Carrie flashed her ID to the security guard and walked in without fanfare.

Welcome back to the jungle; nice of you to come.

The morning hustle and bustle seemed so perfectly ordinary, which paradoxically made it all feel a little eerie. Although there was a heavier-than-usual VA Police presence, Carrie saw no crime scene tape, nothing cordoned off. The evidence, as Detective Kowalski indicated, had been gathered, documented, and photographed in the intervening hours. Life at the VA, for all intents and purposes, had returned to normal.

Carrie's plan for the day was a simple one. With no surgery on the docket, she would spend time examining Dr. Finley's case files, and start to gather evidence. David had the right instincts. Had other vets gone MIA like Abington or Fasciani? If Goodwin wanted to conceal a side effect such as palinacousis, the first step would be to get those patients off the neuro recovery floor, where residents were trained to look for cognitive issues.

Carrie showed up at Dr. Finley's office with two cups of coffee, but when she opened the closed door, she found three people inside. Sandra Goodwin and Evan Navarro sat on those uncomfortable metal chairs facing Dr. Finley.

Carrie's eyes turned to slits as she focused her attention on Goodwin. She fought back the urge to scream, *Did you try to have me killed?* The outburst might have been satisfying, but Carrie knew it would serve no purpose. All that mattered was obtaining proof of Goodwin's wrongdoing. That required tact, not brute force.

Goodwin and Navarro both acted irritated by Carrie's intrusion; no outward signs of empathy there. Dr. Finley's face, by contrast, revealed his deep concern, and it put a walnut-sized lump in Carrie's throat. He was effusive in expressing his utter relief.

Carrie presented Dr. Finley with the coffee she'd bought him. "I know it's not Starbucks, but it's the best we've got here," she said.

"The fact that you could think about me at all is incredible," Dr. Finley said. He took the beverage with a grateful smile. He remained standing beside Carrie, his hire.

Carrie looked over at Goodwin and Navarro. "I hope I'm not inter-rupting anything," she said.

"Coincidentally enough," Goodwin said, "you were the subject of our conversation." The tone of her voice cooled the room a few degrees.

"Oh?"

"We're discussing the DBS program," Navarro said.

Carrie could not help feeling amazed at the lack of empathy. "Well, in case you or Sandra were curious, I'm doing just fine," she said. "Thank you very much for asking."

"I'm glad to hear it," Goodwin said, not sounding glad at all. "But my chief concern, as I was just explaining to Alistair, is the continua-tion of DBS surgeries in light of your incident."

"By 'incident,' I assume you mean my attempted murder." Carrie felt her whole body heat up. It took great restraint not to go at Goodwin the way Adam had threatened David.

"It's my opinion that a trauma such as what you experienced makes you a danger to the patients and to the program."

"Last I checked, I wasn't actually shot," Carrie countered. She saw where this conversation was headed, and she did not like it one bit.

"While you aren't physically injured," Goodwin said, "your mental status is questionable at best. Evan has been studying up on the DBS procedure, and I think he'll be fine to take over for you until a mental health professional clears you to operate."

"Evan?" Carrie could not hide her incredulity. "Is that why he came to the OR? To watch me work? Nice bit of subterfuge there, Sandra. Well played."

"I don't appreciate your innuendos, Carrie," Navarro said.

"I don't appreciate you poaching my job," Carrie snapped back.

"It would only be temporary," Dr. Finley said in a conciliatory tone.

Carrie frowned. "You're not on their side here, are you, Alistair?"

"No," Dr. Finley said. "I'm not. But we have another problem."

Sandra flashed a frigid smile. "I told Alistair that if we don't replace you with Evan, I'll go to the board with a formal complaint about your violating my procedures by interfering with patient care. Given all the scrutiny the VA is under these days, I'm sure you can imagine how poorly that will be received."

"They'll force me to let you go, Carrie," Dr. Finley said in a defeated voice.

"And Evan will continue in your place regardless. So really, Carrie, you have no choice in the matter."

"When is the next surgery?" Carrie asked.

"The day after tomorrow," Navarro said.

Carrie shot Dr. Finley a panicked look. "Is it a PTSD case?" she asked.

"Yes, it is," Navarro answered. "But don't worry, I'm ready, and it'll go just fine."

Dr. Finley cleared his throat, and Carrie noticed how uncomfortable he seemed. "Carrie, Dr. Goodwin has requested that you take a leave of absence until you're medically cleared to operate."

"I've seen how you like to interfere with my processes and procedures. I'm not one to give second chances, and I don't want to risk you inserting yourself where your services are not required."

"Alistair, I can't believe you're letting this happen," Carrie said. "Navarro doesn't know anything about DBS."

"Look at it this way, Carrie," Dr. Finley said. "I have no choice. That's the way it is in the VA. It's the military, and everyone has to take orders, including me. Navarro has a licensed M.D. after his name, and as far as the VA is concerned, that means he can do everything from heart surgery to delivering a baby if the VA says so."

"I strongly disagree with this," Carrie said. "How can you feel comfortable with someone who may be completely incompetent?"

"As I recall, Carrie," Navarro said, "you had no experience when you came on board."

"If you take some time away, I can get you back on the team," Dr. Finley said. "On a permanent basis, if you like. If you don't, Sandra will go to the board, and if she does that, your status here will be entirely out of my hands."

Carrie's arms fell to her sides. "What choice do I have?" she asked.

Goodwin stood. "None," she said.

CHAPTER 53

With a scowl across her face, Carrie leaned against a wall outside Dr. Finley's office, arms folded tightly across her chest, and waited for Goodwin and Navarro to depart. As he walked out, Navarro shot Carrie a smarmy, sidelong glance that made her blood boil once more. But her real anger was saved for Goodwin, who refused to look Carrie in the eyes.

Are you surprised I'm still alive? Carrie wanted to shout.

Goodwin could not have been completely dissatisfied, though. She had played the same blackmail card twice, but this time to greater effect.

Carrie stormed back into Dr. Finley's office as soon as the other two were out of sight.

"I can't believe you let Goodwin do that to me," Carrie snapped as she closed the door behind her.

Seated at his desk, Dr. Finley looked utterly besieged. He let go a loud sigh and ran his fingers through an unruly tangle of hair.

"We can retreat now and regroup later, or Goodwin will put a permanent end to your career," he said. "She'll trash your reputation so that you'll never match for another residency, and I doubt you'll find a situation like this one at some other hospital. Think about what's best for your career here, Carrie. Take the time off. Let the dust settle and hope to allow cooler heads to prevail. The program has to be protected at all costs."

Though it stung to hear, Carrie was not entirely surprised by Dr. Finley's stance. Any threat to the program, in his view, had to be neutralized. He had gone out of his way to hire Carrie in a rather unorthodox manner to avoid significant delays following Rockwell's accident. He would do what was necessary to keep the OR active.

"Speaking of the program, did you know Bob Richardson works for CerebroMed?"

Dr. Finley's brow creased and he looked a little puzzled. "I'd never met Richardson before your demo. But I'm not entirely surprised."

"No? Why?"

"DARPA hired them."

"DARPA contracted with CerebroMed?" Carrie was surprised. "We deal in DBS, Alistair, not neurological drugs."

"I'm well aware," Dr. Finley said. "Cal Trent told me that CerebroMed has been developing software for studying and re-creating traumatic events. DARPA has been partnering with them, but that's all I know. It's part of the VR program, and not really within my area of expertise. How did you learn this, by the way?"

Carrie shrugged off the question. There was no use debating. Carrie knew she had lost her greatest ally. This program was Dr. Finley's greatest love, and it meant more to him than the truth about Goodwin. That much was obvious. Until she could give him definitive proof, he would always find a logical explanation for any concern Carrie raised.

"Well, can I at least review the files I requested?" Carrie asked.

"Yes, of course," Dr. Finley said, and he presented Carrie with a large stack of files. Carrie glanced at them briefly.

"These are neurological reports," she said.

"Yes."

"I'm looking specifically for postoperative complications."

Dr. Finley grimaced a little. "I'm afraid that would require Dr. Goodwin's involvement."

Carrie just smiled and clutched Dr. Finley's files to her chest. "No worries then," she said. "I'll just look over what I have."

CARRIE RETREATED to her office. She set Dr. Finley's files on her desk. From her purse, she dug out Evan Navarro's hospital ID and log-on credentials. They were written on the same piece of scratch paper as the main number for the VA, which Carrie had jotted down the night Eric Fasciani disappeared. Carrie might not be able to view the medical records of DBS patients who had spent time on the neuro recovery floor, but Navarro could.

The electronic medical records system, known as VistA (for Veterans Health Information Systems and Technology Architecture), offered a variety of specialized enterprise applications, including electronic health records. The system, one of the largest in the United States, contained the records of more than eight million veterans, and personal data for hundreds of thousands of medical personnel and operating staff. Carrie was interested in only a handful of patients, specifically vets like Abington and Fasciani who had DBS surgery to combat PTSD symptoms.

Carrie launched the VistA program and entered Navarro's ID into the log-on screen. It took her almost thirty minutes to figure out the system, but eventually Carrie got the hang of it. It was different from the electronic medical records system at BCH, but intuitive enough for her to search for Steve Abington's name. From there, Carrie was a few clicks away from the problem list detailed in the computerized patient record system, abbreviated on the graphical user interface as "CPRS."

Steve Abington's arrhythmia was logged as "inactive," but she could see the onset date, last update, and location of the incident, which was the neuro recovery floor. The application said nothing about Abington's transfer to the med ICU, probably because Navarro did not have access privileges to that part of his medical record. Navarro was a neurosurgeon, and it seemed the walls Goodwin had erected between her department and the rest of the VA applied to this software application as well. No matter. Using Abington's case file, Carrie retrieved the clinic-specific procedure code for DBS and used that to search all DBS patients in the past twelve months.

There they were. Some names Carrie recognized: Steve Abington, Eric Fasciani, Don McCall, Ramón Hernandez, Gerald Wright, and Terry Bushman. Some she did not. Based on the patients who were fully anesthetized during their operation, it was easy to distinguish between DBS patients treated for movement disorders, and those treated for PTSD.

On a piece of paper, Carrie made a two-column table and filled it with information from Abington's patient record. She ignored details such as clinical reminders, recent lab results, patient record flags, postings, and active medications to focus solely on significant problems that might have resulted in a patient being transferred to another unit.

She started with the patients she knew, and in a matter of minutes had a list of four names, with one medical complication post-DBS among them.

Patient Name	Problem List
Abington, Steve	Ventricular Tachycardia
Hernandez, Ramón	None
Fasciani, Eric	None
Bushman, Terry	None

The next patient Carrie looked up was Jim Caldwell. According to the record, Sam Rockwell had done his surgery. Seven hours after the operation, Caldwell's blood sugar levels dropped. Carrie could not see in the VistA system whether he remained on the neuro recovery floor, but now she had another name for her expanding table.

Patient Name	Problem List
Caldwell, Jim	Hypoglycemia

This process went on for several hours. Carrie combed through the records of every vet who had come through the DARPA program seeking a cure for PTSD. Twenty names in total.

By this point Carrie's eyes were like sandpaper. But her mind was reeling, and her whole body pulsed with an intense energy like nothing she'd ever experienced. She scanned the list, utterly incredulous. Of the twenty patients in total, fifteen had experienced complications, eleven of which were not typically associated with the surgery.

Carrie made a second table that summarized her findings.

Complication	Number of instances
Arrhythmia	4
Hypoglycemia	3
Hypotension	4
Severe Nausea	2
Vision Problem/NOS	2
No Complications	5

Once again, Navarro's access restrictions prevented Carrie from seeing what happened to each patient following his medical complication, but she presumed many would have been transferred to the med ICU or some other acute care department within the hospital. Carrie was not certain of the percent of DBS surgeries that resulted in post-op complications, but she knew the number was not 75 percent.

It would be Goodwin's job to bring these astronomical numbers to Dr. Finley's attention—which, of course, she would not do if her intent was to hide them. With Goodwin's philosophy of "turfing" so ingrained, by getting the patients off the floor, she essentially made them disappear.

Carrie tried to come up with ways those complications could be induced. Potassium certainly could produce arrhythmia, and insulin obviously made the blood sugar levels drop. Beta blockers were a possible cause for a sudden drop in blood pressure, but Carrie knew of several drugs that would induce hypotension.

Five patients appeared to have no postoperative side effects whatsoever, but that included Eric Fasciani, who had improbably overcome the effects of Valium to check out AMA. Two of the other five vets Carrie knew: Ramón Hernandez and Terry Bushman. The remaining two must have been the patients Dr. Finley said had results similar to Bushman and Hernandez.

Carrie thought back to the night Fasciani disappeared and recalled that only one nurse was working the floor, the same man she thought she'd recognized in the photograph at Rita Abington's home. If Nurse Taggart were involved, Fasciani could have been removed from the floor without intentionally inducing some medical complication.

Carrie took out her phone to call David, and tried to quell the intense feelings of anger that coursed through her veins.

David picked up on the second ring.

"Do you still have the temporary ID for Michael Stephen?" she asked.

"And hello to you, my dear," David said in a cheery voice. "I've been worried about you all day. How are you?"

"No time to chat. I need to know if you still have that ID."

"I've still got it," David said. "Why?"

"Because I'm now persona non grata on the neuro recovery floor, and in the VA as well, but you're not."

"And what, pray tell, will I be doing on the neuro recovery floor?"

"You'll be helping me figure out what really happens to Evan Navarro's very first DBS patient after his surgery is done."

CHAPTER 54

David's temporary ID was good for the month, and he had no trouble getting inside the VA. He wore his easy-on, easy-off disguise—surgical scrubs and canvas sneakers—and just like that, he was one of the crew.

By now, he guessed, Carrie was parked in the back lot, watching the rear of the building. David flashed on his meeting with Carrie just hours ago at Java du Jour. While it had only been a day since he'd last seen her, his visit marred by that uncomfortable confrontation with Adam, David felt as if it had been weeks. He took in every detail of her, and even though she was grim-faced and tense, David felt exhilarated to be with her again.

They ordered cappuccinos and discussed the plan; just like the last time, their drinks went cold. Carrie might have lost access to the OR, but she still could read the surgical schedule. From that, she got the name of Navarro's first DBS patient: Garrett McGhee.

It was David who came up with the stakeout approach. It made sense to Carrie, because she did not know what happened to the patients after they left the neuro recovery floor. Were they even moved to a different unit?

"I think they get transferred," Carrie had said. "Dr. Finley showed me Abington's patient information from the med ICU."

David was not convinced. "But that was after you went there looking for him," he said.

"So?"

"Maybe he never even made it there," David said.

"Come to think of it, the nurse in the med ICU couldn't trace him when I showed up, but I thought that was some problem with the record system. Should we set up surveillance cameras in McGhee's hospital room?"

David shook his head. "Might be easy to detect. I think we should figure out what happens—*if* anything happens—see it for ourselves, and then we'll improvise how to get the proof we need."

Carrie clutched her arms tightly, as though staving off a sudden chill.

"These are killers, David," Carrie said. "I feel sick I'm so scared. I don't know if I can go through with this."

"I'm just as scared as you are," David said. "And I'll back out, but only if you want to."

It was obvious from Carrie's face that it was not an option.

"I've never wanted to be more wrong about something in my entire life," Carrie said.

"Stats don't lie," David said. "Based on what you found, we have a seventy-five percent chance of proving that you're right."

David wandered the halls of the VA, trying to look like he belonged. He made frequent visits to the cafeteria and the restroom to pass the time until the next shift change. Throughout it all, he remained in constant communication with Carrie using Motorola two-way radios, which he had bought at Walmart for sixty bucks.

Now, thirty minutes before showtime, David had Carrie on his mind as much as the mission. He snuck into an unoccupied quiet room and put the push-to-talk to his mouth.

"Ground control to Major Tom. Can you hear me, Major Tom?"

There was a crackle and he heard Carrie's voice say, "Not funny."

"It was a little funny," David said.

"What's going on? Where are you?"

"Shift change is happening soon. I'm getting ready to move into position. I just wanted to hear your voice before I headed out."

"Be careful, David," Carrie said. "I don't know what is going to happen."

"Careful is my middle name," David said.

"I thought you told me it was Charles."

David's eyes widened. "Wow, that's some steel-trap memory you've got there."

He imagined Carrie's smile and it filled him with joy.

"Just be careful," she repeated. "Radio me when you're in position."

At fifteen minutes before the hour, David headed for the neuro recovery floor. According to Carrie's intel, the unit was already half full with non-DBS surgical patients, but Garrett McGhee was not scheduled to arrive for several more hours. At that moment, Navarro was still doing the job Carrie had done, and Dr. Finley was in the OR with him, guiding his every step.

The double doors to the unit were closed and locked when David arrived, but he did not want to be buzzed inside. Instead, he used his smartphone to look occupied as he waited for the next shift to show up. There would be a little commotion at that point, during which David could more easily slip inside undetected.

At five minutes until three o'clock the new crew emerged from the elevator in a clump, chatting noisily amongst each other. The unit doors buzzed open, and David fell into step right behind them. He walked purposefully down the hall. He was practiced at looking official in places where he did not belong, and from the corner of his eyes it did not appear anybody paid particularly close attention to him.

He was quick to locate the room with McGhee's name written on a whiteboard—the kind of reservation nobody wanted to have. Inside the cubicle space David found an adjustable hospital bed, along with a bunch of medical equipment he could not identify. The glass enclosure left David exposed, but at least there were no direct sight lines to the nurses' station.

As a precaution, David closed the flimsy curtain for privacy and slipped inside the freestanding wardrobe closet that was pushed up against the wall opposite the bed. He closed the doors and plunged into darkness. A thin crack between the closet doors offered some light, but not much.

He had hardly any space to move about, and David already dreaded the many hours he would spend inside waiting for Garrett McGhee's arrival. After five minutes or so, David's legs began to throb, so he removed the two-way from his pants pocket, twisted his body so his back pressed against one of the side walls, and sank to the closet floor. To fit better, David wrapped his arms around his knees, which were nearly in his mouth, but at least he could hold this position for a while, meditate if he had to. He put the two-way to his mouth and called Carrie.

"I'm in a closet on the neuro recovery floor," he said. He had the volume low for when Carrie answered back.

"Okay, I'm outside watching the back entrance. I'll wait to hear from you."

"Roger. Over and out. Or whatever you're supposed to say."

There was a brief period of silence during which David wished he had one more chance to hear Carrie's voice. A second later the radio crackled back to life.

"Thank you, David. I mean it. Thank you for everything."

"Roger, over and out," David said.

And that was enough for him.

TEDIUM.

The walls of David's hideout were made of thin particleboard, so he passed the time by listening to the nurses' chatter, or counting the beeps on whichever machine happened to be loudest. The antiseptic hospital smell, that sickly clean odor, was starting to get to him, making the hours even more unpleasant to endure. Adding to his discomfort, David's body heat had turned the cramped quarters oppressively stuffy, and the slat between the doors offered a limited supply of fresh air. He had checked in with Carrie about a dozen times, but now he had to go dark since McGhee could arrive at any minute.

David's phone battery had run down, but he guessed it was close to 7:00 P.M., going by the last time he spoke with Carrie. Four hours jammed like a pretzel inside a closet; this was becoming a habit for him, it seemed. He felt achy all over, and the throbbing pain in his knees had gone from uncomfortable to deeply unpleasant. He could stretch his arms above his head, and that lessened the soreness somewhat. He wondered when—if—McGhee would finally show up.

The minutes passed slowly and without mercy until maybe another hour had ticked off the clock. What if there were complications? What if McGhee died during surgery? Maybe Navarro was as incompetent as he was devious. At some point during the long stretch of time with nothing happening, David felt pressure building in his bladder.

"Oh, great," he muttered.

I can hold it, was his first thought.

McGhee better get here soon, was the next thing to cross his mind.

A minute passed, then another, and all David could think about was peeing. When the pressure finally got too intense, David pushed open the closet door and clambered out like the Tin Man before he got oiled. The curtain kept David mostly out of sight while he used a portable urinal to relieve himself. The overwhelming feeling of relief extended to his arms and legs, and David absolutely despised the thought of jamming himself back into the wardrobe. But then he heard the squeaky wheels of a stretcher in motion.

David scrambled into the closet and got the doors closed a few seconds before the stretcher came rolling into the room. The portable toilet was a tight fit under his legs, but he could not leave it half full of his urine for the nurses to find. There was a lot of commotion and dialogue as the patient, who David presumed was McGhee, was transferred from the stretcher to the bed. Two nurses took their time getting McGhee's vitals and hooking up his IV.

Now began the waiting game, and with each passing minute, each agonizing hour, David grew more weary. If nothing happened—and statistically that was a 25 percent possibility—he would find a way to sneak out of McGhee's room and get back to Carrie. Mission aborted for the night. His thoughts were dulled from inactivity and waiting.

The nurses came and went. They chatted playfully amongst themselves, but it was obvious they had tremendous competence in their craft, and deep caring for the patients. David was not interested in evaluating their skills as nursing professionals. He was waiting for the complication.

It must have been eleven, because another shift change arrived. He heard them talking, discussing medications, treatment, and such. A doctor poked her head in and did some exam on McGhee, but it was brief.

Thirty minutes after the eleven o'clock shift change took place—it had to be thirty—David heard someone enter the room. That was odd, because the new duty nurse had been in to see McGhee not long ago. The muscles in the back of David's neck tightened to the point he thought they might snap, but he turned his head anyway to get a look out the crack in the closet door. He could see a shape, the outline of a man with dark skin, lurking over McGhee's bed.

"How are we feeling tonight, Garrett?" the male nurse asked while glancing at a clipboard.

David watched the nurse extract something from the pocket of his uniform and had to squint to make out the syringe in the nurse's hand. The nurse inserted the syringe into the IV. Nothing happened for several minutes, until the nurse said, "Open your eyes, Garrett. The drug I gave you should make you less groggy . . . good . . . that's real good. Can you hear my voice?"

McGhee groaned, and then said in a mumbling voice, with almost exaggerated torpidity, "Yeah, yeah, stop saying it. Stop it."

"Oh, good," the nurse said. "I'm going to give you a little something else."

"A little something else . . . little something else . . . little some-thing . . ." McGhee spoke as though in a daze, but he pronounced the words clearly so they were easy to understand.

David thought immediately of the auditory illusion, palinacousis, Carrie had so accurately described. It sounded as though McGhee was acting out her very description. Still peering through that crack in the closet, David watched the nurse inject something else into McGhee's IV, and a minute later he took out a smartphone and made a call.

"Rear entrance twenty minutes," the nurse said. "Keep the van run-ning. It'll be quick."

David felt elated. At last they had proof Carrie was right. Something truly sinister was going on here, even if he had no idea what exactly caused the auditory illusion, or where this nurse was taking McGhee, or what would happen to him once he got there, or why they were do-ing it. Carrie was watching the rear entrance right now, and she needed to know trouble was headed her way.

CHAPTER 55

Hours of doing nothing made it hard to ignore the ever-present fear. It also gave Carrie lots of idle time to think about Adam. Nobody had heard from him since he left in such a rage. Her parents naturally continued to worry, and contemplated canceling evening plans to wait at home for him to show, but Carrie cajoled them into going out. If Adam was going to show, he would do so when he felt ready, she advised. So her parents went out, and soon after, Carrie did the same.

Had Adam returned home, Carrie would not have known. She kept her phone in her purse and the radio off, worried she might miss something of consequence if distracted. But there was a whole lot of nothing going on, and this gave Carrie time to fret and ponder the mission's many open questions. Would McGhee even have a medical complication induced? Would he be transferred to another unit, or moved out of the hospital entirely? Would they bring him back? If so, when?

The plan itself was all a bit "squishy," as Carrie said to David, which ran counter to her ethos of procedures and planning. Then again, she had long ago abandoned her comfort zone and proved to herself, many times over, just how adaptable she had become.

For want of something to do, Carrie ran through the plan's many permutations in her head for the umpteenth time. David was going to trail McGhee off the unit floor, assuming he experienced some sort of medical problem that required transfer. If McGhee left the hospital entirely, it would be Carrie's job to pick David up in her car, unless that maneuver would cause her to lose sight of the patient. For that reason, David had a Zipcar on standby in the visitor parking lot. If they became separated, she and David could communicate their locations via the two-way radios, which had a thirty-five-mile range.

That was the plan.

Squishy.

It had been hours since David made contact, and in that time Carrie's concern had grown—not to panic levels, but close. She knew McGhee must have been on the neuro recovery unit for several hours by now, but how long it would be until somebody might try to sneak him off the floor was anybody's guess.

The crackle of the radio sent Carrie's heart revving. She felt a surge of excitement, like the first tug on a once-slack fishing line.

"Carrie, are you there?" David spoke in a hushed voice.

"I'm here. What's the status?"

"A male nurse just left McGhee's hospital room. I think he injected something into his IV. Said something about a van coming to the rear entrance in about twenty minutes. Do you copy?"

Carrie scanned her surroundings—the rear entrance was in sight of where she was parked. "I got it. Where are you right now?" she asked.

"Um, that would be a closet in McGhee's cubicle."

"David, you've got to get out of there."

"Well, that's my plan. I'll meet you at the rear entrance, and we'll see if that van shows up."

In the background, Carrie heard loud beeping sounds. Right away she understood that one of the machines hooked to McGhee had just gone haywire. Another alarm sounded, this one much louder.

"Oh no, David," Carrie said into the radio. "Get out of there. Get out right now!"

In a matter of seconds, McGhee's cramped quarters had two nurses at his bedside. Through the slat between the closet doors, David watched them work as a team.

McGhee muttered under his breath, "I feel dizzy . . . dizzy . . . dizzy."

After a minute or so of silence, one of the nurses said, "Blood pressure is eighty-five over forty, heart rate hundred twenty bpm, respiratory sixteen breaths."

"He feels clammy to me," the other nurse said. "Shaking, sweating—does he have diabetes?"

"Not according to the EMR."

"Check his blood sugar anyway."

From out of David's view, a new voice spoke up. It was the same person who had earlier injected McGhee with something.

"What's happening?" the male nurse said. "I was just down the hall when I heard the alarm."

"Nurse Taggart, hello. I think our friend here might be having a blood sugar problem."

"Oh," was all Taggart said.

"I can give two milligrams IM glucagon," said one nurse, "and see what that does for him. I'd like a doctor to see him right away, please."

David felt dizzy and sweaty as well. He could pretty much follow the procedures as they took place, and soon after McGhee got the glucagon, a woman showed up, dark skinned, thin, petite, and introduced herself as Dr. Nisha Kapur.

"Fifty cc D50 stat," Dr. Kapur said. "We treat him first and then confirm with the lab results."

"FS zero," said a nurse. "I sent a venous level to the stat lab."

Dr. Kapur performed a battery of tests on McGhee just as David's left leg started to go numb. Prolonged pressure had cut off communication between the nerves in David's leg and his brain, producing an

array of sensations that included warmth, numbness, and a wholly unpleasant tingling.

"How are you feeling, Mr. McGhee?" Kapur said in an overly loud
voice.

"How are you feeling . . . how are you feeling . . . how are you feeling. Stop asking me!"

Sounds of flailing and twisting limbs alerted David that McGhee was
likely quite agitated and might need to be restrained.

"He's a bit delirious from the DBS surgery still," one nurse said.

Somebody else entered the room. "What's going on?"

"Oh, Dr. Goodwin," Dr. Kapur said. "I didn't know you were here."

"Well, I'm helping out Evan because he was doing DBS surgery today."

Dr. Kapur explained the situation to Dr. Goodwin.

"Don't you think we should transfer him to the med ICU?"

"I can do that," Nurse Taggart said. "It's not a problem."

"Great. Thanks. And I'll head down to alert them that he's on his
way," Goodwin said as she rushed out of the room.

While this took place, David's leg became miserably numb. The feeling of pins and needles digging into his skin was agonizing in ways he
had never experienced. He tried everything to stretch the leg, but the
burning sensation only intensified.

David watched the nurses unhook the monitors, and soon enough
Nurse Taggart wheeled Garrett McGhee out of the room. The two
nurses who stayed behind set to work putting the cubicle back together,
which was now down one bed. Massaging his leg, David tried to ease
the torturous sensation, but to no avail. He had to stretch the leg completely to get any relief, and every second the nurses remained inside
the empty unit was excruciating. They chatted pleasantly, taking their
sweet time.

A minute passed . . . then two . . .

The leg had to move. David flexed his hips and lifted the leg up a few inches. The relief was not quite enough, but it was something. He raised the leg a little bit higher, but this time his right leg moved as well. As it did, he knocked over the portable toilet with his urine inside. The plastic container landed with a soft sound that might not have attracted any attention, but the top came open and the liquid spilled out. David watched in horror as his urine trickled out the bottom of the closet door and cascaded to the floor like a golden waterfall. He could not move an inch to create a dam without pushing open the closet doors.

It did not really matter. A few seconds of the River David was enough for a nurse to take notice. The closet doors swung open with force, and David smiled awkwardly at the startled woman, who let fly a thunderous shriek.

David wasted no time. He sprang from the closet like a jack-in-the-box cut loose from its spring. His right leg landed just fine, but with his left leg asleep, his foot buckled from what he hoped was a temporary paralysis. He nearly collapsed to the floor. The nurse closest to him stumbled back and screamed again, a look of shock stretched across her face. Both nurses were frozen in place, which gave David a head start to hop out of the room. He could feel the sensation in his foot slowly return through the pins and needles. The strength came back fully by the time he reached the stairwell.

From behind, David heard tremendous tumult and commotion, but one phrase stuck out above all others.

"He took the stairs! Call the police!"

David descended one level and went out the first exit he came to, entering the hallway directly below the neuro recovery unit. He tried the nearest door, but it was locked. Time was going to run out on him. He put the radio to his lips.

"Carrie, listen, abort! Abort! I've been spotted. Do you hear me? Respond!"

"David, what's going on?"

David could not answer, because footsteps like a stampede could be heard headed his way. Security was heightened in the aftermath of Carrie's lethal encounter, and David was not surprised by the speed and effectiveness of the response.

He retreated back to the stairs, his only way out. The stairwell door boomed shut behind him. Breathless with anxiety, David shouted into the radio, "I've been spotted and they've called the police."

His voice echoed in the stairwell. From below David heard, "You, up there. Come down with your hands up!"

Nobody was going to wait for David to comply. Loud footsteps were on their way up to greet him.

It would be a hell of an escape, but David was not ready to give up just yet. He left the stairwell for a second time, and reentered the hallway he had just exited. This time, two uniformed police officers were running his way. With no available options, David darted back into the stairwell, where another police officer had just come into view.

"Hands up! Hands up!" David heard.

The officer stood five stairs away and removed what looked like a gun from his holster. David had just put the radio to his lips when the officer flicked his wrist. A square-shaped cartridge spat out the front end of what David now saw was a Taser.

"Carrie, abort! Aboooorr—"

A knifelike pain ripped through David's body the instant those contact points penetrated his right thigh. The pain was like nothing he had ever experienced. His skin felt on fire, immolation from the inside out. Maybe a scream escaped his lips. Hard for him to say. His body vibrated so violently it threatened to break apart.

Twitching, David fell to the concrete, landing hard on his back. Through the slits of his eyes, pushing beyond the pain, the burn, the earthquake of his body, David fixed his gaze on the radio that had tumbled from his grasp. He reached for it, but felt another pinch. A second lightning bolt of electricity coursed through him. His teeth knocked together in a violent chatter as his arms went spastic.

The radio, his lifeline to Carrie, was within reach, but miles away.

CHAPTER 56

Carrie was on the two-way, trying to reach David, when a van pulled up to the rear entrance of the VA. The white cargo van without any windows was the kind that gave Carrie shivers anytime she passed one on the road. She set the radio down on the seat beside her and did not move. Twelve thirty in the morning. Floodlights partially illuminated the back lot, but not Carrie's Volvo, which was parked directly opposite the van, maybe a hundred feet away. The van idled for a minute or two. No action. Just waiting.

Even though she was parked in the shadows, Carrie sank lower in her seat and peered out over the car's front dash. She caught a flash of movement near the van. The hospital rear doors had come open, and out stepped Lee Taggart, dressed in street clothes and pushing a wheelchair. Seated in that wheelchair was a limp-looking man covered in a gray blanket, wearing a baseball cap on his head, which was slumped forward onto his chest. He looked unresponsive, likely very sedated.

It had to be Garrett McGhee.

The van's rear doors sprang open and a huge figure emerged out the back. Carrie recognized him right away. It was Ramón Hernandez.

She'd suspected Taggart, but Hernandez? What was he doing here?

Confusion paralyzed Carrie's mind. Pieces were on the table, but she still could not put them all into the puzzle.

Hernandez jumped to the ground and waited for Taggart to reach him. Together, the two men lifted the wheelchair holding McGhee into the back of the van with ease. To Carrie, to anybody, it looked like a hospital discharge, not a kidnapping. Seconds later, the van slipped into reverse and headed for the exit. And just like that, McGhee was gone.

Carrie waited until the van got some distance before she started her car's engine. She was short of breath, but not determination. The van took a left out of the lot and Carrie followed. She glanced at the two-way radio on the seat beside her. No way to reach David now. He was probably in handcuffs by this point.

Sick as she was about David, she could call somebody for help. From her purse, Carrie retrieved her phone without losing sight of the van. At that moment, the van made a sudden left turn and Carrie pulled to a quick stop on the side of the road, confused.

The turn made no sense to her. The van had gone down the access road to the VA's long-abandoned construction project on the hospital annex. The access road was a dead end, not a through street. Nothing was down that way but the boarded-up brick building.

A few seconds of contemplation, nothing more. She had to follow.

Carrie shut off her car's headlights and took the same turn as the van. It was dark, and hard to see, but Carrie managed not to drive off the potholed road and into a ditch. The four-story building loomed large in front of her. Battered chain-link fencing surrounded the annex, a symbolic "keep out" gesture at best. The structure was built on what appeared to be a weed-strewn sandlot dotted with rusted trash barrels. At the rear of the annex, beyond the fencing, was a dense patch of scraggly-looking trees and a sea of unruly brush.

When Carrie reached the halfway point, she let up on the gas and pulled over to the side of the road. She could see the van in front of her, and that meant the people inside would be able to see her.

The van drove up to the fence and Taggart got out. He pried the fence open where there was not any gate, and secured the pliable metal flap using two bungee cords, creating a makeshift entrance wide enough for the van to drive through. They must have cut the fence so from a distance the perimeter would not appear to have been breached.

Hernandez brought the van close to the building, but kept the engine running. Taggart stayed with McGhee, while Hernandez put the van in reverse and drove back through the fence opening. Carrie panicked, thinking he would drive right past her car, but instead he drove off the road and down what appeared to be a path that cut through the growth behind the annex.

Just like that, the van was gone.

A moment later, Hernandez emerged from a thicket of trees and brush. He went back through the fence and undid the bungee cords holding the flap in place. He caught up to Taggart, who waited for him at what must have been a rear entrance into the abandoned building. Sure enough, Taggart opened a door, and soon all three men vanished inside.

Carrie rolled down her window to battle back a sudden wave of nausea. Only then did she realize she was completely soaked in sweat. She watched the building for a few minutes and felt certain nobody was coming out. Why would Hernandez have hidden the van if he planned to go somewhere anytime soon? *The plan,* Carrie thought. *Get the evidence.* Maybe there was a window, some way for her to take a picture without entering the building.

A voice inside her head spoke up. She was unarmed, outnumbered, and untrained, while Hernandez was solid muscle and a skilled combat vet. No contest.

"Be smart here, Carrie," she said aloud.

Then she remembered the call she'd been about to make. Carrie retrieved her smartphone and dialed a number stored in her contacts. The phone rang four times before somebody finally answered.

Dr. Finley sounded logy. "Yeah, hello?"

"Alistair, it's Carrie. There's an emergency. I need your help." Her speech came out hurried and short of breath.

"Carrie, what on earth? What's going on?"

"The VA Police have my friend David Hoffman in custody right now. You have to tell them he's not a threat. He's with me."

"In custody? Why? And what do you mean he's with you? What are you doing?"

"I don't have time to explain, but there's something terrible happening at the VA. Sandra Goodwin and Cal Trent are kidnapping the DBS patients."

"What?" Dr. Finley sounded fully awake now, and appropriately alarmed.

"They've been experimenting on people, Alistair," Carrie said. "It's not DBS that's curing them. It's some sort of drug they've been given, I'm sure of it—something from CerebroMed, but it doesn't always work. There are side effects like palinacousis, maybe others. And Ramón Hernandez, he's involved, same as the nurse from the VA, Lee Taggart. I just watched them take Garrett McGee off of the neuro recovery unit."

"Carrie, you realize you sound absolutely mad."

"It's happening, whether you want to believe me or not. Now, please—help my friend David and call the police."

"Where are you?"

"I'm at the VA hospital annex construction site. That's where they brought McGhee."

"Okay, okay. Just get out of there. Get out now. I'll call the police and I'll call you right back."

Carrie ended the call. She knew the smart thing to do: get out. Of course she should do just that.

But a thought came to her. *What if the van takes off with McGhee inside before the police arrive?* More proof gone. She should at least get the license plate. It might be a vital bit of evidence the police would need.

Carrie scolded herself for not taking video of the two men lifting McGhee into the back of the van. So much had happened so fast she had not been thinking clearly. She could at least get a picture of the license plate, and then get out of there. For Abington, for Fasciani, for all the vets who had been hurt because of Goodwin and Trent—she owed it to them.

Carrie fired up the engine, but kept the lights off as she drove ahead. If anybody saw her coming, she could slam the car into reverse and make a quick escape. A hundred feet from the chain-link fence, Carrie pulled to the side of the road. She kept the engine running as she got out.

Her feet crunched on the hard-packed dirt, and the glow of city lights in the distance shone like an artificial dawn. Blood pounded in her ears, but she could still hear the drone of millions of buzzing insects that infested the woods where the van had been hidden.

Carrie's nerves were crackling. To her left she saw the path down which Hernandez had driven the van. She vanished inside the forest that bordered the access road and reached the van in a matter of feet. Her hands shook violently, but she managed to get a few pictures of the Massachusetts license plate.

The van itself was completely unremarkable, scuffed up some, dented in places. She did not linger and was soon headed down the path, back to her idling car. The whole trip took a few minutes at most. Carrie settled into the driver's seat and let the feeling of relief wash over her.

As soon as her hands found the steering wheel, Carrie felt a presence rise behind her. Her eyes went to the rearview mirror and she took it all in: the short-cropped hair, strong jawline, broad shoulders. Almost immediately Carrie recognized the silhouette of Terry Bushman, the second vet she had examined.

"Never turn your back on a marine," Bushman said. "We're sneaky bastards."

Carrie screamed and tried to get out, but Bushman reached his powerful arm over the seat and brought it down alongside Carrie's neck. Bushman's left hand pushed against his right wrist. He made a muscle with his right arm that bulged into the side of Carrie's neck.

The pressure was directly on her two carotid arteries, thankfully not her larynx or throat.

One second.

Carrie struggled to break free.

Two seconds.

She tried to scream.

Three seconds.

Her world was gone.

CHAPTER 57

The first thing Carrie noticed was the smell. It was damp and mildewed, like the fetid water of a marsh. There was a whiff of urine, too, as well as a rank body-odor smell that made her want to gag. She felt tender soreness on both sides of her neck, but nothing on her throat. A sick, flulike feeling made it hard to focus. She wondered if she'd been drugged. Probably. What had happened?

As her awareness became more acute, Carrie heard moaning and what sounded like people mumbling. The noises came from both her left and right, and it was different men who spoke. They made strange groaning and grunting sounds. Disturbed. Panicked. She could make out some of the words.

"Get down! Get down!"

The voice that spoke was sharp-edged, but muted, and the words were slurred like somebody talking in their sleep.

A different voice said, "We're taking fire from the north side. Where they at? Where they at?"

More voices blended together. The chatter was best described as incessant, like the buzzing of the insects that occupied the woods behind the annex—only these were human voices, maybe half a dozen in total, mumbling simultaneously.

"I'm hit! I'm hit!"

"Talk, talk, talk to me."

"Oscar Mike! Oscar Mike!"

"Go! Go!"

"Clear!"

"The rounds are firing downwind."

On and on it went, without letup, until the chorus of voices became a single droning noise that Carrie could ignore. Her eyes fluttered open and she focused on what appeared to be the stripes of a mattress. It smelled, too—truly foul, just like the rest of this space.

With great effort Carrie managed to push onto her hands and knees. She lifted her head groggily and blinked rapidly. Her vision must not have cleared entirely, because what she saw made no sense to her. It looked like she was inside a dog kennel of some kind. Galvanized tubular frames held in place heavy-duty-gauge chain-link wire. The wire covered all sides of the welded structure, including the top. The single door, framed with galvanized tubes and covered in wire, was secured with a heavy chain and a heavy-duty padlock.

Carrie looked right and saw three additional kennels all in a row. Inside each wired enclosure was a thin and dirty man. Each of the three men sported a different stage of facial hair growth, as if it marked the length of his stay here. One had stubble, one had a full beard, and one looked like the Taliban. The man in the cage closest to Carrie rested on a grimy mattress, while the other two paced about their enclosures like animals at the zoo. Each man had sunken, hollow eyes, and a vacant stare. Those who moved about ambled with a zombie's gait. They wore blue hospital scrubs that were soiled and tattered and in such deplorable condition it made them look like shipwreck survivors. Affixed to each man's arm was an IV drip, secured in place with tape and hooked to a rolling metal IV stand. All three men muttered to themselves and seemed completely oblivious to Carrie's presence.

Inside each kennel was a blue bucket, into which Carrie watched one man urinate. Water bottles were strewn about, and trays with food scraps attracted a large congregation of buzzing flies. The cement floor, the color of rust, was damp with puddles and chipped in spots. Carrie noticed several coiled-up hoses outside the cages—showers, she thought—and drains spaced throughout to capture any excess water.

Lining a concrete wall to Carrie's left was a bank of decrepit-looking washing machines and dryers, some fallen over, some with broken glass and dimpled sides, all industrial strength. She knew then that this was the abandoned laundry facility of the old annex building. A tall pile of industrial laundry machines, like a mini-mountain of junkyard scrap, occupied a sizable area in the center of the cavernous space. Carrie believed she was in a subterranean room, with thick concrete columns peppered throughout to distribute and support the building's substantial weight. Overhead banks of fluorescent lights lit the old laundry facility from above, and flickered on and off as if they were sending Morse code.

"Hey, why are you standing? Get the hell down, or get shot!"

Carrie spun her head in the direction of the voice. Three more kennels stood to her left, but only two had people inside them. The far cage appeared to hold the man Carrie believed to be Garrett McGhee. The person in the cage closest to her, who had ordered her down, caused Carrie's jaw to come unhinged. It was Eric Fasciani! He was skeletal-looking, fierce with his gaze, haunted in every way imaginable.

Like the others, Fasciani wore soiled scrubs. His thin arms were covered in scabbed-over scratches, and Carrie noticed gruesome scratches on his neck as well. His face was bearded like the other men. Nobody shaved them. Nobody took care of them. Lab rats were treated better than this, at least for a while.

"Eric, what are you doing here? What is this place?"

Carrie spoke in a hushed whisper, afraid someone might come for her.

"What are you doing . . . what are you doing . . . stop saying that . . . got Taliban crawling all over this place. We gonna have to shoot our way out."

"Eric, please, talk to me. Tell me what's happening here."

"He can't hear you, Carrie Bryant, not really. Not in the way you understand it."

Carrie's breath caught at the sound of the man's voice. Her heart sank and her spirit cracked wide open. For a few frozen moments, Carrie could not move. She swallowed a jet of bile as the fear set in and anger cooked inside. With gritted teeth, Carrie wheeled and set her frightened gaze on the man who spoke.

Dr. Alistair Finley.

CHAPTER 58

"What the hell are you doing?" Carrie screamed at Dr. Finley. "Let me go! Let me out of here!"

Dressed in his trademark oxford shirt and khaki pants, Dr. Finley had a pressed, clean appearance that made the other men's condition look even more deplorable. He approached with honest sympathy in his eyes. Almost a look of heartache, as though he knew Carrie's fate and deeply regretted it. He came over to her kennel and locked his fingers around the wire.

Meanwhile, Fasciani continued to bark and mutter and speak unintelligibly, but Carrie no longer concentrated on what he said. Her entire focus remained on Dr. Finley and three men who accompanied him into this dank cellar: Terry Bushman, Ramón Hernandez, and Lee Taggart, who held in his hand a long rodlike implement with two pointed prongs on the end. A few of the men in cages took notice of the cattle prod in Taggart's hand, and sank to the back of their kennels as though they'd been conditioned to react that way.

Carrie lunged at the wire, causing Dr. Finley to rip his hands away before she could grab them. With as much force as she could muster, Carrie shook the cage, but managed to make it rattle and nothing more. These kennels were bolted into the cement and would not budge no matter how much she tried. None of the men down here, those inside the cages or out, reacted to Carrie's rage.

"You need to calm down, Carrie," Dr. Finley said. "Nobody can hear you scream. Your outbursts will do you no good, and I have questions to ask. Important questions. If you yell, or don't cooperate, Braxton will administer a painful shock with this livestock prod."

"Braxton?" Carrie said.

Dr. Finley became aware of Carrie's confusion. "Ah, of course, Nurse Lee Taggart is in actuality Braxton Price, and he's as skilled as these other two gentlemen, if not more so. So you'll need to cooperate now, Carrie. It's vital for you."

Carrie focused her thoughts to compartmentalize her fear and terror. "What is this? What is going on here?"

Dr. Finley kept some distance from the cage as he removed his spectacles and rubbed at his eyes.

"This, Carrie," Dr. Finley said, gesturing to the kennels of men, "is how we're going to cure PTSD."

Carrie hated to hear Dr. Finley speak her name. It felt like another violation of her trust. She shook her head, disbelieving. She focused on the words the men in these cages spoke—playacted, it now seemed— and Carrie understood in a way she had not before that they seemed to be trapped inside a virtual reality simulation, one of war and bloodshed, a place where the gunfire never let up.

"What have you done to them?"

Easy does it, Carrie warned herself. *Don't lose your temper. They'll hurt you if you do.*

"I'm helping them," Dr. Finley said. "Well, not them exactly, but others like them. These men are pioneers, Carrie. These are men who will give us a window into the secret world of the traumatized brain. These men are heroes."

Carrie's sense of Dr. Finley's program was coming into sharper focus. A sickly chill overtook her.

"They're all homeless, aren't they?" she whispered. "Like Steve, like Eric, these men are vets who were living on the street, people nobody noticed and nobody missed."

"They fit the criteria we needed."

"And you!" Carrie's eyes turned fierce as she set her gaze on Ramón Hernandez and Terry Bushman. "You were like them, you were on the streets, too. How could you let this happen to these men?"

"Actually," Dr. Finley said, "Ramón and Terry weren't like them at all. They're both former members of Braxton's military squad. And they helped to—oh, let's call it *recruit* vets for our program. I was quite impressed when you discovered Ramón had a connection to Steve Abington that preceded our efforts here. You're a very clever woman."

Carrie gripped the wires again. "But you cured them both," she said.

"No," Dr. Finley answered. "I performed DBS surgery on them, and that's all. These men never had PTSD. And their implants produce no electrical discharge. To be blunt, they are part of our dog-and-pony show for the federal government, to ensure we continue to receive more funding. You see, Cal Trent needed to show progress to the higher-ups at DARPA, and sadly vets like Steve Abington were not going to do the trick. Not yet, anyway."

"What is this?" Carrie said, gesturing to Eric's IV drip. "What is in those IVs?" What had she gotten herself into?

"You actually had it figured out, Carrie," Dr. Finley said. "You just didn't quite put it all together."

"CerebroMed," Carrie said. "Bob Richardson."

"Richardson and CerebroMed," Dr. Finley repeated. "But it's not all Bob's doing, not by a long shot. I had the basis for the chemical properties of Deleritum and brought it to Richardson's attention."

"Deleritum?" Carrie asked.

"From the Latin verb meaning 'to erase.'"

Dr. Finley's ego and overweening pride would keep him talking, revealing secrets Carrie longed to know, but dreaded to hear.

"What is Deleritum?" Carrie spat out the word.

"It's a drug, Carrie, that reconsolidates bad memories causing PTSD symptoms," Dr. Finley answered matter-of-factly. "The drug is a highly modified form of MDMA, which you know better as the street drug ecstasy. Our lab is located down here, but I'm sure you had no idea. There are no nasty fumes, and not a lot of highly suspicious chemicals involved. Richardson is our supplier, and that service can't be undervalued. CerebroMed has been after something like this for years. Richardson stands to make a lot of money from this discovery, but money isn't everything."

Carrie was aware that the compounds found in MDMA had been shown to dampen the amygdala, which would allow people to re-engage with the negative experiences without significant consequence.

"It all has to do with perseverating memory," Dr. Finley continued. "We needed a way to trigger the memory so that it persisted in the amygdala, where we could then use DBS to neutralize the emotion. The problem was getting the memory to perseverate properly."

Carrie's eyes went wide with a look of horror. "Virtual reality didn't work, did it? You needed drugs to make it happen," she said.

"We needed drugs and a way to test them. Animals aren't very good at telling us their feelings. It might not look to you like we're close to a breakthrough here, but we are. A few more trials and we'll have something truly remarkable."

"But these drugs don't work," Carrie said. "These men are lost."

"Well, they do in some ways. It's a process, you see."

Carrie's thoughts were gelling, and those disparate threads Dr. Finley had referenced connected in ways she could not possibly have imagined. The word that flashed in her mind like neon on Broadway was "perseverate." It meant a thought or action repeated long after a stimulus that prompted a response had ceased. For some of these men, Deleritum made the war live on in their minds. Their trauma continued unabated—*perseverated,* in medical parlance—but for some, that perseveration manifested as palinacousis.

Dr. Finley observed Carrie thoughtfully. "So you do understand now, don't you?"

Carrie felt gravely ill, weak throughout her body. "Have you cured anybody?" she asked.

Dr. Finley appeared a bit contrite. "There are flashes of real lucidity, yes, and the length varies—sometimes weeks—but eventually significant deteriorations recur. A few of the patients just have the palinacousis side effect, no lingering PTSD symptoms, but that's happened only a handful of times. Of course those are the ones we're most excited about."

Carrie felt confused. "Steve Abington—he communicated with me. He talked about his friend Roach before he attacked me. Was he one of those men? Is he still alive?"

"No, I'm afraid not. The sedatives we gave him pre-op dampened the effects of Deleritum significantly, but as soon as those drugs wore off he was completely lost. Same as your friend Eric, here."

Carrie looked down the row of cages. None of them appeared to be engaged with reality.

"But you said some people just have the palinacousis side effect. Where are those men?"

"They didn't make it."

"*Make* it? What do you do, Alistair—just execute them?"

"They might have trouble with hearing," Dr. Finley said, "but their mouths work just fine."

"You're a monster," Carrie said. "All of you. Monsters!"

Hernandez took a threatening step toward Carrie's cage. She retreated a few steps, forgetting for a moment the barrier between them.

"These guys were gone anyway," Hernandez said. "Why not put the body and mind to good use?"

"And what do you get out of this deal?" Carrie asked bitterly.

"Me?" Hernandez touched a finger to his chest. "I'm helping to fix one of the biggest problems in the military and make a fortune doing it. What more do you want?"

"Is that it for you, Alistair?" Carrie asked. "Is it about the money?"

"No," Dr. Finley said with a shake of his head. "It's about the results. Think about what a drug like Deleritum can do for the world. The trauma of war, of rape, of child abuse, fatal accidents, death and grief, all of it can be neutralized. I can bring happiness to the world. True peace of mind. What's that worth, Carrie? I think it's worth the sacrifice of these men."

"I think you don't want to go through the proper channels and develop a drug under the guidelines of the FDA. I think you want your glory and you want it now."

Dr. Finley shrugged off the rebuke. "There's a certain truth to what you say," he admitted. "I would like to be alive when I finally get the recognition and respect I deserve. Who wouldn't want to go down in history as the person who unlocked the secrets of the mind?"

"And Sandra Goodwin will have a state-of-the-art neurosurgical practice to run. I guess she gets something out of the deal, too," Carrie said.

"We all have our motivators in life," Dr. Finley said.

Carrie shook on the inside and out. Whether it was hubris or ego, Dr. Finley needed Carrie to understand his motives, to accept them if possible.

"Sam Rockwell knew what you were doing, didn't he?"

Dr. Finley got a distant look in his eyes, almost a pained expression. "Sam was a dear friend. And he supported us from the start. He saw the greater good."

"By 'us,' you mean Navarro and Goodwin."

Dr. Finley scoffed. "Sandra yes, but Evan, no. That boy is a flea whom I utterly despise, as does Sandra. But he's a good soldier and he does as Sandra says. Unlike you."

Carrie felt nauseated all over again. *Turfing.* Sandra Goodwin had fostered the perfect work culture to make these patients disappear. "When these vets leave the floor they become other people's problems," Carrie said, almost to herself. "Navarro never bothered to look at the number of medical complications associated with DBS. To him it was just one less thing to worry about. So you killed Sam because why? He didn't want to play along?"

"So to speak," Dr. Finley said. "But believe me, I did not want to hurt him. Same as I don't want to hurt you. Sam left me no choice. I do have a heart, Carrie. We could have killed him when the accident didn't." Dr. Finley put the word "accident" inside air quotes. "But I told Braxton to leave him be. In his condition his family at least had a sprig of hope for his recovery, and he was no threat to me."

"Until he woke up."

A dark cloud crossed Dr. Finley's face. "If you hadn't been on your way to see him, we might have been able to handle it differently. As it was, you forced us to improvise. Why couldn't you have just done your job and inserted those wires while we did the rest?"

"It's not who I am."

"That, I'm afraid, was my miscalculation. Now I need to know: besides David Hoffman, who else have you told?"

Cold terror seeped into Carrie's bones. "No, no, not David. He doesn't know anything."

Dr. Finley returned an annoyed look. "Don't play me for a fool," he said. "Who else have you told?"

Carrie would not answer.

"Your entire family is in danger now, Carrie. Be honest here. Who else have you told?"

"Go screw yourself." Carrie bent down, grabbed the empty blue bucket beside her, and hurled it as hard as she could against the wire. The bucket bounced back and nearly hit her in the face before it clattered noisily to the ground.

Dr. Finley turned his attention to Braxton. "Come with me to the lab. I'd like to have a word with you in private before we go and deal with Mr. Hoffman."

Braxton showed Carrie a syringe. "I used this to take care of Sam Rockwell after I ran you off the road," he said, a cold glint in his eyes. Ruefully, he added, "Guess I should have taken you out that day, after all."

Dr. Finley took a single step toward the exit, but turned back to address Carrie once more.

"I'm so sorry it's come to this," he said. "I really thought we could continue our efforts with you on board. The thought of landing a top-notch neurosurgeon so soon after we dealt with Sam was simply out of the question. I figured we'd have to go dark for some time. But then you came along. Like a miracle, really. The timing honestly could not have been better. And given your . . . past, well, I assumed you'd follow the rules and just do your job. Insert wires. Go home. Why would you rock the boat? You should have been the ultimate good soldier, Carrie. Sandra was right about you. You really were a loose cannon all along."

Braxton followed Dr. Finley to the exit.

"What are you going to do to me?" Carrie yelled.

Dr. Finley turned to Braxton. "He was your friend."

Braxton looked over at Carrie and then to Bushman. "Shooting an unarmed woman inside a cage isn't really my style. Bushman, kill the bitch."

Bushman's eyes flared as he took a pistol from an ankle holster. "As you wish," he said.

Braxton and Dr. Finley disappeared through an exit door. The vets' mumbling flooded Carrie's ears once again.

Bushman and Hernandez consulted one another for a bit, out of Carrie's earshot. When Bushman approached, he had venom in his eyes. Then he softened. For a second, Carrie thought he was going to let her go.

"It won't hurt, I promise," he said, almost apologetically.

Carrie fell to her knees as tears streamed down her face.

"Any last words?" Hernandez asked.

Carrie began to convulse. The fear, the pure terror of knowing these were her final few seconds, overwhelmed her. She really had no way out. Death had come for her.

In that moment Carrie's resolve thickened. She caught her breath and with great effort, fixed her gaze on Bushman. She would not die with her eyes closed. She would stare into the face of her killer. It was the last bit of humanity she had left.

Bushman's outstretched arm was like a steel rod. The pistol in his hand did not waver.

"Do you have anything to say?" Bushman asked.

"Yeah, get the fuck away from my sister."

Carrie heard an enormous bang, a bright flash of light that came from her right. In the very next instant, Terry Bushman's entire head vanished inside an explosion of blood, brains, and bone.

CHAPTER 59

All Carrie could see was the blur of her brother, Adam, as he charged into the room, his rifle aimed at Ramón Hernandez. Bushman had crumpled to the floor, his face no longer recognizable beneath a gruesome crimson mask. The gun tumbled from Bushman's lifeless hand and skidded close to Fasciani's cage, far out of Carrie's reach. Several flashes erupted from the barrel of Adam's rifle, but Hernandez dropped to the floor with startling quickness, and as he did, removed a pistol from his holster.

"Look out, Adam!" Carrie screamed. As she spoke those words, bright flashes erupted from Hernandez's gun, aimed in Adam's direction.

Trapped inside their cages, the vets reacted to the sudden tumult as though they were part of the action. Some took cover, while others held up their arms and fired make-believe weapons at invisible targets.

With his feet in constant motion, Adam zigzagged using quick cuts that avoided the hail of bullets. The muffled pops from Hernandez's weapon rang out in the hollow enclosure. Feeling helpless beyond measure, Carrie grabbed the chain-link wire of her prison cell and pulled futilely, watching the scene unfold as if in slow motion.

Adam, surefooted and dexterous, veered left, then right in a series of sharp turns that closed the gap between him and Hernandez considerably. Seeking protection, Adam took shelter behind one of the many thick concrete support columns and opened a line of fire at Hernandez, who immediately returned volley. Bright flashes hindered her vision, but Carrie saw a few bullets fired by Hernandez smack into the concrete column that shielded her brother. Several more hit the ground near Adam's feet.

Hernandez's fire paused, during which Adam leaned out and got off several shots. Adam had a pistol strapped to his waist, but he seemed to prefer the accuracy of his rifle.

Of the six or so shots Adam fired, one hit the intended target. A geyser of blood erupted from Hernandez's punctured arm. He let out a savage scream. Clamping his hand over the wound, Hernandez found cover behind the tall pile of detritus laundry machines discarded nearby. For the moment, at least, he was out of Adam's direct firing line.

Adam let fly several shots, but those did nothing against Hernandez's massive steel barricade. To Carrie's horror, Adam unsheathed an enormous bowie knife from an ankle holster and slipped out from behind the protection of the support column. Holding the rifle one-handed, Adam fired several more shots designed to hold Hernandez in place. He set the rifle on the ground without making a sound. His finger went to his lips, urging Carrie's silence.

Adam approached the fortification of laundry machines stealthily, taking quick steps. Hernandez may have been reloading, or recovering, during the short respite, which allowed Adam to reach the barricade without incident. With a sudden burst of motion, Adam shot forward and ascended the metal mountain with the skill and grace of a ram.

Hernandez, sensing imminent danger, came up from his hiding place and raised his weapon to fire. At that same instant, Adam reached the top of the pile, and he leapt down on Hernandez, arms and legs spread-eagled, the knife clutched in his hand like a deadly talon.

The two entangled men vanished behind the metal mound, out of Carrie's sight. When they finally emerged, Adam had the knife poised above Hernandez's head, pressing with all his might. Hernandez grimaced as he parried the knife attack with his right hand, while his left clutched Adam's throat. The two men tussled and spun in a violent ballet.

Adam's color began to change, alarming red to terrifying blue, and the strength in his arm began to fade. Hernandez managed to bend the wrist enough to turn the blade against Adam. Then Hernandez applied tremendous pressure that bent the arm and inched the blade closer to Adam's heart.

Adam grunted and snorted as he tried to battle back.

The blade still moved closer.

"No!" Carrie screamed.

But there was no stopping it now. Hernandez plunged the knife into Adam's chest, burying it up to the hilt. Adam's mouth fell open, but no sound escaped. As he stumbled backward, Adam used his right hand to retrieve the pistol from its holster. He flicked his wrist and fired a shot that struck Hernandez in the stomach. Adam shot again, in the heart this time, and Hernandez went slack as his eyes bugged out. They fell on top of each other and Adam fired two more times, into the stomach area. Those bullets exploded out Hernandez's back and made his body jump as if it had been electrocuted.

Adam rolled Hernandez off of him, and fished a ring full of keys from the dead man's pockets. With great exertion, Adam staggered to his feet, with the knife still protruding from his chest. Tears streamed down Carrie's face as Adam stumbled toward her cage. Blood sputtered from Adam's throat, painting the floor with bright red dots. He fumbled with the keys, but dropped to his knees before he could put one in the lock.

Carrie fell to the floor with him and stuck her hands through the wire to hold her brother upright. She moved her hands up a few holes in the wire to caress Adam's bloodstained face. His body listed from side to side, unsteady in her grasp, as if he were being tossed by waves.

"Adam, Adam, what are you doing here? Oh, Adam."

"I . . . followed . . . you. Been following you." The rasp in Adam's voice, the rattle in his chest, cleaved Carrie's heart.

Carrie recalled the Camaro she had seen in her rearview mirror. She'd thought little of it, but the car *had* belonged to her brother.

"I saw you," Carrie said.

Adam broke into that trademark smile of his, but this time flashed Carrie teeth that were stained bloodred.

"You followed them," Adam managed. "And I followed you. Protect, you—finally got the damn car working. Didn't tell you . . . told nobody, didn't want you to spot me. Guess you did anyway . . ."

There were certainly opportunities for Adam to come and go without anybody at home to notice. Maybe her parents had seen his car was gone, but with her phone shut off they had no way to reach her.

Adam's eyes glazed over.

"No," Carrie whimpered, and she held on tighter. "Don't you die on me. Don't you do it."

"Love you, sis," Adam said. It was obvious that incredible strength was required for Adam to push the key ring toward Carrie's cage. "Get out. Get out of here."

"No, I'm not letting go."

Adam glanced down at the knife buried in his chest. "I am," he said. "I am."

With that, Adam's body went limp. The eyes Carrie had seen full of both laughter and rage turned glassy and vacant. His expression, drained, became nearly serene.

Carrie sobbed and stretched through the wire to clutch her brother in her arms. She was still holding on to him when Braxton Price and Dr. Finley returned to the laundry room and saw the incredible carnage. Price drew his gun and took aim at Carrie, who would not for a second let go of her brother. She put her head up against the wire, desperate to feel more connected to Adam. Her eyes closed and she waited for death to come.

"They don't pay me enough," Price said.

A gunshot rang out, and then another.

Carrie looked just as a bullet lodged dead center into Price's skull. Price went limp, and he dropped to the ground like a marionette separated from its strings. A third gunshot sounded; this one hit Dr. Finley in the neck. Clutching the wound, Dr. Finley spun around in frantic circles, blood spewing through his fingers, spraying in all directions, a look of horror on his face. He tumbled to the floor near Price's inert body, where he convulsed and gurgled on the blood that now filled his throat, until his spasms stopped and he went perfectly still.

Confused by who had fired, Carrie turned her head in the direction of those gunshots. She saw Eric Fasciani, on his feet in a firing stance, IV in his arm, holding Bushman's smoking pistol in his right hand.

Fasciani looked over at Carrie and said, "Sergeant! Sergeant! I got two confirmed kills here, that's two confirmed kills."

EPILOGUE

Only certain sections of the Arlington Cemetery allow private headstone markers to be placed. Adam's marker was a simple design, dignified, and appropriate for a military setting. The inscription was factual: name, rank, date of birth, date of death, and a short phrase that required special approval. It read: *Remember those with invisible wounds.*

Spring days, like this seventy-degree delight in mid April, are seldom so spectacular, and the warm breeze made the freshly bloomed cherry blossoms smell even sweeter. The cemetery was mostly deserted at that midday hour, except for Howard and Irene Bryant, who were walking arm in arm back to their rental car parked nearby—and for David and Carrie, who lingered behind, holding hands, gazing at Adam's gravestone with somber expressions.

Carrie clutched in her hand the qualification number from her recent running of the Boston Marathon. She put the number on the grass in front of Adam's grave and used a rock she'd brought with her to hold it in place. When she stood, her eyes were filled with tears, and she clutched David's hand for comfort.

"I didn't do great, little brother," Carrie said, her voice cracking with emotion. "But I finished. Can't believe we lived in Hopkinton all those years and never bothered to run the big race. Well, I ran it for you. For Steve, for Eric, for all the vets. I raised about two thousand dollars for the Red Sox's Home Base Program, too, which I guess is pretty good. It'll help other vets suffering from PTSD, so I hope you're pleased."

Carrie's throat closed. She tried to take a breath, but a sob came out instead. It took time before she could speak again. When she did, her voice was soft and it trembled.

"I miss you every day, and I love you so very much," Carrie said through her gathering tears. "So here's the big news Mom and Dad told you I was going to share. Sandra Goodwin was finally sentenced today. That's really why we came down. I wanted to be here when it happened so I could tell you personally. It took *a year* for the trial," Carrie said. "Can you believe it's been a year? Well, she's going to spend the rest of her life in prison for what she did. Cal Trent and Bob Richardson— well, their trials are still under way, but they'll get the same, don't you worry about it."

Carrie fished a tissue from her purse and used it to wipe away the tears. She remembered something else to tell her brother.

"They found a burial site."

Buried. Burned.

Carrie had heard all about the gruesome details of the killings, since she became close with the new secretary of Veterans Affairs. There had been eleven killings, they thought, but it could be more. Bodies turned to ash. The former secretary had resigned in disgrace, along with the medical director at the Boston VA, even though he claimed no involvement with Dr. Finley's program, no knowledge that DARPA's blood money funded a nightmare factory.

"Not much new to report on Eric's condition, or the others," Carrie said. "They're still suffering significant neurological damage. But the irony is, Dr. Finley might have been onto something all along. We've gone through his case files and there's something there. Using DBS to cure PTSD is not so far-fetched after all."

Carrie's composure cracked again, and she took a moment to recover. David gripped her hand tighter, but the heavy sadness felt like a boulder on her chest.

"I know it sounds horrible to say, but I'd rather you and the others didn't die in vain. And I guess on that note, I have some more good news to share. I matched with a residency program at the Cleveland Clinic. I'll be starting in September, and they want me to continue work on treating PTSD and other trauma using DBS. I've given this a lot of thought, and I've decided I'm not going to back away. There's an answer to the problem, a way to do the treatment that's safe and effective. It'll take years, and lots of hard work to figure it out, but the effort will pay off one day, I know it. What these people did was horrible, beyond words, but I'm choosing to blame the doctors, not the medicine."

Carrie leaned her head on David's shoulder as a strong wind kicked up. She brushed the hair from her face and gave a strained smile.

"I feel the wind. Is that you talking, Adam? I sure hope so. I hope you approve. Anyway, I think about you every day. Mom and Dad do, too. We all love you so much."

Carrie shut her eyes tight, but those tears leaked out anyway. After a few minutes, she and David turned and walked over to where Howard and Irene stood, and all four embraced.

"We'll meet you for dinner later?" Irene asked, dabbing at her eyes with a handkerchief.

"Yeah," Carrie said. "Just text me the place and the time and we'll be there."

Howard leaned over to kiss Carrie on the forehead, and pulled her into his arms. "I love you so much, kiddo," he said in a shaky voice. "I'm so proud to call you my daughter."

Carrie hugged her father hard as she ever had. Then they were apart, two pairs headed for separate cars. Howard and Irene got into their sedan, while Carrie climbed into the driver's seat of Adam's fire-red Camaro, with David taking the passenger seat beside her. The car had made the long journey from Hopkinton to D.C. without one mechanical problem. Evidently, Adam needed inspiration to get it working right, and watching out for his sister's safety had provided more than enough.

Carrie fired up the engine and started to drive when David's cell phone rang.

"David here," he answered.

There was a long series of pauses as David said things like, "Uh-huh, oh good, yeah, sure, of course, that sounds fine, of course."

He ended the call and said nothing.

Carrie looked over at him. "Well?"

"Well what?" David asked.

"Who called?"

"Anneke from the *Lowell Observer*."

"What about?"

"The Pulitzer," David said. "I won."

Carrie laughed. "That's how you celebrate?"

"Not a real celebratory occasion, and it's a story I wish I didn't have to write."

"David, it's fantastic news. I'm so proud of you. I really am."

Carrie used one hand to drive, and the other to give David's hand a squeeze.

"There's more," David said. "I've apparently been offered an assignment for *The New York Times*. They want me to go to Sierra Leone for a couple months."

"Oh my. That sounds dangerous."

"I'm a stringer, Carrie. I go where the story is."

Carrie pulled her hand away and focused on the road.

"What?" David asked.

"I'm moving to Cleveland soon," Carrie said. "We haven't really talked about us, and now you're going away."

David smiled and touched Carrie's face with much tenderness. "I'm a stringer," he said. "I go where the story is. And you're the story I want to follow for the rest of my life."

Carrie took David's hand and this time gave it a kiss. She pressed down on the gas, and the Camaro shot forward like a rocket ship. For a moment Carrie felt Adam's presence in the seat behind her, his hand resting on her shoulder, a broad grin on his face, that twinkle in his eyes.

And on she drove.

She drove.

A NOTE FROM DANIEL PALMER

Dear Readers:

Every September, after submitting his latest novel to St. Martin's Press, my father would immediately begin to brainstorm. What kind of story would he be sharing with his readers next? Autumn 2013 was no exception. Pop knew he wanted his twentieth thriller to return to the hospital setting that was the hallmark of his earlier works. The protagonist would be a young female resident who encounters a desperate patient with the repeated claim, "I don't belong here." The doctor begins to believe the patient, investigates, and soon descends into a labyrinth of murder and corruption.

Dad's next story was in place. Then, in October of 2013, my father died suddenly.

I don't know how long my dad would have kept writing. He had no plans to stop. He had journals and file folders filled with ideas. With each novel, my father aimed to deliver his very best because he cared deeply for his readers. When news broke of his passing, my inbox flooded with messages from fans around the world.

Even though he was a bestselling novelist published in over thirty languages, the business of writing was sometimes lonely for my dad. It meant blank pages, solitude, and deadlines. But something changed for him in 2009. That was the year I landed my first publishing contract.

I was working from home doing consulting and writing. My dad was at his office, too, some sixty miles to the south. I'd leave my iChat application running all day so whenever Pop wanted a little face time, he could just dial me up online and there I'd be. Or me and his grandkids, or all of us plus his daughter-in-law. We would jawbone about plots until our fingers grew itchy to do some key tapping. I learned the craft of writing from my father during those long talks. Remembering them gave me confidence that I could run with his great premise for TRAUMA.

Working on the book proved to be a remarkable and deeply emotional journey. When the email from Dad's beloved editor Jennifer Enderlin came in accepting the manuscript, I said aloud, "We did it, Pop."

I can't replace my father; nobody can. But I can continue his legacy, and that's a thrill and an honor that leaves me humbled and incredibly grateful.

In friendship,

Daniel Palmer

RECIPROCALS OF BASIC FUNCTIONS

18. $\int \dfrac{1}{1 \pm \sin u}\, du = \tan u \mp \sec u + C$

19. $\int \dfrac{1}{1 \pm \cos u}\, du = -\cot u \pm \csc u + C$

20. $\int \dfrac{1}{1 \pm \tan u}\, du = \frac{1}{2}(u \pm \ln|\cos u \pm \sin u|) + C$

21. $\int \dfrac{1}{\sin u \cos u}\, du = \ln|\tan u| + C$

22. $\int \dfrac{1}{1 \pm \cot u}\, du = \frac{1}{2}(u \mp \ln|\sin u \pm \cos u|) + C$

23. $\int \dfrac{1}{1 \pm \sec u}\, du = u + \cot u \mp \csc u + C$

24. $\int \dfrac{1}{1 \pm \csc u}\, du = u - \tan u \pm \sec u + C$

25. $\int \dfrac{1}{1 \pm e^u}\, du = u - \ln(1 \pm e^u) + C$

POWERS OF TRIGONOMETRIC FUNCTIONS

26. $\int \sin^2 u\, du = \frac{1}{2}u - \frac{1}{4}\sin 2u + C$

27. $\int \cos^2 u\, du = \frac{1}{2}u + \frac{1}{4}\sin 2u + C$

28. $\int \tan^2 u\, du = \tan u - u + C$

29. $\int \sin^n u\, du = -\dfrac{1}{n}\sin^{n-1} u \cos u + \dfrac{n-1}{n}\int \sin^{n-2} u\, du$

30. $\int \cos^n u\, du = \dfrac{1}{n}\cos^{n-1} u \sin u + \dfrac{n-1}{n}\int \cos^{n-2} u\, du$

31. $\int \tan^n u\, du = \dfrac{1}{n-1}\tan^{n-1} u - \int \tan^{n-2} u\, du$

32. $\int \cot^2 u\, du = -\cot u - u + C$

33. $\int \sec^2 u\, du = \tan u + C$

34. $\int \csc^2 u\, du = -\cot u + C$

35. $\int \cot^n u\, du = -\dfrac{1}{n-1}\cot^{n-1} u - \int \cot^{n-2} u\, du$

36. $\int \sec^n u\, du = \dfrac{1}{n-1}\sec^{n-2} u \tan u + \dfrac{n-2}{n-1}\int \sec^{n-2} u\, du$

37. $\int \csc^n u\, du = -\dfrac{1}{n-1}\csc^{n-2} u \cot u + \dfrac{n-2}{n-1}\int \csc^{n-2} u\, du$

PRODUCTS OF TRIGONOMETRIC FUNCTIONS

38. $\int \sin mu \sin nu\, du = -\dfrac{\sin(m+n)u}{2(m+n)} + \dfrac{\sin(m-n)u}{2(m-n)} + C$

39. $\int \cos mu \cos nu\, du = \dfrac{\sin(m+n)u}{2(m+n)} + \dfrac{\sin(m-n)u}{2(m-n)} + C$

40. $\int \sin mu \cos nu\, du = -\dfrac{\cos(m+n)u}{2(m+n)} - \dfrac{\cos(m-n)u}{2(m-n)} + C$

41. $\int \sin^m u \cos^n u\, du = -\dfrac{\sin^{m-1} u \cos^{n+1} u}{m+n} + \dfrac{m-1}{m+n}\int \sin^{m-2} u \cos^n u\, du$

$$= \dfrac{\sin^{m+1} u \cos^{n-1} u}{m+n} + \dfrac{n-1}{m+n}\int \sin^m u \cos^{n-2} u\, du$$

PRODUCTS OF TRIGONOMETRIC AND EXPONENTIAL FUNCTIONS

42. $\int e^{au} \sin bu\, du = \dfrac{e^{au}}{a^2+b^2}(a \sin bu - b \cos bu) + C$

43. $\int e^{au} \cos bu\, du = \dfrac{e^{au}}{a^2+b^2}(a \cos bu + b \sin bu) + C$

POWERS OF u MULTIPLYING OR DIVIDING BASIC FUNCTIONS

44. $\int u \sin u\, du = \sin u - u \cos u + C$

45. $\int u \cos u\, du = \cos u + u \sin u + C$

46. $\int u^2 \sin u\, du = 2u \sin u + (2 - u^2)\cos u + C$

47. $\int u^2 \cos u\, du = 2u \cos u + (u^2 - 2)\sin u + C$

48. $\int u^n \sin u\, du = -u^n \cos u + n\int u^{n-1}\cos u\, du$

49. $\int u^n \cos u\, du = u^n \sin u - n\int u^{n-1}\sin u\, du$

50. $\int u^n \ln u\, du = \dfrac{u^{n+1}}{(n+1)^2}[(n+1)\ln u - 1] + C$

51. $\int u e^u\, du = e^u(u - 1) + C$

52. $\int u^n e^u\, du = u^n e^u - n\int u^{n-1} e^u\, du$

53. $\int u^n a^u\, du = \dfrac{u^n a^u}{\ln a} - \dfrac{n}{\ln a}\int u^{n-1} a^u\, du + C$

54. $\int \dfrac{e^u\, du}{u^n} = -\dfrac{e^u}{(n-1)u^{n-1}} + \dfrac{1}{n-1}\int \dfrac{e^u\, du}{u^{n-1}}$

55. $\int \dfrac{a^u\, du}{u^n} = -\dfrac{a^u}{(n-1)u^{n-1}} + \dfrac{\ln a}{n-1}\int \dfrac{a^u\, du}{u^{n-1}}$

56. $\int \dfrac{du}{u \ln u} = \ln|\ln u| + C$

POLYNOMIALS MULTIPLYING BASIC FUNCTIONS

57. $\int p(u) e^{au}\, du = \dfrac{1}{a}p(u)e^{au} - \dfrac{1}{a^2}p'(u)e^{au} + \dfrac{1}{a^3}p''(u)e^{au} - \cdots$ [signs alternate: $+ - + - \cdots$]

58. $\int p(u) \sin au\, du = -\dfrac{1}{a}p(u)\cos au + \dfrac{1}{a^2}p'(u)\sin au + \dfrac{1}{a^3}p''(u)\cos au - \cdots$ [signs alternate in pairs after first term: $+ + - - + + - - \cdots$]

59. $\int p(u) \cos au\, du = \dfrac{1}{a}p(u)\sin au + \dfrac{1}{a^2}p'(u)\cos au - \dfrac{1}{a^3}p''(u)\sin au - \cdots$ [signs alternate in pairs: $+ + - - + + - - \cdots$]

Calculus provides a way of viewing and analyzing the physical world. As with all mathematics courses, calculus involves equations and formulas. However, if you successfully learn to use all the formulas and solve all of the problems in the text but do not master the underlying *ideas*, you will have missed the most important part of calculus. If you master these ideas, you will have a widely applicable tool that goes far beyond textbook exercises.

Before starting your studies, you may find it helpful to leaf through this text to get a general feeling for its different parts:

■ The opening page of each chapter gives you an overview of what that chapter is about, and the opening page of each section within a chapter gives you an overview of what that section is about. To help you locate specific information, sections are subdivided into topics that are marked with a box like this ■.

■ Each section ends with a set of exercises. The answers to most odd-numbered exercises appear in the back of the book. If you find that your answer to an exercise does not match that in the back of the book, do not assume immediately that yours is incorrect—there may be more than one way to express the answer. For example, if your answer is $\sqrt{2}/2$ and the text answer is $1/\sqrt{2}$, then both are correct since your answer can be obtained by "rationalizing" the text answer. In general, if your answer does not match that in the text, then your best first step is to look for an algebraic manipulation or a trigonometric identity that might help you determine if the two answers are equivalent. If the answer is in the form of a decimal approximation, then your answer might differ from that in the text because of a difference in the number of decimal places used in the computations.

■ The section exercises include regular exercises and four special categories: *Quick Check*, *Focus on Concepts*, *True/False*, and *Writing*.

• The *Quick Check* exercises are intended to give you quick feedback on whether you understand the key ideas in the section; they involve relatively little computation, and have answers provided at the end of the exercise set.

• The *Focus on Concepts* exercises, as their name suggests, key in on the main ideas in the section.

• *True/False* exercises focus on key ideas in a different way. You must decide whether the statement is true in *all possible circumstances*, in which case you would declare it to be "true," or whether there are some circumstances in which it is not true, in which case you would declare it to be "false." In each such exercise you are asked to "Explain your answer." You might do this by noting a

theorem in the text that shows the statement to be true or by finding a particular example in which the statement is not true.

• *Writing* exercises are intended to test your ability to explain mathematical ideas in words rather than relying solely on numbers and symbols. All exercises requiring writing should be answered in complete, correctly punctuated logical sentences—not with fragmented phrases and formulas.

■ Each chapter ends with two additional sets of exercises: *Chapter Review Exercises*, which, as the name suggests, is a select set of exercises that provide a review of the main concepts and techniques in the chapter, and *Making Connections*, in which exercises require you to draw on and combine various ideas developed throughout the chapter.

■ Your instructor may choose to incorporate technology in your calculus course. Exercises whose solution involves the use of some kind of technology are tagged with icons to alert you and your instructor. Those exercises tagged with the icon ∼ require graphing technology—either a graphing calculator or a computer program that can graph equations. Those exercises tagged with the icon C require a computer algebra system (CAS) such as *Mathematica*, *Maple*, or available on some graphing calculators.

■ At the end of the text you will find a set of four appendices covering various topics such as a detailed review of trigonometry and graphing techniques using technology. Inside the front and back covers of the text you will find endpapers that contain useful formulas.

■ The ideas in this text were created by real people with interesting personalities and backgrounds. Pictures and biographical sketches of many of these people appear throughout the book.

■ Notes in the margin are intended to clarify or comment on important points in the text.

A Word of Encouragement

As you work your way through this text you will find some ideas that you understand immediately, some that you don't understand until you have read them several times, and others that you do not seem to understand, even after several readings. Do not become discouraged—some ideas are intrinsically difficult and take time to "percolate." You may well find that a hard idea becomes clear later when you least expect it.

Wiley Web Site for this Text

www.wiley.com/college/anton

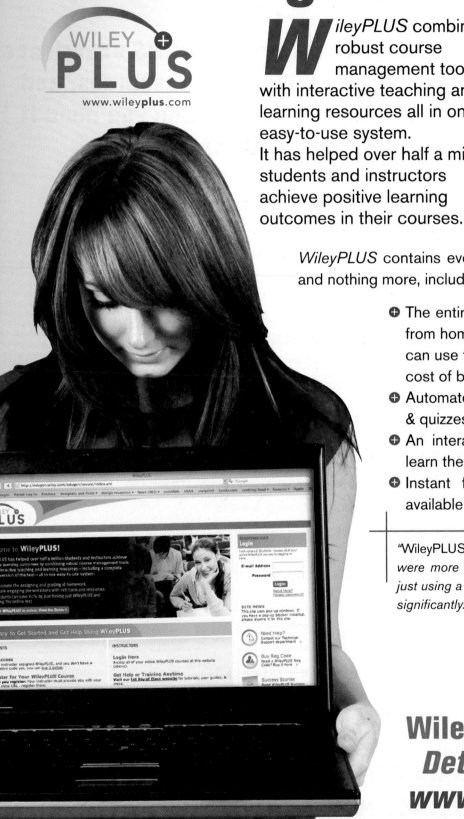

www.wiley**plus**.com

Wiley is committed to making your entire *WileyPLUS* experience productive & enjoyable by providing the help, resources, and personal support you & your students need, when you need it. It's all here: www.wileyplus.com –

TECHNICAL SUPPORT:

⊕ A fully searchable knowledge base of FAQs and help documentation, available 24/7

⊕ Live chat with a trained member of our support staff during business hours

⊕ A form to fill out and submit online to ask any question and get a quick response

⊕ **Instructor-only** phone line during business hours: 1.877.586.0192

FACULTY-LED TRAINING THROUGH THE WILEY FACULTY NETWORK:
Register online: www.wherefacultyconnect.com
Connect with your colleagues in a complimentary virtual seminar, with a personal mentor in your field, or at a live workshop to share best practices for teaching with technology.

1ST DAY OF CLASS...AND BEYOND!
Resources You & Your Students Need to Get Started & Use *WileyPLUS* from the first day forward.

⊕ 2-Minute Tutorials on how to set up & maintain your *WileyPLUS* course

⊕ User guides, links to technical support & training options

⊕ *WileyPLUS for Dummies*: Instructors' quick reference guide to using *WileyPLUS*

⊕ Student tutorials & instruction on how to register, buy, and use *WileyPLUS*

YOUR *WileyPLUS* ACCOUNT MANAGER:
Your personal *WileyPLUS* connection for any assistance you need!

SET UP YOUR *WileyPLUS* COURSE IN MINUTES!
Selected *WileyPLUS* courses with QuickStart contain pre-loaded assignments & presentations created by subject matter experts who are also experienced *WileyPLUS* users.

Interested? See and try WileyPLUS in action!
Details and Demo: www.wileyplus.com

9th EDITION

CALCULUS

MULTIVARIABLE

■ **HOWARD ANTON** *Drexel University*

■ **IRL BIVENS** *Davidson College*

■ **STEPHEN DAVIS** *Davidson College*

with contributions by

Thomas Polaski *Winthrop University*

JOHN WILEY & SONS, INC.

WILEY

Publisher: Laurie Rosatone
Acquisitions Editor: David Dietz
Freelance Developmental Editor: Anne Scanlan-Rohrer
Marketing Manager: Sarah Davis
Associate Editor: Michael Shroff/Will Art/Jeffrey Benson
Editorial Assistant: Pamela Lashbrook
Full Service Production Management: Carol Sawyer/The Perfect Proof
Senior Production Editor: Ken Santor
Senior Designer: Madelyn Lesure
Associate Photo Editor: Sheena Goldstein
Freelance Illustration: Karen Heyt
Cover Photo: NASA Goddard Space Flight Center (NASA-GSFC)

This book was set in LaTeX by Techsetters, Inc., and printed and bound by R.R. Donnelley/Jefferson City. The cover was printed by R.R. Donnelley.

This book is printed on acid-free paper.

The paper in this book was manufactured by a mill whose forest management programs include sustained yield harvesting of its timberlands. Sustained yield harvesting principles ensure that the numbers of trees cut each year does not exceed the amount of new growth.

ISBN 978-0-470-18346-5

Printed in the United States of America

10 9 8 7 6 5 4 3 2 1

About **HOWARD ANTON**

Howard Anton wrote the original version of this text and was the author of the first six editions. He obtained his B.A. from Lehigh University, his M.A. from the University of Illinois, and his Ph.D. from the Polytechnic University of Brooklyn, all in mathematics. In the early 1960s he worked for Burroughs Corporation and Avco Corporation at Cape Canaveral, Florida, where he was involved with the manned space program. In 1968 he joined the Mathematics Department at Drexel University, where he taught full time until 1983. Since that time he has been an adjunct professor at Drexel and has devoted the majority of his time to textbook writing and activities for mathematical associations. Dr. Anton was president of the EPADEL Section of the Mathematical Association of America (MAA), served on the Board of Governors of that organization, and guided the creation of the Student Chapters of the MAA. He has published numerous research papers in functional analysis, approximation theory, and topology, as well as pedagogical papers. He is best known for his textbooks in mathematics, which are among the most widely used in the world. There are currently more than one hundred versions of his books, including translations into Spanish, Arabic, Portuguese, Italian, Indonesian, French, Japanese, Chinese, Hebrew, and German. For relaxation, Dr. Anton enjoys traveling and photography.

About **IRL BIVENS**

Irl C. Bivens, recipient of the George Polya Award and the Merten M. Hasse Prize for Expository Writing in Mathematics, received his A.B. from Pfeiffer College and his Ph.D. from the University of North Carolina at Chapel Hill, both in mathematics. Since 1982, he has taught at Davidson College, where he currently holds the position of professor of mathematics. A typical academic year sees him teaching courses in calculus, topology, and geometry. Dr. Bivens also enjoys mathematical history, and his annual History of Mathematics seminar is a perennial favorite with Davidson mathematics majors. He has published numerous articles on undergraduate mathematics, as well as research papers in his specialty, differential geometry. He has served on the editorial boards of the MAA Problem Book series and *The College Mathematics Journal* and is a reviewer for *Mathematical Reviews*. When he is not pursuing mathematics, Professor Bivens enjoys juggling, swimming, walking, and spending time with his son Robert.

About **STEPHEN DAVIS**

Stephen L. Davis received his B.A. from Lindenwood College and his Ph.D. from Rutgers University in mathematics. Having previously taught at Rutgers University and Ohio State University, Dr. Davis came to Davidson College in 1981, where he is currently a professor of mathematics. He regularly teaches calculus, linear algebra, abstract algebra, and computer science. A sabbatical in 1995–1996 took him to Swarthmore College as a visiting associate professor. Professor Davis has published numerous articles on calculus reform and testing, as well as research papers on finite group theory, his specialty. Professor Davis has held several offices in the Southeastern section of the MAA, including chair and secretary-treasurer. He is currently a faculty consultant for the Educational Testing Service Advanced Placement Calculus Test, a board member of the North Carolina Association of Advanced Placement Mathematics Teachers, and is actively involved in nurturing mathematically talented high school students through leadership in the Charlotte Mathematics Club. He was formerly North Carolina state director for the MAA. For relaxation, he plays basketball, juggles, and travels. Professor Davis and his wife Elisabeth have three children, Laura, Anne, and James, all former calculus students.

About **THOMAS POLASKI,** contributor to the ninth edition

Thomas W. Polaski received his B.S. from Furman University and his Ph.D. in mathematics from Duke University. He is currently a professor at Winthrop University, where he has taught since 1991. He was named Outstanding Junior Professor at Winthrop in 1996. He has published articles on mathematics pedagogy and stochastic processes and has authored a chapter in a forthcoming linear algebra textbook. Professor Polaski is a frequent presenter at mathematics meetings, giving talks on topics ranging from mathematical biology to mathematical models for baseball. He has been an MAA Visiting Lecturer and is a reviewer for *Mathematical Reviews*. Professor Polaski has been a reader for the Advanced Placement Calculus Tests for many years. In addition to calculus, he enjoys travel and hiking. Professor Polaski and his wife, LeDayne, have a daughter, Kate, and live in Charlotte, North Carolina.

To
my wife Pat and my children: Brian, David, and Lauren

In Memory of
my mother Shirley
my father Benjamin
my thesis advisor and inspiration, George Bachman
my benefactor in my time of need, Stephen Girard (1750–1831)
—HA

To
my son Robert
—IB

To
my wife Elisabeth
my children: Laura, Anne, and James
—SD

PREFACE

This ninth edition of *Calculus* maintains those aspects of previous editions that have led to the series' success—we continue to strive for student comprehension without sacrificing mathematical accuracy, and the exercise sets are carefully constructed to avoid unhappy surprises that can derail a calculus class. However, this edition also has many new features that we hope will attract new users and also motivate past users to take a fresh look at our work. We had two main goals for this edition:

- To make those adjustments to the order and content that would align the text more precisely with the most widely followed calculus outlines.
- To add new elements to the text that would provide a wider range of teaching and learning tools.

All of the changes were carefully reviewed by an advisory committee of outstanding teachers comprised of both users and nonusers of the previous edition. The charge of this committee was to ensure that all changes did not alter those aspects of the text that attracted users of the eighth edition and at the same time provide freshness to the new edition that would attract new users. Some of the more substantive changes are described below.

NEW FEATURES IN THIS EDITION

New Elements in the Exercises   We added new true/false exercises, new writing exercises, and new exercise types that were requested by reviewers of the eighth edition.

Making Connections   We added this new element to the end of each chapter. A Making Connections exercise synthesizes concepts drawn across multiple sections of its chapter rather than using ideas from a single section as is expected of a regular or review exercise.

Reorganization of Material on Tangent Planes and Surface Area   Section 13.7 (*Tangent Planes and Normal Vectors*) now begins with a discussion of tangent planes to level surfaces, followed by a treatment of tangent planes to graphs of functions of two variables. This reverses the order of presentation from that of the eighth edition. Section 14.4 (*Surface Area; Parametric Surfaces*) has been reorganized so that surfaces of the form $z = f(x, y)$ are now discussed before surfaces defined parametrically.

OTHER FEATURES

Flexibility   This edition has a built-in flexibility that is designed to serve a broad spectrum of calculus philosophies—from traditional to "reform." Technology can be emphasized or not, and the order of many topics can be permuted freely to accommodate each instructor's specific needs.

Rigor   The challenge of writing a good calculus book is to strike the right balance between rigor and clarity. Our goal is to present precise mathematics to the fullest extent possible in an introductory treatment. Where clarity and rigor conflict, we choose clarity; however, we believe it to be important that the student understand the difference between a careful proof and an informal argument, so we have informed the reader when the arguments being presented are informal or motivational.

Rule of Four   The "rule of four" refers to presenting concepts from the verbal, algebraic, visual, and numerical points of view. In keeping with current pedagogical philosophy, we used this approach whenever appropriate.

Visualization   This edition makes extensive use of modern computer graphics to clarify concepts and to develop the student's ability to visualize mathematical objects, particularly those in 3-space. For those students who are working with graphing technology, there are many exercises that are designed to develop the student's ability to generate and analyze mathematical curves and surfaces.

Quick Check Exercises   Each exercise set begins with approximately five exercises (answers included) that are designed to provide students with an immediate assessment of whether they have mastered key ideas from the section. They require a minimum of computation and are answered by filling in the blanks.

Focus on Concepts Exercises   Each exercise set contains a clearly identified group of problems that focus on the main ideas of the section.

Technology Exercises   Most sections include exercises that are designed to be solved using either a graphing calculator or a computer algebra system such as *Mathematica*, *Maple*, or the open source program *Sage*. These exercises are marked with an icon for easy identification.

Applicability of Calculus   One of the primary goals of this text is to link calculus to the real world and the student's own experience. This theme is carried through in the examples and exercises.

Career Preparation   This text is written at a mathematical level that will prepare students for a wide variety of careers that require a sound mathematics background, including engineering, the various sciences, and business.

Historical Notes   The biographies and historical notes have been a hallmark of this text from its first edition and have been maintained. All of the biographical materials have been distilled from standard sources with the goal of capturing and bringing to life for the student the personalities of history's greatest mathematicians.

Margin Notes and Warnings   These appear in the margins throughout the text to clarify or expand on the text exposition or to alert the reader to some pitfall.

SUPPLEMENTS

Print Supplements

The Student Solutions Manual (978-0470-37964-6) provides students with detailed solutions to odd-numbered exercises from the text. The structure of solutions in the manual matches those of worked examples in the textbook.

Student Companion Site

The Student Companion Site provides access to the following student supplements:

- Web Quizzes, which are short, fill-in-the-blank quizzes that are arranged by chapter and section.
- Additional textbook content, including answers to odd-numbered exercises and appendices.

WileyPLUS

WileyPLUS, Wiley's digital-learning environment, is loaded with all of the supplements above, and also features the following:

- The E-book, which is an exact version of the print text, but also features hyperlinks to questions, definitions, and supplements for quicker and easier support.
- The Student Study Guide provides concise summaries for quick review, checklists, common mistakes/pitfalls, and sample tests for each section and chapter of the text.
- The Graphing Calculator Manual helps students to get the most out of their graphing calculator and shows how they can apply the numerical and graphing functions of their calculators to their study of calculus.
- Guided Online (GO) Exercises prompt students to build solutions step by step. Rather than simply grading an exercise answer as wrong, GO problems show students precisely where they are making a mistake.
- Are You Ready? quizzes gauge student mastery of chapter concepts and techniques and provide feedback on areas that require further attention.

SUPPLEMENTS FOR THE INSTRUCTOR

Print Supplements

The Instructor's Solutions Manual (978-0470-37966-0) contains detailed solutions to all exercises in the text.

The Instructor's Manual (978-0470-37960-8) suggests time allocations and teaching plans for each section in the text. Most of the teaching plans contain a bulleted list of key points to emphasize. The discussion of each section concludes with a sample homework assignment.

Instructor Companion Site

The Instructor Companion Site provides detailed information on the textbook's features, contents, and coverage and provides access to the following instructor supplements:

- The Computerized Test Bank features nearly 7000 questions—mostly algorithmically generated—that allow for varied questions and numerical inputs.
- PowerPoint slides cover the major concepts and themes of each section in a chapter.
- Personal-Response System questions ("Clicker Questions") appear at the end of each PowerPoint presentation and provide an easy way to gauge classroom understanding.
- Additional textbook content, such as Calculus Horizons and Explorations, back-of-the-book appendices, and selected biographies.

WileyPLUS

WileyPLUS, Wiley's digital-learning environment, is loaded with all of the supplements above, and also features the following:

- Homework management tools, which easily allow you to assign and grade questions, as well as gauge student comprehension.
- QuickStart features predesigned reading and homework assignments. Use them as-is or customize them to fit the needs of your classroom.
- The E-book, which is an exact version of the print text but also features hyperlinks to questions, definitions, and supplements for quicker and easier support.
- Animated applets, which can be used in class to present and explore key ideas graphically and dynamically—especially useful for display of three-dimensional graphs in multivariable calculus.

ACKNOWLEDGMENTS

It has been our good fortune to have the advice and guidance of many talented people whose knowledge and skills have enhanced this book in many ways. For their valuable help we thank the following people.

Reviewers and Contributors to the Ninth Edition of Early Transcendentals Calculus

Frederick Adkins, *Indiana University of Pennsylvania*
Bill Allen, *Reedley College–Clovis Center*
Jerry Allison, *Black Hawk College*
Seth Armstrong, *Southern Utah University*
Przemyslaw Bogacki, *Old Dominion University*
Wayne P. Britt, *Louisiana State University*
Kristin Chatas, *Washtenaw Community College*
Michele Clement, *Louisiana State University*
Ray Collings, *Georgia Perimeter College*
David E. Dobbs, *University of Tennessee, Knoxville*
H. Edward Donley, *Indiana University of Pennsylvania*
Jim Edmondson, *Santa Barbara City College*
Michael Filaseta, *University of South Carolina*
Jose Flores, *University of South Dakota*
Mitch Francis, *Horace Mann*
Jerome Heaven, *Indiana Tech*
Patricia Henry, *Drexel University*
Danrun Huang, *St. Cloud State University*
Alvaro Islas, *University of Central Florida*
Bin Jiang, *Portland State University*
Ronald Jorgensen, *Milwaukee School of Engineering*
Raja Khoury, *Collin County Community College*

Carole King Krueger, *The University of Texas at Arlington*
Thomas Leness, *Florida International University*
Kathryn Lesh, *Union College*
Behailu Mammo, *Hofstra University*
John McCuan, *Georgia Tech*
Daryl McGinnis, *Columbus State Community College*
Michael Mears, *Manatee Community College*
John G. Michaels, *SUNY Brockport*
Jason Miner, *Santa Barbara City College*
Darrell Minor, *Columbus State Community College*
Kathleen Miranda, *SUNY Old Westbury*
Carla Monticelli, *Camden County College*
Bryan Mosher, *University of Minnesota*
Ferdinand O. Orock, *Hudson County Community College*
Altay Ozgener, *Manatee Community College*
Chuang Peng, *Morehouse College*
Joni B. Pirnot, *Manatee Community College*
Elise Price, *Tarrant County College*
Holly Puterbaugh, *University of Vermont*
Hah Suey Quan, *Golden West College*
Joseph W. Rody, *Arizona State University*
Constance Schober, *University of Central Florida*

Kurt Sebastian, *United States Coast Guard*
Paul Seeburger, *Monroe Community College*
Bradley Stetson, *Schoolcraft College*
Walter E. Stone, Jr., *North Shore Community College*
Eleanor Storey, *Front Range Community College, Westminster Campus*
Stefania Tracogna, *Arizona State University*
Francis J. Vasko, *Kutztown University*
Jim Voss, *Front Range Community College*
Anke Walz, *Kutztown Community College*
Xian Wu, *University of South Carolina*
Yvonne Yaz, *Milwaukee School of Engineering*
Richard A. Zang, *University of New Hampshire*

The following people read the ninth edition at various stages for mathematical and pedagogical accuracy and/or assisted with the critically important job of preparing answers to exercises:

Dean Hickerson
Ron Jorgensen, *Milwaukee School of Engineering*
Roger Lipsett
Georgia Mederer
Ann Ostberg
David Ryeburn, *Simon Fraser University*
Neil Wigley

Reviewers and Contributors to the Ninth Edition of Late Transcendentals and Multivariable Calculus

David Bradley, *University of Maine*
Dean Burbank, *Gulf Coast Community College*
Jason Cantarella, *University of Georgia*
Yanzhao Cao, *Florida A&M University*
T.J. Duda, *Columbus State Community College*
Nancy Eschen, *Florida Community College, Jacksonville*
Reuben Farley, *Virginia Commonwealth University*
Zhuang-dan Guan, *University of California, Riverside*
Greg Henderson, *Hillsborough Community College*

Micah James, *University of Illinois*
Mohammad Kazemi, *University of North Carolina, Charlotte*
Przemo Kranz, *University of Mississippi*
Steffen Lempp, *University of Wisconsin, Madison*
Wen-Xiu Ma, *University of South Florida*
Vania Mascioni, *Ball State University*
David Price, *Tarrant County College*
Jan Rychtar, *University of North Carolina, Greensboro*
John T. Saccoman, *Seton Hall University*

Charlotte Simmons, *University of Central Oklahoma*
Don Soash, *Hillsborough Community College*
Bryan Stewart, *Tarrant County College*
Helene Tyler, *Manhattan College*
Pavlos Tzermias, *University of Tennessee, Knoxville*
Raja Varatharajah, *North Carolina A&T*
David Voss, *Western Illinois University*
Richard Watkins, *Tidewater Community College*
Xiao-Dong Zhang, *Florida Atlantic University*
Diane Zych, *Erie Community College*

Reviewers and Contributors to the Eighth Edition of Calculus

Gregory Adams, *Bucknell University*

Bill Allen, *Reedley College–Clovis Center*

Jerry Allison, *Black Hawk College*

Stella Ashford, *Southern University and A&M College*

Mary Lane Baggett, *University of Mississippi*

Christopher Barker, *San Joaquin Delta College*

Kbenesh Blayneh, *Florida A&M University*

David Bradley, *University of Maine*

Paul Britt, *Louisiana State University*

Judith Broadwin, *Jericho High School*

Andrew Bulleri, *Howard Community College*

Christopher Butler, *Case Western Reserve University*

Cheryl Cantwell, *Seminole Community College*

Judith Carter, *North Shore Community College*

Miriam Castroconde, *Irvine Valley College*

Neena Chopra, *The Pennsylvania State University*

Gaemus Collins, *University of California, San Diego*

Fielden Cox, *Centennial College*

Danielle Cross, *Northern Essex Community College*

Gary Crown, *Wichita State University*

Larry Cusick, *California State University–Fresno*

Stephan DeLong, *Tidewater Community College–Virginia Beach Campus*

Debbie A. Desrochers, *Napa Valley College*

Ryness Doherty, *Community College of Denver*

T.J. Duda, *Columbus State Community College*

Peter Embalabala, *Lincoln Land Community College*

Phillip Farmer, *Diablo Valley College*

Laurene Fausett, *Georgia Southern University*

Sally E. Fishbeck, *Rochester Institute of Technology*

Bob Grant, *Mesa Community College*

Richard Hall, *Cochise College*

Noal Harbertson, *California State University, Fresno*

Donald Hartig, *California Polytechnic State University*

Karl Havlak, *Angelo State University*

J. Derrick Head, *University of Minnesota–Morris*

Konrad Heuvers, *Michigan Technological University*

Tommie Ann Hill-Natter, *Prairie View A&M University*

Holly Hirst, *Appalachian State University*

Joe Howe, *St. Charles County Community College*

Shirley Huffman, *Southwest Missouri State University*

Gary S. Itzkowitz, *Rowan University*

John Johnson, *George Fox University*

Kenneth Kalmanson, *Montclair State University*

Grant Karamyan, *University of California, Los Angeles*

David Keller, *Kirkwood Community College*

Dan Kemp, *South Dakota State University*

Vesna Kilibarda, *Indiana University Northwest*

Cecilia Knoll, *Florida Institute of Technology*

Carole King Krueger, *The University of Texas at Arlington*

Holly A. Kresch, *Diablo Valley College*

John Kubicek, *Southwest Missouri State University*

Theodore Lai, *Hudson County Community College*

Richard Lane, *University of Montana*

Jeuel LaTorre, *Clemson University*

Marshall Leitman, *Case Western Reserve University*

Phoebe Lutz, *Delta College*

Ernest Manfred, *U.S. Coast Guard Academy*

James Martin, *Wake Technical Community College*

Vania Mascioni, *Ball State University*

Tamra Mason, *Albuquerque TVI Community College*

Thomas W. Mason, *Florida A&M University*

Roy Mathia, *The College of William and Mary*

John Michaels, *SUNY Brockport*

Darrell Minor, *Columbus State Community College*

Darren Narayan, *Rochester Institute of Technology*

Doug Nelson, *Central Oregon Community College*

Lawrence J. Newberry, *Glendale College*

Judith Palagallo, *The University of Akron*

Efton Park, *Texas Christian University*

Joanne Peeples, *El Paso Community College*

Gary L. Peterson, *James Madison University*

Lefkios Petevis, *Kirkwood Community College*

Thomas W. Polaski, *Winthrop University*

Richard Ponticelli, *North Shore Community College*

Holly Puterbaugh, *University of Vermont*

Douglas Quinney, *University of Keele*

B. David Redman, Jr., *Delta College*

William H. Richardson, *Wichita State University*

Lila F. Roberts, *Georgia Southern University*

Robert Rock, *Daniel Webster College*

John Saccoman, *Seton Hall University*

Avinash Sathaye, *University of Kentucky*

George W. Schultz, *St. Petersburg Junior College*

Paul Seeburger, *Monroe Community College*

Richard B. Shad, *Florida Community College–Jacksonville*

Mary Margaret Shoaf-Grubbs, *College of New Rochelle*

Charlotte Simmons, *University of Central Oklahoma*

Ann Sitomer, *Portland Community College*

Jeanne Smith, *Saddleback Community College*

Rajalakshmi Sriram, *Okaloosa-Walton Community College*

Mark Stevenson, *Oakland Community College*

Bryan Stewart, *Tarrant County College*

Bradley Stoll, *The Harker School*

Eleanor Storey, *Front Range Community College*

John A. Suvak, *Memorial University of Newfoundland*

Richard Swanson, *Montana State University*

Skip Thompson, *Radford University*

Helene Tyler, *Manhattan College*

Paramanathan Varatharajah, *North Carolina A&T State University*

David Voss, *Western Illinois University*

Jim Voss, *Front Range Community College*

Richard Watkins, *Tidewater Community College*

Bruce R. Wenner, *University of Missouri–Kansas City*

Jane West, *Trident Technical College*

Ted Wilcox, *Rochester Institute of Technology*

Janine Wittwer, *Williams College*

Diane Zych, *Erie Community College–North Campus*

The following people read the eighth edition at various stages for mathematical and pedagogical accuracy and/or assisted with the critically important job of preparing answers to exercises:

Elka Block, *Twin Prime Editorial*

Dean Hickerson

Ann Ostberg

Thomas Polaski, *Winthrop University*

Frank Purcell, *Twin Prime Editorial*

David Ryeburn, *Simon Fraser University*

CONTENTS

WEB PROJECTS (Expanding the Calculus Horizon)

THE ROOTS OF CALCULUS

Today's exciting applications of calculus have roots that can be traced to the work of the Greek mathematician Archimedes, but the actual discovery of the fundamental principles of calculus was made independently by Isaac Newton (English) and Gottfried Leibniz (German) in the late seventeenth century. The work of Newton and Leibniz was motivated by four major classes of scientific and mathematical problems of the time:

- Find the tangent line to a general curve at a given point.

- Find the area of a general region, the length of a general curve, and the volume of a general solid.

- Find the maximum or minimum value of a quantity—for example, the maximum and minimum distances of a planet from the Sun, or the maximum range attainable for a projectile by varying its angle of fire.

- Given a formula for the distance traveled by a body in any specified amount of time, find the velocity and acceleration of the body at any instant. Conversely, given a formula that specifies the acceleration of velocity at any instant, find the distance traveled by the body in a specified period of time.

Newton and Leibniz found a fundamental relationship between the problem of finding a tangent line to a curve and the problem of determining the area of a region. Their realization of this connection is considered to be the "discovery of calculus." Though Newton saw how these two problems are related ten years before Leibniz did, Leibniz published his work twenty years before Newton. This situation led to a stormy debate over who was the rightful discoverer of calculus. The debate engulfed Europe for half a century, with the scientists of the European continent supporting Leibniz and those from England supporting Newton. The conflict was extremely unfortunate because Newton's inferior notation badly hampered scientific development in England, and the Continent in turn lost the benefit of Newton's discoveries in astronomy and physics for nearly fifty years. In spite of it all, Newton and Leibniz were sincere admirers of each other's work.

ISAAC NEWTON (1642–1727)

Newton was born in the village of Woolsthorpe, England. His father died before he was born and his mother raised him on the family farm. As a youth he showed little evidence of his later brilliance, except for an unusual talent with mechanical devices—he apparently built a working water clock and a toy flour mill powered by a mouse. In 1661 he entered Trinity College in Cambridge with a deficiency in geometry. Fortunately, Newton caught the eye of Isaac Barrow, a gifted mathematician and teacher. Under Barrow's guidance Newton immersed himself in mathematics and science, but he graduated without any special distinction. Because the bubonic plague was spreading rapidly through London, Newton returned to his home in Woolsthorpe and stayed there during the years of 1665 and 1666. In those two momentous years the entire framework of modern science was miraculously created in Newton's mind. He discovered calculus, recognized the underlying principles of planetary motion and gravity, and determined that "white" sunlight was composed of all colors, red to violet. For whatever reasons he kept his discoveries to himself. In 1667 he returned to Cambridge to obtain his Master's degree and upon graduation became a teacher at Trinity. Then in 1669 Newton succeeded his teacher, Isaac Barrow, to the Lucasian chair of mathematics at Trinity, one of the most honored chairs of mathematics in the world.

Thereafter, brilliant discoveries flowed from Newton steadily. He formulated the law of gravitation and used it to explain the motion of the moon, the planets, and the tides; he formulated basic theories of light, thermodynamics, and hydrodynamics; and he devised and constructed the first modern reflecting telescope. Throughout his life Newton was hesitant to publish his major discoveries, revealing them only to a select circle of friends, perhaps because of a fear of criticism or controversy. In 1687, only after intense coaxing by the astronomer, Edmond Halley (discoverer of Halley's comet), did Newton publish his masterpiece, *Philosophiae Naturalis Principia Mathematica* (The Mathematical Principles of Natural Philosophy). This work is generally considered to be the most important and influential scientific book ever written. In it Newton explained the workings of the solar system and formulated the basic laws of motion, which to this day are fundamental in engineering and physics. However, not even the pleas of his friends could convince Newton to publish his discovery of calculus. Only after Leibniz published his results did Newton relent and publish his own work on calculus.

After twenty-five years as a professor, Newton suffered depression and a nervous break-down. He gave up research in 1695 to accept a position as warden and later master of the London mint. During the twenty-five years that he worked at the mint, he did virtually no scientific or mathematical work. He was knighted in 1705 and on his death was buried in Westminster Abbey with all the honors his country could bestow. It is interesting to note that Newton was a learned theologian who viewed the primary value of his work to be its support of the existence of God. Throughout his life he worked passionately to date biblical events by relating them to astronomical phenomena. He was so consumed with this passion that he spent years searching the Book of Daniel for clues to the end of the world and the geography of hell.

Newton described his brilliant accomplishments as follows: "I seem to have been only like a boy playing on the seashore and diverting myself in now and then finding a smoother pebble or prettier shell than ordinary, whilst the great ocean of truth lay all undiscovered before me."

GOTTFRIED WILHELM LEIBNIZ (1646–1716)

This gifted genius was one of the last people to have mastered most major fields of knowledge—an impossible accomplishment in our own era of specialization. He was an expert in law, religion, philosophy, literature, politics, geology, metaphysics, alchemy, history, and mathematics.

Leibniz was born in Leipzig, Germany. His father, a professor of moral philosophy at the University of Leipzig, died when Leibniz was six years old. The precocious boy then gained access to his father's library and began reading voraciously on a wide range of subjects, a habit that he maintained throughout his life. At age fifteen he entered the University of Leipzig as a law student and by the age of twenty received a doctorate from the University of Altdorf. Subsequently, Leibniz followed a career in law and international politics, serving as counsel to kings and princes. During his numerous foreign missions, Leibniz came in contact with outstanding mathematicians and scientists who stimulated his interest in mathematics—most notably, the physicist Christian Huygens. In mathematics Leibniz was self-taught, learning the subject by reading papers and journals. As a result of this fragmented mathematical education, Leibniz often rediscovered the results of others, and this helped to fuel the debate over the discovery of calculus.

Leibniz never married. He was moderate in his habits, quick-tempered but easily appeased, and charitable in his judgment of other people's work. In spite of his great achievements, Leibniz never received the honors showered on Newton, and he spent his final years as a lonely embittered man. At his funeral there was one mourner, his secretary. An eyewitness stated, "He was buried more like a robber than what he really was—an ornament of his country."

Craig Aurness/Corbis Images

11

THREE-DIMENSIONAL SPACE; VECTORS

To describe fully the motion of a boat, one must specify its speed and direction of motion at each instant. Speed and direction together describe a "vector" quantity. We will study vectors in this chapter.

In this chapter we will discuss rectangular coordinate systems in three dimensions, and we will study the analytic geometry of lines, planes, and other basic surfaces. The second theme of this chapter is the study of vectors. These are the mathematical objects that physicists and engineers use to study forces, displacements, and velocities of objects moving on curved paths. More generally, vectors are used to represent all physical entities that involve both a magnitude and a direction for their complete description. We will introduce various algebraic operations on vectors, and we will apply these operations to problems involving force, work, and rotational tendencies in two and three dimensions. Finally, we will discuss cylindrical and spherical coordinate systems, which are appropriate in problems that involve various kinds of symmetries and also have specific applications in navigation and celestial mechanics.

11.1 RECTANGULAR COORDINATES IN 3-SPACE; SPHERES; CYLINDRICAL SURFACES

In this section we will discuss coordinate systems in three-dimensional space and some basic facts about surfaces in three dimensions.

■ RECTANGULAR COORDINATE SYSTEMS

In the remainder of this text we will call three-dimensional space *3-space*, two-dimensional space (a plane) *2-space*, and one-dimensional space (a line) *1-space*. Just as points in 2-space can be placed in one-to-one correspondence with pairs of real numbers using two perpendicular coordinate lines, so points in 3-space can be placed in one-to-one correspondence with triples of real numbers by using three mutually perpendicular coordinate lines, called the *x-axis*, the *y-axis*, and the *z-axis*, positioned so that their origins coincide (Figure 11.1.1). The three coordinate axes form a three-dimensional *rectangular coordinate system* (or *Cartesian coordinate system*). The point of intersection of the coordinate axes is called the *origin* of the coordinate system.

Rectangular coordinate systems in 3-space fall into two categories: *left-handed* and *right-handed*. A right-handed system has the property that when the fingers of the right hand are cupped so that they curve from the positive *x*-axis toward the positive *y*-axis, the thumb points (roughly) in the direction of the positive *z*-axis (Figure 11.1.2). A similar

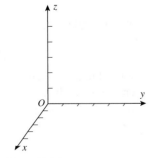

▲ **Figure 11.1.1**

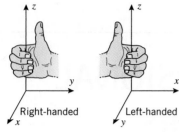

▲ **Figure 11.1.2**

property holds for a left-handed coordinate system (Figure 11.1.2). We will use only right-handed coordinate systems in this text.

The coordinate axes, taken in pairs, determine three *coordinate planes*: the *xy-plane*, the *xz-plane*, and the *yz-plane* (Figure 11.1.3). To each point P in 3-space we can assign a triple of real numbers by passing three planes through P parallel to the coordinate planes and letting a, b, and c be the coordinates of the intersections of those planes with the x-axis, y-axis, and z-axis, respectively (Figure 11.1.4). We call a, b, and c the *x-coordinate*, *y-coordinate*, and *z-coordinate* of P, respectively, and we denote the point P by (a, b, c) or by $P(a, b, c)$. Figure 11.1.5 shows the points $(4, 5, 6)$ and $(-3, 2, -4)$.

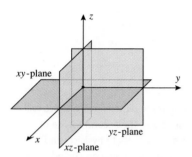

▲ **Figure 11.1.3**

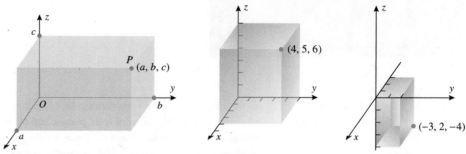

▲ **Figure 11.1.4**   ▲ **Figure 11.1.5**

Just as the coordinate axes in a two-dimensional coordinate system divide 2-space into four quadrants, so the coordinate planes of a three-dimensional coordinate system divide 3-space into eight parts, called *octants*. The set of points with three positive coordinates forms the *first octant*; the remaining octants have no standard numbering.

You should be able to visualize the following facts about three-dimensional rectangular coordinate systems:

REGION	DESCRIPTION
xy-plane	Consists of all points of the form $(x, y, 0)$
xz-plane	Consists of all points of the form $(x, 0, z)$
yz-plane	Consists of all points of the form $(0, y, z)$
x-axis	Consists of all points of the form $(x, 0, 0)$
y-axis	Consists of all points of the form $(0, y, 0)$
z-axis	Consists of all points of the form $(0, 0, z)$

■ **DISTANCE IN 3-SPACE; SPHERES**

Recall that in 2-space the distance d between the points $P_1(x_1, y_1)$ and $P_2(x_2, y_2)$ is

$$d = \sqrt{(x_2 - x_1)^2 + (y_2 - y_1)^2} \tag{1}$$

The distance formula in 3-space has the same form, but it has a third term to account for the added dimension. (We will see that this is a common occurrence in extending formulas from 2-space to 3-space.) The distance between the points $P_1(x_1, y_1, z_1)$ and $P_2(x_2, y_2, z_2)$ is

$$d = \sqrt{(x_2 - x_1)^2 + (y_2 - y_1)^2 + (z_2 - z_1)^2} \tag{2}$$

We leave the proof of (2) as an exercise (Exercise 7).

▶ **Example 1**   Find the distance d between the points $(2, 3, -1)$ and $(4, -1, 3)$.

Solution.   From Formula (2)

$$d = \sqrt{(4 - 2)^2 + (-1 - 3)^2 + (3 + 1)^2} = \sqrt{36} = 6 \quad ◀$$

In an xy-coordinate system, the set of points (x, y) whose coordinates satisfy an equation in x and y is called the *graph* of the equation. Analogously, in an xyz-coordinate system, the set of points (x, y, z) whose coordinates satisfy an equation in x, y, and z is called the *graph* of the equation.

Recall that the standard equation of the circle in 2-space that has center (x_0, y_0) and radius r is

$$(x - x_0)^2 + (y - y_0)^2 = r^2 \tag{3}$$

This follows from distance formula (1) and the fact that the circle consists of all points in 2-space whose distance from (x_0, y_0) is r. Analogously, the ***standard equation of the sphere*** in 3-space that has center (x_0, y_0, z_0) and radius r is

$$(x - x_0)^2 + (y - y_0)^2 + (z - z_0)^2 = r^2 \tag{4}$$

This follows from distance formula (2) and the fact that the sphere consists of all points in 3-space whose distance from (x_0, y_0, z_0) is r. Note that (4) has the same form as the standard equation for the circle in 2-space, but with an additional term to account for the third coordinate. Some examples of the standard equation of the sphere are given in the following table:

EQUATION	GRAPH
$(x - 3)^2 + (y - 2)^2 + (z - 1)^2 = 9$	Sphere with center $(3, 2, 1)$ and radius 3
$(x + 1)^2 + y^2 + (z + 4)^2 = 5$	Sphere with center $(-1, 0, -4)$ and radius $\sqrt{5}$
$x^2 + y^2 + z^2 = 1$	Sphere with center $(0, 0, 0)$ and radius 1

If the terms in (4) are expanded and like terms are collected, then the resulting equation has the form

$$x^2 + y^2 + z^2 + Gx + Hy + Iz + J = 0 \tag{5}$$

The following example shows how the center and radius of a sphere that is expressed in this form can be obtained by completing the squares.

▶ **Example 2**   Find the center and radius of the sphere

$$x^2 + y^2 + z^2 - 2x - 4y + 8z + 17 = 0$$

Solution.   We can put the equation in the form of (4) by completing the squares:

$$(x^2 - 2x) + (y^2 - 4y) + (z^2 + 8z) = -17$$
$$(x^2 - 2x + 1) + (y^2 - 4y + 4) + (z^2 + 8z + 16) = -17 + 21$$
$$(x - 1)^2 + (y - 2)^2 + (z + 4)^2 = 4$$

which is the equation of the sphere with center $(1, 2, -4)$ and radius 2. ◀

In general, completing the squares in (5) produces an equation of the form

$$(x - x_0)^2 + (y - y_0)^2 + (z - z_0)^2 = k$$

If $k > 0$, then the graph of this equation is a sphere with center (x_0, y_0, z_0) and radius $\sqrt{k}$. If $k = 0$, then the sphere has radius zero, so the graph is the single point (x_0, y_0, z_0). If $k < 0$, the equation is not satisfied by any values of x, y, and z (why?), so it has no graph.

11.1.1   THEOREM   *An equation of the form*

$$x^2 + y^2 + z^2 + Gx + Hy + Iz + J = 0$$

represents a sphere, a point, or has no graph.

■ CYLINDRICAL SURFACES

Although it is natural to graph equations in two variables in 2-space and equations in three variables in 3-space, it is also possible to graph equations in two variables in 3-space. For example, the graph of the equation $y = x^2$ in an xy-coordinate system is a parabola; however, there is nothing to prevent us from inquiring about its graph in an xyz-coordinate system. To obtain this graph we need only observe that the equation $y = x^2$ does not impose any restrictions on z. Thus, if we find values of x and y that satisfy this equation, then the coordinates of the point (x, y, z) will also satisfy the equation for *arbitrary* values of z. Geometrically, the point (x, y, z) lies on the vertical line through the point $(x, y, 0)$ in the xy-plane, which means that we can obtain the graph of $y = x^2$ in an xyz-coordinate system by first graphing the equation in the xy-plane and then translating that graph parallel to the z-axis to generate the entire graph (Figure 11.1.6).

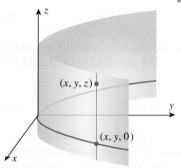

▲ Figure 11.1.6

The process of generating a surface by translating a plane curve parallel to some line is called ***extrusion***, and surfaces that are generated by extrusion are called ***cylindrical surfaces***. A familiar example is the surface of a right circular cylinder, which can be generated by translating a circle parallel to the axis of the cylinder. The following theorem provides basic information about graphing equations in two variables in 3-space:

11.1.2   THEOREM   *An equation that contains only two of the variables x, y, and z represents a cylindrical surface in an xyz-coordinate system. The surface can be obtained by graphing the equation in the coordinate plane of the two variables that appear in the equation and then translating that graph parallel to the axis of the missing variable.*

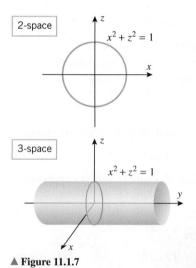

▲ Figure 11.1.7

▶ **Example 3**   Sketch the graph of $x^2 + z^2 = 1$ in 3-space.

Solution.   Since y does not appear in this equation, the graph is a cylindrical surface generated by extrusion parallel to the y-axis. In the xz-plane the graph of the equation $x^2 + z^2 = 1$ is a circle. Thus, in 3-space the graph is a right circular cylinder along the y-axis (Figure 11.1.7). ◀

▶ **Example 4**   Sketch the graph of $z = \sin y$ in 3-space.

Solution.   (See Figure 11.1.8.) ◀

In an xy-coordinate system, the graph of the equation $x = 1$ is a line parallel to the y-axis. What is the graph of this equation in an xyz-coordinate system?

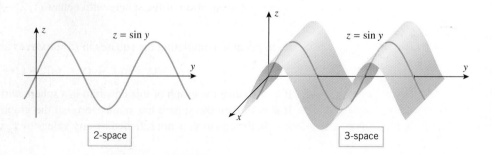

▶ Figure 11.1.8

✔ QUICK CHECK EXERCISES 11.1   (See page 773 for answers.)

1. The distance between the points $(1, -2, 0)$ and $(4, 0, 5)$ is _____.

2. The graph of $(x - 3)^2 + (y - 2)^2 + (z + 1)^2 = 16$ is a _____ of radius _____ centered at _____.

3. The shortest distance from the point $(4, 0, 5)$ to the sphere $(x - 1)^2 + (y + 2)^2 + z^2 = 36$ is _____.

4. Let S be the graph of $x^2 + z^2 + 6z = 16$ in 3-space.
   (a) The intersection of S with the xz-plane is a circle with center _____ and radius _____.
   (b) The intersection of S with the xy-plane is two lines, $x =$ _____ and $x =$ _____.
   (c) The intersection of S with the yz-plane is two lines, $z =$ _____ and $z =$ _____.

EXERCISE SET 11.1   ⌇ Graphing Utility

1. In each part, find the coordinates of the eight corners of the box.

   (a)   (b)

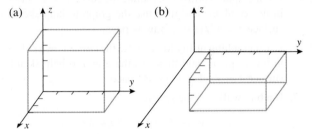

2. A cube of side 4 has its geometric center at the origin and its faces parallel to the coordinate planes. Sketch the cube and give the coordinates of the corners.

FOCUS ON CONCEPTS

3. Suppose that a box has its faces parallel to the coordinate planes and the points $(4, 2, -2)$ and $(-6, 1, 1)$ are endpoints of a diagonal. Sketch the box and give the coordinates of the remaining six corners.

4. Suppose that a box has its faces parallel to the coordinate planes and the points (x_1, y_1, z_1) and (x_2, y_2, z_2) are endpoints of a diagonal.
   (a) Find the coordinates of the remaining six corners.
   (b) Show that the midpoint of the line segment joining (x_1, y_1, z_1) and (x_2, y_2, z_2) is

   $$\left(\tfrac{1}{2}(x_1 + x_2), \tfrac{1}{2}(y_1 + y_2), \tfrac{1}{2}(z_1 + z_2)\right)$$

   [*Suggestion:* Apply Theorem H.2 in Web Appendix H to three appropriate edges of the box.]

5. Interpret the graph of $x = 1$ in the contexts of
   (a) a number line   (b) 2-space   (c) 3-space.

6. Consider the points $P(3, 1, 0)$ and $Q(1, 4, 4)$.
   (a) Sketch the triangle with vertices P, Q, and $(1, 4, 0)$. Without computing distances, explain why this triangle is a right triangle, and then apply the Theorem of Pythagoras twice to find the distance from P to Q.
   (b) Repeat part (a) using the points P, Q, and $(3, 4, 0)$.
   (c) Repeat part (a) using the points P, Q, and $(1, 1, 4)$.

7. (a) Consider a box whose sides have lengths a, b, and c. Use the Theorem of Pythagoras to show that a diagonal of the box has length $d = \sqrt{a^2 + b^2 + c^2}$. [*Hint:* Use the Theorem of Pythagoras to find the length of a diagonal of the base and then again to find the length of a diagonal of the entire box.]
   (b) Use the result of part (a) to derive formula (2).

8. (a) Make a conjecture about the set of points in 3-space that are equidistant from the origin and the point $(1, 0, 0)$.
   (b) Confirm your conjecture in part (a) by using distance formula (2).

9. Find the center and radius of the sphere that has $(1, -2, 4)$ and $(3, 4, -12)$ as endpoints of a diameter. [See Exercise 4.]

10. Show that $(4, 5, 2)$, $(1, 7, 3)$, and $(2, 4, 5)$ are vertices of an equilateral triangle.

11. (a) Show that $(2, 1, 6)$, $(4, 7, 9)$, and $(8, 5, -6)$ are the vertices of a right triangle.
    (b) Which vertex is at the $90°$ angle?
    (c) Find the area of the triangle.

12. Find the distance from the point $(-5, 2, -3)$ to the
    (a) xy-plane   (b) xz-plane   (c) yz-plane
    (d) x-axis   (e) y-axis   (f) z-axis.

13. In each part, find the standard equation of the sphere that satisfies the stated conditions.
    (a) Center $(1, 0, -1)$; diameter $= 8$.
    (b) Center $(-1, 3, 2)$ and passing through the origin.
    (c) A diameter has endpoints $(-1, 2, 1)$ and $(0, 2, 3)$.

14. Find equations of two spheres that are centered at the origin and are tangent to the sphere of radius 1 centered at $(3, -2, 4)$.

15. In each part, find an equation of the sphere with center $(2, -1, -3)$ and satisfying the given condition.
    (a) Tangent to the xy-plane
    (b) Tangent to the xz-plane
    (c) Tangent to the yz-plane

16. (a) Find an equation of the sphere that is inscribed in the cube that is centered at the point $(-2, 1, 3)$ and has sides of length 1 that are parallel to the coordinate planes.

(cont.)

(b) Find an equation of the sphere that is circumscribed about the cube in part (a).

17. A sphere has center in the first octant and is tangent to each of the three coordinate planes. Show that the center of the sphere is at a point of the form (r, r, r), where r is the radius of the sphere.

18. A sphere has center in the first octant and is tangent to each of the three coordinate planes. The distance from the origin to the sphere is $3 - \sqrt{3}$ units. Find an equation for the sphere.

19–22 True–False Determine whether the statement is true or false. Explain your answer. ■

19. By definition, a "cylindrical surface" is a right circular cylinder whose axis is parallel to one of the coordinate axes.

20. The graph of $x^2 + y^2 = 1$ in 3-space is a circle of radius 1 centered at the origin.

21. If a point belongs to both the xy-plane and the xz-plane, then the point lies on the x-axis.

22. A sphere with center $P(x_0, y_0, z_0)$ and radius r consists of all points (x, y, z) that satisfy the inequality

$$(x - x_0)^2 + (y - y_0)^2 + (z - z_0)^2 \leq r^2$$

23–28 Describe the surface whose equation is given. ■

23. $x^2 + y^2 + z^2 + 10x + 4y + 2z - 19 = 0$

24. $x^2 + y^2 + z^2 - y = 0$

25. $2x^2 + 2y^2 + 2z^2 - 2x - 3y + 5z - 2 = 0$

26. $x^2 + y^2 + z^2 + 2x - 2y + 2z + 3 = 0$

27. $x^2 + y^2 + z^2 - 3x + 4y - 8z + 25 = 0$

28. $x^2 + y^2 + z^2 - 2x - 6y - 8z + 1 = 0$

29. In each part, sketch the portion of the surface that lies in the first octant.
(a) $y = x$ (b) $y = z$ (c) $x = z$

30. In each part, sketch the graph of the equation in 3-space.
(a) $x = 1$ (b) $y = 1$ (c) $z = 1$

31. In each part, sketch the graph of the equation in 3-space.
(a) $x^2 + y^2 = 25$ (b) $y^2 + z^2 = 25$ (c) $x^2 + z^2 = 25$

32. In each part, sketch the graph of the equation in 3-space.
(a) $x = y^2$ (b) $z = x^2$ (c) $y = z^2$

33. In each part, write an equation for the surface.
(a) The plane that contains the x-axis and the point $(0, 1, 2)$.
(b) The plane that contains the y-axis and the point $(1, 0, 2)$.
(c) The right circular cylinder that has radius 1 and is centered on the line parallel to the z-axis that passes through the point $(1, 1, 0)$.
(d) The right circular cylinder that has radius 1 and is centered on the line parallel to the y-axis that passes through the point $(1, 0, 1)$.

34. Find equations for the following right circular cylinders. Each cylinder has radius a and is tangent to two coordinate planes.

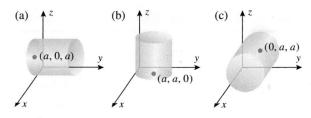

35–44 Sketch the surface in 3-space. ■

35. $y = \sin x$ **36.** $y = e^x$

37. $z = 1 - y^2$ **38.** $z = \cos x$

39. $2x + z = 3$ **40.** $2x + 3y = 6$

41. $4x^2 + 9z^2 = 36$ **42.** $z = \sqrt{3 - x}$

43. $y^2 - 4z^2 = 4$ **44.** $yz = 1$

45. Use a graphing utility to generate the curve $y = x^3/(1 + x^2)$ in the xy-plane, and then use the graph to help sketch the surface $z = y^3/(1 + y^2)$ in 3-space.

46. Use a graphing utility to generate the curve $y = x/(1 + x^4)$ in the xy-plane, and then use the graph to help sketch the surface $z = y/(1 + y^4)$ in 3-space.

47. If a bug walks on the sphere

$$x^2 + y^2 + z^2 + 2x - 2y - 4z - 3 = 0$$

how close and how far can it get from the origin?

48. Describe the set of all points in 3-space whose coordinates satisfy the inequality $x^2 + y^2 + z^2 - 2x + 8z \leq 8$.

49. Describe the set of all points in 3-space whose coordinates satisfy the inequality $y^2 + z^2 + 6y - 4z > 3$.

50. The distance between a point $P(x, y, z)$ and the point $A(1, -2, 0)$ is twice the distance between P and the point $B(0, 1, 1)$. Show that the set of all such points is a sphere, and find the center and radius of the sphere.

51. As shown in the accompanying figure, a bowling ball of radius R is placed inside a box just large enough to hold it, and it is secured for shipping by packing a Styrofoam sphere into each corner of the box. Find the radius of the largest Styrofoam sphere that can be used. [*Hint:* Take the origin of a Cartesian coordinate system at a corner of the box with the coordinate axes along the edges.]

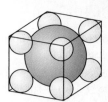

◄ **Figure Ex-51**

52. Consider the equation

$$x^2 + y^2 + z^2 + Gx + Hy + Iz + J = 0$$

and let $K = G^2 + H^2 + I^2 - 4J$.
(a) Prove that the equation represents a sphere if $K > 0$, a point if $K = 0$, and has no graph if $K < 0$.   *(cont.)*

(b) In the case where $K > 0$, find the center and radius of the sphere.

53. (a) The accompanying figure shows a surface of revolution that is generated by revolving the curve $y = f(x)$ in the xy-plane about the x-axis. Show that the equation of this surface is $y^2 + z^2 = [f(x)]^2$. [*Hint:* Each point on the curve traces a circle as it revolves about the x-axis.]

(b) Find an equation of the surface of revolution that is generated by revolving the curve $y = e^x$ in the xy-plane about the x-axis.

(c) Show that the ellipsoid $3x^2 + 4y^2 + 4z^2 = 16$ is a surface of revolution about the x-axis by finding a curve $y = f(x)$ in the xy-plane that generates it.

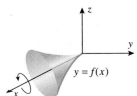

$y = f(x)$

◀ **Figure Ex-53**

54. In each part, use the idea in Exercise 53(a) to derive a formula for the stated surface of revolution.

(a) The surface generated by revolving the curve $x = f(y)$ in the xy-plane about the y-axis.

(b) The surface generated by revolving the curve $y = f(z)$ in the yz-plane about the z-axis.

(c) The surface generated by revolving the curve $z = f(x)$ in the xz-plane about the x-axis.

55. Show that for all values of θ and ϕ, the point

$$(a \sin \phi \cos \theta, a \sin \phi \sin \theta, a \cos \phi)$$

lies on the sphere $x^2 + y^2 + z^2 = a^2$.

56. Writing Explain how you might determine whether a set of points in 3-space is the graph of an equation involving at most two of the variables x, y, and z.

57. Writing Discuss what happens geometrically when equations in x, y, and z are replaced by inequalities. For example, compare the graph of $x^2 + y^2 + z^2 = 1$ with the set of points that satisfy the inequality $x^2 + y^2 + z^2 \leq 1$.

✔ **QUICK CHECK ANSWERS 11.1**

1. $\sqrt{38}$ 2. sphere; 4; $(3, 2, -1)$ 3. $\sqrt{38} - 6$ 4. (a) $(0, 0, -3)$; 5 (b) 4; -4 (c) 2; -8

11.2 VECTORS

Many physical quantities such as area, length, mass, and temperature are completely described once the magnitude of the quantity is given. Such quantities are called "scalars." Other physical quantities, called "vectors," are not completely determined until both a magnitude and a direction are specified. For example, winds are usually described by giving their speed and direction, say 20 mi/h northeast. The wind speed and wind direction together form a vector quantity called the wind velocity. Other examples of vectors are force and displacement. In this section we will develop the basic mathematical properties of vectors.

■ VECTORS IN PHYSICS AND ENGINEERING

A particle that moves along a line can move in only two directions, so its direction of motion can be described by taking one direction to be positive and the other negative. Thus, the *displacement* or *change in position* of the point can be described by a signed real number. For example, a displacement of 3 ($= +3$) describes a position change of 3 units in the positive direction, and a displacement of -3 describes a position change of 3 units in the negative direction. However, for a particle that moves in two dimensions or three dimensions, a plus or minus sign is no longer sufficient to specify the direction of motion—other methods are required. One method is to use an arrow, called a *vector*, that points in the direction of motion and whose length represents the distance from the starting point to the ending point; this is called the ***displacement vector*** for the motion. For example, Figure 11.2.1*a* shows the displacement vector of a particle that moves from point A to point B along a circuitous path. Note that the length of the arrow describes the

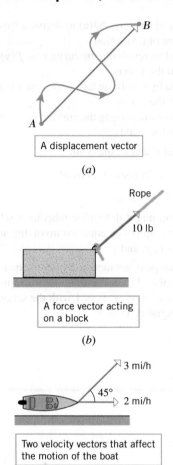

A displacement vector

(a)

Rope

10 lb

A force vector acting on a block

(b)

3 mi/h

45°

2 mi/h

Two velocity vectors that affect the motion of the boat

(c)

▲ **Figure 11.2.1**

distance between the starting and ending points and not the actual distance traveled by the particle.

Arrows are not limited to describing displacements—they can be used to describe any physical quantity that involves both a magnitude and a direction. Two important examples are forces and velocities. For example, the arrow in Figure 11.2.1*b* represents a force vector of 10 lb acting in a specific direction on a block, and the arrows in Figure 11.2.1*c* show the velocity vector of a boat whose motor propels it parallel to the shore at 2 mi/h and the velocity vector of a 3 mi/h wind acting at an angle of 45° with the shoreline. Intuition suggests that the two velocity vectors will combine to produce some net velocity for the boat at an angle to the shoreline. Thus, our first objective in this section is to define mathematical operations on vectors that can be used to determine the combined effect of vectors.

■ **VECTORS VIEWED GEOMETRICALLY**

Vectors can be represented geometrically by arrows in 2-space or 3-space; the direction of the arrow specifies the direction of the vector, and the length of the arrow describes its magnitude. The tail of the arrow is called the ***initial point*** of the vector, and the tip of the arrow the ***terminal point***. We will denote vectors with lowercase boldface type such as **a**, **k**, **v**, **w**, and **x**. When discussing vectors, we will refer to real numbers as ***scalars***. Scalars will be denoted by lowercase italic type such as a, k, v, w, and x. Two vectors, **v** and **w**, are considered to be ***equal*** (also called ***equivalent***) if they have the same length and same direction, in which case we write **v** = **w**. Geometrically, two vectors are equal if they are translations of one another; thus, the three vectors in Figure 11.2.2*a* are equal, even though they are in different positions.

Because vectors are not affected by translation, the initial point of a vector **v** can be moved to any convenient point A by making an appropriate translation. If the initial point of **v** is A and the terminal point is B, then we write $\mathbf{v} = \overrightarrow{AB}$ when we want to emphasize the initial and terminal points (Figure 11.2.2*b*). If the initial and terminal points of a vector coincide, then the vector has length zero; we call this the ***zero vector*** and denote it by **0**. The zero vector does not have a specific direction, so we will agree that it can be assigned any convenient direction in a specific problem.

There are various algebraic operations that are performed on vectors, all of whose definitions originated in physics. We begin with vector addition.

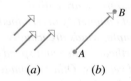

(a)   (b)

▲ **Figure 11.2.2**

> **11.2.1   DEFINITION**   If **v** and **w** are vectors, then the ***sum*** **v** + **w** is the vector from the initial point of **v** to the terminal point of **w** when the vectors are positioned so the initial point of **w** is at the terminal point of **v** (Figure 11.2.3*a*).

In Figure 11.2.3*b* we have constructed two sums, **v** + **w** (from purple arrows) and **w** + **v** (from green arrows). It is evident that

$$\mathbf{v} + \mathbf{w} = \mathbf{w} + \mathbf{v}$$

and that the sum (gray arrow) coincides with the diagonal of the parallelogram determined by **v** and **w** when these vectors are positioned so they have the same initial point.

Since the initial and terminal points of **0** coincide, it follows that

$$\mathbf{0} + \mathbf{v} = \mathbf{v} + \mathbf{0} = \mathbf{v}$$

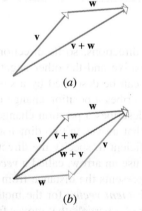

w

v

v + w

(a)

w

v   **v + w**

w + v   **v**

w

(b)

▲ **Figure 11.2.3**

> **11.2.2   DEFINITION**   If **v** is a nonzero vector and k is a nonzero real number (a scalar), then the ***scalar multiple*** $k\mathbf{v}$ is defined to be the vector whose length is $|k|$ times the length of **v** and whose direction is the same as that of **v** if $k > 0$ and opposite to that of **v** if $k < 0$. We define $k\mathbf{v} = \mathbf{0}$ if $k = 0$ or $\mathbf{v} = \mathbf{0}$.

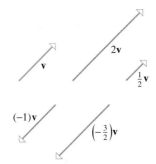

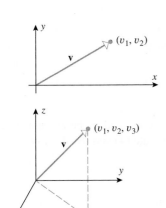

▲ Figure 11.2.4

Figure 11.2.4 shows the geometric relationship between a vector **v** and various scalar multiples of it. Observe that if k and **v** are nonzero, then the vectors **v** and k**v** lie on the same line if their initial points coincide and lie on parallel or coincident lines if they do not. Thus, we say that **v** and k**v** are **parallel vectors**. Observe also that the vector (-1)**v** has the same length as **v** but is oppositely directed. We call (-1)**v** the **negative** of **v** and denote it by $-$**v** (Figure 11.2.5). In particular, $-\mathbf{0} = (-1)\mathbf{0} = \mathbf{0}$.

Vector subtraction is defined in terms of addition and scalar multiplication by

$$\mathbf{v} - \mathbf{w} = \mathbf{v} + (-\mathbf{w})$$

The difference **v** $-$ **w** can be obtained geometrically by first constructing the vector $-$**w** and then adding **v** and $-$**w**, say by the parallelogram method (Figure 11.2.6a). However, if **v** and **w** are positioned so their initial points coincide, then **v** $-$ **w** can be formed more directly, as shown in Figure 11.2.6b, by drawing the vector from the terminal point of **w** (the second term) to the terminal point of **v** (the first term). In the special case where **v** = **w** the terminal points of the vectors coincide, so their difference is **0**; that is,

$$\mathbf{v} + (-\mathbf{v}) = \mathbf{v} - \mathbf{v} = \mathbf{0}$$

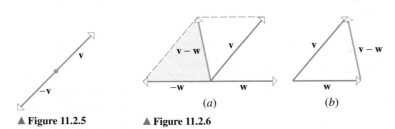

▲ Figure 11.2.5   ▲ Figure 11.2.6

■ VECTORS IN COORDINATE SYSTEMS

Problems involving vectors are often best solved by introducing a rectangular coordinate system. If a vector **v** is positioned with its initial point at the origin of a rectangular coordinate system, then its terminal point will have coordinates of the form (v_1, v_2) or (v_1, v_2, v_3), depending on whether the vector is in 2-space or 3-space (Figure 11.2.7). We call these coordinates the **components** of **v**, and we write **v** in *component form* using the **bracket notation**

$$\mathbf{v} = \langle v_1, v_2 \rangle \quad \text{or} \quad \mathbf{v} = \langle v_1, v_2, v_3 \rangle$$

2-space   3-space

▲ Figure 11.2.7

Note the difference in notation between a *point* (v_1, v_2) and a *vector* $\langle v_1, v_2 \rangle$.

In particular, the zero vectors in 2-space and 3-space are

$$\mathbf{0} = \langle 0, 0 \rangle \quad \text{and} \quad \mathbf{0} = \langle 0, 0, 0 \rangle$$

respectively.

Components provide a simple way of identifying equivalent vectors. For example, consider the vectors $\mathbf{v} = \langle v_1, v_2 \rangle$ and $\mathbf{w} = \langle w_1, w_2 \rangle$ in 2-space. If **v** = **w**, then the vectors have the same length and same direction, and this means that their terminal points coincide when their initial points are placed at the origin. It follows that $v_1 = w_1$ and $v_2 = w_2$, so we have shown that equivalent vectors have the same components. Conversely, if $v_1 = w_1$ and $v_2 = w_2$, then the terminal points of the vectors coincide when their initial points are placed at the origin. It follows that the vectors have the same length and same direction, so we have shown that vectors with the same components are equivalent. A similar argument holds for vectors in 3-space, so we have the following result.

11.2.3 THEOREM *Two vectors are equivalent if and only if their corresponding components are equal.*

For example,

$$\langle a, b, c \rangle = \langle 1, -4, 2 \rangle$$

if and only if $a = 1$, $b = -4$, and $c = 2$.

■ ARITHMETIC OPERATIONS ON VECTORS

The next theorem shows how to perform arithmetic operations on vectors using components.

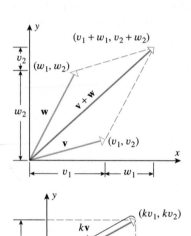

11.2.4 THEOREM *If $\mathbf{v} = \langle v_1, v_2 \rangle$ and $\mathbf{w} = \langle w_1, w_2 \rangle$ are vectors in 2-space and k is any scalar, then*

$$\mathbf{v} + \mathbf{w} = \langle v_1 + w_1, v_2 + w_2 \rangle \tag{1}$$
$$\mathbf{v} - \mathbf{w} = \langle v_1 - w_1, v_2 - w_2 \rangle \tag{2}$$
$$k\mathbf{v} = \langle kv_1, kv_2 \rangle \tag{3}$$

Similarly, if $\mathbf{v} = \langle v_1, v_2, v_3 \rangle$ and $\mathbf{w} = \langle w_1, w_2, w_3 \rangle$ are vectors in 3-space and k is any scalar, then

$$\mathbf{v} + \mathbf{w} = \langle v_1 + w_1, v_2 + w_2, v_3 + w_3 \rangle \tag{4}$$
$$\mathbf{v} - \mathbf{w} = \langle v_1 - w_1, v_2 - w_2, v_3 - w_3 \rangle \tag{5}$$
$$k\mathbf{v} = \langle kv_1, kv_2, kv_3 \rangle \tag{6}$$

▲ Figure 11.2.8

We will not prove this theorem. However, results (1) and (3) should be evident from Figure 11.2.8. Similar figures in 3-space can be used to motivate (4) and (6). Formulas (2) and (5) can be obtained by writing $\mathbf{v} + \mathbf{w} = \mathbf{v} + (-1)\mathbf{w}$.

▶ **Example 1** If $\mathbf{v} = \langle -2, 0, 1 \rangle$ and $\mathbf{w} = \langle 3, 5, -4 \rangle$, then

$$\mathbf{v} + \mathbf{w} = \langle -2, 0, 1 \rangle + \langle 3, 5, -4 \rangle = \langle 1, 5, -3 \rangle$$
$$3\mathbf{v} = \langle -6, 0, 3 \rangle$$
$$-\mathbf{w} = \langle -3, -5, 4 \rangle$$
$$\mathbf{w} - 2\mathbf{v} = \langle 3, 5, -4 \rangle - \langle -4, 0, 2 \rangle = \langle 7, 5, -6 \rangle \ \blacktriangleleft$$

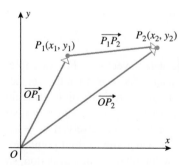

■ VECTORS WITH INITIAL POINT NOT AT THE ORIGIN

Recall that we defined the components of a vector to be the coordinates of its terminal point when its initial point is at the origin. We will now consider the problem of finding the components of a vector whose initial point is not at the origin. To be specific, suppose that $P_1(x_1, y_1)$ and $P_2(x_2, y_2)$ are points in 2-space and we are interested in finding the components of the vector $\overrightarrow{P_1P_2}$. As illustrated in Figure 11.2.9, we can write this vector as

$$\overrightarrow{P_1P_2} = \overrightarrow{OP_2} - \overrightarrow{OP_1} = \langle x_2, y_2 \rangle - \langle x_1, y_1 \rangle = \langle x_2 - x_1, y_2 - y_1 \rangle$$

▲ Figure 11.2.9

Thus, we have shown that the components of the vector $\overrightarrow{P_1P_2}$ can be obtained by subtracting the coordinates of its initial point from the coordinates of its terminal point. Similar computations hold in 3-space, so we have established the following result.

11.2.5 THEOREM *If $\overrightarrow{P_1P_2}$ is a vector in 2-space with initial point $P_1(x_1, y_1)$ and terminal point $P_2(x_2, y_2)$, then*

$$\overrightarrow{P_1P_2} = \langle x_2 - x_1, y_2 - y_1 \rangle \tag{7}$$

Similarly, if $\overrightarrow{P_1P_2}$ is a vector in 3-space with initial point $P_1(x_1, y_1, z_1)$ and terminal point $P_2(x_2, y_2, z_2)$, then

$$\overrightarrow{P_1P_2} = \langle x_2 - x_1, y_2 - y_1, z_2 - z_1 \rangle \tag{8}$$

▶ **Example 2** In 2-space the vector from $P_1(1, 3)$ to $P_2(4, -2)$ is

$$\overrightarrow{P_1P_2} = \langle 4 - 1, -2 - 3 \rangle = \langle 3, -5 \rangle$$

and in 3-space the vector from $A(0, -2, 5)$ to $B(3, 4, -1)$ is

$$\overrightarrow{AB} = \langle 3 - 0, 4 - (-2), -1 - 5 \rangle = \langle 3, 6, -6 \rangle \ ◀$$

■ **RULES OF VECTOR ARITHMETIC**

The following theorem shows that many of the familiar rules of ordinary arithmetic also hold for vector arithmetic.

It follows from part (*b*) of Theorem 11.2.6 that the expression

$$\mathbf{u} + \mathbf{v} + \mathbf{w}$$

is unambiguous since the same vector results no matter how the terms are grouped.

11.2.6 THEOREM *For any vectors $\mathbf{u}$, $\mathbf{v}$, and $\mathbf{w}$ and any scalars k and l, the following relationships hold:*

(*a*) $\mathbf{u} + \mathbf{v} = \mathbf{v} + \mathbf{u}$ (*e*) $k(l\mathbf{u}) = (kl)\mathbf{u}$

(*b*) $(\mathbf{u} + \mathbf{v}) + \mathbf{w} = \mathbf{u} + (\mathbf{v} + \mathbf{w})$ (*f*) $k(\mathbf{u} + \mathbf{v}) = k\mathbf{u} + k\mathbf{v}$

(*c*) $\mathbf{u} + \mathbf{0} = \mathbf{0} + \mathbf{u} = \mathbf{u}$ (*g*) $(k + l)\mathbf{u} = k\mathbf{u} + l\mathbf{u}$

(*d*) $\mathbf{u} + (-\mathbf{u}) = \mathbf{0}$ (*h*) $1\mathbf{u} = \mathbf{u}$

The results in this theorem can be proved either algebraically by using components or geometrically by treating the vectors as arrows. We will prove part (*b*) both ways and leave some of the remaining proofs as exercises.

Observe that in Figure 11.2.10 the vectors $\mathbf{u}$, $\mathbf{v}$, and $\mathbf{w}$ are positioned "tip to tail" and that

$$\mathbf{u} + \mathbf{v} + \mathbf{w}$$

is the vector from the initial point of $\mathbf{u}$ (the first term in the sum) to the terminal point of $\mathbf{w}$ (the last term in the sum). This "tip to tail" method of vector addition also works for four or more vectors (Figure 11.2.11).

PROOF (*b*) (ALGEBRAIC IN 2-SPACE) Let $\mathbf{u} = \langle u_1, u_2 \rangle$, $\mathbf{v} = \langle v_1, v_2 \rangle$, and $\mathbf{w} = \langle w_1, w_2 \rangle$. Then

$$\begin{aligned}
(\mathbf{u} + \mathbf{v}) + \mathbf{w} &= (\langle u_1, u_2 \rangle + \langle v_1, v_2 \rangle) + \langle w_1, w_2 \rangle \\
&= \langle u_1 + v_1, u_2 + v_2 \rangle + \langle w_1, w_2 \rangle \\
&= \langle (u_1 + v_1) + w_1, (u_2 + v_2) + w_2 \rangle \\
&= \langle u_1 + (v_1 + w_1), u_2 + (v_2 + w_2) \rangle \\
&= \langle u_1, u_2 \rangle + \langle v_1 + w_1, v_2 + w_2 \rangle \\
&= \mathbf{u} + (\mathbf{v} + \mathbf{w})
\end{aligned}$$

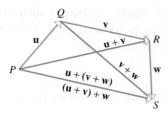

▲ **Figure 11.2.10**

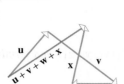

▲ **Figure 11.2.11**

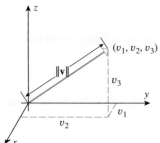

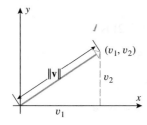

▲ **Figure 11.2.12**

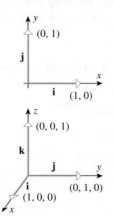

▲ **Figure 11.2.13**

PROOF (b) (GEOMETRIC)   Let **u**, **v**, and **w** be represented by $\overrightarrow{PQ}$, $\overrightarrow{QR}$, and $\overrightarrow{RS}$ as shown in Figure 11.2.10. Then

$$\mathbf{v} + \mathbf{w} = \overrightarrow{QS} \quad \text{and} \quad \mathbf{u} + (\mathbf{v} + \mathbf{w}) = \overrightarrow{PS}$$
$$\mathbf{u} + \mathbf{v} = \overrightarrow{PR} \quad \text{and} \quad (\mathbf{u} + \mathbf{v}) + \mathbf{w} = \overrightarrow{PS}$$

Therefore,

$$(\mathbf{u} + \mathbf{v}) + \mathbf{w} = \mathbf{u} + (\mathbf{v} + \mathbf{w}) \quad \blacksquare$$

■ NORM OF A VECTOR

The distance between the initial and terminal points of a vector **v** is called the *length*, the *norm*, or the *magnitude* of **v** and is denoted by $\|\mathbf{v}\|$. This distance does not change if the vector is translated, so for purposes of calculating the norm we can assume that the vector is positioned with its initial point at the origin (Figure 11.2.12). This makes it evident that the norm of a vector $\mathbf{v} = \langle v_1, v_2 \rangle$ in 2-space is given by

$$\|\mathbf{v}\| = \sqrt{v_1^2 + v_2^2} \tag{9}$$

and the norm of a vector $\mathbf{v} = \langle v_1, v_2, v_3 \rangle$ in 3-space is given by

$$\|\mathbf{v}\| = \sqrt{v_1^2 + v_2^2 + v_3^2} \tag{10}$$

▶ **Example 3**   Find the norms of $\mathbf{v} = \langle -2, 3 \rangle$, $10\mathbf{v} = \langle -20, 30 \rangle$, and $\mathbf{w} = \langle 2, 3, 6 \rangle$.

Solution.   From (9) and (10)

$$\|\mathbf{v}\| = \sqrt{(-2)^2 + 3^2} = \sqrt{13}$$
$$\|10\mathbf{v}\| = \sqrt{(-20)^2 + 30^2} = \sqrt{1300} = 10\sqrt{13}$$
$$\|\mathbf{w}\| = \sqrt{2^2 + 3^2 + 6^2} = \sqrt{49} = 7 \quad ◄$$

Note that $\|10\mathbf{v}\| = 10\|\mathbf{v}\|$ in Example 3. This is consistent with Definition 11.2.2, which stipulated that for any vector **v** and scalar k, the length of $k\mathbf{v}$ must be $|k|$ times the length of **v**; that is,

$$\|k\mathbf{v}\| = |k|\|\mathbf{v}\| \tag{11}$$

Thus, for example,

$$\|3\mathbf{v}\| = |3|\|\mathbf{v}\| = 3\|\mathbf{v}\|$$
$$\|-2\mathbf{v}\| = |-2|\|\mathbf{v}\| = 2\|\mathbf{v}\|$$
$$\|-1\mathbf{v}\| = |-1|\|\mathbf{v}\| = \|\mathbf{v}\|$$

This applies to vectors in 2-space and 3-space.

■ UNIT VECTORS

A vector of length 1 is called a *unit vector*. In an xy-coordinate system the unit vectors along the x- and y-axes are denoted by **i** and **j**, respectively; and in an xyz-coordinate system the unit vectors along the x-, y-, and z-axes are denoted by **i**, **j**, and **k**, respectively (Figure 11.2.13). Thus,

$$\mathbf{i} = \langle 1, 0 \rangle, \qquad \mathbf{j} = \langle 0, 1 \rangle \qquad \boxed{\text{In 2-space}}$$
$$\mathbf{i} = \langle 1, 0, 0 \rangle, \quad \mathbf{j} = \langle 0, 1, 0 \rangle, \quad \mathbf{k} = \langle 0, 0, 1 \rangle \qquad \boxed{\text{In 3-space}}$$

Every vector in 2-space is expressible uniquely in terms of $\mathbf{i}$ and $\mathbf{j}$, and every vector in 3-space is expressible uniquely in terms of $\mathbf{i}$, $\mathbf{j}$, and $\mathbf{k}$ as follows:

$$\mathbf{v} = \langle v_1, v_2 \rangle = \langle v_1, 0 \rangle + \langle 0, v_2 \rangle = v_1 \langle 1, 0 \rangle + v_2 \langle 0, 1 \rangle = v_1 \mathbf{i} + v_2 \mathbf{j}$$

$$\mathbf{v} = \langle v_1, v_2, v_3 \rangle = v_1 \langle 1, 0, 0 \rangle + v_2 \langle 0, 1, 0 \rangle + v_3 \langle 0, 0, 1 \rangle = v_1 \mathbf{i} + v_2 \mathbf{j} + v_3 \mathbf{k}$$

▶ **Example 4** The following table provides some examples of vector notation in 2-space and 3-space.

2-SPACE	3-SPACE
$\langle 2, 3 \rangle = 2\mathbf{i} + 3\mathbf{j}$	$\langle 2, -3, 4 \rangle = 2\mathbf{i} - 3\mathbf{j} + 4\mathbf{k}$
$\langle -4, 0 \rangle = -4\mathbf{i} + 0\mathbf{j} = -4\mathbf{i}$	$\langle 0, 3, 0 \rangle = 3\mathbf{j}$
$\langle 0, 0 \rangle = 0\mathbf{i} + 0\mathbf{j} = \mathbf{0}$	$\langle 0, 0, 0 \rangle = 0\mathbf{i} + 0\mathbf{j} + 0\mathbf{k} = \mathbf{0}$
$(3\mathbf{i} + 2\mathbf{j}) + (4\mathbf{i} + \mathbf{j}) = 7\mathbf{i} + 3\mathbf{j}$	$(3\mathbf{i} + 2\mathbf{j} - \mathbf{k}) - (4\mathbf{i} - \mathbf{j} + 2\mathbf{k}) = -\mathbf{i} + 3\mathbf{j} - 3\mathbf{k}$
$5(6\mathbf{i} - 2\mathbf{j}) = 30\mathbf{i} - 10\mathbf{j}$	$2(\mathbf{i} + \mathbf{j} - \mathbf{k}) + 4(\mathbf{i} - \mathbf{j}) = 6\mathbf{i} - 2\mathbf{j} - 2\mathbf{k}$
$\|2\mathbf{i} - 3\mathbf{j}\| = \sqrt{2^2 + (-3)^2} = \sqrt{13}$	$\|\mathbf{i} + 2\mathbf{j} - 3\mathbf{k}\| = \sqrt{1^2 + 2^2 + (-3)^2} = \sqrt{14}$
$\|v_1\mathbf{i} + v_2\mathbf{j}\| = \sqrt{v_1^2 + v_2^2}$	$\|\langle v_1, v_2, v_3 \rangle\| = \sqrt{v_1^2 + v_2^2 + v_3^2}$

◀

The two notations for vectors illustrated in Example 4 are completely interchangeable, the choice being a matter of convenience or personal preference.

■ NORMALIZING A VECTOR

A common problem in applications is to find a unit vector $\mathbf{u}$ that has the same direction as some given nonzero vector $\mathbf{v}$. This can be done by multiplying $\mathbf{v}$ by the reciprocal of its length; that is,

$$\mathbf{u} = \frac{1}{\|\mathbf{v}\|}\mathbf{v} = \frac{\mathbf{v}}{\|\mathbf{v}\|}$$

is a unit vector with the same direction as $\mathbf{v}$—the direction is the same because $k = 1/\|\mathbf{v}\|$ is a positive scalar, and the length is 1 because

$$\|\mathbf{u}\| = \|k\mathbf{v}\| = |k|\|\mathbf{v}\| = k\|\mathbf{v}\| = \frac{1}{\|\mathbf{v}\|}\|\mathbf{v}\| = 1$$

The process of multiplying a vector $\mathbf{v}$ by the reciprocal of its length to obtain a unit vector with the same direction is called *normalizing* $\mathbf{v}$.

TECHNOLOGY MASTERY

Many calculating utilities can perform vector operations, and some have built-in norm and normalization operations. If your calculator has these capabilities, use it to check the computations in Examples 1, 3, and 5.

▶ **Example 5** Find the unit vector that has the same direction as $\mathbf{v} = 2\mathbf{i} + 2\mathbf{j} - \mathbf{k}$.

Solution. The vector $\mathbf{v}$ has length

$$\|\mathbf{v}\| = \sqrt{2^2 + 2^2 + (-1)^2} = 3$$

so the unit vector $\mathbf{u}$ in the same direction as $\mathbf{v}$ is

$$\mathbf{u} = \tfrac{1}{3}\mathbf{v} = \tfrac{2}{3}\mathbf{i} + \tfrac{2}{3}\mathbf{j} - \tfrac{1}{3}\mathbf{k} \quad ◀$$

■ VECTORS DETERMINED BY LENGTH AND ANGLE

If $\mathbf{v}$ is a nonzero vector with its initial point at the origin of an xy-coordinate system, and if θ is the angle from the positive x-axis to the radial line through $\mathbf{v}$, then the x-component of $\mathbf{v}$ can be written as $\|\mathbf{v}\| \cos\theta$ and the y-component as $\|\mathbf{v}\| \sin\theta$ (Figure 11.2.14); and hence $\mathbf{v}$ can be expressed in trigonometric form as

$$\mathbf{v} = \|\mathbf{v}\| \langle \cos\theta, \sin\theta \rangle \quad \text{or} \quad \mathbf{v} = \|\mathbf{v}\| \cos\theta\, \mathbf{i} + \|\mathbf{v}\| \sin\theta\, \mathbf{j} \tag{12}$$

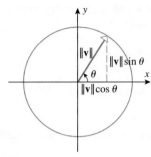

▲ **Figure 11.2.14**

In the special case of a unit vector $\mathbf{u}$ this simplifies to

$$\mathbf{u} = \langle \cos\theta, \sin\theta \rangle \quad \text{or} \quad \mathbf{u} = \cos\theta\,\mathbf{i} + \sin\theta\,\mathbf{j} \tag{13}$$

▶ **Example 6**

(a) Find the vector of length 2 that makes an angle of $\pi/4$ with the positive x-axis.

(b) Find the angle that the vector $\mathbf{v} = -\sqrt{3}\,\mathbf{i} + \mathbf{j}$ makes with the positive x-axis.

Solution (a). From (12)

$$\mathbf{v} = 2\cos\frac{\pi}{4}\mathbf{i} + 2\sin\frac{\pi}{4}\mathbf{j} = \sqrt{2}\,\mathbf{i} + \sqrt{2}\,\mathbf{j}$$

Solution (b). We will normalize $\mathbf{v}$, then use (13) to find $\sin\theta$ and $\cos\theta$, and then use these values to find θ. Normalizing $\mathbf{v}$ yields

$$\frac{\mathbf{v}}{\|\mathbf{v}\|} = \frac{-\sqrt{3}\,\mathbf{i} + \mathbf{j}}{\sqrt{(-\sqrt{3})^2 + 1^2}} = -\frac{\sqrt{3}}{2}\mathbf{i} + \frac{1}{2}\mathbf{j}$$

Thus, $\cos\theta = -\sqrt{3}/2$ and $\sin\theta = 1/2$, from which we conclude that $\theta = 5\pi/6$. ◀

■ **VECTORS DETERMINED BY LENGTH AND A VECTOR IN THE SAME DIRECTION**

It is a common problem in many applications that a direction in 2-space or 3-space is determined by some known unit vector $\mathbf{u}$, and it is of interest to find the components of a vector $\mathbf{v}$ that has the same direction as $\mathbf{u}$ and some specified length $\|\mathbf{v}\|$. This can be done by expressing $\mathbf{v}$ as

$$\mathbf{v} = \|\mathbf{v}\|\mathbf{u} \qquad \boxed{\mathbf{v} \text{ is equal to its length times a unit vector in the same direction.}}$$

and then reading off the components of $\|\mathbf{v}\|\mathbf{u}$.

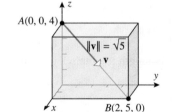

▲ **Figure 11.2.15**

▶ **Example 7** Figure 11.2.15 shows a vector $\mathbf{v}$ of length $\sqrt{5}$ that extends along the line through A and B. Find the components of $\mathbf{v}$.

Solution. First we will find the components of the vector $\overrightarrow{AB}$, then we will normalize this vector to obtain a unit vector in the direction of $\mathbf{v}$, and then we will multiply this unit vector by $\|\mathbf{v}\|$ to obtain the vector $\mathbf{v}$. The computations are as follows:

$$\overrightarrow{AB} = \langle 2, 5, 0 \rangle - \langle 0, 0, 4 \rangle = \langle 2, 5, -4 \rangle$$

$$\|\overrightarrow{AB}\| = \sqrt{2^2 + 5^2 + (-4)^2} = \sqrt{45} = 3\sqrt{5}$$

$$\frac{\overrightarrow{AB}}{\|\overrightarrow{AB}\|} = \left\langle \frac{2}{3\sqrt{5}}, \frac{5}{3\sqrt{5}}, -\frac{4}{3\sqrt{5}} \right\rangle$$

$$\mathbf{v} = \|\mathbf{v}\|\left(\frac{\overrightarrow{AB}}{\|\overrightarrow{AB}\|}\right) = \sqrt{5}\left\langle \frac{2}{3\sqrt{5}}, \frac{5}{3\sqrt{5}}, -\frac{4}{3\sqrt{5}} \right\rangle = \left\langle \frac{2}{3}, \frac{5}{3}, -\frac{4}{3} \right\rangle \quad ◀$$

■ **RESULTANT OF TWO CONCURRENT FORCES**

The effect that a force has on an object depends on the magnitude and direction of the force and the point at which it is applied. Thus, forces are regarded to be vector quantities and, indeed, the algebraic operations on vectors that we have defined in this section have their origin in the study of forces. For example, it is a fact of physics that if two forces $\mathbf{F}_1$ and

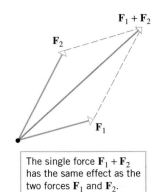

The single force $\mathbf{F}_1 + \mathbf{F}_2$ has the same effect as the two forces $\mathbf{F}_1$ and $\mathbf{F}_2$.

▲ **Figure 11.2.16**

$\mathbf{F}_2$ are applied at the same point on an object, then the two forces have the same effect on the object as the single force $\mathbf{F}_1 + \mathbf{F}_2$ applied at the point (Figure 11.2.16). Physicists and engineers call $\mathbf{F}_1 + \mathbf{F}_2$ the ***resultant*** of $\mathbf{F}_1$ and $\mathbf{F}_2$, and they say that the forces $\mathbf{F}_1$ and $\mathbf{F}_2$ are ***concurrent*** to indicate that they are applied at the same point.

In many applications, the magnitudes of two concurrent forces and the angle between them are known, and the problem is to find the magnitude and direction of the resultant. One approach to solving this problem is to use (12) to find the components of the concurrent forces, and then use (1) to find the components of the resultant. The next example illustrates this method.

▶ **Example 8**   Suppose that two forces are applied to an eye bracket, as shown in Figure 11.2.17. Find the magnitude of the resultant and the angle θ that it makes with the positive x-axis.

Solution.   Note that $\mathbf{F}_1$ makes an angle of $30°$ with the positive x-axis and $\mathbf{F}_2$ makes an angle of $30° + 40° = 70°$ with the positive x-axis. Since we are given that $\|\mathbf{F}_1\| = 200$ N and $\|\mathbf{F}_2\| = 300$ N, (12) yields

$$\mathbf{F}_1 = 200\langle\cos 30°, \sin 30°\rangle = \langle 100\sqrt{3}, 100\rangle$$

and

$$\mathbf{F}_2 = 300\langle\cos 70°, \sin 70°\rangle = \langle 300\cos 70°, 300\sin 70°\rangle$$

Therefore, the resultant $\mathbf{F} = \mathbf{F}_1 + \mathbf{F}_2$ has component form

$$\mathbf{F} = \mathbf{F}_1 + \mathbf{F}_2 = \langle 100\sqrt{3} + 300\cos 70°, 100 + 300\sin 70°\rangle$$
$$= 100\langle\sqrt{3} + 3\cos 70°, 1 + 3\sin 70°\rangle \approx \langle 275.8, 381.9\rangle$$

The magnitude of the resultant is then

$$\|\mathbf{F}\| = 100\sqrt{\left(\sqrt{3} + 3\cos 70°\right)^2 + \left(1 + 3\sin 70°\right)^2} \approx 471 \text{ N}$$

Let θ denote the angle $\mathbf{F}$ makes with the positive x-axis when the initial point of $\mathbf{F}$ is at the origin. Using (12) and equating the x-components of $\mathbf{F}$ yield

$$\|\mathbf{F}\|\cos\theta = 100\sqrt{3} + 300\cos 70° \quad \text{or} \quad \cos\theta = \frac{100\sqrt{3} + 300\cos 70°}{\|\mathbf{F}\|}$$

The resultant of three or more concurrent forces can be found by working in pairs. For example, the resultant of three forces can be found by finding the resultant of any two of the forces and then finding the resultant of that resultant with the third force.

Since the terminal point of $\mathbf{F}$ is in the first quadrant, we have

$$\theta = \cos^{-1}\left(\frac{100\sqrt{3} + 300\cos 70°}{\|\mathbf{F}\|}\right) \approx 54.2°$$

(Figure 11.2.18). ◀

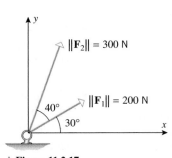

▲ **Figure 11.2.17**

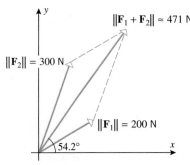

▲ **Figure 11.2.18**

✔**QUICK CHECK EXERCISES 11.2**   *(See page 784 for answers.)*

1. If $\mathbf{v} = \langle 3, -1, 7 \rangle$ and $\mathbf{w} = \langle 4, 10, -5 \rangle$, then
   (a) $\|\mathbf{v}\| = \underline{\hspace{1.5cm}}$ (b) $\mathbf{v} + \mathbf{w} = \underline{\hspace{1.5cm}}$
   (c) $\mathbf{v} - \mathbf{w} = \underline{\hspace{1.5cm}}$ (d) $2\mathbf{v} = \underline{\hspace{1.5cm}}$.

2. The unit vector in the direction of $\mathbf{v} = \langle 3, -1, 7 \rangle$ is
   $\underline{\hspace{1cm}}$.

3. The unit vector in 2-space that makes an angle of $\pi/3$ with the positive x-axis is $\underline{\hspace{1.5cm}}$.

4. Consider points $A(3, 4, 0)$ and $B(0, 0, 5)$.
   (a) $\overrightarrow{AB} = \underline{\hspace{1.5cm}}$
   (b) If $\mathbf{v}$ is a vector in the same direction as $\overrightarrow{AB}$ and the length of $\mathbf{v}$ is $\sqrt{2}$, then $\mathbf{v} = \underline{\hspace{1.5cm}}$.

EXERCISE SET 11.2

1–4 Sketch the vectors with their initial points at the origin. ■

1. (a) $\langle 2, 5 \rangle$ (b) $\langle -5, -4 \rangle$ (c) $\langle 2, 0 \rangle$
   (d) $-5\mathbf{i} + 3\mathbf{j}$ (e) $3\mathbf{i} - 2\mathbf{j}$ (f) $-6\mathbf{j}$

2. (a) $\langle -3, 7 \rangle$ (b) $\langle 6, -2 \rangle$ (c) $\langle 0, -8 \rangle$
   (d) $4\mathbf{i} + 2\mathbf{j}$ (e) $-2\mathbf{i} - \mathbf{j}$ (f) $4\mathbf{i}$

3. (a) $\langle 1, -2, 2 \rangle$ (b) $\langle 2, 2, -1 \rangle$
   (c) $-\mathbf{i} + 2\mathbf{j} + 3\mathbf{k}$ (d) $2\mathbf{i} + 3\mathbf{j} - \mathbf{k}$

4. (a) $\langle -1, 3, 2 \rangle$ (b) $\langle 3, 4, 2 \rangle$
   (c) $2\mathbf{j} - \mathbf{k}$ (d) $\mathbf{i} - \mathbf{j} + 2\mathbf{k}$

5–6 Find the components of the vector, and sketch an equivalent vector with its initial point at the origin. ■

5. (a)   (b)

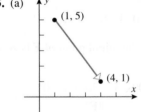
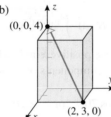

6. (a)   (b)

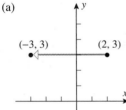
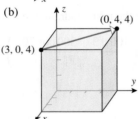

7–8 Find the components of the vector $\overrightarrow{P_1 P_2}$. ■

7. (a) $P_1(3, 5)$, $P_2(2, 8)$ (b) $P_1(7, -2)$, $P_2(0, 0)$
   (c) $P_1(5, -2, 1)$, $P_2(2, 4, 2)$

8. (a) $P_1(-6, -2)$, $P_2(-4, -1)$
   (b) $P_1(0, 0, 0)$, $P_2(-1, 6, 1)$
   (c) $P_1(4, 1, -3)$, $P_2(9, 1, -3)$

9. (a) Find the terminal point of $\mathbf{v} = 3\mathbf{i} - 2\mathbf{j}$ if the initial point is $(1, -2)$.
   (b) Find the initial point of $\mathbf{v} = \langle -3, 1, 2 \rangle$ if the terminal point is $(5, 0, -1)$.

10. (a) Find the terminal point of $\mathbf{v} = \langle 7, 6 \rangle$ if the initial point is $(2, -1)$.
   (b) Find the terminal point of $\mathbf{v} = \mathbf{i} + 2\mathbf{j} - 3\mathbf{k}$ if the initial point is $(-2, 1, 4)$.

11–12 Perform the stated operations on the given vectors $\mathbf{u}$, $\mathbf{v}$, and $\mathbf{w}$. ■

11. $\mathbf{u} = 3\mathbf{i} - \mathbf{k}$, $\mathbf{v} = \mathbf{i} - \mathbf{j} + 2\mathbf{k}$, $\mathbf{w} = 3\mathbf{j}$
   (a) $\mathbf{w} - \mathbf{v}$ (b) $6\mathbf{u} + 4\mathbf{w}$
   (c) $-\mathbf{v} - 2\mathbf{w}$ (d) $4(3\mathbf{u} + \mathbf{v})$
   (e) $-8(\mathbf{v} + \mathbf{w}) + 2\mathbf{u}$ (f) $3\mathbf{w} - (\mathbf{v} - \mathbf{w})$

12. $\mathbf{u} = \langle 2, -1, 3 \rangle$, $\mathbf{v} = \langle 4, 0, -2 \rangle$, $\mathbf{w} = \langle 1, 1, 3 \rangle$
   (a) $\mathbf{u} - \mathbf{w}$ (b) $7\mathbf{v} + 3\mathbf{w}$ (c) $-\mathbf{w} + \mathbf{v}$
   (d) $3(\mathbf{u} - 7\mathbf{v})$ (e) $-3\mathbf{v} - 8\mathbf{w}$ (f) $2\mathbf{v} - (\mathbf{u} + \mathbf{w})$

13–14 Find the norm of $\mathbf{v}$. ■

13. (a) $\mathbf{v} = \langle 1, -1 \rangle$ (b) $\mathbf{v} = -\mathbf{i} + 7\mathbf{j}$
   (c) $\mathbf{v} = \langle -1, 2, 4 \rangle$ (d) $\mathbf{v} = -3\mathbf{i} + 2\mathbf{j} + \mathbf{k}$

14. (a) $\mathbf{v} = \langle 3, 4 \rangle$ (b) $\mathbf{v} = \sqrt{2}\mathbf{i} - \sqrt{7}\mathbf{j}$
   (c) $\mathbf{v} = \langle 0, -3, 0 \rangle$ (d) $\mathbf{v} = \mathbf{i} + \mathbf{j} + \mathbf{k}$

15. Let $\mathbf{u} = \mathbf{i} - 3\mathbf{j} + 2\mathbf{k}$, $\mathbf{v} = \mathbf{i} + \mathbf{j}$, and $\mathbf{w} = 2\mathbf{i} + 2\mathbf{j} - 4\mathbf{k}$. Find
   (a) $\|\mathbf{u} + \mathbf{v}\|$ (b) $\|\mathbf{u}\| + \|\mathbf{v}\|$
   (c) $\|-2\mathbf{u}\| + 2\|\mathbf{v}\|$ (d) $\|3\mathbf{u} - 5\mathbf{v} + \mathbf{w}\|$
   (e) $\dfrac{1}{\|\mathbf{w}\|}\mathbf{w}$ (f) $\left\|\dfrac{1}{\|\mathbf{w}\|}\mathbf{w}\right\|$.

16. Is it possible to have $\|\mathbf{u} - \mathbf{v}\| = \|\mathbf{u} + \mathbf{v}\|$ if $\mathbf{u}$ and $\mathbf{v}$ are nonzero vectors? Justify your conclusion geometrically.

17–20 True–False Determine whether the statement is true or false. Explain your answer. ■

17. The norm of the sum of two vectors is equal to the sum of the norms of the two vectors.

18. If two distinct vectors $\mathbf{v}$ and $\mathbf{w}$ are drawn with the same initial point, then a vector drawn between the terminal points of $\mathbf{v}$ and $\mathbf{w}$ will be either $\mathbf{v} - \mathbf{w}$ or $\mathbf{w} - \mathbf{v}$.

19. There are exactly two unit vectors that are parallel to a given nonzero vector.

20. Given a nonzero scalar c and vectors **b** and **d**, the vector equation $c\mathbf{a} + \mathbf{b} = \mathbf{d}$ has a unique solution **a**.

21–22 Find unit vectors that satisfy the stated conditions.

21. (a) Same direction as $-\mathbf{i} + 4\mathbf{j}$.
(b) Oppositely directed to $6\mathbf{i} - 4\mathbf{j} + 2\mathbf{k}$.
(c) Same direction as the vector from the point $A(-1, 0, 2)$ to the point $B(3, 1, 1)$.

22. (a) Oppositely directed to $3\mathbf{i} - 4\mathbf{j}$.
(b) Same direction as $2\mathbf{i} - \mathbf{j} - 2\mathbf{k}$.
(c) Same direction as the vector from the point $A(-3, 2)$ to the point $B(1, -1)$.

23–24 Find the vectors that satisfy the stated conditions.

23. (a) Oppositely directed to $\mathbf{v} = \langle 3, -4 \rangle$ and half the length of **v**.
(b) Length $\sqrt{17}$ and same direction as $\mathbf{v} = \langle 7, 0, -6 \rangle$.

24. (a) Same direction as $\mathbf{v} = -2\mathbf{i} + 3\mathbf{j}$ and three times the length of **v**.
(b) Length 2 and oppositely directed to $\mathbf{v} = -3\mathbf{i} + 4\mathbf{j} + \mathbf{k}$.

25. In each part, find the component form of the vector **v** in 2-space that has the stated length and makes the stated angle θ with the positive x-axis.
(a) $\|\mathbf{v}\| = 3$; $\theta = \pi/4$ (b) $\|\mathbf{v}\| = 2$; $\theta = 90°$
(c) $\|\mathbf{v}\| = 5$; $\theta = 120°$ (d) $\|\mathbf{v}\| = 1$; $\theta = \pi$

26. Find the component forms of $\mathbf{v} + \mathbf{w}$ and $\mathbf{v} - \mathbf{w}$ in 2-space, given that $\|\mathbf{v}\| = 1$, $\|\mathbf{w}\| = 1$, **v** makes an angle of $\pi/6$ with the positive x-axis, and **w** makes an angle of $3\pi/4$ with the positive x-axis.

27–28 Find the component form of $\mathbf{v} + \mathbf{w}$, given that **v** and **w** are unit vectors.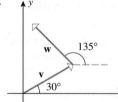

27.
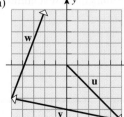

28.
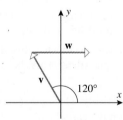

29. In each part, sketch the vector $\mathbf{u} + \mathbf{v} + \mathbf{w}$ and express it in component form.

(a)

(b)

30. In each part of Exercise 29, sketch the vector $\mathbf{u} - \mathbf{v} + \mathbf{w}$ and express it in component form.

31. Let $\mathbf{u} = \langle 1, 3 \rangle$, $\mathbf{v} = \langle 2, 1 \rangle$, $\mathbf{w} = \langle 4, -1 \rangle$. Find the vector **x** that satisfies $2\mathbf{u} - \mathbf{v} + \mathbf{x} = 7\mathbf{x} + \mathbf{w}$.

32. Let $\mathbf{u} = \langle -1, 1 \rangle$, $\mathbf{v} = \langle 0, 1 \rangle$, and $\mathbf{w} = \langle 3, 4 \rangle$. Find the vector **x** that satisfies $\mathbf{u} - 2\mathbf{x} = \mathbf{x} - \mathbf{w} + 3\mathbf{v}$.

33. Find **u** and **v** if $\mathbf{u} + 2\mathbf{v} = 3\mathbf{i} - \mathbf{k}$ and $3\mathbf{u} - \mathbf{v} = \mathbf{i} + \mathbf{j} + \mathbf{k}$.

34. Find **u** and **v** if $\mathbf{u} + \mathbf{v} = \langle 2, -3 \rangle$ and $3\mathbf{u} + 2\mathbf{v} = \langle -1, 2 \rangle$.

35. Use vectors to find the lengths of the diagonals of the parallelogram that has $\mathbf{i} + \mathbf{j}$ and $\mathbf{i} - 2\mathbf{j}$ as adjacent sides.

36. Use vectors to find the fourth vertex of a parallelogram, three of whose vertices are $(0, 0)$, $(1, 3)$, and $(2, 4)$. [*Note:* There is more than one answer.]

37. (a) Given that $\|\mathbf{v}\| = 3$, find all values of k such that $\|k\mathbf{v}\| = 5$.
(b) Given that $k = -2$ and $\|k\mathbf{v}\| = 6$, find $\|\mathbf{v}\|$.

38. What do you know about k and **v** if $\|k\mathbf{v}\| = 0$?

39. In each part, find two unit vectors in 2-space that satisfy the stated condition.
(a) Parallel to the line $y = 3x + 2$
(b) Parallel to the line $x + y = 4$
(c) Perpendicular to the line $y = -5x + 1$

40. In each part, find two unit vectors in 3-space that satisfy the stated condition.
(a) Perpendicular to the xy-plane
(b) Perpendicular to the xz-plane
(c) Perpendicular to the yz-plane

FOCUS ON CONCEPTS

41. Let $\mathbf{r} = \langle x, y \rangle$ be an arbitrary vector. In each part, describe the set of all points (x, y) in 2-space that satisfy the stated condition.
(a) $\|\mathbf{r}\| = 1$ (b) $\|\mathbf{r}\| \le 1$ (c) $\|\mathbf{r}\| > 1$

42. Let $\mathbf{r} = \langle x, y \rangle$ and $\mathbf{r}_0 = \langle x_0, y_0 \rangle$. In each part, describe the set of all points (x, y) in 2-space that satisfy the stated condition.
(a) $\|\mathbf{r} - \mathbf{r}_0\| = 1$ (b) $\|\mathbf{r} - \mathbf{r}_0\| \le 1$ (c) $\|\mathbf{r} - \mathbf{r}_0\| > 1$

43. Let $\mathbf{r} = \langle x, y, z \rangle$ be an arbitrary vector. In each part, describe the set of all points (x, y, z) in 3-space that satisfy the stated condition.
(a) $\|\mathbf{r}\| = 1$ (b) $\|\mathbf{r}\| \le 1$ (c) $\|\mathbf{r}\| > 1$

44. Let $\mathbf{r}_1 = \langle x_1, y_1 \rangle$, $\mathbf{r}_2 = \langle x_2, y_2 \rangle$, and $\mathbf{r} = \langle x, y \rangle$. Assuming that $k > \|\mathbf{r}_2 - \mathbf{r}_1\|$, describe the set of all points (x, y) for which $\|\mathbf{r} - \mathbf{r}_1\| + \|\mathbf{r} - \mathbf{r}_2\| = k$.

45–50 Find the magnitude of the resultant force and the angle that it makes with the positive x-axis.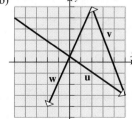

45.
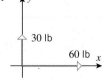

46.
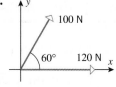

47.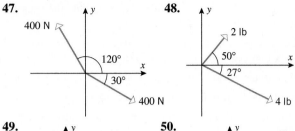

48.

49.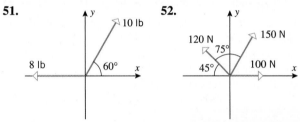

50.

51–52 A particle is said to be in *static equilibrium* if the resultant of all forces applied to it is zero. In these exercises, find the force **F** that must be applied to the point to produce static equilibrium. Describe **F** by specifying its magnitude and the angle that it makes with the positive x-axis. ■

51.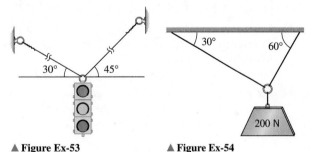

52.

53. The accompanying figure shows a 250 lb traffic light supported by two flexible cables. The magnitudes of the forces that the cables apply to the eye ring are called the cable *tensions*. Find the tensions in the cables if the traffic light is in static equilibrium (defined above Exercise 51).

54. Find the tensions in the cables shown in the accompanying figure if the block is in static equilibrium (see Exercise 53).

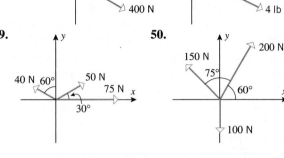

▲ **Figure Ex-53**   ▲ **Figure Ex-54**

55. A vector **w** is said to be a *linear combination* of the vectors $\mathbf{v}_1$ and $\mathbf{v}_2$ if **w** can be expressed as $\mathbf{w} = c_1\mathbf{v}_1 + c_2\mathbf{v}_2$, where c_1 and c_2 are scalars.
   (a) Find scalars c_1 and c_2 to express the vector $4\mathbf{j}$ as a linear combination of the vectors $\mathbf{v}_1 = 2\mathbf{i} - \mathbf{j}$ and $\mathbf{v}_2 = 4\mathbf{i} + 2\mathbf{j}$.
   (b) Show that the vector $\langle 3, 5 \rangle$ cannot be expressed as a linear combination of the vectors $\mathbf{v}_1 = \langle 1, -3 \rangle$ and $\mathbf{v}_2 = \langle -2, 6 \rangle$.

56. A vector **w** is a *linear combination* of the vectors $\mathbf{v}_1$, $\mathbf{v}_2$, and $\mathbf{v}_3$ if **w** can be expressed as $\mathbf{w} = c_1\mathbf{v}_1 + c_2\mathbf{v}_2 + c_3\mathbf{v}_3$, where c_1, c_2, and c_3 are scalars.
   (a) Find scalars c_1, c_2, and c_3 to express $\langle -1, 1, 5 \rangle$ as a linear combination of $\mathbf{v}_1 = \langle 1, 0, 1 \rangle$, $\mathbf{v}_2 = \langle 3, 2, 0 \rangle$, and $\mathbf{v}_3 = \langle 0, 1, 1 \rangle$.
   (b) Show that the vector $2\mathbf{i} + \mathbf{j} - \mathbf{k}$ cannot be expressed as a linear combination of $\mathbf{v}_1 = \mathbf{i} - \mathbf{j}$, $\mathbf{v}_2 = 3\mathbf{i} + \mathbf{k}$, and $\mathbf{v}_3 = 4\mathbf{i} - \mathbf{j} + \mathbf{k}$.

57. Use a theorem from plane geometry to show that if **u** and **v** are vectors in 2-space or 3-space, then

$$\|\mathbf{u} + \mathbf{v}\| \le \|\mathbf{u}\| + \|\mathbf{v}\|$$

which is called the *triangle inequality for vectors*. Give some examples to illustrate this inequality.

58. Prove parts (*a*), (*c*), and (*e*) of Theorem 11.2.6 algebraically in 2-space.

59. Prove parts (*d*), (*g*), and (*h*) of Theorem 11.2.6 algebraically in 2-space.

60. Prove part (*f*) of Theorem 11.2.6 geometrically.

FOCUS ON CONCEPTS

61. Use vectors to prove that the line segment joining the midpoints of two sides of a triangle is parallel to the third side and half as long.

62. Use vectors to prove that the midpoints of the sides of a quadrilateral are the vertices of a parallelogram.

---

63. Writing Do some research and then write a few paragraphs on the early history of the use of vectors in mathematics.

64. Writing Write a paragraph that discusses some of the similarities and differences between the rules of "vector arithmetic" and the rules of arithmetic of real numbers.

✔ **QUICK CHECK ANSWERS 11.2**

1. (a) $\sqrt{59}$ (b) $\langle 7, 9, 2 \rangle$ (c) $\langle -1, -11, 12 \rangle$ (d) $\langle 6, -2, 14 \rangle$ **2.** $\dfrac{1}{\sqrt{59}}\mathbf{v} = \left\langle \dfrac{3}{\sqrt{59}}, -\dfrac{1}{\sqrt{59}}, \dfrac{7}{\sqrt{59}} \right\rangle$ **3.** $\left\langle \dfrac{1}{2}, \dfrac{\sqrt{3}}{2} \right\rangle = \dfrac{1}{2}\mathbf{i} + \dfrac{\sqrt{3}}{2}\mathbf{j}$

4. (a) $\langle -3, -4, 5 \rangle$ (b) $\frac{1}{5}\overrightarrow{AB} = \langle -\frac{3}{5}, -\frac{4}{5}, 1 \rangle$

11.3 DOT PRODUCT; PROJECTIONS

In the last section we defined three operations on vectors—addition, subtraction, and scalar multiplication. In scalar multiplication a vector is multiplied by a scalar and the result is a vector. In this section we will define a new kind of multiplication in which two vectors are multiplied to produce a scalar. This multiplication operation has many uses, some of which we will also discuss in this section.

■ DEFINITION OF THE DOT PRODUCT

> **11.3.1 DEFINITION**   If $\mathbf{u} = \langle u_1, u_2 \rangle$ and $\mathbf{v} = \langle v_1, v_2 \rangle$ are vectors in 2-space, then the *dot product* of $\mathbf{u}$ and $\mathbf{v}$ is written as $\mathbf{u} \cdot \mathbf{v}$ and is defined as
>
> $$\mathbf{u} \cdot \mathbf{v} = u_1 v_1 + u_2 v_2$$
>
> Similarly, if $\mathbf{u} = \langle u_1, u_2, u_3 \rangle$ and $\mathbf{v} = \langle v_1, v_2, v_3 \rangle$ are vectors in 3-space, then their dot product is defined as
>
> $$\mathbf{u} \cdot \mathbf{v} = u_1 v_1 + u_2 v_2 + u_3 v_3$$

In words, the dot product of two vectors is formed by multiplying their corresponding components and adding the resulting products. Note that the dot product of two vectors is a scalar.

▶ **Example 1**

$$\langle 3, 5 \rangle \cdot \langle -1, 2 \rangle = 3(-1) + 5(2) = 7$$
$$\langle 2, 3 \rangle \cdot \langle -3, 2 \rangle = 2(-3) + 3(2) = 0$$
$$\langle 1, -3, 4 \rangle \cdot \langle 1, 5, 2 \rangle = 1(1) + (-3)(5) + 4(2) = -6$$

Here are the same computations expressed another way:

$$(3\mathbf{i} + 5\mathbf{j}) \cdot (-\mathbf{i} + 2\mathbf{j}) = 3(-1) + 5(2) = 7$$
$$(2\mathbf{i} + 3\mathbf{j}) \cdot (-3\mathbf{i} + 2\mathbf{j}) = 2(-3) + 3(2) = 0$$
$$(\mathbf{i} - 3\mathbf{j} + 4\mathbf{k}) \cdot (\mathbf{i} + 5\mathbf{j} + 2\mathbf{k}) = 1(1) + (-3)(5) + 4(2) = -6 \ ◀$$

TECHNOLOGY MASTERY

Many calculating utilities have a built-in dot product operation. If your calculating utility has this capability, use it to check the computations in Example 1.

■ ALGEBRAIC PROPERTIES OF THE DOT PRODUCT

The following theorem provides some of the basic algebraic properties of the dot product.

> **11.3.2 THEOREM**   *If* $\mathbf{u}$, $\mathbf{v}$, *and* $\mathbf{w}$ *are vectors in 2- or 3-space and k is a scalar, then:*
>
> (*a*) $\mathbf{u} \cdot \mathbf{v} = \mathbf{v} \cdot \mathbf{u}$
>
> (*b*) $\mathbf{u} \cdot (\mathbf{v} + \mathbf{w}) = \mathbf{u} \cdot \mathbf{v} + \mathbf{u} \cdot \mathbf{w}$
>
> (*c*) $k(\mathbf{u} \cdot \mathbf{v}) = (k\mathbf{u}) \cdot \mathbf{v} = \mathbf{u} \cdot (k\mathbf{v})$
>
> (*d*) $\mathbf{v} \cdot \mathbf{v} = \|\mathbf{v}\|^2$
>
> (*e*) $\mathbf{0} \cdot \mathbf{v} = 0$

Note the difference between the two zeros that appear in part (e) of Theorem 11.3.2—the zero on the left side is the *zero vector* (boldface), whereas the zero on the right side is the *zero scalar* (lightface).

We will prove parts (*c*) and (*d*) for vectors in 3-space and leave some of the others as exercises.

PROOF (*c*) Let $\mathbf{u} = \langle u_1, u_2, u_3 \rangle$ and $\mathbf{v} = \langle v_1, v_2, v_3 \rangle$. Then

$$k(\mathbf{u} \cdot \mathbf{v}) = k(u_1 v_1 + u_2 v_2 + u_3 v_3) = (ku_1)v_1 + (ku_2)v_2 + (ku_3)v_3 = (k\mathbf{u}) \cdot \mathbf{v}$$

Similarly, $k(\mathbf{u} \cdot \mathbf{v}) = \mathbf{u} \cdot (k\mathbf{v})$.

PROOF (*d*) $\mathbf{v} \cdot \mathbf{v} = v_1 v_1 + v_2 v_2 + v_3 v_3 = v_1^2 + v_2^2 + v_3^2 = \|\mathbf{v}\|^2$. ∎

The following alternative form of the formula in part (*d*) of Theorem 11.3.2 provides a useful way of expressing the norm of a vector in terms of a dot product:

$$\|\mathbf{v}\| = \sqrt{\mathbf{v} \cdot \mathbf{v}} \tag{1}$$

■ ANGLE BETWEEN VECTORS

Suppose that $\mathbf{u}$ and $\mathbf{v}$ are nonzero vectors in 2-space or 3-space that are positioned so their initial points coincide. We define the ***angle between*** $\mathbf{u}$ ***and*** $\mathbf{v}$ to be the angle θ determined by the vectors that satisfies the condition $0 \leq \theta \leq \pi$ (Figure 11.3.1). In 2-space, θ is the smallest counterclockwise angle through which one of the vectors can be rotated until it aligns with the other.

The next theorem provides a way of calculating the angle between two vectors from their components.

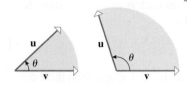
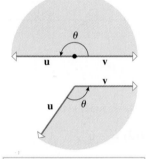
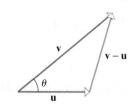

θ is the angle between $\mathbf{u}$ and $\mathbf{v}$.

▲ **Figure 11.3.1**

11.3.3   **THEOREM**   *If* $\mathbf{u}$ *and* $\mathbf{v}$ *are nonzero vectors in 2-space or 3-space, and if* θ *is the angle between them, then*

$$\cos\theta = \frac{\mathbf{u} \cdot \mathbf{v}}{\|\mathbf{u}\|\,\|\mathbf{v}\|} \tag{2}$$

PROOF   Suppose that the vectors $\mathbf{u}$, $\mathbf{v}$, and $\mathbf{v} - \mathbf{u}$ are positioned to form three sides of a triangle, as shown in Figure 11.3.2. It follows from the law of cosines that

$$\|\mathbf{v} - \mathbf{u}\|^2 = \|\mathbf{u}\|^2 + \|\mathbf{v}\|^2 - 2\|\mathbf{u}\|\,\|\mathbf{v}\|\cos\theta \tag{3}$$

Using the properties of the dot product in Theorem 11.3.2, we can rewrite the left side of this equation as

$$\begin{aligned}
\|\mathbf{v} - \mathbf{u}\|^2 &= (\mathbf{v} - \mathbf{u}) \cdot (\mathbf{v} - \mathbf{u}) \\
&= (\mathbf{v} - \mathbf{u}) \cdot \mathbf{v} - (\mathbf{v} - \mathbf{u}) \cdot \mathbf{u} \\
&= \mathbf{v} \cdot \mathbf{v} - \mathbf{u} \cdot \mathbf{v} - \mathbf{v} \cdot \mathbf{u} + \mathbf{u} \cdot \mathbf{u} \\
&= \|\mathbf{v}\|^2 - 2\mathbf{u} \cdot \mathbf{v} + \|\mathbf{u}\|^2
\end{aligned}$$

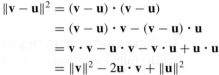

▲ **Figure 11.3.2**

Substituting this back into (3) yields

$$\|\mathbf{v}\|^2 - 2\mathbf{u} \cdot \mathbf{v} + \|\mathbf{u}\|^2 = \|\mathbf{u}\|^2 + \|\mathbf{v}\|^2 - 2\|\mathbf{u}\|\,\|\mathbf{v}\|\cos\theta$$

which we can simplify and rewrite as

$$\mathbf{u} \cdot \mathbf{v} = \|\mathbf{u}\|\,\|\mathbf{v}\|\cos\theta$$

Finally, dividing both sides of this equation by $\|\mathbf{u}\|\,\|\mathbf{v}\|$ yields (2). ∎

▶ **Example 2**   Find the angle between the vector $\mathbf{u} = \mathbf{i} - 2\mathbf{j} + 2\mathbf{k}$ and

(a) $\mathbf{v} = -3\mathbf{i} + 6\mathbf{j} + 2\mathbf{k}$ (b) $\mathbf{w} = 2\mathbf{i} + 7\mathbf{j} + 6\mathbf{k}$ (c) $\mathbf{z} = -3\mathbf{i} + 6\mathbf{j} - 6\mathbf{k}$

Solution (*a*).

$$\cos\theta = \frac{\mathbf{u} \cdot \mathbf{v}}{\|\mathbf{u}\|\,\|\mathbf{v}\|} = \frac{-11}{(3)(7)} = -\frac{11}{21}$$

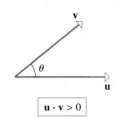

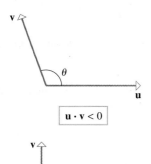

$\mathbf{u} \cdot \mathbf{v} > 0$

$\mathbf{u} \cdot \mathbf{v} < 0$

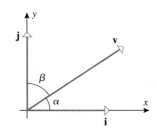

$\mathbf{u} \cdot \mathbf{v} = 0$

▲ Figure 11.3.3

Thus,

$$\theta = \cos^{-1}\left(-\tfrac{11}{21}\right) \approx 2.12 \text{ radians} \approx 121.6°$$

Solution (b).

$$\cos\theta = \frac{\mathbf{u} \cdot \mathbf{w}}{\|\mathbf{u}\| \|\mathbf{w}\|} = \frac{0}{\|\mathbf{u}\| \|\mathbf{w}\|} = 0$$

Thus, $\theta = \pi/2$, which means that the vectors are perpendicular.

Solution (c).

$$\cos\theta = \frac{\mathbf{u} \cdot \mathbf{z}}{\|\mathbf{u}\| \|\mathbf{z}\|} = \frac{-27}{(3)(9)} = -1$$

Thus, $\theta = \pi$, which means that the vectors are oppositely directed. (In retrospect, we could have seen this without computing θ, since $\mathbf{z} = -3\mathbf{u}$.) ◄

■ INTERPRETING THE SIGN OF THE DOT PRODUCT

It will often be convenient to express Formula (2) as

$$\mathbf{u} \cdot \mathbf{v} = \|\mathbf{u}\| \|\mathbf{v}\| \cos\theta \tag{4}$$

which expresses the dot product of $\mathbf{u}$ and $\mathbf{v}$ in terms of the lengths of these vectors and the angle between them. Since $\mathbf{u}$ and $\mathbf{v}$ are assumed to be nonzero vectors, this version of the formula makes it clear that the sign of $\mathbf{u} \cdot \mathbf{v}$ is the same as the sign of $\cos\theta$. Thus, we can tell from the dot product whether the angle between two vectors is acute or obtuse or whether the vectors are perpendicular (Figure 11.3.3).

REMARK | The terms "perpendicular," "orthogonal," and "normal" are all commonly used to describe geometric objects that meet at right angles. For consistency, we will say that two vectors are *orthogonal*, a vector is *normal* to a plane, and two planes are *perpendicular*. Moreover, although the zero vector does not make a well-defined angle with other vectors, we will consider $\mathbf{0}$ to be orthogonal to *all* vectors. This convention allows us to say that $\mathbf{u}$ and $\mathbf{v}$ are orthogonal vectors if and only if $\mathbf{u} \cdot \mathbf{v} = 0$, and makes Formula (4) valid if $\mathbf{u}$ or $\mathbf{v}$ (or both) is zero.

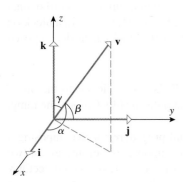

▲ Figure 11.3.4

▲ Figure 11.3.5

■ DIRECTION ANGLES

In an xy-coordinate system, the direction of a nonzero vector $\mathbf{v}$ is completely determined by the angles α and β between $\mathbf{v}$ and the unit vectors $\mathbf{i}$ and $\mathbf{j}$ (Figure 11.3.4), and in an xyz-coordinate system the direction is completely determined by the angles α, β, and γ between $\mathbf{v}$ and the unit vectors $\mathbf{i}$, $\mathbf{j}$, and $\mathbf{k}$ (Figure 11.3.5). In both 2-space and 3-space the angles between a nonzero vector $\mathbf{v}$ and the vectors $\mathbf{i}$, $\mathbf{j}$, and $\mathbf{k}$ are called the *direction angles* of $\mathbf{v}$, and the cosines of those angles are called the *direction cosines* of $\mathbf{v}$. Formulas for the direction cosines of a vector can be obtained from Formula (2). For example, if $\mathbf{v} = v_1\mathbf{i} + v_2\mathbf{j} + v_3\mathbf{k}$, then

$$\cos\alpha = \frac{\mathbf{v} \cdot \mathbf{i}}{\|\mathbf{v}\| \|\mathbf{i}\|} = \frac{v_1}{\|\mathbf{v}\|}, \quad \cos\beta = \frac{\mathbf{v} \cdot \mathbf{j}}{\|\mathbf{v}\| \|\mathbf{j}\|} = \frac{v_2}{\|\mathbf{v}\|}, \quad \cos\gamma = \frac{\mathbf{v} \cdot \mathbf{k}}{\|\mathbf{v}\| \|\mathbf{k}\|} = \frac{v_3}{\|\mathbf{v}\|}$$

Thus, we have the following theorem.

11.3.4 THEOREM *The direction cosines of a nonzero vector* $\mathbf{v} = v_1\mathbf{i} + v_2\mathbf{j} + v_3\mathbf{k}$ *are*

$$\cos\alpha = \frac{v_1}{\|\mathbf{v}\|}, \quad \cos\beta = \frac{v_2}{\|\mathbf{v}\|}, \quad \cos\gamma = \frac{v_3}{\|\mathbf{v}\|}$$

The direction cosines of a vector $\mathbf{v} = v_1\mathbf{i} + v_2\mathbf{j} + v_3\mathbf{k}$ can be computed by normalizing $\mathbf{v}$ and reading off the components of $\mathbf{v}/\|\mathbf{v}\|$, since

$$\frac{\mathbf{v}}{\|\mathbf{v}\|} = \frac{v_1}{\|\mathbf{v}\|}\mathbf{i} + \frac{v_2}{\|\mathbf{v}\|}\mathbf{j} + \frac{v_3}{\|\mathbf{v}\|}\mathbf{k} = (\cos\alpha)\mathbf{i} + (\cos\beta)\mathbf{j} + (\cos\gamma)\mathbf{k}$$

We leave it as an exercise for you to show that the direction cosines of a vector satisfy the equation

$$\cos^2\alpha + \cos^2\beta + \cos^2\gamma = 1 \tag{5}$$

▶ **Example 3**   Find the direction cosines of the vector $\mathbf{v} = 2\mathbf{i} - 4\mathbf{j} + 4\mathbf{k}$, and approximate the direction angles to the nearest degree.

Solution.   First we will normalize the vector $\mathbf{v}$ and then read off the components. We have $\|\mathbf{v}\| = \sqrt{4 + 16 + 16} = 6$, so that $\mathbf{v}/\|\mathbf{v}\| = \frac{1}{3}\mathbf{i} - \frac{2}{3}\mathbf{j} + \frac{2}{3}\mathbf{k}$. Thus,

$$\cos\alpha = \tfrac{1}{3}, \quad \cos\beta = -\tfrac{2}{3}, \quad \cos\gamma = \tfrac{2}{3}$$

With the help of a calculating utility we obtain

$$\alpha = \cos^{-1}\left(\tfrac{1}{3}\right) \approx 71°, \quad \beta = \cos^{-1}\left(-\tfrac{2}{3}\right) \approx 132°, \quad \gamma = \cos^{-1}\left(\tfrac{2}{3}\right) \approx 48° \quad ◀$$

▶ **Example 4**   Find the angle between a diagonal of a cube and one of its edges.

Solution.   Assume that the cube has side a, and introduce a coordinate system as shown in Figure 11.3.6. In this coordinate system the vector

$$\mathbf{d} = a\mathbf{i} + a\mathbf{j} + a\mathbf{k}$$

is a diagonal of the cube and the unit vectors $\mathbf{i}$, $\mathbf{j}$, and $\mathbf{k}$ run along the edges. By symmetry, the diagonal makes the same angle with each edge, so it is sufficient to find the angle between $\mathbf{d}$ and $\mathbf{i}$ (the direction angle α). Thus,

$$\cos\alpha = \frac{\mathbf{d} \cdot \mathbf{i}}{\|\mathbf{d}\|\|\mathbf{i}\|} = \frac{a}{\|\mathbf{d}\|} = \frac{a}{\sqrt{3a^2}} = \frac{1}{\sqrt{3}}$$

and hence

$$\alpha = \cos^{-1}\left(\frac{1}{\sqrt{3}}\right) \approx 0.955 \text{ radian} \approx 54.7° \quad ◀$$

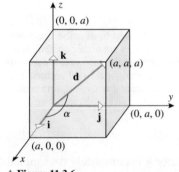

▲ **Figure 11.3.6**

■ DECOMPOSING VECTORS INTO ORTHOGONAL COMPONENTS

In many applications it is desirable to "decompose" a vector into a sum of two orthogonal vectors with convenient specified directions. For example, Figure 11.3.7 shows a block on an inclined plane. The downward force $\mathbf{F}$ that gravity exerts on the block can be decomposed into the sum

$$\mathbf{F} = \mathbf{F}_1 + \mathbf{F}_2$$

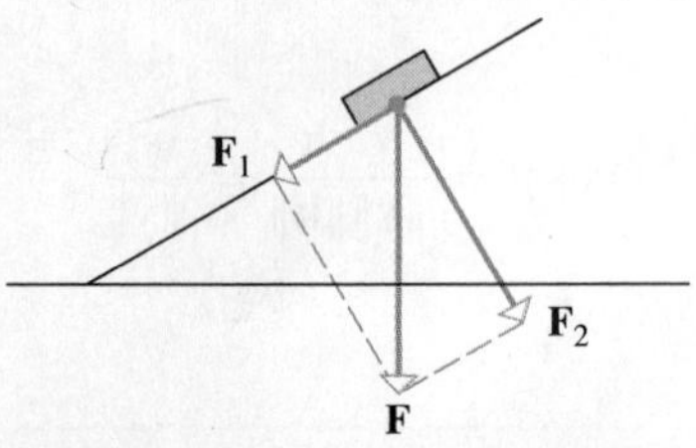

where the force $\mathbf{F}_1$ is parallel to the ramp and the force $\mathbf{F}_2$ is perpendicular to the ramp. The forces $\mathbf{F}_1$ and $\mathbf{F}_2$ are useful because $\mathbf{F}_1$ is the force that pulls the block *along* the ramp, and $\mathbf{F}_2$ is the force that the block exerts *against* the ramp.

Thus, our next objective is to develop a computational procedure for decomposing a vector into a sum of orthogonal vectors. For this purpose, suppose that $\mathbf{e}_1$ and $\mathbf{e}_2$ are two orthogonal *unit* vectors in 2-space, and suppose that we want to express a given vector $\mathbf{v}$ as a sum

$$\mathbf{v} = \mathbf{w}_1 + \mathbf{w}_2$$

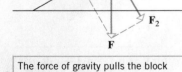

The force of gravity pulls the block against the ramp and down the ramp.

▲ **Figure 11.3.7**

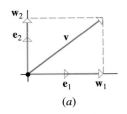

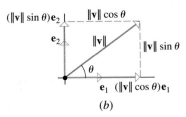

▲ **Figure 11.3.8**

Note that the vector components of v along e_1 and e_2 are *vectors*, whereas the scalar components of v along e_1 and e_2 are *numbers*.

so that $\mathbf{w}_1$ is a scalar multiple of $\mathbf{e}_1$ and $\mathbf{w}_2$ is a scalar multiple of $\mathbf{e}_2$ (Figure 11.3.8a). That is, we want to find scalars k_1 and k_2 such that

$$\mathbf{v} = k_1\mathbf{e}_1 + k_2\mathbf{e}_2 \tag{6}$$

We can find k_1 by taking the dot product of $\mathbf{v}$ with $\mathbf{e}_1$. This yields

$$\begin{aligned}\mathbf{v} \cdot \mathbf{e}_1 &= (k_1\mathbf{e}_1 + k_2\mathbf{e}_2) \cdot \mathbf{e}_1 \\ &= k_1(\mathbf{e}_1 \cdot \mathbf{e}_1) + k_2(\mathbf{e}_2 \cdot \mathbf{e}_1) \\ &= k_1\|\mathbf{e}_1\|^2 + 0 = k_1\end{aligned}$$

Similarly,

$$\mathbf{v} \cdot \mathbf{e}_2 = (k_1\mathbf{e}_1 + k_2\mathbf{e}_2) \cdot \mathbf{e}_2 = k_1(\mathbf{e}_1 \cdot \mathbf{e}_2) + k_2(\mathbf{e}_2 \cdot \mathbf{e}_2) = 0 + k_2\|\mathbf{e}_2\|^2 = k_2$$

Substituting these expressions for k_1 and k_2 in (6) yields

$$\mathbf{v} = (\mathbf{v} \cdot \mathbf{e}_1)\mathbf{e}_1 + (\mathbf{v} \cdot \mathbf{e}_2)\mathbf{e}_2 \tag{7}$$

In this formula we call $(\mathbf{v} \cdot \mathbf{e}_1)\mathbf{e}_1$ and $(\mathbf{v} \cdot \mathbf{e}_2)\mathbf{e}_2$ the *vector components* of $\mathbf{v}$ along $\mathbf{e}_1$ and $\mathbf{e}_2$, respectively; and we call $\mathbf{v} \cdot \mathbf{e}_1$ and $\mathbf{v} \cdot \mathbf{e}_2$ the *scalar components* of $\mathbf{v}$ along $\mathbf{e}_1$ and $\mathbf{e}_2$, respectively. If θ denotes the angle between $\mathbf{v}$ and $\mathbf{e}_1$, and the angle between $\mathbf{v}$ and $\mathbf{e}_2$ is $\pi/2$ or less, then the scalar components of $\mathbf{v}$ can be written in trigonometric form as

$$\mathbf{v} \cdot \mathbf{e}_1 = \|\mathbf{v}\|\cos\theta \quad \text{and} \quad \mathbf{v} \cdot \mathbf{e}_2 = \|\mathbf{v}\|\sin\theta \tag{8}$$

(Figure 11.3.8b). Moreover, the vector components of $\mathbf{v}$ can be expressed as

$$(\mathbf{v} \cdot \mathbf{e}_1)\mathbf{e}_1 = (\|\mathbf{v}\|\cos\theta)\mathbf{e}_1 \quad \text{and} \quad (\mathbf{v} \cdot \mathbf{e}_2)\mathbf{e}_2 = (\|\mathbf{v}\|\sin\theta)\mathbf{e}_2 \tag{9}$$

and the decomposition (6) can be expressed as

$$\mathbf{v} = (\|\mathbf{v}\|\cos\theta)\mathbf{e}_1 + (\|\mathbf{v}\|\sin\theta)\mathbf{e}_2 \tag{10}$$

provided the angle between $\mathbf{v}$ and $\mathbf{e}_2$ is at most $\pi/2$.

▶ **Example 5** Let

$$\mathbf{v} = \langle 2, 3\rangle, \quad \mathbf{e}_1 = \left\langle\frac{1}{\sqrt{2}}, \frac{1}{\sqrt{2}}\right\rangle, \quad \text{and} \quad \mathbf{e}_2 = \left\langle-\frac{1}{\sqrt{2}}, \frac{1}{\sqrt{2}}\right\rangle$$

Find the scalar components of $\mathbf{v}$ along $\mathbf{e}_1$ and $\mathbf{e}_2$ and the vector components of $\mathbf{v}$ along $\mathbf{e}_1$ and $\mathbf{e}_2$.

Solution. The scalar components of $\mathbf{v}$ along $\mathbf{e}_1$ and $\mathbf{e}_2$ are

$$\mathbf{v} \cdot \mathbf{e}_1 = 2\left(\frac{1}{\sqrt{2}}\right) + 3\left(\frac{1}{\sqrt{2}}\right) = \frac{5}{\sqrt{2}}$$

$$\mathbf{v} \cdot \mathbf{e}_2 = 2\left(-\frac{1}{\sqrt{2}}\right) + 3\left(\frac{1}{\sqrt{2}}\right) = \frac{1}{\sqrt{2}}$$

so the vector components are

$$(\mathbf{v} \cdot \mathbf{e}_1)\mathbf{e}_1 = \frac{5}{\sqrt{2}}\left\langle\frac{1}{\sqrt{2}}, \frac{1}{\sqrt{2}}\right\rangle = \left\langle\frac{5}{2}, \frac{5}{2}\right\rangle$$

$$(\mathbf{v} \cdot \mathbf{e}_2)\mathbf{e}_2 = \frac{1}{\sqrt{2}}\left\langle-\frac{1}{\sqrt{2}}, \frac{1}{\sqrt{2}}\right\rangle = \left\langle-\frac{1}{2}, \frac{1}{2}\right\rangle \quad ◀$$

Notice that in Example 5

$(\mathbf{v} \cdot \mathbf{e}_1)\mathbf{e}_1 + (\mathbf{v} \cdot \mathbf{e}_2)\mathbf{e}_2 = \langle 2, 3\rangle = \mathbf{v}$

as guaranteed by (7).

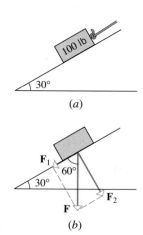

(a)

(b)

▲ **Figure 11.3.9**

▶ **Example 6**   A rope is attached to a 100 lb block on a ramp that is inclined at an angle of 30° with the ground (Figure 11.3.9a). How much force does the block exert against the ramp, and how much force must be applied to the rope in a direction parallel to the ramp to prevent the block from sliding down the ramp? (Assume that the ramp is smooth, that is, exerts no frictional forces.)

Solution.   Let **F** denote the downward force of gravity on the block (so $\|\mathbf{F}\| = 100$ lb), and let $\mathbf{F}_1$ and $\mathbf{F}_2$ be the vector components of **F** parallel and perpendicular to the ramp (as shown in Figure 11.3.9b). The lengths of $\mathbf{F}_1$ and $\mathbf{F}_2$ are

$$\|\mathbf{F}_1\| = \|\mathbf{F}\|\cos 60° = 100\left(\frac{1}{2}\right) = 50 \text{ lb}$$

$$\|\mathbf{F}_2\| = \|\mathbf{F}\|\sin 60° = 100\left(\frac{\sqrt{3}}{2}\right) \approx 86.6 \text{ lb}$$

Thus, the block exerts a force of approximately 86.6 lb against the ramp, and it requires a force of 50 lb to prevent the block from sliding down the ramp. ◀

ORTHOGONAL PROJECTIONS

The vector components of **v** along $\mathbf{e}_1$ and $\mathbf{e}_2$ in (7) are also called the *orthogonal projections* of **v** on $\mathbf{e}_1$ and $\mathbf{e}_2$ and are commonly denoted by

$$\text{proj}_{\mathbf{e}_1}\mathbf{v} = (\mathbf{v} \cdot \mathbf{e}_1)\mathbf{e}_1 \quad \text{and} \quad \text{proj}_{\mathbf{e}_2}\mathbf{v} = (\mathbf{v} \cdot \mathbf{e}_2)\mathbf{e}_2$$

In general, if **e** is a unit vector, then we define the *orthogonal projection of **v** on **e*** to be

$$\text{proj}_{\mathbf{e}}\mathbf{v} = (\mathbf{v} \cdot \mathbf{e})\mathbf{e} \tag{11}$$

The orthogonal projection of **v** on an arbitrary nonzero vector **b** can be obtained by normalizing **b** and then applying Formula (11); that is,

$$\text{proj}_{\mathbf{b}}\mathbf{v} = \left(\mathbf{v} \cdot \frac{\mathbf{b}}{\|\mathbf{b}\|}\right)\left(\frac{\mathbf{b}}{\|\mathbf{b}\|}\right)$$

which can be rewritten as

$$\text{proj}_{\mathbf{b}}\mathbf{v} = \frac{\mathbf{v} \cdot \mathbf{b}}{\|\mathbf{b}\|^2}\mathbf{b} \tag{12}$$

Geometrically, if **b** and **v** have a common initial point, then $\text{proj}_{\mathbf{b}}\mathbf{v}$ is the vector that is determined when a perpendicular is dropped from the terminal point of **v** to the line through **b** (illustrated in Figure 11.3.10 in two cases).

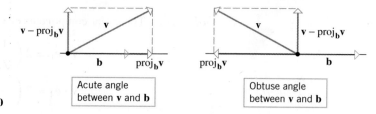

▶ **Figure 11.3.10**

Moreover, it is evident from Figure 11.3.10 that if we subtract $\text{proj}_{\mathbf{b}}\mathbf{v}$ from **v**, then the resulting vector

$$\mathbf{v} - \text{proj}_{\mathbf{b}}\mathbf{v}$$

will be orthogonal to **b**; we call this the *vector component of **v** orthogonal to **b***.

Stated informally, the orthogonal projection $\text{proj}_b v$ is the "shadow" that v casts on the line through b.

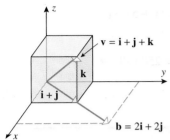

▲ **Figure 11.3.11**

▶ **Example 7** Find the orthogonal projection of $v = i + j + k$ on $b = 2i + 2j$, and then find the vector component of v orthogonal to b.

Solution. We have

$$v \cdot b = (i + j + k) \cdot (2i + 2j) = 2 + 2 + 0 = 4$$
$$\|b\|^2 = 2^2 + 2^2 = 8$$

Thus, the orthogonal projection of v on b is

$$\text{proj}_b v = \frac{v \cdot b}{\|b\|^2} b = \frac{4}{8}(2i + 2j) = i + j$$

and the vector component of v orthogonal to b is

$$v - \text{proj}_b v = (i + j + k) - (i + j) = k$$

These results are consistent with Figure 11.3.11. ◀

■ **WORK**

In Section 6.6 we discussed the work done by a constant force acting on an object that moves along a line. We defined the work W done on the object by a constant force of magnitude F acting in the direction of motion over a distance d to be

$$W = Fd = \text{force} \times \text{distance} \tag{13}$$

If we let $\mathbf{F}$ denote a force vector of magnitude $\|\mathbf{F}\| = F$ *acting in the direction of motion*, then we can write (13) as

$$W = \|\mathbf{F}\|d$$

Furthermore, if we assume that the object moves along a line from point P to point Q, then $d = \|\overrightarrow{PQ}\|$, so that the work can be expressed entirely in vector form as

$$W = \|\mathbf{F}\|\|\overrightarrow{PQ}\|$$

Note that in Formula (14) the quantity $\|\mathbf{F}\|\cos\theta$ is the scalar component of force along the displacement vector. Thus, in the case where $\cos\theta > 0$, a force of magnitude $\|\mathbf{F}\|$ acting at an angle θ does the same work as a force of magnitude $\|\mathbf{F}\|\cos\theta$ acting in the direction of motion.

(Figure 11.3.12a). The vector $\overrightarrow{PQ}$ is called the **displacement vector** for the object. In the case where a constant force $\mathbf{F}$ is not in the direction of motion, but rather makes an angle θ with the displacement vector, then we *define* the work W done by $\mathbf{F}$ to be

$$W = (\|\mathbf{F}\|\cos\theta)\|\overrightarrow{PQ}\| = \mathbf{F} \cdot \overrightarrow{PQ} \tag{14}$$

(Figure 11.3.12b).

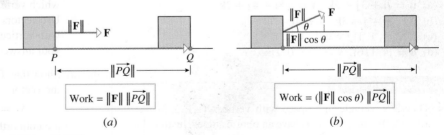

▲ **Figure 11.3.12**

▶ **Example 8** A wagon is pulled horizontally by exerting a constant force of 10 lb on the handle at an angle of 60° with the horizontal. How much work is done in moving the wagon 50 ft?

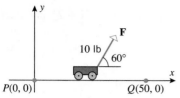

▲ **Figure 11.3.13**

Solution.   Introduce an xy-coordinate system so that the wagon moves from $P(0, 0)$ to $Q(50, 0)$ along the x-axis (Figure 11.3.13). In this coordinate system

$$\overrightarrow{PQ} = 50\mathbf{i}$$

and

$$\mathbf{F} = (10\cos 60°)\mathbf{i} + (10\sin 60°)\mathbf{j} = 5\mathbf{i} + 5\sqrt{3}\,\mathbf{j}$$

so the work done is

$$W = \mathbf{F} \cdot \overrightarrow{PQ} = (5\mathbf{i} + 5\sqrt{3}\,\mathbf{j}) \cdot (50\mathbf{i}) = 250 \text{ ft·lb} \blacktriangleleft$$

✔ **QUICK CHECK EXERCISES 11.3**   (*See page 794 for answers.*)

1. $\langle 3, 1, -2 \rangle \cdot \langle 6, 0, 5 \rangle = $ _____

2. Suppose that $\mathbf{u}$, $\mathbf{v}$, and $\mathbf{w}$ are vectors in 3-space such that $\|\mathbf{u}\| = 5$, $\mathbf{u} \cdot \mathbf{v} = 7$, and $\mathbf{u} \cdot \mathbf{w} = -3$.
   (a) $\mathbf{u} \cdot \mathbf{u} = $ _____   (b) $\mathbf{v} \cdot \mathbf{u} = $ _____
   (c) $\mathbf{u} \cdot (\mathbf{v} - \mathbf{w}) = $ _____   (d) $\mathbf{u} \cdot (2\mathbf{w}) = $ _____

3. For the vectors $\mathbf{u}$ and $\mathbf{v}$ in the preceding exercise, if the angle between $\mathbf{u}$ and $\mathbf{v}$ is $\pi/3$, then $\|\mathbf{v}\| = $ _____.

4. The direction cosines of $\langle 2, -1, 3 \rangle$ are $\cos \alpha = $ _____, $\cos \beta = $ _____, and $\cos \gamma = $ _____.

5. The orthogonal projection of $\mathbf{v} = 10\mathbf{i}$ on $\mathbf{b} = -3\mathbf{i} + \mathbf{j}$ is _____.

EXERCISE SET 11.3   [c] CAS

1. In each part, find the dot product of the vectors and the cosine of the angle between them.
   (a) $\mathbf{u} = \mathbf{i} + 2\mathbf{j}$, $\mathbf{v} = 6\mathbf{i} - 8\mathbf{j}$
   (b) $\mathbf{u} = \langle -7, -3 \rangle$, $\mathbf{v} = \langle 0, 1 \rangle$
   (c) $\mathbf{u} = \mathbf{i} - 3\mathbf{j} + 7\mathbf{k}$, $\mathbf{v} = 8\mathbf{i} - 2\mathbf{j} - 2\mathbf{k}$
   (d) $\mathbf{u} = \langle -3, 1, 2 \rangle$, $\mathbf{v} = \langle 4, 2, -5 \rangle$

2. In each part use the given information to find $\mathbf{u} \cdot \mathbf{v}$.
   (a) $\|\mathbf{u}\| = 1$, $\|\mathbf{v}\| = 2$, the angle between $\mathbf{u}$ and $\mathbf{v}$ is $\pi/6$.
   (b) $\|\mathbf{u}\| = 2$, $\|\mathbf{v}\| = 3$, the angle between $\mathbf{u}$ and $\mathbf{v}$ is $135°$.

3. In each part, determine whether $\mathbf{u}$ and $\mathbf{v}$ make an acute angle, an obtuse angle, or are orthogonal.
   (a) $\mathbf{u} = 7\mathbf{i} + 3\mathbf{j} + 5\mathbf{k}$, $\mathbf{v} = -8\mathbf{i} + 4\mathbf{j} + 2\mathbf{k}$
   (b) $\mathbf{u} = 6\mathbf{i} + \mathbf{j} + 3\mathbf{k}$, $\mathbf{v} = 4\mathbf{i} - 6\mathbf{k}$
   (c) $\mathbf{u} = \langle 1, 1, 1 \rangle$, $\mathbf{v} = \langle -1, 0, 0 \rangle$
   (d) $\mathbf{u} = \langle 4, 1, 6 \rangle$, $\mathbf{v} = \langle -3, 0, 2 \rangle$

FOCUS ON CONCEPTS

4. Does the triangle in 3-space with vertices $(-1, 2, 3)$, $(2, -2, 0)$, and $(3, 1, -4)$ have an obtuse angle? Justify your answer.

5. The accompanying figure shows eight vectors that are equally spaced around a circle of radius 1. Find the dot product of $\mathbf{v}_0$ with each of the other seven vectors.

6. The accompanying figure shows six vectors that are equally spaced around a circle of radius 5. Find the dot product of $\mathbf{v}_0$ with each of the other five vectors.

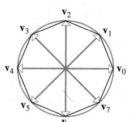

▲ **Figure Ex-5**   ▲ **Figure Ex-6**

7. (a) Use vectors to show that $A(2, -1, 1)$, $B(3, 2, -1)$, and $C(7, 0, -2)$ are vertices of a right triangle. At which vertex is the right angle?
   (b) Use vectors to find the interior angles of the triangle with vertices $(-1, 0)$, $(2, -1)$, and $(1, 4)$. Express your answers to the nearest degree.

8. (a) Show that if $\mathbf{v} = a\mathbf{i} + b\mathbf{j}$ is a vector in 2-space, then the vectors
   $$\mathbf{v}_1 = -b\mathbf{i} + a\mathbf{j} \quad \text{and} \quad \mathbf{v}_2 = b\mathbf{i} - a\mathbf{j}$$
   are both orthogonal to $\mathbf{v}$.
   (b) Use the result in part (a) to find two unit vectors that are orthogonal to the vector $\mathbf{v} = 3\mathbf{i} - 2\mathbf{j}$. Sketch the vectors $\mathbf{v}$, $\mathbf{v}_1$, and $\mathbf{v}_2$.

9. Explain why each of the following expressions makes no sense.
   (a) $\mathbf{u} \cdot (\mathbf{v} \cdot \mathbf{w})$ (b) $(\mathbf{u} \cdot \mathbf{v}) + \mathbf{w}$
   (c) $\|\mathbf{u} \cdot \mathbf{v}\|$ (d) $k \cdot (\mathbf{u} + \mathbf{v})$

10. Explain why each of the following expressions makes sense.
(a) $(\mathbf{u} \cdot \mathbf{v})\mathbf{w}$
(b) $(\mathbf{u} \cdot \mathbf{v})(\mathbf{v} \cdot \mathbf{w})$
(c) $\mathbf{u} \cdot \mathbf{v} + k$
(d) $(k\mathbf{u}) \cdot \mathbf{v}$

11. Verify parts (b) and (c) of Theorem 11.3.2 for the vectors $\mathbf{u} = 6\mathbf{i} - \mathbf{j} + 2\mathbf{k}$, $\mathbf{v} = 2\mathbf{i} + 7\mathbf{j} + 4\mathbf{k}$, $\mathbf{w} = \mathbf{i} + \mathbf{j} - 3\mathbf{k}$ and $k = -5$.

12. Let $\mathbf{u} = \langle 1, 2 \rangle$, $\mathbf{v} = \langle 4, -2 \rangle$, and $\mathbf{w} = \langle 6, 0 \rangle$. Find
(a) $\mathbf{u} \cdot (7\mathbf{v} + \mathbf{w})$
(b) $\|(\mathbf{u} \cdot \mathbf{w})\mathbf{w}\|$
(c) $\|\mathbf{u}\|(\mathbf{v} \cdot \mathbf{w})$
(d) $(\|\mathbf{u}\|\mathbf{v}) \cdot \mathbf{w}$.

13. Find r so that the vector from the point $A(1, -1, 3)$ to the point $B(3, 0, 5)$ is orthogonal to the vector from A to the point $P(r, r, r)$.

14. Find two unit vectors in 2-space that make an angle of $45°$ with $4\mathbf{i} + 3\mathbf{j}$.

15–16 Find the direction cosines of $\mathbf{v}$ and confirm that they satisfy Equation (5). Then use the direction cosines to approximate the direction angles to the nearest degree. ■

15. (a) $\mathbf{v} = \mathbf{i} + \mathbf{j} - \mathbf{k}$
(b) $\mathbf{v} = 2\mathbf{i} - 2\mathbf{j} + \mathbf{k}$

16. (a) $\mathbf{v} = 3\mathbf{i} - 2\mathbf{j} - 6\mathbf{k}$
(b) $\mathbf{v} = 3\mathbf{i} - 4\mathbf{k}$

FOCUS ON CONCEPTS

17. Show that the direction cosines of a vector satisfy
$$\cos^2 \alpha + \cos^2 \beta + \cos^2 \gamma = 1$$

18. Let θ and λ be the angles shown in the accompanying figure. Show that the direction cosines of $\mathbf{v}$ can be expressed as
$$\cos \alpha = \cos \lambda \cos \theta$$
$$\cos \beta = \cos \lambda \sin \theta$$
$$\cos \gamma = \sin \lambda$$
[*Hint:* Express $\mathbf{v}$ in component form and normalize.]

19. The accompanying figure shows a cube.
(a) Find the angle between the vectors $\mathbf{d}$ and $\mathbf{u}$ to the nearest degree.
(b) Make a conjecture about the angle between the vectors $\mathbf{d}$ and $\mathbf{v}$, and confirm your conjecture by computing the angle.

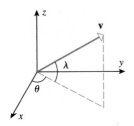

▲ Figure Ex-18

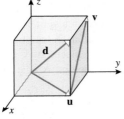

▲ Figure Ex-19

20. Show that two nonzero vectors $\mathbf{v}_1$ and $\mathbf{v}_2$ are orthogonal if and only if their direction cosines satisfy
$$\cos \alpha_1 \cos \alpha_2 + \cos \beta_1 \cos \beta_2 + \cos \gamma_1 \cos \gamma_2 = 0$$

21. Use the result in Exercise 18 to find the direction angles of the vector shown in the accompanying figure to the nearest degree.

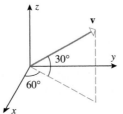

◀ Figure Ex-21

22. Find, to the nearest degree, the acute angle formed by two diagonals of a cube.

23. Find, to the nearest degree, the angles that a diagonal of a box with dimensions 10 cm by 15 cm by 25 cm makes with the edges of the box.

24. In each part, find the vector component of $\mathbf{v}$ along $\mathbf{b}$ and the vector component of $\mathbf{v}$ orthogonal to $\mathbf{b}$. Then sketch the vectors $\mathbf{v}$, $\mathrm{proj}_\mathbf{b}\mathbf{v}$, and $\mathbf{v} - \mathrm{proj}_\mathbf{b}\mathbf{v}$.
(a) $\mathbf{v} = 2\mathbf{i} - \mathbf{j}$, $\mathbf{b} = 3\mathbf{i} + 4\mathbf{j}$
(b) $\mathbf{v} = \langle 4, 5 \rangle$, $\mathbf{b} = \langle 1, -2 \rangle$
(c) $\mathbf{v} = -3\mathbf{i} - 2\mathbf{j}$, $\mathbf{b} = 2\mathbf{i} + \mathbf{j}$

25. In each part, find the vector component of $\mathbf{v}$ along $\mathbf{b}$ and the vector component of $\mathbf{v}$ orthogonal to $\mathbf{b}$.
(a) $\mathbf{v} = 2\mathbf{i} - \mathbf{j} + 3\mathbf{k}$, $\mathbf{b} = \mathbf{i} + 2\mathbf{j} + 2\mathbf{k}$
(b) $\mathbf{v} = \langle 4, -1, 7 \rangle$, $\mathbf{b} = \langle 2, 3, -6 \rangle$

26–27 Express the vector $\mathbf{v}$ as the sum of a vector parallel to $\mathbf{b}$ and a vector orthogonal to $\mathbf{b}$. ■

26. (a) $\mathbf{v} = 2\mathbf{i} - 4\mathbf{j}$, $\mathbf{b} = \mathbf{i} + \mathbf{j}$
(b) $\mathbf{v} = 3\mathbf{i} + \mathbf{j} - 2\mathbf{k}$, $\mathbf{b} = 2\mathbf{i} - \mathbf{k}$
(c) $\mathbf{v} = 4\mathbf{i} - 2\mathbf{j} + 6\mathbf{k}$, $\mathbf{b} = -2\mathbf{i} + \mathbf{j} - 3\mathbf{k}$

27. (a) $\mathbf{v} = \langle -3, 5 \rangle$, $\mathbf{b} = \langle 1, 1 \rangle$
(b) $\mathbf{v} = \langle -2, 1, 6 \rangle$, $\mathbf{b} = \langle 0, -2, 1 \rangle$
(c) $\mathbf{v} = \langle 1, 4, 1 \rangle$, $\mathbf{b} = \langle 3, -2, 5 \rangle$

28–31 True–False Determine whether the statement is true or false. Explain your answer. ■

28. If $\mathbf{a} \cdot \mathbf{b} = \mathbf{a} \cdot \mathbf{c}$ and $\mathbf{a} \neq \mathbf{0}$, then $\mathbf{b} = \mathbf{c}$.

29. If $\mathbf{v}$ and $\mathbf{w}$ are nonzero orthogonal vectors, then $\mathbf{v} + \mathbf{w} \neq \mathbf{0}$.

30. If $\mathbf{u}$ is a unit vector that is parallel to a nonzero vector $\mathbf{v}$, then $\mathbf{u} \cdot \mathbf{v} = \pm\|\mathbf{v}\|$.

31. If $\mathbf{v}$ and $\mathbf{b}$ are nonzero vectors, then the orthogonal projection of $\mathbf{v}$ on $\mathbf{b}$ is a vector that is parallel to $\mathbf{b}$.

32. If L is a line in 2-space or 3-space that passes through the points A and B, then the distance from a point P to the line L is equal to the length of the component of the vector $\overrightarrow{AP}$ that is orthogonal to the vector $\overrightarrow{AB}$ (see the accompanying figure). Use this result to find the distance from the point $P(1, 0)$ to the line through $A(2, -3)$ and $B(5, 1)$.

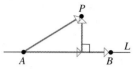

◀ **Figure Ex-32**

33. Use the method of Exercise 32 to find the distance from the point $P(-3, 1, 2)$ to the line through $A(1, 1, 0)$ and $B(-2, 3, -4)$.

34. As shown in the accompanying figure, a child with mass 34 kg is seated on a smooth (frictionless) playground slide that is inclined at an angle of $27°$ with the horizontal. How much force does the child exert on the slide, and how much force must be applied in the direction of **P** to prevent the child from sliding down the slide? Take the acceleration due to gravity to be 9.8 m/s^2.

35. For the child in Exercise 34, how much force must be applied in the direction of **Q** (shown in the accompanying figure) to prevent the child from sliding down the slide?

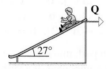

▲ **Figure Ex-34**   ▲ **Figure Ex-35**

36. Find the work done by a force $\mathbf{F} = -3\mathbf{j}$ pounds applied to a point that moves on a line from $(1, 3)$ to $(4, 7)$. Assume that distance is measured in feet.

37. A force of $\mathbf{F} = 4\mathbf{i} - 6\mathbf{j} + \mathbf{k}$ newtons is applied to a point that moves a distance of 15 meters in the direction of the vector $\mathbf{i} + \mathbf{j} + \mathbf{k}$. How much work is done?

38. A boat travels 100 meters due north while the wind exerts a force of 500 newtons toward the northeast. How much work does the wind do?

FOCUS ON CONCEPTS

39. Let **u** and **v** be adjacent sides of a parallelogram. Use vectors to prove that the diagonals of the parallelogram are perpendicular if the sides are equal in length.

40. Let **u** and **v** be adjacent sides of a parallelogram. Use vectors to prove that the parallelogram is a rectangle if the diagonals are equal in length.

41. Prove that
$$\|\mathbf{u} + \mathbf{v}\|^2 + \|\mathbf{u} - \mathbf{v}\|^2 = 2\|\mathbf{u}\|^2 + 2\|\mathbf{v}\|^2$$
and interpret the result geometrically by translating it into a theorem about parallelograms.

42. Prove: $\mathbf{u} \cdot \mathbf{v} = \frac{1}{4}\|\mathbf{u} + \mathbf{v}\|^2 - \frac{1}{4}\|\mathbf{u} - \mathbf{v}\|^2$.

43. Show that if $\mathbf{v}_1$, $\mathbf{v}_2$, and $\mathbf{v}_3$ are mutually orthogonal nonzero vectors in 3-space, and if a vector **v** in 3-space is expressed as
$$\mathbf{v} = c_1\mathbf{v}_1 + c_2\mathbf{v}_2 + c_3\mathbf{v}_3$$
then the scalars c_1, c_2, and c_3 are given by the formulas
$$c_i = (\mathbf{v} \cdot \mathbf{v}_i)/\|\mathbf{v}_i\|^2, \quad i = 1, 2, 3$$

44. Show that the three vectors
$$\mathbf{v}_1 = 3\mathbf{i} - \mathbf{j} + 2\mathbf{k}, \quad \mathbf{v}_2 = \mathbf{i} + \mathbf{j} - \mathbf{k}, \quad \mathbf{v}_3 = \mathbf{i} - 5\mathbf{j} - 4\mathbf{k}$$
are mutually orthogonal, and then use the result of Exercise 43 to find scalars c_1, c_2, and c_3 so that
$$c_1\mathbf{v}_1 + c_2\mathbf{v}_2 + c_3\mathbf{v}_3 = \mathbf{i} - \mathbf{j} + \mathbf{k}$$

C 45. For each x in $(-\infty, +\infty)$, let $\mathbf{u}(x)$ be the vector from the origin to the point $P(x, y)$ on the curve $y = x^2 + 1$, and $\mathbf{v}(x)$ the vector from the origin to the point $Q(x, y)$ on the line $y = -x - 1$.
   (a) Use a CAS to find, to the nearest degree, the minimum angle between $\mathbf{u}(x)$ and $\mathbf{v}(x)$ for x in $(-\infty, +\infty)$.
   (b) Determine whether there are any real values of x for which $\mathbf{u}(x)$ and $\mathbf{v}(x)$ are orthogonal.

C 46. Let **u** be a unit vector in the xy-plane of an xyz-coordinate system, and let **v** be a unit vector in the yz-plane. Let θ_1 be the angle between **u** and **i**, let θ_2 be the angle between **v** and **k**, and let θ be the angle between **u** and **v**.
   (a) Show that $\cos\theta = \pm\sin\theta_1 \sin\theta_2$.
   (b) Find θ if θ is acute and $\theta_1 = \theta_2 = 45°$.
   (c) Use a CAS to find, to the nearest degree, the maximum and minimum values of θ if θ is acute and $\theta_2 = 2\theta_1$.

47. Prove parts (b) and (e) of Theorem 11.3.2 for vectors in 3-space.

48. **Writing** Discuss some of the similarities and differences between the multiplication properties of real numbers and those of the dot product of vectors.

49. **Writing** Discuss the merits of the following claim: "Suppose an algebraic identity involves only the addition, subtraction, and multiplication of real numbers. If the numbers are replaced by vectors, and the multiplication is replaced by the dot product, then an identity involving vectors will result."

✔ **QUICK CHECK ANSWERS 11.3**

1. 8   2. (a) 25 (b) 7 (c) 10 (d) -6 3. $\frac{14}{5}$ 4. $\frac{2}{\sqrt{14}}$; $-\frac{1}{\sqrt{14}}$; $\frac{3}{\sqrt{14}}$ 5. $9\mathbf{i} - 3\mathbf{j}$

11.4   CROSS PRODUCT

In many applications of vectors in mathematics, physics, and engineering, there is a need to find a vector that is orthogonal to two given vectors. In this section we will discuss a new type of vector multiplication that can be used for this purpose.

■ DETERMINANTS

Some of the concepts that we will develop in this section require basic ideas about ***determinants***, which are functions that assign numerical values to square arrays of numbers. For example, if a_1, a_2, b_1, and b_2 are real numbers, then we define a **2 × 2 *determinant*** by

$$\begin{vmatrix} a_1 & a_2 \\ b_1 & b_2 \end{vmatrix} = a_1 b_2 - a_2 b_1 \tag{1}$$

The purpose of the arrows is to help you remember the formula—the determinant is the product of the entries on the rightward arrow minus the product of the entries on the leftward arrow. For example,

$$\begin{vmatrix} 3 & -2 \\ 4 & 5 \end{vmatrix} = (3)(5) - (-2)(4) = 15 + 8 = 23$$

A **3 × 3 *determinant*** is defined in terms of 2 × 2 determinants by

$$\begin{vmatrix} a_1 & a_2 & a_3 \\ b_1 & b_2 & b_3 \\ c_1 & c_2 & c_3 \end{vmatrix} = a_1 \begin{vmatrix} b_2 & b_3 \\ c_2 & c_3 \end{vmatrix} - a_2 \begin{vmatrix} b_1 & b_3 \\ c_1 & c_3 \end{vmatrix} + a_3 \begin{vmatrix} b_1 & b_2 \\ c_1 & c_2 \end{vmatrix} \tag{2}$$

The right side of this formula is easily remembered by noting that a_1, a_2, and a_3 are the entries in the first "row" of the left side, and the 2 × 2 determinants on the right side arise by deleting the first row and an appropriate column from the left side. The pattern is as follows:

$$\begin{vmatrix} a_1 & a_2 & a_3 \\ b_1 & b_2 & b_3 \\ c_1 & c_2 & c_3 \end{vmatrix} = a_1 \begin{vmatrix} a_1 & a_2 & a_3 \\ b_1 & b_2 & b_3 \\ c_1 & c_2 & c_3 \end{vmatrix} - a_2 \begin{vmatrix} a_1 & a_2 & a_3 \\ b_1 & b_2 & b_3 \\ c_1 & c_2 & c_3 \end{vmatrix} + a_3 \begin{vmatrix} a_1 & a_2 & a_3 \\ b_1 & b_2 & b_3 \\ c_1 & c_2 & c_3 \end{vmatrix}$$

For example,

$$\begin{vmatrix} 3 & -2 & -5 \\ 1 & 4 & -4 \\ 0 & 3 & 2 \end{vmatrix} = 3 \begin{vmatrix} 4 & -4 \\ 3 & 2 \end{vmatrix} - (-2) \begin{vmatrix} 1 & -4 \\ 0 & 2 \end{vmatrix} + (-5) \begin{vmatrix} 1 & 4 \\ 0 & 3 \end{vmatrix}$$

$$= 3(20) + 2(2) - 5(3) = 49$$

There are also definitions of 4 × 4 determinants, 5 × 5 determinants, and higher, but we will not need them in this text. Properties of determinants are studied in a branch of mathematics called ***linear algebra***, but we will only need the two properties stated in the following theorem.

11.4.1   THEOREM

(a) *If two rows in the array of a determinant are the same, then the value of the determinant is* 0.

(b) *Interchanging two rows in the array of a determinant multiplies its value by* −1.

We will give the proofs of parts (a) and (b) for 2×2 determinants and leave the proofs for 3×3 determinants as exercises.

PROOF (a)

$$\begin{vmatrix} a_1 & a_2 \\ a_1 & a_2 \end{vmatrix} = a_1 a_2 - a_2 a_1 = 0$$

PROOF (b)

$$\begin{vmatrix} b_1 & b_2 \\ a_1 & a_2 \end{vmatrix} = b_1 a_2 - b_2 a_1 = -(a_1 b_2 - a_2 b_1) = -\begin{vmatrix} a_1 & a_2 \\ b_1 & b_2 \end{vmatrix} \quad \blacksquare$$

■ **CROSS PRODUCT**

We now turn to the main concept in this section.

11.4.2 DEFINITION If $\mathbf{u} = \langle u_1, u_2, u_3 \rangle$ and $\mathbf{v} = \langle v_1, v_2, v_3 \rangle$ are vectors in 3-space, then the *cross product* $\mathbf{u} \times \mathbf{v}$ is the vector defined by

$$\mathbf{u} \times \mathbf{v} = \begin{vmatrix} u_2 & u_3 \\ v_2 & v_3 \end{vmatrix} \mathbf{i} - \begin{vmatrix} u_1 & u_3 \\ v_1 & v_3 \end{vmatrix} \mathbf{j} + \begin{vmatrix} u_1 & u_2 \\ v_1 & v_2 \end{vmatrix} \mathbf{k} \tag{3}$$

or, equivalently,

$$\mathbf{u} \times \mathbf{v} = (u_2 v_3 - u_3 v_2)\mathbf{i} - (u_1 v_3 - u_3 v_1)\mathbf{j} + (u_1 v_2 - u_2 v_1)\mathbf{k} \tag{4}$$

Observe that the right side of Formula (3) has the same form as the right side of Formula (2), the difference being notation and the order of the factors in the three terms. Thus, we can rewrite (3) as

$$\mathbf{u} \times \mathbf{v} = \begin{vmatrix} \mathbf{i} & \mathbf{j} & \mathbf{k} \\ u_1 & u_2 & u_3 \\ v_1 & v_2 & v_3 \end{vmatrix} \tag{5}$$

However, this is just a mnemonic device and not a true determinant since the entries in a determinant are numbers, not vectors.

▶ **Example 1** Let $\mathbf{u} = \langle 1, 2, -2 \rangle$ and $\mathbf{v} = \langle 3, 0, 1 \rangle$. Find

(a) $\mathbf{u} \times \mathbf{v}$ (b) $\mathbf{v} \times \mathbf{u}$

Solution (a).

$$\mathbf{u} \times \mathbf{v} = \begin{vmatrix} \mathbf{i} & \mathbf{j} & \mathbf{k} \\ 1 & 2 & -2 \\ 3 & 0 & 1 \end{vmatrix}$$

$$= \begin{vmatrix} 2 & -2 \\ 0 & 1 \end{vmatrix} \mathbf{i} - \begin{vmatrix} 1 & -2 \\ 3 & 1 \end{vmatrix} \mathbf{j} + \begin{vmatrix} 1 & 2 \\ 3 & 0 \end{vmatrix} \mathbf{k} = 2\mathbf{i} - 7\mathbf{j} - 6\mathbf{k}$$

Solution (b). We could use the method of part (a), but it is really not necessary to perform any computations. We need only observe that reversing $\mathbf{u}$ and $\mathbf{v}$ interchanges the second and third rows in (5), which in turn interchanges the rows in the arrays for the 2×2 determinants in (3). But interchanging the rows in the array of a 2×2 determinant reverses its sign, so the net effect of reversing the factors in a cross product is to reverse the signs of the components. Thus, by inspection

$$\mathbf{v} \times \mathbf{u} = -(\mathbf{u} \times \mathbf{v}) = -2\mathbf{i} + 7\mathbf{j} + 6\mathbf{k} \blacktriangleleft$$

▶ **Example 2** Show that $\mathbf{u} \times \mathbf{u} = \mathbf{0}$ for any vector $\mathbf{u}$ in 3-space.

Solution. We could let $\mathbf{u} = u_1\mathbf{i} + u_2\mathbf{j} + u_3\mathbf{k}$ and apply the method in part (a) of Example 1 to show that

$$\mathbf{u} \times \mathbf{u} = \begin{vmatrix} \mathbf{i} & \mathbf{j} & \mathbf{k} \\ u_1 & u_2 & u_3 \\ u_1 & u_2 & u_3 \end{vmatrix} = \mathbf{0}$$

However, the actual computations are unnecessary. We need only observe that if the two factors in a cross product are the same, then each 2×2 determinant in (3) is zero because its array has identical rows. Thus, $\mathbf{u} \times \mathbf{u} = \mathbf{0}$ by inspection. ◀

■ **ALGEBRAIC PROPERTIES OF THE CROSS PRODUCT**

Our next goal is to establish some of the basic algebraic properties of the cross product. As you read the discussion, keep in mind the essential differences between the cross product and the dot product:

- The cross product is defined only for vectors in 3-space, whereas the dot product is defined for vectors in 2-space and 3-space.

- The cross product of two vectors is a vector, whereas the dot product of two vectors is a scalar.

The main algebraic properties of the cross product are listed in the next theorem.

Whereas the order of the factors does not matter for ordinary multiplication, or for dot products, it does matter for cross products. Specifically, part (*a*) of Theorem 11.4.3 shows that reversing the order of the factors in a cross product reverses the direction of the resulting vector.

11.4.3   THEOREM   *If* $\mathbf{u}$, $\mathbf{v}$, *and* $\mathbf{w}$ *are any vectors in 3-space and* k *is any scalar, then:*

(*a*) $\mathbf{u} \times \mathbf{v} = -(\mathbf{v} \times \mathbf{u})$

(*b*) $\mathbf{u} \times (\mathbf{v} + \mathbf{w}) = (\mathbf{u} \times \mathbf{v}) + (\mathbf{u} \times \mathbf{w})$

(*c*) $(\mathbf{u} + \mathbf{v}) \times \mathbf{w} = (\mathbf{u} \times \mathbf{w}) + (\mathbf{v} \times \mathbf{w})$

(*d*) $k(\mathbf{u} \times \mathbf{v}) = (k\mathbf{u}) \times \mathbf{v} = \mathbf{u} \times (k\mathbf{v})$

(*e*) $\mathbf{u} \times \mathbf{0} = \mathbf{0} \times \mathbf{u} = \mathbf{0}$

(*f*) $\mathbf{u} \times \mathbf{u} = \mathbf{0}$

Parts (*a*) and (*f*) were addressed in Examples 1 and 2. The other proofs are left as exercises.

The following cross products occur so frequently that it is helpful to be familiar with them:

$$\begin{array}{ccc} \mathbf{i} \times \mathbf{j} = \mathbf{k} & \mathbf{j} \times \mathbf{k} = \mathbf{i} & \mathbf{k} \times \mathbf{i} = \mathbf{j} \\ \mathbf{j} \times \mathbf{i} = -\mathbf{k} & \mathbf{k} \times \mathbf{j} = -\mathbf{i} & \mathbf{i} \times \mathbf{k} = -\mathbf{j} \end{array} \tag{6}$$

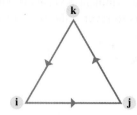

▲ **Figure 11.4.1**

These results are easy to obtain; for example,

$$\mathbf{i} \times \mathbf{j} = \begin{vmatrix} \mathbf{i} & \mathbf{j} & \mathbf{k} \\ 1 & 0 & 0 \\ 0 & 1 & 0 \end{vmatrix} = \begin{vmatrix} 0 & 0 \\ 1 & 0 \end{vmatrix} \mathbf{i} - \begin{vmatrix} 1 & 0 \\ 0 & 0 \end{vmatrix} \mathbf{j} + \begin{vmatrix} 1 & 0 \\ 0 & 1 \end{vmatrix} \mathbf{k} = \mathbf{k}$$

However, rather than computing these cross products each time you need them, you can use the diagram in Figure 11.4.1. In this diagram, the cross product of two consecutive vectors in the counterclockwise direction is the next vector around, and the cross product of two consecutive vectors in the clockwise direction is the negative of the next vector around.

WARNING   We can write a product of three real numbers as uvw since the associative law $u(vw) = (uv)w$ ensures that the same value for the product results no matter how the factors are grouped. However, the associative law *does not* hold for cross products. For example,

$$\mathbf{i} \times (\mathbf{j} \times \mathbf{j}) = \mathbf{i} \times \mathbf{0} = \mathbf{0} \quad \text{and} \quad (\mathbf{i} \times \mathbf{j}) \times \mathbf{j} = \mathbf{k} \times \mathbf{j} = -\mathbf{i}$$

so that $\mathbf{i} \times (\mathbf{j} \times \mathbf{j}) \neq (\mathbf{i} \times \mathbf{j}) \times \mathbf{j}$. Thus, we cannot write a cross product with three vectors as $\mathbf{u} \times \mathbf{v} \times \mathbf{w}$, since this expression is ambiguous without parentheses.

■ GEOMETRIC PROPERTIES OF THE CROSS PRODUCT

The following theorem shows that the cross product of two vectors is orthogonal to both factors. This property of the cross product will be used many times in the following sections.

11.4.4   THEOREM   *If* $\mathbf{u}$ *and* $\mathbf{v}$ *are vectors in 3-space, then:*

(*a*) $\mathbf{u} \cdot (\mathbf{u} \times \mathbf{v}) = 0$ ($\mathbf{u} \times \mathbf{v}$ *is orthogonal to* $\mathbf{u}$)

(*b*) $\mathbf{v} \cdot (\mathbf{u} \times \mathbf{v}) = 0$ ($\mathbf{u} \times \mathbf{v}$ *is orthogonal to* $\mathbf{v}$)

We will prove part (*a*). The proof of part (*b*) is similar.

PROOF (*a*)   Let $\mathbf{u} = \langle u_1, u_2, u_3 \rangle$ and $\mathbf{v} = \langle v_1, v_2, v_3 \rangle$. Then from (4)

$$\mathbf{u} \times \mathbf{v} = \langle u_2 v_3 - u_3 v_2, \; u_3 v_1 - u_1 v_3, \; u_1 v_2 - u_2 v_1 \rangle \tag{7}$$

so that

$$\mathbf{u} \cdot (\mathbf{u} \times \mathbf{v}) = u_1(u_2 v_3 - u_3 v_2) + u_2(u_3 v_1 - u_1 v_3) + u_3(u_1 v_2 - u_2 v_1) = 0 \quad \blacksquare$$

▶ **Example 3**   Find a vector that is orthogonal to both of the vectors $\mathbf{u} = \langle 2, -1, 3 \rangle$ and $\mathbf{v} = \langle -7, 2, -1 \rangle$.

Solution.   By Theorem 11.4.4, the vector $\mathbf{u} \times \mathbf{v}$ will be orthogonal to both $\mathbf{u}$ and $\mathbf{v}$. We compute that

$$\mathbf{u} \times \mathbf{v} = \begin{vmatrix} \mathbf{i} & \mathbf{j} & \mathbf{k} \\ 2 & -1 & 3 \\ -7 & 2 & -1 \end{vmatrix}$$

$$= \begin{vmatrix} -1 & 3 \\ 2 & -1 \end{vmatrix} \mathbf{i} - \begin{vmatrix} 2 & 3 \\ -7 & -1 \end{vmatrix} \mathbf{j} + \begin{vmatrix} 2 & -1 \\ -7 & 2 \end{vmatrix} \mathbf{k} = -5\mathbf{i} - 19\mathbf{j} - 3\mathbf{k} \quad ◀$$

Confirm that $\mathbf{u} \times \mathbf{v}$ in Example 3 is orthogonal to both $\mathbf{u}$ and $\mathbf{v}$ by computing $\mathbf{u} \cdot (\mathbf{u} \times \mathbf{v})$ and $\mathbf{v} \cdot (\mathbf{u} \times \mathbf{v})$.

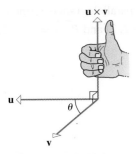

▲ **Figure 11.4.2**

It can be proved that if **u** and **v** are nonzero and nonparallel vectors, then the direction of **u** × **v** relative to **u** and **v** is determined by a right-hand rule;* that is, if the fingers of the right hand are cupped so they curl from **u** toward **v** in the direction of rotation that takes **u** into **v** in less than 180°, then the thumb will point (roughly) in the direction of **u** × **v** (Figure 11.4.2). For example, we stated in (6) that

$$\mathbf{i} \times \mathbf{j} = \mathbf{k}, \quad \mathbf{j} \times \mathbf{k} = \mathbf{i}, \quad \mathbf{k} \times \mathbf{i} = \mathbf{j}$$

all of which are consistent with the right-hand rule (verify).

The next theorem lists some more important geometric properties of the cross product.

11.4.5   THEOREM   *Let* **u** *and* **v** *be nonzero vectors in 3-space, and let* θ *be the angle between these vectors when they are positioned so their initial points coincide.*

(a) $\|\mathbf{u} \times \mathbf{v}\| = \|\mathbf{u}\|\|\mathbf{v}\| \sin\theta$

(b)   *The area A of the parallelogram that has* **u** *and* **v** *as adjacent sides is*

$$A = \|\mathbf{u} \times \mathbf{v}\| \tag{8}$$

(c)   **u** × **v** = **0** *if and only if* **u** *and* **v** *are parallel vectors, that is, if and only if they are scalar multiples of one another.*

PROOF (*a*)

$$\|\mathbf{u}\|\|\mathbf{v}\| \sin\theta = \|\mathbf{u}\|\|\mathbf{v}\| \sqrt{1 - \cos^2\theta}$$

$$= \|\mathbf{u}\|\|\mathbf{v}\| \sqrt{1 - \frac{(\mathbf{u} \cdot \mathbf{v})^2}{\|\mathbf{u}\|^2 \|\mathbf{v}\|^2}} \quad \boxed{\text{Theorem 11.3.3}}$$

$$= \sqrt{\|\mathbf{u}\|^2 \|\mathbf{v}\|^2 - (\mathbf{u} \cdot \mathbf{v})^2}$$

$$= \sqrt{(u_1^2 + u_2^2 + u_3^2)(v_1^2 + v_2^2 + v_3^2) - (u_1 v_1 + u_2 v_2 + u_3 v_3)^2}$$

$$= \sqrt{(u_2 v_3 - u_3 v_2)^2 + (u_1 v_3 - u_3 v_1)^2 + (u_1 v_2 - u_2 v_1)^2}$$

$$= \|\mathbf{u} \times \mathbf{v}\| \quad \boxed{\text{See Formula (4).}}$$

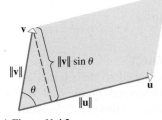

▲ **Figure 11.4.3**

PROOF (*b*)   Referring to Figure 11.4.3, the parallelogram that has **u** and **v** as adjacent sides can be viewed as having base $\|\mathbf{u}\|$ and altitude $\|\mathbf{v}\| \sin\theta$. Thus, its area A is

$$A = (\text{base})(\text{altitude}) = \|\mathbf{u}\|\|\mathbf{v}\| \sin\theta = \|\mathbf{u} \times \mathbf{v}\|$$

PROOF (*c*)   Since **u** and **v** are assumed to be nonzero vectors, it follows from part (*a*) that **u** × **v** = **0** if and only if $\sin\theta = 0$; this is true if and only if $\theta = 0$ or $\theta = \pi$ (since $0 \le \theta \le \pi$). Geometrically, this means that **u** × **v** = **0** if and only if **u** and **v** are parallel vectors. ■

▶ **Example 4**   Find the area of the triangle that is determined by the points $P_1(2, 2, 0)$, $P_2(-1, 0, 2)$, and $P_3(0, 4, 3)$.

---

*Recall that we agreed to consider only right-handed coordinate systems in this text. Had we used left-handed systems instead, a "left-hand rule" would apply here.

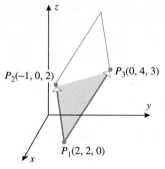

▲ **Figure 11.4.4**

Solution.   The area A of the triangle is half the area of the parallelogram determined by the vectors $\overrightarrow{P_1P_2}$ and $\overrightarrow{P_1P_3}$ (Figure 11.4.4). But $\overrightarrow{P_1P_2} = \langle -3, -2, 2 \rangle$ and $\overrightarrow{P_1P_3} = \langle -2, 2, 3 \rangle$, so

$$\overrightarrow{P_1P_2} \times \overrightarrow{P_1P_3} = \langle -10, 5, -10 \rangle$$

(verify), and consequently

$$A = \tfrac{1}{2} \| \overrightarrow{P_1P_2} \times \overrightarrow{P_1P_3} \| = \tfrac{15}{2} \quad ◄$$

■ **SCALAR TRIPLE PRODUCTS**

If $\mathbf{u} = \langle u_1, u_2, u_3 \rangle$, $\mathbf{v} = \langle v_1, v_2, v_3 \rangle$, and $\mathbf{w} = \langle w_1, w_2, w_3 \rangle$ are vectors in 3-space, then the number

$$\mathbf{u} \cdot (\mathbf{v} \times \mathbf{w})$$

is called the *scalar triple product* of $\mathbf{u}$, $\mathbf{v}$, and $\mathbf{w}$. It is not necessary to compute the dot product and cross product to evaluate a scalar triple product—the value can be obtained directly from the formula

$$\mathbf{u} \cdot (\mathbf{v} \times \mathbf{w}) = \begin{vmatrix} u_1 & u_2 & u_3 \\ v_1 & v_2 & v_3 \\ w_1 & w_2 & w_3 \end{vmatrix} \tag{9}$$

the validity of which can be seen by writing

$$\mathbf{u} \cdot (\mathbf{v} \times \mathbf{w}) = \mathbf{u} \cdot \left(\begin{vmatrix} v_2 & v_3 \\ w_2 & w_3 \end{vmatrix} \mathbf{i} - \begin{vmatrix} v_1 & v_3 \\ w_1 & w_3 \end{vmatrix} \mathbf{j} + \begin{vmatrix} v_1 & v_2 \\ w_1 & w_2 \end{vmatrix} \mathbf{k} \right)$$

$$= u_1 \begin{vmatrix} v_2 & v_3 \\ w_2 & w_3 \end{vmatrix} - u_2 \begin{vmatrix} v_1 & v_3 \\ w_1 & w_3 \end{vmatrix} + u_3 \begin{vmatrix} v_1 & v_2 \\ w_1 & w_2 \end{vmatrix}$$

$$= \begin{vmatrix} u_1 & u_2 & u_3 \\ v_1 & v_2 & v_3 \\ w_1 & w_2 & w_3 \end{vmatrix}$$

TECHNOLOGY MASTERY

Many calculating utilities have built-in cross product and determinant operations. If your calculating utility has these capabilities, use it to check the computations in Examples 1 and 5.

▶ **Example 5**   Calculate the scalar triple product $\mathbf{u} \cdot (\mathbf{v} \times \mathbf{w})$ of the vectors

$$\mathbf{u} = 3\mathbf{i} - 2\mathbf{j} - 5\mathbf{k}, \quad \mathbf{v} = \mathbf{i} + 4\mathbf{j} - 4\mathbf{k}, \quad \mathbf{w} = 3\mathbf{j} + 2\mathbf{k}$$

Solution.

$$\mathbf{u} \cdot (\mathbf{v} \times \mathbf{w}) = \begin{vmatrix} 3 & -2 & -5 \\ 1 & 4 & -4 \\ 0 & 3 & 2 \end{vmatrix} = 49 \quad ◄$$

■ **GEOMETRIC PROPERTIES OF THE SCALAR TRIPLE PRODUCT**

If $\mathbf{u}$, $\mathbf{v}$, and $\mathbf{w}$ are nonzero vectors in 3-space that are positioned so their initial points coincide, then these vectors form the adjacent sides of a parallelepiped (Figure 11.4.5). The following theorem establishes a relationship between the volume of this parallelepiped and the scalar triple product of the sides.

▲ **Figure 11.4.5**

It follows from Formula (10) that

$$\mathbf{u} \cdot (\mathbf{v} \times \mathbf{w}) = \pm V$$

The $+$ occurs when $\mathbf{u}$ makes an acute angle with $\mathbf{v} \times \mathbf{w}$ and the $-$ occurs when it makes an obtuse angle.

11.4.6   THEOREM   *Let $\mathbf{u}$, $\mathbf{v}$, and $\mathbf{w}$ be nonzero vectors in 3-space.*

(a)   The volume V of the parallelepiped that has $\mathbf{u}$, $\mathbf{v}$, and $\mathbf{w}$ as adjacent edges is

$$V = |\mathbf{u} \cdot (\mathbf{v} \times \mathbf{w})| \tag{10}$$

(b) $\mathbf{u} \cdot (\mathbf{v} \times \mathbf{w}) = 0$ if and only if $\mathbf{u}$, $\mathbf{v}$, and $\mathbf{w}$ lie in the same plane.

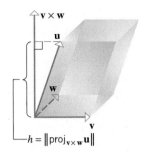

$\mathbf{v} \times \mathbf{w}$

$\mathbf{u}$

$\mathbf{w}$

$\mathbf{v}$

$h = \|\mathrm{proj}_{\mathbf{v} \times \mathbf{w}} \mathbf{u}\|$

▲ **Figure 11.4.6**

PROOF (*a*) Referring to Figure 11.4.6, let us regard the base of the parallelepiped with **u**, **v**, and **w** as adjacent sides to be the parallelogram determined by **v** and **w**. Thus, the area of the base is $\|\mathbf{v} \times \mathbf{w}\|$, and the altitude h of the parallelepiped (shown in the figure) is the length of the orthogonal projection of **u** on the vector $\mathbf{v} \times \mathbf{w}$. Therefore, from Formula (12) of Section 11.3 we have

$$h = \|\mathrm{proj}_{\mathbf{v} \times \mathbf{w}} \mathbf{u}\| = \frac{|\mathbf{u} \cdot (\mathbf{v} \times \mathbf{w})|}{\|\mathbf{v} \times \mathbf{w}\|^2} \|\mathbf{v} \times \mathbf{w}\| = \frac{|\mathbf{u} \cdot (\mathbf{v} \times \mathbf{w})|}{\|\mathbf{v} \times \mathbf{w}\|}$$

It now follows that the volume of the parallelepiped is

$$V = (\text{area of base})(\text{height}) = \|\mathbf{v} \times \mathbf{w}\| h = |\mathbf{u} \cdot (\mathbf{v} \times \mathbf{w})|$$

PROOF (*b*) The vectors **u**, **v**, and **w** lie in the same plane if and only if the parallelepiped with these vectors as adjacent sides has volume zero (why?). Thus, from part (*a*) the vectors lie in the same plane if and only if $\mathbf{u} \cdot (\mathbf{v} \times \mathbf{w}) = 0$. ■

ALGEBRAIC PROPERTIES OF THE SCALAR TRIPLE PRODUCT

We observed earlier in this section that the expression $\mathbf{u} \times \mathbf{v} \times \mathbf{w}$ must be avoided because it is ambiguous without parentheses. However, the expression $\mathbf{u} \cdot \mathbf{v} \times \mathbf{w}$ is not ambiguous—it has to mean $\mathbf{u} \cdot (\mathbf{v} \times \mathbf{w})$ and not $(\mathbf{u} \cdot \mathbf{v}) \times \mathbf{w}$ because we cannot form the cross product of a scalar and a vector. Similarly, the expression $\mathbf{u} \times \mathbf{v} \cdot \mathbf{w}$ must mean $(\mathbf{u} \times \mathbf{v}) \cdot \mathbf{w}$ and not $\mathbf{u} \times (\mathbf{v} \cdot \mathbf{w})$. Thus, when you see an expression of the form $\mathbf{u} \cdot \mathbf{v} \times \mathbf{w}$ or $\mathbf{u} \times \mathbf{v} \cdot \mathbf{w}$, the cross product is formed first and the dot product second.

Since interchanging two rows of a determinant multiplies its value by -1, making two row interchanges in a determinant has no effect on its value. This being the case, it follows that

$$\mathbf{u} \cdot (\mathbf{v} \times \mathbf{w}) = \mathbf{w} \cdot (\mathbf{u} \times \mathbf{v}) = \mathbf{v} \cdot (\mathbf{w} \times \mathbf{u}) \qquad (11)$$

> A good way to remember Formula (11) is to observe that the second expression in the formula can be obtained from the first by leaving the dot, cross, and parentheses fixed, moving the first two vectors to the right, and bringing the third vector to the first position. The same procedure produces the third expression from the second and the first expression from the third (verify).

since the 3×3 determinants that are used to compute these scalar triple products can be obtained from one another by two row interchanges (verify).

Another useful formula can be obtained by rewriting the first equality in (11) as

$$\mathbf{u} \cdot (\mathbf{v} \times \mathbf{w}) = (\mathbf{u} \times \mathbf{v}) \cdot \mathbf{w}$$

and then omitting the superfluous parentheses to obtain

$$\mathbf{u} \cdot \mathbf{v} \times \mathbf{w} = \mathbf{u} \times \mathbf{v} \cdot \mathbf{w} \qquad (12)$$

In words, this formula states that the dot and cross in a scalar triple product can be interchanged (provided the factors are grouped appropriately).

DOT AND CROSS PRODUCTS ARE COORDINATE INDEPENDENT

In Definitions 11.3.1 and 11.4.2 we defined the dot product and the cross product of two vectors in terms of the components of those vectors in a coordinate system. Thus, it is theoretically possible that changing the coordinate system might change $\mathbf{u} \cdot \mathbf{v}$ or $\mathbf{u} \times \mathbf{v}$, since the components of a vector depend on the coordinate system that is chosen. However, the relationships

$$\mathbf{u} \cdot \mathbf{v} = \|\mathbf{u}\| \|\mathbf{v}\| \cos\theta \qquad (13)$$

$$\|\mathbf{u} \times \mathbf{v}\| = \|\mathbf{u}\| \|\mathbf{v}\| \sin\theta \qquad (14)$$

> This independence of a coordinate system is important in applications because it allows us to choose any convenient coordinate system for solving a problem with full confidence that the choice will not affect computations that involve dot products or cross products.

that were obtained in Theorems 11.3.3 and 11.4.5 show that this is not the case. Formula (13) shows that the value of $\mathbf{u} \cdot \mathbf{v}$ depends only on the lengths of the vectors and the angle between them—not on the coordinate system. Similarly, Formula (14), in combination with the right-hand rule and Theorem 11.4.4, shows that $\mathbf{u} \times \mathbf{v}$ does not depend on the coordinate system (as long as it is right-handed).

World Perspectives/Getty Images

Astronauts use tools that are designed to limit forces that would impart unintended rotational motion to a satellite.

■ **MOMENTS AND ROTATIONAL MOTION IN 3-SPACE**

Cross products play an important role in describing rotational motion in 3-space. For example, suppose that an astronaut on a satellite repair mission in space applies a force **F** at a point Q on the surface of a spherical satellite. If the force is directed along a line that passes through the center P of the satellite, then Newton's Second Law of Motion implies that the force will accelerate the satellite in the direction of **F**. However, if the astronaut applies the same force at an angle θ with the vector $\overrightarrow{PQ}$, then **F** will tend to cause a rotation, as well as an acceleration in the direction of **F**. To see why this is so, let us resolve **F** into a sum of orthogonal components $\mathbf{F} = \mathbf{F}_1 + \mathbf{F}_2$, where $\mathbf{F}_1$ is the orthogonal projection of **F** on the vector $\overrightarrow{PQ}$ and $\mathbf{F}_2$ is the component of **F** orthogonal to $\overrightarrow{PQ}$ (Figure 11.4.7). Since the force $\mathbf{F}_1$ acts along the line through the center of the satellite, it contributes to the linear acceleration of the satellite but does not cause any rotation. However, the force $\mathbf{F}_2$ is tangent to the circle around the satellite in the plane of **F** and $\overrightarrow{PQ}$, so it causes the satellite to rotate about an axis that is perpendicular to that plane.

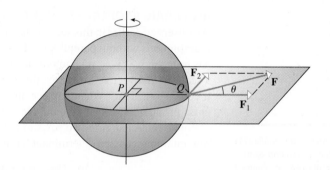

▶ **Figure 11.4.7**

You know from your own experience that the "tendency" for rotation about an axis depends both on the amount of force and how far from the axis it is applied. For example, it is easier to close a door by pushing on its outer edge than applying the same force close to the hinges. In fact, the tendency of rotation of the satellite can be measured by

$$\|\overrightarrow{PQ}\|\,\|\mathbf{F}_2\| \qquad \boxed{\text{distance from the center} \times \text{magnitude of the force}} \tag{15}$$

However, $\|\mathbf{F}_2\| = \|\mathbf{F}\|\sin\theta$, so we can rewrite (15) as

$$\|\overrightarrow{PQ}\|\,\|\mathbf{F}\|\sin\theta = \|\overrightarrow{PQ} \times \mathbf{F}\|$$

This is called the ***scalar moment*** or ***torque*** of **F** about the point P. Scalar moments have units of force times distance—pound-feet or newton-meters, for example. The vector $\overrightarrow{PQ} \times \mathbf{F}$ is called the ***vector moment*** or ***torque vector*** of **F** about P.

Recalling that the direction of $\overrightarrow{PQ} \times \mathbf{F}$ is determined by the right-hand rule, it follows that the direction of rotation about P that results by applying the force **F** at the point Q is counterclockwise looking down the axis of $\overrightarrow{PQ} \times \mathbf{F}$ (Figure 11.4.7). Thus, the vector moment $\overrightarrow{PQ} \times \mathbf{F}$ captures the essential information about the rotational effect of the force—the magnitude of the cross product provides the scalar moment of the force, and the cross product vector itself provides the axis and direction of rotation.

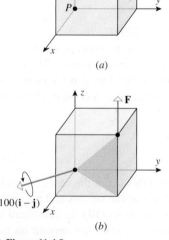

▲ **Figure 11.4.8**

▶ **Example 6**   Figure 11.4.8*a* shows a force **F** of 100 N applied in the positive z-direction at the point $Q(1, 1, 1)$ of a cube whose sides have a length of 1 m. Assuming that the cube is free to rotate about the point $P(0, 0, 0)$ (the origin), find the scalar moment of the force about P, and describe the direction of rotation.

Solution. The force vector is $\mathbf{F} = 100\mathbf{k}$, and the vector from P to Q is $\overrightarrow{PQ} = \mathbf{i} + \mathbf{j} + \mathbf{k}$, so the vector moment of $\mathbf{F}$ about P is

$$\overrightarrow{PQ} \times \mathbf{F} = \begin{vmatrix} \mathbf{i} & \mathbf{j} & \mathbf{k} \\ 1 & 1 & 1 \\ 0 & 0 & 100 \end{vmatrix} = 100\mathbf{i} - 100\mathbf{j}$$

Thus, the scalar moment of $\mathbf{F}$ about P is $\|100\mathbf{i} - 100\mathbf{j}\| = 100\sqrt{2} \approx 141$ N·m, and the direction of rotation is counterclockwise looking along the vector $100\mathbf{i} - 100\mathbf{j} = 100(\mathbf{i} - \mathbf{j})$ toward its initial point (Figure 11.4.8*b*). ◄

✔ QUICK CHECK EXERCISES 11.4   (*See page 805 for answers.*)

1. (a) $\begin{vmatrix} 3 & 2 \\ 4 & 5 \end{vmatrix} = $ _____   (b) $\begin{vmatrix} 3 & 2 & 1 \\ 3 & 2 & 1 \\ 5 & 5 & 5 \end{vmatrix} = $ _____

2. $\langle 1, 2, 0 \rangle \times \langle 3, 0, 4 \rangle = $ _____

3. Suppose that $\mathbf{u}$, $\mathbf{v}$, and $\mathbf{w}$ are vectors in 3-space such that $\mathbf{u} \times \mathbf{v} = \langle 2, 7, 3 \rangle$ and $\mathbf{u} \times \mathbf{w} = \langle -5, 4, 0 \rangle$.
   (a) $\mathbf{u} \times \mathbf{u} = $ _____   (b) $\mathbf{v} \times \mathbf{u} = $ _____

   (c) $\mathbf{u} \times (\mathbf{v} + \mathbf{w}) = $ _____
   (d) $\mathbf{u} \times (2\mathbf{w}) = $ _____

4. Let $\mathbf{u} = \mathbf{i} - 5\mathbf{k}$, $\mathbf{v} = 2\mathbf{i} - 4\mathbf{j} + \mathbf{k}$, and $\mathbf{w} = 3\mathbf{i} - 2\mathbf{j} + 5\mathbf{k}$.
   (a) $\mathbf{u} \cdot (\mathbf{v} \times \mathbf{w}) = $ _____
   (b) The volume of the parallelepiped that has $\mathbf{u}$, $\mathbf{v}$, and $\mathbf{w}$ as adjacent edges is $V = $ _____.

EXERCISE SET 11.4   [C] CAS

1. (a) Use a determinant to find the cross product

   $$\mathbf{i} \times (\mathbf{i} + \mathbf{j} + \mathbf{k})$$

   (b) Check your answer in part (a) by rewriting the cross product as

   $$\mathbf{i} \times (\mathbf{i} + \mathbf{j} + \mathbf{k}) = (\mathbf{i} \times \mathbf{i}) + (\mathbf{i} \times \mathbf{j}) + (\mathbf{i} \times \mathbf{k})$$

   and evaluating each term.

2. In each part, use the two methods in Exercise 1 to find
   (a) $\mathbf{j} \times (\mathbf{i} + \mathbf{j} + \mathbf{k})$ (b) $\mathbf{k} \times (\mathbf{i} + \mathbf{j} + \mathbf{k})$.

3–6 Find $\mathbf{u} \times \mathbf{v}$ and check that it is orthogonal to both $\mathbf{u}$ and $\mathbf{v}$. ▪

3. $\mathbf{u} = \langle 1, 2, -3 \rangle$, $\mathbf{v} = \langle -4, 1, 2 \rangle$

4. $\mathbf{u} = 3\mathbf{i} + 2\mathbf{j} - \mathbf{k}$, $\mathbf{v} = -\mathbf{i} - 3\mathbf{j} + \mathbf{k}$

5. $\mathbf{u} = \langle 0, 1, -2 \rangle$, $\mathbf{v} = \langle 3, 0, -4 \rangle$

6. $\mathbf{u} = 4\mathbf{i} + \mathbf{k}$, $\mathbf{v} = 2\mathbf{i} - \mathbf{j}$

7. Let $\mathbf{u} = \langle 2, -1, 3 \rangle$, $\mathbf{v} = \langle 0, 1, 7 \rangle$, and $\mathbf{w} = \langle 1, 4, 5 \rangle$. Find
   (a) $\mathbf{u} \times (\mathbf{v} \times \mathbf{w})$ (b) $(\mathbf{u} \times \mathbf{v}) \times \mathbf{w}$
   (c) $(\mathbf{u} \times \mathbf{v}) \times (\mathbf{v} \times \mathbf{w})$ (d) $(\mathbf{v} \times \mathbf{w}) \times (\mathbf{u} \times \mathbf{v})$.

[C] 8. Use a CAS or a calculating utility that can compute determinants or cross products to solve Exercise 7.

9. Find the direction cosines of $\mathbf{u} \times \mathbf{v}$ for the vectors $\mathbf{u}$ and $\mathbf{v}$ in the accompanying figure.

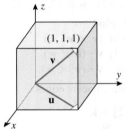

◄ **Figure Ex-9**

10. Find two unit vectors that are orthogonal to both

    $$\mathbf{u} = -7\mathbf{i} + 3\mathbf{j} + \mathbf{k}, \quad \mathbf{v} = 2\mathbf{i} + 4\mathbf{k}$$

11. Find two unit vectors that are normal to the plane determined by the points $A(0, -2, 1)$, $B(1, -1, -2)$, and $C(-1, 1, 0)$.

12. Find two unit vectors that are parallel to the yz-plane and are orthogonal to the vector $3\mathbf{i} - \mathbf{j} + 2\mathbf{k}$.

13–16 True–False Determine whether the statement is true or false. Explain your answer. ▪

13. If the cross product of two nonzero vectors is the zero vector, then each of the two vectors is a scalar multiple of the other.

14. For any three vectors $\mathbf{a}$, $\mathbf{b}$, and $\mathbf{c}$, we have $\mathbf{a} \times (\mathbf{b} \times \mathbf{c}) = (\mathbf{a} \times \mathbf{b}) \times \mathbf{c}$.

15. If $\mathbf{v} \times \mathbf{u} = \mathbf{v} \times \mathbf{w}$ and if $\mathbf{v} \neq \mathbf{0}$, then $\mathbf{u} = \mathbf{w}$.

16. If $\mathbf{u} = a\mathbf{v} + b\mathbf{w}$, then $\mathbf{u} \cdot \mathbf{v} \times \mathbf{w} = 0$.

17–18 Find the area of the parallelogram that has **u** and **v** as adjacent sides. ■

17. $\mathbf{u} = \mathbf{i} - \mathbf{j} + 2\mathbf{k}$, $\mathbf{v} = 3\mathbf{j} + \mathbf{k}$

18. $\mathbf{u} = 2\mathbf{i} + 3\mathbf{j}$, $\mathbf{v} = -\mathbf{i} + 2\mathbf{j} - 2\mathbf{k}$

19–20 Find the area of the triangle with vertices P, Q, and R. ■

19. $P(1, 5, -2)$, $Q(0, 0, 0)$, $R(3, 5, 1)$

20. $P(2, 0, -3)$, $Q(1, 4, 5)$, $R(7, 2, 9)$

21–24 Find $\mathbf{u} \cdot (\mathbf{v} \times \mathbf{w})$. ■

21. $\mathbf{u} = 2\mathbf{i} - 3\mathbf{j} + \mathbf{k}$, $\mathbf{v} = 4\mathbf{i} + \mathbf{j} - 3\mathbf{k}$, $\mathbf{w} = \mathbf{j} + 5\mathbf{k}$

22. $\mathbf{u} = \langle 1, -2, 2 \rangle$, $\mathbf{v} = \langle 0, 3, 2 \rangle$, $\mathbf{w} = \langle -4, 1, -3 \rangle$

23. $\mathbf{u} = \langle 2, 1, 0 \rangle$, $\mathbf{v} = \langle 1, -3, 1 \rangle$, $\mathbf{w} = \langle 4, 0, 1 \rangle$

24. $\mathbf{u} = \mathbf{i}$, $\mathbf{v} = \mathbf{i} + \mathbf{j}$, $\mathbf{w} = \mathbf{i} + \mathbf{j} + \mathbf{k}$

25–26 Use a scalar triple product to find the volume of the parallelepiped that has **u**, **v**, and **w** as adjacent edges. ■

25. $\mathbf{u} = \langle 2, -6, 2 \rangle$, $\mathbf{v} = \langle 0, 4, -2 \rangle$, $\mathbf{w} = \langle 2, 2, -4 \rangle$

26. $\mathbf{u} = 3\mathbf{i} + \mathbf{j} + 2\mathbf{k}$, $\mathbf{v} = 4\mathbf{i} + 5\mathbf{j} + \mathbf{k}$, $\mathbf{w} = \mathbf{i} + 2\mathbf{j} + 4\mathbf{k}$

27. In each part, use a scalar triple product to determine whether the vectors lie in the same plane.
(a) $\mathbf{u} = \langle 1, -2, 1 \rangle$, $\mathbf{v} = \langle 3, 0, -2 \rangle$, $\mathbf{w} = \langle 5, -4, 0 \rangle$
(b) $\mathbf{u} = 5\mathbf{i} - 2\mathbf{j} + \mathbf{k}$, $\mathbf{v} = 4\mathbf{i} - \mathbf{j} + \mathbf{k}$, $\mathbf{w} = \mathbf{i} - \mathbf{j}$
(c) $\mathbf{u} = \langle 4, -8, 1 \rangle$, $\mathbf{v} = \langle 2, 1, -2 \rangle$, $\mathbf{w} = \langle 3, -4, 12 \rangle$

28. Suppose that $\mathbf{u} \cdot (\mathbf{v} \times \mathbf{w}) = 3$. Find
(a) $\mathbf{u} \cdot (\mathbf{w} \times \mathbf{v})$ (b) $(\mathbf{v} \times \mathbf{w}) \cdot \mathbf{u}$
(c) $\mathbf{w} \cdot (\mathbf{u} \times \mathbf{v})$ (d) $\mathbf{v} \cdot (\mathbf{u} \times \mathbf{w})$
(e) $(\mathbf{u} \times \mathbf{w}) \cdot \mathbf{v}$ (f) $\mathbf{v} \cdot (\mathbf{w} \times \mathbf{w})$.

29. Consider the parallelepiped with adjacent edges
$$\mathbf{u} = 3\mathbf{i} + 2\mathbf{j} + \mathbf{k}$$
$$\mathbf{v} = \mathbf{i} + \mathbf{j} + 2\mathbf{k}$$
$$\mathbf{w} = \mathbf{i} + 3\mathbf{j} + 3\mathbf{k}$$
(a) Find the volume.
(b) Find the area of the face determined by **u** and **w**.
(c) Find the angle between **u** and the plane containing the face determined by **v** and **w**.

30. Show that in 3-space the distance d from a point P to the line L through points A and B can be expressed as
$$d = \frac{\|\overrightarrow{AP} \times \overrightarrow{AB}\|}{\|\overrightarrow{AB}\|}$$

31. Use the result in Exercise 30 to find the distance between the point P and the line through the points A and B.
(a) $P(-3, 1, 2)$, $A(1, 1, 0)$, $B(-2, 3, -4)$
(b) $P(4, 3)$, $A(2, 1)$, $B(0, 2)$

32. It is a theorem of solid geometry that the volume of a tetrahedron is $\frac{1}{3}$(area of base) $\cdot$ (height). Use this result to prove that the volume of a tetrahedron with adjacent edges given by the vectors **u**, **v**, and **w** is $\frac{1}{6}|\mathbf{u} \cdot (\mathbf{v} \times \mathbf{w})|$.

33. Use the result of Exercise 32 to find the volume of the tetrahedron with vertices
$$P(-1, 2, 0), \quad Q(2, 1, -3), \quad R(1, 0, 1), \quad S(3, -2, 3)$$

34. Let θ be the angle between the vectors $\mathbf{u} = 2\mathbf{i} + 3\mathbf{j} - 6\mathbf{k}$ and $\mathbf{v} = 2\mathbf{i} + 3\mathbf{j} + 6\mathbf{k}$.
(a) Use the dot product to find $\cos \theta$.
(b) Use the cross product to find $\sin \theta$.
(c) Confirm that $\sin^2 \theta + \cos^2 \theta = 1$.

FOCUS ON CONCEPTS

35. Let A, B, C, and D be four distinct points in 3-space. If $\overrightarrow{AB} \times \overrightarrow{CD} \neq \mathbf{0}$ and $\overrightarrow{AC} \cdot (\overrightarrow{AB} \times \overrightarrow{CD}) = 0$, explain why the line through A and B must intersect the line through C and D.

36. Let A, B, and C be three distinct noncollinear points in 3-space. Describe the set of all points P that satisfy the vector equation $\overrightarrow{AP} \cdot (\overrightarrow{AB} \times \overrightarrow{AC}) = 0$.

37. What can you say about the angle between nonzero vectors **u** and **v** if $\mathbf{u} \cdot \mathbf{v} = \|\mathbf{u} \times \mathbf{v}\|$?

38. Show that if **u** and **v** are vectors in 3-space, then
$$\|\mathbf{u} \times \mathbf{v}\|^2 = \|\mathbf{u}\|^2 \|\mathbf{v}\|^2 - (\mathbf{u} \cdot \mathbf{v})^2$$
[*Note:* This result is sometimes called *Lagrange's identity*.]

39. The accompanying figure shows a force **F** of 10 lb applied in the positive y-direction to the point $Q(1, 1, 1)$ of a cube whose sides have a length of 1 ft. In each part, find the scalar moment of **F** about the point P, and describe the direction of rotation, if any, if the cube is free to rotate about P.
(a) P is the point $(0, 0, 0)$.   (b) P is the point $(1, 0, 0)$.
(c) P is the point $(1, 0, 1)$.

40. The accompanying figure shows a force **F** of 1000 N applied to the corner of a box.
(a) Find the scalar moment of **F** about the point P.
(b) Find the direction angles of the vector moment of **F** about the point P to the nearest degree.

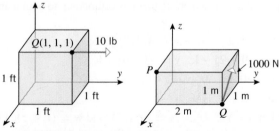

▲ **Figure Ex-39**   ▲ **Figure Ex-40**

41. As shown in the accompanying figure on the next page, a force of 200 N is applied at an angle of 18° to a point near the end of a monkey wrench. Find the scalar moment of the force about the center of the bolt. [*Note:* Treat this as a problem in two dimensions.]

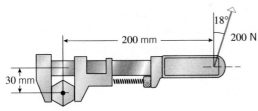

▲ **Figure Ex-41**

42. Prove parts (*b*) and (*c*) of Theorem 11.4.3.

43. Prove parts (*d*) and (*e*) of Theorem 11.4.3.

44. Prove part (*b*) of Theorem 11.4.1 for 3 × 3 determinants. [*Note:* Just give the proof for the first two rows.] Then use (*b*) to prove (*a*).

45. Expressions of the form

$$\mathbf{u} \times (\mathbf{v} \times \mathbf{w}) \quad \text{and} \quad (\mathbf{u} \times \mathbf{v}) \times \mathbf{w}$$

are called **vector triple products**. It can be proved with some effort that

$$\mathbf{u} \times (\mathbf{v} \times \mathbf{w}) = (\mathbf{u} \cdot \mathbf{w})\mathbf{v} - (\mathbf{u} \cdot \mathbf{v})\mathbf{w}$$
$$(\mathbf{u} \times \mathbf{v}) \times \mathbf{w} = (\mathbf{w} \cdot \mathbf{u})\mathbf{v} - (\mathbf{w} \cdot \mathbf{v})\mathbf{u}$$

These expressions can be summarized with the following mnemonic rule:

vector triple product = (outer · remote)adjacent
$$\qquad\qquad\qquad - \text{(outer · adjacent)remote}$$

See if you can figure out what the expressions "outer," "remote," and "adjacent" mean in this rule, and then use the rule to find the two vector triple products of the vectors

$$\mathbf{u} = \mathbf{i} + 3\mathbf{j} - \mathbf{k}, \quad \mathbf{v} = \mathbf{i} + \mathbf{j} + 2\mathbf{k}, \quad \mathbf{w} = 3\mathbf{i} - \mathbf{j} + 2\mathbf{k}$$

46. (a) Use the result in Exercise 45 to show that $\mathbf{u} \times (\mathbf{v} \times \mathbf{w})$ lies in the same plane as $\mathbf{v}$ and $\mathbf{w}$, and $(\mathbf{u} \times \mathbf{v}) \times \mathbf{w}$ lies in the same plane as $\mathbf{u}$ and $\mathbf{v}$.
  (b) Use a geometrical argument to justify the results in part (a).

47. In each part, use the result in Exercise 45 to prove the vector identity.
  (a) $(\mathbf{a} \times \mathbf{b}) \times (\mathbf{c} \times \mathbf{d}) = (\mathbf{a} \times \mathbf{b} \cdot \mathbf{d})\mathbf{c} - (\mathbf{a} \times \mathbf{b} \cdot \mathbf{c})\mathbf{d}$
  (b) $(\mathbf{a} \times \mathbf{b}) \times \mathbf{c} + (\mathbf{b} \times \mathbf{c}) \times \mathbf{a} + (\mathbf{c} \times \mathbf{a}) \times \mathbf{b} = 0$

48. Prove: If $\mathbf{a}$, $\mathbf{b}$, $\mathbf{c}$, and $\mathbf{d}$ lie in the same plane when positioned with a common initial point, then

$$(\mathbf{a} \times \mathbf{b}) \times (\mathbf{c} \times \mathbf{d}) = 0$$

c 49. Use a CAS to approximate the minimum area of a triangle if two of its vertices are $(2, -1, 0)$ and $(3, 2, 2)$ and its third vertex is on the curve $y = \ln x$ in the xy-plane.

50. If a force $\mathbf{F}$ is applied to an object at a point Q, then the line through Q parallel to $\mathbf{F}$ is called the **line of action** of the force. We defined the vector moment of $\mathbf{F}$ about a point P to be $\overrightarrow{PQ} \times \mathbf{F}$. Show that if Q' is any point on the line of action of $\mathbf{F}$, then $\overrightarrow{PQ} \times \mathbf{F} = \overrightarrow{PQ'} \times \mathbf{F}$; that is, it is not essential to use the point of application to compute the vector moment—any point on the line of action will do. [*Hint:* Write $\overrightarrow{PQ'} = \overrightarrow{PQ} + \overrightarrow{QQ'}$ and use properties of the cross product.]

51. Writing Discuss some of the similarities and differences between the multiplication of real numbers and the cross product of vectors.

52. Writing In your own words, describe what it means to say that the cross-product operation is "coordinate independent," and state why this fact is significant.

✔ QUICK CHECK ANSWERS 11.4

1. (a) 7 (b) 0   **2.** $8\mathbf{i} - 4\mathbf{j} - 6\mathbf{k}$ **3.** (a) $\langle 0, 0, 0 \rangle$ (b) $\langle -2, -7, -3 \rangle$ (c) $\langle -3, 11, 3 \rangle$ (d) $\langle -10, 8, 0 \rangle$ **4.** (a) -58 (b) 58

11.5 PARAMETRIC EQUATIONS OF LINES

In this section we will discuss parametric equations of lines in 2-space and 3-space. In 3-space, parametric equations of lines are especially important because they generally provide the most convenient form for representing lines algebraically.

■ LINES DETERMINED BY A POINT AND A VECTOR

A line in 2-space or 3-space can be determined uniquely by specifying a point on the line and a nonzero vector parallel to the line (Figure 11.5.1). For example, consider a line L

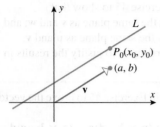

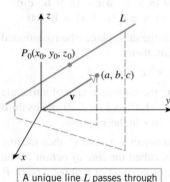

A unique line L passes through P_0 and is parallel to $\mathbf{v}$.

▲ **Figure 11.5.1**

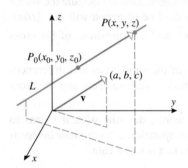

▲ **Figure 11.5.2**

in 3-space that passes through the point $P_0(x_0, y_0, z_0)$ and is parallel to the nonzero vector $\mathbf{v} = \langle a, b, c \rangle$. Then L consists precisely of those points $P(x, y, z)$ for which the vector $\overrightarrow{P_0 P}$ is parallel to $\mathbf{v}$ (Figure 11.5.2). In other words, the point $P(x, y, z)$ is on L if and only if $\overrightarrow{P_0 P}$ is a scalar multiple of $\mathbf{v}$, say

$$\overrightarrow{P_0 P} = t\mathbf{v}$$

This equation can be written as

$$\langle x - x_0, y - y_0, z - z_0 \rangle = \langle ta, tb, tc \rangle$$

which implies that

$$x - x_0 = ta, \quad y - y_0 = tb, \quad z - z_0 = tc$$

Thus, L can be described by the parametric equations

$$x = x_0 + at, \quad y = y_0 + bt, \quad z = z_0 + ct$$

A similar description applies to lines in 2-space. We summarize these descriptions in the following theorem.

11.5.1   THEOREM

(a)   The line in 2-space that passes through the point $P_0(x_0, y_0)$ and is parallel to the nonzero vector $\mathbf{v} = \langle a, b \rangle = a\mathbf{i} + b\mathbf{j}$ has parametric equations

$$x = x_0 + at, \quad y = y_0 + bt \tag{1}$$

(b)   The line in 3-space that passes through the point $P_0(x_0, y_0, z_0)$ and is parallel to the nonzero vector $\mathbf{v} = \langle a, b, c \rangle = a\mathbf{i} + b\mathbf{j} + c\mathbf{k}$ has parametric equations

$$x = x_0 + at, \quad y = y_0 + bt, \quad z = z_0 + ct \tag{2}$$

REMARK   Although it is not stated explicitly, it is understood in Equations (1) and (2) that $-\infty < t < +\infty$, which reflects the fact that lines extend indefinitely.

▶ **Example 1**   Find parametric equations of the line

(a) passing through (4, 2) and parallel to $\mathbf{v} = \langle -1, 5 \rangle$;

(b) passing through (1, 2, −3) and parallel to $\mathbf{v} = 4\mathbf{i} + 5\mathbf{j} - 7\mathbf{k}$;

(c) passing through the origin in 3-space and parallel to $\mathbf{v} = \langle 1, 1, 1 \rangle$.

Solution (a).   From (1) with $x_0 = 4$, $y_0 = 2$, $a = -1$, and $b = 5$ we obtain

$$x = 4 - t, \quad y = 2 + 5t$$

Solution (b).   From (2) we obtain

$$x = 1 + 4t, \quad y = 2 + 5t, \quad z = -3 - 7t$$

Solution (c).   From (2) with $x_0 = 0$, $y_0 = 0$, $z_0 = 0$, $a = 1$, $b = 1$, and $c = 1$ we obtain

$$x = t, \quad y = t, \quad z = t \quad ◀$$

▶ **Example 2**

(a) Find parametric equations of the line L passing through the points $P_1(2, 4, -1)$ and $P_2(5, 0, 7)$.

(b) Where does the line intersect the xy-plane?

Solution (a). The vector $\overrightarrow{P_1P_2} = \langle 3, -4, 8 \rangle$ is parallel to L and the point $P_1(2, 4, -1)$ lies on L, so it follows from (2) that L has parametric equations

$$x = 2 + 3t, \quad y = 4 - 4t, \quad z = -1 + 8t \tag{3}$$

Had we used P_2 as the point on L rather than P_1, we would have obtained the equations

$$x = 5 + 3t, \quad y = -4t, \quad z = 7 + 8t$$

Although these equations look different from those obtained using P_1, the two sets of equations are actually equivalent in that both generate L as t varies from $-\infty$ to $+\infty$. To see this, note that if t_1 gives a point

$$(x, y, z) = (2 + 3t_1, 4 - 4t_1, -1 + 8t_1)$$

on L using the first set of equations, then $t_2 = t_1 - 1$ gives the *same* point

$$\begin{aligned}
(x, y, z) &= (5 + 3t_2, -4t_2, 7 + 8t_2) \\
&= (5 + 3(t_1 - 1), -4(t_1 - 1), 7 + 8(t_1 - 1)) \\
&= (2 + 3t_1, 4 - 4t_1, -1 + 8t_1)
\end{aligned}$$

on L using the second set of equations. Conversely, if t_2 gives a point on L using the second set of equations, then $t_1 = t_2 + 1$ gives the same point using the first set.

Solution (b). It follows from (3) in part (a) that the line intersects the xy-plane at the point where $z = -1 + 8t = 0$, that is, when $t = \frac{1}{8}$. Substituting this value of t in (3) yields the point of intersection $(x, y, z) = \left(\frac{19}{8}, \frac{7}{2}, 0 \right)$. ◀

▶ **Example 3** Let L_1 and L_2 be the lines

$$\begin{aligned}
L_1 &: x = 1 + 4t, \quad y = 5 - 4t, \quad z = -1 + 5t \\
L_2 &: x = 2 + 8t, \quad y = 4 - 3t, \quad z = 5 + t
\end{aligned}$$

(a) Are the lines parallel?

(b) Do the lines intersect?

Solution (a). The line L_1 is parallel to the vector $4\mathbf{i} - 4\mathbf{j} + 5\mathbf{k}$, and the line L_2 is parallel to the vector $8\mathbf{i} - 3\mathbf{j} + \mathbf{k}$. These vectors are not parallel since neither is a scalar multiple of the other. Thus, the lines are not parallel.

Solution (b). For L_1 and L_2 to intersect at some point (x_0, y_0, z_0) these coordinates would have to satisfy the equations of both lines. In other words, there would have to exist values t_1 and t_2 for the parameters such that

$$x_0 = 1 + 4t_1, \quad y_0 = 5 - 4t_1, \quad z_0 = -1 + 5t_1$$

and

$$x_0 = 2 + 8t_2, \quad y_0 = 4 - 3t_2, \quad z_0 = 5 + t_2$$

This leads to three conditions on t_1 and t_2,

$$\begin{aligned} 1+4t_1 &= 2+8t_2 \\ 5-4t_1 &= 4-3t_2 \\ -1+5t_1 &= 5+t_2 \end{aligned} \tag{4}$$

Thus, the lines intersect if there are values of t_1 and t_2 that satisfy all three equations, and the lines do not intersect if there are no such values. You should be familiar with methods for solving systems of two linear equations in two unknowns; however, this is a system of three linear equations in two unknowns. To determine whether this system has a solution we will solve the first two equations for t_1 and t_2 and then check whether these values satisfy the third equation.

We will solve the first two equations by the method of elimination. We can eliminate the unknown t_1 by adding the equations. This yields the equation

$$6 = 6 + 5t_2$$

from which we obtain $t_2 = 0$. We can now find t_1 by substituting this value of t_2 in either the first or second equation. This yields $t_1 = \frac{1}{4}$. However, the values $t_1 = \frac{1}{4}$ and $t_2 = 0$ do not satisfy the third equation in (4), so the lines do not intersect. ◄

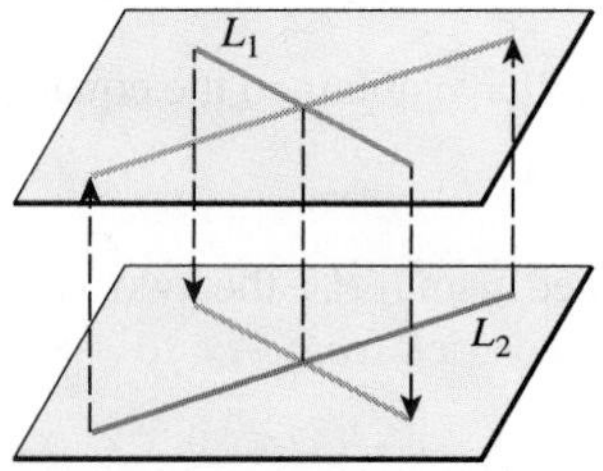

Parallel planes containing skew lines L_1 and L_2 can be determined by translating each line until it intersects the other.

▲ Figure 11.5.3

Two lines in 3-space that are not parallel and do not intersect (such as those in Example 3) are called ***skew*** lines. As illustrated in Figure 11.5.3, any two skew lines lie in parallel planes.

LINE SEGMENTS

Sometimes one is not interested in an entire line, but rather some *segment* of a line. Parametric equations of a line segment can be obtained by finding parametric equations for the entire line, and then restricting the parameter appropriately so that only the desired segment is generated.

► **Example 4** Find parametric equations describing the line segment joining the points $P_1(2, 4, -1)$ and $P_2(5, 0, 7)$.

Solution. From Example 2, the line through the points P_1 and P_2 has parametric equations $x = 2 + 3t$, $y = 4 - 4t$, $z = -1 + 8t$. With these equations, the point P_1 corresponds to $t = 0$ and P_2 to $t = 1$. Thus, the line segment that joins P_1 and P_2 is given by

$$x = 2 + 3t, \quad y = 4 - 4t, \quad z = -1 + 8t \qquad (0 \le t \le 1)$$ ◄

VECTOR EQUATIONS OF LINES

We will now show how vector notation can be used to express the parametric equations of a line more compactly. Because two vectors are equal if and only if their components are equal, (1) and (2) can be written in vector form as

$$\langle x, y\rangle = \langle x_0 + at, y_0 + bt\rangle$$

$$\langle x, y, z\rangle = \langle x_0 + at, y_0 + bt, z_0 + ct\rangle$$

or, equivalently, as

$$\langle x, y\rangle = \langle x_0, y_0\rangle + t\langle a, b\rangle \tag{5}$$

$$\langle x, y, z\rangle = \langle x_0, y_0, z_0\rangle + t\langle a, b, c\rangle \tag{6}$$

For the equation in 2-space we define the vectors $\mathbf{r}$, $\mathbf{r}_0$, and $\mathbf{v}$ as

$$\mathbf{r} = \langle x, y \rangle, \quad \mathbf{r}_0 = \langle x_0, y_0 \rangle, \quad \mathbf{v} = \langle a, b \rangle \tag{7}$$

and for the equation in 3-space we define them as

$$\mathbf{r} = \langle x, y, z \rangle, \quad \mathbf{r}_0 = \langle x_0, y_0, z_0 \rangle, \quad \mathbf{v} = \langle a, b, c \rangle \tag{8}$$

Substituting (7) and (8) in (5) and (6), respectively, yields the equation

$$\mathbf{r} = \mathbf{r}_0 + t\mathbf{v} \tag{9}$$

in both cases. We call this the ***vector equation of a line*** in 2-space or 3-space. In this equation, $\mathbf{v}$ is a nonzero vector parallel to the line, and $\mathbf{r}_0$ is a vector whose components are the coordinates of a point on the line.

We can interpret Equation (9) geometrically by positioning the vectors $\mathbf{r}_0$ and $\mathbf{v}$ with their initial points at the origin and the vector $t\mathbf{v}$ with its initial point at P_0 (Figure 11.5.4). The vector $t\mathbf{v}$ is a scalar multiple of $\mathbf{v}$ and hence is parallel to $\mathbf{v}$ and L. Moreover, since the initial point of $t\mathbf{v}$ is at the point P_0 on L, this vector actually runs along L; hence, the vector $\mathbf{r} = \mathbf{r}_0 + t\mathbf{v}$ can be interpreted as the vector from the origin to a point on L. As the parameter t varies from 0 to $+\infty$, the terminal point of $\mathbf{r}$ traces out the portion of L that extends from P_0 in the direction of $\mathbf{v}$, and as t varies from 0 to $-\infty$, the terminal point of $\mathbf{r}$ traces out the portion of L that extends from P_0 in the direction that is opposite to $\mathbf{v}$. Thus, the entire line is traced as t varies over the interval $(-\infty, +\infty)$, and it is traced in the direction of $\mathbf{v}$ as t increases.

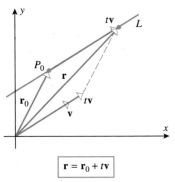

$$\mathbf{r} = \mathbf{r}_0 + t\mathbf{v}$$

▲ **Figure 11.5.4**

▶ **Example 5** The equation

$$\langle x, y, z \rangle = \langle -1, 0, 2 \rangle + t\langle 1, 5, -4 \rangle$$

is of form (9) with

$$\mathbf{r}_0 = \langle -1, 0, 2 \rangle \quad \text{and} \quad \mathbf{v} = \langle 1, 5, -4 \rangle$$

Thus, the equation represents the line in 3-space that passes through the point $(-1, 0, 2)$ and is parallel to the vector $\langle 1, 5, -4 \rangle$. ◀

▶ **Example 6** Find an equation of the line in 3-space that passes through the points $P_1(2, 4, -1)$ and $P_2(5, 0, 7)$.

Solution. The vector

$$\overrightarrow{P_1 P_2} = \langle 3, -4, 8 \rangle$$

is parallel to the line, so it can be used as $\mathbf{v}$ in (9). For $\mathbf{r}_0$ we can use either the vector from the origin to P_1 or the vector from the origin to P_2. Using the former yields

$$\mathbf{r}_0 = \langle 2, 4, -1 \rangle$$

Thus, a vector equation of the line through P_1 and P_2 is

$$\langle x, y, z \rangle = \langle 2, 4, -1 \rangle + t\langle 3, -4, 8 \rangle$$

If needed, we can express the line parametrically by equating corresponding components on the two sides of this vector equation, in which case we obtain the parametric equations in Example 2 (verify). ◀

✔**QUICK CHECK EXERCISES 11.5** *(See page 812 for answers.)*

1. Let L be the line through $(2, 5)$ and parallel to $\mathbf{v} = \langle 3, -1 \rangle$.
   (a) Parametric equations of L are

$$x = \underline{\hspace{1cm}} \qquad y = \underline{\hspace{1cm}}$$

   (b) A vector equation of L is $\langle x, y \rangle = \underline{\hspace{1cm}}$.

2. Parametric equations for the line through $(5, 3, 7)$ and parallel to the line $x = 3 - t$, $y = 2$, $z = 8 + 4t$ are

$$x = \underline{\hspace{1cm}}, \qquad y = \underline{\hspace{1cm}}, \qquad z = \underline{\hspace{1cm}}$$

3. Parametric equations for the line segment joining the points $(3, 0, 11)$ and $(2, 6, 7)$ are

$$x = \underline{\hspace{1cm}}, \qquad y = \underline{\hspace{1cm}}, \qquad z = \underline{\hspace{1cm}} \quad (\underline{\hspace{1cm}})$$

4. The line through the points $(-3, 8, -4)$ and $(1, 0, 8)$ intersects the yz-plane at $\underline{\hspace{1cm}}$.

EXERCISE SET 11.5 ⬚ Graphing Utility ⧉ CAS

1. (a) Find parametric equations for the lines through the corner of the unit square shown in part (a) of the accompanying figure.
   (b) Find parametric equations for the lines through the corner of the unit cube shown in part (b) of the accompanying figure.

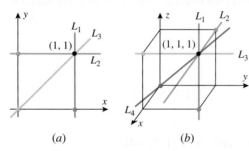

(a)   (b)

▲ **Figure Ex-1**

2. (a) Find parametric equations for the line segments in the unit square in part (a) of the accompanying figure.
   (b) Find parametric equations for the line segments in the unit cube shown in part (b) of the accompanying figure.

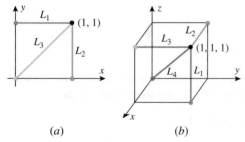

(a)   (b)

▲ **Figure Ex-2**

3–4 Find parametric equations for the line through P_1 and P_2 and also for the line segment joining those points. ■

3. (a) $P_1(3, -2)$, $P_2(5, 1)$ (b) $P_1(5, -2, 1)$, $P_2(2, 4, 2)$
4. (a) $P_1(0, 1)$, $P_2(-3, -4)$
   (b) $P_1(-1, 3, 5)$, $P_2(-1, 3, 2)$

5–6 Find parametric equations for the line whose vector equation is given. ■

5. (a) $\langle x, y \rangle = \langle 2, -3 \rangle + t \langle 1, -4 \rangle$
   (b) $x\mathbf{i} + y\mathbf{j} + z\mathbf{k} = \mathbf{k} + t(\mathbf{i} - \mathbf{j} + \mathbf{k})$
6. (a) $x\mathbf{i} + y\mathbf{j} = (3\mathbf{i} - 4\mathbf{j}) + t(2\mathbf{i} + \mathbf{j})$
   (b) $\langle x, y, z \rangle = \langle -1, 0, 2 \rangle + t \langle -1, 3, 0 \rangle$

7–8 Find a point P on the line and a vector $\mathbf{v}$ parallel to the line by inspection. ■

7. (a) $x\mathbf{i} + y\mathbf{j} = (2\mathbf{i} - \mathbf{j}) + t(4\mathbf{i} - \mathbf{j})$
   (b) $\langle x, y, z \rangle = \langle -1, 2, 4 \rangle + t \langle 5, 7, -8 \rangle$
8. (a) $\langle x, y \rangle = \langle -1, 5 \rangle + t \langle 2, 3 \rangle$
   (b) $x\mathbf{i} + y\mathbf{j} + z\mathbf{k} = (\mathbf{i} + \mathbf{j} - 2\mathbf{k}) + t\mathbf{j}$

9–10 Express the given parametric equations of a line using bracket notation and also using $\mathbf{i}, \mathbf{j}, \mathbf{k}$ notation. ■

9. (a) $x = -3 + t$, $y = 4 + 5t$
   (b) $x = 2 - t$, $y = -3 + 5t$, $z = t$
10. (a) $x = t$, $y = -2 + t$
   (b) $x = 1 + t$, $y = -7 + 3t$, $z = 4 - 5t$

11–14 True–False Determine whether the statement is true or false. Explain your answer. In these exercises L_0 and L_1 are lines in 3-space whose parametric equations are

$$L_0: x = x_0 + a_0 t, \quad y = y_0 + b_0 t, \quad z = z_0 + c_0 t$$
$$L_1: x = x_1 + a_1 t, \quad y = y_1 + b_1 t, \quad z = z_1 + c_1 t \quad ■$$

11. By definition, if L_1 and L_2 do not intersect, then L_1 and L_2 are parallel.

12. If L_1 and L_2 are parallel, then $\mathbf{v}_0 = \langle a_0, b_0, c_0 \rangle$ is a scalar multiple of $\mathbf{v}_1 = \langle a_1, b_1, c_1 \rangle$.

13. If L_1 and L_2 intersect at a point (x, y, z), then there exists a single value of t such that

$$L_0: x = x_0 + a_0 t, \quad y = y_0 + b_0 t, \quad z = z_0 + c_0 t$$
$$L_1: x = x_1 + a_1 t, \quad y = y_1 + b_1 t, \quad z = z_1 + c_1 t$$

are satisfied.

14. If L_0 passes through the origin, then the vectors $\langle a_0, b_0, c_0 \rangle$ and $\langle x_0, y_0, z_0 \rangle$ are parallel.

15–22 Find parametric equations of the line that satisfies the stated conditions. ■

15. The line through $(-5, 2)$ that is parallel to $2\mathbf{i} - 3\mathbf{j}$.

16. The line through $(0, 3)$ that is parallel to the line $x = -5 + t$, $y = 1 - 2t$.

17. The line that is tangent to the circle $x^2 + y^2 = 25$ at the point $(3, -4)$.

18. The line that is tangent to the parabola $y = x^2$ at the point $(-2, 4)$.

19. The line through $(-1, 2, 4)$ that is parallel to $3\mathbf{i} - 4\mathbf{j} + \mathbf{k}$.

20. The line through $(2, -1, 5)$ that is parallel to $\langle -1, 2, 7 \rangle$.

21. The line through $(-2, 0, 5)$ that is parallel to the line given by $x = 1 + 2t$, $y = 4 - t$, $z = 6 + 2t$.

22. The line through the origin that is parallel to the line given by $x = t$, $y = -1 + t$, $z = 2$.

23. Where does the line $x = 1 + 3t$, $y = 2 - t$ intersect
 (a) the x-axis   (b) the y-axis
 (c) the parabola $y = x^2$?

24. Where does the line $\langle x, y \rangle = \langle 4t, 3t \rangle$ intersect the circle $x^2 + y^2 = 25$?

25–26 Find the intersections of the lines with the xy-plane, the xz-plane, and the yz-plane. ■

25. $x = -2$, $y = 4 + 2t$, $z = -3 + t$

26. $x = -1 + 2t$, $y = 3 + t$, $z = 4 - t$

27. Where does the line $x = 1 + t$, $y = 3 - t$, $z = 2t$ intersect the cylinder $x^2 + y^2 = 16$?

28. Where does the line $x = 2 - t$, $y = 3t$, $z = -1 + 2t$ intersect the plane $2y + 3z = 6$?

29–30 Show that the lines L_1 and L_2 intersect, and find their point of intersection. ■

29. $L_1: x = 2 + t$, $y = 2 + 3t$, $z = 3 + t$
 $L_2: x = 2 + t$, $y = 3 + 4t$, $z = 4 + 2t$

30. $L_1: x + 1 = 4t$, $y - 3 = t$, $z - 1 = 0$
 $L_2: x + 13 = 12t$, $y - 1 = 6t$, $z - 2 = 3t$

31–32 Show that the lines L_1 and L_2 are skew. ■

31. $L_1: x = 1 + 7t$, $y = 3 + t$, $z = 5 - 3t$
 $L_2: x = 4 - t$, $y = 6$, $z = 7 + 2t$

32. $L_1: x = 2 + 8t$, $y = 6 - 8t$, $z = 10t$
 $L_2: x = 3 + 8t$, $y = 5 - 3t$, $z = 6 + t$

33–34 Determine whether the lines L_1 and L_2 are parallel. ■

33. $L_1: x = 3 - 2t$, $y = 4 + t$, $z = 6 - t$
 $L_2: x = 5 - 4t$, $y = -2 + 2t$, $z = 7 - 2t$

34. $L_1: x = 5 + 3t$, $y = 4 - 2t$, $z = -2 + 3t$
 $L_2: x = -1 + 9t$, $y = 5 - 6t$, $z = 3 + 8t$

35–36 Determine whether the points P_1, P_2, and P_3 lie on the same line. ■

35. $P_1(6, 9, 7)$, $P_2(9, 2, 0)$, $P_3(0, -5, -3)$

36. $P_1(1, 0, 1)$, $P_2(3, -4, -3)$, $P_3(4, -6, -5)$

37–38 Show that the lines L_1 and L_2 are the same. ■

37. $L_1: x = 3 - t$, $y = 1 + 2t$
 $L_2: x = -1 + 3t$, $y = 9 - 6t$

38. $L_1: x = 1 + 3t$, $y = -2 + t$, $z = 2t$
 $L_2: x = 4 - 6t$, $y = -1 - 2t$, $z = 2 - 4t$

FOCUS ON CONCEPTS

39. Sketch the vectors $\mathbf{r}_0 = \langle -1, 2 \rangle$ and $\mathbf{v} = \langle 1, 1 \rangle$, and then sketch the six vectors $\mathbf{r}_0 \pm \mathbf{v}$, $\mathbf{r}_0 \pm 2\mathbf{v}$, $\mathbf{r}_0 \pm 3\mathbf{v}$. Draw the line $L: x = -1 + t$, $y = 2 + t$, and describe the relationship between L and the vectors you sketched. What is the vector equation of L?

40. Sketch the vectors $\mathbf{r}_0 = \langle 0, 2, 1 \rangle$ and $\mathbf{v} = \langle 1, 0, 1 \rangle$, and then sketch the vectors $\mathbf{r}_0 + \mathbf{v}$, $\mathbf{r}_0 + 2\mathbf{v}$, and $\mathbf{r}_0 + 3\mathbf{v}$. Draw the line $L: x = t$, $y = 2$, $z = 1 + t$, and describe the relationship between L and the vectors you sketched. What is the vector equation of L?

41. Sketch the vectors $\mathbf{r}_0 = \langle -2, 0 \rangle$ and $\mathbf{r}_1 = \langle 1, 3 \rangle$, and then sketch the vectors
 $$\tfrac{1}{3}\mathbf{r}_0 + \tfrac{2}{3}\mathbf{r}_1, \quad \tfrac{1}{2}\mathbf{r}_0 + \tfrac{1}{2}\mathbf{r}_1, \quad \tfrac{2}{3}\mathbf{r}_0 + \tfrac{1}{3}\mathbf{r}_1$$
 Draw the line segment $(1 - t)\mathbf{r}_0 + t\mathbf{r}_1$ $(0 \le t \le 1)$. If n is a positive integer, what is the position of the point on this line segment corresponding to $t = 1/n$, relative to the points $(-2, 0)$ and $(1, 3)$?

42. Sketch the vectors $\mathbf{r}_0 = \langle 2, 0, 4 \rangle$ and $\mathbf{r}_1 = \langle 0, 4, 0 \rangle$, and then sketch the vectors
 $$\tfrac{1}{4}\mathbf{r}_0 + \tfrac{3}{4}\mathbf{r}_1, \quad \tfrac{1}{2}\mathbf{r}_0 + \tfrac{1}{2}\mathbf{r}_1, \quad \tfrac{3}{4}\mathbf{r}_0 + \tfrac{1}{4}\mathbf{r}_1$$
 Draw the line segment $(1 - t)\mathbf{r}_0 + t\mathbf{r}_1$ $(0 \le t \le 1)$. If n is a positive integer, what is the position of the point on this line segment corresponding to $t = 1/n$, relative to the points $(2, 0, 4)$ and $(0, 4, 0)$?

43–44 Describe the line segment represented by the vector equation. ■

43. $\langle x, y \rangle = \langle 1, 0 \rangle + t\langle -2, 3 \rangle$ $(0 \le t \le 2)$

44. $\langle x, y, z \rangle = \langle -2, 1, 4 \rangle + t\langle 3, 0, -1 \rangle$ $(0 \le t \le 3)$

45. Find the point on the line segment joining $P_1(3, 6)$ and $P_2(8, -4)$ that is $\frac{2}{5}$ of the way from P_1 to P_2.

46. Find the point on the line segment joining $P_1(1, 4, -3)$ and $P_2(1, 5, -1)$ that is $\frac{2}{3}$ of the way from P_1 to P_2.

47–48 Use the method in Exercise 32 of Section 11.3 to find the distance from the point P to the line L, and then check your answer using the method in Exercise 30 of Section 11.4. ■

47. $P(-2, 1, 1)$
 $L: x = 3 - t$, $y = t$, $z = 1 + 2t$

48. $P(1, 4, -3)$
$L: x = 2 + t, \; y = -1 - t, \; z = 3t$

49–50 Show that the lines L_1 and L_2 are parallel, and find the distance between them. ■

49. $L_1: x = 2 - t, \; y = 2t, \; z = 1 + t$
$L_2: x = 1 + 2t, \; y = 3 - 4t, \; z = 5 - 2t$

50. $L_1: x = 2t, \; y = 3 + 4t, \; z = 2 - 6t$
$L_2: x = 1 + 3t, \; y = 6t, \; z = -9t$

51. (a) Find parametric equations for the line through the points (x_0, y_0, z_0) and (x_1, y_1, z_1).
(b) Find parametric equations for the line through the point (x_1, y_1, z_1) and parallel to the line
$$x = x_0 + at, \quad y = y_0 + bt, \quad z = z_0 + ct$$

52. Let L be the line that passes through the point (x_0, y_0, z_0) and is parallel to the vector $\mathbf{v} = \langle a, b, c \rangle$, where a, b, and c are nonzero. Show that a point (x, y, z) lies on the line L if and only if
$$\frac{x - x_0}{a} = \frac{y - y_0}{b} = \frac{z - z_0}{c}$$
These equations, which are called the ***symmetric equations*** of L, provide a nonparametric representation of L.

53. (a) Describe the line whose symmetric equations are
$$\frac{x - 1}{2} = \frac{y + 3}{4} = z - 5$$
(see Exercise 52).
(b) Find parametric equations for the line in part (a).

54. Consider the lines L_1 and L_2 whose symmetric equations are
$$L_1: \frac{x - 1}{2} = \frac{y + \frac{3}{2}}{1} = \frac{z + 1}{2}$$
$$L_2: \frac{x - 4}{-1} = \frac{y - 3}{-2} = \frac{z + 4}{2}$$
(see Exercise 52).
(a) Are L_1 and L_2 parallel? Perpendicular?
(b) Find parametric equations for L_1 and L_2.
(c) Do L_1 and L_2 intersect? If so, where?

55. Let L_1 and L_2 be the lines whose parametric equations are
$$L_1: x = 1 + 2t, \quad y = 2 - t, \quad z = 4 - 2t$$
$$L_2: x = 9 + t, \quad y = 5 + 3t, \quad z = -4 - t$$
(a) Show that L_1 and L_2 intersect at the point $(7, -1, -2)$.
(b) Find, to the nearest degree, the acute angle between L_1 and L_2 at their intersection.
(c) Find parametric equations for the line that is perpendicular to L_1 and L_2 and passes through their point of intersection.

56. Let L_1 and L_2 be the lines whose parametric equations are
$$L_1: x = 4t, \qquad y = 1 - 2t, \quad z = 2 + 2t$$
$$L_2: x = 1 + t, \qquad y = 1 - t, \qquad z = -1 + 4t$$
(a) Show that L_1 and L_2 intersect at the point $(2, 0, 3)$.
(b) Find, to the nearest degree, the acute angle between L_1 and L_2 at their intersection.
(c) Find parametric equations for the line that is perpendicular to L_1 and L_2 and passes through their point of intersection.

57–58 Find parametric equations of the line that contains point P and intersects the line L at a right angle, and find the distance between P and L. ■

57. $P(0, 2, 1)$
$L: x = 2t, \; y = 1 - t, \; z = 2 + t$

58. $P(3, 1, -2)$
$L: x = -2 + 2t, \; y = 4 + 2t, \; z = 2 + t$

59. Two bugs are walking along lines in 3-space. At time t bug 1 is at the point (x, y, z) on the line
$$x = 4 - t, \quad y = 1 + 2t, \quad z = 2 + t$$
and at the same time t bug 2 is at the point (x, y, z) on the line
$$x = t, \quad y = 1 + t, \quad z = 1 + 2t$$
Assume that distance is in centimeters and that time is in minutes.
(a) Find the distance between the bugs at time $t = 0$.
(b) Use a graphing utility to graph the distance between the bugs as a function of time from $t = 0$ to $t = 5$.
(c) What does the graph tell you about the distance between the bugs?
(d) How close do the bugs get?

60. Suppose that the temperature T at a point (x, y, z) on the line $x = t, y = 1 + t, z = 3 - 2t$ is $T = 25x^2yz$. Use a CAS or a calculating utility with a root-finding capability to approximate the maximum temperature on that portion of the line that extends from the xz-plane to the xy-plane.

61. **Writing** Give some examples of geometric problems that can be solved using the parametric equations of a line, and describe their solution. For example, how would you find the points of intersection of a line and a sphere?

62. **Writing** Discuss how the vector equation of a line can be used to model the motion of a point that is moving with constant velocity in 3-space.

✔ **QUICK CHECK ANSWERS 11.5**

1. (a) $2 + 3t$; $5 - t$ (b) $\langle 2, 5 \rangle + t \langle 3, -1 \rangle$ **2.** $5 - t$; 3; $7 + 4t$ **3.** $3 - t$; $6t$; $11 - 4t$; $0 \leq t \leq 1$ **4.** $(0, 2, 5)$

11.6 PLANES IN 3-SPACE

In this section we will use vectors to derive equations of planes in 3-space, and then we will use these equations to solve various geometric problems.

■ PLANES PARALLEL TO THE COORDINATE PLANES

The graph of the equation $x = a$ in an xyz-coordinate system consists of all points of the form (a, y, z), where y and z are arbitrary. One such point is $(a, 0, 0)$, and all others are in the plane that passes through this point and is parallel to the yz-plane (Figure 11.6.1). Similarly, the graph of $y = b$ is the plane through $(0, b, 0)$ that is parallel to the xz-plane, and the graph of $z = c$ is the plane through $(0, 0, c)$ that is parallel to the xy-plane.

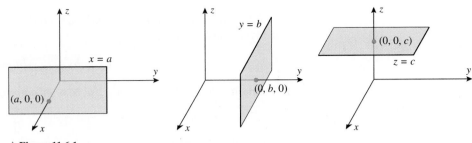

▲ Figure 11.6.1

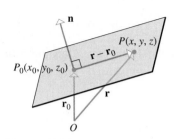

The colored plane is determined uniquely by the point P and the vector **n** perpendicular to the plane.

▲ Figure 11.6.2

■ PLANES DETERMINED BY A POINT AND A NORMAL VECTOR

A plane in 3-space can be determined uniquely by specifying a point in the plane and a vector perpendicular to the plane (Figure 11.6.2). A vector perpendicular to a plane is called a **normal** to the plane.

Suppose that we want to find an equation of the plane passing through $P_0(x_0, y_0, z_0)$ and perpendicular to the vector $\mathbf{n} = \langle a, b, c \rangle$. Define the vectors $\mathbf{r}_0$ and $\mathbf{r}$ as

$$\mathbf{r}_0 = \langle x_0, y_0, z_0 \rangle \quad \text{and} \quad \mathbf{r} = \langle x, y, z \rangle$$

It should be evident from Figure 11.6.3 that the plane consists precisely of those points $P(x, y, z)$ for which the vector $\mathbf{r} - \mathbf{r}_0$ is orthogonal to **n**; or, expressed as an equation,

$$\mathbf{n} \cdot (\mathbf{r} - \mathbf{r}_0) = 0 \tag{1}$$

If preferred, we can express this vector equation in terms of components as

$$\langle a, b, c \rangle \cdot \langle x - x_0, y - y_0, z - z_0 \rangle = 0 \tag{2}$$

from which we obtain

$$a(x - x_0) + b(y - y_0) + c(z - z_0) = 0 \tag{3}$$

This is called the **point-normal form** of the equation of a plane. Formulas (1) and (2) are vector versions of this formula.

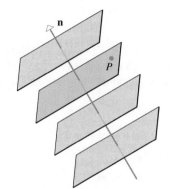

▲ Figure 11.6.3

What does Equation (1) represent if

$$\mathbf{n} = \langle a, b \rangle, \quad \mathbf{r}_0 = \langle x_0, y_0 \rangle, \quad \mathbf{r} = \langle x, y \rangle$$

are vectors in an xy-plane in 2-space? Draw a picture.

▶ **Example 1** Find an equation of the plane passing through the point $(3, -1, 7)$ and perpendicular to the vector $\mathbf{n} = \langle 4, 2, -5 \rangle$.

Solution. From (3), a point-normal form of the equation is

$$4(x - 3) + 2(y + 1) - 5(z - 7) = 0 \tag{4}$$

If preferred, this equation can be written in vector form as

$$\langle 4, 2, -5 \rangle \cdot \langle x - 3, y + 1, z - 7 \rangle = 0 \blacktriangleleft$$

Observe that if we multiply out the terms in (3) and simplify, we obtain an equation of the form

$$ax + by + cz + d = 0 \qquad (5)$$

For example, Equation (4) in Example 1 can be rewritten as

$$4x + 2y - 5z + 25 = 0$$

The following theorem shows that every equation of form (5) represents a plane in 3-space.

11.6.1   **THEOREM**   *If a, b, c, and d are constants, and a, b, and c are not all zero, then the graph of the equation*

$$ax + by + cz + d = 0 \qquad (6)$$

is a plane that has the vector $\mathbf{n} = \langle a, b, c \rangle$ as a normal.

PROOF   Since a, b, and c are not all zero, there is at least one point (x_0, y_0, z_0) whose coordinates satisfy Equation (6). For example, if $a \neq 0$, then such a point is $(-d/a, 0, 0)$, and similarly if $b \neq 0$ or $c \neq 0$ (verify). Thus, let (x_0, y_0, z_0) be any point whose coordinates satisfy (6); that is,

$$ax_0 + by_0 + cz_0 + d = 0$$

Subtracting this equation from (6) yields

$$a(x - x_0) + b(y - y_0) + c(z - z_0) = 0$$

which is the point-normal form of a plane with normal $\mathbf{n} = \langle a, b, c \rangle$. ∎

Equation (6) is called the ***general form*** of the equation of a plane.

▶ **Example 2**   Determine whether the planes

$$3x - 4y + 5z = 0 \quad \text{and} \quad -6x + 8y - 10z - 4 = 0$$

are parallel.

Solution.   It is clear geometrically that two planes are parallel if and only if their normals are parallel vectors. A normal to the first plane is

$$\mathbf{n}_1 = \langle 3, -4, 5 \rangle$$

and a normal to the second plane is

$$\mathbf{n}_2 = \langle -6, 8, -10 \rangle$$

Since $\mathbf{n}_2$ is a scalar multiple of $\mathbf{n}_1$, the normals are parallel, and hence so are the planes. ◀

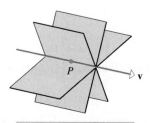

There are infinitely many planes containing P and parallel to **v**.

▲ **Figure 11.6.4**

We have seen that a unique plane is determined by a point in the plane and a nonzero vector normal to the plane. In contrast, a unique plane is not determined by a point in the plane and a nonzero vector *parallel* to the plane (Figure 11.6.4). However, a unique plane

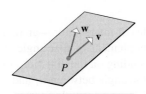

▲ **Figure 11.6.5**

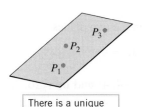

▲ **Figure 11.6.6**

is determined by a point in the plane and two nonparallel vectors that are parallel to the plane (Figure 11.6.5). A unique plane is also determined by three noncollinear points that lie in the plane (Figure 11.6.6).

▶ **Example 3** Find an equation of the plane through the points $P_1(1, 2, -1)$, $P_2(2, 3, 1)$, and $P_3(3, -1, 2)$.

Solution. Since the points P_1, P_2, and P_3 lie in the plane, the vectors $\overrightarrow{P_1P_2} = \langle 1, 1, 2 \rangle$ and $\overrightarrow{P_1P_3} = \langle 2, -3, 3 \rangle$ are parallel to the plane. Therefore,

$$\overrightarrow{P_1P_2} \times \overrightarrow{P_1P_3} = \begin{vmatrix} \mathbf{i} & \mathbf{j} & \mathbf{k} \\ 1 & 1 & 2 \\ 2 & -3 & 3 \end{vmatrix} = 9\mathbf{i} + \mathbf{j} - 5\mathbf{k}$$

is normal to the plane, since it is orthogonal to both $\overrightarrow{P_1P_2}$ and $\overrightarrow{P_1P_3}$. By using this normal and the point $P_1(1, 2, -1)$ in the plane, we obtain the point-normal form

$$9(x - 1) + (y - 2) - 5(z + 1) = 0$$

which can be rewritten as
$$9x + y - 5z - 16 = 0 \blacktriangleleft$$

▶ **Example 4** Determine whether the line

$$x = 3 + 8t, \quad y = 4 + 5t, \quad z = -3 - t$$

is parallel to the plane $x - 3y + 5z = 12$.

Solution. The vector $\mathbf{v} = \langle 8, 5, -1 \rangle$ is parallel to the line and the vector $\mathbf{n} = \langle 1, -3, 5 \rangle$ is normal to the plane. For the line and plane to be parallel, the vectors $\mathbf{v}$ and $\mathbf{n}$ must be orthogonal. But this is not so, since the dot product

$$\mathbf{v} \cdot \mathbf{n} = (8)(1) + (5)(-3) + (-1)(5) = -12$$

is nonzero. Thus, the line and plane are not parallel. ◀

▶ **Example 5** Find the intersection of the line and plane in Example 4.

Solution. If we let (x_0, y_0, z_0) be the point of intersection, then the coordinates of this point satisfy both the equation of the plane and the parametric equations of the line. Thus,

$$x_0 - 3y_0 + 5z_0 = 12 \tag{7}$$

and for some value of t, say $t = t_0$,

$$x_0 = 3 + 8t_0, \quad y_0 = 4 + 5t_0, \quad z_0 = -3 - t_0 \tag{8}$$

Substituting (8) in (7) yields

$$(3 + 8t_0) - 3(4 + 5t_0) + 5(-3 - t_0) = 12$$

Solving for t_0 yields $t_0 = -3$ and on substituting this value in (8), we obtain

$$(x_0, y_0, z_0) = (-21, -11, 0) \blacktriangleleft$$

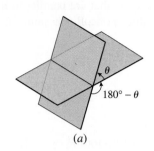

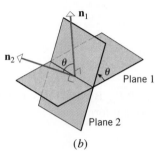

▲ **Figure 11.6.7**

■ INTERSECTING PLANES

Two distinct intersecting planes determine two positive angles of intersection—an (acute) angle θ that satisfies the condition $0 \leq \theta \leq \pi/2$ and the supplement of that angle (Figure 11.6.7a). If $\mathbf{n}_1$ and $\mathbf{n}_2$ are normals to the planes, then depending on the directions of $\mathbf{n}_1$ and $\mathbf{n}_2$, the angle θ is either the angle between $\mathbf{n}_1$ and $\mathbf{n}_2$ or the angle between $\mathbf{n}_1$ and $-\mathbf{n}_2$ (Figure 11.6.7b). In both cases, Theorem 11.3.3 yields the following formula for the *acute angle θ between the planes*:

$$\cos \theta = \frac{|\mathbf{n}_1 \cdot \mathbf{n}_2|}{\|\mathbf{n}_1\| \|\mathbf{n}_2\|} \tag{9}$$

▶ **Example 6**   Find the acute angle of intersection between the two planes

$$2x - 4y + 4z = 6 \quad \text{and} \quad 6x + 2y - 3z = 4$$

Solution.   The given equations yield the normals $\mathbf{n}_1 = \langle 2, -4, 4 \rangle$ and $\mathbf{n}_2 = \langle 6, 2, -3 \rangle$. Thus, Formula (9) yields

$$\cos \theta = \frac{|\mathbf{n}_1 \cdot \mathbf{n}_2|}{\|\mathbf{n}_1\| \|\mathbf{n}_2\|} = \frac{|-8|}{\sqrt{36}\sqrt{49}} = \frac{4}{21}$$

from which we obtain

$$\theta = \cos^{-1}\left(\frac{4}{21}\right) \approx 79° \quad ◀$$

▶ **Example 7**   Find an equation for the line L of intersection of the planes in Example 6.

Solution.   First compute $\mathbf{v} = \mathbf{n}_1 \times \mathbf{n}_2 = \langle 2, -4, 4 \rangle \times \langle 6, 2, -3 \rangle = \langle 4, 30, 28 \rangle$. Since $\mathbf{v}$ is orthogonal to $\mathbf{n}_1$, it is parallel to the first plane, and since $\mathbf{v}$ is orthogonal to $\mathbf{n}_2$, it is parallel to the second plane. That is, $\mathbf{v}$ is parallel to L, the intersection of the two planes. To find a point on L we observe that L must intersect the xy-plane, $z = 0$, since $\mathbf{v} \cdot \langle 0, 0, 1 \rangle = 28 \neq 0$. Substituting $z = 0$ in the equations of both planes yields

$$2x - 4y = 6$$
$$6x + 2y = 4$$

with solution $x = 1$, $y = -1$. Thus, $P(1, -1, 0)$ is a point on L. A vector equation for L is

$$\langle x, y, z \rangle = \langle 1, -1, 0 \rangle + t \langle 4, 30, 28 \rangle \quad ◀$$

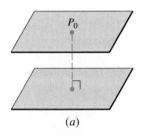

(a)

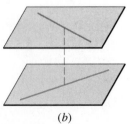

(b)

▲ **Figure 11.6.8**

■ DISTANCE PROBLEMS INVOLVING PLANES

Next we will consider three basic distance problems in 3-space:

- Find the distance between a point and a plane.
- Find the distance between two parallel planes.
- Find the distance between two skew lines.

The three problems are related. If we can find the distance between a point and a plane, then we can find the distance between parallel planes by computing the distance between one of the planes and an arbitrary point P_0 in the other plane (Figure 11.6.8a). Moreover, we can find the distance between two skew lines by computing the distance between parallel planes containing them (Figure 11.6.8b).

11.6.2   THEOREM   *The distance D between a point $P_0(x_0, y_0, z_0)$ and the plane $ax + by + cz + d = 0$ is*

$$D = \frac{|ax_0 + by_0 + cz_0 + d|}{\sqrt{a^2 + b^2 + c^2}} \tag{10}$$

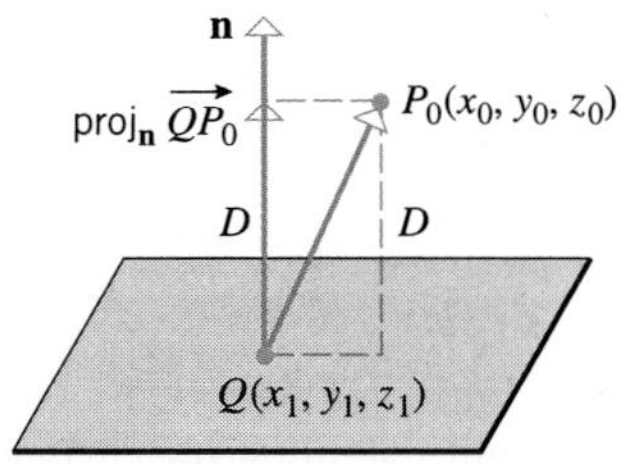

PROOF   Let $Q(x_1, y_1, z_1)$ be any point in the plane, and position the normal $\mathbf{n} = \langle a, b, c \rangle$ so that its initial point is at Q. As illustrated in Figure 11.6.9, the distance D is equal to the length of the orthogonal projection of $\overrightarrow{QP_0}$ on $\mathbf{n}$. Thus, from (12) of Section 11.3,

▲ Figure 11.6.9

$$D = \|\text{proj}_{\mathbf{n}} \overrightarrow{QP_0}\| = \left\| \frac{\overrightarrow{QP_0} \cdot \mathbf{n}}{\|\mathbf{n}\|^2} \mathbf{n} \right\| = \frac{|\overrightarrow{QP_0} \cdot \mathbf{n}|}{\|\mathbf{n}\|^2} \|\mathbf{n}\| = \frac{|\overrightarrow{QP_0} \cdot \mathbf{n}|}{\|\mathbf{n}\|}$$

But

$$\overrightarrow{QP_0} = \langle x_0 - x_1, y_0 - y_1, z_0 - z_1 \rangle$$
$$\overrightarrow{QP_0} \cdot \mathbf{n} = a(x_0 - x_1) + b(y_0 - y_1) + c(z_0 - z_1)$$
$$\|\mathbf{n}\| = \sqrt{a^2 + b^2 + c^2}$$

Thus,

$$D = \frac{|a(x_0 - x_1) + b(y_0 - y_1) + c(z_0 - z_1)|}{\sqrt{a^2 + b^2 + c^2}} \tag{11}$$

Since the point $Q(x_1, y_1, z_1)$ lies in the plane, its coordinates satisfy the equation of the plane; that is,

$$ax_1 + by_1 + cz_1 + d = 0$$

or

$$d = -ax_1 - by_1 - cz_1$$

Combining this expression with (11) yields (10). ■

There is an analog of Formula (10) in 2-space that can be used to compute the distance between a point and a line (see Exercise 52).

▶ **Example 8**   Find the distance D between the point $(1, -4, -3)$ and the plane

$$2x - 3y + 6z = -1$$

Solution.   Formula (10) requires the plane be rewritten in the form $ax + by + cz + d = 0$. Thus, we rewrite the equation of the given plane as

$$2x - 3y + 6z + 1 = 0$$

from which we obtain $a = 2$, $b = -3$, $c = 6$, and $d = 1$. Substituting these values and the coordinates of the given point in (10), we obtain

$$D = \frac{|(2)(1) + (-3)(-4) + 6(-3) + 1|}{\sqrt{2^2 + (-3)^2 + 6^2}} = \frac{|-3|}{7} = \frac{3}{7} \quad ◀$$

▶ **Example 9**   The planes

$$x + 2y - 2z = 3 \quad \text{and} \quad 2x + 4y - 4z = 7$$

are parallel since their normals, $\langle 1, 2, -2 \rangle$ and $\langle 2, 4, -4 \rangle$, are parallel vectors. Find the distance between these planes.

Solution. To find the distance D between the planes, we can select an *arbitrary* point in one of the planes and compute its distance to the other plane. By setting $y = z = 0$ in the equation $x + 2y - 2z = 3$, we obtain the point $P_0(3, 0, 0)$ in this plane. From (10), the distance from P_0 to the plane $2x + 4y - 4z = 7$ is

$$D = \frac{|(2)(3) + 4(0) + (-4)(0) - 7|}{\sqrt{2^2 + 4^2 + (-4)^2}} = \frac{1}{6} \; \blacktriangleleft$$

▶ **Example 10** It was shown in Example 3 of Section 11.5 that the lines

$$L_1: x = 1 + 4t, \quad y = 5 - 4t, \quad z = -1 + 5t$$
$$L_2: x = 2 + 8t, \quad y = 4 - 3t, \quad z = 5 + t$$

are skew. Find the distance between them.

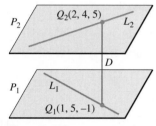

▲ **Figure 11.6.10**

Solution. Let P_1 and P_2 denote parallel planes containing L_1 and L_2, respectively (Figure 11.6.10). To find the distance D between L_1 and L_2, we will calculate the distance from a point in P_1 to the plane P_2. Since L_1 lies in plane P_1, we can find a point in P_1 by finding a point on the line L_1; we can do this by substituting any convenient value of t in the parametric equations of L_1. The simplest choice is $t = 0$, which yields the point $Q_1(1, 5, -1)$.

The next step is to find an equation for the plane P_2. For this purpose, observe that the vector $\mathbf{u}_1 = \langle 4, -4, 5 \rangle$ is parallel to line L_1, and therefore also parallel to planes P_1 and P_2. Similarly, $\mathbf{u}_2 = \langle 8, -3, 1 \rangle$ is parallel to L_2 and hence parallel to P_1 and P_2. Therefore, the cross product

$$\mathbf{n} = \mathbf{u}_1 \times \mathbf{u}_2 = \begin{vmatrix} \mathbf{i} & \mathbf{j} & \mathbf{k} \\ 4 & -4 & 5 \\ 8 & -3 & 1 \end{vmatrix} = 11\mathbf{i} + 36\mathbf{j} + 20\mathbf{k}$$

is normal to both P_1 and P_2. Using this normal and the point $Q_2(2, 4, 5)$ found by setting $t = 0$ in the equations of L_2, we obtain an equation for P_2:

$$11(x - 2) + 36(y - 4) + 20(z - 5) = 0$$

or

$$11x + 36y + 20z - 266 = 0$$

The distance between $Q_1(1, 5, -1)$ and this plane is

$$D = \frac{|(11)(1) + (36)(5) + (20)(-1) - 266|}{\sqrt{11^2 + 36^2 + 20^2}} = \frac{95}{\sqrt{1817}}$$

which is also the distance between L_1 and L_2. ◀

✔ QUICK CHECK EXERCISES 11.6   (See page 821 for answers.)

1. The point-normal form of the equation of the plane through $(0, 3, 5)$ and perpendicular to $\langle -4, 1, 7 \rangle$ is _____.

2. A normal vector for the plane $4x - 2y + 7z - 11 = 0$ is _____.

3. A normal vector for the plane through the points $(2, 5, 1)$, $(3, 7, 0)$, and $(2, 5, 2)$ is _____.

4. The acute angle of intersection of the planes $x + y - 2z = 5$ and $3y - 4z = 6$ is _____.

5. The distance between the point $(9, 8, 3)$ and the plane $x + y - 2z = 5$ is _____.

EXERCISE SET 11.6

1. Find equations of the planes P_1, P_2, and P_3 that are parallel to the coordinate planes and pass through the corner $(3, 4, 5)$ of the box shown in the accompanying figure.

2. Find equations of the planes P_1, P_2, and P_3 that are parallel to the coordinate planes and pass through the corner (x_0, y_0, z_0) of the box shown in the accompanying figure.

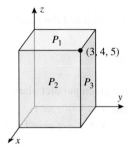
▲ Figure Ex-1

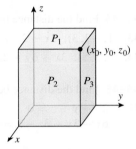
▲ Figure Ex-2

3–6 Find an equation of the plane that passes through the point P and has the vector $\mathbf{n}$ as a normal.

3. $P(2, 6, 1)$; $\mathbf{n} = \langle 1, 4, 2 \rangle$

4. $P(-1, -1, 2)$; $\mathbf{n} = \langle -1, 7, 6 \rangle$

5. $P(1, 0, 0)$; $\mathbf{n} = \langle 0, 0, 1 \rangle$

6. $P(0, 0, 0)$; $\mathbf{n} = \langle 2, -3, -4 \rangle$

7–10 Find an equation of the plane indicated in the figure. ■

7.
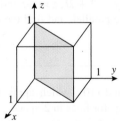

8.
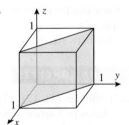

9.
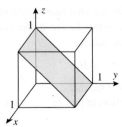

10.
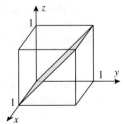

11–12 Find an equation of the plane that passes through the given points. ■

11. $(-2, 1, 1)$, $(0, 2, 3)$, and $(1, 0, -1)$

12. $(3, 2, 1)$, $(2, 1, -1)$, and $(-1, 3, 2)$

13–14 Determine whether the planes are parallel, perpendicular, or neither. ■

13. (a) $2x - 8y - 6z - 2 = 0$
$-x + 4y + 3z - 5 = 0$
(b) $3x - 2y + z = 1$
$4x + 5y - 2z = 4$
(c) $x - y + 3z - 2 = 0$
$2x + z = 1$

14. (a) $3x - 2y + z = 4$
$6x - 4y + 3z = 7$
(b) $y = 4x - 2z + 3$
$x = \frac{1}{4}y + \frac{1}{2}z$
(c) $x + 4y + 7z = 3$
$5x - 3y + z = 0$

15–16 Determine whether the line and plane are parallel, perpendicular, or neither. ■

15. (a) $x = 4 + 2t$, $y = -t$, $z = -1 - 4t$;
$3x + 2y + z - 7 = 0$
(b) $x = t$, $y = 2t$, $z = 3t$;
$x - y + 2z = 5$
(c) $x = -1 + 2t$, $y = 4 + t$, $z = 1 - t$;
$4x + 2y - 2z = 7$

16. (a) $x = 3 - t$, $y = 2 + t$, $z = 1 - 3t$;
$2x + 2y - 5 = 0$
(b) $x = 1 - 2t$, $y = t$, $z = -t$;
$6x - 3y + 3z = 1$
(c) $x = t$, $y = 1 - t$, $z = 2 + t$;
$x + y + z = 1$

17–18 Determine whether the line and plane intersect; if so, find the coordinates of the intersection. ■

17. (a) $x = t$, $y = t$, $z = t$;
$3x - 2y + z - 5 = 0$
(b) $x = 2 - t$, $y = 3 + t$, $z = t$;
$2x + y + z = 1$

18. (a) $x = 3t$, $y = 5t$, $z = -t$;
$2x - y + z + 1 = 0$
(b) $x = 1 + t$, $y = -1 + 3t$, $z = 2 + 4t$;
$x - y + 4z = 7$

19–20 Find the acute angle of intersection of the planes to the nearest degree. ■

19. $x = 0$ and $2x - y + z - 4 = 0$

20. $x + 2y - 2z = 5$ and $6x - 3y + 2z = 8$

21–24 True–False Determine whether the statement is true or false. Explain your answer. ■

21. Every plane has exactly two unit normal vectors.

22. If a plane is parallel to one of the coordinate planes, then its normal vector is parallel to one of the three vectors $\mathbf{i}$, $\mathbf{j}$, or $\mathbf{k}$.

23. If two planes intersect in a line L, then L is parallel to the cross product of the normals to the two planes.

24. If $a^2 + b^2 + c^2 = 1$, then the distance from $P(x_0, y_0, z_0)$ to the plane $ax + by + cz = 0$ is $|\langle a, b, c\rangle \cdot \langle x_0, y_0, z_0\rangle|$.

25–34 Find an equation of the plane that satisfies the stated conditions. ■

25. The plane through the origin that is parallel to the plane $4x - 2y + 7z + 12 = 0$.

26. The plane that contains the line $x = -2 + 3t$, $y = 4 + 2t$, $z = 3 - t$ and is perpendicular to the plane $x - 2y + z = 5$.

27. The plane through the point $(-1, 4, 2)$ that contains the line of intersection of the planes $4x - y + z - 2 = 0$ and $2x + y - 2z - 3 = 0$.

28. The plane through $(-1, 4, -3)$ that is perpendicular to the line $x - 2 = t$, $y + 3 = 2t$, $z = -t$.

29. The plane through $(1, 2, -1)$ that is perpendicular to the line of intersection of the planes $2x + y + z = 2$ and $x + 2y + z = 3$.

30. The plane through the points $P_1(-2, 1, 4)$, $P_2(1, 0, 3)$ that is perpendicular to the plane $4x - y + 3z = 2$.

31. The plane through $(-1, 2, -5)$ that is perpendicular to the planes $2x - y + z = 1$ and $x + y - 2z = 3$.

32. The plane that contains the point $(2, 0, 3)$ and the line $x = -1 + t$, $y = t$, $z = -4 + 2t$.

33. The plane whose points are equidistant from $(2, -1, 1)$ and $(3, 1, 5)$.

34. The plane that contains the line $x = 3t$, $y = 1 + t$, $z = 2t$ and is parallel to the intersection of the planes $y + z = -1$ and $2x - y + z = 0$.

35. Find parametric equations of the line through the point $(5, 0, -2)$ that is parallel to the planes $x - 4y + 2z = 0$ and $2x + 3y - z + 1 = 0$.

36. Let L be the line $x = 3t + 1$, $y = -5t$, $z = t$.
  (a) Show that L lies in the plane $2x + y - z = 2$.
  (b) Show that L is parallel to the plane $x + y + 2z = 0$. Is the line above, below, or on this plane?

37. Show that the lines
$$x = -2 + t, \quad y = 3 + 2t, \quad z = 4 - t$$
$$x = 3 - t, \quad y = 4 - 2t, \quad z = t$$
are parallel and find an equation of the plane they determine.

38. Show that the lines
$$L_1: x + 1 = 4t, \quad y - 3 = t, \quad z - 1 = 0$$
$$L_2: x + 13 = 12t, \quad y - 1 = 6t, \quad z - 2 = 3t$$
intersect and find an equation of the plane they determine.

FOCUS ON CONCEPTS

39. Do the points $(1, 0, -1)$, $(0, 2, 3)$, $(-2, 1, 1)$, and $(4, 2, 3)$ lie in the same plane? Justify your answer two different ways.

40. Show that if a, b, and c are nonzero, then the plane whose intercepts with the coordinate axes are $x = a$,

$y = b$, and $z = c$ is given by the equation
$$\frac{x}{a} + \frac{y}{b} + \frac{z}{c} = 1$$

41–42 Find parametric equations of the line of intersection of the planes. ■

41. $-2x + 3y + 7z + 2 = 0$ **42.** $3x - 5y + 2z = 0$
  $x + 2y - 3z + 5 = 0$ $z = 0$

43–44 Find the distance between the point and the plane. ■

43. $(1, -2, 3)$; $2x - 2y + z = 4$

44. $(0, 1, 5)$; $3x + 6y - 2z - 5 = 0$

45–46 Find the distance between the given parallel planes. ■

45. $-2x + y + z = 0$ **46.** $x + y + z = 1$
  $6x - 3y - 3z - 5 = 0$ $x + y + z = -1$

47–48 Find the distance between the given skew lines. ■

47. $x = 1 + 7t$, $y = 3 + t$, $z = 5 - 3t$
  $x = 4 - t$, $y = 6$, $z = 7 + 2t$

48. $x = 3 - t$, $y = 4 + 4t$, $z = 1 + 2t$
  $x = t$, $y = 3$, $z = 2t$

49. Find an equation of the sphere with center $(2, 1, -3)$ that is tangent to the plane $x - 3y + 2z = 4$.

50. Locate the point of intersection of the plane $2x + y - z = 0$ and the line through $(3, 1, 0)$ that is perpendicular to the plane.

51. Show that the line $x = -1 + t$, $y = 3 + 2t$, $z = -t$ and the plane $2x - 2y - 2z + 3 = 0$ are parallel, and find the distance between them.

FOCUS ON CONCEPTS

52. Formulas (1), (2), (3), (5), and (10), which apply to planes in 3-space, have analogs for lines in 2-space.
  (a) Draw an analog of Figure 11.6.3 in 2-space to illustrate that the equation of the line that passes through the point $P(x_0, y_0)$ and is perpendicular to the vector $\mathbf{n} = \langle a, b\rangle$ can be expressed as
$$\mathbf{n} \cdot (\mathbf{r} - \mathbf{r}_0) = 0$$
  where $\mathbf{r} = \langle x, y\rangle$ and $\mathbf{r}_0 = \langle x_0, y_0\rangle$.
  (b) Show that the vector equation in part (a) can be expressed as
$$a(x - x_0) + b(y - y_0) = 0$$
  This is called the ***point-normal form of a line***.
  (c) Using the proof of Theorem 11.6.1 as a guide, show that if a and b are not both zero, then the graph of the equation
$$ax + by + c = 0$$
  is a line that has $\mathbf{n} = \langle a, b\rangle$ as a normal. (cont.)

(d) Using the proof of Theorem 11.6.2 as a guide, show that the distance D between a point $P(x_0, y_0)$ and the line $ax + by + c = 0$ is

$$D = \frac{|ax_0 + by_0 + c|}{\sqrt{a^2 + b^2}}$$

(e) Use the formula in part (d) to find the distance between the point $P(-3, 5)$ and the line $y = -2x + 1$.

53. (a) Show that the distance D between parallel planes
$$ax + by + cz + d_1 = 0$$
$$ax + by + cz + d_2 = 0$$

is
$$D = \frac{|d_1 - d_2|}{\sqrt{a^2 + b^2 + c^2}}$$

(b) Use the formula in part (a) to solve Exercise 45.

54. **Writing** Explain why any line in 3-space must lie in some vertical plane. Must any line in 3-space also lie in some horizontal plane?

55. **Writing** Given two planes, discuss the various possibilities for the set of points they have in common. Then consider the set of points that three planes can have in common.

✔ **QUICK CHECK ANSWERS 11.6**

1. $-4x + (y - 3) + 7(z - 5) = 0$ 2. $\langle 4, -2, 7 \rangle$ 3. $\langle 2, -1, 0 \rangle$ 4. $\cos^{-1} \dfrac{11}{5\sqrt{6}} \approx 26°$ 5. $\sqrt{6}$

11.7 QUADRIC SURFACES

In this section we will study an important class of surfaces that are the three-dimensional analogs of the conic sections.

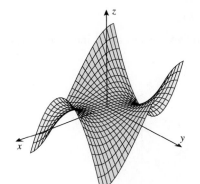

A monkey saddle

▲ **Figure 11.7.1**

The parenthetical part of Equation (2) is a reminder that the z-coordinate of each point in the trace is $z = k$. This needs to be stated explicitly because the variable z does not appear in the equation $x^2 + y^2 = k$.

■ TRACES OF SURFACES

Although the general shape of a curve in 2-space can be obtained by plotting points, this method is not usually helpful for surfaces in 3-space because too many points are required. It is more common to build up the shape of a surface with a network of **mesh lines**, which are curves obtained by cutting the surface with well-chosen planes. For example, Figure 11.7.1, which was generated by a CAS, shows the graph of $z = x^3 - 3xy^2$ rendered with a combination of mesh lines and colorization to produce the surface detail. This surface is called a "monkey saddle" because a monkey sitting astride the surface has a place for its two legs and tail.

The mesh line that results when a surface is cut by a plane is called the **trace** of the surface in the plane (Figure 11.7.2). One way to deduce the shape of a surface is by examining its traces in planes parallel to the coordinate planes. For example, consider the surface

$$z = x^2 + y^2 \tag{1}$$

To find its trace in the plane $z = k$, we substitute this value of z into (1), which yields

$$x^2 + y^2 = k \qquad (z = k) \tag{2}$$

If $k < 0$, this equation has no real solutions, so there is no trace. However, if $k \geq 0$, then the graph of (2) is a circle of radius $\sqrt{k}$ centered at the point $(0, 0, k)$ on the z-axis (Figure 11.7.3a). Thus, for nonnegative values of k the traces parallel to the xy-plane form a family of circles, centered on the z-axis, whose radii start at zero and increase with k. This suggests that the surface has the form shown in Figure 11.7.3b.

To obtain more detailed information about the shape of this surface, we can examine the traces of (1) in planes parallel to the yz-plane. Such planes have equations of the form $x = k$, so we substitute this in (1) to obtain

$$z = k^2 + y^2 \qquad (x = k)$$

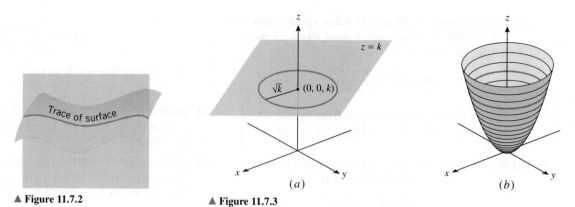

▲ **Figure 11.7.2**

▲ **Figure 11.7.3**

which we can rewrite as

$$z - k^2 = y^2 \qquad (x = k) \tag{3}$$

For simplicity, let us start with the case where $k = 0$ (the trace in the yz-plane), in which case the trace has the equation

$$z = y^2 \qquad (x = 0)$$

You should be able to recognize that this is a parabola in the plane $x = 0$ that has its vertex at the origin, opens in the positive z-direction, and is symmetric about the z-axis (the blue parabola in Figure 11.7.4*a*). You should also be able to recognize that the $-k^2$ term in (3) has the effect of translating the parabola $z = y^2$ in the positive z-direction, so its new vertex in the plane $x = k$ is at the point $(k, 0, k^2)$. This is the red parabola in Figure 11.7.4*a*. Thus, the traces in planes parallel to the yz-plane form a family of parabolas whose vertices move upward as k^2 increases (Figure 11.7.4*b*). Similarly, the traces in planes parallel to the xz-plane have equations of the form

$$z - k^2 = x^2 \qquad (y = k)$$

which again is a family of parabolas whose vertices move upward as k^2 increases (Figure 11.7.4*c*).

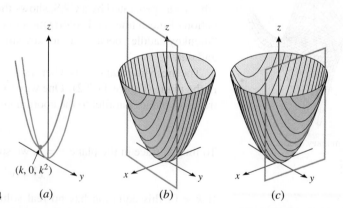

▶ **Figure 11.7.4**　　(*a*)　　　　　　(*b*)　　　　　　(*c*)

■ THE QUADRIC SURFACES

In the discussion of Formula (2) in Section 10.5 we noted that a second-degree equation

$$Ax^2 + Bxy + Cy^2 + Dx + Ey + F = 0$$

represents a conic section (possibly degenerate). The analog of this equation in an xyz-coordinate system is

$$Ax^2 + By^2 + Cz^2 + Dxy + Exz + Fyz + Gx + Hy + Iz + J = 0 \tag{4}$$

which is called a *second-degree equation in x, y, and z*. The graphs of such equations are called *quadric surfaces* or sometimes *quadrics*.

Six common types of quadric surfaces are shown in Table 11.7.1—*ellipsoids, hyperboloids of one sheet, hyperboloids of two sheets, elliptic cones, elliptic paraboloids,* and *hyperbolic paraboloids*. (The constants a, b, and c that appear in the equations in the table are assumed to be positive.) Observe that none of the quadric surfaces in the table have cross-product terms in their equations. This is because of their orientations relative

Table 11.7.1

SURFACE	EQUATION	SURFACE	EQUATION
ELLIPSOID	$$\frac{x^2}{a^2} + \frac{y^2}{b^2} + \frac{z^2}{c^2} = 1$$ The traces in the coordinate planes are ellipses, as are the traces in those planes that are parallel to the coordinate planes and intersect the surface in more than one point.	ELLIPTIC CONE	$$z^2 = \frac{x^2}{a^2} + \frac{y^2}{b^2}$$ The trace in the xy-plane is a point (the origin), and the traces in planes parallel to the xy-plane are ellipses. The traces in the yz- and xz-planes are pairs of lines intersecting at the origin. The traces in planes parallel to these are hyperbolas.
HYPERBOLOID OF ONE SHEET	$$\frac{x^2}{a^2} + \frac{y^2}{b^2} - \frac{z^2}{c^2} = 1$$ The trace in the xy-plane is an ellipse, as are the traces in planes parallel to the xy-plane. The traces in the yz-plane and xz-plane are hyperbolas, as are the traces in those planes that are parallel to these and do not pass through the x- or y-intercepts. At these intercepts the traces are pairs of intersecting lines.	ELLIPTIC PARABOLOID	$$z = \frac{x^2}{a^2} + \frac{y^2}{b^2}$$ The trace in the xy-plane is a point (the origin), and the traces in planes parallel to and above the xy-plane are ellipses. The traces in the yz- and xz-planes are parabolas, as are the traces in planes parallel to these.
HYPERBOLOID OF TWO SHEETS	$$\frac{z^2}{c^2} - \frac{x^2}{a^2} - \frac{y^2}{b^2} = 1$$ There is no trace in the xy-plane. In planes parallel to the xy-plane that intersect the surface in more than one point the traces are ellipses. In the yz- and xz-planes, the traces are hyperbolas, as are the traces in those planes that are parallel to these.	HYPERBOLIC PARABOLOID	$$z = \frac{y^2}{b^2} - \frac{x^2}{a^2}$$ The trace in the xy-plane is a pair of lines intersecting at the origin. The traces in planes parallel to the xy-plane are hyperbolas. The hyperbolas above the xy-plane open in the y-direction, and those below in the x-direction. The traces in the yz- and xz-planes are parabolas, as are the traces in planes parallel to these.

to the coordinate axes. Later in this section we will discuss other possible orientations that produce equations of the quadric surfaces with no cross-product terms. In the special case where the elliptic cross sections of an elliptic cone or an elliptic paraboloid are circles, the terms *circular cone* and *circular paraboloid* are used.

■ TECHNIQUES FOR GRAPHING QUADRIC SURFACES

Accurate graphs of quadric surfaces are best left for graphing utilities. However, the techniques that we will now discuss can be used to generate rough sketches of these surfaces that are useful for various purposes.

A rough sketch of an ellipsoid

$$\frac{x^2}{a^2} + \frac{y^2}{b^2} + \frac{z^2}{c^2} = 1 \qquad (a > 0, b > 0, c > 0) \tag{5}$$

can be obtained by first plotting the intersections with the coordinate axes, and then sketching the elliptical traces in the coordinate planes. Example 1 illustrates this technique.

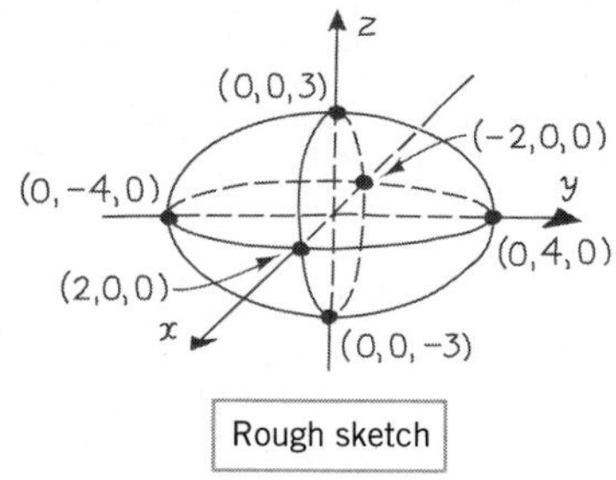

▶ **Example 1**   Sketch the ellipsoid

$$\frac{x^2}{4} + \frac{y^2}{16} + \frac{z^2}{9} = 1 \tag{6}$$

Solution.   The x-intercepts can be obtained by setting $y = 0$ and $z = 0$ in (6). This yields $x = \pm 2$. Similarly, the y-intercepts are $y = \pm 4$, and the z-intercepts are $z = \pm 3$. Sketching the elliptical traces in the coordinate planes yields the graph in Figure 11.7.5. ◀

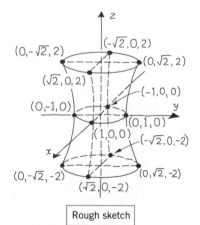

Rough sketch

▲ **Figure 11.7.5**

A rough sketch of a hyperboloid of one sheet

$$\frac{x^2}{a^2} + \frac{y^2}{b^2} - \frac{z^2}{c^2} = 1 \qquad (a > 0, b > 0, c > 0) \tag{7}$$

can be obtained by first sketching the elliptical trace in the xy-plane, then the elliptical traces in the planes $z = \pm c$, and then the hyperbolic curves that join the endpoints of the axes of these ellipses. The next example illustrates this technique.

▶ **Example 2**   Sketch the graph of the hyperboloid of one sheet

$$x^2 + y^2 - \frac{z^2}{4} = 1 \tag{8}$$

Solution.   The trace in the xy-plane, obtained by setting $z = 0$ in (8), is

$$x^2 + y^2 = 1 \qquad (z = 0)$$

which is a circle of radius 1 centered on the z-axis. The traces in the planes $z = 2$ and $z = -2$, obtained by setting $z = \pm 2$ in (8), are given by

$$x^2 + y^2 = 2 \qquad (z = \pm 2)$$

which are circles of radius $\sqrt{2}$ centered on the z-axis. Joining these circles by the hyperbolic traces in the vertical coordinate planes yields the graph in Figure 11.7.6. ◀

Rough sketch

▲ **Figure 11.7.6**

A rough sketch of the hyperboloid of two sheets

$$\frac{z^2}{c^2} - \frac{x^2}{a^2} - \frac{y^2}{b^2} = 1 \qquad (a > 0, b > 0, c > 0) \tag{9}$$

can be obtained by first plotting the intersections with the z-axis, then sketching the elliptical traces in the planes $z = \pm 2c$, and then sketching the hyperbolic traces that connect the z-axis intersections and the endpoints of the axes of the ellipses. (It is not essential to use the planes $z = \pm 2c$, but these are good choices since they simplify the calculations slightly and have the right spacing for a good sketch.) The next example illustrates this technique.

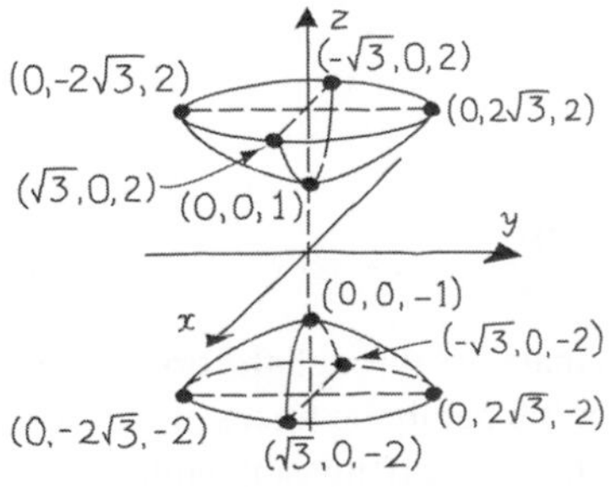

▶ **Example 3** Sketch the graph of the hyperboloid of two sheets

$$z^2 - x^2 - \frac{y^2}{4} = 1 \tag{10}$$

Solution. The z-intercepts, obtained by setting $x = 0$ and $y = 0$ in (10), are $z = \pm 1$. The traces in the planes $z = 2$ and $z = -2$, obtained by setting $z = \pm 2$ in (10), are given by

$$\frac{x^2}{3} + \frac{y^2}{12} = 1 \qquad (z = \pm 2)$$

Sketching these ellipses and the hyperbolic traces in the vertical coordinate planes yields Figure 11.7.7. ◀

(0,-2√3,2)   (-√3,0,2)
(0,2√3,2)
(√3,0,2)   (0,0,1)
(0,0,-1)
(-√3,0,-2)
(0,-2√3,-2)   (0,2√3,-2)
(√3,0,-2)

Rough sketch

▲ **Figure 11.7.7**

A rough sketch of the elliptic cone

$$z^2 = \frac{x^2}{a^2} + \frac{y^2}{b^2} \qquad (a > 0, b > 0) \tag{11}$$

can be obtained by first sketching the elliptical traces in the planes $z = \pm 1$ and then sketching the linear traces that connect the endpoints of the axes of the ellipses. The next example illustrates this technique.

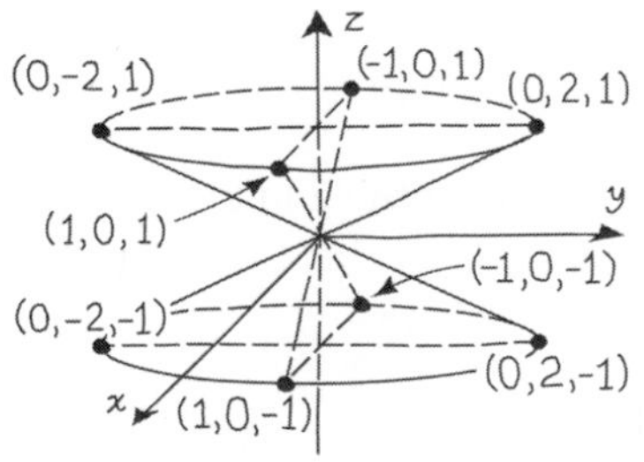

▶ **Example 4** Sketch the graph of the elliptic cone

$$z^2 = x^2 + \frac{y^2}{4} \tag{12}$$

Solution. The traces of (12) in the planes $z = \pm 1$ are given by

$$x^2 + \frac{y^2}{4} = 1 \qquad (z = \pm 1)$$

Sketching these ellipses and the linear traces in the vertical coordinate planes yields the graph in Figure 11.7.8. ◀

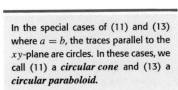

(0,-2,1)   (-1,0,1)
(0,2,1)
(1,0,1)
(-1,0,-1)
(0,-2,-1)
(0,2,-1)
(1,0,-1)

Rough sketch

▲ **Figure 11.7.8**

In the special cases of (11) and (13) where $a = b$, the traces parallel to the xy-plane are circles. In these cases, we call (11) a *circular cone* and (13) a *circular paraboloid.*

A rough sketch of the elliptic paraboloid

$$z = \frac{x^2}{a^2} + \frac{y^2}{b^2} \qquad (a > 0, b > 0) \tag{13}$$

can be obtained by first sketching the elliptical trace in the plane $z = 1$ and then sketching the parabolic traces in the vertical coordinate planes to connect the origin to the ends of the axes of the ellipse. The next example illustrates this technique.

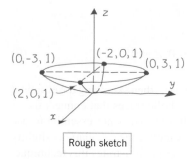

Rough sketch

▲ **Figure 11.7.9**

▶ **Example 5**   Sketch the graph of the elliptic paraboloid

$$z = \frac{x^2}{4} + \frac{y^2}{9} \tag{14}$$

Solution.   The trace of (14) in the plane $z = 1$ is

$$\frac{x^2}{4} + \frac{y^2}{9} = 1 \qquad (z = 1)$$

Sketching this ellipse and the parabolic traces in the vertical coordinate planes yields the graph in Figure 11.7.9. ◀

A rough sketch of the hyperbolic paraboloid

$$z = \frac{y^2}{b^2} - \frac{x^2}{a^2} \qquad (a > 0, b > 0) \tag{15}$$

can be obtained by first sketching the two parabolic traces that pass through the origin (one in the plane $x = 0$ and the other in the plane $y = 0$). After the parabolic traces are drawn, sketch the hyperbolic traces in the planes $z = \pm 1$ and then fill in any missing edges. The next example illustrates this technique.

▶ **Example 6**   Sketch the graph of the hyperbolic paraboloid

$$z = \frac{y^2}{4} - \frac{x^2}{9} \tag{16}$$

Solution.   Setting $x = 0$ in (16) yields

$$z = \frac{y^2}{4} \qquad (x = 0)$$

which is a parabola in the yz-plane with vertex at the origin and opening in the positive z-direction (since $z \geq 0$), and setting $y = 0$ yields

$$z = -\frac{x^2}{9} \qquad (y = 0)$$

which is a parabola in the xz-plane with vertex at the origin and opening in the negative z-direction.

The trace in the plane $z = 1$ is

$$\frac{y^2}{4} - \frac{x^2}{9} = 1 \qquad (z = 1)$$

which is a hyperbola that opens along a line parallel to the y-axis (verify), and the trace in the plane $z = -1$ is

$$\frac{x^2}{9} - \frac{y^2}{4} = 1 \qquad (z = -1)$$

which is a hyperbola that opens along a line parallel to the x-axis. Combining all of the above information leads to the sketch in Figure 11.7.10. ◀

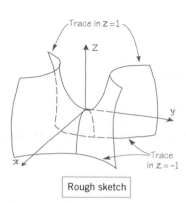

Rough sketch

▲ **Figure 11.7.10**

REMARK   The hyperbolic paraboloid in Figure 11.7.10 has an interesting behavior at the origin—the trace in the xz-plane has a relative maximum at $(0, 0, 0)$, and the trace in the yz-plane has a relative minimum at $(0, 0, 0)$. Thus, a bug walking on the surface may view the origin as a highest point if traveling along one path, or may view the origin as a lowest point if traveling along a different path. A point with this property is commonly called a *saddle point* or a *minimax point*.

Figure 11.7.11 shows two computer-generated views of the hyperbolic paraboloid in Example 6. The first view, which is much like our rough sketch in Figure 11.7.10, has cuts at the top and bottom that are hyperbolic traces parallel to the *xy*-plane. In the second view the top horizontal cut has been omitted; this helps to emphasize the parabolic traces parallel to the *xz*-plane.

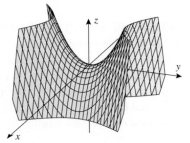 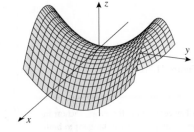

▶ **Figure 11.7.11**

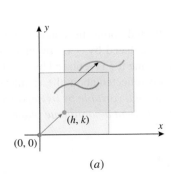

(a)

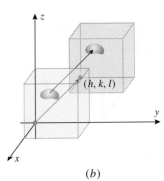

(b)

▲ **Figure 11.7.12**

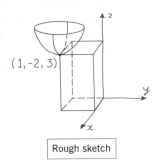

Rough sketch

▲ **Figure 11.7.13**

■ **TRANSLATIONS OF QUADRIC SURFACES**

In Section 10.4 we saw that a conic in an *xy*-coordinate system can be translated by substituting $x - h$ for x and $y - k$ for y in its equation. To understand why this works, think of the *xy*-axes as fixed and think of the plane as a transparent sheet of plastic on which all graphs are drawn. When the coordinates of points are modified by substituting $(x - h, y - k)$ for (x, y), the geometric effect is to translate the sheet of plastic (and hence all curves) so that the point on the plastic that was initially at $(0, 0)$ is moved to the point (h, k) (see Figure 11.7.12*a*).

For the analog in three dimensions, think of the *xyz*-axes as fixed and think of 3-space as a transparent block of plastic in which all surfaces are embedded. When the coordinates of points are modified by substituting $(x - h, y - k, z - l)$ for (x, y, z), the geometric effect is to translate the block of plastic (and hence all surfaces) so that the point in the plastic block that was initially at $(0, 0, 0)$ is moved to the point (h, k, l) (see Figure 11.7.12*b*).

▶ **Example 7**   Describe the surface $z = (x - 1)^2 + (y + 2)^2 + 3$.

Solution.   The equation can be rewritten as

$$z - 3 = (x - 1)^2 + (y + 2)^2$$

This surface is the paraboloid that results by translating the paraboloid

$$z = x^2 + y^2$$

in Figure 11.7.3 so that the new "vertex" is at the point $(1, -2, 3)$. A rough sketch of this paraboloid is shown in Figure 11.7.13. ◀

▶ **Example 8**   Describe the surface

$$4x^2 + 4y^2 + z^2 + 8y - 4z = -4$$

Solution.   Completing the squares yields

$$4x^2 + 4(y + 1)^2 + (z - 2)^2 = -4 + 4 + 4$$

or

$$x^2 + (y + 1)^2 + \frac{(z - 2)^2}{4} = 1$$

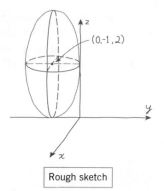

Rough sketch

▲ **Figure 11.7.14**

In Figure 11.7.14, the cross section in the yz-plane is shown tangent to both the y- and z-axes. Confirm that this is correct.

Thus, the surface is the ellipsoid that results when the ellipsoid

$$x^2 + y^2 + \frac{z^2}{4} = 1$$

is translated so that the new "center" is at the point $(0, -1, 2)$. A rough sketch of this ellipsoid is shown in Figure 11.7.14. ◄

■ **REFLECTIONS OF SURFACES IN 3-SPACE**

Recall that in an xy-coordinate system a point (x, y) is reflected about the x-axis if y is replaced by $-y$, and it is reflected about the y-axis if x is replaced by $-x$. In an xyz-coordinate system, a point (x, y, z) is reflected about the xy-plane if z is replaced by $-z$, it is reflected about the yz-plane if x is replaced by $-x$, and it is reflected about the xz-plane if y is replaced by $-y$ (Figure 11.7.15). It follows that *replacing a variable by its negative in the equation of a surface causes that surface to be reflected about a coordinate plane.*

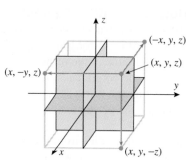

▲ **Figure 11.7.15**

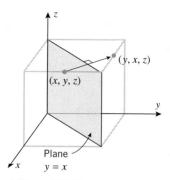

▲ **Figure 11.7.16**

Recall also that in an xy-coordinate system a point (x, y) is reflected about the line $y = x$ if x and y are interchanged. However, in an xyz-coordinate system, interchanging x and y reflects the point (x, y, z) about the plane $y = x$ (Figure 11.7.16). Similarly, interchanging x and z reflects the point about the plane $x = z$, and interchanging y and z reflects it about the plane $y = z$. Thus, it follows that *interchanging two variables in the equation of a surface reflects that surface about a plane that makes a 45° angle with two of the coordinate planes.*

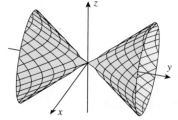

▲ **Figure 11.7.17**

▶ **Example 9** Describe the surfaces

$$\text{(a) } y^2 = x^2 + z^2 \qquad \text{(b) } z = -(x^2 + y^2)$$

Solution (a). The graph of the equation $y^2 = x^2 + z^2$ results from interchanging y and z in the equation $z^2 = x^2 + y^2$. Thus, the graph of the equation $y^2 = x^2 + z^2$ can be obtained by reflecting the graph of $z^2 = x^2 + y^2$ about the plane $y = z$. Since the graph of $z^2 = x^2 + y^2$ is a circular cone opening along the z-axis (see Table 11.7.1), it follows that the graph of $y^2 = x^2 + z^2$ is a circular cone opening along the y-axis (Figure 11.7.17).

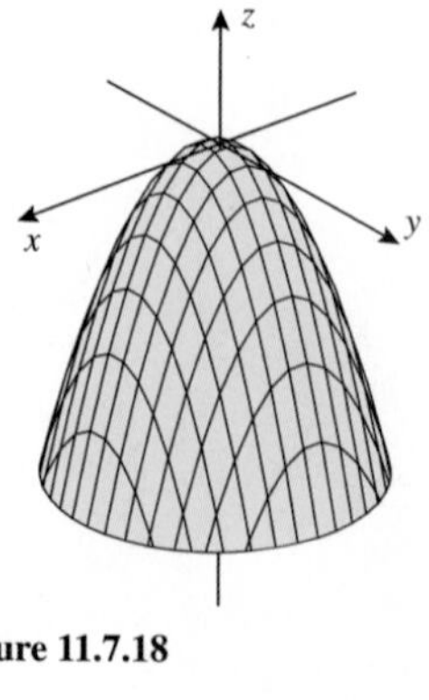

Solution (b). The graph of the equation $z = -(x^2 + y^2)$ can be written as $-z = x^2 + y^2$, which can be obtained by replacing z with $-z$ in the equation $z = x^2 + y^2$. Since the graph of $z = x^2 + y^2$ is a circular paraboloid opening in the positive z-direction (see Table 11.7.1), it follows that the graph of $z = -(x^2 + y^2)$ is a circular paraboloid opening in the negative z-direction (Figure 11.7.18). ◄

▲ **Figure 11.7.18**

■ A TECHNIQUE FOR IDENTIFYING QUADRIC SURFACES

The equations of the quadric surfaces in Table 11.7.1 have certain characteristics that make it possible to identify quadric surfaces that are derived from these equations by reflections. These identifying characteristics, which are shown in Table 11.7.2, are based on writing the equation of the quadric surface so that all of the variable terms are on the left side of the equation and there is a 1 or a 0 on the right side. These characteristics do not change when the surface is reflected about a coordinate plane or planes of the form $x = y$, $x = z$, or $y = z$, thereby making it possible to identify the reflected quadric surface from the form of its equation.

Table 11.7.2

IDENTIFYING A QUADRIC SURFACE FROM THE FORM OF ITS EQUATION

EQUATION	$\dfrac{x^2}{a^2} + \dfrac{y^2}{b^2} + \dfrac{z^2}{c^2} = 1$	$\dfrac{x^2}{a^2} + \dfrac{y^2}{b^2} - \dfrac{z^2}{c^2} = 1$	$\dfrac{z^2}{c^2} - \dfrac{x^2}{a^2} - \dfrac{y^2}{b^2} = 1$	$z^2 - \dfrac{x^2}{a^2} - \dfrac{y^2}{b^2} = 0$	$z - \dfrac{x^2}{a^2} - \dfrac{y^2}{b^2} = 0$	$z - \dfrac{y^2}{b^2} + \dfrac{x^2}{a^2} = 0$
CHARACTERISTIC	No minus signs	One minus sign	Two minus signs	No linear terms	One linear term; two quadratic terms with the same sign	One linear term; two quadratic terms with opposite signs
CLASSIFICATION	Ellipsoid	Hyperboloid of one sheet	Hyperboloid of two sheets	Elliptic cone	Elliptic paraboloid	Hyperbolic paraboloid

▶ **Example 10**   Identify the surfaces

(a) $3x^2 - 4y^2 + 12z^2 + 12 = 0$ (b) $4x^2 - 4y + z^2 = 0$

Solution (a).   The equation can be rewritten as

$$\frac{y^2}{3} - \frac{x^2}{4} - z^2 = 1$$

This equation has a 1 on the right side and two negative terms on the left side, so its graph is a hyperboloid of two sheets.

Solution (b).   The equation has one linear term and two quadratic terms with the same sign, so its graph is an elliptic paraboloid. ◀

✔ **QUICK CHECK EXERCISES 11.7**   *(See page 832 for answers.)*

1. For the surface $4x^2 + y^2 + z^2 = 9$, classify the indicated trace as an ellipse, hyperbola, or parabola.
   (a) $x = 0$ (b) $y = 0$ (c) $z = 1$

2. For the surface $4x^2 + z^2 - y^2 = 9$, classify the indicated trace as an ellipse, hyperbola, or parabola.
   (a) $x = 0$ (b) $y = 0$ (c) $z = 1$

3. For the surface $4x^2 + y^2 - z = 0$, classify the indicated trace as an ellipse, hyperbola, or parabola.
   (a) $x = 0$ (b) $y = 0$ (c) $z = 1$

4. Classify each surface as an ellipsoid, hyperboloid of one sheet, hyperboloid of two sheets, elliptic cone, elliptic paraboloid, or hyperbolic paraboloid.
   (a) $\dfrac{x^2}{36} + \dfrac{y^2}{25} - z = 0$ (b) $\dfrac{x^2}{36} + \dfrac{y^2}{25} + z^2 = 1$

   (c) $\dfrac{x^2}{36} - \dfrac{y^2}{25} + z = 0$ (d) $\dfrac{x^2}{36} + \dfrac{y^2}{25} - z^2 = 1$

   (e) $\dfrac{x^2}{36} + \dfrac{y^2}{25} - z^2 = 0$ (f) $z^2 - \dfrac{x^2}{36} - \dfrac{y^2}{25} = 1$

EXERCISE SET 11.7

1–2 Identify the quadric surface as an ellipsoid, hyperboloid of one sheet, hyperboloid of two sheets, elliptic cone, elliptic paraboloid, or hyperbolic paraboloid by matching the equation with one of the forms given in Table 11.7.1. State the values of a, b, and c in each case. ■

1. (a) $z = \dfrac{x^2}{4} + \dfrac{y^2}{9}$ (b) $z = \dfrac{y^2}{25} - x^2$

  (c) $x^2 + y^2 - z^2 = 16$ (d) $x^2 + y^2 - z^2 = 0$
  (e) $4z = x^2 + 4y^2$ (f) $z^2 - x^2 - y^2 = 1$

2. (a) $6x^2 + 3y^2 + 4z^2 = 12$ (b) $y^2 - x^2 - z = 0$
  (c) $9x^2 + y^2 - 9z^2 = 9$ (d) $4x^2 + y^2 - 4z^2 = -4$
  (e) $2z - x^2 - 4y^2 = 0$ (f) $12z^2 - 3x^2 = 4y^2$

3. Find an equation for and sketch the surface that results when the circular paraboloid $z = x^2 + y^2$ is reflected about the plane

  (a) $z = 0$ (b) $x = 0$ (c) $y = 0$
  (d) $y = x$ (e) $x = z$ (f) $y = z$.

4. Find an equation for and sketch the surface that results when the hyperboloid of one sheet $x^2 + y^2 - z^2 = 1$ is reflected about the plane

  (a) $z = 0$ (b) $x = 0$ (c) $y = 0$
  (d) $y = x$ (e) $x = z$ (f) $y = z$.

FOCUS ON CONCEPTS

5. The given equations represent quadric surfaces whose orientations are different from those in Table 11.7.1. In each part, identify the quadric surface, and give a verbal description of its orientation (e.g., an elliptic cone opening along the z-axis or a hyperbolic paraboloid straddling the y-axis).

  (a) $\dfrac{z^2}{c^2} - \dfrac{y^2}{b^2} + \dfrac{x^2}{a^2} = 1$ (b) $\dfrac{x^2}{a^2} - \dfrac{y^2}{b^2} - \dfrac{z^2}{c^2} = 1$

  (c) $x = \dfrac{y^2}{b^2} + \dfrac{z^2}{c^2}$ (d) $x^2 = \dfrac{y^2}{b^2} + \dfrac{z^2}{c^2}$

  (e) $y = \dfrac{z^2}{c^2} - \dfrac{x^2}{a^2}$ (f) $y = -\left(\dfrac{x^2}{a^2} + \dfrac{z^2}{c^2}\right)$

6. For each of the surfaces in Exercise 5, find the equation of the surface that results if the given surface is reflected about the xz-plane and that surface is then reflected about the plane $z = 0$.

7–8 Find equations of the traces in the coordinate planes and sketch the traces in an xyz-coordinate system. [*Suggestion:* If you have trouble sketching a trace directly in three dimensions, start with a sketch in two dimensions by placing the coordinate plane in the plane of the paper, then transfer the sketch to three dimensions.] ■

7. (a) $\dfrac{x^2}{9} + \dfrac{y^2}{25} + \dfrac{z^2}{4} = 1$ (b) $z = x^2 + 4y^2$

  (c) $\dfrac{x^2}{9} + \dfrac{y^2}{16} - \dfrac{z^2}{4} = 1$

8. (a) $y^2 + 9z^2 = x$ (b) $4x^2 - y^2 + 4z^2 = 4$

  (c) $z^2 = x^2 + \dfrac{y^2}{4}$

9–10 In these exercises, traces of the surfaces in the planes are conic sections. In each part, find an equation of the trace, and state whether it is an ellipse, a parabola, or a hyperbola. ■

9. (a) $4x^2 + y^2 + z^2 = 4$; $y = 1$
  (b) $4x^2 + y^2 + z^2 = 4$; $x = \frac{1}{2}$
  (c) $9x^2 - y^2 - z^2 = 16$; $x = 2$
  (d) $9x^2 - y^2 - z^2 = 16$; $z = 2$
  (e) $z = 9x^2 + 4y^2$; $y = 2$
  (f) $z = 9x^2 + 4y^2$; $z = 4$

10. (a) $9x^2 - y^2 + 4z^2 = 9$; $x = 2$
  (b) $9x^2 - y^2 + 4z^2 = 9$; $y = 4$
  (c) $x^2 + 4y^2 - 9z^2 = 0$; $y = 1$
  (d) $x^2 + 4y^2 - 9z^2 = 0$; $z = 1$
  (e) $z = x^2 - 4y^2$; $x = 1$
  (f) $z = x^2 - 4y^2$; $z = 4$

11–14 True–False Determine whether the statement is true or false. Explain your answer. ■

11. A quadric surface is the graph of a fourth-degree polynomial in x, y, and z.

12. Every ellipsoid will intersect the z-axis in exactly two points.

13. Every ellipsoid is a surface of revolution.

14. The hyperbolic paraboloid

$$z = \dfrac{y^2}{b^2} - \dfrac{x^2}{a^2}$$

intersects the xy-plane in a pair of intersecting lines.

15–26 Identify and sketch the quadric surface. ■

15. $x^2 + \dfrac{y^2}{4} + \dfrac{z^2}{9} = 1$ **16.** $x^2 + 4y^2 + 9z^2 = 36$

17. $\dfrac{x^2}{4} + \dfrac{y^2}{9} - \dfrac{z^2}{16} = 1$ **18.** $x^2 + y^2 - z^2 = 9$

19. $4z^2 = x^2 + 4y^2$ **20.** $9x^2 + 4y^2 - 36z^2 = 0$

21. $9z^2 - 4y^2 - 9x^2 = 36$ **22.** $y^2 - \dfrac{x^2}{4} - \dfrac{z^2}{9} = 1$

23. $z = y^2 - x^2$ **24.** $16z = y^2 - x^2$

25. $4z = x^2 + 2y^2$ **26.** $z - 3x^2 - 3y^2 = 0$

27–32 The given equation represents a quadric surface whose orientation is different from that in Table 11.7.1. Identify and sketch the surface. ■

27. $x^2 - 3y^2 - 3z^2 = 0$ **28.** $x - y^2 - 4z^2 = 0$

29. $2y^2 - x^2 + 2z^2 = 8$ **30.** $x^2 - 3y^2 - 3z^2 = 9$

31. $z = \dfrac{x^2}{4} - \dfrac{y^2}{9}$ **32.** $4x^2 - y^2 + 4z^2 = 16$

33–36 Sketch the surface. ■

33. $z = \sqrt{x^2 + y^2}$
34. $z = \sqrt{1 - x^2 - y^2}$
35. $z = \sqrt{x^2 + y^2 - 1}$
36. $z = \sqrt{1 + x^2 + y^2}$

37–40 Identify the surface and make a rough sketch that shows its position and orientation. ■

37. $z = (x + 2)^2 + (y - 3)^2 - 9$
38. $4x^2 - y^2 + 16(z - 2)^2 = 100$
39. $9x^2 + y^2 + 4z^2 - 18x + 2y + 16z = 10$
40. $z^2 = 4x^2 + y^2 + 8x - 2y + 4z$

41–42 Use the ellipsoid $4x^2 + 9y^2 + 18z^2 = 72$ in these exercises. ■

41. (a) Find an equation of the elliptical trace in the plane $z = \sqrt{2}$.
   (b) Find the lengths of the major and minor axes of the ellipse in part (a).
   (c) Find the coordinates of the foci of the ellipse in part (a).
   (d) Describe the orientation of the focal axis of the ellipse in part (a) relative to the coordinate axes.

42. (a) Find an equation of the elliptical trace in the plane $x = 3$.
   (b) Find the lengths of the major and minor axes of the ellipse in part (a).
   (c) Find the coordinates of the foci of the ellipse in part (a).
   (d) Describe the orientation of the focal axis of the ellipse in part (a) relative to the coordinate axes.

43–46 These exercises refer to the hyperbolic paraboloid $z = y^2 - x^2$. ■

43. (a) Find an equation of the hyperbolic trace in the plane $z = 4$.
   (b) Find the vertices of the hyperbola in part (a).
   (c) Find the foci of the hyperbola in part (a).
   (d) Describe the orientation of the focal axis of the hyperbola in part (a) relative to the coordinate axes.

44. (a) Find an equation of the hyperbolic trace in the plane $z = -4$.
   (b) Find the vertices of the hyperbola in part (a).
   (c) Find the foci of the hyperbola in part (a).
   (d) Describe the orientation of the focal axis of the hyperbola in part (a) relative to the coordinate axes.

45. (a) Find an equation of the parabolic trace in the plane $x = 2$.
   (b) Find the vertices of the parabola in part (a).
   (c) Find the focus of the parabola in part (a).
   (d) Describe the orientation of the focal axis of the parabola in part (a) relative to the coordinate axes.

46. (a) Find an equation of the parabolic trace in the plane $y = 2$.
   (b) Find the vertex of the parabola in part (a).
   (c) Find the focus of the parabola in part (a).

   (d) Describe the orientation of the focal axis of the parabola in part (a) relative to the coordinate axes.

47–48 Sketch the region enclosed between the surfaces and describe their curve of intersection. ■

47. The paraboloids $z = x^2 + y^2$ and $z = 4 - x^2 - y^2$
48. The ellipsoid $2x^2 + 2y^2 + z^2 = 3$ and the paraboloid $z = x^2 + y^2$.

49–50 Find an equation for the surface generated by revolving the curve about the y-axis. ■

49. $y = 4x^2$ ($z = 0$)
50. $y = 2x$ ($z = 0$)

51. Find an equation of the surface consisting of all points $P(x, y, z)$ that are equidistant from the point $(0, 0, 1)$ and the plane $z = -1$. Identify the surface.

52. Find an equation of the surface consisting of all points $P(x, y, z)$ that are twice as far from the plane $z = -1$ as from the point $(0, 0, 1)$. Identify the surface.

53. If a sphere
$$\frac{x^2}{a^2} + \frac{y^2}{a^2} + \frac{z^2}{a^2} = 1$$
of radius a is compressed in the z-direction, then the resulting surface, called an **oblate spheroid**, has an equation of the form
$$\frac{x^2}{a^2} + \frac{y^2}{a^2} + \frac{z^2}{c^2} = 1$$
where $c < a$. Show that the oblate spheroid has a circular trace of radius a in the xy-plane and an elliptical trace in the xz-plane with major axis of length $2a$ along the x-axis and minor axis of length $2c$ along the z-axis.

54. The Earth's rotation causes a flattening at the poles, so its shape is often modeled as an oblate spheroid rather than a sphere (see Exercise 53 for terminology). One of the models used by global positioning satellites is the **World Geodetic System of 1984** (WGS-84), which treats the Earth as an oblate spheroid whose equatorial radius is 6378.1370 km and whose polar radius (the distance from the Earth's center to the poles) is 6356.5231 km. Use the WGS-84 model to find an equation for the surface of the Earth relative to the coordinate system shown in the accompanying figure.

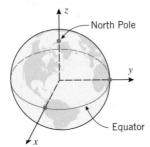
◄ **Figure Ex-54**

55. Use the method of slicing to show that the volume of the ellipsoid
$$\frac{x^2}{a^2} + \frac{y^2}{b^2} + \frac{z^2}{c^2} = 1$$
is $\frac{4}{3}\pi abc$.

56. Writing Discuss some of the connections between conic sections and traces of quadric surfaces.

57. Writing Give a sequence of steps for determining the type of quadric surface that is associated with a quadratic equation in x, y, and z.

✔ **QUICK CHECK ANSWERS 11.7**

1. (a) ellipse (b) ellipse (c) ellipse   2. (a) hyperbola (b) ellipse (c) hyperbola   3. (a) parabola (b) parabola (c) ellipse
4. (a) elliptic paraboloid (b) ellipsoid (c) hyperbolic paraboloid (d) hyperboloid of one sheet (e) elliptic cone
(f) hyperboloid of two sheets

11.8 CYLINDRICAL AND SPHERICAL COORDINATES

In this section we will discuss two new types of coordinate systems in 3-space that are often more useful than rectangular coordinate systems for studying surfaces with symmetries. These new coordinate systems also have important applications in navigation, astronomy, and the study of rotational motion about an axis.

■ **CYLINDRICAL AND SPHERICAL COORDINATE SYSTEMS**
Three coordinates are required to establish the location of a point in 3-space. We have already done this using rectangular coordinates. However, Figure 11.8.1 shows two other possibilities: part (*a*) of the figure shows the ***rectangular coordinates*** (x, y, z) of a point P, part (*b*) shows the ***cylindrical coordinates*** (r, θ, z) of P, and part (*c*) shows the ***spherical coordinates*** (ρ, θ, ϕ) of P. In a rectangular coordinate system the coordinates can be any real numbers, but in cylindrical and spherical coordinate systems there are restrictions on the allowable values of the coordinates (as indicated in Figure 11.8.1).

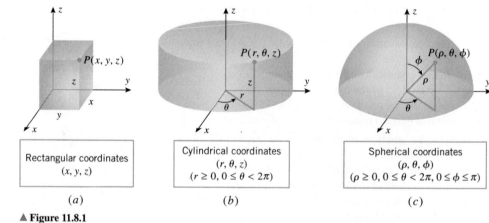

Rectangular coordinates
(x, y, z)

(a)

Cylindrical coordinates
(r, θ, z)
$(r \geq 0, 0 \leq \theta < 2\pi)$

(b)

Spherical coordinates
(ρ, θ, ϕ)
$(\rho \geq 0, 0 \leq \theta < 2\pi, 0 \leq \phi \leq \pi)$

(c)

▲ **Figure 11.8.1**

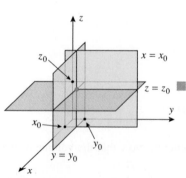

▲ **Figure 11.8.2**

■ **CONSTANT SURFACES**
In rectangular coordinates the surfaces represented by equations of the form

$$x = x_0, \quad y = y_0, \quad \text{and} \quad z = z_0$$

where x_0, y_0, and z_0 are constants, are planes parallel to the yz-plane, xz-plane, and xy-plane, respectively (Figure 11.8.2). In cylindrical coordinates the surfaces represented by equations of the form

$$r = r_0, \quad \theta = \theta_0, \quad \text{and} \quad z = z_0$$

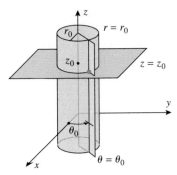

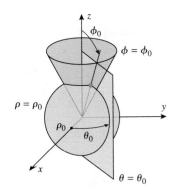

where r_0, θ_0, and z_0 are constants, are shown in Figure 11.8.3:

- The surface $r = r_0$ is a right circular cylinder of radius r_0 centered on the z-axis.
- The surface $\theta = \theta_0$ is a half-plane attached along the z-axis and making an angle θ_0 with the positive x-axis.
- The surface $z = z_0$ is a horizontal plane.

▲ Figure 11.8.3

In spherical coordinates the surfaces represented by equations of the form

$$\rho = \rho_0, \quad \theta = \theta_0, \quad \text{and} \quad \phi = \phi_0$$

where ρ_0, θ_0, and ϕ_0 are constants, are shown in Figure 11.8.4:

- The surface $\rho = \rho_0$ consists of all points whose distance ρ from the origin is ρ_0. Assuming ρ_0 to be nonnegative, this is a sphere of radius ρ_0 centered at the origin.
- As in cylindrical coordinates, the surface $\theta = \theta_0$ is a half-plane attached along the z-axis, making an angle of θ_0 with the positive x-axis.
- The surface $\phi = \phi_0$ consists of all points from which a line segment to the origin makes an angle of ϕ_0 with the positive z-axis. If $0 < \phi_0 < \pi/2$, this will be the nappe of a cone opening up, while if $\pi/2 < \phi_0 < \pi$, this will be the nappe of a cone opening down. (If $\phi_0 = \pi/2$, then the cone is flat, and the surface is the xy-plane.)

▲ Figure 11.8.4

■ CONVERTING COORDINATES

Just as we needed to convert between rectangular and polar coordinates in 2-space, so we will need to be able to convert between rectangular, cylindrical, and spherical coordinates in 3-space. Table 11.8.1 provides formulas for making these conversions.

Table 11.8.1
CONVERSION FORMULAS FOR COORDINATE SYSTEMS

CONVERSION		FORMULAS	RESTRICTIONS
Cylindrical to rectangular	$(r, \theta, z) \rightarrow (x, y, z)$	$x = r\cos\theta, \quad y = r\sin\theta, \quad z = z$	
Rectangular to cylindrical	$(x, y, z) \rightarrow (r, \theta, z)$	$r = \sqrt{x^2 + y^2}, \quad \tan\theta = y/x, \quad z = z$	
Spherical to cylindrical	$(\rho, \theta, \phi) \rightarrow (r, \theta, z)$	$r = \rho\sin\phi, \quad \theta = \theta, \quad z = \rho\cos\phi$	$r \geq 0, \rho \geq 0$
Cylindrical to spherical	$(r, \theta, z) \rightarrow (\rho, \theta, \phi)$	$\rho = \sqrt{r^2 + z^2}, \quad \theta = \theta, \quad \tan\phi = r/z$	$0 \leq \theta < 2\pi$ $0 \leq \phi \leq \pi$
Spherical to rectangular	$(\rho, \theta, \phi) \rightarrow (x, y, z)$	$x = \rho\sin\phi\cos\theta, \quad y = \rho\sin\phi\sin\theta, \quad z = \rho\cos\phi$	
Rectangular to spherical	$(x, y, z) \rightarrow (\rho, \theta, \phi)$	$\rho = \sqrt{x^2 + y^2 + z^2}, \quad \tan\theta = y/x, \quad \cos\phi = z/\sqrt{x^2 + y^2 + z^2}$	

The diagrams in Figure 11.8.5 will help you to understand how the formulas in Table 11.8.1 are derived. For example, part (a) of the figure shows that in converting between rectangular coordinates (x, y, z) and cylindrical coordinates (r, θ, z), we can interpret (r, θ) as polar coordinates of (x, y). Thus, the polar-to-rectangular and rectangular-to-polar

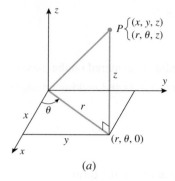

(a)

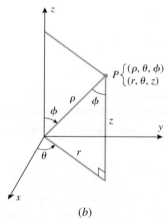

(b)

Comparison of coordinate systems

▲ **Figure 11.8.5**

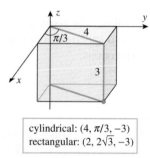

cylindrical: $(4, \pi/3, -3)$
rectangular: $(2, 2\sqrt{3}, -3)$

▲ **Figure 11.8.6**

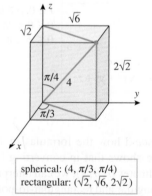

spherical: $(4, \pi/3, \pi/4)$
rectangular: $(\sqrt{2}, \sqrt{6}, 2\sqrt{2})$

▲ **Figure 11.8.7**

conversion formulas (1) and (2) of Section 10.2 provide the conversion formulas between rectangular and cylindrical coordinates in the table.

Part (*b*) of Figure 11.8.5 suggests that the spherical coordinates (ρ, θ, ϕ) of a point P can be converted to cylindrical coordinates (r, θ, z) by the conversion formulas

$$r = \rho \sin \phi, \quad \theta = \theta, \quad z = \rho \cos \phi \tag{1}$$

Moreover, since the cylindrical coordinates (r, θ, z) of P can be converted to rectangular coordinates (x, y, z) by the conversion formulas

$$x = r \cos \theta, \quad y = r \sin \theta, \quad z = z \tag{2}$$

we can obtain direct conversion formulas from spherical coordinates to rectangular coordinates by substituting (1) in (2). This yields

$$x = \rho \sin \phi \cos \theta, \quad y = \rho \sin \phi \sin \theta, \quad z = \rho \cos \phi \tag{3}$$

The other conversion formulas in Table 11.8.1 are left as exercises.

▶ **Example 1**

(a) Find the rectangular coordinates of the point with cylindrical coordinates

$$(r, \theta, z) = (4, \pi/3, -3)$$

(b) Find the rectangular coordinates of the point with spherical coordinates

$$(\rho, \theta, \phi) = (4, \pi/3, \pi/4)$$

Solution (a). Applying the cylindrical-to-rectangular conversion formulas in Table 11.8.1 yields

$$x = r \cos \theta = 4 \cos \frac{\pi}{3} = 2, \quad y = r \sin \theta = 4 \sin \frac{\pi}{3} = 2\sqrt{3}, \quad z = -3$$

Thus, the rectangular coordinates of the point are $(x, y, z) = (2, 2\sqrt{3}, -3)$ (Figure 11.8.6).

Solution (b). Applying the spherical-to-rectangular conversion formulas in Table 12.8.1 yields

$$x = \rho \sin \phi \cos \theta = 4 \sin \frac{\pi}{4} \cos \frac{\pi}{3} = \sqrt{2}$$

$$y = \rho \sin \phi \sin \theta = 4 \sin \frac{\pi}{4} \sin \frac{\pi}{3} = \sqrt{6}$$

$$z = \rho \cos \phi = 4 \cos \frac{\pi}{4} = 2\sqrt{2}$$

The rectangular coordinates of the point are $(x, y, z) = (\sqrt{2}, \sqrt{6}, 2\sqrt{2})$ (Figure 11.8.7). ◀

Since the interval $0 \leq \theta < 2\pi$ covers two periods of the tangent function, the conversion formula $\tan \theta = y/x$ does not completely determine θ. The following example shows how to deal with this ambiguity.

▶ **Example 2** Find the spherical coordinates of the point that has rectangular coordinates

$$(x, y, z) = (4, -4, 4\sqrt{6})$$

How should θ be chosen if $x = 0$?
How should θ be chosen if $y = 0$?

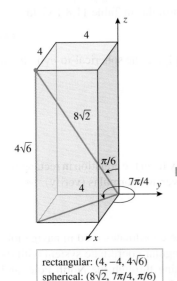

rectangular: $(4, -4, 4\sqrt{6})$
spherical: $(8\sqrt{2}, 7\pi/4, \pi/6)$

▲ **Figure 11.8.8**

Solution. From the rectangular-to-spherical conversion formulas in Table 11.8.1 we obtain

$$\rho = \sqrt{x^2 + y^2 + z^2} = \sqrt{16 + 16 + 96} = \sqrt{128} = 8\sqrt{2}$$

$$\tan \theta = \frac{y}{x} = -1$$

$$\cos \phi = \frac{z}{\sqrt{x^2 + y^2 + z^2}} = \frac{4\sqrt{6}}{8\sqrt{2}} = \frac{\sqrt{3}}{2}$$

From the restriction $0 \leq \theta < 2\pi$ and the computed value of $\tan \theta$, the possibilities for θ are $\theta = 3\pi/4$ and $\theta = 7\pi/4$. However, the given point has a negative y-coordinate, so we must have $\theta = 7\pi/4$. Moreover, from the restriction $0 \leq \phi \leq \pi$ and the computed value of $\cos \phi$, the only possibility for ϕ is $\phi = \pi/6$. Thus, the spherical coordinates of the point are $(\rho, \theta, \phi) = (8\sqrt{2}, 7\pi/4, \pi/6)$ (Figure 11.8.8). ◄

■ **EQUATIONS OF SURFACES IN CYLINDRICAL AND SPHERICAL COORDINATES**

Surfaces of revolution about the z-axis of a rectangular coordinate system usually have simpler equations in cylindrical coordinates than in rectangular coordinates, and the equations of surfaces with symmetry about the origin are usually simpler in spherical coordinates than in rectangular coordinates. For example, consider the upper nappe of the circular cone whose equation in rectangular coordinates is

$$z = \sqrt{x^2 + y^2}$$

(Table 11.8.2). The corresponding equation in cylindrical coordinates can be obtained from the cylindrical-to-rectangular conversion formulas in Table 11.8.1. This yields

$$z = \sqrt{(r \cos \theta)^2 + (r \sin \theta)^2} = \sqrt{r^2} = |r| = r$$

so the equation of the cone in cylindrical coordinates is $z = r$. Going a step further, the equation of the cone in spherical coordinates can be obtained from the spherical-to-cylindrical conversion formulas from Table 11.8.1. This yields

$$\rho \cos \phi = \rho \sin \phi$$

which, if $\rho \neq 0$, can be rewritten as

$$\tan \phi = 1 \quad \text{or} \quad \phi = \frac{\pi}{4}$$

Geometrically, this tells us that the radial line from the origin to any point on the cone makes an angle of $\pi/4$ with the z-axis.

Table 11.8.2

	CONE	CYLINDER	SPHERE	PARABOLOID	HYPERBOLOID
RECTANGULAR	$z = \sqrt{x^2 + y^2}$	$x^2 + y^2 = 1$	$x^2 + y^2 + z^2 = 1$	$z = x^2 + y^2$	$x^2 + y^2 - z^2 = 1$
CYLINDRICAL	$z = r$	$r = 1$	$z^2 = 1 - r^2$	$z = r^2$	$z^2 = r^2 - 1$
SPHERICAL	$\phi = \pi/4$	$\rho = \csc \phi$	$\rho = 1$	$\rho = \cos \phi \csc^2 \phi$	$\rho^2 = -\sec 2\phi$

▶ **Example 3**   Find equations of the paraboloid $z = x^2 + y^2$ in cylindrical and spherical coordinates.

Solution.   The rectangular-to-cylindrical conversion formulas in Table 11.8.1 yield

$$z = r^2 \tag{4}$$

> Verify the equations given in Table 11.8.2 for the cylinder and hyperboloid in cylindrical and spherical coordinates.

which is the equation in cylindrical coordinates. Now applying the spherical-to-cylindrical conversion formulas to (4) yields

$$\rho \cos \phi = \rho^2 \sin^2 \phi$$

which we can rewrite as

$$\rho = \cos \phi \csc^2 \phi$$

Alternatively, we could have obtained this equation directly from the equation in rectangular coordinates by applying the spherical-to-rectangular conversion formulas (verify). ◀

■ SPHERICAL COORDINATES IN NAVIGATION

Spherical coordinates are related to longitude and latitude coordinates used in navigation. To see why this is so, let us construct a right-hand rectangular coordinate system with its origin at the center of the Earth, its positive z-axis passing through the North Pole, and its positive x-axis passing through the prime meridian (Figure 11.8.9). If we assume the Earth to be a sphere of radius $\rho = 4000$ miles, then each point on the Earth has spherical coordinates of the form $(4000, \theta, \phi)$, where ϕ and θ determine the latitude and longitude of the point. It is common to specify longitudes in degrees east or west of the prime meridian and latitudes in degrees north or south of the equator. However, the next example shows that it is a simple matter to determine ϕ and θ from such data.

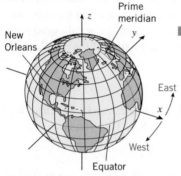

▲ **Figure 11.8.9**

Jon Arnold/Danita Delimont

Modern navigation systems use multiple coordinate representations to calculate position.

▶ **Example 4**   The city of New Orleans is located at 90° west longitude and 30° north latitude. Find its spherical and rectangular coordinates relative to the coordinate axes of Figure 11.8.9. (Assume that distance is in miles.)

Solution.   A longitude of 90° west corresponds to $\theta = 360° - 90° = 270°$ or $\theta = 3\pi/2$ radians; and a latitude of 30° north corresponds to $\phi = 90° - 30° = 60°$ or $\phi = \pi/3$ radians. Thus, the spherical coordinates (ρ, θ, ϕ) of New Orleans are $(4000, 3\pi/2, \pi/3)$.

To find the rectangular coordinates we apply the spherical-to-rectangular conversion formulas in Table 11.8.1. This yields

$$x = 4000 \sin \frac{\pi}{3} \cos \frac{3\pi}{2} = 4000 \frac{\sqrt{3}}{2}(0) = 0 \text{ mi}$$

$$y = 4000 \sin \frac{\pi}{3} \sin \frac{3\pi}{2} = 4000 \frac{\sqrt{3}}{2}(-1) = -2000\sqrt{3} \text{ mi}$$

$$z = 4000 \cos \frac{\pi}{3} = 4000 \left(\frac{1}{2}\right) = 2000 \text{ mi} \blacktriangleleft$$

✔ QUICK CHECK EXERCISES 11.8   *(See page 838 for answers.)*

1. The conversion formulas from cylindrical coordinates (r, θ, z) to rectangular coordinates (x, y, z) are

   $x = $ _____ , $y = $ _____ , $z = $ _____

2. The conversion formulas from spherical coordinates (ρ, θ, ϕ) to rectangular coordinates (x, y, z) are

   $x = $ _____ , $y = $ _____ , $z = $ _____

3. The conversion formulas from spherical coordinates (ρ, θ, ϕ) to cylindrical coordinates (r, θ, z) are

$$r = \underline{\hspace{1cm}}, \quad \theta = \underline{\hspace{1cm}}, \quad z = \underline{\hspace{1cm}}$$

4. Let P be the point in 3-space with rectangular coordinates $(\sqrt{2}, -\sqrt{2}, 2\sqrt{3})$.
   (a) Cylindrical coordinates for P are $(r, \theta, z) = \underline{\hspace{1cm}}$.
   (b) Spherical coordinates for P are $(\rho, \theta, \phi) = \underline{\hspace{1cm}}$.

5. Give an equation of a sphere of radius 5, centered at the origin, in
   (a) rectangular coordinates
   (b) cylindrical coordinates
   (c) spherical coordinates.

EXERCISE SET 11.8   ⌐∿ Graphing Utility   ⌐C⌐ CAS

1–2 Convert from rectangular to cylindrical coordinates. ■

1. (a) $(4\sqrt{3}, 4, -4)$ (b) $(-5, 5, 6)$
   (c) $(0, 2, 0)$ (d) $(4, -4\sqrt{3}, 6)$

2. (a) $(\sqrt{2}, -\sqrt{2}, 1)$ (b) $(0, 1, 1)$
   (c) $(-4, 4, -7)$ (d) $(2, -2, -2)$

3–4 Convert from cylindrical to rectangular coordinates. ■

3. (a) $(4, \pi/6, 3)$ (b) $(8, 3\pi/4, -2)$
   (c) $(5, 0, 4)$ (d) $(7, \pi, -9)$

4. (a) $(6, 5\pi/3, 7)$ (b) $(1, \pi/2, 0)$
   (c) $(3, \pi/2, 5)$ (d) $(4, \pi/2, -1)$

5–6 Convert from rectangular to spherical coordinates. ■

5. (a) $(1, \sqrt{3}, -2)$ (b) $(1, -1, \sqrt{2})$
   (c) $(0, 3\sqrt{3}, 3)$ (d) $(-5\sqrt{3}, 5, 0)$

6. (a) $(4, 4, 4\sqrt{6})$ (b) $(1, -\sqrt{3}, -2)$
   (c) $(2, 0, 0)$ (d) $(\sqrt{3}, 1, 2\sqrt{3})$

7–8 Convert from spherical to rectangular coordinates. ■

7. (a) $(5, \pi/6, \pi/4)$ (b) $(7, 0, \pi/2)$
   (c) $(1, \pi, 0)$ (d) $(2, 3\pi/2, \pi/2)$

8. (a) $(1, 2\pi/3, 3\pi/4)$ (b) $(3, 7\pi/4, 5\pi/6)$
   (c) $(8, \pi/6, \pi/4)$ (d) $(4, \pi/2, \pi/3)$

9–10 Convert from cylindrical to spherical coordinates. ■

9. (a) $(\sqrt{3}, \pi/6, 3)$ (b) $(1, \pi/4, -1)$
   (c) $(2, 3\pi/4, 0)$ (d) $(6, 1, -2\sqrt{3})$

10. (a) $(4, 5\pi/6, 4)$ (b) $(2, 0, -2)$
   (c) $(4, \pi/2, 3)$ (d) $(6, \pi, 2)$

11–12 Convert from spherical to cylindrical coordinates. ■

11. (a) $(5, \pi/4, 2\pi/3)$ (b) $(1, 7\pi/6, \pi)$
   (c) $(3, 0, 0)$ (d) $(4, \pi/6, \pi/2)$

12. (a) $(5, \pi/2, 0)$ (b) $(6, 0, 3\pi/4)$
   (c) $(\sqrt{2}, 3\pi/4, \pi)$ (d) $(5, 2\pi/3, 5\pi/6)$

⌐C⌐ **13.** Use a CAS or a programmable calculating utility to set up the conversion formulas in Table 11.8.1, and then use the CAS or calculating utility to solve the problems in Exercises 1, 3, 5, 7, 9, and 11.

⌐C⌐ **14.** Use a CAS or a programmable calculating utility to set up the conversion formulas in Table 11.8.1, and then use the CAS or calculating utility to solve the problems in Exercises 2, 4, 6, 8, 10, and 12.

15–18 True–False Determine whether the statement is true or false. Explain your answer. ■

15. In cylindrical coordinates for a point, r is the distance from the point to the z-axis.

16. In spherical coordinates for a point, ρ is the distance from the point to the origin.

17. The graph of $\theta = \theta_0$ in cylindrical coordinates is the same as the graph of $\theta = \theta_0$ in spherical coordinates.

18. The graph of $r = f(\theta)$ in cylindrical coordinates can always be obtained by extrusion of the polar graph of $r = f(\theta)$ in the xy-plane.

19–26 An equation is given in cylindrical coordinates. Express the equation in rectangular coordinates and sketch the graph. ■

19. $r = 3$ **20.** $\theta = \pi/4$ **21.** $z = r^2$

22. $z = r \cos\theta$ **23.** $r = 4\sin\theta$ **24.** $r = 2\sec\theta$

25. $r^2 + z^2 = 1$ **26.** $r^2 \cos 2\theta = z$

27–34 An equation is given in spherical coordinates. Express the equation in rectangular coordinates and sketch the graph. ■

27. $\rho = 3$ **28.** $\theta = \pi/3$ **29.** $\phi = \pi/4$

30. $\rho = 2\sec\phi$ **31.** $\rho = 4\cos\phi$ **32.** $\rho \sin\phi = 1$

33. $\rho \sin\phi = 2\cos\theta$ **34.** $\rho - 2\sin\phi\cos\theta = 0$

35–46 An equation of a surface is given in rectangular coordinates. Find an equation of the surface in (a) cylindrical coordinates and (b) spherical coordinates. ■

35. $z = 3$ **36.** $y = 2$

37. $z = 3x^2 + 3y^2$ **38.** $z = \sqrt{3x^2 + 3y^2}$

39. $x^2 + y^2 = 4$ **40.** $x^2 + y^2 - 6y = 0$

41. $x^2 + y^2 + z^2 = 9$ **42.** $z^2 = x^2 - y^2$

43. $2x + 3y + 4z = 1$ **44.** $x^2 + y^2 - z^2 = 1$

45. $x^2 = 16 - z^2$ **46.** $x^2 + y^2 + z^2 = 2z$

FOCUS ON CONCEPTS

47–50 Describe the region in 3-space that satisfies the given inequalities. ■

47. $r^2 \leq z \leq 4$ **48.** $0 \leq r \leq 2\sin\theta, \quad 0 \leq z \leq 3$

49. $1 \leq \rho \leq 3$ **50.** $0 \leq \phi \leq \pi/6, \quad 0 \leq \rho \leq 2$

51. St. Petersburg (Leningrad), Russia, is located at 30° east longitude and 60° north latitude. Find its spherical and rectangular coordinates relative to the coordinate axes of Figure 11.8.9. Take miles as the unit of distance and assume the Earth to be a sphere of radius 4000 miles.

52. (a) Show that the curve of intersection of the surfaces $z = \sin\theta$ and $r = a$ (cylindrical coordinates) is an ellipse.
  (b) Sketch the surface $z = \sin\theta$ for $0 \leq \theta \leq \pi/2$.

53. The accompanying figure shows a right circular cylinder of radius 10 cm spinning at 3 revolutions per minute about the z-axis. At time $t = 0$ s, a bug at the point $(0, 10, 0)$ begins walking straight up the face of the cylinder at the rate of 0.5 cm/min.

(a) Find the cylindrical coordinates of the bug after 2 min.
(b) Find the rectangular coordinates of the bug after 2 min.
(c) Find the spherical coordinates of the bug after 2 min.

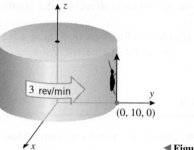

3 rev/min

$(0, 10, 0)$

◀ **Figure Ex-53**

54. Referring to Exercise 53, use a graphing utility to graph the bug's distance from the origin as a function of time.

55. Writing Discuss some practical applications in which non-rectangular coordinate systems are useful.

56. Writing The terms "zenith" and "azimuth" are used in celestial navigation. How do these terms relate to spherical coordinates?

✔ **QUICK CHECK ANSWERS 11.8**

1. $r\cos\theta; \ r\sin\theta; \ z$ **2.** $\rho\sin\phi\cos\theta; \ \rho\sin\phi\sin\theta; \ \rho\cos\phi$ **3.** $\rho\sin\phi; \ \theta; \ \rho\cos\theta$
4. (a) $(2, 7\pi/4, 2\sqrt{3})$ (b) $(4, 7\pi/4, \pi/6)$ **5.** (a) $x^2 + y^2 + z^2 = 25$ (b) $r^2 + z^2 = 25$ (c) $\rho = 5$

CHAPTER 11 REVIEW EXERCISES

1. (a) What is the difference between a vector and a scalar? Give a physical example of each.
  (b) How can you determine whether or not two vectors are orthogonal?
  (c) How can you determine whether or not two vectors are parallel?
  (d) How can you determine whether or not three vectors with a common initial point lie in the same plane in 3-space?

2. (a) Sketch vectors $\mathbf{u}$ and $\mathbf{v}$ for which $\mathbf{u} + \mathbf{v}$ and $\mathbf{u} - \mathbf{v}$ are orthogonal.
  (b) How can you use vectors to determine whether four points in 3-space lie in the same plane?
  (c) If forces $\mathbf{F}_1 = \mathbf{i}$ and $\mathbf{F}_2 = \mathbf{j}$ are applied at a point in 2-space, what force would you apply at that point to cancel the combined effect of $\mathbf{F}_1$ and $\mathbf{F}_2$?
  (d) Write an equation of the sphere with center $(1, -2, 2)$ that passes through the origin.

3. (a) Draw a picture that shows the direction angles α, β, and γ of a vector.

  (b) What are the components of a unit vector in 2-space that makes an angle of 120° with the vector $\mathbf{i}$ (two answers)?
  (c) How can you use vectors to determine whether a triangle with known vertices P_1, P_2, and P_3 has an obtuse angle?
  (d) True or false: The cross product of orthogonal unit vectors is a unit vector. Explain your reasoning.

4. (a) Make a table that shows all possible cross products of the vectors $\mathbf{i}$, $\mathbf{j}$, and $\mathbf{k}$.
  (b) Give a geometric interpretation of $\|\mathbf{u} \times \mathbf{v}\|$.
  (c) Give a geometric interpretation of $|\mathbf{u} \cdot (\mathbf{v} \times \mathbf{w})|$.
  (d) Write an equation of the plane that passes through the origin and is perpendicular to the line $x = t$, $y = 2t$, $z = -t$.

5. In each part, find an equation of the sphere with center $(-3, 5, -4)$ and satisfying the given condition.
  (a) Tangent to the xy-plane
  (b) Tangent to the xz-plane
  (c) Tangent to the yz-plane

6. Find the largest and smallest distances between the point $P(1, 1, 1)$ and the sphere

$$x^2 + y^2 + z^2 - 2y + 6z - 6 = 0$$

7. Given the points $P(3, 4)$, $Q(1, 1)$, and $R(5, 2)$, use vector methods to find the coordinates of the fourth vertex of the parallelogram whose adjacent sides are $\overrightarrow{PQ}$ and $\overrightarrow{QR}$.

8. Let $\mathbf{u} = \langle 3, 5, -1 \rangle$ and $\mathbf{v} = \langle 2, -2, 3 \rangle$. Find

(a) $2\mathbf{u} + 5\mathbf{v}$
(b) $\dfrac{1}{\|\mathbf{v}\|}\mathbf{v}$
(c) $\|\mathbf{u}\|$
(d) $\|\mathbf{u} - \mathbf{v}\|$.

9. Let $\mathbf{a} = c\mathbf{i} + \mathbf{j}$ and $\mathbf{b} = 4\mathbf{i} + 3\mathbf{j}$. Find c so that
(a) $\mathbf{a}$ and $\mathbf{b}$ are orthogonal
(b) the angle between $\mathbf{a}$ and $\mathbf{b}$ is $\pi/4$
(c) the angle between $\mathbf{a}$ and $\mathbf{b}$ is $\pi/6$
(d) $\mathbf{a}$ and $\mathbf{b}$ are parallel.

10. Let $\mathbf{r}_0 = \langle x_0, y_0, z_0 \rangle$ and $\mathbf{r} = \langle x, y, z \rangle$. Describe the set of all points (x, y, z) for which
(a) $\mathbf{r} \cdot \mathbf{r}_0 = 0$
(b) $(\mathbf{r} - \mathbf{r}_0) \cdot \mathbf{r}_0 = 0$.

11. Show that if $\mathbf{u}$ and $\mathbf{v}$ are unit vectors and θ is the angle between them, then $\|\mathbf{u} - \mathbf{v}\| = 2 \sin \frac{1}{2}\theta$.

12. Find the vector with length 5 and direction angles $\alpha = 60°$, $\beta = 120°$, $\gamma = 135°$.

13. Assuming that force is in pounds and distance is in feet, find the work done by a constant force $\mathbf{F} = 3\mathbf{i} - 4\mathbf{j} + \mathbf{k}$ acting on a particle that moves on a straight line from $P(5, 7, 0)$ to $Q(6, 6, 6)$.

14. Assuming that force is in newtons and distance is in meters, find the work done by the resultant of the constant forces $\mathbf{F}_1 = \mathbf{i} - 3\mathbf{j} + \mathbf{k}$ and $\mathbf{F}_2 = \mathbf{i} + 2\mathbf{j} + 2\mathbf{k}$ acting on a particle that moves on a straight line from $P(-1, -2, 3)$ to $Q(0, 2, 0)$.

15. (a) Find the area of the triangle with vertices $A(1, 0, 1)$, $B(0, 2, 3)$, and $C(2, 1, 0)$.
(b) Use the result in part (a) to find the length of the altitude from vertex C to side AB.

16. True or false? Explain your reasoning.
(a) If $\mathbf{u} \cdot \mathbf{v} = 0$, then $\mathbf{u} = \mathbf{0}$ or $\mathbf{v} = \mathbf{0}$.
(b) If $\mathbf{u} \times \mathbf{v} = \mathbf{0}$, then $\mathbf{u} = \mathbf{0}$ or $\mathbf{v} = \mathbf{0}$.
(c) If $\mathbf{u} \cdot \mathbf{v} = 0$ and $\mathbf{u} \times \mathbf{v} = \mathbf{0}$, then $\mathbf{u} = \mathbf{0}$ or $\mathbf{v} = \mathbf{0}$.

17. Consider the points

$$A(1, -1, 2), \quad B(2, -3, 0), \quad C(-1, -2, 0), \quad D(2, 1, -1)$$

(a) Find the volume of the parallelepiped that has the vectors $\overrightarrow{AB}$, $\overrightarrow{AC}$, $\overrightarrow{AD}$ as adjacent edges.
(b) Find the distance from D to the plane containing A, B, and C.

18. Suppose that a force $\mathbf{F}$ with a magnitude of 9 lb is applied to the lever–shaft assembly shown in the accompanying figure.
(a) Express the force $\mathbf{F}$ in component form.
(b) Find the vector moment of $\mathbf{F}$ about the origin.

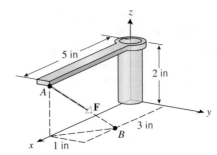

◀ Figure Ex-18

19. Let P be the point $(4, 1, 2)$. Find parametric equations for the line through P and parallel to the vector $\langle 1, -1, 0 \rangle$.

20. (a) Find parametric equations for the intersection of the planes $2x + y - z = 3$ and $x + 2y + z = 3$.
(b) Find the acute angle between the two planes.

21. Find an equation of the plane that is parallel to the plane $x + 5y - z + 8 = 0$ and contains the point $(1, 1, 4)$.

22. Find an equation of the plane through the point $(4, 3, 0)$ and parallel to the vectors $\mathbf{i} + \mathbf{k}$ and $2\mathbf{j} - \mathbf{k}$.

23. What condition must the constants satisfy for the planes

$$a_1x + b_1y + c_1z = d_1 \quad \text{and} \quad a_2x + b_2y + c_2z = d_2$$

to be perpendicular?

24. (a) List six common types of quadric surfaces, and describe their traces in planes parallel to the coordinate planes.
(b) Give the coordinates of the points that result when the point (x, y, z) is reflected about the plane $y = x$, the plane $y = z$, and the plane $x = z$.
(c) Describe the intersection of the surfaces $r = 5$ and $z = 1$ in cylindrical coordinates.
(d) Describe the intersection of the surfaces $\phi = \pi/4$ and $\theta = 0$ in spherical coordinates.

25. In each part, identify the surface by completing the squares.
(a) $x^2 + 4y^2 - z^2 - 6x + 8y + 4z = 0$
(b) $x^2 + y^2 + z^2 + 6x - 4y + 12z = 0$
(c) $x^2 + y^2 - z^2 - 2x + 4y + 5 = 0$

26. In each part, express the equation in cylindrical and spherical coordinates.
(a) $x^2 + y^2 = z$
(b) $x^2 - y^2 - z^2 = 0$

27. In each part, express the equation in rectangular coordinates.
(a) $z = r^2 \cos 2\theta$
(b) $\rho^2 \sin \phi \cos \phi \cos \theta = 1$

28–29 Sketch the solid in 3-space that is described in cylindrical coordinates by the stated inequalities. ■

28. (a) $1 \le r \le 2$ (b) $2 \le z \le 3$ (c) $\pi/6 \le \theta \le \pi/3$
(d) $1 \le r \le 2$, $2 \le z \le 3$, and $\pi/6 \le \theta \le \pi/3$

29. (a) $r^2 + z^2 \le 4$ (b) $r \le 1$
(c) $r^2 + z^2 \le 4$ and $r > 1$

30–31 Sketch the solid in 3-space that is described in spherical coordinates by the stated inequalities. ■

30. (a) $0 \leq \rho \leq 2$ (b) $0 \leq \phi \leq \pi/6$
(c) $0 \leq \rho \leq 2$ and $0 \leq \phi \leq \pi/6$

31. (a) $0 \leq \rho \leq 5$, $0 \leq \phi \leq \pi/2$, and $0 \leq \theta \leq \pi/2$
(b) $0 \leq \phi \leq \pi/3$ and $0 \leq \rho \leq 2 \sec \phi$
(c) $0 \leq \rho \leq 2$ and $\pi/6 \leq \phi \leq \pi/3$

32. Sketch the surface whose equation in spherical coordinates is $\rho = a(1 - \cos \phi)$. [*Hint:* The surface is shaped like a familiar fruit.]

CHAPTER 11 MAKING CONNECTIONS

1. Define a "rotation operator" R on vectors in the xy-plane by the formula
$$R(x\mathbf{i} + y\mathbf{j}) = -y\mathbf{i} + x\mathbf{j}$$

(a) Verify that R rotates vectors $90°$ counterclockwise.
(b) Prove that R has the following linearity properties:
$$R(c\mathbf{v}) = cR(\mathbf{v}) \quad \text{and} \quad R(\mathbf{v} + \mathbf{w}) = R(\mathbf{v}) + R(\mathbf{w})$$

2. (a) Given a triangle in the xy-plane, assign to each side of the triangle an outward normal vector whose length is the same as that of the corresponding side. Prove that the sum of the resulting three normal vectors is the zero vector.
(b) Extend the result of part (a) to a polygon of n sides in the xy-plane. [*Hint:* Use the results of the preceding exercise.]

3. (a) Given a tetrahedron in 3-space, assign to each face of the tetrahedron an outward normal vector whose length is numerically the same as the area of the corresponding face. Prove that the sum of the resulting four normal vectors is the zero vector. [*Hint:* Use cross products.]
(b) Extend your result from part (a) to a pyramid with a four-sided base. [*Hint:* Divide the base into two triangles and use the result from part (a) on each of the two resulting tetrahedra.]
(c) Can you extend the results of parts (a) and (b) to other polyhedra?

4. Given a tetrahedron in 3-space, pick a vertex and label the three faces that meet at that vertex as A, B, and C. Let a, b, and c denote the respective areas of those faces, and let d denote the area of the fourth face of the tetrahedron. Let α denote the (internal) angle between faces A and B, β the angle between B and C, and γ the angle between A and C.
(a) Prove that
$$d^2 = a^2 + b^2 + c^2 - 2ab \cos \alpha - 2bc \cos \beta - 2ac \cos \gamma$$

This result is sometimes referred to as the *law of cosines for a tetrahedron*. [*Hint:* Use the result in part (a) of the preceding exercise.]
(b) With the result in part (a) as motivation, state and prove a "Theorem of Pythagoras for a Tetrahedron."

5. Any circle that lies on a sphere can be realized as the intersection of the sphere and a plane. If the plane passes through the center of the sphere, then the circle is referred to as a *great circle*. Given two points on a sphere, the *great circle distance* between the two points is the length of the smallest arc of a great circle that contains both points. Assume that Σ is a sphere of radius ρ centered at the origin in 3-space. If points P and Q lie on Σ and have spherical coordinates (ρ, θ_1, ϕ_1) and (ρ, θ_2, ϕ_2), respectively, prove that the great circle distance between P and Q is
$$\rho \cos^{-1}(\cos \phi_1 \cos \phi_2 + \cos(\theta_1 - \theta_2) \sin \phi_1 \sin \phi_2)$$

6. A ship at sea is at point A that is $60°$ west longitude and $40°$ north latitude. The ship travels to point B that is $40°$ west longitude and $20°$ north latitude. Assuming that the Earth is a sphere with radius 6370 kilometers, find the shortest distance the ship can travel in going from A to B, given that the shortest distance between two points on a sphere is along the arc of the great circle joining the points. [*Suggestion:* Introduce an xyz-coordinate system as in Figure 11.8.9, and use the result of the preceding exercise.]

Courtesy Cedar Point

12

VECTOR-VALUED FUNCTIONS

The design of a roller coaster requires an understanding of the mathematical principles governing the motion of objects that move with varying speed and direction.

In this chapter we will consider functions whose values are vectors. Such functions provide a unified way of studying parametric curves in 2-space and 3-space and are a basic tool for analyzing the motion of particles along curved paths. We will begin by developing the calculus of vector-valued functions—we will show how to differentiate and integrate such functions, and we will develop some of the basic properties of these operations. We will then apply these calculus tools to define three fundamental vectors that can be used to describe such basic characteristics of curves as curvature and twisting tendencies. Once this is done, we will develop the concepts of velocity and acceleration for such motion, and we will apply these concepts to explain various physical phenomena. Finally, we will use the calculus of vector-valued functions to develop basic principles of gravitational attraction and to derive Kepler's laws of planetary motion.

12.1 INTRODUCTION TO VECTOR-VALUED FUNCTIONS

In Section 11.5 we discussed parametric equations of lines in 3-space. In this section we will discuss more general parametric curves in 3-space, and we will show how vector notation can be used to express parametric equations in 2-space and 3-space in a more compact form. This will lead us to consider a new kind of function—namely, functions that associate vectors with real numbers. Such functions have many important applications in physics and engineering.

■ PARAMETRIC CURVES IN 3-SPACE

Recall from Section 10.1 that if f and g are well-behaved functions, then the pair of parametric equations

$$x = f(t), \quad y = g(t) \tag{1}$$

generates a curve in 2-space that is traced in a specific direction as the parameter t increases. We defined this direction to be the *orientation* of the curve or the *direction of increasing parameter*, and we called the curve together with its orientation the *graph* of the parametric equations or the *parametric curve* represented by the equations. Analogously, if f, g, and h are three well-behaved functions, then the parametric equations

$$x = f(t), \quad y = g(t), \quad z = h(t) \tag{2}$$

generate a curve in 3-space that is traced in a specific direction as t increases. As in 2-space, this direction is called the **orientation** or **direction of increasing parameter**, and

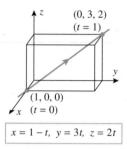

$$x = 1 - t, \quad y = 3t, \quad z = 2t$$

▲ Figure 12.1.1

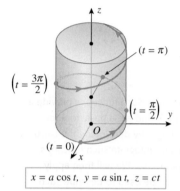

$$x = a\cos t, \quad y = a\sin t, \quad z = ct$$

▲ Figure 12.1.2

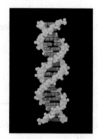

The circular helix described in Example 2 occurs in nature. Above is a computer representation of the twin helix DNA molecule (deoxyribonucleic acid). This structure contains all the inherited instructions necessary for the development of a living organism.

TECHNOLOGY MASTERY

If you have a CAS, use it to generate the tricuspoid in Figure 12.1.3, and show that this parametric curve is oriented counterclockwise.

the curve together with its orientation is called the **graph** of the parametric equations or the **parametric curve** represented by the equations. If no restrictions are stated explicitly or are implied by the equations, then it will be understood that t varies over the interval $(-\infty, +\infty)$.

▶ **Example 1** The parametric equations

$$x = 1 - t, \quad y = 3t, \quad z = 2t$$

represent a line in 3-space that passes through the point $(1, 0, 0)$ and is parallel to the vector $\langle -1, 3, 2 \rangle$. Since x decreases as t increases, the line has the orientation shown in Figure 12.1.1. ◀

▶ **Example 2** Describe the parametric curve represented by the equations

$$x = a\cos t, \quad y = a\sin t, \quad z = ct$$

where a and c are positive constants.

Solution. As the parameter t increases, the value of $z = ct$ also increases, so the point (x, y, z) moves upward. However, as t increases, the point (x, y, z) also moves in a path directly over the circle

$$x = a\cos t, \quad y = a\sin t$$

in the xy-plane. The combination of these upward and circular motions produces a corkscrew-shaped curve that wraps around a right circular cylinder of radius a centered on the z-axis (Figure 12.1.2). This curve is called a **circular helix**. ◀

■ **PARAMETRIC CURVES GENERATED WITH TECHNOLOGY**

Except in the simplest cases, parametric curves can be difficult to visualize and draw without the help of a graphing utility. For example, the **tricuspoid** is the graph of the parametric equations

$$x = 2\cos t + \cos 2t, \quad y = 2\sin t - \sin 2t$$

Although it would be tedious to plot the tricuspoid by hand, a computer rendering is easy to obtain and reveals the significance of the name of the curve (Figure 12.1.3). However, note that the depiction of the tricuspoid in Figure 12.1.3 is incomplete, since the orientation of the curve is not indicated. This is often the case for curves that are generated with a graphing utility. (Some graphing utilities plot parametric curves slowly enough for the orientation to be discerned, or provide a feature for tracing the points along the curve in the direction of increasing parameter.)

Parametric curves in 3-space can be difficult to visualize correctly even with the help of a graphing utility. For example, Figure 12.1.4a shows a parametric curve called a *torus knot* that was produced with a CAS. However, it is unclear from this computer-generated figure whether the points of overlap are intersections or whether one portion of the curve is in front of the other. To resolve the visualization problem, some graphing utilities provide the capability of enclosing the curve within a thin tube, as in Figure 12.1.4b. Such graphs are called **tube plots**.

■ **PARAMETRIC EQUATIONS FOR INTERSECTIONS OF SURFACES**

Curves in 3-space often arise as intersections of surfaces. For example, Figure 12.1.5a shows a portion of the intersection of the cylinders $z = x^3$ and $y = x^2$. One method for finding parametric equations for the curve of intersection is to choose one of the variables as the parameter and use the two equations to express the remaining two variables in terms

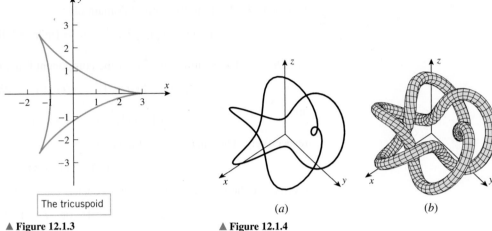

The tricuspoid

▲ **Figure 12.1.3**

(a)   (b)

▲ **Figure 12.1.4**

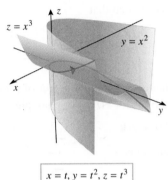

$x = t, y = t^2, z = t^3$

▲ **Figure 12.1.5**

of that parameter. In particular, if we choose $x = t$ as the parameter and substitute this into the equations $z = x^3$ and $y = x^2$, we obtain the parametric equations

$$x = t, \quad y = t^2, \quad z = t^3 \tag{3}$$

This curve, called a ***twisted cubic***, is shown in red in Figure 12.1.5. Also graphed are the surfaces $z = x^3$ and $y = x^2$ of which the twisted cubic is the intersection. The orientation of the twisted cubic can be deduced from (3) by observing that the value of x increases as t increases. Some other examples and techniques for finding intersections of surfaces are discussed in the exercises.

■ VECTOR-VALUED FUNCTIONS

The twisted cubic defined by the equations in (3) is the set of points of the form (t, t^2, t^3) for real values of t. If we view each of these points as a terminal point for a vector $\mathbf{r}$ whose initial point is at the origin,

$$\mathbf{r} = \langle x, y, z \rangle = \langle t, t^2, t^3 \rangle = t\mathbf{i} + t^2\mathbf{j} + t^3\mathbf{k}$$

then we obtain $\mathbf{r}$ as a function of the parameter t, that is, $\mathbf{r} = \mathbf{r}(t)$. Since this function produces a *vector*, we say that $\mathbf{r} = \mathbf{r}(t)$ defines $\mathbf{r}$ as a ***vector-valued function of a real variable***, or more simply, a ***vector-valued function***. The vectors that we will consider in this text are either in 2-space or 3-space, so we will say that a vector-valued function is in 2-space or in 3-space according to the kind of vectors that it produces.

If $\mathbf{r}(t)$ is a vector-valued function in 3-space, then for each allowable value of t the vector $\mathbf{r} = \mathbf{r}(t)$ can be represented in terms of components as

$$\mathbf{r} = \mathbf{r}(t) = \langle x(t), y(t), z(t) \rangle = x(t)\mathbf{i} + y(t)\mathbf{j} + z(t)\mathbf{k} \tag{4}$$

The functions $x(t)$, $y(t)$, and $z(t)$ are called the ***component functions*** or the ***components*** of $\mathbf{r}(t)$.

Whereas a vector-valued function in 3-space, such as (4), has three components, a vector-valued function in 2-space has only two components and hence has the form

$$r(t) = \langle x(t), y(t) \rangle$$
$$= x(t)\mathbf{i} + y(t)\mathbf{j}$$

Find the vector-valued function in 2-space whose component functions are $x(t) = t$ and $y(t) = t^2$.

▶ **Example 3**   The component functions of

$$\mathbf{r}(t) = \langle t, t^2, t^3 \rangle = t\mathbf{i} + t^2\mathbf{j} + t^3\mathbf{k}$$

are

$$x(t) = t, \quad y(t) = t^2, \quad z(t) = t^3 \blacktriangleleft$$

The ***domain*** of a vector-valued function $\mathbf{r}(t)$ is the set of allowable values for t. If $\mathbf{r}(t)$ is defined in terms of component functions and the domain is not specified explicitly, then it will be understood that the domain is the intersection of the natural domains of the component functions; this is called the ***natural domain*** of $\mathbf{r}(t)$.

▶ **Example 4** Find the natural domain of

$$\mathbf{r}(t) = \langle \ln|t-1|, e^t, \sqrt{t} \rangle = (\ln|t-1|)\mathbf{i} + e^t\mathbf{j} + \sqrt{t}\mathbf{k}$$

Solution. The natural domains of the component functions

$$x(t) = \ln|t-1|, \quad y(t) = e^t, \quad z(t) = \sqrt{t}$$

are

$$(-\infty, 1) \cup (1, +\infty), \quad (-\infty, +\infty), \quad [0, +\infty)$$

respectively. The intersection of these sets is

$$[0, 1) \cup (1, +\infty)$$

(verify), so the natural domain of $\mathbf{r}(t)$ consists of all values of t such that

$$0 \le t < 1 \quad \text{or} \quad t > 1 \blacktriangleleft$$

■ **GRAPHS OF VECTOR-VALUED FUNCTIONS**

If $\mathbf{r}(t)$ is a vector-valued function in 2-space or 3-space, then we define the *graph* of $\mathbf{r}(t)$ to be the parametric curve described by the component functions for $\mathbf{r}(t)$. For example, if

$$\mathbf{r}(t) = \langle 1-t, 3t, 2t \rangle = (1-t)\mathbf{i} + 3t\mathbf{j} + 2t\mathbf{k} \qquad (5)$$

then the graph of $\mathbf{r} = \mathbf{r}(t)$ is the graph of the parametric equations

$$x = 1-t, \quad y = 3t, \quad z = 2t$$

Thus, the graph of (5) is the line in Figure 12.1.1.

▶ **Example 5** Describe the graph of the vector-valued function

$$\mathbf{r}(t) = \langle \cos t, \sin t, t \rangle = \cos t\mathbf{i} + \sin t\mathbf{j} + t\mathbf{k}$$

Solution. The corresponding parametric equations are

$$x = \cos t, \quad y = \sin t, \quad z = t$$

Thus, as we saw in Example 2, the graph is a circular helix wrapped around a cylinder of radius 1. ◀

Up to now we have considered parametric curves to be paths traced by moving points. However, if a parametric curve is viewed as the graph of a vector-valued function, then we can also imagine the graph to be traced by the tip of a moving vector. For example, if the curve C in 3-space is the graph of

$$\mathbf{r}(t) = x(t)\mathbf{i} + y(t)\mathbf{j} + z(t)\mathbf{k}$$

and if we position $\mathbf{r}(t)$ so its initial point is at the origin, then its terminal point will fall on the curve C (as shown in Figure 12.1.6). Thus, when $\mathbf{r}(t)$ is positioned with its initial point at the origin, its terminal point will trace out the curve C as the parameter t varies, in which case we call $\mathbf{r}(t)$ the *radius vector* or the *position vector* for C. For simplicity, we will sometimes let the dependence on t be understood and write $\mathbf{r}$ rather than $\mathbf{r}(t)$ for a radius vector.

Strictly speaking, we should write $(\cos t)\mathbf{i}$ and $(\sin t)\mathbf{j}$ rather than $\cos t\mathbf{i}$ and $\sin t\mathbf{j}$ for clarity. However, it is a common practice to omit the parentheses in such cases, since no misinterpretation is possible. Why?

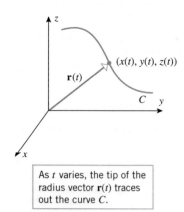

As t varies, the tip of the radius vector $\mathbf{r}(t)$ traces out the curve C.

▲ **Figure 12.1.6**

▶ **Example 6** Sketch the graph and a radius vector of

(a) $\mathbf{r}(t) = \cos t\mathbf{i} + \sin t\mathbf{j}, \quad 0 \le t \le 2\pi$

(b) $\mathbf{r}(t) = \cos t\mathbf{i} + \sin t\mathbf{j} + 2\mathbf{k}, \quad 0 \le t \le 2\pi$

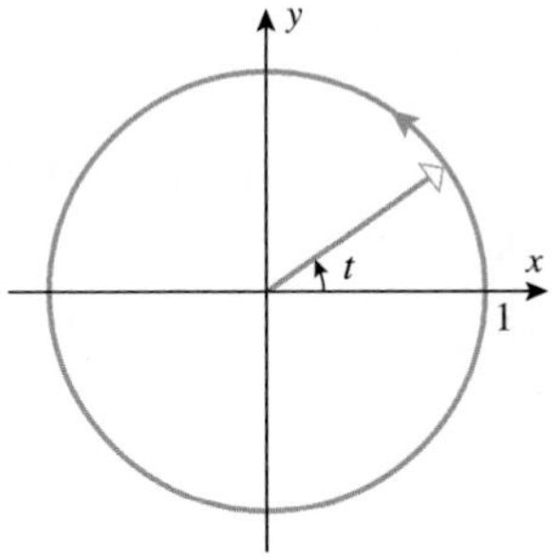

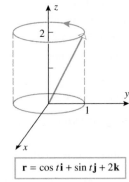

$$\mathbf{r} = \cos t\,\mathbf{i} + \sin t\,\mathbf{j}$$

▲ **Figure 12.1.7**

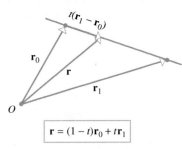

$$\mathbf{r} = \cos t\,\mathbf{i} + \sin t\,\mathbf{j} + 2\mathbf{k}$$

▲ **Figure 12.1.8**

$$\mathbf{r} = (1 - t)\mathbf{r}_0 + t\mathbf{r}_1$$

▲ **Figure 12.1.9**

Solution (a).   The corresponding parametric equations are

$$x = \cos t, \quad y = \sin t \qquad (0 \le t \le 2\pi)$$

so the graph is a circle of radius 1, centered at the origin, and oriented counterclockwise. The graph and a radius vector are shown in Figure 12.1.7.

Solution (b).   The corresponding parametric equations are

$$x = \cos t, \quad y = \sin t, \quad z = 2 \qquad (0 \le t \le 2\pi)$$

From the third equation, the tip of the radius vector traces a curve in the plane $z = 2$, and from the first two equations, the curve is a circle of radius 1 centered at the point $(0, 0, 2)$ and traced counterclockwise looking down the z-axis. The graph and a radius vector are shown in Figure 12.1.8. ◄

■ VECTOR FORM OF A LINE SEGMENT

Recall from Formula (9) of Section 11.5 that if $\mathbf{r}_0$ is a vector in 2-space or 3-space with its initial point at the origin, then the line that passes through the terminal point of $\mathbf{r}_0$ and is parallel to the vector $\mathbf{v}$ can be expressed in vector form as

$$\mathbf{r} = \mathbf{r}_0 + t\mathbf{v}$$

In particular, if $\mathbf{r}_0$ and $\mathbf{r}_1$ are vectors in 2-space or 3-space with their initial points at the origin, then the line that passes through the terminal points of these vectors can be expressed in vector form as

$$\mathbf{r} = \mathbf{r}_0 + t(\mathbf{r}_1 - \mathbf{r}_0) \qquad \text{or} \qquad \mathbf{r} = (1 - t)\mathbf{r}_0 + t\mathbf{r}_1 \qquad (6\text{–}7)$$

as indicated in Figure 12.1.9.

It is common to call either (6) or (7) the *two-point vector form of a line* and to say, for simplicity, that the line passes through the *points* $\mathbf{r}_0$ and $\mathbf{r}_1$ (as opposed to saying that it passes through the *terminal points* of $\mathbf{r}_0$ and $\mathbf{r}_1$).

It is understood in (6) and (7) that t varies from $-\infty$ to $+\infty$. However, if we restrict t to vary over the interval $0 \le t \le 1$, then $\mathbf{r}$ will vary from $\mathbf{r}_0$ to $\mathbf{r}_1$. Thus, the equation

$$\mathbf{r} = (1 - t)\mathbf{r}_0 + t\mathbf{r}_1 \qquad (0 \le t \le 1) \qquad (8)$$

represents the line segment in 2-space or 3-space that is traced from $\mathbf{r}_0$ to $\mathbf{r}_1$.

✔ QUICK CHECK EXERCISES 12.1   *(See page 847 for answers.)*

1. (a) Express the parametric equations

$$x = \frac{1}{t}, \quad y = \sqrt{t}, \quad z = \sin^{-1} t$$

as a single vector equation of the form

$$\mathbf{r} = x(t)\mathbf{i} + y(t)\mathbf{j} + z(t)\mathbf{k}$$

(b) The vector equation in part (a) defines $\mathbf{r} = \mathbf{r}(t)$ as a vector-valued function. The domain of $\mathbf{r}(t)$ is _____ and $\mathbf{r}\left(\frac{1}{2}\right) =$ _____.

2. Describe the graph of $\mathbf{r}(t) = \langle 1 + 2t, -1 + 3t \rangle$.

3. Describe the graph of $\mathbf{r}(t) = \sin^2 t\,\mathbf{i} + \cos^2 t\,\mathbf{j}$.

4. Find a vector equation for the curve of intersection of the surfaces $y = x^2$ and $z = y$ in terms of the parameter $x = t$.

EXERCISE SET 12.1   ⌇ Graphing Utility

1–4 Find the domain of $\mathbf{r}(t)$ and the value of $\mathbf{r}(t_0)$. ■

1. $\mathbf{r}(t) = \cos t\,\mathbf{i} - 3t\,\mathbf{j}; \quad t_0 = \pi$

2. $\mathbf{r}(t) = \langle \sqrt{3t + 1}, t^2 \rangle; \quad t_0 = 1$

3. $\mathbf{r}(t) = \cos \pi t\,\mathbf{i} - \ln t\,\mathbf{j} + \sqrt{t - 2}\,\mathbf{k}; \quad t_0 = 3$

4. $\mathbf{r}(t) = \langle 2e^{-t}, \sin^{-1} t, \ln(1 - t)\rangle;\ t_0 = 0$

5–6 Express the parametric equations as a single vector equation of the form

$$\mathbf{r} = x(t)\mathbf{i} + y(t)\mathbf{j}\quad \text{or}\quad \mathbf{r} = x(t)\mathbf{i} + y(t)\mathbf{j} + z(t)\mathbf{k}\ \blacksquare$$

5. $x = 3\cos t,\ y = t + \sin t$

6. $x = 2t,\ y = 2\sin 3t,\ z = 5\cos 3t$

7–8 Find the parametric equations that correspond to the given vector equation. $\blacksquare$

7. $\mathbf{r} = 3t^2\mathbf{i} - 2\mathbf{j}$

8. $\mathbf{r} = (2t - 1)\mathbf{i} - 3\sqrt{t}\,\mathbf{j} + \sin 3t\,\mathbf{k}$

9–14 Describe the graph of the equation. $\blacksquare$

9. $\mathbf{r} = (3 - 2t)\mathbf{i} + 5t\mathbf{j}$ **10.** $\mathbf{r} = 2\sin 3t\mathbf{i} - 2\cos 3t\,\mathbf{j}$

11. $\mathbf{r} = 2t\mathbf{i} - 3\mathbf{j} + (1 + 3t)\mathbf{k}$

12. $\mathbf{r} = 3\mathbf{i} + 2\cos t\,\mathbf{j} + 2\sin t\mathbf{k}$

13. $\mathbf{r} = 2\cos t\mathbf{i} - 3\sin t\,\mathbf{j} + \mathbf{k}$

14. $\mathbf{r} = -3\mathbf{i} + (1 - t^2)\mathbf{j} + t\mathbf{k}$

15. (a) Find the slope of the line in 2-space that is represented by the vector equation $\mathbf{r} = (1 - 2t)\mathbf{i} - (2 - 3t)\mathbf{j}$.
   (b) Find the coordinates of the point where the line

$$\mathbf{r} = (2 + t)\mathbf{i} + (1 - 2t)\mathbf{j} + 3t\mathbf{k}$$

   intersects the xz-plane.

16. (a) Find the y-intercept of the line in 2-space that is represented by the vector equation $\mathbf{r} = (3 + 2t)\mathbf{i} + 5t\mathbf{j}$.
   (b) Find the coordinates of the point where the line

$$\mathbf{r} = t\mathbf{i} + (1 + 2t)\mathbf{j} - 3t\mathbf{k}$$

   intersects the plane $3x - y - z = 2$.

17–18 Sketch the line segment represented by each vector equation. $\blacksquare$

17. (a) $\mathbf{r} = (1 - t)\mathbf{i} + t\mathbf{j};\ 0 \leq t \leq 1$
   (b) $\mathbf{r} = (1 - t)(\mathbf{i} + \mathbf{j}) + t(\mathbf{i} - \mathbf{j});\ 0 \leq t \leq 1$

18. (a) $\mathbf{r} = (1 - t)(\mathbf{i} + \mathbf{j}) + t\mathbf{k};\ 0 \leq t \leq 1$
   (b) $\mathbf{r} = (1 - t)(\mathbf{i} + \mathbf{j} + \mathbf{k}) + t(\mathbf{i} + \mathbf{j});\ 0 \leq t \leq 1$

19–20 Write a vector equation for the line segment from P to Q. $\blacksquare$

19.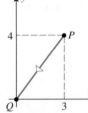

20.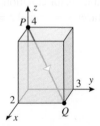

21–30 Sketch the graph of $\mathbf{r}(t)$ and show the direction of increasing t. $\blacksquare$

21. $\mathbf{r}(t) = 2\mathbf{i} + t\mathbf{j}$ **22.** $\mathbf{r}(t) = \langle 3t - 4, 6t + 2\rangle$

23. $\mathbf{r}(t) = (1 + \cos t)\mathbf{i} + (3 - \sin t)\mathbf{j};\ 0 \leq t \leq 2\pi$

24. $\mathbf{r}(t) = \langle 2\cos t, 5\sin t\rangle;\ 0 \leq t \leq 2\pi$

25. $\mathbf{r}(t) = \cosh t\mathbf{i} + \sinh t\mathbf{j}$ **26.** $\mathbf{r}(t) = \sqrt{t}\,\mathbf{i} + (2t + 4)\mathbf{j}$

27. $\mathbf{r}(t) = 2\cos t\mathbf{i} + 2\sin t\mathbf{j} + t\mathbf{k}$

28. $\mathbf{r}(t) = 9\cos t\mathbf{i} + 4\sin t\mathbf{j} + t\mathbf{k}$

29. $\mathbf{r}(t) = t\mathbf{i} + t^2\mathbf{j} + 2\mathbf{k}$

30. $\mathbf{r}(t) = t\mathbf{i} + t\mathbf{j} + \sin t\mathbf{k};\ 0 \leq t \leq 2\pi$

31–34 True–False Determine whether the statement is true or false. Explain your answer. $\blacksquare$

31. The natural domain of a vector-valued function is the union of the domains of its component functions.

32. If $\mathbf{r}(t) = \langle x(t), y(t)\rangle$ is a vector-valued function in 2-space, then the graph of $\mathbf{r}(t)$ is a surface in 3-space.

33. If $\mathbf{r}_0$ and $\mathbf{r}_1$ are vectors in 3-space, then the graph of the vector-valued function

$$\mathbf{r}(t) = (1 - t)\mathbf{r}_0 + t\mathbf{r}_1 \quad (0 \leq t \leq 1)$$

is the straight line segment joining the terminal points of $\mathbf{r}_0$ and $\mathbf{r}_1$.

34. The graph of $\mathbf{r}(t) = \langle 2\cos t, 2\sin t, t\rangle$ is a circular helix.

$\sim$ **35–36** Sketch the curve of intersection of the surfaces, and find parametric equations for the intersection in terms of parameter $x = t$. Check your work with a graphing utility by generating the parametric curve over the interval $-1 \leq t \leq 1$. $\blacksquare$

35. $z = x^2 + y^2,\ x - y = 0$

36. $y + x = 0,\ z = \sqrt{2 - x^2 - y^2}$

37–38 Sketch the curve of intersection of the surfaces, and find a vector equation for the curve in terms of the parameter $x = t$. $\blacksquare$

37. $9x^2 + y^2 + 9z^2 = 81,\ y = x^2 \quad (z > 0)$

38. $y = x,\ x + y + z = 1$

39. Show that the graph of

$$\mathbf{r} = t\sin t\mathbf{i} + t\cos t\mathbf{j} + t^2\mathbf{k}$$

lies on the paraboloid $z = x^2 + y^2$.

40. Show that the graph of

$$\mathbf{r} = t\mathbf{i} + \frac{1 + t}{t}\mathbf{j} + \frac{1 - t^2}{t}\mathbf{k}, \quad t > 0$$

lies in the plane $x - y + z + 1 = 0$.

FOCUS ON CONCEPTS

41. Show that the graph of

$$\mathbf{r} = \sin t\mathbf{i} + 2\cos t\mathbf{j} + \sqrt{3}\sin t\mathbf{k}$$

is a circle, and find its center and radius. [*Hint:* Show that the curve lies on both a sphere and a plane.]

42. Show that the graph of
$$\mathbf{r} = 3\cos t\,\mathbf{i} + 3\sin t\,\mathbf{j} + 3\sin t\,\mathbf{k}$$
is an ellipse, and find the lengths of the major and minor axes. [*Hint:* Show that the graph lies on both a circular cylinder and a plane and use the result in Exercise 42 of Section 10.4.]

43. For the helix $\mathbf{r} = a\cos t\,\mathbf{i} + a\sin t\,\mathbf{j} + ct\,\mathbf{k}$, find the value of c $(c > 0)$ so that the helix will make one complete turn in a distance of 3 units measured along the z-axis.

44. How many revolutions will the circular helix
$$\mathbf{r} = a\cos t\,\mathbf{i} + a\sin t\,\mathbf{j} + 0.2t\,\mathbf{k}$$
make in a distance of 10 units measured along the z-axis?

45. Show that the curve $\mathbf{r} = t\cos t\,\mathbf{i} + t\sin t\,\mathbf{j} + t\,\mathbf{k}$, $t \geq 0$, lies on the cone $z = \sqrt{x^2 + y^2}$. Describe the curve.

46. Describe the curve $\mathbf{r} = a\cos t\,\mathbf{i} + b\sin t\,\mathbf{j} + ct\,\mathbf{k}$, where a, b, and c are positive constants such that $a \neq b$.

47. In each part, match the vector equation with one of the accompanying graphs, and explain your reasoning.
(a) $\mathbf{r} = t\mathbf{i} - t\mathbf{j} + \sqrt{2 - t^2}\,\mathbf{k}$
(b) $\mathbf{r} = \sin \pi t\,\mathbf{i} - t\mathbf{j} + t\mathbf{k}$
(c) $\mathbf{r} = \sin t\,\mathbf{i} + \cos t\,\mathbf{j} + \sin 2t\,\mathbf{k}$
(d) $\mathbf{r} = \frac{1}{2}t\mathbf{i} + \cos 3t\,\mathbf{j} + \sin 3t\,\mathbf{k}$

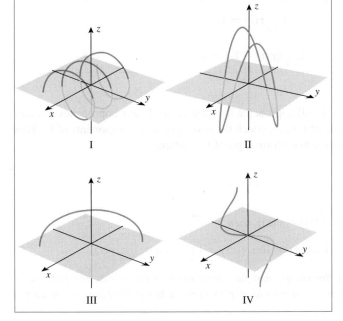

I

II

III

IV

48. Check your conclusions in Exercise 47 by generating the curves with a graphing utility. [*Note:* Your graphing utility may look at the curve from a different viewpoint. Read the documentation for your graphing utility to determine how to control the viewpoint, and see if you can generate a reasonable facsimile of the graphs shown in the figure by adjusting the viewpoint and choosing the interval of t-values appropriately.]

49. (a) Find parametric equations for the curve of intersection of the circular cylinder $x^2 + y^2 = 9$ and the parabolic cylinder $z = x^2$ in terms of a parameter t for which $x = 3\cos t$.
(b) Use a graphing utility to generate the curve of intersection in part (a).

50. (a) Sketch the graph of
$$\mathbf{r}(t) = \left\langle 2t, \frac{2}{1 + t^2}\right\rangle$$
(b) Prove that the curve in part (a) is also the graph of the function
$$y = \frac{8}{4 + x^2}$$
[The graphs of $y = a^3/(a^2 + x^2)$, where a denotes a constant, were first studied by the French mathematician Pierre de Fermat, and later by the Italian mathematicians Guido Grandi and Maria Agnesi. Any such curve is now known as a "witch of Agnesi." There are a number of theories for the origin of this name. Some suggest there was a mistranslation by either Grandi or Agnesi of some less colorful Latin name into Italian. Others lay the blame on a translation into English of Agnesi's 1748 treatise, *Analytical Institutions*.]

51. Writing Consider the curve C of intersection of the cone $z = \sqrt{x^2 + y^2}$ and the plane $z = y + 2$. Sketch and identify the curve C, and describe a procedure for finding a vector-valued function $\mathbf{r}(t)$ whose graph is C.

52. Writing Suppose that $\mathbf{r}_1(t)$ and $\mathbf{r}_2(t)$ are vector-valued functions in 2-space. Explain why solving the equation $\mathbf{r}_1(t) = \mathbf{r}_2(t)$ may not produce all of the points where the graphs of these functions intersect.

✔ QUICK CHECK ANSWERS 12.1

1. (a) $\mathbf{r} = \dfrac{1}{t}\mathbf{i} + \sqrt{t}\mathbf{j} + \sin^{-1} t\,\mathbf{k}$ (b) $0 < t \leq 1$; $2\mathbf{i} + \dfrac{\sqrt{2}}{2}\mathbf{j} + \dfrac{\pi}{6}\mathbf{k}$ **2.** The graph is a line through $(1, -1)$ with direction vector $2\mathbf{i} + 3\mathbf{j}$. **3.** The graph is the line segment in the xy-plane from $(0, 1)$ to $(1, 0)$. **4.** $\mathbf{r} = \langle t, t^2, t^2\rangle$

12.2 CALCULUS OF VECTOR-VALUED FUNCTIONS

In this section we will define limits, derivatives, and integrals of vector-valued functions and discuss their properties.

■ LIMITS AND CONTINUITY

Our first goal in this section is to develop a notion of what it means for a vector-valued function $\mathbf{r}(t)$ in 2-space or 3-space to approach a limiting vector $\mathbf{L}$ as t approaches a number a. That is, we want to define

$$\lim_{t \to a} \mathbf{r}(t) = \mathbf{L} \tag{1}$$

One way to motivate a reasonable definition of (1) is to position $\mathbf{r}(t)$ and $\mathbf{L}$ with their initial points at the origin and interpret this limit to mean that the terminal point of $\mathbf{r}(t)$ approaches the terminal point of $\mathbf{L}$ as t approaches a or, equivalently, that the vector $\mathbf{r}(t)$ approaches the vector $\mathbf{L}$ in both length and direction at t approaches a (Figure 12.2.1). Algebraically, this is equivalent to stating that

$$\lim_{t \to a} \|\mathbf{r}(t) - \mathbf{L}\| = 0 \tag{2}$$

(Figure 12.2.2). Thus, we make the following definition.

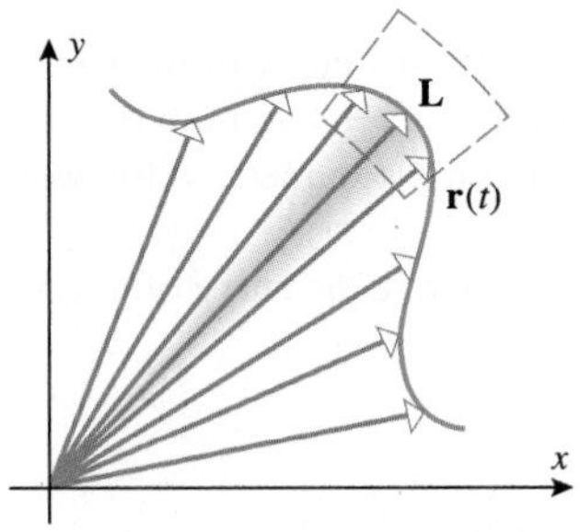

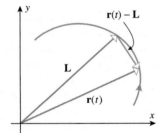

$\mathbf{r}(t)$ approaches $\mathbf{L}$ in length and direction if $\lim_{t \to a} \mathbf{r}(t) = \mathbf{L}$.

▲ **Figure 12.2.1**

$\|\mathbf{r}(t) - \mathbf{L}\|$ is the distance between terminal points for vectors $\mathbf{r}(t)$ and $\mathbf{L}$ when positioned with the same initial points.

▲ **Figure 12.2.2**

Note that $\|\mathbf{r}(t) - \mathbf{L}\|$ is a real number for each value of t, so even though this expression involves a vector-valued function, the limit

$$\lim_{t \to a} \|\mathbf{r}(t) - \mathbf{L}\|$$

is an ordinary limit of a real-valued function.

12.2.1 DEFINITION Let $\mathbf{r}(t)$ be a vector-valued function that is defined for all t in some open interval containing the number a, except that $\mathbf{r}(t)$ need not be defined at a. We will write

$$\lim_{t \to a} \mathbf{r}(t) = \mathbf{L}$$

if and only if

$$\lim_{t \to a} \|\mathbf{r}(t) - \mathbf{L}\| = 0$$

It is clear intuitively that $\mathbf{r}(t)$ will approach a limiting vector $\mathbf{L}$ as t approaches a if and only if the component functions of $\mathbf{r}(t)$ approach the corresponding components of $\mathbf{L}$. This suggests the following theorem, whose formal proof is omitted.

12.2.2 THEOREM

(a) If $\mathbf{r}(t) = \langle x(t), y(t) \rangle = x(t)\mathbf{i} + y(t)\mathbf{j}$, *then*

$$\lim_{t \to a} \mathbf{r}(t) = \left\langle \lim_{t \to a} x(t), \lim_{t \to a} y(t) \right\rangle = \lim_{t \to a} x(t)\mathbf{i} + \lim_{t \to a} y(t)\mathbf{j}$$

provided the limits of the component functions exist. Conversely, the limits of the component functions exist provided $\mathbf{r}(t)$ *approaches a limiting vector as t approaches a.*

(b) If $\mathbf{r}(t) = \langle x(t), y(t), z(t) \rangle = x(t)\mathbf{i} + y(t)\mathbf{j} + z(t)\mathbf{k}$, *then*

$$\lim_{t \to a} \mathbf{r}(t) = \left\langle \lim_{t \to a} x(t), \lim_{t \to a} y(t), \lim_{t \to a} z(t) \right\rangle$$

$$= \lim_{t \to a} x(t)\mathbf{i} + \lim_{t \to a} y(t)\mathbf{j} + \lim_{t \to a} z(t)\mathbf{k}$$

provided the limits of the component functions exist. Conversely, the limits of the component functions exist provided $\mathbf{r}(t)$ *approaches a limiting vector as t approaches a.*

How would you define the one-sided limits

$$\lim_{t \to a^+} \mathbf{r}(t) \quad \text{and} \quad \lim_{t \to a^-} \mathbf{r}(t)?$$

Limits of vector-valued functions have many of the same properties as limits of real-valued functions. For example, assuming that the limits exist, the limit of a sum is the sum of the limits, the limit of a difference is the difference of the limits, and a constant scalar factor can be moved through a limit symbol.

▶ **Example 1** Let $\mathbf{r}(t) = t^2\mathbf{i} + e^t\mathbf{j} - (2\cos \pi t)\mathbf{k}$. Then

$$\lim_{t \to 0} \mathbf{r}(t) = \left(\lim_{t \to 0} t^2\right)\mathbf{i} + \left(\lim_{t \to 0} e^t\right)\mathbf{j} - \left(\lim_{t \to 0} 2\cos \pi t\right)\mathbf{k} = \mathbf{j} - 2\mathbf{k}$$

Alternatively, using the angle bracket notation for vectors,

$$\lim_{t \to 0} \mathbf{r}(t) = \lim_{t \to 0}\langle t^2, e^t, -2\cos \pi t\rangle = \left\langle \lim_{t \to 0} t^2, \lim_{t \to 0} e^t, \lim_{t \to 0}(-2\cos \pi t)\right\rangle = \langle 0, 1, -2\rangle \quad ◀$$

Motivated by the definition of continuity for real-valued functions, we define a vector-valued function $\mathbf{r}(t)$ to be ***continuous*** at $t = a$ if

$$\lim_{t \to a} \mathbf{r}(t) = \mathbf{r}(a) \tag{3}$$

That is, $\mathbf{r}(a)$ is defined, the limit of $\mathbf{r}(t)$ as $t \to a$ exists, and the two are equal. As in the case for real-valued functions, we say that $\mathbf{r}(t)$ is ***continuous on an interval*** I if it is continuous at each point of I [with the understanding that at an endpoint in I the two-sided limit in (3) is replaced by the appropriate one-sided limit]. It follows from Theorem 12.2.2 that a vector-valued function is continuous at $t = a$ if and only if its component functions are continuous at $t = a$.

■ DERIVATIVES

The derivative of a vector-valued function is defined by a limit similar to that for the derivative of a real-valued function.

12.2.3 DEFINITION If $\mathbf{r}(t)$ is a vector-valued function, we define the ***derivative of*** $\mathbf{r}$ ***with respect to*** t to be the vector-valued function $\mathbf{r}'$ given by

$$\mathbf{r}'(t) = \lim_{h \to 0} \frac{\mathbf{r}(t + h) - \mathbf{r}(t)}{h} \tag{4}$$

The domain of $\mathbf{r}'$ consists of all values of t in the domain of $\mathbf{r}(t)$ for which the limit exists.

The function $\mathbf{r}(t)$ is ***differentiable*** at t if the limit in (4) exists. All of the standard notations for derivatives continue to apply. For example, the derivative of $\mathbf{r}(t)$ can be expressed as

$$\frac{d}{dt}[\mathbf{r}(t)], \quad \frac{d\mathbf{r}}{dt}, \quad \mathbf{r}'(t), \quad \text{or} \quad \mathbf{r}'$$

It is important to keep in mind that $\mathbf{r}'(t)$ is a vector, not a number, and hence has a magnitude and a direction for each value of t [except if $\mathbf{r}'(t) = \mathbf{0}$, in which case $\mathbf{r}'(t)$ has magnitude zero but no specific direction]. In the next section we will consider the significance of the magnitude of $\mathbf{r}'(t)$, but for now our goal is to obtain a geometric interpretation of the direction of $\mathbf{r}'(t)$. For this purpose, consider parts (*a*) and (*b*) of Figure 12.2.3. These illustrations show the graph C of $\mathbf{r}(t)$ (with its orientation) and the vectors $\mathbf{r}(t)$, $\mathbf{r}(t + h)$, and $\mathbf{r}(t + h) - \mathbf{r}(t)$ for positive h and for negative h. In both cases, the vector $\mathbf{r}(t + h) - \mathbf{r}(t)$ runs along the secant line joining the terminal points of $\mathbf{r}(t + h)$ and $\mathbf{r}(t)$, but with opposite directions in the two cases. In the case where h is positive the vector $\mathbf{r}(t + h) - \mathbf{r}(t)$ points in the direction of increasing parameter, and in the case where h is

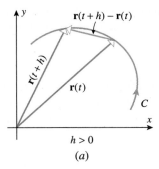

$h > 0$

(*a*)

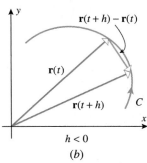

$h < 0$

(*b*)

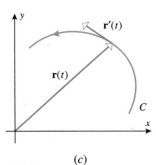

(*c*)

▲ **Figure 12.2.3**

negative it points in the opposite direction. However, in the case where h is negative the direction gets reversed when we multiply by $1/h$, so in both cases the vector

$$\frac{1}{h}[\mathbf{r}(t+h) - \mathbf{r}(t)] = \frac{\mathbf{r}(t+h) - \mathbf{r}(t)}{h}$$

points in the direction of increasing parameter and runs along the secant line. As $h \to 0$, the secant line approaches the tangent line at the terminal point of $\mathbf{r}(t)$, so we can conclude that the limit

$$\mathbf{r}'(t) = \lim_{h \to 0} \frac{\mathbf{r}(t+h) - \mathbf{r}(t)}{h}$$

(if it exists and is nonzero) is a vector that is tangent to the curve C at the tip of $\mathbf{r}(t)$ and points in the direction of increasing parameter (Figure 12.2.3c).

We can summarize all of this as follows.

12.2.4   GEOMETRIC INTERPRETATION OF THE DERIVATIVE   Suppose that C is the graph of a vector-valued function $\mathbf{r}(t)$ in 2-space or 3-space and that $\mathbf{r}'(t)$ exists and is nonzero for a given value of t. If the vector $\mathbf{r}'(t)$ is positioned with its initial point at the terminal point of the radius vector $\mathbf{r}(t)$, then $\mathbf{r}'(t)$ is tangent to C and points in the direction of increasing parameter.

Since limits of vector-valued functions can be computed componentwise, it seems reasonable that we should be able to compute derivatives in terms of component functions as well. This is the result of the next theorem.

12.2.5   THEOREM   *If $\mathbf{r}(t)$ is a vector-valued function, then $\mathbf{r}$ is differentiable at t if and only if each of its component functions is differentiable at t, in which case the component functions of $\mathbf{r}'(t)$ are the derivatives of the corresponding component functions of $\mathbf{r}(t)$.*

PROOF   For simplicity, we give the proof in 2-space; the proof in 3-space is identical, except for the additional component. Assume that $\mathbf{r}(t) = x(t)\mathbf{i} + y(t)\mathbf{j}$. Then

$$\mathbf{r}'(t) = \lim_{h \to 0} \frac{\mathbf{r}(t+h) - \mathbf{r}(t)}{h}$$

$$= \lim_{h \to 0} \frac{[x(t+h)\mathbf{i} + y(t+h)\mathbf{j}] - [x(t)\mathbf{i} + y(t)\mathbf{j}]}{h}$$

$$= \left(\lim_{h \to 0} \frac{x(t+h) - x(t)}{h} \right)\mathbf{i} + \left(\lim_{h \to 0} \frac{y(t+h) - y(t)}{h} \right)\mathbf{j}$$

$$= x'(t)\mathbf{i} + y'_\ast(t)\mathbf{j} \quad \blacksquare$$

▶ **Example 2**   Let $\mathbf{r}(t) = t^2\mathbf{i} + e^t\mathbf{j} - (2\cos \pi t)\mathbf{k}$. Then

$$\mathbf{r}'(t) = \frac{d}{dt}(t^2)\mathbf{i} + \frac{d}{dt}(e^t)\mathbf{j} - \frac{d}{dt}(2\cos \pi t)\mathbf{k}$$

$$= 2t\mathbf{i} + e^t\mathbf{j} + (2\pi \sin \pi t)\mathbf{k} \quad \blacktriangleleft$$

■ **DERIVATIVE RULES**

Many of the rules for differentiating real-valued functions have analogs in the context of differentiating vector-valued functions. We state some of these in the following theorem.

12.2.6 THEOREM (*Rules of Differentiation*) *Let* $\mathbf{r}(t)$, $\mathbf{r}_1(t)$, *and* $\mathbf{r}_2(t)$ *be differentiable vector-valued functions that are all in 2-space or all in 3-space, and let* $f(t)$ *be a differentiable real-valued function, k a scalar, and* $\mathbf{c}$ *a constant vector (that is, a vector whose value does not depend on t). Then the following rules of differentiation hold:*

(a) $\dfrac{d}{dt}[\mathbf{c}] = \mathbf{0}$

(b) $\dfrac{d}{dt}[k\mathbf{r}(t)] = k\dfrac{d}{dt}[\mathbf{r}(t)]$

(c) $\dfrac{d}{dt}[\mathbf{r}_1(t) + \mathbf{r}_2(t)] = \dfrac{d}{dt}[\mathbf{r}_1(t)] + \dfrac{d}{dt}[\mathbf{r}_2(t)]$

(d) $\dfrac{d}{dt}[\mathbf{r}_1(t) - \mathbf{r}_2(t)] = \dfrac{d}{dt}[\mathbf{r}_1(t)] - \dfrac{d}{dt}[\mathbf{r}_2(t)]$

(e) $\dfrac{d}{dt}[f(t)\mathbf{r}(t)] = f(t)\dfrac{d}{dt}[\mathbf{r}(t)] + \dfrac{d}{dt}[f(t)]\mathbf{r}(t)$

The proofs of most of these rules are immediate consequences of Definition 12.2.3, although the last rule can be seen more easily by application of the product rule for real-valued functions to the component functions. The proof of Theorem 12.2.6 is left as an exercise.

■ TANGENT LINES TO GRAPHS OF VECTOR-VALUED FUNCTIONS

Motivated by the discussion of the geometric interpretation of the derivative of a vector-valued function, we make the following definition.

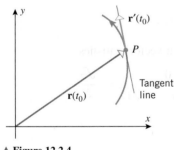

▲ **Figure 12.2.4**

12.2.7 DEFINITION Let P be a point on the graph of a vector-valued function $\mathbf{r}(t)$, and let $\mathbf{r}(t_0)$ be the radius vector from the origin to P (Figure 12.2.4). If $\mathbf{r}'(t_0)$ exists and $\mathbf{r}'(t_0) \neq \mathbf{0}$, then we call $\mathbf{r}'(t_0)$ a *tangent vector* to the graph of $\mathbf{r}(t)$ at $\mathbf{r}(t_0)$, and we call the line through P that is parallel to the tangent vector the *tangent line* to the graph of $\mathbf{r}(t)$ at $\mathbf{r}(t_0)$.

Let $\mathbf{r}_0 = \mathbf{r}(t_0)$ and $\mathbf{v}_0 = \mathbf{r}'(t_0)$. It follows from Formula (9) of Section 11.5 that the tangent line to the graph of $\mathbf{r}(t)$ at $\mathbf{r}_0$ is given by the vector equation

$$\mathbf{r} = \mathbf{r}_0 + t\mathbf{v}_0 \qquad (5)$$

▶ **Example 3** Find parametric equations of the tangent line to the circular helix

$$x = \cos t, \quad y = \sin t, \quad z = t$$

where $t = t_0$, and use that result to find parametric equations for the tangent line at the point where $t = \pi$.

Solution. The vector equation of the helix is

$$\mathbf{r}(t) = \cos t\,\mathbf{i} + \sin t\,\mathbf{j} + t\mathbf{k}$$

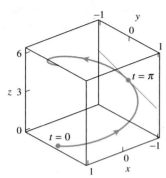

▲ **Figure 12.2.5**

so we have

$$\mathbf{r}_0 = \mathbf{r}(t_0) = \cos t_0\mathbf{i} + \sin t_0\mathbf{j} + t_0\mathbf{k}$$

$$\mathbf{v}_0 = \mathbf{r}'(t_0) = (-\sin t_0)\mathbf{i} + \cos t_0\mathbf{j} + \mathbf{k}$$

It follows from (5) that the vector equation of the tangent line at $t = t_0$ is

$$\mathbf{r} = \cos t_0\mathbf{i} + \sin t_0\mathbf{j} + t_0\mathbf{k} + t[(-\sin t_0)\mathbf{i} + \cos t_0\mathbf{j} + \mathbf{k}]$$

$$= (\cos t_0 - t \sin t_0)\mathbf{i} + (\sin t_0 + t \cos t_0)\mathbf{j} + (t_0 + t)\mathbf{k}$$

Thus, the parametric equations of the tangent line at $t = t_0$ are

$$x = \cos t_0 - t \sin t_0, \quad y = \sin t_0 + t \cos t_0, \quad z = t_0 + t$$

In particular, the tangent line at the point where $t = \pi$ has parametric equations

$$x = -1, \quad y = -t, \quad z = \pi + t$$

The graph of the helix and this tangent line are shown in Figure 12.2.5. ◄

▶ **Example 4** Let

$$\mathbf{r}_1(t) = (\tan^{-1} t)\mathbf{i} + (\sin t)\mathbf{j} + t^2\mathbf{k}$$

and

$$\mathbf{r}_2(t) = (t^2 - t)\mathbf{i} + (2t - 2)\mathbf{j} + (\ln t)\mathbf{k}$$

The graphs of $\mathbf{r}_1(t)$ and $\mathbf{r}_2(t)$ intersect at the origin. Find the degree measure of the acute angle between the tangent lines to the graphs of $\mathbf{r}_1(t)$ and $\mathbf{r}_2(t)$ at the origin.

Solution. The graph of $\mathbf{r}_1(t)$ passes through the origin at $t = 0$, where its tangent vector is

$$\mathbf{r}_1'(0) = \left\langle \frac{1}{1 + t^2}, \cos t, 2t \right\rangle \bigg|_{t=0} = \langle 1, 1, 0 \rangle$$

The graph of $\mathbf{r}_2(t)$ passes through the origin at $t = 1$ (verify), where its tangent vector is

$$\mathbf{r}_2'(1) = \left\langle 2t - 1, 2, \frac{1}{t} \right\rangle \bigg|_{t=1} = \langle 1, 2, 1 \rangle$$

By Theorem 11.3.3, the angle θ between these two tangent vectors satisfies

$$\cos\theta = \frac{\langle 1, 1, 0 \rangle \cdot \langle 1, 2, 1 \rangle}{\|\langle 1, 1, 0 \rangle\| \, \|\langle 1, 2, 1 \rangle\|} = \frac{1 + 2 + 0}{\sqrt{2}\sqrt{6}} = \frac{3}{\sqrt{12}} = \frac{\sqrt{3}}{2}$$

It follows that $\theta = \pi/6$ radians, or 30°. ◄

■ **DERIVATIVES OF DOT AND CROSS PRODUCTS**

The following rules, which are derived in the exercises, provide a method for differentiating dot products in 2-space and 3-space and cross products in 3-space.

Note that in (6) the order of the factors in each term on the right does not matter, but in (7) it does.

$$\frac{d}{dt}[\mathbf{r}_1(t) \cdot \mathbf{r}_2(t)] = \mathbf{r}_1(t) \cdot \frac{d\mathbf{r}_2}{dt} + \frac{d\mathbf{r}_1}{dt} \cdot \mathbf{r}_2(t) \tag{6}$$

$$\frac{d}{dt}[\mathbf{r}_1(t) \times \mathbf{r}_2(t)] = \mathbf{r}_1(t) \times \frac{d\mathbf{r}_2}{dt} + \frac{d\mathbf{r}_1}{dt} \times \mathbf{r}_2(t) \tag{7}$$

In plane geometry one learns that a tangent line to a circle is perpendicular to the radius at the point of tangency. Consequently, if a point moves along a circle in 2-space that is centered at the origin, then one would expect the radius vector and the tangent vector at any point on the circle to be orthogonal. This is the motivation for the following useful theorem, which is applicable in both 2-space and 3-space.

12.2.8   THEOREM   *If $\mathbf{r}(t)$ is a differentiable vector-valued function in 2-space or 3-space and $\|\mathbf{r}(t)\|$ is constant for all t, then*

$$\mathbf{r}(t) \cdot \mathbf{r}'(t) = 0 \qquad (8)$$

that is, $\mathbf{r}(t)$ and $\mathbf{r}'(t)$ are orthogonal vectors for all t.

PROOF   It follows from (6) with $\mathbf{r}_1(t) = \mathbf{r}_2(t) = \mathbf{r}(t)$ that

$$\frac{d}{dt}[\mathbf{r}(t) \cdot \mathbf{r}(t)] = \mathbf{r}(t) \cdot \frac{d\mathbf{r}}{dt} + \frac{d\mathbf{r}}{dt} \cdot \mathbf{r}(t)$$

or, equivalently,

$$\frac{d}{dt}[\|\mathbf{r}(t)\|^2] = 2\mathbf{r}(t) \cdot \frac{d\mathbf{r}}{dt} \qquad (9)$$

But $\|\mathbf{r}(t)\|^2$ is constant, so its derivative is zero. Thus

$$2\mathbf{r}(t) \cdot \frac{d\mathbf{r}}{dt} = 0$$

from which (8) follows. ■

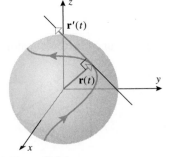

▲ **Figure 12.2.6**

▶ **Example 5**   Just as a tangent line to a circle in 2-space is perpendicular to the radius at the point of tangency, so a tangent vector to a curve on the surface of a sphere in 3-space that is centered at the origin is orthogonal to the radius vector at the point of tangency (Figure 12.2.6). To see that this is so, suppose that the graph of $\mathbf{r}(t)$ lies on the surface of a sphere of positive radius k centered at the origin. For each value of t we have $\|\mathbf{r}(t)\| = k$, so by Theorem 12.2.8

$$\mathbf{r}(t) \cdot \mathbf{r}'(t) = 0$$

and hence the radius vector $\mathbf{r}(t)$ and the tangent vector $\mathbf{r}'(t)$ are orthogonal. ◀

■ DEFINITE INTEGRALS OF VECTOR-VALUED FUNCTIONS

If $\mathbf{r}(t)$ is a vector-valued function that is continuous on the interval $a \le t \le b$, then we define the ***definite integral*** of $\mathbf{r}(t)$ over this interval as a limit of Riemann sums, just as in Definition 5.5.1, except here the integrand is a vector-valued function. Specifically, we define

$$\int_a^b \mathbf{r}(t)\, dt = \lim_{\max \Delta t_k \to 0} \sum_{k=1}^n \mathbf{r}(t_k^*) \Delta t_k \qquad (10)$$

It follows from (10) that the definite integral of $\mathbf{r}(t)$ over the interval $a \le t \le b$ can be expressed as a vector whose components are the definite integrals of the component functions of $\mathbf{r}(t)$. For example, if $\mathbf{r}(t) = x(t)\mathbf{i} + y(t)\mathbf{j}$, then

$$\int_a^b \mathbf{r}(t)\, dt = \lim_{\max \Delta t_k \to 0} \sum_{k=1}^n \mathbf{r}(t_k^*) \Delta t_k$$

$$= \lim_{\max \Delta t_k \to 0} \left[\left(\sum_{k=1}^n x(t_k^*) \Delta t_k \right) \mathbf{i} + \left(\sum_{k=1}^n y(t_k^*) \Delta t_k \right) \mathbf{j} \right]$$

$$= \left(\lim_{\max \Delta t_k \to 0} \sum_{k=1}^n x(t_k^*) \Delta t_k \right) \mathbf{i} + \left(\lim_{\max \Delta t_k \to 0} \sum_{k=1}^n y(t_k^*) \Delta t_k \right) \mathbf{j}$$

$$= \left(\int_a^b x(t)\, dt \right) \mathbf{i} + \left(\int_a^b y(t)\, dt \right) \mathbf{j}$$

Rewrite Formulas (11) and (12) in bracket notation with

$$\mathbf{r}(t) = \langle x(t), y(t) \rangle$$

and

$$\mathbf{r}(t) = \langle x(t), y(t), z(t) \rangle$$

respectively.

In general, we have

$$\int_a^b \mathbf{r}(t)\,dt = \left(\int_a^b x(t)\,dt \right)\mathbf{i} + \left(\int_a^b y(t)\,dt \right)\mathbf{j} \qquad \boxed{\text{2-space}} \qquad (11)$$

$$\int_a^b \mathbf{r}(t)\,dt = \left(\int_a^b x(t)\,dt \right)\mathbf{i} + \left(\int_a^b y(t)\,dt \right)\mathbf{j} + \left(\int_a^b z(t)\,dt \right)\mathbf{k} \qquad \boxed{\text{3-space}} \qquad (12)$$

▶ **Example 6**   Let $\mathbf{r}(t) = t^2\mathbf{i} + e^t\mathbf{j} - (2\cos \pi t)\mathbf{k}$. Then

$$\int_0^1 \mathbf{r}(t)\,dt = \left(\int_0^1 t^2\,dt \right)\mathbf{i} + \left(\int_0^1 e^t\,dt \right)\mathbf{j} - \left(\int_0^1 2\cos \pi t\,dt \right)\mathbf{k}$$

$$= \frac{t^3}{3}\bigg]_0^1 \mathbf{i} + e^t\bigg]_0^1 \mathbf{j} - \frac{2}{\pi}\sin \pi t\bigg]_0^1 \mathbf{k} = \frac{1}{3}\mathbf{i} + (e-1)\mathbf{j} \ \blacktriangleleft$$

■ **RULES OF INTEGRATION**

As with differentiation, many of the rules for integrating real-valued functions have analogs for vector-valued functions.

12.2.9   **THEOREM** (*Rules of Integration*)   *Let $\mathbf{r}(t)$, $\mathbf{r}_1(t)$, and $\mathbf{r}_2(t)$ be vector-valued functions in 2-space or 3-space that are continuous on the interval $a \le t \le b$, and let k be a scalar. Then the following rules of integration hold:*

(a) $\displaystyle \int_a^b k\mathbf{r}(t)\,dt = k \int_a^b \mathbf{r}(t)\,dt$

(b) $\displaystyle \int_a^b [\mathbf{r}_1(t) + \mathbf{r}_2(t)]\,dt = \int_a^b \mathbf{r}_1(t)\,dt + \int_a^b \mathbf{r}_2(t)\,dt$

(c) $\displaystyle \int_a^b [\mathbf{r}_1(t) - \mathbf{r}_2(t)]\,dt = \int_a^b \mathbf{r}_1(t)\,dt - \int_a^b \mathbf{r}_2(t)\,dt$

We omit the proof.

■ **ANTIDERIVATIVES OF VECTOR-VALUED FUNCTIONS**

An **antiderivative** for a vector-valued function $\mathbf{r}(t)$ is a vector-valued function $\mathbf{R}(t)$ such that

$$\mathbf{R}'(t) = \mathbf{r}(t) \qquad (13)$$

As in Chapter 5, we express Equation (13) using integral notation as

$$\int \mathbf{r}(t)\,dt = \mathbf{R}(t) + \mathbf{C} \qquad (14)$$

where $\mathbf{C}$ represents an arbitrary constant *vector*.

Since differentiation of vector-valued functions can be performed componentwise, it follows that antidifferentiation can be done this way as well. This is illustrated in the next example.

▶ **Example 7**

$$\int (2t\mathbf{i} + 3t^2\mathbf{j})\,dt = \left(\int 2t\,dt\right)\mathbf{i} + \left(\int 3t^2\,dt\right)\mathbf{j}$$

$$= (t^2 + C_1)\mathbf{i} + (t^3 + C_2)\mathbf{j}$$

$$= (t^2\mathbf{i} + t^3\mathbf{j}) + (C_1\mathbf{i} + C_2\mathbf{j}) = (t^2\mathbf{i} + t^3\mathbf{j}) + \mathbf{C}$$

where $\mathbf{C} = C_1\mathbf{i} + C_2\mathbf{j}$ is an arbitrary vector constant of integration. ◀

Most of the familiar integration properties have vector counterparts. For example, vector differentiation and integration are inverse operations in the sense that

$$\frac{d}{dt}\left[\int \mathbf{r}(t)\,dt\right] = \mathbf{r}(t) \qquad \text{and} \qquad \int \mathbf{r}'(t)\,dt = \mathbf{r}(t) + \mathbf{C} \tag{15--16}$$

Moreover, if $\mathbf{R}(t)$ is an antiderivative of $\mathbf{r}(t)$ on an interval containing $t = a$ and $t = b$, then we have the following vector form of the Fundamental Theorem of Calculus:

$$\int_a^b \mathbf{r}(t)\,dt = \mathbf{R}(t)\Big]_a^b = \mathbf{R}(b) - \mathbf{R}(a) \tag{17}$$

▶ **Example 8**   Evaluate the definite integral $\displaystyle\int_0^2 (2t\mathbf{i} + 3t^2\mathbf{j})\,dt$.

Solution.   Integrating the components yields

$$\int_0^2 (2t\mathbf{i} + 3t^2\mathbf{j})\,dt = t^2\Big]_0^2 \mathbf{i} + t^3\Big]_0^2 \mathbf{j} = 4\mathbf{i} + 8\mathbf{j}$$

Alternative Solution.   The function $\mathbf{R}(t) = t^2\mathbf{i} + t^3\mathbf{j}$ is an antiderivative of the integrand since $\mathbf{R}'(t) = 2t\mathbf{i} + 3t^2\mathbf{j}$. Thus, it follows from (17) that

$$\int_0^2 (2t\mathbf{i} + 3t^2\mathbf{j})\,dt = \mathbf{R}(t)\Big]_0^2 = t^2\mathbf{i} + t^3\mathbf{j}\Big]_0^2 = (4\mathbf{i} + 8\mathbf{j}) - (0\mathbf{i} + 0\mathbf{j}) = 4\mathbf{i} + 8\mathbf{j} \quad ◀$$

▶ **Example 9**   Find $\mathbf{r}(t)$ given that $\mathbf{r}'(t) = \langle 3, 2t\rangle$ and $\mathbf{r}(1) = \langle 2, 5\rangle$.

Solution.   Integrating $\mathbf{r}'(t)$ to obtain $\mathbf{r}(t)$ yields

$$\mathbf{r}(t) = \int \mathbf{r}'(t)\,dt = \int \langle 3, 2t\rangle\,dt = \langle 3t, t^2\rangle + \mathbf{C}$$

where $\mathbf{C}$ is a vector constant of integration. To find the value of $\mathbf{C}$ we substitute $t = 1$ and use the given value of $\mathbf{r}(1)$ to obtain

$$\mathbf{r}(1) = \langle 3, 1\rangle + \mathbf{C} = \langle 2, 5\rangle$$

so that $\mathbf{C} = \langle -1, 4\rangle$. Thus,

$$\mathbf{r}(t) = \langle 3t, t^2\rangle + \langle -1, 4\rangle = \langle 3t - 1, t^2 + 4\rangle \quad ◀$$

✓ **QUICK CHECK EXERCISES 12.2** (See page 858 for answers.)

1. (a) $\lim_{t \to 3}(t^2\mathbf{i} + 2t\mathbf{j}) = $ _____

   (b) $\lim_{t \to \pi/4}\langle \cos t, \sin t \rangle = $ _____

2. Find $\mathbf{r}'(t)$.
   (a) $\mathbf{r}(t) = (4 + 5t)\mathbf{i} + (t - t^2)\mathbf{j}$

   (b) $\mathbf{r}(t) = \left\langle \dfrac{1}{t}, \tan t, e^{2t} \right\rangle$

3. Suppose that $\mathbf{r}_1(0) = \langle 3, 2, 1 \rangle$, $\mathbf{r}_2(0) = \langle 1, 2, 3 \rangle$, $\mathbf{r}_1'(0) = \langle 0, 0, 0 \rangle$, and $\mathbf{r}_2'(0) = \langle -6, -4, -2 \rangle$. Use this in-

formation to evaluate the derivative of each function at $t = 0$.
   (a) $\mathbf{r}(t) = 2\mathbf{r}_1(t) - \mathbf{r}_2(t)$
   (b) $\mathbf{r}(t) = \cos t\, \mathbf{r}_1(t) + e^{2t}\mathbf{r}_2(t)$
   (c) $\mathbf{r}(t) = \mathbf{r}_1(t) \times \mathbf{r}_2(t)$
   (d) $f(t) = \mathbf{r}_1(t) \cdot \mathbf{r}_2(t)$

4. (a) $\displaystyle\int_0^1 \langle 2t, t^2, \sin \pi t \rangle \, dt = $ _____

   (b) $\displaystyle\int (t\mathbf{i} - 3t^2\mathbf{j} + e^t\mathbf{k}) \, dt = $ _____

EXERCISE SET 12.2 〰 Graphing Utility

1–4 Find the limit. ▪

1. $\displaystyle\lim_{t \to +\infty} \left\langle \dfrac{t^2 + 1}{3t^2 + 2}, \dfrac{1}{t} \right\rangle$ 2. $\displaystyle\lim_{t \to 0^+} \left(\sqrt{t}\,\mathbf{i} + \dfrac{\sin t}{t}\mathbf{j} \right)$

3. $\displaystyle\lim_{t \to 2} (t\mathbf{i} - 3\mathbf{j} + t^2\mathbf{k})$ 4. $\displaystyle\lim_{t \to 1} \left\langle \dfrac{3}{t^2}, \dfrac{\ln t}{t^2 - 1}, \sin 2t \right\rangle$

5–6 Determine whether $\mathbf{r}(t)$ is continuous at $t = 0$. Explain your reasoning. ▪

5. (a) $\mathbf{r}(t) = 3 \sin t\mathbf{i} - 2t\mathbf{j}$ (b) $\mathbf{r}(t) = t^2\mathbf{i} + \dfrac{1}{t}\mathbf{j} + t\mathbf{k}$

6. (a) $\mathbf{r}(t) = e^t\mathbf{i} + \mathbf{j} + \csc t\mathbf{k}$
   (b) $\mathbf{r}(t) = 5\mathbf{i} - \sqrt{3t + 1}\mathbf{j} + e^{2t}\mathbf{k}$

7. Sketch the circle $\mathbf{r}(t) = \cos t\mathbf{i} + \sin t\mathbf{j}$, and in each part draw the vector with its correct length.
   (a) $\mathbf{r}'(\pi/4)$ (b) $\mathbf{r}''(\pi)$ (c) $\mathbf{r}(2\pi) - \mathbf{r}(3\pi/2)$

8. Sketch the circle $\mathbf{r}(t) = \cos t\mathbf{i} - \sin t\mathbf{j}$, and in each part draw the vector with its correct length.
   (a) $\mathbf{r}'(\pi/4)$ (b) $\mathbf{r}''(\pi)$ (c) $\mathbf{r}(2\pi) - \mathbf{r}(3\pi/2)$

9–10 Find $\mathbf{r}'(t)$. ▪

9. $\mathbf{r}(t) = 4\mathbf{i} - \cos t\mathbf{j}$

10. $\mathbf{r}(t) = (\tan^{-1} t)\mathbf{i} + t \cos t\mathbf{j} - \sqrt{t}\mathbf{k}$

11–14 Find the vector $\mathbf{r}'(t_0)$; then sketch the graph of $\mathbf{r}(t)$ in 2-space and draw the tangent vector $\mathbf{r}'(t_0)$. ▪

11. $\mathbf{r}(t) = \langle t, t^2 \rangle$; $t_0 = 2$ 12. $\mathbf{r}(t) = t^3\mathbf{i} + t^2\mathbf{j}$; $t_0 = 1$

13. $\mathbf{r}(t) = \sec t\mathbf{i} + \tan t\mathbf{j}$; $t_0 = 0$

14. $\mathbf{r}(t) = 2 \sin t\mathbf{i} + 3 \cos t\mathbf{j}$; $t_0 = \pi/6$

15–16 Find the vector $\mathbf{r}'(t_0)$; then sketch the graph of $\mathbf{r}(t)$ in 3-space and draw the tangent vector $\mathbf{r}'(t_0)$. ▪

15. $\mathbf{r}(t) = 2 \sin t\mathbf{i} + \mathbf{j} + 2 \cos t\mathbf{k}$; $t_0 = \pi/2$

16. $\mathbf{r}(t) = \cos t\mathbf{i} + \sin t\mathbf{j} + t\mathbf{k}$; $t_0 = \pi/4$

〰 **17–18** Use a graphing utility to generate the graph of $\mathbf{r}(t)$ and the graph of the tangent line at t_0 on the same screen. ▪

17. $\mathbf{r}(t) = \sin \pi t\mathbf{i} + t^2\mathbf{j}$; $t_0 = \frac{1}{2}$

18. $\mathbf{r}(t) = 3 \sin t\mathbf{i} + 4 \cos t\mathbf{j}$; $t_0 = \pi/4$

19–22 Find parametric equations of the line tangent to the graph of $\mathbf{r}(t)$ at the point where $t = t_0$. ▪

19. $\mathbf{r}(t) = t^2\mathbf{i} + (2 - \ln t)\mathbf{j}$; $t_0 = 1$

20. $\mathbf{r}(t) = e^{2t}\mathbf{i} - 2 \cos 3t\mathbf{j}$; $t_0 = 0$

21. $\mathbf{r}(t) = 2 \cos \pi t\mathbf{i} + 2 \sin \pi t\mathbf{j} + 3t\mathbf{k}$; $t_0 = \frac{1}{3}$

22. $\mathbf{r}(t) = \ln t\mathbf{i} + e^{-t}\mathbf{j} + t^3\mathbf{k}$; $t_0 = 2$

23–26 Find a vector equation of the line tangent to the graph of $\mathbf{r}(t)$ at the point P_0 on the curve. ▪

23. $\mathbf{r}(t) = (2t - 1)\mathbf{i} + \sqrt{3t + 4}\mathbf{j}$; $P_0(-1, 2)$

24. $\mathbf{r}(t) = 4 \cos t\mathbf{i} - 3t\mathbf{j}$; $P_0(2, -\pi)$

25. $\mathbf{r}(t) = t^2\mathbf{i} - \dfrac{1}{t + 1}\mathbf{j} + (4 - t^2)\mathbf{k}$; $P_0(4, 1, 0)$

26. $\mathbf{r}(t) = \sin t\mathbf{i} + \cosh t\mathbf{j} + (\tan^{-1} t)\mathbf{k}$; $P_0(0, 1, 0)$

27. Let $\mathbf{r}(t) = \cos t\mathbf{i} + \sin t\mathbf{j} + \mathbf{k}$. Find
   (a) $\displaystyle\lim_{t \to 0} (\mathbf{r}(t) - \mathbf{r}'(t))$ (b) $\displaystyle\lim_{t \to 0} (\mathbf{r}(t) \times \mathbf{r}'(t))$
   (c) $\displaystyle\lim_{t \to 0} (\mathbf{r}(t) \cdot \mathbf{r}'(t))$.

28. Let $\mathbf{r}(t) = t\mathbf{i} + t^2\mathbf{j} + t^3\mathbf{k}$. Find
   $$\lim_{t \to 1} \mathbf{r}(t) \cdot (\mathbf{r}'(t) \times \mathbf{r}''(t))$$

29–30 Calculate
$$\frac{d}{dt}[\mathbf{r}_1(t) \cdot \mathbf{r}_2(t)] \quad \text{and} \quad \frac{d}{dt}[\mathbf{r}_1(t) \times \mathbf{r}_2(t)]$$
first by differentiating the product directly and then by applying Formulas (6) and (7). ▪

29. $\mathbf{r}_1(t) = 2t\mathbf{i} + 3t^2\mathbf{j} + t^3\mathbf{k}$, $\mathbf{r}_2(t) = t^4\mathbf{k}$

30. $\mathbf{r}_1(t) = \cos t\mathbf{i} + \sin t\mathbf{j} + t\mathbf{k}$, $\mathbf{r}_2(t) = \mathbf{i} + t\mathbf{k}$

31–34 Evaluate the indefinite integral. ▪

31. $\int (3\mathbf{i} + 4t\mathbf{j})\, dt$

32. $\int \left(t^2\mathbf{i} - 2t\mathbf{j} + \dfrac{1}{t}\mathbf{k} \right) dt$

33. $\int \langle \sin t, -\cos t \rangle\, dt$

34. $\int \langle e^{-t}, e^t, 3t^2 \rangle\, dt$

35–40 Evaluate the definite integral. ▧

35. $\displaystyle\int_0^{\pi/2} \langle \cos 2t, \sin 2t \rangle\, dt$

36. $\displaystyle\int_0^1 (t^2\mathbf{i} + t^3\mathbf{j})\, dt$

37. $\displaystyle\int_0^2 \| t\mathbf{i} + t^2\mathbf{j} \|\, dt$

38. $\displaystyle\int_{-3}^3 \langle (3-t)^{3/2}, (3+t)^{3/2}, 1 \rangle\, dt$

39. $\displaystyle\int_1^9 (t^{1/2}\mathbf{i} + t^{-1/2}\mathbf{j})\, dt$

40. $\displaystyle\int_0^1 (e^{2t}\mathbf{i} + e^{-t}\mathbf{j} + t\mathbf{k})\, dt$

41–44 True–False Determine whether the statement is true or false. Explain your answer. ▧

41. If a vector-valued function $\mathbf{r}(t)$ is continuous at $t = a$, then the limit
$$\lim_{h \to 0} \frac{\mathbf{r}(a+h) - \mathbf{r}(a)}{h}$$
exists.

42. If $\mathbf{r}(t)$ is a vector-valued function in 2-space and $\|\mathbf{r}(t)\|$ is constant, then $\mathbf{r}(t)$ and $\mathbf{r}'(t)$ are parallel vectors for all t.

43. If $\mathbf{r}(t)$ is a vector-valued function that is continuous on the interval $a \le t \le b$, then
$$\int_a^b \mathbf{r}(t)\, dt$$
is a vector.

44. If $\mathbf{r}(t)$ is a vector-valued function that is continuous on the interval $[a, b]$, then for $a < t < b$,
$$\frac{d}{dt}\left[\int_a^t \mathbf{r}(u)\, du \right] = \mathbf{r}(t)$$

45–48 Solve the vector initial-value problem for $\mathbf{y}(t)$ by integrating and using the initial conditions to find the constants of integration. ▧

45. $\mathbf{y}'(t) = 2t\mathbf{i} + 3t^2\mathbf{j},\ \mathbf{y}(0) = \mathbf{i} - \mathbf{j}$

46. $\mathbf{y}'(t) = \cos t\mathbf{i} + \sin t\mathbf{j},\ \mathbf{y}(0) = \mathbf{i} - \mathbf{j}$

47. $\mathbf{y}''(t) = \mathbf{i} + e^t\mathbf{j},\ \mathbf{y}(0) = 2\mathbf{i},\ \mathbf{y}'(0) = \mathbf{j}$

48. $\mathbf{y}''(t) = 12t^2\mathbf{i} - 2t\mathbf{j},\ \mathbf{y}(0) = 2\mathbf{i} - 4\mathbf{j},\ \mathbf{y}'(0) = \mathbf{0}$

49. (a) Find the points where the curve
$$\mathbf{r} = t\mathbf{i} + t^2\mathbf{j} - 3t\mathbf{k}$$
intersects the plane $2x - y + z = -2$.

(b) For the curve and plane in part (a), find, to the nearest degree, the acute angle that the tangent line to the curve makes with a line normal to the plane at each point of intersection.

50. Find where the tangent line to the curve
$$\mathbf{r} = e^{-2t}\mathbf{i} + \cos t\mathbf{j} + 3 \sin t\mathbf{k}$$
at the point $(1, 1, 0)$ intersects the yz-plane.

51–52 Show that the graphs of $\mathbf{r}_1(t)$ and $\mathbf{r}_2(t)$ intersect at the point P. Find, to the nearest degree, the acute angle between the tangent lines to the graphs of $\mathbf{r}_1(t)$ and $\mathbf{r}_2(t)$ at the point P. ▧

51. $\mathbf{r}_1(t) = t^2\mathbf{i} + t\mathbf{j} + 3t^3\mathbf{k}$
$\mathbf{r}_2(t) = (t-1)\mathbf{i} + \tfrac{1}{4}t^2\mathbf{j} + (5-t)\mathbf{k};\ \ P(1, 1, 3)$

52. $\mathbf{r}_1(t) = 2e^{-t}\mathbf{i} + \cos t\mathbf{j} + (t^2 + 3)\mathbf{k}$
$\mathbf{r}_2(t) = (1-t)\mathbf{i} + t^2\mathbf{j} + (t^3 + 4)\mathbf{k};\ \ P(2, 1, 3)$

FOCUS ON CONCEPTS

53. Use Formula (7) to derive the differentiation formula
$$\frac{d}{dt}[\mathbf{r}(t) \times \mathbf{r}'(t)] = \mathbf{r}(t) \times \mathbf{r}''(t)$$

54. Let $\mathbf{u} = \mathbf{u}(t),\ \mathbf{v} = \mathbf{v}(t)$, and $\mathbf{w} = \mathbf{w}(t)$ be differentiable vector-valued functions. Use Formulas (6) and (7) to show that
$$\frac{d}{dt}[\mathbf{u} \cdot (\mathbf{v} \times \mathbf{w})]$$
$$= \frac{d\mathbf{u}}{dt} \cdot [\mathbf{v} \times \mathbf{w}] + \mathbf{u} \cdot \left[\frac{d\mathbf{v}}{dt} \times \mathbf{w} \right] + \mathbf{u} \cdot \left[\mathbf{v} \times \frac{d\mathbf{w}}{dt} \right]$$

55. Let $u_1, u_2, u_3, v_1, v_2, v_3, w_1, w_2$, and w_3 be differentiable functions of t. Use Exercise 54 to show that
$$\frac{d}{dt} \begin{vmatrix} u_1 & u_2 & u_3 \\ v_1 & v_2 & v_3 \\ w_1 & w_2 & w_3 \end{vmatrix}$$
$$= \begin{vmatrix} u_1' & u_2' & u_3' \\ v_1 & v_2 & v_3 \\ w_1 & w_2 & w_3 \end{vmatrix} + \begin{vmatrix} u_1 & u_2 & u_3 \\ v_1' & v_2' & v_3' \\ w_1 & w_2 & w_3 \end{vmatrix} + \begin{vmatrix} u_1 & u_2 & u_3 \\ v_1 & v_2 & v_3 \\ w_1' & w_2' & w_3' \end{vmatrix}$$

56. Prove Theorem 12.2.6 for 2-space.

57. Derive Formulas (6) and (7) for 3-space.

58. Prove Theorem 12.2.9 for 2-space.

59. Writing Explain what it means for a vector-valued function $\mathbf{r}(t)$ to be differentiable, and discuss geometric interpretations of $\mathbf{r}'(t)$.

60. Writing Let $\mathbf{r}(t) = \langle t^2, t^3 + 1 \rangle$ and define $\theta(t)$ to be the angle between $\mathbf{r}(t)$ and $\mathbf{r}'(t)$. The graph of $\theta = \theta(t)$ is shown in the accompanying figure. Interpret important features of this graph in terms of information about $\mathbf{r}(t)$ and $\mathbf{r}'(t)$. Accompany your discussion with a graph of $\mathbf{r}(t)$, highlighting particular instances of the vectors $\mathbf{r}(t)$ and $\mathbf{r}'(t)$.

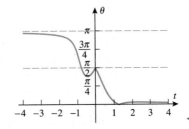

◀ **Figure Ex-60**

12.3   CHANGE OF PARAMETER; ARC LENGTH

We observed in earlier sections that a curve in 2-space or 3-space can be represented parametrically in more than one way. For example, in Section 10.1 we gave two parametric representations of a circle—one in which the circle was traced clockwise and the other in which it was traced counterclockwise. Sometimes it will be desirable to change the parameter for a parametric curve to a different parameter that is better suited for the problem at hand. In this section we will investigate issues associated with changes of parameter, and we will show that arc length plays a special role in parametric representations of curves.

■ **SMOOTH PARAMETRIZATIONS**

Graphs of vector-valued functions range from continuous and smooth to discontinuous and wildly erratic. In this text we will not be concerned with graphs of the latter type, so we will need to impose restrictions to eliminate the unwanted behavior. We will say that a curve represented by $\mathbf{r}(t)$ is *smoothly parametrized* by $\mathbf{r}(t)$, or that $\mathbf{r}(t)$ is a *smooth function* of t if $\mathbf{r}'(t)$ is continuous and $\mathbf{r}'(t) \neq \mathbf{0}$ for any allowable value of t. Geometrically, this means that a smoothly parametrized curve can have no abrupt changes in direction as the parameter increases.

Mathematically, "smoothness" is a property of the *parametrization* and not of the curve itself. Exercise 38 gives an example of a curve that is well-behaved geometrically and has one parametrization that is smooth and another that is not.

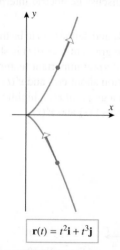

$\mathbf{r}(t) = t^2\mathbf{i} + t^3\mathbf{j}$

▲ **Figure 12.3.1**

▶ **Example 1**   Determine whether the following vector-valued functions are smooth.

(a) $\mathbf{r}(t) = a \cos t\,\mathbf{i} + a \sin t\,\mathbf{j} + ct\,\mathbf{k}$ $(a > 0, c > 0)$

(b) $\mathbf{r}(t) = t^2\mathbf{i} + t^3\mathbf{j}$

Solution (a).   We have

$$\mathbf{r}'(t) = -a \sin t\,\mathbf{i} + a \cos t\,\mathbf{j} + c\mathbf{k}$$

The components are continuous functions, and there is no value of t for which all three of them are zero (verify), so $\mathbf{r}(t)$ is a smooth function. The graph of $\mathbf{r}(t)$ is the circular helix in Figure 12.1.2.

Solution (b).   We have

$$\mathbf{r}'(t) = 2t\mathbf{i} + 3t^2\mathbf{j}$$

Although the components are continuous functions, they are both equal to zero if $t = 0$, so $\mathbf{r}(t)$ is not a smooth function. The graph of $\mathbf{r}(t)$, which is shown in Figure 12.3.1, is a semicubical parabola traced in the upward direction (see Example 6 of Section 10.1). Observe that for values of t slightly less than zero the angle between $\mathbf{r}'(t)$ and $\mathbf{i}$ is near π, and for values of t slightly larger than zero the angle is near 0; hence there is a sudden reversal in the direction of the tangent vector as t increases through $t = 0$ (see Exercise 44). ◀

■ **ARC LENGTH FROM THE VECTOR VIEWPOINT**

Recall from Theorem 10.1.1 that the arc length L of a parametric curve

$$x = x(t), \quad y = y(t) \quad (a \le t \le b) \tag{1}$$

is given by the formula

$$L = \int_a^b \sqrt{\left(\frac{dx}{dt}\right)^2 + \left(\frac{dy}{dt}\right)^2}\, dt \tag{2}$$

Analogously, the arc length L of a parametric curve

$$x = x(t), \quad y = y(t), \quad z = z(t) \quad (a \le t \le b) \tag{3}$$

in 3-space is given by the formula

$$L = \int_a^b \sqrt{\left(\frac{dx}{dt}\right)^2 + \left(\frac{dy}{dt}\right)^2 + \left(\frac{dz}{dt}\right)^2}\, dt \tag{4}$$

Formulas (2) and (4) have vector forms that we can obtain by letting

$$\underbrace{\mathbf{r}(t) = x(t)\mathbf{i} + y(t)\mathbf{j}}_{\text{2-space}} \quad \text{or} \quad \underbrace{\mathbf{r}(t) = x(t)\mathbf{i} + y(t)\mathbf{j} + z(t)\mathbf{k}}_{\text{3-space}}$$

It follows that

$$\underbrace{\frac{d\mathbf{r}}{dt} = \frac{dx}{dt}\mathbf{i} + \frac{dy}{dt}\mathbf{j}}_{\text{2-space}} \quad \text{or} \quad \underbrace{\frac{d\mathbf{r}}{dt} = \frac{dx}{dt}\mathbf{i} + \frac{dy}{dt}\mathbf{j} + \frac{dz}{dt}\mathbf{k}}_{\text{3-space}}$$

and hence

$$\underbrace{\left\| \frac{d\mathbf{r}}{dt} \right\| = \sqrt{\left(\frac{dx}{dt}\right)^2 + \left(\frac{dy}{dt}\right)^2}}_{\text{2-space}} \quad \text{or} \quad \underbrace{\left\| \frac{d\mathbf{r}}{dt} \right\| = \sqrt{\left(\frac{dx}{dt}\right)^2 + \left(\frac{dy}{dt}\right)^2 + \left(\frac{dz}{dt}\right)^2}}_{\text{3-space}}$$

Substituting these expressions in (2) and (4) leads us to the following theorem.

12.3.1   THEOREM   *If C is the graph in 2-space or 3-space of a smooth vector-valued function $\mathbf{r}(t)$, then its arc length L from $t = a$ to $t = b$ is*

$$L = \int_a^b \left\| \frac{d\mathbf{r}}{dt} \right\| dt \tag{5}$$

▶ **Example 2**   Find the arc length of that portion of the circular helix

$$x = \cos t, \quad y = \sin t, \quad z = t$$

from $t = 0$ to $t = \pi$.

Solution.   Set $\mathbf{r}(t) = (\cos t)\mathbf{i} + (\sin t)\mathbf{j} + t\mathbf{k} = \langle \cos t, \sin t, t \rangle$. Then

$$\mathbf{r}'(t) = \langle -\sin t, \cos t, 1 \rangle \quad \text{and} \quad \|\mathbf{r}'(t)\| = \sqrt{(-\sin t)^2 + (\cos t)^2 + 1} = \sqrt{2}$$

From Theorem 12.3.1 the arc length of the helix is

$$L = \int_0^\pi \left\| \frac{d\mathbf{r}}{dt} \right\| dt = \int_0^\pi \sqrt{2}\, dt = \sqrt{2}\pi \blacktriangleleft$$

◼ ARC LENGTH AS A PARAMETER

For many purposes the best parameter to use for representing a curve in 2-space or 3-space parametrically is the length of arc measured along the curve from some fixed reference point. This can be done as follows:

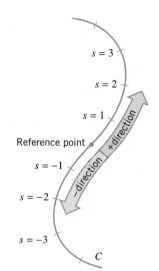

▲ **Figure 12.3.2**

> ### *Using Arc Length as a Parameter*
>
> **Step 1.** Select an arbitrary point on the curve C to serve as a ***reference point***.
>
> **Step 2.** Starting from the reference point, choose one direction along the curve to be the ***positive direction*** and the other to be the ***negative direction***.
>
> **Step 3.** If P is a point on the curve, let s be the "signed" arc length along C from the reference point to P, where s is positive if P is in the positive direction from the reference point and s is negative if P is in the negative direction. Figure 12.3.2 illustrates this idea.

By this procedure, a unique point P on the curve is determined when a value for s is given. For example, $s = 2$ determines the point that is 2 units along the curve in the positive direction from the reference point, and $s = -\frac{3}{2}$ determines the point that is $\frac{3}{2}$ units along the curve in the negative direction from the reference point.

Let us now treat s as a variable. As the value of s changes, the corresponding point P moves along C and the coordinates of P become functions of s. Thus, in 2-space the coordinates of P are $(x(s), y(s))$, and in 3-space they are $(x(s), y(s), z(s))$. Therefore, in 2-space or 3-space the curve C is given by the parametric equations

$$x = x(s), \quad y = y(s) \quad \text{or} \quad x = x(s), \quad y = y(s), \quad z = z(s)$$

A parametric representation of a curve with arc length as the parameter is called an ***arc length parametrization*** of the curve. Note that a given curve will generally have infinitely many different arc length parametrizations, since the reference point and orientation can be chosen arbitrarily.

▶ **Example 3** Find the arc length parametrization of the circle $x^2 + y^2 = a^2$ with counterclockwise orientation and $(a, 0)$ as the reference point.

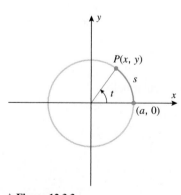

▲ **Figure 12.3.3**

Solution. The circle with counterclockwise orientation can be represented by the parametric equations

$$x = a \cos t, \quad y = a \sin t \qquad (0 \le t \le 2\pi) \tag{6}$$

in which t can be interpreted as the angle in radian measure from the positive x-axis to the radius from the origin to the point $P(x, y)$ (Figure 12.3.3). If we take the positive direction for measuring the arc length to be counterclockwise, and we take $(a, 0)$ to be the reference point, then s and t are related by

$$s = at \quad \text{or} \quad t = s/a$$

Making this change of variable in (6) and noting that s increases from 0 to $2\pi a$ as t increases from 0 to 2π yields the following arc length parametrization of the circle:

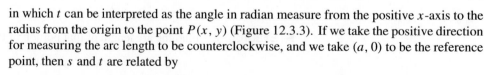

$$x = a \cos(s/a), \quad y = a \sin(s/a) \qquad (0 \le s \le 2\pi a) \blacktriangleleft$$

■ CHANGE OF PARAMETER

In many situations the solution of a problem can be simplified by choosing the parameter in a vector-valued function or a parametric curve in the right way. The two most common parameters for curves in 2-space or 3-space are time and arc length. However, there are other useful possibilities as well. For example, in analyzing the motion of a particle in 2-space, it is often desirable to parametrize its trajectory in terms of the angle ϕ between the tangent vector and the positive x-axis (Figure 12.3.4). Thus, our next objective is to develop methods for changing the parameter in a vector-valued function or parametric curve. This will allow us to move freely between different possible parametrizations.

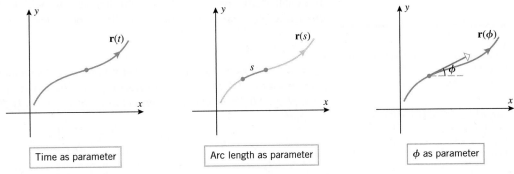

Time as parameter   Arc length as parameter ϕ as parameter

▲ **Figure 12.3.4**

A *change of parameter* in a vector-valued function $\mathbf{r}(t)$ is a substitution $t = g(\tau)$ that produces a new vector-valued function $\mathbf{r}(g(\tau))$ having the same graph as $\mathbf{r}(t)$, but possibly traced differently as the parameter τ increases.

▶ **Example 4**   Find a change of parameter $t = g(\tau)$ for the circle

$$\mathbf{r}(t) = \cos t\,\mathbf{i} + \sin t\,\mathbf{j} \qquad (0 \le t \le 2\pi)$$

such that

(a) the circle is traced counterclockwise as τ increases over the interval $[0, 1]$;

(b) the circle is traced clockwise as τ increases over the interval $[0, 1]$.

***Solution** (a).*   The given circle is traced counterclockwise as t increases. Thus, if we choose g to be an increasing function, then it will follow from the relationship $t = g(\tau)$ that t increases when τ increases, thereby ensuring that the circle will be traced counterclockwise as τ increases. We also want to choose g so that t increases from 0 to 2π as τ increases from 0 to 1. A simple choice of g that satisfies all of the required criteria is the linear function graphed in Figure 12.3.5a. The equation of this line is

$$t = g(\tau) = 2\pi\tau \tag{7}$$

which is the desired change of parameter. The resulting representation of the circle in terms of the parameter τ is

$$\mathbf{r}(g(\tau)) = \cos 2\pi\tau\,\mathbf{i} + \sin 2\pi\tau\,\mathbf{j} \qquad (0 \le \tau \le 1)$$

***Solution** (b).*   To ensure that the circle is traced clockwise, we will choose g to be a decreasing function such that t decreases from 2π to 0 as τ increases from 0 to 1. A simple choice of g that achieves this is the linear function

$$t = g(\tau) = 2\pi(1 - \tau) \tag{8}$$

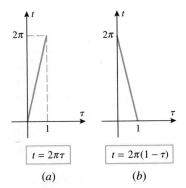

$t = 2\pi\tau$

(a)

$t = 2\pi(1 - \tau)$

(b)

▲ **Figure 12.3.5**

graphed in Figure 12.3.5*b*. The resulting representation of the circle in terms of the parameter τ is

$$\mathbf{r}(g(\tau)) = \cos(2\pi(1 - \tau))\mathbf{i} + \sin(2\pi(1 - \tau))\mathbf{j} \qquad (0 \le \tau \le 1)$$

which simplifies to (verify)

$$\mathbf{r}(g(\tau)) = \cos 2\pi\tau\,\mathbf{i} - \sin 2\pi\tau\,\mathbf{j} \qquad (0 \le \tau \le 1) \blacktriangleleft$$

When making a change of parameter $t = g(\tau)$ in a vector-valued function $\mathbf{r}(t)$, it will be important to ensure that the new vector-valued function $\mathbf{r}(g(\tau))$ is smooth if $\mathbf{r}(t)$ is smooth. To establish conditions under which this happens, we will need the following version of the chain rule for vector-valued functions. The proof is left as an exercise.

Strictly speaking, since $d\mathbf{r}/dt$ is a vector and $dt/d\tau$ is a scalar, Formula (9) should be written in the form

$$\frac{d\mathbf{r}}{d\tau} = \frac{dt}{d\tau}\frac{d\mathbf{r}}{dt}$$

(scalar first). However, reversing the order of the factors makes the formula easier to remember, and we will continue to do so.

> **12.3.2** **THEOREM** (*Chain Rule*) *Let* $\mathbf{r}(t)$ *be a vector-valued function in 2-space or 3-space that is differentiable with respect to* t. *If* $t = g(\tau)$ *is a change of parameter in which* g *is differentiable with respect to* τ, *then* $\mathbf{r}(g(\tau))$ *is differentiable with respect to* τ *and*
>
> $$\frac{d\mathbf{r}}{d\tau} = \frac{d\mathbf{r}}{dt}\frac{dt}{d\tau} \qquad (9)$$

A change of parameter $t = g(\tau)$ in which $\mathbf{r}(g(\tau))$ is smooth if $\mathbf{r}(t)$ is smooth is called a *smooth change of parameter*. It follows from (9) that $t = g(\tau)$ will be a smooth change of parameter if $dt/d\tau$ is continuous and $dt/d\tau \ne 0$ for all values of τ, since these conditions imply that $d\mathbf{r}/d\tau$ is continuous and nonzero if $d\mathbf{r}/dt$ is continuous and nonzero. Smooth changes of parameter fall into two categories—those for which $dt/d\tau > 0$ for all τ (called *positive changes of parameter*) and those for which $dt/d\tau < 0$ for all τ (called *negative changes of parameter*). A positive change of parameter preserves the orientation of a parametric curve, and a negative change of parameter reverses it.

▶ **Example 5** In Example 4 the change of parameter in Formula (7) is positive since $dt/d\tau = 2\pi > 0$, and the change of parameter given by Formula (8) is negative since $dt/d\tau = -2\pi < 0$. The positive change of parameter preserved the orientation of the circle, and the negative change of parameter reversed it. ◀

■ FINDING ARC LENGTH PARAMETRIZATIONS

Next we will consider the problem of finding an arc length parametrization of a vector-valued function that is expressed initially in terms of some other parameter t. The following theorem will provide a general method for doing this.

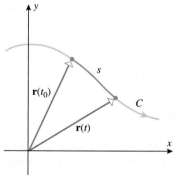

▲ **Figure 12.3.6**

> **12.3.3** **THEOREM** *Let* C *be the graph of a smooth vector-valued function* $\mathbf{r}(t)$ *in 2-space or 3-space, and let* $\mathbf{r}(t_0)$ *be any point on* C. *Then the following formula defines a positive change of parameter from* t *to* s, *where* s *is an arc length parameter having* $\mathbf{r}(t_0)$ *as its reference point (Figure 12.3.6):*
>
> $$s = \int_{t_0}^{t} \left\| \frac{d\mathbf{r}}{du} \right\| du \qquad (10)$$

PROOF   From (5) with u as the variable of integration instead of t, the integral represents the arc length of that portion of C between $\mathbf{r}(t_0)$ and $\mathbf{r}(t)$ if $t > t_0$ and the negative of that arc length if $t < t_0$. Thus, s is the arc length parameter with $\mathbf{r}(t_0)$ as its reference point and its positive direction in the direction of increasing t. ∎

When needed, Formula (10) can be expressed in component form as

$$s = \int_{t_0}^{t} \sqrt{\left(\frac{dx}{du}\right)^2 + \left(\frac{dy}{du}\right)^2}\, du \qquad \boxed{\text{2-space}} \qquad (11)$$

$$s = \int_{t_0}^{t} \sqrt{\left(\frac{dx}{du}\right)^2 + \left(\frac{dy}{du}\right)^2 + \left(\frac{dz}{du}\right)^2}\, du \qquad \boxed{\text{3-space}} \qquad (12)$$

▶ **Example 6**   Find the arc length parametrization of the circular helix

$$\mathbf{r} = \cos t\, \mathbf{i} + \sin t\, \mathbf{j} + t\, \mathbf{k} \qquad (13)$$

that has reference point $\mathbf{r}(0) = (1, 0, 0)$ and the same orientation as the given helix.

Solution.   Replacing t by u in $\mathbf{r}$ for integration purposes and taking $t_0 = 0$ in Formula (10), we obtain

$$\mathbf{r} = \cos u\, \mathbf{i} + \sin u\, \mathbf{j} + u\, \mathbf{k}$$

$$\frac{d\mathbf{r}}{du} = (-\sin u)\mathbf{i} + \cos u\, \mathbf{j} + \mathbf{k}$$

$$\left\|\frac{d\mathbf{r}}{du}\right\| = \sqrt{(-\sin u)^2 + \cos^2 u + 1} = \sqrt{2}$$

$$s = \int_0^t \left\|\frac{d\mathbf{r}}{du}\right\| du = \int_0^t \sqrt{2}\, du = \sqrt{2}u \Big]_0^t = \sqrt{2}t$$

Thus, $t = s/\sqrt{2}$, so (13) can be reparametrized in terms of s as

$$\mathbf{r} = \cos\left(\frac{s}{\sqrt{2}}\right)\mathbf{i} + \sin\left(\frac{s}{\sqrt{2}}\right)\mathbf{j} + \frac{s}{\sqrt{2}}\mathbf{k}$$

We are guaranteed that this reparametrization preserves the orientation of the helix since Formula (10) produces a positive change of parameter. ◀

▶ **Example 7**   A bug walks along the trunk of a tree following a path modeled by the circular helix in Example 6. The bug starts at the reference point $(1, 0, 0)$ and walks up the helix for a distance of 10 units. What are the bug's final coordinates?

Solution.   From Example 6, the arc length parametrization of the helix relative to the reference point $(1, 0, 0)$ is

$$\mathbf{r} = \cos\left(\frac{s}{\sqrt{2}}\right)\mathbf{i} + \sin\left(\frac{s}{\sqrt{2}}\right)\mathbf{j} + \frac{s}{\sqrt{2}}\mathbf{k}$$

or, expressed parametrically,

$$x = \cos\left(\frac{s}{\sqrt{2}}\right), \quad y = \sin\left(\frac{s}{\sqrt{2}}\right), \quad z = \frac{s}{\sqrt{2}}$$

Thus, at $s = 10$ the coordinates are

$$\left(\cos\left(\frac{10}{\sqrt{2}}\right), \sin\left(\frac{10}{\sqrt{2}}\right), \frac{10}{\sqrt{2}}\right) \approx (0.705, 0.709, 7.07) \blacktriangleleft$$

▶ **Example 8**   Recall from Formula (9) of Section 11.5 that the equation

$$\mathbf{r} = \mathbf{r}_0 + t\mathbf{v} \tag{14}$$

is the vector form of the line that passes through the terminal point of $\mathbf{r}_0$ and is parallel to the vector $\mathbf{v}$. Find the arc length parametrization of the line that has reference point $\mathbf{r}_0$ and the same orientation as the given line.

Solution.   Replacing t by u in (14) for integration purposes and taking $t_0 = 0$ in Formula (10), we obtain

$$\mathbf{r} = \mathbf{r}_0 + u\mathbf{v} \quad \text{and} \quad \frac{d\mathbf{r}}{du} = \mathbf{v} \qquad \boxed{\text{Since } \mathbf{r}_0 \text{ is constant}}$$

It follows from this that

$$s = \int_0^t \left\| \frac{d\mathbf{r}}{du} \right\| du = \int_0^t \|\mathbf{v}\|\, du = \|\mathbf{v}\| u \Big]_0^t = t\|\mathbf{v}\|$$

This implies that $t = s/\|\mathbf{v}\|$, so (14) can be reparametrized in terms of s as

$$\mathbf{r} = \mathbf{r}_0 + s\left(\frac{\mathbf{v}}{\|\mathbf{v}\|}\right) \blacktriangleleft \tag{15}$$

In words, Formula (15) tells us that the line represented by Equation (14) can be reparametrized in terms of arc length with $\mathbf{r}_0$ as the reference point by normalizing $\mathbf{v}$ and then replacing t by s.

▶ **Example 9**   Find the arc length parametrization of the line

$$x = 2t + 1, \quad y = 3t - 2$$

that has the same orientation as the given line and uses $(1, -2)$ as the reference point.

Solution.   The line passes through the point $(1, -2)$ and is parallel to $\mathbf{v} = 2\mathbf{i} + 3\mathbf{j}$. To find the arc length parametrization of the line, we need only rewrite the given equations using $\mathbf{v}/\|\mathbf{v}\|$ rather than $\mathbf{v}$ to determine the direction and replace t by s. Since

$$\frac{\mathbf{v}}{\|\mathbf{v}\|} = \frac{2\mathbf{i} + 3\mathbf{j}}{\sqrt{13}} = \frac{2}{\sqrt{13}}\mathbf{i} + \frac{3}{\sqrt{13}}\mathbf{j}$$

it follows that the parametric equations for the line in terms of s are

$$x = \frac{2}{\sqrt{13}} s + 1, \quad y = \frac{3}{\sqrt{13}} s - 2 \blacktriangleleft$$

■ **PROPERTIES OF ARC LENGTH PARAMETRIZATIONS**

Because arc length parameters for a curve C are intimately related to the geometric characteristics of C, arc length parametrizations have properties that are not enjoyed by other parametrizations. For example, the following theorem shows that if a smooth curve is represented parametrically using an arc length parameter, then the tangent vectors all have length 1.

12.3.4 THEOREM

(a) *If C is the graph of a smooth vector-valued function* $\mathbf{r}(t)$ *in 2-space or 3-space, where t is a general parameter, and if s is the arc length parameter for C defined by Formula (10), then for every value of t the tangent vector has length*

$$\left\| \frac{d\mathbf{r}}{dt} \right\| = \frac{ds}{dt} \tag{16}$$

(b) *If C is the graph of a smooth vector-valued function* $\mathbf{r}(s)$ *in 2-space or 3-space, where s is an arc length parameter, then for every value of s the tangent vector to C has length*

$$\left\| \frac{d\mathbf{r}}{ds} \right\| = 1 \tag{17}$$

(c) *If C is the graph of a smooth vector-valued function* $\mathbf{r}(t)$ *in 2-space or 3-space, and if* $\|d\mathbf{r}/dt\| = 1$ *for every value of t, then for any value of* t_0 *in the domain of* $\mathbf{r}$*, the parameter* $s = t - t_0$ *is an arc length parameter that has its reference point at the point on C where* $t = t_0$*.*

PROOF (*a*) This result follows by applying the Fundamental Theorem of Calculus (Theorem 5.6.3) to Formula (10).

PROOF (*b*) Let $t = s$ in part (*a*).

PROOF (*c*) It follows from Theorem 12.3.3 that the formula

$$s = \int_{t_0}^{t} \left\| \frac{d\mathbf{r}}{du} \right\| du$$

defines an arc length parameter for C with reference point $\mathbf{r}(0)$. However, $\|d\mathbf{r}/du\| = 1$ by hypothesis, so we can rewrite the formula for s as

$$s = \int_{t_0}^{t} du = u \Big]_{t_0}^{t} = t - t_0 \quad \blacksquare$$

The component forms of Formulas (16) and (17) will be of sufficient interest in later sections that we provide them here for reference:

$$\frac{ds}{dt} = \left\| \frac{d\mathbf{r}}{dt} \right\| = \sqrt{\left(\frac{dx}{dt} \right)^2 + \left(\frac{dy}{dt} \right)^2} \qquad \boxed{\text{2-space}} \tag{18}$$

$$\frac{ds}{dt} = \left\| \frac{d\mathbf{r}}{dt} \right\| = \sqrt{\left(\frac{dx}{dt} \right)^2 + \left(\frac{dy}{dt} \right)^2 + \left(\frac{dz}{dt} \right)^2} \qquad \boxed{\text{3-space}} \tag{19}$$

$$\left\| \frac{d\mathbf{r}}{ds} \right\| = \sqrt{\left(\frac{dx}{ds} \right)^2 + \left(\frac{dy}{ds} \right)^2} = 1 \qquad \boxed{\text{2-space}} \tag{20}$$

$$\left\| \frac{d\mathbf{r}}{ds} \right\| = \sqrt{\left(\frac{dx}{ds} \right)^2 + \left(\frac{dy}{ds} \right)^2 + \left(\frac{dz}{ds} \right)^2} = 1 \qquad \boxed{\text{3-space}} \tag{21}$$

Note that Formulas (18) and (19) do not involve t_0, and hence do not depend on where the reference point for s is chosen. This is to be expected since changing the reference point shifts s by a constant (the arc length between the two reference points), and this constant drops out on differentiating.

✔ **QUICK CHECK EXERCISES 12.3** (*See page 868 for answers.*)

1. If $\mathbf{r}(t)$ is a smooth vector-valued function, then the integral

$$\int_a^b \left\| \frac{d\mathbf{r}}{dt} \right\| \, dt$$

may be interpreted geometrically as the _____.

2. If $\mathbf{r}(s)$ is a smooth vector-valued function parametrized by arc length s, then

$$\left\| \frac{d\mathbf{r}}{ds} \right\| = \text{_____}$$

and the arc length of the graph of $\mathbf{r}$ over the interval $a \leq s \leq b$ is _____.

3. If $\mathbf{r}(t)$ is a smooth vector-valued function, then the arc length parameter s having $\mathbf{r}(t_0)$ as the reference point may be defined by the integral

$$s = \int_{t_0}^{t} \text{_____} \, du$$

4. Suppose that $\mathbf{r}(t)$ is a smooth vector-valued function of t with $\mathbf{r}'(1) = \langle \sqrt{3}, -\sqrt{3}, -1 \rangle$, and let $\mathbf{r}_1(t)$ be defined by the equation $\mathbf{r}_1(t) = \mathbf{r}(2 \cos t)$. Then $\mathbf{r}_1'(\pi/3) = $ _____.

EXERCISE SET 12.3

1–4 Determine whether $\mathbf{r}(t)$ is a smooth function of the parameter t. ■

1. $\mathbf{r}(t) = t^3 \mathbf{i} + (3t^2 - 2t)\mathbf{j} + t^2 \mathbf{k}$

2. $\mathbf{r}(t) = \cos t^2 \mathbf{i} + \sin t^2 \mathbf{j} + e^{-t} \mathbf{k}$

3. $\mathbf{r}(t) = te^{-t} \mathbf{i} + (t^2 - 2t)\mathbf{j} + \cos \pi t \mathbf{k}$

4. $\mathbf{r}(t) = \sin \pi t \mathbf{i} + (2t - \ln t)\mathbf{j} + (t^2 - t)\mathbf{k}$

5–8 Find the arc length of the parametric curve. ■

5. $x = \cos^3 t, \ y = \sin^3 t, \ z = 2; \ 0 \leq t \leq \pi/2$

6. $x = 3 \cos t, \ y = 3 \sin t, \ z = 4t; \ 0 \leq t \leq \pi$

7. $x = e^t, \ y = e^{-t}, \ z = \sqrt{2} t; \ 0 \leq t \leq 1$

8. $x = \frac{1}{2}t, \ y = \frac{1}{3}(1-t)^{3/2}, \ z = \frac{1}{3}(1+t)^{3/2}; \ -1 \leq t \leq 1$

9–12 Find the arc length of the graph of $\mathbf{r}(t)$. ■

9. $\mathbf{r}(t) = t^3 \mathbf{i} + t\mathbf{j} + \frac{1}{2}\sqrt{6} t^2 \mathbf{k}; \ 1 \leq t \leq 3$

10. $\mathbf{r}(t) = (4 + 3t)\mathbf{i} + (2 - 2t)\mathbf{j} + (5 + t)\mathbf{k}; \ 3 \leq t \leq 4$

11. $\mathbf{r}(t) = 3 \cos t \mathbf{i} + 3 \sin t \mathbf{j} + t\mathbf{k}; \ 0 \leq t \leq 2\pi$

12. $\mathbf{r}(t) = t^2 \mathbf{i} + (\cos t + t \sin t)\mathbf{j} + (\sin t - t \cos t)\mathbf{k};$ $0 \leq t \leq \pi$

13–16 Calculate $d\mathbf{r}/d\tau$ by the chain rule, and then check your result by expressing $\mathbf{r}$ in terms of τ and differentiating. ■

13. $\mathbf{r} = t\mathbf{i} + t^2 \mathbf{j}; \ t = 4\tau + 1$

14. $\mathbf{r} = \langle 3 \cos t, 3 \sin t \rangle; \ t = \pi \tau$

15. $\mathbf{r} = e^t \mathbf{i} + 4e^{-t} \mathbf{j}; \ t = \tau^2$

16. $\mathbf{r} = \mathbf{i} + 3t^{3/2} \mathbf{j} + t\mathbf{k}; \ t = 1/\tau$

17–20 True–False Determine whether the statement is true or false. Explain your answer. ■

17. If $\mathbf{r}(t)$ is a smooth vector-valued function in 2-space, then

$$\int_a^b \|\mathbf{r}'(t)\| \, dt$$

is a vector.

18. If the line $y = x$ is parametrized by the vector-valued function $\mathbf{r}(t)$, then $\mathbf{r}(t)$ is smooth.

19. If $\mathbf{r}(s)$ parametrizes the graph of $y = |x|$ in 2-space by arc length, then $\mathbf{r}(s)$ is smooth.

20. If a curve C in the plane is parametrized by the smooth vector-valued function $\mathbf{r}(s)$, where s is an arc length parameter, then

$$\int_{-1}^{3} \|\mathbf{r}'(s)\| \, ds = 4$$

21. (a) Find the arc length parametrization of the line

$$x = t, \quad y = t$$

that has the same orientation as the given line and has reference point $(0, 0)$.

(b) Find the arc length parametrization of the line

$$x = t, \quad y = t, \quad z = t$$

that has the same orientation as the given line and has reference point $(0, 0, 0)$.

22. Find arc length parametrizations of the lines in Exercise 21 that have the stated reference points but are oriented opposite to the given lines.

23. (a) Find the arc length parametrization of the line

$$x = 1 + t, \quad y = 3 - 2t, \quad z = 4 + 2t$$

that has the same direction as the given line and has reference point $(1, 3, 4)$.

(b) Use the parametric equations obtained in part (a) to find the point on the line that is 25 units from the reference point in the direction of increasing parameter.

24. (a) Find the arc length parametrization of the line
$$x = -5 + 3t, \quad y = 2t, \quad z = 5 + t$$
that has the same direction as the given line and has reference point $(-5, 0, 5)$.

(b) Use the parametric equations obtained in part (a) to find the point on the line that is 10 units from the reference point in the direction of increasing parameter.

25–30 Find an arc length parametrization of the curve that has the same orientation as the given curve and for which the reference point corresponds to $t = 0$. ■

25. $\mathbf{r}(t) = (3 + \cos t)\mathbf{i} + (2 + \sin t)\mathbf{j}; \ 0 \le t \le 2\pi$

26. $\mathbf{r}(t) = \cos^3 t\mathbf{i} + \sin^3 t\mathbf{j}; \ 0 \le t \le \pi/2$

27. $\mathbf{r}(t) = \frac{1}{3}t^3\mathbf{i} + \frac{1}{2}t^2\mathbf{j}; \ t \ge 0$

28. $\mathbf{r}(t) = (1 + t)^2\mathbf{i} + (1 + t)^3\mathbf{j}; \ 0 \le t \le 1$

29. $\mathbf{r}(t) = e^t \cos t\mathbf{i} + e^t \sin t\mathbf{j}; \ 0 \le t \le \pi/2$

30. $\mathbf{r}(t) = \sin e^t\mathbf{i} + \cos e^t\mathbf{j} + \sqrt{3}e^t\mathbf{k}; \ t \ge 0$

31. Show that the arc length of the circular helix $x = a \cos t$, $y = a \sin t$, $z = ct$ for $0 \le t \le t_0$ is $t_0\sqrt{a^2 + c^2}$.

32. Use the result in Exercise 31 to show the circular helix
$$\mathbf{r} = a \cos t\mathbf{i} + a \sin t\mathbf{j} + ct\mathbf{k}$$
can be expressed as
$$\mathbf{r} = \left(a \cos \frac{s}{w}\right)\mathbf{i} + \left(a \sin \frac{s}{w}\right)\mathbf{j} + \frac{cs}{w}\mathbf{k}$$
where $w = \sqrt{a^2 + c^2}$ and s is an arc length parameter with reference point at $(a, 0, 0)$.

33. Find an arc length parametrization of the cycloid
$$x = at - a \sin t$$
$$y = a - a \cos t \qquad (0 \le t \le 2\pi)$$
with $(0, 0)$ as the reference point.

34. Show that in cylindrical coordinates a curve given by the parametric equations $r = r(t)$, $\theta = \theta(t)$, $z = z(t)$ for $a \le t \le b$ has arc length
$$L = \int_a^b \sqrt{\left(\frac{dr}{dt}\right)^2 + r^2\left(\frac{d\theta}{dt}\right)^2 + \left(\frac{dz}{dt}\right)^2} \, dt$$
[*Hint:* Use the relationships $x = r \cos \theta$, $y = r \sin \theta$.]

35. In each part, use the formula in Exercise 34 to find the arc length of the curve.
(a) $r = e^{2t}, \theta = t, z = e^{2t}; \ 0 \le t \le \ln 2$
(b) $r = t^2, \theta = \ln t, z = \frac{1}{3}t^3; \ 1 \le t \le 2$

36. Show that in spherical coordinates a curve given by the parametric equations $\rho = \rho(t)$, $\theta = \theta(t)$, $\phi = \phi(t)$ for $a \le t \le b$ has arc length
$$L = \int_a^b \sqrt{\left(\frac{d\rho}{dt}\right)^2 + \rho^2 \sin^2 \phi \left(\frac{d\theta}{dt}\right)^2 + \rho^2 \left(\frac{d\phi}{dt}\right)^2} \, dt$$
[*Hint:* $x = \rho \sin \phi \cos \theta$, $y = \rho \sin \phi \sin \theta$, $z = \rho \cos \phi$.]

37. In each part, use the formula in Exercise 36 to find the arc length of the curve.

(a) $\rho = e^{-t}, \theta = 2t, \phi = \pi/4; \ 0 \le t \le 2$
(b) $\rho = 2t, \theta = \ln t, \phi = \pi/6; \ 1 \le t \le 5$

FOCUS ON CONCEPTS

38. (a) Sketch the graph of $\mathbf{r}(t) = t\mathbf{i} + t^2\mathbf{j}$. Show that $\mathbf{r}(t)$ is a smooth vector-valued function but the change of parameter $t = \tau^3$ produces a vector-valued function that is not smooth, yet has the same graph as $\mathbf{r}(t)$.

(b) Examine how the two vector-valued functions are traced, and see if you can explain what causes the problem.

39. Find a change of parameter $t = g(\tau)$ for the semicircle
$$\mathbf{r}(t) = \cos t\mathbf{i} + \sin t\mathbf{j} \quad (0 \le t \le \pi)$$
such that
(a) the semicircle is traced counterclockwise as τ varies over the interval $[0, 1]$
(b) the semicircle is traced clockwise as τ varies over the interval $[0, 1]$.

40. What change of parameter $t = g(\tau)$ would you make if you wanted to trace the graph of $\mathbf{r}(t)$ $(0 \le t \le 1)$ in the opposite direction with τ varying from 0 to 1?

41. As illustrated in the accompanying figure, copper cable with a diameter of $\frac{1}{2}$ inch is to be wrapped in a circular helix around a cylinder that has a 12-inch diameter. What length of cable (measured along its centerline) will make one complete turn around the cylinder in a distance of 20 inches (between centerlines) measured parallel to the axis of the cylinder?

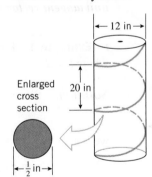

← 12 in →

Enlarged cross section

20 in

← $\frac{1}{2}$ in →

◀ **Figure Ex-41**

42. Let $\mathbf{r}(t) = \langle \cos t, \sin t, t^{3/2} \rangle$. Find
(a) $\|\mathbf{r}'(t)\|$ \quad (b) $\dfrac{ds}{dt}$ \quad (c) $\displaystyle\int_0^2 \|\mathbf{r}'(t)\| \, dt$.

43. Let $\mathbf{r}(t) = \ln t\mathbf{i} + 2t\mathbf{j} + t^2\mathbf{k}$. Find
(a) $\|\mathbf{r}'(t)\|$ \quad (b) $\dfrac{ds}{dt}$ \quad (c) $\displaystyle\int_1^3 \|\mathbf{r}'(t)\| \, dt$.

44. Let $\mathbf{r}(t) = t^2\mathbf{i} + t^3\mathbf{j}$ (see Figure 12.3.1). Let $\theta(t)$ be the angle between $\mathbf{r}'(t)$ and $\mathbf{i}$. Show that
$$\theta(t) \to \pi \text{ as } t \to 0^- \quad \text{and} \quad \theta(t) \to 0 \text{ as } t \to 0^+$$

45. Prove: If $\mathbf{r}(t)$ is a smoothly parametrized function, then the angles between $\mathbf{r}'(t)$ and the vectors $\mathbf{i}$, $\mathbf{j}$, and $\mathbf{k}$ are continuous functions of t.

46. Prove the vector form of the chain rule for 2-space (Theorem 12.3.2) by expressing $\mathbf{r}(t)$ in terms of components.

47. Writing The triangle with vertices $(0, 0)$, $(1, 0)$, and $(0, 1)$ has three "corners." Discuss whether it is possible to have a smooth vector-valued function whose graph is this triangle. Also discuss whether it is possible to have a differentiable vector-valued function whose graph is this triangle.

 QUICK CHECK ANSWERS 12.3

1. arc length of the graph of $\mathbf{r}(t)$ from $t = a$ to $t = b$ **2.** 1; $b - a$ **3.** $\left\| \dfrac{d\mathbf{r}}{du} \right\|$ **4.** $\langle -3, 3, \sqrt{3} \rangle$

12.4 UNIT TANGENT, NORMAL, AND BINORMAL VECTORS

In this section we will discuss some of the fundamental geometric properties of vector-valued functions. Our work here will have important applications to the study of motion along a curved path in 2-space or 3-space and to the study of the geometric properties of curves and surfaces.

UNIT TANGENT VECTORS

Recall that if C is the graph of a *smooth* vector-valued function $\mathbf{r}(t)$ in 2-space or 3-space, then the vector $\mathbf{r}'(t)$ is nonzero, tangent to C, and points in the direction of increasing parameter. Thus, by normalizing $\mathbf{r}'(t)$ we obtain a unit vector

> As a general rule, we will position $\mathbf{T}(t)$ with its initial point at the terminal point of $\mathbf{r}(t)$, as in Figure 12.4.1. This will ensure that $\mathbf{T}(t)$ is actually tangent to the graph of $\mathbf{r}(t)$ and not simply parallel to the tangent line.

$$\mathbf{T}(t) = \frac{\mathbf{r}'(t)}{\|\mathbf{r}'(t)\|} \tag{1}$$

that is tangent to C and points in the direction of increasing parameter. We call $\mathbf{T}(t)$ the **unit tangent vector** to C at t.

▶ **Example 1** Find the unit tangent vector to the graph of $\mathbf{r}(t) = t^2\mathbf{i} + t^3\mathbf{j}$ at the point where $t = 2$.

Solution. Since

$$\mathbf{r}'(t) = 2t\mathbf{i} + 3t^2\mathbf{j}$$

we obtain

$$\mathbf{T}(2) = \frac{\mathbf{r}'(2)}{\|\mathbf{r}'(2)\|} = \frac{4\mathbf{i} + 12\mathbf{j}}{\sqrt{160}} = \frac{4\mathbf{i} + 12\mathbf{j}}{4\sqrt{10}} = \frac{1}{\sqrt{10}}\mathbf{i} + \frac{3}{\sqrt{10}}\mathbf{j}$$

The graph of $\mathbf{r}(t)$ and the vector $\mathbf{T}(2)$ are shown in Figure 12.4.2. ◀

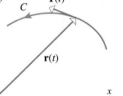

▲ Figure 12.4.1

UNIT NORMAL VECTORS

Recall from Theorem 12.2.8 that if a vector-valued function $\mathbf{r}(t)$ has constant norm, then $\mathbf{r}(t)$ and $\mathbf{r}'(t)$ are orthogonal vectors. In particular, $\mathbf{T}(t)$ has constant norm 1, so $\mathbf{T}(t)$ and $\mathbf{T}'(t)$ are orthogonal vectors. This implies that $\mathbf{T}'(t)$ is perpendicular to the tangent line to C at t, so we say that $\mathbf{T}'(t)$ is **normal** to C at t. It follows that if $\mathbf{T}'(t) \neq \mathbf{0}$, and if we normalize $\mathbf{T}'(t)$, then we obtain a unit vector

$$\mathbf{N}(t) = \frac{\mathbf{T}'(t)}{\|\mathbf{T}'(t)\|} \tag{2}$$

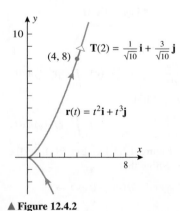

▲ Figure 12.4.2

that is normal to C and points in the same direction as $\mathbf{T}'(t)$. We call $\mathbf{N}(t)$ the ***principal unit normal vector*** to C at t, or more simply, the ***unit normal vector***. Observe that the unit normal vector is defined only at points where $\mathbf{T}'(t) \neq \mathbf{0}$. Unless stated otherwise, we will assume that this condition is satisfied. In particular, this *excludes* straight lines.

REMARK | In 2-space there are two unit vectors that are orthogonal to $\mathbf{T}(t)$, and in 3-space there are infinitely many such vectors (Figure 12.4.3). In both cases the principal unit normal is that particular normal that points in the direction of $\mathbf{T}'(t)$. After the next example we will show that for a nonlinear parametric curve in 2-space the principal unit normal is the one that points "inward" toward the concave side of the curve.

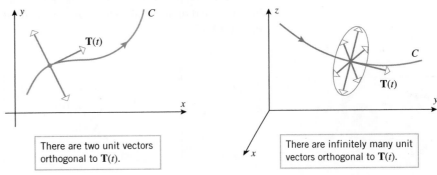

There are two unit vectors orthogonal to $\mathbf{T}(t)$.

There are infinitely many unit vectors orthogonal to $\mathbf{T}(t)$.

▲ **Figure 12.4.3**

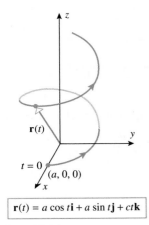

$\mathbf{r}(t) = a \cos t\,\mathbf{i} + a \sin t\,\mathbf{j} + ct\mathbf{k}$

▲ **Figure 12.4.4**

► **Example 2** Find $\mathbf{T}(t)$ and $\mathbf{N}(t)$ for the circular helix

$$x = a \cos t, \quad y = a \sin t, \quad z = ct$$

where $a > 0$.

Solution. The radius vector for the helix is

$$\mathbf{r}(t) = a \cos t\,\mathbf{i} + a \sin t\,\mathbf{j} + ct\mathbf{k}$$

(Figure 12.4.4). Thus,

$$\mathbf{r}'(t) = (-a \sin t)\mathbf{i} + a \cos t\,\mathbf{j} + c\mathbf{k}$$

$$\|\mathbf{r}'(t)\| = \sqrt{(-a \sin t)^2 + (a \cos t)^2 + c^2} = \sqrt{a^2 + c^2}$$

$$\mathbf{T}(t) = \frac{\mathbf{r}'(t)}{\|\mathbf{r}'(t)\|} = -\frac{a \sin t}{\sqrt{a^2 + c^2}}\mathbf{i} + \frac{a \cos t}{\sqrt{a^2 + c^2}}\mathbf{j} + \frac{c}{\sqrt{a^2 + c^2}}\mathbf{k}$$

$$\mathbf{T}'(t) = -\frac{a \cos t}{\sqrt{a^2 + c^2}}\mathbf{i} - \frac{a \sin t}{\sqrt{a^2 + c^2}}\mathbf{j}$$

$$\|\mathbf{T}'(t)\| = \sqrt{\left(-\frac{a \cos t}{\sqrt{a^2 + c^2}}\right)^2 + \left(-\frac{a \sin t}{\sqrt{a^2 + c^2}}\right)^2} = \sqrt{\frac{a^2}{a^2 + c^2}} = \frac{a}{\sqrt{a^2 + c^2}}$$

$$\mathbf{N}(t) = \frac{\mathbf{T}'(t)}{\|\mathbf{T}'(t)\|} = (-\cos t)\mathbf{i} - (\sin t)\mathbf{j} = -(\cos t\,\mathbf{i} + \sin t\,\mathbf{j})$$

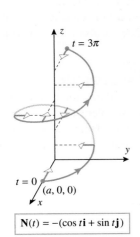

$\mathbf{N}(t) = -(\cos t\,\mathbf{i} + \sin t\,\mathbf{j})$

▲ **Figure 12.4.5**

Note that the $\mathbf{k}$ component of the principal unit normal $\mathbf{N}(t)$ is zero for every value of t, so this vector always lies in a horizontal plane, as illustrated in Figure 12.4.5. We leave it as an exercise to show that this vector actually always points toward the z-axis. ◄

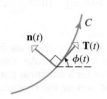

▲ **Figure 12.4.6**

INWARD UNIT NORMAL VECTORS IN 2-SPACE

Our next objective is to show that for a nonlinear parametric curve C in 2-space the unit normal vector always points toward the concave side of C. For this purpose, let $\phi(t)$ be the angle from the positive x-axis to $\mathbf{T}(t)$, and let $\mathbf{n}(t)$ be the unit vector that results when $\mathbf{T}(t)$ is rotated counterclockwise through an angle of $\pi/2$ (Figure 12.4.6). Since $\mathbf{T}(t)$ and $\mathbf{n}(t)$ are unit vectors, it follows from Formula (13) of Section 11.2 that these vectors can be expressed as

$$\mathbf{T}(t) = \cos\phi(t)\mathbf{i} + \sin\phi(t)\mathbf{j} \tag{3}$$

and

$$\mathbf{n}(t) = \cos[\phi(t) + \pi/2]\mathbf{i} + \sin[\phi(t) + \pi/2]\mathbf{j} = -\sin\phi(t)\mathbf{i} + \cos\phi(t)\mathbf{j} \tag{4}$$

Observe that on intervals where $\phi(t)$ is increasing the vector $\mathbf{n}(t)$ points *toward* the concave side of C, and on intervals where $\phi(t)$ is decreasing it points *away* from the concave side (Figure 12.4.7).

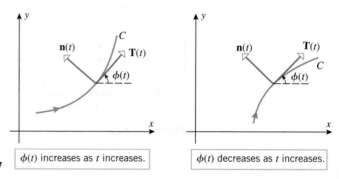

| $\phi(t)$ increases as t increases. | $\phi(t)$ decreases as t increases. |

▶ **Figure 12.4.7**

Now let us differentiate $\mathbf{T}(t)$ by using Formula (3) and applying the chain rule. This yields

$$\frac{d\mathbf{T}}{dt} = \frac{d\mathbf{T}}{d\phi}\frac{d\phi}{dt} = [(-\sin\phi)\mathbf{i} + (\cos\phi)\mathbf{j}]\frac{d\phi}{dt}$$

and thus from (4)

$$\frac{d\mathbf{T}}{dt} = \mathbf{n}(t)\frac{d\phi}{dt} \tag{5}$$

But $d\phi/dt > 0$ on intervals where $\phi(t)$ is increasing and $d\phi/dt < 0$ on intervals where $\phi(t)$ is decreasing. Thus, it follows from (5) that $d\mathbf{T}/dt$ has the same direction as $\mathbf{n}(t)$ on intervals where $\phi(t)$ is increasing and the opposite direction on intervals where $\phi(t)$ is decreasing. Therefore, $\mathbf{T}'(t) = d\mathbf{T}/dt$ points "inward" toward the concave side of the curve in all cases, and hence so does $\mathbf{N}(t)$. For this reason, $\mathbf{N}(t)$ is also called the *inward unit normal* when applied to curves in 2-space.

COMPUTING T AND N FOR CURVES PARAMETRIZED BY ARC LENGTH

In the case where $\mathbf{r}(s)$ is parametrized by arc length, the procedures for computing the unit tangent vector $\mathbf{T}(s)$ and the unit normal vector $\mathbf{N}(s)$ are simpler than in the general case. For example, we showed in Theorem 12.3.4 that if s is an arc length parameter, then $\|\mathbf{r}'(s)\| = 1$. Thus, Formula (1) for the unit tangent vector simplifies to

WARNING

Formulas (6) and (7) are only applicable when the curve is parametrized by an arc length parameter s. For other parametrizations Formulas (1) and (2) can be used.

$$\mathbf{T}(s) = \mathbf{r}'(s) \tag{6}$$

and consequently Formula (2) for the unit normal vector simplifies to

$$\mathbf{N}(s) = \frac{\mathbf{r}''(s)}{\|\mathbf{r}''(s)\|} \tag{7}$$

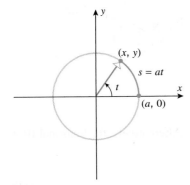

▲ **Figure 12.4.8**

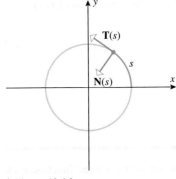

▲ **Figure 12.4.9**

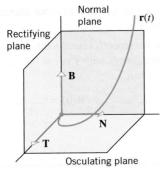

▲ **Figure 12.4.10**

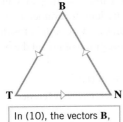

In (10), the vectors **B**, **N**, and **T** are each expressed as the cross product of the other two taken in the counterclockwise direction around the above triangle.

▲ **Figure 12.4.11**

▶ **Example 3** The circle of radius a with counterclockwise orientation and centered at the origin can be represented by the vector-valued function

$$\mathbf{r} = a\cos t\mathbf{i} + a\sin t\mathbf{j} \qquad (0 \le t \le 2\pi) \tag{8}$$

Parametrize this circle by arc length and find $\mathbf{T}(s)$ and $\mathbf{N}(s)$.

Solution. In (8) we can interpret t as the angle in radian measure from the positive x-axis to the radius vector (Figure 12.4.8). This angle subtends an arc of length $s = at$ on the circle, so we can reparametrize the circle in terms of s by substituting s/a for t in (8). This yields
$$\mathbf{r}(s) = a\cos(s/a)\mathbf{i} + a\sin(s/a)\mathbf{j} \qquad (0 \le s \le 2\pi a)$$

To find $\mathbf{T}(s)$ and $\mathbf{N}(s)$ from Formulas (6) and (7), we must compute $\mathbf{r}'(s)$, $\mathbf{r}''(s)$, and $\|\mathbf{r}''(s)\|$. Doing so, we obtain

$$\mathbf{r}'(s) = -\sin(s/a)\mathbf{i} + \cos(s/a)\mathbf{j}$$

$$\mathbf{r}''(s) = -(1/a)\cos(s/a)\mathbf{i} - (1/a)\sin(s/a)\mathbf{j}$$

$$\|\mathbf{r}''(s)\| = \sqrt{(-1/a)^2\cos^2(s/a) + (-1/a)^2\sin^2(s/a)} = 1/a$$

Thus,

$$\mathbf{T}(s) = \mathbf{r}'(s) = -\sin(s/a)\mathbf{i} + \cos(s/a)\mathbf{j}$$

$$\mathbf{N}(s) = \mathbf{r}''(s)/\|\mathbf{r}''(s)\| = -\cos(s/a)\mathbf{i} - \sin(s/a)\mathbf{j}$$

so $\mathbf{N}(s)$ points toward the center of the circle for all s (Figure 12.4.9). This makes sense geometrically and is also consistent with our earlier observation that in 2-space the unit normal vector is the inward normal. ◀

■ **BINORMAL VECTORS IN 3-SPACE**

If C is the graph of a vector-valued function $\mathbf{r}(t)$ in 3-space, then we define the ***binormal vector*** to C at t to be

$$\mathbf{B}(t) = \mathbf{T}(t) \times \mathbf{N}(t) \tag{9}$$

It follows from properties of the cross product that $\mathbf{B}(t)$ is orthogonal to both $\mathbf{T}(t)$ and $\mathbf{N}(t)$ and is oriented relative to $\mathbf{T}(t)$ and $\mathbf{N}(t)$ by the right-hand rule. Moreover, $\mathbf{T}(t) \times \mathbf{N}(t)$ is a unit vector since

$$\|\mathbf{T}(t) \times \mathbf{N}(t)\| = \|\mathbf{T}(t)\|\|\mathbf{N}(t)\|\sin(\pi/2) = 1$$

Thus, $\{\mathbf{T}(t), \mathbf{N}(t), \mathbf{B}(t)\}$ is a set of three mutually orthogonal unit vectors.

Just as the vectors $\mathbf{i}$, $\mathbf{j}$, and $\mathbf{k}$ determine a right-handed coordinate system in 3-space, so do the vectors $\mathbf{T}(t)$, $\mathbf{N}(t)$, and $\mathbf{B}(t)$. At each point on a smooth parametric curve C in 3-space, these vectors determine three mutually perpendicular planes that pass through the point—the TB-plane (called the ***rectifying plane***), the TN-plane (called the ***osculating plane***), and the NB-plane (called the ***normal plane***) (Figure 12.4.10). Moreover, one can show that a coordinate system determined by $\mathbf{T}(t)$, $\mathbf{N}(t)$, and $\mathbf{B}(t)$ is right-handed in the sense that each of these vectors is related to the other two by the right-hand rule (Figure 12.4.11):

$$\mathbf{B}(t) = \mathbf{T}(t) \times \mathbf{N}(t), \quad \mathbf{N}(t) = \mathbf{B}(t) \times \mathbf{T}(t), \quad \mathbf{T}(t) = \mathbf{N}(t) \times \mathbf{B}(t) \tag{10}$$

The coordinate system determined by $\mathbf{T}(t)$, $\mathbf{N}(t)$, and $\mathbf{B}(t)$ is called the ***TNB-frame*** or sometimes the ***Frenet frame*** in honor of the French mathematician Jean Frédéric Frenet (1816–1900) who pioneered its application to the study of space curves. Typically, the xyz-coordinate system determined by the unit vectors $\mathbf{i}$, $\mathbf{j}$, and $\mathbf{k}$ remains fixed, whereas the TNB-frame changes as its origin moves along the curve C (Figure 12.4.12).

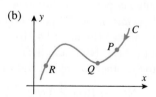

► **Figure 12.4.12**

Formula (9) expresses $\mathbf{B}(t)$ in terms of $\mathbf{T}(t)$ and $\mathbf{N}(t)$. Alternatively, the binormal $\mathbf{B}(t)$ can be expressed directly in terms of $\mathbf{r}(t)$ as

$$\mathbf{B}(t) = \frac{\mathbf{r}'(t) \times \mathbf{r}''(t)}{\|\mathbf{r}'(t) \times \mathbf{r}''(t)\|} \tag{11}$$

and in the case where the parameter is arc length it can be expressed in terms of $\mathbf{r}(s)$ as

$$\mathbf{B}(s) = \frac{\mathbf{r}'(s) \times \mathbf{r}''(s)}{\|\mathbf{r}''(s)\|} \tag{12}$$

We omit the proof.

✔ QUICK CHECK EXERCISES 12.4   *(See page 873 for answers.)*

1. If C is the graph of a smooth vector-valued function $\mathbf{r}(t)$, then the unit tangent, unit normal, and binormal to C at t are defined, respectively, by

$$\mathbf{T}(t) = \underline{\hspace{1cm}}, \quad \mathbf{N}(t) = \underline{\hspace{1cm}}, \quad \mathbf{B}(t) = \underline{\hspace{1cm}}$$

2. If C is the graph of a smooth vector-valued function $\mathbf{r}(s)$ parametrized by arc length, then the definitions of the unit tangent and unit normal to C at s simplify, respectively, to

$$\mathbf{T}(s) = \underline{\hspace{1cm}} \quad \text{and} \quad \mathbf{N}(s) = \underline{\hspace{1cm}}$$

3. If C is the graph of a smooth vector-valued function $\mathbf{r}(t)$, then the unit binormal vector to C at t may be computed directly in terms of $\mathbf{r}'(t)$ and $\mathbf{r}''(t)$ by the formula $\mathbf{B}(t) = \underline{\hspace{1cm}}$. When $t = s$ is the arc length parameter, this formula simplifies to $\mathbf{B}(s) = \underline{\hspace{1cm}}$.

4. Suppose that C is the graph of a smooth vector-valued function $\mathbf{r}(s)$ parametrized by arc length with $\mathbf{r}'(0) = \langle \frac{2}{3}, \frac{1}{3}, \frac{2}{3} \rangle$ and $\mathbf{r}''(0) = \langle -3, 12, -3 \rangle$. Then

$$\mathbf{T}(0) = \underline{\hspace{1cm}}, \quad \mathbf{N}(0) = \underline{\hspace{1cm}}, \quad \mathbf{B}(0) = \underline{\hspace{1cm}}$$

EXERCISE SET 12.4

FOCUS ON CONCEPTS

1. In each part, sketch the unit tangent and normal vectors at the points P, Q, and R, taking into account the orientation of the curve C.

(a) 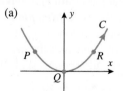 (b)

2. Make a rough sketch that shows the ellipse

$$\mathbf{r}(t) = 3 \cos t\, \mathbf{i} + 2 \sin t\, \mathbf{j}$$

for $0 \le t \le 2\pi$ and the unit tangent and normal vectors at the points $t = 0$, $t = \pi/4$, $t = \pi/2$, and $t = \pi$.

3. In the marginal note associated with Example 8 of Section 12.3, we observed that a line $\mathbf{r} = \mathbf{r}_0 + t\mathbf{v}$ can be parametrized in terms of an arc length parameter s with reference point $\mathbf{r}_0$ by normalizing $\mathbf{v}$. Use this result to show that the tangent line to the graph of $\mathbf{r}(t)$ at the point t_0 can be expressed as

$$\mathbf{r} = \mathbf{r}(t_0) + s\mathbf{T}(t_0)$$

where s is an arc length parameter with reference point $\mathbf{r}(t_0)$.

4. Use the result in Exercise 3 to show that the tangent line to the parabola

$$x = t, \quad y = t^2$$

at the point $(1, 1)$ can be expressed parametrically as

$$x = 1 + \frac{s}{\sqrt{5}}, \quad y = 1 + \frac{2s}{\sqrt{5}}$$

5–12 Find $\mathbf{T}(t)$ and $\mathbf{N}(t)$ at the given point. ■

5. $\mathbf{r}(t) = (t^2 - 1)\mathbf{i} + t\mathbf{j}; \ t = 1$

6. $\mathbf{r}(t) = \frac{1}{2}t^2\mathbf{i} + \frac{1}{3}t^3\mathbf{j}; \ t = 1$

7. $\mathbf{r}(t) = 5\cos t\mathbf{i} + 5\sin t\mathbf{j}; \ t = \pi/3$

8. $\mathbf{r}(t) = \ln t\mathbf{i} + t\mathbf{j}; \ t = e$

9. $\mathbf{r}(t) = 4\cos t\mathbf{i} + 4\sin t\mathbf{j} + t\mathbf{k}; \ t = \pi/2$

10. $\mathbf{r}(t) = t\mathbf{i} + \frac{1}{2}t^2\mathbf{j} + \frac{1}{3}t^3\mathbf{k}; \ t = 0$

11. $x = e^t\cos t, \ y = e^t\sin t, \ z = e^t; \ t = 0$

12. $x = \cosh t, \ y = \sinh t, \ z = t; \ t = \ln 2$

13–14 Use the result in Exercise 3 to find parametric equations for the tangent line to the graph of $\mathbf{r}(t)$ at t_0 in terms of an arc length parameter s. ■

13. $\mathbf{r}(t) = \sin t\mathbf{i} + \cos t\mathbf{j} + \frac{1}{2}t^2\mathbf{k}; \ t_0 = 0$

14. $\mathbf{r}(t) = t\mathbf{i} + t\mathbf{j} + \sqrt{9 - t^2}\mathbf{k}; \ t_0 = 1$

15–18 Use the formula $\mathbf{B}(t) = \mathbf{T}(t) \times \mathbf{N}(t)$ to find $\mathbf{B}(t)$, and then check your answer by using Formula (11) to find $\mathbf{B}(t)$ directly from $\mathbf{r}(t)$. ■

15. $\mathbf{r}(t) = 3\sin t\mathbf{i} + 3\cos t\mathbf{j} + 4t\mathbf{k}$

16. $\mathbf{r}(t) = e^t\sin t\mathbf{i} + e^t\cos t\mathbf{j} + 3\mathbf{k}$

17. $\mathbf{r}(t) = (\sin t - t\cos t)\mathbf{i} + (\cos t + t\sin t)\mathbf{j} + \mathbf{k}$

18. $\mathbf{r}(t) = a\cos t\mathbf{i} + a\sin t\mathbf{j} + ct\mathbf{k} \quad (a \neq 0, c \neq 0)$

19–20 Find $\mathbf{T}(t)$, $\mathbf{N}(t)$, and $\mathbf{B}(t)$ for the given value of t. Then find equations for the osculating, normal, and rectifying planes at the point that corresponds to that value of t. ■

19. $\mathbf{r}(t) = \cos t\mathbf{i} + \sin t\mathbf{j} + \mathbf{k}; \ t = \pi/4$

20. $\mathbf{r}(t) = e^t\mathbf{i} + e^t\cos t\mathbf{j} + e^t\sin t\mathbf{k}; \ t = 0$

21–24 True–False Determine whether the statement is true or false. Explain your answer. ■

21. If C is the graph of a smooth vector-valued function $\mathbf{r}(t)$ in 2-space, then the unit tangent vector $\mathbf{T}(t)$ to C is orthogonal to $\mathbf{r}(t)$ and points in the direction of increasing parameter.

22. If C is the graph of a smooth vector-valued function $\mathbf{r}(t)$ in 2-space, then the angle measured in the counterclockwise direction from the unit tangent vector $\mathbf{T}(t)$ to the unit normal vector $\mathbf{N}(t)$ is $\pi/2$.

23. If the smooth vector-valued function $\mathbf{r}(s)$ is parametrized by arc length and $\mathbf{r}''(s)$ is defined, then $\mathbf{r}'(s)$ and $\mathbf{r}''(s)$ are orthogonal vectors.

24. The binormal vector $\mathbf{B}(t)$ to the graph of a vector-valued function $\mathbf{r}(t)$ in 3-space is the dot product of unit tangent and unit normal vectors, $\mathbf{T}(t)$ and $\mathbf{N}(t)$.

25. Writing Look up the definition of "osculating" in a dictionary and discuss why "osculating plane" is an appropriate term for the **TN**-plane.

26. Writing Discuss some of the advantages of parametrizing a curve by arc length.

✔ **QUICK CHECK ANSWERS 12.4**

1. $\dfrac{\mathbf{r}'(t)}{\|\mathbf{r}'(t)\|}$; $\dfrac{\mathbf{T}'(t)}{\|\mathbf{T}'(t)\|}$; $\mathbf{T}(t) \times \mathbf{N}(t)$ **2.** $\mathbf{r}'(s)$; $\dfrac{\mathbf{r}''(s)}{\|\mathbf{r}''(s)\|}$ **3.** $\dfrac{\mathbf{r}'(t) \times \mathbf{r}''(t)}{\|\mathbf{r}'(t) \times \mathbf{r}''(t)\|}$; $\dfrac{\mathbf{r}'(s) \times \mathbf{r}''(s)}{\|\mathbf{r}''(s)\|}$

4. $\left\langle \dfrac{2}{3}, \dfrac{1}{3}, \dfrac{2}{3} \right\rangle$; $\left\langle -\dfrac{1}{3\sqrt{2}}, \dfrac{4}{3\sqrt{2}}, -\dfrac{1}{3\sqrt{2}} \right\rangle$; $\left\langle -\dfrac{1}{\sqrt{2}}, 0, \dfrac{1}{\sqrt{2}} \right\rangle$

12.5 CURVATURE

In this section we will consider the problem of obtaining a numerical measure of how sharply a curve in 2-space or 3-space bends. Our results will have applications in geometry and in the study of motion along a curved path.

■ DEFINITION OF CURVATURE

Suppose that C is the graph of a smooth vector-valued function in 2-space or 3-space that is parametrized in terms of arc length. Figure 12.5.1 suggests that for a curve in 2-space the "sharpness" of the bend in C is closely related to $d\mathbf{T}/ds$, which is the rate of change of the unit tangent vector $\mathbf{T}$ with respect to s. (Keep in mind that $\mathbf{T}$ has constant length, so only its direction changes.) If C is a straight line (no bend), then the direction of $\mathbf{T}$ remains constant (Figure 12.5.1a); if C bends slightly, then $\mathbf{T}$ undergoes a gradual change of direction (Figure 12.5.1b); and if C bends sharply, then $\mathbf{T}$ undergoes a rapid change of direction (Figure 12.5.1c).

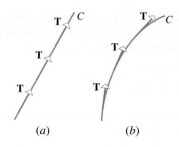

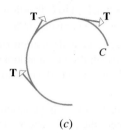

(c)

▲ Figure 12.5.1

The situation in 3-space is more complicated because bends in a curve are not limited to a single plane—they can occur in all directions, as illustrated by the complicated tube plot in Figure 12.1.4. To describe the bending characteristics of a curve in 3-space completely, one must take into account $d\mathbf{T}/ds$, $d\mathbf{N}/ds$, and $d\mathbf{B}/ds$. A complete study of this topic would take us too far afield, so we will limit our discussion to $d\mathbf{T}/ds$, which is the most important of these derivatives in applications.

12.5.1 DEFINITION If C is a smooth curve in 2-space or 3-space that is parametrized by arc length, then the **curvature** of C, denoted by $\kappa = \kappa(s)$ (κ = Greek "kappa"), is defined by

$$\kappa(s) = \left\| \frac{d\mathbf{T}}{ds} \right\| = \|\mathbf{r}''(s)\| \tag{1}$$

Observe that $\kappa(s)$ is a real-valued function of s, since it is the *length* of $d\mathbf{T}/ds$ that measures the curvature. In general, the curvature will vary from point to point along a curve; however, the following example shows that the curvature is constant for circles in 2-space, as you might expect.

▶ **Example 1** In Example 3 of Section 12.4 we showed that the circle of radius a, centered at the origin, can be parametrized in terms of arc length as

$$\mathbf{r}(s) = a \cos \left(\frac{s}{a} \right) \mathbf{i} + a \sin \left(\frac{s}{a} \right) \mathbf{j} \qquad (0 \le s \le 2\pi a)$$

Thus,

$$\mathbf{r}''(s) = -\frac{1}{a} \cos \left(\frac{s}{a} \right) \mathbf{i} - \frac{1}{a} \sin \left(\frac{s}{a} \right) \mathbf{j}$$

and hence from (1)

$$\kappa(s) = \|\mathbf{r}''(s)\| = \sqrt{ \left[-\frac{1}{a} \cos \left(\frac{s}{a} \right) \right]^2 + \left[-\frac{1}{a} \sin \left(\frac{s}{a} \right) \right]^2 } = \frac{1}{a}$$

so the circle has constant curvature $1/a$. ◀

The next example shows that lines have zero curvature, which is consistent with the fact that they do not bend.

▶ **Example 2** Recall from Formula (15) of Section 12.3 that a line in 2-space or 3-space can be parametrized in terms of arc length as

$$\mathbf{r} = \mathbf{r}_0 + s\mathbf{u}$$

where the terminal point of $\mathbf{r}_0$ is a point on the line and $\mathbf{u}$ is a unit vector parallel to the line. Since $\mathbf{u}$ and $\mathbf{r}_0$ are constant, their derivatives with respect to s are zero, and hence

$$\mathbf{r}'(s) = \frac{d\mathbf{r}}{ds} = \frac{d}{ds}[\mathbf{r}_0 + s\mathbf{u}] = \mathbf{0} + \mathbf{u} = \mathbf{u}$$

$$\mathbf{r}''(s) = \frac{d\mathbf{r}'}{ds} = \frac{d}{ds}[\mathbf{u}] = \mathbf{0}$$

Thus,

$$\kappa(s) = \|\mathbf{r}''(s)\| = 0 \quad ◀$$

■ FORMULAS FOR CURVATURE

Formula (1) is only applicable if the curve is parametrized in terms of arc length. The following theorem provides two formulas for curvature in terms of a general parameter t.

12.5.2 THEOREM *If $\mathbf{r}(t)$ is a smooth vector-valued function in 2-space or 3-space, then for each value of t at which $\mathbf{T}'(t)$ and $\mathbf{r}''(t)$ exist, the curvature κ can be expressed as*

$(a) \quad \kappa(t) = \dfrac{\|\mathbf{T}'(t)\|}{\|\mathbf{r}'(t)\|}$ \hfill (2)

$(b) \quad \kappa(t) = \dfrac{\|\mathbf{r}'(t) \times \mathbf{r}''(t)\|}{\|\mathbf{r}'(t)\|^3}$ \hfill (3)

PROOF (a) It follows from Formula (1) and Formula (16) of Section 12.3 that

$$\kappa(t) = \left\| \frac{d\mathbf{T}}{ds} \right\| = \left\| \frac{d\mathbf{T}/dt}{ds/dt} \right\| = \left\| \frac{d\mathbf{T}/dt}{\|d\mathbf{r}/dt\|} \right\| = \frac{\|\mathbf{T}'(t)\|}{\|\mathbf{r}'(t)\|}$$

PROOF (b) It follows from Formula (1) of Section 12.4 that

$$\mathbf{r}'(t) = \|\mathbf{r}'(t)\|\mathbf{T}(t) \tag{4}$$
$$\mathbf{r}''(t) = \|\mathbf{r}'(t)\|'\mathbf{T}(t) + \|\mathbf{r}'(t)\|\mathbf{T}'(t) \tag{5}$$

But from Formula (2) of Section 12.4 and part (a) of this theorem we have

$$\mathbf{T}'(t) = \|\mathbf{T}'(t)\|\mathbf{N}(t) \quad \text{and} \quad \|\mathbf{T}'(t)\| = \kappa(t)\|\mathbf{r}'(t)\|$$

so

$$\mathbf{T}'(t) = \kappa(t)\|\mathbf{r}'(t)\|\mathbf{N}(t)$$

Substituting this into (5) yields

$$\mathbf{r}''(t) = \|\mathbf{r}'(t)\|'\mathbf{T}(t) + \kappa(t)\|\mathbf{r}'(t)\|^2\mathbf{N}(t) \tag{6}$$

Thus, from (4) and (6)

$$\mathbf{r}'(t) \times \mathbf{r}''(t) = \|\mathbf{r}'(t)\|\|\mathbf{r}'(t)\|'(\mathbf{T}(t) \times \mathbf{T}(t)) + \kappa(t)\|\mathbf{r}'(t)\|^3(\mathbf{T}(t) \times \mathbf{N}(t))$$

But the cross product of a vector with itself is zero, so this equation simplifies to

$$\mathbf{r}'(t) \times \mathbf{r}''(t) = \kappa(t)\|\mathbf{r}'(t)\|^3(\mathbf{T}(t) \times \mathbf{N}(t)) = \kappa(t)\|\mathbf{r}'(t)\|^3\mathbf{B}(t)$$

It follows from this equation and the fact that $\mathbf{B}(t)$ is a unit vector that

$$\|\mathbf{r}'(t) \times \mathbf{r}''(t)\| = \kappa(t)\|\mathbf{r}'(t)\|^3$$

Formula (3) now follows. ■

REMARK   Formula (2) is useful if $\mathbf{T}(t)$ is known or is easy to obtain; however, Formula (3) will usually be easier to apply, since it involves only $\mathbf{r}(t)$ and its derivatives. We also note that cross products were defined only for vectors in 3-space, so to use Formula (3) in 2-space we must first write the 2-space function $\mathbf{r}(t) = x(t)\mathbf{i} + y(t)\mathbf{j}$ as the 3-space function $\mathbf{r}(t) = x(t)\mathbf{i} + y(t)\mathbf{j} + 0\mathbf{k}$ with a zero $\mathbf{k}$ component.

▶ **Example 3**   Find $\kappa(t)$ for the circular helix

$$x = a \cos t, \quad y = a \sin t, \quad z = ct$$

where $a > 0$.

Solution. The radius vector for the helix is

$$\mathbf{r}(t) = a\cos t\mathbf{i} + a\sin t\mathbf{j} + ct\mathbf{k}$$

Thus,

$$\mathbf{r}'(t) = (-a\sin t)\mathbf{i} + a\cos t\mathbf{j} + c\mathbf{k}$$
$$\mathbf{r}''(t) = (-a\cos t)\mathbf{i} + (-a\sin t)\mathbf{j}$$

$$\mathbf{r}'(t) \times \mathbf{r}''(t) = \begin{vmatrix} \mathbf{i} & \mathbf{j} & \mathbf{k} \\ -a\sin t & a\cos t & c \\ -a\cos t & -a\sin t & 0 \end{vmatrix} = (ac\sin t)\mathbf{i} - (ac\cos t)\mathbf{j} + a^2\mathbf{k}$$

Therefore,

$$\|\mathbf{r}'(t)\| = \sqrt{(-a\sin t)^2 + (a\cos t)^2 + c^2} = \sqrt{a^2 + c^2}$$

and

$$\|\mathbf{r}'(t) \times \mathbf{r}''(t)\| = \sqrt{(ac\sin t)^2 + (-ac\cos t)^2 + a^4}$$
$$= \sqrt{a^2c^2 + a^4} = a\sqrt{a^2 + c^2}$$

so

$$\kappa(t) = \frac{\|\mathbf{r}'(t) \times \mathbf{r}''(t)\|}{\|\mathbf{r}'(t)\|^3} = \frac{a\sqrt{a^2 + c^2}}{\left(\sqrt{a^2 + c^2}\right)^3} = \frac{a}{a^2 + c^2}$$

Note that κ does not depend on t, which tells us that the helix has constant curvature. ◀

▶ **Example 4** The graph of the vector equation

$$\mathbf{r} = 2\cos t\mathbf{i} + 3\sin t\mathbf{j} \quad (0 \le t \le 2\pi)$$

is the ellipse in Figure 12.5.2. Find the curvature of the ellipse at the endpoints of the major and minor axes, and use a graphing utility to generate the graph of $\kappa(t)$.

Solution. To apply Formula (3), we must treat the ellipse as a curve in the xy-plane of an xyz-coordinate system by adding a zero $\mathbf{k}$ component and writing its equation as

$$\mathbf{r} = 2\cos t\mathbf{i} + 3\sin t\mathbf{j} + 0\mathbf{k}$$

It is not essential to write the zero $\mathbf{k}$ component explicitly as long as you assume it to be there when you calculate a cross product. Thus,

$$\mathbf{r}'(t) = (-2\sin t)\mathbf{i} + 3\cos t\mathbf{j}$$
$$\mathbf{r}''(t) = (-2\cos t)\mathbf{i} + (-3\sin t)\mathbf{j}$$

$$\mathbf{r}'(t) \times \mathbf{r}''(t) = \begin{vmatrix} \mathbf{i} & \mathbf{j} & \mathbf{k} \\ -2\sin t & 3\cos t & 0 \\ -2\cos t & -3\sin t & 0 \end{vmatrix} = [(6\sin^2 t) + (6\cos^2 t)]\mathbf{k} = 6\mathbf{k}$$

Therefore,

$$\|\mathbf{r}'(t)\| = \sqrt{(-2\sin t)^2 + (3\cos t)^2} = \sqrt{4\sin^2 t + 9\cos^2 t}$$
$$\|\mathbf{r}'(t) \times \mathbf{r}''(t)\| = 6$$

so

$$\kappa(t) = \frac{\|\mathbf{r}'(t) \times \mathbf{r}''(t)\|}{\|\mathbf{r}'(t)\|^3} = \frac{6}{[4\sin^2 t + 9\cos^2 t]^{3/2}} \tag{7}$$

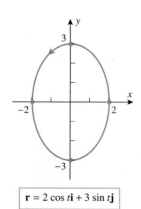

$$\mathbf{r} = 2\cos t\mathbf{i} + 3\sin t\mathbf{j}$$

▲ **Figure 12.5.2**

The endpoints of the minor axis are $(2, 0)$ and $(-2, 0)$, which correspond to $t = 0$ and $t = \pi$, respectively. Substituting these values in (7) yields the same curvature at both points, namely,

$$\kappa = \kappa(0) = \kappa(\pi) = \frac{6}{9^{3/2}} = \frac{6}{27} = \frac{2}{9}$$

The endpoints of the major axis are $(0, 3)$ and $(0, -3)$, which correspond to $t = \pi/2$ and $t = 3\pi/2$, respectively; from (7) the curvature at these points is

$$\kappa = \kappa\left(\frac{\pi}{2}\right) = \kappa\left(\frac{3\pi}{2}\right) = \frac{6}{4^{3/2}} = \frac{3}{4}$$

Observe that the curvature is greater at the ends of the major axis than at the ends of the minor axis, as you might expect. Figure 12.5.3 shows the graph of κ versus t. This graph illustrates clearly that the curvature is minimum at $t = 0$ (the right end of the minor axis), increases to a maximum at $t = \pi/2$ (the top of the major axis), decreases to a minimum again at $t = \pi$ (the left end of the minor axis), and continues cyclically in this manner. Figure 12.5.4 provides another way of picturing the curvature. ◄

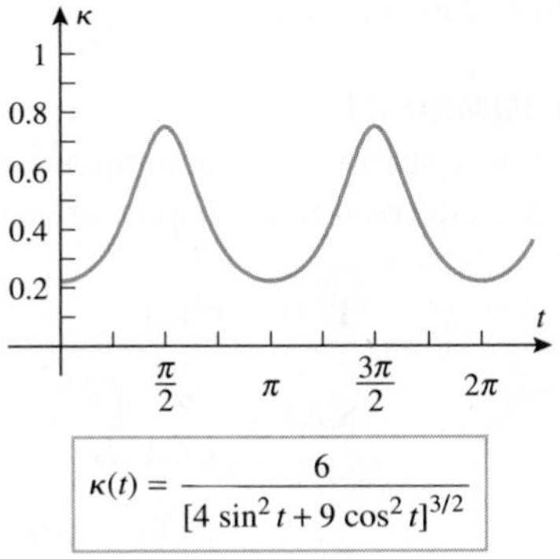

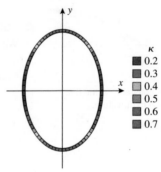

$$\kappa(t) = \frac{6}{[4\sin^2 t + 9\cos^2 t]^{3/2}}$$

▲ Figure 12.5.3

▲ Figure 12.5.4

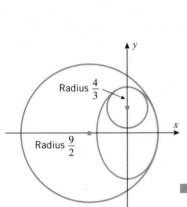

▲ Figure 12.5.5

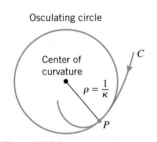

Osculating circle

Center of curvature

$\rho = \dfrac{1}{\kappa}$

▲ Figure 12.5.6

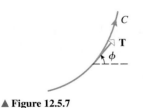

▲ Figure 12.5.7

■ RADIUS OF CURVATURE

In the last example we found the curvature at the ends of the minor axis to be $\frac{2}{9}$ and the curvature at the ends of the major axis to be $\frac{3}{4}$. To obtain a better understanding of the meaning of these numbers, recall from Example 1 that a circle of radius a has a constant curvature of $1/a$; thus, the curvature of the ellipse at the ends of the minor axis is the same as that of a circle of radius $\frac{9}{2}$, and the curvature at the ends of the major axis is the same as that of a circle of radius $\frac{4}{3}$ (Figure 12.5.5).

In general, if a curve C in 2-space has nonzero curvature κ at a point P, then the circle of radius $\rho = 1/\kappa$ sharing a common tangent with C at P, and centered on the concave side of the curve at P, is called the ***osculating circle*** or ***circle of curvature*** at P (Figure 12.5.6). The osculating circle and the curve C not only touch at P but they have equal curvatures at that point. In this sense, the osculating circle is the circle that best approximates the curve C near P. The radius ρ of the osculating circle at P is called the ***radius of curvature*** at P, and the center of the circle is called the ***center of curvature*** at P (Figure 12.5.6).

■ AN INTERPRETATION OF CURVATURE IN 2-SPACE

A useful geometric interpretation of curvature in 2-space can be obtained by considering the angle ϕ measured counterclockwise from the direction of the positive x-axis to the unit tangent vector $\mathbf{T}$ (Figure 12.5.7). By Formula (13) of Section 11.2, we can express $\mathbf{T}$ in terms of ϕ as

$$\mathbf{T}(\phi) = \cos\phi\,\mathbf{i} + \sin\phi\,\mathbf{j}$$

Thus,

$$\frac{d\mathbf{T}}{d\phi} = (-\sin\phi)\mathbf{i} + \cos\phi\,\mathbf{j}$$

$$\frac{d\mathbf{T}}{ds} = \frac{d\mathbf{T}}{d\phi}\frac{d\phi}{ds}$$

from which we obtain

$$\kappa(s) = \left\|\frac{d\mathbf{T}}{ds}\right\| = \left|\frac{d\phi}{ds}\right| \left\|\frac{d\mathbf{T}}{d\phi}\right\| = \left|\frac{d\phi}{ds}\right|\sqrt{(-\sin\phi)^2 + \cos^2\phi} = \left|\frac{d\phi}{ds}\right|$$

In summary, we have shown that

$$\kappa(s) = \left|\frac{d\phi}{ds}\right| \qquad (8)$$

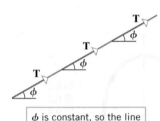

In 2-space, $\kappa(s)$ is the magnitude of the rate of change of ϕ with respect to s.

▲ **Figure 12.5.8**

which tells us that curvature in 2-space can be interpreted as the magnitude of the rate of change of ϕ with respect to s—the greater the curvature, the more rapidly ϕ changes with s (Figure 12.5.8). In the case of a straight line, the angle ϕ is constant (Figure 12.5.9) and consequently $\kappa(s) = |d\phi/ds| = 0$, which is consistent with the fact that a straight line has zero curvature at every point.

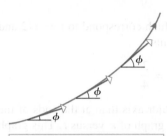

ϕ is constant, so the line has zero curvature.

▲ **Figure 12.5.9**

■ **FORMULA SUMMARY**

We conclude this section with a summary of formulas for **T**, **N**, and **B**. These formulas have either been derived in the text or are easily derivable from formulas we have already established.

$$\mathbf{T}(s) = \mathbf{r}'(s) \qquad (9)$$

$$\mathbf{N}(s) = \frac{1}{\kappa(s)}\frac{d\mathbf{T}}{ds} = \frac{\mathbf{r}''(s)}{\|\mathbf{r}''(s)\|} = \frac{\mathbf{r}''(s)}{\kappa(s)} \qquad (10)$$

$$\mathbf{B}(s) = \frac{\mathbf{r}'(s) \times \mathbf{r}''(s)}{\|\mathbf{r}''(s)\|} = \frac{\mathbf{r}'(s) \times \mathbf{r}''(s)}{\kappa(s)} \qquad (11)$$

$$\mathbf{T}(t) = \frac{\mathbf{r}'(t)}{\|\mathbf{r}'(t)\|} \qquad (12)$$

$$\mathbf{B}(t) = \frac{\mathbf{r}'(t) \times \mathbf{r}''(t)}{\|\mathbf{r}'(t) \times \mathbf{r}''(t)\|} \qquad (13)$$

$$\mathbf{N}(t) = \mathbf{B}(t) \times \mathbf{T}(t) \qquad (14)$$

✔ **QUICK CHECK EXERCISES 12.5**   (See page 881 for answers.)

1. If C is a smooth curve parametrized by arc length, then the curvature is defined by $\kappa(s) = $ _____.

2. Let $\mathbf{r}(t)$ be a smooth vector-valued function with curvature $\kappa(t)$.
   (a) The curvature may be expressed in terms of $\mathbf{T}'(t)$ and $\mathbf{r}'(t)$ as $\kappa(t) = $ _____.
   (b) The curvature may be expressed directly in terms of $\mathbf{r}'(t)$ and $\mathbf{r}''(t)$ as $\kappa(t) = $ _____.

3. Suppose that C is the graph of a smooth vector-valued function $\mathbf{r}(s) = \langle x(s), y(s)\rangle$ parametrized by arc length and that the unit tangent $\mathbf{T}(s) = \langle \cos\phi(s), \sin\phi(s)\rangle$. Then the curvature can be expressed in terms of $\phi(s)$ as $\kappa(s) = $ _____.

4. Suppose that C is a smooth curve and that $x^2 + y^2 = 4$ is the osculating circle to C at $P(1, \sqrt{3})$. Then the curvature of C at P is _____.

EXERCISE SET 12.5   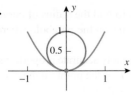 Graphing Utility   [c] CAS

1–2 Use the osculating circle shown in the figure to estimate the curvature at the indicated point. ■

1.   **2.**

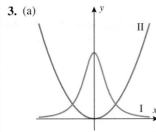

3–4 For a plane curve $y = f(x)$ the curvature at $(x, f(x))$ is a function $\kappa(x)$. In these exercises the graphs of $f(x)$ and $\kappa(x)$ are shown. Determine which is which and explain your reasoning. ■

3. (a)   (b)

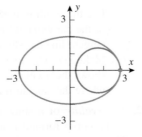

4. (a)   (b)

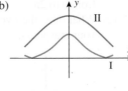

5–12 Use Formula (3) to find $\kappa(t)$. ■

5. $\mathbf{r}(t) = t^2\mathbf{i} + t^3\mathbf{j}$ **6.** $\mathbf{r}(t) = 4\cos t\,\mathbf{i} + \sin t\,\mathbf{j}$

7. $\mathbf{r}(t) = e^{3t}\mathbf{i} + e^{-t}\mathbf{j}$ **8.** $x = 1 - t^3, \ y = t - t^2$

9. $\mathbf{r}(t) = 4\cos t\,\mathbf{i} + 4\sin t\,\mathbf{j} + t\mathbf{k}$

10. $\mathbf{r}(t) = t\mathbf{i} + \frac{1}{2}t^2\mathbf{j} + \frac{1}{3}t^3\mathbf{k}$

11. $x = \cosh t, \ y = \sinh t, \ z = t$

12. $\mathbf{r}(t) = \mathbf{i} + t\mathbf{j} + t^2\mathbf{k}$

13–16 Find the curvature and the radius of curvature at the stated point. ■

13. $\mathbf{r}(t) = 3\cos t\,\mathbf{i} + 4\sin t\,\mathbf{j} + t\mathbf{k}; \ t = \pi/2$

14. $\mathbf{r}(t) = e^t\mathbf{i} + e^{-t}\mathbf{j} + t\mathbf{k}; \ t = 0$

15. $x = e^t\cos t, \ y = e^t\sin t, z = e^t; \ t = 0$

16. $x = \sin t, \ y = \cos t, z = \frac{1}{2}t^2; \ t = 0$

17–18 Confirm that s is an arc length parameter by showing that $\|d\mathbf{r}/ds\| = 1$, and then apply Formula (1) to find $\kappa(s)$. ■

17. $\mathbf{r} = \sin\left(1 + \frac{s}{2}\right)\mathbf{i} + \cos\left(1 + \frac{s}{2}\right)\mathbf{j} + \sqrt{3}\left(1 + \frac{s}{2}\right)\mathbf{k}$

18. $\mathbf{r} = \left(1 - \frac{2}{3}s\right)^{3/2}\mathbf{i} + \left(\frac{2}{3}s\right)^{3/2}\mathbf{j} \quad \left(0 \le s \le \frac{3}{2}\right)$

19–22 True–False Determine whether the statement is true or false. Explain your answer. ■

19. A circle of radius 2 has constant curvature $\frac{1}{2}$.

20. A vertical line in 2-space has undefined curvature.

21. If $\mathbf{r}(s)$ is parametrized by arc length, then the curvature of the graph of $\mathbf{r}(s)$ is the length of $\mathbf{r}'(s)$.

22. If C is a curve in 2-space, then the osculating circle to C at a point P has radius equal to the curvature of C at P.

23. (a) Use Formula (3) to show that in 2-space the curvature of a smooth parametric curve

$$x = x(t), \quad y = y(t)$$

is

$$\kappa(t) = \frac{|x'y'' - y'x''|}{(x'^2 + y'^2)^{3/2}}$$

where primes denote differentiation with respect to t.

(b) Use the result in part (a) to show that in 2-space the curvature of the plane curve given by $y = f(x)$ is

$$\kappa(x) = \frac{|d^2y/dx^2|}{[1 + (dy/dx)^2]^{3/2}}$$

[*Hint:* Express $y = f(x)$ parametrically with $x = t$ as the parameter.]

24. Use part (b) of Exercise 23 to show that the curvature of $y = f(x)$ can be expressed in terms of the angle of inclination of the tangent line as

$$\kappa(\phi) = \left|\frac{d^2y}{dx^2}\cos^3\phi\right|$$

[*Hint:* $\tan\phi = dy/dx$.]

25–28 Use the result in Exercise 23(b) to find the curvature at the stated point. ■

25. $y = \sin x; \ x = \pi/2$ **26.** $y = x^3/3; \ x = 0$

27. $y = e^{-x}; \ x = 1$ **28.** $y^2 - 4x^2 = 9; \ (2, 5)$

29–32 Use the result in Exercise 23(a) to find the curvature at the stated point. ■

29. $x = t^2, y = t^3; \ t = \frac{1}{2}$ **30.** $x = e^{3t}, y = e^{-t}; \ t = 0$

31. $x = t, y = 1/t; \ t = 1$

32. $x = 2\sin 2t, y = 3\sin t; \ t = \pi/2$

33. In each part, use the formulas in Exercise 23 to help find the radius of curvature at the stated points. Then sketch the graph together with the osculating circles at those points.

(a) $y = \cos x$ at $x = 0$ and $x = \pi$

(b) $x = 2\cos t, y = \sin t \ (0 \le t \le 2\pi)$ at $t = 0$ and $t = \pi/2$

34. Use the formula in Exercise 23(a) to find $\kappa(t)$ for the curve $x = e^{-t}\cos t, y = e^{-t}\sin t$. Then sketch the graph of $\kappa(t)$.

35–36 Generate the graph of $y = f(x)$ using a graphing utility, and then make a conjecture about the shape of the graph of $y = \kappa(x)$. Check your conjecture by generating the graph of $y = \kappa(x)$. ■

35. $f(x) = xe^{-x}$ for $0 \leq x \leq 5$

36. $f(x) = x^3 - x$ for $-1 \leq x \leq 1$

c **37.** (a) If you have a CAS, read the documentation on calculating higher-order derivatives. Then use the CAS and part (b) of Exercise 23 to find $\kappa(x)$ for $f(x) = x^4 - 2x^2$.
(b) Use the CAS to generate the graphs of $f(x) = x^4 - 2x^2$ and $\kappa(x)$ on the same screen for $-2 \leq x \leq 2$.
(c) Find the radius of curvature at each relative extremum.
(d) Make a reasonably accurate hand-drawn sketch that shows the graph of $f(x) = x^4 - 2x^2$ and the osculating circles in their correct proportions at the relative extrema.

c **38.** (a) Use a CAS to graph the parametric curve $x = t \cos t$, $y = t \sin t$ for $t \geq 0$.
(b) Make a conjecture about the behavior of the curvature $\kappa(t)$ as $t \to +\infty$.
(c) Use the CAS and part (a) of Exercise 23 to find $\kappa(t)$.
(d) Check your conjecture by finding the limit of $\kappa(t)$ as $t \to +\infty$.

39. Use the formula in Exercise 23(a) to show that for a curve in polar coordinates described by $r = f(\theta)$ the curvature is

$$\kappa(\theta) = \frac{\left| r^2 + 2\left(\dfrac{dr}{d\theta}\right)^2 - r\dfrac{d^2r}{d\theta^2} \right|}{\left[r^2 + \left(\dfrac{dr}{d\theta}\right)^2 \right]^{3/2}}$$

[*Hint:* Let θ be the parameter and use the relationships $x = r \cos\theta$, $y = r \sin\theta$.]

40. Use the result in Exercise 39 to show that a circle has constant curvature.

41–44 Use the formula in Exercise 39 to find the curvature at the indicated point. ■

41. $r = 1 + \cos\theta$; $\theta = \pi/2$ **42.** $r = e^{2\theta}$; $\theta = 1$

43. $r = \sin 3\theta$; $\theta = 0$ **44.** $r = \theta$; $\theta = 1$

45. Find the radius of curvature of the parabola $y^2 = 4px$ at $(0, 0)$.

46. At what point(s) does $y = e^x$ have maximum curvature?

47. At what point(s) does $4x^2 + 9y^2 = 36$ have minimum radius of curvature?

48. Find the maximum and minimum values of the radius of curvature for the curve $x = \cos t$, $y = \sin t$, $z = \cos t$.

49. Use the formula in Exercise 39 to show that the curvature of the polar curve $r = e^{a\theta}$ is inversely proportional to r.

c **50.** Use the formula in Exercise 39 and a CAS to show that the curvature of the lemniscate $r = \sqrt{a \cos 2\theta}$ is directly proportional to r.

51. (a) Use the result in Exercise 24 to show that for the parabola $y = x^2$ the curvature $\kappa(\phi)$ at points where the tangent line has an angle of inclination of ϕ is

$$\kappa(\phi) = |2 \cos^3 \phi|$$

(b) Use the result in part (a) to find the radius of curvature of the parabola at the point on the parabola where the tangent line has slope 1.
(c) Make a sketch with reasonably accurate proportions that shows the osculating circle at the point on the parabola where the tangent line has slope 1.

52. The *evolute* of a smooth parametric curve C in 2-space is the curve formed from the centers of curvature of C. The accompanying figure shows the ellipse $x = 3 \cos t$, $y = 2 \sin t$ ($0 \leq t \leq 2\pi$) and its evolute graphed together.
(a) Which points on the evolute correspond to $t = 0$ and $t = \pi/2$?
(b) In what direction is the evolute traced as t increases from 0 to 2π?
(c) What does the evolute of a circle look like? Explain your reasoning.

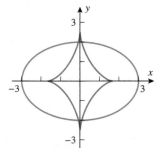

◀ **Figure Ex-52**

FOCUS ON CONCEPTS

53–57 These exercises are concerned with the problem of creating a single smooth curve by piecing together two separate smooth curves. If two smooth curves C_1 and C_2 are joined at a point P to form a curve C, then we will say that C_1 and C_2 make a *smooth transition* at P if the curvature of C is continuous at P. ■

53. Show that the transition at $x = 0$ from the horizontal line $y = 0$ for $x \leq 0$ to the parabola $y = x^2$ for $x > 0$ is not smooth, whereas the transition to $y = x^3$ for $x > 0$ is smooth.

54. (a) Sketch the graph of the curve defined piecewise by $y = x^2$ for $x < 0$, $y = x^4$ for $x \geq 0$.
(b) Show that for the curve in part (a) the transition at $x = 0$ is not smooth.

55. The accompanying figure on the next page shows the arc of a circle of radius r with center at $(0, r)$. Find the value of a so that there is a smooth transition from the circle to the parabola $y = ax^2$ at the point where $x = 0$.

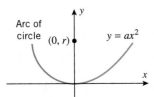

Arc of circle $(0, r)$

$y = ax^2$

◀ **Figure Ex-55**

56. Find a, b, and c so that there is a smooth transition at $x = 0$ from the curve $y = e^x$ for $x \leq 0$ to the parabola $y = ax^2 + bx + c$ for $x > 0$. [*Hint:* The curvature is continuous at those points where y'' is continuous.]

57. Assume that f is a function for which $f'''(x)$ is defined for all $x \leq 0$. Explain why it is always possible to find numbers a, b, and c such that there is a smooth transition at $x = 0$ from the curve $y = f(x)$, $x \leq 0$, to the parabola $y = ax^2 + bx + c$.

58–61 Assume that s is an arc length parameter for a smooth vector-valued function $\mathbf{r}(s)$ in 3-space and that $d\mathbf{T}/ds$ and $d\mathbf{N}/ds$ exist at each point on the curve. (This implies that $d\mathbf{B}/ds$ exists as well, since $\mathbf{B} = \mathbf{T} \times \mathbf{N}$.) ◼

58. Show that
$$\frac{d\mathbf{T}}{ds} = \kappa(s)\mathbf{N}(s)$$
and use this result to obtain the formulas in (10).

59. (a) Show that $d\mathbf{B}/ds$ is perpendicular to $\mathbf{B}(s)$.
   (b) Show that $d\mathbf{B}/ds$ is perpendicular to $\mathbf{T}(s)$. [*Hint:* Use the fact that $\mathbf{B}(s)$ is perpendicular to both $\mathbf{T}(s)$ and $\mathbf{N}(s)$, and differentiate $\mathbf{B} \cdot \mathbf{T}$ with respect to s.]
   (c) Use the results in parts (a) and (b) to show that $d\mathbf{B}/ds$ is a scalar multiple of $\mathbf{N}(s)$. The *negative* of this scalar is called the **torsion** of $\mathbf{r}(s)$ and is denoted by $\tau(s)$. Thus,
$$\frac{d\mathbf{B}}{ds} = -\tau(s)\mathbf{N}(s)$$
   (d) Show that $\tau(s) = 0$ for all s if the graph of $\mathbf{r}(s)$ lies in a plane. [*Note:* For reasons that we cannot discuss here, the torsion is related to the "twisting" properties of the curve, and $\tau(s)$ is regarded as a numerical measure of the tendency for the curve to twist out of the osculating plane.]

60. Let κ be the curvature of C and τ the torsion (defined in Exercise 59). By differentiating $\mathbf{N} = \mathbf{B} \times \mathbf{T}$ with respect to s, show that $d\mathbf{N}/ds = -\kappa\mathbf{T} + \tau\mathbf{B}$.

61. The following derivatives, known as the **Frenet–Serret formulas**, are fundamental in the theory of curves in 3-space:
$$d\mathbf{T}/ds = \kappa\mathbf{N} \qquad \text{[Exercise 58]}$$
$$d\mathbf{N}/ds = -\kappa\mathbf{T} + \tau\mathbf{B} \qquad \text{[Exercise 60]}$$
$$d\mathbf{B}/ds = -\tau\mathbf{N} \qquad \text{[Exercise 59(c)]}$$

Use the first two Frenet–Serret formulas and the fact that $\mathbf{r}'(s) = \mathbf{T}$ if $\mathbf{r} = \mathbf{r}(s)$ to show that
$$\tau = \frac{[\mathbf{r}'(s) \times \mathbf{r}''(s)] \cdot \mathbf{r}'''(s)}{\|\mathbf{r}''(s)\|^2} \quad \text{and} \quad \mathbf{B} = \frac{\mathbf{r}'(s) \times \mathbf{r}''(s)}{\|\mathbf{r}''(s)\|}$$

62. (a) Use the chain rule and the first two Frenet–Serret formulas in Exercise 61 to show that
$$\mathbf{T}' = \kappa s'\mathbf{N} \quad \text{and} \quad \mathbf{N}' = -\kappa s'\mathbf{T} + \tau s'\mathbf{B}$$
where primes denote differentiation with respect to t.
   (b) Show that Formulas (4) and (6) can be written in the form
$$\mathbf{r}'(t) = s'\mathbf{T} \quad \text{and} \quad \mathbf{r}''(t) = s''\mathbf{T} + \kappa(s')^2\mathbf{N}$$
   (c) Use the results in parts (a) and (b) to show that
$$\mathbf{r}'''(t) = [s''' - \kappa^2(s')^3]\mathbf{T}$$
$$+ [3\kappa s's'' + \kappa'(s')^2]\mathbf{N} + \kappa\tau(s')^3\mathbf{B}$$
   (d) Use the results in parts (b) and (c) to show that
$$\tau(t) = \frac{[\mathbf{r}'(t) \times \mathbf{r}''(t)] \cdot \mathbf{r}'''(t)}{\|\mathbf{r}'(t) \times \mathbf{r}''(t)\|^2}$$

63–66 Use the formula in Exercise 62(d) to find the torsion $\tau = \tau(t)$. ◼

63. The twisted cubic $\mathbf{r}(t) = 2t\mathbf{i} + t^2\mathbf{j} + \frac{1}{3}t^3\mathbf{k}$

64. The circular helix $\mathbf{r}(t) = a\cos t\,\mathbf{i} + a\sin t\,\mathbf{j} + ct\mathbf{k}$

65. $\mathbf{r}(t) = e^t\mathbf{i} + e^{-t}\mathbf{j} + \sqrt{2}t\mathbf{k}$

66. $\mathbf{r}(t) = (t - \sin t)\mathbf{i} + (1 - \cos t)\mathbf{j} + t\mathbf{k}$

67. Writing One property of a twice-differentiable function $f(x)$ is that an inflection point on the graph is a point at which the tangent line crosses the graph of f. Consider the analogous issue in 2-space for an osculating circle to a curve C at a point P: What does it mean for the osculating circle to cross (or not to cross) C at P? Investigate this issue through some examples of your own and write a brief essay, with illustrations, supporting your conclusions.

68. Writing The accompanying figure is the graph of the radius of curvature versus θ in rectangular coordinates for the cardioid $r = 1 + \cos\theta$. In words, explain what the graph tells you about the cardioid.

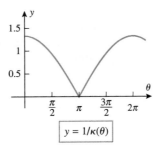

$y = 1/\kappa(\theta)$

◀ **Figure Ex-68**

✔ **QUICK CHECK ANSWERS 12.5**

1. $\left\|\dfrac{d\mathbf{T}}{ds}\right\| = \|\mathbf{r}''(s)\|$ **2.** (a) $\dfrac{\|\mathbf{T}'(t)\|}{\|\mathbf{r}'(t)\|}$ (b) $\dfrac{\|\mathbf{r}'(t) \times \mathbf{r}''(t)\|}{\|\mathbf{r}'(t)\|^3}$ **3.** $\left|\dfrac{d\phi}{ds}\right|$ **4.** $\dfrac{1}{2}$

12.6 MOTION ALONG A CURVE

In earlier sections we considered the motion of a particle along a line. In that situation there are only two directions in which the particle can move—the positive direction or the negative direction. Motion in 2-space or 3-space is more complicated because there are infinitely many directions in which a particle can move. In this section we will show how vectors can be used to analyze motion along curves in 2-space or 3-space.

■ VELOCITY, ACCELERATION, AND SPEED

Let us assume that the motion of a particle in 2-space or 3-space is described by a smooth vector-valued function $\mathbf{r}(t)$ in which the parameter t denotes time; we will call this the *position function* or *trajectory* of the particle. As the particle moves along its trajectory, its direction of motion and its speed can vary from instant to instant. Thus, before we can undertake any analysis of such motion, we must have clear answers to the following questions:

- What is the direction of motion of the particle at an instant of time?
- What is the speed of the particle at an instant of time?

We will define the direction of motion at time t to be the direction of the unit tangent vector $\mathbf{T}(t)$, and we will define the speed to be ds/dt—the instantaneous rate of change of the arc length traveled by the particle from an arbitrary reference point. Taking this a step further, we will combine the speed and the direction of motion to form the vector

$$\mathbf{v}(t) = \frac{ds}{dt}\mathbf{T}(t) \tag{1}$$

which we call the *velocity* of the particle at time t. Thus, at each instant of time the velocity vector $\mathbf{v}(t)$ points in the direction of motion and has a magnitude that is equal to the speed of the particle (Figure 12.6.1).

Recall that for motion along a coordinate line the velocity function is the derivative of the position function. The same is true for motion along a curve, since

$$\frac{d\mathbf{r}}{dt} = \frac{d\mathbf{r}}{ds}\frac{ds}{dt} = \frac{ds}{dt}\mathbf{T}(t) = \mathbf{v}(t)$$

For motion along a coordinate line, the acceleration function was defined to be the derivative of the velocity function. The definition is the same for motion along a curve.

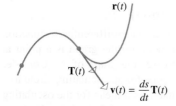

The length of the velocity vector is the speed of the particle, and the direction of the velocity vector is the direction of motion.

▲ **Figure 12.6.1**

12.6.1 DEFINITION If $\mathbf{r}(t)$ is the position function of a particle moving along a curve in 2-space or 3-space, then the *instantaneous velocity*, *instantaneous acceleration*, and *instantaneous speed* of the particle at time t are defined by

$$\text{velocity} = \mathbf{v}(t) = \frac{d\mathbf{r}}{dt} \tag{2}$$

$$\text{acceleration} = \mathbf{a}(t) = \frac{d\mathbf{v}}{dt} = \frac{d^2\mathbf{r}}{dt^2} \tag{3}$$

$$\text{speed} = \|\mathbf{v}(t)\| = \frac{ds}{dt} \tag{4}$$

As shown in Table 12.6.1, the position, velocity, acceleration, and speed can also be expressed in component form.

Table 12.6.1

FORMULAS FOR POSITION, VELOCITY, ACCELERATION, AND SPEED

	2-SPACE	3-SPACE
POSITION	$\mathbf{r}(t) = x(t)\mathbf{i} + y(t)\mathbf{j}$	$\mathbf{r}(t) = x(t)\mathbf{i} + y(t)\mathbf{j} + z(t)\mathbf{k}$
VELOCITY	$\mathbf{v}(t) = \dfrac{dx}{dt}\mathbf{i} + \dfrac{dy}{dt}\mathbf{j}$	$\mathbf{v}(t) = \dfrac{dx}{dt}\mathbf{i} + \dfrac{dy}{dt}\mathbf{j} + \dfrac{dz}{dt}\mathbf{k}$
ACCELERATION	$\mathbf{a}(t) = \dfrac{d^2x}{dt^2}\mathbf{i} + \dfrac{d^2y}{dt^2}\mathbf{j}$	$\mathbf{a}(t) = \dfrac{d^2x}{dt^2}\mathbf{i} + \dfrac{d^2y}{dt^2}\mathbf{j} + \dfrac{d^2z}{dt^2}\mathbf{k}$
SPEED	$\|\mathbf{v}(t)\| = \sqrt{\left(\dfrac{dx}{dt}\right)^2 + \left(\dfrac{dy}{dt}\right)^2}$	$\|\mathbf{v}(t)\| = \sqrt{\left(\dfrac{dx}{dt}\right)^2 + \left(\dfrac{dy}{dt}\right)^2 + \left(\dfrac{dz}{dt}\right)^2}$

▶ **Example 1**   A particle moves along a circular path in such a way that its x- and y-coordinates at time t are

$$x = 2\cos t, \quad y = 2\sin t$$

(a) Find the instantaneous velocity and speed of the particle at time t.

(b) Sketch the path of the particle, and show the position and velocity vectors at time $t = \pi/4$ with the velocity vector drawn so that its initial point is at the tip of the position vector.

(c) Show that at each instant the acceleration vector is perpendicular to the velocity vector.

Solution (a).   At time t, the position vector is

$$\mathbf{r}(t) = 2\cos t\,\mathbf{i} + 2\sin t\,\mathbf{j}$$

so the instantaneous velocity and speed are

$$\mathbf{v}(t) = \frac{d\mathbf{r}}{dt} = -2\sin t\,\mathbf{i} + 2\cos t\,\mathbf{j}$$

$$\|\mathbf{v}(t)\| = \sqrt{(-2\sin t)^2 + (2\cos t)^2} = 2$$

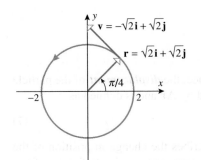

$\mathbf{v} = -\sqrt{2}\,\mathbf{i} + \sqrt{2}\,\mathbf{j}$

$\mathbf{r} = \sqrt{2}\,\mathbf{i} + \sqrt{2}\,\mathbf{j}$

▲ **Figure 12.6.2**

Solution (b).   The graph of the parametric equations is a circle of radius 2 centered at the origin. At time $t = \pi/4$ the position and velocity vectors of the particle are

$$\mathbf{r}(\pi/4) = 2\cos(\pi/4)\mathbf{i} + 2\sin(\pi/4)\mathbf{j} = \sqrt{2}\,\mathbf{i} + \sqrt{2}\,\mathbf{j}$$

$$\mathbf{v}(\pi/4) = -2\sin(\pi/4)\mathbf{i} + 2\cos(\pi/4)\mathbf{j} = -\sqrt{2}\,\mathbf{i} + \sqrt{2}\,\mathbf{j}$$

These vectors and the circle are shown in Figure 12.6.2.

Solution (c).   At time t, the acceleration vector is

$$\mathbf{a}(t) = \frac{d\mathbf{v}}{dt} = -2\cos t\,\mathbf{i} - 2\sin t\,\mathbf{j}$$

One way of showing that $\mathbf{v}(t)$ and $\mathbf{a}(t)$ are perpendicular is to show that their dot product is zero (try it). However, it is easier to observe that $\mathbf{a}(t)$ is the negative of $\mathbf{r}(t)$, which implies that $\mathbf{v}(t)$ and $\mathbf{a}(t)$ are perpendicular, since at each point on a circle the radius and tangent line are perpendicular. ◀

How could you apply Theorem 12.2.8 to answer part (c) of Example 1?

Since $\mathbf{v}(t)$ can be obtained by differentiating $\mathbf{r}(t)$, and since $\mathbf{a}(t)$ can be obtained by differentiating $\mathbf{v}(t)$, it follows that $\mathbf{r}(t)$ can be obtained by integrating $\mathbf{v}(t)$, and $\mathbf{v}(t)$ can be obtained by integrating $\mathbf{a}(t)$. However, such integrations do not produce unique functions because constants of integration occur. Typically, initial conditions are required to determine these constants.

▶ **Example 2**   A particle moves through 3-space in such a way that its velocity is

$$\mathbf{v}(t) = \mathbf{i} + t\mathbf{j} + t^2\mathbf{k}$$

Find the coordinates of the particle at time $t = 1$ given that the particle is at the point $(-1, 2, 4)$ at time $t = 0$.

Solution.   Integrating the velocity function to obtain the position function yields

$$\mathbf{r}(t) = \int \mathbf{v}(t)\, dt = \int (\mathbf{i} + t\mathbf{j} + t^2\mathbf{k})\, dt = t\mathbf{i} + \frac{t^2}{2}\mathbf{j} + \frac{t^3}{3}\mathbf{k} + \mathbf{C} \tag{5}$$

where $\mathbf{C}$ is a vector constant of integration. Since the coordinates of the particle at time $t = 0$ are $(-1, 2, 4)$, the position vector at time $t = 0$ is

$$\mathbf{r}(0) = -\mathbf{i} + 2\mathbf{j} + 4\mathbf{k} \tag{6}$$

It follows on substituting $t = 0$ in (5) and equating the result with (6) that

$$\mathbf{C} = -\mathbf{i} + 2\mathbf{j} + 4\mathbf{k}$$

Substituting this value of $\mathbf{C}$ in (5) and simplifying yields

$$\mathbf{r}(t) = (t - 1)\mathbf{i} + \left(\frac{t^2}{2} + 2\right)\mathbf{j} + \left(\frac{t^3}{3} + 4\right)\mathbf{k}$$

Thus, at time $t = 1$ the position vector of the particle is

$$\mathbf{r}(1) = 0\mathbf{i} + \frac{5}{2}\mathbf{j} + \frac{13}{3}\mathbf{k}$$

so its coordinates at that instant are $\left(0, \frac{5}{2}, \frac{13}{3}\right)$. ◀

■ DISPLACEMENT AND DISTANCE TRAVELED

If a particle travels along a curve C in 2-space or 3-space, the ***displacement*** of the particle over the time interval $t_1 \leq t \leq t_2$ is commonly denoted by $\Delta\mathbf{r}$ and is defined as

$$\Delta\mathbf{r} = \mathbf{r}(t_2) - \mathbf{r}(t_1) \tag{7}$$

(Figure 12.6.3). The displacement vector, which describes the change in position of the particle during the time interval, can be obtained by integrating the velocity function from t_1 to t_2:

$$\Delta\mathbf{r} = \int_{t_1}^{t_2} \mathbf{v}(t)\, dt = \int_{t_1}^{t_2} \frac{d\mathbf{r}}{dt}\, dt = \mathbf{r}(t)\Big]_{t_1}^{t_2} = \mathbf{r}(t_2) - \mathbf{r}(t_1) \qquad \boxed{\text{Displacement}} \tag{8}$$

It follows from Theorem 12.3.1 that we can find the distance s traveled by a particle over a time interval $t_1 \leq t \leq t_2$ by integrating the speed over that interval, since

$$s = \int_{t_1}^{t_2} \left\|\frac{d\mathbf{r}}{dt}\right\| dt = \int_{t_1}^{t_2} \|\mathbf{v}(t)\|\, dt \qquad \boxed{\text{Distance traveled}} \tag{9}$$

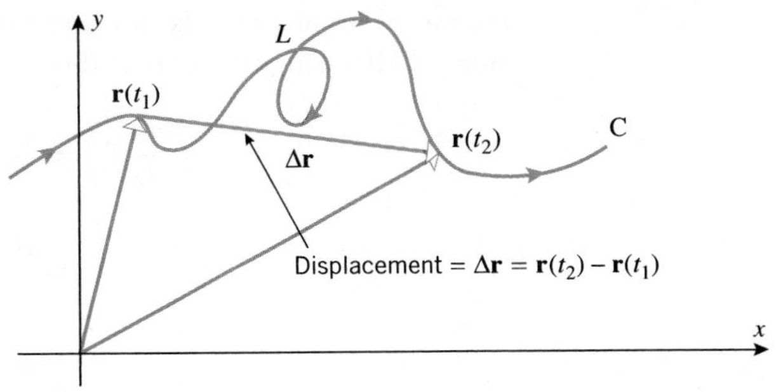

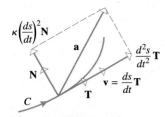

▶ Figure 12.6.3

▶ Example 3 Suppose that a particle moves along a circular helix in 3-space so that its position vector at time t is

$$\mathbf{r}(t) = (4\cos\pi t)\mathbf{i} + (4\sin\pi t)\mathbf{j} + t\mathbf{k}$$

Find the distance traveled and the displacement of the particle during the time interval $1 \leq t \leq 5$.

Solution. We have

$$\mathbf{v}(t) = \frac{d\mathbf{r}}{dt} = (-4\pi\sin\pi t)\mathbf{i} + (4\pi\cos\pi t)\mathbf{j} + \mathbf{k}$$

$$\|\mathbf{v}(t)\| = \sqrt{(-4\pi\sin\pi t)^2 + (4\pi\cos\pi t)^2 + 1} = \sqrt{16\pi^2 + 1}$$

Thus, it follows from (9) that the distance traveled by the particle from time $t = 1$ to $t = 5$ is

$$s = \int_1^5 \sqrt{16\pi^2 + 1}\, dt = 4\sqrt{16\pi^2 + 1}$$

Moreover, it follows from (8) that the displacement over the time interval is

$$\Delta\mathbf{r} = \mathbf{r}(5) - \mathbf{r}(1)$$
$$= (4\cos 5\pi\mathbf{i} + 4\sin 5\pi\mathbf{j} + 5\mathbf{k}) - (4\cos\pi\mathbf{i} + 4\sin\pi\mathbf{j} + \mathbf{k})$$
$$= (-4\mathbf{i} + 5\mathbf{k}) - (-4\mathbf{i} + \mathbf{k}) = 4\mathbf{k}$$

which tells us that the change in the position of the particle over the time interval was 4 units straight up. ◀

■ NORMAL AND TANGENTIAL COMPONENTS OF ACCELERATION

You know from your experience as an automobile passenger that if a car speeds up rapidly, then your body is thrown back against the backrest of the seat. You also know that if the car rounds a turn in the road, then your body is thrown toward the outside of the curve—the greater the curvature in the road, the greater this effect. The explanation of these effects can be understood by resolving the velocity and acceleration components of the motion into vector components that are parallel to the unit tangent and unit normal vectors. The following theorem explains how to do this.

12.6.2 THEOREM *If a particle moves along a smooth curve C in 2-space or 3-space, then at each point on the curve velocity and acceleration vectors can be written as*

$$\mathbf{v} = \frac{ds}{dt}\mathbf{T} \qquad \mathbf{a} = \frac{d^2s}{dt^2}\mathbf{T} + \kappa\left(\frac{ds}{dt}\right)^2\mathbf{N} \qquad (10\text{--}11)$$

where s is an arc length parameter for the curve, and **T**, **N**, *and* κ *denote the unit tangent vector, unit normal vector, and curvature at the point (Figure 12.6.4).*

▲ **Figure 12.6.4**

PROOF   Formula (10) is just a restatement of (1). To obtain (11), we differentiate both sides of (10) with respect to t; this yields

$$\mathbf{a} = \frac{d}{dt}\left(\frac{ds}{dt}\mathbf{T}\right) = \frac{d^2s}{dt^2}\mathbf{T} + \frac{ds}{dt}\frac{d\mathbf{T}}{dt}$$

$$= \frac{d^2s}{dt^2}\mathbf{T} + \frac{ds}{dt}\frac{d\mathbf{T}}{ds}\frac{ds}{dt}$$

$$= \frac{d^2s}{dt^2}\mathbf{T} + \left(\frac{ds}{dt}\right)^2\frac{d\mathbf{T}}{ds}$$

$$= \frac{d^2s}{dt^2}\mathbf{T} + \left(\frac{ds}{dt}\right)^2\kappa\mathbf{N} \qquad \boxed{\text{Formula (10) of Section 12.5}}$$

from which (11) follows. ■

The coefficients of $\mathbf{T}$ and $\mathbf{N}$ in (11) are commonly denoted by

$$a_T = \frac{d^2s}{dt^2} \qquad a_N = \kappa\left(\frac{ds}{dt}\right)^2 \qquad\qquad (12\text{–}13)$$

in which case Formula (11) is expressed as

$$\mathbf{a} = a_T\mathbf{T} + a_N\mathbf{N} \qquad\qquad (14)$$

In this formula the scalars a_T and a_N are called the ***tangential scalar component of acceleration*** and the ***normal scalar component of acceleration***, and the vectors $a_T\mathbf{T}$ and $a_N\mathbf{N}$ are called the ***tangential vector component of acceleration*** and the ***normal vector component of acceleration***.

The scalar components of acceleration explain the effect that you experience when a car speeds up rapidly or rounds a turn. The rapid increase in speed produces a large value for d^2s/dt^2, which results in a large tangential scalar component of acceleration; and by Newton's second law this corresponds to a large tangential force on the car in the direction of motion. To understand the effect of rounding a turn, observe that the normal scalar component of acceleration has the curvature κ and the square of the speed ds/dt as factors. Thus, sharp turns or turns taken at high speed both correspond to large normal forces on the car.

Although Formulas (12) and (13) provide useful insight into the behavior of particles moving along curved paths, they are not always the best formulas for computations. The following theorem provides some more useful formulas that relate a_T, a_N, and κ to the velocity $\mathbf{v}$ and acceleration $\mathbf{a}$.

> Formula (14) applies to motion in both 2-space and 3-space. What is interesting is that the 3-space formula does not involve the binormal vector $\mathbf{B}$, so the acceleration vector always lies in the plane of $\mathbf{T}$ and $\mathbf{N}$ (the osculating plane), even for highly twisting paths of motion (Figure 12.6.5).

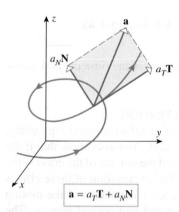

▲ **Figure 12.6.5**

> Theorem 12.6.3 applies to motion in 2-space and 3-space, but for motion in 2-space you will have to add a zero $\mathbf{k}$ component to $\mathbf{v}$ to calculate the cross product.

12.6.3   THEOREM   *If a particle moves along a smooth curve C in 2-space or 3-space, then at each point on the curve the velocity $\mathbf{v}$ and the acceleration $\mathbf{a}$ are related to a_T, a_N, and κ by the formulas*

$$a_T = \frac{\mathbf{v}\cdot\mathbf{a}}{\|\mathbf{v}\|} \qquad a_N = \frac{\|\mathbf{v}\times\mathbf{a}\|}{\|\mathbf{v}\|} \qquad \kappa = \frac{\|\mathbf{v}\times\mathbf{a}\|}{\|\mathbf{v}\|^3} \qquad (15\text{–}17)$$

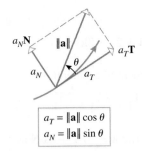

$$a_T = \|\mathbf{a}\|\cos\theta$$
$$a_N = \|\mathbf{a}\|\sin\theta$$

▲ Figure 12.6.6

Recall that for nonlinear smooth curves in 2-space the unit normal vector $\mathbf{N}$ is the inward normal (points toward the concave side of the curve). Explain why the same is true for $a_N \mathbf{N}$.

PROOF As illustrated in Figure 12.6.6, let θ be the angle between the vector $\mathbf{a}$ and the vector $a_T\mathbf{T}$. Thus,
$$a_T = \|\mathbf{a}\|\cos\theta \quad \text{and} \quad a_N = \|\mathbf{a}\|\sin\theta$$
from which we obtain
$$a_T = \|\mathbf{a}\|\cos\theta = \frac{\|\mathbf{v}\|\|\mathbf{a}\|\cos\theta}{\|\mathbf{v}\|} = \frac{\mathbf{v}\cdot\mathbf{a}}{\|\mathbf{v}\|}$$
$$a_N = \|\mathbf{a}\|\sin\theta = \frac{\|\mathbf{v}\|\|\mathbf{a}\|\sin\theta}{\|\mathbf{v}\|} = \frac{\|\mathbf{v}\times\mathbf{a}\|}{\|\mathbf{v}\|}$$
$$\kappa = \frac{a_N}{(ds/dt)^2} = \frac{a_N}{\|\mathbf{v}\|^2} = \frac{1}{\|\mathbf{v}\|^2}\frac{\|\mathbf{v}\times\mathbf{a}\|}{\|\mathbf{v}\|} = \frac{\|\mathbf{v}\times\mathbf{a}\|}{\|\mathbf{v}\|^3} \quad \blacksquare$$

▶ **Example 4**   Suppose that a particle moves through 3-space so that its position vector at time t is
$$\mathbf{r}(t) = t\mathbf{i} + t^2\mathbf{j} + t^3\mathbf{k}$$
(The path is the twisted cubic shown in Figure 12.1.5.)

(a) Find the scalar tangential and normal components of acceleration at time t.

(b) Find the scalar tangential and normal components of acceleration at time $t = 1$.

(c) Find the vector tangential and normal components of acceleration at time $t = 1$.

(d) Find the curvature of the path at the point where the particle is located at time $t = 1$.

Solution (a).   We have
$$\mathbf{v}(t) = \mathbf{r}'(t) = \mathbf{i} + 2t\mathbf{j} + 3t^2\mathbf{k}$$
$$\mathbf{a}(t) = \mathbf{v}'(t) = 2\mathbf{j} + 6t\mathbf{k}$$
$$\|\mathbf{v}(t)\| = \sqrt{1 + 4t^2 + 9t^4}$$
$$\mathbf{v}(t)\cdot\mathbf{a}(t) = 4t + 18t^3$$
$$\mathbf{v}(t)\times\mathbf{a}(t) = \begin{vmatrix} \mathbf{i} & \mathbf{j} & \mathbf{k} \\ 1 & 2t & 3t^2 \\ 0 & 2 & 6t \end{vmatrix} = 6t^2\mathbf{i} - 6t\mathbf{j} + 2\mathbf{k}$$

Thus, from (15) and (16)
$$a_T = \frac{\mathbf{v}\cdot\mathbf{a}}{\|\mathbf{v}\|} = \frac{4t + 18t^3}{\sqrt{1 + 4t^2 + 9t^4}}$$
$$a_N = \frac{\|\mathbf{v}\times\mathbf{a}\|}{\|\mathbf{v}\|} = \frac{\sqrt{36t^4 + 36t^2 + 4}}{\sqrt{1 + 4t^2 + 9t^4}} = 2\sqrt{\frac{9t^4 + 9t^2 + 1}{9t^4 + 4t^2 + 1}}$$

Solution (b).   At time $t = 1$, the components a_T and a_N in part (a) are
$$a_T = \frac{22}{\sqrt{14}} \approx 5.88 \quad \text{and} \quad a_N = 2\sqrt{\frac{19}{14}} \approx 2.33$$

Solution (c).   Since $\mathbf{T}$ and $\mathbf{v}$ have the same direction, $\mathbf{T}$ can be obtained by normalizing $\mathbf{v}$, that is,
$$\mathbf{T}(t) = \frac{\mathbf{v}(t)}{\|\mathbf{v}(t)\|}$$

At time $t = 1$ we have

$$\mathbf{T}(1) = \frac{\mathbf{v}(1)}{\|\mathbf{v}(1)\|} = \frac{\mathbf{i} + 2\mathbf{j} + 3\mathbf{k}}{\|\mathbf{i} + 2\mathbf{j} + 3\mathbf{k}\|} = \frac{1}{\sqrt{14}}(\mathbf{i} + 2\mathbf{j} + 3\mathbf{k})$$

From this and part (b) we obtain the vector tangential component of acceleration:

$$a_T(1)\mathbf{T}(1) = \frac{22}{\sqrt{14}}\mathbf{T}(1) = \frac{11}{7}(\mathbf{i} + 2\mathbf{j} + 3\mathbf{k}) = \frac{11}{7}\mathbf{i} + \frac{22}{7}\mathbf{j} + \frac{33}{7}\mathbf{k}$$

To find the normal vector component of acceleration, we rewrite $\mathbf{a} = a_T\mathbf{T} + a_N\mathbf{N}$ as

$$a_N\mathbf{N} = \mathbf{a} - a_T\mathbf{T}$$

Thus, at time $t = 1$ the normal vector component of acceleration is

$$\begin{aligned}
a_N(1)\mathbf{N}(1) &= \mathbf{a}(1) - a_T(1)\mathbf{T}(1) \\
&= (2\mathbf{j} + 6\mathbf{k}) - \left(\frac{11}{7}\mathbf{i} + \frac{22}{7}\mathbf{j} + \frac{33}{7}\mathbf{k}\right) \\
&= -\frac{11}{7}\mathbf{i} - \frac{8}{7}\mathbf{j} + \frac{9}{7}\mathbf{k}
\end{aligned}$$

Solution (d).   We will apply Formula (17) with $t = 1$. From part (a)

$$\|\mathbf{v}(1)\| = \sqrt{14} \quad \text{and} \quad \mathbf{v}(1) \times \mathbf{a}(1) = 6\mathbf{i} - 6\mathbf{j} + 2\mathbf{k}$$

Thus, at time $t = 1$

$$\kappa = \frac{\|\mathbf{v} \times \mathbf{a}\|}{\|\mathbf{v}\|^3} = \frac{\sqrt{76}}{(\sqrt{14})^3} = \frac{1}{14}\sqrt{\frac{38}{7}} \approx 0.17 \;\blacktriangleleft$$

In the case where $\|\mathbf{a}\|$ and a_T are known, there is a useful alternative to Formula (16) for a_N that does not require the calculation of a cross product. It follows algebraically from Formula (14) (see Exercise 51) or geometrically from Figure 12.6.6 and the Theorem of Pythagoras that

$$a_N = \sqrt{\|\mathbf{a}\|^2 - a_T^2} \tag{18}$$

Confirm that the value of a_N computed in Example 4 agrees with the value that results by applying Formula (18).

■ A MODEL OF PROJECTILE MOTION

Earlier in this text we examined various problems concerned with objects moving *vertically* in the Earth's gravitational field (see the subsection of Section 5.7 entitled Free-Fall Model and the subsection of Section 8.4 entitled A Model of Free-Fall Motion Retarded by Air Resistance). Now we will consider the motion of a projectile launched along a *curved* path in the Earth's gravitational field. For this purpose we will need the following *vector version* of Newton's Second Law of Motion (6.6.4)

$$\mathbf{F} = m\mathbf{a} \tag{19}$$

and we will need to make three modeling assumptions:

- The mass m of the object is constant.
- The only force acting on the object after it is launched is the force of the Earth's gravity. (Thus, air resistance and the gravitational effect of other planets and celestial objects are ignored.)
- The object remains sufficiently close to the Earth that we can assume the force of gravity to be constant.

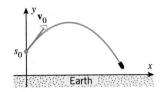

▲ Figure 12.6.7

Let us assume that at time $t = 0$ an object of mass m is launched from a height of s_0 above the Earth with an initial velocity vector of $\mathbf{v}_0$. Furthermore, let us introduce an xy-coordinate system as shown in Figure 12.6.7. In this coordinate system the positive y-direction is up, the origin is at the surface of the Earth, and the initial location of the object is $(0, s_0)$. Our objective is to use basic principles of physics to derive the velocity function $\mathbf{v}(t)$ and the position function $\mathbf{r}(t)$ from the acceleration function $\mathbf{a}(t)$ of the object. Our starting point is the physical observation that the downward force $\mathbf{F}$ of the Earth's gravity on an object of mass m is

$$\mathbf{F} = -mg\mathbf{j}$$

where g is the acceleration due to gravity. It follows from this fact and Newton's second law (19) that

$$m\mathbf{a} = -mg\mathbf{j}$$

or on canceling m from both sides

$$\mathbf{a} = -g\mathbf{j} \tag{20}$$

Observe that this acceleration function does not involve t and hence is constant. We can now obtain the velocity function $\mathbf{v}(t)$ by integrating this acceleration function and using the initial condition $\mathbf{v}(0) = \mathbf{v}_0$ to find the constant of integration. Integrating (20) with respect to t and keeping in mind that $-g\mathbf{j}$ is constant yields

$$\mathbf{v}(t) = \int -g\mathbf{j}\, dt = -gt\mathbf{j} + \mathbf{c}_1$$

where $\mathbf{c}_1$ is a vector constant of integration. Substituting $t = 0$ in this equation and using the initial condition $\mathbf{v}(0) = \mathbf{v}_0$ yields $\mathbf{v}_0 = \mathbf{c}_1$. Thus, the velocity function of the object is

$$\mathbf{v}(t) = -gt\mathbf{j} + \mathbf{v}_0 \tag{21}$$

To obtain the position function $\mathbf{r}(t)$ of the object, we will integrate the velocity function and use the known initial position of the object to find the constant of integration. For this purpose observe that the object has coordinates $(0, s_0)$ at time $t = 0$, so the position vector at that time is

$$\mathbf{r}(0) = 0\mathbf{i} + s_0\mathbf{j} = s_0\mathbf{j} \tag{22}$$

This is the initial condition that we will need to find the constant of integration. Integrating (21) with respect to t yields

$$\mathbf{r}(t) = \int (-gt\mathbf{j} + \mathbf{v}_0)\, dt = -\tfrac{1}{2}gt^2\mathbf{j} + t\mathbf{v}_0 + \mathbf{c}_2 \tag{23}$$

where $\mathbf{c}_2$ is another vector constant of integration. Substituting $t = 0$ in (23) and using initial condition (22) yields

$$s_0\mathbf{j} = \mathbf{c}_2$$

so that (23) can be written as

$$\mathbf{r}(t) = \left(-\tfrac{1}{2}gt^2 + s_0\right)\mathbf{j} + t\mathbf{v}_0 \tag{24}$$

This formula expresses the position function of the object in terms of its known initial position and velocity.

Observe that the mass m does not appear in Formulas (21) and (24) and hence has no influence on the velocity or the trajectory of the object. This explains the famous observation of Galileo that two objects of different mass that are released from the same height reach the ground at the same time if air resistance is neglected.

■ PARAMETRIC EQUATIONS OF PROJECTILE MOTION

Formulas (21) and (24) can be used to obtain parametric equations for the position and velocity in terms of the initial speed of the object and the angle that the initial velocity vector makes with the positive x-axis. For this purpose, let $v_0 = \|\mathbf{v}_0\|$ be the initial speed, let α be the angle that the initial velocity vector $\mathbf{v}_0$ makes with the positive x-axis, let v_x and v_y be the horizontal and vertical scalar components of $\mathbf{v}(t)$ at time t, and let x and y

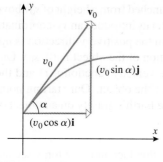

▲ **Figure 12.6.8**

be the horizontal and vertical components of $\mathbf{r}(t)$ at time t. As illustrated in Figure 12.6.8, the initial velocity vector can be expressed as

$$\mathbf{v}_0 = (v_0 \cos \alpha)\mathbf{i} + (v_0 \sin \alpha)\mathbf{j} \tag{25}$$

Substituting this expression in (24) and combining like components yields (verify)

$$\mathbf{r}(t) = (v_0 \cos \alpha)t\mathbf{i} + \left(s_0 + (v_0 \sin \alpha)t - \tfrac{1}{2}gt^2\right)\mathbf{j} \tag{26}$$

which is equivalent to the parametric equations

$$x = (v_0 \cos \alpha)t, \quad y = s_0 + (v_0 \sin \alpha)t - \tfrac{1}{2}gt^2 \tag{27}$$

Similarly, substituting (25) in (21) and combining like components yields

$$\mathbf{v}(t) = (v_0 \cos \alpha)\mathbf{i} + (v_0 \sin \alpha - gt)\mathbf{j}$$

which is equivalent to the parametric equations

$$v_x = v_0 \cos \alpha, \quad v_y = v_0 \sin \alpha - gt \tag{28}$$

The parameter t can be eliminated in (27) by solving the first equation for t and substituting in the second equation. We leave it for you to show that this yields

$$y = s_0 + (\tan \alpha)x - \left(\frac{g}{2v_0^2 \cos^2 \alpha}\right)x^2 \tag{29}$$

which is the equation of a parabola, since the right side is a quadratic polynomial in x. Thus, we have shown that the trajectory of the projectile is a parabolic arc.

▶ **Example 5**   A shell, fired from a cannon, has a muzzle speed (the speed as it leaves the barrel) of 800 ft/s. The barrel makes an angle of 45° with the horizontal and, for simplicity, the barrel opening is assumed to be at ground level.

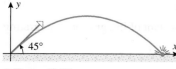

▲ **Figure 12.6.9**

(a) Find parametric equations for the shell's trajectory relative to the coordinate system in Figure 12.6.9.

(b) How high does the shell rise?

(c) How far does the shell travel horizontally?

(d) What is the speed of the shell at its point of impact with the ground?

Solution (a).   From (27) with $v_0 = 800$ ft/s, $\alpha = 45°$, $s_0 = 0$ ft (since the shell starts at ground level), and $g = 32$ ft/s², we obtain the parametric equations

$$x = (800 \cos 45°)t, \quad y = (800 \sin 45°)t - 16t^2 \quad (t \geq 0)$$

which simplify to

$$x = 400\sqrt{2}t, \quad y = 400\sqrt{2}t - 16t^2 \quad (t \geq 0) \tag{30}$$

Solution (b).   The maximum height of the shell is the maximum value of y in (30), which occurs when $dy/dt = 0$, that is, when

$$400\sqrt{2} - 32t = 0 \quad \text{or} \quad t = \frac{25\sqrt{2}}{2}$$

Substituting this value of t in (30) yields

$$y = 5000 \text{ ft}$$

as the maximum height of the shell.

Solution (c). The shell will hit the ground when $y = 0$. From (30), this occurs when

$$400\sqrt{2}\,t - 16t^2 = 0 \quad \text{or} \quad t(400\sqrt{2} - 16t) = 0$$

The solution $t = 0$ corresponds to the initial position of the shell and the solution $t = 25\sqrt{2}$ to the time of impact. Substituting the latter value in the equation for x in (30) yields

$$x = 20{,}000 \text{ ft}$$

as the horizontal distance traveled by the shell.

Solution (d). From (30), the position function of the shell is

$$\mathbf{r}(t) = 400\sqrt{2}\,t\mathbf{i} + (400\sqrt{2}\,t - 16t^2)\mathbf{j}$$

so that the velocity function is

$$\mathbf{v}(t) = \mathbf{r}'(t) = 400\sqrt{2}\,\mathbf{i} + (400\sqrt{2} - 32t)\mathbf{j}$$

From part (c), impact occurs when $t = 25\sqrt{2}$, so the velocity vector at this point is

$$\mathbf{v}(25\sqrt{2}) = 400\sqrt{2}\,\mathbf{i} + [400\sqrt{2} - 32(25\sqrt{2})]\mathbf{j} = 400\sqrt{2}\,\mathbf{i} - 400\sqrt{2}\,\mathbf{j}$$

Thus, the speed at impact is

$$\|\mathbf{v}(25\sqrt{2})\| = \sqrt{(400\sqrt{2})^2 + (-400\sqrt{2})^2} = 800 \text{ ft/s} \blacktriangleleft$$

> The speed at impact and the muzzle speed of the shell in Example 5 are the same. Is this an expected result? Explain.

✔ QUICK CHECK EXERCISES 12.6   (See page 895 for answers.)

1. If $\mathbf{r}(t)$ is the position function of a particle, then the velocity, acceleration, and speed of the particle at time t are given, respectively, by

$$\mathbf{v}(t) = \underline{\hspace{1.5cm}}, \quad \mathbf{a}(t) = \underline{\hspace{1.5cm}}, \quad \frac{ds}{dt} = \underline{\hspace{1.5cm}}$$

2. If $\mathbf{r}(t)$ is the position function of a particle, then the displacement of the particle over the time interval $t_1 \le t \le t_2$ is $\underline{\hspace{1.5cm}}$, and the distance s traveled by the particle during this time interval is given by the integral $\underline{\hspace{1.5cm}}$.

3. The tangential scalar component of acceleration is given by the formula $\underline{\hspace{1.5cm}}$, and the normal scalar component of acceleration is given by the formula $\underline{\hspace{1.5cm}}$.

4. The projectile motion model

$$\mathbf{r}(t) = \left(-\tfrac{1}{2}gt^2 + s_0\right)\mathbf{j} + t\mathbf{v}_0$$

describes the motion of an object with constant acceleration $\mathbf{a} = \underline{\hspace{1.5cm}}$ and velocity function $\mathbf{v}(t) = \underline{\hspace{1.5cm}}$. The initial position of the object is $\underline{\hspace{1.5cm}}$ and its initial velocity is $\underline{\hspace{1.5cm}}$.

EXERCISE SET 12.6   ⌇ Graphing Utility   [C] CAS

1–4 In these exercises $\mathbf{r}(t)$ is the position vector of a particle moving in the plane. Find the velocity, acceleration, and speed at an arbitrary time t. Then sketch the path of the particle together with the velocity and acceleration vectors at the indicated time t. ▨

1. $\mathbf{r}(t) = 3\cos t\mathbf{i} + 3\sin t\mathbf{j}; \quad t = \pi/3$

2. $\mathbf{r}(t) = t\mathbf{i} + t^2\mathbf{j}; \quad t = 2$

3. $\mathbf{r}(t) = e^t\mathbf{i} + e^{-t}\mathbf{j}; \quad t = 0$

4. $\mathbf{r}(t) = (2 + 4t)\mathbf{i} + (1 - t)\mathbf{j}; \quad t = 1$

5–8 Find the velocity, speed, and acceleration at the given time t of a particle moving along the given curve. ▨

5. $\mathbf{r}(t) = t\mathbf{i} + \tfrac{1}{2}t^2\mathbf{j} + \tfrac{1}{3}t^3\mathbf{k}; \quad t = 1$

6. $x = 1 + 3t, \ y = 2 - 4t, \ z = 7 + t; \quad t = 2$

7. $x = 2\cos t, \ y = 2\sin t, \ z = t; \quad t = \pi/4$

8. $\mathbf{r}(t) = e^t\sin t\mathbf{i} + e^t\cos t\mathbf{j} + t\mathbf{k}; \quad t = \pi/2$

FOCUS ON CONCEPTS

9. As illustrated in the accompanying figure on the next page, suppose that the equations of motion of a particle moving along an elliptic path are $x = a\cos\omega t$, $y = b\sin\omega t$.
   (a) Show that the acceleration is directed toward the origin. *(cont.)*

(b) Show that the magnitude of the acceleration is proportional to the distance from the particle to the origin.

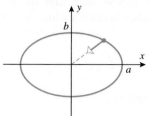

◀ **Figure Ex-9**

10. Suppose that a particle vibrates in such a way that its position function is $\mathbf{r}(t) = 16 \sin \pi t \mathbf{i} + 4 \cos 2\pi t \mathbf{j}$, where distance is in millimeters and t is in seconds.
    (a) Find the velocity and acceleration at time $t = 1$ s.
    (b) Show that the particle moves along a parabolic curve.
    (c) Show that the particle moves back and forth along the curve.

11. What can you say about the trajectory of a particle that moves in 2-space or 3-space with zero acceleration? Justify your answer.

12. Recall from Theorem 12.2.8 that if $\mathbf{r}(t)$ is a vector-valued function in 2-space or 3-space, and if $\|\mathbf{r}(t)\|$ is constant for all t, then $\mathbf{r}(t) \cdot \mathbf{r}'(t) = 0$.
    (a) Translate this theorem into a statement about the motion of a particle in 2-space or 3-space.
    (b) Replace $\mathbf{r}(t)$ by $\mathbf{r}'(t)$ in the theorem, and translate the result into a statement about the motion of a particle in 2-space or 3-space.

13. Suppose that the position vector of a particle moving in the plane is $\mathbf{r} = 12\sqrt{t}\,\mathbf{i} + t^{3/2}\mathbf{j}$, $t > 0$. Find the minimum speed of the particle and its location when it has this speed.

14. Suppose that the motion of a particle is described by the position vector $\mathbf{r} = (t - t^2)\mathbf{i} - t^2\mathbf{j}$. Find the minimum speed of the particle and its location when it has this speed.

15. Suppose that the position function of a particle moving in 2-space is $\mathbf{r} = \sin 3t\mathbf{i} - 2 \cos 3t\mathbf{j}$, $0 \le t \le 2\pi/3$.
    (a) Use a graphing utility to graph the speed of the particle versus time from $t = 0$ to $t = 2\pi/3$.
    (b) What are the maximum and minimum speeds of the particle?
    (c) Use the graph to estimate the time at which the maximum speed first occurs.
    (d) Find the exact time at which the maximum speed first occurs.

16. Suppose that the position function of a particle moving in 3-space is $\mathbf{r} = 3 \cos 2t\mathbf{i} + \sin 2t\mathbf{j} + 4t\mathbf{k}$.
    (a) Use a graphing utility to graph the speed of the particle versus time from $t = 0$ to $t = \pi$.

(b) Use the graph to estimate the maximum and minimum speeds of the particle.
(c) Use the graph to estimate the time at which the maximum speed first occurs.
(d) Find the exact values of the maximum and minimum speeds and the exact time at which the maximum speed first occurs.

17–20 Use the given information to find the position and velocity vectors of the particle. ■

17. $\mathbf{a}(t) = -\cos t\mathbf{i} - \sin t\mathbf{j}$; $\mathbf{v}(0) = \mathbf{i}$; $\mathbf{r}(0) = \mathbf{j}$

18. $\mathbf{a}(t) = \mathbf{i} + e^{-t}\mathbf{j}$; $\mathbf{v}(0) = 2\mathbf{i} + \mathbf{j}$; $\mathbf{r}(0) = \mathbf{i} - \mathbf{j}$

19. $\mathbf{a}(t) = \sin t\mathbf{i} + \cos t\mathbf{j} + e^t\mathbf{k}$; $\mathbf{v}(0) = \mathbf{k}$; $\mathbf{r}(0) = -\mathbf{i} + \mathbf{k}$

20. $\mathbf{a}(t) = (t + 1)^{-2}\mathbf{j} - e^{-2t}\mathbf{k}$; $\mathbf{v}(0) = 3\mathbf{i} - \mathbf{j}$; $\mathbf{r}(0) = 2\mathbf{k}$

21. Find, to the nearest degree, the angle between $\mathbf{v}$ and $\mathbf{a}$ for $\mathbf{r} = t^3\mathbf{i} + t^2\mathbf{j}$ when $t = 1$.

22. Show that the angle between $\mathbf{v}$ and $\mathbf{a}$ is constant for the position vector $\mathbf{r} = e^t \cos t\mathbf{i} + e^t \sin t\mathbf{j}$. Find the angle.

23. (a) Suppose that at time $t = t_0$ an electron has a position vector of $\mathbf{r} = 3.5\mathbf{i} - 1.7\mathbf{j} + \mathbf{k}$, and at a later time $t = t_1$ it has a position vector of $\mathbf{r} = 4.2\mathbf{i} + \mathbf{j} - 2.4\mathbf{k}$. What is the displacement of the electron during the time interval from t_0 to t_1?
    (b) Suppose that during a certain time interval a proton has a displacement of $\Delta\mathbf{r} = 0.7\mathbf{i} + 2.9\mathbf{j} - 1.2\mathbf{k}$ and its final position vector is known to be $\mathbf{r} = 3.6\mathbf{k}$. What was the initial position vector of the proton?

24. Suppose that the position function of a particle moving along a circle in the xy-plane is $\mathbf{r} = 5 \cos 2\pi t\mathbf{i} + 5 \sin 2\pi t\mathbf{j}$.
    (a) Sketch some typical displacement vectors over the time interval from $t = 0$ to $t = 1$.
    (b) What is the distance traveled by the particle during the time interval?

25–28 Find the displacement and the distance traveled over the indicated time interval. ■

25. $\mathbf{r} = t^2\mathbf{i} + \frac{1}{3}t^3\mathbf{j}$; $1 \le t \le 3$

26. $\mathbf{r} = (1 - 3 \sin t)\mathbf{i} + 3 \cos t\mathbf{j}$; $0 \le t \le 3\pi/2$

27. $\mathbf{r} = e^t\mathbf{i} + e^{-t}\mathbf{j} + \sqrt{2}t\mathbf{k}$; $0 \le t \le \ln 3$

28. $\mathbf{r} = \cos 2t\mathbf{i} + (1 - \cos 2t)\mathbf{j} + \left(3 + \frac{1}{2}\cos 2t\right)\mathbf{k}$; $0 \le t \le \pi$

29–30 The position vectors $\mathbf{r}_1$ and $\mathbf{r}_2$ of two particles are given. Show that the particles move along the same path but the speed of the first is constant and the speed of the second is not. ■

29. $\mathbf{r}_1 = 2 \cos 3t\mathbf{i} + 2 \sin 3t\mathbf{j}$
    $\mathbf{r}_2 = 2 \cos(t^2)\mathbf{i} + 2 \sin(t^2)\mathbf{j}$ $(t \ge 0)$

30. $\mathbf{r}_1 = (3 + 2t)\mathbf{i} + t\mathbf{j} + (1 - t)\mathbf{k}$
    $\mathbf{r}_2 = (5 - 2t^3)\mathbf{i} + (1 - t^3)\mathbf{j} + t^3\mathbf{k}$

31–36 The position function of a particle is given. Use Theorem 12.6.3 to find
(a) the scalar tangential and normal components of acceleration at the stated time t;
(b) the vector tangential and normal components of acceleration at the stated time t;
(c) the curvature of the path at the point where the particle is located at the stated time t. ◼

31. $\mathbf{r} = e^{-t}\mathbf{i} + e^{t}\mathbf{j}; \ t = 0$

32. $\mathbf{r} = \cos(t^2)\mathbf{i} + \sin(t^2)\mathbf{j}; \ t = \sqrt{\pi}/2$

33. $\mathbf{r} = (t^3 - 2t)\mathbf{i} + (t^2 - 4)\mathbf{j}; \ t = 1$

34. $\mathbf{r} = e^{t}\cos t\,\mathbf{i} + e^{t}\sin t\,\mathbf{j}; \ t = \pi/4$

35. $\mathbf{r} = e^{t}\mathbf{i} + e^{-2t}\mathbf{j} + t\mathbf{k}; \ t = 0$

36. $\mathbf{r} = 3\sin t\,\mathbf{i} + 2\cos t\,\mathbf{j} - \sin 2t\,\mathbf{k}; \ t = \pi/2$

37–38 In these exercises $\mathbf{v}$ and $\mathbf{a}$ are given at a certain instant of time. Find a_T, a_N, $\mathbf{T}$, and $\mathbf{N}$ at this instant. ◼

37. $\mathbf{v} = -4\mathbf{j}, \ \mathbf{a} = 2\mathbf{i} + 3\mathbf{j}$

38. $\mathbf{v} = 3\mathbf{i} - 4\mathbf{k}, \ \mathbf{a} = \mathbf{i} - \mathbf{j} + 2\mathbf{k}$

39–40 The speed $\|\mathbf{v}\|$ of a particle at an arbitrary time t is given. Find the scalar tangential component of acceleration at the indicated time. ◼

39. $\|\mathbf{v}\| = \sqrt{t^2 + e^{-3t}}; \ t = 0$

40. $\|\mathbf{v}\| = \sqrt{(4t-1)^2 + \cos^2 \pi t}; \ t = \frac{1}{4}$

41. The nuclear accelerator at the Enrico Fermi Laboratory is circular with a radius of 1 km. Find the scalar normal component of acceleration of a proton moving around the accelerator with a constant speed of 2.9×10^5 km/s.

42. Suppose that a particle moves with nonzero acceleration along the curve $y = f(x)$. Use part (b) of Exercise 23 in Section 12.5 to show that the acceleration vector is tangent to the curve at each point where $f''(x) = 0$.

43–44 Use the given information and Exercise 23 of Section 12.5 to find the normal scalar component of acceleration as a function of x. ◼

43. A particle moves along the parabola $y = x^2$ with a constant speed of 3 units per second.

44. A particle moves along the curve $x = \ln y$ with a constant speed of 2 units per second.

45–46 Use the given information to find the normal scalar component of acceleration at time $t = 1$. ◼

45. $\mathbf{a}(1) = \mathbf{i} + 2\mathbf{j} - 2\mathbf{k}; \ a_T(1) = 3$

46. $\|\mathbf{a}(1)\| = 9; \ a_T(1)\mathbf{T}(1) = 2\mathbf{i} - 2\mathbf{j} + \mathbf{k}$

47–50 True–False Determine whether the statement is true or false. Explain your answer. ◼

47. The velocity and unit tangent vectors for a moving particle are parallel.

48. If a particle moves along a smooth curve C in 3-space, then at each point on C the normal scalar component of acceleration for the particle is the product of the curvature of C and speed of the particle at the point.

49. If a particle is moving along a smooth curve C and passes through a point at which the curvature is zero, then the velocity and acceleration vectors have the same direction at that point.

50. The distance traveled by a particle over a time interval is the magnitude of the displacement vector for the particle during that time interval.

51. Derive Formula (18) from Formula (14).

52. An automobile travels at a constant speed around a curve whose radius of curvature is 1000 m. What is the maximum allowable speed if the maximum acceptable value for the normal scalar component of acceleration is 1.5 m/s²?

53. If an automobile of mass m rounds a curve, then its inward vector component of acceleration $a_N\mathbf{N}$ is caused by the frictional force $\mathbf{F}$ of the road. Thus, it follows from the vector form of Newton's second law [Equation (19)] that the frictional force and the normal scalar component of acceleration are related by the equation $\mathbf{F} = ma_N\mathbf{N}$. Thus,

$$\|\mathbf{F}\| = m\kappa \left(\frac{ds}{dt}\right)^2$$

Use this result to find the magnitude of the frictional force in newtons exerted by the road on a 500 kg go-cart driven at a speed of 10 km/h around a circular track of radius 15 m. [*Note:* 1 N = 1 kg·m/s².]

54. A shell is fired from ground level with a muzzle speed of 320 ft/s and elevation angle of 60°. Find
(a) parametric equations for the shell's trajectory
(b) the maximum height reached by the shell
(c) the horizontal distance traveled by the shell
(d) the speed of the shell at impact.

55. A rock is thrown downward from the top of a building, 168 ft high, at an angle of 60° with the horizontal. How far from the base of the building will the rock land if its initial speed is 80 ft/s?

56. Solve Exercise 55 assuming that the rock is thrown horizontally at a speed of 80 ft/s.

57. A shell is to be fired from ground level at an elevation angle of 30°. What should the muzzle speed be in order for the maximum height of the shell to be 2500 ft?

58. A shell, fired from ground level at an elevation angle of 45°, hits the ground 24,500 m away. Calculate the muzzle speed of the shell.

59. Find two elevation angles that will enable a shell, fired from ground level with a muzzle speed of 800 ft/s, to hit a ground-level target 10,000 ft away.

60. A ball rolls off a table 4 ft high while moving at a constant speed of 5 ft/s. *(cont.)*

(a) How long does it take for the ball to hit the floor after it leaves the table?

(b) At what speed does the ball hit the floor?

(c) If a ball were dropped from rest at table height just as the rolling ball leaves the table, which ball would hit the ground first? Justify your answer.

61. As illustrated in the accompanying figure, a fire hose sprays water with an initial velocity of 40 ft/s at an angle of 60° with the horizontal.

(a) Confirm that the water will clear corner point A.

(b) Confirm that the water will hit the roof.

(c) How far from corner point A will the water hit the roof?

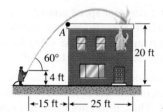

|←15 ft→|←— 25 ft —→| ◀ **Figure Ex-61**

62. What is the minimum initial velocity that will allow the water in Exercise 61 to hit the roof?

63. As shown in the accompanying figure, water is sprayed from a hose with an initial velocity of 35 m/s at an angle of 45° with the horizontal.

(a) What is the radius of curvature of the stream at the point where it leaves the hose?

(b) What is the maximum height of the stream above the nozzle of the hose?

64. As illustrated in the accompanying figure, a train is traveling on a curved track. At a point where the train is traveling at a speed of 132 ft/s and the radius of curvature of the track is 3000 ft, the engineer hits the brakes to make the train slow down at a constant rate of 7.5 ft/s^2.

(a) Find the magnitude of the acceleration vector at the instant the engineer hits the brakes.

(b) Approximate the angle between the acceleration vector and the unit tangent vector $\mathbf{T}$ at the instant the engineer hits the brakes.

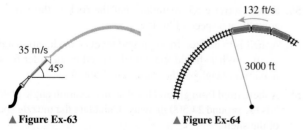

▲ **Figure Ex-63**   ▲ **Figure Ex-64**

65. A shell is fired from ground level at an elevation angle of α and a muzzle speed of v_0.

(a) Show that the maximum height reached by the shell is

$$\text{maximum height} = \frac{(v_0 \sin \alpha)^2}{2g}$$

(b) The **horizontal range** R of the shell is the horizontal distance traveled when the shell returns to ground level. Show that $R = (v_0^2 \sin 2\alpha)/g$. For what elevation angle will the range be maximum? What is the maximum range?

66. A shell is fired from ground level with an elevation angle α and a muzzle speed of v_0. Find two angles that can be used to hit a target at ground level that is a distance of three-fourths the maximum range of the shell. Express your answer to the nearest tenth of a degree. [*Hint:* See Exercise 65(b).]

67. At time $t = 0$ a baseball that is 5 ft above the ground is hit with a bat. The ball leaves the bat with a speed of 80 ft/s at an angle of 30° above the horizontal.

(a) How long will it take for the baseball to hit the ground? Express your answer to the nearest hundredth of a second.

(b) Use the result in part (a) to find the horizontal distance traveled by the ball. Express your answer to the nearest tenth of a foot.

68. Repeat Exercise 67, assuming that the ball leaves the bat with a speed of 70 ft/s at an angle of 60° above the horizontal.

C **69.** At time $t = 0$ a skier leaves the end of a ski jump with a speed of v_0 ft/s at an angle α with the horizontal (see the accompanying figure). The skier lands 259 ft down the incline 2.9 s later.

(a) Approximate v_0 to the nearest ft/s and α to the nearest degree. [*Note:* Use $g = 32$ ft/s^2 as the acceleration due to gravity.]

(b) Use a CAS or a calculating utility with a numerical integration capability to approximate the distance traveled by the skier.

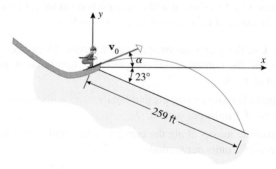

▲ **Figure Ex-69**

70. At time $t = 0$ a projectile is fired from a height h above level ground at an elevation angle of α with a speed v. Let R be the horizontal distance to the point where the projectile hits the ground.

(a) Show that α and R must satisfy the equation

$$g(\sec^2 \alpha)R^2 - 2v^2(\tan \alpha)R - 2v^2h = 0 \qquad \text{\small(cont.)}$$

(b) If g, h, and v are constant, then the equation in part (a) defines R implicitly as a function of α. Let R_0 be the maximum value of R and α_0 the value of α when $R = R_0$. Use implicit differentiation to find $dR/d\alpha$ and show that
$$\tan \alpha_0 = \frac{v^2}{g R_0}$$
[*Hint:* Assume that $dR/d\alpha = 0$ when R attains a maximum.]

(c) Use the results in parts (a) and (b) to show that
$$R_0 = \frac{v}{g}\sqrt{v^2 + 2gh}$$
and
$$\alpha_0 = \tan^{-1} \frac{v}{\sqrt{v^2 + 2gh}}$$

71. Writing Consider the various forces that a passenger in a car would sense while traveling over the crest of a hill or around a curve. Relate these sensations to the tangential and normal vector components of the acceleration vector for the car's motion. Discuss how speeding up or slowing down (e.g., doubling or halving the car's speed) affects these components.

72. Writing The formula
$$\mathbf{r}(t) = (v_0 \cos \alpha)t\mathbf{i} + (s_0 + (v_0 \sin \alpha)t - \tfrac{1}{2}gt^2)\mathbf{j}$$
models a position function for projectile motion [Formula (26)]. Identify the various quantities (v_0, α, s_0, and g) in this formula and discuss how the formula is derived, including any assumptions that are made.

✔ **QUICK CHECK ANSWERS 12.6**

1. $\dfrac{d\mathbf{r}}{dt}$; $\dfrac{d\mathbf{v}}{dt} = \dfrac{d^2\mathbf{r}}{dt^2}$; $\|\mathbf{v}(t)\|$ 2. $\mathbf{r}(t_2) - \mathbf{r}(t_1)$; $\displaystyle\int_{t_1}^{t_2} \|\mathbf{v}(t)\|\,dt$ 3. $\dfrac{d^2s}{dt^2}$; $\kappa(ds/dt)^2$ 4. $-g\mathbf{j}$; $-gt\mathbf{j} + \mathbf{v}_0$; $s_0\mathbf{j}$; $\mathbf{v}_0$

12.7 KEPLER'S LAWS OF PLANETARY MOTION

One of the great advances in the history of astronomy occurred in the early 1600s when Johannes Kepler deduced from empirical data that all planets in our solar system move in elliptical orbits with the Sun at a focus. Subsequently, Isaac Newton showed mathematically that such planetary motion is the consequence of an inverse-square law of gravitational attraction. In this section we will use the concepts developed in the preceding sections of this chapter to derive three basic laws of planetary motion, known as **Kepler's laws**.*

■ KEPLER'S LAWS
In Section 10.6 we stated the following laws of planetary motion that were published by Johannes Kepler in 1609 in his book known as *Astronomia Nova*.

© Science Photo Library
The planets in our solar system move in accordance with Kepler's three laws.

12.7.1 KEPLER'S LAWS

- First law (**Law of Orbits**). Each planet moves in an elliptical orbit with the Sun at a focus.

- Second law (**Law of Areas**). Equal areas are swept out in equal times by the line from the Sun to a planet.

- Third law (**Law of Periods**). The square of a planet's period (the time it takes the planet to complete one orbit about the Sun) is proportional to the cube of the semimajor axis of its orbit.

---

*See biography on p. 759.

CENTRAL FORCES

If a particle moves under the influence of a *single* force that is always directed toward a fixed point O, then the particle is said to be moving in a ***central force field***. The force is called a ***central force***, and the point O is called the ***center of force***. For example, in the simplest model of planetary motion, it is assumed that the only force acting on a planet is the force of the Sun's gravity, directed toward the center of the Sun. This model, which produces Kepler's laws, ignores the forces that other celestial objects exert on the planet as well as the minor effect that the planet's gravity has on the Sun. Central force models are also used to study the motion of comets, asteroids, planetary moons, and artificial satellites. They also have important applications in electromagnetics. Our objective in this section is to develop some basic principles about central force fields and then use those results to derive Kepler's laws.

Suppose that a particle P of mass m moves in a central force field due to a force $\mathbf{F}$ that is directed toward a fixed point O, and let $\mathbf{r} = \mathbf{r}(t)$ be the position vector from O to P (Figure 12.7.1). Let $\mathbf{v} = \mathbf{v}(t)$ and $\mathbf{a} = \mathbf{a}(t)$ be the velocity and acceleration functions of the particle, and assume that $\mathbf{F}$ and $\mathbf{a}$ are related by Newton's second law ($\mathbf{F} = m\mathbf{a}$).

Our first objective is to show that the particle P moves in a plane containing the point O. For this purpose observe that $\mathbf{a}$ has the same direction as $\mathbf{F}$ by Newton's second law, and this implies that $\mathbf{a}$ and $\mathbf{r}$ are oppositely directed vectors. Thus, it follows from part (c) of Theorem 11.4.5 that

$$\mathbf{r} \times \mathbf{a} = \mathbf{0}$$

Since the velocity and acceleration of the particle are given by $\mathbf{v} = d\mathbf{r}/dt$ and $\mathbf{a} = d\mathbf{v}/dt$, respectively, we have

$$\frac{d}{dt}(\mathbf{r} \times \mathbf{v}) = \mathbf{r} \times \frac{d\mathbf{v}}{dt} + \frac{d\mathbf{r}}{dt} \times \mathbf{v} = (\mathbf{r} \times \mathbf{a}) + (\mathbf{v} \times \mathbf{v}) = \mathbf{0} + \mathbf{0} = \mathbf{0} \quad (1)$$

Integrating the left and right sides of this equation with respect to t yields

$$\mathbf{r} \times \mathbf{v} = \mathbf{b} \quad (2)$$

where $\mathbf{b}$ is a constant (independent of t). However, $\mathbf{b}$ is orthogonal to both $\mathbf{r}$ and $\mathbf{v}$, so we can conclude that $\mathbf{r} = \mathbf{r}(t)$ and $\mathbf{v} = \mathbf{v}(t)$ lie in a fixed plane containing the point O.

NEWTON'S LAW OF UNIVERSAL GRAVITATION

Our next objective is to derive the position function of a particle moving under a central force in a polar coordinate system. For this purpose we will need the following result, known as ***Newton's Law of Universal Gravitation***.

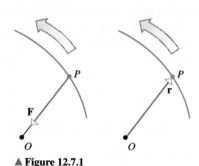
▲ **Figure 12.7.1**

Astronomers call the plane containing the orbit of a planet the *ecliptic* of the planet.

12.7.2 NEWTON'S LAW OF UNIVERSAL GRAVITATION   Every particle of matter in the Universe attracts every other particle of matter in the Universe with a force that is proportional to the product of their masses and inversely proportional to the square of the distance between them. Specifically, if a particle of mass M and a particle of mass m are at a distance r from each other, then they attract each other with equal and opposite forces, $\mathbf{F}$ and $-\mathbf{F}$, of magnitude

$$\|\mathbf{F}\| = \frac{GMm}{r^2} \quad (3)$$

where G is a constant called the ***universal gravitational constant***.

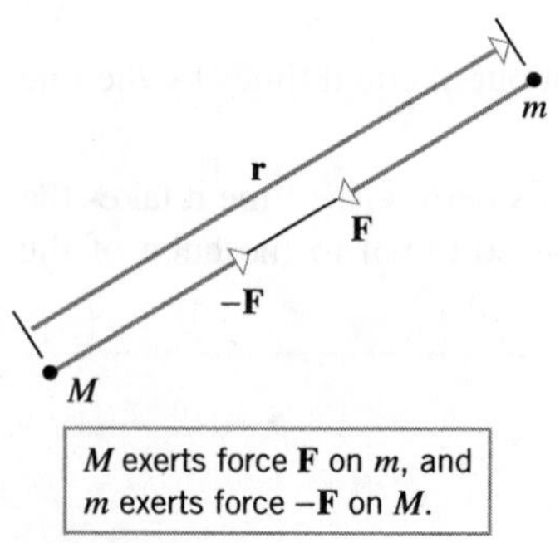

M exerts force $\mathbf{F}$ on m, and m exerts force $-\mathbf{F}$ on M.

▲ **Figure 12.7.2**

To obtain a formula for the vector force $\mathbf{F}$ that mass M exerts on mass m, we will let $\mathbf{r}$ be the radius vector from mass M to mass m (Figure 12.7.2). Thus, the distance r between the masses is $\|\mathbf{r}\|$, and the force $\mathbf{F}$ can be expressed in terms of $\mathbf{r}$ as

$$\mathbf{F} = \|\mathbf{F}\| \left(-\frac{\mathbf{r}}{\|\mathbf{r}\|} \right) = \|\mathbf{F}\| \left(-\frac{\mathbf{r}}{r} \right)$$

which from (3) can be expressed as

$$\mathbf{F} = -\frac{GMm}{r^3}\mathbf{r} \tag{4}$$

We start by finding a formula for the acceleration function. To do this we use Formula (4) and Newton's second law to obtain

$$m\mathbf{a} = -\frac{GMm}{r^3}\mathbf{r}$$

from which we obtain

$$\mathbf{a} = -\frac{GM}{r^3}\mathbf{r} \tag{5}$$

> Observe in Formula (5) that the acceleration $\mathbf{a}$ does not involve m. Thus, the mass of a planet has no effect on its acceleration.

To obtain a formula for the position function of the mass m, we will need to introduce a coordinate system and make some assumptions about the initial conditions:

- The distance r from m to M is minimum at time $t = 0$.
- The mass m has nonzero position and velocity vectors $\mathbf{r}_0$ and $\mathbf{v}_0$ at time $t = 0$.
- A polar coordinate system is introduced with its pole at mass M and oriented so $\theta = 0$ at time $t = 0$.
- The vector $\mathbf{v}_0$ is perpendicular to the polar axis at time $t = 0$.

Moreover, to ensure that the polar angle θ increases with t, let us agree to observe this polar coordinate system looking toward the pole from the terminal point of the vector $\mathbf{b} = \mathbf{r}_0 \times \mathbf{v}_0$. We will also find it useful to superimpose an xyz-coordinate system on the polar coordinate system with the positive z-axis in the direction of $\mathbf{b}$ (Figure 12.7.3).

For computational purposes, it will be helpful to denote $\|\mathbf{r}_0\|$ by r_0 and $\|\mathbf{v}_0\|$ by v_0, in which case we can express the vectors $\mathbf{r}_0$ and $\mathbf{v}_0$ in xyz-coordinates as

$$\mathbf{r}_0 = r_0\mathbf{i} \quad \text{and} \quad \mathbf{v}_0 = v_0\mathbf{j}$$

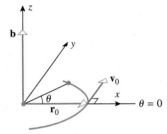

▲ Figure 12.7.3

and the vector $\mathbf{b}$ as

$$\mathbf{b} = \mathbf{r}_0 \times \mathbf{v}_0 = r_0\mathbf{i} \times v_0\mathbf{j} = r_0 v_0 \mathbf{k} \tag{6}$$

(Figure 12.7.4). It will also be useful to introduce the unit vector

$$\mathbf{u} = \cos\theta\,\mathbf{i} + \sin\theta\,\mathbf{j} \tag{7}$$

which will allow us to express the polar form of the position vector $\mathbf{r}$ as

$$\mathbf{r} = r\cos\theta\,\mathbf{i} + r\sin\theta\,\mathbf{j} = r(\cos\theta\,\mathbf{i} + \sin\theta\,\mathbf{j}) = r\mathbf{u} \tag{8}$$

and to express the acceleration vector $\mathbf{a}$ in terms of $\mathbf{u}$ by rewriting (5) as

$$\mathbf{a} = -\frac{GM}{r^2}\mathbf{u} \tag{9}$$

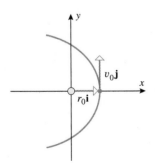

▲ Figure 12.7.4

We are now ready to derive the position function of the mass m in polar coordinates. For this purpose, recall from (2) that the vector $\mathbf{b} = \mathbf{r} \times \mathbf{v}$ is constant, so it follows from (6) that the relationship

$$\mathbf{b} = \mathbf{r} \times \mathbf{v} = r_0 v_0 \mathbf{k} \tag{10}$$

holds for *all* values of t. Now let us examine $\mathbf{b}$ from another point of view. It follows from (8) that

$$\mathbf{v} = \frac{d\mathbf{r}}{dt} = \frac{d}{dt}(r\mathbf{u}) = r\frac{d\mathbf{u}}{dt} + \frac{dr}{dt}\mathbf{u}$$

and hence

$$\mathbf{b} = \mathbf{r} \times \mathbf{v} = (r\mathbf{u}) \times \left(r\frac{d\mathbf{u}}{dt} + \frac{dr}{dt}\mathbf{u}\right) = r^2\mathbf{u} \times \frac{d\mathbf{u}}{dt} + r\frac{dr}{dt}\mathbf{u} \times \mathbf{u} = r^2\mathbf{u} \times \frac{d\mathbf{u}}{dt} \quad (11)$$

But (7) implies that

$$\frac{d\mathbf{u}}{dt} = \frac{d\mathbf{u}}{d\theta}\frac{d\theta}{dt} = (-\sin\theta\,\mathbf{i} + \cos\theta\,\mathbf{j})\frac{d\theta}{dt}$$

so

$$\mathbf{u} \times \frac{d\mathbf{u}}{dt} = \frac{d\theta}{dt}\mathbf{k} \quad (12)$$

Substituting (12) in (11) yields

$$\mathbf{b} = r^2\frac{d\theta}{dt}\mathbf{k} \quad (13)$$

Thus, it follows from (7), (9), and (13) that

$$\mathbf{a} \times \mathbf{b} = -\frac{GM}{r^2}(\cos\theta\,\mathbf{i} + \sin\theta\,\mathbf{j}) \times \left(r^2\frac{d\theta}{dt}\mathbf{k}\right)$$

$$= GM(-\sin\theta\,\mathbf{i} + \cos\theta\,\mathbf{j})\frac{d\theta}{dt} = GM\frac{d\mathbf{u}}{dt} \quad (14)$$

From this formula and the fact that $d\mathbf{b}/dt = \mathbf{0}$ (since $\mathbf{b}$ is constant), we obtain

$$\frac{d}{dt}(\mathbf{v} \times \mathbf{b}) = \mathbf{v} \times \frac{d\mathbf{b}}{dt} + \frac{d\mathbf{v}}{dt} \times \mathbf{b} = \mathbf{a} \times \mathbf{b} = GM\frac{d\mathbf{u}}{dt}$$

Integrating both sides of this equation with respect to t yields

$$\mathbf{v} \times \mathbf{b} = GM\mathbf{u} + \mathbf{C} \quad (15)$$

where $\mathbf{C}$ is a vector constant of integration. This constant can be obtained by evaluating both sides of the equation at $t = 0$. We leave it as an exercise to show that

$$\mathbf{C} = (r_0 v_0^2 - GM)\mathbf{i} \quad (16)$$

from which it follows that

$$\mathbf{v} \times \mathbf{b} = GM\mathbf{u} + (r_0 v_0^2 - GM)\mathbf{i} \quad (17)$$

We can now obtain the position function by computing the scalar triple product $\mathbf{r} \cdot (\mathbf{v} \times \mathbf{b})$ in two ways. First we use (10) and property (11) of Section 11.4 to obtain

$$\mathbf{r} \cdot (\mathbf{v} \times \mathbf{b}) = (\mathbf{r} \times \mathbf{v}) \cdot \mathbf{b} = \mathbf{b} \cdot \mathbf{b} = r_0^2 v_0^2 \quad (18)$$

and next we use (17) to obtain

$$\mathbf{r} \cdot (\mathbf{v} \times \mathbf{b}) = \mathbf{r} \cdot (GM\mathbf{u}) + \mathbf{r} \cdot (r_0 v_0^2 - GM)\mathbf{i}$$

$$= \mathbf{r} \cdot \left(GM\frac{\mathbf{r}}{r}\right) + r\mathbf{u} \cdot (r_0 v_0^2 - GM)\mathbf{i}$$

$$= GMr + r(r_0 v_0^2 - GM)\cos\theta$$

If we now equate this to (18), we obtain

$$r_0^2 v_0^2 = GMr + r(r_0 v_0^2 - GM)\cos\theta$$

which when solved for r gives

$$r = \frac{r_0^2 v_0^2}{GM + (r_0 v_0^2 - GM)\cos\theta} = \frac{\dfrac{r_0^2 v_0^2}{GM}}{1 + \left(\dfrac{r_0 v_0^2}{GM} - 1\right)\cos\theta} \quad (19)$$

or more simply

$$r = \frac{k}{1 + e\cos\theta} \quad (20)$$

where

$$k = \frac{r_0^2 v_0^2}{GM} \quad \text{and} \quad e = \frac{r_0 v_0^2}{GM} - 1 \tag{21-22}$$

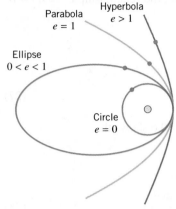

Parabola
$e = 1$

Hyperbola
$e > 1$

Ellipse
$0 < e < 1$

Circle
$e = 0$

▲ **Figure 12.7.5**

We will leave it as an exercise to show that $e \geq 0$. Accepting this to be so, it follows by comparing (20) to Formula (3) of Section 10.6 that the trajectory is a conic section with eccentricity e, the focus at the pole, and $d = k/e$. Thus, depending on whether $e < 1$, $e = 1$, or $e > 1$, the trajectory will be, respectively, an ellipse, a parabola, or a hyperbola (Figure 12.7.5).

Note from Formula (22) that e depends on r_0 and v_0, so the exact form of the trajectory is determined by the mass M and the initial conditions. If the initial conditions are such that $e < 1$, then the mass m becomes trapped in an elliptical orbit; otherwise the mass m "escapes" and never returns to its initial position. Accordingly, the initial velocity that produces an eccentricity of $e = 1$ is called the ***escape speed*** and is denoted by v_{esc}. Thus, it follows from (22) that

$$v_{esc} = \sqrt{\frac{2GM}{r_0}} \tag{23}$$

(verify).

KEPLER'S FIRST AND SECOND LAWS

It follows from our general discussion of central force fields that the planets have elliptical orbits with the Sun at the focus, which is Kepler's first law. To derive Kepler's second law, we begin by equating (10) and (13) to obtain

$$r^2 \frac{d\theta}{dt} = r_0 v_0 \tag{24}$$

To prove that the radial line from the center of the Sun to the center of a planet sweeps out equal areas in equal times, let $r = f(\theta)$ denote the polar equation of the planet, and let A denote the area swept out by the radial line as it varies from any fixed angle θ_0 to an angle θ. It follows from the area formula in 10.3.4 that A can be expressed as

$$A = \int_{\theta_0}^{\theta} \frac{1}{2} [f(\phi)]^2 \, d\phi$$

where the dummy variable ϕ is introduced for the integration to reserve θ for the upper limit. It now follows from Part 2 of the Fundamental Theorem of Calculus and the chain rule that

$$\frac{dA}{dt} = \frac{dA}{d\theta} \frac{d\theta}{dt} = \frac{1}{2} [f(\theta)]^2 \frac{d\theta}{dt} = \frac{1}{2} r^2 \frac{d\theta}{dt}$$

Thus, it follows from (24) that

$$\frac{dA}{dt} = \frac{1}{2} r_0 v_0 \tag{25}$$

which shows that A changes at a constant rate. This implies that equal areas are swept out in equal times.

KEPLER'S THIRD LAW

To derive Kepler's third law, we let a and b be the semimajor and semiminor axes of the elliptical orbit, and we recall that the area of this ellipse is πab. It follows by integrating (25) that in t units of time the radial line will sweep out an area of $A = \frac{1}{2} r_0 v_0 t$. Thus, if T denotes the time required for the planet to make one revolution around the Sun (the period), then the radial line will sweep out the area of the entire ellipse during that time and hence

$$\pi ab = \frac{1}{2} r_0 v_0 T$$

from which we obtain

$$T^2 = \frac{4\pi^2 a^2 b^2}{r_0^2 v_0^2} \tag{26}$$

However, it follows from Formula (1) of Section 10.6 and the relationship $c^2 = a^2 - b^2$ for an ellipse that

$$e = \frac{c}{a} = \frac{\sqrt{a^2 - b^2}}{a}$$

Thus, $b^2 = a^2(1 - e^2)$ and hence (26) can be written as

$$T^2 = \frac{4\pi^2 a^4 (1 - e^2)}{r_0^2 v_0^2} \tag{27}$$

But comparing Equation (20) to Equation (17) of Section 10.6 shows that

$$k = a(1 - e^2)$$

Finally, substituting this expression and (21) in (27) yields

$$T^2 = \frac{4\pi^2 a^3}{r_0^2 v_0^2} k = \frac{4\pi^2 a^3}{r_0^2 v_0^2} \frac{r_0^2 v_0^2}{GM} = \frac{4\pi^2}{GM} a^3 \tag{28}$$

Thus, we have proved that T^2 is proportional to a^3, which is Kepler's third law. When convenient, Formula (28) can also be expressed as

$$T = \frac{2\pi}{\sqrt{GM}} a^{3/2} \tag{29}$$

■ **ARTIFICIAL SATELLITES**

Kepler's second and third laws and Formula (23) also apply to satellites that orbit a celestial body; we need only interpret M to be the mass of the body exerting the force and m to be the mass of the satellite. Values of GM that are required in many of the formulas in this section have been determined experimentally for various attracting bodies (Table 12.7.1).

Table 12.7.1

ATTRACTING BODY	INTERNATIONAL SYSTEM	BRITISH ENGINEERING SYSTEM
Earth	$GM = 3.99 \times 10^{14}$ m³/s² $GM = 3.99 \times 10^5$ km³/s²	$GM = 1.41 \times 10^{16}$ ft³/s² $GM = 1.24 \times 10^{12}$ mi³/h²
Sun	$GM = 1.33 \times 10^{20}$ m³/s² $GM = 1.33 \times 10^{11}$ km³/s²	$GM = 4.69 \times 10^{21}$ ft³/s² $GM = 4.13 \times 10^{17}$ mi³/h²
Moon	$GM = 4.90 \times 10^{12}$ m³/s² $GM = 4.90 \times 10^3$ km³/s²	$GM = 1.73 \times 10^{14}$ ft³/s² $GM = 1.53 \times 10^{10}$ mi³/h²

Recall that for orbits of planets around the Sun, the point at which the distance between the center of the planet and the center of the Sun is maximum is called the *aphelion* and the point at which it is minimum the *perihelion*. For satellites orbiting the Earth, the point at which the maximum distance occurs is called the ***apogee***, and the point at which the minimum distance occurs is called the ***perigee*** (Figure 12.7.6). The actual distances between the centers at apogee and perigee are called the ***apogee distance*** and the ***perigee distance***.

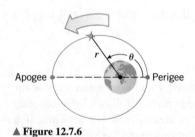

▲ Figure 12.7.6

▶ **Example 1**   A geosynchronous orbit for a satellite is a circular orbit about the equator of the Earth in which the satellite stays fixed over a point on the equator. Use the fact that the Earth makes one revolution about its axis every 24 hours to find the altitude in miles of a communications satellite in geosynchronous orbit. Assume the Earth to be a sphere of radius 4000 mi.

Solution. To remain fixed over a point on the equator, the satellite must have a period of $T = 24$ h. It follows from (28) or (29) and the Earth value of $GM = 1.24 \times 10^{12}$ mi^3/h^2 from Table 12.7.1 that

$$a = \sqrt[3]{\frac{GMT^2}{4\pi^2}} = \sqrt[3]{\frac{(1.24 \times 10^{12})(24)^2}{4\pi^2}} \approx 26{,}250 \text{ mi}$$

and hence the altitude h of the satellite is

$$h \approx 26{,}250 - 4000 = 22{,}250 \text{ mi} \blacktriangleleft$$

✔ **QUICK CHECK EXERCISES 12.7** *(See page 902 for answers.)*

1. Let G denote the universal gravitational constant and let M and m denote masses a distance r apart.
   (a) According to Newton's Law of Universal Gravitation, M and m attract each other with a force of magnitude _____.
   (b) If $\mathbf{r}$ is the radius vector from M to m, then the force of attraction that mass M exerts on mass m is _____.

2. Suppose that a mass m is in an orbit about a mass M and that r_0 is the minimum distance from m to M. If G is the universal gravitational constant, then the "escape" speed of m is _____.

3. For a planet in an elliptical orbit about the Sun, the square of the planet's period is proportional to what power of the semimajor axis of its orbit?

4. Suppose that a mass m is in an orbit about a mass M and that r_0 is the minimum distance from m to M. If v_0 is the speed of mass m when it is a distance r_0 from M, and if G denotes the universal gravitational constant, then the eccentricity of the orbit is _____.

EXERCISE SET 12.7

1–14 In exercises that require numerical values, use Table 12.7.1 and the following values, where needed:

   radius of Earth = 4000 mi = 6440 km
   radius of Moon = 1080 mi = 1740 km
   1 year (Earth year) = 365 days ■

FOCUS ON CONCEPTS

1. (a) Obtain the value of $\mathbf{C}$ given in Formula (16) by setting $t = 0$ in (15).
   (b) Use Formulas (7), (17), and (22) to show that
   $$\mathbf{v} \times \mathbf{b} = GM[(e + \cos\theta)\mathbf{i} + \sin\theta\,\mathbf{j}]$$
   (c) Show that $\|\mathbf{v} \times \mathbf{b}\| = \|\mathbf{v}\|\|\mathbf{b}\|$.
   (d) Use the results in parts (b) and (c) to show that the speed of a particle in an elliptical orbit is
   $$v = \frac{v_0}{1+e}\sqrt{e^2 + 2e\cos\theta + 1}$$
   (e) Suppose that a particle is in an elliptical orbit. Use part (d) to conclude that the distance from the particle to the center of force is a minimum if and only if the speed of the particle is a maximum. Similarly,

argue that the distance from the particle to the center of force is a maximum if and only if the speed of the particle is a minimum.

2. Use the result in Exercise 1(d) to show that when a particle in an elliptical orbit with eccentricity e reaches an end of the minor axis, its speed is
   $$v = v_0\sqrt{\frac{1-e}{1+e}}$$

3. Use the result in Exercise 1(d) to show that for a particle in an elliptical orbit with eccentricity e, the maximum and minimum speeds are related by
   $$v_{\max} = v_{\min}\frac{1+e}{1-e}$$

4. Use Formula (22) and the result in Exercise 1(d) to show that the speed v of a particle in a circular orbit of radius r_0 is constant and is given by
   $$v = \sqrt{\frac{GM}{r_0}}$$

5. Suppose that a particle is in an elliptical orbit in a central force field in which the center of force is at a focus, and let $\mathbf{r} = \mathbf{r}(t)$ and $\mathbf{v} = \mathbf{v}(t)$ be the position and velocity functions of the particle, respectively. Let r_{min} and r_{max} denote the minimum and maximum distances from the particle to the center of force, and let v_{min} and v_{max} denote the minimum and maximum speeds of the particle.

   (a) Review the discussion of ellipses in polar coordinates in Section 10.6, and show that if the ellipse has eccentricity e and semimajor axis a, then $r_{min} = a(1 - e)$ and $r_{max} = a(1 + e)$.

   (b) Explain why r_{min} and r_{max} occur at points at which $\mathbf{r}$ and $\mathbf{v}$ are orthogonal. [*Hint:* First argue that the extreme values of $\|\mathbf{r}\|$ occur at critical points of the function $\|\mathbf{r}\|^2 = \mathbf{r} \cdot \mathbf{r}$.]

   (c) Explain why v_{min} and v_{max} occur at points at which $\mathbf{r}$ and $\mathbf{v}$ are orthogonal. [*Hint:* First argue that the extreme values of $\|\mathbf{v}\|$ occur at critical points of the function $\|\mathbf{v}\|^2 = \mathbf{v} \cdot \mathbf{v}$. Then use Equation (5).]

   (d) Use Equation (2) and parts (b) and (c) to conclude that $r_{max}v_{min} = r_{min}v_{max}$.

6. Use the results in parts (a) and (d) of Exercise 5 to give a derivation of the equation in Exercise 3.

7. Use the result in Exercise 4 to find the speed in km/s of a satellite in a circular orbit that is 200 km above the surface of the Earth.

8. Use the result in Exercise 4 to find the speed in mi/h of a communications satellite that is in geosynchronous orbit around the Earth (see Example 1).

9. Find the escape speed in km/s for a space probe in a circular orbit that is 300 km above the surface of the Earth.

10. The universal gravitational constant is approximately

$$G = 6.67 \times 10^{-11} \text{ m}^3/\text{kg·s}^2$$

and the semimajor axis of the Earth's orbit is approximately

$$a = 149.6 \times 10^6 \text{ km}$$

Estimate the mass of the Sun in kg.

11. (a) The eccentricity of the Moon's orbit around the Earth is 0.055, and its semimajor axis is $a = 238{,}900$ mi. Find the maximum and minimum distances between the surface of the Earth and the surface of the Moon.

   (b) Find the period of the Moon's orbit in days.

12. (a) *Vanguard 1* was launched in March 1958 with perigee and apogee altitudes above the Earth of 649 km and 4340 km, respectively. Find the length of the semimajor axis of its orbit.

   (b) Use the result in part (a) of Exercise 16 in Section 10.6 to find the eccentricity of its orbit.

   (c) Find the period of *Vanguard 1* in minutes.

13. (a) Suppose that a space probe is in a circular orbit at an altitude of 180 mi above the surface of the Earth. Use the result in Exercise 4 to find its speed.

   (b) During a very short period of time, a thruster rocket on the space probe is fired to increase the speed of the probe by 600 mi/h in its direction of motion. Find the eccentricity of the resulting elliptical orbit, and use the result in part (a) of Exercise 5 to find the apogee altitude.

14. Show that the quantity e defined by Formula (22) is non-negative. [*Hint:* The polar axis was chosen so that r is minimum when $\theta = 0$.]

✔ QUICK CHECK ANSWERS 12.7

1. (a) $\dfrac{GMm}{r^2}$ (b) $-\dfrac{GMm}{r^3}\mathbf{r}$ 2. $\sqrt{\dfrac{2GM}{r_0}}$ 3. 3   4. $e = \dfrac{r_0v_0^2}{GM} - 1$

CHAPTER 12 REVIEW EXERCISES

1. In words, what is meant by the graph of a vector-valued function?

2–5 Describe the graph of the equation. ■

2. $\mathbf{r} = (2 - 3t)\mathbf{i} - 4t\mathbf{j}$ 3. $\mathbf{r} = 3 \sin 2t\,\mathbf{i} + 3 \cos 2t\,\mathbf{j}$

4. $\mathbf{r} = 3 \cos t\,\mathbf{i} + 2 \sin t\,\mathbf{j} - \mathbf{k}$ 5. $\mathbf{r} = -2\mathbf{i} + t\mathbf{j} + (t^2 - 1)\mathbf{k}$

6. Describe the graph of the vector-valued function.

   (a) $\mathbf{r} = \mathbf{r}_0 + t(\mathbf{r}_1 - \mathbf{r}_0)$

   (b) $\mathbf{r} = \mathbf{r}_0 + t(\mathbf{r}_1 - \mathbf{r}_0)$ $(0 \le t \le 1)$

   (c) $\mathbf{r} = \mathbf{r}_0 + t\mathbf{r}'(t_0)$

7. Show that the graph of $\mathbf{r}(t) = t \sin \pi t\,\mathbf{i} + t\mathbf{j} + t \cos \pi t\,\mathbf{k}$ lies on the surface of a cone, and sketch the cone.

8. Find parametric equations for the intersection of the surfaces

$$y = x^2 \quad \text{and} \quad 2x^2 + y^2 + 6z^2 = 24$$

and sketch the intersection.

9. In words, give a geometric description of the statement $\lim\limits_{t \to a} \mathbf{r}(t) = \mathbf{L}$.

10. Evaluate $\lim\limits_{t \to 0} \left(e^{-t}\mathbf{i} + \dfrac{1 - \cos t}{t}\mathbf{j} + t^2\mathbf{k} \right)$.

11. Find parametric equations of the line tangent to the graph of
$$\mathbf{r}(t) = (t + \cos 2t)\mathbf{i} - (t^2 + t)\mathbf{j} + \sin t\mathbf{k}$$
at the point where $t = 0$.

12. Suppose that $\mathbf{r}_1(t)$ and $\mathbf{r}_2(t)$ are smooth vector-valued functions such that $\mathbf{r}_1(0) = \langle -1, 1, 2 \rangle$, $\mathbf{r}_2(0) = \langle 1, 2, 1 \rangle$, $\mathbf{r}_1'(0) = \langle 1, 0, 1 \rangle$, and $\mathbf{r}_2'(0) = \langle 4, 0, 2 \rangle$. Use this information to evaluate the derivative at $t = 0$ of each function.
    (a) $\mathbf{r}(t) = 3\mathbf{r}_1(t) + 2\mathbf{r}_2(t)$ (b) $\mathbf{r}(t) = [\ln(t + 1)]\mathbf{r}_1(t)$
    (c) $\mathbf{r}(t) = \mathbf{r}_1(t) \times \mathbf{r}_2(t)$ (d) $f(t) = \mathbf{r}_1(t) \cdot \mathbf{r}_2(t)$

13. Evaluate $\displaystyle\int (\cos t\mathbf{i} + \sin t\mathbf{j}) \, dt$.

14. Evaluate $\displaystyle\int_0^{\pi/3} \langle \cos 3t, -\sin 3t \rangle \, dt$.

15. Solve the vector initial-value problem
$$\mathbf{y}'(t) = t^2\mathbf{i} + 2t\mathbf{j}, \quad \mathbf{y}(0) = \mathbf{i} + \mathbf{j}$$

16. Solve the vector initial-value problem
$$\frac{d\mathbf{r}}{dt} = \mathbf{r}, \quad \mathbf{r}(0) = \mathbf{r}_0$$
for the unknown vector-valued function $\mathbf{r}(t)$.

17. Find the arc length of the graph of
$$\mathbf{r}(t) = e^{\sqrt{2}t}\mathbf{i} + e^{-\sqrt{2}t}\mathbf{j} + 2t\mathbf{k} \quad (0 \le t \le \sqrt{2}\ln 2)$$

18. Suppose that $\mathbf{r}(t)$ is a smooth vector-valued function of t with $\mathbf{r}'(0) = 3\mathbf{i} - \mathbf{j} + \mathbf{k}$ and that $\mathbf{r}_1(t) = \mathbf{r}(2 - e^{t \ln 2})$. Find $\mathbf{r}_1'(1)$.

19. Find the arc length parametrization of the line through $P(-1, 4, 3)$ and $Q(0, 2, 5)$ that has reference point P and orients the line in the direction from P to Q.

20. Find an arc length parametrization of the curve
$$\mathbf{r}(t) = \langle e^t \cos t, -e^t \sin t \rangle \quad (0 \le t \le \pi/2)$$
which has the same orientation and has $\mathbf{r}(0)$ as the reference point.

21. Suppose that $\mathbf{r}(t)$ is a smooth vector-valued function. State the definitions of $\mathbf{T}(t)$, $\mathbf{N}(t)$, and $\mathbf{B}(t)$.

22. Find $\mathbf{T}(0)$, $\mathbf{N}(0)$, and $\mathbf{B}(0)$ for the curve
$$\mathbf{r}(t) = \left\langle 2\cos t, 2\cos t + \frac{3}{\sqrt{5}}\sin t, \cos t - \frac{6}{\sqrt{5}}\sin t \right\rangle$$

23. State the definition of "curvature" and explain what it means geometrically.

24. Suppose that $\mathbf{r}(t)$ is a smooth curve with $\mathbf{r}'(0) = \mathbf{i}$ and $\mathbf{r}''(0) = \mathbf{i} + 2\mathbf{j}$. Find the curvature at $t = 0$.

25-28 Find the curvature of the curve at the stated point. ▨

25. $\mathbf{r}(t) = 2\cos t\mathbf{i} + 3\sin t\mathbf{j} - t\mathbf{k}$; $t = \pi/2$

26. $\mathbf{r}(t) = \langle 2t, e^{2t}, e^{-2t} \rangle$; $t = 0$

27. $y = \cos x$; $x = \pi/2$ 28. $y = \ln x$; $x = 1$

29. Suppose that $\mathbf{r}(t)$ is the position function of a particle moving in 2-space or 3-space. In each part, explain what the given quantity represents physically.
    (a) $\left\| \dfrac{d\mathbf{r}}{dt} \right\|$ (b) $\displaystyle\int_{t_0}^{t_1} \left\| \dfrac{d\mathbf{r}}{dt} \right\| dt$ (c) $\| \mathbf{r}(t) \|$

30. (a) What does Theorem 12.2.8 tell you about the velocity vector of a particle that moves over a sphere?
    (b) What does Theorem 12.2.8 tell you about the acceleration vector of a particle that moves with constant speed?
    (c) Show that the particle with position function
$$\mathbf{r}(t) = \sqrt{1 - \tfrac{1}{4}\cos^2 t}\,\cos t\mathbf{i} + \sqrt{1 - \tfrac{1}{4}\cos^2 t}\,\sin t\mathbf{j} + \tfrac{1}{2}\cos t\mathbf{k}$$
    moves over a sphere.

31. As illustrated in the accompanying figure, suppose that a particle moves counterclockwise around a circle of radius R centered at the origin at a constant rate of ω radians per second. This is called **uniform circular motion**. If we assume that the particle is at the point $(R, 0)$ at time $t = 0$, then its position function will be
$$\mathbf{r}(t) = R\cos \omega t\mathbf{i} + R\sin \omega t\mathbf{j}$$
    (a) Show that the velocity vector $\mathbf{v}(t)$ is always tangent to the circle and that the particle has constant speed v given by
$$v = R\omega$$
    (b) Show that the acceleration vector $\mathbf{a}(t)$ is always directed toward the center of the circle and has constant magnitude a given by
$$a = R\omega^2$$
    (c) Show that the time T required for the particle to make one complete revolution is
$$T = \frac{2\pi}{\omega} = \frac{2\pi R}{v}$$

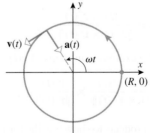

◀ **Figure Ex-31**

32. If a particle of mass m has uniform circular motion (see Exercise 31), then the acceleration vector $\mathbf{a}(t)$ is called the **centripetal acceleration**. According to Newton's second law, this acceleration must be produced by some force $\mathbf{F}(t)$, called the **centripetal force**, that is related to $\mathbf{a}(t)$ by the equation $\mathbf{F}(t) = m\mathbf{a}(t)$. If this force is not present, then the particle cannot undergo uniform circular motion. *(cont.)*

(a) Show that the direction of the centripetal force varies with time but that it has constant magnitude F given by

$$F = \frac{mv^2}{R}$$

(b) An astronaut with a mass of $m = 60$ kg orbits the Earth at an altitude of $h = 3200$ km with a constant speed of $v = 6.43$ km/s. Find her centripetal acceleration assuming that the radius of the Earth is 6440 km.

(c) What centripetal gravitational force in newtons does the Earth exert on the astronaut?

33. At time $t = 0$ a particle at the origin of an xyz-coordinate system has a velocity vector of $\mathbf{v}_0 = \mathbf{i} + 2\mathbf{j} - \mathbf{k}$. The acceleration function of the particle is $\mathbf{a}(t) = 2t^2\mathbf{i} + \mathbf{j} + \cos 2t\mathbf{k}$.
(a) Find the position function of the particle.
(b) Find the speed of the particle at time $t = 1$.

34. Let $\mathbf{v} = \mathbf{v}(t)$ and $\mathbf{a} = \mathbf{a}(t)$ be the velocity and acceleration vectors for a particle moving in 2-space or 3-space. Show that the rate of change of its speed can be expressed as

$$\frac{d}{dt}(\|\mathbf{v}\|) = \frac{1}{\|\mathbf{v}\|}(\mathbf{v} \cdot \mathbf{a})$$

35. Use Formula (23) in Section 12.7 and refer to Table 12.7.1 to find the escape speed (in km/s) for a space probe 600 km above the surface of the Earth.

36. As illustrated in the accompanying figure, the polar coordinates of a rocket are tracked by radar from a point that is b units from the launching pad. Show that the speed v of the rocket can be expressed in terms b, θ, and $d\theta/dt$ as

$$v = b \sec^2 \theta \frac{d\theta}{dt}$$

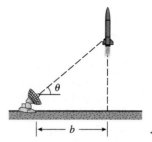

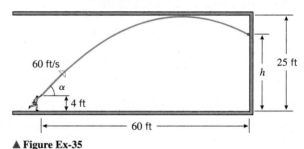

◀ **Figure Ex-34**

37. A player throws a ball with an initial speed of 60 ft/s at an unknown angle α with the horizontal from a point that is 4 ft above the floor of a gymnasium. Given that the ceiling of the gymnasium is 25 ft high, determine the maximum height h at which the ball can hit a wall that is 60 ft away (see the accompanying figure).

▲ **Figure Ex-35**

CHAPTER 12 MAKING CONNECTIONS C CAS

1. (a) Use the formulas

$$\mathbf{N}(t) = \mathbf{B}(t) \times \mathbf{T}(t)$$
$$\mathbf{T}(t) = \mathbf{r}'(t)/\|\mathbf{r}'(t)\|$$

and

$$\mathbf{B}(t) = \frac{\mathbf{r}'(t) \times \mathbf{r}''(t)}{\|\mathbf{r}'(t) \times \mathbf{r}''(t)\|}$$

to show that $\mathbf{N}(t)$ can be expressed in terms of $\mathbf{r}(t)$ as

$$\mathbf{N}(t) = \frac{\mathbf{r}'(t) \times \mathbf{r}''(t)}{\|\mathbf{r}'(t) \times \mathbf{r}''(t)\|} \times \frac{\mathbf{r}'(t)}{\|\mathbf{r}'(t)\|}$$

(b) Use properties of cross products to show that the formula in part (a) can be expressed as

$$\mathbf{N}(t) = \frac{(\mathbf{r}'(t) \times \mathbf{r}''(t)) \times \mathbf{r}'(t)}{\|(\mathbf{r}'(t) \times \mathbf{r}''(t)) \times \mathbf{r}'(t)\|}$$

(c) Use the result in part (b) to find $\mathbf{N}(t)$ at the given point.
(i) $\mathbf{r}(t) = (t^2 - 1)\mathbf{i} + t\mathbf{j}$; $t = 1$
(ii) $\mathbf{r}(t) = 4\cos t\mathbf{i} + 4\sin t\mathbf{j} + t\mathbf{k}$; $t = \pi/2$

2. (a) Use the result in Exercise 1(b) and Exercise 45 of Section 11.4 to show that $\mathbf{N}(t)$ can be expressed directly in terms of $\mathbf{r}(t)$ as

$$\mathbf{N}(t) = \frac{\mathbf{u}(t)}{\|\mathbf{u}(t)\|}$$

where

$$\mathbf{u}(t) = \|\mathbf{r}'(t)\|^2\mathbf{r}''(t) - (\mathbf{r}'(t) \cdot \mathbf{r}''(t))\mathbf{r}'(t)$$

(b) Use the result in part (a) to find $\mathbf{N}(t)$.
(i) $\mathbf{r}(t) = \sin t\mathbf{i} + \cos t\mathbf{j} + t\mathbf{k}$
(ii) $\mathbf{r}(t) = t\mathbf{i} + t^2\mathbf{j} + t^3\mathbf{k}$

3. In Making Connections Exercise 1 of Chapter 10 we defined the Cornu spiral parametrically as

$$x = \int_0^t \cos\left(\frac{\pi u^2}{2}\right) du, \quad y = \int_0^t \sin\left(\frac{\pi u^2}{2}\right) du$$

This curve, which is graphed in the accompanying figure, is used in highway design to create a gradual transition from a straight road (zero curvature) to an exit ramp with positive curvature. *(cont.)*

(a) Express the Cornu spiral as a vector-valued function $\mathbf{r}(t)$, and then use Theorem 12.3.4 to show that $s = t$ is the arc length parameter with reference point $(0, 0)$.

(b) Replace t by s and use Formula (1) of Section 12.5 to show that $\kappa(s) = \pi|s|$. [*Note:* If $s \geq 0$, then the curvature $\kappa(s) = \pi s$ increases from 0 at a constant rate with respect to s. This makes the spiral ideal for joining a curved road to a straight road.]

(c) What happens to the curvature of the Cornu spiral as $s \to +\infty$? In words, explain why this is consistent with the graph.

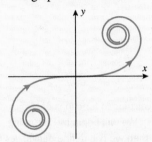

◀ **Figure Ex-3**

c 4. In 1975, German engineer Werner Stengel pioneered the use of Cornu spirals (see Exercise 3) in the design of loops for roller coasters with the *Revolution* at Six Flags Magic Mountain in California. For this design, the top of the loop is a circular arc, joined at either end to Cornu spirals that ease the transitions to horizontal track. The accompanying figure illustrates this design when the circular arc (in red) is a semicircle, quarter-circle, or a single point, respectively. Suppose that a roller-coaster loop is designed to be 45 feet across at its widest point. For each case in Figure Ex-4, find the vertical distance between the level of the horizontal track and the top of the loop. Use the numerical integration capability of your CAS to estimate integrals, as necessary.

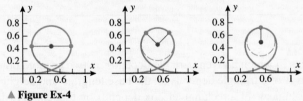

▲ **Figure Ex-4**

5. Use the results in Exercise 61 of Section 12.5 and the results in Exercise 32 of Section 12.3 to show that for the circular helix
$$\mathbf{r} = a \cos t\,\mathbf{i} + a \sin t\,\mathbf{j} + ct\,\mathbf{k}$$
with $a > 0$, the torsion and the binormal vector are
$$\tau = \frac{c}{w^2}$$

and
$$\mathbf{B} = \left(\frac{c}{w}\sin\frac{s}{w}\right)\mathbf{i} - \left(\frac{c}{w}\cos\frac{s}{w}\right)\mathbf{j} + \left(\frac{a}{w}\right)\mathbf{k}$$

where $w = \sqrt{a^2 + c^2}$ and s has reference point $(a, 0, 0)$.

6. Suppose that the position function of a point moving in the xy-plane is
$$\mathbf{r} = x(t)\mathbf{i} + y(t)\mathbf{j}$$

This equation can be expressed in polar coordinates by making the substitution
$$x(t) = r(t)\cos\theta(t), \quad y(t) = r(t)\sin\theta(t)$$

This yields
$$\mathbf{r} = r(t)\cos\theta(t)\mathbf{i} + r(t)\sin\theta(t)\mathbf{j}$$

which can be expressed as
$$\mathbf{r} = r(t)\mathbf{e}_r(t)$$

where $\mathbf{e}_r(t) = \cos\theta(t)\mathbf{i} + \sin\theta(t)\mathbf{j}$.

(a) Show that $\mathbf{e}_r(t)$ is a unit vector in the same direction as the radius vector $\mathbf{r}$ if $r(t) > 0$. Also, show that $\mathbf{e}_\theta(t) = -\sin\theta(t)\mathbf{i} + \cos\theta(t)\mathbf{j}$ is the unit vector that results when $\mathbf{e}_r(t)$ is rotated counterclockwise through an angle of $\pi/2$. The vector $\mathbf{e}_r(t)$ is called the ***radial unit vector*** and the vector $\mathbf{e}_\theta(t)$ is called the ***transverse unit vector*** (see the accompanying figure).

(b) Show that the velocity function $\mathbf{v} = \mathbf{v}(t)$ can be expressed in terms of radial and transverse components as
$$\mathbf{v} = \frac{dr}{dt}\mathbf{e}_r + r\frac{d\theta}{dt}\mathbf{e}_\theta$$

(c) Show that the acceleration function $\mathbf{a} = \mathbf{a}(t)$ can be expressed in terms of radial and transverse components as
$$\mathbf{a} = \left[\frac{d^2r}{dt^2} - r\left(\frac{d\theta}{dt}\right)^2\right]\mathbf{e}_r + \left[r\frac{d^2\theta}{dt^2} + 2\frac{dr}{dt}\frac{d\theta}{dt}\right]\mathbf{e}_\theta$$

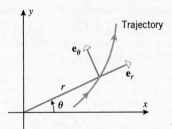

◀ **Figure Ex-6**

EXPANDING THE CALCULUS HORIZON

For a practical application of projectile motion in a whimsical setting, see the module entitled **Blammo the Human Cannonball** at:

www.wiley.com/college/anton

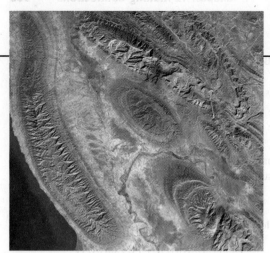

© Science Photo Library

13

PARTIAL DERIVATIVES

Three-dimensional surfaces have high points and low points that are analogous to the peaks and valleys of a mountain range. In this chapter we will use derivatives to locate these points and to study other features of such surfaces.

In this chapter we will extend many of the basic concepts of calculus to functions of two or more variables, commonly called functions of several variables. We will begin by discussing limits and continuity for functions of two and three variables, then we will define derivatives of such functions, and then we will use these derivatives to study tangent planes, rates of change, slopes of surfaces, and maximization and minimization problems. Although many of the basic ideas that we developed for functions of one variable will carry over in a natural way, functions of several variables are intrinsically more complicated than functions of one variable, so we will need to develop new tools and new ideas to deal with such functions.

13.1 FUNCTIONS OF TWO OR MORE VARIABLES

In previous sections we studied real-valued functions of a real variable and vector-valued functions of a real variable. In this section we will consider real-valued functions of two or more real variables.

◾ NOTATION AND TERMINOLOGY

There are many familiar formulas in which a given variable depends on two or more other variables. For example, the area A of a triangle depends on the base length b and height h by the formula $A = \frac{1}{2}bh$; the volume V of a rectangular box depends on the length l, the width w, and the height h by the formula $V = lwh$; and the arithmetic average $\bar{x}$ of n real numbers, $x_1, x_2, \ldots, x_n$, depends on those numbers by the formula

$$\bar{x} = \frac{1}{n}(x_1 + x_2 + \cdots + x_n)$$

Thus, we say that

A is a function of the two variables b and h;

V is a function of the three variables l, w, and h;

$\bar{x}$ is a function of the n variables $x_1, x_2, \ldots, x_n$.

The terminology and notation for functions of two or more variables is similar to that for functions of one variable. For example, the expression

$$z = f(x, y)$$

means that z is a function of x and y in the sense that a unique value of the dependent variable z is determined by specifying values for the independent variables x and y. Similarly,

$$w = f(x, y, z)$$

expresses w as a function of x, y, and z, and

$$u = f(x_1, x_2, \ldots, x_n)$$

expresses u as a function of $x_1, x_2, \ldots, x_n$.

As with functions of one variable, the independent variables of a function of two or more variables may be restricted to lie in some set D, which we call the ***domain*** of f. Sometimes the domain will be determined by physical restrictions on the variables. If the function is defined by a formula and if there are no physical restrictions or other restrictions stated explicitly, then it is understood that the domain consists of all points for which the formula yields a real value for the dependent variable. We call this the ***natural domain*** of the function. The following definitions summarize this discussion.

By extension, one can define the notion of "n-dimensional space" in which a "point" is a sequence of n real numbers $(x_1, x_2, \ldots, x_n)$, and a function of n real variables is a rule that assigns a unique real number $f(x_1, x_2, \ldots, x_n)$ to each point in some set in this space.

13.1.1 **DEFINITION** A ***function f of two variables***, x and y, is a rule that assigns a unique real number $f(x, y)$ to each point (x, y) in some set D in the xy-plane.

13.1.2 **DEFINITION** A ***function f of three variables***, x, y, and z, is a rule that assigns a unique real number $f(x, y, z)$ to each point (x, y, z) in some set D in three-dimensional space.

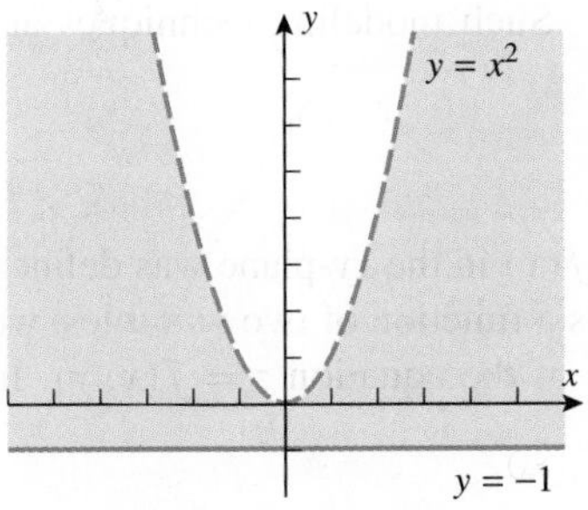

The solid boundary line is included in the domain, while the dashed boundary is not included in the domain.

▲ **Figure 13.1.1**

▶ **Example 1** Let $f(x, y) = \sqrt{y + 1} + \ln(x^2 - y)$. Find $f(e, 0)$ and sketch the natural domain of f.

Solution. By substitution,

$$f(e, 0) = \sqrt{0 + 1} + \ln(e^2 - 0) = \sqrt{1} + \ln(e^2) = 1 + 2 = 3$$

To find the natural domain of f, we note that $\sqrt{y + 1}$ is defined only when $y \geq -1$, while $\ln(x^2 - y)$ is defined only when $0 < x^2 - y$ or $y < x^2$. Thus, the natural domain of f consists of all points in the xy-plane for which $-1 \leq y < x^2$. To sketch the natural domain, we first sketch the parabola $y = x^2$ as a "dashed" curve and the line $y = -1$ as a solid curve. The natural domain of f is then the region lying above or on the line $y = -1$ and below the parabola $y = x^2$ (Figure 13.1.1.) ◀

▶ **Example 2** Let

$$f(x, y, z) = \sqrt{1 - x^2 - y^2 - z^2}$$

Find $f\left(0, \frac{1}{2}, -\frac{1}{2}\right)$ and the natural domain of f.

Solution. By substitution,

$$f\left(0, \tfrac{1}{2}, -\tfrac{1}{2}\right) = \sqrt{1 - (0)^2 - \left(\tfrac{1}{2}\right)^2 - \left(-\tfrac{1}{2}\right)^2} = \sqrt{\tfrac{1}{2}}$$

Because of the square root sign, we must have $0 \leq 1 - x^2 - y^2 - z^2$ in order to have a real value for $f(x, y, z)$. Rewriting this inequality in the form

$$x^2 + y^2 + z^2 \leq 1$$

we see that the natural domain of f consists of all points on or within the sphere

$$x^2 + y^2 + z^2 = 1 \quad \blacktriangleleft$$

■ FUNCTIONS DESCRIBED BY TABLES

The wind chill index is that temperature (in °F) which would produce the same sensation on exposed skin at a wind speed of 3 mi/h as the temperature and wind speed combination in current weather conditions.

Sometimes it is either desirable or necessary to represent a function of two variables in table form, rather than as an explicit formula. For example, the U.S. National Weather Service uses the formula

$$W = 35.74 + 0.6215T + (0.4275T - 35.75)v^{0.16} \tag{1}$$

to model the wind chill index W (in °F) as a function of the temperature T (in °F) and the wind speed v (in mi/h) for wind speeds greater than 3 mi/h. This formula is sufficiently complex that it is difficult to get an intuitive feel for the relationship between the variables. One can get a clearer sense of the relationship by selecting sample values of T and v and constructing a table, such as Table 13.1.1, in which we have rounded the values of W to the nearest integer. For example, if the temperature is 30°F and the wind speed is 5 mi/h, it feels as if the temperature is 25°F. If the wind speed increases to 15 mi/h, the temperature then feels as if it has dropped to 19°F. Note that in this case, an increase in wind speed of 10 mi/h causes a 6°F decrease in the wind chill index. To estimate wind chill values not displayed in the table, we can use *linear interpolation*. For example, suppose that the temperature is 30°F and the wind speed is 7 mi/h. A reasonable estimate for the drop in the wind chill index from its value when the wind speed is 5 mi/h would be $\frac{2}{10} \cdot 6°F = 1.2°F$. (Why?) The resulting estimate in wind chill would then be $25° - 1.2° = 23.8°F$.

In some cases, tables for functions of two variables arise directly from experimental data, in which case one must either work directly with the table or else use some technique to construct a formula that models the data in the table. Such modeling techniques are developed in statistics and numerical analysis texts.

Table 13.1.1

TEMPERATURE T (°F)

WIND SPEED v (mi/h)	20	25	30	35
5	13	19	25	31
15	6	13	19	25
25	3	9	16	23
35	0	7	14	21
45	-2	5	12	19

■ GRAPHS OF FUNCTIONS OF TWO VARIABLES

Recall that for a function f of one variable, the graph of $f(x)$ in the xy-plane was defined to be the graph of the equation $y = f(x)$. Similarly, if f is a function of two variables, we define the *graph* of $f(x, y)$ in xyz-space to be the graph of the equation $z = f(x, y)$. In general, such a graph will be a surface in 3-space.

▶ **Example 3** In each part, describe the graph of the function in an xyz-coordinate system.

(a) $f(x, y) = 1 - x - \frac{1}{2}y$ (b) $f(x, y) = \sqrt{1 - x^2 - y^2}$
(c) $f(x, y) = -\sqrt{x^2 + y^2}$

Solution (a). By definition, the graph of the given function is the graph of the equation

$$z = 1 - x - \frac{1}{2}y$$

which is a plane. A triangular portion of the plane can be sketched by plotting the intersections with the coordinate axes and joining them with line segments (Figure 13.1.2a).

Solution (b). By definition, the graph of the given function is the graph of the equation

$$z = \sqrt{1 - x^2 - y^2} \tag{2}$$

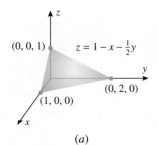

(a)

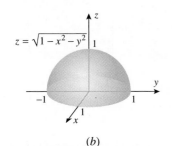

(b)

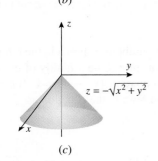

(c)

▲ **Figure 13.1.2**

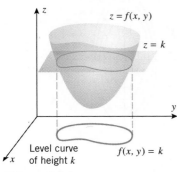

Level curve of height k $f(x, y) = k$

▲ **Figure 13.1.4**

After squaring both sides, this can be rewritten as

$$x^2 + y^2 + z^2 = 1$$

which represents a sphere of radius 1, centered at the origin. Since (2) imposes the added condition that $z \geq 0$, the graph is just the upper hemisphere (Figure 13.1.2b).

Solution (c).   The graph of the given function is the graph of the equation

$$z = -\sqrt{x^2 + y^2} \tag{3}$$

After squaring, we obtain

$$z^2 = x^2 + y^2$$

which is the equation of a circular cone (see Table 11.7.1). Since (3) imposes the condition that $z \leq 0$, the graph is just the lower nappe of the cone (Figure 13.1.2c). ◄

■ **LEVEL CURVES**

We are all familiar with the topographic (or contour) maps in which a three-dimensional landscape, such as a mountain range, is represented by two-dimensional contour lines or curves of constant elevation. Consider, for example, the model hill and its contour map shown in Figure 13.1.3. The contour map is constructed by passing planes of constant elevation through the hill, projecting the resulting contours onto a flat surface, and labeling the contours with their elevations. In Figure 13.1.3, note how the two gullies appear as indentations in the contour lines and how the curves are close together on the contour map where the hill has a steep slope and become more widely spaced where the slope is gradual.

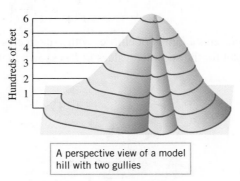

A perspective view of a model hill with two gullies

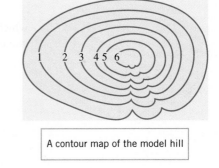

A contour map of the model hill

▲ **Figure 13.1.3**

Contour maps are also useful for studying functions of two variables. If the surface $z = f(x, y)$ is cut by the horizontal plane $z = k$, then at all points on the intersection we have $f(x, y) = k$. The projection of this intersection onto the xy-plane is called the ***level curve of height*** k or the ***level curve with constant*** k (Figure 13.1.4). A set of level curves for $z = f(x, y)$ is called a ***contour plot*** or ***contour map*** of f.

▶ **Example 4**   The graph of the function $f(x, y) = y^2 - x^2$ in xyz-space is the hyperbolic paraboloid (saddle surface) shown in Figure 13.1.5a. The level curves have equations of the form $y^2 - x^2 = k$. For $k > 0$ these curves are hyperbolas opening along lines parallel to the y-axis; for $k < 0$ they are hyperbolas opening along lines parallel to the x-axis; and for $k = 0$ the level curve consists of the intersecting lines $y + x = 0$ and $y - x = 0$ (Figure 13.1.5b). ◄

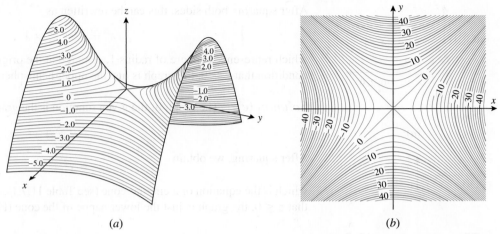

(a)

(b)

▲ **Figure 13.1.5**

▶ **Example 5** Sketch the contour plot of $f(x, y) = 4x^2 + y^2$ using level curves of height $k = 0, 1, 2, 3, 4, 5$.

Solution. The graph of the surface $z = 4x^2 + y^2$ is the paraboloid shown in the left part of Figure 13.1.6, so we can reasonably expect the contour plot to be a family of ellipses centered at the origin. The level curve of height k has the equation $4x^2 + y^2 = k$. If $k = 0$, then the graph is the single point $(0, 0)$. For $k > 0$ we can rewrite the equation as

$$\frac{x^2}{k/4} + \frac{y^2}{k} = 1$$

which represents a family of ellipses with x-intercepts $\pm\sqrt{k}/2$ and y-intercepts $\pm\sqrt{k}$. The contour plot for the specified values of k is shown in the right part of Figure 13.1.6. ◀

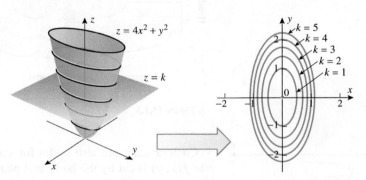

▶ **Figure 13.1.6**

▶ **Example 6** Sketch the contour plot of $f(x, y) = 2 - x - y$ using level curves of height $k = -6, -4, -2, 0, 2, 4, 6$.

Solution. The graph of the surface $z = 2 - x - y$ is the plane shown in the left part of Figure 13.1.7, so we can reasonably expect the contour plot to be a family of parallel lines. The level curve of height k has the equation $2 - x - y = k$, which we can rewrite as

$$y = -x + (2 - k)$$

This represents a family of parallel lines of slope -1. The contour plot for the specified values of k is shown in the right part of Figure 13.1.7. ◀

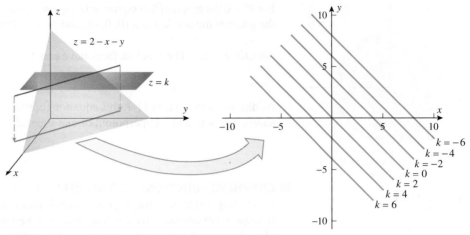

▲ **Figure 13.1.7**

■ CONTOUR PLOTS USING TECHNOLOGY

Except in the simplest cases, contour plots can be difficult to produce without the help of a graphing utility. Figure 13.1.8 illustrates how graphing technology can be used to display level curves. The table shows two graphical representations of the level curves of the function $f(x, y) = |\sin x \sin y|$ produced with a CAS over the domain $0 \leq x \leq 2\pi$, $0 \leq y \leq 2\pi$.

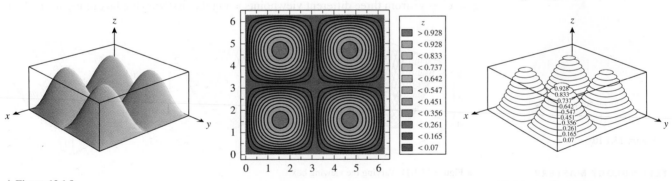

▲ **Figure 13.1.8**

■ LEVEL SURFACES

The term "level surface" is standard but confusing, since a level surface need *not* be level in the sense of being horizontal—it is simply a surface on which all values of f are the same.

Observe that the graph of $y = f(x)$ is a curve in 2-space, and the graph of $z = f(x, y)$ is a surface in 3-space, so the number of dimensions required for these graphs is one greater than the number of independent variables. Accordingly, there is no "direct" way to graph a function of three variables since four dimensions are required. However, if k is a constant, then the graph of the equation $f(x, y, z) = k$ will generally be a surface in 3-space (e.g., the graph of $x^2 + y^2 + z^2 = 1$ is a sphere), which we call the *level surface with constant k*. Some geometric insight into the behavior of the function f can sometimes be obtained by graphing these level surfaces for various values of k.

▶ **Example 7**   Describe the level surfaces of

(a) $f(x, y, z) = x^2 + y^2 + z^2$ (b) $f(x, y, z) = z^2 - x^2 - y^2$

Solution (a).   The level surfaces have equations of the form

$$x^2 + y^2 + z^2 = k$$

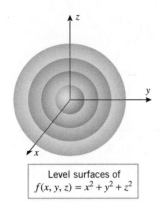

Level surfaces of
$f(x, y, z) = x^2 + y^2 + z^2$

▲ **Figure 13.1.9**

For $k > 0$ the graph of this equation is a sphere of radius $\sqrt{k}$, centered at the origin; for $k = 0$ the graph is the single point $(0, 0, 0)$; and for $k < 0$ there is no level surface (Figure 13.1.9).

Solution (b). The level surfaces have equations of the form

$$z^2 - x^2 - y^2 = k$$

As discussed in Section 11.7, this equation represents a cone if $k = 0$, a hyperboloid of two sheets if $k > 0$, and a hyperboloid of one sheet if $k < 0$ (Figure 13.1.10). ◄

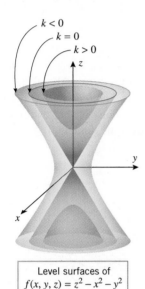

Level surfaces of
$f(x, y, z) = z^2 - x^2 - y^2$

▲ **Figure 13.1.10**

TECHNOLOGY MASTERY

If you have a graphing utility that can generate surfaces in 3-space, read the documentation and try to duplicate some of the surfaces in Figures 13.1.11 and 13.1.12 and Table 13.1.2.

■ GRAPHING FUNCTIONS OF TWO VARIABLES USING TECHNOLOGY

Generating surfaces with a graphing utility is more complicated than generating plane curves because there are more factors that must be taken into account. We can only touch on the ideas here, so if you want to use a graphing utility, its documentation will be your main source of information.

Graphing utilities can only show a portion of xyz-space in a viewing screen, so the first step in graphing a surface is to determine which portion of xyz-space you want to display. This region is called the *viewing box* or *viewing window*. For example, Figure 13.1.11 shows the effect of graphing the paraboloid $z = x^2 + y^2$ in three different viewing windows. However, within a fixed viewing box, the appearance of the surface is also affected by the *viewpoint*, that is, the direction from which the surface is viewed, and the distance from the viewer to the surface. For example, Figure 13.1.12 shows the graph of the paraboloid $z = x^2 + y^2$ from three different viewpoints using the first viewing box in Figure 13.1.11.

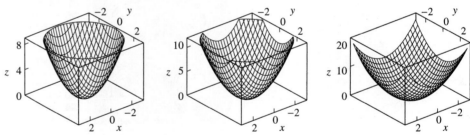

▲ **Figure 13.1.11** Varying the viewing box.

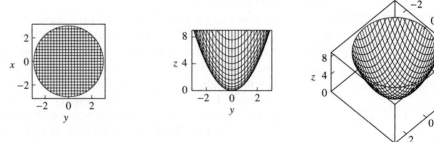

▲ **Figure 13.1.12** Varying the viewpoint.

Table 13.1.2 shows six surfaces in 3-space along with their associated contour plots. Note that the mesh lines on the surface are traces in vertical planes, whereas the level curves correspond to traces in horizontal planes. In these contour plots the color gradation varies from purple through green to red as z increases.

Table 13.1.2

SURFACE	CONTOUR PLOT	SURFACE	CONTOUR PLOT
$z = \cos y$		$z = 5e^x \sin y$	
$z = \sin\left(\sqrt{x^2 + y^2}\right)$		$z = xye^{-\frac{1}{2}(x^2 + y^2)}$	
$z = \cos(xy)$		$z = xy$	

✔ **QUICK CHECK EXERCISES 13.1**   *(See page 917 for answers.)*

1. The domain of $f(x, y) = \ln xy$ is _____ and the domain of $g(x, y) = \ln x + \ln y$ is _____.

2. Let $f(x, y) = \dfrac{x - y}{x + y + 1}$.
   (a) $f(2, 1) =$ _____   (b) $f(1, 2) =$ _____
   (c) $f(a, a) =$ _____   (d) $f(y + 1, y) =$ _____

3. Let $f(x, y) = e^{x+y}$.
   (a) For what values of k will the graph of the level curve $f(x, y) = k$ be nonempty?

   (b) Describe the level curves $f(x, y) = k$ for the values of k obtained in part (a).

4. Let $f(x, y, z) = \dfrac{1}{x^2 + y^2 + z^2 + 1}$.
   (a) For what values of k will the graph of the level surface $f(x, y, z) = k$ be nonempty?
   (b) Describe the level surfaces $f(x, y, z) = k$ for the values of k obtained in part (a).

EXERCISE SET 13.1 ◺ Graphing Utility [c] CAS

1–8 These exercises are concerned with functions of two variables. ■

1. Let $f(x, y) = x^2y + 1$. Find
(a) $f(2, 1)$ (b) $f(1, 2)$ (c) $f(0, 0)$
(d) $f(1, -3)$ (e) $f(3a, a)$ (f) $f(ab, a - b)$.

2. Let $f(x, y) = x + \sqrt[3]{xy}$. Find
(a) $f(t, t^2)$ (b) $f(x, x^2)$ (c) $f(2y^2, 4y)$.

3. Let $f(x, y) = xy + 3$. Find
(a) $f(x + y, x - y)$ (b) $f(xy, 3x^2y^3)$.

4. Let $g(x) = x \sin x$. Find
(a) $g(x/y)$ (b) $g(xy)$ (c) $g(x - y)$.

5. Find $F(g(x), h(y))$ if $F(x, y) = xe^{xy}$, $g(x) = x^3$, and $h(y) = 3y + 1$.

6. Find $g(u(x, y), v(x, y))$ if $g(x, y) = y \sin(x^2y)$, $u(x, y) = x^2y^3$, and $v(x, y) = \pi xy$.

7. Let $f(x, y) = x + 3x^2y^2$, $x(t) = t^2$, and $y(t) = t^3$. Find
(a) $f(x(t), y(t))$ (b) $f(x(0), y(0))$
(c) $f(x(2), y(2))$.

8. Let $g(x, y) = ye^{-3x}$, $x(t) = \ln(t^2 + 1)$, and $y(t) = \sqrt{t}$. Find $g(x(t), y(t))$.

9. Refer to Table 13.1.1 to estimate the wind chill index when
(a) the temperature is $25°$F and the wind speed is 7 mi/h.
(b) the temperature is $28°$F and the wind speed is 5 mi/h.

10. Refer to Table 13.1.1 to estimate the wind chill index when
(a) the temperature is $35°$F and the wind speed is 14 mi/h.
(b) the temperature is $32°$F and the wind speed is 15 mi/h.

11. One method for determining relative humidity is to wet the bulb of a thermometer, whirl it through the air, and then compare the thermometer reading with the actual air temperature. If the relative humidity is less than 100%, the reading on the thermometer will be less than the temperature of the air. This difference in temperature is known as the *wet-bulb depression*. The accompanying table gives the relative humidity as a function of the air temperature and the wet-bulb depression. Use the table to complete parts (a)–(c).
(a) What is the relative humidity if the air temperature is $20°$C and the wet-bulb thermometer reads $16°$C?
(b) Estimate the relative humidity if the air temperature is $25°$C and the wet-bulb depression is $3.5°$C.
(c) Estimate the relative humidity if the air temperature is $22°$C and the wet-bulb depression is $5°$C.

AIR TEMPERATURE (°C)

		15	20	25	30
WET-BULB DEPRESSION (°C)	3	71	74	77	79
	4	62	66	70	73
	5	53	59	63	67

▲ **Table Ex-11**

12. Use the table in Exercise 11 to complete parts (a)–(c).
(a) What is the wet-bulb depression if the air temperature is $30°$C and the relative humidity is 73%?
(b) Estimate the relative humidity if the air temperature is $15°$C and the wet-bulb depression is $4.25°$C.
(c) Estimate the relative humidity if the air temperature is $26°$C and the wet-bulb depression is $3°$C.

13–16 These exercises involve functions of three variables. ■

13. Let $f(x, y, z) = xy^2z^3 + 3$. Find
(a) $f(2, 1, 2)$ (b) $f(-3, 2, 1)$
(c) $f(0, 0, 0)$ (d) $f(a, a, a)$
(e) $f(t, t^2, -t)$ (f) $f(a + b, a - b, b)$.

14. Let $f(x, y, z) = zxy + x$. Find
(a) $f(x + y, x - y, x^2)$ (b) $f(xy, y/x, xz)$.

15. Find $F(f(x), g(y), h(z))$ if $F(x, y, z) = ye^{xyz}$, $f(x) = x^2$, $g(y) = y + 1$, and $h(z) = z^2$.

16. Find $g(u(x, y, z), v(x, y, z), w(x, y, z))$ if $g(x, y, z) = z \sin xy$, $u(x, y, z) = x^2z^3$, $v(x, y, z) = \pi xyz$, and $w(x, y, z) = xy/z$.

17–18 These exercises are concerned with functions of four or more variables. ■

17. (a) Let $f(x, y, z, t) = x^2y^3\sqrt{z + t}$. Find $f(\sqrt{5}, 2, \pi, 3\pi)$.
(b) Let $f(x_1, x_2, \ldots, x_n) = \sum_{k=1}^{n} kx_k$. Find $f(1, 1, \ldots, 1)$.

18. (a) Let $f(u, v, \lambda, \phi) = e^{u+v} \cos \lambda \tan \phi$. Find $f(-2, 2, 0, \pi/4)$.
(b) Let $f(x_1, x_2, \ldots, x_n) = x_1^2 + x_2^2 + \cdots + x_n^2$. Find $f(1, 2, \ldots, n)$.

19–22 Sketch the domain of f. Use solid lines for portions of the boundary included in the domain and dashed lines for portions not included. ■

19. $f(x, y) = \ln(1 - x^2 - y^2)$ **20.** $f(x, y) = \sqrt{x^2 + y^2 - 4}$

21. $f(x, y) = \dfrac{1}{x - y^2}$ **22.** $f(x, y) = \ln xy$

23–24 Describe the domain of f in words. ■

23. (a) $f(x, y) = xe^{-\sqrt{y+2}}$
(b) $f(x, y, z) = \sqrt{25 - x^2 - y^2 - z^2}$
(c) $f(x, y, z) = e^{xyz}$

24. (a) $f(x, y) = \dfrac{\sqrt{4 - x^2}}{y^2 + 3}$ (b) $f(x, y) = \ln(y - 2x)$
(c) $f(x, y, z) = \dfrac{xyz}{x + y + z}$

25–28 True–False Determine whether the statement is true or false. Explain your answer. ■

25. If the domain of $f(x, y)$ is the xy-plane, then the domain of $f(\sin^{-1} t, \sqrt{t})$ is the interval $[0, 1]$.

26. If $f(x, y) = y/x$, then a contour $f(x, y) = m$ is the straight line $y = mx$.

27. The natural domain of $f(x, y, z) = \sqrt{1 - x^2 - y^2}$ is a disk of radius 1 centered at the origin in the xy-plane.

28. Every level surface of $f(x, y, z) = x + 2y + 3z$ is a plane.

29–38 Sketch the graph of f. ■

29. $f(x, y) = 3$

30. $f(x, y) = \sqrt{9 - x^2 - y^2}$

31. $f(x, y) = \sqrt{x^2 + y^2}$

32. $f(x, y) = x^2 + y^2$

33. $f(x, y) = x^2 - y^2$

34. $f(x, y) = 4 - x^2 - y^2$

35. $f(x, y) = \sqrt{x^2 + y^2 + 1}$

36. $f(x, y) = \sqrt{x^2 + y^2 - 1}$

37. $f(x, y) = y + 1$

38. $f(x, y) = x^2$

FOCUS ON CONCEPTS

39. In each part, match the contour plot with one of the functions

$$f(x, y) = \sqrt{x^2 + y^2}, \quad f(x, y) = x^2 + y^2,$$
$$f(x, y) = 1 - x^2 - y^2$$

by inspection, and explain your reasoning. Larger values of z are indicated by lighter colors in the contour plot, and the concentric contours correspond to equally spaced values of z.

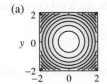 (a)

 (b)

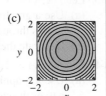 (c)

40. In each part, match the contour plot with one of the surfaces in the accompanying figure by inspection, and explain your reasoning. The larger the value of z, the lighter the color in the contour plot.

(a)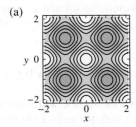

(b)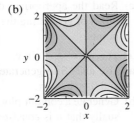

(c)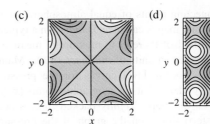

(d)

(I) (II)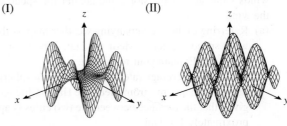

(III) (IV)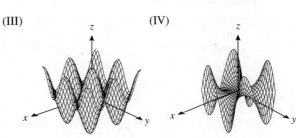

▲ **Figure Ex-40**

41. In each part, the questions refer to the contour map in the accompanying figure.

(a) Is A or B the higher point? Explain your reasoning.

(b) Is the slope steeper at point A or at point B? Explain your reasoning.

(c) Starting at A and moving so that y remains constant and x increases, will the elevation begin to increase or decrease?

(d) Starting at B and moving so that y remains constant and x increases, will the elevation begin to increase or decrease?

(e) Starting at A and moving so that x remains constant and y decreases, will the elevation begin to increase or decrease?

(f) Starting at B and moving so that x remains constant and y decreases, will the elevation begin to increase or decrease?

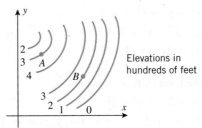

Elevations in hundreds of feet

◀ **Figure Ex-41**

42. A curve connecting points of equal atmospheric pressure on a weather map is called an *isobar*. On a typical weather map the isobars refer to pressure at mean sea level and are given in units of *millibars* (mb). Mathematically, isobars are level curves for the pressure function $p(x, y)$ defined at the geographic points (x, y) represented on the map. Tightly packed isobars correspond to steep slopes on the graph of the pressure function, and these are usually associated with strong winds—the steeper the slope, the greater the speed of the wind.

(a) Referring to the accompanying weather map, is the wind speed greater in Medicine Hat, Alberta or in Chicago? Explain your reasoning.

(b) Estimate the average rate of change in atmospheric pressure (in mb/mi) from Medicine Hat to Chicago, given that the distance between the two cities is approximately 1400 mi.

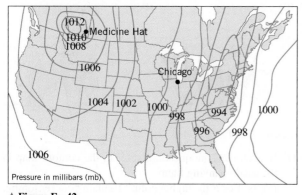

▲ **Figure Ex-42**

43–48 Sketch the level curve $z = k$ for the specified values of k. ■

43. $z = x^2 + y^2$; $k = 0, 1, 2, 3, 4$

44. $z = y/x$; $k = -2, -1, 0, 1, 2$

45. $z = x^2 + y$; $k = -2, -1, 0, 1, 2$

46. $z = x^2 + 9y^2$; $k = 0, 1, 2, 3, 4$

47. $z = x^2 - y^2$; $k = -2, -1, 0, 1, 2$

48. $z = y \csc x$; $k = -2, -1, 0, 1, 2$

49–52 Sketch the level surface $f(x, y, z) = k$. ■

49. $f(x, y, z) = 4x^2 + y^2 + 4z^2$; $k = 16$

50. $f(x, y, z) = x^2 + y^2 - z^2$; $k = 0$

51. $f(x, y, z) = z - x^2 - y^2 + 4$; $k = 7$

52. $f(x, y, z) = 4x - 2y + z$; $k = 1$

53–56 Describe the level surfaces in words. ■

53. $f(x, y, z) = (x - 2)^2 + y^2 + z^2$

54. $f(x, y, z) = 3x - y + 2z$ **55.** $f(x, y, z) = x^2 + z^2$

56. $f(x, y, z) = z - x^2 - y^2$

57. Let $f(x, y) = x^2 - 2x^3 + 3xy$. Find an equation of the level curve that passes through the point
(a) $(-1, 1)$ (b) $(0, 0)$ (c) $(2, -1)$.

58. Let $f(x, y) = ye^x$. Find an equation of the level curve that passes through the point
(a) $(\ln 2, 1)$ (b) $(0, 3)$ (c) $(1, -2)$.

59. Let $f(x, y, z) = x^2 + y^2 - z$. Find an equation of the level surface that passes through the point
(a) $(1, -2, 0)$ (b) $(1, 0, 3)$ (c) $(0, 0, 0)$.

60. Let $f(x, y, z) = xyz + 3$. Find an equation of the level surface that passes through the point
(a) $(1, 0, 2)$ (b) $(-2, 4, 1)$ (c) $(0, 0, 0)$.

61. If $T(x, y)$ is the temperature at a point (x, y) on a thin metal plate in the xy-plane, then the level curves of T are called *isothermal curves*. All points on such a curve are at the same temperature. Suppose that a plate occupies the first quadrant and $T(x, y) = xy$.
(a) Sketch the isothermal curves on which $T = 1$, $T = 2$, and $T = 3$.
(b) An ant, initially at $(1, 4)$, wants to walk on the plate so that the temperature along its path remains constant. What path should the ant take and what is the temperature along that path?

62. If $V(x, y)$ is the voltage or potential at a point (x, y) in the xy-plane, then the level curves of V are called *equipotential curves*. Along such a curve, the voltage remains constant. Given that
$$V(x, y) = \frac{8}{\sqrt{16 + x^2 + y^2}}$$
sketch the equipotential curves at which $V = 2.0$, $V = 1.0$, and $V = 0.5$.

63. Let $f(x, y) = x^2 + y^3$.
(a) Use a graphing utility to generate the level curve that passes through the point $(2, -1)$.
(b) Generate the level curve of height 1.

64. Let $f(x, y) = 2\sqrt{xy}$.
(a) Use a graphing utility to generate the level curve that passes through the point $(2, 2)$.
(b) Generate the level curve of height 8.

65. Let $f(x, y) = xe^{-(x^2+y^2)}$.
(a) Use a CAS to generate the graph of f for $-2 \le x \le 2$ and $-2 \le y \le 2$.
(b) Generate a contour plot for the surface, and confirm visually that it is consistent with the surface obtained in part (a).
(c) Read the appropriate documentation and explore the effect of generating the graph of f from various viewpoints.

66. Let $f(x, y) = \frac{1}{10}e^x \sin y$.
(a) Use a CAS to generate the graph of f for $0 \le x \le 4$ and $0 \le y \le 2\pi$.
(b) Generate a contour plot for the surface, and confirm visually that it is consistent with the surface obtained in part (a).

(cont.)

(c) Read the appropriate documentation and explore the effect of generating the graph of f from various viewpoints.

67. In each part, describe in words how the graph of g is related to the graph of f.
 (a) $g(x, y) = f(x - 1, y)$ (b) $g(x, y) = 1 + f(x, y)$
 (c) $g(x, y) = -f(x, y + 1)$

68. (a) Sketch the graph of $f(x, y) = e^{-(x^2+y^2)}$.
 (b) Describe in words how the graph of the function $g(x, y) = e^{-a(x^2+y^2)}$ is related to the graph of f for positive values of a.

69. Writing Find a few practical examples of functions of two and three variables, and discuss how physical considerations affect their domains.

70. Writing Describe two different ways in which a function $f(x, y)$ can be represented geometrically. Discuss some of the advantages and disadvantages of each representation.

✔ **QUICK CHECK ANSWERS 13.1**

1. points (x, y) in the first or third quadrants; points (x, y) in the first quadrant   **2.** (a) $\frac{1}{4}$ (b) $-\frac{1}{4}$ (c) 0 (d) $1/(2y + 2)$
3. (a) $k > 0$ (b) the lines $x + y = \ln k$ **4.** (a) $0 < k \le 1$ (b) spheres of radius $\sqrt{(1-k)/k}$ for $0 < k < 1$, the single point $(0, 0, 0)$ for $k = 1$

13.2 LIMITS AND CONTINUITY

In this section we will introduce the notions of limit and continuity for functions of two or more variables. We will not go into great detail—our objective is to develop the basic concepts accurately and to obtain results needed in later sections. A more extensive study of these topics is usually given in advanced calculus.

■ LIMITS ALONG CURVES

For a function of one variable there are two one-sided limits at a point x_0, namely,

$$\lim_{x \to x_0^+} f(x) \quad \text{and} \quad \lim_{x \to x_0^-} f(x)$$

reflecting the fact that there are only two directions from which x can approach x_0, the right or the left. For functions of two or three variables the situation is more complicated because there are infinitely many different curves along which one point can approach another (Figure 13.2.1). Our first objective in this section is to define the limit of $f(x, y)$ as (x, y) approaches a point (x_0, y_0) along a curve C (and similarly for functions of three variables).

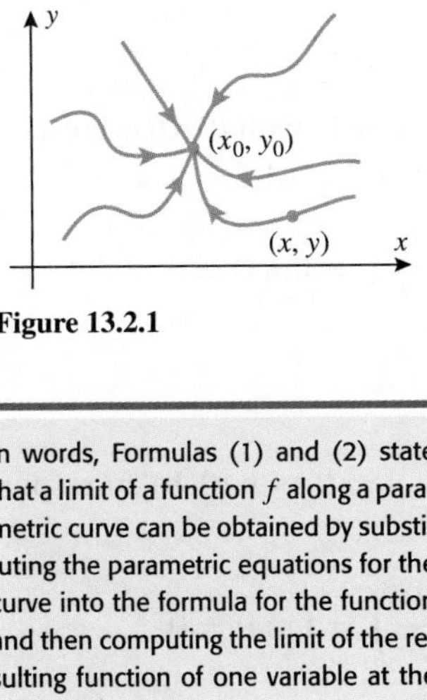

If C is a smooth parametric curve in 2-space or 3-space that is represented by the equations

$$x = x(t), \quad y = y(t) \quad \text{or} \quad x = x(t), \quad y = y(t), \quad z = z(t)$$

and if $x_0 = x(t_0)$, $y_0 = y(t_0)$, and $z_0 = z(t_0)$, then the limits

$$\lim_{\substack{(x, y) \to (x_0, y_0) \\ \text{(along } C)}} f(x, y) \quad \text{and} \quad \lim_{\substack{(x, y, z) \to (x_0, y_0, z_0) \\ \text{(along } C)}} f(x, y, z)$$

are defined by

$$\lim_{\substack{(x, y) \to (x_0, y_0) \\ \text{(along } C)}} f(x, y) = \lim_{t \to t_0} f(x(t), y(t)) \tag{1}$$

$$\lim_{\substack{(x, y, z) \to (x_0, y_0, z_0) \\ \text{(along } C)}} f(x, y, z) = \lim_{t \to t_0} f(x(t), y(t), z(t)) \tag{2}$$

▲ **Figure 13.2.1**

In words, Formulas (1) and (2) state that a limit of a function f along a parametric curve can be obtained by substituting the parametric equations for the curve into the formula for the function and then computing the limit of the resulting function of one variable at the appropriate point.

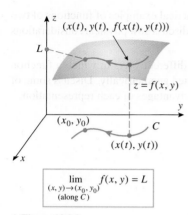

$$\lim_{\substack{(x, y) \to (x_0, y_0) \\ (\text{along } C)}} f(x, y) = L$$

▲ **Figure 13.2.2**

In these formulas the limit of the function of t must be treated as a one-sided limit if (x_0, y_0) or (x_0, y_0, z_0) is an endpoint of C.

A geometric interpretation of the limit along a curve for a function of two variables is shown in Figure 13.2.2: As the point $(x(t), y(t))$ moves along the curve C in the xy-plane toward (x_0, y_0), the point $(x(t), y(t), f(x(t), y(t)))$ moves directly above it along the graph of $z = f(x, y)$ with $f(x(t), y(t))$ approaching the limiting value L. In the figure we followed a common practice of omitting the zero z-coordinate for points in the xy-plane.

▶ **Example 1** Figure 13.2.3a shows a computer-generated graph of the function

$$f(x, y) = -\frac{xy}{x^2 + y^2}$$

The graph reveals that the surface has a ridge above the line $y = -x$, which is to be expected since $f(x, y)$ has a constant value of $\frac{1}{2}$ for $y = -x$, except at $(0, 0)$ where f is undefined (verify). Moreover, the graph suggests that the limit of $f(x, y)$ as $(x, y) \to (0, 0)$ along a line through the origin varies with the direction of the line. Find this limit along

(a) the x-axis   (b) the y-axis   (c) the line $y = x$

(d) the line $y = -x$ (e) the parabola $y = x^2$

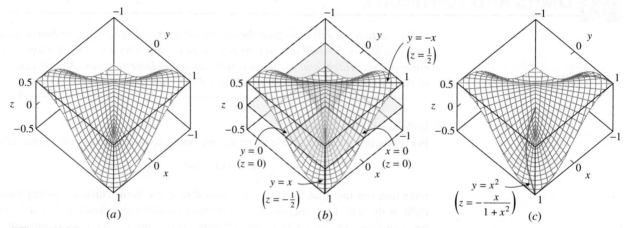

▲ **Figure 13.2.3**

Solution (a). The x-axis has parametric equations $x = t$, $y = 0$, with $(0, 0)$ corresponding to $t = 0$, so

$$\lim_{\substack{(x, y) \to (0, 0) \\ (\text{along } y = 0)}} f(x, y) = \lim_{t \to 0} f(t, 0) = \lim_{t \to 0} \left(-\frac{0}{t^2}\right) = \lim_{t \to 0} 0 = 0$$

which is consistent with Figure 13.2.3b.

Solution (b). The y-axis has parametric equations $x = 0$, $y = t$, with $(0, 0)$ corresponding to $t = 0$, so

$$\lim_{\substack{(x, y) \to (0, 0) \\ (\text{along } x = 0)}} f(x, y) = \lim_{t \to 0} f(0, t) = \lim_{t \to 0} \left(-\frac{0}{t^2}\right) = \lim_{t \to 0} 0 = 0$$

which is consistent with Figure 13.2.3b.

Solution (c).   The line $y = x$ has parametric equations $x = t$, $y = t$, with $(0, 0)$ corresponding to $t = 0$, so

$$\lim_{\substack{(x, y) \to (0, 0) \\ \text{(along } y = x)}} f(x, y) = \lim_{t \to 0} f(t, t) = \lim_{t \to 0} \left(-\frac{t^2}{2t^2} \right) = \lim_{t \to 0} \left(-\frac{1}{2} \right) = -\frac{1}{2}$$

which is consistent with Figure 13.2.3*b*.

Solution (d).   The line $y = -x$ has parametric equations $x = t$, $y = -t$, with $(0, 0)$ corresponding to $t = 0$, so

$$\lim_{\substack{(x, y) \to (0, 0) \\ \text{(along } y = -x)}} f(x, y) = \lim_{t \to 0} f(t, -t) = \lim_{t \to 0} \frac{t^2}{2t^2} = \lim_{t \to 0} \frac{1}{2} = \frac{1}{2}$$

which is consistent with Figure 13.2.3*b*.

Solution (e).   The parabola $y = x^2$ has parametric equations $x = t$, $y = t^2$, with $(0, 0)$ corresponding to $t = 0$, so

$$\lim_{\substack{(x, y) \to (0, 0) \\ \text{(along } y = x^2)}} f(x, y) = \lim_{t \to 0} f(t, t^2) = \lim_{t \to 0} \left(-\frac{t^3}{t^2 + t^4} \right) = \lim_{t \to 0} \left(-\frac{t}{1 + t^2} \right) = 0$$

This is consistent with Figure 13.2.3*c*, which shows the parametric curve

$$x = t, \quad y = t^2, \quad z = -\frac{t}{1 + t^2}$$

superimposed on the surface. ◄

For uniformity, we have chosen the same parameter t in each part of Example 1. We could have used x or y as the parameter, according to the context. For example, part (b) could be computed using

$$\lim_{y \to 0} f(0, y)$$

and part (e) could be computed using

$$\lim_{x \to 0} f(x, x^2)$$

■ OPEN AND CLOSED SETS

Although limits along specific curves are useful for many purposes, they do not always tell the complete story about the limiting behavior of a function at a point; what is required is a limit concept that accounts for the behavior of the function in an *entire vicinity* of a point, not just along smooth curves passing through the point. For this purpose, we start by introducing some terminology.

Let C be a circle in 2-space that is centered at (x_0, y_0) and has positive radius δ. The set of points that are enclosed by the circle, but do not lie on the circle, is called the ***open disk*** of radius δ centered at (x_0, y_0), and the set of points that lie on the circle together with those enclosed by the circle is called the ***closed disk*** of radius δ centered at (x_0, y_0) (Figure 13.2.4). Analogously, if S is a sphere in 3-space that is centered at (x_0, y_0, z_0) and has positive radius δ, then the set of points that are enclosed by the sphere, but do not lie on the sphere, is called the ***open ball*** of radius δ centered at (x_0, y_0, z_0), and the set of points that lie on the sphere together with those enclosed by the sphere is called the ***closed ball*** of radius δ centered at (x_0, y_0, z_0). Disks and balls are the two-dimensional and three-dimensional analogs of intervals on a line.

The notions of "open" and "closed" can be extended to more general sets in 2-space and 3-space. If D is a set of points in 2-space, then a point (x_0, y_0) is called an ***interior point*** of D if there is *some* open disk centered at (x_0, y_0) that contains only points of D, and (x_0, y_0) is called a ***boundary point*** of D if *every* open disk centered at (x_0, y_0) contains both points in D and points not in D. The same terminology applies to sets in 3-space, but in that case the definitions use balls rather than disks (Figure 13.2.5).

For a set D in either 2-space or 3-space, the set of all interior points is called the ***interior*** of D and the set of all boundary points is called the ***boundary*** of D. Moreover, just as for disks, we say that D is ***closed*** if it contains all of its boundary points and ***open*** if it contains *none* of its boundary points. The set of all points in 2-space and the set of all points in

A closed disk includes all of the points on its bounding circle.

An open disk contains none of the points on its bounding circle.

▲ **Figure 13.2.4**

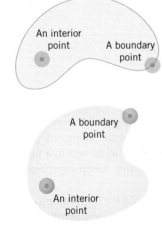

An interior point

A boundary point

A boundary point

An interior point

▲ **Figure 13.2.5**

3-space have no boundary points (why?), so by agreement they are regarded to be both open and closed.

■ GENERAL LIMITS OF FUNCTIONS OF TWO VARIABLES

The statement

$$\lim_{(x,y)\to(x_0,y_0)} f(x, y) = L$$

is intended to convey the idea that the value of $f(x, y)$ can be made as close as we like to the number L by restricting the point (x, y) to be sufficiently close to (but different from) the point (x_0, y_0). This idea has a formal expression in the following definition and is illustrated in Figure 13.2.6.

13.2.1   DEFINITION   Let f be a function of two variables, and assume that f is defined at all points of some open disk centered at (x_0, y_0), except possibly at (x_0, y_0). We will write

$$\lim_{(x,y)\to(x_0,y_0)} f(x, y) = L \tag{3}$$

if given any number $\epsilon > 0$, we can find a number $\delta > 0$ such that $f(x, y)$ satisfies

$$|f(x, y) - L| < \epsilon$$

whenever the distance between (x, y) and (x_0, y_0) satisfies

$$0 < \sqrt{(x - x_0)^2 + (y - y_0)^2} < \delta$$

When convenient, (3) can also be written as

$$\lim_{\substack{x \to x_0 \\ y \to y_0}} f(x, y) = L$$

or as

$$f(x, y) \to L \quad \text{as} \quad (x, y) \to (x_0, y_0)$$

In Figure 13.2.6, the condition

$$|f(x, y) - L| < \epsilon$$

is satisfied at each point (x, y) within the circular region. However, the fact that this condition is satisfied at the center of the circular region is not relevant to the limit.

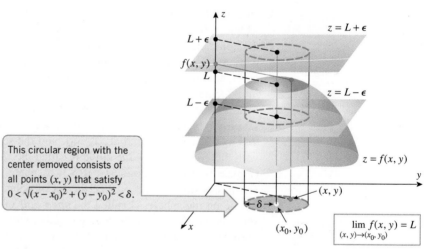

This circular region with the center removed consists of all points (x, y) that satisfy $0 < \sqrt{(x - x_0)^2 + (y - y_0)^2} < \delta$.

$$\lim_{(x,y)\to(x_0,y_0)} f(x, y) = L$$

▲ **Figure 13.2.6**

Another illustration of Definition 13.2.1 is shown in the "arrow diagram" of Figure 13.2.7. As in Figure 13.2.6, this figure is intended to convey the idea that the values of $f(x, y)$ can be forced within ϵ units of L on the z-axis by restricting (x, y) to lie within δ units of (x_0, y_0) in the xy-plane. We used a white dot at (x_0, y_0) to suggest that the epsilon condition need not hold at this point.

We note without proof that the standard properties of limits hold for limits along curves and for general limits of functions of two variables, so that computations involving such limits can be performed in the usual way.

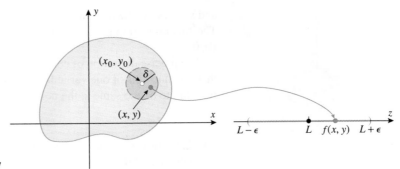

▶ **Figure 13.2.7**

▶ **Example 2**

$$\lim_{(x,y) \to (1,4)} [5x^3y^2 - 9] = \lim_{(x,y) \to (1,4)} [5x^3y^2] - \lim_{(x,y) \to (1,4)} 9$$

$$= 5 \left[\lim_{(x,y) \to (1,4)} x \right]^3 \left[\lim_{(x,y) \to (1,4)} y \right]^2 - 9$$

$$= 5(1)^3(4)^2 - 9 = 71 \quad ◄$$

■ **RELATIONSHIPS BETWEEN GENERAL LIMITS AND LIMITS ALONG SMOOTH CURVES**

Stated informally, if $f(x, y)$ has limit L as (x, y) approaches (x_0, y_0), then the value of $f(x, y)$ gets closer and closer to L as the distance between (x, y) and (x_0, y_0) approaches zero. Since this statement imposes no restrictions on the direction in which (x, y) approaches (x_0, y_0), it is plausible that the function $f(x, y)$ will also have the limit L as (x, y) approaches (x_0, y_0) along *any* smooth curve C. This is the implication of the following theorem, which we state without proof.

WARNING

In general, one cannot show that

$$\lim_{(x,y) \to (x_0, y_0)} f(x, y) = L$$

by showing that this limit holds along a specific curve, or even some specific family of curves. The problem is there may be some other curve along which the limit does not exist or has a value different from L (see Exercise 34, for example).

13.2.2 THEOREM

(a) *If $f(x, y) \to L$ as $(x, y) \to (x_0, y_0)$, then $f(x, y) \to L$ as $(x, y) \to (x_0, y_0)$ along any smooth curve.*

(b) *If the limit of $f(x, y)$ fails to exist as $(x, y) \to (x_0, y_0)$ along some smooth curve, or if $f(x, y)$ has different limits as $(x, y) \to (x_0, y_0)$ along two different smooth curves, then the limit of $f(x, y)$ does not exist as $(x, y) \to (x_0, y_0)$.*

▶ **Example 3** The limit

$$\lim_{(x,y) \to (0,0)} -\frac{xy}{x^2 + y^2}$$

does not exist because in Example 1 we found two different smooth curves along which this limit had different values. Specifically,

$$\lim_{\substack{(x, y) \to (0, 0) \\ (\text{along } x = 0)}} -\frac{xy}{x^2 + y^2} = 0 \quad \text{and} \quad \lim_{\substack{(x, y) \to (0, 0) \\ (\text{along } y = x)}} -\frac{xy}{x^2 + y^2} = -\frac{1}{2} \quad ◄$$

■ **CONTINUITY**

Stated informally, a function of one variable is continuous if its graph is an unbroken curve without jumps or holes. To extend this idea to functions of two variables, imagine that the graph of $z = f(x, y)$ is formed from a thin sheet of clay that has been molded into peaks

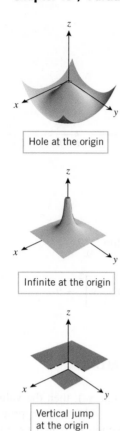

Hole at the origin

Infinite at the origin

Vertical jump at the origin

▲ **Figure 13.2.8**

and valleys. We will regard f as being continuous if the clay surface has no tears or holes. The functions graphed in Figure 13.2.8 fail to be continuous because of their behavior at $(0, 0)$.

The precise definition of continuity at a point for functions of two variables is similar to that for functions of one variable—we require the limit of the function and the value of the function to be the same at the point.

13.2.3   **DEFINITION**   A function $f(x, y)$ is said to be ***continuous at*** (x_0, y_0) if $f(x_0, y_0)$ is defined and if

$$\lim_{(x, y) \to (x_0, y_0)} f(x, y) = f(x_0, y_0)$$

In addition, if f is continuous at every point in an open set D, then we say that f is ***continuous on*** D, and if f is continuous at every point in the xy-plane, then we say that f is ***continuous everywhere***.

The following theorem, which we state without proof, illustrates some of the ways in which continuous functions can be combined to produce new continuous functions.

13.2.4   **THEOREM**

(a) *If $g(x)$ is continuous at x_0 and $h(y)$ is continuous at y_0, then $f(x, y) = g(x)h(y)$ is continuous at (x_0, y_0).*

(b) *If $h(x, y)$ is continuous at (x_0, y_0) and $g(u)$ is continuous at $u = h(x_0, y_0)$, then the composition $f(x, y) = g(h(x, y))$ is continuous at (x_0, y_0).*

(c) *If $f(x, y)$ is continuous at (x_0, y_0), and if $x(t)$ and $y(t)$ are continuous at t_0 with $x(t_0) = x_0$ and $y(t_0) = y_0$, then the composition $f(x(t), y(t))$ is continuous at t_0.*

▶ **Example 4**   Use Theorem 13.2.4 to show that the functions $f(x, y) = 3x^2y^5$ and $f(x, y) = \sin(3x^2y^5)$ are continuous everywhere.

Solution.   The polynomials $g(x) = 3x^2$ and $h(y) = y^5$ are continuous at every real number, and therefore by part (a) of Theorem 13.2.4, the function $f(x, y) = 3x^2y^5$ is continuous at every point (x, y) in the xy-plane. Since $3x^2y^5$ is continuous at every point in the xy-plane and $\sin u$ is continuous at every real number u, it follows from part (b) of Theorem 13.2.4 that the composition $f(x, y) = \sin(3x^2y^5)$ is continuous everywhere. ◀

Theorem 13.2.4 is one of a whole class of theorems about continuity of functions in two or more variables. The content of these theorems can be summarized informally with three basic principles:

Recognizing Continuous Functions

- A composition of continuous functions is continuous.

- A sum, difference, or product of continuous functions is continuous.

- A quotient of continuous functions is continuous, except where the denominator is zero.

By using these principles and Theorem 13.2.4, you should be able to confirm that the following functions are all continuous everywhere:

$$xe^{xy} + y^{2/3}, \quad \cosh(xy^3) - |xy|, \quad \frac{xy}{1 + x^2 + y^2}$$

▶ **Example 5**   Evaluate $\displaystyle\lim_{(x,y)\to(-1,2)} \frac{xy}{x^2 + y^2}$.

Solution.   Since $f(x, y) = xy/(x^2 + y^2)$ is continuous at $(-1, 2)$ (why?), it follows from the definition of continuity for functions of two variables that

$$\lim_{(x,y)\to(-1,2)} \frac{xy}{x^2 + y^2} = \frac{(-1)(2)}{(-1)^2 + (2)^2} = -\frac{2}{5} \quad ◀$$

▶ **Example 6**   Since the function

$$f(x, y) = \frac{x^3 y^2}{1 - xy}$$

is a quotient of continuous functions, it is continuous except where $1 - xy = 0$. Thus, $f(x, y)$ is continuous everywhere except on the hyperbola $xy = 1$. ◀

■ LIMITS AT DISCONTINUITIES

Sometimes it is easy to recognize when a limit does not exist. For example, it is evident that

$$\lim_{(x,y)\to(0,0)} \frac{1}{x^2 + y^2} = +\infty$$

which implies that the values of the function approach $+\infty$ as $(x, y) \to (0, 0)$ along any smooth curve (Figure 13.2.9). However, it is not evident whether the limit

$$\lim_{(x,y)\to(0,0)} (x^2 + y^2) \ln(x^2 + y^2)$$

exists because it is an indeterminate form of type $0 \cdot \infty$. Although L'Hôpital's rule cannot be applied directly, the following example illustrates a method for finding this limit by converting to polar coordinates.

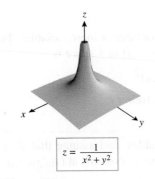

$$z = \frac{1}{x^2 + y^2}$$

▲ **Figure 13.2.9**

▶ **Example 7**   Find $\displaystyle\lim_{(x,y)\to(0,0)} (x^2 + y^2) \ln(x^2 + y^2)$.

Solution.   Let (r, θ) be polar coordinates of the point (x, y) with $r \geq 0$. Then we have

$$x = r\cos\theta, \quad y = r\sin\theta, \quad r^2 = x^2 + y^2$$

Moreover, since $r \geq 0$ we have $r = \sqrt{x^2 + y^2}$, so that $r \to 0^+$ if and only if $(x, y) \to (0, 0)$. Thus, we can rewrite the given limit as

$$\lim_{(x,y)\to(0,0)} (x^2 + y^2) \ln(x^2 + y^2) = \lim_{r\to 0^+} r^2 \ln r^2$$

$$= \lim_{r\to 0^+} \frac{2\ln r}{1/r^2} \qquad \boxed{\text{This converts the limit to an indeterminate form of type } \infty/\infty.}$$

$$= \lim_{r\to 0^+} \frac{2/r}{-2/r^3} \qquad \boxed{\text{L'Hôpital's rule}}$$

$$= \lim_{r\to 0^+} (-r^2) = 0 \quad ◀$$

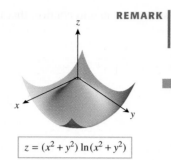

$$z = (x^2 + y^2)\ln(x^2 + y^2)$$

▲ **Figure 13.2.10**

REMARK | The graph of $f(x, y) = (x^2 + y^2)\ln(x^2 + y^2)$ in Example 7 is a surface with a hole (sometimes called a *puncture*) at the origin (Figure 13.2.10). We can remove this discontinuity by *defining* $f(0, 0)$ to be 0. (See Exercises 39 and 40, which also deal with the notion of a "removable" discontinuity.)

■ CONTINUITY AT BOUNDARY POINTS

Recall that in our study of continuity for functions of one variable, we first defined continuity at a point, then continuity on an open interval, and then, by using one-sided limits, we extended the notion of continuity to include the boundary points of the interval. Similarly, for functions of two variables one can extend the notion of continuity of $f(x, y)$ to the boundary of its domain by modifying Definition 13.2.1 appropriately so that (x, y) is restricted to approach (x_0, y_0) through points lying wholly in the domain of f. We will omit the details.

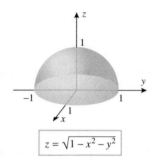

$$z = \sqrt{1 - x^2 - y^2}$$

▲ **Figure 13.2.11**

▶ **Example 8** The graph of the function $f(x, y) = \sqrt{1 - x^2 - y^2}$ is the upper hemisphere shown in Figure 13.2.11, and the natural domain of f is the closed unit disk

$$x^2 + y^2 \leq 1$$

The graph of f has no tears or holes, so it passes our "intuitive test" of continuity. In this case the continuity at a point (x_0, y_0) on the boundary reflects the fact that

$$\lim_{(x,y)\to(x_0,y_0)} \sqrt{1 - x^2 - y^2} = \sqrt{1 - x_0^2 - y_0^2} = 0$$

when (x, y) is restricted to points on the closed unit disk $x^2 + y^2 \leq 1$. It follows that f is continuous on its domain. ◀

■ EXTENSIONS TO THREE VARIABLES

All of the results in this section can be extended to functions of three or more variables. For example, the distance between the points (x, y, z) and (x_0, y_0, z_0) in 3-space is

$$\sqrt{(x - x_0)^2 + (y - y_0)^2 + (z - z_0)^2}$$

so the natural extension of Definition 13.2.1 to 3-space is as follows:

13.2.5 DEFINITION Let f be a function of three variables, and assume that f is defined at all points within a ball centered at (x_0, y_0, z_0), except possibly at (x_0, y_0, z_0). We will write

$$\lim_{(x,y,z)\to(x_0,y_0,z_0)} f(x, y, z) = L \tag{4}$$

if given any number $\epsilon > 0$, we can find a number $\delta > 0$ such that $f(x, y, z)$ satisfies

$$|f(x, y, z) - L| < \epsilon$$

whenever the distance between (x, y, z) and (x_0, y_0, z_0) satisfies

$$0 < \sqrt{(x - x_0)^2 + (y - y_0)^2 + (z - z_0)^2} < \delta$$

As with functions of one and two variables, we define a function $f(x, y, z)$ of three variables to be continuous at a point (x_0, y_0, z_0) if the limit of the function and the value of the function are the same at this point; that is,

$$\lim_{(x,y,z)\to(x_0,y_0,z_0)} f(x, y, z) = f(x_0, y_0, z_0)$$

Although we will omit the details, the properties of limits and continuity that we discussed for functions of two variables, including the notion of continuity at boundary points, carry over to functions of three variables.

✓ QUICK CHECK EXERCISES 13.2   (See page 927 for answers.)

1. Let
$$f(x, y) = \frac{x^2 - y^2}{x^2 + y^2}$$

Determine the limit of $f(x, y)$ as (x, y) approaches $(0, 0)$ along the curve C.
(a) $C: x = 0$ (b) $C: y = 0$
(c) $C: y = x$ (d) $C: y = x^2$

2. (a) $\lim\limits_{(x,y) \to (3,2)} x \cos \pi y = $ _____

(b) $\lim\limits_{(x,y) \to (0,1)} e^{xy^2} = $ _____

(c) $\lim\limits_{(x,y) \to (0,0)} (x^2 + y^2) \sin\left(\dfrac{1}{x^2 + y^2}\right) = $ _____

3. A function $f(x, y)$ is continuous at (x_0, y_0) provided $f(x_0, y_0)$ exists and provided $f(x, y)$ has limit _____ as (x, y) approaches _____.

4. Determine all values of the constant a such that the function $f(x, y) = \sqrt{x^2 - ay^2 + 1}$ is continuous everywhere.

EXERCISE SET 13.2

1–6 Use limit laws and continuity properties to evaluate the limit. ■

1. $\lim\limits_{(x,y) \to (1,3)} (4xy^2 - x)$ 2. $\lim\limits_{(x,y) \to (1/2,\pi)} (xy^2 \sin xy)$

3. $\lim\limits_{(x,y) \to (-1,2)} \dfrac{xy^3}{x + y}$ 4. $\lim\limits_{(x,y) \to (1,-3)} e^{2x-y^2}$

5. $\lim\limits_{(x,y) \to (0,0)} \ln(1 + x^2 y^3)$ 6. $\lim\limits_{(x,y) \to (4,-2)} x \sqrt[3]{y^3 + 2x}$

7–8 Show that the limit does not exist by considering the limits as $(x, y) \to (0, 0)$ along the coordinate axes. ■

7. (a) $\lim\limits_{(x,y) \to (0,0)} \dfrac{3}{x^2 + 2y^2}$ (b) $\lim\limits_{(x,y) \to (0,0)} \dfrac{x + y}{2x^2 + y^2}$

8. (a) $\lim\limits_{(x,y) \to (0,0)} \dfrac{x - y}{x^2 + y^2}$ (b) $\lim\limits_{(x,y) \to (0,0)} \dfrac{\cos xy}{x^2 + y^2}$

9–12 Evaluate the limit using the substitution $z = x^2 + y^2$ and observing that $z \to 0^+$ if and only if $(x, y) \to (0, 0)$. ■

9. $\lim\limits_{(x,y) \to (0,0)} \dfrac{\sin(x^2 + y^2)}{x^2 + y^2}$ 10. $\lim\limits_{(x,y) \to (0,0)} \dfrac{1 - \cos(x^2 + y^2)}{x^2 + y^2}$

11. $\lim\limits_{(x,y) \to (0,0)} e^{-1/(x^2+y^2)}$ 12. $\lim\limits_{(x,y) \to (0,0)} \dfrac{e^{-1/\sqrt{x^2+y^2}}}{\sqrt{x^2 + y^2}}$

13–22 Determine whether the limit exists. If so, find its value. ■

13. $\lim\limits_{(x,y) \to (0,0)} \dfrac{x^4 - y^4}{x^2 + y^2}$ 14. $\lim\limits_{(x,y) \to (0,0)} \dfrac{x^4 - 16y^4}{x^2 + 4y^2}$

15. $\lim\limits_{(x,y) \to (0,0)} \dfrac{xy}{3x^2 + 2y^2}$ 16. $\lim\limits_{(x,y) \to (0,0)} \dfrac{1 - x^2 - y^2}{x^2 + y^2}$

17. $\lim\limits_{(x,y,z) \to (2,-1,2)} \dfrac{xz^2}{\sqrt{x^2 + y^2 + z^2}}$

18. $\lim\limits_{(x,y,z) \to (2,0,-1)} \ln(2x + y - z)$

19. $\lim\limits_{(x,y,z) \to (0,0,0)} \dfrac{\sin(x^2 + y^2 + z^2)}{\sqrt{x^2 + y^2 + z^2}}$

20. $\lim\limits_{(x,y,z) \to (0,0,0)} \dfrac{\sin\sqrt{x^2 + y^2 + z^2}}{x^2 + y^2 + z^2}$

21. $\lim\limits_{(x,y,z) \to (0,0,0)} \dfrac{e^{\sqrt{x^2+y^2+z^2}}}{\sqrt{x^2 + y^2 + z^2}}$

22. $\lim\limits_{(x,y,z) \to (0,0,0)} \tan^{-1}\left[\dfrac{1}{x^2 + y^2 + z^2}\right]$

23–26 Evaluate the limits by converting to polar coordinates, as in Example 7. ■

23. $\lim\limits_{(x,y) \to (0,0)} \sqrt{x^2 + y^2} \ln(x^2 + y^2)$

24. $\lim\limits_{(x,y) \to (0,0)} y \ln(x^2 + y^2)$ 25. $\lim\limits_{(x,y) \to (0,0)} \dfrac{x^2 y^2}{\sqrt{x^2 + y^2}}$

26. $\lim\limits_{(x,y) \to (0,0)} \dfrac{xy}{\sqrt{x^2 + 2y^2}}$

27–28 Evaluate the limits by converting to spherical coordinates (ρ, θ, ϕ) and by observing that $\rho \to 0^+$ if and only if $(x, y, z) \to (0, 0, 0)$. ■

27. $\lim\limits_{(x,y,z) \to (0,0,0)} \dfrac{xyz}{x^2 + y^2 + z^2}$

28. $\lim\limits_{(x,y,z) \to (0,0,0)} \dfrac{\sin x \sin y}{\sqrt{x^2 + 2y^2 + 3z^2}}$

29–32 True–False Determine whether the statement is true or false. Explain your answer. ■

29. If D is an open set in 2-space or in 3-space, then every point in D is an interior point of D.

30. If $f(x, y) \to L$ as (x, y) approaches $(0, 0)$ along the x-axis, and if $f(x, y) \to L$ as (x, y) approaches $(0, 0)$ along the y-axis, then $\lim_{(x,y) \to (0,0)} f(x, y) = L$.

31. If f and g are functions of two variables such that $f + g$ and fg are both continuous, then f and g are themselves continuous.

32. If $\lim_{x \to 0^+} f(x) = L \neq 0$, then

$$\lim_{(x,y) \to (0,0)} \frac{x^2 + y^2}{f(x^2 + y^2)} = 0$$

FOCUS ON CONCEPTS

33. The accompanying figure shows a portion of the graph of

$$f(x, y) = \frac{x^2 y}{x^4 + y^2}$$

(a) Based on the graph in the figure, does $f(x, y)$ have a limit as $(x, y) \to (0, 0)$? Explain your reasoning.

(b) Show that $f(x, y) \to 0$ as $(x, y) \to (0, 0)$ along any line $y = mx$. Does this imply that $f(x, y) \to 0$ as $(x, y) \to (0, 0)$? Explain.

(c) Show that $f(x, y) \to \frac{1}{2}$ as $(x, y) \to (0, 0)$ along the parabola $y = x^2$, and confirm visually that this is consistent with the graph of $f(x, y)$.

(d) Based on parts (b) and (c), does $f(x, y)$ have a limit as $(x, y) \to (0, 0)$? Is this consistent with your answer to part (a)?

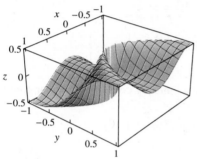

◀ **Figure Ex-33**

34. (a) Show that the value of

$$\frac{x^3 y}{2x^6 + y^2}$$

approaches 0 as $(x, y) \to (0, 0)$ along any straight line $y = mx$, or along any parabola $y = kx^2$.

(b) Show that

$$\lim_{(x,y) \to (0,0)} \frac{x^3 y}{2x^6 + y^2}$$

does not exist by letting $(x, y) \to (0, 0)$ along the curve $y = x^3$.

35. (a) Show that the value of

$$\frac{xyz}{x^2 + y^4 + z^4}$$

approaches 0 as $(x, y, z) \to (0, 0, 0)$ along any line $x = at$, $y = bt$, $z = ct$.

(b) Show that the limit

$$\lim_{(x,y,z) \to (0,0,0)} \frac{xyz}{x^2 + y^4 + z^4}$$

does not exist by letting $(x, y, z) \to (0, 0, 0)$ along the curve $x = t^2$, $y = t$, $z = t$.

36. Find $\lim\limits_{(x,y) \to (0,1)} \tan^{-1}\left[\dfrac{x^2 + 1}{x^2 + (y-1)^2} \right]$.

37. Find $\lim\limits_{(x,y) \to (0,1)} \tan^{-1}\left[\dfrac{x^2 - 1}{x^2 + (y-1)^2} \right]$.

38. Let $f(x, y) = \begin{cases} \dfrac{\sin(x^2 + y^2)}{x^2 + y^2}, & (x, y) \neq (0, 0) \\ 1, & (x, y) = (0, 0). \end{cases}$

Show that f is continuous at $(0, 0)$.

39–40 A function $f(x, y)$ is said to have a ***removable discontinuity*** at (x_0, y_0) if $\lim_{(x,y) \to (x_0, y_0)} f(x, y)$ exists but f is not continuous at (x_0, y_0), either because f is not defined at (x_0, y_0) or because $f(x_0, y_0)$ differs from the value of the limit. Determine whether $f(x, y)$ has a removable discontinuity at $(0, 0)$. ■

39. $f(x, y) = \dfrac{x^2}{x^2 + y^2}$ ⠀⠀⠀ **40.** $f(x, y) = xy \ln(x^2 + y^2)$

41–48 Sketch the largest region on which the function f is continuous. ■

41. $f(x, y) = y \ln(1 + x)$ ⠀⠀⠀ **42.** $f(x, y) = \sqrt{x - y}$

43. $f(x, y) = \dfrac{x^2 y}{\sqrt{25 - x^2 - y^2}}$

44. $f(x, y) = \ln(2x - y + 1)$

45. $f(x, y) = \cos\left(\dfrac{xy}{1 + x^2 + y^2} \right)$

46. $f(x, y) = e^{1 - xy}$ ⠀⠀⠀ **47.** $f(x, y) = \sin^{-1}(xy)$

48. $f(x, y) = \tan^{-1}(y - x)$

49–52 Describe the largest region on which the function f is continuous. ■

49. $f(x, y, z) = 3x^2 e^{yz} \cos(xyz)$

50. $f(x, y, z) = \ln(4 - x^2 - y^2 - z^2)$

51. $f(x, y, z) = \dfrac{y + 1}{x^2 + z^2 - 1}$

52. $f(x, y, z) = \sin\sqrt{x^2 + y^2 + 3z^2}$

53. Writing Describe the procedure you would use to determine whether or not the limit

$$\lim_{(x,y) \to (x_0, y_0)} f(x, y)$$

exists.

54. Writing In your own words, state the geometric interpretations of ϵ and δ in the definition of

$$\lim_{(x,y) \to (x_0, y_0)} f(x, y) = L$$

given in Definition 13.2.1.

1. (a) -1 (b) 1 (c) 0 (d) 1 2. (a) 3 (b) 1 (c) 0 3. $f(x_0, y_0)$; (x_0, y_0) 4. $a \leq 0$

13.3 PARTIAL DERIVATIVES

In this section we will develop the mathematical tools for studying rates of change that involve two or more independent variables.

■ PARTIAL DERIVATIVES OF FUNCTIONS OF TWO VARIABLES

If $z = f(x, y)$, then one can inquire how the value of z changes if y is held fixed and x is allowed to vary, or if x is held fixed and y is allowed to vary. For example, the ideal gas law in physics states that under appropriate conditions the pressure exerted by a gas is a function of the volume of the gas and its temperature. Thus, a physicist studying gases might be interested in the rate of change of the pressure if the volume is held fixed and the temperature is allowed to vary, or if the temperature is held fixed and the volume is allowed to vary. We now define a derivative that describes such rates of change.

Suppose that (x_0, y_0) is a point in the domain of a function $f(x, y)$. If we fix $y = y_0$, then $f(x, y_0)$ is a function of the variable x alone. The value of the derivative

$$\frac{d}{dx}[f(x, y_0)]$$

at x_0 then gives us a measure of the instantaneous rate of change of f with respect to x at the point (x_0, y_0). Similarly, the value of the derivative

$$\frac{d}{dy}[f(x_0, y)]$$

at y_0 gives us a measure of the instantaneous rate of change of f with respect to y at the point (x_0, y_0). These derivatives are so basic to the study of differential calculus of multivariable functions that they have their own name and notation.

13.3.1   DEFINITION   If $z = f(x, y)$ and (x_0, y_0) is a point in the domain of f, then the ***partial derivative of f with respect to x*** at (x_0, y_0) [also called the ***partial derivative of z with respect to x*** at (x_0, y_0)] is the derivative at x_0 of the function that results when $y = y_0$ is held fixed and x is allowed to vary. This partial derivative is denoted by $f_x(x_0, y_0)$ and is given by

$$f_x(x_0, y_0) = \frac{d}{dx}[f(x, y_0)]\Big|_{x=x_0} = \lim_{\Delta x \to 0} \frac{f(x_0 + \Delta x, y_0) - f(x_0, y_0)}{\Delta x} \tag{1}$$

Similarly, the ***partial derivative of f with respect to y*** at (x_0, y_0) [also called the ***partial derivative of z with respect to y*** at (x_0, y_0)] is the derivative at y_0 of the function that results when $x = x_0$ is held fixed and y is allowed to vary. This partial derivative is denoted by $f_y(x_0, y_0)$ and is given by

$$f_y(x_0, y_0) = \frac{d}{dy}[f(x_0, y)]\Big|_{y=y_0} = \lim_{\Delta y \to 0} \frac{f(x_0, y_0 + \Delta y) - f(x_0, y_0)}{\Delta y} \tag{2}$$

The limits in (1) and (2) show the relationship between partial derivatives and derivatives of functions of one variable. In practice, our usual method for computing partial derivatives is to hold one variable fixed and then differentiate the resulting function using the derivative rules for functions of one variable.

▶ **Example 1**   Find $f_x(1, 3)$ and $f_y(1, 3)$ for the function $f(x, y) = 2x^3 y^2 + 2y + 4x$.

Solution.   Since

$$f_x(x, 3) = \frac{d}{dx}[f(x, 3)] = \frac{d}{dx}[18x^3 + 4x + 6] = 54x^2 + 4$$

we have $f_x(1, 3) = 54 + 4 = 58$. Also, since

$$f_y(1, y) = \frac{d}{dy}[f(1, y)] = \frac{d}{dy}[2y^2 + 2y + 4] = 4y + 2$$

we have $f_y(1, 3) = 4(3) + 2 = 14$. ◀

THE PARTIAL DERIVATIVE FUNCTIONS

Formulas (1) and (2) define the partial derivatives of a function at a specific point (x_0, y_0). However, often it will be desirable to omit the subscripts and think of the partial derivatives as functions of the variables x and y. These functions are

$$f_x(x, y) = \lim_{\Delta x \to 0} \frac{f(x + \Delta x, y) - f(x, y)}{\Delta x} \qquad f_y(x, y) = \lim_{\Delta y \to 0} \frac{f(x, y + \Delta y) - f(x, y)}{\Delta y}$$

The following example gives an alternative way of performing the computations in Example 1.

▶ **Example 2**   Find $f_x(x, y)$ and $f_y(x, y)$ for $f(x, y) = 2x^3 y^2 + 2y + 4x$, and use those partial derivatives to compute $f_x(1, 3)$ and $f_y(1, 3)$.

Solution.   Keeping y fixed and differentiating with respect to x yields

$$f_x(x, y) = \frac{d}{dx}[2x^3 y^2 + 2y + 4x] = 6x^2 y^2 + 4$$

and keeping x fixed and differentiating with respect to y yields

$$f_y(x, y) = \frac{d}{dy}[2x^3 y^2 + 2y + 4x] = 4x^3 y + 2$$

Thus,

$$f_x(1, 3) = 6(1^2)(3^2) + 4 = 58 \quad \text{and} \quad f_y(1, 3) = 4(1^3)3 + 2 = 14$$

which agree with the results in Example 1. ◀

TECHNOLOGY MASTERY

Computer algebra systems have specific commands for calculating partial derivatives. If you have a CAS, use it to find the partial derivatives $f_x(x, y)$ and $f_y(x, y)$ in Example 2.

PARTIAL DERIVATIVE NOTATION

If $z = f(x, y)$, then the partial derivatives f_x and f_y are also denoted by the symbols

$$\frac{\partial f}{\partial x}, \quad \frac{\partial z}{\partial x} \qquad \text{and} \qquad \frac{\partial f}{\partial y}, \quad \frac{\partial z}{\partial y}$$

The symbol ∂ is called a partial derivative sign. It is derived from the Cyrillic alphabet.

Some typical notations for the partial derivatives of $z = f(x, y)$ at a point (x_0, y_0) are

$$\left.\frac{\partial f}{\partial x}\right|_{x=x_0, y=y_0}, \quad \left.\frac{\partial z}{\partial x}\right|_{(x_0, y_0)}, \quad \left.\frac{\partial f}{\partial x}\right|_{(x_0, y_0)}, \quad \frac{\partial f}{\partial x}(x_0, y_0), \quad \frac{\partial z}{\partial x}(x_0, y_0)$$

▶ **Example 3** Find $\partial z/\partial x$ and $\partial z/\partial y$ if $z = x^4 \sin(xy^3)$.

Solution.

$$\frac{\partial z}{\partial x} = \frac{\partial}{\partial x}[x^4 \sin(xy^3)] = x^4 \frac{\partial}{\partial x}[\sin(xy^3)] + \sin(xy^3) \cdot \frac{\partial}{\partial x}(x^4)$$

$$= x^4 \cos(xy^3) \cdot y^3 + \sin(xy^3) \cdot 4x^3 = x^4 y^3 \cos(xy^3) + 4x^3 \sin(xy^3)$$

$$\frac{\partial z}{\partial y} = \frac{\partial}{\partial y}[x^4 \sin(xy^3)] = x^4 \frac{\partial}{\partial y}[\sin(xy^3)] + \sin(xy^3) \cdot \frac{\partial}{\partial y}(x^4)$$

$$= x^4 \cos(xy^3) \cdot 3xy^2 + \sin(xy^3) \cdot 0 = 3x^5 y^2 \cos(xy^3) \quad ◀$$

■ PARTIAL DERIVATIVES VIEWED AS RATES OF CHANGE AND SLOPES

Recall that if $y = f(x)$, then the value of $f'(x_0)$ can be interpreted either as the rate of change of y with respect to x at x_0 or as the slope of the tangent line to the graph of f at x_0. Partial derivatives have analogous interpretations. To see that this is so, suppose that C_1 is the intersection of the surface $z = f(x, y)$ with the plane $y = y_0$ and that C_2 is its intersection with the plane $x = x_0$ (Figure 13.3.1). Thus, $f_x(x, y_0)$ can be interpreted as the rate of change of z with respect to x along the curve C_1, and $f_y(x_0, y)$ can be interpreted as the rate of change of z with respect to y along the curve C_2. In particular, $f_x(x_0, y_0)$ is the rate of change of z with respect to x along the curve C_1 at the point (x_0, y_0), and $f_y(x_0, y_0)$ is the rate of change of z with respect to y along the curve C_2 at the point (x_0, y_0).

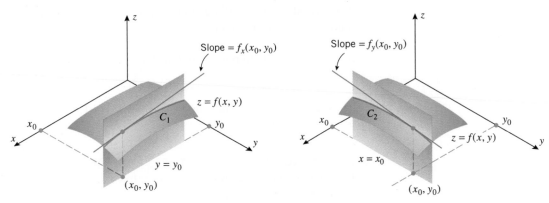

▲ **Figure 13.3.1**

In an applied problem, the interpretations of $f_x(x_0, y_0)$ and $f_y(x_0, y_0)$ must be accompanied by the proper units. See Example 4.

▶ **Example 4** Recall that the wind chill temperature index is given by the formula

$$W = 35.74 + 0.6215T + (0.4275T - 35.75)v^{0.16}$$

Compute the partial derivative of W with respect to v at the point $(T, v) = (25, 10)$ and interpret this partial derivative as a rate of change.

Solution. Holding T fixed and differentiating with respect to v yields

$$\frac{\partial W}{\partial v}(T, v) = 0 + 0 + (0.4275T - 35.75)(0.16)v^{0.16-1} = (0.4275T - 35.75)(0.16)v^{-0.84}$$

Since W is in degrees Fahrenheit and v is in miles per hour, a rate of change of W with respect to v will have units $°\text{F}/(\text{mi}/\text{h})$ (which may also be written as $°\text{F·h}/\text{mi}$). Substituting

$T = 25$ and $v = 10$ gives

$$\frac{\partial W}{\partial v}(25, 10) = (-4.01)10^{-0.84} \approx -0.58 \ \frac{°F}{mi/h}$$

as the instantaneous rate of change of W with respect to v at $(T, v) = (25, 10)$. We conclude that if the air temperature is a constant $25°F$ and the wind speed changes by a small amount from an initial speed of 10 mi/h, then the ratio of the change in the wind chill index to the change in wind speed should be about $-0.58°F/(mi/h)$. ◄

Geometrically, $f_x(x_0, y_0)$ can be viewed as the slope of the tangent line to the curve C_1 at the point (x_0, y_0), and $f_y(x_0, y_0)$ can be viewed as the slope of the tangent line to the curve C_2 at the point (x_0, y_0) (Figure 13.3.1). We will call $f_x(x_0, y_0)$ the **slope of the surface in the x-direction** at (x_0, y_0) and $f_y(x_0, y_0)$ the **slope of the surface in the y-direction** at (x_0, y_0).

► **Example 5**   Let $f(x, y) = x^2y + 5y^3$.

(a) Find the slope of the surface $z = f(x, y)$ in the x-direction at the point $(1, -2)$.

(b) Find the slope of the surface $z = f(x, y)$ in the y-direction at the point $(1, -2)$.

Solution (a).   Differentiating f with respect to x with y held fixed yields

$$f_x(x, y) = 2xy$$

Thus, the slope in the x-direction is $f_x(1, -2) = -4$; that is, z is decreasing at the rate of 4 units per unit increase in x.

Solution (b).   Differentiating f with respect to y with x held fixed yields

$$f_y(x, y) = x^2 + 15y^2$$

Thus, the slope in the y-direction is $f_y(1, -2) = 61$; that is, z is increasing at the rate of 61 units per unit increase in y. ◄

■ **ESTIMATING PARTIAL DERIVATIVES FROM TABULAR DATA**

For functions that are presented in tabular form, we can estimate partial derivatives by using adjacent entries within the table.

► **Example 6**   Use the values of the wind chill index function $W(T, v)$ displayed in Table 13.3.1 to estimate the partial derivative of W with respect to v at $(T, v) = (25, 10)$. Compare this estimate with the value of the partial derivative obtained in Example 4.

Table 13.3.1

TEMPERATURE T (°F)

WIND SPEED v (mi/h)

	20	25	30	35
5	13	19	25	31
10	9	15	21	27
15	6	13	19	25
20	4	11	17	24

Solution.   Since

$$\frac{\partial W}{\partial v}(25, 10) = \lim_{\Delta v \to 0} \frac{W(25, 10 + \Delta v) - W(25, 10)}{\Delta v} = \lim_{\Delta v \to 0} \frac{W(25, 10 + \Delta v) - 15}{\Delta v}$$

we can approximate the partial derivative by

$$\frac{\partial W}{\partial v}(25, 10) \approx \frac{W(25, 10 + \Delta v) - 15}{\Delta v}$$

With $\Delta v = 5$ this approximation is

$$\frac{\partial W}{\partial v}(25, 10) \approx \frac{W(25, 10 + 5) - 15}{5} = \frac{W(25, 15) - 15}{5} = \frac{13 - 15}{5} = -\frac{2}{5} \ \frac{°F}{mi/h}$$

and with $\Delta v = -5$ this approximation is

$$\frac{\partial W}{\partial v}(25, 10) \approx \frac{W(25, 10-5) - 15}{-5} = \frac{W(25, 5) - 15}{-5} = \frac{19 - 15}{-5} = -\frac{4}{5}\frac{°F}{mi/h}$$

We will take the average, $-\frac{3}{5} = -0.6°F/(mi/h)$, of these two approximations as our estimate of $(\partial W/\partial v)(25, 10)$. This is close to the value

$$\frac{\partial W}{\partial v}(25, 10) = (-4.01)10^{-0.84} \approx -0.58 \frac{°F}{mi/h}$$

found in Example 4. ◄

■ IMPLICIT PARTIAL DIFFERENTIATION

▶ **Example 7** Find the slope of the sphere $x^2 + y^2 + z^2 = 1$ in the y-direction at the points $\left(\frac{2}{3}, \frac{1}{3}, \frac{2}{3}\right)$ and $\left(\frac{2}{3}, \frac{1}{3}, -\frac{2}{3}\right)$ (Figure 13.3.2).

Solution. The point $\left(\frac{2}{3}, \frac{1}{3}, \frac{2}{3}\right)$ lies on the upper hemisphere $z = \sqrt{1 - x^2 - y^2}$, and the point $\left(\frac{2}{3}, \frac{1}{3}, -\frac{2}{3}\right)$ lies on the lower hemisphere $z = -\sqrt{1 - x^2 - y^2}$. We could find the slopes by differentiating each expression for z separately with respect to y and then evaluating the derivatives at $x = \frac{2}{3}$ and $y = \frac{1}{3}$. However, it is more efficient to differentiate the given equation

$$x^2 + y^2 + z^2 = 1$$

implicitly with respect to y, since this will give us both slopes with one differentiation. To perform the implicit differentiation, we view z as a function of x and y and differentiate both sides with respect to y, taking x to be fixed. The computations are as follows:

$$\frac{\partial}{\partial y}[x^2 + y^2 + z^2] = \frac{\partial}{\partial y}[1]$$

$$0 + 2y + 2z\frac{\partial z}{\partial y} = 0$$

$$\frac{\partial z}{\partial y} = -\frac{y}{z}$$

Substituting the y- and z-coordinates of the points $\left(\frac{2}{3}, \frac{1}{3}, \frac{2}{3}\right)$ and $\left(\frac{2}{3}, \frac{1}{3}, -\frac{2}{3}\right)$ in this expression, we find that the slope at the point $\left(\frac{2}{3}, \frac{1}{3}, \frac{2}{3}\right)$ is $-\frac{1}{2}$ and the slope at $\left(\frac{2}{3}, \frac{1}{3}, -\frac{2}{3}\right)$ is $\frac{1}{2}$. ◄

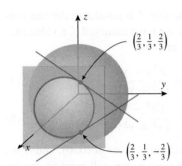

▲ Figure 13.3.2

Check the results in Example 7 by differentiating the functions

$$z = \sqrt{1 - x^2 - y^2}$$

and

$$z = -\sqrt{1 - x^2 - y^2}$$

directly.

▶ **Example 8** Suppose that $D = \sqrt{x^2 + y^2}$ is the length of the diagonal of a rectangle whose sides have lengths x and y that are allowed to vary. Find a formula for the rate of change of D with respect to x if x varies with y held constant, and use this formula to find the rate of change of D with respect to x at the point where $x = 3$ and $y = 4$.

Solution. Differentiating both sides of the equation $D^2 = x^2 + y^2$ with respect to x yields

$$2D\frac{\partial D}{\partial x} = 2x \quad \text{and thus} \quad D\frac{\partial D}{\partial x} = x$$

Since $D = 5$ when $x = 3$ and $y = 4$, it follows that

$$5\left.\frac{\partial D}{\partial x}\right|_{x=3, y=4} = 3 \quad \text{or} \quad \left.\frac{\partial D}{\partial x}\right|_{x=3, y=4} = \frac{3}{5}$$

Thus, D is increasing at a rate of $\frac{3}{5}$ unit per unit increase in x at the point $(3, 4)$. ◄

■ **PARTIAL DERIVATIVES AND CONTINUITY**

In contrast to the case of functions of a single variable, the existence of partial derivatives for a multivariable function does not guarantee the continuity of the function. This fact is shown in the following example.

▶ **Example 9** Let

$$f(x, y) = \begin{cases} -\dfrac{xy}{x^2 + y^2}, & (x, y) \neq (0, 0) \\ 0, & (x, y) = (0, 0) \end{cases} \tag{3}$$

(a) Show that $f_x(x, y)$ and $f_y(x, y)$ exist at all points (x, y).

(b) Explain why f is not continuous at $(0, 0)$.

Solution (a). Figure 13.3.3 shows the graph of f. Note that f is similar to the function considered in Example 1 of Section 13.2, except that here we have assigned f a value of 0 at $(0, 0)$. Except at this point, the partial derivatives of f are

$$f_x(x, y) = -\frac{(x^2 + y^2)y - xy(2x)}{(x^2 + y^2)^2} = \frac{x^2 y - y^3}{(x^2 + y^2)^2} \tag{4}$$

$$f_y(x, y) = -\frac{(x^2 + y^2)x - xy(2y)}{(x^2 + y^2)^2} = \frac{xy^2 - x^3}{(x^2 + y^2)^2} \tag{5}$$

It is not evident from Formula (3) whether f has partial derivatives at $(0, 0)$, and if so, what the values of those derivatives are. To answer that question we will have to use the definitions of the partial derivatives (Definition 13.3.1). Applying Formulas (1) and (2) to (3) we obtain

$$f_x(0, 0) = \lim_{\Delta x \to 0} \frac{f(\Delta x, 0) - f(0, 0)}{\Delta x} = \lim_{\Delta x \to 0} \frac{0 - 0}{\Delta x} = 0$$

$$f_y(0, 0) = \lim_{\Delta y \to 0} \frac{f(0, \Delta y) - f(0, 0)}{\Delta y} = \lim_{\Delta y \to 0} \frac{0 - 0}{\Delta y} = 0$$

This shows that f has partial derivatives at $(0, 0)$ and the values of both partial derivatives are 0 at that point.

Solution (b). We saw in Example 3 of Section 13.2 that

$$\lim_{(x, y) \to (0,0)} -\frac{xy}{x^2 + y^2}$$

does not exist. Thus, f is not continuous at $(0, 0)$. ◀

We will study the relationship between the continuity of a function and the properties of its partial derivatives in the next section.

■ **PARTIAL DERIVATIVES OF FUNCTIONS WITH MORE THAN TWO VARIABLES**

For a function $f(x, y, z)$ of three variables, there are three *partial derivatives*:

$$f_x(x, y, z), \quad f_y(x, y, z), \quad f_z(x, y, z)$$

The partial derivative f_x is calculated by holding y and z constant and differentiating with respect to x. For f_y the variables x and z are held constant, and for f_z the variables x and y are held constant. If a dependent variable

$$w = f(x, y, z)$$

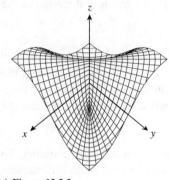

▲ **Figure 13.3.3**

is used, then the three partial derivatives of f can be denoted by

$$\frac{\partial w}{\partial x}, \quad \frac{\partial w}{\partial y}, \quad \text{and} \quad \frac{\partial w}{\partial z}$$

▶ **Example 10** If $f(x, y, z) = x^3 y^2 z^4 + 2xy + z$, then

$$f_x(x, y, z) = 3x^2 y^2 z^4 + 2y$$
$$f_y(x, y, z) = 2x^3 y z^4 + 2x$$
$$f_z(x, y, z) = 4x^3 y^2 z^3 + 1$$
$$f_z(-1, 1, 2) = 4(-1)^3 (1)^2 (2)^3 + 1 = -31 \quad ◀$$

▶ **Example 11** If $f(\rho, \theta, \phi) = \rho^2 \cos \phi \sin \theta$, then

$$f_\rho(\rho, \theta, \phi) = 2\rho \cos \phi \sin \theta$$
$$f_\theta(\rho, \theta, \phi) = \rho^2 \cos \phi \cos \theta$$
$$f_\phi(\rho, \theta, \phi) = -\rho^2 \sin \phi \sin \theta \quad ◀$$

In general, if $f(v_1, v_2, \ldots, v_n)$ is a function of n variables, there are n partial derivatives of f, each of which is obtained by holding $n - 1$ of the variables fixed and differentiating the function f with respect to the remaining variable. If $w = f(v_1, v_2, \ldots, v_n)$, then these partial derivatives are denoted by

$$\frac{\partial w}{\partial v_1}, \frac{\partial w}{\partial v_2}, \ldots, \frac{\partial w}{\partial v_n}$$

where $\partial w / \partial v_i$ is obtained by holding all variables except v_i fixed and differentiating with respect to v_i.

■ HIGHER-ORDER PARTIAL DERIVATIVES

Suppose that f is a function of two variables x and y. Since the partial derivatives $\partial f / \partial x$ and $\partial f / \partial y$ are also functions of x and y, these functions may themselves have partial derivatives. This gives rise to four possible **second-order** partial derivatives of f, which are defined by

$$\frac{\partial^2 f}{\partial x^2} = \frac{\partial}{\partial x} \left(\frac{\partial f}{\partial x} \right) = f_{xx} \qquad \frac{\partial^2 f}{\partial y^2} = \frac{\partial}{\partial y} \left(\frac{\partial f}{\partial y} \right) = f_{yy}$$

Differentiate twice with respect to x. | Differentiate twice with respect to y.

$$\frac{\partial^2 f}{\partial y \partial x} = \frac{\partial}{\partial y} \left(\frac{\partial f}{\partial x} \right) = f_{xy} \qquad \frac{\partial^2 f}{\partial x \partial y} = \frac{\partial}{\partial x} \left(\frac{\partial f}{\partial y} \right) = f_{yx}$$

Differentiate first with respect to x and then with respect to y. | Differentiate first with respect to y and then with respect to x.

The last two cases are called the **mixed second-order partial derivatives** or the **mixed second partials**. Also, the derivatives $\partial f / \partial x$ and $\partial f / \partial y$ are often called the **first-order partial derivatives** when it is necessary to distinguish them from higher-order partial derivatives. Similar conventions apply to the second-order partial derivatives of a function of three variables.

WARNING

Observe that the two notations for the mixed second partials have opposite conventions for the order of differentiation. In the "∂" notation the derivatives are taken right to left, and in the "subscript" notation they are taken left to right. The conventions are logical if you insert parentheses:

$$\frac{\partial^2 f}{\partial y \partial x} = \frac{\partial}{\partial y}\left(\frac{\partial f}{\partial x}\right) \quad \boxed{\begin{array}{l}\text{Right to left. Differentiate} \\ \text{inside the parentheses first.}\end{array}} \qquad f_{xy} = (f_x)_y \quad \boxed{\begin{array}{l}\text{Left to right. Differentiate} \\ \text{inside the parentheses first.}\end{array}}$$

▶ **Example 12** Find the second-order partial derivatives of $f(x, y) = x^2 y^3 + x^4 y$.

Solution. We have

$$\frac{\partial f}{\partial x} = 2xy^3 + 4x^3 y \quad \text{and} \quad \frac{\partial f}{\partial y} = 3x^2 y^2 + x^4$$

so that

$$\frac{\partial^2 f}{\partial x^2} = \frac{\partial}{\partial x}\left(\frac{\partial f}{\partial x}\right) = \frac{\partial}{\partial x}(2xy^3 + 4x^3 y) = 2y^3 + 12x^2 y$$

$$\frac{\partial^2 f}{\partial y^2} = \frac{\partial}{\partial y}\left(\frac{\partial f}{\partial y}\right) = \frac{\partial}{\partial y}(3x^2 y^2 + x^4) = 6x^2 y$$

$$\frac{\partial^2 f}{\partial x \partial y} = \frac{\partial}{\partial x}\left(\frac{\partial f}{\partial y}\right) = \frac{\partial}{\partial x}(3x^2 y^2 + x^4) = 6xy^2 + 4x^3$$

$$\frac{\partial^2 f}{\partial y \partial x} = \frac{\partial}{\partial y}\left(\frac{\partial f}{\partial x}\right) = \frac{\partial}{\partial y}(2xy^3 + 4x^3 y) = 6xy^2 + 4x^3 \quad ◀$$

Third-order, fourth-order, and higher-order partial derivatives can be obtained by successive differentiation. Some possibilities are

$$\frac{\partial^3 f}{\partial x^3} = \frac{\partial}{\partial x}\left(\frac{\partial^2 f}{\partial x^2}\right) = f_{xxx} \qquad \frac{\partial^4 f}{\partial y^4} = \frac{\partial}{\partial y}\left(\frac{\partial^3 f}{\partial y^3}\right) = f_{yyyy}$$

$$\frac{\partial^3 f}{\partial y^2 \partial x} = \frac{\partial}{\partial y}\left(\frac{\partial^2 f}{\partial y \partial x}\right) = f_{xyy} \qquad \frac{\partial^4 f}{\partial y^2 \partial x^2} = \frac{\partial}{\partial y}\left(\frac{\partial^3 f}{\partial y \partial x^2}\right) = f_{xxyy}$$

▶ **Example 13** Let $f(x, y) = y^2 e^x + y$. Find f_{xyy}.

Solution.

$$f_{xyy} = \frac{\partial^3 f}{\partial y^2 \partial x} = \frac{\partial^2}{\partial y^2}\left(\frac{\partial f}{\partial x}\right) = \frac{\partial^2}{\partial y^2}(y^2 e^x) = \frac{\partial}{\partial y}(2ye^x) = 2e^x \quad ◀$$

■ **EQUALITY OF MIXED PARTIALS**

For a function $f(x, y)$ it might be expected that there would be four distinct second-order partial derivatives: f_{xx}, f_{xy}, f_{yx}, and f_{yy}. However, observe that the mixed second-order partial derivatives in Example 12 are equal. The following theorem (proved in Web Appendix D) explains why this is so.

If f is a function of three variables, then the analog of Theorem 13.3.2 holds for each pair of mixed second-order partials if we replace "open disk" by "open ball." How many second-order partials does $f(x, y, z)$ have?

13.3.2 THEOREM *Let f be a function of two variables. If f_{xy} and f_{yx} are continuous on some open disk, then $f_{xy} = f_{yx}$ on that disk.*

It follows from this theorem that if $f_{xy}(x, y)$ and $f_{yx}(x, y)$ are continuous everywhere, then $f_{xy}(x, y) = f_{yx}(x, y)$ for all values of x and y. Since polynomials are continuous everywhere, this explains why the mixed second-order partials in Example 12 are equal.

■ THE WAVE EQUATION

Consider a string of length L that is stretched taut between $x = 0$ and $x = L$ on an x-axis, and suppose that the string is set into vibratory motion by "plucking" it at time $t = 0$ (Figure 13.3.4a). The displacement of a point on the string depends both on its coordinate x and the elapsed time t, and hence is described by a function $u(x, t)$ of two variables. For a fixed value t, the function $u(x, t)$ depends on x alone, and the graph of u versus x describes the shape of the string—think of it as a "snapshot" of the string at time t (Figure 13.3.4b). It follows that at a fixed time t, the partial derivative $\partial u / \partial x$ represents the slope of the string at x, and the sign of the second partial derivative $\partial^2 u / \partial x^2$ tells us whether the string is concave up or concave down at x (Figure 13.3.4c).

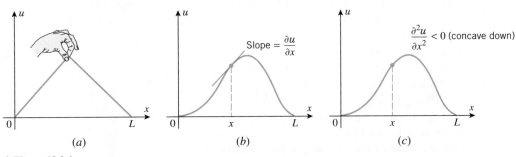

(a) $\qquad\qquad$ (b) $\qquad\qquad$ (c)

▲ **Figure 13.3.4**

Leverett Bradley/Getty Images
The vibration of a plucked string is governed by the wave equation.

For a fixed value of x, the function $u(x, t)$ depends on t alone, and the graph of u versus t is the position versus time curve of the point on the string with coordinate x. Thus, for a fixed value of x, the partial derivative $\partial u / \partial t$ is the velocity of the point with coordinate x, and $\partial^2 u / \partial t^2$ is the acceleration of that point.

It can be proved that under appropriate conditions the function $u(x, t)$ satisfies an equation of the form

$$\frac{\partial^2 u}{\partial t^2} = c^2 \frac{\partial^2 u}{\partial x^2} \tag{6}$$

where c is a positive constant that depends on the physical characteristics of the string. This equation, which is called the ***one-dimensional wave equation***, involves partial derivatives of the unknown function $u(x, t)$ and hence is classified as a ***partial differential equation***. Techniques for solving partial differential equations are studied in advanced courses and will not be discussed in this text.

▶ **Example 14** Show that the function $u(x, t) = \sin(x - ct)$ is a solution of Equation (6).

Solution. We have

$$\frac{\partial u}{\partial x} = \cos(x - ct), \qquad \frac{\partial^2 u}{\partial x^2} = -\sin(x - ct)$$

$$\frac{\partial u}{\partial t} = -c \cos(x - ct), \qquad \frac{\partial^2 u}{\partial t^2} = -c^2 \sin(x - ct)$$

Thus, $u(x, t)$ satisfies (6). ◀

✔**QUICK CHECK EXERCISES 13.3** (See page 940 for answers.)

1. Let $f(x, y) = x \sin xy$. Then $f_x(x, y) =$ _____ and $f_y(x, y) =$ _____.

2. The slope of the surface $z = xy^2$ in the x-direction at the point $(2, 3)$ is _____, and the slope of this surface in the y-direction at the point $(2, 3)$ is _____.

3. The volume V of a right circular cone of radius r and height h is given by $V = \frac{1}{3}\pi r^2 h$.

(a) Find a formula for the instantaneous rate of change of V with respect to r if r changes and h remains constant.

(b) Find a formula for the instantaneous rate of change of V with respect to h if h changes and r remains constant.

4. Find all second-order partial derivatives for the function $f(x, y) = x^2 y^3$.

EXERCISE SET 13.3 ⬨ Graphing Utility

1. Let $f(x, y) = 3x^3 y^2$. Find
(a) $f_x(x, y)$ (b) $f_y(x, y)$ (c) $f_x(1, y)$
(d) $f_x(x, 1)$ (e) $f_y(1, y)$ (f) $f_y(x, 1)$
(g) $f_x(1, 2)$ (h) $f_y(1, 2)$.

2. Let $z = e^{2x} \sin y$. Find
(a) $\partial z/\partial x$ (b) $\partial z/\partial y$ (c) $\partial z/\partial x|_{(0,y)}$
(d) $\partial z/\partial x|_{(x,0)}$ (e) $\partial z/\partial y|_{(0,y)}$ (f) $\partial z/\partial y|_{(x,0)}$
(g) $\partial z/\partial x|_{(\ln 2,0)}$ (h) $\partial z/\partial y|_{(\ln 2,0)}$.

3. Let $f(x, y) = \sqrt{3x + 2y}$.
(a) Find the slope of the surface $z = f(x, y)$ in the x-direction at the point $(4, 2)$.
(b) Find the slope of the surface $z = f(x, y)$ in the y-direction at the point $(4, 2)$.

4. Let $f(x, y) = xe^{-y} + 5y$.
(a) Find the slope of the surface $z = f(x, y)$ in the x-direction at the point $(3, 0)$.
(b) Find the slope of the surface $z = f(x, y)$ in the y-direction at the point $(3, 0)$.

5. Let $z = \sin(y^2 - 4x)$.
(a) Find the rate of change of z with respect to x at the point $(2, 1)$ with y held fixed.
(b) Find the rate of change of z with respect to y at the point $(2, 1)$ with x held fixed.

6. Let $z = (x + y)^{-1}$.
(a) Find the rate of change of z with respect to x at the point $(-2, 4)$ with y held fixed.
(b) Find the rate of change of z with respect to y at the point $(-2, 4)$ with x held fixed.

FOCUS ON CONCEPTS

7. Use the information in the accompanying figure to find the values of the first-order partial derivatives of f at the point $(1, 2)$.

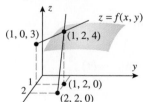

◀ **Figure Ex-7**

8. The accompanying figure shows a contour plot for an unspecified function $f(x, y)$. Make a conjecture about the signs of the partial derivatives $f_x(x_0, y_0)$ and $f_y(x_0, y_0)$, and explain your reasoning.

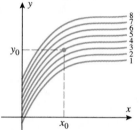

◀ **Figure Ex-8**

9. Suppose that Nolan throws a baseball to Ryan and that the baseball leaves Nolan's hand at the same height at which it is caught by Ryan. It we ignore air resistance, the horizontal range r of the baseball is a function of the initial speed v of the ball when it leaves Nolan's hand and the angle θ above the horizontal at which it is thrown. Use the accompanying table and the method of Example 6 to estimate
(a) the partial derivative of r with respect to v when $v = 80$ ft/s and $\theta = 40°$
(b) the partial derivative of r with respect to θ when $v = 80$ ft/s and $\theta = 40°$.

SPEED v (ft/s)

		75	80	85	90
ANGLE θ (degrees)	35	165	188	212	238
	40	173	197	222	249
	45	176	200	226	253
	50	173	197	222	249

◀ **Table Ex-9**

10. Use the table in Exercise 9 and the method of Example 6 to estimate
(a) the partial derivative of r with respect to v when $v = 85$ ft/s and $\theta = 45°$
(b) the partial derivative of r with respect to θ when $v = 85$ ft/s and $\theta = 45°$.

11. The accompanying figure shows the graphs of an unspecified function $f(x, y)$ and its partial derivatives $f_x(x, y)$ and $f_y(x, y)$. Determine which is which, and explain your reasoning.

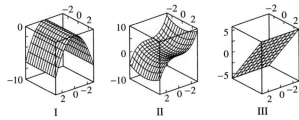

I   II   III

▲ **Figure Ex-11**

12. What can you say about the signs of $\partial z/\partial x$, $\partial^2 z/\partial x^2$, $\partial z/\partial y$, and $\partial^2 z/\partial y^2$ at the point P in the accompanying figure? Explain your reasoning.

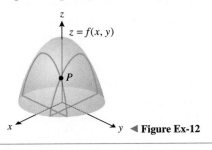

◀ **Figure Ex-12**

13–16 True–False Determine whether the statement is true or false. Explain your answer. ■

13. If the line $y = 2$ is a contour of $f(x, y)$ through $(4, 2)$, then $f_x(4, 2) = 0$.

14. If the plane $x = 3$ intersects the surface $z = f(x, y)$ in a curve that passes through $(3, 4, 16)$ and satisfies $z = y^2$, then $f_y(3, 4) = 8$.

15. If the graph of $z = f(x, y)$ is a plane in 3-space, then both f_x and f_y are constant functions.

16. There exists a polynomial $f(x, y)$ that satisfies the equations $f_x(x, y) = 3x^2 + y^2 + 2y$ and $f_y(x, y) = 2xy + 2y$.

17–22 Find $\partial z/\partial x$ and $\partial z/\partial y$. ■

17. $z = 4e^{x^2 y^3}$

18. $z = \cos(x^5 y^4)$

19. $z = x^3 \ln(1 + xy^{-3/5})$

20. $z = e^{xy} \sin 4y^2$

21. $z = \dfrac{xy}{x^2 + y^2}$

22. $z = \dfrac{x^2 y^3}{\sqrt{x + y}}$

23–28 Find $f_x(x, y)$ and $f_y(x, y)$. ■

23. $f(x, y) = \sqrt{3x^5 y - 7x^3 y}$

24. $f(x, y) = \dfrac{x + y}{x - y}$

25. $f(x, y) = y^{-3/2} \tan^{-1}(x/y)$

26. $f(x, y) = x^3 e^{-y} + y^3 \sec \sqrt{x}$

27. $f(x, y) = (y^2 \tan x)^{-4/3}$

28. $f(x, y) = \cosh(\sqrt{x}) \sinh^2(xy^2)$

29–32 Evaluate the indicated partial derivatives. ■

29. $f(x, y) = 9 - x^2 - 7y^3$; $f_x(3, 1)$, $f_y(3, 1)$

30. $f(x, y) = x^2 y e^{xy}$; $\partial f/\partial x(1, 1)$, $\partial f/\partial y(1, 1)$

31. $z = \sqrt{x^2 + 4y^2}$; $\partial z/\partial x(1, 2)$, $\partial z/\partial y(1, 2)$

32. $w = x^2 \cos xy$; $\partial w/\partial x \left(\frac{1}{2}, \pi\right)$, $\partial w/\partial y \left(\frac{1}{2}, \pi\right)$

33. Let $f(x, y, z) = x^2 y^4 z^3 + xy + z^2 + 1$. Find
   (a) $f_x(x, y, z)$ (b) $f_y(x, y, z)$ (c) $f_z(x, y, z)$
   (d) $f_x(1, y, z)$ (e) $f_y(1, 2, z)$ (f) $f_z(1, 2, 3)$.

34. Let $w = x^2 y \cos z$. Find
   (a) $\partial w/\partial x(x, y, z)$ (b) $\partial w/\partial y(x, y, z)$
   (c) $\partial w/\partial z(x, y, z)$ (d) $\partial w/\partial x(2, y, z)$
   (e) $\partial w/\partial y(2, 1, z)$ (f) $\partial w/\partial z(2, 1, 0)$.

35–38 Find f_x, f_y, and f_z. ■

35. $f(x, y, z) = z \ln(x^2 y \cos z)$

36. $f(x, y, z) = y^{-3/2} \sec\left(\dfrac{xz}{y}\right)$

37. $f(x, y, z) = \tan^{-1}\left(\dfrac{1}{xy^2 z^3}\right)$

38. $f(x, y, z) = \cosh(\sqrt{z}) \sinh^2(x^2 yz)$

39–42 Find $\partial w/\partial x$, $\partial w/\partial y$, and $\partial w/\partial z$. ■

39. $w = ye^z \sin xz$

40. $w = \dfrac{x^2 - y^2}{y^2 + z^2}$

41. $w = \sqrt{x^2 + y^2 + z^2}$

42. $w = y^3 e^{2x + 3z}$

43. Let $f(x, y, z) = y^2 e^{xz}$. Find
   (a) $\partial f/\partial x|_{(1,1,1)}$ (b) $\partial f/\partial y|_{(1,1,1)}$ (c) $\partial f/\partial z|_{(1,1,1)}$.

44. Let $w = \sqrt{x^2 + 4y^2 - z^2}$. Find
   (a) $\partial w/\partial x|_{(2,1,-1)}$ (b) $\partial w/\partial y|_{(2,1,-1)}$
   (c) $\partial w/\partial z|_{(2,1,-1)}$.

45. Let $f(x, y) = e^x \cos y$. Use a graphing utility to graph the functions $f_x(0, y)$ and $f_y(x, \pi/2)$.

46. Let $f(x, y) = e^x \sin y$. Use a graphing utility to graph the functions $f_x(0, y)$ and $f_y(x, 0)$.

47. A point moves along the intersection of the elliptic paraboloid $z = x^2 + 3y^2$ and the plane $y = 1$. At what rate is z changing with respect to x when the point is at $(2, 1, 7)$?

48. A point moves along the intersection of the elliptic paraboloid $z = x^2 + 3y^2$ and the plane $x = 2$. At what rate is z changing with respect to y when the point is at $(2, 1, 7)$?

49. A point moves along the intersection of the plane $y = 3$ and the surface $z = \sqrt{29 - x^2 - y^2}$. At what rate is z changing with respect to x when the point is at $(4, 3, 2)$?

50. Find the slope of the tangent line at $(-1, 1, 5)$ to the curve of intersection of the surface $z = x^2 + 4y^2$ and
   (a) the plane $x = -1$ (b) the plane $y = 1$.

51. The volume V of a right circular cylinder is given by the formula $V = \pi r^2 h$, where r is the radius and h is the height.
   (a) Find a formula for the instantaneous rate of change of V with respect to r if r changes and h remains constant.

(cont.)

(b) Find a formula for the instantaneous rate of change of V with respect to h if h changes and r remains constant.

(c) Suppose that h has a constant value of 4 in, but r varies. Find the rate of change of V with respect to r at the point where $r = 6$ in.

(d) Suppose that r has a constant value of 8 in, but h varies. Find the instantaneous rate of change of V with respect to h at the point where $h = 10$ in.

52. The volume V of a right circular cone is given by

$$V = \frac{\pi}{24} d^2 \sqrt{4s^2 - d^2}$$

where s is the slant height and d is the diameter of the base.

(a) Find a formula for the instantaneous rate of change of V with respect to s if d remains constant.

(b) Find a formula for the instantaneous rate of change of V with respect to d if s remains constant.

(c) Suppose that d has a constant value of 16 cm, but s varies. Find the rate of change of V with respect to s when $s = 10$ cm.

(d) Suppose that s has a constant value of 10 cm, but d varies. Find the rate of change of V with respect to d when $d = 16$ cm.

53. According to the ideal gas law, the pressure, temperature, and volume of a gas are related by $P = kT/V$, where k is a constant of proportionality. Suppose that V is measured in cubic inches (in³), T is measured in kelvins (K), and that for a certain gas the constant of proportionality is $k = 10$ in·lb/K.

(a) Find the instantaneous rate of change of pressure with respect to temperature if the temperature is 80 K and the volume remains fixed at 50 in³.

(b) Find the instantaneous rate of change of volume with respect to pressure if the volume is 50 in³ and the temperature remains fixed at 80 K.

54. The temperature at a point (x, y) on a metal plate in the xy-plane is $T(x, y) = x^3 + 2y^2 + x$ degrees Celsius. Assume that distance is measured in centimeters and find the rate at which temperature changes with respect to distance if we start at the point $(1, 2)$ and move

(a) to the right and parallel to the x-axis

(b) upward and parallel to the y-axis.

55. The length, width, and height of a rectangular box are $l = 5$, $w = 2$, and $h = 3$, respectively.

(a) Find the instantaneous rate of change of the volume of the box with respect to the length if w and h are held constant.

(b) Find the instantaneous rate of change of the volume of the box with respect to the width if l and h are held constant.

(c) Find the instantaneous rate of change of the volume of the box with respect to the height if l and w are held constant.

56. The area A of a triangle is given by $A = \frac{1}{2}ab \sin\theta$, where a and b are the lengths of two sides and θ is the angle between these sides. Suppose that $a = 5$, $b = 10$, and $\theta = \pi/3$.

(a) Find the rate at which A changes with respect to a if b and θ are held constant.

(b) Find the rate at which A changes with respect to θ if a and b are held constant.

(c) Find the rate at which b changes with respect to a if A and θ are held constant.

57. The volume of a right circular cone of radius r and height h is $V = \frac{1}{3}\pi r^2 h$. Show that if the height remains constant while the radius changes, then the volume satisfies

$$\frac{\partial V}{\partial r} = \frac{2V}{r}$$

58. Find parametric equations for the tangent line at $(1, 3, 3)$ to the curve of intersection of the surface $z = x^2 y$ and

(a) the plane $x = 1$ (b) the plane $y = 3$.

59. (a) By differentiating implicitly, find the slope of the hyperboloid $x^2 + y^2 - z^2 = 1$ in the x-direction at the points $(3, 4, 2\sqrt{6})$ and $(3, 4, -2\sqrt{6})$.

(b) Check the results in part (a) by solving for z and differentiating the resulting functions directly.

60. (a) By differentiating implicitly, find the slope of the hyperboloid $x^2 + y^2 - z^2 = 1$ in the y-direction at the points $(3, 4, 2\sqrt{6})$ and $(3, 4, -2\sqrt{6})$.

(b) Check the results in part (a) by solving for z and differentiating the resulting functions directly.

61–64 Calculate $\partial z/\partial x$ and $\partial z/\partial y$ using implicit differentiation. Leave your answers in terms of x, y, and z. ■

61. $(x^2 + y^2 + z^2)^{3/2} = 1$ **62.** $\ln(2x^2 + y - z^3) = x$

63. $x^2 + z \sin xyz = 0$ **64.** $e^{xy} \sinh z - z^2 x + 1 = 0$

65–66 Find $\partial w/\partial x$, $\partial w/\partial y$, and $\partial w/\partial z$ using implicit differentiation. Leave your answers in terms of x, y, z, and w. ■

65. $(x^2 + y^2 + z^2 + w^2)^{3/2} = 4$

66. $\ln(2x^2 + y - z^3 + 3w) = z$

67. $w^2 + w \sin xyz = 1$

68. $e^{xy} \sinh w - z^2 w + 1 = 0$

69–72 Find f_x and f_y. ■

69. $f(x, y) = \displaystyle\int_y^x e^{t^2}\, dt$ **70.** $f(x, y) = \displaystyle\int_1^{xy} e^{t^2}\, dt$

71. $f(x, y) = \displaystyle\int_0^{x^2 y^3} \sin t^3\, dt$ **72.** $f(x, y) = \displaystyle\int_{x+y}^{x-y} \sin t^3\, dt$

73. Let $z = \sqrt{x} \cos y$. Find

(a) $\partial^2 z/\partial x^2$ (b) $\partial^2 z/\partial y^2$

(c) $\partial^2 z/\partial x \partial y$ (d) $\partial^2 z/\partial y \partial x$.

74. Let $f(x, y) = 4x^2 - 2y + 7x^4 y^5$. Find

(a) f_{xx} (b) f_{yy} (c) f_{xy} (d) f_{yx}.

75–82 Confirm that the mixed second-order partial derivatives of f are the same. ■

75. $f(x, y) = 4x^2 - 8xy^4 + 7y^5 - 3$

76. $f(x, y) = \sqrt{x^2 + y^2}$ **77.** $f(x, y) = e^x \cos y$

78. $f(x, y) = e^{x-y^2}$ **79.** $f(x, y) = \ln(4x - 5y)$

80. $f(x, y) = \ln(x^2 + y^2)$

81. $f(x, y) = (x - y)/(x + y)$

82. $f(x, y) = (x^2 - y^2)/(x^2 + y^2)$

83. Express the following derivatives in "∂" notation.
   (a) f_{xxx} (b) f_{xyy} (c) f_{yyxx} (d) f_{xyyy}

84. Express the derivatives in "subscript" notation.
   (a) $\dfrac{\partial^3 f}{\partial y^2 \partial x}$ (b) $\dfrac{\partial^4 f}{\partial x^4}$ (c) $\dfrac{\partial^4 f}{\partial y^2 \partial x^2}$ (d) $\dfrac{\partial^5 f}{\partial x^2 \partial y^3}$

85. Given $f(x, y) = x^3 y^5 - 2x^2 y + x$, find
   (a) f_{xxy} (b) f_{yxy} (c) f_{yyy}.

86. Given $z = (2x - y)^5$, find
   (a) $\dfrac{\partial^3 z}{\partial y \partial x \partial y}$ (b) $\dfrac{\partial^3 z}{\partial x^2 \partial y}$ (c) $\dfrac{\partial^4 z}{\partial x^2 \partial y^2}$.

87. Given $f(x, y) = y^3 e^{-5x}$, find
   (a) $f_{xyy}(0, 1)$ (b) $f_{xxx}(0, 1)$ (c) $f_{yyxx}(0, 1)$.

88. Given $w = e^y \cos x$, find
   (a) $\dfrac{\partial^3 w}{\partial y^2 \partial x}\bigg|_{(\pi/4, 0)}$ (b) $\dfrac{\partial^3 w}{\partial x^2 \partial y}\bigg|_{(\pi/4, 0)}$

89. Let $f(x, y, z) = x^3 y^5 z^7 + xy^2 + y^3 z$. Find
   (a) f_{xy} (b) f_{yz} (c) f_{xz} (d) f_{zz}
   (e) f_{zyy} (f) f_{xxy} (g) f_{zyx} (h) f_{xxyz}.

90. Let $w = (4x - 3y + 2z)^5$. Find
   (a) $\dfrac{\partial^2 w}{\partial x \partial z}$ (b) $\dfrac{\partial^3 w}{\partial x \partial y \partial z}$ (c) $\dfrac{\partial^4 w}{\partial z^2 \partial y \partial x}$.

91. Show that the function satisfies **Laplace's equation**
$$\frac{\partial^2 z}{\partial x^2} + \frac{\partial^2 z}{\partial y^2} = 0$$
   (a) $z = x^2 - y^2 + 2xy$
   (b) $z = e^x \sin y + e^y \cos x$
   (c) $z = \ln(x^2 + y^2) + 2\tan^{-1}(y/x)$

92. Show that the function satisfies the **heat equation**
$$\frac{\partial z}{\partial t} = c^2 \frac{\partial^2 z}{\partial x^2} \quad (c > 0, \text{ constant})$$
   (a) $z = e^{-t} \sin(x/c)$ (b) $z = e^{-t} \cos(x/c)$

93. Show that the function $u(x, t) = \sin c\omega t \sin \omega x$ satisfies the wave equation [Equation (6)] for all real values of ω.

94. In each part, show that $u(x, y)$ and $v(x, y)$ satisfy the **Cauchy–Riemann equations**
$$\frac{\partial u}{\partial x} = \frac{\partial v}{\partial y} \quad \text{and} \quad \frac{\partial u}{\partial y} = -\frac{\partial v}{\partial x}$$
   (a) $u = x^2 - y^2$, $v = 2xy$
   (b) $u = e^x \cos y$, $v = e^x \sin y$
   (c) $u = \ln(x^2 + y^2)$, $v = 2\tan^{-1}(y/x)$

95. Show that if $u(x, y)$ and $v(x, y)$ each have equal mixed second partials, and if u and v satisfy the Cauchy–Riemann equations (Exercise 94), then u, v, and $u + v$ satisfy Laplace's equation (Exercise 91).

96. When two resistors having resistances R_1 ohms and R_2 ohms are connected in parallel, their combined resistance R in ohms is $R = R_1 R_2/(R_1 + R_2)$. Show that
$$\frac{\partial^2 R}{\partial R_1^2} \frac{\partial^2 R}{\partial R_2^2} = \frac{4R^2}{(R_1 + R_2)^4}$$

97–100 Find the indicated partial derivatives. ■

97. $f(v, w, x, y) = 4v^2 w^3 x^4 y^5$;
   $\partial f/\partial v, \ \partial f/\partial w, \ \partial f/\partial x, \ \partial f/\partial y$

98. $w = r \cos st + e^u \sin ur$;
   $\partial w/\partial r, \ \partial w/\partial s, \ \partial w/\partial t, \ \partial w/\partial u$

99. $f(v_1, v_2, v_3, v_4) = \dfrac{v_1^2 - v_2^2}{v_3^2 + v_4^2}$;
   $\partial f/\partial v_1, \ \partial f/\partial v_2, \ \partial f/\partial v_3, \ \partial f/\partial v_4$

100. $V = xe^{2x-y} + we^{zw} + yw$;
   $\partial V/\partial x, \ \partial V/\partial y, \ \partial V/\partial z, \ \partial V/\partial w$

101. Let $u(w, x, y, z) = xe^{yw} \sin^2 z$. Find
   (a) $\dfrac{\partial u}{\partial x}(0, 0, 1, \pi)$ (b) $\dfrac{\partial u}{\partial y}(0, 0, 1, \pi)$
   (c) $\dfrac{\partial u}{\partial w}(0, 0, 1, \pi)$ (d) $\dfrac{\partial u}{\partial z}(0, 0, 1, \pi)$
   (e) $\dfrac{\partial^4 u}{\partial x \partial y \partial w \partial z}$ (f) $\dfrac{\partial^4 u}{\partial w \partial z \partial y^2}$.

102. Let $f(v, w, x, y) = 2v^{1/2} w^4 x^{1/2} y^{2/3}$. Find $f_v(1, -2, 4, 8)$, $f_w(1, -2, 4, 8)$, $f_x(1, -2, 4, 8)$, and $f_y(1, -2, 4, 8)$.

103–104 Find $\partial w/\partial x_i$ for $i = 1, 2, \ldots, n$. ■

103. $w = \cos(x_1 + 2x_2 + \cdots + nx_n)$

104. $w = \left(\displaystyle\sum_{k=1}^{n} x_k\right)^{1/n}$

105–106 Describe the largest set on which Theorem 13.3.2 can be used to prove that f_{xy} and f_{yx} are equal on that set. Then confirm by direct computation that $f_{xy} = f_{yx}$ on the given set. ■

105. (a) $f(x, y) = 4x^3 y + 3x^2 y$ (b) $f(x, y) = x^3/y$

106. (a) $f(x, y) = \sqrt{x^2 + y^2 - 1}$
   (b) $f(x, y) = \sin(x^2 + y^3)$

107. Let $f(x, y) = 2x^2 - 3xy + y^2$. Find $f_x(2, -1)$ and $f_y(2, -1)$ by evaluating the limits in Definition 13.3.1. Then check your work by calculating the derivative in the usual way.

108. Let $f(x, y) = (x^2 + y^2)^{2/3}$. Show that

$$f_x(x, y) = \begin{cases} \dfrac{4x}{3(x^2 + y^2)^{1/3}}, & (x, y) \neq (0, 0) \\ 0, & (x, y) = (0, 0) \end{cases}$$

Source: This problem, due to Don Cohen, appeared in *Mathematics and Computer Education*, Vol. 25, No. 2, 1991, p. 179.

109. Let $f(x, y) = (x^3 + y^3)^{1/3}$.
  (a) Show that $f_y(0, 0) = 1$.
  (b) At what points, if any, does $f_y(x, y)$ fail to exist?

110. Writing Explain how one might use the graph of the equation $z = f(x, y)$ to determine the signs of $f_x(x_0, y_0)$ and $f_y(x_0, y_0)$ by inspection.

111. Writing Explain how one might use the graphs of some appropriate contours of $z = f(x, y)$ to determine the signs of $f_x(x_0, y_0)$ and $f_y(x_0, y_0)$ by inspection.

✔ **QUICK CHECK ANSWERS 13.3**

1. $\sin xy + xy \cos xy$; $x^2 \cos xy$ 2. 9; 12   3. (a) $\frac{2}{3}\pi rh$ (b) $\frac{1}{3}\pi r^2 s$
4. $f_{xx}(x, y) = 2y^3$, $f_{yy}(x, y) = 6x^2 y$, $f_{xy}(x, y) = f_{yx}(x, y) = 6xy^2$

13.4 DIFFERENTIABILITY, DIFFERENTIALS, AND LOCAL LINEARITY

In this section we will extend the notion of differentiability to functions of two or three variables. Our definition of differentiability will be based on the idea that a function is differentiable at a point provided it can be very closely approximated by a linear function near that point. In the process, we will expand the concept of a "differential" to functions of more than one variable and define the "local linear approximation" of a function.

■ DIFFERENTIABILITY

Recall that a function f of one variable is called differentiable at x_0 if it has a derivative at x_0, that is, if the limit

$$f'(x_0) = \lim_{\Delta x \to 0} \frac{f(x_0 + \Delta x) - f(x_0)}{\Delta x} \qquad (1)$$

exists. As a consequence of (1) a differentiable function enjoys a number of other important properties:

- The graph of $y = f(x)$ has a nonvertical tangent line at the point $(x_0, f(x_0))$;
- f may be closely approximated by a linear function near x_0 (Section 3.5);
- f is continuous at x_0.

Our primary objective in this section is to extend the notion of differentiability to functions of two or three variables in such a way that the natural analogs of these properties hold. For example, if a function $f(x, y)$ of two variables is differentiable at a point (x_0, y_0), we want it to be the case that

- the surface $z = f(x, y)$ has a nonvertical tangent plane at the point $(x_0, y_0, f(x_0, y_0))$ (Figure 13.4.1);
- the values of f at points near (x_0, y_0) can be very closely approximated by the values of a linear function;
- f is continuous at (x_0, y_0).

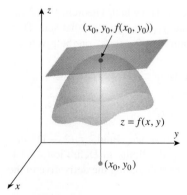

▲ **Figure 13.4.1**

One could reasonably conjecture that a function f of two or three variables should be called differentiable at a point if all the first-order partial derivatives of the function exist at that point. Unfortunately, this condition is not strong enough to guarantee that the properties above hold. For instance, we saw in Example 9 of Section 13.3 that the mere existence of both first-order partial derivatives for a function is not sufficient to guarantee the continuity of the function. To determine what else we should include in our definition, it will be helpful to reexamine one of the consequences of differentiability for a *single-variable* function $f(x)$. Suppose that $f(x)$ is differentiable at $x = x_0$ and let

$$\Delta f = f(x_0 + \Delta x) - f(x_0)$$

denote the change in f that corresponds to the change Δx in x from x_0 to $x_0 + \Delta x$. We saw in Section 3.5 that

$$\Delta f \approx f'(x_0)\Delta x$$

provided Δx is close to 0. In fact, for Δx close to 0 the error $\Delta f - f'(x_0)\Delta x$ in this approximation will have magnitude much smaller than that of Δx because

$$\lim_{\Delta x \to 0} \frac{\Delta f - f'(x_0)\Delta x}{\Delta x} = \lim_{\Delta x \to 0} \left(\frac{f(x_0 + \Delta x) - f(x_0)}{\Delta x} - f'(x_0) \right) = f'(x_0) - f'(x_0) = 0$$

Since the magnitude of Δx is just the distance between the points x_0 and $x_0 + \Delta x$, we see that when the two points are close together, the magnitude of the error in the approximation will be much smaller than the distance between the two points (Figure 13.4.2). The extension of this idea to functions of two or three variables is the "extra ingredient" needed in our definition of differentiability for multivariable functions.

For a function $f(x, y)$, the symbol Δf, called the **increment** of f, denotes the change in the value of $f(x, y)$ that results when (x, y) varies from some initial position (x_0, y_0) to some new position $(x_0 + \Delta x, y_0 + \Delta y)$; thus

$$\Delta f = f(x_0 + \Delta x, y_0 + \Delta y) - f(x_0, y_0) \tag{2}$$

(see Figure 13.4.3). [If a dependent variable $z = f(x, y)$ is used, then we will sometimes write Δz rather than Δf.] Let us assume that both $f_x(x_0, y_0)$ and $f_y(x_0, y_0)$ exist and (by analogy with the one-variable case) make the approximation

$$\Delta f \approx f_x(x_0, y_0)\Delta x + f_y(x_0, y_0)\Delta y \tag{3}$$

> Show that if $f(x, y)$ is a linear function, then (3) becomes an equality.

For Δx and Δy close to 0, we would like the error

$$\Delta f - f_x(x_0, y_0)\Delta x - f_y(x_0, y_0)\Delta y$$

in this approximation to be much smaller than the distance $\sqrt{(\Delta x)^2 + (\Delta y)^2}$ between (x_0, y_0) and $(x_0 + \Delta x, y_0 + \Delta y)$. We can guarantee this by requiring that

$$\lim_{(\Delta x, \Delta y) \to (0,0)} \frac{\Delta f - f_x(x_0, y_0)\Delta x - f_y(x_0, y_0)\Delta y}{\sqrt{(\Delta x)^2 + (\Delta y)^2}} = 0$$

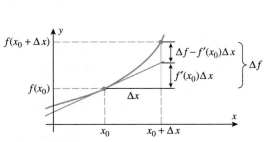

▲ Figure 13.4.2

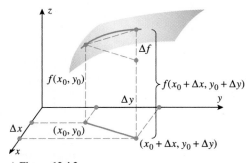

▲ Figure 13.4.3

Based on these ideas, we can now give our definition of differentiability for functions of two variables.

13.4.1 DEFINITION A function f of two variables is said to be **differentiable** at (x_0, y_0) provided $f_x(x_0, y_0)$ and $f_y(x_0, y_0)$ both exist and

$$\lim_{(\Delta x, \Delta y) \to (0,0)} \frac{\Delta f - f_x(x_0, y_0)\Delta x - f_y(x_0, y_0)\Delta y}{\sqrt{(\Delta x)^2 + (\Delta y)^2}} = 0 \qquad (4)$$

As with the one-variable case, verification of differentiability using this definition involves the computation of a limit.

▶ **Example 1** Use Definition 13.4.1 to prove that $f(x, y) = x^2 + y^2$ is differentiable at $(0, 0)$.

Solution. The increment is

$$\Delta f = f(0 + \Delta x, 0 + \Delta y) - f(0, 0) = (\Delta x)^2 + (\Delta y)^2$$

Since $f_x(x, y) = 2x$ and $f_y(x, y) = 2y$, we have $f_x(0, 0) = f_y(0, 0) = 0$, and (4) becomes

$$\lim_{(\Delta x, \Delta y) \to (0,0)} \frac{(\Delta x)^2 + (\Delta y)^2}{\sqrt{(\Delta x)^2 + (\Delta y)^2}} = \lim_{(\Delta x, \Delta y) \to (0,0)} \sqrt{(\Delta x)^2 + (\Delta y)^2} = 0$$

Therefore, f is differentiable at $(0, 0)$. ◀

We now derive an important consequence of limit (4). Define a function

$$\epsilon = \epsilon(\Delta x, \Delta y) = \frac{\Delta f - f_x(x_0, y_0)\Delta x - f_y(x_0, y_0)\Delta y}{\sqrt{(\Delta x)^2 + (\Delta y)^2}} \quad \text{for } (\Delta x, \Delta y) \neq (0, 0)$$

and define $\epsilon(0, 0)$ to be 0. Equation (4) then implies that

$$\lim_{(\Delta x, \Delta y) \to (0,0)} \epsilon(\Delta x, \Delta y) = 0$$

Furthermore, it immediately follows from the definition of ϵ that

$$\Delta f = f_x(x_0, y_0)\Delta x + f_y(x_0, y_0)\Delta y + \epsilon \sqrt{(\Delta x)^2 + (\Delta y)^2} \qquad (5)$$

In other words, if f is differentiable at (x_0, y_0), then Δf may be expressed as shown in (5), where $\epsilon \to 0$ as $(\Delta x, \Delta y) \to (0, 0)$ and where $\epsilon = 0$ if $(\Delta x, \Delta y) = (0, 0)$.

For functions of three variables we have an analogous definition of differentiability in terms of the increment

$$\Delta f = f(x_0 + \Delta x, y_0 + \Delta y, z_0 + \Delta z) - f(x_0, y_0, z_0)$$

13.4.2 DEFINITION A function f of three variables is said to be **differentiable** at (x_0, y_0, z_0) provided $f_x(x_0, y_0, z_0)$, $f_y(x_0, y_0, z_0)$, and $f_z(x_0, y_0, z_0)$ exist and

$$\lim_{(\Delta x, \Delta y, \Delta z) \to (0,0,0)} \frac{\Delta f - f_x(x_0, y_0, z_0)\Delta x - f_y(x_0, y_0, z_0)\Delta y - f_z(x_0, y_0, z_0)\Delta z}{\sqrt{(\Delta x)^2 + (\Delta y)^2 + (\Delta z)^2}} = 0$$

$$(6)$$

In a manner similar to the two-variable case, we can express the limit (6) in terms of a function $\epsilon(\Delta x, \Delta y, \Delta z)$ that vanishes at $(\Delta x, \Delta y, \Delta z) = (0, 0, 0)$ and is continuous there. The details are left as an exercise for the reader.

If a function f of two variables is differentiable at each point of a region R in the xy-plane, then we say that f is **differentiable on R**; and if f is differentiable at every point in the xy-plane, then we say that f is **differentiable everywhere**. For a function f of three variables we have corresponding conventions.

■ DIFFERENTIABILITY AND CONTINUITY

Recall that we want a function to be continuous at every point at which it is differentiable. The next result shows this to be the case.

13.4.3   THEOREM   *If a function is differentiable at a point, then it is continuous at that point.*

PROOF   We will give the proof for $f(x, y)$, a function of two variables, since that will reveal the essential ideas. Assume that f is differentiable at (x_0, y_0). To prove that f is continuous at (x_0, y_0) we must show that

$$\lim_{(x,y) \to (x_0,y_0)} f(x, y) = f(x_0, y_0)$$

which, on letting $x = x_0 + \Delta x$ and $y = y_0 + \Delta y$, is equivalent to

$$\lim_{(\Delta x, \Delta y) \to (0,0)} f(x_0 + \Delta x, y_0 + \Delta y) = f(x_0, y_0)$$

By Equation (2) this is equivalent to

$$\lim_{(\Delta x, \Delta y) \to (0,0)} \Delta f = 0$$

However, from Equation (5)

$$\lim_{(\Delta x, \Delta y) \to (0,0)} \Delta f = \lim_{(\Delta x, \Delta y) \to (0,0)} \left[f_x(x_0, y_0)\Delta x + f_y(x_0, y_0)\Delta y \right.$$
$$\left. + \epsilon(\Delta x, \Delta y)\sqrt{(\Delta x)^2 + (\Delta y)^2} \right]$$
$$= 0 + 0 + 0 \cdot 0 = 0 \quad ■$$

> The converse of Theorem 13.4.3 is false. For example, the function
> $$f(x, y) = \sqrt{x^2 + y^2}$$
> is continuous at $(0, 0)$ but is not differentiable at $(0, 0)$. Why not?

It can be difficult to verify that a function is differentiable at a point directly from the definition. The next theorem, whose proof is usually studied in more advanced courses, provides simple conditions for a function to be differentiable at a point.

13.4.4   THEOREM   *If all first-order partial derivatives of f exist and are continuous at a point, then f is differentiable at that point.*

For example, consider the function

$$f(x, y, z) = x + yz$$

Since $f_x(x, y, z) = 1$, $f_y(x, y, z) = z$, and $f_z(x, y, z) = y$ are defined and continuous everywhere, we conclude from Theorem 13.4.4 that f is differentiable everywhere.

■ DIFFERENTIALS

As with the one-variable case, the approximations

$$\Delta f \approx f_x(x_0, y_0)\Delta x + f_y(x_0, y_0)\Delta y$$

for a function of two variables and the approximation

$$\Delta f \approx f_x(x_0, y_0, z_0)\Delta x + f_y(x_0, y_0, z_0)\Delta y + f_z(x_0, y_0, z_0)\Delta z \tag{7}$$

for a function of three variables have a convenient formulation in the language of differentials. If $z = f(x, y)$ is differentiable at a point (x_0, y_0), we let

$$dz = f_x(x_0, y_0)\,dx + f_y(x_0, y_0)\,dy \tag{8}$$

denote a new function with dependent variable dz and independent variables dx and dy. We refer to this function (also denoted df) as the **total differential of z** at (x_0, y_0) or as the **total differential of f** at (x_0, y_0). Similarly, for a function $w = f(x, y, z)$ of three variables we have the **total differential of w** at (x_0, y_0, z_0),

$$dw = f_x(x_0, y_0, z_0)\,dx + f_y(x_0, y_0, z_0)\,dy + f_z(x_0, y_0, z_0)\,dz \tag{9}$$

which is also referred to as the **total differential of f** at (x_0, y_0, z_0). It is common practice to omit the subscripts and write Equations (8) and (9) as

$$dz = f_x(x, y)\,dx + f_y(x, y)\,dy \tag{10}$$

and

$$dw = f_x(x, y, z)\,dx + f_y(x, y, z)\,dy + f_z(x, y, z)\,dz \tag{11}$$

In the two-variable case, the approximation

$$\Delta f \approx f_x(x_0, y_0)\Delta x + f_y(x_0, y_0)\Delta y$$

can be written in the form

$$\Delta f \approx df \tag{12}$$

for $dx = \Delta x$ and $dy = \Delta y$. Equivalently, we can write approximation (12) as

$$\Delta z \approx dz \tag{13}$$

In other words, we can estimate the change Δz in z by the value of the differential dz where dx is the change in x and dy is the change in y. Furthermore, it follows from (4) that if Δx and Δy are close to 0, then the magnitude of the error in approximation (13) will be much smaller than the distance $\sqrt{(\Delta x)^2 + (\Delta y)^2}$ between (x_0, y_0) and $(x_0 + \Delta x, y_0 + \Delta y)$.

▶ **Example 2** Use (13) to approximate the change in $z = xy^2$ from its value at $(0.5, 1.0)$ to its value at $(0.503, 1.004)$. Compare the magnitude of the error in this approximation with the distance between the points $(0.5, 1.0)$ and $(0.503, 1.004)$.

Solution. For $z = xy^2$ we have $dz = y^2\,dx + 2xy\,dy$. Evaluating this differential at $(x, y) = (0.5, 1.0), dx = \Delta x = 0.503 - 0.5 = 0.003$, and $dy = \Delta y = 1.004 - 1.0 = 0.004$ yields

$$dz = 1.0^2(0.003) + 2(0.5)(1.0)(0.004) = 0.007$$

Since $z = 0.5$ at $(x, y) = (0.5, 1.0)$ and $z = 0.507032048$ at $(x, y) = (0.503, 1.004)$, we have

$$\Delta z = 0.507032048 - 0.5 = 0.007032048$$

and the error in approximating Δz by dz has magnitude

$$|dz - \Delta z| = |0.007 - 0.007032048| = 0.000032048$$

Since the distance between $(0.5, 1.0)$ and $(0.503, 1.004) = (0.5 + \Delta x, 1.0 + \Delta y)$ is

$$\sqrt{(\Delta x)^2 + (\Delta y)^2} = \sqrt{(0.003)^2 + (0.004)^2} = \sqrt{0.000025} = 0.005$$

we have

$$\frac{|dz - \Delta z|}{\sqrt{(\Delta x)^2 + (\Delta y)^2}} = \frac{0.000032048}{0.005} = 0.0064096 < \frac{1}{150}$$

Thus, the magnitude of the error in our approximation is less than $\frac{1}{150}$ of the distance between the two points. ◄

With the appropriate changes in notation, the preceding analysis can be extended to functions of three or more variables.

▶ **Example 3**   The length, width, and height of a rectangular box are measured with an error of at most 5%. Use a total differential to estimate the maximum percentage error that results if these quantities are used to calculate the diagonal of the box.

Solution.   The diagonal D of a box with length x, width y, and height z is given by

$$D = \sqrt{x^2 + y^2 + z^2}$$

Let x_0, y_0, z_0, and $D_0 = \sqrt{x_0^2 + y_0^2 + z_0^2}$ denote the actual values of the length, width, height, and diagonal of the box. The total differential dD of D at (x_0, y_0, z_0) is given by

$$dD = \frac{x_0}{\sqrt{x_0^2 + y_0^2 + z_0^2}}\, dx + \frac{y_0}{\sqrt{x_0^2 + y_0^2 + z_0^2}}\, dy + \frac{z_0}{\sqrt{x_0^2 + y_0^2 + z_0^2}}\, dz$$

If x, y, z, and $D = \sqrt{x^2 + y^2 + z^2}$ are the measured and computed values of the length, width, height, and diagonal, respectively, then

$$\Delta x = x - x_0, \quad \Delta y = y - y_0, \quad \Delta z = z - z_0$$

and

$$\left|\frac{\Delta x}{x_0}\right| \le 0.05, \quad \left|\frac{\Delta y}{y_0}\right| \le 0.05, \quad \left|\frac{\Delta z}{z_0}\right| \le 0.05$$

We are seeking an estimate for the maximum size of $\Delta D / D_0$. With the aid of Equation (11) we have

$$\frac{\Delta D}{D_0} \approx \frac{dD}{D_0} = \frac{1}{x_0^2 + y_0^2 + z_0^2}[x_0\Delta x + y_0\Delta y + z_0\Delta z]$$

$$= \frac{1}{x_0^2 + y_0^2 + z_0^2}\left[x_0^2\frac{\Delta x}{x_0} + y_0^2\frac{\Delta y}{y_0} + z_0^2\frac{\Delta z}{z_0}\right]$$

Since

$$\left|\frac{dD}{D_0}\right| = \frac{1}{x_0^2 + y_0^2 + z_0^2}\left|x_0^2\frac{\Delta x}{x_0} + y_0^2\frac{\Delta y}{y_0} + z_0^2\frac{\Delta z}{z_0}\right|$$

$$\le \frac{1}{x_0^2 + y_0^2 + z_0^2}\left(x_0^2\left|\frac{\Delta x}{x_0}\right| + y_0^2\left|\frac{\Delta y}{y_0}\right| + z_0^2\left|\frac{\Delta z}{z_0}\right|\right)$$

$$\le \frac{1}{x_0^2 + y_0^2 + z_0^2}\left(x_0^2(0.05) + y_0^2(0.05) + z_0^2(0.05)\right) = 0.05$$

we estimate the maximum percentage error in D to be 5%. ◄

■ **LOCAL LINEAR APPROXIMATIONS**

We now show that if a function f is differentiable at a point, then it can be very closely approximated by a linear function near that point. For example, suppose that $f(x, y)$ is differentiable at the point (x_0, y_0). Then approximation (3) can be written in the form

$$f(x_0 + \Delta x, y_0 + \Delta y) \approx f(x_0, y_0) + f_x(x_0, y_0)\Delta x + f_y(x_0, y_0)\Delta y$$

If we let $x = x_0 + \Delta x$ and $y = x_0 + \Delta y$, this approximation becomes

$$f(x, y) \approx f(x_0, y_0) + f_x(x_0, y_0)(x - x_0) + f_y(x_0, y_0)(y - y_0) \tag{14}$$

> Show that if $f(x, y)$ is a linear function, then (14) becomes an equality.

which yields a linear approximation of $f(x, y)$. Since the error in this approximation is equal to the error in approximation (3), we conclude that for (x, y) close to (x_0, y_0), the error in (14) will be much smaller than the distance between these two points. When $f(x, y)$ is differentiable at (x_0, y_0) we get

> Explain why the error in approximation (14) is the same as the error in approximation (3).

$$L(x, y) = f(x_0, y_0) + f_x(x_0, y_0)(x - x_0) + f_y(x_0, y_0)(y - y_0) \tag{15}$$

and refer to $L(x, y)$ as the ***local linear approximation to f at*** (x_0, y_0).

▶ **Example 4** Let $L(x, y)$ denote the local linear approximation to $f(x, y) = \sqrt{x^2 + y^2}$ at the point $(3, 4)$. Compare the error in approximating

$$f(3.04, 3.98) = \sqrt{(3.04)^2 + (3.98)^2}$$

by $L(3.04, 3.98)$ with the distance between the points $(3, 4)$ and $(3.04, 3.98)$.

Solution. We have

$$f_x(x, y) = \frac{x}{\sqrt{x^2 + y^2}} \quad \text{and} \quad f_y(x, y) = \frac{y}{\sqrt{x^2 + y^2}}$$

with $f_x(3, 4) = \frac{3}{5}$ and $f_y(3, 4) = \frac{4}{5}$. Therefore, the local linear approximation to f at $(3, 4)$ is given by

$$L(x, y) = 5 + \tfrac{3}{5}(x - 3) + \tfrac{4}{5}(y - 4)$$

Consequently,

$$f(3.04, 3.98) \approx L(3.04, 3.98) = 5 + \tfrac{3}{5}(0.04) + \tfrac{4}{5}(-0.02) = 5.008$$

Since

$$f(3.04, 3.98) = \sqrt{(3.04)^2 + (3.98)^2} \approx 5.00819$$

the error in the approximation is about $5.00819 - 5.008 = 0.00019$. This is less than $\frac{1}{200}$ of the distance

$$\sqrt{(3.04 - 3)^2 + (3.98 - 4)^2} \approx 0.045$$

between the points $(3, 4)$ and $(3.04, 3.98)$. ◀

For a function $f(x, y, z)$ that is differentiable at (x_0, y_0, z_0), the local linear approximation is

$$\begin{aligned} L(x, y, z) = {}& f(x_0, y_0, z_0) + f_x(x_0, y_0, z_0)(x - x_0) \\ &+ f_y(x_0, y_0, z_0)(y - y_0) + f_z(x_0, y_0, z_0)(z - z_0) \end{aligned} \tag{16}$$

We have formulated our definitions in this section in such a way that continuity and local linearity are consequences of differentiability. In Section 13.7 we will show that if a function $f(x, y)$ is differentiable at a point (x_0, y_0), then the graph of $L(x, y)$ is a nonvertical tangent plane to the graph of f at the point $(x_0, y_0, f(x_0, y_0))$.

✔ **QUICK CHECK EXERCISES 13.4**   *(See page 949 for answers.)*

1. Assume that $f(x, y)$ is differentiable at (x_0, y_0) and let Δf denote the change in f from its value at (x_0, y_0) to its value at $(x_0 + \Delta x, y_0 + \Delta y)$.
   (a) $\Delta f \approx$ _____
   (b) The limit that guarantees the error in the approximation in part (a) is very small when both Δx and Δy are close to 0 is _____.

2. Compute the differential of each function.
   (a) $z = xe^{y^2}$ (b) $w = x\sin(yz)$

3. If f is differentiable at (x_0, y_0), then the local linear approximation to f at (x_0, y_0) is $L(x) =$ _____.

4. Assume that $f(1, -2) = 4$ and $f(x, y)$ is differentiable at $(1, -2)$ with $f_x(1, -2) = 2$ and $f_y(1, -2) = -3$. Estimate the value of $f(0.9, -1.950)$.

EXERCISE SET 13.4

FOCUS ON CONCEPTS

1. Suppose that a function $f(x, y)$ is differentiable at the point $(3, 4)$ with $f_x(3, 4) = 2$ and $f_y(3, 4) = -1$. If $f(3, 4) = 5$, estimate the value of $f(3.01, 3.98)$.

2. Suppose that a function $f(x, y)$ is differentiable at the point $(-1, 2)$ with $f_x(-1, 2) = 1$ and $f_y(-1, 2) = 3$. If $f(-1, 2) = 2$, estimate the value of $f(-0.99, 2.02)$.

3. Suppose that a function $f(x, y, z)$ is differentiable at the point $(1, 2, 3)$ with $f_x(1, 2, 3) = 1$, $f_y(1, 2, 3) = 2$, and $f_z(1, 2, 3) = 3$. If $f(1, 2, 3) = 4$, estimate the value of $f(1.01, 2.02, 3.03)$.

4. Suppose that a function $f(x, y, z)$ is differentiable at the point $(2, 1, -2)$, $f_x(2, 1, -2) = -1$, $f_y(2, 1, -2) = 1$, and $f_z(2, 1, -2) = -2$. If $f(2, 1, -2) = 0$, estimate the value of $f(1.98, 0.99, -1.97)$.

5. Use Definitions 13.4.1 and 13.4.2 to prove that a constant function of two or three variables is differentiable everywhere.

6. Use Definitions 13.4.1 and 13.4.2 to prove that a linear function of two or three variables is differentiable everywhere.

7. Use Definition 13.4.2 to prove that
   $$f(x, y, z) = x^2 + y^2 + z^2$$
   is differentiable at $(0, 0, 0)$.

8. Use Definition 13.4.2 to determine all values of r such that $f(x, y, z) = (x^2 + y^2 + z^2)^r$ is differentiable at $(0, 0, 0)$.

9–20 Compute the differential dz or dw of the function. ■

9. $z = 7x - 2y$ 10. $z = e^{xy}$ 11. $z = x^3 y^2$
12. $z = 5x^2 y^5 - 2x + 4y + 7$
13. $z = \tan^{-1} xy$ 14. $z = \sec^2(x - 3y)$

15. $w = 8x - 3y + 4z$ 16. $w = e^{xyz}$
17. $w = x^3 y^2 z$
18. $w = 4x^2 y^3 z^7 - 3xy + z + 5$
19. $w = \tan^{-1}(xyz)$ 20. $w = \sqrt{x} + \sqrt{y} + \sqrt{z}$

21–26 Use a total differential to approximate the change in the values of f from P to Q. Compare your estimate with the actual change in f. ■

21. $f(x, y) = x^2 + 2xy - 4x$; $P(1, 2)$, $Q(1.01, 2.04)$
22. $f(x, y) = x^{1/3} y^{1/2}$; $P(8, 9)$, $Q(7.78, 9.03)$
23. $f(x, y) = \dfrac{x + y}{xy}$; $P(-1, -2)$, $Q(-1.02, -2.04)$
24. $f(x, y) = \ln\sqrt{1 + xy}$; $P(0, 2)$, $Q(-0.09, 1.98)$
25. $f(x, y, z) = 2xy^2 z^3$; $P(1, -1, 2)$, $Q(0.99, -1.02, 2.02)$
26. $f(x, y, z) = \dfrac{xyz}{x + y + z}$; $P(-1, -2, 4)$,
    $Q(-1.04, -1.98, 3.97)$

27–30 True–False Determine whether the statement is true or false. Explain your answer. ■

27. By definition, a function $f(x, y)$ is differentiable at (x_0, y_0) provided both $f_x(x_0, y_0)$ and $f_y(x_0, y_0)$ are defined.

28. For any point (x_0, y_0) in the domain of a function $f(x, y)$, we have
    $$\lim_{(\Delta x, \Delta y) \to (0,0)} \Delta f = 0$$
    where
    $$\Delta f = f(x_0 + \Delta x, y_0 + \Delta y) - f(x_0, y_0)$$

29. If f_x and f_y are both continuous at (x_0, y_0), then so is f.

30. The graph of a local linear approximation to a function $f(x, y)$ is a plane.

31. In the accompanying figure a rectangle with initial length x_0 and initial width y_0 has been enlarged, resulting in a rectangle with length $x_0 + \Delta x$ and width $y_0 + \Delta y$. What portion of the figure represents the increase in the area of the rectangle? What portion of the figure represents an approximation of the increase in area by a total differential?

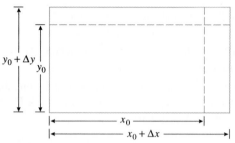

▲ **Figure Ex-31**

32. The volume V of a right circular cone of radius r and height h is given by $V = \frac{1}{3}\pi r^2 h$. Suppose that the height decreases from 20 in to 19.95 in and the radius increases from 4 in to 4.05 in. Compare the change in volume of the cone with an approximation of this change using a total differential.

33–40 (a) Find the local linear approximation L to the specified function f at the designated point P. (b) Compare the error in approximating f by L at the specified point Q with the distance between P and Q. ■

33. $f(x, y) = \dfrac{1}{\sqrt{x^2 + y^2}}$; $P(4, 3)$, $Q(3.92, 3.01)$

34. $f(x, y) = x^{0.5} y^{0.3}$; $P(1, 1)$, $Q(1.05, 0.97)$

35. $f(x, y) = x \sin y$; $P(0, 0)$, $Q(0.003, 0.004)$

36. $f(x, y) = \ln xy$; $P(1, 2)$, $Q(1.01, 2.02)$

37. $f(x, y, z) = xyz$; $P(1, 2, 3)$, $Q(1.001, 2.002, 3.003)$

38. $f(x, y, z) = \dfrac{x + y}{y + z}$; $P(-1, 1, 1)$, $Q(-0.99, 0.99, 1.01)$

39. $f(x, y, z) = xe^{yz}$; $P(1, -1, -1)$, $Q(0.99, -1.01, -0.99)$

40. $f(x, y, z) = \ln(x + yz)$; $P(2, 1, -1)$, $Q(2.02, 0.97, -1.01)$

41. In each part, confirm that the stated formula is the local linear approximation at $(0, 0)$.

(a) $e^x \sin y \approx y$ (b) $\dfrac{2x + 1}{y + 1} \approx 1 + 2x - y$

42. Show that the local linear approximation of the function $f(x, y) = x^\alpha y^\beta$ at $(1, 1)$ is
$$x^\alpha y^\beta \approx 1 + \alpha(x - 1) + \beta(y - 1)$$

43. In each part, confirm that the stated formula is the local linear approximation at $(1, 1, 1)$.

(a) $xyz + 2 \approx x + y + z$ (b) $\dfrac{4x}{y + z} \approx 2x - y - z + 2$

44. Based on Exercise 42, what would you conjecture is the local linear approximation to $x^\alpha y^\beta z^\gamma$ at $(1, 1, 1)$? Verify your conjecture by finding this local linear approximation.

45. Suppose that a function $f(x, y)$ is differentiable at the point $(1, 1)$ with $f_x(1, 1) = 2$ and $f(1, 1) = 3$. Let $L(x, y)$ denote the local linear approximation of f at $(1, 1)$. If $L(1.1, 0.9) = 3.15$, find the value of $f_y(1, 1)$.

46. Suppose that a function $f(x, y)$ is differentiable at the point $(0, -1)$ with $f_y(0, -1) = -2$ and $f(0, -1) = 3$. Let $L(x, y)$ denote the local linear approximation of f at $(0, -1)$. If $L(0.1, -1.1) = 3.3$, find the value of $f_x(0, -1)$.

47. Suppose that a function $f(x, y, z)$ is differentiable at the point $(3, 2, 1)$ and $L(x, y, z) = x - y + 2z - 2$ is the local linear approximation to f at $(3, 2, 1)$. Find $f(3, 2, 1)$, $f_x(3, 2, 1)$, $f_y(3, 2, 1)$, and $f_z(3, 2, 1)$.

48. Suppose that a function $f(x, y, z)$ is differentiable at the point $(0, -1, -2)$ and $L(x, y, z) = x + 2y + 3z + 4$ is the local linear approximation to f at $(0, -1, -2)$. Find $f(0, -1, -2)$, $f_x(0, -1, -2)$, $f_y(0, -1, -2)$, and $f_z(0, -1, -2)$.

49–52 A function f is given along with a local linear approximation L to f at a point P. Use the information given to determine point P. ■

49. $f(x, y) = x^2 + y^2$; $L(x, y) = 2y - 2x - 2$

50. $f(x, y) = x^2 y$; $L(x, y) = 4y - 4x + 8$

51. $f(x, y, z) = xy + z^2$; $L(x, y, z) = y + 2z - 1$

52. $f(x, y, z) = xyz$; $L(x, y, z) = x - y - z - 2$

53. The length and width of a rectangle are measured with errors of at most 3% and 5%, respectively. Use differentials to approximate the maximum percentage error in the calculated area.

54. The radius and height of a right circular cone are measured with errors of at most 1% and 4%, respectively. Use differentials to approximate the maximum percentage error in the calculated volume.

55. The length and width of a rectangle are measured with errors of at most $r\%$, where r is small. Use differentials to approximate the maximum percentage error in the calculated length of the diagonal.

56. The legs of a right triangle are measured to be 3 cm and 4 cm, with a maximum error of 0.05 cm in each measurement. Use differentials to approximate the maximum possible error in the calculated value of (a) the hypotenuse and (b) the area of the triangle.

57. The period T of a simple pendulum with small oscillations is calculated from the formula $T = 2\pi\sqrt{L/g}$, where L is the length of the pendulum and g is the acceleration due to gravity. Suppose that measured values of L and g have errors of at most 0.5% and 0.1%, respectively. Use differentials to approximate the maximum percentage error in the calculated value of T.

58. According to the ideal gas law, the pressure, temperature, and volume of a confined gas are related by $P = kT/V$, where k is a constant. Use differentials to approximate the percentage change in pressure if the temperature of a gas is increased 3% and the volume is increased 5%.

59. Suppose that certain measured quantities x and y have errors of at most $r\%$ and $s\%$, respectively. For each of the following formulas in x and y, use differentials to approximate the maximum possible error in the calculated result.
(a) xy (b) x/y (c) $x^2 y^3$ (d) $x^3 \sqrt{y}$

60. The total resistance R of three resistances R_1, R_2, and R_3, connected in parallel, is given by
$$\frac{1}{R} = \frac{1}{R_1} + \frac{1}{R_2} + \frac{1}{R_3}$$
Suppose that R_1, R_2, and R_3 are measured to be 100 ohms, 200 ohms, and 500 ohms, respectively, with a maximum error of 10% in each. Use differentials to approximate the maximum percentage error in the calculated value of R.

61. The area of a triangle is to be computed from the formula $A = \frac{1}{2}ab\sin\theta$, where a and b are the lengths of two sides and θ is the included angle. Suppose that a, b, and θ are measured to be 40 ft, 50 ft, and 30°, respectively. Use differentials to approximate the maximum error in the calculated value of A if the maximum errors in a, b, and θ are $\frac{1}{2}$ ft, $\frac{1}{4}$ ft, and 2°, respectively.

62. The length, width, and height of a rectangular box are measured with errors of at most $r\%$ (where r is small). Use differentials to approximate the maximum percentage error in the computed value of the volume.

63. Use Theorem 13.4.4 to prove that $f(x, y) = x^2 \sin y$ is differentiable everywhere.

64. Use Theorem 13.4.4 to prove that $f(x, y, z) = xy\sin z$ is differentiable everywhere.

65. Suppose that $f(x, y)$ is differentiable at the point (x_0, y_0) and let $z_0 = f(x_0, y_0)$. Prove that $g(x, y, z) = z - f(x, y)$ is differentiable at (x_0, y_0, z_0).

66. Suppose that Δf satisfies an equation in the form of (5), where $\epsilon(\Delta x, \Delta y)$ is continuous at $(\Delta x, \Delta y) = (0, 0)$ with $\epsilon(0, 0) = 0$. Prove that f is differentiable at (x_0, y_0).

67. Writing Discuss the similarities and differences between the definition of "differentiability" for a function of a single variable and the definition of "differentiability" for a function of two variables.

68. Writing Discuss the use of differentials in the approximation of increments and in the estimation of errors.

QUICK CHECK ANSWERS 13.4

1. (a) $f_x(x_0, y_0)\Delta x + f_y(x_0, y_0)\Delta y$ (b) $\lim_{(\Delta x, \Delta y) \to (0,0)} \dfrac{\Delta f - f_x(x_0, y_0)\Delta x - f_y(x_0, y_0)\Delta y}{\sqrt{(\Delta x)^2 + (\Delta y)^2}} = 0$ **2.** (a) $dz = e^{y^2}dx + 2xye^{y^2}dy$
(b) $dw = \sin(yz)\,dx + xz\cos(yz)\,dy + xy\cos(yz)\,dz$ **3.** $f(x_0, y_0) + f_x(x_0, y_0)(x - x_0) + f_y(x_0, y_0)(y - y_0)$ **4.** 3.65

13.5 THE CHAIN RULE

In this section we will derive versions of the chain rule for functions of two or three variables. These new versions will allow us to generate useful relationships among the derivatives and partial derivatives of various functions.

CHAIN RULES FOR DERIVATIVES

If y is a differentiable function of x and x is a differentiable function of t, then the chain rule for functions of one variable states that, under composition, y becomes a differentiable function of t with
$$\frac{dy}{dt} = \frac{dy}{dx}\frac{dx}{dt}$$

We will now derive a version of the chain rule for functions of two variables.

Assume that $z = f(x, y)$ is a function of x and y, and suppose that x and y are in turn functions of a single variable t, say
$$x = x(t), \quad y = y(t)$$

The composition $z = f(x(t), y(t))$ then expresses z as a function of the single variable t. Thus, we can ask for the derivative dz/dt and we can inquire about its relationship to the derivatives $\partial z/\partial x$, $\partial z/\partial y$, dx/dt, and dy/dt. Letting Δx, Δy, and Δz denote the changes in x, y, and z, respectively, that correspond to a change of Δt in t, we have

$$\frac{dz}{dt} = \lim_{\Delta t \to 0} \frac{\Delta z}{\Delta t}, \quad \frac{dx}{dt} = \lim_{\Delta t \to 0} \frac{\Delta x}{\Delta t}, \quad \text{and} \quad \frac{dy}{dt} = \lim_{\Delta t \to 0} \frac{\Delta y}{\Delta t}$$

It follows from (3) of Section 13.4 that

$$\Delta z \approx \frac{\partial z}{\partial x} \Delta x + \frac{\partial z}{\partial y} \Delta y \tag{1}$$

where the partial derivatives are evaluated at $(x(t), y(t))$. Dividing both sides of (1) by Δt yields

$$\frac{\Delta z}{\Delta t} \approx \frac{\partial z}{\partial x} \frac{\Delta x}{\Delta t} + \frac{\partial z}{\partial y} \frac{\Delta y}{\Delta t} \tag{2}$$

Similarly, we can produce the analog of (2) for functions of three variables as follows: assume that $w = f(x, y, z)$ is a function of x, y, and z, and suppose that x, y, and z are functions of a single variable t. As above we define Δw, Δx, Δy, and Δz to be the changes in w, x, y, and z that correspond to a change of Δt in t. Then (7) in Section 13.4 implies that

$$\Delta w \approx \frac{\partial w}{\partial x} \Delta x + \frac{\partial w}{\partial y} \Delta y + \frac{\partial w}{\partial z} \Delta z \tag{3}$$

and dividing both sides of (3) by Δt yields

$$\frac{\Delta w}{\Delta t} \approx \frac{\partial w}{\partial x} \frac{\Delta x}{\Delta t} + \frac{\partial w}{\partial y} \frac{\Delta y}{\Delta t} + \frac{\partial w}{\partial z} \frac{\Delta z}{\Delta t} \tag{4}$$

Taking the limit as $\Delta t \to 0$ of both sides of (2) and (4) suggests the following results. (A complete proof of the two-variable case can be found in Web Appendix D.)

13.5.1 THEOREM (*Chain Rules for Derivatives*) *If $x = x(t)$ and $y = y(t)$ are differentiable at t, and if $z = f(x, y)$ is differentiable at the point $(x, y) = (x(t), y(t))$, then $z = f(x(t), y(t))$ is differentiable at t and*

$$\frac{dz}{dt} = \frac{\partial z}{\partial x} \frac{dx}{dt} + \frac{\partial z}{\partial y} \frac{dy}{dt} \tag{5}$$

where the ordinary derivatives are evaluated at t and the partial derivatives are evaluated at (x, y).

If each of the functions $x = x(t)$, $y = y(t)$, and $z = z(t)$ is differentiable at t, and if $w = f(x, y, z)$ is differentiable at the point $(x, y, z) = (x(t), y(t), z(t))$, then the function $w = f(x(t), y(t), z(t))$ is differentiable at t and

$$\frac{dw}{dt} = \frac{\partial w}{\partial x} \frac{dx}{dt} + \frac{\partial w}{\partial y} \frac{dy}{dt} + \frac{\partial w}{\partial z} \frac{dz}{dt} \tag{6}$$

where the ordinary derivatives are evaluated at t and the partial derivatives are evaluated at (x, y, z).

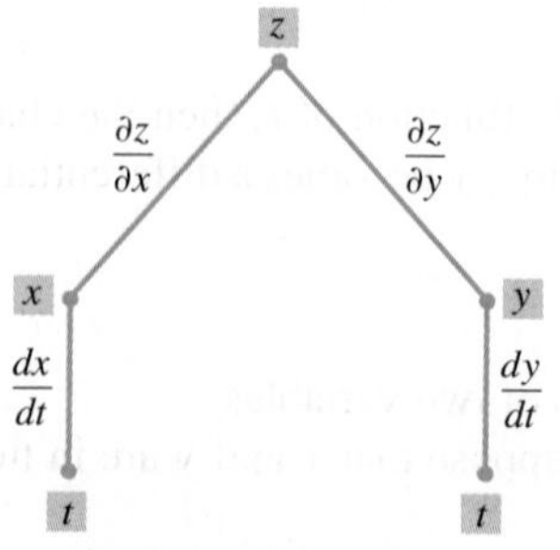

$$\frac{dz}{dt} = \frac{\partial z}{\partial x} \frac{dx}{dt} + \frac{\partial z}{\partial y} \frac{dy}{dt}$$

▲ **Figure 13.5.1**

Formula (5) can be represented schematically by a "tree diagram" that is constructed as follows (Figure 13.5.1). Starting with z at the top of the tree and moving downward, join each variable by lines (or branches) to those variables on which it depends *directly*. Thus, z is joined to x and y and these in turn are joined to t. Next, label each branch with a derivative whose "numerator" contains the variable at the top end of that branch and whose "denominator" contains the variable at the bottom end of that branch. This completes the "tree." To find the formula for dz/dt, follow the two paths through the tree that start with z and end with t. Each such path corresponds to a term in Formula (5).

> Create a tree diagram for Formula (6).

▶ **Example 1** Suppose that

$$z = x^2 y, \quad x = t^2, \quad y = t^3$$

Use the chain rule to find dz/dt, and check the result by expressing z as a function of t and differentiating directly.

Solution. By the chain rule [Formula (5)],

$$\frac{dz}{dt} = \frac{\partial z}{\partial x}\frac{dx}{dt} + \frac{\partial z}{\partial y}\frac{dy}{dt} = (2xy)(2t) + (x^2)(3t^2)$$

$$= (2t^5)(2t) + (t^4)(3t^2) = 7t^6$$

Alternatively, we can express z directly as a function of t,

$$z = x^2 y = (t^2)^2 (t^3) = t^7$$

and then differentiate to obtain $dz/dt = 7t^6$. However, this procedure may not always be convenient. ◀

▶ **Example 2** Suppose that

$$w = \sqrt{x^2 + y^2 + z^2}, \quad x = \cos\theta, \quad y = \sin\theta, \quad z = \tan\theta$$

Use the chain rule to find $dw/d\theta$ when $\theta = \pi/4$.

Solution. From Formula (6) with θ in the place of t, we obtain

$$\frac{dw}{d\theta} = \frac{\partial w}{\partial x}\frac{dx}{d\theta} + \frac{\partial w}{\partial y}\frac{dy}{d\theta} + \frac{\partial w}{\partial z}\frac{dz}{d\theta}$$

$$= \frac{1}{2}(x^2 + y^2 + z^2)^{-1/2}(2x)(-\sin\theta) + \frac{1}{2}(x^2 + y^2 + z^2)^{-1/2}(2y)(\cos\theta)$$

$$+ \frac{1}{2}(x^2 + y^2 + z^2)^{-1/2}(2z)(\sec^2\theta)$$

When $\theta = \pi/4$, we have

$$x = \cos\frac{\pi}{4} = \frac{1}{\sqrt{2}}, \quad y = \sin\frac{\pi}{4} = \frac{1}{\sqrt{2}}, \quad z = \tan\frac{\pi}{4} = 1$$

Substituting $x = 1/\sqrt{2}$, $y = 1/\sqrt{2}$, $z = 1$, $\theta = \pi/4$ in the formula for $dw/d\theta$ yields

> Confirm the result of Example 2 by expressing w directly as a function of θ.

$$\frac{dw}{d\theta}\bigg|_{\theta=\pi/4} = \frac{1}{2}\left(\frac{1}{\sqrt{2}}\right)(\sqrt{2})\left(-\frac{1}{\sqrt{2}}\right) + \frac{1}{2}\left(\frac{1}{\sqrt{2}}\right)(\sqrt{2})\left(\frac{1}{\sqrt{2}}\right) + \frac{1}{2}\left(\frac{1}{\sqrt{2}}\right)(2)(2)$$

$$= \sqrt{2} \quad ◀$$

REMARK   There are many variations in derivative notations, each of which gives the chain rule a different look. If $z = f(x, y)$, where x and y are functions of t, then some possibilities are

$$\frac{dz}{dt} = f_x \frac{dx}{dt} + f_y \frac{dy}{dt}$$

$$\frac{df}{dt} = \frac{\partial f}{\partial x} \frac{dx}{dt} + \frac{\partial f}{\partial y} \frac{dy}{dt}$$

$$\frac{df}{dt} = f_x x'(t) + f_y y'(t)$$

■ CHAIN RULES FOR PARTIAL DERIVATIVES

In Formula (5) the variables x and y are each functions of a single variable t. We now consider the case where x and y are each functions of two variables. Let $z = f(x, y)$ and suppose that x and y are functions of u and v, say

$$x = x(u, v), \quad y = y(u, v)$$

The composition $z = f(x(u, v), y(u, v))$ expresses z as a function of the two variables u and v. Thus, we can ask for the partial derivatives $\partial z/\partial u$ and $\partial z/\partial v$; and we can inquire about the relationship between these derivatives and the derivatives $\partial z/\partial x$, $\partial z/\partial y$, $\partial x/\partial u$, $\partial x/\partial v$, $\partial y/\partial u$, and $\partial y/\partial v$.

Similarly, if $w = f(x, y, z)$ and x, y, and z are each functions of u and v, then the composition $w = f(x(u, v), y(u, v), z(u, v))$ expresses w as a function of u and v. Thus we can also ask for the derivatives $\partial w/\partial u$ and $\partial w/\partial v$; and we can investigate the relationship between these derivatives, the partial derivatives $\partial w/\partial x$, $\partial w/\partial y$, and $\partial w/\partial z$, and the partial derivatives of x, y, and z with respect to u and v.

13.5.2   THEOREM (*Chain Rules for Partial Derivatives*)   *If $x = x(u, v)$ and $y = y(u, v)$ have first-order partial derivatives at the point (u, v), and if $z = f(x, y)$ is differentiable at the point $(x, y) = (x(u, v), y(u, v))$, then $z = f(x(u, v), y(u, v))$ has first-order partial derivatives at the point (u, v) given by*

$$\frac{\partial z}{\partial u} = \frac{\partial z}{\partial x} \frac{\partial x}{\partial u} + \frac{\partial z}{\partial y} \frac{\partial y}{\partial u} \quad \text{and} \quad \frac{\partial z}{\partial v} = \frac{\partial z}{\partial x} \frac{\partial x}{\partial v} + \frac{\partial z}{\partial y} \frac{\partial y}{\partial v} \qquad (7\text{–}8)$$

If each function $x = x(u, v)$, $y = y(u, v)$, and $z = z(u, v)$ has first-order partial derivatives at the point (u, v), and if the function $w = f(x, y, z)$ is differentiable at the point $(x, y, z) = (x(u, v), y(u, v), z(u, v))$, then $w = f(x(u, v), y(u, v), z(u, v))$ has first-order partial derivatives at the point (u, v) given by

$$\frac{\partial w}{\partial u} = \frac{\partial w}{\partial x} \frac{\partial x}{\partial u} + \frac{\partial w}{\partial y} \frac{\partial y}{\partial u} + \frac{\partial w}{\partial z} \frac{\partial z}{\partial u} \quad \text{and} \quad \frac{\partial w}{\partial v} = \frac{\partial w}{\partial x} \frac{\partial x}{\partial v} + \frac{\partial w}{\partial y} \frac{\partial y}{\partial v} + \frac{\partial w}{\partial z} \frac{\partial z}{\partial v}$$

$$(9\text{–}10)$$

PROOF   We will prove Formula (7); the other formulas are derived similarly. If v is held fixed, then $x = x(u, v)$ and $y = y(u, v)$ become functions of u alone. Thus, we are back to the case of Theorem 13.5.1. If we apply that theorem with u in place of t, and if we use ∂ rather than d to indicate that the variable v is fixed, we obtain

$$\frac{\partial z}{\partial u} = \frac{\partial z}{\partial x} \frac{\partial x}{\partial u} + \frac{\partial z}{\partial y} \frac{\partial y}{\partial u} \quad \blacksquare$$

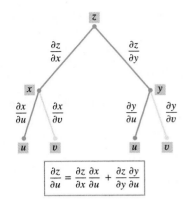

$$\frac{\partial z}{\partial u} = \frac{\partial z}{\partial x}\frac{\partial x}{\partial u} + \frac{\partial z}{\partial y}\frac{\partial y}{\partial u}$$

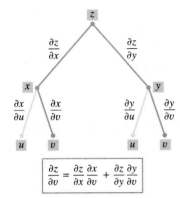

$$\frac{\partial z}{\partial v} = \frac{\partial z}{\partial x}\frac{\partial x}{\partial v} + \frac{\partial z}{\partial y}\frac{\partial y}{\partial v}$$

▲ **Figure 13.5.2**

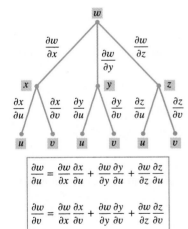

$$\frac{\partial w}{\partial u} = \frac{\partial w}{\partial x}\frac{\partial x}{\partial u} + \frac{\partial w}{\partial y}\frac{\partial y}{\partial u} + \frac{\partial w}{\partial z}\frac{\partial z}{\partial u}$$

$$\frac{\partial w}{\partial v} = \frac{\partial w}{\partial x}\frac{\partial x}{\partial v} + \frac{\partial w}{\partial y}\frac{\partial y}{\partial v} + \frac{\partial w}{\partial z}\frac{\partial z}{\partial v}$$

▲ **Figure 13.5.3**

Figures 13.5.2 and 13.5.3 show tree diagrams for the formulas in Theorem 13.5.2. As illustrated in Figure 13.5.2, the formula for $\partial z/\partial u$ can be obtained by tracing all paths through the tree that start with z and end with u, and the formula for $\partial z/\partial v$ can be obtained by tracing all paths through the tree that start with z and end with v. Figure 13.5.3 displays analogous results for $\partial w/\partial u$ and $\partial w/\partial v$.

▶ **Example 3** Given that

$$z = e^{xy}, \quad x = 2u + v, \quad y = u/v$$

find $\partial z/\partial u$ and $\partial z/\partial v$ using the chain rule.

Solution.

$$\frac{\partial z}{\partial u} = \frac{\partial z}{\partial x}\frac{\partial x}{\partial u} + \frac{\partial z}{\partial y}\frac{\partial y}{\partial u} = (ye^{xy})(2) + (xe^{xy})\left(\frac{1}{v}\right) = \left[2y + \frac{x}{v}\right]e^{xy}$$

$$= \left[\frac{2u}{v} + \frac{2u+v}{v}\right]e^{(2u+v)(u/v)} = \left[\frac{4u}{v} + 1\right]e^{(2u+v)(u/v)}$$

$$\frac{\partial z}{\partial v} = \frac{\partial z}{\partial x}\frac{\partial x}{\partial v} + \frac{\partial z}{\partial y}\frac{\partial y}{\partial v} = (ye^{xy})(1) + (xe^{xy})\left(-\frac{u}{v^2}\right)$$

$$= \left[y - x\left(\frac{u}{v^2}\right)\right]e^{xy} = \left[\frac{u}{v} - (2u+v)\left(\frac{u}{v^2}\right)\right]e^{(2u+v)(u/v)}$$

$$= -\frac{2u^2}{v^2}e^{(2u+v)(u/v)} \quad ◀$$

▶ **Example 4** Suppose that

$$w = e^{xyz}, \quad x = 3u + v, \quad y = 3u - v, \quad z = u^2v$$

Use appropriate forms of the chain rule to find $\partial w/\partial u$ and $\partial w/\partial v$.

Solution. From the tree diagram and corresponding formulas in Figure 13.5.3 we obtain

$$\frac{\partial w}{\partial u} = yze^{xyz}(3) + xze^{xyz}(3) + xye^{xyz}(2uv) = e^{xyz}(3yz + 3xz + 2xyuv)$$

and

$$\frac{\partial w}{\partial v} = yze^{xyz}(1) + xze^{xyz}(-1) + xye^{xyz}(u^2) = e^{xyz}(yz - xz + xyu^2)$$

If desired, we can express $\partial w/\partial u$ and $\partial w/\partial v$ in terms of u and v alone by replacing x, y, and z by their expressions in terms of u and v. ◀

■ **OTHER VERSIONS OF THE CHAIN RULE**

Although we will not prove it, the chain rule extends to functions $w = f(v_1, v_2, \ldots, v_n)$ of n variables. For example, if each v_i is a function of t, $i = 1, 2, \ldots, n$, the relevant formula is

$$\frac{dw}{dt} = \frac{\partial w}{\partial v_1}\frac{dv_1}{dt} + \frac{\partial w}{\partial v_2}\frac{dv_2}{dt} + \cdots + \frac{\partial w}{\partial v_n}\frac{dv_n}{dt} \tag{11}$$

Note that (11) is a natural extension of Formulas (5) and (6) in Theorem 13.5.1.

There are infinitely many variations of the chain rule, depending on the number of variables and the choice of independent and dependent variables. A good working procedure is to use tree diagrams to derive new versions of the chain rule as needed.

▶ **Example 5** Suppose that $w = x^2 + y^2 - z^2$ and

$$x = \rho \sin \phi \cos \theta, \quad y = \rho \sin \phi \sin \theta, \quad z = \rho \cos \phi$$

Use appropriate forms of the chain rule to find $\partial w / \partial \rho$ and $\partial w / \partial \theta$.

Solution. From the tree diagram and corresponding formulas in Figure 13.5.4 we obtain

$$\frac{\partial w}{\partial \rho} = 2x \sin \phi \cos \theta + 2y \sin \phi \sin \theta - 2z \cos \phi$$

$$= 2\rho \sin^2 \phi \cos^2 \theta + 2\rho \sin^2 \phi \sin^2 \theta - 2\rho \cos^2 \phi$$

$$= 2\rho \sin^2 \phi (\cos^2 \theta + \sin^2 \theta) - 2\rho \cos^2 \phi$$

$$= 2\rho (\sin^2 \phi - \cos^2 \phi)$$

$$= -2\rho \cos 2\phi$$

$$\frac{\partial w}{\partial \theta} = (2x)(-\rho \sin \phi \sin \theta) + (2y)\rho \sin \phi \cos \theta$$

$$= -2\rho^2 \sin^2 \phi \sin \theta \cos \theta + 2\rho^2 \sin^2 \phi \sin \theta \cos \theta$$

$$= 0$$

This result is explained by the fact that w does not vary with θ. You can see this directly by expressing the variables x, y, and z in terms of ρ, ϕ, and θ in the formula for w. (Verify that $w = -\rho^2 \cos 2\phi$.) ◀

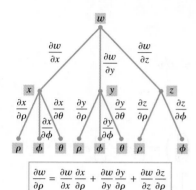

$$\frac{\partial w}{\partial \rho} = \frac{\partial w}{\partial x}\frac{\partial x}{\partial \rho} + \frac{\partial w}{\partial y}\frac{\partial y}{\partial \rho} + \frac{\partial w}{\partial z}\frac{\partial z}{\partial \rho}$$

$$\frac{\partial w}{\partial \theta} = \frac{\partial w}{\partial x}\frac{\partial x}{\partial \theta} + \frac{\partial w}{\partial y}\frac{\partial y}{\partial \theta}$$

▲ **Figure 13.5.4**

▶ **Example 6** Suppose that

$$w = xy + yz, \quad y = \sin x, \quad z = e^x$$

Use an appropriate form of the chain rule to find dw/dx.

Solution. From the tree diagram and corresponding formulas in Figure 13.5.5 we obtain

$$\frac{dw}{dx} = y + (x + z) \cos x + ye^x$$

$$= \sin x + (x + e^x) \cos x + e^x \sin x$$

This result can also be obtained by first expressing w explicitly in terms of x as

$$w = x \sin x + e^x \sin x$$

and then differentiating with respect to x; however, such direct substitution is not always possible. ◀

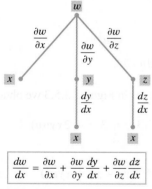

$$\frac{dw}{dx} = \frac{\partial w}{\partial x} + \frac{\partial w}{\partial y}\frac{dy}{dx} + \frac{\partial w}{\partial z}\frac{dz}{dx}$$

▲ **Figure 13.5.5**

WARNING The symbol ∂z, unlike the differential dz, has no meaning of its own. For example, if we were to "cancel" partial symbols in the chain-rule formula

$$\frac{\partial z}{\partial u} = \frac{\partial z}{\partial x}\frac{\partial x}{\partial u} + \frac{\partial z}{\partial y}\frac{\partial y}{\partial u}$$

we would obtain

$$\frac{\partial z}{\partial u} = \frac{\partial z}{\partial u} + \frac{\partial z}{\partial u}$$

which is false in cases where $\partial z / \partial u \neq 0$.

One of the principal uses of the chain rule for functions of a *single* variable was to compute formulas for the derivatives of compositions of functions. Theorems 13.5.1 and 13.5.2 are important not so much for the computation of formulas but because they allow us to express *relationships* among various derivatives. As an illustration, we revisit the topic of implicit differentiation.

■ IMPLICIT DIFFERENTIATION

Consider the special case where $z = f(x, y)$ is a function of x and y and y is a differentiable function of x. Equation (5) then becomes

$$\frac{dz}{dx} = \frac{\partial f}{\partial x}\frac{dx}{dx} + \frac{\partial f}{\partial y}\frac{dy}{dx} = \frac{\partial f}{\partial x} + \frac{\partial f}{\partial y}\frac{dy}{dx} \tag{12}$$

This result can be used to find derivatives of functions that are defined implicitly. For example, suppose that the equation

$$f(x, y) = c \tag{13}$$

defines y implicitly as a differentiable function of x and we are interested in finding dy/dx. Differentiating both sides of (13) with respect to x and applying (12) yields

$$\frac{\partial f}{\partial x} + \frac{\partial f}{\partial y}\frac{dy}{dx} = 0$$

Thus, if $\partial f/\partial y \neq 0$, we obtain

$$\frac{dy}{dx} = -\frac{\partial f/\partial x}{\partial f/\partial y}$$

In summary, we have the following result.

Show that the function $y = x$ is defined implicitly by the equation

$$x^2 - 2xy + y^2 = 0$$

but that Theorem 13.5.3 is not applicable for finding dy/dx.

> **13.5.3 THEOREM** *If the equation $f(x, y) = c$ defines y implicitly as a differentiable function of x, and if $\partial f/\partial y \neq 0$, then*
>
> $$\frac{dy}{dx} = -\frac{\partial f/\partial x}{\partial f/\partial y} \tag{14}$$

▶ **Example 7** Given that

$$x^3 + y^2x - 3 = 0$$

find dy/dx using (14), and check the result using implicit differentiation.

Solution. By (14) with $f(x, y) = x^3 + y^2x - 3$,

$$\frac{dy}{dx} = -\frac{\partial f/\partial x}{\partial f/\partial y} = -\frac{3x^2 + y^2}{2yx}$$

Alternatively, differentiating implicitly yields

$$3x^2 + y^2 + x\left(2y\frac{dy}{dx}\right) - 0 = 0 \quad \text{or} \quad \frac{dy}{dx} = -\frac{3x^2 + y^2}{2yx}$$

which agrees with the result obtained by (14). ◀

The chain rule also applies to implicit partial differentiation. Consider the case where $w = f(x, y, z)$ is a function of x, y, and z and z is a differentiable function of x and y. It follows from Theorem 13.5.2 that

$$\frac{\partial w}{\partial x} = \frac{\partial f}{\partial x} + \frac{\partial f}{\partial z}\frac{\partial z}{\partial x} \tag{15}$$

If the equation

$$f(x, y, z) = c \tag{16}$$

defines z implicitly as a differentiable function of x and y, then taking the partial derivative of each side of (16) with respect to x and applying (15) gives

$$\frac{\partial f}{\partial x} + \frac{\partial f}{\partial z}\frac{\partial z}{\partial x} = 0$$

If $\partial f/\partial z \neq 0$, then

$$\frac{\partial z}{\partial x} = -\frac{\partial f/\partial x}{\partial f/\partial z}$$

A similar result holds for $\partial z/\partial y$.

13.5.4 **THEOREM** *If the equation $f(x, y, z) = c$ defines z implicitly as a differentiable function of x and y, and if $\partial f/\partial z \neq 0$, then*

$$\frac{\partial z}{\partial x} = -\frac{\partial f/\partial x}{\partial f/\partial z} \qquad and \qquad \frac{\partial z}{\partial y} = -\frac{\partial f/\partial y}{\partial f/\partial z}$$

▶ **Example 8** Consider the sphere $x^2 + y^2 + z^2 = 1$. Find $\partial z/\partial x$ and $\partial z/\partial y$ at the point $\left(\frac{2}{3}, \frac{1}{3}, \frac{2}{3}\right)$.

Solution. By Theorem 13.5.4 with $f(x, y, z) = x^2 + y^2 + z^2$,

Note the similarity between the expression for $\partial z/\partial y$ found in Example 8 and that found in Example 7 of Section 13.3.

$$\frac{\partial z}{\partial x} = -\frac{\partial f/\partial x}{\partial f/\partial z} = -\frac{2x}{2z} = -\frac{x}{z} \quad \text{and} \quad \frac{\partial z}{\partial y} = -\frac{\partial f/\partial y}{\partial f/\partial z} = -\frac{2y}{2z} = -\frac{y}{z}$$

At the point $\left(\frac{2}{3}, \frac{1}{3}, \frac{2}{3}\right)$, evaluating these derivatives gives $\partial z/\partial x = -1$ and $\partial z/\partial y = -\frac{1}{2}$. ◀

✔ **QUICK CHECK EXERCISES 13.5** (*See page 959 for answers.*)

1. Suppose that $z = xy^2$ and x and y are differentiable functions of t with $x = 1$, $y = -1$, $dx/dt = -2$, and $dy/dt = 3$ when $t = -1$. Then $dz/dt =$ _____ when $t = -1$.

2. Suppose that C is the graph of the equation $f(x, y) = 1$ and that this equation defines y implicitly as a differentiable function of x. If the point $(2, 1)$ belongs to C with $f_x(2, 1) = 3$ and $f_y(2, 1) = -1$, then the tangent line to C at the point $(2, 1)$ has slope _____.

3. A rectangle is growing in such a way that when its length is 5 ft and its width is 2 ft, the length is increasing at a rate

of 3 ft/s and its width is increasing at a rate of 4 ft/s. At this instant the area of the rectangle is growing at a rate of _____.

4. Suppose that $z = x/y$, where x and y are differentiable functions of u and v such that $x = 3$, $y = 1$, $\partial x/\partial u = 4$, $\partial x/\partial v = -2$, $\partial y/\partial u = 1$, and $\partial y/\partial v = -1$ when $u = 2$ and $v = 1$. When $u = 2$ and $v = 1$, $\partial z/\partial u =$ _____ and $\partial z/\partial v =$ _____.

EXERCISE SET 13.5

1–6 Use an appropriate form of the chain rule to find dz/dt. ■

1. $z = 3x^2 y^3$; $x = t^4$, $y = t^2$

2. $z = \ln(2x^2 + y)$; $x = \sqrt{t}$, $y = t^{2/3}$

3. $z = 3\cos x - \sin xy$; $x = 1/t$, $y = 3t$

4. $z = \sqrt{1 + x - 2xy^4}$; $x = \ln t$, $y = t$

5. $z = e^{1-xy}$; $x = t^{1/3}$, $y = t^3$

6. $z = \cosh^2 xy$; $x = t/2$, $y = e^t$

7–10 Use an appropriate form of the chain rule to find dw/dt.

7. $w = 5x^2 y^3 z^4$; $x = t^2$, $y = t^3$, $z = t^5$

8. $w = \ln(3x^2 - 2y + 4z^3)$; $x = t^{1/2}$, $y = t^{2/3}$, $z = t^{-2}$

9. $w = 5\cos xy - \sin xz$; $x = 1/t$, $y = t$, $z = t^3$

10. $w = \sqrt{1 + x - 2yz^4 x}$; $x = \ln t$, $y = t$, $z = 4t$

FOCUS ON CONCEPTS

11. Suppose that
$$w = x^3 y^2 z^4; \quad x = t^2, \quad y = t + 2, \quad z = 2t^4$$
Find the rate of change of w with respect to t at $t = 1$ by using the chain rule, and then check your work by expressing w as a function of t and differentiating.

12. Suppose that
$$w = x \sin yz^2; \quad x = \cos t, \quad y = t^2, \quad z = e^t$$
Find the rate of change of w with respect to t at $t = 0$ by using the chain rule, and then check your work by expressing w as a function of t and differentiating.

13. Suppose that $z = f(x, y)$ is differentiable at the point $(4, 8)$ with $f_x(4, 8) = 3$ and $f_y(4, 8) = -1$. If $x = t^2$ and $y = t^3$, find dz/dt when $t = 2$.

14. Suppose that $w = f(x, y, z)$ is differentiable at the point $(1, 0, 2)$ with $f_x(1, 0, 2) = 1$, $f_y(1, 0, 2) = 2$, and $f_z(1, 0, 2) = 3$. If $x = t$, $y = \sin(\pi t)$, and $z = t^2 + 1$, find dw/dt when $t = 1$.

15. Explain how the product rule for functions of a single variable may be viewed as a consequence of the chain rule applied to a particular function of two variables.

16. A student attempts to differentiate the function x^x using the power rule, mistakenly getting $x \cdot x^{x-1}$. A second student attempts to differentiate x^x by treating it as an exponential function, mistakenly getting $(\ln x)x^x$. Use the chain rule to explain why the correct derivative is the sum of these two incorrect results.

17–22 Use appropriate forms of the chain rule to find $\partial z/\partial u$ and $\partial z/\partial v$.

17. $z = 8x^2 y - 2x + 3y$; $x = uv$, $y = u - v$

18. $z = x^2 - y \tan x$; $x = u/v$, $y = u^2 v^2$

19. $z = x/y$; $x = 2\cos u$, $y = 3\sin v$

20. $z = 3x - 2y$; $x = u + v \ln u$, $y = u^2 - v \ln v$

21. $z = e^{x^2 y}$; $x = \sqrt{uv}$, $y = 1/v$

22. $z = \cos x \sin y$; $x = u - v$, $y = u^2 + v^2$

23–30 Use appropriate forms of the chain rule to find the derivatives.

23. Let $T = x^2 y - xy^3 + 2$; $x = r\cos\theta$, $y = r\sin\theta$. Find $\partial T/\partial r$ and $\partial T/\partial\theta$.

24. Let $R = e^{2s-t^2}$; $s = 3\phi$, $t = \phi^{1/2}$. Find $dR/d\phi$.

25. Let $t = u/v$; $u = x^2 - y^2$, $v = 4xy^3$. Find $\partial t/\partial x$ and $\partial t/\partial y$.

26. Let $w = rs/(r^2 + s^2)$; $r = uv$, $s = u - 2v$. Find $\partial w/\partial u$ and $\partial w/\partial v$.

27. Let $z = \ln(x^2 + 1)$, where $x = r\cos\theta$. Find $\partial z/\partial r$ and $\partial z/\partial\theta$.

28. Let $u = rs^2 \ln t$, $r = x^2$, $s = 4y + 1$, $t = xy^3$. Find $\partial u/\partial x$ and $\partial u/\partial y$.

29. Let $w = 4x^2 + 4y^2 + z^2$, $x = \rho \sin\phi\cos\theta$, $y = \rho\sin\phi\sin\theta$, $z = \rho\cos\phi$. Find $\partial w/\partial\rho$, $\partial w/\partial\phi$, and $\partial w/\partial\theta$.

30. Let $w = 3xy^2 z^3$, $y = 3x^2 + 2$, $z = \sqrt{x - 1}$. Find dw/dx.

31. Use a chain rule to find the value of $\dfrac{dw}{ds}\bigg|_{s=1/4}$ if $w = r^2 - r\tan\theta$; $r = \sqrt{s}$, $\theta = \pi s$.

32. Use a chain rule to find the values of
$$\frac{\partial f}{\partial u}\bigg|_{u=1, v=-2} \quad \text{and} \quad \frac{\partial f}{\partial v}\bigg|_{u=1, v=-2}$$
if $f(x, y) = x^2 y^2 - x + 2y$; $x = \sqrt{u}$, $y = uv^3$.

33. Use a chain rule to find the values of
$$\frac{\partial z}{\partial r}\bigg|_{r=2, \theta=\pi/6} \quad \text{and} \quad \frac{\partial z}{\partial\theta}\bigg|_{r=2, \theta=\pi/6}$$
if $z = xye^{x/y}$; $x = r\cos\theta$, $y = r\sin\theta$.

34. Use a chain rule to find $\dfrac{dz}{dt}\bigg|_{t=3}$ if $z = x^2 y$; $x = t^2$, $y = t + 7$.

35–38 True–False Determine whether the statement is true or false. Explain your answer.

35. The symbols ∂z and ∂x are defined in such a way that the partial derivative $\partial z/\partial x$ can be interpreted as a ratio.

36. If z is a differentiable function of x_1, x_2, and x_3, and if x_i is a differentiable function of t for $i = 1, 2, 3$, then z is a differentiable function of t and
$$\frac{dz}{dt} = \sum_{i=1}^{3} \frac{\partial z}{\partial x_i} \frac{dx_i}{dt}$$

37. If z is a differentiable function of x and y, and if x and y are twice differentiable functions of t, then z is a twice differentiable function of t and
$$\frac{d^2 z}{dt^2} = \frac{\partial z}{\partial x} \frac{d^2 x}{dt^2} + \frac{\partial z}{\partial y} \frac{d^2 y}{dt^2}$$

38. If z is a differentiable function of x and y such that $z = 2$ when $x = y = 1$ and such that
$$x\frac{\partial z}{\partial x} - y\frac{\partial z}{\partial y} = 0$$
then $z = 2xy$.

39–42 Use Theorem 13.5.3 to find dy/dx and check your result using implicit differentiation. ■

39. $x^2 y^3 + \cos y = 0$

40. $x^3 - 3xy^2 + y^3 = 5$

41. $e^{xy} + ye^y = 1$

42. $x - \sqrt{xy} + 3y = 4$

43–46 Find $\partial z/\partial x$ and $\partial z/\partial y$ by implicit differentiation, and confirm that the results obtained agree with those predicted by the formulas in Theorem 13.5.4. ■

43. $x^2 - 3yz^2 + xyz - 2 = 0$

44. $\ln(1+z) + xy^2 + z = 1$

45. $ye^x - 5\sin 3z = 3z$

46. $e^{xy}\cos yz - e^{yz}\sin xz + 2 = 0$

47. (a) Suppose that $z = f(u)$ and $u = g(x, y)$. Draw a tree diagram, and use it to construct chain rules that express $\partial z/\partial x$ and $\partial z/\partial y$ in terms of dz/du, $\partial u/\partial x$, and $\partial u/\partial y$.

(b) Show that
$$\frac{\partial^2 z}{\partial x^2} = \frac{dz}{du}\frac{\partial^2 u}{\partial x^2} + \frac{d^2 z}{du^2}\left(\frac{\partial u}{\partial x}\right)^2$$
$$\frac{\partial^2 z}{\partial y^2} = \frac{dz}{du}\frac{\partial^2 u}{\partial y^2} + \frac{d^2 z}{du^2}\left(\frac{\partial u}{\partial y}\right)^2$$
$$\frac{\partial^2 z}{\partial y\partial x} = \frac{dz}{du}\frac{\partial^2 u}{\partial y\partial x} + \frac{d^2 z}{du^2}\frac{\partial u}{\partial x}\frac{\partial u}{\partial y}$$

48. (a) Let $z = f(x^2 - y^2)$. Use the result in Exercise 47(a) to show that
$$y\frac{\partial z}{\partial x} + x\frac{\partial z}{\partial y} = 0$$

(b) Let $z = f(xy)$. Use the result in Exercise 47(a) to show that
$$x\frac{\partial z}{\partial x} - y\frac{\partial z}{\partial y} = 0$$

(c) Confirm the result in part (a) in the case where $z = \sin(x^2 - y^2)$.

(d) Confirm the result in part (b) in the case where $z = e^{xy}$.

49. Let f be a differentiable function of one variable, and let $z = f(x + 2y)$. Show that
$$2\frac{\partial z}{\partial x} - \frac{\partial z}{\partial y} = 0$$

50. Let f be a differentiable function of one variable, and let $z = f(x^2 + y^2)$. Show that
$$y\frac{\partial z}{\partial x} - x\frac{\partial z}{\partial y} = 0$$

51. Let f be a differentiable function of one variable, and let $w = f(u)$, where $u = x + 2y + 3z$. Show that
$$\frac{\partial w}{\partial x} + \frac{\partial w}{\partial y} + \frac{\partial w}{\partial z} = 6\frac{dw}{du}$$

52. Let f be a differentiable function of one variable, and let $w = f(\rho)$, where $\rho = (x^2 + y^2 + z^2)^{1/2}$. Show that
$$\left(\frac{\partial w}{\partial x}\right)^2 + \left(\frac{\partial w}{\partial y}\right)^2 + \left(\frac{\partial w}{\partial z}\right)^2 = \left(\frac{dw}{d\rho}\right)^2$$

53. Let $z = f(x - y, y - x)$. Show that $\partial z/\partial x + \partial z/\partial y = 0$.

54. Let f be a differentiable function of three variables and suppose that $w = f(x - y, y - z, z - x)$. Show that
$$\frac{\partial w}{\partial x} + \frac{\partial w}{\partial y} + \frac{\partial w}{\partial z} = 0$$

55. Suppose that the equation $z = f(x, y)$ is expressed in the polar form $z = g(r, \theta)$ by making the substitution $x = r\cos\theta$ and $y = r\sin\theta$.

(a) View r and θ as functions of x and y and use implicit differentiation to show that
$$\frac{\partial r}{\partial x} = \cos\theta \quad \text{and} \quad \frac{\partial\theta}{\partial x} = -\frac{\sin\theta}{r}$$

(b) View r and θ as functions of x and y and use implicit differentiation to show that
$$\frac{\partial r}{\partial y} = \sin\theta \quad \text{and} \quad \frac{\partial\theta}{\partial y} = \frac{\cos\theta}{r}$$

(c) Use the results in parts (a) and (b) to show that
$$\frac{\partial z}{\partial x} = \frac{\partial z}{\partial r}\cos\theta - \frac{1}{r}\frac{\partial z}{\partial\theta}\sin\theta$$
$$\frac{\partial z}{\partial y} = \frac{\partial z}{\partial r}\sin\theta + \frac{1}{r}\frac{\partial z}{\partial\theta}\cos\theta$$

(d) Use the result in part (c) to show that
$$\left(\frac{\partial z}{\partial x}\right)^2 + \left(\frac{\partial z}{\partial y}\right)^2 = \left(\frac{\partial z}{\partial r}\right)^2 + \frac{1}{r^2}\left(\frac{\partial z}{\partial\theta}\right)^2$$

(e) Use the result in part (c) to show that if $z = f(x, y)$ satisfies Laplace's equation
$$\frac{\partial^2 z}{\partial x^2} + \frac{\partial^2 z}{\partial y^2} = 0$$

then $z = g(r, \theta)$ satisfies the equation
$$\frac{\partial^2 z}{\partial r^2} + \frac{1}{r^2}\frac{\partial^2 z}{\partial\theta^2} + \frac{1}{r}\frac{\partial z}{\partial r} = 0$$

and conversely. The latter equation is called the **polar form of Laplace's equation**.

56. Show that the function
$$z = \tan^{-1}\frac{2xy}{x^2 - y^2}$$

satisfies Laplace's equation; then make the substitution $x = r\cos\theta$, $y = r\sin\theta$, and show that the resulting function of r and θ satisfies the polar form of Laplace's equation given in part (e) of Exercise 55.

57. (a) Show that if $u(x, y)$ and $v(x, y)$ satisfy the Cauchy–Riemann equations (Exercise 94, Section 13.3), and if $x = r\cos\theta$ and $y = r\sin\theta$, then
$$\frac{\partial u}{\partial r} = \frac{1}{r}\frac{\partial v}{\partial\theta} \quad \text{and} \quad \frac{\partial v}{\partial r} = -\frac{1}{r}\frac{\partial u}{\partial\theta}$$

This is called the **polar form of the Cauchy–Riemann equations**.

(b) Show that the functions
$$u = \ln(x^2 + y^2), \quad v = 2\tan^{-1}(y/x)$$

satisfy the Cauchy–Riemann equations; then make the substitution $x = r\cos\theta$, $y = r\sin\theta$, and show that the resulting functions of r and θ satisfy the polar form of the Cauchy–Riemann equations.

58. Recall from Formula (6) of Section 13.3 that under appropriate conditions a plucked string satisfies the wave equation

$$\frac{\partial^2 u}{\partial t^2} = c^2 \frac{\partial^2 u}{\partial x^2}$$

where c is a positive constant.

(a) Show that a function of the form $u(x, t) = f(x + ct)$ satisfies the wave equation.

(b) Show that a function of the form $u(x, t) = g(x - ct)$ satisfies the wave equation.

(c) Show that a function of the form

$$u(x, t) = f(x + ct) + g(x - ct)$$

satisfies the wave equation.

(d) It can be proved that every solution of the wave equation is expressible in the form stated in part (c). Confirm that $u(x, t) = \sin t \sin x$ satisfies the wave equation in which $c = 1$, and then use appropriate trigonometric identities to express this function in the form $f(x + t) + g(x - t)$.

59. Let f be a differentiable function of three variables, and let $w = f(x, y, z), x = \rho \sin \phi \cos \theta, y = \rho \sin \phi \sin \theta$, and $z = \rho \cos \phi$. Express $\partial w/\partial \rho$, $\partial w/\partial \phi$, and $\partial w/\partial \theta$ in terms of $\partial w/\partial x$, $\partial w/\partial y$, and $\partial w/\partial z$.

60. Let $w = f(x, y, z)$ be differentiable, where $z = g(x, y)$. Taking x and y as the independent variables, express each of the following in terms of $\partial f/\partial x$, $\partial f/\partial y$, $\partial f/\partial z$, $\partial z/\partial x$, and $\partial z/\partial y$.

(a) $\partial w/\partial x$ (b) $\partial w/\partial y$

61. Let $w = \ln(e^r + e^s + e^t + e^u)$. Show that

$$w_{rstu} = -6e^{r+s+t+u-4w}$$

[*Hint:* Take advantage of the relationship $e^w = e^r + e^s + e^t + e^u$.]

62. Suppose that w is a differentiable function of x_1, x_2, and x_3, and

$$x_1 = a_1 y_1 + b_1 y_2$$
$$x_2 = a_2 y_1 + b_2 y_2$$
$$x_3 = a_3 y_1 + b_3 y_2$$

where the a's and b's are constants. Express $\partial w/\partial y_1$ and $\partial w/\partial y_2$ in terms of $\partial w/\partial x_1$, $\partial w/\partial x_2$, and $\partial w/\partial x_3$.

63. (a) Let w be a differentiable function of x_1, x_2, x_3, and x_4, and let each x_i be a differentiable function of t. Find a chain-rule formula for dw/dt.

(b) Let w be a differentiable function of x_1, x_2, x_3, and x_4, and let each x_i be a differentiable function of v_1, v_2, and v_3. Find chain-rule formulas for $\partial w/\partial v_1$, $\partial w/\partial v_2$, and $\partial w/\partial v_3$.

64. Let $w = (x_1^2 + x_2^2 + \cdots + x_n^2)^k$, where $n \geq 2$. For what values of k does

$$\frac{\partial^2 w}{\partial x_1^2} + \frac{\partial^2 w}{\partial x_2^2} + \cdots + \frac{\partial^2 w}{\partial x_n^2} = 0$$

hold?

65. We showed in Exercise 28 of Section 5.10 that

$$\frac{d}{dx} \int_{h(x)}^{g(x)} f(t)\, dt = f(g(x))g'(x) - f(h(x))h'(x)$$

Derive this same result by letting $u = g(x)$ and $v = h(x)$ and then differentiating the function

$$F(u, v) = \int_v^u f(t)\, dt$$

with respect to x.

66. Prove: If f, f_x, and f_y are continuous on a circular region containing $A(x_0, y_0)$ and $B(x_1, y_1)$, then there is a point (x^*, y^*) on the line segment joining A and B such that

$$f(x_1, y_1) - f(x_0, y_0)$$
$$= f_x(x^*, y^*)(x_1 - x_0) + f_y(x^*, y^*)(y_1 - y_0)$$

This result is the two-dimensional version of the Mean-Value Theorem. [*Hint:* Express the line segment joining A and B in parametric form and use the Mean-Value Theorem for functions of one variable.]

67. Prove: If $f_x(x, y) = 0$ and $f_y(x, y) = 0$ throughout a circular region, then $f(x, y)$ is constant on that region. [*Hint:* Use the result of Exercise 66.]

68. Writing Use differentials to give an informal justification for the chain rules for derivatives.

69. Writing Compare the use of the formula

$$\frac{dy}{dx} = -\frac{\partial f/\partial x}{\partial f/\partial y}$$

with the process of implicit differentiation.

✔ **QUICK CHECK ANSWERS 13.5**

1. -8 **2.** 3   **3.** 26 ft^2/s   **4.** 1; 1

13.6 DIRECTIONAL DERIVATIVES AND GRADIENTS

The partial derivatives $f_x(x, y)$ and $f_y(x, y)$ represent the rates of change of $f(x, y)$ in directions parallel to the x- and y-axes. In this section we will investigate rates of change of $f(x, y)$ in other directions.

■ DIRECTIONAL DERIVATIVES

In this section we extend the concept of a *partial* derivative to the more general notion of a *directional* derivative. We have seen that the partial derivatives of a function give the instantaneous rates of change of that function in directions parallel to the coordinate axes. Directional derivatives allow us to compute the rates of change of a function with respect to distance in *any* direction.

Suppose that we wish to compute the instantaneous rate of change of a function $f(x, y)$ with respect to distance from a point (x_0, y_0) in some direction. Since there are infinitely many different directions from (x_0, y_0) in which we could move, we need a convenient method for describing a specific direction starting at (x_0, y_0). One way to do this is to use a unit vector

$$\mathbf{u} = u_1\mathbf{i} + u_2\mathbf{j}$$

that has its initial point at (x_0, y_0) and points in the desired direction (Figure 13.6.1). This vector determines a line l in the xy-plane that can be expressed parametrically as

$$x = x_0 + su_1, \quad y = y_0 + su_2 \tag{1}$$

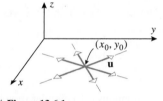
▲ **Figure 13.6.1**

Since u is a unit vector, s is the arc length parameter that has its reference point at (x_0, y_0) and has positive values in the direction of $\mathbf{u}$. For $s = 0$, the point (x, y) is at the reference point (x_0, y_0), and as s increases, the point (x, y) moves along l in the direction of $\mathbf{u}$. On the line l the variable $z = f(x_0 + su_1, y_0 + su_2)$ is a function of the parameter s. The value of the derivative dz/ds at $s = 0$ then gives an instantaneous rate of change of $f(x, y)$ with respect to distance from (x_0, y_0) in the direction of $\mathbf{u}$.

13.6.1 DEFINITION If $f(x, y)$ is a function of x and y, and if $\mathbf{u} = u_1\mathbf{i} + u_2\mathbf{j}$ is a unit vector, then the ***directional derivative of f in the direction of*** $\mathbf{u}$ at (x_0, y_0) is denoted by $D_\mathbf{u}f(x_0, y_0)$ and is defined by

$$D_\mathbf{u}f(x_0, y_0) = \frac{d}{ds}\left[f(x_0 + su_1, y_0 + su_2)\right]_{s=0} \tag{2}$$

provided this derivative exists.

Slope in **u** direction = rate of change of z with respect to s

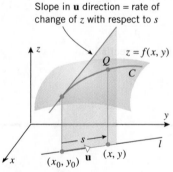
▲ **Figure 13.6.2**

Geometrically, $D_\mathbf{u}f(x_0, y_0)$ can be interpreted as the ***slope of the surface $z = f(x, y)$ in the direction of*** $\mathbf{u}$ at the point $(x_0, y_0, f(x_0, y_0))$ (Figure 13.6.2). Usually the value of $D_\mathbf{u}f(x_0, y_0)$ will depend on both the point (x_0, y_0) and the direction $\mathbf{u}$. Thus, at a fixed point the slope of the surface may vary with the direction (Figure 13.6.3). Analytically, the directional derivative represents the ***instantaneous rate of change of $f(x, y)$ with respect to distance in the direction of*** $\mathbf{u}$ at the point (x_0, y_0).

▶ **Example 1** Let $f(x, y) = xy$. Find and interpret $D_\mathbf{u}f(1, 2)$ for the unit vector

$$\mathbf{u} = \frac{\sqrt{3}}{2}\mathbf{i} + \frac{1}{2}\mathbf{j}$$

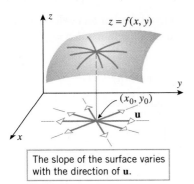

$z = f(x, y)$

(x_0, y_0)

u

The slope of the surface varies with the direction of **u**.

▲ Figure 13.6.3

Solution. It follows from Equation (2) that

$$D_{\mathbf{u}} f(1, 2) = \frac{d}{ds} \left[f \left(1 + \frac{\sqrt{3}s}{2}, 2 + \frac{s}{2} \right) \right]_{s=0}$$

Since

$$f \left(1 + \frac{\sqrt{3}s}{2}, 2 + \frac{s}{2} \right) = \left(1 + \frac{\sqrt{3}s}{2} \right) \left(2 + \frac{s}{2} \right) = \frac{\sqrt{3}}{4} s^2 + \left(\frac{1}{2} + \sqrt{3} \right) s + 2$$

we have

$$D_{\mathbf{u}} f(1, 2) = \frac{d}{ds} \left[\frac{\sqrt{3}}{4} s^2 + \left(\frac{1}{2} + \sqrt{3} \right) s + 2 \right]_{s=0}$$

$$= \left[\frac{\sqrt{3}}{2} s + \frac{1}{2} + \sqrt{3} \right]_{s=0} = \frac{1}{2} + \sqrt{3}$$

Since $\frac{1}{2} + \sqrt{3} \approx 2.23$, we conclude that if we move a small distance from the point $(1, 2)$ in the direction of **u**, the function $f(x, y) = xy$ will increase by about 2.23 times the distance moved. ◄

The definition of a directional derivative for a function $f(x, y, z)$ of three variables is similar to Definition 13.6.1.

13.6.2 **DEFINITION** If $\mathbf{u} = u_1 \mathbf{i} + u_2 \mathbf{j} + u_3 \mathbf{k}$ is a unit vector, and if $f(x, y, z)$ is a function of x, y, and z, then the *directional derivative of f in the direction of* **u** at (x_0, y_0, z_0) is denoted by $D_{\mathbf{u}} f(x_0, y_0, z_0)$ and is defined by

$$D_{\mathbf{u}} f(x_0, y_0, z_0) = \frac{d}{ds} \left[f(x_0 + su_1, y_0 + su_2, z_0 + su_3) \right]_{s=0} \tag{3}$$

provided this derivative exists.

Although Equation (3) does not have a convenient geometric interpretation, we can still interpret directional derivatives for functions of three variables in terms of instantaneous rates of change in a specified direction.

For a function that is differentiable at a point, directional derivatives exist in every direction from the point and can be computed directly in terms of the first-order partial derivatives of the function.

13.6.3 **THEOREM**

(a) *If $f(x, y)$ is differentiable at (x_0, y_0), and if $\mathbf{u} = u_1 \mathbf{i} + u_2 \mathbf{j}$ is a unit vector, then the directional derivative $D_{\mathbf{u}} f(x_0, y_0)$ exists and is given by*

$$D_{\mathbf{u}} f(x_0, y_0) = f_x(x_0, y_0)u_1 + f_y(x_0, y_0)u_2 \tag{4}$$

(b) *If $f(x, y, z)$ is differentiable at (x_0, y_0, z_0), and if $\mathbf{u} = u_1 \mathbf{i} + u_2 \mathbf{j} + u_3 \mathbf{k}$ is a unit vector, then the directional derivative $D_{\mathbf{u}} f(x_0, y_0, z_0)$ exists and is given by*

$$D_{\mathbf{u}} f(x_0, y_0, z_0) = f_x(x_0, y_0, z_0)u_1 + f_y(x_0, y_0, z_0)u_2 + f_z(x_0, y_0, z_0)u_3 \tag{5}$$

PROOF   We will give the proof of part (*a*); the proof of part (*b*) is similar and will be omitted. The function $z = f(x_0 + su_1, y_0 + su_2)$ is the composition of the function $z = f(x, y)$ with the functions

$$x = x(s) = x_0 + su_1 \quad \text{and} \quad y = y(s) = y_0 + su_2$$

As such, the chain rule in Formula (5) of Section 13.5 immediately gives

$$D_{\mathbf{u}} f(x_0, y_0) = \frac{d}{ds} \big[f(x_0 + su_1, y_0 + su_2) \big]_{s=0}$$

$$= \frac{dz}{ds}\bigg|_{s=0} = f_x(x_0, y_0)u_1 + f_y(x_0, y_0)u_2 \ \blacksquare$$

We can use Theorem 13.6.3 to confirm the result of Example 1. For $f(x, y) = xy$ we have $f_x(1, 2) = 2$ and $f_y(1, 2) = 1$ (verify). With

$$\mathbf{u} = \frac{\sqrt{3}}{2}\mathbf{i} + \frac{1}{2}\mathbf{j}$$

Equation (4) becomes

$$D_{\mathbf{u}} f(1, 2) = 2\left(\frac{\sqrt{3}}{2} \right) + \frac{1}{2} = \sqrt{3} + \frac{1}{2}$$

which agrees with our solution in Example 1.

Recall from Formula (13) of Section 11.2 that a unit vector $\mathbf{u}$ in the xy-plane can be expressed as

$$\mathbf{u} = \cos\phi\,\mathbf{i} + \sin\phi\,\mathbf{j} \tag{6}$$

where ϕ is the angle from the positive x-axis to $\mathbf{u}$. Thus, Formula (4) can also be expressed as

$$D_{\mathbf{u}} f(x_0, y_0) = f_x(x_0, y_0) \cos\phi + f_y(x_0, y_0) \sin\phi \tag{7}$$

▶ **Example 2**   Find the directional derivative of $f(x, y) = e^{xy}$ at $(-2, 0)$ in the direction of the unit vector that makes an angle of $\pi/3$ with the positive x-axis.

Solution.   The partial derivatives of f are

$$f_x(x, y) = ye^{xy}, \quad f_y(x, y) = xe^{xy}$$
$$f_x(-2, 0) = 0, \quad f_y(-2, 0) = -2$$

The unit vector $\mathbf{u}$ that makes an angle of $\pi/3$ with the positive x-axis is

$$\mathbf{u} = \cos(\pi/3)\mathbf{i} + \sin(\pi/3)\mathbf{j} = \frac{1}{2}\mathbf{i} + \frac{\sqrt{3}}{2}\mathbf{j}$$

Thus, from (7)

$$D_{\mathbf{u}} f(-2, 0) = f_x(-2, 0) \cos(\pi/3) + f_y(-2, 0) \sin(\pi/3)$$
$$= 0(1/2) + (-2)(\sqrt{3}/2) = -\sqrt{3} \ \blacktriangleleft$$

Note that in Example 3 we used a *unit vector* to specify the direction of the directional derivative. This is required in order to apply either Formula (4) or Formula (5).

▶ **Example 3**   Find the directional derivative of $f(x, y, z) = x^2y - yz^3 + z$ at the point $(1, -2, 0)$ in the direction of the vector $\mathbf{a} = 2\mathbf{i} + \mathbf{j} - 2\mathbf{k}$.

Solution.   The partial derivatives of f are

$$f_x(x, y, z) = 2xy, \quad f_y(x, y, z) = x^2 - z^3, \quad f_z(x, y, z) = -3yz^2 + 1$$
$$f_x(1, -2, 0) = -4, \quad f_y(1, -2, 0) = 1, \quad f_z(1, -2, 0) = 1$$

Since **a** is not a unit vector, we normalize it, getting

$$\mathbf{u} = \frac{\mathbf{a}}{\|\mathbf{a}\|} = \frac{1}{\sqrt{9}}(2\mathbf{i} + \mathbf{j} - 2\mathbf{k}) = \frac{2}{3}\mathbf{i} + \frac{1}{3}\mathbf{j} - \frac{2}{3}\mathbf{k}$$

Formula (5) then yields

$$D_{\mathbf{u}} f(1, -2, 0) = (-4)\left(\frac{2}{3}\right) + \frac{1}{3} - \frac{2}{3} = -3 \blacktriangleleft$$

■ **THE GRADIENT**

Formula (4) can be expressed in the form of a dot product as

$$D_{\mathbf{u}} f(x_0, y_0) = (f_x(x_0, y_0)\mathbf{i} + f_y(x_0, y_0)\mathbf{j}) \cdot (u_1\mathbf{i} + u_2\mathbf{j})$$
$$= (f_x(x_0, y_0)\mathbf{i} + f_y(x_0, y_0)\mathbf{j}) \cdot \mathbf{u}$$

Similarly, Formula (5) can be expressed as

$$D_{\mathbf{u}} f(x_0, y_0, z_0) = (f_x(x_0, y_0, z_0)\mathbf{i} + f_y(x_0, y_0, z_0)\mathbf{j} + f_z(x_0, y_0, z_0)\mathbf{k}) \cdot \mathbf{u}$$

In both cases the directional derivative is obtained by dotting the direction vector **u** with a new vector constructed from the first-order partial derivatives of f.

> **13.6.4   DEFINITION**
>
> (a)   If f is a function of x and y, then the *gradient of* f is defined by
>
> $$\nabla f(x, y) = f_x(x, y)\mathbf{i} + f_y(x, y)\mathbf{j} \qquad (8)$$
>
> (b)   If f is a function of x, y, and z, then the *gradient of* f is defined by
>
> $$\nabla f(x, y, z) = f_x(x, y, z)\mathbf{i} + f_y(x, y, z)\mathbf{j} + f_z(x, y, z)\mathbf{k} \qquad (9)$$

Remember that ∇f is not a product of ∇ and f. Think of ∇ as an "operator" that acts on a function f to produce the gradient ∇f.

The symbol ∇ (read "del") is an inverted delta. (It is sometimes called a "nabla" because of its similarity in form to an ancient Hebrew ten-stringed harp of that name.)

Formulas (4) and (5) can now be written as

$$D_{\mathbf{u}} f(x_0, y_0) = \nabla f(x_0, y_0) \cdot \mathbf{u} \qquad (10)$$

and

$$D_{\mathbf{u}} f(x_0, y_0, z_0) = \nabla f(x_0, y_0, z_0) \cdot \mathbf{u} \qquad (11)$$

respectively. For example, using Formula (11) our solution to Example 3 would take the form

$$D_{\mathbf{u}} f(1, -2, 0) = \nabla f(1, -2, 0) \cdot \mathbf{u} = (-4\mathbf{i} + \mathbf{j} + \mathbf{k}) \cdot \left(\tfrac{2}{3}\mathbf{i} + \tfrac{1}{3}\mathbf{j} - \tfrac{2}{3}\mathbf{k}\right)$$
$$= (-4)\left(\tfrac{2}{3}\right) + \tfrac{1}{3} - \tfrac{2}{3} = -3$$

Formula (10) can be interpreted to mean that the slope of the surface $z = f(x, y)$ at the point (x_0, y_0) in the direction of **u** is the dot product of the gradient with **u** (Figure 13.6.4).

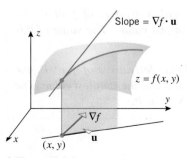

Slope $= \nabla f \cdot \mathbf{u}$

$z = f(x, y)$

∇f

(x, y)

▲ Figure 13.6.4

■ PROPERTIES OF THE GRADIENT

The gradient is not merely a notational device to simplify the formula for the directional derivative; we will see that the length and direction of the gradient ∇f provide important information about the function f and the surface $z = f(x, y)$. For example, suppose that $\nabla f(x, y) \neq \mathbf{0}$, and let us use Formula (4) of Section 11.3 to rewrite (10) as

$$D_{\mathbf{u}} f(x, y) = \nabla f(x, y) \cdot \mathbf{u} = \|\nabla f(x, y)\| \|\mathbf{u}\| \cos \theta = \|\nabla f(x, y)\| \cos \theta \qquad (12)$$

where θ is the angle between $\nabla f(x, y)$ and $\mathbf{u}$. Equation (12) tells us that the maximum value of $D_{\mathbf{u}} f$ at the point (x, y) is $\|\nabla f(x, y)\|$, and this maximum occurs when $\theta = 0$, that is, when $\mathbf{u}$ is in the direction of $\nabla f(x, y)$. Geometrically, this means:

> *At (x, y), the surface $z = f(x, y)$ has its maximum slope in the direction of the gradient, and the maximum slope is $\|\nabla f(x, y)\|$.*

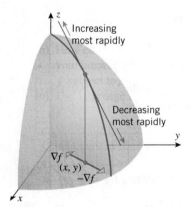

That is, the function $f(x, y)$ increases most rapidly in the direction of its gradient (Figure 13.6.5).

Similarly, (12) tells us that the minimum value of $D_{\mathbf{u}} f$ at the point (x, y) is $-\|\nabla f(x, y)\|$, and this minimum occurs when $\theta = \pi$, that is, when $\mathbf{u}$ is oppositely directed to $\nabla f(x, y)$. Geometrically, this means:

> *At (x, y), the surface $z = f(x, y)$ has its minimum slope in the direction that is opposite to the gradient, and the minimum slope is $-\|\nabla f(x, y)\|$.*

▲ **Figure 13.6.5**

That is, the function $f(x, y)$ decreases most rapidly in the direction opposite to its gradient (Figure 13.6.5).

Finally, in the case where $\nabla f(x, y) = \mathbf{0}$, it follows from (12) that $D_{\mathbf{u}} f(x, y) = 0$ in all directions at the point (x, y). This typically occurs where the surface $z = f(x, y)$ has a "relative maximum," a "relative minimum," or a saddle point.

A similar analysis applies to functions of three variables. As a consequence, we have the following result.

> **13.6.5 THEOREM** *Let f be a function of either two variables or three variables, and let P denote the point $P(x_0, y_0)$ or $P(x_0, y_0, z_0)$, respectively. Assume that f is differentiable at P.*
>
> *(a) If $\nabla f = \mathbf{0}$ at P, then all directional derivatives of f at P are zero.*
>
> *(b) If $\nabla f \neq \mathbf{0}$ at P, then among all possible directional derivatives of f at P, the derivative in the direction of ∇f at P has the largest value. The value of this largest directional derivative is $\|\nabla f\|$ at P.*
>
> *(c) If $\nabla f \neq \mathbf{0}$ at P, then among all possible directional derivatives of f at P, the derivative in the direction opposite to that of ∇f at P has the smallest value. The value of this smallest directional derivative is $-\|\nabla f\|$ at P.*

▶ **Example 4**   Let $f(x, y) = x^2 e^y$. Find the maximum value of a directional derivative at $(-2, 0)$, and find the unit vector in the direction in which the maximum value occurs.

Solution. Since
$$\nabla f(x, y) = f_x(x, y)\mathbf{i} + f_y(x, y)\mathbf{j} = 2xe^y\mathbf{i} + x^2e^y\mathbf{j}$$
the gradient of f at $(-2, 0)$ is
$$\nabla f(-2, 0) = -4\mathbf{i} + 4\mathbf{j}$$
By Theorem 13.6.5, the maximum value of the directional derivative is
$$\|\nabla f(-2, 0)\| = \sqrt{(-4)^2 + 4^2} = \sqrt{32} = 4\sqrt{2}$$
This maximum occurs in the direction of $\nabla f(-2, 0)$. The unit vector in this direction is
$$\mathbf{u} = \frac{\nabla f(-2, 0)}{\|\nabla f(-2, 0)\|} = \frac{1}{4\sqrt{2}}(-4\mathbf{i} + 4\mathbf{j}) = -\frac{1}{\sqrt{2}}\mathbf{i} + \frac{1}{\sqrt{2}}\mathbf{j} \blacktriangleleft$$

> What would be the minimum value of a directional derivative of
> $$f(x, y) = x^2e^y$$
> at $(-2, 0)$?

■ GRADIENTS ARE NORMAL TO LEVEL CURVES

We have seen that the gradient points in the direction in which a function increases most rapidly. For a function $f(x, y)$ of two variables, we will now consider how this direction of maximum rate of increase can be determined from a contour map of the function. Suppose that (x_0, y_0) is a point on a level curve $f(x, y) = c$ of f, and assume that this curve can be smoothly parametrized as
$$x = x(s), \quad y = y(s) \tag{13}$$
where s is an arc length parameter. Recall from Formula (6) of Section 12.4 that the unit tangent vector to (13) is
$$\mathbf{T} = \mathbf{T}(s) = \left(\frac{dx}{ds}\right)\mathbf{i} + \left(\frac{dy}{ds}\right)\mathbf{j}$$

Since $\mathbf{T}$ gives a direction along which f is nearly constant, we would expect the instantaneous rate of change of f with respect to distance in the direction of $\mathbf{T}$ to be 0. That is, we would expect that
$$D_{\mathbf{T}}f(x, y) = \nabla f(x, y) \cdot \mathbf{T}(s) = 0$$
To show this to be the case, we differentiate both sides of the equation $f(x, y) = c$ with respect to s. Assuming that f is differentiable at (x, y), we can use the chain rule to obtain
$$\frac{\partial f}{\partial x}\frac{dx}{ds} + \frac{\partial f}{\partial y}\frac{dy}{ds} = 0$$
which we can rewrite as
$$\left(\frac{\partial f}{\partial x}\mathbf{i} + \frac{\partial f}{\partial y}\mathbf{j}\right) \cdot \left(\frac{dx}{ds}\mathbf{i} + \frac{dy}{ds}\mathbf{j}\right) = 0$$
or, alternatively, as
$$\nabla f(x, y) \cdot \mathbf{T} = 0$$
Therefore, if $\nabla f(x, y) \neq \mathbf{0}$, then $\nabla f(x, y)$ should be normal to the level curve $f(x, y) = c$ at any point (x, y) on the curve.

It is proved in advanced courses that if $f(x, y)$ has continuous first-order partial derivatives, and if $\nabla f(x_0, y_0) \neq \mathbf{0}$, then near (x_0, y_0) the graph of $f(x, y) = c$ is indeed a smooth curve through (x_0, y_0). Furthermore, we also know from Theorem 13.4.4 that f will be differentiable at (x_0, y_0). We therefore have the following result.

> Show that the level curves for
> $$f(x, y) = x^2 + y^2$$
> are circles and verify Theorem 13.6.6 at $(x_0, y_0) = (3, 4)$.

> **13.6.6 THEOREM** *Assume that $f(x, y)$ has continuous first-order partial derivatives in an open disk centered at (x_0, y_0) and that $\nabla f(x_0, y_0) \neq \mathbf{0}$. Then $\nabla f(x_0, y_0)$ is normal to the level curve of f through (x_0, y_0).*

When we examine a contour map, we instinctively regard the distance between adjacent contours to be measured in a normal direction. If the contours correspond to equally spaced values of f, then the closer together the contours appear to be, the more rapidly the values of f will be changing in that normal direction. It follows from Theorems 13.6.5 and 13.6.6 that this rate of change of f is given by $\|\nabla f(x, y)\|$. Thus, the closer together the contours appear to be, the greater the length of the gradient of f.

▶ **Example 5** A contour plot of a function f is given in Figure 13.6.6*a*. Sketch the directions of the gradient of f at the points P, Q, and R. At which of these three points does the gradient vector have maximum length? Minimum length?

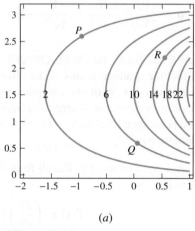 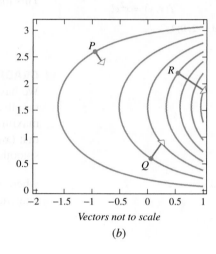

Vectors not to scale

(*a*)   (*b*)

▲ **Figure 13.6.6**

Solution. It follows from Theorems 13.6.5 and 13.6.6 that the directions of the gradient vectors will be as given in Figure 13.6.6*b*. Based on the density of the contour lines, we would guess that the gradient of f has maximum length at R and minimum length at P, with the length at Q somewhere in between. ◀

REMARK

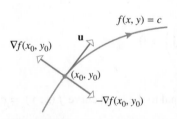

▲ **Figure 13.6.7**

If (x_0, y_0) is a point on the level curve $f(x, y) = c$, then the slope of the surface $z = f(x, y)$ at that point in the direction of **u** is

$$D_{\mathbf{u}} f(x_0, y_0) = \nabla f(x_0, y_0) \cdot \mathbf{u}$$

If **u** is tangent to the level curve at (x_0, y_0), then $f(x, y)$ is neither increasing nor decreasing in that direction, so $D_{\mathbf{u}} f(x_0, y_0) = 0$. Thus, $\nabla f(x_0, y_0)$, $-\nabla f(x_0, y_0)$, and the tangent vector **u** mark the directions of maximum slope, minimum slope, and zero slope at a point (x_0, y_0) on a level curve (Figure 13.6.7). Good skiers use these facts intuitively to control their speed by zigzagging down ski slopes—they ski across the slope with their skis tangential to a level curve to stop their downhill motion, and they point their skis down the slope and normal to the level curve to obtain the most rapid descent.

■ **AN APPLICATION OF GRADIENTS**

There are numerous applications in which the motion of an object must be controlled so that it moves toward a heat source. For example, in medical applications the operation of certain diagnostic equipment is designed to locate heat sources generated by tumors or infections, and in military applications the trajectories of heat-seeking missiles are controlled to seek and destroy enemy aircraft. The following example illustrates how gradients are used to solve such problems.

Heat-seeking missiles such as "Stinger" and "Sidewinder" use infrared sensors to measure gradients.

▶ **Example 6** A heat-seeking particle is located at the point $(2, 3)$ on a flat metal plate whose temperature at a point (x, y) is

$$T(x, y) = 10 - 8x^2 - 2y^2$$

Find an equation for the trajectory of the particle if it moves continuously in the direction of maximum temperature increase.

Solution. Assume that the trajectory is represented parametrically by the equations

$$x = x(t), \quad y = y(t)$$

where the particle is at the point $(2, 3)$ at time $t = 0$. Because the particle moves in the direction of maximum temperature increase, its direction of motion at time t is in the direction of the gradient of $T(x, y)$, and hence its velocity vector $\mathbf{v}(t)$ at time t points in the direction of the gradient. Thus, there is a scalar k that depends on t such that

$$\mathbf{v}(t) = k\nabla T(x, y)$$

from which we obtain

$$\frac{dx}{dt}\mathbf{i} + \frac{dy}{dt}\mathbf{j} = k(-16x\mathbf{i} - 4y\mathbf{j})$$

Equating components yields

$$\frac{dx}{dt} = -16kx, \quad \frac{dy}{dt} = -4ky$$

and dividing to eliminate k yields

$$\frac{dy}{dx} = \frac{-4ky}{-16kx} = \frac{y}{4x}$$

Thus, we can obtain the trajectory by solving the initial-value problem

$$\frac{dy}{dx} - \frac{y}{4x} = 0, \quad y(2) = 3$$

The differential equation is a separable first-order equation and hence can be solved by the method of separation of variables discussed in Section 8.2. We leave it for you to show that the solution of the initial-value problem is

$$y = \frac{3}{\sqrt[4]{2}}x^{1/4}$$

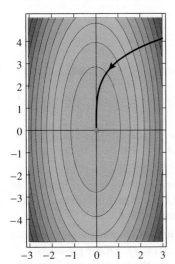
▲ **Figure 13.6.8**

The graph of the trajectory and a contour plot of the temperature function are shown in Figure 13.6.8. ◄

✔ **QUICK CHECK EXERCISES 13.6**   *(See page 971 for answers.)*

1. The gradient of $f(x, y, z) = xy^2z^3$ at the point $(1, 1, 1)$ is _____.

2. Suppose that the differentiable function $f(x, y)$ has the property that

$$f\left(2 + \frac{s\sqrt{3}}{2}, 1 + \frac{s}{2}\right) = 3se^s$$

The directional derivative of f in the direction of

$$\mathbf{u} = \frac{\sqrt{3}}{2}\mathbf{i} + \frac{1}{2}\mathbf{j}$$

at $(2, 1)$ is _____.

3. If the gradient of $f(x, y)$ at the origin is $6\mathbf{i} + 8\mathbf{j}$, then the directional derivative of f in the direction of $\mathbf{a} = 3\mathbf{i} + 4\mathbf{j}$ at the origin is _____. The slope of the tangent line to the level curve of f through the origin at $(0, 0)$ is _____.

4. If the gradient of $f(x, y, z)$ at $(1, 2, 3)$ is $2\mathbf{i} - 2\mathbf{j} + \mathbf{k}$, then the maximum value for a directional derivative of f at $(1, 2, 3)$ is _____ and the minimum value for a directional derivative at this point is _____.

EXERCISE SET 13.6   Graphing Utility   [c] CAS

1–8 Find $D_{\mathbf{u}} f$ at P. ■

1. $f(x, y) = (1 + xy)^{3/2}$; $P(3, 1)$; $\mathbf{u} = \dfrac{1}{\sqrt{2}}\mathbf{i} + \dfrac{1}{\sqrt{2}}\mathbf{j}$

2. $f(x, y) = e^{2xy}$; $P(4, 0)$; $\mathbf{u} = -\frac{3}{5}\mathbf{i} + \frac{4}{5}\mathbf{j}$

3. $f(x, y) = \ln(1 + x^2 + y)$; $P(0, 0)$;
$\mathbf{u} = -\dfrac{1}{\sqrt{10}}\mathbf{i} - \dfrac{3}{\sqrt{10}}\mathbf{j}$

4. $f(x, y) = \dfrac{cx + dy}{x - y}$; $P(3, 4)$; $\mathbf{u} = \frac{4}{5}\mathbf{i} + \frac{3}{5}\mathbf{j}$

5. $f(x, y, z) = 4x^5 y^2 z^3$; $P(2, -1, 1)$; $\mathbf{u} = \frac{1}{3}\mathbf{i} + \frac{2}{3}\mathbf{j} - \frac{2}{3}\mathbf{k}$

6. $f(x, y, z) = ye^{xz} + z^2$; $P(0, 2, 3)$; $\mathbf{u} = \frac{2}{7}\mathbf{i} - \frac{3}{7}\mathbf{j} + \frac{6}{7}\mathbf{k}$

7. $f(x, y, z) = \ln(x^2 + 2y^2 + 3z^2)$; $P(-1, 2, 4)$;
$\mathbf{u} = -\frac{3}{13}\mathbf{i} - \frac{4}{13}\mathbf{j} - \frac{12}{13}\mathbf{k}$

8. $f(x, y, z) = \sin xyz$; $P\left(\frac{1}{2}, \frac{1}{3}, \pi\right)$;
$\mathbf{u} = \dfrac{1}{\sqrt{3}}\mathbf{i} - \dfrac{1}{\sqrt{3}}\mathbf{j} + \dfrac{1}{\sqrt{3}}\mathbf{k}$

9–18 Find the directional derivative of f at P in the direction of $\mathbf{a}$. ■

9. $f(x, y) = 4x^3 y^2$; $P(2, 1)$; $\mathbf{a} = 4\mathbf{i} - 3\mathbf{j}$

10. $f(x, y) = x^2 - 3xy + 4y^3$; $P(-2, 0)$; $\mathbf{a} = \mathbf{i} + 2\mathbf{j}$

11. $f(x, y) = y^2 \ln x$; $P(1, 4)$; $\mathbf{a} = -3\mathbf{i} + 3\mathbf{j}$

12. $f(x, y) = e^x \cos y$; $P(0, \pi/4)$; $\mathbf{a} = 5\mathbf{i} - 2\mathbf{j}$

13. $f(x, y) = \tan^{-1}(y/x)$; $P(-2, 2)$; $\mathbf{a} = -\mathbf{i} - \mathbf{j}$

14. $f(x, y) = xe^y - ye^x$; $P(0, 0)$; $\mathbf{a} = 5\mathbf{i} - 2\mathbf{j}$

15. $f(x, y, z) = x^3 z - yx^2 + z^2$; $P(2, -1, 1)$;
$\mathbf{a} = 3\mathbf{i} - \mathbf{j} + 2\mathbf{k}$

16. $f(x, y, z) = y - \sqrt{x^2 + z^2}$; $P(-3, 1, 4)$;
$\mathbf{a} = 2\mathbf{i} - 2\mathbf{j} - \mathbf{k}$

17. $f(x, y, z) = \dfrac{z - x}{z + y}$; $P(1, 0, -3)$; $\mathbf{a} = -6\mathbf{i} + 3\mathbf{j} - 2\mathbf{k}$

18. $f(x, y, z) = e^{x+y+3z}$; $P(-2, 2, -1)$; $\mathbf{a} = 20\mathbf{i} - 4\mathbf{j} + 5\mathbf{k}$

19–22 Find the directional derivative of f at P in the direction of a vector making the counterclockwise angle θ with the positive x-axis. ■

19. $f(x, y) = \sqrt{xy}$; $P(1, 4)$; $\theta = \pi/3$

20. $f(x, y) = \dfrac{x - y}{x + y}$; $P(-1, -2)$; $\theta = \pi/2$

21. $f(x, y) = \tan(2x + y)$; $P(\pi/6, \pi/3)$; $\theta = 7\pi/4$

22. $f(x, y) = \sinh x \cosh y$; $P(0, 0)$; $\theta = \pi$

23. Find the directional derivative of
$$f(x, y) = \dfrac{x}{x + y}$$
at $P(1, 0)$ in the direction of $Q(-1, -1)$.

24. Find the directional derivative of $f(x, y) = e^{-x} \sec y$ at $P(0, \pi/4)$ in the direction of the origin.

25. Find the directional derivative of $f(x, y) = \sqrt{xy}e^y$ at $P(1, 1)$ in the direction of the negative y-axis.

26. Let
$$f(x, y) = \dfrac{y}{x + y}$$
Find a unit vector $\mathbf{u}$ for which $D_{\mathbf{u}} f(2, 3) = 0$.

27. Find the directional derivative of
$$f(x, y, z) = \dfrac{y}{x + z}$$
at $P(2, 1, -1)$ in the direction from P to $Q(-1, 2, 0)$.

28. Find the directional derivative of the function
$$f(x, y, z) = x^3 y^2 z^5 - 2xz + yz + 3x$$
at $P(-1, -2, 1)$ in the direction of the negative z-axis.

FOCUS ON CONCEPTS

29. Suppose that $D_{\mathbf{u}} f(1, 2) = -5$ and $D_{\mathbf{v}} f(1, 2) = 10$, where $\mathbf{u} = \frac{3}{5}\mathbf{i} - \frac{4}{5}\mathbf{j}$ and $\mathbf{v} = \frac{4}{5}\mathbf{i} + \frac{3}{5}\mathbf{j}$. Find
(a) $f_x(1, 2)$ (b) $f_y(1, 2)$
(c) the directional derivative of f at $(1, 2)$ in the direction of the origin.

30. Given that $f_x(-5, 1) = -3$ and $f_y(-5, 1) = 2$, find the directional derivative of f at $P(-5, 1)$ in the direction of the vector from P to $Q(-4, 3)$.

31. The accompanying figure shows some level curves of an unspecified function $f(x, y)$. Which of the three vectors shown in the figure is most likely to be ∇f? Explain.

32. The accompanying figure shows some level curves of an unspecified function $f(x, y)$. Of the gradients at P and Q, which probably has the greater length? Explain.

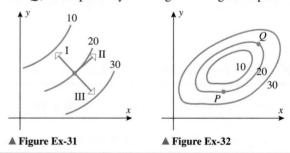

▲ **Figure Ex-31**   ▲ **Figure Ex-32**

33–36 Find ∇z or ∇w. ■

33. $z = 4x - 8y$ **34.** $z = e^{-3y} \cos 4x$

35. $w = \ln \sqrt{x^2 + y^2 + z^2}$ **36.** $w = e^{-5x} \sec x^2 yz$

37–40 Find the gradient of f at the indicated point. ■

37. $f(x, y) = (x^2 + xy)^3$; $(-1, -1)$

38. $f(x, y) = (x^2 + y^2)^{-1/2}$; $(3, 4)$

39. $f(x, y, z) = y \ln(x + y + z)$; $(-3, 4, 0)$

40. $f(x, y, z) = y^2 z \tan^3 x$; $(\pi/4, -3, 1)$

41–44 Sketch the level curve of $f(x, y)$ that passes through P and draw the gradient vector at P. ■

41. $f(x, y) = 4x - 2y + 3$; $P(1, 2)$

42. $f(x, y) = y/x^2$; $P(-2, 2)$

43. $f(x, y) = x^2 + 4y^2$; $P(-2, 0)$

44. $f(x, y) = x^2 - y^2$; $P(2, -1)$

45. Find a unit vector $\mathbf{u}$ that is normal at $P(1, -2)$ to the level curve of $f(x, y) = 4x^2 y$ through P.

46. Find a unit vector $\mathbf{u}$ that is normal at $P(2, -3)$ to the level curve of $f(x, y) = 3x^2 y - xy$ through P.

47–54 Find a unit vector in the direction in which f increases most rapidly at P, and find the rate of change of f at P in that direction. ■

47. $f(x, y) = 4x^3 y^2$; $P(-1, 1)$

48. $f(x, y) = 3x - \ln y$; $P(2, 4)$

49. $f(x, y) = \sqrt{x^2 + y^2}$; $P(4, -3)$

50. $f(x, y) = \dfrac{x}{x + y}$; $P(0, 2)$

51. $f(x, y, z) = x^3 z^2 + y^3 z + z - 1$; $P(1, 1, -1)$

52. $f(x, y, z) = \sqrt{x - 3y + 4z}$; $P(0, -3, 0)$

53. $f(x, y, z) = \dfrac{x}{z} + \dfrac{z}{y^2}$; $P(1, 2, -2)$

54. $f(x, y, z) = \tan^{-1}\left(\dfrac{x}{y + z}\right)$; $P(4, 2, 2)$

55–60 Find a unit vector in the direction in which f decreases most rapidly at P, and find the rate of change of f at P in that direction. ■

55. $f(x, y) = 20 - x^2 - y^2$; $P(-1, -3)$

56. $f(x, y) = e^{xy}$; $P(2, 3)$

57. $f(x, y) = \cos(3x - y)$; $P(\pi/6, \pi/4)$

58. $f(x, y) = \sqrt{\dfrac{x - y}{x + y}}$; $P(3, 1)$

59. $f(x, y, z) = \dfrac{x + z}{z - y}$; $P(5, 7, 6)$

60. $f(x, y, z) = 4e^{xy} \cos z$; $P(0, 1, \pi/4)$

61–64 True–False Determine whether the statement is true or false. Explain your answer. In each exercise, assume that f denotes a differentiable function of two variables whose domain is the xy-plane. ■

61. If $\mathbf{v} = 2\mathbf{u}$, then the directional derivative of f in the direction of $\mathbf{v}$ at a point (x_0, y_0) is twice the directional derivative of f in the direction of $\mathbf{u}$ at the point (x_0, y_0).

62. If $y = x^2$ is a contour of f, then $f_x(0, 0) = 0$.

63. If $\mathbf{u}$ is a fixed unit vector and $D_{\mathbf{u}} f(x, y) = 0$ for all points (x, y), then f is a constant function.

64. If the displacement vector from (x_0, y_0) to (x_1, y_1) is a positive multiple of $\nabla f(x_0, y_0)$, then $f(x_0, y_0) \le f(x_1, y_1)$.

FOCUS ON CONCEPTS

65. Given that $\nabla f(4, -5) = 2\mathbf{i} - \mathbf{j}$, find the directional derivative of the function f at the point $(4, -5)$ in the direction of $\mathbf{a} = 5\mathbf{i} + 2\mathbf{j}$.

66. Given that $\nabla f(x_0, y_0) = \mathbf{i} - 2\mathbf{j}$ and $D_{\mathbf{u}} f(x_0, y_0) = -2$, find $\mathbf{u}$ (two answers).

67. The accompanying figure shows some level curves of an unspecified function $f(x, y)$.
(a) Use the available information to approximate the length of the vector $\nabla f(1, 2)$, and sketch the approximation. Explain how you approximated the length and determined the direction of the vector.
(b) Sketch an approximation of the vector $-\nabla f(4, 4)$.

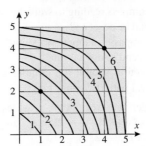

◀ **Figure Ex-67**

68. The accompanying figure shows a topographic map of a hill and a point P at the bottom of the hill. Suppose that you want to climb from the point P toward the top of the hill in such a way that you are always ascending in the direction of steepest slope. Sketch the projection of your path on the contour map. This is called the **path of steepest ascent**. Explain how you determined the path.

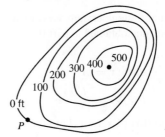

◀ **Figure Ex-68**

69. Let $z = 3x^2 - y^2$. Find all points at which $\|\nabla z\| = 6$.

70. Given that $z = 3x + y^2$, find $\nabla \|\nabla z\|$ at the point $(5, 2)$.

71. A particle moves along a path C given by the equations $x = t$ and $y = -t^2$. If $z = x^2 + y^2$, find dz/ds along C at the instant when the particle is at the point $(2, -4)$.

72. The temperature (in degrees Celsius) at a point (x, y) on a metal plate in the xy-plane is

$$T(x, y) = \frac{xy}{1 + x^2 + y^2}$$

(cont.)

(a) Find the rate of change of temperature at $(1, 1)$ in the direction of $\mathbf{a} = 2\mathbf{i} - \mathbf{j}$.

(b) An ant at $(1, 1)$ wants to walk in the direction in which the temperature drops most rapidly. Find a unit vector in that direction.

73. If the electric potential at a point (x, y) in the xy-plane is $V(x, y)$, then the **electric intensity vector** at the point (x, y) is $\mathbf{E} = -\nabla V(x, y)$. Suppose that $V(x, y) = e^{-2x} \cos 2y$.

(a) Find the electric intensity vector at $(\pi/4, 0)$.

(b) Show that at each point in the plane, the electric potential decreases most rapidly in the direction of the vector $\mathbf{E}$.

74. On a certain mountain, the elevation z above a point (x, y) in an xy-plane at sea level is $z = 2000 - 0.02x^2 - 0.04y^2$, where x, y, and z are in meters. The positive x-axis points east, and the positive y-axis north. A climber is at the point $(-20, 5, 1991)$.

(a) If the climber uses a compass reading to walk due west, will she begin to ascend or descend?

(b) If the climber uses a compass reading to walk northeast, will she ascend or descend? At what rate?

(c) In what compass direction should the climber begin walking to travel a level path (two answers)?

75. Given that the directional derivative of $f(x, y, z)$ at the point $(3, -2, 1)$ in the direction of $\mathbf{a} = 2\mathbf{i} - \mathbf{j} - 2\mathbf{k}$ is -5 and that $\|\nabla f(3, -2, 1)\| = 5$, find $\nabla f(3, -2, 1)$.

76. The temperature (in degrees Celsius) at a point (x, y, z) in a metal solid is

$$T(x, y, z) = \frac{xyz}{1 + x^2 + y^2 + z^2}$$

(a) Find the rate of change of temperature with respect to distance at $(1, 1, 1)$ in the direction of the origin.

(b) Find the direction in which the temperature rises most rapidly at the point $(1, 1, 1)$. (Express your answer as a unit vector.)

(c) Find the rate at which the temperature rises moving from $(1, 1, 1)$ in the direction obtained in part (b).

77. Let $r = \sqrt{x^2 + y^2}$.

(a) Show that $\nabla r = \dfrac{\mathbf{r}}{r}$, where $\mathbf{r} = x\mathbf{i} + y\mathbf{j}$.

(b) Show that $\nabla f(r) = f'(r) \nabla r = \dfrac{f'(r)}{r} \mathbf{r}$.

78. Use the formula in part (b) of Exercise 77 to find

(a) $\nabla f(r)$ if $f(r) = re^{-3r}$

(b) $f(r)$ if $\nabla f(r) = 3r^2 \mathbf{r}$ and $f(2) = 1$.

79. Let $\mathbf{u}_r$ be a unit vector whose counterclockwise angle from the positive x-axis is θ, and let $\mathbf{u}_\theta$ be a unit vector $90°$ counterclockwise from $\mathbf{u}_r$. Show that if $z = f(x, y)$, $x = r \cos \theta$, and $y = r \sin \theta$, then

$$\nabla z = \frac{\partial z}{\partial r} \mathbf{u}_r + \frac{1}{r} \frac{\partial z}{\partial \theta} \mathbf{u}_\theta$$

[*Hint:* Use part (c) of Exercise 55, Section 13.5.]

80. Prove: If f and g are differentiable, then

(a) $\nabla(f + g) = \nabla f + \nabla g$

(b) $\nabla(cf) = c\nabla f$ (c constant)

(c) $\nabla(fg) = f\nabla g + g\nabla f$

(d) $\nabla\left(\dfrac{f}{g}\right) = \dfrac{g\nabla f - f\nabla g}{g^2}$

(e) $\nabla(f^n) = nf^{n-1}\nabla f$.

81–82 A heat-seeking particle is located at the point P on a flat metal plate whose temperature at a point (x, y) is $T(x, y)$. Find parametric equations for the trajectory of the particle if it moves continuously in the direction of maximum temperature increase.

81. $T(x, y) = 5 - 4x^2 - y^2$; $P(1, 4)$

82. $T(x, y) = 100 - x^2 - 2y^2$; $P(5, 3)$

83. Use a graphing utility to generate the trajectory of the particle together with some representative level curves of the temperature function in Exercise 81.

84. Use a graphing utility to generate the trajectory of the particle together with some representative level curves of the temperature function in Exercise 82.

85. (a) Use a CAS to graph $f(x, y) = (x^2 + 3y^2)e^{-(x^2+y^2)}$.

(b) At how many points do you think it is true that $D_{\mathbf{u}} f(x, y) = 0$ for all unit vectors $\mathbf{u}$?

(c) Use a CAS to find ∇f.

(d) Use a CAS to solve the equation $\nabla f(x, y) = 0$ for x and y.

(e) Use the result in part (d) together with Theorem 13.6.5 to check your conjecture in part (b).

86. Prove: If $x = x(t)$ and $y = y(t)$ are differentiable at t, and if $z = f(x, y)$ is differentiable at the point $(x(t), y(t))$, then

$$\frac{dz}{dt} = \nabla z \cdot \mathbf{r}'(t)$$

where $\mathbf{r}(t) = x(t)\mathbf{i} + y(t)\mathbf{j}$.

87. Prove: If f, f_x, and f_y are continuous on a circular region, and if $\nabla f(x, y) = \mathbf{0}$ throughout the region, then $f(x, y)$ is constant on the region. [*Hint:* See Exercise 67, Section 13.5.]

88. Prove: If the function f is differentiable at the point (x, y) and if $D_{\mathbf{u}} f(x, y) = 0$ in two nonparallel directions, then $D_{\mathbf{u}} f(x, y) = 0$ in all directions.

89. Given that the functions $u = u(x, y, z)$, $v = v(x, y, z)$, $w = w(x, y, z)$, and $f(u, v, w)$ are all differentiable, show that

$$\nabla f(u, v, w) = \frac{\partial f}{\partial u} \nabla u + \frac{\partial f}{\partial v} \nabla v + \frac{\partial f}{\partial w} \nabla w$$

90. Writing Let f denote a differentiable function of two variables. Write a short paragraph that discusses the connections between directional derivatives of f and slopes of tangent lines to the graph of f.

91. Writing Let f denote a differentiable function of two variables. Although we have defined what it means to say that f is differentiable, we have not defined the "derivative" of f. Write a short paragraph that discusses the merits of defining the derivative of f to be the gradient ∇f.

13.7 TANGENT PLANES AND NORMAL VECTORS

In this section we will discuss tangent planes to surfaces in three-dimensional space. We will be concerned with three main questions: What is a tangent plane? When do tangent planes exist? How do we find equations of tangent planes?

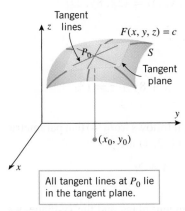

▲ **Figure 13.7.1**

■ TANGENT PLANES AND NORMAL VECTORS TO LEVEL SURFACES $F(x, y, z) = c$

We begin by considering the problem of finding tangent planes to level surfaces of a function $F(x, y, z)$. These surfaces are represented by equations of the form $F(x, y, z) = c$. We will assume that F has continuous first-order partial derivatives, since this has an important geometric consequence. Fix c, and suppose that $P_0(x_0, y_0, z_0)$ satisfies the equation $F(x, y, z) = c$. In advanced courses it is proved that if F has continuous first-order partial derivatives, and if $\nabla F(x_0, y_0, z_0) \neq \mathbf{0}$, then near P_0 the graph of $F(x, y, z) = c$ is indeed a "surface" rather than some possibly exotic-looking set of points in 3-space.

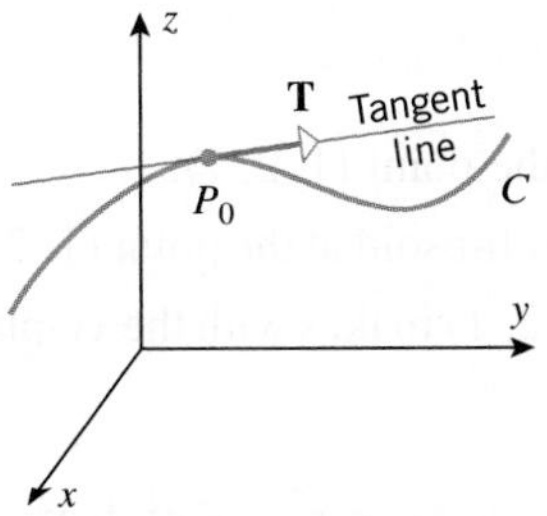

We will base our concept of a tangent plane to a level surface $S: F(x, y, z) = c$ on the more elementary notion of a tangent line to a curve C in 3-space (Figure 13.7.1). Intuitively, we would expect a tangent plane to S at a point P_0 to be composed of the tangent lines at P_0 of all curves on S that pass through P_0 (Figure 13.7.2). Suppose C is a curve on S through P_0 that is parametrized by $x = x(t)$, $y = y(t)$, $z = z(t)$ with $x_0 = x(t_0)$, $y_0 = y(t_0)$, and $z_0 = z(t_0)$. The tangent line l to C through P_0 is then parallel to the vector

$$\mathbf{r}' = x'(t_0)\mathbf{i} + y'(t_0)\mathbf{j} + z'(t_0)\mathbf{k}$$

where we assume that $\mathbf{r}' \neq \mathbf{0}$ (Definition 12.2.7). Since C is on the surface $F(x, y, z) = c$, we have

$$c = F(x(t), y(t), z(t)) \tag{1}$$

Computing the derivative at t_0 of both sides of (1), we have by the chain rule that

$$0 = F_x(x_0, y_0, z_0)x'(t_0) + F_y(x_0, y_0, z_0)y'(t_0) + F_z(x_0, y_0, z_0)z'(t_0)$$

We can write this equation in vector form as

$$0 = (F_x(x_0, y_0, z_0)\mathbf{i} + F_y(x_0, y_0, z_0)\mathbf{j} + F_z(x_0, y_0, z_0)\mathbf{k}) \cdot (x'(t_0)\mathbf{i} + y'(t_0)\mathbf{j} + z'(t_0)\mathbf{k})$$

or

$$0 = \nabla F(x_0, y_0, z_0) \cdot \mathbf{r}' \tag{2}$$

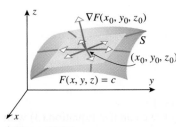

It follows that if $\nabla F(x_0, y_0, z_0) \neq \mathbf{0}$, then $\nabla F(x_0, y_0, z_0)$ is normal to line l. Therefore, the tangent line l to C at P_0 is contained in the plane through P_0 with normal vector $\nabla F(x_0, y_0, z_0)$. Since C was *arbitrary*, we conclude that the same is true for any curve on S through P_0 (Figure 13.7.3). Thus, it makes sense to define the tangent plane to S at P_0 to be the plane through P_0 whose normal vector is

$$\mathbf{n} = \nabla F(x_0, y_0, z_0) = \langle F_x(x_0, y_0, z_0), F_y(x_0, y_0, z_0), F_z(x_0, y_0, z_0) \rangle$$

Using the point-normal form [see Formula (3) in Section 11.6], we have the following definition.

▲ **Figure 13.7.2**

All tangent lines at P_0 lie in the tangent plane.

▲ **Figure 13.7.3**

13.7.1   DEFINITION   Assume that $F(x, y, z)$ has continuous first-order partial derivatives and that $P_0(x_0, y_0, z_0)$ is a point on the level surface $S: F(x, y, z) = c$. If $\nabla F(x_0, y_0, z_0) \neq \mathbf{0}$, then $\mathbf{n} = \nabla F(x_0, y_0, z_0)$ is a ***normal vector*** to S at P_0 and the ***tangent plane*** to S at P_0 is the plane with equation

$$F_x(x_0, y_0, z_0)(x - x_0) + F_y(x_0, y_0, z_0)(y - y_0) + F_z(x_0, y_0, z_0)(z - z_0) = 0 \quad (3)$$

Definition 13.7.1 can be viewed as an extension of Theorem 13.6.6 from curves to surfaces.

The line through the point P_0 parallel to the normal vector $\mathbf{n}$ is perpendicular to the tangent plane (3). We will call this the ***normal line***, or sometimes more simply the ***normal*** to the surface $F(x, y, z) = c$ at P_0. It follows that this line can be expressed parametrically as

$$x = x_0 + F_x(x_0, y_0, z_0)t, \quad y = y_0 + F_y(x_0, y_0, z_0)t, \quad z = z_0 + F_z(x_0, y_0, z_0)t \quad (4)$$

▶ **Example 1**   Consider the ellipsoid $x^2 + 4y^2 + z^2 = 18$.

(a) Find an equation of the tangent plane to the ellipsoid at the point $(1, 2, 1)$.

(b) Find parametric equations of the line that is normal to the ellipsoid at the point $(1, 2, 1)$.

(c) Find the acute angle that the tangent plane at the point $(1, 2, 1)$ makes with the xy-plane.

Solution (a).   We apply Definition 13.7.1 with $F(x, y, z) = x^2 + 4y^2 + z^2$ and $(x_0, y_0, z_0) = (1, 2, 1)$. Since

$$\nabla F(x, y, z) = \langle F_x(x, y, z), F_y(x, y, z), F_z(x, y, z) \rangle = \langle 2x, 8y, 2z \rangle$$

we have

$$\mathbf{n} = \nabla F(1, 2, 1) = \langle 2, 16, 2 \rangle$$

Hence, from (3) the equation of the tangent plane is

$$2(x - 1) + 16(y - 2) + 2(z - 1) = 0 \quad \text{or} \quad x + 8y + z = 18$$

Solution (b).   Since $\mathbf{n} = \langle 2, 16, 2 \rangle$ at the point $(1, 2, 1)$, it follows from (4) that parametric equations for the normal line to the ellipsoid at the point $(1, 2, 1)$ are

$$x = 1 + 2t, \quad y = 2 + 16t, \quad z = 1 + 2t$$

Solution (c).   To find the acute angle θ between the tangent plane and the xy-plane, we will apply Formula (9) of Section 11.6 with $\mathbf{n}_1 = \mathbf{n} = \langle 2, 16, 2 \rangle$ and $\mathbf{n}_2 = \langle 0, 0, 1 \rangle$. This yields

$$\cos \theta = \frac{|\langle 2, 16, 2 \rangle \cdot \langle 0, 0, 1 \rangle|}{\|\langle 2, 16, 2 \rangle\| \, \|\langle 0, 0, 1 \rangle\|} = \frac{2}{(2\sqrt{66})(1)} = \frac{1}{\sqrt{66}}$$

Thus,

$$\theta = \cos^{-1}\left(\frac{1}{\sqrt{66}}\right) \approx 83°$$

(Figure 13.7.4). ◀

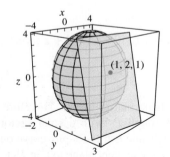

▲ **Figure 13.7.4**

■ **TANGENT PLANES TO SURFACES OF THE FORM** $z = f(x, y)$

To find a tangent plane to a surface of the form $z = f(x, y)$, we can use Equation (3) with the function $F(x, y, z) = z - f(x, y)$.

▶ **Example 2** Find an equation for the tangent plane and parametric equations for the normal line to the surface $z = x^2 y$ at the point $(2, 1, 4)$.

Solution. Let $F(x, y, z) = z - x^2 y$. Then $F(x, y, z) = 0$ on the surface, so we can find the find the gradient of F at the point $(2, 1, 4)$:

$$\nabla F(x, y, z) = -2xy\mathbf{i} - x^2\mathbf{j} + \mathbf{k}$$

$$\nabla F(2, 1, 4) = -4\mathbf{i} - 4\mathbf{j} + \mathbf{k}$$

From (3) the tangent plane has equation

$$-4(x - 2) - 4(y - 1) + 1(z - 4) = 0 \quad \text{or} \quad -4x - 4y + z = -8$$

and the normal line has equations

$$x = 2 - 4t, \qquad y = 1 - 4t, \qquad z = 4 + t \quad \blacktriangleleft$$

Suppose that $f(x, y)$ is differentiable at a point (x_0, y_0) and that $z_0 = f(x_0, y_0)$. It can be shown that the procedure of Example 2 can be used to find the tangent plane to the surface $z = f(x, y)$ at the point (x_0, y_0, z_0). This yields an alternative equation for a tangent plane to the graph of a differentiable function.

13.7.2 **THEOREM** *If $f(x, y)$ is differentiable at the point (x_0, y_0), then the tangent plane to the surface $z = f(x, y)$ at the point $P_0(x_0, y_0, f(x_0, y_0))$ [or (x_0, y_0)] is the plane*

$$z = f(x_0, y_0) + f_x(x_0, y_0)(x - x_0) + f_y(x_0, y_0)(y - y_0) \tag{5}$$

PROOF Consider the function $F(x, y, z) = z - f(x, y)$. Since $F(x, y, z) = 0$ on the surface, we will apply (3) to this function. The partial derivatives of F are

$$F_x(x, y, z) = -f_x(x, y), \quad F_y(x, y, z) = -f_y(x, y), \quad F_z(x, y, z) = 1$$

Since the point at which we evaluate these derivatives lies on the surface, it will have the form $(x_0, y_0, f(x_0, y_0))$. Thus, (3) gives

$$0 = F_x(x_0, y_0, z_0)(x - x_0) + F_y(x_0, y_0, z_0)(y - y_0) + F_z(x_0, y_0, z_0)(z - f(x_0, y_0))$$

$$= -f_x(x_0, y_0)(x - x_0) - f_y(x_0, y_0)(y - y_0) + 1(z - f(x_0, y_0))$$

which is equivalent to (5). ∎

Recall from Section 13.4 that if a function $f(x, y)$ is differentiable at a point (x_0, y_0), then the local linear approximation $L(x, y)$ to f at (x_0, y_0) has the equation

$$L(x, y) = f(x_0, y_0) + f_x(x_0, y_0)(x - x_0) + f_y(x_0, y_0)(y - y_0)$$

Notice that the equation $z = L(x, y)$ is identical to that of the tangent plane to $f(x, y)$ at the point (x_0, y_0). Thus, the graph of the local linear approximation to $f(x, y)$ at the point (x_0, y_0) is the tangent plane to the surface $z = f(x, y)$ at the point (x_0, y_0).

■ **TANGENT PLANES AND TOTAL DIFFERENTIALS**

Recall that for a function $z = f(x, y)$ of two variables, the approximation by differentials is

$$\Delta z = \Delta f = f(x, y) - f(x_0, y_0) \approx dz = f_x(x_0, y_0)(x - x_0) + f_y(x_0, y_0)(y - y_0)$$

Note that the tangent plane in Figure 13.7.5 is analogous to the tangent line in Figure 13.4.2.

The tangent plane provides a geometric interpretation of this approximation. We see in Figure 13.7.5 that Δz is the change in z *along the surface* $z = f(x, y)$ from the point $P_0(x_0, y_0, f(x_0, y_0))$ to the point $P(x, y, f(x, y))$, and dz is the change in z *along the tangent plane* from P_0 to $Q(x, y, L(x, y))$. The small vertical displacement at (x, y) between the surface and the plane represents the error in the local linear approximation to f at (x_0, y_0). We have seen that near (x_0, y_0) this error term has magnitude much smaller than the distance between (x, y) and (x_0, y_0).

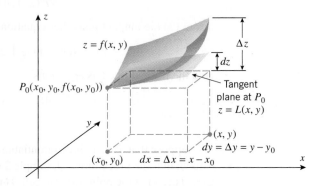

▶ **Figure 13.7.5**

USING GRADIENTS TO FIND TANGENT LINES TO INTERSECTIONS OF SURFACES

In general, the intersection of two surfaces $F(x, y, z) = 0$ and $G(x, y, z) = 0$ will be a curve in 3-space. If (x_0, y_0, z_0) is a point on this curve, then $\nabla F(x_0, y_0, z_0)$ will be normal to the surface $F(x, y, z) = 0$ at (x_0, y_0, z_0) and $\nabla G(x_0, y_0, z_0)$ will be normal to the surface $G(x, y, z) = 0$ at (x_0, y_0, z_0). Thus, if the curve of intersection can be smoothly parametrized, then its unit tangent vector $\mathbf{T}$ at (x_0, y_0, z_0) will be orthogonal to both $\nabla F(x_0, y_0, z_0)$ and $\nabla G(x_0, y_0, z_0)$ (Figure 13.7.6). Consequently, if

$$\nabla F(x_0, y_0, z_0) \times \nabla G(x_0, y_0, z_0) \neq \mathbf{0}$$

then this cross product will be parallel to $\mathbf{T}$ and hence will be tangent to the curve of intersection. This tangent vector can be used to determine the direction of the tangent line to the curve of intersection at the point (x_0, y_0, z_0).

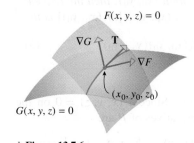

▲ **Figure 13.7.6**

▶ **Example 3**   Find parametric equations of the tangent line to the curve of intersection of the paraboloid $z = x^2 + y^2$ and the ellipsoid $3x^2 + 2y^2 + z^2 = 9$ at the point $(1, 1, 2)$ (Figure 13.7.7).

Solution.   We begin by rewriting the equations of the surfaces as

$$x^2 + y^2 - z = 0 \quad \text{and} \quad 3x^2 + 2y^2 + z^2 - 9 = 0$$

and we take

$$F(x, y, z) = x^2 + y^2 - z \quad \text{and} \quad G(x, y, z) = 3x^2 + 2y^2 + z^2 - 9$$

We will need the gradients of these functions at the point $(1, 1, 2)$. The computations are

$$\nabla F(x, y, z) = 2x\mathbf{i} + 2y\mathbf{j} - \mathbf{k}, \quad \nabla G(x, y, z) = 6x\mathbf{i} + 4y\mathbf{j} + 2z\mathbf{k}$$
$$\nabla F(1, 1, 2) = 2\mathbf{i} + 2\mathbf{j} - \mathbf{k}, \quad \nabla G(1, 1, 2) = 6\mathbf{i} + 4\mathbf{j} + 4\mathbf{k}$$

Thus, a tangent vector at $(1, 1, 2)$ to the curve of intersection is

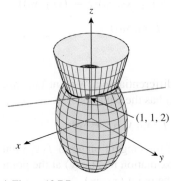

▲ **Figure 13.7.7**

$$\nabla F(1, 1, 2) \times \nabla G(1, 1, 2) = \begin{vmatrix} \mathbf{i} & \mathbf{j} & \mathbf{k} \\ 2 & 2 & -1 \\ 6 & 4 & 4 \end{vmatrix} = 12\mathbf{i} - 14\mathbf{j} - 4\mathbf{k}$$

Since any scalar multiple of this vector will do just as well, we can multiply by $\frac{1}{2}$ to reduce the size of the coefficients and use the vector of $6\mathbf{i} - 7\mathbf{j} - 2\mathbf{k}$ to determine the direction of the tangent line. This vector and the point $(1, 1, 2)$ yield the parametric equations

$$x = 1 + 6t, \quad y = 1 - 7t, \quad z = 2 - 2t \blacktriangleleft$$

✔ QUICK CHECK EXERCISES 13.7   (See page 977 for answers.)

1. Suppose that $f(1, 0, -1) = 2$, and $f(x, y, z)$ is differentiable at $(1, 0, -1)$ with $\nabla f(1, 0, -1) = \langle 2, 1, 1 \rangle$. An equation for the tangent plane to the level surface $f(x, y, z) = 2$ at the point $(1, 0, -1)$ is _____, and parametric equations for the normal line to the level surface through the point $(1, 0, -1)$ are

   $x = $ _____, $y = $ _____, $z = $ _____

2. Suppose that $f(x, y)$ is differentiable at the point $(3, 1)$ with $f(3, 1) = 4$, $f_x(3, 1) = 2$, and $f_y(3, 1) = -3$. An equation for the tangent plane to the graph of f at the point $(3, 1, 4)$ is _____, and parametric equations for the normal line to the graph of f through the point $(3, 1, 4)$ are

   $x = $ _____, $y = $ _____, $z = $ _____

3. An equation for the tangent plane to the graph of $z = x^2\sqrt{y}$ at the point $(2, 4, 8)$ is _____, and parametric equations for the normal line to the graph of $z = x^2\sqrt{y}$ through the point $(2, 4, 8)$ are

   $x = $ _____, $y = $ _____, $z = $ _____

4. The sphere $x^2 + y^2 + z^2 = 9$ and the plane $x + y + z = 5$ intersect in a circle that passes through the point $(2, 1, 2)$. Parametric equations for the tangent line to this circle at $(2, 1, 2)$ are

   $x = $ _____, $y = $ _____, $z = $ _____

EXERCISE SET 13.7   ⃞C CAS

1. Consider the ellipsoid $x^2 + y^2 + 4z^2 = 12$.
   (a) Find an equation of the tangent plane to the ellipsoid at the point $(2, 2, 1)$.
   (b) Find parametric equations of the line that is normal to the ellipsoid at the point $(2, 2, 1)$.
   (c) Find the acute angle that the tangent plane at the point $(2, 2, 1)$ makes with the xy-plane.

2. Consider the surface $xz - yz^3 + yz^2 = 2$.
   (a) Find an equation of the tangent plane to the surface at the point $(2, -1, 1)$.
   (b) Find parametric equations of the line that is normal to the surface at the point $(2, -1, 1)$.
   (c) Find the acute angle that the tangent plane at the point $(2, -1, 1)$ makes with the xy-plane.

3–10 Find an equation for the tangent plane and parametric equations for the normal line to the surface at the point P. ◾

3. $x^2 + y^2 + z^2 = 25$; $P(-3, 0, 4)$
4. $x^2y - 4z^2 = -7$; $P(-3, 1, -2)$
5. $z = 4x^3y^2 + 2y$; $P(1, -2, 12)$
6. $z = \frac{1}{2}x^7y^{-2}$; $P(2, 4, 4)$
7. $z = xe^{-y}$; $P(1, 0, 1)$
8. $z = \ln\sqrt{x^2 + y^2}$; $P(-1, 0, 0)$
9. $z = e^{3y}\sin 3x$; $P(\pi/6, 0, 1)$
10. $z = x^{1/2} + y^{1/2}$; $P(4, 9, 5)$

FOCUS ON CONCEPTS

11. Find all points on the surface at which the tangent plane is horizontal.
    (a) $z = x^3y^2$
    (b) $z = x^2 - xy + y^2 - 2x + 4y$

12. Find a point on the surface $z = 3x^2 - y^2$ at which the tangent plane is parallel to the plane $6x + 4y - z = 5$.

13. Find a point on the surface $z = 8 - 3x^2 - 2y^2$ at which the tangent plane is perpendicular to the line $x = 2 - 3t$, $y = 7 + 8t$, $z = 5 - t$.

14. Show that the surfaces
    $$z = \sqrt{x^2 + y^2} \quad \text{and} \quad z = \tfrac{1}{10}(x^2 + y^2) + \tfrac{5}{2}$$
    intersect at $(3, 4, 5)$ and have a common tangent plane at that point.

15. (a) Find all points of intersection of the line
    $$x = -1 + t, \quad y = 2 + t, \quad z = 2t + 7$$
    and the surface
    $$z = x^2 + y^2$$
    (b) At each point of intersection, find the cosine of the acute angle between the given line and the line normal to the surface.

16. Show that if f is differentiable and $z = xf(x/y)$, then all tangent planes to the graph of this equation pass through the origin.

17–20 True–False Determine whether the statement is true or false. Explain your answer. ■

17. If the tangent plane to the level surface of $F(x, y, z)$ at the point $P_0(x_0, y_0, z_0)$ is also tangent to a level surface of $G(x, y, z)$ at P_0, then $\nabla F(x_0, y_0, z_0) = \nabla G(x_0, y_0, z_0)$.

18. If the tangent plane to the graph of $z = f(x, y)$ at the point $(1, 1, 2)$ has equation $x - y + 2z = 4$, then $f_x(1, 1) = 1$ and $f_y(1, 1) = -1$.

19. If the tangent plane to the graph of $z = f(x, y)$ at the point $(1, 2, 1)$ has equation $2x + y - z = 3$, then the local linear approximation to f at $(1, 2)$ is given by the function $L(x, y) = 1 + 2(x - 1) + (y - 2)$.

20. The normal line to the surface $z = f(x, y)$ at the point $P_0(x_0, y_0, f(x_0, y_0))$ has a direction vector given by $f_x(x_0, y_0)\mathbf{i} + f_y(x_0, y_0)\mathbf{j} - \mathbf{k}$.

21–22 Find two unit vectors that are normal to the given surface at the point P. ■

21. $\sqrt{\dfrac{z + x}{y - 1}} = z^2$; $P(3, 5, 1)$

22. $\sin xz - 4\cos yz = 4$; $P(\pi, \pi, 1)$

23. Show that every line that is normal to the sphere

$$x^2 + y^2 + z^2 = 1$$

passes through the origin.

24. Find all points on the ellipsoid $2x^2 + 3y^2 + 4z^2 = 9$ at which the plane tangent to the ellipsoid is parallel to the plane $x - 2y + 3z = 5$.

25. Find all points on the surface $x^2 + y^2 - z^2 = 1$ at which the normal line is parallel to the line through $P(1, -2, 1)$ and $Q(4, 0, -1)$.

26. Show that the ellipsoid $2x^2 + 3y^2 + z^2 = 9$ and the sphere

$$x^2 + y^2 + z^2 - 6x - 8y - 8z + 24 = 0$$

have a common tangent plane at the point $(1, 1, 2)$.

27. Find parametric equations for the tangent line to the curve of intersection of the paraboloid $z = x^2 + y^2$ and the ellipsoid $x^2 + 4y^2 + z^2 = 9$ at the point $(1, -1, 2)$.

28. Find parametric equations for the tangent line to the curve of intersection of the cone $z = \sqrt{x^2 + y^2}$ and the plane $x + 2y + 2z = 20$ at the point $(4, 3, 5)$.

29. Find parametric equations for the tangent line to the curve of intersection of the cylinders $x^2 + z^2 = 25$ and $y^2 + z^2 = 25$ at the point $(3, -3, 4)$.

c **30.** The accompanying figure shows the intersection of the surfaces $z = 8 - x^2 - y^2$ and $4x + 2y - z = 0$.
 (a) Find parametric equations for the tangent line to the curve of intersection at the point $(0, 2, 4)$.
 (b) Use a CAS to generate a reasonable facsimile of the figure. You need not generate the colors, but try to obtain a similar viewpoint.

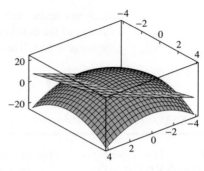

◀ **Figure Ex-30**

31. Show that the equation of the plane that is tangent to the ellipsoid

$$\frac{x^2}{a^2} + \frac{y^2}{b^2} + \frac{z^2}{c^2} = 1$$

at (x_0, y_0, z_0) can be written in the form

$$\frac{x_0 x}{a^2} + \frac{y_0 y}{b^2} + \frac{z_0 z}{c^2} = 1$$

32. Show that the equation of the plane that is tangent to the paraboloid

$$z = \frac{x^2}{a^2} + \frac{y^2}{b^2}$$

at (x_0, y_0, z_0) can be written in the form

$$z + z_0 = \frac{2x_0 x}{a^2} + \frac{2y_0 y}{b^2}$$

33. Prove: If the surfaces $z = f(x, y)$ and $z = g(x, y)$ intersect at $P(x_0, y_0, z_0)$, and if f and g are differentiable at (x_0, y_0), then the normal lines at P are perpendicular if and only if

$$f_x(x_0, y_0)g_x(x_0, y_0) + f_y(x_0, y_0)g_y(x_0, y_0) = -1$$

34. Use the result in Exercise 33 to show that the normal lines to the cones $z = \sqrt{x^2 + y^2}$ and $z = -\sqrt{x^2 + y^2}$ are perpendicular to the normal lines to the sphere $x^2 + y^2 + z^2 = a^2$ at every point of intersection (see Figure Ex-36).

35. Two surfaces $f(x, y, z) = 0$ and $g(x, y, z) = 0$ are said to be **orthogonal** at a point P of intersection if ∇f and ∇g are nonzero at P and the normal lines to the surfaces are perpendicular at P. Show that if $\nabla f(x_0, y_0, z_0) \neq \mathbf{0}$ and $\nabla g(x_0, y_0, z_0) \neq \mathbf{0}$, then the surfaces $f(x, y, z) = 0$ and $g(x, y, z) = 0$ are orthogonal at the point (x_0, y_0, z_0) if and only if

$$f_x g_x + f_y g_y + f_z g_z = 0$$

at this point. [*Note:* This is a more general version of the result in Exercise 33.]

36. Use the result of Exercise 35 to show that the sphere $x^2 + y^2 + z^2 = a^2$ and the cone $z^2 = x^2 + y^2$ are orthogonal at every point of intersection (see the accompanying figure).

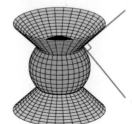

◀ **Figure Ex-36**

37. Show that the volume of the solid bounded by the coordinate planes and a plane tangent to the portion of the surface $xyz = k$, $k > 0$, in the first octant does not depend on the point of tangency.

38. Writing Discuss the role of the chain rule in defining a tangent plane to a level surface.

39. Writing Discuss the relationship between tangent planes and local linear approximations for functions of two variables.

✔ **QUICK CHECK ANSWERS 13.7**

1. $2(x - 1) + y + (z + 1) = 0$; $x = 1 + 2t$; $y = t$; $z = -1 + t$
2. $z = 4 + 2(x - 3) - 3(y - 1)$; $x = 3 + 2t$; $y = 1 - 3t$; $z = 4 - t$
3. $z = 8 + 8(x - 2) + (y - 4)$; $x = 2 + 8t$; $y = 4 + t$; $z = 8 - t$ 4. $x = 2 + t$; $y = 1$; $z = 2 - t$

13.8   MAXIMA AND MINIMA OF FUNCTIONS OF TWO VARIABLES

Earlier in this text we learned how to find maximum and minimum values of a function of one variable. In this section we will develop similar techniques for functions of two variables.

■ **EXTREMA**

If we imagine the graph of a function f of two variables to be a mountain range (Figure 13.8.1), then the mountaintops, which are the high points in their immediate vicinity, are called *relative maxima* of f, and the valley bottoms, which are the low points in their immediate vicinity, are called *relative minima* of f.

Just as a geologist might be interested in finding the highest mountain and deepest valley in an entire mountain range, so a mathematician might be interested in finding the largest and smallest values of $f(x, y)$ over the *entire* domain of f. These are called the *absolute maximum* and *absolute minimum values* of f. The following definitions make these informal ideas precise.

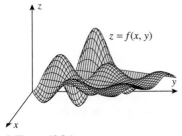

▲ **Figure 13.8.1**

13.8.1   DEFINITION   A function f of two variables is said to have a ***relative maximum*** at a point (x_0, y_0) if there is a disk centered at (x_0, y_0) such that $f(x_0, y_0) \geq f(x, y)$ for all points (x, y) that lie inside the disk, and f is said to have an ***absolute maximum*** at (x_0, y_0) if $f(x_0, y_0) \geq f(x, y)$ for all points (x, y) in the domain of f.

13.8.2   DEFINITION   A function f of two variables is said to have a ***relative minimum*** at a point (x_0, y_0) if there is a disk centered at (x_0, y_0) such that $f(x_0, y_0) \leq f(x, y)$ for all points (x, y) that lie inside the disk, and f is said to have an ***absolute minimum*** at (x_0, y_0) if $f(x_0, y_0) \leq f(x, y)$ for all points (x, y) in the domain of f.

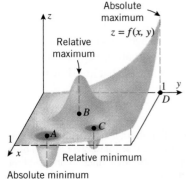

▲ **Figure 13.8.2**

If f has a relative maximum or a relative minimum at (x_0, y_0), then we say that f has a ***relative extremum*** at (x_0, y_0), and if f has an absolute maximum or absolute minimum at (x_0, y_0), then we say that f has an ***absolute extremum*** at (x_0, y_0).

Figure 13.8.2 shows the graph of a function f whose domain is the square region in the xy-plane whose points satisfy the inequalities $0 \leq x \leq 1$, $0 \leq y \leq 1$. The function f has relative minima at the points A and C and a relative maximum at B. There is an absolute minimum at A and an absolute maximum at D.

For functions of two variables we will be concerned with two important questions:

- Are there any relative or absolute extrema?
- If so, where are they located?

BOUNDED SETS

Just as we distinguished between finite intervals and infinite intervals on the real line, so we will want to distinguish between regions of "finite extent" and regions of "infinite extent" in 2-space and 3-space. A set of points in 2-space is called **bounded** if the entire set can be contained within some rectangle, and is called **unbounded** if there is no rectangle that contains all the points of the set. Similarly, a set of points in 3-space is **bounded** if the entire set can be contained within some box, and is unbounded otherwise (Figure 13.8.3).

> Explain why any subset of a bounded set is also bounded.

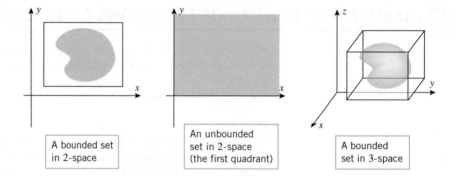

A bounded set in 2-space

An unbounded set in 2-space (the first quadrant)

A bounded set in 3-space

▶ **Figure 13.8.3**

THE EXTREME-VALUE THEOREM

For functions of one variable that are continuous on a closed interval, the Extreme-Value Theorem (Theorem 4.4.2) answered the existence question for absolute extrema. The following theorem, which we state without proof, is the corresponding result for functions of two variables.

13.8.3 **THEOREM** (*Extreme-Value Theorem*) *If $f(x, y)$ is continuous on a closed and bounded set R, then f has both an absolute maximum and an absolute minimum on R.*

▶ **Example 1** The square region R whose points satisfy the inequalities

$$0 \le x \le 1 \quad \text{and} \quad 0 \le y \le 1$$

is a closed and bounded set in the xy-plane. The function f whose graph is shown in Figure 13.8.2 is continuous on R; thus, it is guaranteed to have an absolute maximum and minimum on R by the last theorem. These occur at points D and A that are shown in the figure. ◀

REMARK   If any of the conditions in the Extreme-Value Theorem fail to hold, then there is no guarantee that an absolute maximum or absolute minimum exists on the region R. Thus, a discontinuous function on a closed and bounded set need not have any absolute extrema, and a continuous function on a set that is not closed and bounded also need not have any absolute extrema.

■ FINDING RELATIVE EXTREMA

Recall that if a function g of one variable has a relative extremum at a point x_0 where g is differentiable, then $g'(x_0) = 0$. To obtain the analog of this result for functions of two variables, suppose that $f(x, y)$ has a relative maximum at a point (x_0, y_0) and that the partial derivatives of f exist at (x_0, y_0). It seems plausible geometrically that the traces of the surface $z = f(x, y)$ on the planes $x = x_0$ and $y = y_0$ have horizontal tangent lines at (x_0, y_0) (Figure 13.8.4), so

$$f_x(x_0, y_0) = 0 \quad \text{and} \quad f_y(x_0, y_0) = 0$$

The same conclusion holds if f has a relative minimum at (x_0, y_0), all of which suggests the following result, which we state without formal proof.

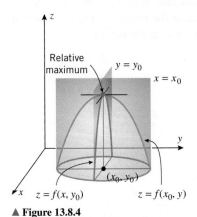

$z = f(x, y_0)$ $z = f(x_0, y)$

▲ **Figure 13.8.4**

13.8.4   THEOREM   *If f has a relative extremum at a point (x_0, y_0), and if the first-order partial derivatives of f exist at this point, then*

$$f_x(x_0, y_0) = 0 \quad \text{and} \quad f_y(x_0, y_0) = 0$$

Recall that the *critical points* of a function f of one variable are those values of x in the domain of f at which $f'(x) = 0$ or f is not differentiable. The following definition is the analog for functions of two variables.

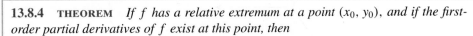

Explain why

$$D_{\mathbf{u}} f(x_0, y_0) = 0$$

for all **u** if (x_0, y_0) is a critical point of f and f is differentiable at (x_0, y_0).

13.8.5   DEFINITION   A point (x_0, y_0) in the domain of a function $f(x, y)$ is called a ***critical point*** of the function if $f_x(x_0, y_0) = 0$ and $f_y(x_0, y_0) = 0$ or if one or both partial derivatives do not exist at (x_0, y_0).

It follows from this definition and Theorem 13.8.4 that relative extrema occur at critical points, just as for a function of one variable. However, recall that for a function of one variable a relative extremum need not occur at *every* critical point. For example, the function might have an inflection point with a horizontal tangent line at the critical point (see Figure 4.2.6). Similarly, a function of two variables need not have a relative extremum at every critical point. For example, consider the function

$$f(x, y) = y^2 - x^2$$

This function, whose graph is the hyperbolic paraboloid shown in Figure 13.8.5, has a critical point at $(0, 0)$, since

$$f_x(x, y) = -2x \quad \text{and} \quad f_y(x, y) = 2y$$

from which it follows that

$$f_x(0, 0) = 0 \quad \text{and} \quad f_y(0, 0) = 0$$

However, the function f has neither a relative maximum nor a relative minimum at $(0, 0)$. For obvious reasons, the point $(0, 0)$ is called a *saddle point* of f. In general, we will say that a surface $z = f(x, y)$ has a ***saddle point*** at (x_0, y_0) if there are two distinct vertical planes through this point such that the trace of the surface in one of the planes has a relative maximum at (x_0, y_0) and the trace in the other has a relative minimum at (x_0, y_0).

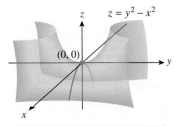

The function $f(x, y) = y^2 - x^2$ has neither a relative maximum nor a relative minimum at the critical point $(0, 0)$.

▲ **Figure 13.8.5**

▶ **Example 2**   The three functions graphed in Figure 13.8.6 all have critical points at $(0, 0)$. For the paraboloids, the partial derivatives at the origin are zero. You can check this algebraically by evaluating the partial derivatives at $(0, 0)$, but you can see it geometrically by observing that the traces in the xz-plane and yz-plane have horizontal tangent lines at $(0, 0)$. For the cone neither partial derivative exists at the origin because the traces in the xz-plane and the yz-plane have corners there. The paraboloid in part (a) and the cone in part (c) have a relative minimum and absolute minimum at the origin, and the paraboloid in part (b) has a relative maximum and an absolute maximum at the origin. ◄

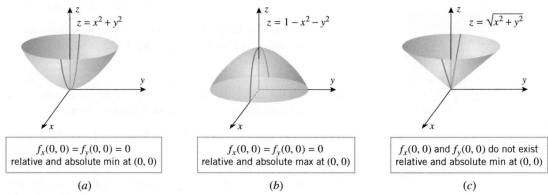

$$z = x^2 + y^2$$

$f_x(0, 0) = f_y(0, 0) = 0$
relative and absolute min at $(0, 0)$

(a)

$$z = 1 - x^2 - y^2$$

$f_x(0, 0) = f_y(0, 0) = 0$
relative and absolute max at $(0, 0)$

(b)

$$z = \sqrt{x^2 + y^2}$$

$f_x(0, 0)$ and $f_y(0, 0)$ do not exist
relative and absolute min at $(0, 0)$

(c)

▲ **Figure 13.8.6**

■ THE SECOND PARTIALS TEST

For functions of one variable the second derivative test (Theorem 4.2.4) was used to determine the behavior of a function at a critical point. The following theorem, which is usually proved in advanced calculus, is the analog of that theorem for functions of two variables.

13.8.6 THEOREM (*The Second Partials Test*) *Let f be a function of two variables with continuous second-order partial derivatives in some disk centered at a critical point (x_0, y_0), and let*

$$D = f_{xx}(x_0, y_0) f_{yy}(x_0, y_0) - f_{xy}^2(x_0, y_0)$$

(a) *If $D > 0$ and $f_{xx}(x_0, y_0) > 0$, then f has a relative minimum at (x_0, y_0).*

(b) *If $D > 0$ and $f_{xx}(x_0, y_0) < 0$, then f has a relative maximum at (x_0, y_0).*

(c) *If $D < 0$, then f has a saddle point at (x_0, y_0).*

(d) *If $D = 0$, then no conclusion can be drawn.*

With the notation of Theorem 13.8.6, show that if $D > 0$, then $f_{xx}(x_0, y_0)$ and $f_{yy}(x_0, y_0)$ have the same sign. Thus, we can replace $f_{xx}(x_0, y_0)$ by $f_{yy}(x_0, y_0)$ in parts (a) and (b) of the theorem.

▶ **Example 3** Locate all relative extrema and saddle points of

$$f(x, y) = 3x^2 - 2xy + y^2 - 8y$$

Solution. Since $f_x(x, y) = 6x - 2y$ and $f_y(x, y) = -2x + 2y - 8$, the critical points of f satisfy the equations

$$6x - 2y = 0$$
$$-2x + 2y - 8 = 0$$

Solving these for x and y yields $x = 2$, $y = 6$ (verify), so $(2, 6)$ is the only critical point. To apply Theorem 13.8.6 we need the second-order partial derivatives

$$f_{xx}(x, y) = 6, \quad f_{yy}(x, y) = 2, \quad f_{xy}(x, y) = -2$$

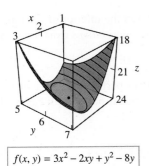

$$f(x, y) = 3x^2 - 2xy + y^2 - 8y$$

▲ **Figure 13.8.7**

At the point $(2, 6)$ we have

$$D = f_{xx}(2, 6) f_{yy}(2, 6) - f_{xy}^2(2, 6) = (6)(2) - (-2)^2 = 8 > 0$$

and

$$f_{xx}(2, 6) = 6 > 0$$

so f has a relative minimum at $(2, 6)$ by part (a) of the second partials test. Figure 13.8.7 shows a graph of f in the vicinity of the relative minimum. ◄

▶ **Example 4** Locate all relative extrema and saddle points of

$$f(x, y) = 4xy - x^4 - y^4$$

Solution. Since

$$\begin{aligned} f_x(x, y) &= 4y - 4x^3 \\ f_y(x, y) &= 4x - 4y^3 \end{aligned} \tag{1}$$

the critical points of f have coordinates satisfying the equations

$$\begin{array}{ccc} 4y - 4x^3 = 0 & & y = x^3 \\ & \text{or} & \\ 4x - 4y^3 = 0 & & x = y^3 \end{array} \tag{2}$$

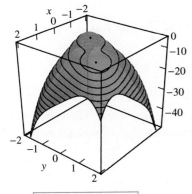

$$f(x, y) = 4xy - x^4 - y^4$$

Substituting the top equation in the bottom yields $x = (x^3)^3$ or, equivalently, $x^9 - x = 0$ or $x(x^8 - 1) = 0$, which has solutions $x = 0$, $x = 1$, $x = -1$. Substituting these values in the top equation of (2), we obtain the corresponding y-values $y = 0$, $y = 1$, $y = -1$. Thus, the critical points of f are $(0, 0)$, $(1, 1)$, and $(-1, -1)$.

From (1),

$$f_{xx}(x, y) = -12x^2, \quad f_{yy}(x, y) = -12y^2, \quad f_{xy}(x, y) = 4$$

which yields the following table:

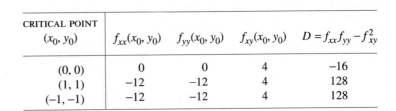

CRITICAL POINT (x_0, y_0)	$f_{xx}(x_0, y_0)$	$f_{yy}(x_0, y_0)$	$f_{xy}(x_0, y_0)$	$D = f_{xx}f_{yy} - f_{xy}^2$
$(0, 0)$	0	0	4	-16
$(1, 1)$	-12	-12	4	128
$(-1, -1)$	-12	-12	4	128

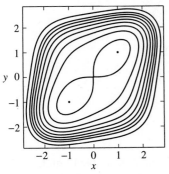

▲ **Figure 13.8.8**

At the points $(1, 1)$ and $(-1, -1)$, we have $D > 0$ and $f_{xx} < 0$, so relative maxima occur at these critical points. At $(0, 0)$ there is a saddle point since $D < 0$. The surface and a contour plot are shown in Figure 13.8.8. ◄

The following theorem, which is the analog for functions of two variables of Theorem 4.4.3, will lead to an important method for finding absolute extrema.

The "figure eight" pattern at $(0, 0)$ in the contour plot for the surface in Figure 13.8.8 is typical for level curves that pass through a saddle point. If a bug starts at the point $(0, 0, 0)$ on the surface, in how many directions can it walk and remain in the xy-plane?

13.8.7 THEOREM *If a function f of two variables has an absolute extremum (either an absolute maximum or an absolute minimum) at an interior point of its domain, then this extremum occurs at a critical point.*

PROOF   If f has an absolute maximum at the point (x_0, y_0) in the interior of the domain of f, then f has a relative maximum at (x_0, y_0). If both partial derivatives exist at (x_0, y_0), then

$$f_x(x_0, y_0) = 0 \quad \text{and} \quad f_y(x_0, y_0) = 0$$

by Theorem 13.8.4, so (x_0, y_0) is a critical point of f. If either partial derivative does not exist, then again (x_0, y_0) is a critical point, so (x_0, y_0) is a critical point in all cases. The proof for an absolute minimum is similar. ■

■ FINDING ABSOLUTE EXTREMA ON CLOSED AND BOUNDED SETS

If $f(x, y)$ is continuous on a closed and bounded set R, then the Extreme-Value Theorem (Theorem 13.8.3) guarantees the existence of an absolute maximum and an absolute minimum of f on R. These absolute extrema can occur either on the boundary of R or in the interior of R, but if an absolute extremum occurs in the interior, then it occurs at a critical point by Theorem 13.8.7. Thus, we are led to the following procedure for finding absolute extrema:

> Compare this procedure with that in Section 4.4 for finding the extreme values of $f(x)$ on a closed interval.

> *How to Find the Absolute Extrema of a Continuous Function f of Two Variables on a Closed and Bounded Set R*
>
> **Step 1.** Find the critical points of f that lie in the interior of R.
>
> **Step 2.** Find all boundary points at which the absolute extrema can occur.
>
> **Step 3.** Evaluate $f(x, y)$ at the points obtained in the preceding steps. The largest of these values is the absolute maximum and the smallest the absolute minimum.

▶ **Example 5**   Find the absolute maximum and minimum values of

$$f(x, y) = 3xy - 6x - 3y + 7 \tag{3}$$

on the closed triangular region R with vertices $(0, 0)$, $(3, 0)$, and $(0, 5)$.

Solution.   The region R is shown in Figure 13.8.9. We have

$$\frac{\partial f}{\partial x} = 3y - 6 \quad \text{and} \quad \frac{\partial f}{\partial y} = 3x - 3$$

so all critical points occur where

$$3y - 6 = 0 \quad \text{and} \quad 3x - 3 = 0$$

Solving these equations yields $x = 1$ and $y = 2$, so $(1, 2)$ is the only critical point. As shown in Figure 13.8.9, this critical point is in the interior of R.

Next we want to determine the locations of the points on the boundary of R at which the absolute extrema might occur. The boundary of R consists of three line segments, each of which we will treat separately:

The line segment between $(0, 0)$ *and* $(3, 0)$: On this line segment we have $y = 0$, so (3) simplifies to a function of the single variable x,

$$u(x) = f(x, 0) = -6x + 7, \quad 0 \le x \le 3$$

This function has no critical points because $u'(x) = -6$ is nonzero for all x. Thus the extreme values of $u(x)$ occur at the endpoints $x = 0$ and $x = 3$, which correspond to the points $(0, 0)$ and $(3, 0)$ of R.

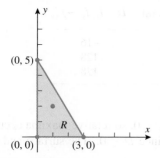

▲ **Figure 13.8.9**

The line segment between (0, 0) *and* (0, 5): On this line segment we have $x = 0$, so (3) simplifies to a function of the single variable y,

$$v(y) = f(0, y) = -3y + 7, \quad 0 \leq y \leq 5$$

This function has no critical points because $v'(y) = -3$ is nonzero for all y. Thus, the extreme values of $v(y)$ occur at the endpoints $y = 0$ and $y = 5$, which correspond to the points (0, 0) and (0, 5) of R.

The line segment between (3, 0) *and* (0, 5): In the xy-plane, an equation for this line segment is

$$y = -\tfrac{5}{3}x + 5, \quad 0 \leq x \leq 3 \tag{4}$$

so (3) simplifies to a function of the single variable x,

$$\begin{aligned} w(x) = f\left(x, -\tfrac{5}{3}x + 5\right) &= 3x\left(-\tfrac{5}{3}x + 5\right) - 6x - 3\left(-\tfrac{5}{3}x + 5\right) + 7 \\ &= -5x^2 + 14x - 8, \quad 0 \leq x \leq 3 \end{aligned}$$

Since $w'(x) = -10x + 14$, the equation $w'(x) = 0$ yields $x = \tfrac{7}{5}$ as the only critical point of w. Thus, the extreme values of w occur either at the critical point $x = \tfrac{7}{5}$ or at the endpoints $x = 0$ and $x = 3$. The endpoints correspond to the points (0, 5) and (3, 0) of R, and from (4) the critical point corresponds to $\left(\tfrac{7}{5}, \tfrac{8}{3}\right)$.

Finally, Table 13.8.1 lists the values of $f(x, y)$ at the interior critical point and at the points on the boundary where an absolute extremum can occur. From the table we conclude that the absolute maximum value of f is $f(0, 0) = 7$ and the absolute minimum value is $f(3, 0) = -11$. ◄

Table 13.8.1

(x, y)	$(0, 0)$	$(3, 0)$	$(0, 5)$	$\left(\tfrac{7}{5}, \tfrac{8}{3}\right)$	$(1, 2)$
$f(x, y)$	7	−11	−8	$\tfrac{9}{5}$	1

► **Example 6** Determine the dimensions of a rectangular box, open at the top, having a volume of 32 ft³, and requiring the least amount of material for its construction.

Solution. Let

$$x = \text{length of the box (in feet)}$$
$$y = \text{width of the box (in feet)}$$
$$z = \text{height of the box (in feet)}$$
$$S = \text{surface area of the box (in square feet)}$$

We may reasonably assume that the box with least surface area requires the least amount of material, so our objective is to minimize the surface area

$$S = xy + 2xz + 2yz \tag{5}$$

(Figure 13.8.10) subject to the volume requirement

$$xyz = 32 \tag{6}$$

From (6) we obtain $z = 32/xy$, so (5) can be rewritten as

$$S = xy + \frac{64}{y} + \frac{64}{x} \tag{7}$$

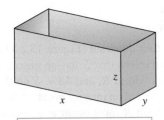

Two sides each have area xz.
Two sides each have area yz.
The base has area xy.

▲ **Figure 13.8.10**

which expresses S as a function of two variables. The dimensions x and y in this formula must be positive, but otherwise have no limitation, so our problem reduces to finding the absolute minimum value of S over the open first quadrant: $x > 0$, $y > 0$. Because this region is neither closed nor bounded, we have no mathematical guarantee at this stage that an absolute minimum exists. However, if S has an absolute minimum value in the open first quadrant, then it must occur at a critical point of S. Thus, our next step is to find the critical points of S.

Differentiating (7) we obtain

$$\frac{\partial S}{\partial x} = y - \frac{64}{x^2}, \quad \frac{\partial S}{\partial y} = x - \frac{64}{y^2} \qquad (8)$$

so the coordinates of the critical points of S satisfy

$$y - \frac{64}{x^2} = 0, \quad x - \frac{64}{y^2} = 0$$

Solving the first equation for y yields

$$y = \frac{64}{x^2} \qquad (9)$$

and substituting this expression in the second equation yields

$$x - \frac{64}{(64/x^2)^2} = 0$$

which can be rewritten as

$$x\left(1 - \frac{x^3}{64}\right) = 0$$

The solutions of this equation are $x = 0$ and $x = 4$. Since we require $x > 0$, the only solution of significance is $x = 4$. Substituting this value into (9) yields $y = 4$. We conclude that the point $(x, y) = (4, 4)$ is the only critical point of S in the first quadrant. Since $S = 48$ if $x = y = 4$, this suggests we try to show that the minimum value of S on the open first quadrant is 48.

It immediately follows from Equation (7) that $48 < S$ at any point in the first quadrant for which at least one of the inequalities

$$xy > 48, \quad \frac{64}{y} > 48, \quad \frac{64}{x} > 48$$

is satisfied. Therefore, to prove that $48 \leq S$, we can restrict attention to the set of points in the first quadrant that satisfy the three inequalities

$$xy \leq 48, \quad \frac{64}{y} \leq 48, \quad \frac{64}{x} \leq 48$$

These inequalities can be rewritten as

$$xy \leq 48, \quad y \geq \frac{4}{3}, \quad x \geq \frac{4}{3}$$

and they define a closed and bounded region R within the first quadrant (Figure 13.8.11). The function S is continuous on R, so Theorem 13.8.3 guarantees that S has an absolute minimum value somewhere on R. Since the point $(4, 4)$ lies within R, and $48 < S$ on the boundary of R (why?), the minimum value of S on R must occur at an interior point. It then follows from Theorem 13.8.7 that the mimimum value of S on R must occur at a critical point of S. Hence, the absolute minimum of S on R (and therefore on the entire open first quadrant) is $S = 48$ at the point $(4, 4)$. Substituting $x = 4$ and $y = 4$ into (6) yields $z = 2$, so the box using the least material has a height of 2 ft and a square base whose edges are 4 ft long. ◀

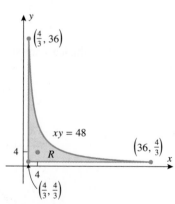

▲ **Figure 13.8.11**

REMARK Fortunately, in our solution to Example 6 we were able to prove the existence of an absolute minimum of S in the first quadrant. The general problem of finding the absolute extrema of a function on an unbounded region, or on a region that is not closed, can be difficult and will not be considered in this text. However, in applied problems we can sometimes use physical considerations to deduce that an absolute extremum has been found. For example, the graph of Equation (7) in Figure 13.8.12 strongly suggests that the relative minimum at $x = 4$ and $y = 4$ is also an absolute minimum.

▲ **Figure 13.8.12**

✔ **QUICK CHECK EXERCISES 13.8**   *(See page 989 for answers.)*

1. The critical points of the function $f(x, y) = x^3 + xy + y^2$ are _____.

2. Suppose that $f(x, y)$ has continuous second-order partial derivatives everywhere and that the origin is a critical point for f. State what information (if any) is provided by the second partials test if
   (a) $f_{xx}(0, 0) = 2$, $f_{xy}(0, 0) = 2$, $f_{yy}(0, 0) = 2$
   (b) $f_{xx}(0, 0) = -2$, $f_{xy}(0, 0) = 2$, $f_{yy}(0, 0) = 2$
   (c) $f_{xx}(0, 0) = 3$, $f_{xy}(0, 0) = 2$, $f_{yy}(0, 0) = 2$

   (d) $f_{xx}(0, 0) = -3$, $f_{xy}(0, 0) = 2$, $f_{yy}(0, 0) = -2$.

3. For the function $f(x, y) = x^3 - 3xy + y^3$, state what information (if any) is provided by the second partials test at the point
   (a) $(0, 0)$ (b) $(-1, -1)$ (c) $(1, 1)$.

4. A rectangular box has total surface area of 2 ft^2. Express the volume of the box as a function of the dimensions x and y of the base of the box.

EXERCISE SET 13.8   ⬚ Graphing Utility   [c] CAS

1–2 Locate all absolute maxima and minima, if any, by inspection. Then check your answers using calculus. ◼

1. (a) $f(x, y) = (x - 2)^2 + (y + 1)^2$
   (b) $f(x, y) = 1 - x^2 - y^2$
   (c) $f(x, y) = x + 2y - 5$

2. (a) $f(x, y) = 1 - (x + 1)^2 - (y - 5)^2$
   (b) $f(x, y) = e^{xy}$
   (c) $f(x, y) = x^2 - y^2$

3–4 Complete the squares and locate all absolute maxima and minima, if any, by inspection. Then check your answers using calculus. ◼

3. $f(x, y) = 13 - 6x + x^2 + 4y + y^2$
4. $f(x, y) = 1 - 2x - x^2 + 4y - 2y^2$

FOCUS ON CONCEPTS

5–8 The contour plots show all significant features of the function. Make a conjecture about the number and the location of all relative extrema and saddle points, and then use calculus to check your conjecture. ◼

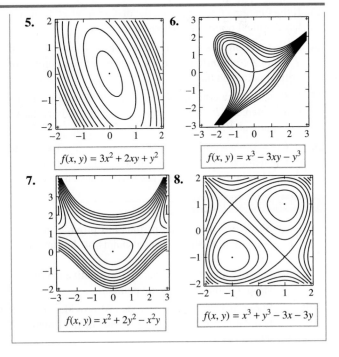

5. $f(x, y) = 3x^2 + 2xy + y^2$

6. $f(x, y) = x^3 - 3xy - y^3$

7. $f(x, y) = x^2 + 2y^2 - x^2 y$

8. $f(x, y) = x^3 + y^3 - 3x - 3y$

9–20 Locate all relative maxima, relative minima, and saddle points, if any. ■

9. $f(x, y) = y^2 + xy + 3y + 2x + 3$

10. $f(x, y) = x^2 + xy - 2y - 2x + 1$

11. $f(x, y) = x^2 + xy + y^2 - 3x$

12. $f(x, y) = xy - x^3 - y^2$ 13. $f(x, y) = x^2 + y^2 + \dfrac{2}{xy}$

14. $f(x, y) = xe^y$ 15. $f(x, y) = x^2 + y - e^y$

16. $f(x, y) = xy + \dfrac{2}{x} + \dfrac{4}{y}$ 17. $f(x, y) = e^x \sin y$

18. $f(x, y) = y \sin x$ 19. $f(x, y) = e^{-(x^2 + y^2 + 2x)}$

20. $f(x, y) = xy + \dfrac{a^3}{x} + \dfrac{b^3}{y}$ $(a \neq 0, b \neq 0)$

[C] **21.** Use a CAS to generate a contour plot of
$$f(x, y) = 2x^2 - 4xy + y^4 + 2$$
for $-2 \leq x \leq 2$ and $-2 \leq y \leq 2$, and use the plot to approximate the locations of all relative extrema and saddle points in the region. Check your answer using calculus, and identify the relative extrema as relative maxima or minima.

[C] **22.** Use a CAS to generate a contour plot of
$$f(x, y) = 2y^2 x - yx^2 + 4xy$$
for $-5 \leq x \leq 5$ and $-5 \leq y \leq 5$, and use the plot to approximate the locations of all relative extrema and saddle points in the region. Check your answer using calculus, and identify the relative extrema as relative maxima or minima.

23–26 True–False Determine whether the statement is true or false. Explain your answer. In these exercises, assume that $f(x, y)$ has continuous second-order partial derivatives and that
$$D(x, y) = f_{xx}(x, y) f_{yy}(x, y) - f_{xy}^2(x, y) ■$$

23. If the function f is defined on the disk $x^2 + y^2 \leq 1$, then f has a critical point somewhere on this disk.

24. If the function f is defined on the disk $x^2 + y^2 \leq 1$, and if f is not a constant function, then f has a finite number of critical points on this disk.

25. If $P(x_0, y_0)$ is a critical point of f, and if f is defined on a disk centered at P with $D(x_0, y_0) > 0$, then f has a relative extremum at P.

26. If $P(x_0, y_0)$ is a critical point of f with $f(x_0, y_0) = 0$, and if f is defined on a disk centered at P with $D(x_0, y_0) < 0$, then f has both positive and negative values on this disk.

FOCUS ON CONCEPTS

27. (a) Show that the second partials test provides no information about the critical points of the function $f(x, y) = x^4 + y^4$.
   (b) Classify all critical points of f as relative maxima, relative minima, or saddle points.

28. (a) Show that the second partials test provides no information about the critical points of the function $f(x, y) = x^4 - y^4$.

(b) Classify all critical points of f as relative maxima, relative minima, or saddle points.

29. Recall from Theorem 4.4.4 that if a continuous function of one variable has exactly one relative extremum on an interval, then that relative extremum is an absolute extremum on the interval. This exercise shows that this result does not extend to functions of two variables.
   (a) Show that $f(x, y) = 3xe^y - x^3 - e^{3y}$ has only one critical point and that a relative maximum occurs there. (See the accompanying figure.)
   (b) Show that f does not have an absolute maximum.

Source: This exercise is based on the article "The Only Critical Point in Town Test" by Ira Rosenholtz and Lowell Smylie, *Mathematics Magazine*, Vol. 58, No. 3, May 1985, pp. 149–150.

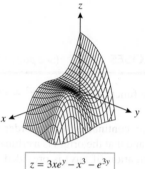

$z = 3xe^y - x^3 - e^{3y}$

◀ **Figure Ex-29**

30. If f is a continuous function of one variable with two relative maxima on an interval, then there must be a relative minimum between the relative maxima. (Convince yourself of this by drawing some pictures.) The purpose of this exercise is to show that this result does not extend to functions of two variables. Show that $f(x, y) = 4x^2 e^y - 2x^4 - e^{4y}$ has two relative maxima but no other critical points (see Figure Ex-30).

Source: This exercise is based on the problem "Two Mountains Without a Valley" proposed and solved by Ira Rosenholtz, *Mathematics Magazine*, Vol. 60, No. 1, February 1987, p. 48.

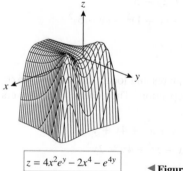

$z = 4x^2 e^y - 2x^4 - e^{4y}$

◀ **Figure Ex-30**

31–36 Find the absolute extrema of the given function on the indicated closed and bounded set R. ■

31. $f(x, y) = xy - x - 3y$; R is the triangular region with vertices $(0, 0)$, $(0, 4)$, and $(5, 0)$.

32. $f(x, y) = xy - 2x$; R is the triangular region with vertices $(0, 0)$, $(0, 4)$, and $(4, 0)$.

33. $f(x, y) = x^2 - 3y^2 - 2x + 6y$; R is the region bounded by the square with vertices $(0, 0)$, $(0, 2)$, $(2, 2)$, and $(2, 0)$.

34. $f(x, y) = xe^y - x^2 - e^y$; R is the rectangular region with vertices $(0, 0)$, $(0, 1)$, $(2, 1)$, and $(2, 0)$.

35. $f(x, y) = x^2 + 2y^2 - x$; R is the disk $x^2 + y^2 \leq 4$.

36. $f(x, y) = xy^2$; R is the region that satisfies the inequalities $x \geq 0$, $y \geq 0$, and $x^2 + y^2 \leq 1$.

37. Find three positive numbers whose sum is 48 and such that their product is as large as possible.

38. Find three positive numbers whose sum is 27 and such that the sum of their squares is as small as possible.

39. Find all points on the portion of the plane $x + y + z = 5$ in the first octant at which $f(x, y, z) = xy^2z^2$ has a maximum value.

40. Find the points on the surface $x^2 - yz = 5$ that are closest to the origin.

41. Find the dimensions of the rectangular box of maximum volume that can be inscribed in a sphere of radius a.

42. Find the maximum volume of a rectangular box with three faces in the coordinate planes and a vertex in the first octant on the plane $x + y + z = 1$.

43. A closed rectangular box with a volume of 16 ft³ is made from two kinds of materials. The top and bottom are made of material costing 10¢ per square foot and the sides from material costing 5¢ per square foot. Find the dimensions of the box so that the cost of materials is minimized.

44. A manufacturer makes two models of an item, standard and deluxe. It costs $40 to manufacture the standard model and $60 for the deluxe. A market research firm estimates that if the standard model is priced at x dollars and the deluxe at y dollars, then the manufacturer will sell $500(y - x)$ of the standard items and $45,000 + 500(x - 2y)$ of the deluxe each year. How should the items be priced to maximize the profit?

45. Consider the function

$$f(x, y) = 4x^2 - 3y^2 + 2xy$$

over the unit square $0 \leq x \leq 1, 0 \leq y \leq 1$.
   (a) Find the maximum and minimum values of f on each edge of the square.
   (b) Find the maximum and minimum values of f on each diagonal of the square.
   (c) Find the maximum and minimum values of f on the entire square.

46. Show that among all parallelograms with perimeter l, a square with sides of length $l/4$ has maximum area. [*Hint:* The area of a parallelogram is given by the formula $A = ab \sin \alpha$, where a and b are the lengths of two adjacent sides and α is the angle between them.]

47. Determine the dimensions of a rectangular box, open at the top, having volume V, and requiring the least amount of material for its construction.

48. A length of sheet metal 27 inches wide is to be made into a water trough by bending up two sides as shown in the accompanying figure. Find x and ϕ so that the trapezoid-shaped cross section has a maximum area.

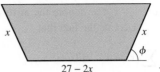

$27 - 2x$ ◀ **Figure Ex-48**

49–50 A common problem in experimental work is to obtain a mathematical relationship $y = f(x)$ between two variables x and y by "fitting" a curve to points in the plane that correspond to experimentally determined values of x and y, say

$$(x_1, y_1), (x_2, y_2), \ldots, (x_n, y_n)$$

The curve $y = f(x)$ is called a *mathematical model* of the data. The general form of the function f is commonly determined by some underlying physical principle, but sometimes it is just determined by the pattern of the data. We are concerned with fitting a straight line $y = mx + b$ to data. Usually, the data will not lie on a line (possibly due to experimental error or variations in experimental conditions), so the problem is to find a line that fits the data "best" according to some criterion. One criterion for selecting the line of best fit is to choose m and b to minimize the function

$$g(m, b) = \sum_{i=1}^{n} (mx_i + b - y_i)^2$$

This is called the *method of least squares*, and the resulting line is called the *regression line* or the *least squares line of best fit*. Geometrically, $|mx_i + b - y_i|$ is the vertical distance between the data point (x_i, y_i) and the line $y = mx + b$.

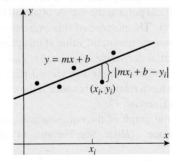

These vertical distances are called the *residuals* of the data points, so the effect of minimizing $g(m, b)$ is to minimize the sum of the squares of the residuals. In these exercises, we will derive a formula for the regression line. ◼

49. The purpose of this exercise is to find the values of m and b that produce the regression line.
   (a) To minimize $g(m, b)$, we start by finding values of m and b such that $\partial g/\partial m = 0$ and $\partial g/\partial b = 0$. Show

that these equations are satisfied if m and b satisfy the conditions

$$\left(\sum_{i=1}^{n} x_i^2\right) m + \left(\sum_{i=1}^{n} x_i\right) b = \sum_{i=1}^{n} x_i y_i$$

$$\left(\sum_{i=1}^{n} x_i\right) m + nb = \sum_{i=1}^{n} y_i$$

(b) Let $\bar{x} = (x_1 + x_2 + \cdots + x_n)/n$ denote the arithmetic average of $x_1, x_2, \ldots, x_n$. Use the fact that

$$\sum_{i=1}^{n} (x_i - \bar{x})^2 \geq 0$$

to show that

$$n\left(\sum_{i=1}^{n} x_i^2\right) - \left(\sum_{i=1}^{n} x_i\right)^2 \geq 0$$

with equality if and only if all the x_i's are the same.

(c) Assuming that not all the x_i's are the same, prove that the equations in part (a) have the unique solution

$$m = \frac{n \sum_{i=1}^{n} x_i y_i - \sum_{i=1}^{n} x_i \sum_{i=1}^{n} y_i}{n \sum_{i=1}^{n} x_i^2 - \left(\sum_{i=1}^{n} x_i\right)^2}$$

$$b = \frac{1}{n}\left(\sum_{i=1}^{n} y_i - m \sum_{i=1}^{n} x_i\right)$$

[*Note:* We have shown that g has a critical point at these values of m and b. In the next exercise we will show that g has an absolute minimum at this critical point. Accepting this to be so, we have shown that the line $y = mx + b$ is the regression line for these values of m and b.]

50. Assume that not all the x_i's are the same, so that $g(m, b)$ has a unique critical point at the values of m and b obtained in Exercise 49(c). The purpose of this exercise is to show that g has an absolute minimum value at this point.

(a) Find the partial derivatives $g_{mm}(m, b)$, $g_{bb}(m, b)$, and $g_{mb}(m, b)$, and then apply the second partials test to show that g has a relative minimum at the critical point obtained in Exercise 49.

(b) Show that the graph of the equation $z = g(m, b)$ is a quadric surface. [*Hint:* See Formula (4) of Section 11.7.]

(c) It can be proved that the graph of $z = g(m, b)$ is an elliptic paraboloid. Accepting this to be so, show that this paraboloid opens in the positive z-direction, and explain how this shows that g has an absolute minimum at the critical point obtained in Exercise 49.

51–54 Use the formulas obtained in Exercise 49 to find and draw the regression line. If you have a calculating utility that can calculate regression lines, use it to check your work. ■

51.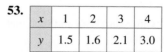

52.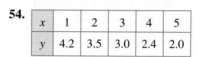

53.

x	1	2	3	4
y	1.5	1.6	2.1	3.0

54.

x	1	2	3	4	5
y	4.2	3.5	3.0	2.4	2.0

55. The following table shows the life expectancy by year of birth of females in the United States:

YEAR OF BIRTH	1930	1940	1950	1960	1970	1980	1990	2000
LIFE EXPECTANCY	61.6	65.2	71.1	73.1	74.7	77.5	78.8	79.7

(a) Take $t = 0$ to be the year 1930, and let y be the life expectancy for birth year t. Use the regression capability of a calculating utility to find the regression line of y as a function of t.

(b) Use a graphing utility to make a graph that shows the data points and the regression line.

(c) Use the regression line to make a conjecture about the life expectancy of females born in the year 2010.

56. A company manager wants to establish a relationship between the sales of a certain product and the price. The company research department provides the following data:

PRICE (x) IN DOLLARS	$35.00	$40.00	$45.00	$48.00	$50.00
DAILY SALES VOLUME (y) IN UNITS	80	75	68	66	63

(a) Use a calculating utility to find the regression line of y as a function of x.

(b) Use a graphing utility to make a graph that shows the data points and the regression line.

(c) Use the regression line to make a conjecture about the number of units that would be sold at a price of $60.00.

57. If a gas is cooled with its volume held constant, then it follows from the **ideal gas law** in physics that its pressure drops proportionally to the drop in temperature. The temperature that, in theory, corresponds to a pressure of zero is called **absolute zero**. Suppose that an experiment produces the following data for pressure P versus temperature T with the volume held constant:

(cont.)

P (KILOPASCALS)	134	142	155	160	171	184
T (°CELSIUS)	0	20	40	60	80	100

(a) Use a calculating utility to find the regression line of P as a function of T.

(b) Use a graphing utility to make a graph that shows the data points and the regression line.

(c) Use the regression line to estimate the value of absolute zero in degrees Celsius.

58. Find

(a) a continuous function $f(x, y)$ that is defined on the entire xy-plane and has no absolute extrema on the xy-plane;

(b) a function $f(x, y)$ that is defined everywhere on the rectangle $0 \le x \le 1, 0 \le y \le 1$ and has no absolute extrema on the rectangle.

59. Show that if f has a relative maximum at (x_0, y_0), then $G(x) = f(x, y_0)$ has a relative maximum at $x = x_0$ and $H(y) = f(x_0, y)$ has a relative maximum at $y = y_0$.

60. Writing Explain how to determine the location of relative extrema or saddle points of $f(x, y)$ by examining the contours of f.

61. Writing Suppose that the second partials test gives no information about a certain critical point (x_0, y_0) because $D(x_0, y_0) = 0$. Discuss what other steps you might take to determine whether there is a relative extremum at that critical point.

✔ **QUICK CHECK ANSWERS 13.8**

1. $(0, 0)$ and $\left(\frac{1}{6}, -\frac{1}{12}\right)$ **2.** (a) no information (b) a saddle point at $(0, 0)$ (c) a relative minimum at $(0, 0)$
(d) a relative maximum at $(0, 0)$ **3.** (a) a saddle point at $(0, 0)$ (b) no information, since $(-1, -1)$ is not a critical point
(c) a relative minimum at $(1, 1)$ **4.** $V = \dfrac{xy(1 - xy)}{x + y}$

13.9 LAGRANGE MULTIPLIERS

In this section we will study a powerful new method for maximizing or minimizing a function subject to constraints on the variables. This method will help us to solve certain optimization problems that are difficult or impossible to solve using the methods studied in the last section.

■ **EXTREMUM PROBLEMS WITH CONSTRAINTS**

In Example 6 of the last section, we solved the problem of minimizing

$$S = xy + 2xz + 2yz \tag{1}$$

subject to the constraint

$$xyz - 32 = 0 \tag{2}$$

This is a special case of the following general problem:

13.9.1 Three-Variable Extremum Problem with One Constraint
Maximize or minimize the function $f(x, y, z)$ subject to the constraint $g(x, y, z) = 0$.

We will also be interested in the following two-variable version of this problem:

13.9.2 Two-Variable Extremum Problem with One Constraint
Maximize or minimize the function $f(x, y)$ subject to the constraint $g(x, y) = 0$.

■ **LAGRANGE MULTIPLIERS**

One way to attack problems of these types is to solve the constraint equation for one of the variables in terms of the others and substitute the result into f. This produces a new function of one or two variables that incorporates the constraint and can be maximized or minimized by applying standard methods. For example, to solve the problem in Example 6 of the last section we substituted (2) into (1) to obtain

$$S = xy + \frac{64}{y} + \frac{64}{x}$$

which we then minimized by finding the critical points and applying the second partials test. However, this approach hinges on our ability to solve the constraint equation for one of the variables in terms of the others. If this cannot be done, then other methods must be used. One such method, called the *method of Lagrange multipliers*, will be discussed in this section.

To motivate the method of Lagrange multipliers, suppose that we are trying to maximize a function $f(x, y)$ subject to the constraint $g(x, y) = 0$. Geometrically, this means that we are looking for a point (x_0, y_0) on the graph of the constraint curve at which $f(x, y)$ is as large as possible. To help locate such a point, let us construct a contour plot of $f(x, y)$ in the same coordinate system as the graph of $g(x, y) = 0$. For example, Figure 13.9.1a shows some typical level curves of $f(x, y) = c$, which we have labeled $c = 100, 200, 300, 400$, and 500 for purposes of illustration. In this figure, each point of intersection of $g(x, y) = 0$ with a level curve is a candidate for a solution, since these points lie on the constraint curve. Among the seven such intersections shown in the figure, the maximum value of $f(x, y)$ occurs at the intersection (x_0, y_0) where $f(x, y)$ has a value of 400. Note that at (x_0, y_0) the constraint curve and the level curve just touch and thus have a *common* tangent line at this point. Since $\nabla f(x_0, y_0)$ is normal to the level curve $f(x, y) = 400$ at (x_0, y_0), and since $\nabla g(x_0, y_0)$ is normal to the constraint curve $g(x, y) = 0$ at (x_0, y_0), we conclude that the vectors $\nabla f(x_0, y_0)$ and $\nabla g(x_0, y_0)$ must be parallel. That is,

$$\nabla f(x_0, y_0) = \lambda \nabla g(x_0, y_0) \tag{3}$$

for some scalar λ. The same condition holds at points on the constraint curve where $f(x, y)$ has a minimum. For example, if the level curves are as shown in Figure 13.9.1b, then the minimum value of $f(x, y)$ occurs where the constraint curve just touches a level curve.

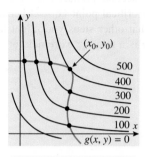

Maximum of $f(x, y)$ is 400

(a)

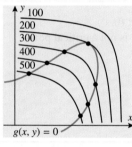

Minimum of $f(x, y)$ is 200

(b)

▲ **Figure 13.9.1**

Joseph Louis Lagrange (1736–1813) French–Italian mathematician and astronomer. Lagrange, the son of a public official, was born in Turin, Italy. (Baptismal records list his name as Giuseppe Lodovico Lagrangia.) Although his father wanted him to be a lawyer, Lagrange was attracted to mathematics and astronomy after reading a memoir by the astronomer Halley. At age 16 he began to study mathematics on his own and by age 19 was appointed to a professorship at the Royal Artillery School in Turin. The following year Lagrange sent Euler solutions to some famous problems using new methods that eventually blossomed into a branch of mathematics called calculus of variations. These methods and Lagrange's applications of them to problems in celestial mechanics were so monumental that by age 25 he was regarded by many of his contemporaries as the greatest living mathematician.

In 1776, on the recommendations of Euler, he was chosen to succeed Euler as the director of the Berlin Academy. During his stay in Berlin, Lagrange distinguished himself not only in celestial mechanics, but also in algebraic equations and the theory of numbers. After twenty years in Berlin, he moved to Paris at the invitation of Louis XVI. He was given apartments in the Louvre and treated with great honor, even during the revolution.

Napoleon was a great admirer of Lagrange and showered him with honors—count, senator, and Legion of Honor. The years Lagrange spent in Paris were devoted primarily to didactic treatises summarizing his mathematical conceptions. One of Lagrange's most famous works is a memoir, *Mécanique Analytique*, in which he reduced the theory of mechanics to a few general formulas from which all other necessary equations could be derived.

It is an interesting historical fact that Lagrange's father speculated unsuccessfully in several financial ventures, so his family was forced to live quite modestly. Lagrange himself stated that if his family had money, he would not have made mathematics his vocation. In spite of his fame, Lagrange was always a shy and modest man. On his death, he was buried with honor in the Pantheon.

Thus, to find the maximum or minimum of $f(x, y)$ subject to the constraint $g(x, y) = 0$, we look for points at which (3) holds—this is the method of Lagrange multipliers.

Our next objective in this section is to make the preceding intuitive argument more precise. For this purpose it will help to begin with some terminology about the problem of maximizing or minimizing a function $f(x, y)$ subject to a constraint $g(x, y) = 0$. As with other kinds of maximization and minimization problems, we need to distinguish between relative and absolute extrema. We will say that f has a *constrained absolute maximum* (*minimum*) at (x_0, y_0) if $f(x_0, y_0)$ is the largest (smallest) value of f on the constraint curve, and we will say that f has a *constrained relative maximum* (*minimum*) at (x_0, y_0) if $f(x_0, y_0)$ is the largest (smallest) value of f on some segment of the constraint curve that extends on both sides of the point (x_0, y_0) (Figure 13.9.2).

Let us assume that a constrained relative maximum or minimum occurs at the point (x_0, y_0), and for simplicity let us further assume that the equation $g(x, y) = 0$ can be smoothly parametrized as

$$x = x(s), \quad y = y(s)$$

where s is an arc length parameter with reference point (x_0, y_0) at $s = 0$. Thus, the quantity

$$z = f(x(s), y(s))$$

has a relative maximum or minimum at $s = 0$, and this implies that $dz/ds = 0$ at that point. From the chain rule, this equation can be expressed as

$$\frac{dz}{ds} = \frac{\partial f}{\partial x}\frac{dx}{ds} + \frac{\partial f}{\partial y}\frac{dy}{ds} = \left(\frac{\partial f}{\partial x}\mathbf{i} + \frac{\partial f}{\partial y}\mathbf{j}\right) \cdot \left(\frac{dx}{ds}\mathbf{i} + \frac{dy}{ds}\mathbf{j}\right) = 0$$

where the derivatives are all evaluated at $s = 0$. However, the first factor in the dot product is the gradient of f, and the second factor is the unit tangent vector to the constraint curve. Since the point (x_0, y_0) corresponds to $s = 0$, it follows from this equation that

$$\nabla f(x_0, y_0) \cdot \mathbf{T}(0) = 0$$

which implies that the gradient is either $\mathbf{0}$ or is normal to the constraint curve at a constrained relative extremum. However, the constraint curve $g(x, y) = 0$ is a level curve for the function $g(x, y)$, so that if $\nabla g(x_0, y_0) \neq \mathbf{0}$, then $\nabla g(x_0, y_0)$ is normal to this curve at (x_0, y_0). It then follows that there is some scalar λ such that

$$\nabla f(x_0, y_0) = \lambda \nabla g(x_0, y_0) \tag{4}$$

This scalar is called a *Lagrange multiplier*. Thus, the *method of Lagrange multipliers* for finding constrained relative extrema is to look for points on the constraint curve $g(x, y) = 0$ at which Equation (4) is satisfied for some scalar λ.

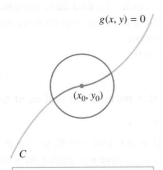

A constrained relative maximum occurs at (x_0, y_0) if $f(x_0, y_0) \geq f(x, y)$ on some segment of C that extends on both sides of (x_0, y_0).

▲ **Figure 13.9.2**

13.9.3   THEOREM (*Constrained-Extremum Principle for Two Variables and One Constraint*)   *Let f and g be functions of two variables with continuous first partial derivatives on some open set containing the constraint curve $g(x, y) = 0$, and assume that $\nabla g \neq \mathbf{0}$ at any point on this curve. If f has a constrained relative extremum, then this extremum occurs at a point (x_0, y_0) on the constraint curve at which the gradient vectors $\nabla f(x_0, y_0)$ and $\nabla g(x_0, y_0)$ are parallel; that is, there is some number λ such that*

$$\nabla f(x_0, y_0) = \lambda \nabla g(x_0, y_0)$$

▶ **Example 1**   At what point or points on the circle $x^2 + y^2 = 1$ does $f(x, y) = xy$ have an absolute maximum, and what is that maximum?

Solution. The circle $x^2 + y^2 = 1$ is a closed and bounded set and $f(x, y) = xy$ is a continuous function, so it follows from the Extreme-Value Theorem (Theorem 13.8.3) that f has an absolute maximum and an absolute minimum on the circle. To find these extrema, we will use Lagrange multipliers to find the constrained relative extrema, and then we will evaluate f at those relative extrema to find the absolute extrema.

We want to maximize $f(x, y) = xy$ subject to the constraint

$$g(x, y) = x^2 + y^2 - 1 = 0 \qquad (5)$$

First we will look for constrained *relative* extrema. For this purpose we will need the gradients
$$\nabla f = y\mathbf{i} + x\mathbf{j} \quad \text{and} \quad \nabla g = 2x\mathbf{i} + 2y\mathbf{j}$$

From the formula for ∇g we see that $\nabla g = \mathbf{0}$ if and only if $x = 0$ and $y = 0$, so $\nabla g \neq \mathbf{0}$ at any point on the circle $x^2 + y^2 = 1$. Thus, at a constrained relative extremum we must have
$$\nabla f = \lambda \nabla g \quad \text{or} \quad y\mathbf{i} + x\mathbf{j} = \lambda(2x\mathbf{i} + 2y\mathbf{j})$$

which is equivalent to the pair of equations

$$y = 2x\lambda \quad \text{and} \quad x = 2y\lambda$$

It follows from these equations that if $x = 0$, then $y = 0$, and if $y = 0$, then $x = 0$. In either case we have $x^2 + y^2 = 0$, so the constraint equation $x^2 + y^2 = 1$ is not satisfied. Thus, we can assume that x and y are nonzero, and we can rewrite the equations as

$$\lambda = \frac{y}{2x} \quad \text{and} \quad \lambda = \frac{x}{2y}$$

from which we obtain

$$\frac{y}{2x} = \frac{x}{2y}$$

or

$$y^2 = x^2 \qquad (6)$$

Substituting this in (5) yields

$$2x^2 - 1 = 0$$

from which we obtain $x = \pm 1/\sqrt{2}$. Each of these values, when substituted in Equation (6), produces y-values of $y = \pm 1/\sqrt{2}$. Thus, constrained relative extrema occur at the points $(1/\sqrt{2}, 1/\sqrt{2})$, $(1/\sqrt{2}, -1/\sqrt{2})$, $(-1/\sqrt{2}, 1/\sqrt{2})$, and $(-1/\sqrt{2}, -1/\sqrt{2})$. The values of xy at these points are as follows:

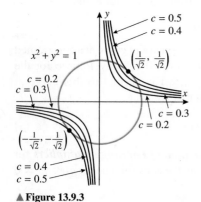

$x^2 + y^2 = 1$

$c = 0.5$
$c = 0.4$
$\left(\frac{1}{\sqrt{2}}, \frac{1}{\sqrt{2}}\right)$
$c = 0.2$
$c = 0.3$
$c = 0.3$
$c = 0.2$
$\left(-\frac{1}{\sqrt{2}}, -\frac{1}{\sqrt{2}}\right)$
$c = 0.4$
$c = 0.5$

▲ **Figure 13.9.3**

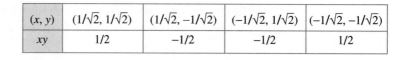

(x, y)	$(1/\sqrt{2}, 1/\sqrt{2})$	$(1/\sqrt{2}, -1/\sqrt{2})$	$(-1/\sqrt{2}, 1/\sqrt{2})$	$(-1/\sqrt{2}, -1/\sqrt{2})$
xy	$1/2$	$-1/2$	$-1/2$	$1/2$

Thus, the function $f(x, y) = xy$ has an absolute maximum of $\frac{1}{2}$ occurring at the two points $(1/\sqrt{2}, 1/\sqrt{2})$ and $(-1/\sqrt{2}, -1/\sqrt{2})$. Although it was not asked for, we can also see that f has an absolute minimum of $-\frac{1}{2}$ occurring at the points $(1/\sqrt{2}, -1/\sqrt{2})$ and $(-1/\sqrt{2}, 1/\sqrt{2})$. Figure 13.9.3 shows some level curves $xy = c$ and the constraint curve in the vicinity of the maxima. A similar figure for the minima can be obtained using negative values of c for the level curves $xy = c$. ◄

Give another solution to Example 1 using the parametrization

$$x = \cos\theta, \quad y = \sin\theta$$

and the identity

$$\sin 2\theta = 2\sin\theta\cos\theta$$

REMARK | If c is a constant, then the functions $g(x, y)$ and $g(x, y) - c$ have the same gradient since the constant c drops out when we differentiate. Consequently, it is *not* essential to rewrite a constraint of the form $g(x, y) = c$ as $g(x, y) - c = 0$ in order to apply the constrained-extremum principle. Thus, in the last example, we could have kept the constraint in the form $x^2 + y^2 = 1$ and then taken $g(x, y) = x^2 + y^2$ rather than $g(x, y) = x^2 + y^2 - 1$.

▶ **Example 2** Use the method of Lagrange multipliers to find the dimensions of a rectangle with perimeter p and maximum area.

Solution. Let

$x =$ length of the rectangle, $y =$ width of the rectangle, $A =$ area of the rectangle

We want to maximize $A = xy$ on the line segment

$$2x + 2y = p, \quad 0 \le x, y \qquad (7)$$

that corresponds to the perimeter constraint. This segment is a closed and bounded set, and since $f(x, y) = xy$ is a continuous function, it follows from the Extreme-Value Theorem (Theorem 13.8.3) that f has an absolute maximum on this segment. This absolute maximum must also be a constrained relative maximum since f is 0 at the endpoints of the segment and positive elsewhere on the segment. If $g(x, y) = 2x + 2y$, then we have

$$\nabla f = y\mathbf{i} + x\mathbf{j} \quad \text{and} \quad \nabla g = 2\mathbf{i} + 2\mathbf{j}$$

Noting that $\nabla g \ne \mathbf{0}$, it follows from (4) that

$$y\mathbf{i} + x\mathbf{j} = \lambda(2\mathbf{i} + 2\mathbf{j})$$

at a constrained relative maximum. This is equivalent to the two equations

$$y = 2\lambda \quad \text{and} \quad x = 2\lambda$$

Eliminating λ from these equations we obtain $x = y$, which shows that the rectangle is actually a square. Using this condition and constraint (7), we obtain $x = p/4, y = p/4$. ◀

■ **THREE VARIABLES AND ONE CONSTRAINT**

The method of Lagrange multipliers can also be used to maximize or minimize a function of three variables $f(x, y, z)$ subject to a constraint $g(x, y, z) = 0$. As a rule, the graph of $g(x, y, z) = 0$ will be some surface S in 3-space. Thus, from a geometric viewpoint, the problem is to maximize or minimize $f(x, y, z)$ as (x, y, z) varies over the surface S (Figure 13.9.4). As usual, we distinguish between relative and absolute extrema. We will say that f has a **constrained absolute maximum (minimum)** at (x_0, y_0, z_0) if $f(x_0, y_0, z_0)$ is the largest (smallest) value of $f(x, y, z)$ on S, and we will say that f has a **constrained relative maximum (minimum)** at (x_0, y_0, z_0) if $f(x_0, y_0, z_0)$ is the largest (smallest) value of $f(x, y, z)$ at all points of S "near" (x_0, y_0, z_0).

The following theorem, which we state without proof, is the three-variable analog of Theorem 13.9.3.

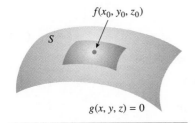

$f(x_0, y_0, z_0)$

S

$g(x, y, z) = 0$

A constrained relative maximum occurs at (x_0, y_0, z_0) if $f(x_0, y_0, z_0) \ge f(x, y, z)$ at all points of S near (x_0, y_0, z_0).

▲ **Figure 13.9.4**

13.9.4   **THEOREM** (*Constrained-Extremum Principle for Three Variables and One Constraint*)   *Let f and g be functions of three variables with continuous first partial derivatives on some open set containing the constraint surface $g(x, y, z) = 0$, and assume that $\nabla g \ne \mathbf{0}$ at any point on this surface. If f has a constrained relative extremum, then this extremum occurs at a point (x_0, y_0, z_0) on the constraint surface at which the gradient vectors $\nabla f(x_0, y_0, z_0)$ and $\nabla g(x_0, y_0, z_0)$ are parallel; that is, there is some number λ such that*

$$\nabla f(x_0, y_0, z_0) = \lambda \nabla g(x_0, y_0, z_0)$$

▶ **Example 3** Find the points on the sphere $x^2 + y^2 + z^2 = 36$ that are closest to and farthest from the point $(1, 2, 2)$.

Solution. To avoid radicals, we will find points on the sphere that minimize and maximize the *square* of the distance to (1, 2, 2). Thus, we want to find the relative extrema of

$$f(x, y, z) = (x - 1)^2 + (y - 2)^2 + (z - 2)^2$$

subject to the constraint

$$x^2 + y^2 + z^2 = 36 \tag{8}$$

If we let $g(x, y, z) = x^2 + y^2 + z^2$, then $\nabla g = 2x\mathbf{i} + 2y\mathbf{j} + 2z\mathbf{k}$. Thus, $\nabla g = \mathbf{0}$ if and only if $x = y = z = 0$. It follows that $\nabla g \neq \mathbf{0}$ at any point of the sphere (8), and hence the constrained relative extrema must occur at points where

$$\nabla f(x, y, z) = \lambda \nabla g(x, y, z)$$

That is,

$$2(x - 1)\mathbf{i} + 2(y - 2)\mathbf{j} + 2(z - 2)\mathbf{k} = \lambda(2x\mathbf{i} + 2y\mathbf{j} + 2z\mathbf{k})$$

which leads to the equations

$$2(x - 1) = 2x\lambda, \quad 2(y - 2) = 2y\lambda, \quad 2(z - 2) = 2z\lambda \tag{9}$$

We may assume that x, y, and z are nonzero since $x = 0$ does not satisfy the first equation, $y = 0$ does not satisfy the second, and $z = 0$ does not satisfy the third. Thus, we can rewrite (9) as

$$\frac{x - 1}{x} = \lambda, \quad \frac{y - 2}{y} = \lambda, \quad \frac{z - 2}{z} = \lambda$$

The first two equations imply that

$$\frac{x - 1}{x} = \frac{y - 2}{y}$$

from which it follows that

$$y = 2x \tag{10}$$

Similarly, the first and third equations imply that

$$z = 2x \tag{11}$$

Substituting (10) and (11) in the constraint equation (8), we obtain

$$9x^2 = 36 \quad \text{or} \quad x = \pm 2$$

Substituting these values in (10) and (11) yields two points:

$$(2, 4, 4) \quad \text{and} \quad (-2, -4, -4)$$

Since $f(2, 4, 4) = 9$ and $f(-2, -4, -4) = 81$, it follows that (2, 4, 4) is the point on the sphere closest to (1, 2, 2), and (−2, −4, −4) is the point that is farthest (Figure 13.9.5). ◄

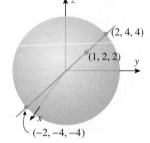

(2, 4, 4)

(1, 2, 2)

(−2, −4, −4)

▲ **Figure 13.9.5**

REMARK Solving nonlinear systems such as (9) usually involves trial and error. A technique that sometimes works is demonstrated in Example 3. In that example the equations were solved for a common variable (λ), and we then derived relationships between the remaining variables (x, y, and z). Substituting those relationships in the constraint equation led to the value of one of the variables, and the values of the other variables were then computed.

Next we will use Lagrange multipliers to solve the problem of Example 6 in the last section.

▶ **Example 4** Use Lagrange multipliers to determine the dimensions of a rectangular box, open at the top, having a volume of 32 ft³, and requiring the least amount of material for its construction.

Solution. With the notation introduced in Example 6 of the last section, the problem is to minimize the surface area

$$S = xy + 2xz + 2yz$$

subject to the volume constraint

$$xyz = 32 \tag{12}$$

If we let $f(x, y, z) = xy + 2xz + 2yz$ and $g(x, y, z) = xyz$, then

$$\nabla f = (y + 2z)\mathbf{i} + (x + 2z)\mathbf{j} + (2x + 2y)\mathbf{k} \quad \text{and} \quad \nabla g = yz\mathbf{i} + xz\mathbf{j} + xy\mathbf{k}$$

It follows that $\nabla g \neq \mathbf{0}$ at any point on the surface $xyz = 32$, since x, y, and z are all nonzero on this surface. Thus, at a constrained relative extremum we must have $\nabla f = \lambda \nabla g$, that is,

$$(y + 2z)\mathbf{i} + (x + 2z)\mathbf{j} + (2x + 2y)\mathbf{k} = \lambda(yz\mathbf{i} + xz\mathbf{j} + xy\mathbf{k})$$

This condition yields the three equations

$$y + 2z = \lambda yz, \quad x + 2z = \lambda xz, \quad 2x + 2y = \lambda xy$$

Because x, y, and z are nonzero, these equations can be rewritten as

$$\frac{1}{z} + \frac{2}{y} = \lambda, \quad \frac{1}{z} + \frac{2}{x} = \lambda, \quad \frac{2}{y} + \frac{2}{x} = \lambda$$

From the first two equations,

$$y = x \tag{13}$$

and from the first and third equations,

$$z = \tfrac{1}{2}x \tag{14}$$

Substituting (13) and (14) in the volume constraint (12) yields

$$\tfrac{1}{2}x^3 = 32$$

This equation, together with (13) and (14), yields

$$x = 4, \quad y = 4, \quad z = 2$$

which agrees with the result that was obtained in Example 6 of the last section. ◄

There are variations in the method of Lagrange multipliers that can be used to solve problems with two or more constraints. However, we will not discuss that topic here.

✔ **QUICK CHECK EXERCISES 13.9** *(See page 997 for answers.)*

---

1. (a) Suppose that $f(x, y)$ and $g(x, y)$ are differentiable at the origin and have nonzero gradients there, and that $g(0, 0) = 0$. If the maximum value of $f(x, y)$ subject to the constraint $g(x, y) = 0$ occurs at the origin, how is the tangent line to the graph of $g(x, y) = 0$ related to the tangent line at the origin to the level curve of f through $(0, 0)$?

(b) Suppose that $f(x, y, z)$ and $g(x, y, z)$ are differentiable at the origin and have nonzero gradients there, and that $g(0, 0, 0) = 0$. If the maximum value of $f(x, y, z)$ subject to the constraint $g(x, y, z) = 0$ occurs at the origin,

how is the tangent plane to the graph of the constraint $g(x, y, z) = 0$ related to the tangent plane at the origin to the level surface of f through $(0, 0, 0)$?

2. The maximum value of $x + y$ subject to the constraint $x^2 + y^2 = 1$ is _____.

3. The maximum value of $x + y + z$ subject to the constraint $x^2 + y^2 + z^2 = 1$ is _____.

4. The maximum and minimum values of $2x + 3y$ subject to the constraint $x + y = 1$, where $0 \leq x, 0 \leq y$, are _____ and _____, respectively.

EXERCISE SET 13.9   Graphing Utility   C CAS

FOCUS ON CONCEPTS

1. The accompanying figure shows graphs of the line $x + y = 4$ and the level curves of height $c = 2, 4, 6$, and 8 for the function $f(x, y) = xy$.
   (a) Use the figure to find the maximum value of the function $f(x, y) = xy$ subject to $x + y = 4$, and explain your reasoning.
   (b) How can you tell from the figure that your answer to part (a) is not the minimum value of f subject to the constraint?
   (c) Use Lagrange multipliers to check your work.

2. The accompanying figure shows the graphs of the line $3x + 4y = 25$ and the level curves of height $c = 9, 16, 25, 36$, and 49 for the function $f(x, y) = x^2 + y^2$.
   (a) Use the accompanying figure to find the minimum value of the function $f(x, y) = x^2 + y^2$ subject to $3x + 4y = 25$, and explain your reasoning.
   (b) How can you tell from the accompanying figure that your answer to part (a) is not the maximum value of f subject to the constraint?
   (c) Use Lagrange multipliers to check your work.

▲ Figure Ex-1

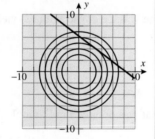

▲ Figure Ex-2

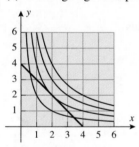 3. (a) On a graphing utility, graph the circle $x^2 + y^2 = 25$ and two distinct level curves of $f(x, y) = x^2 - y$ that just touch the circle in a single point.
   (b) Use the results you obtained in part (a) to approximate the maximum and minimum values of f subject to the constraint $x^2 + y^2 = 25$.
   (c) Check your approximations in part (b) using Lagrange multipliers.

C 4. (a) If you have a CAS with implicit plotting capability, use it to graph the circle $(x - 4)^2 + (y - 4)^2 = 4$ and two level curves of $f(x, y) = x^3 + y^3 - 3xy$ that just touch the circle.
   (b) Use the result you obtained in part (a) to approximate the minimum value of f subject to the constraint $(x - 4)^2 + (y - 4)^2 = 4$.
   (c) Confirm graphically that you have found a minimum and not a maximum.
   (d) Check your approximation using Lagrange multipliers and solving the required equations numerically.

5–12 Use Lagrange multipliers to find the maximum and minimum values of f subject to the given constraint. Also, find the points at which these extreme values occur. ■

5. $f(x, y) = xy$; $4x^2 + 8y^2 = 16$
6. $f(x, y) = x^2 - y^2$; $x^2 + y^2 = 25$
7. $f(x, y) = 4x^3 + y^2$; $2x^2 + y^2 = 1$
8. $f(x, y) = x - 3y - 1$; $x^2 + 3y^2 = 16$
9. $f(x, y, z) = 2x + y - 2z$; $x^2 + y^2 + z^2 = 4$
10. $f(x, y, z) = 3x + 6y + 2z$; $2x^2 + 4y^2 + z^2 = 70$
11. $f(x, y, z) = xyz$; $x^2 + y^2 + z^2 = 1$
12. $f(x, y, z) = x^4 + y^4 + z^4$; $x^2 + y^2 + z^2 = 1$

13–16 True–False Determine whether the statement is true or false. Explain your answer. ■

13. A "Lagrange multiplier" is a special type of gradient vector.
14. The extrema of $f(x, y)$ subject to the constraint $g(x, y) = 0$ occur at those points for which $\nabla f = \nabla g$.
15. In the method of Lagrange multipliers it is necessary to solve a constraint equation $g(x, y) = 0$ for y in terms of x.
16. The extrema of $f(x, y)$ subject to the constraint $g(x, y) = 0$ occur at those points at which a contour of f is tangent to the constraint curve $g(x, y) = 0$.

17–24 Solve using Lagrange multipliers. ■

17. Find the point on the line $2x - 4y = 3$ that is closest to the origin.
18. Find the point on the line $y = 2x + 3$ that is closest to $(4, 2)$.
19. Find the point on the plane $x + 2y + z = 1$ that is closest to the origin.
20. Find the point on the plane $4x + 3y + z = 2$ that is closest to $(1, -1, 1)$.
21. Find the points on the circle $x^2 + y^2 = 45$ that are closest to and farthest from $(1, 2)$.
22. Find the points on the surface $xy - z^2 = 1$ that are closest to the origin.
23. Find a vector in 3-space whose length is 5 and whose components have the largest possible sum.
24. Suppose that the temperature at a point (x, y) on a metal plate is $T(x, y) = 4x^2 - 4xy + y^2$. An ant, walking on the plate, traverses a circle of radius 5 centered at the origin. What are the highest and lowest temperatures encountered by the ant?

25–32 Use Lagrange multipliers to solve the indicated problems from Section 13.8. ■

25. Exercise 38
26. Exercise 39

27. Exercise 40

28. Exercise 41

29. Exercise 43

30. Exercises 45(a) and (b)

31. Exercise 46

32. Exercise 47

⊂ **33.** Let α, β, and γ be the angles of a triangle.
   (a) Use Lagrange multipliers to find the maximum value of $f(\alpha, \beta, \gamma) = \cos\alpha \cos\beta \cos\gamma$, and determine the angles for which the maximum occurs.
   (b) Express $f(\alpha, \beta, \gamma)$ as a function of α and β alone, and use a CAS to graph this function of two variables. Confirm that the result obtained in part (a) is consistent with the graph.

34. The accompanying figure shows the intersection of the elliptic paraboloid $z = x^2 + 4y^2$ and the right circular cylinder $x^2 + y^2 = 1$. Use Lagrange multipliers to find the highest and lowest points on the curve of intersection.

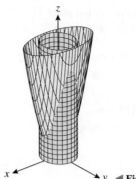

◄ Figure Ex-34

35. **Writing** List a sequence of steps for solving a two-variable extremum problem with one constraint using the method of Lagrange multipliers. Interpret each step geometrically.

36. **Writing** Redo Example 2 using the methods of Section 4.5, and compare your solution with that of Example 2. For example, how is the perimeter constraint used in each approach?

✔ **QUICK CHECK ANSWERS 13.9**

1. (a) They are the same line. (b) They are the same plane.   **2.** $\sqrt{2}$ **3.** $\sqrt{3}$ **4.** 3; 2

CHAPTER 13 REVIEW EXERCISES   〜 Graphing Utility

1. Let $f(x, y) = e^x \ln y$. Find
   (a) $f(\ln y, e^x)$ (b) $f(r + s, rs)$.

2. Sketch the domain of f using solid lines for portions of the boundary included in the domain and dashed lines for portions not included.
   (a) $f(x, y) = \ln(xy - 1)$ (b) $f(x, y) = (\sin^{-1} x)/e^y$

3. Show that the level curves of the cone $z = \sqrt{x^2 + y^2}$ and the paraboloid $z = x^2 + y^2$ are circles, and make a sketch that illustrates the difference between the contour plots of the two functions.

4. (a) In words, describe the level surfaces of the function $f(x, y, z) = a^2 x^2 + a^2 y^2 + z^2$, where $a > 0$.
   (b) Find a function $f(x, y, z)$ whose level surfaces form a family of circular paraboloids that open in the positive z-direction.

5–6 (a) Find the limit of $f(x, y)$ as $(x, y) \to (0, 0)$ if it exists, and (b) determine whether f is continuous at $(0, 0)$. ■

5. $f(x, y) = \dfrac{x^4 - x + y - x^3 y}{x - y}$

6. $f(x, y) = \begin{cases} \dfrac{x^4 - y^4}{x^2 + y^2} & \text{if } (x, y) \neq (0, 0) \\ 0 & \text{if } (x, y) = (0, 0) \end{cases}$

7. (a) A company manufactures two types of computer monitors: standard monitors and high resolution monitors. Suppose that $P(x, y)$ is the profit that results from producing and selling x standard monitors and y high-resolution monitors. What do the two partial derivatives $\partial P/\partial x$ and $\partial P/\partial y$ represent?
   (b) Suppose that the temperature at time t at a point (x, y) on the surface of a lake is $T(x, y, t)$. What do the partial derivatives $\partial T/\partial x$, $\partial T/\partial y$, and $\partial T/\partial t$ represent?

8. Let $z = f(x, y)$.
   (a) Express $\partial z/\partial x$ and $\partial z/\partial y$ as limits.
   (b) In words, what do the derivatives $f_x(x_0, y_0)$ and $f_y(x_0, y_0)$ tell you about the surface $z = f(x, y)$?
   (c) In words, what do the derivatives $\partial z/\partial x(x_0, y_0)$ and $\partial z/\partial y(x_0, y_0)$ tell you about the rates of change of z with respect to x and y?

9. The pressure in newtons per square meter (N/m^2) of a gas in a cylinder is given by $P = 10T/V$ with T in kelvins (K) and V in cubic meters (m^3).
   (a) If T is increasing at a rate of 3 K/min with V held fixed at 2.5 m^3, find the rate at which the pressure is changing when $T = 50$ K.
   (b) If T is held fixed at 50 K while V is decreasing at the rate of 3 m^3/min, find the rate at which the pressure is changing when $V = 2.5$ m^3.

10. Find the slope of the tangent line at the point $(1, -2, -3)$ on the curve of intersection of the surface $z = 5 - 4x^2 - y^2$ with
(a) the plane $x = 1$ (b) the plane $y = -2$.

11–14 Verify the assertion. ■

11. If $w = \tan(x^2 + y^2) + x\sqrt{y}$, then $w_{xy} = w_{yx}$.

12. If $w = \ln(3x - 3y) + \cos(x + y)$, then $\partial^2 w/\partial x^2 = \partial^2 w/\partial y^2$.

13. If $F(x, y, z) = 2z^3 - 3(x^2 + y^2)z$, then F satisfies the equation $F_{xx} + F_{yy} + F_{zz} = 0$.

14. If $f(x, y, z) = xyz + x^2 + \ln(y/z)$, then $f_{xyzx} = f_{zxxy}$.

15. What do Δf and df represent, and how are they related?

16. If $w = x^2 y - 2xy + y^2 x$, find the increment Δw and the differential dw if (x, y) varies from $(1, 0)$ to $(1.1, -0.1)$.

17. Use differentials to estimate the change in the volume $V = \frac{1}{3}x^2 h$ of a pyramid with a square base when its height h is increased from 2 to 2.2 m and its base dimension x is decreased from 1 to 0.9 m. Compare this to ΔV.

18. Find the local linear approximation of $f(x, y) = \sin(xy)$ at $(\frac{1}{3}, \pi)$.

19. Suppose that z is a differentiable function of x and y with

$$\frac{\partial z}{\partial x}(1, 2) = 4 \quad \text{and} \quad \frac{\partial z}{\partial y}(1, 2) = 2$$

If $x = x(t)$ and $y = y(t)$ are differentiable functions of t with $x(0) = 1$, $y(0) = 2$, $x'(0) = -\frac{1}{2}$, and (under composition) $z'(0) = 2$, find $y'(0)$.

20. In each part, use Theorem 13.5.3 to find dy/dx.
(a) $3x^2 - 5xy + \tan xy = 0$
(b) $x \ln y + \sin(x - y) = \pi$

21. Given that $f(x, y) = 0$, use Theorem 13.5.3 to express $d^2 y/dx^2$ in terms of partial derivatives of f.

22. Let $z = f(x, y)$, where $x = g(t)$ and $y = h(t)$.
(a) Show that

$$\frac{d}{dt}\left(\frac{\partial z}{\partial x}\right) = \frac{\partial^2 z}{\partial x^2}\frac{dx}{dt} + \frac{\partial^2 z}{\partial y \partial x}\frac{dy}{dt}$$

and

$$\frac{d}{dt}\left(\frac{\partial z}{\partial y}\right) = \frac{\partial^2 z}{\partial x \partial y}\frac{dx}{dt} + \frac{\partial^2 z}{\partial y^2}\frac{dy}{dt}$$

(b) Use the formulas in part (a) to help find a formula for $d^2 z/dt^2$.

23. (a) How are the directional derivative and the gradient of a function related?
(b) Under what conditions is the directional derivative of a differentiable function 0?
(c) In what direction does the directional derivative of a differentiable function have its maximum value? Its minimum value?

24. In words, what does the derivative $D_{\mathbf{u}} f(x_0, y_0)$ tell you about the surface $z = f(x, y)$?

25. Find $D_{\mathbf{u}} f(-3, 5)$ for $f(x, y) = y \ln(x + y)$ if $\mathbf{u} = \frac{3}{5}\mathbf{i} + \frac{4}{5}\mathbf{j}$.

26. Suppose that $\nabla f(0, 0) = 2\mathbf{i} + \frac{3}{2}\mathbf{j}$.
(a) Find a unit vector $\mathbf{u}$ such that $D_{\mathbf{u}} f(0, 0)$ is a maximum. What is this maximum value?
(b) Find a unit vector $\mathbf{u}$ such that $D_{\mathbf{u}} f(0, 0)$ is a minimum. What is this minimum value?

27. At the point $(1, 2)$, the directional derivative $D_{\mathbf{u}} f$ is $2\sqrt{2}$ toward $P_1(2, 3)$ and -3 toward $P_2(1, 0)$. Find $D_{\mathbf{u}} f(1, 2)$ toward the origin.

28. Find equations for the tangent plane and normal line to the given surface at P_0.
(a) $z = x^2 e^{2y}$; $P_0(1, \ln 2, 4)$
(b) $x^2 y^3 z^4 + xyz = 2$; $P_0(2, 1, -1)$

29. Find all points P_0 on the surface $z = 2 - xy$ at which the normal line passes through the origin.

30. Show that for all tangent planes to the surface

$$x^{2/3} + y^{2/3} + z^{2/3} = 1$$

the sum of the squares of the x-, y-, and z-intercepts is 1.

31. Find all points on the paraboloid $z = 9x^2 + 4y^2$ at which the normal line is parallel to the line through the points $P(4, -2, 5)$ and $Q(-2, -6, 4)$.

32. Suppose the equations of motion of a particle are $x = t - 1$, $y = 4e^{-t}$, $z = 2 - \sqrt{t}$, where $t > 0$. Find, to the nearest tenth of a degree, the acute angle between the velocity vector and the normal line to the surface $(x^2/4) + y^2 + z^2 = 1$ at the points where the particle collides with the surface. Use a calculating utility with a root-finding capability where needed.

33–36 Locate all relative minima, relative maxima, and saddle points. ■

33. $f(x, y) = x^2 + 3xy + 3y^2 - 6x + 3y$

34. $f(x, y) = x^2 y - 6y^2 - 3x^2$

35. $f(x, y) = x^3 - 3xy + \frac{1}{2}y^2$

36. $f(x, y) = 4x^2 - 12xy + 9y^2$

37–39 Solve these exercises two ways:
(a) Use the constraint to eliminate a variable.
(b) Use Lagrange multipliers. ■

37. Find all relative extrema of $x^2 y^2$ subject to the constraint $4x^2 + y^2 = 8$.

38. Find the dimensions of the rectangular box of maximum volume that can be inscribed in the ellipsoid

$$(x/a)^2 + (y/b)^2 + (z/c)^2 = 1$$

39. As illustrated in the accompanying figure on the next page, suppose that a current I branches into currents I_1, I_2, and I_3 through resistors R_1, R_2, and R_3 in such a way that the total power dissipated in the three resistors is a minimum. Find the ratios $I_1 : I_2 : I_3$ if the power dissipated in R_i is $I_i^2 R_i (i = 1, 2, 3)$ and $I_1 + I_2 + I_3 = I$.

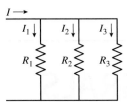

◀ **Figure Ex-39**

40–42 In economics, a ***production model*** is a mathematical relationship between the output of a company or a country and the labor and capital equipment required to produce that output. Much of the pioneering work in the field of production models occurred in the 1920s when Paul Douglas of the University of Chicago and his collaborator Charles Cobb proposed that the output P can be expressed in terms of the labor L and the capital equipment K by an equation of the form

$$P = cL^\alpha K^\beta$$

where c is a constant of proportionality and α and β are constants such that $0 < \alpha < 1$ and $0 < \beta < 1$. This is called the ***Cobb–Douglas production model***. Typically, P, L, and K are all expressed in terms of their equivalent monetary values. These exercises explore properties of this model. ▪

40. (a) Consider the Cobb–Douglas production model given by the formula $P = L^{0.75}K^{0.25}$. Sketch the level curves $P(L, K) = 1$, $P(L, K) = 2$, and $P(L, K) = 3$ in an LK-coordinate system (L horizontal and K vertical). Your sketch need not be accurate numerically, but it should show the general shape of the curves and their relative positions.

  (b) Use a graphing utility to make a more extensive contour plot of the model.

41. (a) Find $\partial P/\partial L$ and $\partial P/\partial K$ for the Cobb–Douglas production model $P = cL^\alpha K^\beta$.

  (b) The derivative $\partial P/\partial L$ is called the ***marginal productivity of labor***, and the derivative $\partial P/\partial K$ is called the ***marginal productivity of capital***. Explain what these quantities mean in practical terms.

  (c) Show that if $\beta = 1 - \alpha$, then P satisfies the partial differential equation

$$K\frac{\partial P}{\partial K} + L\frac{\partial P}{\partial L} = P$$

42. Consider the Cobb–Douglas production model

$$P = 1000L^{0.6}K^{0.4}$$

  (a) Find the maximum output value of P if labor costs $\$50.00$ per unit, capital costs $\$100.00$ per unit, and the total cost of labor and capital is set at $\$200,000$.

  (b) How should the $\$200,000$ be allocated between labor and capital to achieve the maximum?

CHAPTER 13 MAKING CONNECTIONS

1. Suppose that a function $z = f(x, y)$ is expressed in polar form by making the substitutions $x = r\cos\theta$ and $y = r\sin\theta$. Show that

$$r\frac{\partial z}{\partial r} = x\frac{\partial z}{\partial x} + y\frac{\partial z}{\partial y}$$

$$\frac{\partial z}{\partial \theta} = -y\frac{\partial z}{\partial x} + x\frac{\partial z}{\partial y}$$

2. A function $f(x, y)$ is said to be ***homogeneous of degree n*** if $f(tx, ty) = t^n f(x, y)$ for $t > 0$. In each part, show that the function is homogeneous, and find its degree.

  (a) $f(x, y) = 3x^2 + y^2$ (b) $f(x, y) = \sqrt{x^2 + y^2}$

  (c) $f(x, y) = x^2y - 2y^3$ (d) $f(x, y) = \dfrac{5}{(x^2 + 2y^2)^2}$

3. Suppose that a function $f(x, y)$ is defined for all points $(x, y) \neq (0, 0)$. Prove that f is homogeneous of degree n if and only if there exists a function $g(\theta)$ that is 2π periodic such that in polar form the equation $z = f(x, y)$ becomes

$$z = r^n g(\theta)$$

for $r > 0$ and $-\infty < \theta < +\infty$.

4. (a) Use the chain rule to show that if $f(x, y)$ is a homogeneous function of degree n, then

$$x\frac{\partial f}{\partial x} + y\frac{\partial f}{\partial y} = nf$$

  [*Hint:* Let $u = tx$ and $v = ty$ in $f(tx, ty)$, and differentiate both sides of $f(u, v) = t^n f(x, y)$ with respect to t.]

  (b) Use the results of Exercise 1 and 3 to give another derivation of the equation in part (a).

  (c) Confirm that the functions in Exercise 2 satisfy the equation in part (a).

5. Suppose that a function $f(x, y)$ is defined for all points $(x, y) \neq (0, 0)$ and satisfies

$$x\frac{\partial f}{\partial x} + y\frac{\partial f}{\partial y} = nf$$

Prove that f is homogeneous of degree n. [*Hint:* Express the function $z = f(x, y)$ in polar form and use Exercise 1 to conclude that

$$r\frac{\partial z}{\partial r} - nz = 0$$

Divide both sides of this equation by r^{n+1} and interpret the left-hand side of the resulting equation as the partial derivative with respect to r of a product of two functions.]

14

MULTIPLE INTEGRALS

Stone/Getty Images

Finding the areas of complex surfaces such as those used in the design of the Denver International Airport require integration methods studied in this chapter.

In this chapter we will extend the concept of a definite integral to functions of two and three variables. Whereas functions of one variable are usually integrated over intervals, functions of two variables are usually integrated over regions in 2-space and functions of three variables over regions in 3-space. Calculating such integrals will require some new techniques that will be a central focus in this chapter. Once we have developed the basic methods for integrating functions of two and three variables, we will show how such integrals can be used to calculate surface areas and volumes of solids; and we will also show how they can be used to find masses and centers of gravity of flat plates and three-dimensional solids. In addition to our study of integration, we will generalize the concept of a parametric curve in 2-space to a parametric surface in 3-space. This will allow us to work with a wider variety of surfaces than previously possible and will provide a powerful tool for generating surfaces using computers and other graphing utilities.

14.1 DOUBLE INTEGRALS

The notion of a definite integral can be extended to functions of two or more variables. In this section we will discuss the double integral, which is the extension to functions of two variables.

■ VOLUME

Recall that the definite integral of a function of one variable

$$\int_a^b f(x)\,dx = \lim_{\max \Delta x_k \to 0} \sum_{k=1}^n f(x_k^*)\Delta x_k = \lim_{n \to +\infty} \sum_{k=1}^n f(x_k^*)\Delta x_k \qquad (1)$$

arose from the problem of finding areas under curves. [In the rightmost expression in (1), we use the "limit as $n \to +\infty$" to encapsulate the process by which we increase the number of subintervals of $[a, b]$ in such a way that the lengths of the subintervals approach zero.] Integrals of functions of two variables arise from the problem of finding volumes under surfaces.

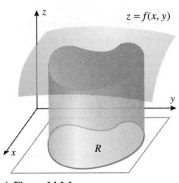

$z = f(x, y)$

▲ **Figure 14.1.1**

14.1.1 **THE VOLUME PROBLEM**   Given a function f of two variables that is continuous and nonnegative on a region R in the xy-plane, find the volume of the solid enclosed between the surface $z = f(x, y)$ and the region R (Figure 14.1.1).

Later, we will place more restrictions on the region R, but for now we will just assume that the entire region can be enclosed within some suitably large rectangle with sides parallel to the coordinate axes. This ensures that R does not extend indefinitely in any direction.

The procedure for finding the volume V of the solid in Figure 14.1.1 will be similar to the limiting process used for finding areas, except that now the approximating elements will be rectangular parallelepipeds rather than rectangles. We proceed as follows:

- Using lines parallel to the coordinate axes, divide the rectangle enclosing the region R into subrectangles, and exclude from consideration all those subrectangles that contain any points outside of R. This leaves only rectangles that are subsets of R (Figure 14.1.2). Assume that there are n such rectangles, and denote the area of the kth such rectangle by ΔA_k.

- Choose any arbitrary point in each subrectangle, and denote the point in the kth subrectangle by (x_k^*, y_k^*). As shown in Figure 14.1.3, the product $f(x_k^*, y_k^*)\Delta A_k$ is the volume of a rectangular parallelepiped with base area ΔA_k and height $f(x_k^*, y_k^*)$, so the sum

$$\sum_{k=1}^{n} f(x_k^*, y_k^*)\Delta A_k$$

can be viewed as an approximation to the volume V of the entire solid.

- There are two sources of error in the approximation: first, the parallelepipeds have flat tops, whereas the surface $z = f(x, y)$ may be curved; second, the rectangles that form the bases of the parallelepipeds may not completely cover the region R. However, if we repeat the above process with more and more subdivisions in such a way that both the lengths and the widths of the subrectangles approach zero, then it is plausible that the errors of both types approach zero, and the exact volume of the solid will be

$$V = \lim_{n \to +\infty} \sum_{k=1}^{n} f(x_k^*, y_k^*)\Delta A_k$$

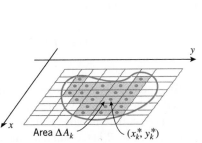

Area ΔA_k (x_k^*, y_k^*)

▲ **Figure 14.1.2**

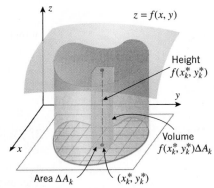

$z = f(x, y)$

Height $f(x_k^*, y_k^*)$

Volume $f(x_k^*, y_k^*)\Delta A_k$

Area ΔA_k (x_k^*, y_k^*)

▲ **Figure 14.1.3**

This suggests the following definition.

Definition 14.1.2 is satisfactory for our present purposes, but some issues would have to be resolved before it could be regarded as rigorous. For example, we would have to prove that the limit actually exists and that its value does not depend on how the points $(x_1^*, y_1^*), (x_2^*, y_2^*), \ldots, (x_n^*, y_n^*)$ are chosen. These facts are true if the region R is not too "complicated" and if f is continuous on R. The details are beyond the scope of this text.

14.1.2 DEFINITION (*Volume Under a Surface*) If f is a function of two variables that is continuous and nonnegative on a region R in the xy-plane, then the volume of the solid enclosed between the surface $z = f(x, y)$ and the region R is defined by

$$V = \lim_{n \to +\infty} \sum_{k=1}^{n} f(x_k^*, y_k^*) \Delta A_k \qquad (2)$$

Here, $n \to +\infty$ indicates the process of increasing the number of subrectangles of the rectangle enclosing R in such a way that both the lengths and the widths of the subrectangles approach zero.

It is assumed in Definition 14.1.2 that f is nonnegative on the region R. If f is continuous on R and has both positive and negative values, then the limit

$$\lim_{n \to +\infty} \sum_{k=1}^{n} f(x_k^*, y_k^*) \Delta A_k \qquad (3)$$

no longer represents the volume between R and the surface $z = f(x, y)$; rather, it represents a *difference* of volumes—the volume between R and the portion of the surface that is above the xy-plane minus the volume between R and the portion of the surface below the xy-plane. We call this the ***net signed volume*** between the region R and the surface $z = f(x, y)$.

■ DEFINITION OF A DOUBLE INTEGRAL

As in Definition 14.1.2, the notation $n \to +\infty$ in (3) encapsulates a process in which the enclosing rectangle for R is repeatedly subdivided in such a way that both the lengths and the widths of the subrectangles approach zero. Note that subdividing so that the subrectangle lengths approach zero forces the mesh of the partition of the length of the enclosing rectangle for R to approach zero. Similarly, subdividing so that the subrectangle widths approach zero forces the mesh of the partition of the width of the enclosing rectangle for R to approach zero. Thus, we have extended the notion conveyed by Formula (1) where the definite integral of a one-variable function is expressed as a limit of Riemann sums. By extension, the sums in (3) are also called ***Riemann sums***, and the limit of the Riemann sums is denoted by

$$\iint\limits_{R} f(x, y)\, dA = \lim_{n \to +\infty} \sum_{k=1}^{n} f(x_k^*, y_k^*) \Delta A_k \qquad (4)$$

which is called the ***double integral*** of $f(x, y)$ over R.

If f is continuous and nonnegative on the region R, then the volume formula in (2) can be expressed as

$$V = \iint\limits_{R} f(x, y)\, dA \qquad (5)$$

If f has both positive and negative values on R, then a positive value for the double integral of f over R means that there is more volume above R than below, a negative value for the double integral means that there is more volume below R than above, and a value of zero means that the volume above R is the same as the volume below R.

■ EVALUATING DOUBLE INTEGRALS

Except in the simplest cases, it is impractical to obtain the value of a double integral from the limit in (4). However, we will now show how to evaluate double integrals by calculating two successive single integrals. For the rest of this section we will limit our discussion to the case where R is a rectangle; in the next section we will consider double integrals over more complicated regions.

The partial derivatives of a function $f(x, y)$ are calculated by holding one of the variables fixed and differentiating with respect to the other variable. Let us consider the reverse of this process, *partial integration*. The symbols

$$\int_a^b f(x, y)\, dx \quad \text{and} \quad \int_c^d f(x, y)\, dy$$

denote *partial definite integrals*; the first integral, called the *partial definite integral with respect to x*, is evaluated by holding y fixed and integrating with respect to x, and the second integral, called the *partial definite integral with respect to y*, is evaluated by holding x fixed and integrating with respect to y. As the following example shows, the partial definite integral with respect to x is a function of y, and the partial definite integral with respect to y is a function of x.

▶ **Example 1**

$$\int_0^1 xy^2\, dx = y^2 \int_0^1 x\, dx = \left.\frac{y^2 x^2}{2}\right]_{x=0}^1 = \frac{y^2}{2}$$

$$\int_0^1 xy^2\, dy = x \int_0^1 y^2\, dy = \left.\frac{xy^3}{3}\right]_{y=0}^1 = \frac{x}{3} \quad ◀$$

A partial definite integral with respect to x is a function of y and hence can be integrated with respect to y; similarly, a partial definite integral with respect to y can be integrated with respect to x. This two-stage integration process is called *iterated* (or *repeated*) *integration*. We introduce the following notation:

$$\int_c^d \int_a^b f(x, y)\, dx\, dy = \int_c^d \left[\int_a^b f(x, y)\, dx \right] dy \tag{6}$$

$$\int_a^b \int_c^d f(x, y)\, dy\, dx = \int_a^b \left[\int_c^d f(x, y)\, dy \right] dx \tag{7}$$

These integrals are called *iterated integrals*.

▶ **Example 2** Evaluate

(a) $\displaystyle\int_1^3 \int_2^4 (40 - 2xy)\, dy\, dx$ (b) $\displaystyle\int_2^4 \int_1^3 (40 - 2xy)\, dx\, dy$

Solution (a).

$$\int_1^3 \int_2^4 (40 - 2xy)\, dy\, dx = \int_1^3 \left[\int_2^4 (40 - 2xy)\, dy \right] dx$$

$$= \int_1^3 (40y - xy^2)\big]_{y=2}^4\, dx$$

$$= \int_1^3 [(160 - 16x) - (80 - 4x)]\, dx$$

$$= \int_1^3 (80 - 12x)\, dx$$

$$= (80x - 6x^2)\big]_1^3 = 112$$

Solution (b).

$$\int_2^4 \int_1^3 (40 - 2xy)\,dx\,dy = \int_2^4 \left[\int_1^3 (40 - 2xy)\,dx \right] dy$$

$$= \int_2^4 (40x - x^2 y)\Big]_{x=1}^3 \, dy$$

$$= \int_2^4 [(120 - 9y) - (40 - y)]\,dy$$

$$= \int_2^4 (80 - 8y)\,dy$$

$$= (80y - 4y^2)\Big]_2^4 = 112 \ \blacktriangleleft$$

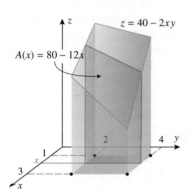

▲ **Figure 14.1.4**

It is no accident that both parts of Example 2 produced the same answer. Consider the solid S bounded above by the surface $z = 40 - 2xy$ and below by the rectangle R defined by $1 \le x \le 3$ and $2 \le y \le 4$. By the method of slicing discussed in Section 6.2, the volume of S is given by

$$V = \int_1^3 A(x)\,dx$$

where $A(x)$ is the area of a vertical cross section of S taken perpendicular to the x-axis (Figure 14.1.4). For a fixed value of x, $1 \le x \le 3$, $z = 40 - 2xy$ is a function of y, so the integral

$$A(x) = \int_2^4 (40 - 2xy)\,dy$$

represents the area under the graph of this function of y. Thus,

$$V = \int_1^3 \left[\int_2^4 (40 - 2xy)\,dy \right] dx = \int_1^3 \int_2^4 (40 - 2xy)\,dy\,dx$$

is the volume of S. Similarly, by the method of slicing with cross sections of S taken perpendicular to the y-axis, the volume of S is given by

$$V = \int_2^4 A(y)\,dy = \int_2^4 \left[\int_1^3 (40 - 2xy)\,dx \right] dy = \int_2^4 \int_1^3 (40 - 2xy)\,dx\,dy$$

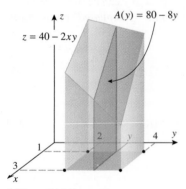

▲ **Figure 14.1.5**

(Figure 14.1.5). Thus, the iterated integrals in parts (a) and (b) of Example 2 both measure the volume of S, which by Formula (5) is the double integral of $z = 40 - 2xy$ over R. That is,

$$\int_1^3 \int_2^4 (40 - 2xy)\,dy\,dx = \iint\limits_R (40 - 2xy)\,dA = \int_2^4 \int_1^3 (40 - 2xy)\,dx\,dy$$

> We will often denote the rectangle
>
> $\{(x, y) : a \le x \le b, c \le y \le d\}$
>
> as $[a, b] \times [c, d]$ for simplicity.

The geometric argument above applies to any continuous function $f(x, y)$ that is nonnegative on a rectangle $R = [a, b] \times [c, d]$, as is the case for $f(x, y) = 40 - 2xy$ on $[1, 3] \times [2, 4]$. The conclusion that the double integral of $f(x, y)$ over R has the same value as either of the two possible iterated integrals is true even when f is negative at some points in R. We state this result in the following theorem and omit a formal proof.

14.1.3   **THEOREM** (*Fubini's Theorem*)   *Let R be the rectangle defined by the inequalities*

$$a \le x \le b, \quad c \le y \le d$$

If $f(x, y)$ is continuous on this rectangle, then

$$\iint\limits_R f(x, y)\,dA = \int_c^d \int_a^b f(x, y)\,dx\,dy = \int_a^b \int_c^d f(x, y)\,dy\,dx$$

Theorem 14.1.3 allows us to evaluate a double integral over a rectangle by converting it to an iterated integral. This can be done in two ways, both of which produce the value of the double integral.

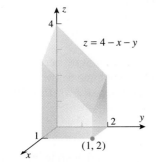

$z = 4 - x - y$

$(1, 2)$

▲ Figure 14.1.6

▶ **Example 3**   Use a double integral to find the volume of the solid that is bounded above by the plane $z = 4 - x - y$ and below by the rectangle $R = [0, 1] \times [0, 2]$ (Figure 14.1.6).

Solution.   The volume is the double integral of $z = 4 - x - y$ over R. Using Theorem 14.1.3, this can be obtained from either of the iterated integrals

$$\int_0^2 \int_0^1 (4 - x - y)\, dx\, dy \quad \text{or} \quad \int_0^1 \int_0^2 (4 - x - y)\, dy\, dx \tag{8}$$

Using the first of these, we obtain

$$V = \iint_R (4 - x - y)\, dA = \int_0^2 \int_0^1 (4 - x - y)\, dx\, dy$$

$$= \int_0^2 \left[4x - \frac{x^2}{2} - xy \right]_{x=0}^1 dy = \int_0^2 \left(\frac{7}{2} - y \right) dy$$

$$= \left[\frac{7}{2}y - \frac{y^2}{2} \right]_0^2 = 5$$

You can check this result by evaluating the second integral in (8). ◀

TECHNOLOGY MASTERY

If you have a CAS with a built-in capability for computing iterated double integrals, use it to check Example 3.

Theorem 14.1.3 guarantees that the double integral in Example 4 can also be evaluated by integrating first with respect to y and then with respect to x. Verify this.

▶ **Example 4**   Evaluate the double integral

$$\iint_R y^2 x\, dA$$

over the rectangle $R = \{(x, y) : -3 \le x \le 2, 0 \le y \le 1\}$.

Solution.   In view of Theorem 14.1.3, the value of the double integral can be obtained by evaluating one of two possible iterated double integrals. We choose to integrate first with

Guido Fubini (1879–1943) Italian mathematician. Fubini, the son of a mathematician, showed brilliance in mathematics as a young pupil in Venice. He entered college at the Scuola Normale Superiore di Pisa in 1896 and presented his doctoral thesis on the subject of elliptic geometry in 1900 at the young age of 20. He subsequently had teaching positions at various universities, finally settling at the University of Turin where he remained for several decades. His mathematical work was diverse, and he made major contributions to many branches of mathematics. At the outbreak of World War I he shifted his attention to the accuracy of artillery fire, and following the war he worked on other applied subjects such as electrical circuits and acoustics. In 1939, as he neared age 60 and retirement, Benito Mussolini's Fascists adopted Hitler's anti-Jewish policies, so Fubini, who was Jewish, accepted a position at Princeton University, where he stayed until his death four years later. Fubini was well liked by his colleagues at Princeton and stories about him abound. He once gave a lecture on ballistics in which he showed that if you fired a projectile of a certain shape, then under the right conditions it could double back on itself and hit your own troops. Then, tongue in cheek, he suggested that one could fool the enemy by aiming this "Fubini Gun" at one's own troops and hit the unsuspecting enemy after the projectile reversed direction.

Fubini was exceptionally short, which occasionally caused problems. The story goes that one day his worried landlady called his friends to report that he had not come home. After searching everywhere, including the area near the local lake, it was discovered that Fubini was trapped in a stalled elevator and was unable to reach any of the buttons. Fubini celebrated his rescue with a party and later left a sign in his room that said, "To my landlady: When I am not home at 6:30 at night, please check the elevator...."

(photo by Wendy Wray)

respect to x and then with respect to y.

$$\iint_R y^2 x \, dA = \int_0^1 \int_{-3}^2 y^2 x \, dx \, dy = \int_0^1 \left[\frac{1}{2} y^2 x^2 \right]_{x=-3}^2 dy$$

$$= \int_0^1 \left(-\frac{5}{2} y^2 \right) dy = -\frac{5}{6} y^3 \Big]_0^1 = -\frac{5}{6} \blacktriangleleft$$

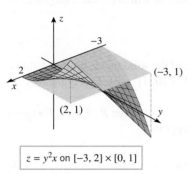

$z = y^2 x$ on $[-3, 2] \times [0, 1]$

▲ **Figure 14.1.7**

The integral in Example 4 can be interpreted as the net signed volume between the rectangle $[-3, 2] \times [0, 1]$ and the surface $z = y^2 x$. That is, it is the volume below $z = y^2 x$ and above $[0, 2] \times [0, 1]$ minus the volume above $z = y^2 x$ and below $[-3, 0] \times [0, 1]$ (Figure 14.1.7).

■ **PROPERTIES OF DOUBLE INTEGRALS**

To distinguish between double integrals of functions of two variables and definite integrals of functions of one variable, we will refer to the latter as ***single integrals***. Because double integrals, like single integrals, are defined as limits, they inherit many of the properties of limits. The following results, which we state without proof, are analogs of those in Theorem 5.5.4.

$$\iint_R cf(x, y) \, dA = c \iint_R f(x, y) \, dA \quad (c \text{ a constant}) \tag{9}$$

$$\iint_R [f(x, y) + g(x, y)] \, dA = \iint_R f(x, y) \, dA + \iint_R g(x, y) \, dA \tag{10}$$

$$\iint_R [f(x, y) - g(x, y)] \, dA = \iint_R f(x, y) \, dA - \iint_R g(x, y) \, dA \tag{11}$$

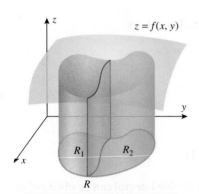

The volume of the entire solid is the sum of the volumes of the solids above R_1 and R_2.

▲ **Figure 14.1.8**

It is evident intuitively that if $f(x, y)$ is nonnegative on a region R, then subdividing R into two regions R_1 and R_2 has the effect of subdividing the solid between R and $z = f(x, y)$ into two solids, the sum of whose volumes is the volume of the entire solid (Figure 14.1.8). This suggests the following result, which holds even if f has negative values:

$$\iint_R f(x, y) \, dA = \iint_{R_1} f(x, y) \, dA + \iint_{R_2} f(x, y) \, dA \tag{12}$$

The proof of this result will be omitted.

✔ **QUICK CHECK EXERCISES 14.1**   *(See page 1008 for answers.)*

1. The double integral is defined as a limit of Riemann sums by
$$\iint_R f(x, y) \, dA = \underline{\hspace{2cm}}$$

2. The iterated integral
$$\int_1^5 \int_2^4 f(x, y) \, dx \, dy$$
integrates f over the rectangle defined by
$$\underline{\hspace{1.5cm}} \le x \le \underline{\hspace{1.5cm}}, \quad \underline{\hspace{1.5cm}} \le y \le \underline{\hspace{1.5cm}}$$

3. Supply the missing integrand and limits of integration.
$$\int_1^5 \int_2^4 (3x^2 - 2xy + y^2) \, dx \, dy = \int_\square^\square \underline{\hspace{1.5cm}} \, dy$$

4. The volume of the solid enclosed by the surface $z = x/y$ and the rectangle $0 \le x \le 4$, $1 \le y \le e^2$ in the xy-plane is $\underline{\hspace{1cm}}$.

EXERCISE SET 14.1   C CAS

1–12 Evaluate the iterated integrals.

1. $\displaystyle\int_0^1\int_0^2 (x+3)\,dy\,dx$

2. $\displaystyle\int_1^3\int_{-1}^1 (2x-4y)\,dy\,dx$

3. $\displaystyle\int_2^4\int_0^1 x^2y\,dx\,dy$

4. $\displaystyle\int_{-2}^0\int_{-1}^2 (x^2+y^2)\,dx\,dy$

5. $\displaystyle\int_0^{\ln 3}\int_0^{\ln 2} e^{x+y}\,dy\,dx$

6. $\displaystyle\int_0^2\int_0^1 y\sin x\,dy\,dx$

7. $\displaystyle\int_{-1}^0\int_2^5 dx\,dy$

8. $\displaystyle\int_4^6\int_{-3}^7 dy\,dx$

9. $\displaystyle\int_0^1\int_0^1 \frac{x}{(xy+1)^2}\,dy\,dx$

10. $\displaystyle\int_{\pi/2}^\pi\int_1^2 x\cos xy\,dy\,dx$

11. $\displaystyle\int_0^{\ln 2}\int_0^1 xye^{y^2x}\,dy\,dx$

12. $\displaystyle\int_3^4\int_1^2 \frac{1}{(x+y)^2}\,dy\,dx$

13–16 Evaluate the double integral over the rectangular region R.

13. $\displaystyle\iint_R 4xy^3\,dA; \quad R=\{(x,y): -1\le x\le 1,\ -2\le y\le 2\}$

14. $\displaystyle\iint_R \frac{xy}{\sqrt{x^2+y^2+1}}\,dA;$
$R=\{(x,y): 0\le x\le 1,\ 0\le y\le 1\}$

15. $\displaystyle\iint_R x\sqrt{1-x^2}\,dA; \quad R=\{(x,y): 0\le x\le 1,\ 2\le y\le 3\}$

16. $\displaystyle\iint_R (x\sin y - y\sin x)\,dA;$
$R=\{(x,y): 0\le x\le \pi/2,\ 0\le y\le \pi/3\}$

FOCUS ON CONCEPTS

17. (a) Let $f(x,y)=x^2+y$, and as shown in the accompanying figure, let the rectangle $R=[0,2]\times[0,2]$ be subdivided into 16 subrectangles. Take (x_k^*,y_k^*) to be the center of the kth rectangle, and approximate the double integral of f over R by the resulting Riemann sum.
(b) Compare the result in part (a) to the exact value of the integral.

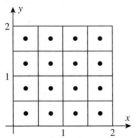

◀ **Figure Ex-17**

18. (a) Let $f(x,y)=x-2y$, and as shown in Exercise 17, let the rectangle $R=[0,2]\times[0,2]$ be subdivided into 16 subrectangles. Take (x_k^*,y_k^*) to be the center of the kth rectangle, and approximate the double integral of f over R by the resulting Riemann sum.
(b) Compare the result in part (a) to the exact value of the integral.

19–20 Each iterated integral represents the volume of a solid. Make a sketch of the solid. Use geometry to find the volume of the solid, and then evaluate the iterated integral.

19. $\displaystyle\int_0^5\int_1^2 4\,dx\,dy$

20. $\displaystyle\int_0^1\int_0^1 (2-x-y)\,dx\,dy$

21–22 Each iterated integral represents the volume of a solid. Make a sketch of the solid. (You do *not* have to find the volume.)

21. $\displaystyle\int_0^3\int_0^4 \sqrt{25-x^2-y^2}\,dy\,dx$

22. $\displaystyle\int_{-2}^2\int_{-2}^2 (x^2+y^2)\,dx\,dy$

23–26 True–False Determine whether the statement is true or false. Explain your answer.

23. In the definition of a double integral
$$\iint_R f(x,y)\,dA = \lim_{n\to+\infty}\sum_{k=1}^n f(x_k^*,y_k^*)\Delta A_k$$
the symbol ΔA_k represents a rectangular region within R from which the point (x_k^*,y_k^*) is taken.

24. If R is the rectangle $\{(x,y): 1\le x\le 4,\ 0\le y\le 3\}$ and $\int_0^3 f(x,y)\,dy = 2x$, then
$$\iint_R f(x,y)\,dA = 15$$

25. If R is the rectangle $\{(x,y): 1\le x\le 5,\ 2\le y\le 4\}$, then
$$\iint_R f(x,y)\,dA = \int_1^5\int_2^4 f(x,y)\,dx\,dy$$

26. Suppose that for some region R in the xy-plane
$$\iint_R f(x,y)\,dA = 0$$
If R is subdivided into two regions R_1 and R_2, then
$$\iint_{R_1} f(x,y)\,dA = -\iint_{R_2} f(x,y)\,dA$$

27. In this exercise, suppose that $f(x,y)=g(x)h(y)$ and $R=\{(x,y): a\le x\le b,\ c\le y\le d\}$. Show that
$$\iint_R f(x,y)\,dA = \left[\int_a^b g(x)\,dx\right]\left[\int_c^d h(y)\,dy\right]$$

28. Use the result in Exercise 27 evaluate the integral

$$\int_0^{\ln 2} \int_{-1}^1 \sqrt{e^y + 1} \tan x \, dx \, dy$$

by inspection. Explain your reasoning.

29–32 Use a double integral to find the volume. ■

29. The volume under the plane $z = 2x + y$ and over the rectangle $R = \{(x, y) : 3 \le x \le 5, 1 \le y \le 2\}$.

30. The volume under the surface $z = 3x^3 + 3x^2 y$ and over the rectangle $R = \{(x, y) : 1 \le x \le 3, 0 \le y \le 2\}$.

31. The volume of the solid enclosed by the surface $z = x^2$ and the planes $x = 0$, $x = 2$, $y = 3$, $y = 0$, and $z = 0$.

32. The volume in the first octant bounded by the coordinate planes, the plane $y = 4$, and the plane $(x/3) + (z/5) = 1$.

33. Evaluate the integral by choosing a convenient order of integration:

$$\iint_R x \cos(xy) \cos^2 \pi x \, dA; \ R = \left[0, \tfrac{1}{2}\right] \times [0, \pi]$$

34. (a) Sketch the solid in the first octant that is enclosed by the planes $x = 0$, $z = 0$, $x = 5$, $z - y = 0$, and $z = -2y + 6$.
    (b) Find the volume of the solid by breaking it into two parts.

35–38 The *average value* or *mean value* of a continuous function $f(x, y)$ over a rectangle $R = [a, b] \times [c, d]$ is defined as

$$f_{\text{ave}} = \frac{1}{A(R)} \iint_R f(x, y) \, dA$$

where $A(R) = (b - a)(d - c)$ is the area of the rectangle R (compare to Definition 5.8.1). Use this definition in these exercises. ■

35. Find the average value of $f(x, y) = y \sin xy$ over the rectangle $[0, 1] \times [0, \pi/2]$.

36. Find the average value of $f(x, y) = x(x^2 + y)^{1/2}$ over the rectangle $[0, 1] \times [0, 3]$.

37. Suppose that the temperature in degrees Celsius at a point (x, y) on a flat metal plate is $T(x, y) = 10 - 8x^2 - 2y^2$,

where x and y are in meters. Find the average temperature of the rectangular portion of the plate for which $0 \le x \le 1$ and $0 \le y \le 2$.

38. Show that if $f(x, y)$ is constant on the rectangle $R = [a, b] \times [c, d]$, say $f(x, y) = k$, then $f_{\text{ave}} = k$ over R.

39–40 Most computer algebra systems have commands for approximating double integrals numerically. Read the relevant documentation and use a CAS to find a numerical approximation of the double integral in these exercises. ■

39. $\boxed{\text{c}}$ $\displaystyle\int_0^2 \int_0^1 \sin \sqrt{x^3 + y^3} \, dx \, dy$

40. $\boxed{\text{c}}$ $\displaystyle\int_{-1}^1 \int_{-1}^1 e^{-(x^2 + y^2)} \, dx \, dy$

41. $\boxed{\text{c}}$ Use a CAS to evaluate the iterated integrals

$$\int_0^1 \int_0^1 \frac{y - x}{(x + y)^3} \, dx \, dy \quad \text{and} \quad \int_0^1 \int_0^1 \frac{y - x}{(x + y)^3} \, dy \, dx$$

Does this contradict Theorem 14.1.3? Explain.

42. $\boxed{\text{c}}$ Use a CAS to show that the volume V under the surface $z = xy^3 \sin xy$ over the rectangle shown in the accompanying figure is $V = 3/\pi$.

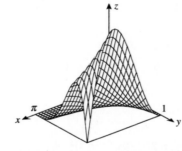

◀ **Figure Ex-42**

43. **Writing** Discuss how computing a volume using an iterated double integral corresponds to the method of computing a volume by slicing (Section 6.2).

44. **Writing** Discuss how the double integral property given in Formula (12) generalizes the single integral property in Theorem 5.5.5.

✔ **QUICK CHECK ANSWERS 14.1**

1. $\displaystyle\lim_{n \to +\infty} \sum_{k=1}^n f(x_k^*, y_k^*) \Delta A_k$ **2.** $2 \le x \le 4$, $1 \le y \le 5$ **3.** $\displaystyle\int_1^5 (56 - 12y + 2y^2) \, dy$ **4.** 16

14.2 DOUBLE INTEGRALS OVER NONRECTANGULAR REGIONS

In this section we will show how to evaluate double integrals over regions other than rectangles.

■ ITERATED INTEGRALS WITH NONCONSTANT LIMITS OF INTEGRATION

Later in this section we will see that double integrals over nonrectangular regions can often be evaluated as iterated integrals of the following types:

Note that in (1) and (2) the limits of integration in the outer integral are constants. This is consistent with the fact that the value of each iterated integral is a number that represents a net signed volume.

$$\int_a^b \int_{g_1(x)}^{g_2(x)} f(x, y)\, dy\, dx = \int_a^b \left[\int_{g_1(x)}^{g_2(x)} f(x, y)\, dy \right] dx \qquad (1)$$

$$\int_c^d \int_{h_1(y)}^{h_2(y)} f(x, y)\, dx\, dy = \int_c^d \left[\int_{h_1(y)}^{h_2(y)} f(x, y)\, dx \right] dy \qquad (2)$$

We begin with an example that illustrates how to evaluate such integrals.

▶ **Example 1**   Evaluate

$$\text{(a)} \quad \int_0^1 \int_{-x}^{x^2} y^2 x\, dy\, dx \qquad\qquad \text{(b)} \quad \int_0^{\pi/3} \int_0^{\cos y} x \sin y\, dx\, dy$$

Solution (a).

$$\int_0^1 \int_{-x}^{x^2} y^2 x\, dy\, dx = \int_0^1 \left[\int_{-x}^{x^2} y^2 x\, dy \right] dx = \int_0^1 \frac{y^3 x}{3} \Big]_{y=-x}^{x^2} dx$$

$$= \int_0^1 \left[\frac{x^7}{3} + \frac{x^4}{3} \right] dx = \left(\frac{x^8}{24} + \frac{x^5}{15} \right) \Big]_0^1 = \frac{13}{120}$$

Solution (b).

$$\int_0^{\pi/3} \int_0^{\cos y} x \sin y\, dx\, dy = \int_0^{\pi/3} \left[\int_0^{\cos y} x \sin y\, dx \right] dy = \int_0^{\pi/3} \frac{x^2}{2} \sin y \Big]_{x=0}^{\cos y} dy$$

$$= \int_0^{\pi/3} \left[\frac{1}{2} \cos^2 y \sin y \right] dy = -\frac{1}{6} \cos^3 y \Big]_0^{\pi/3} = \frac{7}{48} \quad ◀$$

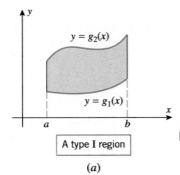

A type I region

(a)

■ DOUBLE INTEGRALS OVER NONRECTANGULAR REGIONS

Plane regions can be extremely complex, and the theory of double integrals over very general regions is a topic for advanced courses in mathematics. We will limit our study of double integrals to two basic types of regions, which we will call *type I* and *type II*; they are defined as follows.

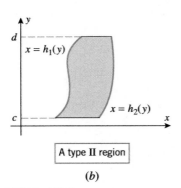

A type II region

(b)

▲ Figure 14.2.1

14.2.1   DEFINITION

(a)   A *type I region* is bounded on the left and right by vertical lines $x = a$ and $x = b$ and is bounded below and above by continuous curves $y = g_1(x)$ and $y = g_2(x)$, where $g_1(x) \le g_2(x)$ for $a \le x \le b$ (Figure 14.2.1a).

(b)   A *type II region* is bounded below and above by horizontal lines $y = c$ and $y = d$ and is bounded on the left and right by continuous curves $x = h_1(y)$ and $x = h_2(y)$ satisfying $h_1(y) \le h_2(y)$ for $c \le y \le d$ (Figure 14.2.1b).

The following theorem will enable us to evaluate double integrals over type I and type II regions using iterated integrals.

14.2.2   THEOREM

(a) *If R is a type I region on which $f(x, y)$ is continuous, then*

$$\iint\limits_{R} f(x, y)\, dA = \int_{a}^{b} \int_{g_1(x)}^{g_2(x)} f(x, y)\, dy\, dx \tag{3}$$

(b) *If R is a type II region on which $f(x, y)$ is continuous, then*

$$\iint\limits_{R} f(x, y)\, dA = \int_{c}^{d} \int_{h_1(y)}^{h_2(y)} f(x, y)\, dx\, dy \tag{4}$$

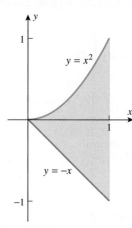

▲ **Figure 14.2.2**

▶ **Example 2**   Each of the iterated integrals in Example 1 is equal to a double integral over a region R. Identify the region R in each case.

Solution.   Using Theorem 14.2.2, the integral in Example 1(a) is the double integral of the function $f(x, y) = y^2 x$ over the type I region R bounded on the left and right by the vertical lines $x = 0$ and $x = 1$ and bounded below and above by the curves $y = -x$ and $y = x^2$ (Figure 14.2.2). The integral in Example 1(b) is the double integral of the function $f(x, y) = x \sin y$ over the type II region R bounded below and above by the horizontal lines $y = 0$ and $y = \pi/3$ and bounded on the left and right by the curves $x = 0$ and $x = \cos y$ (Figure 14.2.3). ◀

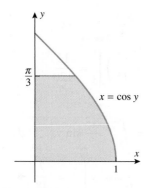

▲ **Figure 14.2.3**

We will not prove Theorem 14.2.2, but for the case where $f(x, y)$ is nonnegative on the region R, it can be made plausible by a geometric argument that is similar to that given for Theorem 14.1.3. Since $f(x, y)$ is nonnegative, the double integral can be interpreted as the volume of the solid S that is bounded above by the surface $z = f(x, y)$ and below by the region R, so it suffices to show that the iterated integrals also represent this volume. Consider the iterated integral in (3), for example. For a fixed value of x, the function $f(x, y)$ is a function of y, and hence the integral

$$A(x) = \int_{g_1(x)}^{g_2(x)} f(x, y)\, dy$$

represents the area under the graph of this function of y between $y = g_1(x)$ and $y = g_2(x)$. This area, shown in yellow in Figure 14.2.4, is the cross-sectional area at x of the solid S, and hence by the method of slicing, the volume V of the solid S is

$$V = \int_{a}^{b} \int_{g_1(x)}^{g_2(x)} f(x, y)\, dy\, dx$$

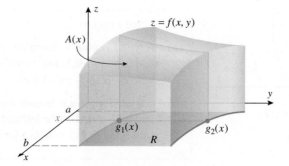

▶ **Figure 14.2.4**

which shows that in (3) the iterated integral is equal to the double integral. Similarly, the iterated integral in (4) is equal to the corresponding double integral.

■ SETTING UP LIMITS OF INTEGRATION FOR EVALUATING DOUBLE INTEGRALS

To apply Theorem 14.2.2, it is helpful to start with a two-dimensional sketch of the region R. [It is not necessary to graph $f(x, y)$.] For a type I region, the limits of integration in Formula (3) can be obtained as follows:

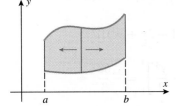

Determining Limits of Integration: Type I Region

Step 1. Since x is held fixed for the first integration, we draw a vertical line through the region R at an arbitrary fixed value x (Figure 14.2.5). This line crosses the boundary of R twice. The lower point of intersection is on the curve $y = g_1(x)$ and the higher point is on the curve $y = g_2(x)$. These two intersections determine the lower and upper y-limits of integration in Formula (3).

Step 2. Imagine moving the line drawn in Step 1 first to the left and then to the right (Figure 14.2.5). The leftmost position where the line intersects the region R is $x = a$, and the rightmost position where the line intersects the region R is $x = b$. This yields the limits for the x-integration in Formula (3).

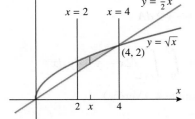

▲ **Figure 14.2.5**

▶ **Example 3** Evaluate

$$\iint\limits_R xy \, dA$$

over the region R enclosed between $y = \frac{1}{2}x$, $y = \sqrt{x}$, $x = 2$, and $x = 4$.

Solution. We view R as a type I region. The region R and a vertical line corresponding to a fixed x are shown in Figure 14.2.6. This line meets the region R at the lower boundary $y = \frac{1}{2}x$ and the upper boundary $y = \sqrt{x}$. These are the y-limits of integration. Moving this line first left and then right yields the x-limits of integration, $x = 2$ and $x = 4$. Thus,

$$\iint\limits_R xy \, dA = \int_2^4 \int_{x/2}^{\sqrt{x}} xy \, dy \, dx = \int_2^4 \left[\frac{xy^2}{2} \right]_{y=x/2}^{\sqrt{x}} dx = \int_2^4 \left(\frac{x^2}{2} - \frac{x^3}{8} \right) dx$$

$$= \left[\frac{x^3}{6} - \frac{x^4}{32} \right]_2^4 = \left(\frac{64}{6} - \frac{256}{32} \right) - \left(\frac{8}{6} - \frac{16}{32} \right) = \frac{11}{6} \quad ◀$$

▲ **Figure 14.2.6**

If R is a type II region, then the limits of integration in Formula (4) can be obtained as follows:

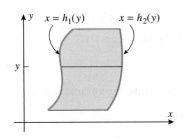

Determining Limits of Integration: Type II Region

Step 1. Since y is held fixed for the first integration, we draw a horizontal line through the region R at a fixed value y (Figure 14.2.7). This line crosses the boundary of R twice. The leftmost point of intersection is on the curve $x = h_1(y)$ and the rightmost point is on the curve $x = h_2(y)$. These intersections determine the x-limits of integration in (4).

Step 2. Imagine moving the line drawn in Step 1 first down and then up (Figure 14.2.7). The lowest position where the line intersects the region R is $y = c$, and the highest position where the line intersects the region R is $y = d$. This yields the y-limits of integration in (4).

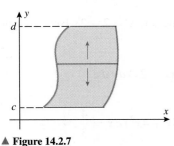

▲ **Figure 14.2.7**

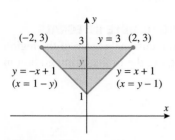

▲ **Figure 14.2.8**

To integrate over a type II region, the left- and right-hand boundaries must be expressed in the form $x = h_1(y)$ and $x = h_2(y)$. This is why we rewrote the boundary equations

$$y = -x + 1 \quad \text{and} \quad y = x + 1$$

as

$$x = 1 - y \quad \text{and} \quad x = y - 1$$

in Example 4.

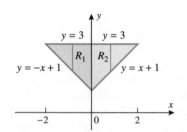

▲ **Figure 14.2.9**

▶ **Example 4**   Evaluate

$$\iint_R (2x - y^2)\, dA$$

over the triangular region R enclosed between the lines $y = -x + 1$, $y = x + 1$, and $y = 3$.

Solution.   We view R as a type II region. The region R and a horizontal line corresponding to a fixed y are shown in Figure 14.2.8. This line meets the region R at its left-hand boundary $x = 1 - y$ and its right-hand boundary $x = y - 1$. These are the x-limits of integration. Moving this line first down and then up yields the y-limits, $y = 1$ and $y = 3$. Thus,

$$\iint_R (2x - y^2)\, dA = \int_1^3 \int_{1-y}^{y-1} (2x - y^2)\, dx\, dy = \int_1^3 \left[x^2 - y^2 x \right]_{x=1-y}^{y-1} dy$$

$$= \int_1^3 [(1 - 2y + 2y^2 - y^3) - (1 - 2y + y^3)]\, dy$$

$$= \int_1^3 (2y^2 - 2y^3)\, dy = \left[\frac{2y^3}{3} - \frac{y^4}{2} \right]_1^3 = -\frac{68}{3} \quad ◀$$

In Example 4 we could have treated R as a type I region, but with an added complication. Viewed as a type I region, the upper boundary of R is the line $y = 3$ (Figure 14.2.9) and the lower boundary consists of two parts, the line $y = -x + 1$ to the left of the y-axis and the line $y = x + 1$ to the right of the y-axis. To carry out the integration it is necessary to decompose the region R into two parts, R_1 and R_2, as shown in Figure 14.2.9, and write

$$\iint_R (2x - y^2)\, dA = \iint_{R_1} (2x - y^2)\, dA + \iint_{R_2} (2x - y^2)\, dA$$

$$= \int_{-2}^0 \int_{-x+1}^3 (2x - y^2)\, dy\, dx + \int_0^2 \int_{x+1}^3 (2x - y^2)\, dy\, dx$$

This will yield the same result that was obtained in Example 4. (Verify.)

▶ **Example 5**   Use a double integral to find the volume of the tetrahedron bounded by the coordinate planes and the plane $z = 4 - 4x - 2y$.

Solution.   The tetrahedron in question is bounded above by the plane

$$z = 4 - 4x - 2y \tag{5}$$

and below by the triangular region R shown in Figure 14.2.10. Thus, the volume is given by

$$V = \iint_R (4 - 4x - 2y)\, dA$$

The region R is bounded by the x-axis, the y-axis, and the line $y = 2 - 2x$ [set $z = 0$ in (5)], so that treating R as a type I region yields

$$V = \iint_R (4 - 4x - 2y)\, dA = \int_0^1 \int_0^{2-2x} (4 - 4x - 2y)\, dy\, dx$$

$$= \int_0^1 \left[4y - 4xy - y^2 \right]_{y=0}^{2-2x} dx = \int_0^1 (4 - 8x + 4x^2)\, dx = \frac{4}{3} \quad ◀$$

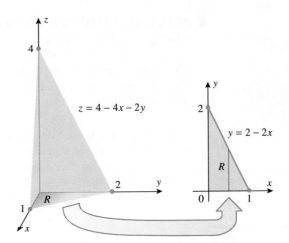

▶ **Figure 14.2.10**

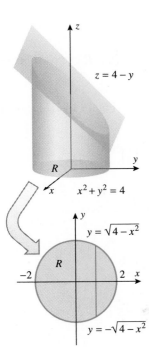

▲ **Figure 14.2.11**

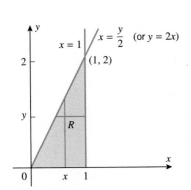

▲ **Figure 14.2.12**

▶ **Example 6** Find the volume of the solid bounded by the cylinder $x^2 + y^2 = 4$ and the planes $y + z = 4$ and $z = 0$.

Solution. The solid shown in Figure 14.2.11 is bounded above by the plane $z = 4 - y$ and below by the region R within the circle $x^2 + y^2 = 4$. The volume is given by

$$V = \iint_R (4 - y)\, dA$$

Treating R as a type I region we obtain

$$V = \int_{-2}^{2} \int_{-\sqrt{4-x^2}}^{\sqrt{4-x^2}} (4 - y)\, dy\, dx = \int_{-2}^{2} \left[4y - \frac{1}{2} y^2 \right]_{y=-\sqrt{4-x^2}}^{\sqrt{4-x^2}} dx$$

$$= \int_{-2}^{2} 8\sqrt{4 - x^2}\, dx = 8(2\pi) = 16\pi \qquad \boxed{\text{See Formula (3) of Section 7.4.}} \quad ◀$$

■ **REVERSING THE ORDER OF INTEGRATION**

Sometimes the evaluation of an iterated integral can be simplified by reversing the order of integration. The next example illustrates how this is done.

▶ **Example 7** Since there is no elementary antiderivative of e^{x^2}, the integral

$$\int_0^2 \int_{y/2}^1 e^{x^2}\, dx\, dy$$

cannot be evaluated by performing the x-integration first. Evaluate this integral by expressing it as an equivalent iterated integral with the order of integration reversed.

Solution. For the inside integration, y is fixed and x varies from the line $x = y/2$ to the line $x = 1$ (Figure 14.2.12). For the outside integration, y varies from 0 to 2, so the given iterated integral is equal to a double integral over the triangular region R in Figure 14.2.12.

To reverse the order of integration, we treat R as a type I region, which enables us to write the given integral as

$$\int_0^2 \int_{y/2}^1 e^{x^2}\, dx\, dy = \iint_R e^{x^2}\, dA = \int_0^1 \int_0^{2x} e^{x^2}\, dy\, dx = \int_0^1 \left[e^{x^2} y \right]_{y=0}^{2x} dx$$

$$= \int_0^1 2x e^{x^2}\, dx = e^{x^2} \Big]_0^1 = e - 1 \quad ◀$$

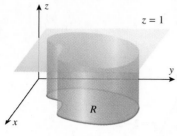

Cylinder with base R and height 1

▲ **Figure 14.2.13**

Formula (7) can be confusing because it equates an area and a volume; the formula is intended to equate only the *numerical values* of the area and volume and not the units, which must, of course, be different.

■ AREA CALCULATED AS A DOUBLE INTEGRAL

Although double integrals arose in the context of calculating volumes, they can also be used to calculate areas. To see why this is so, recall that a *right cylinder* is a solid that is generated when a plane region is translated along a line that is perpendicular to the region. In Formula (2) of Section 6.2 we stated that the volume V of a right cylinder with cross-sectional area A and height h is

$$V = A \cdot h \tag{6}$$

Now suppose that we are interested in finding the area A of a region R in the xy-plane. If we translate the region R upward 1 unit, then the resulting solid will be a right cylinder that has cross-sectional area A, base R, and the plane $z = 1$ as its top (Figure 14.2.13). Thus, it follows from (6) that

$$\iint_R 1\, dA = (\text{area of } R) \cdot 1$$

which we can rewrite as

$$\text{area of } R = \iint_R 1\, dA = \iint_R dA \tag{7}$$

▶ **Example 8** Use a double integral to find the area of the region R enclosed between the parabola $y = \frac{1}{2}x^2$ and the line $y = 2x$.

Solution. The region R may be treated equally well as type I (Figure 14.2.14*a*) or type II (Figure 14.2.14*b*). Treating R as type I yields

$$\text{area of } R = \iint_R dA = \int_0^4 \int_{x^2/2}^{2x} dy\, dx = \int_0^4 \left[y\right]_{y=x^2/2}^{2x} dx$$

$$= \int_0^4 \left(2x - \frac{1}{2}x^2\right) dx = \left[x^2 - \frac{x^3}{6}\right]_0^4 = \frac{16}{3}$$

Treating R as type II yields

$$\text{area of } R = \iint_R dA = \int_0^8 \int_{y/2}^{\sqrt{2y}} dx\, dy = \int_0^8 \left[x\right]_{x=y/2}^{\sqrt{2y}} dy$$

$$= \int_0^8 \left(\sqrt{2y} - \frac{1}{2}y\right) dy = \left[\frac{2\sqrt{2}}{3}y^{3/2} - \frac{y^2}{4}\right]_0^8 = \frac{16}{3} \quad ◀$$

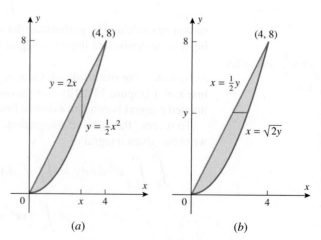

▶ **Figure 14.2.14** (a) (b)

✔ QUICK CHECK EXERCISES 14.2   *(See page 1018 for answers.)*

1. Supply the missing integrand and limits of integration.

   (a) $\displaystyle\int_1^5 \int_2^{y/2} 6x^2y\, dx\, dy = \int_\square^\square \underline{\hspace{1.5cm}}\, dy$

   (b) $\displaystyle\int_1^5 \int_2^{x/2} 6x^2y\, dy\, dx = \int_\square^\square \underline{\hspace{1.5cm}}\, dx$

2. Let R be the triangular region in the xy-plane with vertices $(0, 0)$, $(3, 0)$, and $(0, 4)$. Supply the missing portions of the integrals.

   (a) Treating R as a type I region,

   $$\iint_R f(x, y)\, dA = \int_\square^\square \int_\square^\square f(x, y)\underline{\hspace{1.5cm}}$$

3. Let R be the triangular region in the xy-plane with vertices $(0, 0)$, $(3, 3)$, and $(0, 4)$. Expressed as an iterated double integral, the area of R is $A(R) = \underline{\hspace{1.5cm}}$.

4. The line $y = 2 - x$ and the parabola $y = x^2$ intersect at the points $(-2, 4)$ and $(1, 1)$. If R is the region enclosed by $y = 2 - x$ and $y = x^2$, then

   $$\iint_R (1 + 2y)\, dA = \underline{\hspace{1.5cm}}$$

(b) Treating R as a type II region,

   $$\iint_R f(x, y)\, dA = \int_\square^\square \int_\square^\square f(x, y)\underline{\hspace{1.5cm}}$$

EXERCISE SET 14.2   ⬚ Graphing Utility   🄲 CAS

1–8 Evaluate the iterated integral. ■

1. $\displaystyle\int_0^1 \int_{x^2}^x xy^2\, dy\, dx$

2. $\displaystyle\int_1^{3/2} \int_y^{3-y} y\, dx\, dy$

3. $\displaystyle\int_0^3 \int_0^{\sqrt{9-y^2}} y\, dx\, dy$

4. $\displaystyle\int_{1/4}^1 \int_{x^2}^x \sqrt{\frac{x}{y}}\, dy\, dx$

5. $\displaystyle\int_{\sqrt{\pi}}^{\sqrt{2\pi}} \int_0^{x^3} \sin\frac{y}{x}\, dy\, dx$

6. $\displaystyle\int_{-1}^1 \int_{-x^2}^{x^2} (x^2 - y)\, dy\, dx$

7. $\displaystyle\int_0^1 \int_0^x y\sqrt{x^2 - y^2}\, dy\, dx$

8. $\displaystyle\int_1^2 \int_0^{y^2} e^{x/y^2}\, dx\, dy$

FOCUS ON CONCEPTS

9. Let R be the region shown in the accompanying figure. Fill in the missing limits of integration.

   (a) $\displaystyle\iint_R f(x, y)\, dA = \int_\square^\square \int_\square^\square f(x, y)\, dy\, dx$

   (b) $\displaystyle\iint_R f(x, y)\, dA = \int_\square^\square \int_\square^\square f(x, y)\, dx\, dy$

10. Let R be the region shown in the accompanying figure. Fill in the missing limits of integration.

    (a) $\displaystyle\iint_R f(x, y)\, dA = \int_\square^\square \int_\square^\square f(x, y)\, dy\, dx$

    (b) $\displaystyle\iint_R f(x, y)\, dA = \int_\square^\square \int_\square^\square f(x, y)\, dx\, dy$

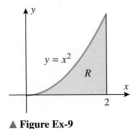

▲ **Figure Ex-9**

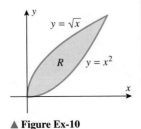

▲ **Figure Ex-10**

11. Let R be the region shown in the accompanying figure. Fill in the missing limits of integration.

    (a) $\displaystyle\iint_R f(x, y)\, dA = \int_1^2 \int_\square^\square f(x, y)\, dy\, dx$

    $$+ \int_2^4 \int_\square^\square f(x, y)\, dy\, dx$$

    $$+ \int_4^5 \int_\square^\square f(x, y)\, dy\, dx$$

    (b) $\displaystyle\iint_R f(x, y)\, dA = \int_\square^\square \int_\square^\square f(x, y)\, dx\, dy$

12. Let R be the region shown in the accompanying figure. Fill in the missing limits of integration.

    (a) $\displaystyle\iint_R f(x, y)\, dA = \int_\square^\square \int_\square^\square f(x, y)\, dy\, dx$

    (b) $\displaystyle\iint_R f(x, y)\, dA = \int_\square^\square \int_\square^\square f(x, y)\, dx\, dy$

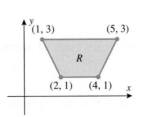

▲ **Figure Ex-11**

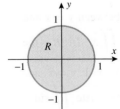

▲ **Figure Ex-12**

13. Evaluate $\displaystyle\iint_R xy\, dA$, where R is the region in

    (a) Exercise 9   (b) Exercise 11.

14. Evaluate $\iint\limits_R (x + y)\, dA$, where R is the region in

(a) Exercise 10   (b) Exercise 12.

15–18 Evaluate the double integral in two ways using iterated integrals: (a) viewing R as a type I region, and (b) viewing R as a type II region. ■

15. $\iint\limits_R x^2\, dA$; R is the region bounded by $y = 16/x$, $y = x$, and $x = 8$.

16. $\iint\limits_R xy^2\, dA$; R is the region enclosed by $y = 1$, $y = 2$, $x = 0$, and $y = x$.

17. $\iint\limits_R (3x - 2y)\, dA$; R is the region enclosed by the circle $x^2 + y^2 = 1$.

18. $\iint\limits_R y\, dA$; R is the region in the first quadrant enclosed between the circle $x^2 + y^2 = 25$ and the line $x + y = 5$.

19–24 Evaluate the double integral. ■

19. $\iint\limits_R x(1 + y^2)^{-1/2}\, dA$; R is the region in the first quadrant enclosed by $y = x^2$, $y = 4$, and $x = 0$.

20. $\iint\limits_R x \cos y\, dA$; R is the triangular region bounded by the lines $y = x$, $y = 0$, and $x = \pi$.

21. $\iint\limits_R xy\, dA$; R is the region enclosed by $y = \sqrt{x}$, $y = 6 - x$, and $y = 0$.

22. $\iint\limits_R x\, dA$; R is the region enclosed by $y = \sin^{-1} x$, $x = 1/\sqrt{2}$, and $y = 0$.

23. $\iint\limits_R (x - 1)\, dA$; R is the region in the first quadrant enclosed between $y = x$ and $y = x^3$.

24. $\iint\limits_R x^2\, dA$; R is the region in the first quadrant enclosed by $xy = 1$, $y = x$, and $y = 2x$.

25. Evaluate $\iint\limits_R \sin(y^3)\, dA$, where R is the region bounded by $y = \sqrt{x}$, $y = 2$, and $x = 0$. [*Hint:* Choose the order of integration carefully.]

26. Evaluate $\iint\limits_R x\, dA$, where R is the region bounded by $x = \ln y$, $x = 0$, and $y = e$.

27. (a) By hand or with the help of a graphing utility, make a sketch of the region R enclosed between the curves $y = x + 2$ and $y = e^x$.

(b) Estimate the intersections of the curves in part (a).

(c) Viewing R as a type I region, estimate $\iint\limits_R x\, dA$.

(d) Viewing R as a type II region, estimate $\iint\limits_R x\, dA$.

28. (a) By hand or with the help of a graphing utility, make a sketch of the region R enclosed between the curves $y = 4x^3 - x^4$ and $y = 3 - 4x + 4x^2$.

(b) Find the intersections of the curves in part (a).

(c) Find $\iint\limits_R x\, dA$.

29–32 Use double integration to find the area of the plane region enclosed by the given curves. ■

29. $y = \sin x$ and $y = \cos x$, for $0 \le x \le \pi/4$.

30. $y^2 = -x$ and $3y - x = 4$.

31. $y^2 = 9 - x$ and $y^2 = 9 - 9x$.

32. $y = \cosh x$, $y = \sinh x$, $x = 0$, and $x = 1$.

33–36 True–False Determine whether the statement is true or false. Explain your answer. ■

33. $\displaystyle\int_0^1 \int_{x^2}^{2x} f(x, y)\, dy\, dx = \int_{x^2}^{2x} \int_0^1 f(x, y)\, dx\, dy$

34. If a region R is bounded below by $y = g_1(x)$ and above by $y = g_2(x)$ for $a \le x \le b$, then

$$\iint\limits_R f(x, y)\, dA = \int_a^b \int_{g_1(x)}^{g_2(x)} f(x, y)\, dy\, dx$$

35. If R is the region in the xy-plane enclosed by $y = x^2$ and $y = 1$, then

$$\iint\limits_R f(x, y)\, dA = 2 \int_0^1 \int_{x^2}^1 f(x, y)\, dy\, dx$$

36. The area of a region R in the xy-plane is given by $\iint\limits_R xy\, dA$.

37–38 Use double integration to find the volume of the solid. ■

37.   **38.**

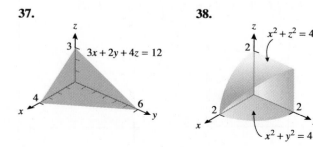

39–44 Use double integration to find the volume of each solid. ■

39. The solid bounded by the cylinder $x^2 + y^2 = 9$ and the planes $z = 0$ and $z = 3 - x$.

40. The solid in the first octant bounded above by the paraboloid $z = x^2 + 3y^2$, below by the plane $z = 0$, and laterally by $y = x^2$ and $y = x$.

41. The solid bounded above by the paraboloid $z = 9x^2 + y^2$, below by the plane $z = 0$, and laterally by the planes $x = 0$, $y = 0$, $x = 3$, and $y = 2$.

42. The solid enclosed by $y^2 = x$, $z = 0$, and $x + z = 1$.

43. The wedge cut from the cylinder $4x^2 + y^2 = 9$ by the planes $z = 0$ and $z = y + 3$.

44. The solid in the first octant bounded above by $z = 9 - x^2$, below by $z = 0$, and laterally by $y^2 = 3x$.

C **45–46** Use a double integral and a CAS to find the volume of the solid. ■

45. The solid bounded above by the paraboloid $z = 1 - x^2 - y^2$ and below by the xy-plane.

46. The solid in the first octant that is bounded by the paraboloid $z = x^2 + y^2$, the cylinder $x^2 + y^2 = 4$, and the coordinate planes.

47–52 Express the integral as an equivalent integral with the order of integration reversed. ■

47. $\displaystyle\int_0^2 \int_0^{\sqrt{x}} f(x, y)\, dy\, dx$ **48.** $\displaystyle\int_0^4 \int_{2y}^8 f(x, y)\, dx\, dy$

49. $\displaystyle\int_0^2 \int_1^{e^y} f(x, y)\, dx\, dy$ **50.** $\displaystyle\int_1^e \int_0^{\ln x} f(x, y)\, dy\, dx$

51. $\displaystyle\int_0^1 \int_{\sin^{-1} y}^{\pi/2} f(x, y)\, dx\, dy$ **52.** $\displaystyle\int_0^1 \int_{y^2}^{\sqrt{y}} f(x, y)\, dx\, dy$

53–56 Evaluate the integral by first reversing the order of integration. ■

53. $\displaystyle\int_0^1 \int_{4x}^4 e^{-y^2}\, dy\, dx$ **54.** $\displaystyle\int_0^2 \int_{y/2}^1 \cos(x^2)\, dx\, dy$

55. $\displaystyle\int_0^4 \int_{\sqrt{y}}^2 e^{x^3}\, dx\, dy$ **56.** $\displaystyle\int_1^3 \int_0^{\ln x} x\, dy\, dx$

C **57.** Try to evaluate the integral with a CAS using the stated order of integration, and then by reversing the order of integration.

(a) $\displaystyle\int_0^4 \int_{\sqrt{x}}^2 \sin \pi y^3\, dy\, dx$

(b) $\displaystyle\int_0^1 \int_{\sin^{-1} y}^{\pi/2} \sec^2(\cos x)\, dx\, dy$

58. Use the appropriate Wallis formula (see Exercise Set 7.3) to find the volume of the solid enclosed between the circular paraboloid $z = x^2 + y^2$, the right circular cylinder $x^2 + y^2 = 4$, and the xy-plane (see the accompanying figure for cut view).

59. Evaluate $\displaystyle\iint_R xy^2\, dA$ over the region R shown in the accompanying figure.

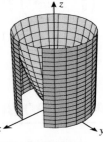
▲ **Figure Ex-58**

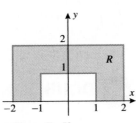
▲ **Figure Ex-59**

60. Give a geometric argument to show that
$$\int_0^1 \int_0^{\sqrt{1-y^2}} \sqrt{1 - x^2 - y^2}\, dx\, dy = \frac{\pi}{6}$$

61–62 The *average value* or *mean value* of a continuous function $f(x, y)$ over a region R in the xy-plane is defined as
$$f_{\text{ave}} = \frac{1}{A(R)} \iint_R f(x, y)\, dA$$
where $A(R)$ is the area of the region R (compare to the definition preceding Exercise 35 in Section 14.1). Use this definition in these exercises. ■

61. Find the average value of $1/(1 + x^2)$ over the triangular region with vertices $(0, 0)$, $(1, 1)$, and $(0, 1)$.

62. Find the average value of $f(x, y) = x^2 - xy$ over the region enclosed by $y = x$ and $y = 3x - x^2$.

63. Suppose that the temperature in degrees Celsius at a point (x, y) on a flat metal plate is $T(x, y) = 5xy + x^2$, where x and y are in meters. Find the average temperature of the diamond-shaped portion of the plate for which $|2x + y| \le 4$ and $|2x - y| \le 4$.

64. A circular lens of radius 2 inches has thickness $1 - (r^2/4)$ inches at all points r inches from the center of the lens. Find the average thickness of the lens.

C **65.** Use a CAS to approximate the intersections of the curves $y = \sin x$ and $y = x/2$, and then approximate the volume of the solid in the first octant that is below the surface $z = \sqrt{1 + x + y}$ and above the region in the xy-plane that is enclosed by the curves.

66. Writing Describe the steps you would follow to find the limits of integration that express a double integral over a nonrectangular region as an iterated double integral. Illustrate your discussion with an example.

67. Writing Describe the steps you would follow to reverse the order of integration in an iterated double integral. Illustrate your discussion with an example.

✔ **QUICK CHECK ANSWERS 14.2**

1. (a) $\displaystyle\int_1^5 \left(\frac{1}{4}y^4 - 16y\right) dy$ (b) $\displaystyle\int_1^5 \left(\frac{3}{4}x^4 - 12x^2\right) dx$ 2. (a) $\displaystyle\int_0^3 \int_0^{-\frac{4}{3}x+4} f(x, y)\, dy\, dx$ (b) $\displaystyle\int_0^4 \int_0^{-\frac{3}{4}y+3} f(x, y)\, dx\, dy$

3. $\displaystyle\int_0^3 \int_x^{-\frac{1}{3}x+4} dy\, dx$ 4. $\displaystyle\int_{-2}^1 \int_{x^2}^{2-x} (1 + 2y)\, dy\, dx = 18.9$

14.3   DOUBLE INTEGRALS IN POLAR COORDINATES

In this section we will study double integrals in which the integrand and the region of integration are expressed in polar coordinates. Such integrals are important for two reasons: first, they arise naturally in many applications, and second, many double integrals in rectangular coordinates can be evaluated more easily if they are converted to polar coordinates.

■ **SIMPLE POLAR REGIONS**

Some double integrals are easier to evaluate if the region of integration is expressed in polar coordinates. This is usually true if the region is bounded by a cardioid, a rose curve, a spiral, or, more generally, by any curve whose equation is simpler in polar coordinates than in rectangular coordinates. For example, the quarter-disk in Figure 14.3.1 is described in rectangular coordinates by

$$0 \le y \le \sqrt{4 - x^2}, \quad 0 \le x \le 2$$

However, in polar coordinates the region is described more simply by

$$0 \le r \le 2, \quad 0 \le \theta \le \pi/2$$

Moreover, double integrals whose integrands involve $x^2 + y^2$ also tend to be easier to evaluate in polar coordinates because this sum simplifies to r^2 when the conversion formulas $x = r \cos \theta$ and $y = r \sin \theta$ are applied.

Figure 14.3.2a shows a region R in a polar coordinate system that is enclosed between two rays, $\theta = \alpha$ and $\theta = \beta$, and two polar curves, $r = r_1(\theta)$ and $r = r_2(\theta)$. If, as shown in the figure, the functions $r_1(\theta)$ and $r_2(\theta)$ are continuous and their graphs do not cross, then the region R is called a *simple polar region*. If $r_1(\theta)$ is identically zero, then the boundary $r = r_1(\theta)$ reduces to a point (the origin), and the region has the general shape shown in Figure 14.3.2b. If, in addition, $\beta = \alpha + 2\pi$, then the rays coincide, and the region has the

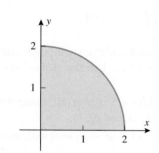

▶ **Figure 14.3.1**

An overview of polar coordinates can be found in Section 10.2.

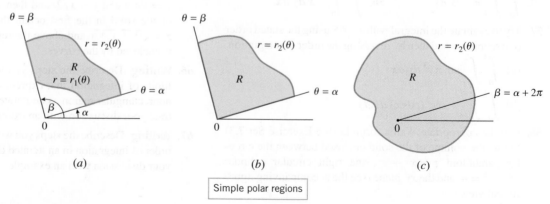

Simple polar regions

▲ **Figure 14.3.2**

general shape shown in Figure 14.3.2c. The following definition expresses these geometric ideas algebraically.

14.3.1 DEFINITION   A *simple polar region* in a polar coordinate system is a region that is enclosed between two rays, $\theta = \alpha$ and $\theta = \beta$, and two continuous polar curves, $r = r_1(\theta)$ and $r = r_2(\theta)$, where the equations of the rays and the polar curves satisfy the following conditions:

(i) $\alpha \leq \beta$ (ii) $\beta - \alpha \leq 2\pi$ (iii) $0 \leq r_1(\theta) \leq r_2(\theta)$

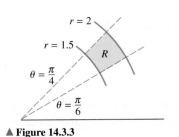

▲ **Figure 14.3.3**

REMARK | Conditions (i) and (ii) together imply that the ray $\theta = \beta$ can be obtained by rotating the ray $\theta = \alpha$ counterclockwise through an angle that is at most 2π radians. This is consistent with Figure 14.3.2. Condition (iii) implies that the boundary curves $r = r_1(\theta)$ and $r = r_2(\theta)$ can touch but cannot actually cross over one another (why?). Thus, in keeping with Figure 14.3.2, it is appropriate to describe $r = r_1(\theta)$ as the ***inner boundary*** of the region and $r = r_2(\theta)$ as the ***outer boundary***.

A *polar rectangle* is a simple polar region for which the bounding polar curves are circular arcs. For example, Figure 14.3.3 shows the polar rectangle R given by

$$1.5 \leq r \leq 2, \quad \frac{\pi}{6} \leq \theta \leq \frac{\pi}{4}$$

■ **DOUBLE INTEGRALS IN POLAR COORDINATES**
Next we will consider the polar version of Problem 14.1.1.

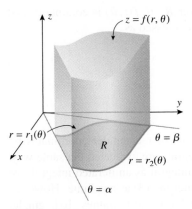

▲ **Figure 14.3.4**

14.3.2   THE VOLUME PROBLEM IN POLAR COORDINATES   Given a function $f(r, \theta)$ that is continuous and nonnegative on a simple polar region R, find the volume of the solid that is enclosed between the region R and the surface whose equation in cylindrical coordinates is $z = f(r, \theta)$ (Figure 14.3.4).

To motivate a formula for the volume V of the solid in Figure 14.3.4, we will use a limit process similar to that used to obtain Formula (2) of Section 14.1, except that here we will use circular arcs and rays to subdivide the region R into polar rectangles. As shown in Figure 14.3.5, we will exclude from consideration all polar rectangles that contain any points outside of R, leaving only polar rectangles that are subsets of R. Assume that there are n such polar rectangles, and denote the area of the kth polar rectangle by ΔA_k. Let (r_k^*, θ_k^*) be any point in this polar rectangle. As shown in Figure 14.3.6, the product $f(r_k^*, \theta_k^*)\Delta A_k$ is the volume of a solid with base area ΔA_k and height $f(r_k^*, \theta_k^*)$, so the sum

$$\sum_{k=1}^{n} f(r_k^*, \theta_k^*)\Delta A_k$$

can be viewed as an approximation to the volume V of the entire solid.

If we now increase the number of subdivisions in such a way that the dimensions of the polar rectangles approach zero, then it seems plausible that the errors in the approximations approach zero, and the exact volume of the solid is

$$V = \lim_{n \to +\infty} \sum_{k=1}^{n} f(r_k^*, \theta_k^*)\Delta A_k \tag{1}$$

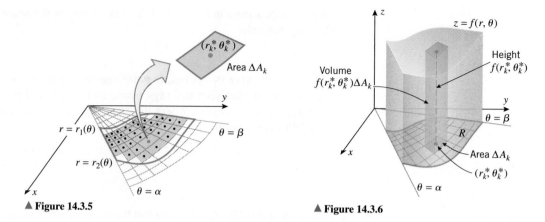

▲ Figure 14.3.5   ▲ Figure 14.3.6

If $f(r, \theta)$ is continuous on R and has both positive and negative values, then the limit

$$\lim_{n \to +\infty} \sum_{k=1}^{n} f(r_k^*, \theta_k^*)\Delta A_k \tag{2}$$

represents the net signed volume between the region R and the surface $z = f(r, \theta)$ (as with double integrals in rectangular coordinates). The sums in (2) are called **polar Riemann sums**, and the limit of the polar Riemann sums is denoted by

$$\iint\limits_{R} f(r, \theta)\, dA = \lim_{n \to +\infty} \sum_{k=1}^{n} f(r_k^*, \theta_k^*)\Delta A_k \tag{3}$$

Polar double integrals are also called **double integrals in polar coordinates** to distinguish them from double integrals over regions in the xy-plane; the latter are called **double integrals in rectangular coordinates**. Double integrals in polar coordinates have the usual integral properties, such as those stated in Formulas (9), (10), and (11) of Section 14.1.

which is called the **polar double integral** of $f(r, \theta)$ over R. If $f(r, \theta)$ is continuous and nonnegative on R, then the volume formula (1) can be expressed as

$$V = \iint\limits_{R} f(r, \theta)\, dA \tag{4}$$

■ EVALUATING POLAR DOUBLE INTEGRALS

In Sections 14.1 and 14.2 we evaluated double integrals in rectangular coordinates by expressing them as iterated integrals. Polar double integrals are evaluated the same way. To motivate the formula that expresses a double polar integral as an iterated integral, we will assume that $f(r, \theta)$ is nonnegative so that we can interpret (3) as a volume. However, the results that we will obtain will also be applicable if f has negative values. To begin, let us choose the arbitrary point (r_k^*, θ_k^*) in (3) to be at the "center" of the kth polar rectangle as shown in Figure 14.3.7. Suppose also that this polar rectangle has a central angle $\Delta\theta_k$ and a "radial thickness" Δr_k. Thus, the inner radius of this polar rectangle is $r_k^* - \frac{1}{2}\Delta r_k$ and the outer radius is $r_k^* + \frac{1}{2}\Delta r_k$. Treating the area ΔA_k of this polar rectangle as the difference in area of two sectors, we obtain

$$\Delta A_k = \tfrac{1}{2}\left(r_k^* + \tfrac{1}{2}\Delta r_k\right)^2 \Delta\theta_k - \tfrac{1}{2}\left(r_k^* - \tfrac{1}{2}\Delta r_k\right)^2 \Delta\theta_k$$

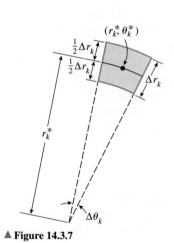

▲ Figure 14.3.7

which simplifies to

$$\Delta A_k = r_k^* \Delta r_k \Delta\theta_k \tag{5}$$

Thus, from (3) and (4)

$$V = \iint\limits_{R} f(r, \theta)\, dA = \lim_{n \to +\infty} \sum_{k=1}^{n} f(r_k^*, \theta_k^*) r_k^* \Delta r_k \Delta\theta_k$$

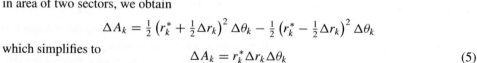

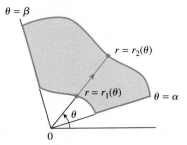

▲ **Figure 14.3.8**

which suggests that the volume V can be expressed as the iterated integral

$$V = \iint\limits_{R} f(r, \theta)\, dA = \int_{\alpha}^{\beta} \int_{r_1(\theta)}^{r_2(\theta)} f(r, \theta)r\, dr\, d\theta \tag{6}$$

in which the limits of integration are chosen to cover the region R; that is, with θ fixed between α and β, the value of r varies from $r_1(\theta)$ to $r_2(\theta)$ (Figure 14.3.8).

Although we assumed $f(r, \theta)$ to be nonnegative in deriving Formula (6), it can be proved that the relationship between the polar double integral and the iterated integral in this formula also holds if f has negative values. Accepting this to be so, we obtain the following theorem, which we state without formal proof.

Note the extra factor of r that appears in the integrand when expressing a polar double integral as an iterated integral in polar coordinates.

14.3.3   THEOREM   *If R is a simple polar region whose boundaries are the rays $\theta = \alpha$ and $\theta = \beta$ and the curves $r = r_1(\theta)$ and $r = r_2(\theta)$ shown in Figure 14.3.8, and if $f(r, \theta)$ is continuous on R, then*

$$\iint\limits_{R} f(r, \theta)\, dA = \int_{\alpha}^{\beta} \int_{r_1(\theta)}^{r_2(\theta)} f(r, \theta)r\, dr\, d\theta \tag{7}$$

To apply this theorem you will need to be able to find the rays and the curves that form the boundary of the region R, since these determine the limits of integration in the iterated integral. This can be done as follows:

Determining Limits of Integration for a Polar Double Integral: Simple Polar Region

Step 1. Since θ is held fixed for the first integration, draw a radial line from the origin through the region R at a fixed angle θ (Figure 14.3.9a). This line crosses the boundary of R at most twice. The innermost point of intersection is on the inner boundary curve $r = r_1(\theta)$ and the outermost point is on the outer boundary curve $r = r_2(\theta)$. These intersections determine the r-limits of integration in (7).

Step 2. Imagine rotating the radial line from Step 1 about the origin, thus sweeping out the region R. The least angle at which the radial line intersects the region R is $\theta = \alpha$ and the greatest angle is $\theta = \beta$ (Figure 14.3.9b). This determines the θ-limits of integration.

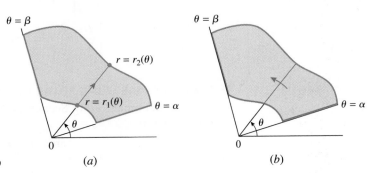

▶ **Figure 14.3.9**   (*a*)   (*b*)

► **Example 1** Evaluate

$$\iint_R \sin\theta \, dA$$

where R is the region in the first quadrant that is outside the circle $r = 2$ and inside the cardioid $r = 2(1 + \cos\theta)$.

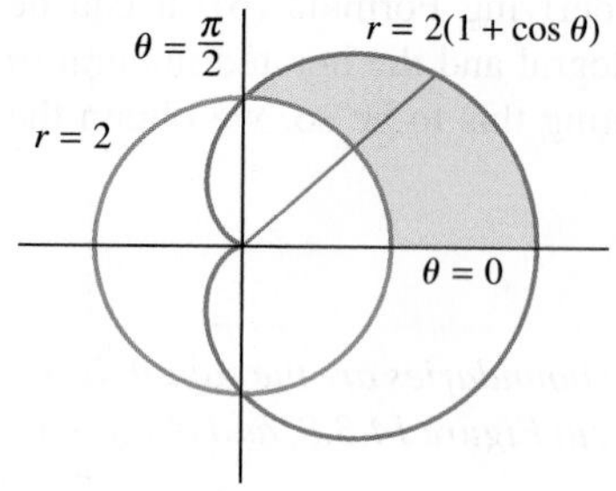

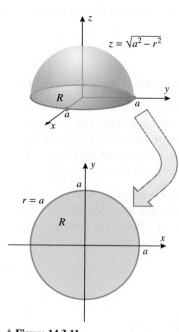

▲ **Figure 14.3.10**

Solution. The region R is sketched in Figure 14.3.10. Following the two steps outlined above we obtain

$$\begin{aligned}
\iint_R \sin\theta \, dA &= \int_0^{\pi/2} \int_2^{2(1+\cos\theta)} (\sin\theta) r \, dr \, d\theta \\
&= \int_0^{\pi/2} \left[\frac{1}{2} r^2 \sin\theta\right]_{r=2}^{2(1+\cos\theta)} d\theta \\
&= 2\int_0^{\pi/2} [(1+\cos\theta)^2 \sin\theta - \sin\theta] \, d\theta \\
&= 2\left[-\frac{1}{3}(1+\cos\theta)^3 + \cos\theta\right]_0^{\pi/2} \\
&= 2\left[-\frac{1}{3} - \left(-\frac{5}{3}\right)\right] = \frac{8}{3} \blacktriangleleft
\end{aligned}$$

► **Example 2** The sphere of radius a centered at the origin is expressed in rectangular coordinates as $x^2 + y^2 + z^2 = a^2$, and hence its equation in cylindrical coordinates is $r^2 + z^2 = a^2$. Use this equation and a polar double integral to find the volume of the sphere.

▲ **Figure 14.3.11**

Solution. In cylindrical coordinates the upper hemisphere is given by the equation

$$z = \sqrt{a^2 - r^2}$$

so the volume enclosed by the entire sphere is

$$V = 2\iint_R \sqrt{a^2 - r^2} \, dA$$

where R is the circular region shown in Figure 14.3.11. Thus,

$$\begin{aligned}
V = 2\iint_R \sqrt{a^2 - r^2} \, dA &= \int_0^{2\pi} \int_0^a \sqrt{a^2 - r^2}(2r) \, dr \, d\theta \\
&= \int_0^{2\pi} \left[-\frac{2}{3}(a^2 - r^2)^{3/2}\right]_{r=0}^a d\theta = \int_0^{2\pi} \frac{2}{3} a^3 \, d\theta \\
&= \left[\frac{2}{3} a^3 \theta\right]_0^{2\pi} = \frac{4}{3}\pi a^3 \blacktriangleleft
\end{aligned}$$

FINDING AREAS USING POLAR DOUBLE INTEGRALS

Recall from Formula (7) of Section 14.2 that the area of a region R in the xy-plane can be expressed as

$$\text{area of } R = \iint_R 1 \, dA = \iint_R dA \tag{8}$$

The argument used to derive this result can also be used to show that the formula applies to polar double integrals over regions in polar coordinates.

▶ **Example 3** Use a polar double integral to find the area enclosed by the three-petaled rose $r = \sin 3\theta$.

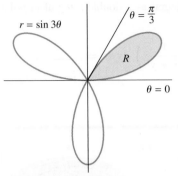

$r = \sin 3\theta$

$\theta = \dfrac{\pi}{3}$

R

$\theta = 0$

▲ **Figure 14.3.12**

Solution. The rose is sketched in Figure 14.3.12. We will use Formula (8) to calculate the area of the petal R in the first quadrant and multiply by three.

$$A = 3 \iint\limits_{R} dA = 3 \int_0^{\pi/3} \int_0^{\sin 3\theta} r\, dr\, d\theta$$

$$= \frac{3}{2} \int_0^{\pi/3} \sin^2 3\theta\, d\theta = \frac{3}{4} \int_0^{\pi/3} (1 - \cos 6\theta)\, d\theta$$

$$= \frac{3}{4} \left[\theta - \frac{\sin 6\theta}{6} \right]_0^{\pi/3} = \frac{1}{4}\pi \quad \blacktriangleleft$$

■ **CONVERTING DOUBLE INTEGRALS FROM RECTANGULAR TO POLAR COORDINATES**

Sometimes a double integral that is difficult to evaluate in rectangular coordinates can be evaluated more easily in polar coordinates by making the substitution $x = r\cos\theta$, $y = r\sin\theta$ and expressing the region of integration in polar form; that is, we rewrite the double integral in rectangular coordinates as

$$\iint\limits_{R} f(x, y)\, dA = \iint\limits_{R} f(r\cos\theta, r\sin\theta)\, dA = \iint\limits_{\substack{\text{appropriate}\\\text{limits}}} f(r\cos\theta, r\sin\theta) r\, dr\, d\theta \quad (9)$$

▶ **Example 4** Use polar coordinates to evaluate $\displaystyle\int_{-1}^{1} \int_0^{\sqrt{1-x^2}} (x^2 + y^2)^{3/2}\, dy\, dx$.

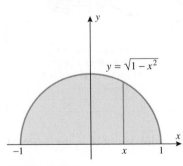

y

$y = \sqrt{1-x^2}$

-1 x 1 x

▲ **Figure 14.3.13**

Solution. In this problem we are starting with an iterated integral in rectangular coordinates rather than a double integral, so before we can make the conversion to polar coordinates we will have to identify the region of integration. To do this, we observe that for fixed x the y-integration runs from $y = 0$ to $y = \sqrt{1 - x^2}$, which tells us that the lower boundary of the region is the x-axis and the upper boundary is a semicircle of radius 1 centered at the origin. From the x-integration we see that x varies from -1 to 1, so we conclude that the region of integration is as shown in Figure 14.3.13. In polar coordinates, this is the region swept out as r varies between 0 and 1 and θ varies between 0 and π. Thus,

$$\int_{-1}^{1} \int_0^{\sqrt{1-x^2}} (x^2 + y^2)^{3/2}\, dy\, dx = \iint\limits_{R} (x^2 + y^2)^{3/2}\, dA$$

$$= \int_0^{\pi} \int_0^1 (r^3) r\, dr\, d\theta = \int_0^{\pi} \frac{1}{5}\, d\theta = \frac{\pi}{5} \quad \blacktriangleleft$$

REMARK | The reason the conversion to polar coordinates worked so nicely in Example 4 is that the substitution $x = r\cos\theta$, $y = r\sin\theta$ collapsed the sum $x^2 + y^2$ into the single term r^2, thereby simplifying the integrand. Whenever you see an expression involving $x^2 + y^2$ in the integrand, you should consider the possibility of converting to polar coordinates.

✔**QUICK CHECK EXERCISES 14.3**   (*See page 1025 for answers.*)

1. The polar region inside the circle $r = 2 \sin \theta$ and outside the circle $r = 1$ is a simple polar region given by the inequalities

   ____ $\leq r \leq$ ____ ,   ____ $\leq \theta \leq$ ____

2. Let R be the region in the first quadrant enclosed between the circles $x^2 + y^2 = 9$ and $x^2 + y^2 = 100$. Supply the missing limits of integration.

   $$\iint\limits_{R} f(r, \theta)\, dA = \int_{\square}^{\square} \int_{\square}^{\square} f(r, \theta) r\, dr\, d\theta$$

3. Let V be the volume of the solid bounded above by the hemisphere $z = \sqrt{1 - r^2}$ and bounded below by the disk enclosed within the circle $r = \sin \theta$. Expressed as a double integral in polar coordinates, $V = $ ____ .

4. Express the iterated integral as a double integral in polar coordinates.

   $$\int_{1/\sqrt{2}}^{1} \int_{\sqrt{1-x^2}}^{x} \left(\frac{1}{x^2 + y^2} \right) dy\, dx = \text{\_\_\_\_}$$

EXERCISE SET 14.3

1–6 Evaluate the iterated integral. ■

1. $\displaystyle\int_{0}^{\pi/2} \int_{0}^{\sin \theta} r \cos \theta\, dr\, d\theta$

2. $\displaystyle\int_{0}^{\pi} \int_{0}^{1+\cos \theta} r\, dr\, d\theta$

3. $\displaystyle\int_{0}^{\pi/2} \int_{0}^{a \sin \theta} r^2\, dr\, d\theta$

4. $\displaystyle\int_{0}^{\pi/6} \int_{0}^{\cos 3\theta} r\, dr\, d\theta$

5. $\displaystyle\int_{0}^{\pi} \int_{0}^{1-\sin \theta} r^2 \cos \theta\, dr\, d\theta$

6. $\displaystyle\int_{0}^{\pi/2} \int_{0}^{\cos \theta} r^3\, dr\, d\theta$

7–10 Use a double integral in polar coordinates to find the area of the region described. ■

7. The region enclosed by the cardioid $r = 1 - \cos \theta$.

8. The region enclosed by the rose $r = \sin 2\theta$.

9. The region in the first quadrant bounded by $r = 1$ and $r = \sin 2\theta$, with $\pi/4 \leq \theta \leq \pi/2$.

10. The region inside the circle $x^2 + y^2 = 4$ and to the right of the line $x = 1$.

FOCUS ON CONCEPTS

11–12 Let R be the region described. Sketch the region R and fill in the missing limits of integration. ■

$$\iint\limits_{R} f(r, \theta)\, dA = \int_{\square}^{\square} \int_{\square}^{\square} f(r, \theta) r\, dr\, d\theta \quad ■$$

11. The region inside the circle $r = 4 \sin \theta$ and outside the circle $r = 2$.

12. The region inside the circle $r = 1$ and outside the cardioid $r = 1 + \cos \theta$.

13–16 Express the volume of the solid described as a double integral in polar coordinates. ■

13.

Inside of $x^2 + y^2 + z^2 = 9$
Outside of $x^2 + y^2 = 1$

14.

Below $z = \sqrt{x^2 + y^2}$
Inside of $x^2 + y^2 = 2y$
Above $z = 0$

15.

Below $z = 1 - x^2 - y^2$
Inside of $x^2 + y^2 - x = 0$
Above $z = 0$

16.

Below $z = (x^2 + y^2)^{-1/2}$
Outside of $x^2 + y^2 = 1$
Inside of $x^2 + y^2 = 9$
Above $z = 0$

17–20 Find the volume of the solid described in the indicated exercise. ■

17. Exercise 13

18. Exercise 14

19. Exercise 15

20. Exercise 16

21. Find the volume of the solid in the first octant bounded above by the surface $z = r \sin \theta$, below by the xy-plane, and laterally by the plane $x = 0$ and the surface $r = 3 \sin \theta$.

22. Find the volume of the solid inside the surface $r^2 + z^2 = 4$ and outside the surface $r = 2 \cos \theta$.

23–26 Use polar coordinates to evaluate the double integral.
■

23. $\iint\limits_{R} e^{-(x^2+y^2)} \, dA$, where R is the region enclosed by the circle $x^2 + y^2 = 1$.

24. $\iint\limits_{R} \sqrt{9 - x^2 - y^2} \, dA$, where R is the region in the first quadrant within the circle $x^2 + y^2 = 9$.

25. $\iint\limits_{R} \dfrac{1}{1 + x^2 + y^2} \, dA$, where R is the sector in the first quadrant bounded by $y = 0$, $y = x$, and $x^2 + y^2 = 4$.

26. $\iint\limits_{R} 2y \, dA$, where R is the region in the first quadrant bounded above by the circle $(x - 1)^2 + y^2 = 1$ and below by the line $y = x$.

27–34 Evaluate the iterated integral by converting to polar coordinates. ■

27. $\displaystyle\int_0^1 \int_0^{\sqrt{1-x^2}} (x^2 + y^2) \, dy \, dx$

28. $\displaystyle\int_{-2}^2 \int_{-\sqrt{4-y^2}}^{\sqrt{4-y^2}} e^{-(x^2+y^2)} \, dx \, dy$

29. $\displaystyle\int_0^2 \int_0^{\sqrt{2x-x^2}} \sqrt{x^2 + y^2} \, dy \, dx$

30. $\displaystyle\int_0^1 \int_0^{\sqrt{1-y^2}} \cos(x^2 + y^2) \, dx \, dy$

31. $\displaystyle\int_0^a \int_0^{\sqrt{a^2-x^2}} \dfrac{dy \, dx}{(1 + x^2 + y^2)^{3/2}} \quad (a > 0)$

32. $\displaystyle\int_0^1 \int_y^{\sqrt{y}} \sqrt{x^2 + y^2} \, dx \, dy$

33. $\displaystyle\int_0^{\sqrt{2}} \int_y^{\sqrt{4-y^2}} \dfrac{1}{\sqrt{1 + x^2 + y^2}} \, dx \, dy$

34. $\displaystyle\int_0^4 \int_3^{\sqrt{25-x^2}} dy \, dx$

35–38 True–False Determine whether the statement is true or false. Explain your answer. ■

35. The disk of radius 2 that is centered at the origin is a polar rectangle.

36. If f is continuous and nonnegative on a simple polar region R, then the volume of the solid enclosed between R and the surface $z = f(r, \theta)$ is expressed as
$$\iint\limits_{R} f(r, \theta) r \, dA$$

37. If R is the region in the first quadrant between the circles $r = 1$ and $r = 2$, and if f is continuous on R, then
$$\iint\limits_{R} f(r, \theta) \, dA = \int_0^{\pi/2} \int_1^2 f(r, \theta) \, dr \, d\theta$$

38. The area enclosed by the circle $r = \sin \theta$ is given by
$$A = \int_0^{2\pi} \int_0^{\sin \theta} r \, dr \, d\theta$$

39. Use a double integral in polar coordinates to find the volume of a cylinder of radius a and height h.

40. Suppose that a geyser, centered at the origin of a polar coordinate system, sprays water in a circular pattern in such a way that the depth D of water that reaches a point at a distance of r feet from the origin in 1 hour is $D = ke^{-r}$. Find the total volume of water that the geyser sprays inside a circle of radius R centered at the origin.

41. Evaluate $\iint\limits_{R} x^2 \, dA$ over the region R shown in the accompanying figure.

42. Show that the shaded area in the accompanying figure is $a^2 \phi - \frac{1}{2} a^2 \sin 2\phi$.

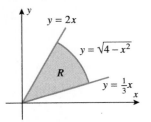

▲ Figure Ex-41

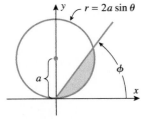

▲ Figure Ex-42

43. (a) Use a double integral in polar coordinates to find the volume of the oblate spheroid
$$\frac{x^2}{a^2} + \frac{y^2}{a^2} + \frac{z^2}{c^2} = 1 \quad (0 < c < a)$$
   (b) Use the result in part (a) and the World Geodetic System of 1984 (WGS-84) discussed in Exercise 54 of Section 11.7 to find the volume of the Earth in cubic meters.

44. Use polar coordinates to find the volume of the solid that is above the xy-plane, inside the cylinder $x^2 + y^2 - ay = 0$, and inside the ellipsoid
$$\frac{x^2}{a^2} + \frac{y^2}{a^2} + \frac{z^2}{c^2} = 1$$

45. Find the area of the region enclosed by the lemniscate $r^2 = 2a^2 \cos 2\theta$.

46. Find the area in the first quadrant that is inside the circle $r = 4 \sin \theta$ and outside the lemniscate $r^2 = 8 \cos 2\theta$.

✓ QUICK CHECK ANSWERS 14.3

1. $1 \le r \le 2 \sin \theta$, $\pi/6 \le \theta \le 5\pi/6$ **2.** $\displaystyle\int_0^{\pi/2} \int_3^{10} f(r, \theta) r \, dr \, d\theta$ **3.** $\displaystyle\int_0^{\pi} \int_0^{\sin \theta} r\sqrt{1 - r^2} \, dr \, d\theta$ **4.** $\displaystyle\int_0^{\pi/4} \int_1^{\sec \theta} \frac{1}{r} \, dr \, d\theta$

14.4   SURFACE AREA; PARAMETRIC SURFACES

In Section 6.5 we showed how to find the surface area of a surface of revolution. In this section we will derive area formulas for surfaces with equations of the form $z = f(x, y)$ and for surfaces that are represented by parametric equations.

■ SURFACE AREA FOR SURFACES OF THE FORM $z = f(x, y)$

In Section 6.5 we obtained formulas for the surface area of a surface of revolution [see Formulas (4) and (5) of that section]. We now obtain a formula for the surface area S of a surface of the form $z = f(x, y)$.

Consider a surface σ of the form $z = f(x, y)$ defined over a region R in the xy-plane (Figure 14.4.1a). We will assume that f has continuous first partial derivatives at the interior points of R. (Geometrically, this means that the surface will have a nonvertical tangent plane at each interior point of R.) We begin by subdividing R into rectangular regions by lines parallel to the x- and y-axes and by discarding any nonrectangular portions that contain points on the boundary of R. Assume that what remains are n rectangles labeled $R_1, R_2, \ldots, R_n$.

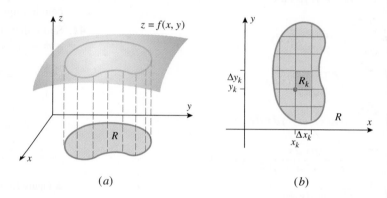

▶ **Figure 14.4.1**   (a)   (b)

Let (x_k, y_k) be the lower left corner of the kth rectangle R_k, and assume that R_k has area $\Delta A_k = \Delta x_k \Delta y_k$, where Δx_k and Δy_k are the dimensions of R_k (Figure 14.4.1b). The portion of σ that lies over R_k will be some *curvilinear patch* on the surface that has a corner at $P_k(x_k, y_k, f(x_k, y_k))$; denote the area of this patch by ΔS_k (Figure 14.4.2a). To obtain an approximation of ΔS_k, we will replace σ by the tangent plane to σ at P_k. The equation of this tangent plane is

$$z = f(x_k, y_k) + f_x(x_k, y_k)(x - x_k) + f_y(x_k, y_k)(y - y_k)$$

(see Theorem 13.7.2). The portion of the tangent plane that lies over R_k will be a parallelogram τ_k. This parallelogram will have a vertex at P_k and adjacent sides determined by the

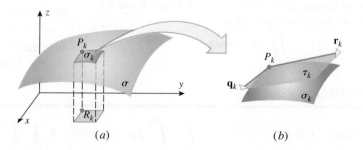

▶ **Figure 14.4.2**   (a)   (b)

vectors

$$\mathbf{q}_k = \left\langle \Delta x_k, 0, \frac{\partial z}{\partial x} \Delta x_k \right\rangle \quad \text{and} \quad \mathbf{r}_k = \left\langle 0, \Delta y_k, \frac{\partial z}{\partial y} \Delta y_k \right\rangle$$

as illustrated in Figure 14.4.2b. [Here we use $\partial z / \partial x$ to represent $f_x(x_k, y_k)$ and $\partial z / \partial y$ to represent $f_y(x_k, y_k)$.]

If the dimensions of R_k are small, then τ_k should provide a good approximation to the curvilinear patch σ_k. By Theorem 11.4.5(b), the area of the parallelogram τ_k is the length of the cross product of $\mathbf{q}_k$ and $\mathbf{r}_k$. Thus, we expect the approximation

$$\Delta S_k \approx \text{area } \tau_k = \|\mathbf{q}_k \times \mathbf{r}_k\|$$

to be good when Δx_k and Δy_k are close to 0. Computing the cross product yields

$$\|\mathbf{q}_k \times \mathbf{r}_k\| = \begin{vmatrix} \mathbf{i} & \mathbf{j} & \mathbf{k} \\ \Delta x_k & 0 & \dfrac{\partial z}{\partial x} \Delta x_k \\ 0 & \Delta y_k & \dfrac{\partial z}{\partial y} \Delta y_k \end{vmatrix} = \left(-\frac{\partial z}{\partial x} \mathbf{i} - \frac{\partial z}{\partial y} \mathbf{j} + \mathbf{k} \right) \Delta x_k \Delta y_k$$

so

$$\Delta S_k \approx \left\| \left(-\frac{\partial z}{\partial x} \mathbf{i} - \frac{\partial z}{\partial y} \mathbf{j} + \mathbf{k} \right) \Delta x_k \Delta y_k \right\| = \left\| -\frac{\partial z}{\partial x} \mathbf{i} - \frac{\partial z}{\partial y} \mathbf{j} + \mathbf{k} \right\| \Delta x_k \Delta y_k$$

$$= \sqrt{\left(\frac{\partial z}{\partial x} \right)^2 + \left(\frac{\partial z}{\partial y} \right)^2 + 1} \; \Delta A_k \tag{1}$$

It follows that the surface area of the entire surface can be approximated as

$$S \approx \sum_{k=1}^{n} \sqrt{\left(\frac{\partial z}{\partial x} \right)^2 + \left(\frac{\partial z}{\partial y} \right)^2 + 1} \; \Delta A_k$$

If we assume that the errors in the approximations approach zero as n increases in such a way that the dimensions of the rectangles approach zero, then it is plausible that the exact value of S is

$$S = \lim_{n \to +\infty} \sum_{k=1}^{n} \sqrt{\left(\frac{\partial z}{\partial x} \right)^2 + \left(\frac{\partial z}{\partial y} \right)^2 + 1} \; \Delta A_k$$

or, equivalently,

$$S = \iint_R \sqrt{\left(\frac{\partial z}{\partial x} \right)^2 + \left(\frac{\partial z}{\partial y} \right)^2 + 1} \; dA \tag{2}$$

▶ **Example 1** Find the surface area of that portion of the surface $z = \sqrt{4 - x^2}$ that lies above the rectangle R in the xy-plane whose coordinates satisfy $0 \le x \le 1$ and $0 \le y \le 4$.

Solution. As shown in Figure 14.4.3, the surface is a portion of the cylinder $x^2 + z^2 = 4$. It follows from (2) that the surface area is

$$S = \iint_R \sqrt{\left(\frac{\partial z}{\partial x} \right)^2 + \left(\frac{\partial z}{\partial y} \right)^2 + 1} \; dA$$

$$= \iint_R \sqrt{\left(-\frac{x}{\sqrt{4-x^2}} \right)^2 + 0 + 1} \; dA = \int_0^4 \int_0^1 \frac{2}{\sqrt{4-x^2}} \, dx \, dy$$

$$= 2 \int_0^4 \left[\sin^{-1}\left(\frac{1}{2}x \right) \right]_{x=0}^1 dy = 2 \int_0^4 \frac{\pi}{6} \, dy = \frac{4}{3}\pi \; ◀$$

Formula 21 of Section 7.1

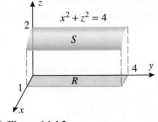

▲ Figure 14.4.3

▶ **Example 2**   Find the surface area of the portion of the paraboloid $z = x^2 + y^2$ below the plane $z = 1$.

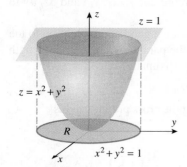

▲ Figure 14.4.4

Solution.   The surface $z = x^2 + y^2$ is the circular paraboloid shown in Figure 14.4.4. The trace of the paraboloid in the plane $z = 1$ projects onto the circle $x^2 + y^2 = 1$ in the xy-plane, and the portion of the paraboloid that lies below the plane $z = 1$ projects onto the region R that is enclosed by this circle. Thus, it follows from (2) that the surface area is

$$S = \iint_R \sqrt{4x^2 + 4y^2 + 1}\, dA$$

The expression $4x^2 + 4y^2 + 1 = 4(x^2 + y^2) + 1$ in the integrand suggests that we evaluate the integral in polar coordinates. In accordance with Formula (9) of Section 14.3, we substitute $x = r\cos\theta$ and $y = r\sin\theta$ in the integrand, replace dA by $r\, dr\, d\theta$, and find the limits of integration by expressing the region R in polar coordinates. This yields

$$S = \int_0^{2\pi}\int_0^1 \sqrt{4r^2 + 1}\, r\, dr\, d\theta = \int_0^{2\pi}\left[\frac{1}{12}(4r^2 + 1)^{3/2}\right]_{r=0}^1 d\theta$$
$$= \int_0^{2\pi} \frac{1}{12}(5\sqrt{5} - 1)\, d\theta = \frac{1}{6}\pi(5\sqrt{5} - 1) \ \blacktriangleleft$$

Some surfaces can't be described conveniently in terms of a function $z = f(x, y)$. For such surfaces, a parametric description may provide a simpler approach. We pause for a discussion of surfaces represented parametrically, with the ultimate goal of deriving a formula for the area of a parametric surface.

■ PARAMETRIC REPRESENTATION OF SURFACES

We have seen that curves in 3-space can be represented by three equations involving one parameter, say

$$x = x(t), \quad y = y(t), \quad z = z(t)$$

Surfaces in 3-space can be represented parametrically by three equations involving two parameters, say

$$x = x(u, v), \quad y = y(u, v), \quad z = z(u, v) \tag{3}$$

To visualize why such equations represent a surface, think of (u, v) as a point that varies over some region in a uv-plane. If u is held constant, then v is the only varying parameter in (3), and hence these equations represent a curve in 3-space. We call this a **constant u-curve** (Figure 14.4.5). Similarly, if v is held constant, then u is the only varying parameter in (3), so again these equations represent a curve in 3-space. We call this a **constant v-curve**. By varying the constants we generate a family of u-curves and a family of v-curves that together form a surface.

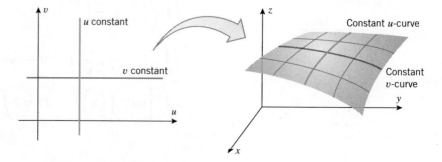

▶ **Figure 14.4.5**

▶ **Example 3** Consider the paraboloid $z = 4 - x^2 - y^2$. One way to parametrize this surface is to take $x = u$ and $y = v$ as the parameters, in which case the surface is represented by the parametric equations

$$x = u, \quad y = v, \quad z = 4 - u^2 - v^2 \tag{4}$$

Figure 14.4.6a shows a computer-generated graph of this surface. The constant u-curves correspond to constant x-values and hence appear on the surface as traces parallel to the yz-plane. Similarly, the constant v-curves correspond to constant y-values and hence appear on the surface as traces parallel to the xz-plane. ◀

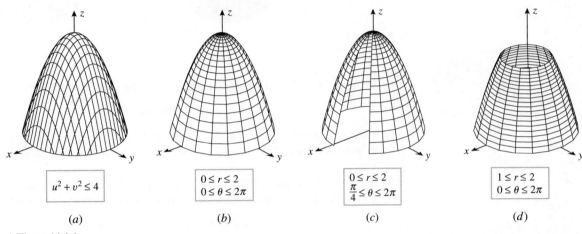

$u^2 + v^2 \leq 4$	$\begin{array}{l} 0 \leq r \leq 2 \\ 0 \leq \theta \leq 2\pi \end{array}$	$\begin{array}{l} 0 \leq r \leq 2 \\ \frac{\pi}{4} \leq \theta \leq 2\pi \end{array}$	$\begin{array}{l} 1 \leq r \leq 2 \\ 0 \leq \theta \leq 2\pi \end{array}$
(a)	(b)	(c)	(d)

▲ **Figure 14.4.6**

TECHNOLOGY MASTERY

If you have a graphing utility that can generate parametric surfaces, consult the relevant documentation and then try to generate the surfaces in Figure 14.4.6.

▶ **Example 4** The paraboloid $z = 4 - x^2 - y^2$ that was considered in Example 3 can also be parametrized by first expressing the equation in cylindrical coordinates. For this purpose, we make the substitution $x = r\cos\theta$, $y = r\sin\theta$, which yields $z = 4 - r^2$. Thus, the paraboloid can be represented parametrically in terms of r and θ as

$$x = r\cos\theta, \quad y = r\sin\theta, \quad z = 4 - r^2 \tag{5}$$

A computer-generated graph of this surface for $0 \leq r \leq 2$ and $0 \leq \theta \leq 2\pi$ is shown in Figure 14.4.6b. The constant r-curves correspond to constant z-values and hence appear on the surface as traces parallel to the xy-plane. The constant θ-curves appear on the surface as traces from vertical planes through the origin at varying angles with the x-axis. Parts (c) and (d) of Figure 14.4.6 show the effect of restrictions on the parameters r and θ. ◀

▶ **Example 5** One way to generate the sphere $x^2 + y^2 + z^2 = 1$ with a graphing utility is to graph the upper and lower hemispheres

$$z = \sqrt{1 - x^2 - y^2} \quad \text{and} \quad z = -\sqrt{1 - x^2 - y^2}$$

on the same screen. However, this sometimes produces a fragmented sphere (Figure 14.4.7a) because roundoff error sporadically produces negative values inside the radical when $1 - x^2 - y^2$ is near zero. A better graph can be generated by first expressing the sphere in spherical coordinates as $\rho = 1$ and then using the spherical-to-rectangular conversion formulas in Table 11.8.1 to obtain the parametric equations

$$x = \sin\phi\cos\theta, \quad y = \sin\phi\sin\theta, \quad z = \cos\phi$$

with parameters θ and ϕ. Figure 14.4.7b shows the graph of this parametric surface for

$0 \leq \theta \leq 2\pi$ and $0 \leq \phi \leq \pi$. In the language of cartographers, the constant ϕ-curves are the *lines of latitude* and the constant θ-curves are the *lines of longitude*. ◄

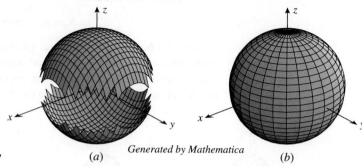

▶ **Figure 14.4.7**   (*a*)   *Generated by Mathematica*   (*b*)

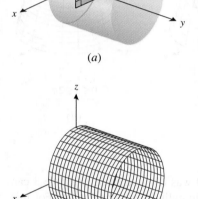

(*a*)

(*b*)

▲ **Figure 14.4.8**

▶ **Example 6**   Find parametric equations for the portion of the right circular cylinder

$$x^2 + z^2 = 9 \quad \text{for which} \quad 0 \leq y \leq 5$$

in terms of the parameters u and v shown in Figure 14.4.8*a*. The parameter u is the y-coordinate of a point $P(x, y, z)$ on the surface, and v is the angle shown in the figure.

Solution.   The radius of the cylinder is 3, so it is evident from the figure that $y = u$, $x = 3\cos v$, and $z = 3\sin v$. Thus, the surface can be represented parametrically as

$$x = 3\cos v, \quad y = u, \quad z = 3\sin v$$

To obtain the portion of the surface from $y = 0$ to $y = 5$, we let the parameter u vary over the interval $0 \leq u \leq 5$, and to ensure that the entire lateral surface is covered, we let the parameter v vary over the interval $0 \leq v \leq 2\pi$. Figure 14.4.8*b* shows a computer-generated graph of the surface in which u and v vary over these intervals. Constant u-curves appear as circular traces parallel to the xz-plane, and constant v-curves appear as lines parallel to the y-axis. ◄

■ **REPRESENTING SURFACES OF REVOLUTION PARAMETRICALLY**

The basic idea of Example 6 can be adapted to obtain parametric equations for surfaces of revolution. For example, suppose that we want to find parametric equations for the surface generated by revolving the plane curve $y = f(x)$ about the x-axis. Figure 14.4.9 suggests that the surface can be represented parametrically as

$$x = u, \quad y = f(u)\cos v, \quad z = f(u)\sin v \tag{6}$$

where v is the angle shown.

In the exercises we will discuss formulas analogous to (6) for surfaces of revolution about other axes.

▶ **Example 7**   Find parametric equations for the surface generated by revolving the curve $y = 1/x$ about the x-axis.

Solution.   From (6) this surface can be represented parametrically as

$$x = u, \quad y = \frac{1}{u}\cos v, \quad z = \frac{1}{u}\sin v$$

A general principle for representing surfaces of revolution parametrically is to let the variable about whose axis the curve is revolving be equal to u and let the other variables be $f(u)\cos v$ and $f(u)\sin v$.

Figure 14.4.10 shows a computer-generated graph of the surface in which $0.7 \leq u \leq 5$ and $0 \leq v \leq 2\pi$. This surface is a portion of Gabriel's horn, which was discussed in Exercise 55 of Section 7.8. ◄

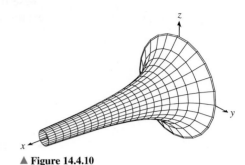

▲ **Figure 14.4.9**   ▲ **Figure 14.4.10**

▨ VECTOR-VALUED FUNCTIONS OF TWO VARIABLES

Recall that the parametric equations

$$x = x(t), \quad y = y(t), \quad z = z(t)$$

can be expressed in vector form as

$$\mathbf{r} = x(t)\mathbf{i} + y(t)\mathbf{j} + z(t)\mathbf{k}$$

where $\mathbf{r} = x\mathbf{i} + y\mathbf{j} + z\mathbf{k}$ is the radius vector and $\mathbf{r}(t) = x(t)\mathbf{i} + y(t)\mathbf{j} + z(t)\mathbf{k}$ is a vector-valued function of one variable. Similarly, the parametric equations

$$x = x(u, v), \quad y = y(u, v), \quad z = z(u, v)$$

can be expressed in vector form as

$$\mathbf{r} = x(u, v)\mathbf{i} + y(u, v)\mathbf{j} + z(u, v)\mathbf{k}$$

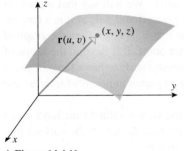

▲ **Figure 14.4.11**

Here the function $\mathbf{r}(u, v) = x(u, v)\mathbf{i} + y(u, v)\mathbf{j} + z(u, v)\mathbf{k}$ is a ***vector-valued function of two variables***. We define the ***graph*** of $\mathbf{r}(u, v)$ to be the graph of the corresponding parametric equations. Geometrically, we can view $\mathbf{r}$ as a vector from the origin to a point (x, y, z) that moves over the surface $\mathbf{r} = \mathbf{r}(u, v)$ as u and v vary (Figure 14.4.11). As with vector-valued functions of one variable, we say that $\mathbf{r}(u, v)$ is ***continuous*** if each component is continuous.

▶ **Example 8** The paraboloid in Example 3 was expressed parametrically as

$$x = u, \quad y = v, \quad z = 4 - u^2 - v^2$$

These equations can be expressed in vector form as

$$\mathbf{r} = u\mathbf{i} + v\mathbf{j} + (4 - u^2 - v^2)\mathbf{k} \quad ◀$$

▨ PARTIAL DERIVATIVES OF VECTOR-VALUED FUNCTIONS

Partial derivatives of vector-valued functions of two variables are obtained by taking partial derivatives of the components. For example, if

$$\mathbf{r}(u, v) = x(u, v)\mathbf{i} + y(u, v)\mathbf{j} + z(u, v)\mathbf{k}$$

then

$$\frac{\partial \mathbf{r}}{\partial u} = \frac{\partial x}{\partial u}\mathbf{i} + \frac{\partial y}{\partial u}\mathbf{j} + \frac{\partial z}{\partial u}\mathbf{k}$$

$$\frac{\partial \mathbf{r}}{\partial v} = \frac{\partial x}{\partial v}\mathbf{i} + \frac{\partial y}{\partial v}\mathbf{j} + \frac{\partial z}{\partial v}\mathbf{k}$$

These derivatives can also be written as $\mathbf{r}_u$ and $\mathbf{r}_v$ or $\mathbf{r}_u(u, v)$ and $\mathbf{r}_v(u, v)$ and can be expressed as the limits

$$\frac{\partial \mathbf{r}}{\partial u} = \lim_{\Delta u \to 0} \frac{\mathbf{r}(u + \Delta u, v) - \mathbf{r}(u, v)}{\Delta u} = \lim_{w \to u} \frac{\mathbf{r}(w, v) - \mathbf{r}(u, v)}{w - u} \tag{7}$$

$$\frac{\partial \mathbf{r}}{\partial v} = \lim_{\Delta v \to 0} \frac{\mathbf{r}(u, v + \Delta v) - \mathbf{r}(u, v)}{\Delta v} = \lim_{w \to v} \frac{\mathbf{r}(u, w) - \mathbf{r}(u, v)}{w - v} \tag{8}$$

▶ **Example 9**   Find the partial derivatives of the vector-valued function $\mathbf{r}$ in Example 8.

Solution.

$$\frac{\partial \mathbf{r}}{\partial u} = \frac{\partial}{\partial u}[u\mathbf{i} + v\mathbf{j} + (4 - u^2 - v^2)\mathbf{k}] = \mathbf{i} - 2u\mathbf{k}$$

$$\frac{\partial \mathbf{r}}{\partial v} = \frac{\partial}{\partial v}[u\mathbf{i} + v\mathbf{j} + (4 - u^2 - v^2)\mathbf{k}] = \mathbf{j} - 2v\mathbf{k} \quad \blacktriangleleft$$

■ TANGENT PLANES TO PARAMETRIC SURFACES

Our next objective is to show how to find tangent planes to parametric surfaces. Let σ denote a parametric surface in 3-space, with P_0 a point on σ. We will say that a plane is *tangent* to σ at P_0 provided a line through P_0 lies in the plane if and only if it is a tangent line at P_0 to a curve on σ. We showed in Section 13.7 that if $z = f(x, y)$, then the graph of f has a tangent plane at a point if f is differentiable at that point. It is beyond the scope of this text to obtain precise conditions under which a parametric surface has a tangent plane at a point, so we will simply assume the existence of tangent planes at points of interest and focus on finding their equations.

Suppose that the parametric surface σ is the graph of the vector-valued function $\mathbf{r}(u, v)$ and that we are interested in the tangent plane at the point (x_0, y_0, z_0) on the surface that corresponds to the parameter values $u = u_0$ and $v = v_0$; that is,

$$\mathbf{r}(u_0, v_0) = x_0\mathbf{i} + y_0\mathbf{j} + z_0\mathbf{k}$$

If $v = v_0$ is kept fixed and u is allowed to vary, then $\mathbf{r}(u, v_0)$ is a vector-valued function of one variable whose graph is the constant v-curve through the point (u_0, v_0); similarly, if $u = u_0$ is kept fixed and v is allowed to vary, then $\mathbf{r}(u_0, v)$ is a vector-valued function of one variable whose graph is the constant u-curve through the point (u_0, v_0). Moreover, it follows from the geometric interpretation of the derivative developed in Section 12.2 that if $\partial \mathbf{r}/\partial u \neq \mathbf{0}$ at (u_0, v_0), then this vector is tangent to the constant v-curve through (u_0, v_0); and if $\partial \mathbf{r}/\partial v \neq \mathbf{0}$ at (u_0, v_0), then this vector is tangent to the constant u-curve through (u_0, v_0) (Figure 14.4.12). Thus, if $\partial \mathbf{r}/\partial u \times \partial \mathbf{r}/\partial v \neq \mathbf{0}$ at (u_0, v_0), then the vector

$$\frac{\partial \mathbf{r}}{\partial u} \times \frac{\partial \mathbf{r}}{\partial v} = \begin{vmatrix} \mathbf{i} & \mathbf{j} & \mathbf{k} \\ \dfrac{\partial x}{\partial u} & \dfrac{\partial y}{\partial u} & \dfrac{\partial z}{\partial u} \\ \dfrac{\partial x}{\partial v} & \dfrac{\partial y}{\partial v} & \dfrac{\partial z}{\partial v} \end{vmatrix} \tag{9}$$

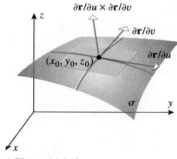

▲ **Figure 14.4.12**

is orthogonal to both tangent vectors at the point (u_0, v_0) and hence is normal to the tangent plane and the surface at this point (Figure 14.4.12). Accordingly, we make the following definition.

14.4.1   DEFINITION   If a parametric surface σ is the graph of $\mathbf{r} = \mathbf{r}(u, v)$, and if $\partial\mathbf{r}/\partial u \times \partial\mathbf{r}/\partial v \neq \mathbf{0}$ at a point on the surface, then the **principal unit normal vector** to the surface at that point is denoted by $\mathbf{n}$ or $\mathbf{n}(u, v)$ and is defined as

$$\mathbf{n} = \frac{\dfrac{\partial\mathbf{r}}{\partial u} \times \dfrac{\partial\mathbf{r}}{\partial v}}{\left\|\dfrac{\partial\mathbf{r}}{\partial u} \times \dfrac{\partial\mathbf{r}}{\partial v}\right\|} \qquad (10)$$

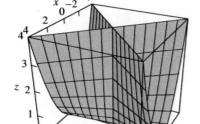

▲ **Figure 14.4.13**

▶ **Example 10**   Find an equation of the tangent plane to the parametric surface

$$x = uv, \quad y = u, \quad z = v^2$$

at the point where $u = 2$ and $v = -1$. This surface, called **Whitney's umbrella**, is an example of a self-intersecting parametric surface (Figure 14.4.13).

Solution.   We start by writing the equations in the vector form

$$\mathbf{r} = uv\mathbf{i} + u\mathbf{j} + v^2\mathbf{k}$$

The partial derivatives of $\mathbf{r}$ are

$$\frac{\partial\mathbf{r}}{\partial u}(u, v) = v\mathbf{i} + \mathbf{j}$$

$$\frac{\partial\mathbf{r}}{\partial v}(u, v) = u\mathbf{i} + 2v\mathbf{k}$$

and at $u = 2$ and $v = -1$ these partial derivatives are

$$\frac{\partial\mathbf{r}}{\partial u}(2, -1) = -\mathbf{i} + \mathbf{j}$$

$$\frac{\partial\mathbf{r}}{\partial v}(2, -1) = 2\mathbf{i} - 2\mathbf{k}$$

Thus, from (9) and (10) a normal to the surface at this point is

$$\frac{\partial\mathbf{r}}{\partial u}(2, -1) \times \frac{\partial\mathbf{r}}{\partial v}(2, -1) = \begin{vmatrix} \mathbf{i} & \mathbf{j} & \mathbf{k} \\ -1 & 1 & 0 \\ 2 & 0 & -2 \end{vmatrix} = -2\mathbf{i} - 2\mathbf{j} - 2\mathbf{k}$$

Since any normal will suffice to find the tangent plane, it makes sense to multiply this vector by $-\frac{1}{2}$ and use the simpler normal $\mathbf{i} + \mathbf{j} + \mathbf{k}$. It follows from the given parametric equations that the point on the surface corresponding to $u = 2$ and $v = -1$ is $(-2, 2, 1)$, so the tangent plane at this point can be expressed in point-normal form as

$$(x + 2) + (y - 2) + (z - 1) = 0 \quad \text{or} \quad x + y + z = 1 \quad ◀$$

Convince yourself that the result obtained in Example 10 is consistent with Figure 14.4.13.

▶ **Example 11**   The sphere $x^2 + y^2 + z^2 = a^2$ can be expressed in spherical coordinates as $\rho = a$, and the spherical-to-rectangular conversion formulas in Table 11.8.1 can then be used to express the sphere as the graph of the vector-valued function

$$\mathbf{r}(\phi, \theta) = a\sin\phi\cos\theta\mathbf{i} + a\sin\phi\sin\theta\mathbf{j} + a\cos\phi\mathbf{k}$$

where $0 \leq \phi \leq \pi$ and $0 \leq \theta \leq 2\pi$ (verify). Use this function to show that the radius vector is normal to the tangent plane at each point on the sphere.

Solution.   We will show that at each point of the sphere the unit normal vector $\mathbf{n}$ is a scalar multiple of $\mathbf{r}$ (and hence is parallel to $\mathbf{r}$). We have

$$\frac{\partial \mathbf{r}}{\partial \phi} \times \frac{\partial \mathbf{r}}{\partial \theta} = \begin{vmatrix} \mathbf{i} & \mathbf{j} & \mathbf{k} \\ \frac{\partial x}{\partial \phi} & \frac{\partial y}{\partial \phi} & \frac{\partial z}{\partial \phi} \\ \frac{\partial x}{\partial \theta} & \frac{\partial y}{\partial \theta} & \frac{\partial z}{\partial \theta} \end{vmatrix} = \begin{vmatrix} \mathbf{i} & \mathbf{j} & \mathbf{k} \\ a \cos\phi\cos\theta & a\cos\phi\sin\theta & -a\sin\phi \\ -a\sin\phi\sin\theta & a\sin\phi\cos\theta & 0 \end{vmatrix}$$

$$= a^2 \sin^2\phi\cos\theta\,\mathbf{i} + a^2\sin^2\phi\sin\theta\,\mathbf{j} + a^2\sin\phi\cos\phi\,\mathbf{k}$$

and hence

$$\left\| \frac{\partial \mathbf{r}}{\partial \phi} \times \frac{\partial \mathbf{r}}{\partial \theta} \right\| = \sqrt{a^4\sin^4\phi\cos^2\theta + a^4\sin^4\phi\sin^2\theta + a^4\sin^2\phi\cos^2\phi}$$

$$= \sqrt{a^4\sin^4\phi + a^4\sin^2\phi\cos^2\phi}$$

$$= a^2\sqrt{\sin^2\phi} = a^2|\sin\phi| = a^2\sin\phi$$

For $\phi \neq 0$ or π, it follows from (10) that

$$\mathbf{n} = \sin\phi\cos\theta\,\mathbf{i} + \sin\phi\sin\theta\,\mathbf{j} + \cos\phi\,\mathbf{k} = \frac{1}{a}\mathbf{r}$$

Furthermore, the tangent planes at $\phi \neq 0$ or π are horizontal, to which $\mathbf{r} = \pm a\mathbf{k}$ is clearly normal. ◄

■ SURFACE AREA OF PARAMETRIC SURFACES

We now obtain a formula for the surface area S of a parametric surface σ. Let σ be a parametric surface whose vector equation is

$$\mathbf{r} = x(u, v)\mathbf{i} + y(u, v)\mathbf{j} + z(u, v)\mathbf{k}$$

Our discussion will be analogous to the case for surfaces of the form $z = f(x, y)$. Here, R will be a region in the uv-plane that we subdivide into n rectangular regions as shown in Figure 14.4.14a. Let R_k be the kth rectangular region, and denote its area by ΔA_k. The patch σ_k is the image of R_k on σ. The patch will have a corner at $\mathbf{r}(u_k, v_k)$; denote the area of σ_k by ΔS_k (Figure 14.4.14b).

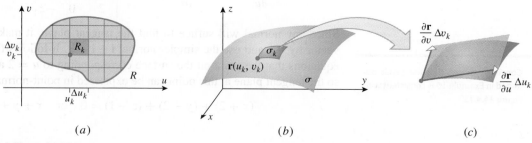

(a)   (b)   (c)

▲ **Figure 14.4.14**

Recall that in the case of $z = f(x, y)$ we used the area of a parallelogram in a tangent plane to the surface to approximate the area of the patch. In the parametric case, the desired parallelogram is spanned by the tangent vectors

$$\frac{\partial \mathbf{r}}{\partial u}\Delta u_k \quad \text{and} \quad \frac{\partial \mathbf{r}}{\partial v}\Delta v_k$$

where the partial derivatives are evaluated at (u_k, v_k) (Figure 14.4.14c). Thus,

$$\Delta S_k \approx \left\| \frac{\partial \mathbf{r}}{\partial u} \Delta u_k \times \frac{\partial \mathbf{r}}{\partial v} \Delta v_k \right\| = \left\| \frac{\partial \mathbf{r}}{\partial u} \times \frac{\partial \mathbf{r}}{\partial v} \right\| \Delta u_k \Delta v_k = \left\| \frac{\partial \mathbf{r}}{\partial u} \times \frac{\partial \mathbf{r}}{\partial v} \right\| \Delta A_k \qquad (11)$$

The surface area of the entire surface is the sum of the areas ΔS_k. If we assume that the errors in the approximations in (11) approach zero as n increases in such a way that the dimensions of the rectangles R_k approach zero, then it is plausible that the exact value of S is

$$S = \lim_{n \to +\infty} \sum_{k=1}^{n} \left\| \frac{\partial \mathbf{r}}{\partial u} \times \frac{\partial \mathbf{r}}{\partial v} \right\| \Delta A_k$$

or, equivalently,

$$S = \iint_R \left\| \frac{\partial \mathbf{r}}{\partial u} \times \frac{\partial \mathbf{r}}{\partial v} \right\| dA \qquad (12)$$

▶ **Example 12**   It follows from (6) that the parametric equations

$$x = u, \quad y = u \cos v, \quad z = u \sin v$$

represent the cone that results when the line $y = x$ in the xy-plane is revolved about the x-axis. Use Formula (12) to find the surface area of that portion of the cone for which $0 \le u \le 2$ and $0 \le v \le 2\pi$ (Figure 14.4.15).

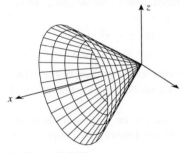

▲ **Figure 14.4.15**

Solution.   The surface can be expressed in vector form as

$$\mathbf{r} = u\mathbf{i} + u \cos v\mathbf{j} + u \sin v\mathbf{k} \quad (0 \le u \le 2, \ 0 \le v \le 2\pi)$$

Thus,

$$\frac{\partial \mathbf{r}}{\partial u} = \mathbf{i} + \cos v\mathbf{j} + \sin v\mathbf{k}$$

$$\frac{\partial \mathbf{r}}{\partial v} = -u \sin v\mathbf{j} + u \cos v\mathbf{k}$$

$$\frac{\partial \mathbf{r}}{\partial u} \times \frac{\partial \mathbf{r}}{\partial v} = \begin{vmatrix} \mathbf{i} & \mathbf{j} & \mathbf{k} \\ 1 & \cos v & \sin v \\ 0 & -u \sin v & u \cos v \end{vmatrix} = u\mathbf{i} - u \cos v\mathbf{j} - u \sin v\mathbf{k}$$

$$\left\| \frac{\partial \mathbf{r}}{\partial u} \times \frac{\partial \mathbf{r}}{\partial v} \right\| = \sqrt{u^2 + (-u \cos v)^2 + (-u \sin v)^2} = |u|\sqrt{2} = u\sqrt{2}$$

Thus, from (12)

$$S = \iint_R \left\| \frac{\partial \mathbf{r}}{\partial u} \times \frac{\partial \mathbf{r}}{\partial v} \right\| dA = \int_0^{2\pi} \int_0^2 \sqrt{2}\,u \, du \, dv = 2\sqrt{2} \int_0^{2\pi} dv = 4\pi\sqrt{2} \ \blacktriangleleft$$

✔ **QUICK CHECK EXERCISES 14.4**   *(See page 1039 for answers.)*

1. The surface area of a surface of the form $z = f(x, y)$ over a region R in the xy-plane is given by

$$S = \iint_R \underline{\hspace{2cm}} dA$$

2. Consider the surface represented parametrically by
$$x = 1 - u$$
$$y = (1 - u) \cos v \qquad (0 \le u \le 1, 0 \le v \le 2\pi)$$
$$z = (1 - u) \sin v$$

   (a) Describe the constant u-curves.
   (b) Describe the constant v-curves.

3. If

$$\mathbf{r}(u, v) = (1 - u)\mathbf{i} + [(1 - u)\cos v]\mathbf{j} + [(1 - u)\sin v]\mathbf{k}$$

then

$$\frac{\partial \mathbf{r}}{\partial u} = \underline{\qquad} \quad \text{and} \quad \frac{\partial \mathbf{r}}{\partial v} = \underline{\qquad}$$

4. If

$$\mathbf{r}(u, v) = (1 - u)\mathbf{i} + [(1 - u)\cos v]\mathbf{j} + [(1 - u)\sin v]\mathbf{k}$$

the principal unit normal to the graph of $\mathbf{r}$ at the point where $u = 1/2$ and $v = \pi/6$ is given by _____.

5. Suppose σ is a parametric surface with vector equation

$$\mathbf{r}(u, v) = x(u, v)\mathbf{i} + y(u, v)\mathbf{j} + z(u, v)\mathbf{k}$$

If σ has no self-intersections and σ is smooth on a region R in the uv-plane, then the surface area of σ is given by

$$S = \iint\limits_{R} \underline{\qquad} \, dA$$

EXERCISE SET 14.4    Graphing Utility   CAS

1–4 Express the area of the given surface as an iterated double integral, and then find the surface area. ■

1. The portion of the cylinder $y^2 + z^2 = 9$ that is above the rectangle $R = \{(x, y) : 0 \le x \le 2, -3 \le y \le 3\}$.

2. The portion of the plane $2x + 2y + z = 8$ in the first octant.

3. The portion of the cone $z^2 = 4x^2 + 4y^2$ that is above the region in the first quadrant bounded by the line $y = x$ and the parabola $y = x^2$.

4. The portion of the surface $z = 2x + y^2$ that is above the triangular region with vertices $(0, 0)$, $(0, 1)$, and $(1, 1)$.

5–10 Express the area of the given surface as an iterated double integral in polar coordinates, and then find the surface area. ■

5. The portion of the cone $z = \sqrt{x^2 + y^2}$ that lies inside the cylinder $x^2 + y^2 = 2x$.

6. The portion of the paraboloid $z = 1 - x^2 - y^2$ that is above the xy-plane.

7. The portion of the surface $z = xy$ that is above the sector in the first quadrant bounded by the lines $y = x/\sqrt{3}$, $y = 0$, and the circle $x^2 + y^2 = 9$.

8. The portion of the paraboloid $2z = x^2 + y^2$ that is inside the cylinder $x^2 + y^2 = 8$.

9. The portion of the sphere $x^2 + y^2 + z^2 = 16$ between the planes $z = 1$ and $z = 2$.

10. The portion of the sphere $x^2 + y^2 + z^2 = 8$ that is inside the cone $z = \sqrt{x^2 + y^2}$.

11–12 Sketch the parametric surface. ■

11. (a) $x = u$, $y = v$, $z = \sqrt{u^2 + v^2}$
    (b) $x = u$, $y = \sqrt{u^2 + v^2}$, $z = v$
    (c) $x = \sqrt{u^2 + v^2}$, $y = u$, $z = v$

12. (a) $x = u$, $y = v$, $z = u^2 + v^2$
    (b) $x = u$, $y = u^2 + v^2$, $z = v$
    (c) $x = u^2 + v^2$, $y = u$, $z = v$

13–14 Find a parametric representation of the surface in terms of the parameters $u = x$ and $v = y$. ■

13. (a) $2z - 3x + 4y = 5$ (b) $z = x^2$

14. (a) $z + zx^2 - y = 0$ (b) $y^2 - 3z = 5$

15. (a) Find parametric equations for the portion of the cylinder $x^2 + y^2 = 5$ that extends between the planes $z = 0$ and $z = 1$.
    (b) Find parametric equations for the portion of the cylinder $x^2 + z^2 = 4$ that extends between the planes $y = 1$ and $y = 3$.

16. (a) Find parametric equations for the portion of the plane $x + y = 1$ that extends between the planes $z = -1$ and $z = 1$.
    (b) Find parametric equations for the portion of the plane $y - 2z = 5$ that extends between the planes $x = 0$ and $x = 3$.

17. Find parametric equations for the surface generated by revolving the curve $y = \sin x$ about the x-axis.

18. Find parametric equations for the surface generated by revolving the curve $y - e^x = 0$ about the x-axis.

19–24 Find a parametric representation of the surface in terms of the parameters r and θ, where (r, θ, z) are the cylindrical coordinates of a point on the surface. ■

19. $z = \dfrac{1}{1 + x^2 + y^2}$ **20.** $z = e^{-(x^2 + y^2)}$

21. $z = 2xy$ **22.** $z = x^2 - y^2$

23. The portion of the sphere $x^2 + y^2 + z^2 = 9$ on or above the plane $z = 2$.

24. The portion of the cone $z = \sqrt{x^2 + y^2}$ on or below the plane $z = 3$.

25. Find a parametric representation of the cone

$$z = \sqrt{3x^2 + 3y^2}$$

in terms of parameters ρ and θ, where (ρ, θ, ϕ) are spherical coordinates of a point on the surface.

26. Describe the cylinder $x^2 + y^2 = 9$ in terms of parameters θ and ϕ, where (ρ, θ, ϕ) are spherical coordinates of a point on the surface.

FOCUS ON CONCEPTS

27–32 Eliminate the parameters to obtain an equation in rectangular coordinates, and describe the surface. ▪

27. $x = 2u + v$, $y = u - v$, $z = 3v$ for $-\infty < u < +\infty$ and $-\infty < v < +\infty$.

28. $x = u \cos v$, $y = u^2$, $z = u \sin v$ for $0 \le u \le 2$ and $0 \le v < 2\pi$.

29. $x = 3 \sin u$, $y = 2 \cos u$, $z = 2v$ for $0 \le u < 2\pi$ and $1 \le v \le 2$.

30. $x = \sqrt{u} \cos v$, $y = \sqrt{u} \sin v$, $z = u$ for $0 \le u \le 4$ and $0 \le v < 2\pi$.

31. $\mathbf{r}(u, v) = 3u \cos v \mathbf{i} + 4u \sin v \mathbf{j} + u \mathbf{k}$ for $0 \le u \le 1$ and $0 \le v < 2\pi$.

32. $\mathbf{r}(u, v) = \sin u \cos v \mathbf{i} + 2 \sin u \sin v \mathbf{j} + 3 \cos u \mathbf{k}$ for $0 \le u \le \pi$ and $0 \le v < 2\pi$.

33. The accompanying figure shows the graphs of two parametric representations of the cone $z = \sqrt{x^2 + y^2}$ for $0 \le z \le 2$.
   (a) Find parametric equations that produce reasonable facsimiles of these surfaces.
   (b) Use a graphing utility to check your answer in part (a).

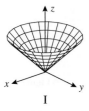 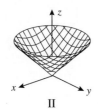

I   II   ◀ **Figure Ex-33**

34. The accompanying figure shows the graphs of two parametric representations of the paraboloid $z = x^2 + y^2$ for $0 \le z \le 2$.
   (a) Find parametric equations that produce reasonable facsimiles of these surfaces.
   (b) Use a graphing utility to check your answer in part (a).

 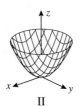

I   II   ◀ **Figure Ex-34**

35. In each part, the figure shows a portion of the parametric surface $x = 3 \cos v$, $y = u$, $z = 3 \sin v$. Find restrictions on u and v that produce the surface, and check your answer with a graphing utility.

(a)   (b)

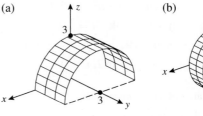

36. In each part, the figure shows a portion of the parametric surface $x = 3 \cos v$, $y = 3 \sin v$, $z = u$. Find restrictions on u and v that produce the surface, and check your answer with a graphing utility.

(a)   (b)

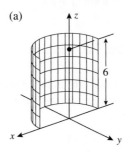 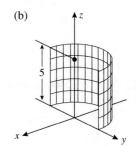

37. In each part, the figure shows a hemisphere that is a portion of the sphere $x = \sin \phi \cos \theta$, $y = \sin \phi \sin \theta$, $z = \cos \phi$. Find restrictions on ϕ and θ that produce the hemisphere, and check your answer with a graphing utility.

(a)   (b)

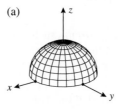 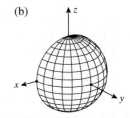

38. In each part, the figure shows a portion of the sphere $x = \sin \phi \cos \theta$, $y = \sin \phi \sin \theta$, $z = \cos \phi$. Find restrictions on ϕ and θ that produce the surface, and check your answer with a graphing utility.

(a)   (b)

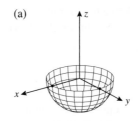 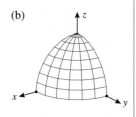

39–44 Find an equation of the tangent plane to the parametric surface at the stated point. ∎

39. $x = u$, $y = v$, $z = u^2 + v^2$; $(1, 2, 5)$

40. $x = u^2$, $y = v^2$, $z = u + v$; $(1, 4, 3)$

41. $x = 3v \sin u$, $y = 2v \cos u$, $z = u^2$; $(0, 2, 0)$

42. $\mathbf{r} = uv\mathbf{i} + (u - v)\mathbf{j} + (u + v)\mathbf{k}$; $u = 1$, $v = 2$

43. $\mathbf{r} = u \cos v\mathbf{i} + u \sin v\mathbf{j} + v\mathbf{k}$; $u = 1/2$, $v = \pi/4$

44. $\mathbf{r} = uv\mathbf{i} + ue^v\mathbf{j} + ve^u\mathbf{k}$; $u = \ln 2$, $v = 0$

45–46 Find the area of the given surface. ∎

45. The portion of the paraboloid

$$\mathbf{r}(u, v) = u \cos v\mathbf{i} + u \sin v\mathbf{j} + u^2\mathbf{k}$$

for which $1 \leq u \leq 2$, $0 \leq v \leq 2\pi$.

46. The portion of the cone

$$\mathbf{r}(u, v) = u \cos v\mathbf{i} + u \sin v\mathbf{j} + u\mathbf{k}$$

for which $0 \leq u \leq 2v$, $0 \leq v \leq \pi/2$.

47–50 True–False Determine whether the statement is true or false. Explain your answer. ∎

47. If f has continuous first partial derivatives in the interior of a region R in the xy-plane, then the surface area of the surface $z = f(x, y)$ over R is

$$\iint\limits_R \sqrt{[f(x, y)]^2 + 1}\, dA$$

48. Suppose that $z = f(x, y)$ has continuous first partial derivatives in the interior of a region R in the xy-plane, and set $\mathbf{q} = \langle 1, 0, \partial z/\partial x \rangle$ and $\mathbf{r} = \langle 0, 1, \partial z/\partial y \rangle$. Then the surface area of the surface $z = f(x, y)$ over R is

$$\iint\limits_R \|\mathbf{q} \times \mathbf{r}\|\, dA$$

49. If $\mathbf{r}(u, v) = x(u, v)\mathbf{i} + y(u, v)\mathbf{j} + z(u, v)\mathbf{k}$ such that $\partial\mathbf{r}/\partial u$ and $\partial\mathbf{r}/\partial v$ are nonzero vectors at (u_0, v_0), then

$$\frac{\partial\mathbf{r}}{\partial u} \times \frac{\partial\mathbf{r}}{\partial v}$$

is normal to the graph of $\mathbf{r} = \mathbf{r}(u, v)$ at (u_0, v_0).

50. For the function $f(x, y) = ax + by$, the area of the surface $z = f(x, y)$ over a rectangle R in the xy-plane is the product of $\|\langle 1, 0, a \rangle \times \langle 0, 1, b \rangle\|$ and the area of R.

51. Use parametric equations to derive the formula for the surface area of a sphere of radius a.

52. Use parametric equations to derive the formula for the lateral surface area of a right circular cylinder of radius r and height h.

53. The portion of the surface

$$z = \frac{h}{a}\sqrt{x^2 + y^2} \quad (a, h > 0)$$

between the xy-plane and the plane $z = h$ is a right circular

cone of height h and radius a. Use a double integral to show that the lateral surface area of this cone is $S = \pi a\sqrt{a^2 + h^2}$.

54. The accompanying figure shows the **torus** that is generated by revolving the circle

$$(x - a)^2 + z^2 = b^2 \quad (0 < b < a)$$

in the xz-plane about the z-axis.

(a) Show that this torus can be expressed parametrically as

$$x = (a + b \cos v) \cos u$$
$$y = (a + b \cos v) \sin u$$
$$z = b \sin v$$

where u and v are the parameters shown in the figure and $0 \leq u \leq 2\pi$, $0 \leq v \leq 2\pi$.

(b) Use a graphing utility to generate a torus.

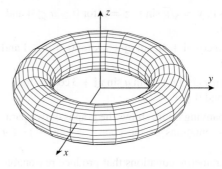

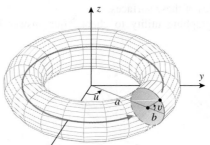

◀ **Figure Ex-54**

55. Find the surface area of the torus in Exercise 54(a).

C **56.** Use a CAS to graph the **helicoid**

$$x = u \cos v, \quad y = u \sin v, \quad z = v$$

for $0 \leq u \leq 5$ and $0 \leq v \leq 4\pi$ (see the accompanying figure), and then use the numerical double integration operation of the CAS to approximate the surface area.

C **57.** Use a CAS to graph the **pseudosphere**

$$x = \cos u \sin v$$
$$y = \sin u \sin v$$
$$z = \cos v + \ln\left(\tan\frac{v}{2}\right)$$

for $0 \leq u \leq 2\pi$, $0 < v < \pi$ (see the accompanying figure on the next page), and then use the numerical double integration operation of the CAS to approximate the surface area between the planes $z = -1$ and $z = 1$.

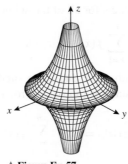

▲ **Figure Ex-56**

▲ **Figure Ex-57**

this image cannot be parsed

58. (a) Find parametric equations for the surface of revolution that is generated by revolving the curve $z = f(x)$ in the xz-plane about the z-axis.

(b) Use the result obtained in part (a) to find parametric equations for the surface of revolution that is generated by revolving the curve $z = 1/x^2$ in the xz-plane about the z-axis.

(c) Use a graphing utility to check your work by graphing the parametric surface.

59–61 The parametric equations in these exercises represent a quadric surface for positive values of a, b, and c. Identify the type of surface by eliminating the parameters u and v. Check your conclusion by choosing specific values for the constants and generating the surface with a graphing utility. ■

59. $x = a \cos u \cos v$, $y = b \sin u \cos v$, $z = c \sin v$

60. $x = a \cos u \cosh v$, $y = b \sin u \cosh v$, $z = c \sinh v$

61. $x = a \sinh v$, $y = b \sinh u \cosh v$, $z = c \cosh u \cosh v$

62. **Writing** An early popular approach to defining surface area was to take a limit of surface areas of inscribed polyhedra, but an example in which this approach fails was published in 1890 by H. A. Schwartz. Frieda Zames discusses Schwartz's example in her article "Surface Area and the Cylinder Area Paradox," *The Two-Year College Mathematics Journal*, Vol. 8, No. 4, September 1977, pp. 207–211. Read the article and write a short summary.

✔ **QUICK CHECK ANSWERS 14.4**

1. $\sqrt{\left(\dfrac{\partial z}{\partial x}\right)^2 + \left(\dfrac{\partial z}{\partial y}\right)^2 + 1}$ **2.** (a) The constant u-curves are circles of radius $1 - u$ centered at $(1 - u, 0, 0)$ and parallel to the yz-plane. (b) The constant v-curves are line segments joining the points $(1, \cos v, \sin v)$ and $(0, 0, 0)$.
3. $\dfrac{\partial \mathbf{r}}{\partial u} = -\mathbf{i} - (\cos v)\mathbf{j} - (\sin v)\mathbf{k}$; $\dfrac{\partial \mathbf{r}}{\partial v} = -[(1 - u)\sin v]\mathbf{j} + [(1 - u)\cos v]\mathbf{k}$ **4.** $\dfrac{1}{\sqrt{8}}(-2\mathbf{i} + \sqrt{3}\mathbf{j} + \mathbf{k})$ **5.** $\left\| \dfrac{\partial \mathbf{r}}{\partial u} \times \dfrac{\partial \mathbf{r}}{\partial v} \right\|$

14.5 TRIPLE INTEGRALS

In the preceding sections we defined and discussed properties of double integrals for functions of two variables. In this section we will define triple integrals for functions of three variables.

■ **DEFINITION OF A TRIPLE INTEGRAL**

A single integral of a function $f(x)$ is defined over a finite closed interval on the x-axis, and a double integral of a function $f(x, y)$ is defined over a finite closed region R in the xy-plane. Our first goal in this section is to define what is meant by a *triple integral* of $f(x, y, z)$ over a closed solid region G in an xyz-coordinate system. To ensure that G does not extend indefinitely in some direction, we will assume that it can be enclosed in a suitably large box whose sides are parallel to the coordinate planes (Figure 14.5.1). In this case we say that G is a *finite solid*.

To define the triple integral of $f(x, y, z)$ over G, we first divide the box into n "subboxes" by planes parallel to the coordinate planes. We then discard those subboxes that contain any points outside of G and choose an arbitrary point in each of the remaining subboxes. As shown in Figure 14.5.1, we denote the volume of the kth remaining subbox by ΔV_k and the point selected in the kth subbox by (x_k^*, y_k^*, z_k^*). Next we form the product

$$f(x_k^*, y_k^*, z_k^*)\Delta V_k$$

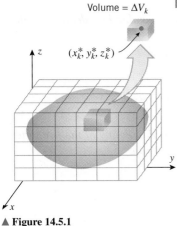

Volume $= \Delta V_k$

(x_k^*, y_k^*, z_k^*)

▲ **Figure 14.5.1**

for each subbox, then add the products for all of the subboxes to obtain the **Riemann sum**

$$\sum_{k=1}^{n} f(x_k^*, y_k^*, z_k^*) \Delta V_k$$

Finally, we repeat this process with more and more subdivisions in such a way that the length, width, and height of each subbox approach zero, and n approaches $+\infty$. The limit

$$\iiint_G f(x, y, z)\, dV = \lim_{n \to +\infty} \sum_{k=1}^{n} f(x_k^*, y_k^*, z_k^*) \Delta V_k \tag{1}$$

is called the **triple integral** of $f(x, y, z)$ over the region G. Conditions under which the triple integral exists are studied in advanced calculus. However, for our purposes it suffices to say that existence is ensured when f is continuous on G and the region G is not too "complicated."

■ PROPERTIES OF TRIPLE INTEGRALS

Triple integrals enjoy many properties of single and double integrals:

$$\iiint_G cf(x, y, z)\, dV = c \iiint_G f(x, y, z)\, dV \quad (c \text{ a constant})$$

$$\iiint_G [f(x, y, z) + g(x, y, z)]\, dV = \iiint_G f(x, y, z)\, dV + \iiint_G g(x, y, z)\, dV$$

$$\iiint_G [f(x, y, z) - g(x, y, z)]\, dV = \iiint_G f(x, y, z)\, dV - \iiint_G g(x, y, z)\, dV$$

Moreover, if the region G is subdivided into two subregions G_1 and G_2 (Figure 14.5.2), then

$$\iiint_G f(x, y, z)\, dV = \iiint_{G_1} f(x, y, z)\, dV + \iiint_{G_2} f(x, y, z)\, dV$$

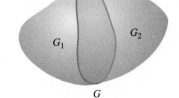

▲ **Figure 14.5.2**

We omit the proofs.

■ EVALUATING TRIPLE INTEGRALS OVER RECTANGULAR BOXES

Just as a double integral can be evaluated by two successive single integrations, so a triple integral can be evaluated by three successive integrations. The following theorem, which we state without proof, is the analog of Theorem 14.1.3.

There are two possible orders of integration for the iterated integrals in Theorem 14.1.3:

$$dx\, dy, \quad dy\, dx$$

Six orders of integration are possible for the iterated integral in Theorem 14.5.1:

$$dx\, dy\, dz, \quad dy\, dz\, dx, \quad dz\, dx\, dy$$
$$dx\, dz\, dy, \quad dz\, dy\, dx, \quad dy\, dx\, dz$$

14.5.1   THEOREM (Fubini's Theorem[*])   *Let G be the rectangular box defined by the inequalities*
$$a \le x \le b, \quad c \le y \le d, \quad k \le z \le l$$
If f is continuous on the region G, then

$$\iiint_G f(x, y, z)\, dV = \int_a^b \int_c^d \int_k^l f(x, y, z)\, dz\, dy\, dx \tag{2}$$

Moreover, the iterated integral on the right can be replaced with any of the five other iterated integrals that result by altering the order of integration.

---

[*]See the Fubini biography on p. 1005.

▶ **Example 1**   Evaluate the triple integral

$$\iiint\limits_{G} 12xy^2z^3 \, dV$$

over the rectangular box G defined by the inequalities $-1 \le x \le 2, 0 \le y \le 3, 0 \le z \le 2$.

Solution.   Of the six possible iterated integrals we might use, we will choose the one in (2). Thus, we will first integrate with respect to z, holding x and y fixed, then with respect to y, holding x fixed, and finally with respect to x.

$$\iiint\limits_{G} 12xy^2z^3 \, dV = \int_{-1}^{2} \int_{0}^{3} \int_{0}^{2} 12xy^2z^3 \, dz \, dy \, dx$$

$$= \int_{-1}^{2} \int_{0}^{3} \left[3xy^2z^4\right]_{z=0}^{2} dy \, dx = \int_{-1}^{2} \int_{0}^{3} 48xy^2 \, dy \, dx$$

$$= \int_{-1}^{2} \left[16xy^3\right]_{y=0}^{3} dx = \int_{-1}^{2} 432x \, dx$$

$$= 216x^2\Big]_{-1}^{2} = 648 \quad \blacktriangleleft$$

■ EVALUATING TRIPLE INTEGRALS OVER MORE GENERAL REGIONS

Next we will consider how triple integrals can be evaluated over solids that are not rectangular boxes. For the moment we will limit our discussion to solids of the type shown in Figure 14.5.3. Specifically, we will assume that the solid G is bounded above by a surface $z = g_2(x, y)$ and below by a surface $z = g_1(x, y)$ and that the projection of the solid on the xy-plane is a type I or type II region R (see Definition 14.2.1). In addition, we will assume that $g_1(x, y)$ and $g_2(x, y)$ are continuous on R and that $g_1(x, y) \le g_2(x, y)$ on R. Geometrically, this means that the surfaces may touch but cannot cross. We call a solid of this type a ***simple xy-solid***.

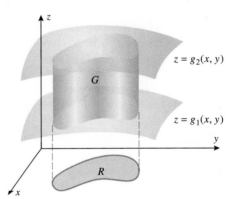

▶ **Figure 14.5.3**

The following theorem, which we state without proof, will enable us to evaluate triple integrals over simple xy-solids.

14.5.2   THEOREM   *Let G be a simple xy-solid with upper surface $z = g_2(x, y)$ and lower surface $z = g_1(x, y)$, and let R be the projection of G on the xy-plane. If $f(x, y, z)$ is continuous on G, then*

$$\iiint\limits_{G} f(x, y, z) \, dV = \iint\limits_{R} \left[\int_{g_1(x,y)}^{g_2(x,y)} f(x, y, z) \, dz \right] dA \qquad (3)$$

In (3), the first integration is with respect to z, after which a function of x and y remains. This function of x and y is then integrated over the region R in the xy-plane. To apply (3), it is helpful to begin with a three-dimensional sketch of the solid G. The limits of integration can be obtained from the sketch as follows:

Determining Limits of Integration: Simple xy-Solid

Step 1. Find an equation $z = g_2(x, y)$ for the upper surface and an equation $z = g_1(x, y)$ for the lower surface of G. The functions $g_1(x, y)$ and $g_2(x, y)$ determine the lower and upper z-limits of integration.

Step 2. Make a two-dimensional sketch of the projection R of the solid on the xy-plane. From this sketch determine the limits of integration for the double integral over R in (3).

▶ **Example 2**   Let G be the wedge in the first octant that is cut from the cylindrical solid $y^2 + z^2 \leq 1$ by the planes $y = x$ and $x = 0$. Evaluate

$$\iiint\limits_G z\, dV$$

Solution.   The solid G and its projection R on the xy-plane are shown in Figure 14.5.4. The upper surface of the solid is formed by the cylinder and the lower surface by the xy-plane. Since the portion of the cylinder $y^2 + z^2 = 1$ that lies above the xy-plane has the equation $z = \sqrt{1 - y^2}$, and the xy-plane has the equation $z = 0$, it follows from (3) that

$$\iiint\limits_G z\, dV = \iint\limits_R \left[\int_0^{\sqrt{1-y^2}} z\, dz \right] dA \qquad (4)$$

For the double integral over R, the x- and y-integrations can be performed in either order, since R is both a type I and type II region. We will integrate with respect to x first. With this choice, (4) yields

$$\iiint\limits_G z\, dV = \int_0^1 \int_0^y \int_0^{\sqrt{1-y^2}} z\, dz\, dx\, dy = \int_0^1 \int_0^y \frac{1}{2} z^2 \bigg]_{z=0}^{\sqrt{1-y^2}} dx\, dy$$

$$= \int_0^1 \int_0^y \frac{1}{2}(1 - y^2)\, dx\, dy = \frac{1}{2} \int_0^1 (1 - y^2)x \bigg]_{x=0}^{y} dy$$

$$= \frac{1}{2} \int_0^1 (y - y^3)\, dy = \frac{1}{2} \left[\frac{1}{2}y^2 - \frac{1}{4}y^4 \right]_0^1 = \frac{1}{8} \blacktriangleleft$$

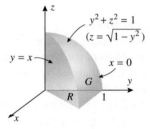

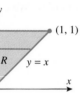

▲ **Figure 14.5.4**

TECHNOLOGY MASTERY

Most computer algebra systems have a built-in capability for computing iterated triple integrals. If you have a CAS, consult the relevant documentation and use the CAS to check Examples 1 and 2.

■ **VOLUME CALCULATED AS A TRIPLE INTEGRAL**

Triple integrals have many physical interpretations, some of which we will consider in Section 14.8. However, in the special case where $f(x, y, z) = 1$, Formula (1) yields

$$\iiint\limits_G dV = \lim_{n \to +\infty} \sum_{k=1}^n \Delta V_k$$

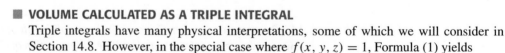

which Figure 14.5.1 suggests is the volume of G; that is,

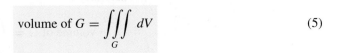

$$\text{volume of } G = \iiint\limits_{G} dV \tag{5}$$

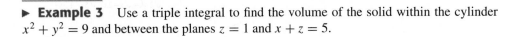

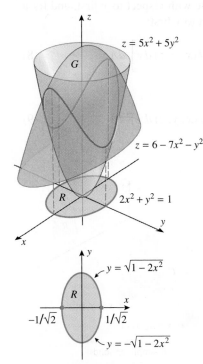

$x + z = 5$

$x^2 + y^2 = 9$

$z = 1$

R

$x^2 + y^2 = 9$

$y = \sqrt{9 - x^2}$

R

-3 3

$y = -\sqrt{9 - x^2}$

▲ Figure 14.5.5

▶ **Example 3**   Use a triple integral to find the volume of the solid within the cylinder $x^2 + y^2 = 9$ and between the planes $z = 1$ and $x + z = 5$.

Solution.   The solid G and its projection R on the xy-plane are shown in Figure 14.5.5. The lower surface of the solid is the plane $z = 1$ and the upper surface is the plane $x + z = 5$ or, equivalently, $z = 5 - x$. Thus, from (3) and (5)

$$\text{volume of } G = \iiint\limits_{G} dV = \iint\limits_{R} \left[\int_{1}^{5-x} dz \right] dA \tag{6}$$

For the double integral over R, we will integrate with respect to y first. Thus, (6) yields

$$\text{volume of } G = \int_{-3}^{3} \int_{-\sqrt{9-x^2}}^{\sqrt{9-x^2}} \int_{1}^{5-x} dz\, dy\, dx = \int_{-3}^{3} \int_{-\sqrt{9-x^2}}^{\sqrt{9-x^2}} z \Big]_{z=1}^{5-x} dy\, dx$$

$$= \int_{-3}^{3} \int_{-\sqrt{9-x^2}}^{\sqrt{9-x^2}} (4 - x)\, dy\, dx = \int_{-3}^{3} (8 - 2x)\sqrt{9 - x^2}\, dx$$

$$= 8 \int_{-3}^{3} \sqrt{9 - x^2}\, dx - \int_{-3}^{3} 2x\sqrt{9 - x^2}\, dx \qquad \boxed{\text{For the first integral, see Formula (3) of Section 7.4.}}$$

$$= 8 \left(\frac{9}{2}\pi \right) - \int_{-3}^{3} 2x\sqrt{9 - x^2}\, dx \qquad \boxed{\text{The second integral is 0 because the integrand is an odd function.}}$$

$$= 8 \left(\frac{9}{2}\pi \right) - 0 = 36\pi \quad ◀$$

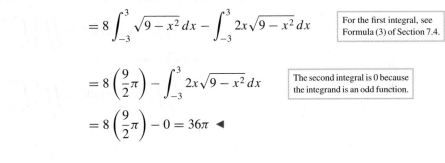

$z = 5x^2 + 5y^2$

G

$z = 6 - 7x^2 - y^2$

R $2x^2 + y^2 = 1$

$y = \sqrt{1 - 2x^2}$

R

$-1/\sqrt{2}$ $1/\sqrt{2}$

$y = -\sqrt{1 - 2x^2}$

▲ Figure 14.5.6

▶ **Example 4**   Find the volume of the solid enclosed between the paraboloids

$$z = 5x^2 + 5y^2 \quad \text{and} \quad z = 6 - 7x^2 - y^2$$

Solution.   The solid G and its projection R on the xy-plane are shown in Figure 14.5.6. The projection R is obtained by solving the given equations simultaneously to determine where the paraboloids intersect. We obtain

$$5x^2 + 5y^2 = 6 - 7x^2 - y^2$$

or

$$2x^2 + y^2 = 1 \tag{7}$$

which tells us that the paraboloids intersect in a curve on the elliptic cylinder given by (7).

The projection of this intersection on the xy-plane is an ellipse with this same equation. Therefore,

$$
\begin{aligned}
\text{volume of } G &= \iiint\limits_{G} dV = \iint\limits_{R} \left[\int_{5x^2+5y^2}^{6-7x^2-y^2} dz \right] dA \\
&= \int_{-1/\sqrt{2}}^{1/\sqrt{2}} \int_{-\sqrt{1-2x^2}}^{\sqrt{1-2x^2}} \int_{5x^2+5y^2}^{6-7x^2-y^2} dz \, dy \, dx \\
&= \int_{-1/\sqrt{2}}^{1/\sqrt{2}} \int_{-\sqrt{1-2x^2}}^{\sqrt{1-2x^2}} (6 - 12x^2 - 6y^2) \, dy \, dx \\
&= \int_{-1/\sqrt{2}}^{1/\sqrt{2}} \left[6(1 - 2x^2)y - 2y^3 \right]_{y=-\sqrt{1-2x^2}}^{\sqrt{1-2x^2}} dx \\
&= 8 \int_{-1/\sqrt{2}}^{1/\sqrt{2}} (1 - 2x^2)^{3/2} \, dx = \frac{8}{\sqrt{2}} \int_{-\pi/2}^{\pi/2} \cos^4 \theta \, d\theta = \frac{3\pi}{\sqrt{2}} \;\blacktriangleleft
\end{aligned}
$$

| Let $x = \dfrac{1}{\sqrt{2}} \sin\theta$. | Use the Wallis cosine formula in Exercise 70 of Section 7.3. |

■ INTEGRATION IN OTHER ORDERS

In Formula (3) for integrating over a simple xy-solid, the z-integration was performed first. However, there are situations in which it is preferable to integrate in a different order. For example, Figure 14.5.7a shows a **simple xz-solid**, and Figure 14.5.7b shows a **simple yz-solid**. For a simple xz-solid it is usually best to integrate with respect to y first, and for a simple yz-solid it is usually best to integrate with respect to x first:

$$
\iiint\limits_{\substack{G \\ \text{simple } xz\text{-solid}}} f(x, y, z) \, dV = \iint\limits_{R} \left[\int_{g_1(x,z)}^{g_2(x,z)} f(x, y, z) \, dy \right] dA \tag{8}
$$

$$
\iiint\limits_{\substack{G \\ \text{simple } yz\text{-solid}}} f(x, y, z) \, dV = \iint\limits_{R} \left[\int_{g_1(y,z)}^{g_2(y,z)} f(x, y, z) \, dx \right] dA \tag{9}
$$

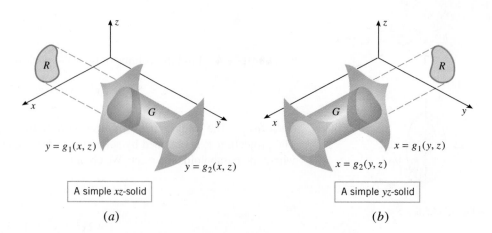

$y = g_1(x, z)$

$y = g_2(x, z)$

A simple xz-solid

$x = g_1(y, z)$

$x = g_2(y, z)$

A simple yz-solid

▶ **Figure 14.5.7** (a) (b)

Sometimes a solid G can be viewed as a simple xy-solid, a simple xz-solid, and a simple yz-solid, in which case the order of integration can be chosen to simplify the computations.

▶ **Example 5**   In Example 2 we evaluated

$$\iiint_G z \, dV$$

over the wedge in Figure 14.5.4 by integrating first with respect to z. Evaluate this integral by integrating first with respect to x.

Solution.   The solid is bounded in the back by the plane $x = 0$ and in the front by the plane $x = y$, so

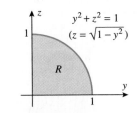

▲ **Figure 14.5.8**

$$\iiint_G z \, dV = \iint_R \left[\int_0^y z \, dx \right] dA$$

where R is the projection of G on the yz-plane (Figure 14.5.8). The integration over R can be performed first with respect to z and then y or vice versa. Performing the z-integration first yields

$$\iiint_G z \, dV = \int_0^1 \int_0^{\sqrt{1-y^2}} \int_0^y z \, dx \, dz \, dy = \int_0^1 \int_0^{\sqrt{1-y^2}} zx \Big]_{x=0}^y dz \, dy$$

$$= \int_0^1 \int_0^{\sqrt{1-y^2}} zy \, dz \, dy = \int_0^1 \frac{1}{2} z^2 y \Big]_{z=0}^{\sqrt{1-y^2}} dy = \int_0^1 \frac{1}{2}(1 - y^2)y \, dy = \frac{1}{8}$$

which agrees with the result in Example 2.   ◀

✔ **QUICK CHECK EXERCISES 14.5**   (See page 1048 for answers.)

1. The iterated integral

$$\int_1^5 \int_2^4 \int_3^6 f(x, y, z) \, dx \, dz \, dy$$

integrates f over the rectangular box defined by

_____ $\leq x \leq$ _____,   _____ $\leq y \leq$ _____,
_____ $\leq z \leq$ _____

2. Let G be the solid in the first octant bounded below by the surface $z = y + x^2$ and bounded above by the plane $z = 4$. Supply the missing limits of integration.

(a) $\displaystyle\iiint_G f(x, y, z) \, dA = \int_\Box^\Box \int_\Box^\Box \int_{y+x^2}^4 f(x, y, z) \, dz \, dx \, dy$

(b) $\displaystyle\iiint_G f(x, y, z) \, dA = \int_\Box^\Box \int_\Box^\Box \int_{y+x^2}^4 f(x, y, z) \, dz \, dy \, dx$

(c) $\displaystyle\iiint_G f(x, y, z) \, dA = \int_\Box^\Box \int_\Box^\Box \int_\Box^\Box f(x, y, z) \, dy \, dz \, dx$

3. The volume of the solid G in Quick Check Exercise 2 is _____.

EXERCISE SET 14.5   [C] CAS

1–8 Evaluate the iterated integral. ▪

1. $\displaystyle\int_{-1}^1 \int_0^2 \int_0^1 (x^2 + y^2 + z^2) \, dx \, dy \, dz$

2. $\displaystyle\int_{1/3}^{1/2} \int_0^\pi \int_0^1 zx \sin xy \, dz \, dy \, dx$

3. $\displaystyle\int_0^2 \int_{-1}^{y^2} \int_{-1}^z yz \, dx \, dz \, dy$

4. $\displaystyle\int_0^{\pi/4} \int_0^1 \int_0^{x^2} x \cos y \, dz \, dx \, dy$

5. $\displaystyle\int_0^3 \int_0^{\sqrt{9-z^2}} \int_0^x xy \, dy \, dx \, dz$

6. $\displaystyle\int_1^3 \int_x^{x^2} \int_0^{\ln z} xe^y \, dy \, dz \, dx$

7. $\displaystyle\int_0^2 \int_0^{\sqrt{4-x^2}} \int_{-5+x^2+y^2}^{3-x^2-y^2} x \, dz \, dy \, dx$

8. $\displaystyle\int_1^2 \int_z^2 \int_0^{\sqrt{3}y} \frac{y}{x^2 + y^2} \, dx \, dy \, dz$

9–12 Evaluate the triple integral. ■

9. $\iiint\limits_{G} xy \sin yz \, dV$, where G is the rectangular box defined by the inequalities $0 \le x \le \pi, 0 \le y \le 1, 0 \le z \le \pi/6$.

10. $\iiint\limits_{G} y \, dV$, where G is the solid enclosed by the plane $z = y$, the xy-plane, and the parabolic cylinder $y = 1 - x^2$.

11. $\iiint\limits_{G} xyz \, dV$, where G is the solid in the first octant that is bounded by the parabolic cylinder $z = 2 - x^2$ and the planes $z = 0$, $y = x$, and $y = 0$.

12. $\iiint\limits_{G} \cos(z/y) \, dV$, where G is the solid defined by the inequalities $\pi/6 \le y \le \pi/2, y \le x \le \pi/2, 0 \le z \le xy$.

c **13.** Use the numerical triple integral operation of a CAS to approximate
$$\iiint\limits_{G} \frac{\sqrt{x + z^2}}{y} \, dV$$
where G is the rectangular box defined by the inequalities $0 \le x \le 3, 1 \le y \le 2, -2 \le z \le 1$.

c **14.** Use the numerical triple integral operation of a CAS to approximate
$$\iiint\limits_{G} e^{-x^2 - y^2 - z^2} \, dV$$
where G is the spherical region $x^2 + y^2 + z^2 \le 1$.

15–18 Use a triple integral to find the volume of the solid. ■

15. The solid in the first octant bounded by the coordinate planes and the plane $3x + 6y + 4z = 12$.

16. The solid bounded by the surface $z = \sqrt{y}$ and the planes $x + y = 1$, $x = 0$, and $z = 0$.

17. The solid bounded by the surface $y = x^2$ and the planes $y + z = 4$ and $z = 0$.

18. The wedge in the first octant that is cut from the solid cylinder $y^2 + z^2 \le 1$ by the planes $y = x$ and $x = 0$.

FOCUS ON CONCEPTS

19. Let G be the solid enclosed by the surfaces in the accompanying figure. Fill in the missing limits of integration.

(a) $\iiint\limits_{G} f(x, y, z) \, dV$
$$= \int_{\square}^{\square} \int_{\square}^{\square} \int_{\square}^{\square} f(x, y, z) \, dz \, dy \, dx$$

(b) $\iiint\limits_{G} f(x, y, z) \, dV$
$$= \int_{\square}^{\square} \int_{\square}^{\square} \int_{\square}^{\square} f(x, y, z) \, dz \, dx \, dy$$

20. Let G be the solid enclosed by the surfaces in the accompanying figure. Fill in the missing limits of integration.

(a) $\iiint\limits_{G} f(x, y, z) \, dV$
$$= \int_{\square}^{\square} \int_{\square}^{\square} \int_{\square}^{\square} f(x, y, z) \, dz \, dy \, dx$$

(b) $\iiint\limits_{G} f(x, y, z) \, dV$
$$= \int_{\square}^{\square} \int_{\square}^{\square} \int_{\square}^{\square} f(x, y, z) \, dz \, dx \, dy$$

$z = 4x^2 + y^2$
$z = 4 - 3y^2$

▲ **Figure Ex-19**

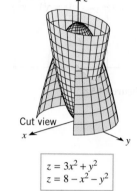

Cut view

$z = 3x^2 + y^2$
$z = 8 - x^2 - y^2$

▲ **Figure Ex-20**

21–24 Set up (but do not evaluate) an iterated triple integral for the volume of the solid enclosed between the given surfaces. ■

21. The surfaces in Exercise 19.

22. The surfaces in Exercise 20.

23. The elliptic cylinder $x^2 + 9y^2 = 9$ and the planes $z = 0$ and $z = x + 3$.

24. The cylinders $x^2 + y^2 = 1$ and $x^2 + z^2 = 1$.

25–26 In each part, sketch the solid whose volume is given by the integral. ■

25. (a) $\int_{-1}^{1} \int_{-\sqrt{1-x^2}}^{\sqrt{1-x^2}} \int_{0}^{y+1} dz \, dy \, dx$

(b) $\int_{0}^{9} \int_{0}^{y/3} \int_{0}^{\sqrt{y^2 - 9x^2}} dz \, dx \, dy$

(c) $\int_{0}^{1} \int_{0}^{\sqrt{1-x^2}} \int_{0}^{2} dy \, dz \, dx$

26. (a) $\int_{0}^{3} \int_{x^2}^{9} \int_{0}^{2} dz \, dy \, dx$

(b) $\int_{0}^{2} \int_{0}^{2-y} \int_{0}^{2-x-y} dz \, dx \, dy$

(c) $\int_{-2}^{2} \int_{0}^{4-y^2} \int_{0}^{2} dx \, dz \, dy$

27–30 True–False Determine whether the statement is true or false. Explain your answer. ■

27. If G is the rectangular solid that is defined by $1 \le x \le 3$, $2 \le y \le 5$, $-1 \le z \le 1$, and if $f(x, y, z)$ is continuous on G, then

$$\iiint\limits_G f(x, y, z)\,dV = \int_1^3 \int_{-1}^1 \int_2^5 f(x, y, z)\,dy\,dz\,dx$$

28. If G is a simple xy-solid and $f(x, y, z)$ is continuous on G, then the triple integral of f over G can be expressed as an iterated integral whose outermost integration is performed with respect to z.

29. If G is the portion of the unit ball in the first octant, then

$$\iiint\limits_G f(x, y, z)\,dV = \int_0^1 \int_0^1 \int_0^{\sqrt{1-x^2-y^2}} f(x, y, z)\,dz\,dy\,dx$$

30. If G is a simple xy-solid and

$$\text{volume of } G = \iiint\limits_G f(x, y, z)\,dV$$

then $f(x, y, z) = 1$ at every point in G.

31. Let G be the rectangular box defined by the inequalities $a \le x \le b$, $c \le y \le d$, $k \le z \le l$. Show that

$$\iiint\limits_G f(x)g(y)h(z)\,dV$$
$$= \left[\int_a^b f(x)\,dx \right]\left[\int_c^d g(y)\,dy \right]\left[\int_k^l h(z)\,dz \right]$$

32. Use the result of Exercise 31 to evaluate

(a) $\displaystyle\iiint\limits_G xy^2 \sin z\,dV$, where G is the set of points satisfying $-1 \le x \le 1$, $0 \le y \le 1$, $0 \le z \le \pi/2$;

(b) $\displaystyle\iiint\limits_G e^{2x+y-z}\,dV$, where G is the set of points satisfying $0 \le x \le 1$, $0 \le y \le \ln 3$, $0 \le z \le \ln 2$.

33–36 The *average value* or *mean value* of a continuous function $f(x, y, z)$ over a solid G is defined as

$$f_{\text{ave}} = \frac{1}{V(G)} \iiint\limits_G f(x, y, z)\,dV$$

where $V(G)$ is the volume of the solid G (compare to the definition preceding Exercise 61 of Section 14.2). Use this definition in these exercises. ■

33. Find the average value of $f(x, y, z) = x + y + z$ over the tetrahedron shown in the accompanying figure.

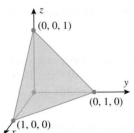

◀ **Figure Ex-33**

34. Find the average value of $f(x, y, z) = xyz$ over the spherical region $x^2 + y^2 + z^2 \le 1$.

C 35. Use the numerical triple integral operation of a CAS to approximate the average distance from the origin to a point in the solid of Example 4.

C 36. Let $d(x, y, z)$ be the distance from the point (z, z, z) to the point $(x, y, 0)$. Use the numerical triple integral operation of a CAS to approximate the average value of d for $0 \le x \le 1$, $0 \le y \le 1$, and $0 \le z \le 1$. Write a short explanation as to why this value may be considered to be the average distance between a point on the diagonal from $(0, 0, 0)$ to $(1, 1, 1)$ and a point on the face in the xy-plane for the unit cube $0 \le x \le 1$, $0 \le y \le 1$, and $0 \le z \le 1$.

37. Let G be the tetrahedron in the first octant bounded by the coordinate planes and the plane

$$\frac{x}{a} + \frac{y}{b} + \frac{z}{c} = 1 \quad (a > 0, b > 0, c > 0)$$

(a) List six different iterated integrals that represent the volume of G.

(b) Evaluate any one of the six to show that the volume of G is $\frac{1}{6}abc$.

38. Use a triple integral to derive the formula for the volume of the ellipsoid

$$\frac{x^2}{a^2} + \frac{y^2}{b^2} + \frac{z^2}{c^2} = 1$$

FOCUS ON CONCEPTS

39–40 Express each integral as an equivalent integral in which the z-integration is performed first, the y-integration second, and the x-integration last. ■

39. (a) $\displaystyle\int_0^5 \int_0^2 \int_0^{\sqrt{4-y^2}} f(x, y, z)\,dx\,dy\,dz$

(b) $\displaystyle\int_0^9 \int_0^{3-\sqrt{x}} \int_0^z f(x, y, z)\,dy\,dz\,dx$

(c) $\displaystyle\int_0^4 \int_y^{8-y} \int_0^{\sqrt{4-y}} f(x, y, z)\,dx\,dz\,dy$

40. (a) $\displaystyle\int_0^3 \int_0^{\sqrt{9-z^2}} \int_0^{\sqrt{9-y^2-z^2}} f(x, y, z)\,dx\,dy\,dz$

(b) $\displaystyle\int_0^4 \int_0^2 \int_0^{x/2} f(x, y, z)\,dy\,dz\,dx$

(c) $\displaystyle\int_0^4 \int_0^{4-y} \int_0^{\sqrt{z}} f(x, y, z)\,dx\,dz\,dy$

41. Writing The following initial steps can be used to express a triple integral over a solid G as an iterated triple integral: First project G onto one of the coordinate planes to obtain a region R, and then project R onto one of the coordinate axes. Describe how you would use these steps to find the limits of integration. Illustrate your discussion with an example.

1. $3 \le x \le 6,\ 1 \le y \le 5,\ 2 \le z \le 4$ **2.** (a) $\displaystyle\int_0^4 \int_0^{\sqrt{4-y}} \int_{y+x^2}^4 f(x, y, z)\, dz\, dx\, dy$ (b) $\displaystyle\int_0^2 \int_0^{4-x^2} \int_{y+x^2}^4 f(x, y, z)\, dz\, dy\, dx$

(c) $\displaystyle\int_0^2 \int_{x^2}^4 \int_0^{z-x^2} f(x, y, z)\, dy\, dz\, dx$ **3.** $\dfrac{128}{15}$

14.6 TRIPLE INTEGRALS IN CYLINDRICAL AND SPHERICAL COORDINATES

In Section 14.3 we saw that some double integrals are easier to evaluate in polar coordinates than in rectangular coordinates. Similarly, some triple integrals are easier to evaluate in cylindrical or spherical coordinates than in rectangular coordinates. In this section we will study triple integrals in these coordinate systems.

■ **TRIPLE INTEGRALS IN CYLINDRICAL COORDINATES**
Recall that in rectangular coordinates the triple integral of a continuous function f over a solid region G is defined as

$$\iiint_G f(x, y, z)\, dV = \lim_{n \to +\infty} \sum_{k=1}^n f(x_k^*, y_k^*, z_k^*)\Delta V_k$$

where ΔV_k denotes the volume of a rectangular parallelepiped interior to G and (x_k^*, y_k^*, z_k^*) is a point in this parallelepiped (see Figure 14.5.1). Triple integrals in cylindrical and spherical coordinates are defined similarly, except that the region G is divided not into rectangular parallelepipeds but into regions more appropriate to these coordinate systems.

In cylindrical coordinates, the simplest equations are of the form

$$r = \text{constant}, \quad \theta = \text{constant}, \quad z = \text{constant}$$

The first equation represents a right circular cylinder centered on the z-axis, the second a vertical half-plane hinged on the z-axis, and the third a horizontal plane. (See Figure 11.8.3.) These surfaces can be paired up to determine solids called *cylindrical wedges* or *cylindrical elements of volume*. To be precise, a cylindrical wedge is a solid enclosed between six surfaces of the following form:

two cylinders (blue)	$r = r_1, \quad r = r_2$	$(r_1 < r_2)$
two vertical half-planes (yellow)	$\theta = \theta_1, \quad \theta = \theta_2$	$(\theta_1 < \theta_2)$
two horizontal planes (gray)	$z = z_1, \quad z = z_2$	$(z_1 < z_2)$

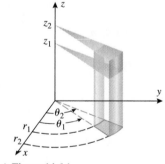

▲ **Figure 14.6.1**

(Figure 14.6.1). The dimensions $\theta_2 - \theta_1$, $r_2 - r_1$, and $z_2 - z_1$ are called the *central angle*, *thickness*, and *height* of the wedge.

To define the triple integral over G of a function $f(r, \theta, z)$ in cylindrical coordinates we proceed as follows:

- Subdivide G into pieces by a three-dimensional grid consisting of concentric circular cylinders centered on the z-axis, half-planes hinged on the z-axis, and horizontal planes. Exclude from consideration all pieces that contain any points outside of G, thereby leaving only cylindrical wedges that are subsets of G.

- Assume that there are n such cylindrical wedges, and denote the volume of the kth cylindrical wedge by ΔV_k. As indicated in Figure 14.6.2, let $(r_k^*, \theta_k^*, z_k^*)$ be any point in the kth cylindrical wedge.

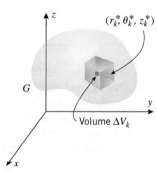

▲ **Figure 14.6.2**

- Repeat this process with more and more subdivisions so that as n increases, the height, thickness, and central angle of the cylindrical wedges approach zero. Define

$$\iiint\limits_{G} f(r, \theta, z)\, dV = \lim_{n \to +\infty} \sum_{k=1}^{n} f(r_k^*, \theta_k^*, z_k^*)\Delta V_k \qquad (1)$$

For computational purposes, it will be helpful to express (1) as an iterated integral. Toward this end we note that the volume ΔV_k of the kth cylindrical wedge can be expressed as

$$\Delta V_k = [\text{area of base}] \cdot [\text{height}] \qquad (2)$$

If we denote the thickness, central angle, and height of this wedge by Δr_k, $\Delta \theta_k$, and Δz_k, and if we choose the arbitrary point $(r_k^*, \theta_k^*, z_k^*)$ to lie above the "center" of the base (Figures 14.3.6 and 14.6.3), then it follows from (5) of Section 14.3 that the base has area $\Delta A_k = r_k^* \Delta r_k \Delta \theta_k$. Thus, (2) can be written as

$$\Delta V_k = r_k^* \Delta r_k \Delta \theta_k \Delta z_k = r_k^* \Delta z_k \Delta r_k \Delta \theta_k$$

Substituting this expression in (1) yields

$$\iiint\limits_{G} f(r, \theta, z)\, dV = \lim_{n \to +\infty} \sum_{k=1}^{n} f(r_k^*, \theta_k^*, z_k^*) r_k^* \Delta z_k \Delta r_k \Delta \theta_k$$

which suggests that a triple integral in cylindrical coordinates can be evaluated as an iterated integral of the form

$$\iiint\limits_{G} f(r, \theta, z)\, dV = \iiint\limits_{\substack{\text{appropriate} \\ \text{limits}}} f(r, \theta, z)\, r\, dz\, dr\, d\theta \qquad (3)$$

In this formula the integration with respect to z is done first, then with respect to r, and then with respect to θ, but any order of integration is allowable.

The following theorem, which we state without proof, makes the preceding ideas more precise.

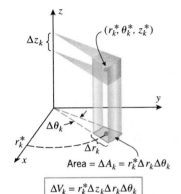

▲ Figure 14.6.3

Note the extra factor of r that appears in the integrand on converting a triple integral to an iterated integral in cylindrical coordinates.

14.6.1 THEOREM *Let G be a solid region whose upper surface has the equation $z = g_2(r, \theta)$ and whose lower surface has the equation $z = g_1(r, \theta)$ in cylindrical coordinates. If the projection of the solid on the xy-plane is a simple polar region R, and if $f(r, \theta, z)$ is continuous on G, then*

$$\iiint\limits_{G} f(r, \theta, z)\, dV = \iint\limits_{R} \left[\int_{g_1(r,\theta)}^{g_2(r,\theta)} f(r, \theta, z)\, dz \right] dA \qquad (4)$$

where the double integral over R is evaluated in polar coordinates. In particular, if the projection R is as shown in Figure 14.6.4, then (4) can be written as

$$\iiint\limits_{G} f(r, \theta, z)\, dV = \int_{\theta_1}^{\theta_2} \int_{r_1(\theta)}^{r_2(\theta)} \int_{g_1(r,\theta)}^{g_2(r,\theta)} f(r, \theta, z)\, r\, dz\, dr\, d\theta \qquad (5)$$

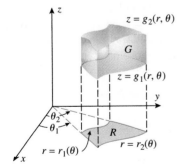

▲ Figure 14.6.4

The type of solid to which Formula (5) applies is illustrated in Figure 14.6.4. To apply (4) and (5) it is best to begin with a three-dimensional sketch of the solid G, from which the limits of integration can be obtained as follows:

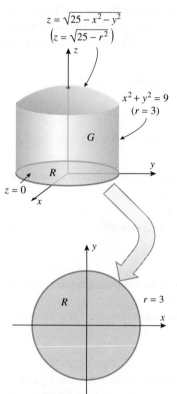

▲ Figure 14.6.5

Determining Limits of Integration: Cylindrical Coordinates

Step 1. Identify the upper surface $z = g_2(r, \theta)$ and the lower surface $z = g_1(r, \theta)$ of the solid. The functions $g_1(r, \theta)$ and $g_2(r, \theta)$ determine the z-limits of integration. (If the upper and lower surfaces are given in rectangular coordinates, convert them to cylindrical coordinates.)

Step 2. Make a two-dimensional sketch of the projection R of the solid on the xy-plane. From this sketch the r- and θ-limits of integration may be obtained exactly as with double integrals in polar coordinates.

▶ **Example 1** Use triple integration in cylindrical coordinates to find the volume of the solid G that is bounded above by the hemisphere $z = \sqrt{25 - x^2 - y^2}$, below by the xy-plane, and laterally by the cylinder $x^2 + y^2 = 9$.

Solution. The solid G and its projection R on the xy-plane are shown in Figure 14.6.5. In cylindrical coordinates, the upper surface of G is the hemisphere $z = \sqrt{25 - r^2}$ and the lower surface is the plane $z = 0$. Thus, from (4), the volume of G is

$$V = \iiint\limits_{G} dV = \iint\limits_{R} \left[\int_0^{\sqrt{25-r^2}} dz \right] dA$$

For the double integral over R, we use polar coordinates:

$$V = \int_0^{2\pi} \int_0^3 \int_0^{\sqrt{25-r^2}} r \, dz \, dr \, d\theta = \int_0^{2\pi} \int_0^3 \left[rz \right]_{z=0}^{\sqrt{25-r^2}} dr \, d\theta$$

$$= \int_0^{2\pi} \int_0^3 r\sqrt{25 - r^2} \, dr \, d\theta = \int_0^{2\pi} \left[-\frac{1}{3}(25 - r^2)^{3/2} \right]_{r=0}^3 d\theta$$

$$= \int_0^{2\pi} \frac{61}{3} \, d\theta = \frac{122}{3}\pi \blacktriangleleft$$

$$\boxed{\begin{aligned} u &= 25 - r^2 \\ du &= -2r \, dr \end{aligned}}$$

■ CONVERTING TRIPLE INTEGRALS FROM RECTANGULAR TO CYLINDRICAL COORDINATES

Sometimes a triple integral that is difficult to integrate in rectangular coordinates can be evaluated more easily by making the substitution $x = r\cos\theta$, $y = r\sin\theta$, $z = z$ to convert it to an integral in cylindrical coordinates. Under such a substitution, a rectangular triple integral can be expressed as an iterated integral in cylindrical coordinates as

The order of integration on the right side of (6) can be changed, provided the limits of integration are adjusted accordingly.

$$\iiint\limits_{G} f(x, y, z) \, dV = \iiint\limits_{\substack{\text{appropriate} \\ \text{limits}}} f(r\cos\theta, r\sin\theta, z) r \, dz \, dr \, d\theta \tag{6}$$

▶ **Example 2** Use cylindrical coordinates to evaluate

$$\int_{-3}^3 \int_{-\sqrt{9-x^2}}^{\sqrt{9-x^2}} \int_0^{9-x^2-y^2} x^2 \, dz \, dy \, dx$$

Solution.   In problems of this type, it is helpful to sketch the region of integration G and its projection R on the xy-plane. From the z-limits of integration, the upper surface of G is the paraboloid $z = 9 - x^2 - y^2$ and the lower surface is the xy-plane $z = 0$. From the x- and y-limits of integration, the projection R is the region in the xy-plane enclosed by the circle $x^2 + y^2 = 9$ (Figure 14.6.6). Thus,

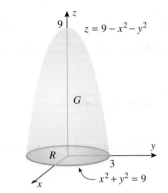

▲ Figure 14.6.6

$$\int_{-3}^{3} \int_{-\sqrt{9-x^2}}^{\sqrt{9-x^2}} \int_{0}^{9-x^2-y^2} x^2 \, dz \, dy \, dx = \iiint_G x^2 \, dV$$

$$= \iint_R \left[\int_{0}^{9-r^2} r^2 \cos^2 \theta \, dz \right] dA = \int_{0}^{2\pi} \int_{0}^{3} \int_{0}^{9-r^2} (r^2 \cos^2 \theta) r \, dz \, dr \, d\theta$$

$$= \int_{0}^{2\pi} \int_{0}^{3} \int_{0}^{9-r^2} r^3 \cos^2 \theta \, dz \, dr \, d\theta = \int_{0}^{2\pi} \int_{0}^{3} \left[zr^3 \cos^2 \theta \right]_{z=0}^{9-r^2} dr \, d\theta$$

$$= \int_{0}^{2\pi} \int_{0}^{3} (9r^3 - r^5) \cos^2 \theta \, dr \, d\theta = \int_{0}^{2\pi} \left[\left(\frac{9r^4}{4} - \frac{r^6}{6} \right) \cos^2 \theta \right]_{r=0}^{3} d\theta$$

$$= \frac{243}{4} \int_{0}^{2\pi} \cos^2 \theta \, d\theta = \frac{243}{4} \int_{0}^{2\pi} \frac{1}{2} (1 + \cos 2\theta) \, d\theta = \frac{243\pi}{4} \quad \blacktriangleleft$$

■ TRIPLE INTEGRALS IN SPHERICAL COORDINATES

In spherical coordinates, the simplest equations are of the form

$$\rho = \text{constant}, \quad \theta = \text{constant}, \quad \phi = \text{constant}$$

As indicated in Figure 11.8.4, the first equation represents a sphere centered at the origin and the second a half-plane hinged on the z-axis. The graph of the third equation is a right circular cone nappe with its vertex at the origin and its line of symmetry along the z-axis for $\phi \neq \pi/2$, and is the xy-plane if $\phi = \pi/2$. By a *spherical wedge* or *spherical element of volume* we mean a solid enclosed between six surfaces of the following form:

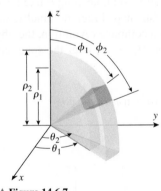

▲ Figure 14.6.7

two spheres (green)	$\rho = \rho_1, \quad \rho = \rho_2 \quad (\rho_1 < \rho_2)$
two vertical half-planes (yellow)	$\theta = \theta_1, \quad \theta = \theta_2 \quad (\theta_1 < \theta_2)$
nappes of two circular cones (pink)	$\phi = \phi_1, \quad \phi = \phi_2 \quad (\phi_1 < \phi_2)$

(Figure 14.6.7). We will refer to the numbers $\rho_2 - \rho_1$, $\theta_2 - \theta_1$, and $\phi_2 - \phi_1$ as the *dimensions* of a spherical wedge.

If G is a solid region in three-dimensional space, then the triple integral over G of a continuous function $f(\rho, \theta, \phi)$ in spherical coordinates is similar in definition to the triple integral in cylindrical coordinates, except that the solid G is partitioned into *spherical wedges* by a three-dimensional grid consisting of spheres centered at the origin, half-planes hinged on the z-axis, and nappes of right circular cones with vertices at the origin and lines of symmetry along the z-axis (Figure 14.6.8).

The defining equation of a triple integral in spherical coordinates is

$$\iiint_G f(\rho, \theta, \phi) \, dV = \lim_{n \to +\infty} \sum_{k=1}^{n} f(\rho_k^*, \theta_k^*, \phi_k^*) \Delta V_k \tag{7}$$

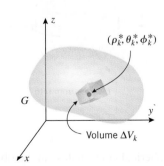

▲ Figure 14.6.8

where ΔV_k is the volume of the kth spherical wedge that is interior to G, $(\rho_k^*, \theta_k^*, \phi_k^*)$ is an arbitrary point in this wedge, and n increases in such a way that the dimensions of each interior spherical wedge tend to zero.

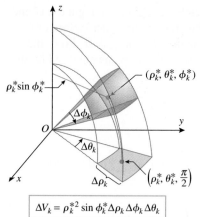

$$\Delta V_k = \rho_k^{*2} \sin \phi_k^* \Delta \rho_k \Delta \phi_k \Delta \theta_k$$

▲ **Figure 14.6.9**

Note the extra factor of $\rho^2 \sin \phi$ that appears in the integrand on converting a triple integral to an iterated integral in spherical coordinates. This is analogous to the extra factor of r that appears in an iterated integral in cylindrical coordinates.

For computational purposes, it will be desirable to express (7) as an iterated integral. In Exercise 30 we will help you to show that if the point $(\rho_k^*, \theta_k^*, \phi_k^*)$ is suitably chosen, then the volume ΔV_k in (7) can be written as

$$\Delta V_k = \rho_k^{*2} \sin \phi_k^* \Delta \rho_k \Delta \phi_k \Delta \theta_k \tag{8}$$

where $\Delta \rho_k$, $\Delta \phi_k$, and $\Delta \theta_k$ are the dimensions of the wedge (Figure 14.6.9). Substituting this in (7) we obtain

$$\iiint_G f(\rho, \theta, \phi) \, dV = \lim_{n \to +\infty} \sum_{k=1}^{n} f(\rho_k^*, \theta_k^*, \phi_k^*) \rho_k^{*2} \sin \phi_k^* \Delta \rho_k \Delta \phi_k \Delta \theta_k$$

which suggests that a triple integral in spherical coordinates can be evaluated as an iterated integral of the form

$$\iiint_G f(\rho, \theta, \phi) \, dV = \iiint_{\substack{\text{appropriate} \\ \text{limits}}} f(\rho, \theta, \phi) \rho^2 \sin \phi \, d\rho \, d\phi \, d\theta \tag{9}$$

The analog of Theorem 14.6.1 for triple integrals in spherical coordinates is tedious to state, so instead we will give some examples that illustrate techniques for obtaining the limits of integration. In all of our examples we will use the same order of integration—first with respect to ρ, then ϕ, and then θ. Once you have mastered the basic ideas, there should be no trouble using other orders of integration.

Suppose that we want to integrate $f(\rho, \theta, \phi)$ over the spherical solid G enclosed by the sphere $\rho = \rho_0$. The basic idea is to choose the limits of integration so that every point of the solid is accounted for in the integration process. Figure 14.6.10 illustrates one way of doing this. Holding θ and ϕ fixed for the first integration, we let ρ vary from 0 to ρ_0. This covers a radial line from the origin to the surface of the sphere. Next, keeping θ fixed, we let ϕ vary from 0 to π so that the radial line sweeps out a fan-shaped region. Finally, we let θ vary from 0 to 2π so that the fan-shaped region makes a complete revolution, thereby sweeping out the entire sphere. Thus, the triple integral of $f(\rho, \theta, \phi)$ over the spherical solid G can be evaluated by writing

$$\iiint_G f(\rho, \theta, \phi) \, dV = \int_0^{2\pi} \int_0^{\pi} \int_0^{\rho_0} f(\rho, \theta, \phi) \rho^2 \sin \phi \, d\rho \, d\phi \, d\theta$$

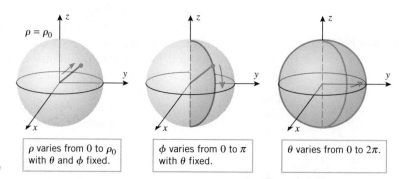

▶ **Figure 14.6.10**

Table 14.6.1 suggests how the limits of integration in spherical coordinates can be obtained for some other common solids.

Table 14.6.1

DETERMINATION OF LIMITS	INTEGRAL

This is the portion of the sphere of radius ρ_0 that lies in the first octant.

$$\int_0^{\pi/2} \int_0^{\pi/2} \int_0^{\rho_0} f(\rho, \theta, \phi)\rho^2 \sin\phi \, d\rho \, d\phi \, d\theta$$

ρ varies from 0 to ρ_0 with θ and ϕ held fixed.

ϕ varies from 0 to $\pi/2$ with θ held fixed.

θ varies from 0 to $\pi/2$.

This ice-cream-cone-shaped solid is cut from the sphere of radius ρ_0 by the cone $\phi = \phi_0$.

$$\int_0^{2\pi} \int_0^{\phi_0} \int_0^{\rho_0} f(\rho, \theta, \phi)\rho^2 \sin\phi \, d\rho \, d\phi \, d\theta$$

ρ varies from 0 to ρ_0 with θ and ϕ held fixed.

ϕ varies from 0 to ϕ_0 with θ held fixed.

θ varies from 0 to 2π.

This solid is cut from the sphere of radius ρ_0 by two cones, $\phi = \phi_1$ and $\phi = \phi_2$, where $\phi_1 < \phi_2$.

$$\int_0^{2\pi} \int_{\phi_1}^{\phi_2} \int_0^{\rho_0} f(\rho, \theta, \phi)\rho^2 \sin\phi \, d\rho \, d\phi \, d\theta$$

ρ varies from 0 to ρ_0 with θ and ϕ held fixed.

ϕ varies from ϕ_1 to ϕ_2 with θ held fixed.

θ varies from 0 to 2π.

Table 14.6.1 (*continued*)

DETERMINATION OF LIMITS	INTEGRAL

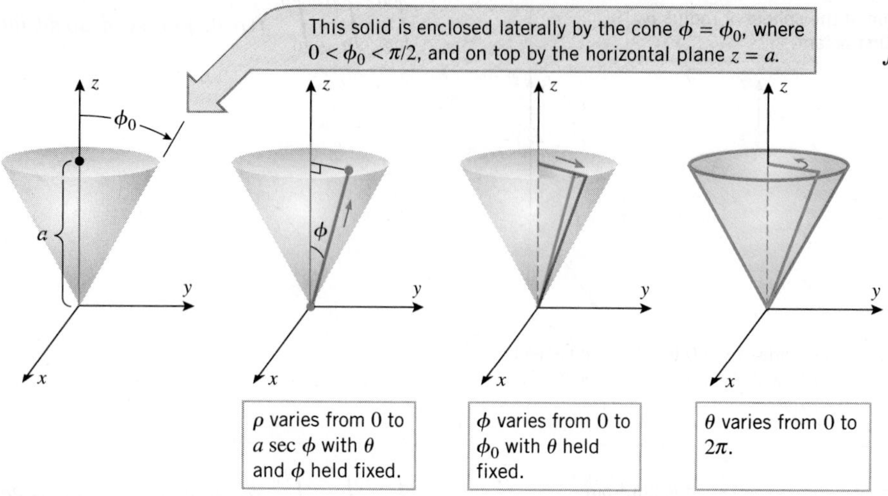

This solid is enclosed laterally by the cone $\phi = \phi_0$, where $0 < \phi_0 < \pi/2$, and on top by the horizontal plane $z = a$.

$$\int_0^{2\pi} \int_0^{\phi_0} \int_0^{a \sec \phi} f(\rho, \theta, \phi)\rho^2 \sin \phi \, d\rho \, d\phi \, d\theta$$

ρ varies from 0 to $a \sec \phi$ with θ and ϕ held fixed.

ϕ varies from 0 to ϕ_0 with θ held fixed.

θ varies from 0 to 2π.

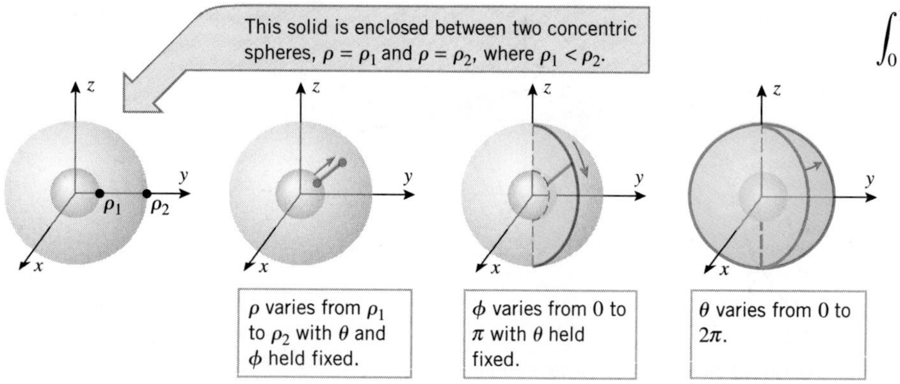

This solid is enclosed between two concentric spheres, $\rho = \rho_1$ and $\rho = \rho_2$, where $\rho_1 < \rho_2$.

$$\int_0^{2\pi} \int_0^{\pi} \int_{\rho_1}^{\rho_2} f(\rho, \theta, \phi)\rho^2 \sin \phi \, d\rho \, d\phi \, d\theta$$

ρ varies from ρ_1 to ρ_2 with θ and ϕ held fixed.

ϕ varies from 0 to π with θ held fixed.

θ varies from 0 to 2π.

▶ **Example 3** Use spherical coordinates to find the volume of the solid G bounded above by the sphere $x^2 + y^2 + z^2 = 16$ and below by the cone $z = \sqrt{x^2 + y^2}$.

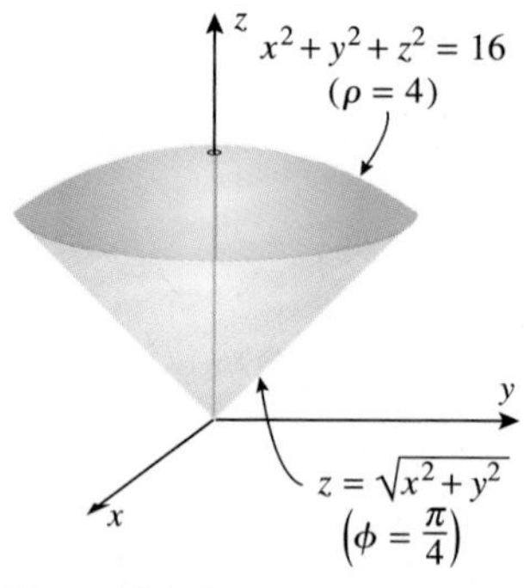

Solution. The solid G is sketched in Figure 14.6.11. In spherical coordinates, the equation of the sphere $x^2 + y^2 + z^2 = 16$ is $\rho = 4$ and the equation of the cone $z = \sqrt{x^2 + y^2}$ is

$$\rho \cos \phi = \sqrt{\rho^2 \sin^2 \phi \cos^2 \theta + \rho^2 \sin^2 \phi \sin^2 \theta}$$

which simplifies to

$$\rho \cos \phi = \rho \sin \phi$$

Dividing both sides of this equation by $\rho \cos \phi$ yields $\tan \phi = 1$, from which it follows that

$$\phi = \pi/4$$

$x^2 + y^2 + z^2 = 16$
$(\rho = 4)$

$z = \sqrt{x^2 + y^2}$
$\left(\phi = \frac{\pi}{4}\right)$

▲ Figure 14.6.11

Thus, it follows from the second entry in Table 14.6.1 that the volume of G is

$$V = \iiint\limits_{G} dV = \int_0^{2\pi} \int_0^{\pi/4} \int_0^4 \rho^2 \sin\phi \, d\rho \, d\phi \, d\theta$$

$$= \int_0^{2\pi} \int_0^{\pi/4} \left[\frac{\rho^3}{3} \sin\phi \right]_{\rho=0}^4 d\phi \, d\theta$$

$$= \int_0^{2\pi} \int_0^{\pi/4} \frac{64}{3} \sin\phi \, d\phi \, d\theta$$

$$= \frac{64}{3} \int_0^{2\pi} \left[-\cos\phi \right]_{\phi=0}^{\pi/4} d\theta = \frac{64}{3} \int_0^{2\pi} \left(1 - \frac{\sqrt{2}}{2} \right) d\theta$$

$$= \frac{64\pi}{3}(2 - \sqrt{2}) \approx 39.26 \blacktriangleleft$$

■ **CONVERTING TRIPLE INTEGRALS FROM RECTANGULAR TO SPHERICAL COORDINATES**

Referring to Table 11.8.1, triple integrals can be converted from rectangular coordinates to spherical coordinates by making the substitution $x = \rho \sin\phi \cos\theta$, $y = \rho \sin\phi \sin\theta$, $z = \rho \cos\phi$. The two integrals are related by the equation

$$\iiint\limits_{G} f(x, y, z) \, dV = \iiint\limits_{\substack{\text{appropriate} \\ \text{limits}}} f(\rho \sin\phi \cos\theta, \rho \sin\phi \sin\theta, \rho \cos\phi)\rho^2 \sin\phi \, d\rho \, d\phi \, d\theta \qquad (10)$$

▶ **Example 4** Use spherical coordinates to evaluate

$$\int_{-2}^2 \int_{-\sqrt{4-x^2}}^{\sqrt{4-x^2}} \int_0^{\sqrt{4-x^2-y^2}} z^2 \sqrt{x^2 + y^2 + z^2} \, dz \, dy \, dx$$

Solution. In problems like this, it is helpful to begin (when possible) with a sketch of the region G of integration. From the z-limits of integration, the upper surface of G is the hemisphere $z = \sqrt{4 - x^2 - y^2}$ and the lower surface is the xy-plane $z = 0$. From the x- and y-limits of integration, the projection of the solid G on the xy-plane is the region enclosed by the circle $x^2 + y^2 = 4$. From this information we obtain the sketch of G in Figure 14.6.12. Thus,

$$\int_{-2}^2 \int_{-\sqrt{4-x^2}}^{\sqrt{4-x^2}} \int_0^{\sqrt{4-x^2-y^2}} z^2 \sqrt{x^2 + y^2 + z^2} \, dz \, dy \, dx$$

$$= \iiint\limits_{G} z^2 \sqrt{x^2 + y^2 + z^2} \, dV$$

$$= \int_0^{2\pi} \int_0^{\pi/2} \int_0^2 \rho^5 \cos^2\phi \sin\phi \, d\rho \, d\phi \, d\theta$$

$$= \int_0^{2\pi} \int_0^{\pi/2} \frac{32}{3} \cos^2\phi \sin\phi \, d\phi \, d\theta$$

$$= \frac{32}{3} \int_0^{2\pi} \left[-\frac{1}{3} \cos^3\phi \right]_{\phi=0}^{\pi/2} d\theta = \frac{32}{9} \int_0^{2\pi} d\theta = \frac{64}{9}\pi \blacktriangleleft$$

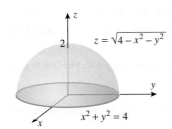

▲ **Figure 14.6.12**

✔ **QUICK CHECK EXERCISES 14.6**   *(See page 1058 for answers.)*

1. (a) The cylindrical wedge $1 \le r \le 3$, $\pi/6 \le \theta \le \pi/2$,
   $0 \le z \le 5$ has volume $V =$ _____.
   (b) The spherical wedge $1 \le \rho \le 3$, $\pi/6 \le \theta \le \pi/2$,
   $0 \le \phi \le \pi/3$ has volume $V =$ _____.

2. Let G be the solid region inside the sphere of radius 2 centered at the origin and above the plane $z = 1$. In each part, supply the missing integrand and limits of integration for the iterated integral in cylindrical coordinates.
   (a) The volume of G is

$$\iiint\limits_{G} dV = \int_{\square}^{\square} \int_{\square}^{\square} \int_{\square}^{\square} \underline{\qquad} \, dz \, dr \, d\theta$$

   (b) $\displaystyle \iiint\limits_{G} \frac{z}{x^2 + y^2 + z^2} \, dV$

$$= \int_{\square}^{\square} \int_{\square}^{\square} \int_{\square}^{\square} \underline{\qquad} \, dz \, dr \, d\theta$$

3. Let G be the solid region described in Quick Check Exercise 2. In each part, supply the missing integrand and limits of integration for the iterated integral in spherical coordinates.
   (a) The volume of G is

$$\iiint\limits_{G} dV = \int_{\square}^{\square} \int_{\square}^{\square} \int_{\square}^{\square} \underline{\qquad} \, d\rho \, d\phi \, d\theta$$

   (b) $\displaystyle \iiint\limits_{G} \frac{z}{x^2 + y^2 + z^2} \, dV$

$$= \int_{\square}^{\square} \int_{\square}^{\square} \int_{\square}^{\square} \underline{\qquad} \, d\rho \, d\phi \, d\theta$$

EXERCISE SET 14.6   □ CAS

1–4 Evaluate the iterated integral. ▪

1. $\displaystyle \int_{0}^{2\pi} \int_{0}^{1} \int_{0}^{\sqrt{1-r^2}} zr \, dz \, dr \, d\theta$

2. $\displaystyle \int_{0}^{\pi/2} \int_{0}^{\cos\theta} \int_{0}^{r^2} r \sin\theta \, dz \, dr \, d\theta$

3. $\displaystyle \int_{0}^{\pi/2} \int_{0}^{\pi/2} \int_{0}^{1} \rho^3 \sin\phi \cos\phi \, d\rho \, d\phi \, d\theta$

4. $\displaystyle \int_{0}^{2\pi} \int_{0}^{\pi/4} \int_{0}^{a \sec\phi} \rho^2 \sin\phi \, d\rho \, d\phi \, d\theta$ $(a > 0)$

FOCUS ON CONCEPTS

5. Sketch the region G and identify the function f so that

$$\iiint\limits_{G} f(r, \theta, z) \, dV$$

corresponds to the iterated integral in Exercise 1.

6. Sketch the region G and identify the function f so that

$$\iiint\limits_{G} f(r, \theta, z) \, dV$$

corresponds to the iterated integral in Exercise 2.

7. Sketch the region G and identify the function f so that

$$\iiint\limits_{G} f(\rho, \theta, \phi) \, dV$$

corresponds to the iterated integral in Exercise 3.

8. Sketch the region G and identify the function f so that

$$\iiint\limits_{G} f(\rho, \theta, \phi) \, dV$$

corresponds to the iterated integral in Exercise 4.

9–12 Use cylindrical coordinates to find the volume of the solid. ▪

9. The solid enclosed by the paraboloid $z = x^2 + y^2$ and the plane $z = 9$.

10. The solid that is bounded above and below by the sphere $x^2 + y^2 + z^2 = 9$ and inside the cylinder $x^2 + y^2 = 4$.

11. The solid that is inside the surface $r^2 + z^2 = 20$ but not above the surface $z = r^2$.

12. The solid enclosed between the cone $z = (hr)/a$ and the plane $z = h$.

13–16 Use spherical coordinates to find the volume of the solid. ▪

13. The solid bounded above by the sphere $\rho = 4$ and below by the cone $\phi = \pi/3$.

14. The solid within the cone $\phi = \pi/4$ and between the spheres $\rho = 1$ and $\rho = 2$.

15. The solid enclosed by the sphere $x^2 + y^2 + z^2 = 4a^2$ and the planes $z = 0$ and $z = a$.

16. The solid within the sphere $x^2 + y^2 + z^2 = 9$, outside the cone $z = \sqrt{x^2 + y^2}$, and above the xy-plane.

17–20 Use cylindrical or spherical coordinates to evaluate the integral. ■

17. $\displaystyle\int_0^a \int_0^{\sqrt{a^2-x^2}} \int_0^{a^2-x^2-y^2} x^2 \, dz \, dy \, dx \quad (a > 0)$

18. $\displaystyle\int_{-1}^1 \int_0^{\sqrt{1-x^2}} \int_0^{\sqrt{1-x^2-y^2}} e^{-(x^2+y^2+z^2)^{3/2}} \, dz \, dy \, dx$

19. $\displaystyle\int_0^2 \int_0^{\sqrt{4-y^2}} \int_{\sqrt{x^2+y^2}}^{\sqrt{8-x^2-y^2}} z^2 \, dz \, dx \, dy$

20. $\displaystyle\int_{-3}^3 \int_{-\sqrt{9-y^2}}^{\sqrt{9-y^2}} \int_{-\sqrt{9-x^2-y^2}}^{\sqrt{9-x^2-y^2}} \sqrt{x^2+y^2+z^2} \, dz \, dx \, dy$

21–24 True–False Determine whether the statement is true or false. Explain your answer. ■

21. A rectangular triple integral can be expressed as an iterated integral in cylindrical coordinates as

$$\iiint_G f(x, y, z) \, dV = \iiint_{\substack{\text{appropriate} \\ \text{limits}}} f(r\cos\theta, r\sin\theta, z)r^2 \, dz \, dr \, d\theta$$

22. If $0 \le \rho_1 < \rho_2$, $0 \le \theta_1 < \theta_2 \le 2\pi$, and $0 \le \phi_1 < \phi_2 \le \pi$, then the volume of the spherical wedge bounded by the spheres $\rho = \rho_1$ and $\rho = \rho_2$, the half-planes $\theta = \theta_1$ and $\theta = \theta_2$, and the cones $\phi = \phi_1$ and $\phi = \phi_2$ is

$$\int_{\theta_1}^{\theta_2} \int_{\phi_1}^{\phi_2} \int_{\rho_1}^{\rho_2} \rho^2 \sin\phi \, d\rho \, d\phi \, d\theta$$

23. Let G be the solid region in 3-space between the spheres of radius 1 and 3 centered at the origin and above the cone $z = \sqrt{x^2+y^2}$. The volume of G equals

$$\int_0^{\pi/4} \int_0^{2\pi} \int_1^3 \rho^2 \sin\phi \, d\rho \, d\theta \, d\phi$$

24. If G is the solid in Exercise 23 and $f(x, y, z)$ is continuous on G, then

$$\iiint_G f(x, y, z) \, dV = \int_0^{\pi/4} \int_0^{2\pi} \int_1^3 F(\rho, \theta, \phi)\rho^2 \sin\phi \, d\rho \, d\theta \, d\phi$$

where $F(\rho, \theta, \phi) = f(\rho\sin\phi\sin\theta, \rho\sin\phi\cos\theta, \rho\cos\phi)$.

c **25.** (a) Use a CAS to evaluate

$$\int_{-2}^2 \int_1^4 \int_{\pi/6}^{\pi/3} \frac{r\tan^3\theta}{\sqrt{1+z^2}} \, d\theta \, dr \, dz$$

(b) Find a function $f(x, y, z)$ and sketch a region G in 3-space so that the triple integral in rectangular coordinates

$$\iiint_G f(x, y, z) \, dV$$

matches the iterated integral in cylindrical coordinates given in part (a).

c **26.** Use a CAS to evaluate

$$\int_0^{\pi/2} \int_0^{\pi/4} \int_0^{\cos\theta} \rho^{17} \cos\phi \cos^{19}\theta \, d\rho \, d\phi \, d\theta$$

27. Find the volume enclosed by $x^2 + y^2 + z^2 = a^2$ using
(a) cylindrical coordinates
(b) spherical coordinates.

28. Let G be the solid in the first octant bounded by the sphere $x^2 + y^2 + z^2 = 4$ and the coordinate planes. Evaluate

$$\iiint_G xyz \, dV$$

(a) using rectangular coordinates
(b) using cylindrical coordinates
(c) using spherical coordinates.

29. Find the volume of the solid in the first octant bounded by the sphere $\rho = 2$, the coordinate planes, and the cones $\phi = \pi/6$ and $\phi = \pi/3$.

30. In this exercise we will obtain a formula for the volume of the spherical wedge illustrated in Figures 14.6.7 and 14.6.9.
(a) Use a triple integral in cylindrical coordinates to show that the volume of the solid bounded above by a sphere $\rho = \rho_0$, below by a cone $\phi = \phi_0$, and on the sides by $\theta = \theta_1$ and $\theta = \theta_2$ ($\theta_1 < \theta_2$) is

$$V = \tfrac{1}{3}\rho_0^3(1 - \cos\phi_0)(\theta_2 - \theta_1)$$

[*Hint:* In cylindrical coordinates, the sphere has the equation $r^2 + z^2 = \rho_0^2$ and the cone has the equation $z = r\cot\phi_0$. For simplicity, consider only the case $0 < \phi_0 < \pi/2$.]

(b) Subtract appropriate volumes and use the result in part (a) to deduce that the volume ΔV of the spherical wedge is

$$\Delta V = \frac{\rho_2^3 - \rho_1^3}{3}(\cos\phi_1 - \cos\phi_2)(\theta_2 - \theta_1)$$

(c) Apply the Mean-Value Theorem to the functions $\cos\phi$ and ρ^3 to deduce that the formula in part (b) can be written as

$$\Delta V = \rho^{*2} \sin\phi^* \, \Delta\rho \, \Delta\phi \, \Delta\theta$$

where ρ^* is between ρ_1 and ρ_2, ϕ^* is between ϕ_1 and ϕ_2, and $\Delta\rho = \rho_2 - \rho_1$, $\Delta\phi = \phi_2 - \phi_1$, $\Delta\theta = \theta_2 - \theta_1$.

31. Writing Suppose that a triple integral is expressed in cylindrical or spherical coordinates in such a way that the outermost variable of integration is θ and none of the limits of integration involves θ. Discuss what this says about the region of integration for the integral.

✔ **QUICK CHECK ANSWERS 14.6**

1. (a) $\dfrac{20}{3}\pi$ (b) $\dfrac{13}{9}\pi$ 2. (a) $\displaystyle\int_0^{2\pi}\int_0^{\sqrt{3}}\int_1^{\sqrt{4-r^2}} r\,dz\,dr\,d\theta$ (b) $\displaystyle\int_0^{2\pi}\int_0^{\sqrt{3}}\int_1^{\sqrt{4-r^2}} \dfrac{rz}{r^2+z^2}\,dz\,dr\,d\theta$

3. (a) $\displaystyle\int_0^{2\pi}\int_0^{\pi/3}\int_{\sec\phi}^2 \rho^2\sin\phi\,d\rho\,d\phi\,d\theta$ (b) $\displaystyle\int_0^{2\pi}\int_0^{\pi/3}\int_{\sec\phi}^2 \rho\cos\phi\sin\phi\,d\rho\,d\phi\,d\theta$

14.7 CHANGE OF VARIABLES IN MULTIPLE INTEGRALS; JACOBIANS

In this section we will discuss a general method for evaluating double and triple integrals by substitution. Most of the results in this section are very difficult to prove, so our approach will be informal and motivational. Our goal is to provide a geometric understanding of the basic principles and an exposure to computational techniques.

■ CHANGE OF VARIABLE IN A SINGLE INTEGRAL

To motivate techniques for evaluating double and triple integrals by substitution, it will be helpful to consider the effect of a substitution $x = g(u)$ on a single integral over an interval $[a, b]$. If g is differentiable and either increasing or decreasing, then g is one-to-one and

$$\int_a^b f(x)\,dx = \int_{g^{-1}(a)}^{g^{-1}(b)} f(g(u))g'(u)\,du$$

In this relationship $f(x)$ and dx are expressed in terms of u, and the u-limits of integration result from solving the equations

$$a = g(u) \quad \text{and} \quad b = g(u)$$

In the case where g is decreasing we have $g^{-1}(b) < g^{-1}(a)$, which is contrary to our usual convention of writing definite integrals with the larger limit of integration at the top. We can remedy this by reversing the limits of integration and writing

$$\int_a^b f(x)\,dx = -\int_{g^{-1}(b)}^{g^{-1}(a)} f(g(u))g'(u)\,du = \int_{g^{-1}(b)}^{g^{-1}(a)} f(g(u))|g'(u)|\,du$$

where the absolute value results from the fact that $g'(u)$ is negative. Thus, regardless of whether g is increasing or decreasing we can write

$$\int_a^b f(x)\,dx = \int_\alpha^\beta f(g(u))|g'(u)|\,du \tag{1}$$

where α and β are the u-limits of integration and $\alpha < \beta$.

The expression $g'(u)$ that appears in (1) is called the **Jacobian** of the change of variable $x = g(u)$ in honor of C. G. J. Jacobi, who made the first serious study of change of variables in multiple integrals in the mid-1800s. Formula (1) reveals three effects of the change of variable $x = g(u)$:

- The new integrand becomes $f(g(u))$ times the absolute value of the Jacobian.
- dx becomes du.
- The x-interval of integration is transformed into a u-interval of integration.

Our goal in this section is to show that analogous results hold for changing variables in double and triple integrals.

■ **TRANSFORMATIONS OF THE PLANE**

In earlier sections we considered parametric equations of three kinds:

$$x = x(t), \quad y = y(t)$$

> A curve in the plane

$$x = x(t), \quad y = y(t), \quad z = z(t)$$

> A curve in 3-space

$$x = x(u, v), \quad y = y(u, v), \quad z = z(u, v)$$

> A surface in 3-space

Now we will consider parametric equations of the form

$$x = x(u, v), \quad y = y(u, v) \tag{2}$$

Parametric equations of this type associate points in the xy-plane with points in the uv-plane. These equations can be written in vector form as

$$\mathbf{r} = \mathbf{r}(u, v) = x(u, v)\mathbf{i} + y(u, v)\mathbf{j}$$

where $\mathbf{r} = x\mathbf{i} + y\mathbf{j}$ is a position vector in the xy-plane and $\mathbf{r}(u, v)$ is a vector-valued function of the variables u and v.

It will also be useful in this section to think of the parametric equations in (2) in terms of inputs and outputs. If we think of the pair of numbers (u, v) as an input, then the two equations, in combination, produce a unique output (x, y), and hence define a function T that associates points in the xy-plane with points in the uv-plane. This function is described by the formula

$$T(u, v) = (x(u, v), y(u, v))$$

We call T a **transformation** from the uv-plane to the xy-plane and (x, y) the **image** of (u, v) under the transformation T. We also say that T **maps** (u, v) into (x, y). The set R of all images in the xy-plane of a set S in the uv-plane is called the **image of S under T**. If distinct points in the uv-plane have distinct images in the xy-plane, then T is said to be **one-to-one**. In this case the equations in (2) define u and v as functions of x and y, say

$$u = u(x, y), \quad v = v(x, y)$$

These equations, which can often be obtained by solving (2) for u and v in terms of x and y, define a transformation from the xy-plane to the uv-plane that maps the image of (u, v) under T back into (u, v). This transformation is denoted by T^{-1} and is called the **inverse of T** (Figure 14.7.1).

Carl Gustav Jacob Jacobi (1804–1851) German mathematician. Jacobi, the son of a banker, grew up in a background of wealth and culture and showed brilliance in mathematics early. He resisted studying mathematics by rote, preferring instead to learn general principles from the works of the masters, Euler and Lagrange. He entered the University of Berlin at age 16 as a student of mathematics and classical studies. However, he soon realized that he could not do both and turned fully to mathematics with a blazing intensity that he would maintain throughout his life. He received his Ph.D. in 1825 and was able to secure a position as a lecturer at the University of Berlin by giving up Judaism and becoming a Christian. However, his promotion opportunities remained limited and he moved on to the University of Königsberg. Jacobi was born to teach—he had a dynamic personality and delivered his lectures with a clarity and enthusiasm that frequently left his audience spellbound. In spite of extensive teaching commitments, he was able to publish volumes of revolutionary mathematical research that eventually made him the leading European mathematician after Gauss. His main body of research was in the area of elliptic functions, a branch of mathematics with important applications in astronomy and physics as well as in other fields of mathematics. Because of his family wealth, Jacobi was not dependent on his teaching salary in his early years. However, his comfortable world eventually collapsed. In 1840 his family went bankrupt and he was wiped out financially. In 1842 he had a nervous breakdown from overwork. In 1843 he became seriously ill with diabetes and moved to Berlin with the help of a government grant to defray his medical expenses. In 1848 he made an injudicious political speech that caused the government to withdraw the grant, eventually resulting in the loss of his home. His health continued to decline and in 1851 he finally succumbed to successive bouts of influenza and smallpox. In spite of all his problems, Jacobi was a tireless worker to the end. When a friend expressed concern about the effect of the hard work on his health, Jacobi replied, "Certainly, I have sometimes endangered my health by overwork, but what of it? Only cabbages have no nerves, no worries. And what do they get out of their perfect well-being?"

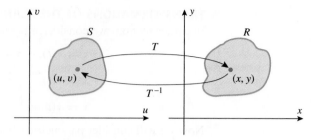

► **Figure 14.7.1**

One way to visualize the geometric effect of a transformation T is to determine the images in the xy-plane of the vertical and horizontal lines in the uv-plane. Following the discussion in Section 14.4, sets of points in the xy-plane that are images of horizontal lines (v constant) are called ***constant v-curves***, and sets of points that are images of vertical lines (u constant) are called ***constant u-curves*** (Figure 14.7.2).

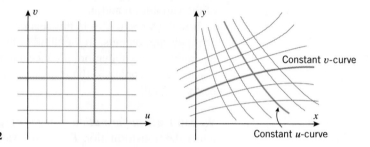

► **Figure 14.7.2**

► **Example 1**   Let T be the transformation from the uv-plane to the xy-plane defined by the equations

$$x = \tfrac{1}{4}(u + v), \quad y = \tfrac{1}{2}(u - v) \tag{3}$$

(a) Find $T(1, 3)$.

(b) Sketch the constant v-curves corresponding to $v = -2, -1, 0, 1, 2$.

(c) Sketch the constant u-curves corresponding to $u = -2, -1, 0, 1, 2$.

(d) Sketch the image under T of the square region in the uv-plane bounded by the lines $u = -2, u = 2, v = -2$, and $v = 2$.

Solution (a).   Substituting $u = 1$ and $v = 3$ in (3) yields $T(1, 3) = (1, -1)$.

Solutions (b and c).   In these parts it will be convenient to express the transformation equations with u and v as functions of x and y. From (3)

$$4x = u + v, \quad 2y = u - v$$

Combining these equations gives

$$4x + 2y = 2u, \quad 4x - 2y = 2v$$

or

$$2x + y = u, \quad 2x - y = v$$

Thus, the constant v-curves corresponding to $v = -2, -1, 0, 1$, and 2 are

$$2x - y = -2, \quad 2x - y = -1, \quad 2x - y = 0, \quad 2x - y = 1, \quad 2x - y = 2$$

and the constant u-curves corresponding to $u = -2, -1, 0, 1$, and 2 are

$$2x + y = -2, \quad 2x + y = -1, \quad 2x + y = 0, \quad 2x + y = 1, \quad 2x + y = 2$$

In Figure 14.7.3 the constant v-curves are shown in purple and the constant u-curves in blue.

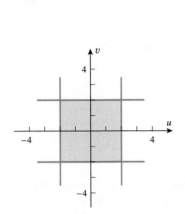

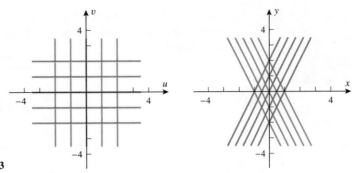

▶ **Figure 14.7.3**

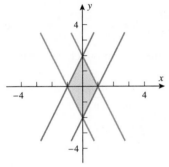

▲ **Figure 14.7.4**

Solution (*d*). The image of a region can often be found by finding the image of its boundary. In this case the images of the boundary lines $u = -2$, $u = 2$, $v = -2$, and $v = 2$ enclose the diamond-shaped region in the xy-plane shown in Figure 14.7.4. ◀

■ JACOBIANS IN TWO VARIABLES

To derive the change of variables formula for double integrals, we will need to understand the relationship between the area of a *small* rectangular region in the uv-plane and the area of its image in the xy-plane under a transformation T given by the equations

$$x = x(u, v), \quad y = y(u, v)$$

For this purpose, suppose that Δu and Δv are positive, and consider a rectangular region S in the uv-plane enclosed by the lines

$$u = u_0, \quad u = u_0 + \Delta u, \quad v = v_0, \quad v = v_0 + \Delta v$$

If the functions $x(u, v)$ and $y(u, v)$ are continuous, and if Δu and Δv are not too large, then the image of S in the xy-plane will be a region R that looks like a slightly distorted parallelogram (Figure 14.7.5). The sides of R are the constant u-curves and v-curves that correspond to the sides of S.

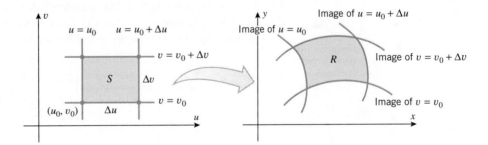

▶ **Figure 14.7.5**

If we let

$$\mathbf{r} = \mathbf{r}(u, v) = x(u, v)\mathbf{i} + y(u, v)\mathbf{j}$$

be the position vector of the point in the xy-plane that corresponds to the point (u, v) in the uv-plane, then the constant v-curve corresponding to $v = v_0$ and the constant u-curve corresponding to $u = u_0$ can be represented in vector form as

$$\mathbf{r}(u, v_0) = x(u, v_0)\mathbf{i} + y(u, v_0)\mathbf{j} \quad \boxed{\text{Constant } v\text{-curve}}$$

$$\mathbf{r}(u_0, v) = x(u_0, v)\mathbf{i} + y(u_0, v)\mathbf{j} \quad \boxed{\text{Constant } u\text{-curve}}$$

Since we are assuming Δu and Δv to be small, the region R can be approximated by a parallelogram determined by the "secant vectors"

$$\mathbf{a} = \mathbf{r}(u_0 + \Delta u, v_0) - \mathbf{r}(u_0, v_0) \tag{4}$$

$$\mathbf{b} = \mathbf{r}(u_0, v_0 + \Delta v) - \mathbf{r}(u_0, v_0) \tag{5}$$

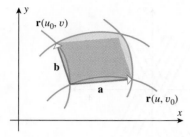

▲ **Figure 14.7.6**

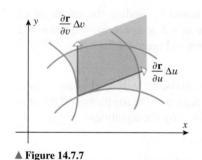

▲ **Figure 14.7.7**

shown in Figure 14.7.6. A more useful approximation of R can be obtained by using Formulas (7) and (8) of Section 14.4 to approximate these secant vectors by tangent vectors as follows:

$$\mathbf{a} = \frac{\mathbf{r}(u_0 + \Delta u, v_0) - \mathbf{r}(u_0, v_0)}{\Delta u} \Delta u$$

$$\approx \frac{\partial \mathbf{r}}{\partial u} \Delta u = \left(\frac{\partial x}{\partial u} \mathbf{i} + \frac{\partial y}{\partial u} \mathbf{j} \right) \Delta u$$

$$\mathbf{b} = \frac{\mathbf{r}(u_0, v_0 + \Delta v) - \mathbf{r}(u_0, v_0)}{\Delta v} \Delta v$$

$$\approx \frac{\partial \mathbf{r}}{\partial v} \Delta v = \left(\frac{\partial x}{\partial v} \mathbf{i} + \frac{\partial y}{\partial v} \mathbf{j} \right) \Delta v$$

where the partial derivatives are evaluated at (u_0, v_0) (Figure 14.7.7). Hence, it follows that the area of the region R, which we will denote by ΔA, can be approximated by the area of the parallelogram determined by these vectors. Thus, from Theorem 11.4.5(b) we have

$$\Delta A \approx \left\| \frac{\partial \mathbf{r}}{\partial u} \Delta u \times \frac{\partial \mathbf{r}}{\partial v} \Delta v \right\| = \left\| \frac{\partial \mathbf{r}}{\partial u} \times \frac{\partial \mathbf{r}}{\partial v} \right\| \Delta u \, \Delta v \tag{6}$$

where the derivatives are evaluated at (u_0, v_0). Computing the cross product, we obtain

$$\frac{\partial \mathbf{r}}{\partial u} \times \frac{\partial \mathbf{r}}{\partial v} = \begin{vmatrix} \mathbf{i} & \mathbf{j} & \mathbf{k} \\ \dfrac{\partial x}{\partial u} & \dfrac{\partial y}{\partial u} & 0 \\ \dfrac{\partial x}{\partial v} & \dfrac{\partial y}{\partial v} & 0 \end{vmatrix} = \begin{vmatrix} \dfrac{\partial x}{\partial u} & \dfrac{\partial y}{\partial u} \\ \dfrac{\partial x}{\partial v} & \dfrac{\partial y}{\partial v} \end{vmatrix} \mathbf{k} = \begin{vmatrix} \dfrac{\partial x}{\partial u} & \dfrac{\partial x}{\partial v} \\ \dfrac{\partial y}{\partial u} & \dfrac{\partial y}{\partial v} \end{vmatrix} \mathbf{k} \tag{7}$$

The determinant in (7) is sufficiently important that it has its own terminology and notation.

14.7.1 **DEFINITION** If T is the transformation from the uv-plane to the xy-plane defined by the equations $x = x(u, v)$, $y = y(u, v)$, then the ***Jacobian of T*** is denoted by $J(u, v)$ or by $\partial(x, y)/\partial(u, v)$ and is defined by

$$J(u, v) = \frac{\partial(x, y)}{\partial(u, v)} = \begin{vmatrix} \dfrac{\partial x}{\partial u} & \dfrac{\partial x}{\partial v} \\ \dfrac{\partial y}{\partial u} & \dfrac{\partial y}{\partial v} \end{vmatrix} = \frac{\partial x}{\partial u} \frac{\partial y}{\partial v} - \frac{\partial y}{\partial u} \frac{\partial x}{\partial v}$$

Using the notation in this definition, it follows from (6) and (7) that

$$\Delta A \approx \left\| \frac{\partial(x, y)}{\partial(u, v)} \mathbf{k} \right\| \Delta u \, \Delta v$$

or, since $\mathbf{k}$ is a unit vector,

$$\Delta A \approx \left| \frac{\partial(x, y)}{\partial(u, v)} \right| \Delta u \, \Delta v \tag{8}$$

At the point (u_0, v_0) this important formula relates the areas of the regions R and S in Figure 14.7.5; it tells us that *for small values of Δu and Δv, the area of R is approximately the absolute value of the Jacobian times the area of S*. Moreover, it is proved in advanced calculus courses that the relative error in the approximation approaches zero as $\Delta u \to 0$ and $\Delta v \to 0$.

■ **CHANGE OF VARIABLES IN DOUBLE INTEGRALS**
Our next objective is to provide a geometric motivation for the following result.

14.7.2   CHANGE OF VARIABLES FORMULA FOR DOUBLE INTEGRALS   If the transformation $x = x(u, v)$, $y = y(u, v)$ maps the region S in the uv-plane into the region R in the xy-plane, and if the Jacobian $\partial(x, y)/\partial(u, v)$ is nonzero and does not change sign on S, then with appropriate restrictions on the transformation and the regions it follows that

$$\iint\limits_{R} f(x, y)\, dA_{xy} = \iint\limits_{S} f(x(u, v), y(u, v)) \left| \frac{\partial(x, y)}{\partial(u, v)} \right| dA_{uv} \qquad (9)$$

where we have attached subscripts to the dA's to help identify the associated variables.

A precise statement of conditions under which Formula (9) holds is beyond the scope of this course. Suffice it to say that the formula holds if T is a one-to-one transformation, $f(x, y)$ is continuous on R, the partial derivatives of $x(u, v)$ and $y(u, v)$ exist and are continuous on S, and the regions R and S are not complicated.

To motivate Formula (9), we proceed as follows:

- Subdivide the region S in the uv-plane into pieces by lines parallel to the coordinate axes, and exclude from consideration any pieces that contain points outside of S. This leaves only rectangular regions that are subsets of S. Assume that there are n such regions and denote the kth such region by S_k. Assume that S_k has dimensions Δu_k by Δv_k and, as shown in Figure 14.7.8a, let (u_k^*, v_k^*) be its "lower left corner."

- As shown in Figure 14.7.8b, the transformation T defined by the coordinate equations $x = x(u, v)$, $y = y(u, v)$ maps S_k into a curvilinear parallelogram R_k in the xy-plane and maps the point (u_k^*, v_k^*) into the point $(x_k^*, y_k^*) = (x(u_k^*, v_k^*), y(u_k^*, v_k^*))$ in R_k. Denote the area of R_k by ΔA_k.

- In rectangular coordinates the double integral of $f(x, y)$ over a region R is defined as a limit of Riemann sums in which R is subdivided into *rectangular* subregions. It is proved in advanced calculus courses that under appropriate conditions subdivisions into *curvilinear* parallelograms can be used instead. Accepting this to be so, we can approximate the double integral of $f(x, y)$ over R as

$$\iint\limits_{R} f(x, y)\, dA_{xy} \approx \sum_{k=1}^{n} f(x_k^*, y_k^*)\, \Delta A_k$$

$$\approx \sum_{k=1}^{n} f(x(u_k^*, v_k^*), y(u_k^*, v_k^*)) \left| \frac{\partial(x, y)}{\partial(u, v)} \right| \Delta u_k\, \Delta v_k$$

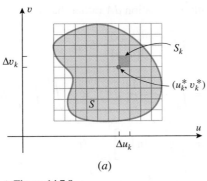

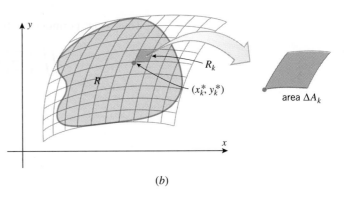

(a) (b)

▲ **Figure 14.7.8**

where the Jacobian is evaluated at (u_k^*, v_k^*). But the last expression is a Riemann sum for the integral

$$\iint\limits_{S} f(x(u, v), y(u, v)) \left| \frac{\partial(x, y)}{\partial(u, v)} \right| dA_{uv}$$

so Formula (9) follows if we assume that the errors in the approximations approach zero as $n \to +\infty$.

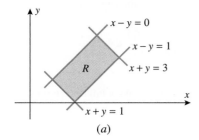

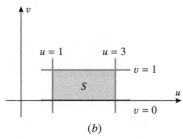

▲ **Figure 14.7.9**

▶ **Example 2**   Evaluate

$$\iint\limits_{R} \frac{x - y}{x + y} \, dA$$

where R is the region enclosed by $x - y = 0$, $x - y = 1$, $x + y = 1$, and $x + y = 3$ (Figure 14.7.9a).

Solution.   This integral would be tedious to evaluate directly because the region R is oriented in such a way that we would have to subdivide it and integrate over each part separately. However, the occurrence of the expressions $x - y$ and $x + y$ in the equations of the boundary suggests that the transformation

$$u = x + y, \quad v = x - y \tag{10}$$

would be helpful, since with this transformation the boundary lines

$$x + y = 1, \quad x + y = 3, \quad x - y = 0, \quad x - y = 1$$

are constant u-curves and constant v-curves corresponding to the lines

$$u = 1, \quad u = 3, \quad v = 0, \quad v = 1$$

in the uv-plane. These lines enclose the rectangular region S shown in Figure 14.7.9b. To find the Jacobian $\partial(x, y)/\partial(u, v)$ of this transformation, we first solve (10) for x and y in terms of u and v. This yields

$$x = \tfrac{1}{2}(u + v), \quad y = \tfrac{1}{2}(u - v)$$

from which we obtain

$$\frac{\partial(x, y)}{\partial(u, v)} = \begin{vmatrix} \dfrac{\partial x}{\partial u} & \dfrac{\partial x}{\partial v} \\[2mm] \dfrac{\partial y}{\partial u} & \dfrac{\partial y}{\partial v} \end{vmatrix} = \begin{vmatrix} \tfrac{1}{2} & \tfrac{1}{2} \\[2mm] \tfrac{1}{2} & -\tfrac{1}{2} \end{vmatrix} = -\tfrac{1}{4} - \tfrac{1}{4} = -\tfrac{1}{2}$$

Thus, from Formula (9), but with the notation dA rather than dA_{xy},

$$\iint\limits_{R} \frac{x - y}{x + y} \, dA = \iint\limits_{S} \frac{v}{u} \left| \frac{\partial(x, y)}{\partial(u, v)} \right| dA_{uv}$$

$$= \iint\limits_{S} \frac{v}{u} \left| -\frac{1}{2} \right| dA_{uv} = \frac{1}{2} \int_0^1 \int_1^3 \frac{v}{u} \, du \, dv$$

$$= \frac{1}{2} \int_0^1 v \ln|u| \Big]_{u=1}^{3} dv$$

$$= \frac{1}{2} \ln 3 \int_0^1 v \, dv = \frac{1}{4} \ln 3 \quad ◀$$

The underlying idea illustrated in Example 2 is to find a one-to-one transformation that maps a rectangle S in the uv-plane into the region R of integration, and then use that transformation as a substitution in the integral to produce an equivalent integral over S.

▶ **Example 3**   Evaluate

$$\iint_R e^{xy}\, dA$$

where R is the region enclosed by the lines $y = \frac{1}{2}x$ and $y = x$ and the hyperbolas $y = 1/x$ and $y = 2/x$ (Figure 14.7.10a).

Solution.   As in the last example, we look for a transformation in which the boundary curves in the xy-plane become constant v-curves and constant u-curves. For this purpose we rewrite the four boundary curves as

$$\frac{y}{x} = \frac{1}{2}, \quad \frac{y}{x} = 1, \quad xy = 1, \quad xy = 2$$

which suggests the transformation

$$u = \frac{y}{x}, \quad v = xy \tag{11}$$

With this transformation the boundary curves in the xy-plane are constant u-curves and constant v-curves corresponding to the lines

$$u = \tfrac{1}{2}, \quad u = 1, \quad v = 1, \quad v = 2$$

in the uv-plane. These lines enclose the region S shown in Figure 14.7.10b. To find the Jacobian $\partial(x, y)/\partial(u, v)$ of this transformation, we first solve (11) for x and y in terms of u and v. This yields

$$x = \sqrt{v/u}, \quad y = \sqrt{uv}$$

from which we obtain

$$\frac{\partial(x, y)}{\partial(u, v)} = \begin{vmatrix} \dfrac{\partial x}{\partial u} & \dfrac{\partial x}{\partial v} \\ \dfrac{\partial y}{\partial u} & \dfrac{\partial y}{\partial v} \end{vmatrix} = \begin{vmatrix} -\dfrac{1}{2u}\sqrt{\dfrac{v}{u}} & \dfrac{1}{2\sqrt{uv}} \\ \dfrac{1}{2}\sqrt{\dfrac{v}{u}} & \dfrac{1}{2}\sqrt{\dfrac{u}{v}} \end{vmatrix} = -\dfrac{1}{4u} - \dfrac{1}{4u} = -\dfrac{1}{2u}$$

Thus, from Formula (9), but with the notation dA rather than dA_{xy},

$$\iint_R e^{xy}\, dA = \iint_S e^{v} \left| -\frac{1}{2u} \right| dA_{uv} = \frac{1}{2} \iint_S \frac{1}{u} e^{v}\, dA_{uv}$$

$$= \frac{1}{2} \int_1^2 \int_{1/2}^1 \frac{1}{u} e^{v}\, du\, dv = \frac{1}{2} \int_1^2 e^{v} \ln |u| \Big]_{u=1/2}^1 dv$$

$$= \frac{1}{2} \ln 2 \int_1^2 e^{v}\, dv = \frac{1}{2}(e^2 - e) \ln 2 \; ◀$$

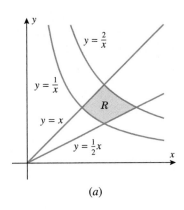

$y = \frac{2}{x}$

$y = \frac{1}{x}$

$y = x$

$y = \frac{1}{2}x$

R

(a)

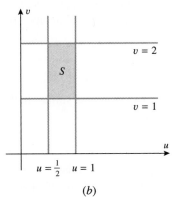

$v = 2$

S

$v = 1$

$u = \frac{1}{2}$ $u = 1$

(b)

▲ **Figure 14.7.10**

■ **CHANGE OF VARIABLES IN TRIPLE INTEGRALS**
Equations of the form

$$x = x(u, v, w), \quad y = y(u, v, w), \quad z = z(u, v, w) \tag{12}$$

define a **transformation** T from uvw-space to xyz-space. Just as a transformation $x = x(u, v)$, $y = y(u, v)$ in two variables maps small rectangles in the uv-plane into curvilinear parallelograms in the xy-plane, so (12) maps small rectangular parallelepipeds

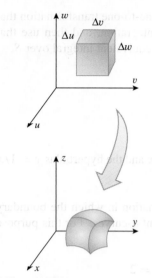

▲ **Figure 14.7.11**

in uvw-space into curvilinear parallelepipeds in xyz-space (Figure 14.7.11). The definition of the Jacobian of (12) is similar to Definition 14.7.1.

14.7.3   **DEFINITION**   If T is the transformation from uvw-space to xyz-space defined by the equations $x = x(u, v, w)$, $y = y(u, v, w)$, $z = z(u, v, w)$, then the ***Jacobian of T*** is denoted by $J(u, v, w)$ or $\partial(x, y, z)/\partial(u, v, w)$ and is defined by

$$J(u, v, w) = \frac{\partial(x, y, z)}{\partial(u, v, w)} = \begin{vmatrix} \dfrac{\partial x}{\partial u} & \dfrac{\partial x}{\partial v} & \dfrac{\partial x}{\partial w} \\[2mm] \dfrac{\partial y}{\partial u} & \dfrac{\partial y}{\partial v} & \dfrac{\partial y}{\partial w} \\[2mm] \dfrac{\partial z}{\partial u} & \dfrac{\partial z}{\partial v} & \dfrac{\partial z}{\partial w} \end{vmatrix}$$

For small values of Δu, Δv, and Δw, the volume ΔV of the curvilinear parallelepiped in Figure 14.7.11 is related to the volume $\Delta u \, \Delta v \, \Delta w$ of the rectangular parallelepiped by

$$\Delta V \approx \left| \frac{\partial(x, y, z)}{\partial(u, v, w)} \right| \Delta u \, \Delta v \, \Delta w \tag{13}$$

which is the analog of Formula (8). Using this relationship and an argument similar to the one that led to Formula (9), we can obtain the following result.

14.7.4   **CHANGE OF VARIABLES FORMULA FOR TRIPLE INTEGRALS**   If the transformation $x = x(u, v, w)$, $y = y(u, v, w)$, $z = z(u, v, w)$ maps the region S in uvw-space into the region R in xyz-space, and if the Jacobian $\partial(x, y, z)/\partial(u, v, w)$ is nonzero and does not change sign on S, then with appropriate restrictions on the transformation and the regions it follows that

$$\iiint\limits_R f(x, y, z) \, dV_{xyz} = \iiint\limits_S f(x(u, v, w), y(u, v, w), z(u, v, w)) \left| \frac{\partial(x, y, z)}{\partial(u, v, w)} \right| dV_{uvw}$$

$$\tag{14}$$

▶ **Example 4**   Find the volume of the region G enclosed by the ellipsoid

$$\frac{x^2}{a^2} + \frac{y^2}{b^2} + \frac{z^2}{c^2} = 1$$

Solution.   The volume V is given by the triple integral

$$V = \iiint\limits_G dV$$

To evaluate this integral, we make the change of variables

$$x = au, \quad y = bv, \quad z = cw \tag{15}$$

which maps the region S in uvw-space enclosed by a sphere of radius 1 into the region G in xyz-space. This can be seen from (15) by noting that

$$\frac{x^2}{a^2} + \frac{y^2}{b^2} + \frac{z^2}{c^2} = 1 \quad \text{becomes} \quad u^2 + v^2 + w^2 = 1$$

The Jacobian of (15) is

$$\frac{\partial(x, y, z)}{\partial(u, v, w)} = \begin{vmatrix} \dfrac{\partial x}{\partial u} & \dfrac{\partial x}{\partial v} & \dfrac{\partial x}{\partial w} \\[2mm] \dfrac{\partial y}{\partial u} & \dfrac{\partial y}{\partial v} & \dfrac{\partial y}{\partial w} \\[2mm] \dfrac{\partial z}{\partial u} & \dfrac{\partial z}{\partial v} & \dfrac{\partial z}{\partial w} \end{vmatrix} = \begin{vmatrix} a & 0 & 0 \\ 0 & b & 0 \\ 0 & 0 & c \end{vmatrix} = abc$$

Thus, from Formula (14), but with the notation dV rather than dV_{xyz},

$$V = \iiint\limits_G dV = \iiint\limits_S \left| \frac{\partial(x, y, z)}{\partial(u, v, w)} \right| dV_{uvw} = abc \iiint\limits_S dV_{uvw}$$

The last integral is the volume enclosed by a sphere of radius 1, which we know to be $\frac{4}{3}\pi$. Thus, the volume enclosed by the ellipsoid is $V = \frac{4}{3}\pi abc$. ◄

Jacobians also arise in converting triple integrals in rectangular coordinates to iterated integrals in cylindrical and spherical coordinates. For example, we will ask you to show in Exercise 48 that the Jacobian of the transformation

$$x = r\cos\theta, \quad y = r\sin\theta, \quad z = z$$

is

$$\frac{\partial(x, y, z)}{\partial(r, \theta, z)} = r$$

and the Jacobian of the transformation

$$x = \rho\sin\phi\cos\theta, \quad y = \rho\sin\phi\sin\theta, \quad z = \rho\cos\phi$$

is

$$\frac{\partial(x, y, z)}{\partial(\rho, \phi, \theta)} = \rho^2\sin\phi$$

Thus, Formulas (6) and (10) of Section 14.6 can be expressed in terms of Jacobians as

$$\iiint\limits_G f(x, y, z)\, dV = \iiint\limits_{\substack{\text{appropriate} \\ \text{limits}}} f(r\cos\theta, r\sin\theta, z)\frac{\partial(x, y, z)}{\partial(r, \theta, z)}\, dz\, dr\, d\theta \tag{16}$$

The absolute-value signs are omitted from Formulas (16) and (17) because the Jacobians are nonnegative (see the restrictions in Table 11.8.1).

$$\iiint\limits_G f(x, y, z)\, dV = \iiint\limits_{\substack{\text{appropriate} \\ \text{limits}}} f(\rho\sin\phi\cos\theta, \rho\sin\phi\sin\theta, \rho\cos\phi)\frac{\partial(x, y, z)}{\partial(\rho, \phi, \theta)}\, d\rho\, d\phi\, d\theta$$

$$\tag{17}$$

✔ **QUICK CHECK EXERCISES 14.7**   *(See page 1071 for answers.)*

1. Let T be the transformation from the uv-plane to the xy-plane defined by the equations

$$x = u - 2v, \quad y = 3u + v$$

(a) Sketch the image under T of the rectangle $1 \le u \le 3$, $0 \le v \le 2$.

(b) Solve for u and v in terms of x and y:

$$u = \underline{\hspace{1cm}}, \quad v = \underline{\hspace{1cm}}$$

2. State the relationship between R and S in the change of variables formula

$$\iint\limits_{R} f(x, y) \, dA_{xy} = \iint\limits_{S} f(x(u, v), y(u, v)) \left| \frac{\partial(x, y)}{\partial(u, v)} \right| dA_{uv}$$

3. Let T be the transformation in Quick Check Exercise 1.

(a) The Jacobian $\partial(x, y)/\partial(u, v)$ of T is \underline{\hspace{1cm}}.

(b) Let R be the region in Quick Check Exercise 1(a). Fill in the missing integrand and limits of integration for the change of variables given by T.

$$\iint\limits_{R} e^{x+2y} \, dA = \int_{\square}^{\square} \int_{\square}^{\square} \underline{\hspace{1cm}} \, du \, dv$$

4. The Jacobian of the transformation

$$x = uv, \quad y = vw, \quad z = 2w$$

is

$$\frac{\partial(x, y, z)}{\partial(u, v, w)} = \underline{\hspace{1cm}}$$

EXERCISE SET 14.7

1–4 Find the Jacobian $\partial(x, y)/\partial(u, v)$. ■

1. $x = u + 4v, \ y = 3u - 5v$

2. $x = u + 2v^2, \ y = 2u^2 - v$

3. $x = \sin u + \cos v, \ y = -\cos u + \sin v$

4. $x = \dfrac{2u}{u^2 + v^2}, \ y = -\dfrac{2v}{u^2 + v^2}$

5–8 Solve for x and y in terms of u and v, and then find the Jacobian $\partial(x, y)/\partial(u, v)$. ■

5. $u = 2x - 5y, \ v = x + 2y$

6. $u = e^x, \ v = ye^{-x}$

7. $u = x^2 - y^2, \ v = x^2 + y^2 \quad (x > 0, y > 0)$

8. $u = xy, \ v = xy^3 \quad (x > 0, y > 0)$

9–12 Find the Jacobian $\partial(x, y, z)/\partial(u, v, w)$. ■

9. $x = 3u + v, \ y = u - 2w, \ z = v + w$

10. $x = u - uv, \ y = uv - uvw, \ z = uvw$

11. $u = xy, \ v = y, \ w = x + z$

12. $u = x + y + z, \ v = x + y - z, \ w = x - y + z$

13–16 True–False Determine whether the statement is true or false. Explain your answer. ■

13. If $\mathbf{r} = x(u, v)\mathbf{i} + y(u, v)\mathbf{j}$, then evaluating $|\partial(x, y)/\partial(u, v)|$ at a point (u_0, v_0) gives the perimeter of the parallelogram generated by the vectors $\partial\mathbf{r}/\partial u$ and $\partial\mathbf{r}/\partial v$ at (u_0, v_0).

14. If $\mathbf{r} = x(u, v)\mathbf{i} + y(u, v)\mathbf{j}$ maps the rectangle $0 \le u \le 2$, $1 \le v \le 5$ to a region R in the xy-plane, then the area of R is given by

$$\int_{1}^{5} \int_{0}^{2} \left| \frac{\partial(x, y)}{\partial(u, v)} \right| du \, dv$$

15. The Jacobian of the transformation $x = r\cos\theta, \ y = r\sin\theta$ is

$$\frac{\partial(x, y)}{\partial(r, \theta)} = r^2$$

16. The Jacobian of the transformation $x = \rho\sin\phi\cos\theta$, $y = \rho\sin\phi\sin\theta, \ z = \rho\cos\phi$ is

$$\frac{\partial(x, y, z)}{\partial(\rho, \phi, \theta)} = \rho^2\sin\phi$$

FOCUS ON CONCEPTS

17–20 Sketch the image in the xy-plane of the set S under the given transformation. ■

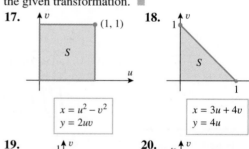

17.

$x = u^2 - v^2$
$y = 2uv$

18.

$x = 3u + 4v$
$y = 4u$

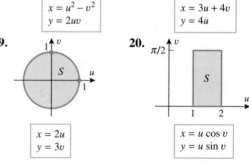

19.

$x = 2u$
$y = 3v$

20.

$x = u\cos v$
$y = u\sin v$

21. Use the transformation $u = x - 2y, \ v = 2x + y$ to find

$$\iint\limits_{R} \frac{x - 2y}{2x + y} \, dA \qquad \text{(cont.)}$$

where R is the rectangular region enclosed by the lines $x - 2y = 1$, $x - 2y = 4$, $2x + y = 1$, $2x + y = 3$.

22. Use the transformation $u = x + y$, $v = x - y$ to find

$$\iint\limits_{R} (x - y)e^{x^2 - y^2} \, dA$$

over the rectangular region R enclosed by the lines $x + y = 0$, $x + y = 1$, $x - y = 1$, $x - y = 4$.

23. Use the transformation $u = \frac{1}{2}(x + y)$, $v = \frac{1}{2}(x - y)$ to find

$$\iint\limits_{R} \sin \tfrac{1}{2}(x + y) \cos \tfrac{1}{2}(x - y) \, dA$$

over the triangular region R with vertices $(0, 0)$, $(2, 0)$, $(1, 1)$.

24. Use the transformation $u = y/x$, $v = xy$ to find

$$\iint\limits_{R} xy^3 \, dA$$

over the region R in the first quadrant enclosed by $y = x$, $y = 3x$, $xy = 1$, $xy = 4$.

25–27 The transformation $x = au$, $y = bv$ $(a > 0, b > 0)$ can be rewritten as $x/a = u$, $y/b = v$, and hence it maps the circular region
$$u^2 + v^2 \leq 1$$
into the elliptical region
$$\frac{x^2}{a^2} + \frac{y^2}{b^2} \leq 1$$
In these exercises, perform the integration by transforming the elliptical region of integration into a circular region of integration and then evaluating the transformed integral in polar coordinates. ◼

25. $\displaystyle\iint\limits_{R} \sqrt{16x^2 + 9y^2} \, dA$, where R is the region enclosed by the ellipse $(x^2/9) + (y^2/16) = 1$.

26. $\displaystyle\iint\limits_{R} e^{-(x^2 + 4y^2)} \, dA$, where R is the region enclosed by the ellipse $(x^2/4) + y^2 = 1$.

27. $\displaystyle\iint\limits_{R} \sin(4x^2 + 9y^2) \, dA$, where R is the region in the first quadrant enclosed by the ellipse $4x^2 + 9y^2 = 1$ and the coordinate axes.

28. Show that the area of the ellipse
$$\frac{x^2}{a^2} + \frac{y^2}{b^2} = 1$$
is πab.

29–30 If a, b, and c are positive constants, then the transformation $x = au$, $y = bv$, $z = cw$ can be rewritten as $x/a = u$, $y/b = v$, $z/c = w$, and hence it maps the spherical region
$$u^2 + v^2 + w^2 \leq 1$$
into the ellipsoidal region
$$\frac{x^2}{a^2} + \frac{y^2}{b^2} + \frac{z^2}{c^2} \leq 1$$
In these exercises, perform the integration by transforming the ellipsoidal region of integration into a spherical region of integration and then evaluating the transformed integral in spherical coordinates. ◼

29. $\displaystyle\iiint\limits_{G} x^2 \, dV$, where G is the region enclosed by the ellipsoid $9x^2 + 4y^2 + z^2 = 36$.

30. $\displaystyle\iiint\limits_{G} (y^2 + z^2) \, dV$, where G is the region enclosed by the ellipsoid
$$\frac{x^2}{a^2} + \frac{y^2}{b^2} + \frac{z^2}{c^2} = 1$$

FOCUS ON CONCEPTS

31–34 Find a transformation
$$u = f(x, y), \quad v = g(x, y)$$
that when applied to the region R in the xy-plane has as its image the region S in the uv-plane. ◼

31.

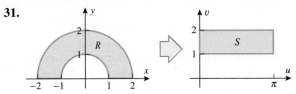

32.

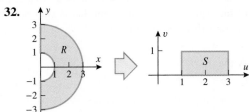

33.

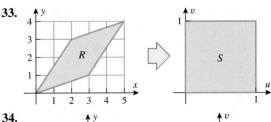

34.

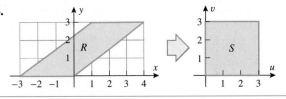

35–38 Evaluate the integral by making an appropriate change of variables. ■

35. $\iint\limits_{R} \dfrac{y - 4x}{y + 4x}\, dA$, where R is the region enclosed by the lines $y = 4x$, $y = 4x + 2$, $y = 2 - 4x$, $y = 5 - 4x$.

36. $\iint\limits_{R} (x^2 - y^2)\, dA$, where R is the rectangular region enclosed by the lines $y = -x$, $y = 1 - x$, $y = x$, $y = x + 2$.

37. $\iint\limits_{R} \dfrac{\sin(x - y)}{\cos(x + y)}\, dA$, where R is the triangular region enclosed by the lines $y = 0$, $y = x$, $x + y = \pi/4$.

38. $\iint\limits_{R} e^{(y-x)/(y+x)}\, dA$, where R is the region in the first quadrant enclosed by the trapezoid with vertices $(0, 1)$, $(1, 0)$, $(0, 4)$, $(4, 0)$.

39. Use an appropriate change of variables to find the area of the region in the first quadrant enclosed by the curves $y = x$, $y = 2x$, $x = y^2$, $x = 4y^2$.

40. Use an appropriate change of variables to find the volume of the solid bounded above by the plane $x + y + z = 9$, below by the xy-plane, and laterally by the elliptic cylinder $4x^2 + 9y^2 = 36$. [*Hint:* Express the volume as a double integral in xy-coordinates, then use polar coordinates to evaluate the transformed integral.]

41. Use the transformation $u = x$, $v = z - y$, $w = xy$ to find

$$\iiint\limits_{G} (z - y)^2 xy\, dV$$

where G is the region enclosed by the surfaces $x = 1$, $x = 3$, $z = y$, $z = y + 1$, $xy = 2$, $xy = 4$.

42. Use the transformation $u = xy$, $v = yz$, $w = xz$ to find the volume of the region in the first octant that is enclosed by the hyperbolic cylinders $xy = 1$, $xy = 2$, $yz = 1$, $yz = 3$, $xz = 1$, $xz = 4$.

43. (a) Verify that

$$\begin{vmatrix} a_1 & b_1 \\ c_1 & d_1 \end{vmatrix} \begin{vmatrix} a_2 & b_2 \\ c_2 & d_2 \end{vmatrix} = \begin{vmatrix} a_1 a_2 + b_1 c_2 & a_1 b_2 + b_1 d_2 \\ c_1 a_2 + d_1 c_2 & c_1 b_2 + d_1 d_2 \end{vmatrix}$$

(b) If $x = x(u, v)$, $y = y(u, v)$ is a one-to-one transformation, then $u = u(x, y)$, $v = v(x, y)$. Assuming the necessary differentiability, use the result in part (a) and the chain rule to show that
$$\dfrac{\partial(x, y)}{\partial(u, v)} \cdot \dfrac{\partial(u, v)}{\partial(x, y)} = 1$$

44–46 The formula obtained in part (b) of Exercise 43 is useful in integration problems where it is inconvenient or impossible to solve the transformation equations $u = f(x, y)$, $v = g(x, y)$ explicitly for x and y in terms of u and v. In these exercises, use the relationship
$$\dfrac{\partial(x, y)}{\partial(u, v)} = \dfrac{1}{\partial(u, v)/\partial(x, y)}$$
to avoid solving for x and y in terms of u and v. ■

44. Use the transformation $u = xy$, $v = xy^4$ to find

$$\iint\limits_{R} \sin(xy)\, dA$$

where R is the region enclosed by the curves $xy = \pi$, $xy = 2\pi$, $xy^4 = 1$, $xy^4 = 2$.

45. Use the transformation $u = x^2 - y^2$, $v = x^2 + y^2$ to find

$$\iint\limits_{R} xy\, dA$$

where R is the region in the first quadrant that is enclosed by the hyperbolas $x^2 - y^2 = 1$, $x^2 - y^2 = 4$ and the circles $x^2 + y^2 = 9$, $x^2 + y^2 = 16$.

46. Use the transformation $u = xy$, $v = x^2 - y^2$ to find

$$\iint\limits_{R} (x^4 - y^4)e^{xy}\, dA$$

where R is the region in the first quadrant enclosed by the hyperbolas $xy = 1$, $xy = 3$, $x^2 - y^2 = 3$, $x^2 - y^2 = 4$.

47. The three-variable analog of the formula derived in part (b) of Exercise 43 is

$$\dfrac{\partial(x, y, z)}{\partial(u, v, w)} \cdot \dfrac{\partial(u, v, w)}{\partial(x, y, z)} = 1$$

Use this result to show that the volume V of the oblique parallelepiped that is bounded by the planes $x + y + 2z = \pm 3$, $x - 2y + z = \pm 2$, $4x + y + z = \pm 6$ is $V = 16$.

48. (a) Consider the transformation

$$x = r\cos\theta, \quad y = r\sin\theta, \quad z = z$$

from cylindrical to rectangular coordinates, where $r \geq 0$. Show that
$$\dfrac{\partial(x, y, z)}{\partial(r, \theta, z)} = r$$

(b) Consider the transformation

$$x = \rho\sin\phi\cos\theta, \quad y = \rho\sin\phi\sin\theta, \quad z = \rho\cos\phi$$

from spherical to rectangular coordinates, where $0 \leq \phi \leq \pi$. Show that
$$\dfrac{\partial(x, y, z)}{\partial(\rho, \phi, \theta)} = \rho^2\sin\phi$$

49. Writing For single-variable definite integrals, the technique of substitution was generally used to simplify the integrand. Discuss some motivations for using a change of variables in a multiple integral.

50. Writing Suppose that the boundary curves of a region R in the xy-plane can be described as level curves of various functions. Discuss how this information can be used to choose an appropriate change of variables for a double integral over R. Illustrate your discussion with an example.

✔ **QUICK CHECK ANSWERS 14.7**

1. (a) The image is the region in the xy-plane enclosed by the parallelogram with vertices $(1, 3)$, $(-3, 5)$, $(-1, 11)$, and $(3, 9)$.
(b) $u = \frac{1}{7}(x + 2y)$, $v = \frac{1}{7}(y - 3x)$.   **2.** S is a region in the uv-plane and R is the image of S in the xy-plane under the
transformation $x = x(u, v)$, $y = y(u, v)$.   **3.** (a) 7 (b) $\int_0^2 \int_1^3 7e^{7u}\,du\,dv$ **4.** $2vw$

14.8 CENTERS OF GRAVITY USING MULTIPLE INTEGRALS

In Section 6.7 we showed how to find the mass and center of gravity of a homogeneous lamina using single integrals. In this section we will show how double and triple integrals can be used to find the mass and center of gravity of inhomogeneous laminas and three-dimensional solids.

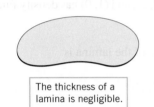

The thickness of a lamina is negligible.

▲ **Figure 14.8.1**

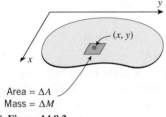

(x, y)

Area $= \Delta A$
Mass $= \Delta M$

▲ **Figure 14.8.2**

■ **DENSITY AND MASS OF AN INHOMOGENEOUS LAMINA**

An idealized flat object that is thin enough to be viewed as a two-dimensional plane region is called a **lamina** (Figure 14.8.1). A lamina is called **homogeneous** if its composition is uniform throughout and **inhomogeneous** otherwise. The **density** of a *homogeneous* lamina was defined in Section 6.7 to be its mass per unit area. Thus, the density δ of a homogeneous lamina of mass M and area A is given by $\delta = M/A$.

For an inhomogeneous lamina the composition may vary from point to point, and hence an appropriate definition of "density" must reflect this. To motivate such a definition, suppose that the lamina is placed in an xy-plane. The density at a point (x, y) can be specified by a function $\delta(x, y)$, called the **density function**, which can be interpreted as follows: Construct a small rectangle centered at (x, y) and let ΔM and ΔA be the mass and area of the portion of the lamina enclosed by this rectangle (Figure 14.8.2). If the ratio $\Delta M/\Delta A$ approaches a limiting value as the dimensions (and hence the area) of the rectangle approach zero, then this limit is considered to be the density of the lamina at (x, y). Symbolically,

$$\delta(x, y) = \lim_{\Delta A \to 0} \frac{\Delta M}{\Delta A} \tag{1}$$

From this relationship we obtain the approximation

$$\Delta M \approx \delta(x, y)\Delta A \tag{2}$$

which relates the mass and area of a small rectangular portion of the lamina centered at (x, y). It is assumed that as the dimensions of the rectangle tend to zero, the error in this approximation also tends to zero.

The following result shows how to find the mass of a lamina from its density function.

14.8.1 MASS OF A LAMINA If a lamina with a continuous density function $\delta(x, y)$ occupies a region R in the xy-plane, then its total mass M is given by

$$M = \iint_R \delta(x, y)\,dA \tag{3}$$

This formula can be motivated by a familiar limiting process that can be outlined as follows: Imagine the lamina to be subdivided into rectangular pieces using lines parallel to the

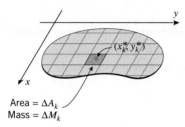

Area = ΔA_k
Mass = ΔM_k

▲ **Figure 14.8.3**

coordinate axes and excluding from consideration any nonrectangular parts at the boundary (Figure 14.8.3). Assume that there are n such rectangular pieces, and suppose that the kth piece has area ΔA_k. If we let (x_k^*, y_k^*) denote the center of the kth piece, then from Formula (2), the mass ΔM_k of this piece can be approximated by

$$\Delta M_k \approx \delta(x_k^*, y_k^*)\Delta A_k \qquad (4)$$

and hence the mass M of the entire lamina can be approximated by

$$M \approx \sum_{k=1}^{n} \delta(x_k^*, y_k^*)\Delta A_k$$

If we now increase n in such a way that the dimensions of the rectangles tend to zero, then it is plausible that the errors in our approximations will approach zero, so

$$M = \lim_{n \to +\infty} \sum_{k=1}^{n} \delta(x_k^*, y_k^*)\Delta A_k = \iint\limits_{R} \delta(x, y)\, dA$$

▶ **Example 1** A triangular lamina with vertices $(0, 0)$, $(0, 1)$, and $(1, 0)$ has density function $\delta(x, y) = xy$. Find its total mass.

Solution. Referring to (3) and Figure 14.8.4, the mass M of the lamina is

$$M = \iint\limits_{R} \delta(x, y)\, dA = \iint\limits_{R} xy\, dA = \int_0^1 \int_0^{-x+1} xy\, dy\, dx$$

$$= \int_0^1 \left[\frac{1}{2}xy^2\right]_{y=0}^{-x+1} dx = \int_0^1 \left[\frac{1}{2}x^3 - x^2 + \frac{1}{2}x\right] dx = \frac{1}{24} \text{ (unit of mass)} \quad ◀$$

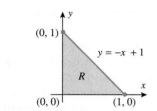

▲ **Figure 14.8.4**

■ **CENTER OF GRAVITY OF AN INHOMOGENEOUS LAMINA**

Recall that the ***center of gravity*** of a lamina occupying a region R in the horizontal xy-plane is the point $(\bar{x}, \bar{y})$ such that the effect of gravity on the lamina is "equivalent" to that of a single force acting at $(\bar{x}, \bar{y})$. If $(\bar{x}, \bar{y})$ is in R, then the lamina will balance horizontally on a point of support placed at $(\bar{x}, \bar{y})$. In Section 6.7 we showed how to locate the center of gravity of a homogeneous lamina. We now turn to this problem for an inhomogeneous lamina.

14.8.2 PROBLEM   Suppose that a lamina with a continuous density function $\delta(x, y)$ occupies a region R in a horizontal xy-plane. Find the coordinates $(\bar{x}, \bar{y})$ of the center of gravity.

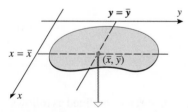

▲ **Figure 14.8.5**

To motivate the solution of Problem 14.8.2, consider what happens if we try to place the lamina in Figure 14.8.5 on a knife-edge running along the line $y = \bar{y}$. Since the lamina behaves as if its entire mass is concentrated at $(\bar{x}, \bar{y})$, the lamina will be in perfect balance. Similarly, the lamina will be in perfect balance if the knife-edge runs along the line $x = \bar{x}$. To find these lines of balance we begin by reviewing some results from Section 6.7 about rotations.

Recall that if a point-mass m is located at the point (x, y), then the moment of m about $x = a$ measures the tendency of the mass to produce a rotation about the line $x = a$, and the moment of m about $y = c$ measures the tendency of the mass to produce a rotation about the line $y = c$. The moments are given by the following formulas:

$$\begin{bmatrix} \text{moment of } m \\ \text{about the} \\ \text{line } x = a \end{bmatrix} = m(x - a) \quad \text{and} \quad \begin{bmatrix} \text{moment of } m \\ \text{about the} \\ \text{line } y = c \end{bmatrix} = m(y - c) \qquad (5\text{--}6)$$

If a number of point-masses are distributed throughout the xy-plane, the sum of their moments about $x = a$ is a measure of the tendency of the masses to produce a rotation of the plane (viewed as a weightless sheet) about the line $x = a$. If the sum of these moments is zero, the collective masses will produce no net rotational effect about the line. (Intuitively, this means that the plane would balance on a knife-edge along the line $x = a$. Similarly, if the sum of the moments of the masses about $y = c$ is zero, the plane would balance on a knife-edge along the line $y = c$.)

We are now ready to solve Problem 14.8.2. We imagine the lamina to be subdivided into rectangular pieces using lines parallel to the coordinate axes and excluding from consideration any nonrectangular pieces at the boundary (Figure 14.8.3). We assume that there are n such rectangular pieces and that the kth piece has area ΔA_k and mass ΔM_k. We will let (x_k^*, y_k^*) be the center of the kth piece, and we will assume that the entire mass of the kth piece is concentrated at its center. From (4), the mass of the kth piece can be approximated by

$$\Delta M_k \approx \delta(x_k^*, y_k^*)\Delta A_k$$

Since the lamina balances on the lines $x = \bar{x}$ and $y = \bar{y}$, the sum of the moments of the rectangular pieces about those lines should be close to zero; that is,

$$\sum_{k=1}^{n}(x_k^* - \bar{x})\Delta M_k = \sum_{k=1}^{n}(x_k^* - \bar{x})\delta(x_k^*, y_k^*)\Delta A_k \approx 0$$

$$\sum_{k=1}^{n}(y_k^* - \bar{y})\Delta M_k = \sum_{k=1}^{n}(y_k^* - \bar{y})\delta(x_k^*, y_k^*)\Delta A_k \approx 0$$

If we now increase n in such a way that the dimensions of the rectangles tend to zero, then it is plausible that the errors in our approximations will approach zero, so that

$$\lim_{n \to +\infty} \sum_{k=1}^{n}(x_k^* - \bar{x})\delta(x_k^*, y_k^*)\Delta A_k = 0$$

$$\lim_{n \to +\infty} \sum_{k=1}^{n}(y_k^* - \bar{y})\delta(x_k^*, y_k^*)\Delta A_k = 0$$

from which we obtain

$$\iint\limits_{R} (x - \bar{x})\delta(x, y)\, dA = \iint\limits_{R} x\delta(x, y)\, dA - \bar{x}\iint\limits_{R} \delta(x, y)\, dA = 0 \qquad (7)$$

$$\iint\limits_{R} (y - \bar{y})\delta(x, y)\, dA = \iint\limits_{R} y\delta(x, y)\, dA - \bar{y}\iint\limits_{R} \delta(x, y)\, dA = 0 \qquad (8)$$

Solving (7) and (8) respectively for $\bar{x}$ and $\bar{y}$ gives formulas for the center of gravity of a lamina:

> **Center of Gravity $(\bar{x}, \bar{y})$ of a Lamina**
>
> $$\bar{x} = \frac{\displaystyle\iint\limits_{R} x\delta(x, y)\, dA}{\displaystyle\iint\limits_{R} \delta(x, y)\, dA}, \qquad \bar{y} = \frac{\displaystyle\iint\limits_{R} y\delta(x, y)\, dA}{\displaystyle\iint\limits_{R} \delta(x, y)\, dA} \qquad (9\text{--}10)$$

In both formulas the denominator is the mass M of the lamina [see (3)]. Following the terminology of Section 6.7, the numerator in the formula for $\bar{x}$ is denoted by M_y and is called the ***first moment of the lamina about the y-axis***; the numerator of the formula for $\bar{y}$ is denoted by M_x and is called the ***first moment of the lamina about the x-axis***. Thus, Formulas (9) and (10) can be expressed as

Alternative Formulas for Center of Gravity $(\bar{x}, \bar{y})$ ***of a Lamina***

$$\bar{x} = \frac{M_y}{M} = \frac{1}{\text{mass of } R} \iint\limits_R x\delta(x, y)\, dA \tag{11}$$

$$\bar{y} = \frac{M_x}{M} = \frac{1}{\text{mass of } R} \iint\limits_R y\delta(x, y)\, dA \tag{12}$$

▶ **Example 2** Find the center of gravity of the triangular lamina with vertices $(0, 0)$, $(0, 1)$, and $(1, 0)$ and density function $\delta(x, y) = xy$.

Solution. The lamina is shown in Figure 14.8.4. In Example 1 we found the mass of the lamina to be

$$M = \iint\limits_R \delta(x, y)\, dA = \iint\limits_R xy\, dA = \frac{1}{24}$$

The moment of the lamina about the y-axis is

$$M_y = \iint\limits_R x\delta(x, y)\, dA = \iint\limits_R x^2 y\, dA = \int_0^1 \int_0^{-x+1} x^2 y\, dy\, dx$$

$$= \int_0^1 \left[\frac{1}{2}x^2 y^2\right]_{y=0}^{-x+1} dx = \int_0^1 \left(\frac{1}{2}x^4 - x^3 + \frac{1}{2}x^2\right) dx = \frac{1}{60}$$

and the moment about the x-axis is

$$M_x = \iint\limits_R y\delta(x, y)\, dA = \iint\limits_R xy^2\, dA = \int_0^1 \int_0^{-x+1} xy^2\, dy\, dx$$

$$= \int_0^1 \left[\frac{1}{3}xy^3\right]_{y=0}^{-x+1} dx = \int_0^1 \left(-\frac{1}{3}x^4 + x^3 - x^2 + \frac{1}{3}x\right) dx = \frac{1}{60}$$

From (11) and (12),

$$\bar{x} = \frac{M_y}{M} = \frac{1/60}{1/24} = \frac{2}{5}, \quad \bar{y} = \frac{M_x}{M} = \frac{1/60}{1/24} = \frac{2}{5}$$

so the center of gravity is $\left(\frac{2}{5}, \frac{2}{5}\right)$. ◀

Recall that the center of gravity of a *homogeneous* lamina is called the ***centroid of the lamina*** or sometimes the ***centroid of the region R***. Because the density function δ is constant for a homogeneous lamina, the factor δ may be moved through the integral signs in (9) and (10) and canceled. Thus, the centroid $(\bar{x}, \bar{y})$ is a geometric property of the region R and is given by the following formulas:

Centroid of a Region R

$$\bar{x} = \frac{\iint\limits_{R} x\, dA}{\iint\limits_{R} dA} = \frac{1}{\text{area of } R} \iint\limits_{R} x\, dA \tag{13}$$

$$\bar{y} = \frac{\iint\limits_{R} y\, dA}{\iint\limits_{R} dA} = \frac{1}{\text{area of } R} \iint\limits_{R} y\, dA \tag{14}$$

▶ **Example 3** Find the centroid of the semicircular region in Figure 14.8.6.

Solution. By symmetry, $\bar{x} = 0$ since the y-axis is obviously a line of balance. From (14),

$$\bar{y} = \frac{1}{\text{area of } R} \iint\limits_{R} y\, dA = \frac{1}{\frac{1}{2}\pi a^2} \iint\limits_{R} y\, dA$$

$$= \frac{1}{\frac{1}{2}\pi a^2} \int_0^\pi \int_0^a (r\sin\theta)r\, dr\, d\theta \qquad \boxed{\text{Evaluating in polar coordinates}}$$

$$= \frac{1}{\frac{1}{2}\pi a^2} \int_0^\pi \left[\frac{1}{3}r^3\sin\theta\right]_{r=0}^a d\theta$$

$$= \frac{1}{\frac{1}{2}\pi a^2}\left(\frac{1}{3}a^3\right)\int_0^\pi \sin\theta\, d\theta = \frac{1}{\frac{1}{2}\pi a^2}\left(\frac{2}{3}a^3\right) = \frac{4a}{3\pi}$$

so the centroid is $\left(0, \dfrac{4a}{3\pi}\right)$. ◀

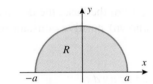

▲ **Figure 14.8.6**

Compare the calculation in Example 3 to that of Example 3 in Section 6.7.

■ **CENTER OF GRAVITY AND CENTROID OF A SOLID**

For a three-dimensional solid G, the formulas for moments, center of gravity, and centroid are similar to those for laminas. If G is *homogeneous*, then its **density** is defined to be its mass per unit volume. Thus, if G is a homogeneous solid of mass M and volume V, then its density δ is given by $\delta = M/V$. If G is inhomogeneous and is in an xyz-coordinate system, then its density at a general point (x, y, z) is specified by a **density function** $\delta(x, y, z)$ whose value at a point can be viewed as a limit:

$$\delta(x, y, z) = \lim_{\Delta V \to 0} \frac{\Delta M}{\Delta V}$$

where ΔM and ΔV represent the mass and volume of a rectangular parallelepiped, centered at (x, y, z), whose dimensions tend to zero (Figure 14.8.7).

Using the discussion of laminas as a model, you should be able to show that the mass M of a solid with a continuous density function $\delta(x, y, z)$ is

$$M = \text{mass of } G = \iiint\limits_{G} \delta(x, y, z)\, dV \tag{15}$$

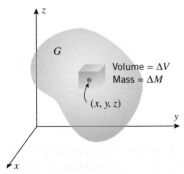

▲ **Figure 14.8.7**

The formulas for center of gravity and centroid are as follows:

Center of Gravity $(\bar{x}, \bar{y}, \bar{z})$ of a Solid G	**Centroid $(\bar{x}, \bar{y}, \bar{z})$ of a Solid G**
$$\bar{x} = \frac{1}{M} \iiint\limits_{G} x\delta(x, y, z)\, dV$$	$$\bar{x} = \frac{1}{V} \iiint\limits_{G} x\, dV$$
$$\bar{y} = \frac{1}{M} \iiint\limits_{G} y\delta(x, y, z)\, dV$$	$$\bar{y} = \frac{1}{V} \iiint\limits_{G} y\, dV$$
$$\bar{z} = \frac{1}{M} \iiint\limits_{G} z\delta(x, y, z)\, dV$$	$$\bar{z} = \frac{1}{V} \iiint\limits_{G} z\, dV$$

(16–17)

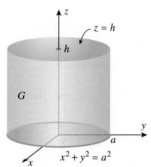

▲ **Figure 14.8.8**

▶ **Example 4** Find the mass and the center of gravity of a cylindrical solid of height h and radius a (Figure 14.8.8), assuming that the density at each point is proportional to the distance between the point and the base of the solid.

Solution. Since the density is proportional to the distance z from the base, the density function has the form $\delta(x, y, z) = kz$, where k is some (unknown) positive constant of proportionality. From (15) the mass of the solid is

$$M = \iiint\limits_{G} \delta(x, y, z)\, dV = \int_{-a}^{a} \int_{-\sqrt{a^2-x^2}}^{\sqrt{a^2-x^2}} \int_{0}^{h} kz\, dz\, dy\, dx$$

$$= k \int_{-a}^{a} \int_{-\sqrt{a^2-x^2}}^{\sqrt{a^2-x^2}} \frac{1}{2}h^2\, dy\, dx$$

$$= kh^2 \int_{-a}^{a} \sqrt{a^2 - x^2}\, dx$$

$$= \tfrac{1}{2}kh^2\pi a^2 \qquad \boxed{\text{Interpret the integral as the area of a semicircle.}}$$

Without additional information, the constant k cannot be determined. However, as we will now see, the value of k does not affect the center of gravity.

From (16),

$$\bar{z} = \frac{1}{M} \iiint\limits_{G} z\delta(x, y, z)\, dV = \frac{1}{\frac{1}{2}kh^2\pi a^2} \iiint\limits_{G} z\delta(x, y, z)\, dV$$

$$= \frac{1}{\frac{1}{2}kh^2\pi a^2} \int_{-a}^{a} \int_{-\sqrt{a^2-x^2}}^{\sqrt{a^2-x^2}} \int_{0}^{h} z(kz)\, dz\, dy\, dx$$

$$= \frac{k}{\frac{1}{2}kh^2\pi a^2} \int_{-a}^{a} \int_{-\sqrt{a^2-x^2}}^{\sqrt{a^2-x^2}} \frac{1}{3}h^3\, dy\, dx$$

$$= \frac{\frac{1}{3}kh^3}{\frac{1}{2}kh^2\pi a^2} \int_{-a}^{a} 2\sqrt{a^2 - x^2}\, dx$$

$$= \frac{\frac{1}{3}kh^3\pi a^2}{\frac{1}{2}kh^2\pi a^2} = \frac{2}{3}h$$

Similar calculations using (16) will yield $\bar{x} = \bar{y} = 0$. However, this is evident by inspection, since it follows from the symmetry of the solid and the form of its density function that the center of gravity is on the z-axis. Thus, the center of gravity is $\left(0, 0, \frac{2}{3}h\right)$. ◀

▶ **Example 5**   Find the centroid of the solid G bounded below by the cone $z = \sqrt{x^2 + y^2}$ and above by the sphere $x^2 + y^2 + z^2 = 16$.

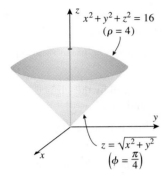

Solution.   The solid G is sketched in Figure 14.8.9. In Example 3 of Section 14.6, spherical coordinates were used to find that the volume of G is

$$V = \frac{64\pi}{3}(2 - \sqrt{2})$$

By symmetry, the centroid $(\bar{x}, \bar{y}, \bar{z})$ is on the z-axis, so $\bar{x} = \bar{y} = 0$. In spherical coordinates, the equation of the sphere $x^2 + y^2 + z^2 = 16$ is $\rho = 4$ and the equation of the cone $z = \sqrt{x^2 + y^2}$ is $\phi = \pi/4$, so from (17) we have

$$\bar{z} = \frac{1}{V} \iiint\limits_{G} z \, dV = \frac{1}{V} \int_0^{2\pi} \int_0^{\pi/4} \int_0^4 (\rho \cos\phi)\rho^2 \sin\phi \, d\rho \, d\phi \, d\theta$$

$$= \frac{1}{V} \int_0^{2\pi} \int_0^{\pi/4} \left[\frac{\rho^4}{4} \cos\phi \sin\phi \right]_{\rho=0}^4 d\phi \, d\theta$$

$$= \frac{64}{V} \int_0^{2\pi} \int_0^{\pi/4} \sin\phi \cos\phi \, d\phi \, d\theta = \frac{64}{V} \int_0^{2\pi} \left[\frac{1}{2} \sin^2\phi \right]_{\phi=0}^{\pi/4} d\theta$$

$$= \frac{16}{V} \int_0^{2\pi} d\theta = \frac{32\pi}{V} = \frac{3}{2(2 - \sqrt{2})}$$

The centroid of G is

$$(\bar{x}, \bar{y}, \bar{z}) = \left(0, 0, \frac{3}{2(2 - \sqrt{2})} \right) \approx (0, 0, 2.561) \blacktriangleleft$$

Figure 14.8.9

✔ **QUICK CHECK EXERCISES 14.8**   *(See page 1080 for answers.)*

1. The total mass of a lamina with continuous density function $\delta(x, y)$ that occupies a region R in the xy-plane is given by $M = $ _____.

2. Consider a lamina with mass M and continuous density function $\delta(x, y)$ that occupies a region R in the xy-plane. The x-coordinate of the center of gravity of the lamina is M_y/M, where M_y is called the _____ and is given by the double integral _____.

3. Let R be the region between the graphs of $y = x^2$ and $y = 2 - x$ for $0 \leq x \leq 1$. The area of R is $\frac{7}{6}$ and the centroid of R is _____.

EXERCISE SET 14.8   Graphing Utility   [C] CAS

1–4 Find the mass and center of gravity of the lamina.

1. A lamina with density $\delta(x, y) = x + y$ is bounded by the x-axis, the line $x = 1$, and the curve $y = \sqrt{x}$.

2. A lamina with density $\delta(x, y) = y$ is bounded by $y = \sin x$, $y = 0$, $x = 0$, and $x = \pi$.

3. A lamina with density $\delta(x, y) = xy$ is in the first quadrant and is bounded by the circle $x^2 + y^2 = a^2$ and the coordinate axes.

4. A lamina with density $\delta(x, y) = x^2 + y^2$ is bounded by the x-axis and the upper half of the circle $x^2 + y^2 = 1$.

FOCUS ON CONCEPTS

5–6 For the given density function, make a conjecture about the coordinates of the center of gravity and confirm your conjecture by integrating.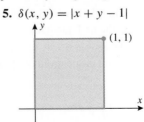

5. $\delta(x, y) = |x + y - 1|$

6. $\delta(x, y) = 1 + x^2 + y^2$

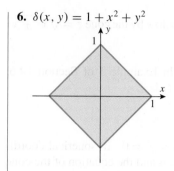

7–8 Make a conjecture about the coordinates of the centroid of the region and confirm your conjecture by integrating. ■

7.   **8.**

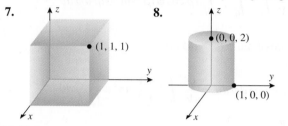

9–12 True–False Determine whether the statement is true or false. Explain your answer. ■

9. The center of gravity of a homogeneous lamina in a plane is located at the lamina's centroid.

10. The mass of a two-dimensional lamina is the product of its area and the density of the lamia at its centroid.

11. The coordinates of the center of gravity of a two-dimensional lamina are the lamina's first moments about the y- and x-axes, respectively.

12. The density of a solid in 3-space is measured in units of mass per unit area.

13. Show that in polar coordinates the formulas for the centroid $(\bar{x}, \bar{y})$ of a region R are

$$\bar{x} = \frac{1}{\text{area of } R} \iint\limits_R r^2 \cos\theta \, dr \, d\theta$$

$$\bar{y} = \frac{1}{\text{area of } R} \iint\limits_R r^2 \sin\theta \, dr \, d\theta$$

14. Use the result of Exercise 13 to find the centroid $(\bar{x}, \bar{y})$ of the region enclosed by the cardioid $r = a(1 + \sin\theta)$.

15. Use the result of Exercise 13 to find the centroid $(\bar{x}, \bar{y})$ of the petal of the rose $r = \sin 2\theta$ in the first quadrant.

16. Let R be the rectangle bounded by the lines $x = 0$, $x = 3$, $y = 0$, and $y = 2$. By inspection, find the centroid of R and use it to evaluate

$$\iint\limits_R x \, dA \quad \text{and} \quad \iint\limits_R y \, dA$$

17–22 Find the centroid of the solid. ■

17. The tetrahedron in the first octant enclosed by the coordinate planes and the plane $x + y + z = 1$.

18. The solid bounded by the parabolic cylinder $z = 1 - y^2$ and the planes $x + z = 1$, $x = 0$, and $z = 0$.

19. The solid bounded by the surface $z = y^2$ and the planes $x = 0$, $x = 1$, and $z = 1$.

20. The solid in the first octant bounded by the surface $z = xy$ and the planes $z = 0$, $x = 2$, and $y = 2$.

21. The solid in the first octant that is bounded by the sphere $x^2 + y^2 + z^2 = a^2$ and the coordinate planes.

22. The solid enclosed by the xy-plane and the hemisphere $z = \sqrt{a^2 - x^2 - y^2}$.

23–26 Find the mass and center of gravity of the solid. ■

23. The cube that has density $\delta(x, y, z) = a - x$ and is defined by the inequalities $0 \le x \le a$, $0 \le y \le a$, and $0 \le z \le a$.

24. The cylindrical solid that has density $\delta(x, y, z) = h - z$ and is enclosed by $x^2 + y^2 = a^2$, $z = 0$, and $z = h$.

25. The solid that has density $\delta(x, y, z) = yz$ and is enclosed by $z = 1 - y^2$ (for $y \ge 0$), $z = 0$, $y = 0$, $x = -1$, and $x = 1$.

26. The solid that has density $\delta(x, y, z) = xz$ and is enclosed by $y = 9 - x^2$ (for $x \ge 0$), $x = 0$, $y = 0$, $z = 0$, and $z = 1$.

27. Find the center of gravity of the square lamina with vertices $(0, 0)$, $(1, 0)$, $(0, 1)$, and $(1, 1)$ if
 (a) the density is proportional to the square of the distance from the origin;
 (b) the density is proportional to the distance from the y-axis.

28. Find the center of gravity of the cube that is determined by the inequalities $0 \le x \le 1$, $0 \le y \le 1$, $0 \le z \le 1$ if
 (a) the density is proportional to the square of the distance to the origin;
 (b) the density is proportional to the sum of the distances to the faces that lie in the coordinate planes.

c **29.** Use the numerical triple integral capability of a CAS to approximate the location of the centroid of the solid that is bounded above by the surface $z = 1/(1 + x^2 + y^2)$, below by the xy-plane, and laterally by the plane $y = 0$ and the surface $y = \sin x$ for $0 \le x \le \pi$ (see the accompanying figure on the next page).

30. The accompanying figure on the next page shows the solid that is bounded above by the surface $z = 1/(x^2 + y^2 + 1)$, below by the xy-plane, and laterally by the cylindrical surface $x^2 + y^2 = a^2$.
 (a) By symmetry, the centroid of the solid lies on the z-axis. Make a conjecture about the behavior of the z-coordinate of the centroid as $a \to 0^+$ and as $a \to +\infty$.
 (b) Find the z-coordinate of the centroid, and check your conjecture by calculating the appropriate limits. *(cont.)*

(c) Use a graphing utility to plot the z-coordinate of the centroid versus a, and use the graph to estimate the value of a for which the centroid is $(0, 0, 0.25)$.

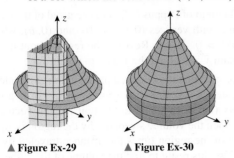

▲ **Figure Ex-29**   ▲ **Figure Ex-30**

31–32 Use cylindrical coordinates. ■

31. Find the mass of the solid with density $\delta(x, y, z) = 3 - z$ that is bounded by the cone $z = \sqrt{x^2 + y^2}$ and the plane $z = 3$.

32. Find the mass of a right circular cylinder of radius a and height h if the density is proportional to the distance from the base. (Let k be the constant of proportionality.)

33–34 Use spherical coordinates. ■

33. Find the mass of a spherical solid of radius a if the density is proportional to the distance from the center. (Let k be the constant of proportionality.)

34. Find the mass of the solid enclosed between the spheres $x^2 + y^2 + z^2 = 1$ and $x^2 + y^2 + z^2 = 4$ if the density is $\delta(x, y, z) = (x^2 + y^2 + z^2)^{-1/2}$.

35–36 Use cylindrical coordinates to find the centroid of the solid. ■

35. The solid that is bounded above by the sphere

$$x^2 + y^2 + z^2 = 2$$

and below by the paraboloid $z = x^2 + y^2$.

36. The solid that is bounded by the cone $z = \sqrt{x^2 + y^2}$ and the plane $z = 2$.

37–38 Use spherical coordinates to find the centroid of the solid. ■

37. The solid in the first octant bounded by the coordinate planes and the sphere $x^2 + y^2 + z^2 = a^2$.

38. The solid bounded above by the sphere $\rho = 4$ and below by the cone $\phi = \pi/3$.

39. Find the mass of the solid that is enclosed by the sphere $x^2 + y^2 + z^2 = 1$ and lies above the cone $z = \sqrt{x^2 + y^2}$ if the density is $\delta(x, y, z) = \sqrt{x^2 + y^2 + z^2}$.

40. Find the center of gravity of the solid bounded by the paraboloid $z = 1 - x^2 - y^2$ and the xy-plane, assuming the density to be $\delta(x, y, z) = x^2 + y^2 + z^2$.

41. Find the center of gravity of the solid that is bounded by the cylinder $x^2 + y^2 = 1$, the cone $z = \sqrt{x^2 + y^2}$, and the xy-plane if the density is $\delta(x, y, z) = z$.

42. Find the center of gravity of the solid hemisphere bounded by $z = \sqrt{a^2 - x^2 - y^2}$ and $z = 0$ if the density is proportional to the distance from the origin.

43. Find the centroid of the solid that is enclosed by the hemispheres $y = \sqrt{9 - x^2 - z^2}$, $y = \sqrt{4 - x^2 - z^2}$, and the plane $y = 0$.

44. Suppose that the density at a point in a gaseous spherical star is modeled by the formula

$$\delta = \delta_0 e^{-(\rho/R)^3}$$

where δ_0 is a positive constant, R is the radius of the star, and ρ is the distance from the point to the star's center. Find the mass of the star.

45–46 The tendency of a lamina to resist a change in rotational motion about an axis is measured by its ***moment of inertia*** about that axis. If a lamina occupies a region R of the xy-plane, and if its density function $\delta(x, y)$ is continuous on R, then the moments of inertia about the x-axis, the y-axis, and the z-axis are denoted by I_x, I_y, and I_z, respectively, and are defined by

$$I_x = \iint_R y^2\, \delta(x, y)\, dA, \quad I_y = \iint_R x^2\, \delta(x, y)\, dA,$$

$$I_z = \iint_R (x^2 + y^2)\, \delta(x, y)\, dA$$

Use these definitions in Exercises 45 and 46. ■

45. Consider the rectangular lamina that occupies the region described by the inequalities $0 \le x \le a$ and $0 \le y \le b$. Assuming that the lamina has constant density δ, show that

$$I_x = \frac{\delta a b^3}{3}, \quad I_y = \frac{\delta a^3 b}{3}, \quad I_z = \frac{\delta a b (a^2 + b^2)}{3}$$

46. Consider the circular lamina that occupies the region described by the inequalities $0 \le x^2 + y^2 \le a^2$. Assuming that the lamina has constant density δ, show that

$$I_x = I_y = \frac{\delta \pi a^4}{4}, \quad I_z = \frac{\delta \pi a^4}{2}$$

47–50 The tendency of a solid to resist a change in rotational motion about an axis is measured by its ***moment of inertia*** about that axis. If the solid occupies a region G in an xyz-coordinate system, and if its density function $\delta(x, y, z)$ is continuous on G, then the moments of inertia about the x-axis, the y-axis, and the z-axis are denoted by I_x, I_y, and I_z, respectively, and are defined by

$$I_x = \iiint_G (y^2 + z^2)\, \delta(x, y, z)\, dV$$

$$I_y = \iiint_G (x^2 + z^2)\, \delta(x, y, z)\, dV$$

$$I_z = \iiint_G (x^2 + y^2)\, \delta(x, y, z)\, dV$$

In these exercises, find the indicated moments of inertia of the solid, assuming that it has constant density δ. ■

47. I_z for the solid cylinder $x^2 + y^2 \leq a^2, 0 \leq z \leq h$.

48. I_y for the solid cylinder $x^2 + y^2 \leq a^2, 0 \leq z \leq h$.

49. I_z for the hollow cylinder $a_1^2 \leq x^2 + y^2 \leq a_2^2, 0 \leq z \leq h$.

50. I_z for the solid sphere $x^2 + y^2 + z^2 \leq a^2$.

51–55 These exercises reference the **Theorem of Pappus**:
If R is a bounded plane region and L is a line that lies in the plane of R such that R is entirely on one side of L, then the volume of the solid formed by revolving R about L is given by

$$volume = (\ area\ of\ R) \cdot \begin{pmatrix} distance\ traveled \\ by\ the\ centroid \end{pmatrix} \blacksquare$$

51. Perform the following steps to prove the Theorem of Pappus:

(a) Introduce an xy-coordinate system so that L is along the y-axis and the region R is in the first quadrant. Partition R into rectangular subregions in the usual way and let R_k be a typical subregion of R with center (x_k^*, y_k^*) and area $\Delta A_k = \Delta x_k \Delta y_k$. Show that the volume generated by R_k as it revolves about L is

$$2\pi x_k^* \Delta x_k \Delta y_k = 2\pi x_k^* \Delta A_k$$

(b) Show that the volume generated by R as it revolves about L is

$$V = \iint\limits_R 2\pi x\, dA = 2\pi \cdot \bar{x} \cdot [area\ of\ R]$$

52. Use the Theorem of Pappus and the result of Example 3 to find the volume of the solid generated when the region bounded by the x-axis and the semicircle $y = \sqrt{a^2 - x^2}$ is revolved about

(a) the line $y = -a$ (b) the line $y = x - a$.

53. Use the Theorem of Pappus and the fact that the area of an ellipse with semiaxes a and b is πab to find the volume of the elliptical torus generated by revolving the ellipse

$$\frac{(x-k)^2}{a^2} + \frac{y^2}{b^2} = 1$$

about the y-axis. Assume that $k > a$.

54. Use the Theorem of Pappus to find the volume of the solid that is generated when the region enclosed by $y = x^2$ and $y = 8 - x^2$ is revolved about the x-axis.

55. Use the Theorem of Pappus to find the centroid of the triangular region with vertices $(0, 0)$, $(a, 0)$, and $(0, b)$, where $a > 0$ and $b > 0$. [*Hint:* Revolve the region about the x-axis to obtain $\bar{y}$ and about the y-axis to obtain $\bar{x}$.]

56. It can be proved that if a bounded plane region slides along a helix in such a way that the region is always orthogonal to the helix (i.e., orthogonal to the unit tangent vector to the helix), then the volume swept out by the region is equal to the area of the region times the distance traveled by its centroid. Use this result to find the volume of the "tube" in the accompanying figure that is swept out by sliding a circle of radius $\frac{1}{2}$ along the helix

$$x = \cos t, \quad y = \sin t, \quad z = \frac{t}{4} \quad (0 \leq t \leq 4\pi)$$

in such a way that the circle is always centered on the helix and lies in the plane perpendicular to the helix.

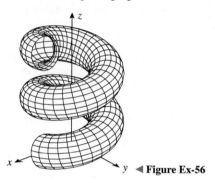

◀ **Figure Ex-56**

57. Writing   Give a physical interpretation of the "center of gravity" of a lamina.

✔ QUICK CHECK ANSWERS 14.8

1. $\iint\limits_R \delta(x, y)\, dA$ **2.** first moment about the y-axis; $\iint\limits_R x\delta(x, y)\, dA$ **3.** $\left(\dfrac{5}{14}, \dfrac{32}{35} \right)$

CHAPTER 14 REVIEW EXERCISES

1. The double integral over a region R in the xy-plane is defined as

$$\iint\limits_R f(x, y)\, dA = \lim_{n \to +\infty} \sum_{k=1}^{n} f(x_k^*, y_k^*)\, \Delta A_k$$

Describe the procedure on which this definition is based.

2. The triple integral over a solid G in an xyz-coordinate system is defined as

$$\iiint\limits_G f(x, y, z)\, dV = \lim_{n \to +\infty} \sum_{k=1}^{n} f(x_k^*, y_k^*, z_k^*)\, \Delta V_k$$

Describe the procedure on which this definition is based.

3. (a) Express the area of a region R in the xy-plane as a double integral.
   (b) Express the volume of a region G in an xyz-coordinate system as a triple integral.
   (c) Express the area of the portion of the surface $z = f(x, y)$ that lies above the region R in the xy-plane as a double integral.

4. (a) Write down parametric equations for a sphere of radius a centered at the origin.
   (b) Write down parametric equations for the right circular cylinder of radius a and height h that is centered on the z-axis, has its base in the xy-plane, and extends in the positive z-direction.

5. Let R be the region in the accompanying figure. Fill in the missing limits of integration in the iterated integral

$$\int_{\square}^{\square} \int_{\square}^{\square} f(x, y)\, dx\, dy$$

over R.

6. Let R be the region shown in the accompanying figure. Fill in the missing limits of integration in the sum of the iterated integrals

$$\int_{0}^{2} \int_{\square}^{\square} f(x, y)\, dy\, dx + \int_{2}^{3} \int_{\square}^{\square} f(x, y)\, dy\, dx$$

over R.

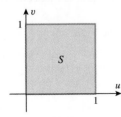

▲ Figure Ex-5

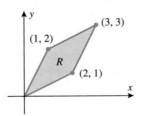

▲ Figure Ex-6

7. (a) Find constants a, b, c, and d such that the transformation $x = au + bv$, $y = cu + dv$ maps the region S in the accompanying figure into the region R.
   (b) Find the area of the parallelogram R by integrating over the region S, and check your answer using a formula from geometry.

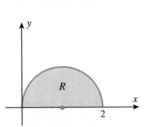

▲ Figure Ex-7

8. Give a geometric argument to show that

$$0 < \int_{0}^{\pi} \int_{0}^{\pi} \sin \sqrt{xy}\, dy\, dx < \pi^2$$

9–10 Evaluate the iterated integral. ■

9. $\displaystyle\int_{1/2}^{1} \int_{0}^{2x} \cos(\pi x^2)\, dy\, dx$ **10.** $\displaystyle\int_{0}^{2} \int_{-y}^{2y} xe^{y^3}\, dx\, dy$

11–12 Express the iterated integral as an equivalent integral with the order of integration reversed. ■

11. $\displaystyle\int_{0}^{2} \int_{0}^{x/2} e^{x} e^{y}\, dy\, dx$ **12.** $\displaystyle\int_{0}^{\pi} \int_{y}^{\pi} \frac{\sin x}{x}\, dx\, dy$

13–14 Sketch the region whose area is represented by the iterated integral. ■

13. $\displaystyle\int_{0}^{\pi/2} \int_{\tan(x/2)}^{\sin x} dy\, dx$

14. $\displaystyle\int_{\pi/6}^{\pi/2} \int_{a}^{a(1+\cos\theta)} r\, dr\, d\theta$ $(a > 0)$

15–16 Evaluate the double integral. ■

15. $\displaystyle\iint_{R} x^2 \sin y^2\, dA$; R is the region that is bounded by $y = x^3$, $y = -x^3$, and $y = 8$.

16. $\displaystyle\iint_{R} (4 - x^2 - y^2)\, dA$; R is the sector in the first quadrant bounded by the circle $x^2 + y^2 = 4$ and the coordinate axes.

17. Convert to rectangular coordinates and evaluate:

$$\int_{0}^{\pi/2} \int_{0}^{2a\sin\theta} r \sin 2\theta\, dr\, d\theta$$

18. Convert to polar coordinates and evaluate:

$$\int_{0}^{\sqrt{2}} \int_{x}^{\sqrt{4-x^2}} 4xy\, dy\, dx$$

19–20 Find the area of the region using a double integral. ■

19. The region bounded by $y = 2x^3$, $2x + y = 4$, and the x-axis.

20. The region enclosed by the rose $r = \cos 3\theta$.

21. Convert to cylindrical coordinates and evaluate:

$$\int_{-2}^{2} \int_{-\sqrt{4-x^2}}^{\sqrt{4-x^2}} \int_{(x^2+y^2)^2}^{16} x^2\, dz\, dy\, dx$$

22. Convert to spherical coordinates and evaluate:

$$\int_{0}^{1} \int_{0}^{\sqrt{1-x^2}} \int_{0}^{\sqrt{1-x^2-y^2}} \frac{1}{1 + x^2 + y^2 + z^2}\, dz\, dy\, dx$$

23. Let G be the region bounded above by the sphere $\rho = a$ and below by the cone $\phi = \pi/3$. Express

$$\iiint_{G} (x^2 + y^2)\, dV$$

as an iterated integral in

(a) spherical coordinates   (b) cylindrical coordinates
(c) rectangular coordinates.

24. Let $G = \{(x, y, z) : x^2 + y^2 \leq z \leq 4x\}$. Express the volume of G as an iterated integral in
(a) rectangular coordinates   (b) cylindrical coordinates.

25–26 Find the volume of the solid using a triple integral. ■

25. The solid bounded below by the cone $\phi = \pi/6$ and above by the plane $z = a$.

26. The solid enclosed between the surfaces $x = y^2 + z^2$ and $x = 1 - y^2$.

27. Find the area of the portion of the surface $z = 3y + 2x^2 + 4$ that is above the triangular region with vertices $(0, 0), (1, 1)$, and $(1, -1)$.

28. Find the surface area of the portion of the spiral ramp

$$\mathbf{r}(u, v) = u \cos v\mathbf{i} + u \sin v\mathbf{j} + v\mathbf{k}$$

for which $0 \leq u \leq 2, 0 \leq v \leq 3u$.

29–30 Find the equation of the tangent plane to the surface at the specified point. ■

29. $\mathbf{r} = u\mathbf{i} + v\mathbf{j} + (u^2 + v^2)\mathbf{k}$; $u = 1, v = 2$

30. $x = u \cosh v, y = u \sinh v, z = u^2$; $(-3, 0, 9)$

31. Suppose that you have a double integral over a region R in the xy-plane and you want to transform that integral into an equivalent double integral over a region S in the uv-plane. Describe the procedure you would use.

32. Use the transformation $u = x - 3y, v = 3x + y$ to find

$$\iint\limits_R \frac{x - 3y}{(3x + y)^2} \, dA$$

where R is the rectangular region enclosed by the lines $x - 3y = 0, x - 3y = 4, 3x + y = 1$, and $3x + y = 3$.

33. Let G be the solid in 3-space defined by the inequalities

$$1 - e^x \leq y \leq 3 - e^x, \quad 1 - y \leq 2z \leq 2 - y, \quad y \leq e^x \leq y + 4$$

(a) Using the coordinate transformation

$$u = e^x + y, \quad v = y + 2z, \quad w = e^x - y$$

calculate the Jacobian $\partial(x, y, z)/\partial(u, v, w)$. Express your answer in terms of u, v, and w.
(b) Using a triple integral and the change of variables given in part (a), find the volume of G.

34. Find the average distance from a point inside a sphere of radius a to the center. [See the definition preceding Exercise 33 of Section 14.5.]

35–36 Find the centroid of the region. ■

35. The region bounded by $y^2 = 4x$ and $y^2 = 8(x - 2)$.

36. The upper half of the ellipse $(x/a)^2 + (y/b)^2 = 1$.

37–38 Find the centroid of the solid. ■

37. The solid cone with vertex $(0, 0, h)$ and with base the disk $x^2 + y^2 \leq a^2$ in the xy-plane.

38. The solid bounded by $y = x^2, z = 0$, and $y + z = 4$.

CHAPTER 14 MAKING CONNECTIONS   [C] CAS

1. The integral $\int_0^{+\infty} e^{-x^2} \, dx$, which arises in probability theory, can be evaluated using the following method. Let the value of the integral be I. Thus,

$$I = \int_0^{+\infty} e^{-x^2} \, dx = \int_0^{+\infty} e^{-y^2} \, dy$$

since the letter used for the variable of integration in a definite integral does not matter.
(a) Give a reasonable argument to show that

$$I^2 = \int_0^{+\infty} \int_0^{+\infty} e^{-(x^2 + y^2)} \, dx \, dy$$

(b) Evaluate the iterated integral in part (a) by converting to polar coordinates.
(c) Use the result in part (b) to show that $I = \sqrt{\pi}/2$.

2. Show that

$$\int_0^{+\infty} \int_0^{+\infty} \frac{1}{(1 + x^2 + y^2)^2} \, dx \, dy = \frac{\pi}{4}$$

[*Hint:* See Exercise 1.]

[C] **3.** (a) Use the numerical integration capability of a CAS to approximate the value of the double integral

$$\int_{-1}^1 \int_0^{\sqrt{1 - x^2}} e^{-(x^2 + y^2)^2} \, dy \, dx$$

(b) Compare the approximation obtained in part (a) to the approximation that results if the integral is first converted to polar coordinates.

[C] **4.** (a) Find the region G over which the triple integral

$$\iiint\limits_G (1 - x^2 - y^2 - z^2) \, dV$$

has its maximum value.
(b) Use the numerical triple integral operation of a CAS to approximate the maximum value.
(c) Find the exact maximum value.

5–6 The accompanying figure shows the graph of an *astroidal sphere*

$$x^{2/3} + y^{2/3} + z^{2/3} = a^{2/3} \quad \blacksquare$$

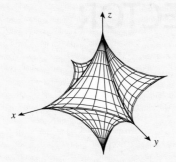

C **5.** (a) Show that the astroidal sphere can be represented parametrically as

$$x = a(\sin u \cos v)^3$$
$$y = a(\sin u \sin v)^3 \qquad (0 \le u \le \pi, \ 0 \le v \le 2\pi)$$
$$z = a(\cos u)^3$$

(b) Use a CAS to approximate the surface area in the case where $a = 1$.

6. Find the volume of the astroidal sphere using a triple integral and the transformation

$$x = \rho(\sin\phi\cos\theta)^3$$
$$y = \rho(\sin\phi\sin\theta)^3$$
$$z = \rho(\cos\phi)^3$$

for which $0 \le \rho \le a, 0 \le \phi \le \pi, 0 \le \theta \le 2\pi$.

NASA Goddard Space Flight Center (NASA/GSFC)

15

TOPICS IN VECTOR CALCULUS

Results in this chapter provide tools for analyzing and understanding the behavior of hurricanes and other fluid flows.

The main theme of this chapter is the concept of a "flow." The body of mathematics that we will study here is concerned with analyzing flows of various types—the flow of a fluid or the flow of electricity, for example. Indeed, the early writings of Isaac Newton on calculus are replete with such nouns as "fluxion" and "fluent," which are rooted in the Latin *fluere* (to flow). We will begin this chapter by introducing the concept of a vector field, which is the mathematical description of a flow. In subsequent sections, we will introduce two new kinds of integrals that are used in a variety of applications to analyze properties of vector fields and flows. Finally, we conclude with three major theorems, Green's Theorem, the Divergence Theorem, and Stokes' Theorem. These theorems provide a deep insight into the nature of flows and are the basis for many of the most important principles in physics and engineering.

15.1 VECTOR FIELDS

In this section we will consider functions that associate vectors with points in 2-space or 3-space. We will see that such functions play an important role in the study of fluid flow, gravitational force fields, electromagnetic force fields, and a wide range of other applied problems.

▲ Figure 15.1.1

■ VECTOR FIELDS

To motivate the mathematical ideas in this section, consider a *unit* point-mass located at any point in the universe. According to Newton's Law of Universal Gravitation, the Earth exerts an attractive force on the mass that is directed toward the center of the Earth and has a magnitude that is inversely proportional to the square of the distance from the mass to the Earth's center (Figure 15.1.1). This association of force vectors with points in space is called the Earth's *gravitational field*. A similar idea arises in fluid flow. Imagine a stream in which the water flows horizontally at every level, and consider the layer of water at a specific depth. At each point of the layer, the water has a certain velocity, which we can represent by a vector at that point (Figure 15.1.2). This association of velocity vectors with points in the two-dimensional layer is called the *velocity field* at that layer. These ideas are captured in the following definition.

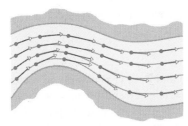

▲ **Figure 15.1.2**

Notice that a vector field is really just a vector-valued function. The term "vector field" is commonly used in physics and engineering.

> **15.1.1   DEFINITION**   A ***vector field*** in a plane is a function that associates with each point P in the plane a unique vector $\mathbf{F}(P)$ parallel to the plane. Similarly, a vector field in 3-space is a function that associates with each point P in 3-space a unique vector $\mathbf{F}(P)$ in 3-space.

Observe that in this definition there is no reference to a coordinate system. However, for computational purposes it is usually desirable to introduce a coordinate system so that vectors can be assigned components. Specifically, if $\mathbf{F}(P)$ is a vector field in an xy-coordinate system, then the point P will have some coordinates (x, y) and the associated vector will have components that are functions of x and y. Thus, the vector field $\mathbf{F}(P)$ can be expressed as

$$\mathbf{F}(x, y) = f(x, y)\mathbf{i} + g(x, y)\mathbf{j}$$

Similarly, in 3-space with an xyz-coordinate system, a vector field $\mathbf{F}(P)$ can be expressed as

$$\mathbf{F}(x, y, z) = f(x, y, z)\mathbf{i} + g(x, y, z)\mathbf{j} + h(x, y, z)\mathbf{k}$$

■ GRAPHICAL REPRESENTATIONS OF VECTOR FIELDS

A vector field in 2-space can be pictured geometrically by drawing representative field vectors $\mathbf{F}(x, y)$ at some well-chosen points in the xy-plane. But, just as it is usually not possible to describe a plane curve completely by plotting finitely many points, so it is usually not possible to describe a vector field completely by drawing finitely many vectors. Nevertheless, such graphical representations can provide useful information about the general behavior of the field if the vectors are chosen appropriately. However, graphical representations of vector fields require a substantial amount of computation, so they are usually created using computers. Figure 15.1.3 shows four computer-generated vector fields. The vector field in part (*a*) might describe the velocity of the current in a stream at various depths. At the bottom of the stream the velocity is zero, but the speed of the current increases as the depth decreases. Points at the same depth have the same speed. The vector field in part (*b*) might describe the velocity at points on a rotating wheel. At the center of the wheel the velocity is zero, but the speed increases with the distance from the center. Points at the same distance from the center have the same speed. The vector field in part (*c*) might describe the repulsive force of an electrical charge—the closer to the charge, the greater the force of repulsion. Part (*d*) shows a vector field in 3-space. Such pictures tend to be cluttered and hence are of lesser value than graphical representations of vector fields in 2-space. Note also that the

TECHNOLOGY MASTERY

If you have a graphing utility that can generate vector fields, read the relevant documentation and try to make reasonable duplicates of parts (*a*) and (*b*) of Figure 15.1.3.

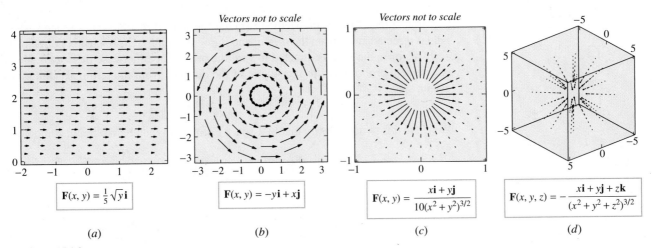

$$(a) \quad \mathbf{F}(x, y) = \tfrac{1}{5}\sqrt{y}\,\mathbf{i}$$

$$(b) \quad \mathbf{F}(x, y) = -y\mathbf{i} + x\mathbf{j}$$

$$(c) \quad \mathbf{F}(x, y) = \frac{x\mathbf{i} + y\mathbf{j}}{10(x^2 + y^2)^{3/2}}$$

$$(d) \quad \mathbf{F}(x, y, z) = -\frac{x\mathbf{i} + y\mathbf{j} + z\mathbf{k}}{(x^2 + y^2 + z^2)^{3/2}}$$

▲ **Figure 15.1.3**

vectors in parts (*b*) and (*c*) are not to scale—their lengths have been compressed for clarity. We will follow this procedure throughout this chapter.

■ A COMPACT NOTATION FOR VECTOR FIELDS

Sometimes it is helpful to denote the vector fields $\mathbf{F}(x, y)$ and $\mathbf{F}(x, y, z)$ entirely in vector notation by identifying (x, y) with the radius vector $\mathbf{r} = x\mathbf{i} + y\mathbf{j}$ and (x, y, z) with the radius vector $\mathbf{r} = x\mathbf{i} + y\mathbf{j} + z\mathbf{k}$. With this notation a vector field in either 2-space or 3-space can be written as $\mathbf{F}(\mathbf{r})$. When no confusion is likely to arise, we will sometimes omit the $\mathbf{r}$ altogether and denote the vector field as $\mathbf{F}$.

■ INVERSE-SQUARE FIELDS

According to Newton's Law of Universal Gravitation, particles with masses m and M attract each other with a force $\mathbf{F}$ of magnitude

$$\|\mathbf{F}\| = \frac{GmM}{r^2} \tag{1}$$

where r is the distance between the particles and G is a constant. If we assume that the particle of mass M is located at the origin of an xyz-coordinate system and $\mathbf{r}$ is the radius vector to the particle of mass m, then $r = \|\mathbf{r}\|$, and the force $\mathbf{F}(\mathbf{r})$ exerted by the particle of mass M on the particle of mass m is in the direction of the unit vector $-\mathbf{r}/\|\mathbf{r}\|$. Thus, it follows from (1) that

$$\mathbf{F}(\mathbf{r}) = -\frac{GmM}{\|\mathbf{r}\|^2}\frac{\mathbf{r}}{\|\mathbf{r}\|} = -\frac{GmM}{\|\mathbf{r}\|^3}\mathbf{r} \tag{2}$$

If m and M are constant, and we let $c = -GmM$, then this formula can be expressed as

$$\mathbf{F}(\mathbf{r}) = \frac{c}{\|\mathbf{r}\|^3}\mathbf{r}$$

Vector fields of this form arise in electromagnetic as well as gravitational problems. Such fields are so important that they have their own terminology.

15.1.2   DEFINITION   If $\mathbf{r}$ is a radius vector in 2-space or 3-space, and if c is a constant, then a vector field of the form
$$\mathbf{F}(\mathbf{r}) = \frac{c}{\|\mathbf{r}\|^3}\mathbf{r} \tag{3}$$

is called an ***inverse-square field***.

Observe that if $c > 0$ in (3), then $\mathbf{F}(\mathbf{r})$ has the same direction as $\mathbf{r}$, so each vector in the field is directed away from the origin; and if $c < 0$, then $\mathbf{F}(\mathbf{r})$ is oppositely directed to $\mathbf{r}$, so each vector in the field is directed toward the origin. In either case the magnitude of $\mathbf{F}(\mathbf{r})$ is inversely proportional to the square of the distance from the terminal point of $\mathbf{r}$ to the origin, since

$$\|\mathbf{F}(\mathbf{r})\| = \frac{|c|}{\|\mathbf{r}\|^3}\|\mathbf{r}\| = \frac{|c|}{\|\mathbf{r}\|^2}$$

We leave it for you to verify that in 2-space Formula (3) can be written in component form as

$$\mathbf{F}(x, y) = \frac{c}{(x^2 + y^2)^{3/2}}(x\mathbf{i} + y\mathbf{j}) \tag{4}$$

and in 3-space as

$$\mathbf{F}(x, y, z) = \frac{c}{(x^2 + y^2 + z^2)^{3/2}}(x\mathbf{i} + y\mathbf{j} + z\mathbf{k}) \tag{5}$$

[see parts (*c*) and (*d*) of Figure 15.1.3].

▶ **Example 1** *Coulomb's law* states that *the electrostatic force exerted by one charged particle on another is directly proportional to the product of the charges and inversely proportional to the square of the distance between them.* This has the same form as Newton's Law of Universal Gravitation, so the electrostatic force field exerted by a charged particle is an inverse-square field. Specifically, if a particle of charge Q is at the origin of a coordinate system, and if $\mathbf{r}$ is the radius vector to a particle of charge q, then the force $\mathbf{F}(\mathbf{r})$ that the particle of charge Q exerts on the particle of charge q is of the form

$$\mathbf{F}(\mathbf{r}) = \frac{qQ}{4\pi\epsilon_0 \|\mathbf{r}\|^3}\mathbf{r}$$

where ϵ_0 is a positive constant (called the ***permittivity constant***). This formula is of form (3) with $c = qQ/4\pi\epsilon_0$. ◀

■ GRADIENT FIELDS

An important class of vector fields arises from the process of finding gradients. Recall that if ϕ is a function of three variables, then the gradient of ϕ is defined as

$$\nabla\phi = \frac{\partial\phi}{\partial x}\mathbf{i} + \frac{\partial\phi}{\partial y}\mathbf{j} + \frac{\partial\phi}{\partial z}\mathbf{k}$$

This formula defines a vector field in 3-space called the ***gradient field of*** $\boldsymbol{\phi}$. Similarly, the gradient of a function of two variables defines a gradient field in 2-space. At each point in a gradient field where the gradient is nonzero, the vector points in the direction in which the rate of increase of ϕ is maximum.

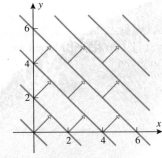

▲ **Figure 15.1.4**

▶ **Example 2** Sketch the gradient field of $\phi(x, y) = x + y$.

Solution. The gradient of ϕ is

$$\nabla\phi = \frac{\partial\phi}{\partial x}\mathbf{i} + \frac{\partial\phi}{\partial y}\mathbf{j} = \mathbf{i} + \mathbf{j}$$

which is constant [i.e., is the same vector at each point (x, y)]. A portion of the vector field is sketched in Figure 15.1.4 together with some level curves of ϕ. Note that at each point, $\nabla\phi$ is normal to the level curve of ϕ through the point (Theorem 13.6.6). ◀

■ CONSERVATIVE FIELDS AND POTENTIAL FUNCTIONS

If $\mathbf{F}(\mathbf{r})$ is an arbitrary vector field in 2-space or 3-space, we can ask whether it is the gradient field of some function ϕ, and if so, how we can find ϕ. This is an important problem in various applications, and we will study it in more detail later. However, there is some terminology for such fields that we will introduce now.

15.1.3 **DEFINITION** A vector field $\mathbf{F}$ in 2-space or 3-space is said to be ***conservative*** in a region if it is the gradient field for some function ϕ in that region, that is, if

$$\mathbf{F} = \nabla\phi$$

The function ϕ is called a ***potential function*** for $\mathbf{F}$ in the region.

▶ **Example 3** Inverse-square fields are conservative in any region that does not contain the origin. For example, in the two-dimensional case the function

$$\phi(x, y) = -\frac{c}{(x^2 + y^2)^{1/2}} \tag{6}$$

is a potential function for (4) in any region not containing the origin, since

$$
\begin{aligned}
\nabla \phi(x, y) &= \frac{\partial \phi}{\partial x}\mathbf{i} + \frac{\partial \phi}{\partial y}\mathbf{j} \\
&= \frac{cx}{(x^2 + y^2)^{3/2}}\mathbf{i} + \frac{cy}{(x^2 + y^2)^{3/2}}\mathbf{j} \\
&= \frac{c}{(x^2 + y^2)^{3/2}}(x\mathbf{i} + y\mathbf{j}) \\
&= \mathbf{F}(x, y)
\end{aligned}
$$

In a later section we will discuss methods for finding potential functions for conservative vector fields. ◀

DIVERGENCE AND CURL

We will now define two important operations on vector fields in 3-space—the *divergence* and the *curl* of the field. These names originate in the study of fluid flow, in which case the divergence relates to the way in which fluid flows toward or away from a point and the curl relates to the rotational properties of the fluid at a point. We will investigate the physical interpretations of these operations in more detail later, but for now we will focus only on their computation.

15.1.4 **DEFINITION** If $\mathbf{F}(x, y, z) = f(x, y, z)\mathbf{i} + g(x, y, z)\mathbf{j} + h(x, y, z)\mathbf{k}$, then we define the *divergence of* $\mathbf{F}$, written div $\mathbf{F}$, to be the function given by

$$\text{div } \mathbf{F} = \frac{\partial f}{\partial x} + \frac{\partial g}{\partial y} + \frac{\partial h}{\partial z} \tag{7}$$

15.1.5 **DEFINITION** If $\mathbf{F}(x, y, z) = f(x, y, z)\mathbf{i} + g(x, y, z)\mathbf{j} + h(x, y, z)\mathbf{k}$, then we define the *curl of* $\mathbf{F}$, written curl $\mathbf{F}$, to be the vector field given by

$$\text{curl } \mathbf{F} = \left(\frac{\partial h}{\partial y} - \frac{\partial g}{\partial z}\right)\mathbf{i} + \left(\frac{\partial f}{\partial z} - \frac{\partial h}{\partial x}\right)\mathbf{j} + \left(\frac{\partial g}{\partial x} - \frac{\partial f}{\partial y}\right)\mathbf{k} \tag{8}$$

REMARK | Observe that div $\mathbf{F}$ and curl $\mathbf{F}$ depend on the point at which they are computed, and hence are more properly written as div $\mathbf{F}(x, y, z)$ and curl $\mathbf{F}(x, y, z)$. However, even though these functions are expressed in terms of x, y, and z, it can be proved that their values at a fixed point depend only on the point and not on the coordinate system selected. This is important in applications, since it allows physicists and engineers to compute the curl and divergence in any convenient coordinate system.

Before proceeding to some examples, we note that div $\mathbf{F}$ has scalar values, whereas curl $\mathbf{F}$ has vector values (i.e., curl $\mathbf{F}$ is itself a vector field). Moreover, for computational purposes it is useful to note that the formula for the curl can be expressed in the determinant form

$$\text{curl } \mathbf{F} = \begin{vmatrix} \mathbf{i} & \mathbf{j} & \mathbf{k} \\ \dfrac{\partial}{\partial x} & \dfrac{\partial}{\partial y} & \dfrac{\partial}{\partial z} \\ f & g & h \end{vmatrix} \tag{9}$$

You should verify that Formula (8) results if the determinant is computed by interpreting a "product" such as $(\partial/\partial x)(g)$ to mean $\partial g/\partial x$. Keep in mind, however, that (9) is just a mnemonic device and not a true determinant, since the entries in a determinant must be numbers, not vectors and partial derivative symbols.

▶ **Example 4** Find the divergence and the curl of the vector field

$$\mathbf{F}(x, y, z) = x^2 y\mathbf{i} + 2y^3 z\mathbf{j} + 3z\mathbf{k}$$

Solution. From (7)

$$\text{div } \mathbf{F} = \frac{\partial}{\partial x}(x^2 y) + \frac{\partial}{\partial y}(2y^3 z) + \frac{\partial}{\partial z}(3z)$$

$$= 2xy + 6y^2 z + 3$$

and from (9)

TECHNOLOGY MASTERY

Most computer algebra systems can compute gradient fields, divergence, and curl. If you have a CAS with these capabilities, read the relevant documentation, and use your CAS to check the computations in Examples 2 and 4.

$$\text{curl } \mathbf{F} = \begin{vmatrix} \mathbf{i} & \mathbf{j} & \mathbf{k} \\ \dfrac{\partial}{\partial x} & \dfrac{\partial}{\partial y} & \dfrac{\partial}{\partial z} \\ x^2 y & 2y^3 z & 3z \end{vmatrix}$$

$$= \left[\frac{\partial}{\partial y}(3z) - \frac{\partial}{\partial z}(2y^3 z) \right] \mathbf{i} + \left[\frac{\partial}{\partial z}(x^2 y) - \frac{\partial}{\partial x}(3z) \right] \mathbf{j} + \left[\frac{\partial}{\partial x}(2y^3 z) - \frac{\partial}{\partial y}(x^2 y) \right] \mathbf{k}$$

$$= -2y^3\mathbf{i} - x^2\mathbf{k} \ \blacktriangleleft$$

▶ **Example 5** Show that the divergence of the inverse-square field

$$\mathbf{F}(x, y, z) = \frac{c}{(x^2 + y^2 + z^2)^{3/2}} (x\mathbf{i} + y\mathbf{j} + z\mathbf{k})$$

is zero.

Solution. The computations can be simplified by letting $r = (x^2 + y^2 + z^2)^{1/2}$, in which case $\mathbf{F}$ can be expressed as

$$\mathbf{F}(x, y, z) = \frac{cx\mathbf{i} + cy\mathbf{j} + cz\mathbf{k}}{r^3} = \frac{cx}{r^3}\mathbf{i} + \frac{cy}{r^3}\mathbf{j} + \frac{cz}{r^3}\mathbf{k}$$

We leave it for you to show that

$$\frac{\partial r}{\partial x} = \frac{x}{r}, \quad \frac{\partial r}{\partial y} = \frac{y}{r}, \quad \frac{\partial r}{\partial z} = \frac{z}{r}$$

Thus

$$\text{div } \mathbf{F} = c\left[\frac{\partial}{\partial x}\left(\frac{x}{r^3}\right) + \frac{\partial}{\partial y}\left(\frac{y}{r^3}\right) + \frac{\partial}{\partial z}\left(\frac{z}{r^3}\right)\right] \tag{10}$$

But

$$\frac{\partial}{\partial x}\left(\frac{x}{r^3}\right) = \frac{r^3 - x(3r^2)(x/r)}{(r^3)^2} = \frac{1}{r^3} - \frac{3x^2}{r^5}$$

$$\frac{\partial}{\partial y}\left(\frac{y}{r^3}\right) = \frac{1}{r^3} - \frac{3y^2}{r^5}$$

$$\frac{\partial}{\partial z}\left(\frac{z}{r^3}\right) = \frac{1}{r^3} - \frac{3z^2}{r^5}$$

Substituting these expressions in (10) yields

$$\text{div } \mathbf{F} = c\left[\frac{3}{r^3} - \frac{3x^2 + 3y^2 + 3z^2}{r^5}\right] = c\left[\frac{3}{r^3} - \frac{3r^2}{r^5}\right] = 0 \blacktriangleleft$$

■ THE ∇ OPERATOR

Thus far, the symbol ∇ that appears in the gradient expression $\nabla\phi$ has not been given a meaning of its own. However, it is often convenient to view ∇ as an operator

$$\nabla = \frac{\partial}{\partial x}\mathbf{i} + \frac{\partial}{\partial y}\mathbf{j} + \frac{\partial}{\partial z}\mathbf{k} \tag{11}$$

which when applied to $\phi(x, y, z)$ produces the gradient

$$\nabla\phi = \frac{\partial\phi}{\partial x}\mathbf{i} + \frac{\partial\phi}{\partial y}\mathbf{j} + \frac{\partial\phi}{\partial z}\mathbf{k}$$

We call (11) the **del operator**. This is analogous to the derivative operator d/dx, which when applied to $f(x)$ produces the derivative $f'(x)$.

The del operator allows us to express the divergence of a vector field

$$\mathbf{F} = f(x, y, z)\mathbf{i} + g(x, y, z)\mathbf{j} + h(x, y, z)\mathbf{k}$$

in dot product notation as

$$\text{div } \mathbf{F} = \nabla \cdot \mathbf{F} = \frac{\partial f}{\partial x} + \frac{\partial g}{\partial y} + \frac{\partial h}{\partial z} \tag{12}$$

and the curl of this field in cross-product notation as

$$\text{curl } \mathbf{F} = \nabla \times \mathbf{F} = \begin{vmatrix} \mathbf{i} & \mathbf{j} & \mathbf{k} \\ \frac{\partial}{\partial x} & \frac{\partial}{\partial y} & \frac{\partial}{\partial z} \\ f & g & h \end{vmatrix} \tag{13}$$

■ THE LAPLACIAN ∇²

The operator that results by taking the dot product of the del operator with itself is denoted by ∇^2 and is called the **Laplacian operator**. This operator has the form

$$\nabla^2 = \nabla \cdot \nabla = \frac{\partial^2}{\partial x^2} + \frac{\partial^2}{\partial y^2} + \frac{\partial^2}{\partial z^2} \tag{14}$$

When applied to $\phi(x, y, z)$ the Laplacian operator produces the function

$$\nabla^2 \phi = \frac{\partial^2 \phi}{\partial x^2} + \frac{\partial^2 \phi}{\partial y^2} + \frac{\partial^2 \phi}{\partial z^2}$$

Note that $\nabla^2 \phi$ can also be expressed as div $(\nabla \phi)$. The equation $\nabla^2 \phi = 0$ or, equivalently,

$$\frac{\partial^2 \phi}{\partial x^2} + \frac{\partial^2 \phi}{\partial y^2} + \frac{\partial^2 \phi}{\partial z^2} = 0$$

is known as **Laplace's equation**. This partial differential equation plays an important role in a wide variety of applications, resulting from the fact that it is satisfied by the potential function for the inverse-square field.

✔ QUICK CHECK EXERCISES 15.1   *(See page 1093 for answers.)*

1. The function $\phi(x, y, z) = xy + yz + xz$ is a potential for the vector field $\mathbf{F} =$ _____.

2. The vector field $\mathbf{F}(x, y, z) =$ _____, defined for $(x, y, z) \neq (0, 0, 0)$, is always directed toward the origin and is of length equal to the distance from (x, y, z) to the origin.

3. An inverse-square field is one that can be written in the form $\mathbf{F}(\mathbf{r}) =$ _____.

4. The vector field

$$\mathbf{F}(x, y, z) = yz\mathbf{i} + xy^2\mathbf{j} + yz^2\mathbf{k}$$

has divergence _____ and curl _____.

Pierre-Simon de Laplace (1749–1827) French mathematician and physicist. Laplace is sometimes referred to as the French Isaac Newton because of his work in celestial mechanics. In a five-volume treatise entitled *Traité de Mécanique Céleste*, he solved extremely difficult problems involving gravitational interactions between the planets. In particular, he was able to show that our solar system is stable and not prone to catastrophic collapse as a result of these interactions. This was an issue of major concern at the time because Jupiter's orbit appeared to be shrinking and Saturn's expanding; Laplace showed that these were expected periodic anomalies. In addition to his work in celestial mechanics, he founded modern probability theory, showed with Lavoisier that respiration is a form of combustion, and developed methods that fostered many new branches of pure mathematics.

Laplace was born to moderately successful parents in Normandy, his father being a farmer and cider merchant. He matriculated in the theology program at the University of Caen at age 16 but left for Paris at age 18 with a letter of introduction to the influential mathematician d'Alembert, who eventually helped him undertake a career in mathematics. Laplace was a prolific writer, and after his election to the Academy of Sciences in 1773, the secretary wrote that the Academy had never received so many important research papers by so young a person in such a short time. Laplace had little interest in pure mathematics—he regarded mathematics merely as a tool for solving applied problems. In his impatience with mathematical detail, he frequently omitted complicated arguments with the statement, "It is easy to show that...." He admitted, however, that as time passed he often had trouble reconstructing the omitted details himself!

At the height of his fame, Laplace served on many government committees and held the posts of Minister of the Interior and Chancellor of the Senate. He barely escaped imprisonment and execution during the period of the Revolution, probably because he was able to convince each opposing party that he sided with them. Napoleon described him as a great mathematician but a poor administrator who "sought subtleties everywhere, had only doubtful ideas, and ... carried the spirit of the infinitely small into administration." In spite of his genius, Laplace was both egotistic and insecure, attempting to ensure his place in history by conveniently failing to crédit mathematicians whose work he used—an unnecessary pettiness since his own work was so brilliant. However, on the positive side he was supportive of young mathematicians, often treating them as his own children. Laplace ranks as one of the most influential mathematicians in history.

EXERCISE SET 15.1 ～ Graphing Utility [c] CAS

1–2 Match the vector field $\mathbf{F}(x, y)$ with one of the plots, and explain your reasoning. ∎

1. (a) $\mathbf{F}(x, y) = x\mathbf{i}$ (b) $\mathbf{F}(x, y) = \sin x\,\mathbf{i} + \mathbf{j}$

2. (a) $\mathbf{F}(x, y) = \mathbf{i} + \mathbf{j}$
   (b) $\mathbf{F}(x, y) = \dfrac{x}{\sqrt{x^2 + y^2}}\mathbf{i} + \dfrac{y}{\sqrt{x^2 + y^2}}\mathbf{j}$

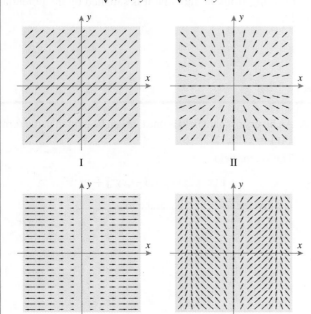

I

II

III

IV

3–4 Determine whether the statement about the vector field $\mathbf{F}(x, y)$ is true or false. If false, explain why. ∎

3. $\mathbf{F}(x, y) = x^2\mathbf{i} - y\mathbf{j}$.
   (a) $\|\mathbf{F}(x, y)\| \to 0$ as $(x, y) \to (0, 0)$.
   (b) If (x, y) is on the positive y-axis, then the vector points in the negative y-direction.
   (c) If (x, y) is in the first quadrant, then the vector points down and to the right.

4. $\mathbf{F}(x, y) = \dfrac{x}{\sqrt{x^2 + y^2}}\mathbf{i} - \dfrac{y}{\sqrt{x^2 + y^2}}\mathbf{j}$.
   (a) As (x, y) moves away from the origin, the lengths of the vectors decrease.
   (b) If (x, y) is a point on the positive x-axis, then the vector points up.
   (c) If (x, y) is a point on the positive y-axis, the vector points to the right.

5–8 Sketch the vector field by drawing some representative nonintersecting vectors. The vectors need not be drawn to scale, but they should be in reasonably correct proportion relative to each other. ∎

5. $\mathbf{F}(x, y) = 2\mathbf{i} - \mathbf{j}$ **6.** $\mathbf{F}(x, y) = y\mathbf{j}, \quad y > 0$

7. $\mathbf{F}(x, y) = y\mathbf{i} - x\mathbf{j}$. [*Note:* Each vector in the field is perpendicular to the position vector $\mathbf{r} = x\mathbf{i} + y\mathbf{j}$.]

8. $\mathbf{F}(x, y) = \dfrac{x\mathbf{i} + y\mathbf{j}}{\sqrt{x^2 + y^2}}$. [*Note:* Each vector in the field is a unit vector in the same direction as the position vector $\mathbf{r} = x\mathbf{i} + y\mathbf{j}$.]

～ 9–10 Use a graphing utility to generate a plot of the vector field. ∎

9. $\mathbf{F}(x, y) = \mathbf{i} + \cos y\,\mathbf{j}$ **10.** $\mathbf{F}(x, y) = y\mathbf{i} - x\mathbf{j}$

11–14 True–False Determine whether the statement is true or false. Explain your answer. ∎

11. The vector-valued function
$$\mathbf{F}(x, y) = y\mathbf{i} + x^2\mathbf{j} + xy\mathbf{k}$$
is an example of a vector field in the xy-plane.

12. If $\mathbf{r}$ is a radius vector in 3-space, then a vector field of the form
$$\mathbf{F}(\mathbf{r}) = \dfrac{1}{\|\mathbf{r}\|^2}\mathbf{r}$$
is an example of an inverse-square field.

13. If $\mathbf{F}$ is a vector field, then so is $\nabla \times \mathbf{F}$.

14. If $\mathbf{F}$ is a vector field and $\nabla \cdot \mathbf{F} = \phi$, then ϕ is a potential function for $\mathbf{F}$.

15–16 Confirm that ϕ is a potential function for $\mathbf{F}(\mathbf{r})$ on some region, and state the region. ∎

15. (a) $\phi(x, y) = \tan^{-1} xy$
   $\mathbf{F}(x, y) = \dfrac{y}{1 + x^2y^2}\mathbf{i} + \dfrac{x}{1 + x^2y^2}\mathbf{j}$
   (b) $\phi(x, y, z) = x^2 - 3y^2 + 4z^2$
   $\mathbf{F}(x, y, z) = 2x\mathbf{i} - 6y\mathbf{j} + 8z\mathbf{k}$

16. (a) $\phi(x, y) = 2y^2 + 3x^2y - xy^3$
   $\mathbf{F}(x, y) = (6xy - y^3)\mathbf{i} + (4y + 3x^2 - 3xy^2)\mathbf{j}$
   (b) $\phi(x, y, z) = x \sin z + y \sin x + z \sin y$
   $\mathbf{F}(x, y, z) = (\sin z + y \cos x)\mathbf{i} + (\sin x + z \cos y)\mathbf{j}$
      $+ (\sin y + x \cos z)\mathbf{k}$

17–22 Find div $\mathbf{F}$ and curl $\mathbf{F}$. ∎

17. $\mathbf{F}(x, y, z) = x^2\mathbf{i} - 2\mathbf{j} + yz\mathbf{k}$

18. $\mathbf{F}(x, y, z) = xz^3\mathbf{i} + 2y^4x^2\mathbf{j} + 5z^2y\mathbf{k}$

19. $\mathbf{F}(x, y, z) = 7y^3z^2\mathbf{i} - 8x^2z^5\mathbf{j} - 3xy^4\mathbf{k}$

20. $\mathbf{F}(x, y, z) = e^{xy}\mathbf{i} - \cos y\,\mathbf{j} + \sin^2 z\,\mathbf{k}$

21. $\mathbf{F}(x, y, z) = \dfrac{1}{\sqrt{x^2 + y^2 + z^2}}(x\mathbf{i} + y\mathbf{j} + z\mathbf{k})$

22. $\mathbf{F}(x, y, z) = \ln x\,\mathbf{i} + e^{xyz}\mathbf{j} + \tan^{-1}(z/x)\mathbf{k}$

23–24 Find $\nabla \cdot (\mathbf{F} \times \mathbf{G})$. ∎

23. $\mathbf{F}(x, y, z) = 2x\mathbf{i} + \mathbf{j} + 4y\mathbf{k}$
   $\mathbf{G}(x, y, z) = x\mathbf{i} + y\mathbf{j} - z\mathbf{k}$

24. $\mathbf{F}(x, y, z) = yz\mathbf{i} + xz\mathbf{j} + xy\mathbf{k}$
$\mathbf{G}(x, y, z) = xy\mathbf{j} + xyz\mathbf{k}$

25–26 Find $\nabla \cdot (\nabla \times \mathbf{F})$. ▩

25. $\mathbf{F}(x, y, z) = \sin x\mathbf{i} + \cos(x - y)\mathbf{j} + z\mathbf{k}$

26. $\mathbf{F}(x, y, z) = e^{xz}\mathbf{i} + 3xe^y\mathbf{j} - e^{yz}\mathbf{k}$

27–28 Find $\nabla \times (\nabla \times \mathbf{F})$. ▩

27. $\mathbf{F}(x, y, z) = xy\mathbf{j} + xyz\mathbf{k}$

28. $\mathbf{F}(x, y, z) = y^2x\mathbf{i} - 3yz\mathbf{j} + xy\mathbf{k}$

c 29. Use a CAS to check the calculations in Exercises 23, 25, and 27.

c 30. Use a CAS to check the calculations in Exercises 24, 26, and 28.

31–38 Let k be a constant, $\mathbf{F} = \mathbf{F}(x, y, z)$, $\mathbf{G} = \mathbf{G}(x, y, z)$, and $\phi = \phi(x, y, z)$. Prove the following identities, assuming that all derivatives involved exist and are continuous. ▩

31. $\operatorname{div}(k\mathbf{F}) = k \operatorname{div} \mathbf{F}$ **32.** $\operatorname{curl}(k\mathbf{F}) = k \operatorname{curl} \mathbf{F}$

33. $\operatorname{div}(\mathbf{F} + \mathbf{G}) = \operatorname{div} \mathbf{F} + \operatorname{div} \mathbf{G}$

34. $\operatorname{curl}(\mathbf{F} + \mathbf{G}) = \operatorname{curl} \mathbf{F} + \operatorname{curl} \mathbf{G}$

35. $\operatorname{div}(\phi\mathbf{F}) = \phi \operatorname{div} \mathbf{F} + \nabla\phi \cdot \mathbf{F}$

36. $\operatorname{curl}(\phi\mathbf{F}) = \phi \operatorname{curl} \mathbf{F} + \nabla\phi \times \mathbf{F}$

37. $\operatorname{div}(\operatorname{curl} \mathbf{F}) = 0$ **38.** $\operatorname{curl}(\nabla\phi) = \mathbf{0}$

39. Rewrite the identities in Exercises 31, 33, 35, and 37 in an equivalent form using the notation $\nabla \cdot$ for divergence and $\nabla \times$ for curl.

40. Rewrite the identities in Exercises 32, 34, 36, and 38 in an equivalent form using the notation $\nabla \cdot$ for divergence and $\nabla \times$ for curl.

41–42 Verify that the radius vector $\mathbf{r} = x\mathbf{i} + y\mathbf{j} + z\mathbf{k}$ has the stated property. ▩

41. (a) $\operatorname{curl} \mathbf{r} = \mathbf{0}$ (b) $\nabla \|\mathbf{r}\| = \dfrac{\mathbf{r}}{\|\mathbf{r}\|}$

42. (a) $\operatorname{div} \mathbf{r} = 3$ (b) $\nabla \dfrac{1}{\|\mathbf{r}\|} = -\dfrac{\mathbf{r}}{\|\mathbf{r}\|^3}$

43–44 Let $\mathbf{r} = x\mathbf{i} + y\mathbf{j} + z\mathbf{k}$, let $r = \|\mathbf{r}\|$, let f be a differentiable function of one variable, and let $\mathbf{F}(\mathbf{r}) = f(r)\mathbf{r}$. ▩

43. (a) Use the chain rule and Exercise 41(b) to show that
$$\nabla f(r) = \frac{f'(r)}{r}\mathbf{r}$$
(b) Use the result in part (a) and Exercises 35 and 42(a) to show that $\operatorname{div} \mathbf{F} = 3f(r) + rf'(r)$.

44. (a) Use part (a) of Exercise 43, Exercise 36, and Exercise 41(a) to show that curl $\mathbf{F} = \mathbf{0}$.
(b) Use the result in part (a) of Exercise 43 and Exercises 35 and 42(a) to show that
$$\nabla^2 f(r) = 2\frac{f'(r)}{r} + f''(r)$$

45. Use the result in Exercise 43(b) to show that the divergence of the inverse-square field $\mathbf{F} = \mathbf{r}/\|\mathbf{r}\|^3$ is zero.

46. Use the result of Exercise 43(b) to show that if $\mathbf{F}$ is a vector field of the form $\mathbf{F} = f(\|\mathbf{r}\|)\mathbf{r}$ and if div $\mathbf{F} = 0$, then $\mathbf{F}$ is an inverse-square field. [*Suggestion:* Let $r = \|\mathbf{r}\|$ and multiply $3f(r) + rf'(r) = 0$ through by r^2. Then write the result as a derivative of a product.]

47. A curve C is called a **flow line** of a vector field $\mathbf{F}$ if $\mathbf{F}$ is a tangent vector to C at each point along C (see the accompanying figure).
(a) Let C be a flow line for $\mathbf{F}(x, y) = -y\mathbf{i} + x\mathbf{j}$, and let (x, y) be a point on C for which $y \neq 0$. Show that the flow lines satisfy the differential equation
$$\frac{dy}{dx} = -\frac{x}{y}$$
(b) Solve the differential equation in part (a) by separation of variables, and show that the flow lines are concentric circles centered at the origin.

C
Flow lines of a vector field
◀ **Figure Ex-47**

48–50 Find a differential equation satisfied by the flow lines of $\mathbf{F}$ (see Exercise 47), and solve it to find equations for the flow lines of $\mathbf{F}$. Sketch some typical flow lines and tangent vectors. ▩

48. $\mathbf{F}(x, y) = \mathbf{i} + x\mathbf{j}$ **49.** $\mathbf{F}(x, y) = x\mathbf{i} + \mathbf{j}$, $x > 0$

50. $\mathbf{F}(x, y) = x\mathbf{i} - y\mathbf{j}$, $x > 0$ and $y > 0$

51. Writing Discuss the similarities and differences between the concepts "vector field" and "slope field."

52. Writing In physical applications it is often necessary to deal with vector quantities that depend not only on position in space but also on time. Give some examples and discuss how the concept of a vector field would need to be modified to apply to such situations.

✔ **QUICK CHECK ANSWERS 15.1**

1. $(y + z)\mathbf{i} + (x + z)\mathbf{j} + (x + y)\mathbf{k}$ **2.** $-\mathbf{r} = -x\mathbf{i} - y\mathbf{j} - z\mathbf{k}$ **3.** $\dfrac{c}{\|\mathbf{r}\|^3}\mathbf{r}$ **4.** $2xy + 2yz$; $z^2\mathbf{i} + y\mathbf{j} + (y^2 - z)\mathbf{k}$

15.2 LINE INTEGRALS

In earlier chapters we considered three kinds of integrals in rectangular coordinates: single integrals over intervals, double integrals over two-dimensional regions, and triple integrals over three-dimensional regions. In this section we will discuss integrals along curves in two- or three-dimensional space.

■ LINE INTEGRALS

The first goal of this section is to define what it means to integrate a function along a curve. To motivate the definition we will consider the problem of finding the mass of a very thin wire whose linear density function (mass per unit length) is known. We assume that we can model the wire by a smooth curve C between two points P and Q in 3-space (Figure 15.2.1). Given any point (x, y, z) on C, we let $f(x, y, z)$ denote the corresponding value of the density function. To compute the mass of the wire, we proceed as follows:

▲ **Figure 15.2.1**   A bent thin wire modeled by a smooth curve

- Divide C into n very small sections using a succession of distinct partition points

$$P = P_0, P_1, P_2, \ldots, P_{n-1}, P_n = Q$$

as illustrated on the left side of Figure 15.2.2. Let ΔM_k be the mass of the kth section, and let Δs_k be the length of the arc between P_{k-1} and P_k.

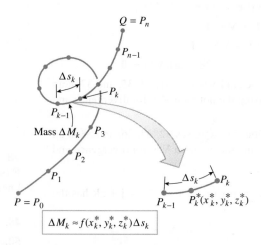

▶ **Figure 15.2.2**

- Choose an arbitrary sampling point $P_k^*(x_k^*, y_k^*, z_k^*)$ on the kth arc, as illustrated on the right side of Figure 15.2.2. If Δs_k is very small, the value of f will not vary much along the kth section and we can approximate f along this section by the value $f(x_k^*, y_k^*, z_k^*)$. It follows that the mass of the kth section can be approximated by

$$\Delta M_k \approx f(x_k^*, y_k^*, z_k^*)\Delta s_k$$

- The mass M of the entire wire can then be approximated by

$$M = \sum_{k=1}^{n} \Delta M_k \approx \sum_{k=1}^{n} f(x_k^*, y_k^*, z_k^*)\Delta s_k \tag{1}$$

- We will use the expression max $\Delta s_k \to 0$ to indicate the process of increasing n in such a way that the lengths of all the sections approach 0. It is plausible that the error in (1) will approach 0 as max $\Delta s_k \to 0$ and the exact value of M will be given by

$$M = \lim_{\max \Delta s_k \to 0} \sum_{k=1}^{n} f(x_k^*, y_k^*, z_k^*)\Delta s_k \tag{2}$$

The limit in (2) is similar to the limit of Riemann sums used to define the definite integral of a function over an interval (Definition 5.5.1). With this similarity in mind, we make the following definition.

15.2.1   DEFINITION   If C is a smooth curve in 2-space or 3-space, then the *line integral of f with respect to s along C* is

$$\int_C f(x, y)\, ds = \lim_{\max \Delta s_k \to 0} \sum_{k=1}^{n} f(x_k^*, y_k^*) \Delta s_k \qquad \boxed{\text{2-space}} \qquad (3)$$

or

$$\int_C f(x, y, z)\, ds = \lim_{\max \Delta s_k \to 0} \sum_{k=1}^{n} f(x_k^*, y_k^*, z_k^*) \Delta s_k \qquad \boxed{\text{3-space}} \qquad (4)$$

provided this limit exists and does not depend on the choice of partition or on the choice of sample points.

Although the term "curve integrals" is more descriptive, the integrals in Definition 15.2.1 are called "line integrals" for historical reasons.

It is usually impractical to evaluate line integrals directly from Definition 15.2.1. However, the definition is important in the application and interpretation of line integrals. For example:

- If C is a curve in 3-space that models a thin wire, and if $f(x, y, z)$ is the linear density function of the wire, then it follows from (2) and Definition 15.2.1 that the mass M of the wire is given by

$$M = \int_C f(x, y, z)\, ds \qquad (5)$$

That is, to obtain the mass of a thin wire, we integrate the linear density function over the smooth curve that models the wire.

- If C is a smooth curve of arc length L, and f is identically 1, then it immediately follows from Definition 15.2.1 that

$$\int_C ds = \lim_{\max \Delta s_k \to 0} \sum_{k=1}^{n} \Delta s_k = \lim_{\max \Delta s_k \to 0} L = L \qquad (6)$$

- If C is a curve in the xy-plane and $f(x, y)$ is a nonnegative continuous function defined on C, then $\int_C f(x, y)\, ds$ can be interpreted as the area A of the "sheet" that is swept out by a vertical line segment that extends upward from the point (x, y) to a height of $f(x, y)$ and moves along C from one endpoint to the other (Figure 15.2.3). To see why this is so, refer to Figure 15.2.4 in which $f(x_k^*, y_k^*)$ is the value of f at an arbitrary point P_k^* on the kth arc of the partition and note the approximation

$$\Delta A_k \approx f(x_k^*, y_k^*) \Delta s_k$$

It follows that

$$A = \sum_{k=1}^{n} \Delta A_k \approx \sum_{k=1}^{n} f(x_k^*, y_k^*) \Delta s_k$$

It is then plausible that

$$A = \lim_{\max \Delta s_k \to 0} \sum_{k=1}^{n} f(x_k^*, y_k^*) \Delta s_k = \int_C f(x, y)\, ds \qquad (7)$$

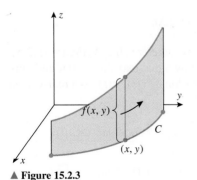

▲ Figure 15.2.3

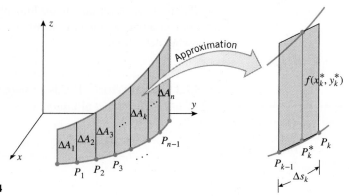

▶ Figure 15.2.4

Since Definition 15.2.1 is closely modeled on Definition 5.5.1, it should come as no surprise that line integrals share many of the common properties of ordinary definite integrals. For example, we have

$$\int_C [f(x, y) + g(x, y)] \, ds = \int_C f(x, y) \, ds + \int_C g(x, y) \, ds$$

provided both line integrals on the right-hand side of this equation exist. Similarly, it can be shown that if f is continuous on C, then the line integral of f with respect to s along C exists.

■ **EVALUATING LINE INTEGRALS**

Except in simple cases, it will not be feasible to evaluate a line integral directly from (3) or (4). However, we will now show that it is possible to express a line integral as an ordinary definite integral, so that no special methods of evaluation are required. For example, suppose that C is a curve in the xy-plane that is smoothly parametrized by

$$\mathbf{r}(t) = x(t)\mathbf{i} + y(t)\mathbf{j} \qquad (a \le t \le b)$$

Moreover, suppose that each partition point P_k of C corresponds to a parameter value of t_k in $[a, b]$. The arc length of C between points P_{k-1} and P_k is then given by

$$\Delta s_k = \int_{t_{k-1}}^{t_k} \|\mathbf{r}'(t)\| \, dt \tag{8}$$

(Theorem 12.3.1). If we let $\Delta t_k = t_k - t_{k-1}$, then it follows from (8) and the Mean-Value Theorem for Integrals (Theorem 5.6.2) that there exists a point t_k^* in $[t_{k-1}, t_k]$ such that

$$\Delta s_k = \int_{t_{k-1}}^{t_k} \|\mathbf{r}'(t)\| \, dt = \|\mathbf{r}'(t_k^*)\| \Delta t_k$$

We let $P_k^*(x_k^*, y_k^*) = P_k^*(x(t_k^*), y(t_k^*))$ correspond to the parameter value t_k^* (Figure 15.2.5).

Since the parametrization of C is smooth, it can be shown that $\max \Delta s_k \to 0$ if and only if $\max \Delta t_k \to 0$ (Exercise 53). Furthermore, the composition $f(x(t), y(t))$ is a real-valued function defined on $[a, b]$ and we have

$$\int_C f(x, y) \, ds = \lim_{\max \Delta s_k \to 0} \sum_{k=1}^n f(x_k^*, y_k^*) \, \Delta s_k \qquad \boxed{\text{Definition 15.2.1}}$$

$$= \lim_{\max \Delta s_k \to 0} \sum_{k=1}^n f(x(t_k^*), y(t_k^*)) \|\mathbf{r}'(t_k^*)\| \Delta t_k \qquad \boxed{\text{Substitution}}$$

$$= \lim_{\max \Delta t_k \to 0} \sum_{k=1}^n f(x(t_k^*), y(t_k^*)) \|\mathbf{r}'(t_k^*)\| \Delta t_k$$

$$= \int_a^b f(x(t), y(t)) \|\mathbf{r}'(t)\| \, dt \qquad \boxed{\text{Definition 5.5.1}}$$

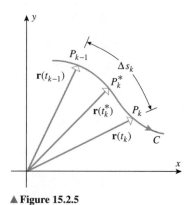

▲ Figure 15.2.5

Therefore, if C is smoothly parametrized by

$$\mathbf{r}(t) = x(t)\mathbf{i} + y(t)\mathbf{j} \qquad (a \leq t \leq b)$$

then

$$\int_C f(x, y)\, ds = \int_a^b f(x(t), y(t))\|\mathbf{r}'(t)\|\, dt \tag{9}$$

Similarly, if C is a curve in 3-space that is smoothly parametrized by

$$\mathbf{r}(t) = x(t)\mathbf{i} + y(t)\mathbf{j} + z(t)\mathbf{k} \qquad (a \leq t \leq b)$$

then

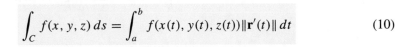

$$\int_C f(x, y, z)\, ds = \int_a^b f(x(t), y(t), z(t))\|\mathbf{r}'(t)\|\, dt \tag{10}$$

Explain how Formulas (9) and (10) confirm Formula (6) for arc length.

► **Example 1**   Using the given parametrization, evaluate the line integral $\int_C (1 + xy^2)\, ds$.

(a) $C : \mathbf{r}(t) = t\mathbf{i} + 2t\mathbf{j}$ $(0 \leq t \leq 1)$ (see Figure 15.2.6a)
(b) $C : \mathbf{r}(t) = (1 - t)\mathbf{i} + (2 - 2t)\mathbf{j}$ $(0 \leq t \leq 1)$ (see Figure 15.2.6b)

Solution (a).   Since $\mathbf{r}'(t) = \mathbf{i} + 2\mathbf{j}$, we have $\|\mathbf{r}'(t)\| = \sqrt{5}$ and it follows from Formula (9) that

$$\int_C (1 + xy^2)\, ds = \int_0^1 [1 + t(2t)^2]\sqrt{5}\, dt$$

$$= \int_0^1 (1 + 4t^3)\sqrt{5}\, dt$$

$$= \sqrt{5}\left[t + t^4\right]_0^1 = 2\sqrt{5}$$

Solution (b).   Since $\mathbf{r}'(t) = -\mathbf{i} - 2\mathbf{j}$, we have $\|\mathbf{r}'(t)\| = \sqrt{5}$ and it follows from Formula (9) that

$$\int_C (1 + xy^2)\, ds = \int_0^1 [1 + (1 - t)(2 - 2t)^2]\sqrt{5}\, dt$$

$$= \int_0^1 [1 + 4(1 - t)^3]\sqrt{5}\, dt$$

$$= \sqrt{5}\left[t - (1 - t)^4\right]_0^1 = 2\sqrt{5} \blacktriangleleft$$

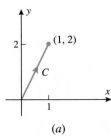

(a)

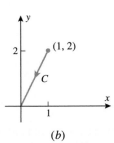

(b)

▲ **Figure 15.2.6**

Note that the integrals in parts (a) and (b) of Example 1 agree, even though the corresponding parametrizations of C have opposite orientations. This illustrates the important result that the value of a line integral of f with respect to s along C *does not depend on an orientation of* C. (This is because Δs_k is always positive; therefore, it does not matter in which *direction* along C we list the partition points of the curve in Definition 15.2.1.) Later in this section we will discuss line integrals that are defined only for oriented curves.

Formula (9) has an alternative expression for a curve C in the xy-plane that is given by parametric equations

$$x = x(t), \quad y = y(t) \qquad (a \leq t \leq b)$$

In this case, we write (9) in the expanded form

$$\int_C f(x, y)\, ds = \int_a^b f(x(t), y(t)) \sqrt{\left(\frac{dx}{dt}\right)^2 + \left(\frac{dy}{dt}\right)^2}\, dt \tag{11}$$

Similarly, if C is a curve in 3-space that is parametrized by

$$x = x(t), \quad y = y(t), \quad z = z(t) \qquad (a \le t \le b)$$

then we write (10) in the form

$$\int_C f(x, y, z)\, ds = \int_a^b f(x(t), y(t), z(t)) \sqrt{\left(\frac{dx}{dt}\right)^2 + \left(\frac{dy}{dt}\right)^2 + \left(\frac{dz}{dt}\right)^2}\, dt \tag{12}$$

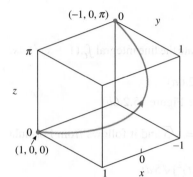

(−1, 0, π)

(1, 0, 0)

▲ **Figure 15.2.7**

▶ **Example 2**   Evaluate the line integral $\int_C (xy + z^3)\, ds$ from $(1, 0, 0)$ to $(-1, 0, \pi)$ along the helix C that is represented by the parametric equations

$$x = \cos t, \quad y = \sin t, \quad z = t \qquad (0 \le t \le \pi)$$

(Figure 15.2.7).

Solution.   From (12)

$$\int_C (xy + z^3)\, ds = \int_0^\pi (\cos t \sin t + t^3) \sqrt{\left(\frac{dx}{dt}\right)^2 + \left(\frac{dy}{dt}\right)^2 + \left(\frac{dz}{dt}\right)^2}\, dt$$

$$= \int_0^\pi (\cos t \sin t + t^3) \sqrt{(-\sin t)^2 + (\cos t)^2 + 1}\, dt$$

$$= \sqrt{2} \int_0^\pi (\cos t \sin t + t^3)\, dt$$

$$= \sqrt{2} \left[\frac{\sin^2 t}{2} + \frac{t^4}{4} \right]_0^\pi = \frac{\sqrt{2}\pi^4}{4} \quad \blacktriangleleft$$

If $\delta(x, y)$ is the linear density function of a wire that is modeled by a smooth curve C in the xy-plane, then an argument similar to the derivation of Formula (5) shows that the mass of the wire is given by $\int_C \delta(x, y)\, ds$.

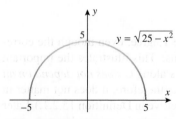

$y = \sqrt{25 - x^2}$

▲ **Figure 15.2.8**

▶ **Example 3**   Suppose that a semicircular wire has the equation $y = \sqrt{25 - x^2}$ and that its mass density is $\delta(x, y) = 15 - y$ (Figure 15.2.8). Physically, this means the wire has a maximum density of 15 units at the base $(y = 0)$ and that the density of the wire decreases linearly with respect to y to a value of 10 units at the top $(y = 5)$. Find the mass of the wire.

Solution.   The mass M of the wire can be expressed as the line integral

$$M = \int_C \delta(x, y)\, ds = \int_C (15 - y)\, ds$$

along the semicircle C. To evaluate this integral we will express C parametrically as

$$x = 5 \cos t, \quad y = 5 \sin t \qquad (0 \le t \le \pi)$$

Thus, it follows from (11) that

$$M = \int_C (15 - y)\, ds = \int_0^{\pi} (15 - 5\sin t)\sqrt{\left(\frac{dx}{dt}\right)^2 + \left(\frac{dy}{dt}\right)^2}\, dt$$

$$= \int_0^{\pi} (15 - 5\sin t)\sqrt{(-5\sin t)^2 + (5\cos t)^2}\, dt$$

$$= 5\int_0^{\pi} (15 - 5\sin t)\, dt$$

$$= 5\left[15t + 5\cos t\right]_0^{\pi}$$

$$= 75\pi - 50 \approx 185.6 \text{ units of mass} \quad \blacktriangleleft$$

In the special case where t is an arc length parameter, say $t = s$, it follows from Formulas (20) and (21) in Section 12.3 that the radicals in (11) and (12) reduce to 1 and the equations simplify to

$$\int_C f(x,\, y)\, ds = \int_a^b f(x(s),\, y(s))\, ds \tag{13}$$

and

$$\int_C f(x,\, y,\, z)\, ds = \int_a^b f(x(s),\, y(s),\, z(s))\, ds \tag{14}$$

respectively.

▶ **Example 4**   Find the area of the surface extending upward from the circle $x^2 + y^2 = 1$ in the xy-plane to the parabolic cylinder $z = 1 - x^2$ (Figure 15.2.9).

Solution.   It follows from (7) that the area A of the surface can be expressed as the line integral

$$A = \int_C (1 - x^2)\, ds \tag{15}$$

where C is the circle $x^2 + y^2 = 1$. This circle can be parametrized in terms of arc length as

$$x = \cos s, \quad y = \sin s \quad (0 \le s \le 2\pi)$$

Thus, it follows from (13) and (15) that

$$A = \int_C (1 - x^2)\, ds = \int_0^{2\pi} (1 - \cos^2 s)\, ds$$

$$= \int_0^{2\pi} \sin^2 s\, ds = \frac{1}{2}\int_0^{2\pi} (1 - \cos 2s)\, ds = \pi \quad \blacktriangleleft$$

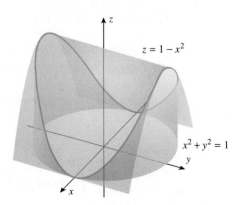

$z = 1 - x^2$

$x^2 + y^2 = 1$

▶ **Figure 15.2.9**

■ **LINE INTEGRALS WITH RESPECT TO x, y, AND z**

We now describe a second type of line integral in which we replace the "ds" in the integral by dx, dy, or dz. For example, suppose that f is a function defined on a smooth curve C in the xy-plane and that partition points of C are denoted by $P_k(x_k, y_k)$. Letting

$$\Delta x_k = x_k - x_{k-1} \quad \text{and} \quad \Delta y_k = y_k - y_{k-1}$$

we would like to define

$$\int_C f(x, y)\, dx = \lim_{\max \Delta s_k \to 0} \sum_{k=1}^{n} f(x_k^*, y_k^*)\Delta x_k \tag{16}$$

$$\int_C f(x, y)\, dy = \lim_{\max \Delta s_k \to 0} \sum_{k=1}^{n} f(x_k^*, y_k^*)\Delta y_k \tag{17}$$

However, unlike Δs_k, the values of Δx_k and Δy_k change sign if the order of the partition points along C is reversed. Therefore, in order to define the line integrals using Formulas (16) and (17), we must restrict ourselves to *oriented* curves C and to partitions of C in which the partition points are ordered in the direction of the curve. With this restriction, if the limit in (16) exists and does not depend on the choice of partition or sampling points, then we refer to (16) as the **line integral of f with respect to x along C**. Similarly, (17) defines the **line integral of f with respect to y along C**. If C is a smooth curve in 3-space, we can have **line integrals of f with respect to x, y, and z along C**. For example,

$$\int_C f(x, y, z)\, dx = \lim_{\max \Delta s_k \to 0} \sum_{k=1}^{n} f(x_k^*, y_k^*, z_k^*)\Delta x_k$$

and so forth. As was the case with line integrals with respect to s, line integrals of f with respect to x, y, and z exist if f is continuous on C.

The basic procedure for evaluating these line integrals is to find parametric equations for C, say

$$x = x(t), \quad y = y(t), \quad z = z(t) \quad (a \le t \le b)$$

in which the orientation of C is in the direction of increasing t, and then express the integrand in terms of t. For example,

$$\int_C f(x, y, z)\, dz = \int_a^b f(x(t), y(t), z(t))z'(t)\, dt$$

[Such a formula is easy to remember—just substitute for x, y, and z using the parametric equations and recall that $dz = z'(t)\, dt$.]

> **Explain why Formula (16) implies that $\int_C dx = x_f - x_i$, where x_f and x_i are the respective x-coordinates of the final and initial points of C. What about $\int_C dy$?**

> **Explain why Formula (16) implies that $\int_C f(x, y)\, dx = 0$ on any oriented segment parallel to the y-axis. What can you say about $\int_C f(x, y)\, dy$ on any oriented segment parallel to the x-axis?**

▶ **Example 5**   Evaluate $\int_C 3xy\, dy$, where C is the line segment joining $(0, 0)$ and $(1, 2)$ with the given orientation.

(a) Oriented from $(0, 0)$ to $(1, 2)$ as in Figure 15.2.6a.

(b) Oriented from $(1, 2)$ to $(0, 0)$ as in Figure 15.2.6b.

Solution (a).   Using the parametrization

$$x = t, \quad y = 2t \quad (0 \le t \le 1)$$

we have

$$\int_C 3xy\, dy = \int_0^1 3(t)(2t)(2)\, dt = \int_0^1 12t^2\, dt = 4t^3 \Big]_0^1 = 4$$

Solution (b).   Using the parametrization

$$x = 1 - t, \quad y = 2 - 2t \qquad (0 \le t \le 1)$$

we have

$$\int_C 3xy\, dy = \int_0^1 3(1-t)(2-2t)(-2)\, dt = \int_0^1 -12(1-t)^2\, dt = 4(1-t)^3 \Big]_0^1 = -4 \quad \blacktriangleleft$$

In Example 5, note that reversing the orientation of the curve changed the sign of the line integral. This is because reversing the orientation of a curve changes the sign of Δx_k in definition (16). Thus, unlike line integrals of functions with respect to s along C, reversing the orientation of C changes the sign of a line integral with respect to x, y, and z. If C is a smooth oriented curve, we will let $-C$ denote the oriented curve consisting of the same points as C but with the opposite orientation (Figure 15.2.10). We then have

$$\int_{-C} f(x, y)\, dx = -\int_C f(x, y)\, dx \quad \text{and} \quad \int_{-C} g(x, y)\, dy = -\int_C g(x, y)\, dy$$
$$(18\text{–}19)$$

while

$$\int_{-C} f(x, y)\, ds = \int_C f(x, y)\, ds \tag{20}$$

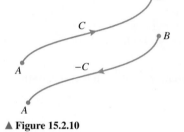

▲ **Figure 15.2.10**

Similar identities hold for line integrals in 3-space. Unless indicated otherwise, we will assume that parametric curves are oriented in the direction of increasing parameter.

Frequently, the line integrals with respect to x and y occur in combination, in which case we will dispense with one of the integral signs and write

$$\int_C f(x, y)\, dx + g(x, y)\, dy = \int_C f(x, y)\, dx + \int_C g(x, y)\, dy \tag{21}$$

We will use a similar convention for combinations of line integrals with respect to x, y, and z along curves in 3-space.

▶ **Example 6**   Evaluate

$$\int_C 2xy\, dx + (x^2 + y^2)\, dy$$

along the circular arc C given by $x = \cos t$, $y = \sin t$ $(0 \le t \le \pi/2)$ (Figure 15.2.11).

Solution.   We have

$$\int_C 2xy\, dx = \int_0^{\pi/2} (2\cos t \sin t)\left[\frac{d}{dt}(\cos t)\right] dt$$

$$= -2\int_0^{\pi/2} \sin^2 t \cos t\, dt = -\frac{2}{3}\sin^3 t \Big]_0^{\pi/2} = -\frac{2}{3}$$

$$\int_C (x^2 + y^2)\, dy = \int_0^{\pi/2} (\cos^2 t + \sin^2 t)\left[\frac{d}{dt}(\sin t)\right] dt$$

$$= \int_0^{\pi/2} \cos t\, dt = \sin t \Big]_0^{\pi/2} = 1$$

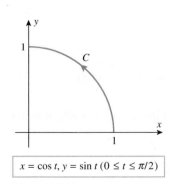

$x = \cos t, y = \sin t \ (0 \le t \le \pi/2)$

▲ **Figure 15.2.11**

Thus, from (21)

$$\int_C 2xy\,dx + (x^2 + y^2)\,dy = \int_C 2xy\,dx + \int_C (x^2 + y^2)\,dy$$

$$= -\frac{2}{3} + 1 = \frac{1}{3} \blacktriangleleft$$

It can be shown that if f and g are continuous functions on C, then combinations of line integrals with respect to x and y can be expressed in terms of a limit and can be evaluated together in a single step. For example, we have

$$\int_C f(x, y)\,dx + g(x, y)\,dy = \lim_{\max \Delta s_k \to 0} \sum_{k=1}^{n} [f(x_k^*, y_k^*)\Delta x_k + g(x_k^*, y_k^*)\,\Delta y_k] \qquad (22)$$

and

$$\int_C f(x, y)\,dx + g(x, y)\,dy = \int_a^b [f(x(t), y(t))x'(t) + g(x(t), y(t))y'(t)]\,dt \qquad (23)$$

Similar results hold for line integrals in 3-space. The evaluation of a line integral can sometimes be simplified by using Formula (23).

▶ **Example 7**   Evaluate

$$\int_C (3x^2 + y^2)\,dx + 2xy\,dy$$

along the circular arc C given by $x = \cos t$, $y = \sin t$ ($0 \le t \le \pi/2$) (Figure 15.2.11).

Solution.   From (23) we have

$$\int_C (3x^2 + y^2)\,dx + 2xy\,dy = \int_0^{\pi/2} [(3\cos^2 t + \sin^2 t)(-\sin t) + 2(\cos t)(\sin t)(\cos t)]\,dt$$

$$= \int_0^{\pi/2} (-3\cos^2 t \sin t - \sin^3 t + 2\cos^2 t \sin t)\,dt$$

$$= \int_0^{\pi/2} (-\cos^2 t - \sin^2 t)(\sin t)\,dt = \int_0^{\pi/2} -\sin t\,dt$$

$$= \cos t\Big]_0^{\pi/2} = -1 \blacktriangleleft$$

Compare the computations in Example 7 with those involved in computing

$$\int_C (3x^2 + y^2)\,dx + \int_C 2xy\,dy$$

It follows from (18) and (19) that

$$\int_{-C} f(x, y)\,dx + g(x, y)\,dy = -\int_C f(x, y)\,dx + g(x, y)\,dy \qquad (24)$$

so that reversing the orientation of C changes the sign of a line integral in which x and y occur in combination. Similarly,

$$\int_{-C} f(x, y, z)\,dx + g(x, y, z)\,dy + h(x, y, z)\,dz$$

$$= -\int_C f(x, y, z)\,dx + g(x, y, z)\,dy + h(x, y, z)\,dz \qquad (25)$$

■ INTEGRATING A VECTOR FIELD ALONG A CURVE

There is an alternative notation for line integrals with respect to x, y, and z that is particularly appropriate for dealing with problems involving vector fields. We will interpret $d\mathbf{r}$ as

$$d\mathbf{r} = dx\mathbf{i} + dy\mathbf{j} \quad \text{or} \quad d\mathbf{r} = dx\mathbf{i} + dy\mathbf{j} + dz\mathbf{k}$$

depending on whether C is in 2-space or 3-space. For an oriented curve C in 2-space and a vector field

$$\mathbf{F}(x, y) = f(x, y)\mathbf{i} + g(x, y)\mathbf{j}$$

we will write

$$\int_C \mathbf{F} \cdot d\mathbf{r} = \int_C (f(x, y)\mathbf{i} + g(x, y)\mathbf{j}) \cdot (dx\mathbf{i} + dy\mathbf{j}) = \int_C f(x, y)\, dx + g(x, y)\, dy \quad (26)$$

Similarly, for a curve C in 3-space and vector field

$$\mathbf{F}(x, y, z) = f(x, y, z)\mathbf{i} + g(x, y, z)\mathbf{j} + h(x, y, z)\mathbf{k}$$

we will write

$$\int_C \mathbf{F} \cdot d\mathbf{r} = \int_C (f(x, y, z)\mathbf{i} + g(x, y, z)\mathbf{j} + h(x, y, z)\mathbf{k}) \cdot (dx\mathbf{i} + dy\mathbf{j} + dz\mathbf{k})$$

$$= \int_C f(x, y, z)\, dx + g(x, y, z)\, dy + h(x, y, z)\, dz \quad (27)$$

With these conventions, we are led to the following definition.

15.2.2   DEFINITION   If $\mathbf{F}$ is a continuous vector field and C is a smooth oriented curve, then the **line integral of $\mathbf{F}$ along C** is

$$\int_C \mathbf{F} \cdot d\mathbf{r} \quad (28)$$

The notation in Definition 15.2.2 makes it easy to remember the formula for evaluating the line integral of $\mathbf{F}$ along C. For example, suppose that C is an oriented curve in the plane given in vector form by

$$\mathbf{r} = \mathbf{r}(t) = x(t)\mathbf{i} + y(t)\mathbf{j} \quad (a \leq t \leq b)$$

If we write

$$\mathbf{F}(\mathbf{r}(t)) = f(x(t), y(t))\mathbf{i} + g(x(t), y(t))\mathbf{j}$$

then

$$\int_C \mathbf{F} \cdot d\mathbf{r} = \int_a^b \mathbf{F}(\mathbf{r}(t)) \cdot \mathbf{r}'(t)\, dt \quad (29)$$

Formula (29) is also valid for oriented curves in 3-space.

▶ **Example 8**   Evaluate $\int_C \mathbf{F} \cdot d\mathbf{r}$ where $\mathbf{F}(x, y) = \cos x\mathbf{i} + \sin x\mathbf{j}$ and where C is the given oriented curve.

(a) $C : \mathbf{r}(t) = -\dfrac{\pi}{2}\mathbf{i} + t\mathbf{j} \quad (1 \leq t \leq 2)$ (see Figure 15.2.12a)

(b) $C : \mathbf{r}(t) = t\mathbf{i} + t^2\mathbf{j} \quad (-1 \leq t \leq 2)$ (see Figure 15.2.12b)

Vectors not to scale

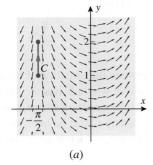

(a)

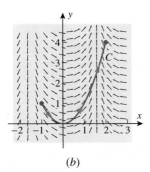

(b)

▲ **Figure 15.2.12**

Solution (a).   Using (29) we have

$$\int_C \mathbf{F} \cdot d\mathbf{r} = \int_1^2 \mathbf{F}(\mathbf{r}(t)) \cdot \mathbf{r}'(t)\, dt = \int_1^2 (-\mathbf{j}) \cdot \mathbf{j}\, dt = \int_1^2 (-1)\, dt = -1$$

Solution (b).   Using (29) we have

$$\int_C \mathbf{F} \cdot d\mathbf{r} = \int_{-1}^2 \mathbf{F}(\mathbf{r}(t)) \cdot \mathbf{r}'(t)\, dt = \int_{-1}^2 (\cos t\, \mathbf{i} + \sin t\, \mathbf{j}) \cdot (\mathbf{i} + 2t\mathbf{j})\, dt$$

$$= \int_{-1}^2 (\cos t + 2t \sin t)\, dt = (-2t \cos t + 3 \sin t)\Big]_{-1}^2$$

$$= -2 \cos 1 - 4 \cos 2 + 3(\sin 1 + \sin 2) \approx 5.83629 \blacktriangleleft$$

If we let t denote an arc length parameter, say $t = s$, with $\mathbf{T} = \mathbf{r}'(s)$ the unit tangent vector field along C, then

$$\int_C \mathbf{F} \cdot d\mathbf{r} = \int_a^b \mathbf{F}(\mathbf{r}(s)) \cdot \mathbf{r}'(s)\, ds = \int_a^b \mathbf{F}(\mathbf{r}(s)) \cdot \mathbf{T}\, ds = \int_C \mathbf{F} \cdot \mathbf{T}\, ds$$

which shows that

$$\int_C \mathbf{F} \cdot d\mathbf{r} = \int_C \mathbf{F} \cdot \mathbf{T}\, ds \tag{30}$$

In words, the integral of a vector field along a curve has the same value as the integral of the tangential component of the vector field along the curve.

We can use (30) to interpret $\int_C \mathbf{F} \cdot d\mathbf{r}$ geometrically. If θ is the angle between $\mathbf{F}$ and $\mathbf{T}$ at a point on C, then at this point

$$\mathbf{F} \cdot \mathbf{T} = \|\mathbf{F}\|\|\mathbf{T}\| \cos \theta \qquad \boxed{\text{Formula (4) in Section 11.3}}$$

$$= \|\mathbf{F}\| \cos \theta \qquad \boxed{\text{Since } \|\mathbf{T}\| = 1}$$

Thus,

$$-\|\mathbf{F}\| \le \mathbf{F} \cdot \mathbf{T} \le \|\mathbf{F}\|$$

and if $\mathbf{F} \ne \mathbf{0}$, then the sign of $\mathbf{F} \cdot \mathbf{T}$ will depend on the angle between the direction of $\mathbf{F}$ and the direction of C (Figure 15.2.13). That is, $\mathbf{F} \cdot \mathbf{T}$ will be positive where $\mathbf{F}$ has the same general direction as C, it will be 0 if $\mathbf{F}$ is normal to C, and it will be negative where $\mathbf{F}$ and C have more or less opposite directions. The line integral of $\mathbf{F}$ along C can be interpreted as the accumulated effect of the magnitude of $\mathbf{F}$ along C, the extent to which $\mathbf{F}$ and C have the same direction, and the arc length of C.

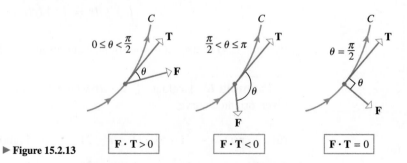

▶ **Figure 15.2.13**

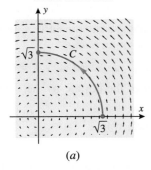

Vectors not to scale

(a)

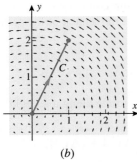

(b)

▲ **Figure 15.2.14**

Refer to Figure 15.2.12 and explain the sign of each line integral in Example 8 geometrically. Exercises 5 and 6 take this geometric analysis further.

▶ **Example 9**   Use (30) to evaluate $\int_C \mathbf{F} \cdot d\mathbf{r}$ where $\mathbf{F}(x, y) = -y\mathbf{i} + x\mathbf{j}$ and where C is the given oriented curve.

(a) $C : x^2 + y^2 = 3$ $(0 \le x, y;$ oriented as in Figure 15.2.14$a)$
(b) $C : \mathbf{r}(t) = t\mathbf{i} + 2t\mathbf{j}$ $(0 \le t \le 1;$ see Figure 15.2.14$b)$

Solution (a).   At every point on C the direction of $\mathbf{F}$ and the direction of C are the same. (Why?) In addition, at every point on C

$$\|\mathbf{F}\| = \sqrt{(-y)^2 + x^2} = \sqrt{x^2 + y^2} = \sqrt{3}$$

Therefore, $\mathbf{F} \cdot \mathbf{T} = \|\mathbf{F}\| \cos(0) = \|\mathbf{F}\| = \sqrt{3}$, and

$$\int_C \mathbf{F} \cdot d\mathbf{r} = \int_C \mathbf{F} \cdot \mathbf{T}\, ds = \int_C \sqrt{3}\, ds = \sqrt{3} \int_C ds = \frac{3\pi}{2}$$

Solution (b).   The vector field $\mathbf{F}$ is normal to C at every point. (Why?) Therefore,

$$\int_C \mathbf{F} \cdot d\mathbf{r} = \int_C \mathbf{F} \cdot \mathbf{T}\, ds = \int_C 0\, ds = 0 \quad ◀$$

In light of (20) and (30), you might expect that reversing the orientation of C in $\int_C \mathbf{F} \cdot d\mathbf{r}$ would have no effect on the value of the line integral. However, reversing the orientation of C reverses the orientation of $\mathbf{T}$ in the integrand and hence reverses the sign of the integral; that is,

$$\int_{-C} \mathbf{F} \cdot \mathbf{T}\, ds = -\int_C \mathbf{F} \cdot \mathbf{T}\, ds \qquad (31)$$

$$\int_{-C} \mathbf{F} \cdot d\mathbf{r} = -\int_C \mathbf{F} \cdot d\mathbf{r} \qquad (32)$$

■ **WORK AS A LINE INTEGRAL**

An important application of line integrals with respect to x, y, and z is to the problem of defining the work performed by a variable force moving a particle along a curved path. In Section 6.6 we defined the work W performed by a force of constant magnitude acting on an object in the direction of motion (Definition 6.6.1), and later in that section we extended the definition to allow for a force of variable magnitude acting in the direction of motion (Definition 6.6.3). In Section 11.3 we took the concept of work a step further by defining the work W performed by a constant force $\mathbf{F}$ moving a particle in a straight line from point P to point Q. We defined the work to be

$$W = \mathbf{F} \cdot \overrightarrow{PQ} \qquad (33)$$

[Formula (14) in Section 11.3]. Our next goal is to define a more general concept of work —the work performed by a variable force acting on a particle that moves along a curved path in 2-space or 3-space.

In many applications variable forces arise from force fields (gravitational fields, electromagnetic fields, and so forth), so we will consider the problem of work in that context. To motivate an appropriate definition for work performed by a force field, we will use a limit process, and since the procedure is the same for 2-space and 3-space, we will discuss it in detail for 2-space only. The idea is as follows:

- Assume that a force field $\mathbf{F} = \mathbf{F}(x, y)$ moves a particle along a smooth curve C from a point P to a point Q. Divide C into n arcs using the partition points

$$P = P_0(x_0, y_0),\ P_1(x_1, y_1),\ P_2(x_2, y_2),\ \ldots,\ P_{n-1}(x_{n-1}, y_{n-1}),\ P_n(x_n, y_n) = Q$$

directed along C from P to Q, and denote the length of the kth arc by Δs_k. Let (x_k^*, y_k^*) be any point on the kth arc, and let

$$\mathbf{F}_k^* = \mathbf{F}(x_k^*, y_k^*) = f(x_k^*, y_k^*)\mathbf{i} + g(x_k^*, y_k^*)\mathbf{j}$$

be the force vector at this point (Figure 15.2.15).

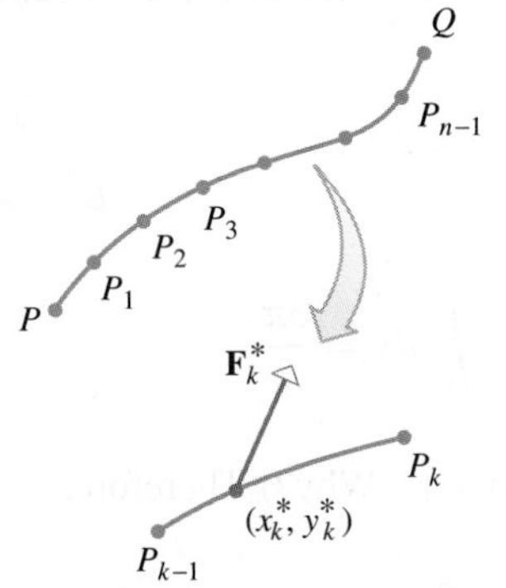

- If the kth arc is small, then the force will not vary much, so we can approximate the force by the constant value $\mathbf{F}_k^*$ on this arc. Moreover, the direction of motion will not vary much over this small arc, so we can approximate the movement of the particle by the displacement vector

$$\overrightarrow{P_{k-1}P_k} = (\Delta x_k)\mathbf{i} + (\Delta y_k)\mathbf{j}$$

where $\Delta x_k = x_k - x_{k-1}$ and $\Delta y_k = y_k - y_{k-1}$.

- Since the work done by a constant force $\mathbf{F}_k^*$ moving a particle along a straight line from P_{k-1} to P_k is

$$\mathbf{F}_k^* \cdot \overrightarrow{P_{k-1}P_k} = (f(x_k^*, y_k^*)\mathbf{i} + g(x_k^*, y_k^*)\mathbf{j}) \cdot ((\Delta x_k)\mathbf{i} + (\Delta y_k)\mathbf{j})$$
$$= f(x_k^*, y_k^*)\Delta x_k + g(x_k^*, y_k^*)\Delta y_k$$

[Formula (33)], the work ΔW_k performed by the force field along the kth arc of C can be approximated by

$$\Delta W_k \approx f(x_k^*, y_k^*)\Delta x_k + g(x_k^*, y_k^*)\Delta y_k$$

The total work W performed by the force moving the particle over the entire curve C can then be approximated as

$$W = \sum_{k=1}^{n} \Delta W_k \approx \sum_{k=1}^{n} [f(x_k^*, y_k^*)\Delta x_k + g(x_k^*, y_k^*)\Delta y_k]$$

- As max $\Delta s_k \to 0$, it is plausible that the error in this approximation approaches 0 and the exact work performed by the force field is

$$W = \lim_{\max \Delta s_k \to 0} \sum_{k=1}^{n} [f(x_k^*, y_k^*)\Delta x_k + g(x_k^*, y_k^*)\Delta y_k]$$

$$= \int_C f(x, y)\, dx + g(x, y)\, dy \qquad \boxed{\text{Formula (22)}}$$

$$= \int_C \mathbf{F} \cdot d\mathbf{r} \qquad \boxed{\text{Formula (26)}}$$

Thus, we are led to the following definition.

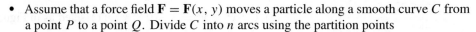

Q

P_{n-1}

P_3

P_2

P_1

P

$\mathbf{F}_k^*$

P_k

(x_k^*, y_k^*)

P_{k-1}

▲ **Figure 15.2.15**

Note from Formula (30) that the work performed by a force field on a particle moving along a smooth curve C is obtained by integrating the scalar tangential component of force along C. This implies that the component of force orthogonal to the direction of motion of the particle has no effect on the work done.

15.2.3 DEFINITION Suppose that under the influence of a continuous force field $\mathbf{F}$ a particle moves along a smooth curve C and that C is oriented in the direction of motion of the particle. Then the *work performed by the force field* on the particle is

$$\int_C \mathbf{F} \cdot d\mathbf{r} \qquad (34)$$

For example, suppose that force is measured in pounds and distance is measured in feet. It follows from part (a) of Example 9 that the work done by a force $\mathbf{F}(x, y) = -y\mathbf{i} + x\mathbf{j}$ acting on a particle moving along the circle $x^2 + y^2 = 3$ from $(\sqrt{3}, 0)$ to $(0, \sqrt{3})$ is $3\pi/2$ foot-pounds.

■ LINE INTEGRALS ALONG PIECEWISE SMOOTH CURVES

Thus far, we have only considered line integrals along smooth curves. However, the notion of a line integral can be extended to curves formed from finitely many smooth curves $C_1, C_2, \ldots, C_n$ joined end to end. Such a curve is called *piecewise smooth* (Figure 15.2.16). We define a line integral along a piecewise smooth curve C to be the sum of the integrals along the sections:

$$\int_C = \int_{C_1} + \int_{C_2} + \cdots + \int_{C_n}$$

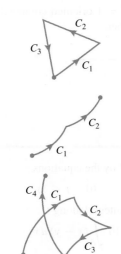

▲ **Figure 15.2.16**

▶ **Example 10**   Evaluate

$$\int_C x^2 y\, dx + x\, dy$$

where C is the triangular path shown in Figure 15.2.17.

Solution.   We will integrate over C_1, C_2, and C_3 separately and add the results. For each of the three integrals we must find parametric equations that trace the path of integration in the correct direction. For this purpose recall from Formula (7) of Section 12.1 that the graph of the vector-valued function

$$\mathbf{r}(t) = (1 - t)\mathbf{r}_0 + t\mathbf{r}_1 \qquad (0 \le t \le 1)$$

is the line segment joining $\mathbf{r}_0$ and $\mathbf{r}_1$, oriented in the direction from $\mathbf{r}_0$ to $\mathbf{r}_1$. Thus, the line segments C_1, C_2, and C_3 can be represented in vector notation as

$$C_1: \mathbf{r}(t) = (1 - t)\langle 0, 0 \rangle + t\langle 1, 0 \rangle = \langle t, 0 \rangle$$
$$C_2: \mathbf{r}(t) = (1 - t)\langle 1, 0 \rangle + t\langle 1, 2 \rangle = \langle 1, 2t \rangle$$
$$C_3: \mathbf{r}(t) = (1 - t)\langle 1, 2 \rangle + t\langle 0, 0 \rangle = \langle 1 - t, 2 - 2t \rangle$$

where t varies from 0 to 1 in each case. From these equations we obtain

$$\int_{C_1} x^2 y\, dx + x\, dy = \int_{C_1} x^2 y\, dx = \int_0^1 (t^2)(0)\frac{d}{dt}[t]\, dt = 0$$

$$\int_{C_2} x^2 y\, dx + x\, dy = \int_{C_2} x\, dy = \int_0^1 (1)\frac{d}{dt}[2t]\, dt = 2$$

$$\int_{C_3} x^2 y\, dx + x\, dy = \int_0^1 (1 - t)^2 (2 - 2t)\frac{d}{dt}[1 - t]\, dt + \int_0^1 (1 - t)\frac{d}{dt}[2 - 2t]\, dt$$

$$= 2\int_0^1 (t - 1)^3\, dt + 2\int_0^1 (t - 1)\, dt = -\tfrac{1}{2} - 1 = -\tfrac{3}{2}$$

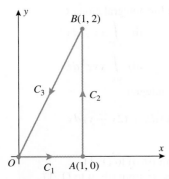

▲ **Figure 15.2.17**

Thus,

$$\int_C x^2 y\, dx + x\, dy = 0 + 2 + \left(-\tfrac{3}{2}\right) = \tfrac{1}{2} \quad ◀$$

✔ **QUICK CHECK EXERCISES 15.2** *(See page 1111 for answers.)*

1. The area of the surface extending upward from the line segment $y = x$ $(0 \le x \le 1)$ in the xy-plane to the plane $z = 2x + 1$ is _____.

2. Suppose that a wire has equation $y = 1 - x$ $(0 \le x \le 1)$ and that its mass density is $\delta(x, y) = 2 - x$. The mass of the wire is _____.

3. If C is the curve represented by the equations
$$x = \sin t, \quad y = \cos t, \quad z = t \quad (0 \le t \le 2\pi)$$
then $\int_C y\,dx - x\,dy + dz =$ _____.

4. If C is the unit circle $x^2 + y^2 = 1$ oriented counterclockwise and $\mathbf{F}(x, y) = x\mathbf{i} + y\mathbf{j}$, then
$$\int_C \mathbf{F} \cdot d\mathbf{r} = \underline{\hspace{2cm}}$$

EXERCISE SET 15.2  Graphing Utility [C] CAS

FOCUS ON CONCEPTS

1. Let C be the line segment from $(0, 0)$ to $(0, 1)$. In each part, evaluate the line integral along C by inspection, and explain your reasoning.
   (a) $\int_C ds$　　　　(b) $\int_C \sin xy\,dy$

2. Let C be the line segment from $(0, 2)$ to $(0, 4)$. In each part, evaluate the line integral along C by inspection, and explain your reasoning.
   (a) $\int_C ds$　　　　(b) $\int_C e^{xy}\,dx$

3–4 Evaluate $\int_C \mathbf{F} \cdot d\mathbf{r}$ by inspection for the force field $\mathbf{F}(x, y) = \mathbf{i} + \mathbf{j}$ and the curve C shown in the figure. Explain your reasoning. [*Note:* For clarity, the vectors in the force field are shown at less than true scale.] ▨

3.　　　　　　　　　　4.

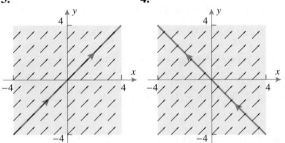

5. Use (30) to explain why the line integral in part (a) of Example 8 can be found by multiplying the length of the line segment C by -1.

 6. (a) Use (30) to explain why the line integral in part (b) of Example 8 should be close to, but somewhat less than, the length of the parabolic curve C.
   (b) Verify the conclusion in part (a) of this exercise by computing the length of C and comparing the length with the value of the line integral.

7. Let C be the curve represented by the equations
$$x = 2t, \quad y = 3t^2 \quad (0 \le t \le 1)$$
In each part, evaluate the line integral along C.
   (a) $\int_C (x - y)\,ds$　　　　(b) $\int_C (x - y)\,dx$
   (c) $\int_C (x - y)\,dy$

8. Let C be the curve represented by the equations
$$x = t, \quad y = 3t^2, \quad z = 6t^3 \quad (0 \le t \le 1)$$
In each part, evaluate the line integral along C.
   (a) $\int_C xyz^2\,ds$　　　　(b) $\int_C xyz^2\,dx$
   (c) $\int_C xyz^2\,dy$　　　　(d) $\int_C xyz^2\,dz$

9. In each part, evaluate the integral
$$\int_C (3x + 2y)\,dx + (2x - y)\,dy$$
along the stated curve.
   (a) The line segment from $(0, 0)$ to $(1, 1)$.
   (b) The parabolic arc $y = x^2$ from $(0, 0)$ to $(1, 1)$.
   (c) The curve $y = \sin(\pi x/2)$ from $(0, 0)$ to $(1, 1)$.
   (d) The curve $x = y^3$ from $(0, 0)$ to $(1, 1)$.

10. In each part, evaluate the integral
$$\int_C y\,dx + z\,dy - x\,dz$$
along the stated curve.
   (a) The line segment from $(0, 0, 0)$ to $(1, 1, 1)$.
   (b) The twisted cubic $x = t, y = t^2, z = t^3$ from $(0, 0, 0)$ to $(1, 1, 1)$.
   (c) The helix $x = \cos \pi t, y = \sin \pi t, z = t$ from $(1, 0, 0)$ to $(-1, 0, 1)$.

11–14 True–False Determine whether the statement is true or false. Explain your answer. ▨

11. If C is a smooth oriented curve in the xy-plane and $f(x, y)$ is a continuous function defined on C, then

$$\int_C f(x, y)\, ds = -\int_{-C} f(x, y)\, ds$$

12. The line integral of a continuous vector field along a smooth curve C is a vector.

13. If $\mathbf{F}(x, y) = f(x, y)\mathbf{i} + g(x, y)\mathbf{j}$ along a smooth oriented curve C in the xy-plane, then

$$\int_C \mathbf{F} \cdot d\mathbf{r} = \int_C f(x, y)\, dx + g(x, y)\, dy$$

14. If a smooth oriented curve C in the xy-plane is a contour for a differentiable function $f(x, y)$, then

$$\int_C \nabla f \cdot d\mathbf{r} = 0$$

15–18 Evaluate the line integral with respect to s along the curve C. ▪

15. $\displaystyle\int_C \frac{1}{1+x}\, ds$
$C : \mathbf{r}(t) = t\mathbf{i} + \frac{2}{3}t^{3/2}\mathbf{j} \quad (0 \le t \le 3)$

16. $\displaystyle\int_C \frac{x}{1+y^2}\, ds$
$C : x = 1 + 2t, \ y = t \quad (0 \le t \le 1)$

17. $\displaystyle\int_C 3x^2yz\, ds$
$C : x = t, \ y = t^2, \ z = \frac{2}{3}t^3 \quad (0 \le t \le 1)$

18. $\displaystyle\int_C \frac{e^{-z}}{x^2 + y^2}\, ds$
$C : \mathbf{r}(t) = 2\cos t\mathbf{i} + 2\sin t\mathbf{j} + t\mathbf{k} \quad (0 \le t \le 2\pi)$

19–26 Evaluate the line integral along the curve C. ▪

19. $\displaystyle\int_C (x + 2y)\, dx + (x - y)\, dy$
$C : x = 2\cos t, \ y = 4\sin t \quad (0 \le t \le \pi/4)$

20. $\displaystyle\int_C (x^2 - y^2)\, dx + x\, dy$
$C : x = t^{2/3}, \ y = t \quad (-1 \le t \le 1)$

21. $\displaystyle\int_C -y\, dx + x\, dy$
$C : y^2 = 3x$ from $(3, 3)$ to $(0, 0)$

22. $\displaystyle\int_C (y - x)\, dx + x^2 y\, dy$
$C : y^2 = x^3$ from $(1, -1)$ to $(1, 1)$

23. $\displaystyle\int_C (x^2 + y^2)\, dx - x\, dy$
$C : x^2 + y^2 = 1$, counterclockwise from $(1, 0)$ to $(0, 1)$

24. $\displaystyle\int_C (y - x)\, dx + xy\, dy$
$C :$ the line segment from $(3, 4)$ to $(2, 1)$

25. $\displaystyle\int_C yz\, dx - xz\, dy + xy\, dz$
$C : x = e^t, \ y = e^{3t}, \ z = e^{-t} \quad (0 \le t \le 1)$

26. $\displaystyle\int_C x^2\, dx + xy\, dy + z^2\, dz$
$C : x = \sin t, \ y = \cos t, \ z = t^2 \quad (0 \le t \le \pi/2)$

c 27–28 Use a CAS to evaluate the line integrals along the given curves. ▪

27. (a) $\displaystyle\int_C (x^3 + y^3)\, ds$
$C : \mathbf{r}(t) = e^t\mathbf{i} + e^{-t}\mathbf{j} \quad (0 \le t \le \ln 2)$

   (b) $\displaystyle\int_C xe^z\, dx + (x - z)\, dy + (x^2 + y^2 + z^2)\, dz$
$C : x = \sin t, \ y = \cos t, \ z = t \quad (0 \le t \le \pi/2)$

28. (a) $\displaystyle\int_C x^7 y^3\, ds$
$C : x = \cos^3 t, \ y = \sin^3 t \quad (0 \le t \le \pi/2)$

   (b) $\displaystyle\int_C x^5 z\, dx + 7y\, dy + y^2 z\, dz$
$C : \mathbf{r}(t) = t\mathbf{i} + t^2\mathbf{j} + \ln t\mathbf{k} \quad (1 \le t \le e)$

29–30 Evaluate $\int_C y\, dx - x\, dy$ along the curve C shown in the figure. ▪

29. (a) 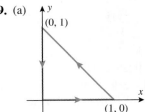 (b)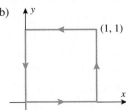

30. (a) 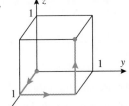 (b)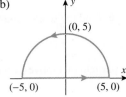

31–32 Evaluate $\int_C x^2 z\, dx - yx^2\, dy + 3\, dz$ along the curve C shown in the figure. ▪

31. 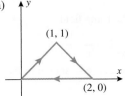 **32.**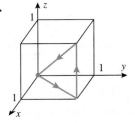

33–36 Evaluate $\int_C \mathbf{F} \cdot d\mathbf{r}$ along the curve C. ▪

33. $\mathbf{F}(x, y) = x^2\mathbf{i} + xy\mathbf{j}$
$C : \mathbf{r}(t) = 2\cos t\mathbf{i} + 2\sin t\mathbf{j} \quad (0 \le t \le \pi)$

34. $\mathbf{F}(x, y) = x^2 y \mathbf{i} + 4 \mathbf{j}$
$C : \mathbf{r}(t) = e^t \mathbf{i} + e^{-t} \mathbf{j} \quad (0 \le t \le 1)$

35. $\mathbf{F}(x, y) = (x^2 + y^2)^{-3/2}(x \mathbf{i} + y \mathbf{j})$
$C : \mathbf{r}(t) = e^t \sin t \mathbf{i} + e^t \cos t \mathbf{j} \quad (0 \le t \le 1)$

36. $\mathbf{F}(x, y, z) = z \mathbf{i} + x \mathbf{j} + y \mathbf{k}$
$C : \mathbf{r}(t) = \sin t \mathbf{i} + 3 \sin t \mathbf{j} + \sin^2 t \mathbf{k} \quad (0 \le t \le \pi/2)$

37. Find the mass of a thin wire shaped in the form of the circular arc $y = \sqrt{9 - x^2} \ (0 \le x \le 3)$ if the density function is $\delta(x, y) = x \sqrt{y}$.

38. Find the mass of a thin wire shaped in the form of the curve $x = e^t \cos t, \ y = e^t \sin t \ (0 \le t \le 1)$ if the density function δ is proportional to the distance from the origin.

39. Find the mass of a thin wire shaped in the form of the helix $x = 3 \cos t, \ y = 3 \sin t, \ z = 4t \ (0 \le t \le \pi/2)$ if the density function is $\delta = kx/(1 + y^2) \ (k > 0)$.

40. Find the mass of a thin wire shaped in the form of the curve $x = 2t, \ y = \ln t, \ z = 4\sqrt{t} \ (1 \le t \le 4)$ if the density function is proportional to the distance above the xy-plane.

41–44 Find the work done by the force field $\mathbf{F}$ on a particle that moves along the curve C. ■

41. $\mathbf{F}(x, y) = xy \mathbf{i} + x^2 \mathbf{j}$
$C : x = y^2$ from $(0, 0)$ to $(1, 1)$

42. $\mathbf{F}(x, y) = (x^2 + xy) \mathbf{i} + (y - x^2 y) \mathbf{j}$
$C : x = t, \ y = 1/t \quad (1 \le t \le 3)$

43. $\mathbf{F}(x, y, z) = xy \mathbf{i} + yz \mathbf{j} + xz \mathbf{k}$
$C : \mathbf{r}(t) = t \mathbf{i} + t^2 \mathbf{j} + t^3 \mathbf{k} \quad (0 \le t \le 1)$

44. $\mathbf{F}(x, y, z) = (x + y) \mathbf{i} + xy \mathbf{j} - z^2 \mathbf{k}$
$C :$ along line segments from $(0, 0, 0)$ to $(1, 3, 1)$ to $(2, -1, 4)$

45–46 Find the work done by the force field

$$\mathbf{F}(x, y) = \frac{1}{x^2 + y^2} \mathbf{i} + \frac{4}{x^2 + y^2} \mathbf{j}$$

on a particle that moves along the curve C shown in the figure. ■

45.

46.

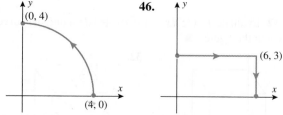

47–48 Use a line integral to find the area of the surface. ■

47. The surface that extends upward from the parabola $y = x^2 \ (0 \le x \le 2)$ in the xy-plane to the plane $z = 3x$.

48. The surface that extends upward from the semicircle $y = \sqrt{4 - x^2}$ in the xy-plane to the surface $z = x^2 y$.

49. As illustrated in the accompanying figure, a sinusoidal cut is made in the top of a cylindrical tin can. Suppose that the base is modeled by the parametric equations $x = \cos t$, $y = \sin t, z = 0 \ (0 \le t \le 2\pi)$, and the height of the cut as a function of t is $z = 2 + 0.5 \sin 3t$.

(a) Use a geometric argument to find the lateral surface area of the cut can.

(b) Write down a line integral for the surface area.

(c) Use the line integral to calculate the surface area.

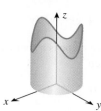

◀ **Figure Ex-49**

50. Evaluate the integral $\displaystyle \int_{-C} \frac{x \, dy - y \, dx}{x^2 + y^2}$, where C is the circle $x^2 + y^2 = a^2$ traversed counterclockwise.

51. Suppose that a particle moves through the force field $\mathbf{F}(x, y) = xy \mathbf{i} + (x - y) \mathbf{j}$ from the point $(0, 0)$ to the point $(1, 0)$ along the curve $x = t, \ y = \lambda t(1 - t)$. For what value of λ will the work done by the force field be 1?

52. A farmer weighing 150 lb carries a sack of grain weighing 20 lb up a circular helical staircase around a silo of radius 25 ft. As the farmer climbs, grain leaks from the sack at a rate of 1 lb per 10 ft of ascent. How much work is performed by the farmer in climbing through a vertical distance of 60 ft in exactly four revolutions? [*Hint:* Find a vector field that represents the force exerted by the farmer in lifting his own weight plus the weight of the sack upward at each point along his path.]

53. Suppose that a curve C in the xy-plane is smoothly parametrized by

$$\mathbf{r}(t) = x(t) \mathbf{i} + y(t) \mathbf{j} \qquad (a \le t \le b)$$

In each part, refer to the notation used in the derivation of Formula (9).

(a) Let m and M denote the respective minimum and maximum values of $\|\mathbf{r}'(t)\|$ on $[a, b]$. Prove that

$$0 \le m(\max \Delta t_k) \le \max \Delta s_k \le M(\max \Delta t_k)$$

(b) Use part (a) to prove that $\max \Delta s_k \to 0$ if and only if $\max \Delta t_k \to 0$.

54. Writing Discuss the similarities and differences between the definition of a definite integral over an interval (Definition 5.5.1) and the definition of the line integral with respect to arc length along a curve (Definition 15.2.1).

55. Writing Describe the different types of line integrals, and discuss how they are related.

1. $2\sqrt{2}$ 2. $\dfrac{3\sqrt{2}}{2}$ 3. 4π 4. 0

15.3 INDEPENDENCE OF PATH; CONSERVATIVE VECTOR FIELDS

In this section we will show that for certain kinds of vector fields **F** *the line integral of* **F** *along a curve depends only on the endpoints of the curve and not on the curve itself. Vector fields with this property, which include gravitational and electrostatic fields, are of special importance in physics and engineering.*

■ WORK INTEGRALS

We saw in the last section that if **F** is a force field in 2-space or 3-space, then the work performed by the field on a particle moving along a parametric curve C from an initial point P to a final point Q is given by the integral

$$\int_C \mathbf{F} \cdot d\mathbf{r} \quad \text{or equivalently} \quad \int_C \mathbf{F} \cdot \mathbf{T}\, ds$$

Accordingly, we call an integral of this type a ***work integral***. Recall that a work integral can also be expressed in scalar form as

$$\int_C \mathbf{F} \cdot d\mathbf{r} = \int_C f(x, y)\, dx + g(x, y)\, dy \qquad \boxed{\text{2-space}} \tag{1}$$

$$\int_C \mathbf{F} \cdot d\mathbf{r} = \int_C f(x, y, z)\, dx + g(x, y, z)\, dy + h(x, y, z)\, dz \qquad \boxed{\text{3-space}} \tag{2}$$

where f, g, and h are the component functions of **F**.

■ INDEPENDENCE OF PATH

The parametric curve C in a work integral is called the ***path of integration***. One of the important problems in applications is to determine how the path of integration affects the work performed by a force field on a particle that moves from a fixed point P to a fixed point Q. We will show shortly that if the force field **F** is conservative (i.e., is the gradient of some potential function ϕ), then the work that the field performs on a particle that moves from P to Q does not depend on the particular path C that the particle follows. This is illustrated in the following example.

▶ **Example 1** The force field $\mathbf{F}(x, y) = y\mathbf{i} + x\mathbf{j}$ is conservative since it is the gradient of $\phi(x, y) = xy$ (verify). Thus, the preceding discussion suggests that the work performed by the field on a particle that moves from the point $(0, 0)$ to the point $(1, 1)$ should be the same along different paths. Confirm that the value of the work integral

$$\int_C \mathbf{F} \cdot d\mathbf{r}$$

is the same along the following paths (Figure 15.3.1):

(a) The line segment $y = x$ from $(0, 0)$ to $(1, 1)$.

(b) The parabola $y = x^2$ from $(0, 0)$ to $(1, 1)$.

(c) The cubic $y = x^3$ from $(0, 0)$ to $(1, 1)$.

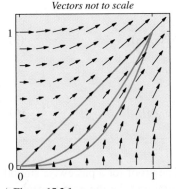

Vectors not to scale

▲ **Figure 15.3.1**

Solution (a).   With $x = t$ as the parameter, the path of integration is given by

$$x = t, \quad y = t \qquad (0 \le t \le 1)$$

Thus,

$$\int_C \mathbf{F} \cdot d\mathbf{r} = \int_C (y\mathbf{i} + x\mathbf{j}) \cdot (dx\mathbf{i} + dy\mathbf{j}) = \int_C y \, dx + x \, dy$$

$$= \int_0^1 2t \, dt = 1$$

Solution (b).   With $x = t$ as the parameter, the path of integration is given by

$$x = t, \quad y = t^2 \qquad (0 \le t \le 1)$$

Thus,

$$\int_C \mathbf{F} \cdot d\mathbf{r} = \int_C y \, dx + x \, dy = \int_0^1 3t^2 \, dt = 1$$

Solution (c).   With $x = t$ as the parameter, the path of integration is given by

$$x = t, \quad y = t^3 \qquad (0 \le t \le 1)$$

Thus,

$$\int_C \mathbf{F} \cdot d\mathbf{r} = \int_C y \, dx + x \, dy = \int_0^1 4t^3 \, dt = 1 \quad \blacktriangleleft$$

■ **THE FUNDAMENTAL THEOREM OF LINE INTEGRALS**

Recall from the Fundamental Theorem of Calculus (Theorem 5.6.1) that if F is an antiderivative of f, then

$$\int_a^b f(x) \, dx = F(b) - F(a)$$

The following result is the analog of that theorem for line integrals in 2-space.

15.3.1   **THEOREM (*The Fundamental Theorem of Line Integrals*)**   *Suppose that*

$$\mathbf{F}(x, y) = f(x, y)\mathbf{i} + g(x, y)\mathbf{j}$$

is a conservative vector field in some open region D containing the points (x_0, y_0) and (x_1, y_1) and that $f(x, y)$ and $g(x, y)$ are continuous in this region. If

$$\mathbf{F}(x, y) = \nabla\phi(x, y)$$

and if C is any piecewise smooth parametric curve that starts at (x_0, y_0), ends at (x_1, y_1), and lies in the region D, then

$$\int_C \mathbf{F}(x, y) \cdot d\mathbf{r} = \phi(x_1, y_1) - \phi(x_0, y_0) \tag{3}$$

or, equivalently,

$$\int_C \nabla\phi \cdot d\mathbf{r} = \phi(x_1, y_1) - \phi(x_0, y_0) \tag{4}$$

The value of

$$\int_C \mathbf{F} \cdot d\mathbf{r} = \int_C \mathbf{F} \cdot \mathbf{T} \, ds$$

depends on the magnitude of $\mathbf{F}$ along C, the alignment of $\mathbf{F}$ with the direction of C at each point, and the length of C. If $\mathbf{F}$ is conservative, these various factors always "balance out" so that the value of $\int_C \mathbf{F} \cdot d\mathbf{r}$ depends only on the initial and final points of C.

PROOF   We will give the proof for a smooth curve C. The proof for a piecewise smooth curve, which is left as an exercise, can be obtained by applying the theorem to each individual smooth piece and adding the results. Suppose that C is given parametrically by $x = x(t)$, $y = y(t)$ ($a \leq t \leq b$), so that the initial and final points of the curve are

$$(x_0, y_0) = (x(a), y(a)) \quad \text{and} \quad (x_1, y_1) = (x(b), y(b))$$

Since $\mathbf{F}(x, y) = \nabla\phi$, it follows that

$$\mathbf{F}(x, y) = \frac{\partial\phi}{\partial x}\mathbf{i} + \frac{\partial\phi}{\partial y}\mathbf{j}$$

so

$$\int_C \mathbf{F}(x, y) \cdot d\mathbf{r} = \int_C \frac{\partial\phi}{\partial x} dx + \frac{\partial\phi}{\partial y} dy = \int_a^b \left[\frac{\partial\phi}{\partial x}\frac{dx}{dt} + \frac{\partial\phi}{\partial y}\frac{dy}{dt} \right] dt$$

$$= \int_a^b \frac{d}{dt}[\phi(x(t), y(t))] \, dt = \phi(x(t), y(t)) \Big]_{t=a}^b$$

$$= \phi(x(b), y(b)) - \phi(x(a), y(a))$$

$$= \phi(x_1, y_1) - \phi(x_0, y_0) \quad \blacksquare$$

Stated informally, this theorem shows that *the value of a line integral of a conservative vector field along a piecewise smooth path is **independent of the path**;* that is, the value of the integral depends on the endpoints and not on the actual path C. Accordingly, for line integrals of conservative vector fields, it is common to express (3) and (4) as

$$\int_{(x_0, y_0)}^{(x_1, y_1)} \mathbf{F} \cdot d\mathbf{r} = \int_{(x_0, y_0)}^{(x_1, y_1)} \nabla\phi \cdot d\mathbf{r} = \phi(x_1, y_1) - \phi(x_0, y_0) \tag{5}$$

▶ **Example 2**

(a) Confirm that the force field $\mathbf{F}(x, y) = y\mathbf{i} + x\mathbf{j}$ in Example 1 is conservative by showing that $\mathbf{F}(x, y)$ is the gradient of $\phi(x, y) = xy$.

> If **F** is conservative, then you have a choice of methods for evaluating $\int_C \mathbf{F} \cdot d\mathbf{r}$. You can work directly with the curve C, you can replace C with another curve that has the same endpoints as C, or you can apply Formula (3).

(b) Use the Fundamental Theorem of Line Integrals to evaluate $\displaystyle\int_{(0,0)}^{(1,1)} \mathbf{F} \cdot d\mathbf{r}$.

Solution (a).

$$\nabla\phi = \frac{\partial\phi}{\partial x}\mathbf{i} + \frac{\partial\phi}{\partial y}\mathbf{j} = y\mathbf{i} + x\mathbf{j}$$

Solution (b).   From (5) we obtain

$$\int_{(0,0)}^{(1,1)} \mathbf{F} \cdot d\mathbf{r} = \phi(1, 1) - \phi(0, 0) = 1 - 0 = 1$$

which agrees with the results obtained in Example 1 by integrating from $(0, 0)$ to $(1, 1)$ along specific paths. ◀

■ **LINE INTEGRALS ALONG CLOSED PATHS**

Parametric curves that begin and end at the same point play an important role in the study of vector fields, so there is some special terminology associated with them. A parametric curve C that is represented by the vector-valued function $\mathbf{r}(t)$ for $a \leq t \leq b$ is said to be *closed* if the initial point $\mathbf{r}(a)$ and the terminal point $\mathbf{r}(b)$ coincide; that is, $\mathbf{r}(a) = \mathbf{r}(b)$ (Figure 15.3.2).

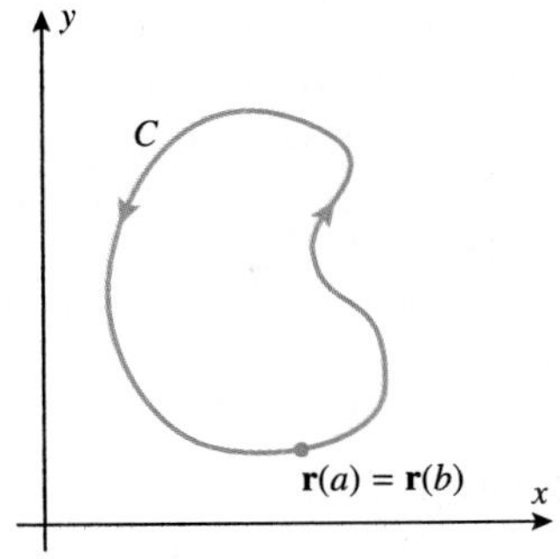

▲ **Figure 15.3.2**

It follows from (5) that the line integral of a conservative vector field along a closed path C that begins and ends at (x_0, y_0) is zero. This is because the point (x_1, y_1) in (5) is the same as (x_0, y_0) and hence

$$\int_C \mathbf{F} \cdot d\mathbf{r} = \phi(x_1, y_1) - \phi(x_0, y_0) = 0$$

Our next objective is to show that the converse of this result is also true. That is, we want to show that under appropriate conditions a vector field whose line integral is zero along *all* closed paths must be conservative. For this to be true we will need to require that the domain D of the vector field be **connected**, by which we mean that any two points in D can be joined by some piecewise smooth curve that lies entirely in D. Stated informally, D is connected if it does not consist of two or more separate pieces (Figure 15.3.3).

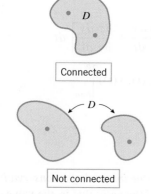

Connected

Not connected

▲ Figure 15.3.3

15.3.2 THEOREM   *If $f(x, y)$ and $g(x, y)$ are continuous on some open connected region D, then the following statements are equivalent (all true or all false):*

(a) $\mathbf{F}(x, y) = f(x, y)\mathbf{i} + g(x, y)\mathbf{j}$ *is a conservative vector field on the region D.*

(b) $\displaystyle\int_C \mathbf{F} \cdot d\mathbf{r} = 0$ *for every piecewise smooth closed curve C in D.*

(c) $\displaystyle\int_C \mathbf{F} \cdot d\mathbf{r}$ *is independent of the path from any point P in D to any point Q in D for every piecewise smooth curve C in D.*

This theorem can be established by proving three implications: $(a) \Rightarrow (b)$, $(b) \Rightarrow (c)$, and $(c) \Rightarrow (a)$. Since we showed above that $(a) \Rightarrow (b)$, we need only prove the last two implications. We will prove $(c) \Rightarrow (a)$ and leave the other implication as an exercise.

PROOF $(c) \Rightarrow (a)$. We are assuming that $\int_C \mathbf{F} \cdot d\mathbf{r}$ is independent of the path for every piecewise smooth curve C in the region, and we want to show that there is a function $\phi = \phi(x, y)$ such that $\nabla\phi = \mathbf{F}(x, y)$ at each point of the region; that is,

$$\frac{\partial \phi}{\partial x} = f(x, y) \quad \text{and} \quad \frac{\partial \phi}{\partial y} = g(x, y) \tag{6}$$

Now choose a fixed point (a, b) in D, let (x, y) be any point in D, and define

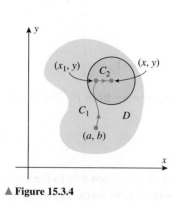

▲ Figure 15.3.4

$$\phi(x, y) = \int_{(a,b)}^{(x,y)} \mathbf{F} \cdot d\mathbf{r} \tag{7}$$

This is an unambiguous definition because we have assumed that the integral is independent of the path. We will show that $\nabla\phi = \mathbf{F}$. Since D is open, we can find a circular disk centered at (x, y) whose points lie entirely in D. As shown in Figure 15.3.4, choose any point (x_1, y) in this disk that lies on the same horizontal line as (x, y) such that $x_1 < x$. Because the integral in (7) is independent of path, we can evaluate it by first integrating from (a, b) to (x_1, y) along an arbitrary piecewise smooth curve C_1 in D, and then continuing along the horizontal line segment C_2 from (x_1, y) to (x, y). This yields

$$\phi(x, y) = \int_{C_1} \mathbf{F} \cdot d\mathbf{r} + \int_{C_2} \mathbf{F} \cdot d\mathbf{r} = \int_{(a,b)}^{(x_1,y)} \mathbf{F} \cdot d\mathbf{r} + \int_{C_2} \mathbf{F} \cdot d\mathbf{r}$$

Since the first term does not depend on x, its partial derivative with respect to x is zero and hence

$$\frac{\partial \phi}{\partial x} = \frac{\partial}{\partial x} \int_{C_2} \mathbf{F} \cdot d\mathbf{r} = \frac{\partial}{\partial x} \int_{C_2} f(x, y)\, dx + g(x, y)\, dy$$

However, the line integral with respect to y is zero along the horizontal line segment C_2, so this equation simplifies to

$$\frac{\partial \phi}{\partial x} = \frac{\partial}{\partial x} \int_{C_2} f(x, y)\, dx \tag{8}$$

To evaluate the integral in this expression, we treat y as a constant and express the line C_2 parametrically as

$$x = t, \quad y = y \quad (x_1 \le t \le x)$$

At the risk of confusion, but to avoid complicating the notation, we have used x both as the dependent variable in the parametric equations and as the endpoint of the line segment. With the latter interpretation of x, it follows that (8) can be expressed as

$$\frac{\partial \phi}{\partial x} = \frac{\partial}{\partial x} \int_{x_1}^{x} f(t, y)\, dt$$

Now we apply Part 2 of the Fundamental Theorem of Calculus (Theorem 5.6.3), treating y as constant. This yields

$$\frac{\partial \phi}{\partial x} = f(x, y)$$

which proves the first part of (6). The proof that $\partial \phi / \partial y = g(x, y)$ can be obtained in a similar manner by joining (x, y) to a point (x, y_1) with a vertical line segment (Exercise 39). ■

A TEST FOR CONSERVATIVE VECTOR FIELDS

Although Theorem 15.3.2 is an important characterization of conservative vector fields, it is not an effective computational tool because it is usually not possible to evaluate the line integral over all possible piecewise smooth curves in D, as required in parts (b) and (c). To develop a method for determining whether a vector field is conservative, we will need to introduce some new concepts about parametric curves and connected sets. We will say that a parametric curve is *simple* if it does not intersect itself between its endpoints. A simple parametric curve may or may not be closed (Figure 15.3.5). In addition, we will say that a connected set D in 2-space is *simply connected* if no simple closed curve in D encloses points that are not in D. Stated informally, a connected set D is simply connected if it has no holes; a connected set with one or more holes is said to be *multiply connected* (Figure 15.3.6).

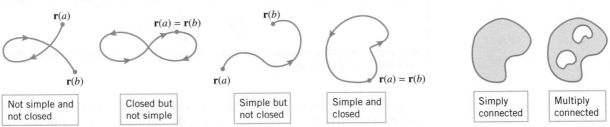

| Not simple and not closed | Closed but not simple | Simple but not closed | Simple and closed | Simply connected | Multiply connected |

▲ Figure 15.3.5   ▲ Figure 15.3.6

The following theorem is the primary tool for determining whether a vector field in 2-space is conservative.

15.3.3 **THEOREM** (*Conservative Field Test*) *If $f(x, y)$ and $g(x, y)$ are continuous and have continuous first partial derivatives on some open region D, and if the vector field $\mathbf{F}(x, y) = f(x, y)\mathbf{i} + g(x, y)\mathbf{j}$ is conservative on D, then*

$$\frac{\partial f}{\partial y} = \frac{\partial g}{\partial x} \tag{9}$$

at each point in D. Conversely, if D is simply connected and (9) holds at each point in D, then $\mathbf{F}(x, y) = f(x, y)\mathbf{i} + g(x, y)\mathbf{j}$ is conservative.

WARNING

In (9), the **i**-component of **F** is differentiated with respect to y and the **j**-component with respect to x. It is easy to get this backwards by mistake.

A complete proof of this theorem requires results from advanced calculus and will be omitted. However, it is not hard to see why (9) must hold if $\mathbf{F}$ is conservative. For this purpose suppose that $\mathbf{F} = \nabla\phi$, in which case we can express the functions f and g as

$$\frac{\partial \phi}{\partial x} = f \quad \text{and} \quad \frac{\partial \phi}{\partial y} = g \tag{10}$$

Thus,

$$\frac{\partial f}{\partial y} = \frac{\partial}{\partial y}\left(\frac{\partial \phi}{\partial x}\right) = \frac{\partial^2 \phi}{\partial y \partial x} \quad \text{and} \quad \frac{\partial g}{\partial x} = \frac{\partial}{\partial x}\left(\frac{\partial \phi}{\partial y}\right) = \frac{\partial^2 \phi}{\partial x \partial y}$$

But the mixed partial derivatives in these equations are equal (Theorem 13.3.2), so (9) follows.

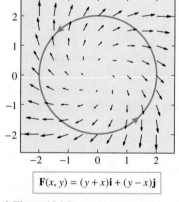

Vectors not to scale

$$\mathbf{F}(x, y) = (y + x)\mathbf{i} + (y - x)\mathbf{j}$$

▲ **Figure 15.3.7**

▶ **Example 3** Use Theorem 15.3.3 to determine whether the vector field

$$\mathbf{F}(x, y) = (y + x)\mathbf{i} + (y - x)\mathbf{j}$$

is conservative on some open set.

Solution. Let $f(x, y) = y + x$ and $g(x, y) = y - x$. Then

$$\frac{\partial f}{\partial y} = 1 \quad \text{and} \quad \frac{\partial g}{\partial x} = -1$$

Thus, there are no points in the xy-plane at which condition (9) holds, and hence $\mathbf{F}$ is not conservative on any open set. ◀

REMARK | Since the vector field $\mathbf{F}$ in Example 3 is not conservative, it follows from Theorem 15.3.2 that there must exist piecewise smooth closed curves in every open connected set in the xy-plane on which

$$\int_C \mathbf{F} \cdot d\mathbf{r} = \int_C \mathbf{F} \cdot \mathbf{T}\, ds \neq 0$$

One such curve is the oriented circle shown in Figure 15.3.7. The figure suggests that $\mathbf{F} \cdot \mathbf{T} < 0$ at each point of C (why?), so $\int_C \mathbf{F} \cdot \mathbf{T}\, ds < 0$.

Once it is established that a vector field is conservative, a potential function for the field can be obtained by first integrating either of the equations in (10). This is illustrated in the following example.

▶ **Example 4**   Let $\mathbf{F}(x, y) = 2xy^3\mathbf{i} + (1 + 3x^2y^2)\mathbf{j}$.

(a) Show that $\mathbf{F}$ is a conservative vector field on the entire xy-plane.
(b) Find ϕ by first integrating $\partial\phi/\partial x$.
(c) Find ϕ by first integrating $\partial\phi/\partial y$.

Solution (a).   Since $f(x, y) = 2xy^3$ and $g(x, y) = 1 + 3x^2y^2$, we have

$$\frac{\partial f}{\partial y} = 6xy^2 = \frac{\partial g}{\partial x}$$

so (9) holds for all (x, y).

Solution (b).   Since the field $\mathbf{F}$ is conservative, there is a potential function ϕ such that

$$\frac{\partial\phi}{\partial x} = 2xy^3 \quad \text{and} \quad \frac{\partial\phi}{\partial y} = 1 + 3x^2y^2 \tag{11}$$

Integrating the first of these equations with respect to x (and treating y as a constant) yields

$$\phi = \int 2xy^3 \, dx = x^2y^3 + k(y) \tag{12}$$

where $k(y)$ represents the "constant" of integration. We are justified in treating the constant of integration as a function of y, since y is held constant in the integration process. To find $k(y)$ we differentiate (12) with respect to y and use the second equation in (11) to obtain

$$\frac{\partial\phi}{\partial y} = 3x^2y^2 + k'(y) = 1 + 3x^2y^2$$

from which it follows that $k'(y) = 1$. Thus,

$$k(y) = \int k'(y) \, dy = \int 1 \, dy = y + K$$

where K is a (numerical) constant of integration. Substituting in (12) we obtain

$$\phi = x^2y^3 + y + K$$

The appearance of the arbitrary constant K tells us that ϕ is not unique. As a check on the computations, you may want to verify that $\nabla\phi = \mathbf{F}$.

Solution (c).   Integrating the second equation in (11) with respect to y (and treating x as a constant) yields

$$\phi = \int (1 + 3x^2y^2) \, dy = y + x^2y^3 + k(x) \tag{13}$$

where $k(x)$ is the "constant" of integration. Differentiating (13) with respect to x and using the first equation in (11) yields

$$\frac{\partial\phi}{\partial x} = 2xy^3 + k'(x) = 2xy^3$$

from which it follows that $k'(x) = 0$ and consequently that $k(x) = K$, where K is a numerical constant of integration. Substituting this in (13) yields

$$\phi = y + x^2y^3 + K$$

which agrees with the solution in part (b). ◀

You can also use (7) to find a potential function for a conservative vector field. For example, find a potential function for the vector field in Example 4 by evaluating (7) on the line segment

$$\mathbf{r}(t) = t(x\mathbf{i}) + t(y\mathbf{j}) \quad (0 \le t \le 1)$$

from $(0, 0)$ to (x, y).

▶ **Example 5**   Use the potential function obtained in Example 4 to evaluate the integral

$$\int_{(1,4)}^{(3,1)} 2xy^3\,dx + (1 + 3x^2y^2)\,dy$$

Solution.   The integrand can be expressed as $\mathbf{F} \cdot d\mathbf{r}$, where $\mathbf{F}$ is the vector field in Example 4. Thus, using Formula (3) and the potential function $\phi = y + x^2y^3 + K$ for $\mathbf{F}$, we obtain

$$\int_{(1,4)}^{(3,1)} 2xy^3\,dx + (1 + 3x^2y^2)\,dy = \int_{(1,4)}^{(3,1)} \mathbf{F} \cdot d\mathbf{r} = \phi(3,1) - \phi(1,4)$$

$$= (10 + K) - (68 + K) = -58 \;\blacktriangleleft$$

In the solution to Example 5, note that the constant K drops out. In future integration problems of the type in this example, we will often omit K from the computations. See Exercise 7 for other ways to evaluate this integral.

▶ **Example 6**   Let $\mathbf{F}(x, y) = e^y\mathbf{i} + xe^y\mathbf{j}$ denote a force field in the xy-plane.

(a) Verify that the force field $\mathbf{F}$ is conservative on the entire xy-plane.

(b) Find the work done by the field on a particle that moves from $(1, 0)$ to $(-1, 0)$ along the semicircular path C shown in Figure 15.3.8.

Solution (a).   For the given field we have $f(x, y) = e^y$ and $g(x, y) = xe^y$. Thus,

$$\frac{\partial}{\partial y}(e^y) = e^y = \frac{\partial}{\partial x}(xe^y)$$

so (9) holds for all (x, y) and hence $\mathbf{F}$ is conservative on the entire xy-plane.

Solution (b).   From Formula (34) of Section 15.2, the work done by the field is

$$W = \int_C \mathbf{F} \cdot d\mathbf{r} = \int_C e^y\,dx + xe^y\,dy \tag{14}$$

However, the calculations involved in integrating along C are tedious, so it is preferable to apply Theorem 15.3.1, taking advantage of the fact that the field is conservative and the integral is independent of path. Thus, we write (14) as

$$W = \int_{(1,0)}^{(-1,0)} e^y\,dx + xe^y\,dy = \phi(-1, 0) - \phi(1, 0) \tag{15}$$

As illustrated in Example 4, we can find ϕ by integrating either of the equations

$$\frac{\partial\phi}{\partial x} = e^y \quad \text{and} \quad \frac{\partial\phi}{\partial y} = xe^y \tag{16}$$

We will integrate the first. We obtain

$$\phi = \int e^y\,dx = xe^y + k(y) \tag{17}$$

Differentiating this equation with respect to y and using the second equation in (16) yields

$$\frac{\partial\phi}{\partial y} = xe^y + k'(y) = xe^y$$

from which it follows that $k'(y) = 0$ or $k(y) = K$. Thus, from (17)

$$\phi = xe^y + K$$

and hence from (15)

$$W = \phi(-1, 0) - \phi(1, 0) = (-1)e^0 - 1e^0 = -2 \;\blacktriangleleft$$

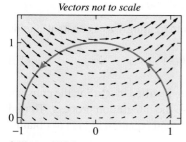

Vectors not to scale

▲ **Figure 15.3.8**

■ **CONSERVATIVE VECTOR FIELDS IN 3-SPACE**
All of the results in this section have analogs in 3-space: Theorems 15.3.1 and 15.3.2 can be extended to vector fields in 3-space simply by adding a third variable and modifying the hypotheses appropriately. For example, in 3-space, Formula (3) becomes

$$\int_C \mathbf{F}(x, y, z) \cdot d\mathbf{r} = \phi(x_1, y_1, z_1) - \phi(x_0, y_0, z_0) \tag{18}$$

Theorem 15.3.3 can also be extended to vector fields in 3-space. We leave it for the exercises to show that if $\mathbf{F}(x, y, z) = f(x, y, z)\mathbf{i} + g(x, y, z)\mathbf{j} + h(x, y, z)\mathbf{k}$ is a conservative field, then

$$\frac{\partial f}{\partial y} = \frac{\partial g}{\partial x}, \quad \frac{\partial f}{\partial z} = \frac{\partial h}{\partial x}, \quad \frac{\partial g}{\partial z} = \frac{\partial h}{\partial y} \tag{19}$$

that is, curl $\mathbf{F} = \mathbf{0}$. Conversely, a vector field satisfying these conditions on a suitably restricted region is conservative on that region if f, g, and h are continuous and have continuous first partial derivatives in the region. Some problems involving Formulas (18) and (19) are given in the review exercises at the end of this chapter.

■ **CONSERVATION OF ENERGY**
If $\mathbf{F}(x, y, z)$ is a conservative force field with a potential function $\phi(x, y, z)$, then we call $V(x, y, z) = -\phi(x, y, z)$ the *potential energy* of the field at the point (x, y, z). Thus, it follows from the 3-space version of Theorem 15.3.1 that the work W done by $\mathbf{F}$ on a particle that moves along any path C from a point (x_0, y_0, z_0) to a point (x_1, y_1, z_1) is related to the potential energy by the equation

$$W = \int_C \mathbf{F} \cdot d\mathbf{r} = \phi(x_1, y_1, z_1) - \phi(x_0, y_0, z_0) = -[V(x_1, y_1, z_1) - V(x_0, y_0, z_0)] \tag{20}$$

That is, the work done by the field is the negative of the change in potential energy. In particular, it follows from the 3-space analog of Theorem 15.3.2 that if a particle traverses a piecewise smooth closed path in a conservative vector field, then the work done by the field is zero, and there is no change in potential energy. To take this a step further, suppose that a particle of mass m moves along any piecewise smooth curve (not necessarily closed) in a conservative force field $\mathbf{F}$, starting at (x_0, y_0, z_0) with speed v_i and ending at (x_1, y_1, z_1) with speed v_f. If $\mathbf{F}$ is the only force acting on the particle, then an argument similar to the derivation of Equation (6) in Section 6.6 shows that the work done on the particle by $\mathbf{F}$ is equal to the change in kinetic energy $\frac{1}{2}mv_f^2 - \frac{1}{2}mv_i^2$ of the particle. (An argument for smooth curves appears in the Making Connections exercises.) If we let V_i denote the potential energy at the starting point and V_f the potential energy at the final point, then it follows from (20) that

$$\tfrac{1}{2}mv_f^2 - \tfrac{1}{2}mv_i^2 = -[V_f - V_i]$$

which we can rewrite as

$$\tfrac{1}{2}mv_f^2 + V_f = \tfrac{1}{2}mv_i^2 + V_i$$

This equation states that the total energy of the particle (kinetic energy + potential energy) does not change as the particle moves along a path in a conservative vector field. This result, called the *conservation of energy principle*, explains the origin of the term "conservative vector field."

✓ **QUICK CHECK EXERCISES 15.3**   *(See page 1121 for answers.)*

1. If C is a piecewise smooth curve from $(1, 2, 3)$ to $(4, 5, 6)$, then
$$\int_C dx + 2\,dy + 3\,dz = \underline{\hspace{1.5cm}}$$

2. If C is the portion of the circle $x^2 + y^2 = 1$ where $0 \le x$, oriented counterclockwise, and $f(x, y) = ye^x$, then
$$\int_C \nabla f \cdot d\mathbf{r} = \underline{\hspace{1.5cm}}$$

3. A potential function for the vector field
$$\mathbf{F}(x, y, z) = yz\mathbf{i} + (xz + z)\mathbf{j} + (xy + y + 1)\mathbf{k}$$
is $\phi(x, y, z) = \underline{\hspace{1.5cm}}$.

4. If a, b, and c are nonzero real numbers such that the vector field $x^5 y^a \mathbf{i} + x^b y^c \mathbf{j}$ is a conservative vector field, then
$$a = \underline{\hspace{1cm}}, \quad b = \underline{\hspace{1cm}}, \quad c = \underline{\hspace{1cm}}$$

EXERCISE SET 15.3   [c] CAS

1–6 Determine whether $\mathbf{F}$ is a conservative vector field. If so, find a potential function for it. ◼

1. $\mathbf{F}(x, y) = x\mathbf{i} + y\mathbf{j}$ **2.** $\mathbf{F}(x, y) = 3y^2\mathbf{i} + 6xy\mathbf{j}$

3. $\mathbf{F}(x, y) = x^2 y\mathbf{i} + 5xy^2\mathbf{j}$

4. $\mathbf{F}(x, y) = e^x \cos y\mathbf{i} - e^x \sin y\mathbf{j}$

5. $\mathbf{F}(x, y) = (\cos y + y \cos x)\mathbf{i} + (\sin x - x \sin y)\mathbf{j}$

6. $\mathbf{F}(x, y) = x \ln y\mathbf{i} + y \ln x\mathbf{j}$

7. In each part, evaluate $\int_C 2xy^3\,dx + (1 + 3x^2 y^2)\,dy$ over the curve C, and compare your answer with the result of Example 5.
   (a) C is the line segment from $(1, 4)$ to $(3, 1)$.
   (b) C consists of the line segment from $(1, 4)$ to $(1, 1)$, followed by the line segment from $(1, 1)$ to $(3, 1)$.

8. (a) Show that the line integral $\int_C y \sin x\,dx - \cos x\,dy$ is independent of the path.
   (b) Evaluate the integral in part (a) along the line segment from $(0, 1)$ to $(\pi, -1)$.
   (c) Evaluate the integral $\int_{(0,1)}^{(\pi,-1)} y \sin x\,dx - \cos x\,dy$ using Theorem 15.3.1, and confirm that the value is the same as that obtained in part (b).

9–14 Show that the integral is independent of the path, and use Theorem 15.3.1 to find its value. ◼

9. $\displaystyle\int_{(1,2)}^{(4,0)} 3y\,dx + 3x\,dy$

10. $\displaystyle\int_{(0,0)}^{(1,\pi/2)} e^x \sin y\,dx + e^x \cos y\,dy$

11. $\displaystyle\int_{(0,0)}^{(3,2)} 2xe^y\,dx + x^2 e^y\,dy$

12. $\displaystyle\int_{(-1,2)}^{(0,1)} (3x - y + 1)\,dx - (x + 4y + 2)\,dy$

13. $\displaystyle\int_{(2,-2)}^{(-1,0)} 2xy^3\,dx + 3y^2 x^2\,dy$

14. $\displaystyle\int_{(1,1)}^{(3,3)} \left(e^x \ln y - \frac{e^y}{x}\right) dx + \left(\frac{e^x}{y} - e^y \ln x\right) dy$, where x and y are positive.

15–18 Confirm that the force field $\mathbf{F}$ is conservative in some open connected region containing the points P and Q, and then find the work done by the force field on a particle moving along an arbitrary smooth curve in the region from P to Q. ◼

15. $\mathbf{F}(x, y) = xy^2\mathbf{i} + x^2 y\mathbf{j}$; $P(1, 1)$, $Q(0, 0)$

16. $\mathbf{F}(x, y) = 2xy^3\mathbf{i} + 3x^2 y^2\mathbf{j}$; $P(-3, 0)$, $Q(4, 1)$

17. $\mathbf{F}(x, y) = ye^{xy}\mathbf{i} + xe^{xy}\mathbf{j}$; $P(-1, 1)$, $Q(2, 0)$

18. $\mathbf{F}(x, y) = e^{-y} \cos x\mathbf{i} - e^{-y} \sin x\mathbf{j}$; $P(\pi/2, 1)$, $Q(-\pi/2, 0)$

19–22 True–False Determine whether the statement is true or false. Explain your answer. ◼

19. If $\mathbf{F}$ is a vector field and there exists a closed curve C such that $\int_C \mathbf{F} \cdot d\mathbf{r} = 0$, then $\mathbf{F}$ is conservative.

20. If $\mathbf{F}(x, y) = a y\mathbf{i} + bx\mathbf{j}$ is a conservative vector field, then $a = b$.

21. If $\phi(x, y)$ is a potential function for a constant vector field, then the graph of $z = \phi(x, y)$ is a plane.

22. If $f(x, y)$ and $g(x, y)$ are differentiable functions defined on the xy-plane, and if $f_y(x, y) = g_x(x, y)$ for all (x, y), then there exists a function $\phi(x, y)$ such that $\phi_x(x, y) = f(x, y)$ and $\phi_y(x, y) = g(x, y)$.

23–24 Find the exact value of $\int_C \mathbf{F} \cdot d\mathbf{r}$ using any method. ◼

23. $\mathbf{F}(x, y) = (e^y + ye^x)\mathbf{i} + (xe^y + e^x)\mathbf{j}$
   $C : \mathbf{r}(t) = \sin(\pi t/2)\mathbf{i} + \ln t\mathbf{j}$ $(1 \le t \le 2)$

24. $\mathbf{F}(x, y) = 2xy\mathbf{i} + (x^2 + \cos y)\mathbf{j}$
   $C : \mathbf{r}(t) = t\mathbf{i} + t \cos(t/3)\mathbf{j}$ $(0 \le t \le \pi)$

[c] **25.** Use the numerical integration capability of a CAS or other calculating utility to approximate the value of the integral in Exercise 23 by direct integration. Confirm that the numerical approximation is consistent with the exact value.

[c] **26.** Use the numerical integration capability of a CAS or other calculating utility to approximate the value of the integral in Exercise 24 by direct integration. Confirm that the numerical approximation is consistent with the exact value.

27–28 Is the vector field conservative? Explain. ■

27.   **28.**

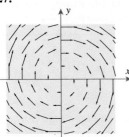   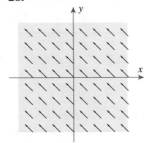

29. Suppose that C is a circle in the domain of a conservative vector field in the xy-plane whose component functions are continuous. Explain why there must be at least two points on C at which the vector field is normal to the circle.

30. Does the result in Exercise 29 remain true if the circle C is replaced by a square? Explain.

31. Prove: If

$$\mathbf{F}(x, y, z) = f(x, y, z)\mathbf{i} + g(x, y, z)\mathbf{j} + h(x, y, z)\mathbf{k}$$

is a conservative field and f, g, and h are continuous and have continuous first partial derivatives in a region, then

$$\frac{\partial f}{\partial y} = \frac{\partial g}{\partial x}, \quad \frac{\partial f}{\partial z} = \frac{\partial h}{\partial x}, \quad \frac{\partial g}{\partial z} = \frac{\partial h}{\partial y}$$

in the region.

32. Use the result in Exercise 31 to show that the integral

$$\int_C yz \, dx + xz \, dy + yx^2 \, dz$$

is not independent of the path.

33. Find a nonzero function h for which

$$\mathbf{F}(x, y) = h(x)[x \sin y + y \cos y]\mathbf{i}$$
$$+ h(x)[x \cos y - y \sin y]\mathbf{j}$$

is conservative.

34. (a) In Example 3 of Section 15.1 we showed that

$$\phi(x, y) = -\frac{c}{(x^2 + y^2)^{1/2}}$$

is a potential function for the two-dimensional inverse-square field

$$\mathbf{F}(x, y) = \frac{c}{(x^2 + y^2)^{3/2}}(x\mathbf{i} + y\mathbf{j})$$

but we did not explain how the potential function $\phi(x, y)$ was obtained. Use Theorem 15.3.3 to show

that the two-dimensional inverse-square field is conservative everywhere except at the origin, and then use the method of Example 4 to derive the formula for $\phi(x, y)$.

(b) Use an appropriate generalization of the method of Example 4 to derive the potential function

$$\phi(x, y, z) = -\frac{c}{(x^2 + y^2 + z^2)^{1/2}}$$

for the three-dimensional inverse-square field given by Formula (5) of Section 15.1.

35–36 Use the result in Exercise 34(b). ■

35. In each part, find the work done by the three-dimensional inverse-square field

$$\mathbf{F}(\mathbf{r}) = \frac{1}{\|\mathbf{r}\|^3}\mathbf{r}$$

on a particle that moves along the curve C.
(a) C is the line segment from $P(1, 1, 2)$ to $Q(3, 2, 1)$.
(b) C is the curve

$$\mathbf{r}(t) = (2t^2 + 1)\mathbf{i} + (t^3 + 1)\mathbf{j} + (2 - \sqrt{t})\mathbf{k}$$

where $0 \leq t \leq 1$.
(c) C is the circle in the xy-plane of radius 1 centered at $(2, 0, 0)$ traversed counterclockwise.

36. Let $\mathbf{F}(x, y) = \dfrac{y}{x^2 + y^2}\mathbf{i} - \dfrac{x}{x^2 + y^2}\mathbf{j}$.
(a) Show that

$$\int_{C_1} \mathbf{F} \cdot d\mathbf{r} \neq \int_{C_2} \mathbf{F} \cdot d\mathbf{r}$$

if C_1 and C_2 are the semicircular paths from $(1, 0)$ to $(-1, 0)$ given by

$$C_1 : x = \cos t, \quad y = \sin t \qquad (0 \leq t \leq \pi)$$
$$C_2 : x = \cos t, \quad y = -\sin t \qquad (0 \leq t \leq \pi)$$

(b) Show that the components of $\mathbf{F}$ satisfy Formula (9).
(c) Do the results in parts (a) and (b) contradict Theorem 15.3.3? Explain.

37. Prove Theorem 15.3.1 if C is a piecewise smooth curve composed of smooth curves $C_1, C_2, \ldots, C_n$.

38. Prove that (*b*) implies (*c*) in Theorem 15.3.2. [*Hint:* Consider any two piecewise smooth oriented curves C_1 and C_2 in the region from a point P to a point Q, and integrate around the closed curve consisting of C_1 and $-C_2$.]

39. Complete the proof of Theorem 15.3.2 by showing that $\partial\phi/\partial y = g(x, y)$, where $\phi(x, y)$ is the function in (7).

40. **Writing** Describe the different methods available for evaluating the integral of a conservative vector field over a smooth curve.

41. **Writing** Discuss some of the ways that you can show a vector field is *not* conservative.

✔ **QUICK CHECK ANSWERS 15.3**

1. 18   **2.** 2   **3.** $xyz + yz + z$ **4.** 6, 6, 5

15.4 GREEN'S THEOREM

In this section we will discuss a remarkable and beautiful theorem that expresses a double integral over a plane region in terms of a line integral around its boundary.

■ GREEN'S THEOREM

15.4.1 THEOREM (*Green's Theorem*)   *Let R be a simply connected plane region whose boundary is a simple, closed, piecewise smooth curve C oriented counterclockwise. If $f(x, y)$ and $g(x, y)$ are continuous and have continuous first partial derivatives on some open set containing R, then*

$$\int_C f(x, y)\, dx + g(x, y)\, dy = \iint\limits_R \left(\frac{\partial g}{\partial x} - \frac{\partial f}{\partial y} \right) dA \tag{1}$$

PROOF   For simplicity, we will prove the theorem for regions that are simultaneously type I and type II (see Definition 14.2.1). Such a region is shown in Figure 15.4.1. The crux of the proof is to show that

$$\int_C f(x, y)\, dx = -\iint\limits_R \frac{\partial f}{\partial y}\, dA \quad \text{and} \quad \int_C g(x, y)\, dy = \iint\limits_R \frac{\partial g}{\partial x}\, dA \tag{2-3}$$

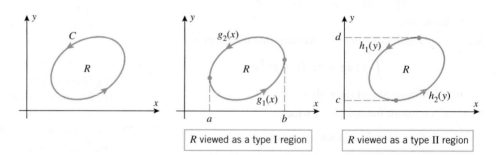

R viewed as a type I region   R viewed as a type II region

▶ **Figure 15.4.1**

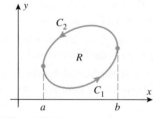

▲ **Figure 15.4.2**

To prove (2), view R as a type I region and let C_1 and C_2 be the lower and upper boundary curves, oriented as in Figure 15.4.2. Then

$$\int_C f(x, y)\, dx = \int_{C_1} f(x, y)\, dx + \int_{C_2} f(x, y)\, dx$$

or, equivalently,

$$\int_C f(x, y)\, dx = \int_{C_1} f(x, y)\, dx - \int_{-C_2} f(x, y)\, dx \tag{4}$$

(This step will help simplify our calculations since C_1 and $-C_2$ are then both oriented left to right.) The curves C_1 and $-C_2$ can be expressed parametrically as

$$C_1 : x = t, \quad y = g_1(t) \quad (a \le t \le b)$$
$$-C_2 : x = t, \quad y = g_2(t) \quad (a \le t \le b)$$

Thus, we can rewrite (4) as

$$\int_C f(x, y)\, dx = \int_a^b f(t, g_1(t))x'(t)\, dt - \int_a^b f(t, g_2(t))x'(t)\, dt$$

$$= \int_a^b f(t, g_1(t))\, dt - \int_a^b f(t, g_2(t))\, dt$$

$$= -\int_a^b [f(t, g_2(t)) - f(t, g_1(t))]\, dt$$

$$= -\int_a^b \left[f(t, y) \right]_{y=g_1(t)}^{y=g_2(t)} dt = -\int_a^b \left[\int_{g_1(t)}^{g_2(t)} \frac{\partial f}{\partial y}\, dy \right] dt$$

$$= -\int_a^b \int_{g_1(x)}^{g_2(x)} \frac{\partial f}{\partial y}\, dy\, dx = -\iint_R \frac{\partial f}{\partial y}\, dA$$

Since $x = t$

The proof of (3) is obtained similarly by treating R as a type II region. We omit the details. ∎

Supply the details for the proof of (3).

▶ **Example 1**   Use Green's Theorem to evaluate

$$\int_C x^2 y\, dx + x\, dy$$

along the triangular path shown in Figure 15.4.3.

Solution.   Since $f(x, y) = x^2 y$ and $g(x, y) = x$, it follows from (1) that

$$\int_C x^2 y\, dx + x\, dy = \iint_R \left[\frac{\partial}{\partial x}(x) - \frac{\partial}{\partial y}(x^2 y) \right] dA = \int_0^1 \int_0^{2x} (1 - x^2)\, dy\, dx$$

$$= \int_0^1 (2x - 2x^3)\, dx = \left[x^2 - \frac{x^4}{2} \right]_0^1 = \frac{1}{2}$$

This agrees with the result obtained in Example 10 of Section 15.2, where we evaluated the line integral directly. Note how much simpler this solution is. ◀

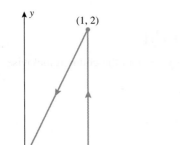

▲ **Figure 15.4.3**

George Green (1793–1841) English mathematician and physicist. Green left school at an early age to work in his father's bakery and consequently had little early formal education. When his father opened a mill, the boy used the top room as a study in which he taught himself physics and mathematics from library books. In 1828 Green published his most important work, *An Essay on the Application of Mathematical Analysis to the Theories of Electricity and Magnetism.* Although Green's Theorem appeared in that paper, the result went virtually unnoticed because of the small pressrun and local distribution. Following the death of his father in 1829, Green was urged by friends to seek a college education. In 1833, after four years of self-study to close the gaps in his elementary education, Green was admitted to Caius College, Cambridge. He graduated four years later, but with a disappointing performance on his final examinations—possibly because he was more interested in his own research. After a succession of works on light and sound, he was named to be Perse Fellow at Caius College. Two years later he died. In 1845, four years after his death, his paper of 1828 was published and the theories developed therein by this obscure, self-taught baker's son helped pave the way to the modern theories of electricity and magnetism.

■ A NOTATION FOR LINE INTEGRALS AROUND SIMPLE CLOSED CURVES

It is common practice to denote a line integral around a simple closed curve by an integral sign with a superimposed circle. With this notation Formula (1) would be written as

$$\oint_C f(x, y)\, dx + g(x, y)\, dy = \iint\limits_R \left(\frac{\partial g}{\partial x} - \frac{\partial f}{\partial y} \right) dA$$

Sometimes a direction arrow is added to the circle to indicate whether the integration is clockwise or counterclockwise. Thus, if we wanted to emphasize the counterclockwise direction of integration required by Theorem 15.4.1, we could express (1) as

$$\oint_C f(x, y)\, dx + g(x, y)\, dy = \iint\limits_R \left(\frac{\partial g}{\partial x} - \frac{\partial f}{\partial y} \right) dA \tag{5}$$

■ FINDING WORK USING GREEN'S THEOREM

It follows from Formula (26) of Section 15.2 that the integral on the left side of (5) is the work performed by the force field $\mathbf{F}(x, y) = f(x, y)\mathbf{i} + g(x, y)\mathbf{j}$ on a particle moving counterclockwise around the simple closed curve C. In the case where this vector field is conservative, it follows from Theorem 15.3.2 that the integrand in the double integral on the right side of (5) is zero, so the work performed by the field is zero, as expected. For vector fields that are not conservative, it is often more efficient to calculate the work around simple closed curves by using Green's Theorem than by parametrizing the curve.

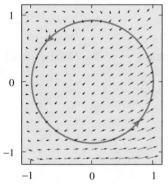

▲ Figure 15.4.4

▶ **Example 2** Find the work done by the force field

$$\mathbf{F}(x, y) = (e^x - y^3)\mathbf{i} + (\cos y + x^3)\mathbf{j}$$

on a particle that travels once around the unit circle $x^2 + y^2 = 1$ in the counterclockwise direction (Figure 15.4.4).

Solution. The work W performed by the field is

$$W = \oint_C \mathbf{F} \cdot d\mathbf{r} = \oint_C (e^x - y^3)\, dx + (\cos y + x^3)\, dy$$

$$= \iint\limits_R \left[\frac{\partial}{\partial x}(\cos y + x^3) - \frac{\partial}{\partial y}(e^x - y^3) \right] dA \qquad \boxed{\text{Green's Theorem}}$$

$$= \iint\limits_R (3x^2 + 3y^2)\, dA = 3 \iint\limits_R (x^2 + y^2)\, dA$$

$$= 3 \int_0^{2\pi} \int_0^1 (r^2) r\, dr\, d\theta = \frac{3}{4} \int_0^{2\pi} d\theta = \frac{3\pi}{2} \quad ◀$$

$\underset{\displaystyle \boxed{\text{We converted to polar coordinates.}}}{}$

■ FINDING AREAS USING GREEN'S THEOREM

Green's Theorem leads to some useful new formulas for the area A of a region R that satisfies the conditions of the theorem. Two such formulas can be obtained as follows:

$$A = \iint\limits_R dA = \oint_C x\, dy \quad \text{and} \quad A = \iint\limits_R dA = \oint_C (-y)\, dx$$

$\boxed{\text{Set } f(x, y) = 0 \text{ and } g(x, y) = x \text{ in (1).}}$ $\qquad$ $\boxed{\text{Set } f(x, y) = -y \text{ and } g(x, y) = 0 \text{ in (1).}}$

A third formula can be obtained by adding these two equations together. Thus, we have the following three formulas that express the area A of a region R in terms of line integrals around the boundary:

Although the third formula in (6) looks more complicated than the other two, it often leads to simpler integrations. Each has advantages in certain situations.

$$A = \oint_C x\, dy = -\oint_C y\, dx = \frac{1}{2}\oint_C -y\, dx + x\, dy \qquad (6)$$

▶ **Example 3**   Use a line integral to find the area enclosed by the ellipse

$$\frac{x^2}{a^2} + \frac{y^2}{b^2} = 1$$

Solution.   The ellipse, with counterclockwise orientation, can be represented parametrically by

$$x = a\cos t, \quad y = b\sin t \qquad (0 \le t \le 2\pi)$$

If we denote this curve by C, then from the third formula in (6) the area A enclosed by the ellipse is

$$A = \frac{1}{2}\oint_C -y\, dx + x\, dy$$

$$= \frac{1}{2}\int_0^{2\pi} [(-b\sin t)(-a\sin t) + (a\cos t)(b\cos t)]\, dt$$

$$= \frac{1}{2} ab \int_0^{2\pi} (\sin^2 t + \cos^2 t)\, dt = \frac{1}{2} ab \int_0^{2\pi} dt = \pi ab \blacktriangleleft$$

■ **GREEN'S THEOREM FOR MULTIPLY CONNECTED REGIONS**

Recall that a plane region is said to be simply connected if it has no holes and is said to be multiply connected if it has one or more holes (see Figure 15.3.6). At the beginning of this section we stated Green's Theorem for a counterclockwise integration around the boundary of a simply connected region R (Theorem 15.4.1). Our next goal is to extend this theorem to multiply connected regions. To make this extension we will need to assume that *the region lies on the left when any portion of the boundary is traversed in the direction of its orientation.* This implies that the outer boundary curve of the region is oriented counterclockwise and the boundary curves that enclose holes have clockwise orientation (Figure 15.4.5a). If all portions of the boundary of a multiply connected region R are oriented in this way, then we say that the boundary of R has ***positive orientation***.

We will now derive a version of Green's Theorem that applies to multiply connected regions with positively oriented boundaries. For simplicity, we will consider a multiply connected region R with one hole, and we will assume that $f(x, y)$ and $g(x, y)$ have continuous first partial derivatives on some open set containing R. As shown in Figure 15.4.5b, let us divide R into two regions R' and R'' by introducing two "cuts" in R. The cuts are shown as line segments, but any piecewise smooth curves will suffice. If we assume that f and g satisfy the hypotheses of Green's Theorem on R (and hence on R' and R''), then we can apply this theorem to both R' and R'' to obtain

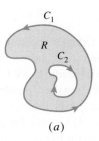

(a)

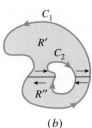

(b)

▲ **Figure 15.4.5**

$$\iint_R \left(\frac{\partial g}{\partial x} - \frac{\partial f}{\partial y}\right) dA = \iint_{R'} \left(\frac{\partial g}{\partial x} - \frac{\partial f}{\partial y}\right) dA + \iint_{R''} \left(\frac{\partial g}{\partial x} - \frac{\partial f}{\partial y}\right) dA$$

$$= \underset{\substack{\text{Boundary} \\ \text{of } R'}}{\oint} f(x, y)\, dx + g(x, y)\, dy + \underset{\substack{\text{Boundary} \\ \text{of } R''}}{\oint} f(x, y)\, dx + g(x, y)\, dy$$

However, the two line integrals are taken in opposite directions along the cuts, and hence cancel there, leaving only the contributions along C_1 and C_2. Thus,

$$\iint\limits_{R} \left(\frac{\partial g}{\partial x} - \frac{\partial f}{\partial y} \right) dA = \oint_{C_1} f(x, y)\, dx + g(x, y)\, dy + \oint_{C_2} f(x, y)\, dx + g(x, y)\, dy \qquad (7)$$

which is an extension of Green's Theorem to a multiply connected region with one hole. Observe that the integral around the outer boundary is taken counterclockwise and the integral around the hole is taken clockwise. More generally, if R is a multiply connected region with n holes, then the analog of (7) involves a sum of $n + 1$ integrals, one taken counterclockwise around the outer boundary of R and the rest taken clockwise around the holes.

▶ **Example 4**   Evaluate the integral

$$\oint_{C} \frac{-y\, dx + x\, dy}{x^2 + y^2}$$

if C is a piecewise smooth simple closed curve oriented counterclockwise such that (a) C does not enclose the origin and (b) C encloses the origin.

Solution (a).   Let

$$f(x, y) = -\frac{y}{x^2 + y^2}, \qquad g(x, y) = \frac{x}{x^2 + y^2} \qquad (8)$$

so that

$$\frac{\partial g}{\partial x} = \frac{y^2 - x^2}{(x^2 + y^2)^2} = \frac{\partial f}{\partial y}$$

if x and y are not both zero. Thus, if C does not enclose the origin, we have

$$\frac{\partial g}{\partial x} - \frac{\partial f}{\partial y} = 0 \qquad (9)$$

on the simply connected region enclosed by C, and hence the given integral is zero by Green's Theorem.

Solution (b).   Unlike the situation in part (a), we cannot apply Green's Theorem directly because the functions $f(x, y)$ and $g(x, y)$ in (8) are discontinuous at the origin. Our problems are further compounded by the fact that we do not have a specific curve C that we can parametrize to evaluate the integral. Our strategy for circumventing these problems will be to replace C with a specific curve that produces the same value for the integral and then use that curve for the evaluation. To obtain such a curve, we will apply Green's Theorem for multiply connected regions to a region that does not contain the origin. For this purpose we construct a circle C_a with *clockwise* orientation, centered at the origin, and with sufficiently small radius a that it lies inside the region enclosed by C (Figure 15.4.6). This creates a multiply connected region R whose boundary curves C and C_a have the orientations required by Formula (7) and such that within R the functions $f(x, y)$ and $g(x, y)$ in (8) satisfy the hypotheses of Green's Theorem (the origin does not belong to R). Thus, it follows from (7) and (9) that

$$\oint_{C} \frac{-y\, dx + x\, dy}{x^2 + y^2} + \oint_{C_a} \frac{-y\, dx + x\, dy}{x^2 + y^2} = \iint\limits_{R} 0\, dA = 0$$

It follows from this equation that

$$\oint_{C} \frac{-y\, dx + x\, dy}{x^2 + y^2} = -\oint_{C_a} \frac{-y\, dx + x\, dy}{x^2 + y^2}$$

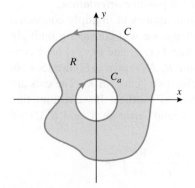

▲ **Figure 15.4.6**

which we can rewrite as

$$\oint_C \frac{-y\,dx + x\,dy}{x^2 + y^2} = \oint_{-C_a} \frac{-y\,dx + x\,dy}{x^2 + y^2}$$

> Reversing the orientation of C_a reverses the sign of the integral.

But C_a has clockwise orientation, so $-C_a$ has counterclockwise orientation. Thus, we have shown that the original integral can be evaluated by integrating counterclockwise around a circle of radius a that is centered at the origin and lies within the region enclosed by C. Such a circle can be expressed parametrically as $x = a\cos t$, $y = a\sin t$ $(0 \le t \le 2\pi)$; and hence

$$\oint_C \frac{-y\,dx + x\,dy}{x^2 + y^2} = \int_0^{2\pi} \frac{(-a\sin t)(-a\sin t)\,dt + (a\cos t)(a\cos t)\,dt}{(a\cos t)^2 + (a\sin t)^2}$$

$$= \int_0^{2\pi} 1\,dt = 2\pi$$

✔ **QUICK CHECK EXERCISES 15.4**   *(See page 1129 for answers.)*

1. If C is the square with vertices $(\pm 1, \pm 1)$ oriented counterclockwise, then

$$\int_C -y\,dx + x\,dy = \underline{\qquad}$$

2. If C is the triangle with vertices $(0,0)$, $(1,0)$, and $(1,1)$ oriented counterclockwise, then

$$\int_C 2xy\,dx + (x^2 + x)\,dy = \underline{\qquad}$$

3. If C is the unit circle centered at the origin and oriented counterclockwise, then

$$\int_C (y^3 - y - x)\,dx + (x^3 + x + y)\,dy = \underline{\qquad}$$

4. What region R and choice of functions $f(x,y)$ and $g(x,y)$ allow us to use Formula (1) of Theorem 15.4.1 to claim that

$$\int_0^1 \int_0^{\sqrt{1-x^2}} (2x + 2y)\,dy\,dx = \int_0^{\pi/2} (\sin^3 t + \cos^3 t)\,dt?$$

EXERCISE SET 15.4   ⃞C CAS

1–2 Evaluate the line integral using Green's Theorem and check the answer by evaluating it directly.

1. $\oint_C y^2\,dx + x^2\,dy$, where C is the square with vertices $(0,0)$, $(1,0)$, $(1,1)$, and $(0,1)$ oriented counterclockwise.

2. $\oint_C y\,dx + x\,dy$, where C is the unit circle oriented counterclockwise.

3–13 Use Green's Theorem to evaluate the integral. In each exercise, assume that the curve C is oriented counterclockwise. ▨

3. $\oint_C 3xy\,dx + 2xy\,dy$, where C is the rectangle bounded by $x = -2$, $x = 4$, $y = 1$, and $y = 2$.

4. $\oint_C (x^2 - y^2)\,dx + x\,dy$, where C is the circle $x^2 + y^2 = 9$.

5. $\oint_C x\cos y\,dx - y\sin x\,dy$, where C is the square with vertices $(0,0)$, $(\pi/2, 0)$, $(\pi/2, \pi/2)$, and $(0, \pi/2)$.

6. $\oint_C y\tan^2 x\,dx + \tan x\,dy$, where C is the circle $x^2 + (y+1)^2 = 1$.

7. $\oint_C (x^2 - y)\,dx + x\,dy$, where C is the circle $x^2 + y^2 = 4$.

8. $\oint_C (e^x + y^2)\,dx + (e^y + x^2)\,dy$, where C is the boundary of the region between $y = x^2$ and $y = x$.

9. $\oint_C \ln(1 + y)\,dx - \frac{xy}{1 + y}\,dy$, where C is the triangle with vertices $(0,0)$, $(2,0)$, and $(0,4)$.

10. $\oint_C x^2 y\,dx - y^2 x\,dy$, where C is the boundary of the region in the first quadrant, enclosed between the coordinate axes and the circle $x^2 + y^2 = 16$.

11. $\oint_C \tan^{-1} y\,dx - \frac{y^2 x}{1 + y^2}\,dy$, where C is the square with vertices $(0,0)$, $(1,0)$, $(1,1)$, and $(0,1)$.

12. $\oint_C \cos x \sin y \, dx + \sin x \cos y \, dy$, where C is the triangle with vertices $(0, 0)$, $(3, 3)$, and $(0, 3)$.

13. $\oint_C x^2 y \, dx + (y + xy^2) \, dy$, where C is the boundary of the region enclosed by $y = x^2$ and $x = y^2$.

14. Let C be the boundary of the region enclosed between $y = x^2$ and $y = 2x$. Assuming that C is oriented counterclockwise, evaluate the following integrals by Green's Theorem:

(a) $\oint_C (6xy - y^2) \, dx$ (b) $\oint_C (6xy - y^2) \, dy$.

15–18 True–False Determine whether the statement is true or false. Explain your answer. (In Exercises 16–18, assume that C is a simple, smooth, closed curve, oriented counterclockwise.) ■

15. Green's Theorem allows us to replace any line integral by a double integral.

16. If

$$\int_C f(x, y) \, dx + g(x, y) \, dy = 0$$

then $\partial g / \partial x = \partial f / \partial y$ at all points in the region bounded by C.

17. It must be the case that

$$\int_C x \, dy > 0$$

18. It must be the case that

$$\int_C e^{x^2} \, dx + \sin y^3 \, dy = 0$$

C 19. Use a CAS to check Green's Theorem by evaluating both integrals in the equation

$$\oint_C e^y \, dx + y e^x \, dy = \iint_R \left[\frac{\partial}{\partial x} (y e^x) - \frac{\partial}{\partial y} (e^y) \right] dA$$

where
(a) C is the circle $x^2 + y^2 = 1$
(b) C is the boundary of the region enclosed by $y = x^2$ and $x = y^2$.

20. In Example 3, we used Green's Theorem to obtain the area of an ellipse. Obtain this area using the first and then the second formula in (6).

21. Use a line integral to find the area of the region enclosed by the astroid

$$x = a \cos^3 \phi, \quad y = a \sin^3 \phi \quad (0 \le \phi \le 2\pi)$$

22. Use a line integral to find the area of the triangle with vertices $(0, 0)$, $(a, 0)$, and $(0, b)$, where $a > 0$ and $b > 0$.

23. Use the formula

$$A = \frac{1}{2} \oint_C -y \, dx + x \, dy$$

to find the area of the region swept out by the line from the origin to the ellipse $x = a \cos t$, $y = b \sin t$ if t varies from $t = 0$ to $t = t_0$ $(0 \le t_0 \le 2\pi)$.

24. Use the formula

$$A = \frac{1}{2} \oint_C -y \, dx + x \, dy$$

to find the area of the region swept out by the line from the origin to the hyperbola $x = a \cosh t$, $y = b \sinh t$ if t varies from $t = 0$ to $t = t_0$ $(t_0 \ge 0)$.

FOCUS ON CONCEPTS

25. Suppose that $\mathbf{F}(x, y) = f(x, y)\mathbf{i} + g(x, y)\mathbf{j}$ is a vector field whose component functions f and g have continuous first partial derivatives. Let C denote a simple, closed, piecewise smooth curve oriented counterclockwise that bounds a region R contained in the domain of $\mathbf{F}$. We can think of $\mathbf{F}$ as a vector field in 3-space by writing it as

$$\mathbf{F}(x, y, z) = f(x, y)\mathbf{i} + g(x, y)\mathbf{j} + 0\mathbf{k}$$

With this convention, explain why

$$\int_C \mathbf{F} \cdot d\mathbf{r} = \iint_R \operatorname{curl} \mathbf{F} \cdot \mathbf{k} \, dA$$

26. Suppose that $\mathbf{F}(x, y) = f(x, y)\mathbf{i} + g(x, y)\mathbf{j}$ is a vector field on the xy-plane and that f and g have continuous first partial derivatives with $f_y = g_x$ everywhere. Use Green's Theorem to explain why

$$\int_{C_1} \mathbf{F} \cdot d\mathbf{r} = \int_{C_2} \mathbf{F} \cdot d\mathbf{r}$$

where C_1 and C_2 are the oriented curves in the accompanying figure. [*Note:* Compare this result with Theorems 15.3.2 and 15.3.3.]

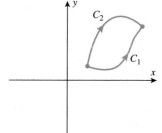

◀ **Figure Ex-26**

27. Suppose that $f(x)$ and $g(x)$ are continuous functions with $g(x) \le f(x)$. Let R denote the region bounded by the graph of f, the graph of g, and the vertical lines $x = a$ and $x = b$. Let C denote the boundary of R oriented counterclockwise. What familiar formula results from applying Green's Theorem to $\int_C (-y) \, dx$?

28. In the accompanying figure on the next page, C is a smooth oriented curve from $P(x_0, y_0)$ to $Q(x_1, y_1)$ that is contained inside the rectangle with corners at the origin and Q and outside the rectangle with corners at the origin and P.
(a) What region in the figure has area $\int_C x \, dy$?
(b) What region in the figure has area $\int_C y \, dx$?
(c) Express $\int_C x \, dy + \int_C y \, dx$ in terms of the coordinates of P and Q.   *(cont.)*

(d) Interpret the result of part (c) in terms of the Fundamental Theorem of Line Integrals.

(e) Interpret the result in part (c) in terms of integration by parts.

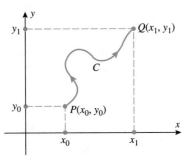

◀ **Figure Ex-28**

29–30 Use Green's Theorem to find the work done by the force field **F** on a particle that moves along the stated path. ▪

29. $\mathbf{F}(x, y) = xy\mathbf{i} + \left(\frac{1}{2}x^2 + xy\right)\mathbf{j}$; the particle starts at $(5, 0)$, traverses the upper semicircle $x^2 + y^2 = 25$, and returns to its starting point along the x-axis.

30. $\mathbf{F}(x, y) = \sqrt{y}\,\mathbf{i} + \sqrt{x}\,\mathbf{j}$; the particle moves counterclockwise one time around the closed curve given by the equations $y = 0$, $x = 2$, and $y = x^3/4$.

31. Evaluate $\oint_C y\,dx - x\,dy$, where C is the cardioid

$$r = a(1 + \cos\theta) \quad (0 \leq \theta \leq 2\pi)$$

32. Let R be a plane region with area A whose boundary is a piecewise smooth, simple, closed curve C. Use Green's Theorem to prove that the centroid $(\bar{x}, \bar{y})$ of R is given by

$$\bar{x} = \frac{1}{2A}\oint_C x^2\,dy, \quad \bar{y} = -\frac{1}{2A}\oint_C y^2\,dx$$

33–36 Use the result in Exercise 32 to find the centroid of the region. ▪

33.

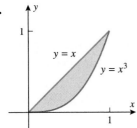

34.

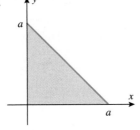

35.

36.

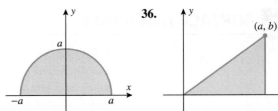

37. Find a simple closed curve C with counterclockwise orientation that maximizes the value of

$$\oint_C \frac{1}{3}y^3\,dx + \left(x - \frac{1}{3}x^3\right)\,dy$$

and explain your reasoning.

38. (a) Let C be the line segment from a point (a, b) to a point (c, d). Show that

$$\int_C -y\,dx + x\,dy = ad - bc$$

(b) Use the result in part (a) to show that the area A of a triangle with successive vertices (x_1, y_1), (x_2, y_2), and (x_3, y_3) going counterclockwise is

$$A = \frac{1}{2}[(x_1y_2 - x_2y_1) \\ + (x_2y_3 - x_3y_2) + (x_3y_1 - x_1y_3)]$$

(c) Find a formula for the area of a polygon with successive vertices (x_1, y_1), (x_2, y_2), ..., (x_n, y_n) going counterclockwise.

(d) Use the result in part (c) to find the area of a quadrilateral with vertices $(0, 0)$, $(3, 4)$, $(-2, 2)$, $(-1, 0)$.

39–40 Evaluate the integral $\int_C \mathbf{F} \cdot d\mathbf{r}$, where C is the boundary of the region R and C is oriented so that the region is on the left when the boundary is traversed in the direction of its orientation. ▪

39. $\mathbf{F}(x, y) = (x^2 + y)\mathbf{i} + (4x - \cos y)\mathbf{j}$; C is the boundary of the region R that is inside the square with vertices $(0, 0)$, $(5, 0)$, $(5, 5)$, $(0, 5)$ but is outside the rectangle with vertices $(1, 1)$, $(3, 1)$, $(3, 2)$, $(1, 2)$.

40. $\mathbf{F}(x, y) = (e^{-x} + 3y)\mathbf{i} + x\mathbf{j}$; C is the boundary of the region R inside the circle $x^2 + y^2 = 16$ and outside the circle $x^2 - 2x + y^2 = 3$.

41. Writing Discuss the role of the Fundamental Theorem of Calculus in the proof of Green's Theorem.

42. Writing Use the Internet or other sources to find information about "planimeters," and then write a paragraph that describes the relationship between these devices and Green's Theorem.

✔ **QUICK CHECK ANSWERS 15.4**

1. 8   **2.** $\frac{1}{2}$ **3.** 2π **4.** R is the region $x^2 + y^2 \leq 1$ ($0 \leq x, 0 \leq y$) and $f(x, y) = -y^2$, $g(x, y) = x^2$.

15.5 SURFACE INTEGRALS

In previous sections we considered four kinds of integrals—integrals over intervals, double integrals over two-dimensional regions, triple integrals over three-dimensional solids, and line integrals along curves in two- or three-dimensional space. In this section we will discuss integrals over surfaces in three-dimensional space. Such integrals occur in problems involving fluid and heat flow, electricity, magnetism, mass, and center of gravity.

■ DEFINITION OF A SURFACE INTEGRAL

In this section we will define what it means to integrate a function $f(x, y, z)$ over a smooth parametric surface σ. To motivate the definition we will consider the problem of finding the mass of a curved lamina whose density function (mass per unit area) is known. Recall that in Section 6.7 we defined a *lamina* to be an idealized flat object that is thin enough to be viewed as a plane region. Analogously, a **curved lamina** is an idealized object that is thin enough to be viewed as a surface in 3-space. A curved lamina may look like a bent plate, as in Figure 15.5.1, or it may enclose a region in 3-space, like the shell of an egg. We will model the lamina by a smooth parametric surface σ. Given any point (x, y, z) on σ, we let $f(x, y, z)$ denote the corresponding value of the density function. To compute the mass of the lamina, we proceed as follows:

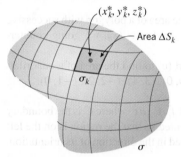

The thickness of a curved lamina is negligible.

▲ **Figure 15.5.1**

- As shown in Figure 15.5.2, we divide σ into n very small patches $\sigma_1, \sigma_2, \ldots, \sigma_n$ with areas $\Delta S_1, \Delta S_2, \ldots, \Delta S_n$, respectively. Let (x_k^*, y_k^*, z_k^*) be a sample point in the kth patch with ΔM_k the mass of the corresponding section.

- If the dimensions of σ_k are very small, the value of f will not vary much along the kth section and we can approximate f along this section by the value $f(x_k^*, y_k^*, z_k^*)$. It follows that the mass of the kth section can be approximated by

$$\Delta M_k \approx f(x_k^*, y_k^*, z_k^*)\Delta S_k$$

- The mass M of the entire lamina can then be approximated by

$$M = \sum_{k=1}^{n} \Delta M_k \approx \sum_{k=1}^{n} f(x_k^*, y_k^*, z_k^*)\Delta S_k \tag{1}$$

- We will use the expression $n \to \infty$ to indicate the process of increasing n in such a way that the maximum dimension of each patch approaches 0. It is plausible that the error in (1) will approach 0 as $n \to \infty$ and the exact value of M will be given by

$$M = \lim_{n \to \infty} \sum_{k=1}^{n} f(x_k^*, y_k^*, z_k^*)\Delta S_k \tag{2}$$

▲ **Figure 15.5.2**

The limit in (2) is very similar to the limit used to find the mass of a thin wire [Formula (2) in Section 15.2]. By analogy to Definition 15.2.1, we make the following definition.

15.5.1 DEFINITION If σ is a smooth parametric surface, then the **surface integral** of $f(x, y, z)$ over σ is

$$\iint_{\sigma} f(x, y, z)\, dS = \lim_{n \to \infty} \sum_{k=1}^{n} f(x_k^*, y_k^*, z_k^*)\Delta S_k \tag{3}$$

provided this limit exists and does not depend on the way the subdivisions of σ are made or how the sample points (x_k^*, y_k^*, z_k^*) are chosen.

It can be shown that the integral of f over σ exists if f is continuous on σ.

We see from (2) and Definition 15.5.1 that if σ models a lamina and if $f(x, y, z)$ is the density function of the lamina, then the mass M of the lamina is given by

$$M = \iint_\sigma f(x, y, z)\, dS \tag{4}$$

That is, to obtain the mass of a lamina, we integrate the density function over the smooth surface that models the lamina.

Note that if σ is a smooth surface of surface area S, and f is identically 1, then it immediately follows from Definition 15.5.1 that

$$\iint_\sigma dS = \lim_{n \to \infty} \sum_{k=1}^{n} \Delta S_k = \lim_{n \to \infty} S = S \tag{5}$$

■ EVALUATING SURFACE INTEGRALS

There are various procedures for evaluating surface integrals that depend on how the surface σ is represented. The following theorem provides a method for evaluating a surface integral when σ is represented parametrically.

15.5.2 THEOREM *Let σ be a smooth parametric surface whose vector equation is*

$$\mathbf{r} = x(u, v)\mathbf{i} + y(u, v)\mathbf{j} + z(u, v)\mathbf{k}$$

where (u, v) varies over a region R in the uv-plane. If $f(x, y, z)$ is continuous on σ, then

$$\iint_\sigma f(x, y, z)\, dS = \iint_R f(x(u, v), y(u, v), z(u, v)) \left\| \frac{\partial \mathbf{r}}{\partial u} \times \frac{\partial \mathbf{r}}{\partial v} \right\| dA \tag{6}$$

Explain how to use Formula (6) to confirm Formula (5).

To motivate this result, suppose that the parameter domain R is subdivided as in Figure 14.4.14, and suppose that the point (x_k^*, y_k^*, z_k^*) in (3) corresponds to parameter values of u_k^* and v_k^*. If we use Formula (11) of Section 14.4 to approximate ΔS_k, and if we assume that the errors in the approximations approach zero as $n \to +\infty$, then it follows from (3) that

$$\iint_\sigma f(x, y, z)\, dS = \lim_{n \to +\infty} \sum_{k=1}^{n} f(x(u_k^*, v_k^*), y(u_k^*, v_k^*), z(u_k^*, v_k^*)) \left\| \frac{\partial \mathbf{r}}{\partial u} \times \frac{\partial \mathbf{r}}{\partial v} \right\| \Delta A_k$$

which suggests Formula (6).

Although Theorem 15.5.2 is stated for *smooth* parametric surfaces, Formula (6) remains valid even if $\partial \mathbf{r}/\partial u \times \partial \mathbf{r}/\partial v$ is allowed to equal $\mathbf{0}$ on the boundary of R.

▶ **Example 1** Evaluate the surface integral $\displaystyle\iint_\sigma x^2 \, dS$ over the sphere $x^2 + y^2 + z^2 = 1$.

Solution. As in Example 11 of Section 14.4 (with $a = 1$), the sphere is the graph of the vector-valued function

$$\mathbf{r}(\phi, \theta) = \sin\phi\cos\theta\,\mathbf{i} + \sin\phi\sin\theta\,\mathbf{j} + \cos\phi\,\mathbf{k} \quad (0 \le \phi \le \pi, \ 0 \le \theta \le 2\pi) \tag{7}$$

and

$$\left\| \frac{\partial\mathbf{r}}{\partial\phi} \times \frac{\partial\mathbf{r}}{\partial\theta} \right\| = \sin\phi$$

Explain why the function $\mathbf{r}(\phi, \theta)$ given in (7) fails to be smooth on its domain.

From the **i**-component of **r**, the integrand in the surface integral can be expressed in terms of ϕ and θ as $x^2 = \sin^2\phi\cos^2\theta$. Thus, it follows from (6) with ϕ and θ in place of u and v and R as the rectangular region in the $\phi\theta$-plane determined by the inequalities in (7) that

$$\iint_\sigma x^2 \, dS = \iint_R (\sin^2\phi\cos^2\theta)\left\| \frac{\partial\mathbf{r}}{\partial\phi} \times \frac{\partial\mathbf{r}}{\partial\theta} \right\| dA$$

$$= \int_0^{2\pi}\int_0^\pi \sin^3\phi\cos^2\theta \, d\phi \, d\theta$$

$$= \int_0^{2\pi}\left[\int_0^\pi \sin^3\phi \, d\phi\right]\cos^2\theta \, d\theta$$

$$= \int_0^{2\pi}\left[\frac{1}{3}\cos^3\phi - \cos\phi\right]_0^\pi \cos^2\theta \, d\theta \qquad \text{Formula (11), Section 7.3}$$

$$= \frac{4}{3}\int_0^{2\pi}\cos^2\theta \, d\theta$$

$$= \frac{4}{3}\left[\frac{1}{2}\theta + \frac{1}{4}\sin 2\theta\right]_0^{2\pi} = \frac{4\pi}{3} \qquad \text{Formula (8), Section 7.3} \quad ◀$$

■ **SURFACE INTEGRALS OVER $z = g(x, y)$, $y = g(x, z)$, AND $x = g(y, z)$**

In the case where σ is a surface of the form $z = g(x, y)$, we can take $x = u$ and $y = v$ as parameters and express the equation of the surface as

$$\mathbf{r} = u\mathbf{i} + v\mathbf{j} + g(u, v)\mathbf{k}$$

in which case we obtain

$$\left\| \frac{\partial\mathbf{r}}{\partial u} \times \frac{\partial\mathbf{r}}{\partial v} \right\| = \sqrt{\left(\frac{\partial z}{\partial x}\right)^2 + \left(\frac{\partial z}{\partial y}\right)^2 + 1}$$

(verify). Thus, it follows from (6) that

$$\iint_\sigma f(x, y, z) \, dS = \iint_R f(x, y, g(x, y))\sqrt{\left(\frac{\partial z}{\partial x}\right)^2 + \left(\frac{\partial z}{\partial y}\right)^2 + 1} \, dA$$

Note that in this formula the region R lies in the xy-plane because the parameters are x and y. Geometrically, this region is the projection of σ on the xy-plane. The following theorem summarizes this result and gives analogous formulas for surface integrals over surfaces of the form $y = g(x, z)$ and $x = g(y, z)$.

15.5.3   THEOREM

(a)   *Let σ be a surface with equation $z = g(x, y)$ and let R be its projection on the xy-plane. If g has continuous first partial derivatives on R and $f(x, y, z)$ is continuous on σ, then*

$$\iint\limits_{\sigma} f(x, y, z)\, dS = \iint\limits_{R} f(x, y, g(x, y))\sqrt{\left(\frac{\partial z}{\partial x}\right)^2 + \left(\frac{\partial z}{\partial y}\right)^2 + 1}\, dA \qquad (8)$$

(b)   *Let σ be a surface with equation $y = g(x, z)$ and let R be its projection on the xz-plane. If g has continuous first partial derivatives on R and $f(x, y, z)$ is continuous on σ, then*

$$\iint\limits_{\sigma} f(x, y, z)\, dS = \iint\limits_{R} f(x, g(x, z), z)\sqrt{\left(\frac{\partial y}{\partial x}\right)^2 + \left(\frac{\partial y}{\partial z}\right)^2 + 1}\, dA \qquad (9)$$

(c)   *Let σ be a surface with equation $x = g(y, z)$ and let R be its projection on the yz-plane. If g has continuous first partial derivatives on R and $f(x, y, z)$ is continuous on σ, then*

$$\iint\limits_{\sigma} f(x, y, z)\, dS = \iint\limits_{R} f(g(y, z), y, z)\sqrt{\left(\frac{\partial x}{\partial y}\right)^2 + \left(\frac{\partial x}{\partial z}\right)^2 + 1}\, dA \qquad (10)$$

Formulas (9) and (10) can be recovered from Formula (8). Explain how.

▶ **Example 2**   Evaluate the surface integral

$$\iint\limits_{\sigma} xz\, dS$$

where σ is the part of the plane $x + y + z = 1$ that lies in the first octant.

Solution.   The equation of the plane can be written as

$$z = 1 - x - y$$

Consequently, we can apply Formula (8) with $z = g(x, y) = 1 - x - y$ and $f(x, y, z) = xz$. We have

$$\frac{\partial z}{\partial x} = -1 \quad \text{and} \quad \frac{\partial z}{\partial y} = -1$$

so (8) becomes

$$\iint\limits_{\sigma} xz\, dS = \iint\limits_{R} x(1 - x - y)\sqrt{(-1)^2 + (-1)^2 + 1}\, dA \qquad (11)$$

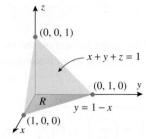

▲ **Figure 15.5.3**

where R is the projection of σ on the xy-plane (Figure 15.5.3). Rewriting the double integral in (11) as an iterated integral yields

$$\iint_\sigma xz\, dS = \sqrt{3} \int_0^1 \int_0^{1-x} (x - x^2 - xy)\, dy\, dx$$

$$= \sqrt{3} \int_0^1 \left[xy - x^2 y - \frac{xy^2}{2} \right]_{y=0}^{1-x} dx$$

$$= \sqrt{3} \int_0^1 \left(\frac{x}{2} - x^2 + \frac{x^3}{2} \right) dx$$

$$= \sqrt{3} \left[\frac{x^2}{4} - \frac{x^3}{3} + \frac{x^4}{8} \right]_0^1 = \frac{\sqrt{3}}{24} \quad \blacktriangleleft$$

▶ **Example 3**   Evaluate the surface integral

$$\iint_\sigma y^2 z^2\, dS$$

where σ is the part of the cone $z = \sqrt{x^2 + y^2}$ that lies between the planes $z = 1$ and $z = 2$ (Figure 15.5.4).

Solution.   We will apply Formula (8) with

$$z = g(x, y) = \sqrt{x^2 + y^2} \quad \text{and} \quad f(x, y, z) = y^2 z^2$$

Thus,

$$\frac{\partial z}{\partial x} = \frac{x}{\sqrt{x^2 + y^2}} \quad \text{and} \quad \frac{\partial z}{\partial y} = \frac{y}{\sqrt{x^2 + y^2}}$$

so

$$\sqrt{ \left(\frac{\partial z}{\partial x} \right)^2 + \left(\frac{\partial z}{\partial y} \right)^2 + 1 } = \sqrt{2}$$

(verify), and (8) yields

$$\iint_\sigma y^2 z^2\, dS = \iint_R y^2 \left(\sqrt{x^2 + y^2} \right)^2 \sqrt{2}\, dA = \sqrt{2} \iint_R y^2 (x^2 + y^2)\, dA$$

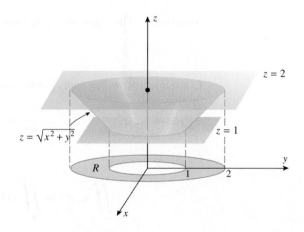

▶ **Figure 15.5.4**

where R is the annulus enclosed between $x^2 + y^2 = 1$ and $x^2 + y^2 = 4$ (Figure 15.5.4). Using polar coordinates to evaluate this double integral over the annulus R yields

$$\iint\limits_{\sigma} y^2 z^2 \, dS = \sqrt{2} \int_0^{2\pi} \int_1^2 (r \sin \theta)^2 (r^2)^2 r \, dr \, d\theta$$

$$= \sqrt{2} \int_0^{2\pi} \int_1^2 r^5 \sin^2 \theta \, dr \, d\theta$$

$$= \sqrt{2} \int_0^{2\pi} \left[\frac{r^6}{6} \sin^2 \theta \right]_{r=1}^2 d\theta = \frac{21}{\sqrt{2}} \int_0^{2\pi} \sin^2 \theta \, d\theta$$

$$= \frac{21}{\sqrt{2}} \left[\frac{1}{2}\theta - \frac{1}{4} \sin 2\theta \right]_0^{2\pi} = \frac{21\pi}{\sqrt{2}} \qquad \boxed{\text{Formula (7), Section 7.3}} \blacktriangleleft$$

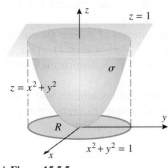

▲ **Figure 15.5.5**

▶ **Example 4** Suppose that a curved lamina σ with constant density $\delta(x, y, z) = \delta_0$ is the portion of the paraboloid $z = x^2 + y^2$ below the plane $z = 1$ (Figure 15.5.5). Find the mass of the lamina.

Solution. Since $z = g(x, y) = x^2 + y^2$, it follows that

$$\frac{\partial z}{\partial x} = 2x \quad \text{and} \quad \frac{\partial z}{\partial y} = 2y$$

Therefore,

$$M = \iint\limits_{\sigma} \delta_0 \, dS = \iint\limits_{R} \delta_0 \sqrt{(2x)^2 + (2y)^2 + 1} \, dA = \delta_0 \iint\limits_{R} \sqrt{4x^2 + 4y^2 + 1} \, dA \qquad (12)$$

where R is the circular region enclosed by $x^2 + y^2 = 1$. To evaluate (12) we use polar coordinates:

$$M = \delta_0 \int_0^{2\pi} \int_0^1 \sqrt{4r^2 + 1} \, r \, dr \, d\theta = \frac{\delta_0}{12} \int_0^{2\pi} (4r^2 + 1)^{3/2} \Big]_{r=0}^1 d\theta$$

$$= \frac{\delta_0}{12} \int_0^{2\pi} (5^{3/2} - 1) \, d\theta = \frac{\pi\delta_0}{6} (5\sqrt{5} - 1) \blacktriangleleft$$

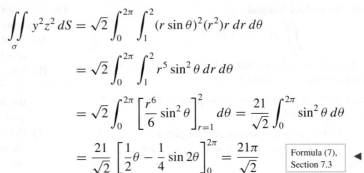

Evaluate the integral in Example 3 with the help of Formula (6) and the parametrization

$$\mathbf{r} = \langle r \cos \theta, r \sin \theta, r \rangle$$

$$(1 \le r \le 2, 0 \le \theta \le 2\pi)$$

✔**QUICK CHECK EXERCISES 15.5**   (*See page 1138 for answers.*)

1. Consider the surface integral $\iint_{\sigma} f(x, y, z) \, dS$.
   (a) If σ is a parametric surface whose vector equation is
   $$\mathbf{r} = x(u, v)\mathbf{i} + y(u, v)\mathbf{j} + z(u, v)\mathbf{k}$$
   to evaluate the integral replace dS by _____.
   (b) If σ is the graph of a function $z = g(x, y)$ with continuous first partial derivatives, to evaluate the integral replace dS by _____.

2. If σ is the triangular region with vertices $(1, 0, 0)$, $(0, 1, 0)$, and $(0, 0, 1)$, then
   $$\iint\limits_{\sigma} (x + y + z) \, dS = \underline{\qquad}$$

3. If σ is the sphere of radius 2 centered at the origin, then
   $$\iint\limits_{\sigma} (x^2 + y^2 + z^2) \, dS = \underline{\qquad}$$

4. If $f(x, y, z)$ is the mass density function of a curved lamina σ, then the mass of σ is given by the integral _____.

EXERCISE SET 15.5 　[C] CAS

1–8 Evaluate the surface integral

$$\iint_\sigma f(x, y, z)\, dS$$ ∎

1. $f(x, y, z) = z^2$; σ is the portion of the cone $z = \sqrt{x^2 + y^2}$ between the planes $z = 1$ and $z = 2$.

2. $f(x, y, z) = xy$; σ is the portion of the plane $x + y + z = 1$ lying in the first octant.

3. $f(x, y, z) = x^2 y$; σ is the portion of the cylinder $x^2 + z^2 = 1$ between the planes $y = 0$, $y = 1$, and above the xy-plane.

4. $f(x, y, z) = (x^2 + y^2)z$; σ is the portion of the sphere $x^2 + y^2 + z^2 = 4$ above the plane $z = 1$.

5. $f(x, y, z) = x - y - z$; σ is the portion of the plane $x + y = 1$ in the first octant between $z = 0$ and $z = 1$.

6. $f(x, y, z) = x + y$; σ is the portion of the plane $z = 6 - 2x - 3y$ in the first octant.

7. $f(x, y, z) = x + y + z$; σ is the surface of the cube defined by the inequalities $0 \le x \le 1, 0 \le y \le 1, 0 \le z \le 1$. [*Hint:* Integrate over each face separately.]

8. $f(x, y, z) = x^2 + y^2$; σ is the surface of the sphere $x^2 + y^2 + z^2 = a^2$.

9–12 True–False Determine whether the statement is true or false. Explain your answer. ∎

9. If $f(x, y, z) \ge 0$ on σ, then

$$\iint_\sigma f(x, y, z)\, dS \ge 0$$

10. If σ has surface area S, and if

$$\iint_\sigma f(x, y, z)\, dS = S$$

then $f(x, y, z)$ is equal to 1 identically on σ.

11. If σ models a curved lamina, and if $f(x, y, z)$ is the density function of the lamina, then

$$\iint_\sigma f(x, y, z)\, dS$$

represents the total density of the lamina.

12. If σ is the portion of a plane $z = c$ over a region R in the xy-plane, then

$$\iint_\sigma f(x, y, z)\, dS = \iint_R f(x, y, c)\, dA$$

for every continuous function f on σ.

13–14 Sometimes evaluating a surface integral results in an improper integral. When this happens, one can either attempt to determine the value of the integral using an appropriate limit or one can try another method. These exercises explore both approaches. ∎

13. Consider the integral of $f(x, y, z) = z + 1$ over the upper hemisphere σ: $z = \sqrt{1 - x^2 - y^2}$ $(0 \le x^2 + y^2 \le 1)$.
   (a) Explain why evaluating this surface integral using (8) results in an improper integral.
   (b) Use (8) to evaluate the integral of f over the surface σ_r: $z = \sqrt{1 - x^2 - y^2}$ $(0 \le x^2 + y^2 \le r^2 < 1)$. Take the limit of this result as $r \to 1^-$ to determine the integral of f over σ.
   (c) Parametrize σ using spherical coordinates and evaluate the integral of f over σ using (6). Verify that your answer agrees with the result in part (b).

14. Consider the integral of $f(x, y, z) = \sqrt{x^2 + y^2 + z^2}$ over the cone $\sigma : z = \sqrt{x^2 + y^2}$ $(0 \le z \le 1)$.
   (a) Explain why evaluating this surface integral using (8) results in an improper integral.
   (b) Use (8) to evaluate the integral of f over the surface σ_r: $z = \sqrt{x^2 + y^2}$ $(0 < r^2 \le x^2 + y^2 \le 1)$. Take the limit of this result as $r \to 0^+$ to determine the integral of f over σ.
   (c) Parametrize σ using spherical coordinates and evaluate the integral of f over σ using (6). Verify that your answer agrees with the result in part (b).

FOCUS ON CONCEPTS

15–18 In some cases it is possible to use Definition 15.5.1 along with symmetry considerations to evaluate a surface integral without reference to a parametrization of the surface. In these exercises, σ denotes the unit sphere centered at the origin. ∎

15. (a) Explain why it is possible to subdivide σ into patches and choose corresponding sample points (x_k^*, y_k^*, z_k^*) such that (i) the dimensions of each patch are as small as desired and (ii) for each sample point (x_k^*, y_k^*, z_k^*), there exists a sample point (x_j^*, y_j^*, z_j^*) with

$$x_k = -x_j, \quad y_k = y_j, \quad z_k = z_j$$

and with $\Delta S_k = \Delta S_j$.
   (b) Use Definition 15.5.1, the result in part (a), and the fact that surface integrals exist for continuous functions to prove that $\iint_\sigma x^n\, dS = 0$ for n an odd positive integer.

16. Use the argument in Exercise 15 to prove that if $f(x)$ is a continuous odd function of x, and if $g(y, z)$ is a continuous function, then

$$\iint_\sigma f(x)g(y, z)\, dS = 0$$

17. (a) Explain why

$$\iint_\sigma x^2\, dS = \iint_\sigma y^2\, dS = \iint_\sigma z^2\, dS \quad \text{(cont.)}$$

(b) Conclude from part (a) that

$$\iint_\sigma x^2\, dS = \frac{1}{3}\left[\iint_\sigma x^2\, dS + \iint_\sigma y^2\, dS + \iint_\sigma y^2\, dS\right]$$

(c) Use part (b) to evaluate

$$\iint_\sigma x^2\, dS$$

without performing an integration.

18. Use the results of Exercises 16 and 17 to evaluate

$$\iint_\sigma (x - y)^2\, dS$$

without performing an integration.

19–20 Set up, but do not evaluate, an iterated integral equal to the given surface integral by projecting σ on (a) the xy-plane, (b) the yz-plane, and (c) the xz-plane. ■

19. $\displaystyle\iint_\sigma xyz\, dS$, where σ is the portion of the plane

$2x + 3y + 4z = 12$ in the first octant.

20. $\displaystyle\iint_\sigma xz\, dS$, where σ is the portion of the sphere

$x^2 + y^2 + z^2 = a^2$ in the first octant.

C 21. Use a CAS to confirm that the three integrals you obtained in Exercise 19 are equal, and find the exact value of the surface integral.

C 22. Try to confirm with a CAS that the three integrals you obtained in Exercise 20 are equal. If you did not succeed, what was the difficulty?

23–24 Set up, but do not evaluate, two different iterated integrals equal to the given integral. ■

23. $\displaystyle\iint_\sigma xyz\, dS$, where σ is the portion of the surface $y^2 = x$

between the planes $z = 0$, $z = 4$, $y = 1$, and $y = 2$.

24. $\displaystyle\iint_\sigma x^2 y\, dS$, where σ is the portion of the cylinder

$y^2 + z^2 = a^2$ in the first octant between the planes
$x = 0$, $x = 9$, $z = y$, and $z = 2y$.

C 25. Use a CAS to confirm that the two integrals you obtained in Exercise 23 are equal, and find the exact value of the surface integral.

C 26. Use a CAS to find the value of the surface integral

$$\iint_\sigma x^2 yz\, dS$$

where the surface σ is the portion of the elliptic paraboloid $z = 5 - 3x^2 - 2y^2$ that lies above the xy-plane.

27–28 Find the mass of the lamina with constant density δ_0. ■

27. The lamina that is the portion of the circular cylinder $x^2 + z^2 = 4$ that lies directly above the rectangle $R = \{(x, y) : 0 \le x \le 1, 0 \le y \le 4\}$ in the xy-plane.

28. The lamina that is the portion of the paraboloid $2z = x^2 + y^2$ inside the cylinder $x^2 + y^2 = 8$.

29. Find the mass of the lamina that is the portion of the surface $y^2 = 4 - z$ between the planes $x = 0$, $x = 3$, $y = 0$, and $y = 3$ if the density is $\delta(x, y, z) = y$.

30. Find the mass of the lamina that is the portion of the cone $z = \sqrt{x^2 + y^2}$ between $z = 1$ and $z = 4$ if the density is $\delta(x, y, z) = x^2 z$.

31. If a curved lamina has constant density δ_0, what relationship must exist between its mass and surface area? Explain your reasoning.

32. Show that if the density of the lamina $x^2 + y^2 + z^2 = a^2$ at each point is equal to the distance between that point and the xy-plane, then the mass of the lamina is $2\pi a^3$.

33–34 The centroid of a surface σ is defined by

$$\bar{x} = \frac{\displaystyle\iint_\sigma x\, dS}{\text{area of } \sigma}, \qquad \bar{y} = \frac{\displaystyle\iint_\sigma y\, dS}{\text{area of } \sigma}, \qquad \bar{z} = \frac{\displaystyle\iint_\sigma z\, dS}{\text{area of } \sigma}$$

Find the centroid of the surface. ■

33. The portion of the paraboloid $z = \frac{1}{2}(x^2 + y^2)$ below the plane $z = 4$.

34. The portion of the sphere $x^2 + y^2 + z^2 = 4$ above the plane $z = 1$.

35–38 Evaluate the integral $\iint_\sigma f(x, y, z)\, dS$ over the surface σ represented by the vector-valued function $\mathbf{r}(u, v)$. ■

35. $f(x, y, z) = xyz$; $\mathbf{r}(u, v) = u\cos v\,\mathbf{i} + u\sin v\,\mathbf{j} + 3u\,\mathbf{k}$
$(1 \le u \le 2,\ 0 \le v \le \pi/2)$

36. $f(x, y, z) = \dfrac{x^2 + z^2}{y}$; $\mathbf{r}(u, v) = 2\cos v\,\mathbf{i} + u\,\mathbf{j} + 2\sin v\,\mathbf{k}$
$(1 \le u \le 3,\ 0 \le v \le 2\pi)$

37. $f(x, y, z) = \dfrac{1}{\sqrt{1 + 4x^2 + 4y^2}}$;
$\mathbf{r}(u, v) = u\cos v\,\mathbf{i} + u\sin v\,\mathbf{j} + u^2\,\mathbf{k}$
$(0 \le u \le \sin v,\ 0 \le v \le \pi)$

38. $f(x, y, z) = e^{-z}$;
$\mathbf{r}(u, v) = 2\sin u\cos v\,\mathbf{i} + 2\sin u\sin v\,\mathbf{j} + 2\cos u\,\mathbf{k}$
$(0 \le u \le \pi/2, 0 \le v \le 2\pi)$

C 39. Use a CAS to approximate the mass of the curved lamina $z = e^{-x^2 - y^2}$ that lies above the region in the xy-plane enclosed by $x^2 + y^2 = 9$ given that the density function is $\delta(x, y, z) = \sqrt{x^2 + y^2}$.

C **40.** The surface σ shown in the accompanying figure, called a *Möbius strip*, is represented by the parametric equations

$$x = (5 + u\cos(v/2))\cos v$$
$$y = (5 + u\cos(v/2))\sin v$$
$$z = u\sin(v/2)$$

where $-1 \le u \le 1$ and $0 \le v \le 2\pi$.

(a) Use a CAS to generate a reasonable facsimile of this surface.

(b) Use a CAS to approximate the location of the centroid of σ (see the definition preceding Exercise 33).

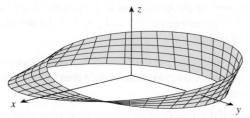

▲ **Figure Ex-40**

41. Writing Discuss the similarities and differences between the definition of a surface integral and the definition of a double integral.

42. Writing Suppose that a surface σ in 3-space and a function $f(x, y, z)$ are described geometrically. For example, σ might be the sphere of radius 1 centered at the origin and $f(x, y, z)$ might be the distance from the point (x, y, z) to the z-axis. How would you explain to a classmate a procedure for evaluating the surface integral of f over σ?

✔ **QUICK CHECK ANSWERS 15.5**

1. (a) $\left\| \dfrac{\partial \mathbf{r}}{\partial u} \times \dfrac{\partial \mathbf{r}}{\partial v} \right\| dA$ (b) $\sqrt{\left(\dfrac{\partial z}{\partial x}\right)^2 + \left(\dfrac{\partial z}{\partial y}\right)^2 + 1}\, dA$ **2.** $\dfrac{\sqrt{3}}{2}$ **3.** 64π **4.** $\displaystyle\iint\limits_{\sigma} f(x, y, z)\, dS$

15.6 APPLICATIONS OF SURFACE INTEGRALS; FLUX

In this section we will discuss applications of surface integrals to vector fields associated with fluid flow and electrostatic forces. However, the ideas that we will develop will be general in nature and applicable to other kinds of vector fields as well.

■ **FLOW FIELDS**

We will be concerned in this section with vector fields in 3-space that involve some type of "flow"—the flow of a fluid or the flow of charged particles in an electrostatic field, for example. In the case of fluid flow, the vector field $\mathbf{F}(x, y, z)$ represents the velocity of a fluid particle at the point (x, y, z), and the fluid particles flow along "streamlines" that are tangential to the velocity vectors (Figure 15.6.1a). In the case of an electrostatic field, $\mathbf{F}(x, y, z)$ is the force that the field exerts on a small unit of positive charge at the point (x, y, z), and such charges have acceleration in the directions of "electric lines" that are tangential to the force vectors (Figures 15.6.1b and 15.6.1c).

■ **ORIENTED SURFACES**

Our main goal in this section is to study flows of vector fields through permeable surfaces placed in the field. For this purpose we will need to consider some basic ideas about surfaces. Most surfaces that we encounter in applications have two sides—a sphere has an inside and an outside, and an infinite horizontal plane has a top side and a bottom side, for example. However, there exist mathematical surfaces with only one side. For example, Figure 15.6.2a shows the construction of a surface called a *Möbius strip* [in honor of the German mathematician August Möbius (1790–1868)]. The Möbius strip has only one side in the sense that a bug can traverse the *entire* surface without crossing an edge (Figure 15.6.2b). In contrast,

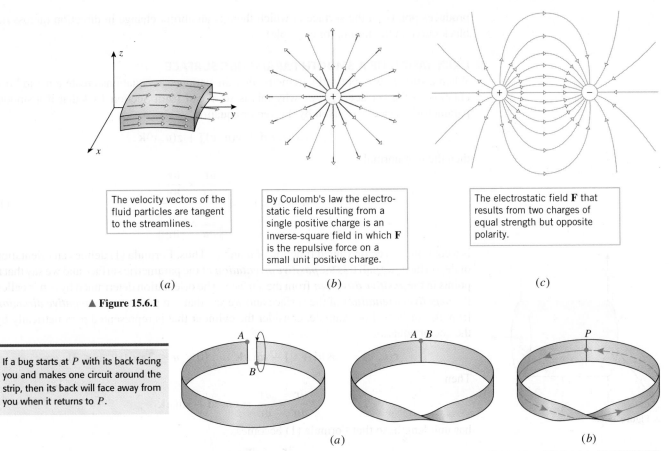

The velocity vectors of the fluid particles are tangent to the streamlines.

By Coulomb's law the electrostatic field resulting from a single positive charge is an inverse-square field in which **F** is the repulsive force on a small unit positive charge.

The electrostatic field **F** that results from two charges of equal strength but opposite polarity.

(a)   *(b)*   *(c)*

▲ **Figure 15.6.1**

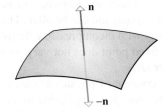

If a bug starts at P with its back facing you and makes one circuit around the strip, then its back will face away from you when it returns to P.

(a)   *(b)*

▲ **Figure 15.6.2**

a sphere is two-sided in the sense that a bug walking on the sphere can traverse the inside surface or the outside surface but cannot traverse both without somehow passing through the sphere. A two-sided surface is said to be ***orientable***, and a one-sided surface is said to be ***nonorientable***. In the rest of this text we will only be concerned with orientable surfaces.

In applications, it is important to have some way of distinguishing between the two sides of an orientable surface. For this purpose let us suppose that σ is an orientable surface that has a unit normal vector **n** at each point. As illustrated in Figure 15.6.3, the vectors **n** and $-$**n** point to opposite sides of the surface and hence serve to distinguish between the two sides. It can be proved that if σ is a smooth orientable surface, then it is always possible to choose the direction of **n** at each point so that $\mathbf{n} = \mathbf{n}(x, y, z)$ varies continuously over the surface. These unit vectors are then said to form an ***orientation*** of the surface. It can also be proved that a smooth orientable surface has only two possible orientations. For example, the surface in Figure 15.6.4 is oriented up by the purple vectors and down by the green vectors. However, we cannot create a third orientation by mixing the two since this

▲ **Figure 15.6.3**

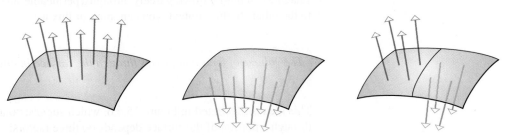

▲ **Figure 15.6.4**

produces points on the surface at which there is an abrupt change in direction (across the black curve in the figure, for example).

ORIENTATION OF A SMOOTH PARAMETRIC SURFACE

When a surface is expressed parametrically, the parametric equations create a natural orientation of the surface. To see why this is so, recall from Section 14.4 that if a smooth parametric surface σ is given by the vector equation

$$\mathbf{r} = x(u, v)\mathbf{i} + y(u, v)\mathbf{j} + z(u, v)\mathbf{k}$$

then the unit normal

$$\mathbf{n} = \mathbf{n}(u, v) = \frac{\dfrac{\partial \mathbf{r}}{\partial u} \times \dfrac{\partial \mathbf{r}}{\partial v}}{\left\| \dfrac{\partial \mathbf{r}}{\partial u} \times \dfrac{\partial \mathbf{r}}{\partial v} \right\|} \tag{1}$$

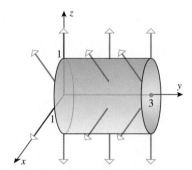

▲ Figure 15.6.5

See if you can find a parametrization of the cylinder in which the positive direction is inward.

is a continuous vector-valued function of u and v. Thus, Formula (1) defines an orientation of the surface; we call this the **positive orientation** of the parametric surface and we say that $\mathbf{n}$ points in the **positive direction** from the surface. The orientation determined by $-\mathbf{n}$ is called the **negative orientation** of the surface and we say that $-\mathbf{n}$ points in the **negative direction** from the surface. For example, consider the cylinder that is represented parametrically by the vector equation

$$\mathbf{r}(u, v) = \cos u\,\mathbf{i} + v\mathbf{j} - \sin u\,\mathbf{k} \qquad (0 \le u \le 2\pi, \;\; 0 \le v \le 3)$$

Then

$$\frac{\partial \mathbf{r}}{\partial u} \times \frac{\partial \mathbf{r}}{\partial v} = \cos u\,\mathbf{i} - \sin u\,\mathbf{k}$$

has unit length, so that Formula (1) becomes

$$\mathbf{n} = \frac{\partial \mathbf{r}}{\partial u} \times \frac{\partial \mathbf{r}}{\partial v} = \cos u\,\mathbf{i} - \sin u\,\mathbf{k}$$

Since $\mathbf{n}$ has the same $\mathbf{i}$- and $\mathbf{k}$-components as $\mathbf{r}$, the positive orientation of the cylinder is *outward* and the negative orientation is *inward* (Figure 15.6.5).

FLUX

In physics, the term *fluid* is used to describe both liquids and gases. Liquids are usually regarded to be **incompressible**, meaning that the liquid has a uniform density (mass per unit volume) that cannot be altered by compressive forces. Gases are regarded to be **compressible**, meaning that the density may vary from point to point and can be altered by compressive forces. In this text we will be concerned primarily with incompressible fluids. Moreover, we will assume that the velocity of the fluid at a fixed point does not vary with time. Fluid flows with this property are said to be in a **steady state**.

Our next goal in this section is to define a fundamental concept of physics known as *flux* (from the Latin word *fluxus*, meaning "flowing"). This concept is applicable to any vector field, but we will motivate it in the context of steady-state incompressible fluid flow. Imagine that fluid is flowing freely through a permeable surface, from one side of the surface to the other. In this context, you can think of flux as:

The volume of fluid that passes through the surface in one unit of time.

This idea is illustrated in Figure 15.6.6, which suggests that the volume of fluid that flows through a portion of the surface depends on three factors:

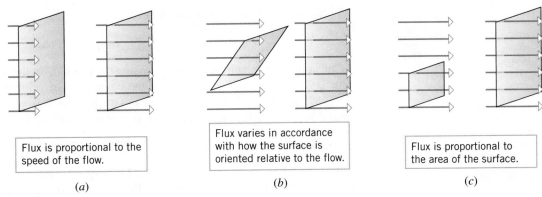

Flux is proportional to the speed of the flow.

Flux varies in accordance with how the surface is oriented relative to the flow.

Flux is proportional to the area of the surface.

(a)　　　　　　　　　　　　　　(b)　　　　　　　　　　　　　(c)

▲ **Figure 15.6.6**

- The speed of the fluid; the greater the speed, the greater the volume (Figure 15.6.6a).
- How the surface is oriented relative to the flow; the more nearly orthogonal the flow is to the surface, the greater the volume (Figure 15.6.6b).
- The area of the portion of the surface; the greater the area, the greater the volume (Figure 15.6.6c).

These ideas lead us to the following problem.

> **15.6.1 PROBLEM** Suppose that an oriented surface σ is immersed in an incompressible, steady-state fluid flow and that the surface is permeable so that the fluid can flow through it freely in either direction. Find the net volume of fluid Φ that passes through the surface per unit of time, where the net volume is interpreted to mean the volume that passes through the surface in the positive direction minus the volume that passes through the surface in the negative direction.

To solve this problem, suppose that the velocity of the fluid at a point (x, y, z) on the surface σ is given by

$$\mathbf{F}(x, y, z) = f(x, y, z)\mathbf{i} + g(x, y, z)\mathbf{j} + h(x, y, z)\mathbf{k}$$

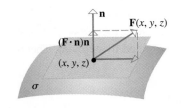

▲ **Figure 15.6.7**

Let $\mathbf{n}$ be the unit normal toward the positive side of σ at the point (x, y, z). As illustrated in Figure 15.6.7, the velocity vector $\mathbf{F}$ can be resolved into two orthogonal components—a component $(\mathbf{F} \cdot \mathbf{n})\mathbf{n}$ that is perpendicular to the surface σ and a second component that is along the "face" of σ. The component of velocity along the face of the surface does not contribute to the flow through σ and hence can be ignored in our computations. Moreover, observe that the sign of $\mathbf{F} \cdot \mathbf{n}$ determines the direction of flow—a positive value means the flow is in the direction of $\mathbf{n}$ and a negative value means that it is opposite to $\mathbf{n}$.

To solve Problem 15.6.1, we subdivide σ into n patches $\sigma_1, \sigma_2, \ldots, \sigma_n$ with areas

$$\Delta S_1, \Delta S_2, \ldots, \Delta S_n$$

If the patches are small and the flow is not too erratic, it is reasonable to assume that the velocity does not vary much on each patch. Thus, if (x_k^*, y_k^*, z_k^*) is any point in the kth patch, we can assume that $\mathbf{F}(x, y, z)$ is constant and equal to $\mathbf{F}(x_k^*, y_k^*, z_k^*)$ throughout the patch and that the component of velocity across the surface σ_k is

$$\mathbf{F}(x_k^*, y_k^*, z_k^*) \cdot \mathbf{n}(x_k^*, y_k^*, z_k^*) \tag{2}$$

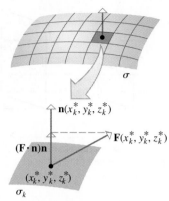

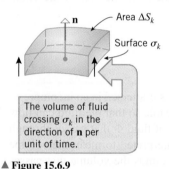

▲ **Figure 15.6.8**

▲ **n**   Area ΔS_k

Surface σ_k

The volume of fluid crossing σ_k in the direction of **n** per unit of time.

▲ **Figure 15.6.9**

If the fluid has mass density δ, then $\Phi\delta$ (volume/time × density) represents the net mass of fluid that passes through σ per unit of time.

(Figure 15.6.8). Thus, we can interpret

$$\mathbf{F}(x_k^*, y_k^*, z_k^*) \cdot \mathbf{n}(x_k^*, y_k^*, z_k^*)\Delta S_k$$

as the approximate volume of fluid crossing the patch σ_k in the direction of **n** per unit of time (Figure 15.6.9). For example, if the component of velocity in the direction of **n** is $\mathbf{F}(x_k^*, y_k^*, z_k^*) \cdot \mathbf{n} = 25$ cm/s, and the area of the patch is $\Delta S_k = 2$ cm^2, then the volume of fluid ΔV_k crossing the patch in the direction of **n** per unit of time is approximately

$$\Delta V_k \approx \mathbf{F}(x_k^*, y_k^*, z_k^*) \cdot \mathbf{n}(x_k^*, y_k^*, z_k^*)\Delta S_k = 25 \text{ cm/s} \cdot 2 \text{ cm}^2 = 50 \text{ cm}^3/\text{s}$$

In the case where the velocity component $\mathbf{F}(x_k^*, y_k^*, z_k^*) \cdot \mathbf{n}(x_k^*, y_k^*, z_k^*)$ is negative, the flow is in the direction opposite to **n**, so that $-\mathbf{F}(x_k^*, y_k^*, z_k^*) \cdot \mathbf{n}(x_k^*, y_k^*, z_k^*)\Delta S_k$ is the approximate volume of fluid crossing the patch σ_k in the direction opposite to **n** per unit time. Thus, the sum

$$\sum_{k=1}^{n} \mathbf{F}(x_k^*, y_k^*, z_k^*) \cdot \mathbf{n}(x_k^*, y_k^*, z_k^*)\Delta S_k$$

measures the approximate net volume of fluid that crosses the surface σ in the direction of its orientation **n** per unit of time.

If we now increase n in such a way that the maximum dimension of each patch approaches zero, then it is plausible that the errors in the approximations approach zero, and the limit

$$\Phi = \lim_{n \to +\infty} \sum_{k=1}^{n} \mathbf{F}(x_k^*, y_k^*, z_k^*) \cdot \mathbf{n}(x_k^*, y_k^*, z_k^*)\Delta S_k \tag{3}$$

represents the exact net volume of fluid that crosses the surface σ in the direction of its orientation **n** per unit of time. The quantity Φ defined by Equation (3) is called the **flux of F across σ**. The flux can also be expressed as the surface integral

$$\Phi = \iint_{\sigma} \mathbf{F}(x, y, z) \cdot \mathbf{n}(x, y, z) \, dS \tag{4}$$

A positive flux means that in one unit of time a greater volume of fluid passes through σ in the positive direction than in the negative direction, a negative flux means that a greater volume passes through the surface in the negative direction than in the positive direction, and a zero flux means that the same volume passes through the surface in each direction. Integrals of form (4) arise in other contexts as well and are called **flux integrals**.

■ EVALUATING FLUX INTEGRALS

An effective formula for evaluating flux integrals can be obtained by applying Theorem 15.5.2 and using Formula (1) for **n**. This yields

$$\iint_{\sigma} \mathbf{F} \cdot \mathbf{n} \, dS = \iint_{R} \mathbf{F} \cdot \mathbf{n} \left\| \frac{\partial \mathbf{r}}{\partial u} \times \frac{\partial \mathbf{r}}{\partial v} \right\| dA$$

$$= \iint_{R} \mathbf{F} \cdot \frac{\dfrac{\partial \mathbf{r}}{\partial u} \times \dfrac{\partial \mathbf{r}}{\partial v}}{\left\| \dfrac{\partial \mathbf{r}}{\partial u} \times \dfrac{\partial \mathbf{r}}{\partial v} \right\|} \left\| \frac{\partial \mathbf{r}}{\partial u} \times \frac{\partial \mathbf{r}}{\partial v} \right\| dA$$

$$= \iint_{R} \mathbf{F} \cdot \left(\frac{\partial \mathbf{r}}{\partial u} \times \frac{\partial \mathbf{r}}{\partial v} \right) dA$$

In summary, we have the following result.

15.6.2   THEOREM   *Let σ be a smooth parametric surface represented by the vector equation $\mathbf{r} = \mathbf{r}(u, v)$ in which (u, v) varies over a region R in the uv-plane. If the component functions of the vector field $\mathbf{F}$ are continuous on σ, and if $\mathbf{n}$ determines the positive orientation of σ, then*

$$\Phi = \iint\limits_{\sigma} \mathbf{F} \cdot \mathbf{n}\, dS = \iint\limits_{R} \mathbf{F} \cdot \left(\frac{\partial \mathbf{r}}{\partial u} \times \frac{\partial \mathbf{r}}{\partial v} \right) dA \qquad (5)$$

where it is understood that the integrand on the right side of the equation is expressed in terms of u and v.

Although Theorem 15.6.2 was derived for smooth parametric surfaces, Formula (5) is valid more generally. For example, as long as σ has a continuous normal vector field $\mathbf{n}$ and the component functions of $\mathbf{r}(u, v)$ have continuous first partial derivatives, Formula (5) can be applied whenever $\partial \mathbf{r}/\partial u \times \partial \mathbf{r}/\partial v$ is a positive multiple of $\mathbf{n}$ in the *interior* of R. (That is, $\partial \mathbf{r}/\partial u \times \partial \mathbf{r}/\partial v$ is allowed to equal $\mathbf{0}$ on the boundary of R.)

▶ **Example 1**   Find the flux of the vector field $\mathbf{F}(x, y, z) = z\mathbf{k}$ across the outward-oriented sphere $x^2 + y^2 + z^2 = a^2$.

Solution.   The sphere with outward positive orientation can be represented by the vector-valued function

$$\mathbf{r}(\phi, \theta) = a \sin \phi \cos \theta\, \mathbf{i} + a \sin \phi \sin \theta\, \mathbf{j} + a \cos \phi\, \mathbf{k} \qquad (0 \le \phi \le \pi, \ 0 \le \theta \le 2\pi)$$

From this formula we obtain (see Example 11 of Section 14.4 for the computations)

$$\frac{\partial \mathbf{r}}{\partial \phi} \times \frac{\partial \mathbf{r}}{\partial \theta} = a^2 \sin^2 \phi \cos \theta\, \mathbf{i} + a^2 \sin^2 \phi \sin \theta\, \mathbf{j} + a^2 \sin \phi \cos \phi\, \mathbf{k}$$

Moreover, for points on the sphere we have $\mathbf{F} = z\mathbf{k} = a \cos \phi\, \mathbf{k}$; hence,

$$\mathbf{F} \cdot \left(\frac{\partial \mathbf{r}}{\partial \phi} \times \frac{\partial \mathbf{r}}{\partial \theta} \right) = a^3 \sin \phi \cos^2 \phi$$

Thus, it follows from (5) with the parameters u and v replaced by ϕ and θ that

$$\Phi = \iint\limits_{\sigma} \mathbf{F} \cdot \mathbf{n}\, dS$$

$$= \iint\limits_{R} \mathbf{F} \cdot \left(\frac{\partial \mathbf{r}}{\partial \phi} \times \frac{\partial \mathbf{r}}{\partial \theta} \right) dA$$

$$= \int_{0}^{2\pi} \int_{0}^{\pi} a^3 \sin \phi \cos^2 \phi\, d\phi\, d\theta$$

$$= a^3 \int_{0}^{2\pi} \left[-\frac{\cos^3 \phi}{3} \right]_{0}^{\pi} d\theta$$

$$= \frac{2a^3}{3} \int_{0}^{2\pi} d\theta = \frac{4\pi a^3}{3} \quad ◀$$

Solve Example 1 using symmetry: First argue that the vector fields $x\mathbf{i}$, $y\mathbf{j}$, and $z\mathbf{k}$ will have the same flux across the sphere. Then define

$$\mathbf{H} = x\mathbf{i} + y\mathbf{j} + z\mathbf{k}$$

and explain why

$$\mathbf{H} \cdot \mathbf{n} = a$$

Use this to compute Φ.

REMARK | Reversing the orientation of the surface σ in (5) reverses the sign of $\mathbf{n}$, hence the sign of $\mathbf{F} \cdot \mathbf{n}$, and hence reverses the sign of Φ. This can also be seen physically by interpreting the flux integral as the volume of fluid per unit time that crosses σ in the positive direction minus the volume per unit time that crosses in the negative direction—reversing the orientation of σ changes the sign of the difference. Thus, in Example 1 an inward orientation of the sphere would produce a flux of $-4\pi a^3/3$.

ORIENTATION OF NONPARAMETRIC SURFACES

Nonparametric surfaces of the form $z = g(x, y)$, $y = g(z, x)$, and $x = g(y, z)$ can be expressed parametrically using the independent variables as parameters. More precisely, these surfaces can be represented by the vector equations

$$\mathbf{r} = u\mathbf{i} + v\mathbf{j} + g(u, v)\mathbf{k}, \quad \mathbf{r} = v\mathbf{i} + g(u, v)\mathbf{j} + u\mathbf{k}, \quad \mathbf{r} = g(u, v)\mathbf{i} + u\mathbf{j} + v\mathbf{k} \quad (6\text{–}8)$$

$$\boxed{z = g(x, y)} \qquad\qquad \boxed{y = g(z, x)} \qquad\qquad \boxed{x = g(y, z)}$$

These representations impose positive and negative orientations on the surfaces in accordance with Formula (1). We leave it as an exercise to calculate $\mathbf{n}$ and $-\mathbf{n}$ in each case and to show that the positive and negative orientations are as shown in Table 15.6.1. (To assist with perspective, each graph is pictured as a portion of the surface of a small solid region.)

Table 15.6.1

$z = g(x, y)$	$y = g(z, x)$	$x = g(y, z)$
$\mathbf{n} = \dfrac{-\dfrac{\partial z}{\partial x}\mathbf{i} - \dfrac{\partial z}{\partial y}\mathbf{j} + \mathbf{k}}{\sqrt{\left(\dfrac{\partial z}{\partial x}\right)^2 + \left(\dfrac{\partial z}{\partial y}\right)^2 + 1}}$ Positive k-component — Positive orientation	$\mathbf{n} = \dfrac{-\dfrac{\partial y}{\partial x}\mathbf{i} + \mathbf{j} - \dfrac{\partial y}{\partial z}\mathbf{k}}{\sqrt{\left(\dfrac{\partial y}{\partial x}\right)^2 + \left(\dfrac{\partial y}{\partial z}\right)^2 + 1}}$ Positive j-component — Positive orientation	$\mathbf{n} = \dfrac{\mathbf{i} - \dfrac{\partial x}{\partial y}\mathbf{j} - \dfrac{\partial x}{\partial z}\mathbf{k}}{\sqrt{\left(\dfrac{\partial x}{\partial y}\right)^2 + \left(\dfrac{\partial x}{\partial z}\right)^2 + 1}}$ Positive i-component — Positive orientation
$-\mathbf{n} = \dfrac{\dfrac{\partial z}{\partial x}\mathbf{i} + \dfrac{\partial z}{\partial y}\mathbf{j} - \mathbf{k}}{\sqrt{\left(\dfrac{\partial z}{\partial x}\right)^2 + \left(\dfrac{\partial z}{\partial y}\right)^2 + 1}}$ Negative k-component — Negative orientation	$-\mathbf{n} = \dfrac{\dfrac{\partial y}{\partial x}\mathbf{i} - \mathbf{j} + \dfrac{\partial y}{\partial z}\mathbf{k}}{\sqrt{\left(\dfrac{\partial y}{\partial x}\right)^2 + \left(\dfrac{\partial y}{\partial z}\right)^2 + 1}}$ Negative j-component — Negative orientation	$-\mathbf{n} = \dfrac{-\mathbf{i} + \dfrac{\partial x}{\partial y}\mathbf{j} + \dfrac{\partial x}{\partial z}\mathbf{k}}{\sqrt{\left(\dfrac{\partial x}{\partial y}\right)^2 + \left(\dfrac{\partial x}{\partial z}\right)^2 + 1}}$ Negative i-component — Negative orientation

The results in Table 15.6.1 can also be obtained using gradients. To see how this can be done, rewrite the equations of the surfaces as

$$z - g(x, y) = 0, \quad y - g(z, x) = 0, \quad x - g(y, z) = 0$$

Each of these equations has the form $G(x, y, z) = 0$ and hence can be viewed as a level surface of a function $G(x, y, z)$. Since the gradient of G is normal to the level surface, it follows that the unit normal $\mathbf{n}$ is either $\nabla G/\|\nabla G\|$ or $-\nabla G/\|\nabla G\|$. However, if $G(x, y, z) = z - g(x, y)$, then ∇G has a $\mathbf{k}$-component of 1; if $G(x, y, z) = y - g(z, x)$,

The dependent variable will increase as you move away from a surface

$$z = g(x, y), \quad y = g(z, x)$$

or

$$x = g(y, z)$$

in the direction of positive orientation.

then ∇G has a **j**-component of 1; and if $G(x, y, z) = x - g(y, z)$, then ∇G has an **i**-component of 1. Thus, it is evident from Table 15.6.1 that in all three cases we have

$$\mathbf{n} = \frac{\nabla G}{\|\nabla G\|} \tag{9}$$

Moreover, we leave it as an exercise to show that if the surfaces $z = g(x, y)$, $y = g(z, x)$, and $x = g(y, z)$ are expressed in vector forms (6), (7), and (8), then

$$\nabla G = \frac{\partial \mathbf{r}}{\partial u} \times \frac{\partial \mathbf{r}}{\partial v} \tag{10}$$

[compare (1) and (9)]. Thus, we are led to the following version of Theorem 15.6.2 for non-parametric surfaces.

15.6.3   THEOREM   *Let σ be a smooth surface of the form $z = g(x, y)$, $y = g(z, x)$, or $x = g(y, z)$, and suppose that the component functions of the vector field **F** are continuous on σ. Suppose also that the equation for σ is rewritten as $G(x, y, z) = 0$ by taking g to the left side of the equation, and let R be the projection of σ on the coordinate plane determined by the independent variables of g. If σ has positive orientation, then*

$$\Phi = \iint_{\sigma} \mathbf{F} \cdot \mathbf{n}\, dS = \iint_{R} \mathbf{F} \cdot \nabla G\, dA \tag{11}$$

Formula (11) can either be used directly for computations or to derive some more specific formulas for each of the three surface types. For example, if $z = g(x, y)$, then we have $G(x, y, z) = z - g(x, y)$, so

$$\nabla G = -\frac{\partial g}{\partial x}\mathbf{i} - \frac{\partial g}{\partial y}\mathbf{j} + \mathbf{k} = -\frac{\partial z}{\partial x}\mathbf{i} - \frac{\partial z}{\partial y}\mathbf{j} + \mathbf{k}$$

Substituting this expression for ∇G in (11) and taking R to be the projection of the surface $z = g(x, y)$ on the xy-plane yields

$$\iint_{\sigma} \mathbf{F} \cdot \mathbf{n}\, dS = \iint_{R} \mathbf{F} \cdot \left(-\frac{\partial z}{\partial x}\mathbf{i} - \frac{\partial z}{\partial y}\mathbf{j} + \mathbf{k}\right)\, dA \qquad \boxed{\begin{array}{l}\sigma \text{ of the form } z = g(x, y) \\ \text{and oriented up}\end{array}} \tag{12}$$

$$\iint_{\sigma} \mathbf{F} \cdot \mathbf{n}\, dS = \iint_{R} \mathbf{F} \cdot \left(\frac{\partial z}{\partial x}\mathbf{i} + \frac{\partial z}{\partial y}\mathbf{j} - \mathbf{k}\right)\, dA \qquad \boxed{\begin{array}{l}\sigma \text{ of the form } z = g(x, y) \\ \text{and oriented down}\end{array}} \tag{13}$$

The derivations of the corresponding formulas when $y = g(z, x)$ and $x = g(y, z)$ are left as exercises.

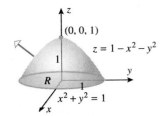

▲ **Figure 15.6.10**

▶ **Example 2**   Let σ be the portion of the surface $z = 1 - x^2 - y^2$ that lies above the xy-plane, and suppose that σ is oriented up, as shown in Figure 15.6.10. Find the flux of the vector field $\mathbf{F}(x, y, z) = x\mathbf{i} + y\mathbf{j} + z\mathbf{k}$ across σ.

Solution. From (12) the flux Φ is given by

$$\Phi = \iint_{\sigma} \mathbf{F} \cdot \mathbf{n}\, dS = \iint_{R} \mathbf{F} \cdot \left(-\frac{\partial z}{\partial x}\mathbf{i} - \frac{\partial z}{\partial y}\mathbf{j} + \mathbf{k} \right) dA$$

$$= \iint_{R} (x\mathbf{i} + y\mathbf{j} + z\mathbf{k}) \cdot (2x\mathbf{i} + 2y\mathbf{j} + \mathbf{k})\, dA$$

$$= \iint_{R} (x^2 + y^2 + 1)\, dA \qquad \boxed{\begin{array}{l}\text{Since } z = 1 - x^2 - y^2 \\ \text{on the surface}\end{array}}$$

$$= \int_{0}^{2\pi} \int_{0}^{1} (r^2 + 1)r\, dr\, d\theta \qquad \boxed{\begin{array}{l}\text{Using polar coordinates} \\ \text{to evaluate the integral}\end{array}}$$

$$= \int_{0}^{2\pi} \left(\frac{3}{4} \right) d\theta = \frac{3\pi}{2} \ \blacktriangleleft$$

✔ **QUICK CHECK EXERCISES 15.6**   *(See page 1148 for answers.)*

In these exercises, $\mathbf{F}(x, y, z)$ denotes a vector field defined on a surface σ oriented by a unit normal vector field $\mathbf{n}(x, y, z)$, and Φ denotes the flux of $\mathbf{F}$ across σ.

1. (a) Φ is the value of the surface integral _____.
   (b) If σ is the unit sphere and $\mathbf{n}$ is the outward unit normal, then the flux of

$$\mathbf{F}(x, y, z) = x\mathbf{i} + y\mathbf{j} + z\mathbf{k}$$

   across σ is $\Phi =$ _____.

2. (a) Assume that σ is parametrized by a vector-valued function $\mathbf{r}(u, v)$ whose domain is a region R in the uv-plane and that $\mathbf{n}$ is a positive multiple of

$$\frac{\partial \mathbf{r}}{\partial u} \times \frac{\partial \mathbf{r}}{\partial v}$$

   Then the double integral over R whose value is Φ is _____.

   (b) Suppose that σ is the parametric surface

$$\mathbf{r}(u, v) = u\mathbf{i} + v\mathbf{j} + (u + v)\mathbf{k} \qquad (0 \le u^2 + v^2 \le 1)$$

and that $\mathbf{n}$ is a positive multiple of

$$\frac{\partial \mathbf{r}}{\partial u} \times \frac{\partial \mathbf{r}}{\partial v}$$

Then the flux of $\mathbf{F}(x, y, z) = x\mathbf{i} + y\mathbf{j} + z\mathbf{k}$ across σ is $\Phi =$ _____.

3. (a) Assume that σ is the graph of a function $z = g(x, y)$ over a region R in the xy-plane and that $\mathbf{n}$ has a positive $\mathbf{k}$-component for every point on σ. Then a double integral over R whose value is Φ is _____.

   (b) Suppose that σ is the triangular region with vertices $(1, 0, 0)$, $(0, 1, 0)$, and $(0, 0, 1)$ with upward orientation. Then the flux of

$$\mathbf{F}(x, y, z) = x\mathbf{i} + y\mathbf{j} + z\mathbf{k}$$

   across σ is $\Phi =$ _____.

4. In the case of steady-state incompressible fluid flow, with $\mathbf{F}(x, y, z)$ the fluid velocity at (x, y, z) on σ, Φ can be interpreted as _____.

EXERCISE SET 15.6   □ CAS

1. Suppose that the surface σ of the unit cube in the accompanying figure has an outward orientation. In each part, determine whether the flux of the vector field $\mathbf{F}(x, y, z) = z\mathbf{j}$ across the specified face is positive, negative, or zero.
   (a) The face $x = 1$ (b) The face $x = 0$
   (c) The face $y = 1$ (d) The face $y = 0$
   (e) The face $z = 1$ (f) The face $z = 0$

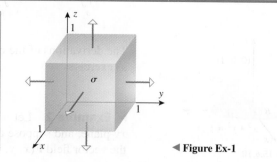

◀ **Figure Ex-1**

2. Answer the questions posed in Exercise 1 for the vector field $\mathbf{F}(x, y, z) = x\mathbf{i} - z\mathbf{k}$.

3. Answer the questions posed in Exercise 1 for the vector field $\mathbf{F}(x, y, z) = x\mathbf{i} + y\mathbf{j} + z\mathbf{k}$.

4. Find the flux of the constant vector field $\mathbf{F}(x, y, z) = \mathbf{i}$ across the entire surface σ in Figure Ex-1. Explain your reasoning.

5. Let σ be the cylindrical surface that is represented by the vector-valued function $\mathbf{r}(u, v) = \cos v\mathbf{i} + \sin v\mathbf{j} + u\mathbf{k}$ with $0 \le u \le 1$ and $0 \le v \le 2\pi$.
   (a) Find the unit normal $\mathbf{n} = \mathbf{n}(u, v)$ that defines the positive orientation of σ.
   (b) Is the positive orientation inward or outward? Justify your answer.

6. Let σ be the conical surface that is represented by the parametric equations $x = r\cos\theta$, $y = r\sin\theta$, $z = r$ with $1 \le r \le 2$ and $0 \le \theta \le 2\pi$.
   (a) Find the unit normal $\mathbf{n} = \mathbf{n}(r, \theta)$ that defines the positive orientation of σ.
   (b) Is the positive orientation upward or downward? Justify your answer.

7–12 Find the flux of the vector field $\mathbf{F}$ across σ. ■

7. $\mathbf{F}(x, y, z) = x\mathbf{i} + y\mathbf{j} + 2z\mathbf{k}$; σ is the portion of the surface $z = 1 - x^2 - y^2$ above the xy-plane, oriented by upward normals.

8. $\mathbf{F}(x, y, z) = (x + y)\mathbf{i} + (y + z)\mathbf{j} + (z + x)\mathbf{k}$; σ is the portion of the plane $x + y + z = 1$ in the first octant, oriented by unit normals with positive components.

9. $\mathbf{F}(x, y, z) = x\mathbf{i} + y\mathbf{j} + 2z\mathbf{k}$; σ is the portion of the cone $z^2 = x^2 + y^2$ between the planes $z = 1$ and $z = 2$, oriented by upward unit normals.

10. $\mathbf{F}(x, y, z) = y\mathbf{j} + \mathbf{k}$; σ is the portion of the paraboloid $z = x^2 + y^2$ below the plane $z = 4$, oriented by downward unit normals.

11. $\mathbf{F}(x, y, z) = x\mathbf{k}$; the surface σ is the portion of the paraboloid $z = x^2 + y^2$ below the plane $z = y$, oriented by downward unit normals.

12. $\mathbf{F}(x, y, z) = x^2\mathbf{i} + yx\mathbf{j} + zx\mathbf{k}$; σ is the portion of the plane $6x + 3y + 2z = 6$ in the first octant, oriented by unit normals with positive components.

13–16 Find the flux of the vector field $\mathbf{F}$ across σ in the direction of positive orientation. ■

13. $\mathbf{F}(x, y, z) = x\mathbf{i} + y\mathbf{j} + \mathbf{k}$; σ is the portion of the paraboloid
$$\mathbf{r}(u, v) = u\cos v\mathbf{i} + u\sin v\mathbf{j} + (1 - u^2)\mathbf{k}$$
with $1 \le u \le 2$, $0 \le v \le 2\pi$.

14. $\mathbf{F}(x, y, z) = e^{-y}\mathbf{i} - y\mathbf{j} + x\sin z\mathbf{k}$; σ is the portion of the elliptic cylinder
$$\mathbf{r}(u, v) = 2\cos v\mathbf{i} + \sin v\mathbf{j} + u\mathbf{k}$$
with $0 \le u \le 5$, $0 \le v \le 2\pi$.

15. $\mathbf{F}(x, y, z) = \sqrt{x^2 + y^2}\,\mathbf{k}$; σ is the portion of the cone
$$\mathbf{r}(u, v) = u\cos v\mathbf{i} + u\sin v\mathbf{j} + 2u\mathbf{k}$$
with $0 \le u \le \sin v$, $0 \le v \le \pi$.

16. $\mathbf{F}(x, y, z) = x\mathbf{i} + y\mathbf{j} + z\mathbf{k}$; σ is the portion of the sphere
$$\mathbf{r}(u, v) = 2\sin u\cos v\mathbf{i} + 2\sin u\sin v\mathbf{j} + 2\cos u\mathbf{k}$$
with $0 \le u \le \pi/3$, $0 \le v \le 2\pi$.

17. Let σ be the surface of the cube bounded by the planes $x = \pm 1$, $y = \pm 1$, $z = \pm 1$, oriented by outward unit normals. In each part, find the flux of $\mathbf{F}$ across σ.
   (a) $\mathbf{F}(x, y, z) = x\mathbf{i}$
   (b) $\mathbf{F}(x, y, z) = x\mathbf{i} + y\mathbf{j} + z\mathbf{k}$
   (c) $\mathbf{F}(x, y, z) = x^2\mathbf{i} + y^2\mathbf{j} + z^2\mathbf{k}$

18. Let σ be the closed surface consisting of the portion of the paraboloid $z = x^2 + y^2$ for which $0 \le z \le 1$ and capped by the disk $x^2 + y^2 \le 1$ in the plane $z = 1$. Find the flux of the vector field $\mathbf{F}(x, y, z) = z\mathbf{j} - y\mathbf{k}$ in the outward direction across σ.

19–22 True–False Determine whether the statement is true or false. Explain your answer. ■

19. The Möbius strip is a surface that has two orientations.

20. The flux of a vector field is another vector field.

21. If the net volume of fluid that passes through a surface per unit time in the positive direction is zero, then the velocity of the fluid is everywhere tangent to the surface.

22. If a surface σ is oriented by a unit normal vector field $\mathbf{n}$, the flux of $\mathbf{n}$ across σ is numerically equal to the surface area of σ.

23–24 Find the flux of $\mathbf{F}$ across the surface σ by expressing σ parametrically. ■

23. $\mathbf{F}(x, y, z) = \mathbf{i} + \mathbf{j} + \mathbf{k}$; the surface σ is the portion of the cone $z = \sqrt{x^2 + y^2}$ between the planes $z = 1$ and $z = 2$, oriented by downward unit normals.

24. $\mathbf{F}(x, y, z) = x\mathbf{i} + y\mathbf{j} + z\mathbf{k}$; σ is the portion of the cylinder $x^2 + z^2 = 1$ between the planes $y = 1$ and $y = -2$, oriented by outward unit normals.

25. Let x, y, and z be measured in meters, and suppose that $\mathbf{F}(x, y, z) = 2x\mathbf{i} - 3y\mathbf{j} + z\mathbf{k}$ is the velocity vector (in m/s) of a fluid particle at the point (x, y, z) in a steady-state incompressible fluid flow.
   (a) Find the net volume of fluid that passes in the upward direction through the portion of the plane $x + y + z = 1$ in the first octant in 1 s.
   (b) Assuming that the fluid has a mass density of 806 kg/m³, find the net mass of fluid that passes in the upward direction through the surface in part (a) in 1 s.

26. Let x, y, and z be measured in meters, and suppose that $\mathbf{F}(x, y, z) = -y\mathbf{i} + z\mathbf{j} + 3x\mathbf{k}$ is the velocity vector (in m/s) of a fluid particle at the point (x, y, z) in a steady-state incompressible fluid flow. *(cont.)*

(a) Find the net volume of fluid that passes in the upward direction through the hemisphere $z = \sqrt{9 - x^2 - y^2}$ in 1 s.

(b) Assuming that the fluid has a mass density of 1060 kg/m^3, find the net mass of fluid that passes in the upward direction through the surface in part (a) in 1 s.

27. (a) Derive the analogs of Formulas (12) and (13) for surfaces of the form $x = g(y, z)$.

(b) Let σ be the portion of the paraboloid $x = y^2 + z^2$ for $x \leq 1$ and $z \geq 0$ oriented by unit normals with negative x-components. Use the result in part (a) to find the flux of
$$\mathbf{F}(x, y, z) = y\mathbf{i} - z\mathbf{j} + 8\mathbf{k}$$
across σ.

28. (a) Derive the analogs of Formulas (12) and (13) for surfaces of the form $y = g(z, x)$.

(b) Let σ be the portion of the paraboloid $y = z^2 + x^2$ for $y \leq 1$ and $z \geq 0$ oriented by unit normals with positive y-components. Use the result in part (a) to find the flux of
$$\mathbf{F}(x, y, z) = x\mathbf{i} + y\mathbf{j} + z\mathbf{k}$$
across σ.

29. Let $\mathbf{F} = \|\mathbf{r}\|^k \mathbf{r}$, where $\mathbf{r} = x\mathbf{i} + y\mathbf{j} + z\mathbf{k}$ and k is a constant. (Note that if $k = -3$, this is an inverse-square field.) Let σ

be the sphere of radius a centered at the origin and oriented by the outward normal $\mathbf{n} = \mathbf{r}/\|\mathbf{r}\| = \mathbf{r}/a$.

(a) Find the flux of $\mathbf{F}$ across σ without performing any integrations. [*Hint:* The surface area of a sphere of radius a is $4\pi a^2$.]

(b) For what value of k is the flux independent of the radius of the sphere?

c 30. Let
$$\mathbf{F}(x, y, z) = a^2 x\mathbf{i} + (y/a)\mathbf{j} + az^2\mathbf{k}$$
and let σ be the sphere of radius 1 centered at the origin and oriented outward. Use a CAS to find all values of a such that the flux of $\mathbf{F}$ across σ is 3π.

c 31. Let
$$\mathbf{F}(x, y, z) = \left(\frac{6}{a} + 1\right) x\mathbf{i} - 4ay\mathbf{j} + a^2 z\mathbf{k}$$
and let σ be the sphere of radius a centered at the origin and oriented outward. Use a CAS to find all values of a such that the flux of $\mathbf{F}$ across σ is zero.

32. **Writing** Discuss the similarities and differences between the flux of a vector field across a surface and the line integral of a vector field along a curve.

33. **Writing** Write a paragraph explaining the concept of flux to someone unfamiliar with its meaning.

✔ **QUICK CHECK ANSWERS 15.6**

1. (a) $\displaystyle\iint_\sigma \mathbf{F} \cdot \mathbf{n}\, dS$ (b) 4π 2. (a) $\displaystyle\iint_R \mathbf{F} \cdot \left(\frac{\partial \mathbf{r}}{\partial u} \times \frac{\partial \mathbf{r}}{\partial v}\right) dA$ (b) 0 3. (a) $\displaystyle\iint_R \mathbf{F} \cdot \left(-\frac{\partial z}{\partial x}\mathbf{i} - \frac{\partial z}{\partial y}\mathbf{j} + \mathbf{k}\right) dA$ (b) $\frac{1}{2}$

4. the net volume of fluid crossing σ in the positive direction per unit time

---

15.7 THE DIVERGENCE THEOREM

In this section we will be concerned with flux across surfaces, such as spheres, that "enclose" a region of space. We will show that the flux across such surfaces can be expressed in terms of the divergence of the vector field, and we will use this result to give a physical interpretation of the concept of divergence.

■ **ORIENTATION OF PIECEWISE SMOOTH CLOSED SURFACES**

In the last section we studied flux across general surfaces. Here we will be concerned exclusively with surfaces that are boundaries of finite solids—the surface of a solid sphere, the surface of a solid box, or the surface of a solid cylinder, for example. Such surfaces are said to be *closed*. A closed surface may or may not be smooth, but most of the surfaces that arise in applications are *piecewise smooth*; that is, they consist of finitely many smooth surfaces joined together at the edges (a box, for example). We will limit our discussion to piecewise smooth surfaces that can be assigned an *inward orientation* (toward the interior of the solid) and an *outward orientation* (away from the interior). It is very difficult to make this concept mathematically precise, but the basic idea is that each piece of the surface is orientable, and oriented pieces fit together in such a way that the entire surface can be assigned an orientation (Figure 15.7.1).

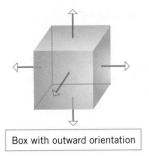

Box with outward orientation

▲ **Figure 15.7.1**

■ **THE DIVERGENCE THEOREM**

In Section 15.1 we defined the divergence of a vector field

$$\mathbf{F}(x, y, z) = f(x, y, z)\mathbf{i} + g(x, y, z)\mathbf{j} + h(x, y, z)\mathbf{k}$$

as

$$\text{div } \mathbf{F} = \frac{\partial f}{\partial x} + \frac{\partial g}{\partial y} + \frac{\partial h}{\partial z}$$

but we did not attempt to give a physical explanation of its meaning at that time. The following result, known as the *Divergence Theorem* or *Gauss's Theorem*, will provide us with a physical interpretation of divergence in the context of fluid flow.

15.7.1 THEOREM (*The Divergence Theorem*) *Let G be a solid whose surface σ is oriented outward. If*

$$\mathbf{F}(x, y, z) = f(x, y, z)\mathbf{i} + g(x, y, z)\mathbf{j} + h(x, y, z)\mathbf{k}$$

where f, g, and h have continuous first partial derivatives on some open set containing G, and if **n** *is the outward unit normal on σ, then*

$$\iint_{\sigma} \mathbf{F} \cdot \mathbf{n}\, dS = \iiint_{G} \text{div } \mathbf{F}\, dV \tag{1}$$

The proof of this theorem for a general solid G is too difficult to present here. However, we can give a proof for the special case where G is simultaneously a simple xy-solid, a simple yz-solid, and a simple zx-solid (see Figure 14.5.3 and the related discussion for terminology).

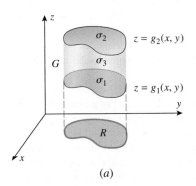

σ_2 $z = g_2(x, y)$

G

σ_3

σ_1 $z = g_1(x, y)$

R

(a)

PROOF Formula (1) can be expressed as

$$\iint_{\sigma} [f(x, y, z)\mathbf{i} + g(x, y, z)\mathbf{j} + h(x, y, z)\mathbf{k}] \cdot \mathbf{n}\, dS = \iiint_{G} \left(\frac{\partial f}{\partial x} + \frac{\partial g}{\partial y} + \frac{\partial h}{\partial z} \right) dV$$

so it suffices to prove the three equalities

$$\iint_{\sigma} f(x, y, z)\mathbf{i} \cdot \mathbf{n}\, dS = \iiint_{G} \frac{\partial f}{\partial x}\, dV \tag{2a}$$

$$\iint_{\sigma} g(x, y, z)\mathbf{j} \cdot \mathbf{n}\, dS = \iiint_{G} \frac{\partial g}{\partial y}\, dV \tag{2b}$$

$$\iint_{\sigma} h(x, y, z)\mathbf{k} \cdot \mathbf{n}\, dS = \iiint_{G} \frac{\partial h}{\partial z}\, dV \tag{2c}$$

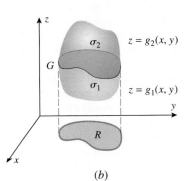

σ_2 $z = g_2(x, y)$

G

σ_1 $z = g_1(x, y)$

R

(b)

▲ **Figure 15.7.2**

Since the proofs of all three equalities are similar, we will prove only the third.

Suppose that G has upper surface $z = g_2(x, y)$, lower surface $z = g_1(x, y)$, and projection R on the xy-plane. Let σ_1 denote the lower surface, σ_2 the upper surface, and σ_3 the lateral surface (Figure 15.7.2a). If the upper surface and lower surface meet as in

Figure 15.7.2*b*, then there is no lateral surface σ_3. Our proof will allow for both cases shown in those figures.

It follows from Theorem 14.5.2 that

$$\iiint_G \frac{\partial h}{\partial z} \, dV = \iint_R \left[\int_{g_1(x,y)}^{g_2(x,y)} \frac{\partial h}{\partial z} \, dz \right] dA = \iint_R \left[h(x, y, z) \right]_{z=g_1(x,y)}^{g_2(x,y)} dA$$

so

$$\iiint_G \frac{\partial h}{\partial z} \, dV = \iint_R [h(x, y, g_2(x, y)) - h(x, y, g_1(x, y))] \, dA \qquad (3)$$

Carl Friedrich Gauss (1777–1855) German mathematician and scientist. Sometimes called the "prince of mathematicians," Gauss ranks with Newton and Archimedes as one of the three greatest mathematicians who ever lived. His father, a laborer, was an uncouth but honest man who would have liked Gauss to take up a trade such as gardening or bricklaying; but the boy's genius for mathematics was not to be denied. In the entire history of mathematics there may never have been a child so precocious as Gauss—by his own account he worked out the rudiments of arithmetic before he could talk. One day, before he was even three years old, his genius became apparent to his parents in a very dramatic way. His father was preparing the weekly payroll for the laborers under his charge while the boy watched quietly from a corner. At the end of the long and tedious calculation, Gauss informed his father that there was an error in the result and stated the answer, which he had worked out in his head. To the astonishment of his parents, a check of the computations showed Gauss to be correct!

For his elementary education Gauss was enrolled in a squalid school run by a man named Büttner whose main teaching technique was thrashing. Büttner was in the habit of assigning long addition problems which, unknown to his students, were arithmetic progressions that he could sum up using formulas. On the first day that Gauss entered the arithmetic class, the students were asked to sum the numbers from 1 to 100. But no sooner had Büttner stated the problem than Gauss turned over his slate and exclaimed in his peasant dialect, "Ligget se'." (Here it lies.) For nearly an hour Büttner glared at Gauss, who sat with folded hands while his classmates toiled away. When Büttner examined the slates at the end of the period, Gauss's slate contained a single number, 5050—the only correct solution in the class. To his credit, Büttner recognized the genius of Gauss and with the help of his assistant, John Bartels, had him brought to the attention of Karl Wilhelm Ferdinand, Duke of Brunswick. The shy and awkward boy, who was then fourteen, so captivated the Duke that he subsidized him through preparatory school, college, and the early part of his career.

From 1795 to 1798 Gauss studied mathematics at the University of Göttingen, receiving his degree in absentia from the University of Helmstadt. For his dissertation, he gave the first complete proof of the fundamental theorem of algebra, which states that every polynomial equation has as many solutions as its degree. At age 19 he solved a problem that baffled Euclid, inscribing a regular polygon of 17 sides in a circle using straightedge and compass; and in 1801, at age 24, he published his first masterpiece, *Disquisitiones Arithmeticae*, considered by many to be one of the most brilliant achievements in mathematics. In that book Gauss systematized the study of number theory (properties of the integers) and formulated the basic concepts that form the foundation of that subject.

In the same year that the *Disquisitiones* was published, Gauss again applied his phenomenal computational skills in a dramatic way. The astronomer Giuseppi Piazzi had observed the asteroid Ceres for $\frac{1}{40}$ of its orbit, but lost it in the Sun. Using only three observations and the "method of least squares" that he had developed in 1795, Gauss computed the orbit with such accuracy that astronomers had no trouble relocating it the following year. This achievement brought him instant recognition as the premier mathematician in Europe, and in 1807 he was made Professor of Astronomy and head of the astronomical observatory at Göttingen.

In the years that followed, Gauss revolutionized mathematics by bringing to it standards of precision and rigor undreamed of by his predecessors. He had a passion for perfection that drove him to polish and rework his papers rather than publish less finished work in greater numbers—his favorite saying was "Pauca, sed matura" (Few, but ripe). As a result, many of his important discoveries were squirreled away in diaries that remained unpublished until years after his death.

Among his myriad achievements, Gauss discovered the Gaussian or "bell-shaped" error curve fundamental in probability, gave the first geometric interpretation of complex numbers and established their fundamental role in mathematics, developed methods of characterizing surfaces intrinsically by means of the curves that they contain, developed the theory of conformal (angle-preserving) maps, and discovered non-Euclidean geometry 30 years before the ideas were published by others. In physics he made major contributions to the theory of lenses and capillary action, and with Wilhelm Weber he did fundamental work in electromagnetism. Gauss invented the heliotrope, bifilar magnetometer, and an electrotelegraph.

Gauss was deeply religious and aristocratic in demeanor. He mastered foreign languages with ease, read extensively, and enjoyed mineralogy and botany as hobbies. He disliked teaching and was usually cool and discouraging to other mathematicians, possibly because he had already anticipated their work. It has been said that if Gauss had published all of his discoveries, the current state of mathematics would be advanced by 50 years. He was without a doubt the greatest mathematician of the modern era.

Next we will evaluate the surface integral in (2c) by integrating over each surface of G separately. If there is a lateral surface σ_3, then at each point of this surface $\mathbf{k} \cdot \mathbf{n} = 0$ since $\mathbf{n}$ is horizontal and $\mathbf{k}$ is vertical. Thus,

$$\iint_{\sigma_3} h(x, y, z)\mathbf{k} \cdot \mathbf{n}\, dS = 0$$

Therefore, regardless of whether G has a lateral surface, we can write

$$\iint_{\sigma} h(x, y, z)\mathbf{k} \cdot \mathbf{n}\, dS = \iint_{\sigma_1} h(x, y, z)\mathbf{k} \cdot \mathbf{n}\, dS + \iint_{\sigma_2} h(x, y, z)\mathbf{k} \cdot \mathbf{n}\, dS \qquad (4)$$

On the upper surface σ_2, the outer normal is an upward normal, and on the lower surface σ_1, the outer normal is a downward normal. Thus, Formulas (12) and (13) of Section 15.6 imply that

$$\iint_{\sigma_2} h(x, y, z)\mathbf{k} \cdot \mathbf{n}\, dS = \iint_R h(x, y, g_2(x, y))\mathbf{k} \cdot \left(-\frac{\partial z}{\partial x}\mathbf{i} - \frac{\partial z}{\partial y}\mathbf{j} + \mathbf{k}\right) dA$$

$$= \iint_R h(x, y, g_2(x, y))\, dA \qquad (5)$$

and

$$\iint_{\sigma_1} h(x, y, z)\mathbf{k} \cdot \mathbf{n}\, dS = \iint_R h(x, y, g_1(x, y))\mathbf{k} \cdot \left(\frac{\partial z}{\partial x}\mathbf{i} + \frac{\partial z}{\partial y}\mathbf{j} - \mathbf{k}\right) dA$$

$$= -\iint_R h(x, y, g_1(x, y))\, dA \qquad (6)$$

Substituting (5) and (6) into (4) and combining the terms into a single integral yields

$$\iint_{\sigma} h(x, y, z)\mathbf{k} \cdot \mathbf{n}\, dS = \iint_R [h(x, y, g_2(x, y)) - h(x, y, g_1(x, y))]\, dA \qquad (7)$$

Equation (2c) now follows from (3) and (7). ∎

Explain how the derivation of (2c) should be modified to yield a proof of (2a) or (2b).

The flux of a vector field across a closed surface with outward orientation is sometimes called the *outward flux* across the surface. In words, the Divergence Theorem states:

The outward flux of a vector field across a closed surface is equal to the triple integral of the divergence over the region enclosed by the surface.

■ USING THE DIVERGENCE THEOREM TO FIND FLUX

Sometimes it is easier to find the flux across a closed surface by using the Divergence Theorem than by evaluating the flux integral directly. This is illustrated in the following example.

▶ **Example 1** Use the Divergence Theorem to find the outward flux of the vector field $\mathbf{F}(x, y, z) = z\mathbf{k}$ across the sphere $x^2 + y^2 + z^2 = a^2$.

Solution.   Let σ denote the outward-oriented spherical surface and G the region that it encloses. The divergence of the vector field is

$$\text{div } \mathbf{F} = \frac{\partial z}{\partial z} = 1$$

so from (1) the flux across σ is

$$\Phi = \iint\limits_{\sigma} \mathbf{F} \cdot \mathbf{n} \, dS = \iiint\limits_{G} dV = \text{volume of } G = \frac{4\pi a^3}{3}$$

Note how much simpler this calculation is than that in Example 1 of Section 15.6. ◄

The Divergence Theorem is usually the method of choice for finding the flux across closed piecewise smooth surfaces with multiple sections, since it eliminates the need for a separate integral evaluation over each section. This is illustrated in the next three examples.

▶ **Example 2**   Use the Divergence Theorem to find the outward flux of the vector field

$$\mathbf{F}(x, y, z) = 2x\mathbf{i} + 3y\mathbf{j} + z^2\mathbf{k}$$

across the unit cube in Figure 15.7.3.

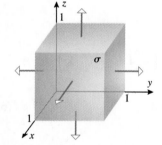

▲ **Figure 15.7.3**

Solution.   Let σ denote the outward-oriented surface of the cube and G the region that it encloses. The divergence of the vector field is

$$\text{div } \mathbf{F} = \frac{\partial}{\partial x}(2x) + \frac{\partial}{\partial y}(3y) + \frac{\partial}{\partial z}(z^2) = 5 + 2z$$

so from (1) the flux across σ is

$$\Phi = \iint\limits_{\sigma} \mathbf{F} \cdot \mathbf{n} \, dS = \iiint\limits_{G} (5 + 2z) \, dV = \int_0^1 \int_0^1 \int_0^1 (5 + 2z) \, dz \, dy \, dx$$

$$= \int_0^1 \int_0^1 \left[5z + z^2\right]_{z=0}^1 dy \, dx = \int_0^1 \int_0^1 6 \, dy \, dx = 6 \; ◄$$

Let $\mathbf{F}(x, y, z)$ be the vector field in Example 2 and show that $\mathbf{F} \cdot \mathbf{n}$ is constant on each of the six faces of the cube in Figure 15.7.3. Use your computations to confirm the result in Example 2.

▶ **Example 3**   Use the Divergence Theorem to find the outward flux of the vector field

$$\mathbf{F}(x, y, z) = x^3\mathbf{i} + y^3\mathbf{j} + z^2\mathbf{k}$$

across the surface of the region that is enclosed by the circular cylinder $x^2 + y^2 = 9$ and the planes $z = 0$ and $z = 2$ (Figure 15.7.4).

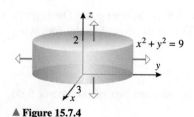

▲ **Figure 15.7.4**

Solution.   Let σ denote the outward-oriented surface and G the region that it encloses. The divergence of the vector field is

$$\text{div } \mathbf{F} = \frac{\partial}{\partial x}(x^3) + \frac{\partial}{\partial y}(y^3) + \frac{\partial}{\partial z}(z^2) = 3x^2 + 3y^2 + 2z$$

so from (1) the flux across σ is

$$\Phi = \iint_\sigma \mathbf{F} \cdot \mathbf{n} \, dS = \iiint_G (3x^2 + 3y^2 + 2z) \, dV$$

$$= \int_0^{2\pi} \int_0^3 \int_0^2 (3r^2 + 2z) r \, dz \, dr \, d\theta \qquad \text{Using cylindrical coordinates}$$

$$= \int_0^{2\pi} \int_0^3 \left[3r^3 z + z^2 r \right]_{z=0}^2 dr \, d\theta$$

$$= \int_0^{2\pi} \int_0^3 (6r^3 + 4r) \, dr \, d\theta$$

$$= \int_0^{2\pi} \left[\frac{3r^4}{2} + 2r^2 \right]_0^3 d\theta$$

$$= \int_0^{2\pi} \frac{279}{2} \, d\theta = 279\pi \quad \blacktriangleleft$$

▶ **Example 4** Use the Divergence Theorem to find the outward flux of the vector field

$$\mathbf{F}(x, y, z) = x^3 \mathbf{i} + y^3 \mathbf{j} + z^3 \mathbf{k}$$

across the surface of the region that is enclosed by the hemisphere $z = \sqrt{a^2 - x^2 - y^2}$ and the plane $z = 0$ (Figure 15.7.5).

Solution. Let σ denote the outward-oriented surface and G the region that it encloses. The divergence of the vector field is

$$\text{div } \mathbf{F} = \frac{\partial}{\partial x}(x^3) + \frac{\partial}{\partial y}(y^3) + \frac{\partial}{\partial z}(z^3) = 3x^2 + 3y^2 + 3z^2$$

so from (1) the flux across σ is

$$\Phi = \iint_\sigma \mathbf{F} \cdot \mathbf{n} \, dS = \iiint_G (3x^2 + 3y^2 + 3z^2) \, dV$$

$$= \int_0^{2\pi} \int_0^{\pi/2} \int_0^a (3\rho^2)\rho^2 \sin \phi \, d\rho \, d\phi \, d\theta \qquad \text{Using spherical coordinates}$$

$$= 3 \int_0^{2\pi} \int_0^{\pi/2} \int_0^a \rho^4 \sin \phi \, d\rho \, d\phi \, d\theta$$

$$= 3 \int_0^{2\pi} \int_0^{\pi/2} \left[\frac{\rho^5}{5} \sin \phi \right]_{\rho=0}^a d\phi \, d\theta$$

$$= \frac{3a^5}{5} \int_0^{2\pi} \int_0^{\pi/2} \sin \phi \, d\phi \, d\theta$$

$$= \frac{3a^5}{5} \int_0^{2\pi} \left[-\cos \phi \right]_0^{\pi/2} d\theta$$

$$= \frac{3a^5}{5} \int_0^{2\pi} d\theta = \frac{6\pi a^5}{5} \quad \blacktriangleleft$$

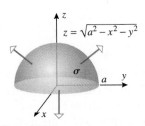

▲ **Figure 15.7.5**

DIVERGENCE VIEWED AS FLUX DENSITY

The Divergence Theorem provides a way of interpreting the divergence of a vector field $\mathbf{F}$. Suppose that G is a *small* spherical region centered at the point P_0 and that its surface, denoted by $\sigma(G)$, is oriented outward. Denote the volume of the region by $\text{vol}(G)$ and the flux of $\mathbf{F}$ across $\sigma(G)$ by $\Phi(G)$. If div $\mathbf{F}$ is continuous on G, then across the small region G the value of div $\mathbf{F}$ will not vary much from its value div $\mathbf{F}(P_0)$ at the center, and we can reasonably approximate div $\mathbf{F}$ by the constant div $\mathbf{F}(P_0)$ on G. Thus, the Divergence Theorem implies that the flux $\Phi(G)$ of $\mathbf{F}$ across $\sigma(G)$ can be approximated by

$$\Phi(G) = \iint\limits_{\sigma(G)} \mathbf{F} \cdot \mathbf{n}\, dS = \iiint\limits_{G} \text{div } \mathbf{F}\, dV \approx \text{div } \mathbf{F}(P_0) \iiint\limits_{G} dV = \text{div } \mathbf{F}(P_0)\, \text{vol}(G)$$

from which we obtain the approximation

$$\text{div } \mathbf{F}(P_0) \approx \frac{\Phi(G)}{\text{vol}(G)} \tag{8}$$

The expression on the right side of (8) is called the ***outward flux density of*** $\mathbf{F}$ ***across*** G. If we now let the radius of the sphere approach zero [so that $\text{vol}(G)$ approaches zero], then it is plausible that the error in this approximation will approach zero, and the divergence of $\mathbf{F}$ at the point P_0 will be given exactly by

$$\text{div } \mathbf{F}(P_0) = \lim_{\text{vol}(G) \to 0} \frac{\Phi(G)}{\text{vol}(G)}$$

which we can express as

> Formula (9) is sometimes taken as the definition of divergence. This is a useful alternative to Definition 15.1.4 because it does not require a coordinate system.

$$\text{div } \mathbf{F}(P_0) = \lim_{\text{vol}(G) \to 0} \frac{1}{\text{vol}(G)} \iint\limits_{\sigma(G)} \mathbf{F} \cdot \mathbf{n}\, dS \tag{9}$$

This limit, which is called the ***outward flux density of*** $\mathbf{F}$ ***at*** P_0, tells us that if $\mathbf{F}$ denotes the velocity field of a fluid, then *in a steady-state fluid flow* div $\mathbf{F}$ *can be interpreted as the limiting flux per unit volume at a point*. Moreover, it follows from (8) that for a small spherical region G centered at a point P_0 in the flow, the outward flux across the surface of G can be approximated by

$$\Phi(G) \approx (\text{div } \mathbf{F}(P_0))(\text{vol}(G)) \tag{10}$$

SOURCES AND SINKS

If P_0 is a point in an incompressible fluid at which div $\mathbf{F}(P_0) > 0$, then it follows from (8) that $\Phi(G) > 0$ for a sufficiently small sphere G centered at P_0. Thus, there is a greater volume of fluid going out through the surface of G than coming in. But this can only happen if there is some point *inside* the sphere at which fluid is entering the flow (say by condensation, melting of a solid, or a chemical reaction); otherwise the net outward flow through the surface would result in a decrease in density within the sphere, contradicting the incompressibility assumption. Similarly, if div $\mathbf{F}(P_0) < 0$, there would have to be a point *inside* the sphere at which fluid is leaving the flow (say by evaporation); otherwise the net inward flow through the surface would result in an increase in density within the sphere. In an incompressible fluid, points at which div $\mathbf{F}(P_0) > 0$ are called ***sources*** and points at which div $\mathbf{F}(P_0) < 0$ are called ***sinks***. Fluid enters the flow at a source and drains out at a sink. In an incompressible fluid without sources or sinks we must have

$$\text{div } \mathbf{F}(P) = 0$$

at every point P. In hydrodynamics this is called the ***continuity equation for incompressible fluids*** and is sometimes taken as the defining characteristic of an incompressible fluid.

■ GAUSS'S LAW FOR INVERSE-SQUARE FIELDS

The Divergence Theorem applied to inverse-square fields (see Definition 15.1.2) produces a result called *Gauss's Law for Inverse-Square Fields*. This result is the basis for many important principles in physics.

***

15.7.2   GAUSS'S LAW FOR INVERSE-SQUARE FIELDS   If

$$\mathbf{F(r)} = \frac{c}{\|\mathbf{r}\|^3}\mathbf{r}$$

is an inverse-square field in 3-space, and if σ is a closed orientable surface that surrounds the origin, then the outward flux of $\mathbf{F}$ across σ is

$$\Phi = \iint_{\sigma} \mathbf{F} \cdot \mathbf{n}\, dS = 4\pi c \tag{11}$$

***

To derive this result, recall from Formula (5) of Section 15.1 that $\mathbf{F}$ can be expressed in component form as

$$\mathbf{F}(x, y, z) = \frac{c}{(x^2 + y^2 + z^2)^{3/2}}(x\mathbf{i} + y\mathbf{j} + z\mathbf{k}) \tag{12}$$

Since the components of $\mathbf{F}$ are not continuous at the origin, we cannot apply the Divergence Theorem across the solid enclosed by σ. However, we can circumvent this difficulty by constructing a sphere of radius a centered at the origin, where the radius is sufficiently small that the sphere lies entirely within the region enclosed by σ (Figure 15.7.6). We will denote the surface of this sphere by σ_a. The solid G enclosed between σ_a and σ is an example of a three-dimensional solid with an internal "cavity." Just as we were able to extend Green's Theorem to multiply connected regions in the plane (regions with holes), so it is possible to extend the Divergence Theorem to solids in 3-space with internal cavities, provided the surface integral in the theorem is taken over the *entire* boundary with the outside boundary of the solid oriented outward and the boundaries of the cavities oriented inward. Thus, if $\mathbf{F}$ is the inverse-square field in (12), and if σ_a is oriented inward, then the Divergence Theorem yields

$$\iiint_G \operatorname{div} \mathbf{F}\, dV = \iint_{\sigma} \mathbf{F} \cdot \mathbf{n}\, dS + \iint_{\sigma_a} \mathbf{F} \cdot \mathbf{n}\, dS \tag{13}$$

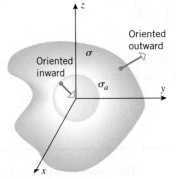

▲ **Figure 15.7.6**

But we showed in Example 5 of Section 15.1 that $\operatorname{div} \mathbf{F} = 0$, so (13) yields

$$\iint_{\sigma} \mathbf{F} \cdot \mathbf{n}\, dS = -\iint_{\sigma_a} \mathbf{F} \cdot \mathbf{n}\, dS \tag{14}$$

We can evaluate the surface integral over σ_a by expressing the integrand in terms of components; however, it is easier to leave it in vector form. At each point on the sphere the unit normal $\mathbf{n}$ points inward along a radius from the origin, and hence $\mathbf{n} = -\mathbf{r}/\|\mathbf{r}\|$. Thus, (14) yields

$$\iint_{\sigma} \mathbf{F} \cdot \mathbf{n}\, dS = -\iint_{\sigma_a} \frac{c}{\|\mathbf{r}\|^3} \mathbf{r} \cdot \left(-\frac{\mathbf{r}}{\|\mathbf{r}\|}\right) dS$$

$$= \iint_{\sigma_a} \frac{c}{\|\mathbf{r}\|^4} (\mathbf{r} \cdot \mathbf{r})\, dS$$

$$= \iint_{\sigma_a} \frac{c}{\|\mathbf{r}\|^2}\, dS$$

$$= \frac{c}{a^2} \iint_{\sigma_a} dS \qquad \boxed{\|\mathbf{r}\| = a \text{ on } \sigma_a}$$

$$= \frac{c}{a^2} (4\pi a^2) \qquad \boxed{\begin{array}{l}\text{The integral is the surface}\\ \text{area of the sphere.}\end{array}}$$

$$= 4\pi c$$

which establishes (11).

■ GAUSS'S LAW IN ELECTROSTATICS

It follows from Example 1 of Section 15.1 with $q = 1$ that a single charged particle of charge Q located at the origin creates an inverse-square field

$$\mathbf{F}(\mathbf{r}) = \frac{Q}{4\pi\epsilon_0 \|\mathbf{r}\|^3} \mathbf{r}$$

in which $\mathbf{F}(\mathbf{r})$ is the electrical force exerted by Q on a unit positive charge ($q = 1$) located at the point with position vector $\mathbf{r}$. In this case Gauss's law (15.7.2) states that the outward flux Φ across any closed orientable surface σ that surrounds Q is

$$\Phi = \iint_{\sigma} \mathbf{F} \cdot \mathbf{n}\, dS = 4\pi \left(\frac{Q}{4\pi\epsilon_0}\right) = \frac{Q}{\epsilon_0}$$

This result, which is called *Gauss's Law for Electric Fields*, can be extended to more than one charge. It is one of the fundamental laws in electricity and magnetism.

✔ QUICK CHECK EXERCISES 15.7   (See page 1158 for answers.)

1. Let G be a solid whose surface σ is oriented outward by the unit normal $\mathbf{n}$, and let $\mathbf{F}(x, y, z)$ denote a vector field whose component functions have continuous first partial derivatives on some open set containing G. The Divergence Theorem states that the surface integral _____ and the triple integral _____ have the same value.

2. The outward flux of $\mathbf{F}(x, y, z) = x\mathbf{i} + y\mathbf{j} + z\mathbf{k}$ across any unit cube is _____.

3. If $\mathbf{F}(x, y, z)$ is the velocity vector field for a steady-state incompressible fluid flow, then a point at which div $\mathbf{F}$ is positive is called a _____ and a point at which div $\mathbf{F}$ is negative is called a _____. The continuity equation for an incompressible fluid states that _____.

4. If

$$\mathbf{F}(\mathbf{r}) = \frac{c}{\|\mathbf{r}\|^3} \mathbf{r}$$

is an inverse-square field, and if σ is a closed orientable surface that surrounds the origin, then Gauss's law states that the outward flux of $\mathbf{F}$ across σ is _____. On the other hand, if σ does not surround the origin, then it follows from the Divergence Theorem that the outward flux of $\mathbf{F}$ across σ is _____.

EXERCISE SET 15.7 C CAS

1–4 Verify Formula (1) in the Divergence Theorem by evaluating the surface integral and the triple integral. ■

1. $\mathbf{F}(x, y, z) = x\mathbf{i} + y\mathbf{j} + z\mathbf{k}$; σ is the surface of the cube bounded by the planes $x = 0$, $x = 1$, $y = 0$, $y = 1$, $z = 0$, $z = 1$.

2. $\mathbf{F}(x, y, z) = x\mathbf{i} + y\mathbf{j} + z\mathbf{k}$; σ is the spherical surface $x^2 + y^2 + z^2 = 1$.

3. $\mathbf{F}(x, y, z) = 2x\mathbf{i} - yz\mathbf{j} + z^2\mathbf{k}$; the surface σ is the paraboloid $z = x^2 + y^2$ capped by the disk $x^2 + y^2 \le 1$ in the plane $z = 1$.

4. $\mathbf{F}(x, y, z) = xy\mathbf{i} + yz\mathbf{j} + xz\mathbf{k}$; σ is the surface of the cube bounded by the planes $x = 0$, $x = 2$, $y = 0$, $y = 2$, $z = 0$, $z = 2$.

5–8 True–False Determine whether the statement is true or false. Explain your answer. ■

5. The Divergence Theorem equates a surface integral and a line integral.

6. If G is a solid whose surface σ is oriented outward, and if $\text{div }\mathbf{F} > 0$ at all points of G, then the flux of $\mathbf{F}$ across σ is positive.

7. The continuity equation for incompressible fluids states that the divergence of the velocity vector field of the fluid is zero.

8. Since the divergence of an inverse-square field is zero, the flux of an inverse-square field across any closed orientable surface must be zero as well.

9–19 Use the Divergence Theorem to find the flux of $\mathbf{F}$ across the surface σ with outward orientation. ■

9. $\mathbf{F}(x, y, z) = (x^2 + y)\mathbf{i} + z^2\mathbf{j} + (e^y - z)\mathbf{k}$; σ is the surface of the rectangular solid bounded by the coordinate planes and the planes $x = 3$, $y = 1$, and $z = 2$.

10. $\mathbf{F}(x, y, z) = z^3\mathbf{i} - x^3\mathbf{j} + y^3\mathbf{k}$, where σ is the sphere $x^2 + y^2 + z^2 = a^2$.

11. $\mathbf{F}(x, y, z) = (x - z)\mathbf{i} + (y - x)\mathbf{j} + (z - y)\mathbf{k}$; σ is the surface of the cylindrical solid bounded by $x^2 + y^2 = a^2$, $z = 0$, and $z = 1$.

12. $\mathbf{F}(x, y, z) = x\mathbf{i} + y\mathbf{j} + z\mathbf{k}$; σ is the surface of the solid bounded by the paraboloid $z = 1 - x^2 - y^2$ and the xy-plane.

13. $\mathbf{F}(x, y, z) = x^3\mathbf{i} + y^3\mathbf{j} + z^3\mathbf{k}$; σ is the surface of the cylindrical solid bounded by $x^2 + y^2 = 4$, $z = 0$, and $z = 3$.

14. $\mathbf{F}(x, y, z) = (x^2 + y)\mathbf{i} + xy\mathbf{j} - (2xz + y)\mathbf{k}$; σ is the surface of the tetrahedron in the first octant bounded by $x + y + z = 1$ and the coordinate planes.

15. $\mathbf{F}(x, y, z) = (x^3 - e^y)\mathbf{i} + (y^3 + \sin z)\mathbf{j} + (z^3 - xy)\mathbf{k}$, where σ is the surface of the solid bounded above by $z = \sqrt{4 - x^2 - y^2}$ and below by the xy-plane. [*Hint:* Use spherical coordinates.]

16. $\mathbf{F}(x, y, z) = 2xz\mathbf{i} + yz\mathbf{j} + z^2\mathbf{k}$, where σ is the surface of the solid bounded above by $z = \sqrt{a^2 - x^2 - y^2}$ and below by the xy-plane.

17. $\mathbf{F}(x, y, z) = x^2\mathbf{i} + y^2\mathbf{j} + z^2\mathbf{k}$; σ is the surface of the conical solid bounded by $z = \sqrt{x^2 + y^2}$ and $z = 1$.

18. $\mathbf{F}(x, y, z) = x^2 y\mathbf{i} - xy^2\mathbf{j} + (z + 2)\mathbf{k}$; σ is the surface of the solid bounded above by the plane $z = 2x$ and below by the paraboloid $z = x^2 + y^2$.

19. $\mathbf{F}(x, y, z) = x^3\mathbf{i} + x^2 y\mathbf{j} + xy\mathbf{k}$; σ is the surface of the solid bounded by $z = 4 - x^2$, $y + z = 5$, $z = 0$, and $y = 0$.

20. Prove that if $\mathbf{r} = x\mathbf{i} + y\mathbf{j} + z\mathbf{k}$ and σ is the surface of a solid G oriented by outward unit normals, then
$$\text{vol}(G) = \frac{1}{3}\iint_\sigma \mathbf{r} \cdot \mathbf{n}\, dS$$
where $\text{vol}(G)$ is the volume of G.

21. Use the result in Exercise 20 to find the outward flux of the vector field $\mathbf{F}(x, y, z) = x\mathbf{i} + y\mathbf{j} + z\mathbf{k}$ across the surface σ of the cylindrical solid bounded by $x^2 + 4x + y^2 = 5$, $z = -1$, and $z = 4$.

FOCUS ON CONCEPTS

22. Let $\mathbf{F}(x, y, z) = a\mathbf{i} + b\mathbf{j} + c\mathbf{k}$ be a constant vector field and let σ be the surface of a solid G. Use the Divergence Theorem to show that the flux of $\mathbf{F}$ across σ is zero. Give an informal physical explanation of this result.

23. Find a vector field $\mathbf{F}(x, y, z)$ that has
    (a) positive divergence everywhere
    (b) negative divergence everywhere.

24. In each part, the figure shows a horizontal layer of the vector field of a fluid flow in which the flow is parallel to the xy-plane at every point and is identical in each layer (i.e., is independent of z). For each flow, what can you say about the sign of the divergence at the origin? Explain your reasoning.

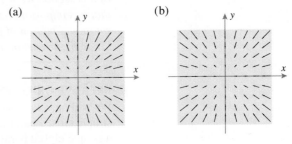

25. Let $\mathbf{F}(x, y, z)$ be a nonzero vector field in 3-space whose component functions have continuous first partial derivatives, and assume that $\text{div }\mathbf{F} = 0$ everywhere. If σ is any sphere in 3-space, explain why there are infinitely many points on σ at which $\mathbf{F}$ is tangent to the sphere.

26. Does the result in Exercise 25 remain true if the sphere σ is replaced by a cube? Explain.

27–31 Prove the identity, assuming that $\mathbf{F}$, σ, and G satisfy the hypotheses of the Divergence Theorem and that all necessary differentiability requirements for the functions $f(x, y, z)$ and $g(x, y, z)$ are met. ■

27. $\iint\limits_{\sigma} \text{curl } \mathbf{F} \cdot \mathbf{n}\, dS = 0$ [*Hint:* See Exercise 37, Section 15.1.]

28. $\iint\limits_{\sigma} \nabla f \cdot \mathbf{n}\, dS = \iiint\limits_{G} \nabla^2 f\, dV$

$$\left(\nabla^2 f = \frac{\partial^2 f}{\partial x^2} + \frac{\partial^2 f}{\partial y^2} + \frac{\partial^2 f}{\partial z^2}\right)$$

29. $\iint\limits_{\sigma} (f \nabla g) \cdot \mathbf{n}\, dS = \iiint\limits_{G} (f \nabla^2 g + \nabla f \cdot \nabla g)\, dV$

30. $\iint\limits_{\sigma} (f \nabla g - g \nabla f) \cdot \mathbf{n}\, dS = \iiint\limits_{G} (f \nabla^2 g - g \nabla^2 f)\, dV$

[*Hint:* Interchange f and g in 29.]

31. $\iint\limits_{\sigma} (f\mathbf{n}) \cdot \mathbf{v}\, dS = \iiint\limits_{G} \nabla f \cdot \mathbf{v}\, dV$ ($\mathbf{v}$ a fixed vector)

32. Use the Divergence Theorem to find all positive values of k such that

$$\mathbf{F(r)} = \frac{\mathbf{r}}{\|\mathbf{r}\|^k}$$

satisfies the condition div $\mathbf{F} = 0$ when $\mathbf{r} \neq \mathbf{0}$.
[*Hint:* Modify the proof of (11).]

33–36 Determine whether the vector field $\mathbf{F}(x, y, z)$ is free of sources and sinks. If it is not, locate them. ■

33. $\mathbf{F}(x, y, z) = (y + z)\mathbf{i} - xz^3\mathbf{j} + (x^2 \sin y)\mathbf{k}$

34. $\mathbf{F}(x, y, z) = xy\mathbf{i} - xy\mathbf{j} + y^2\mathbf{k}$

35. $\mathbf{F}(x, y, z) = x^3\mathbf{i} + y^3\mathbf{j} + z^3\mathbf{k}$

36. $\mathbf{F}(x, y, z) = (x^3 - x)\mathbf{i} + (y^3 - y)\mathbf{j} + (z^3 - z)\mathbf{k}$

C **37.** Let σ be the surface of the solid G that is enclosed by the paraboloid $z = 1 - x^2 - y^2$ and the plane $z = 0$. Use a CAS to verify Formula (1) in the Divergence Theorem for the vector field

$$\mathbf{F} = (x^2 y - z^2)\mathbf{i} + (y^3 - x)\mathbf{j} + (2x + 3z - 1)\mathbf{k}$$

by evaluating the surface integral and the triple integral.

38. Writing Discuss what it means to say that the divergence of a vector field is independent of a coordinate system. Explain how we know this to be true.

39. Writing Describe some geometrical and physical applications of the Divergence Theorem.

✔**QUICK CHECK ANSWERS 15.7**

1. $\iint\limits_{\sigma} \mathbf{F} \cdot \mathbf{n}\, dS$; $\iiint\limits_{G} \text{div } \mathbf{F}\, dV$ **2.** 3   **3.** source; sink; div $\mathbf{F} = 0$ **4.** $4\pi c$; 0

15.8   STOKES' THEOREM

In this section we will discuss a generalization of Green's Theorem to three dimensions that has important applications in the study of vector fields, particularly in the analysis of rotational motion of fluids. This theorem will also provide us with a physical interpretation of the curl of a vector field.

■ **RELATIVE ORIENTATION OF CURVES AND SURFACES**

We will be concerned in this section with oriented surfaces in 3-space that are bounded by simple closed parametric curves (Figure 15.8.1a). If σ is an oriented surface bounded by a simple closed parametric curve C, then there are two possible relationships between the orientations of σ and C, which can be described as follows. Imagine a person walking along the curve C with his or her head in the direction of the orientation of σ. The person is said to be walking in the ***positive direction*** of C relative to the orientation of σ if the surface is on the person's left (Figure 15.8.1b), and the person is said to be walking in the ***negative direction*** of C relative to the orientation of σ if the surface is on the person's right (Figure 15.8.1c). The positive direction of C establishes a right-hand relationship between the orientations of σ and C in the sense that if the fingers of the right hand are curled from the direction of C toward σ, then the thumb points (roughly) in the direction of the orientation of σ.

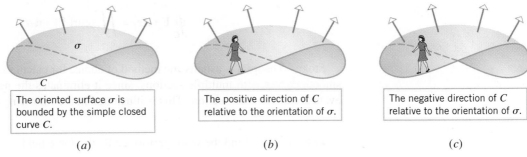

The oriented surface σ is bounded by the simple closed curve C.

The positive direction of C relative to the orientation of σ.

The negative direction of C relative to the orientation of σ.

(a)   (b)   (c)

▲ **Figure 15.8.1**

◼ STOKES' THEOREM

In Section 15.1 we defined the curl of a vector field

$$\mathbf{F}(x, y, z) = f(x, y, z)\mathbf{i} + g(x, y, z)\mathbf{j} + h(x, y, z)\mathbf{k}$$

as

$$\operatorname{curl} \mathbf{F} = \left(\frac{\partial h}{\partial y} - \frac{\partial g}{\partial z}\right)\mathbf{i} + \left(\frac{\partial f}{\partial z} - \frac{\partial h}{\partial x}\right)\mathbf{j} + \left(\frac{\partial g}{\partial x} - \frac{\partial f}{\partial y}\right)\mathbf{k} = \begin{vmatrix} \mathbf{i} & \mathbf{j} & \mathbf{k} \\ \dfrac{\partial}{\partial x} & \dfrac{\partial}{\partial y} & \dfrac{\partial}{\partial z} \\ f & g & h \end{vmatrix} \quad (1)$$

but we did not attempt to give a physical explanation of its meaning at that time. The following result, known as *Stokes' Theorem*, will provide us with a physical interpretation of the curl in the context of fluid flow.

15.8.1   THEOREM (*Stokes' Theorem*)   *Let σ be a piecewise smooth oriented surface that is bounded by a simple, closed, piecewise smooth curve C with positive orientation. If the components of the vector field*

$$\mathbf{F}(x, y, z) = f(x, y, z)\mathbf{i} + g(x, y, z)\mathbf{j} + h(x, y, z)\mathbf{k}$$

are continuous and have continuous first partial derivatives on some open set containing σ, and if $\mathbf{T}$ is the unit tangent vector to C, then

$$\oint_C \mathbf{F} \cdot \mathbf{T}\, ds = \iint_\sigma (\operatorname{curl} \mathbf{F}) \cdot \mathbf{n}\, dS \quad (2)$$

The proof of this theorem is beyond the scope of this text, so we will focus on its applications.

Recall from Formulas (30) and (34) in Section 15.2 that if $\mathbf{F}$ is a force field, the integral on the left side of (2) represents the work performed by the force field on a particle that traverses the curve C. Thus, loosely phrased, Stokes' Theorem states:

The work performed by a force field on a particle that traverses a simple, closed, piecewise smooth curve C in the positive direction can be obtained by integrating the normal component of the curl over an oriented surface σ bounded by C.

■ USING STOKES' THEOREM TO CALCULATE WORK

For computational purposes it is usually preferable to use Formula (30) in Section 15.2 to rewrite the formula in Stokes' Theorem as

$$\oint_C \mathbf{F} \cdot d\mathbf{r} = \iint_\sigma (\text{curl } \mathbf{F}) \cdot \mathbf{n} \, dS \tag{3}$$

Stokes' Theorem is usually the method of choice for calculating work around piecewise smooth curves with multiple sections, since it eliminates the need for a separate integral evaluation over each section. This is illustrated in the following example.

▶ **Example 1**   Find the work performed by the force field

$$\mathbf{F}(x, y, z) = x^2\mathbf{i} + 4xy^3\mathbf{j} + y^2x\mathbf{k}$$

on a particle that traverses the rectangle C in the plane $z = y$ shown in Figure 15.8.2.

Solution.   The work performed by the field is

$$W = \oint_C \mathbf{F} \cdot d\mathbf{r}$$

However, to evaluate this integral directly would require four separate integrations, one over each side of the rectangle. Instead, we will use Formula (3) to express the work as the surface integral

$$W = \iint_\sigma (\text{curl } \mathbf{F}) \cdot \mathbf{n} \, dS$$

in which the plane surface σ enclosed by C is assigned a *downward* orientation to make the orientation of C positive, as required by Stokes' Theorem.

Since the surface σ has equation $z = y$ and

$$\text{curl } \mathbf{F} = \begin{vmatrix} \mathbf{i} & \mathbf{j} & \mathbf{k} \\ \dfrac{\partial}{\partial x} & \dfrac{\partial}{\partial y} & \dfrac{\partial}{\partial z} \\ x^2 & 4xy^3 & xy^2 \end{vmatrix} = 2xy\mathbf{i} - y^2\mathbf{j} + 4y^3\mathbf{k}$$

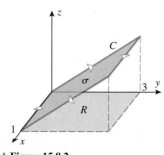

▲ **Figure 15.8.2**

George Gabriel Stokes (1819–1903) Irish mathematician and physicist. Born in Skreen, Ireland, Stokes came from a family deeply rooted in the Church of Ireland. His father was a rector, his mother the daughter of a rector, and three of his brothers took holy orders. He received his early education from his father and a local parish clerk. In 1837, he entered Pembroke College and after graduating with top honors accepted a fellowship at the college. In 1847 he was appointed Lucasian professor of mathematics at Cambridge, a position once held by Isaac Newton (and now held by the British physicist, Stephen Hawking), but one that had lost its esteem through the years. By virtue of his accomplishments, Stokes ultimately restored the position to the eminence it once held. Unfortunately, the position paid very little and Stokes was forced to teach at the Government School of Mines during the 1850s to supplement his income.

Stokes was one of several outstanding nineteenth century scientists who helped turn the physical sciences in a more empirical direction. He systematically studied hydrodynamics, elasticity of solids, behavior of waves in elastic solids, and diffraction of light. For Stokes, mathematics was a tool for his physical studies. He wrote classic papers on the motion of viscous fluids that laid the foundation for modern hydrodynamics; he elaborated on the wave theory of light; and he wrote papers on gravitational variation that established him as a founder of the modern science of geodesy.

Stokes was honored in his later years with degrees, medals, and memberships in foreign societies. He was knighted in 1889. Throughout his life, Stokes gave generously of his time to learned societies and readily assisted those who sought his help in solving problems. He was deeply religious and vitally concerned with the relationship between science and religion.

it follows from Formula (13) of Section 15.6 with curl **F** replacing **F** that

$$W = \iint_\sigma (\text{curl } \mathbf{F}) \cdot \mathbf{n} \, dS = \iint_R (\text{curl } \mathbf{F}) \cdot \left(\frac{\partial z}{\partial x}\mathbf{i} + \frac{\partial z}{\partial y}\mathbf{j} - \mathbf{k} \right) dA$$

$$= \iint_R (2xy\mathbf{i} - y^2\mathbf{j} + 4y^3\mathbf{k}) \cdot (0\mathbf{i} + \mathbf{j} - \mathbf{k}) \, dA$$

$$= \int_0^1 \int_0^3 (-y^2 - 4y^3) \, dy \, dx$$

$$= -\int_0^1 \left[\frac{y^3}{3} + y^4 \right]_{y=0}^3 dx$$

$$= -\int_0^1 90 \, dx = -90 \blacktriangleleft$$

Explain how the result in Example 1 shows that the given force field is not conservative.

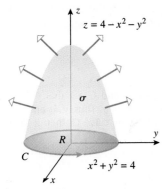

▲ **Figure 15.8.3**

► **Example 2** Verify Stokes' Theorem for the vector field $\mathbf{F}(x, y, z) = 2z\mathbf{i} + 3x\mathbf{j} + 5y\mathbf{k}$, taking σ to be the portion of the paraboloid $z = 4 - x^2 - y^2$ for which $z \geq 0$ with upward orientation, and C to be the positively oriented circle $x^2 + y^2 = 4$ that forms the boundary of σ in the xy-plane (Figure 15.8.3).

Solution. We will verify Formula (3). Since σ is oriented up, the positive orientation of C is counterclockwise looking down the positive z-axis. Thus, C can be represented parametrically (with positive orientation) by

$$x = 2\cos t, \quad y = 2\sin t, \quad z = 0 \qquad (0 \leq t \leq 2\pi) \qquad (4)$$

Therefore,

$$\oint_C \mathbf{F} \cdot d\mathbf{r} = \oint_C 2z \, dx + 3x \, dy + 5y \, dz$$

$$= \int_0^{2\pi} [0 + (6\cos t)(2\cos t) + 0] \, dt$$

$$= \int_0^{2\pi} 12\cos^2 t \, dt = 12 \left[\frac{1}{2}t + \frac{1}{4}\sin 2t \right]_0^{2\pi} = 12\pi$$

To evaluate the right side of (3), we start by finding curl **F**. We obtain

$$\text{curl } \mathbf{F} = \begin{vmatrix} \mathbf{i} & \mathbf{j} & \mathbf{k} \\ \dfrac{\partial}{\partial x} & \dfrac{\partial}{\partial y} & \dfrac{\partial}{\partial z} \\ 2z & 3x & 5y \end{vmatrix} = 5\mathbf{i} + 2\mathbf{j} + 3\mathbf{k}$$

Since σ is oriented up and is expressed in the form $z = g(x, y) = 4 - x^2 - y^2$, it follows from Formula (12) of Section 15.6 with curl $\mathbf{F}$ replacing $\mathbf{F}$ that

$$\iint\limits_{\sigma} (\text{curl } \mathbf{F}) \cdot \mathbf{n}\, dS = \iint\limits_{R} (\text{curl } \mathbf{F}) \cdot \left(-\frac{\partial z}{\partial x}\mathbf{i} - \frac{\partial z}{\partial y}\mathbf{j} + \mathbf{k} \right) dA$$

$$= \iint\limits_{R} (5\mathbf{i} + 2\mathbf{j} + 3\mathbf{k}) \cdot (2x\mathbf{i} + 2y\mathbf{j} + \mathbf{k})\, dA$$

$$= \iint\limits_{R} (10x + 4y + 3)\, dA$$

$$= \int_{0}^{2\pi} \int_{0}^{2} (10r\cos\theta + 4r\sin\theta + 3)r\, dr\, d\theta$$

$$= \int_{0}^{2\pi} \left[\frac{10r^3}{3}\cos\theta + \frac{4r^3}{3}\sin\theta + \frac{3r^2}{2} \right]_{r=0}^{2} d\theta$$

$$= \int_{0}^{2\pi} \left(\frac{80}{3}\cos\theta + \frac{32}{3}\sin\theta + 6 \right) d\theta$$

$$= \left[\frac{80}{3}\sin\theta - \frac{32}{3}\cos\theta + 6\theta \right]_{0}^{2\pi} = 12\pi$$

As guaranteed by Stokes' Theorem, the value of this surface integral is the same as the value obtained for the line integral. Note, however, that the line integral was simpler to evaluate and hence would be the method of choice in this case. ◄

REMARK   Observe that in Formula (3) the only relationships required between σ and C are that C be the boundary of σ and that C be positively oriented relative to the orientation of σ. Thus, if σ_1 and σ_2 are *different* oriented surfaces but have the *same* positively oriented boundary curve C, then it follows from (3) that

$$\iint\limits_{\sigma_1} \text{curl } \mathbf{F} \cdot \mathbf{n}\, dS = \iint\limits_{\sigma_2} \text{curl } \mathbf{F} \cdot \mathbf{n}\, dS$$

For example, the parabolic surface in Example 2 has the same positively oriented boundary C as the disk R in Figure 15.8.3 with upper orientation. Thus, the value of the surface integral in that example would not change if σ is replaced by R (or by any other oriented surface that has the positively oriented circle C as its boundary). This can be useful in computations because it is sometimes possible to circumvent a difficult integration by changing the surface of integration.

■ **RELATIONSHIP BETWEEN GREEN'S THEOREM AND STOKES' THEOREM**

It is sometimes convenient to regard a vector field

$$\mathbf{F}(x, y) = f(x, y)\mathbf{i} + g(x, y)\mathbf{j}$$

in 2-space as a vector field in 3-space by expressing it as

$$\mathbf{F}(x, y) = f(x, y)\mathbf{i} + g(x, y)\mathbf{j} + 0\mathbf{k} \tag{5}$$

If R is a region in the xy-plane enclosed by a simple, closed, piecewise smooth curve C, then we can treat R as a *flat* surface, and we can treat a surface integral over R as an ordinary double integral over R. Thus, if we orient R up and C counterclockwise looking down the positive z-axis, then Formula (3) applied to (5) yields

$$\oint_{C} \mathbf{F} \cdot d\mathbf{r} = \iint\limits_{R} \text{curl } \mathbf{F} \cdot \mathbf{k}\, dA \tag{6}$$

But

$$\text{curl }\mathbf{F} = \begin{vmatrix} \mathbf{i} & \mathbf{j} & \mathbf{k} \\ \dfrac{\partial}{\partial x} & \dfrac{\partial}{\partial y} & \dfrac{\partial}{\partial z} \\ f & g & 0 \end{vmatrix} = -\frac{\partial g}{\partial z}\mathbf{i} + \frac{\partial f}{\partial z}\mathbf{j} + \left(\frac{\partial g}{\partial x} - \frac{\partial f}{\partial y}\right)\mathbf{k} = \left(\frac{\partial g}{\partial x} - \frac{\partial f}{\partial y}\right)\mathbf{k}$$

since $\partial g/\partial z = \partial f/\partial z = 0$. Substituting this expression in (6) and expressing the integrals in terms of components yields

$$\oint_C f\,dx + g\,dy = \iint_R \left(\frac{\partial g}{\partial x} - \frac{\partial f}{\partial y}\right) dA$$

which is Green's Theorem [Formula (1) of Section 15.4]. Thus, we have shown that Green's Theorem can be viewed as a special case of Stokes' Theorem.

■ CURL VIEWED AS CIRCULATION

Stokes' Theorem provides a way of interpreting the curl of a vector field $\mathbf{F}$ in the context of fluid flow. For this purpose let σ_a be a small oriented disk of radius a centered at a point P_0 in a steady-state fluid flow, and let $\mathbf{n}$ be a unit normal vector at the center of the disk that points in the direction of orientation. Let us assume that the flow of liquid past the disk causes it to spin around the axis through $\mathbf{n}$, and let us try to find the direction of $\mathbf{n}$ that will produce the maximum rotation rate in the positive direction of the boundary curve C_a (Figure 15.8.4). For convenience, we will denote the area of the disk σ_a by $A(\sigma_a)$; that is, $A(\sigma_a) = \pi a^2$.

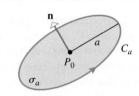

▲ **Figure 15.8.4**

If the direction of $\mathbf{n}$ is fixed, then at each point of C_a the only component of $\mathbf{F}$ that contributes to the rotation of the disk about $\mathbf{n}$ is the component $\mathbf{F} \cdot \mathbf{T}$ tangent to C_a (Figure 15.8.5). Thus, for a fixed $\mathbf{n}$ the integral

$$\oint_{C_a} \mathbf{F} \cdot \mathbf{T}\,ds \tag{7}$$

can be viewed as a measure of the tendency for the fluid to flow in the positive direction around C_a. Accordingly, (7) is called the ***circulation of*** $\mathbf{F}$ ***around*** C_a. For example, in the extreme case where the flow is normal to the circle at each point, the circulation around C_a is zero, since $\mathbf{F} \cdot \mathbf{T} = 0$ at each point. The more closely that $\mathbf{F}$ aligns with $\mathbf{T}$ along the circle, the larger the value of $\mathbf{F} \cdot \mathbf{T}$ and the larger the value of the circulation.

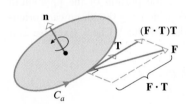

▲ **Figure 15.8.5**

To see the relationship between circulation and curl, suppose that curl $\mathbf{F}$ is continuous on σ_a, so that when σ_a is small the value of curl $\mathbf{F}$ at any point of σ_a will not vary much from the value of curl $\mathbf{F}(P_0)$ at the center. Thus, for a small disk σ_a we can reasonably approximate curl $\mathbf{F}$ on σ_a by the constant value curl $\mathbf{F}(P_0)$. Moreover, because the surface σ_a is flat, the unit normal vectors that orient σ_a are all equal. Thus, the vector quantity $\mathbf{n}$ in Formula (3) can be treated as a constant, and we can write

$$\oint_{C_a} \mathbf{F} \cdot \mathbf{T}\,ds = \iint_{\sigma_a} (\text{curl }\mathbf{F}) \cdot \mathbf{n}\,dS \approx \text{curl }\mathbf{F}(P_0) \cdot \mathbf{n} \iint_{\sigma_a} dS$$

where the line integral is taken in the positive direction of C_a. But the last double integral in this equation represents the surface area of σ_a, so

$$\oint_{C_a} \mathbf{F} \cdot \mathbf{T}\,ds \approx [\text{curl }\mathbf{F}(P_0) \cdot \mathbf{n}]A(\sigma_a)$$

from which we obtain

$$\text{curl }\mathbf{F}(P_0) \cdot \mathbf{n} \approx \frac{1}{A(\sigma_a)} \oint_{C_a} \mathbf{F} \cdot \mathbf{T}\,ds \tag{8}$$

> Formula (9) is sometimes taken as a definition of curl. This is a useful alternative to Definition 15.1.5 because it does not require a coordinate system.

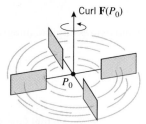

▲ **Figure 15.8.6**

The quantity on the right side of (8) is called the ***circulation density of*** **F** ***around*** C_a. If we now let the radius a of the disk approach zero (with **n** fixed), then it is plausible that the error in this approximation will approach zero and the exact value of curl $\mathbf{F}(P_0) \cdot \mathbf{n}$ will be given by

$$\operatorname{curl} \mathbf{F}(P_0) \cdot \mathbf{n} = \lim_{a \to 0} \frac{1}{A(\sigma_a)} \oint_{C_a} \mathbf{F} \cdot \mathbf{T}\, ds \qquad (9)$$

We call curl $\mathbf{F}(P_0) \cdot \mathbf{n}$ the ***circulation density of*** **F** ***at*** P_0 ***in the direction of*** **n**. This quantity has its maximum value when **n** is in the same direction as curl $\mathbf{F}(P_0)$; this tells us that *at each point in a steady-state fluid flow the maximum circulation density occurs in the direction of the curl*. Physically, this means that if a small paddle wheel is immersed in the fluid so that the pivot point is at P_0, then the paddles will turn most rapidly when the spindle is aligned with curl $\mathbf{F}(P_0)$ (Figure 15.8.6). If curl $\mathbf{F} = \mathbf{0}$ at each point of a region, then **F** is said to be ***irrotational*** in that region, since no circulation occurs about any point of the region.

✔ QUICK CHECK EXERCISES 15.8   (See page 1166 for answers.)

1. Let σ be a piecewise smooth oriented surface that is bounded by a simple, closed, piecewise smooth curve C with positive orientation. If the component functions of the vector field $\mathbf{F}(x, y, z)$ have continuous first partial derivatives on some open set containing σ, and if **T** is the unit tangent vector to C, then Stokes' Theorem states that the line integral _____ and the surface integral _____ are equal.

2. We showed in Example 2 that the vector field
$$\mathbf{F}(x, y, z) = 2z\mathbf{i} + 3x\mathbf{j} + 5y\mathbf{k}$$
satisfies the equation curl $\mathbf{F} = 5\mathbf{i} + 2\mathbf{j} + 3\mathbf{k}$. It follows from Stokes' Theorem that if C is any circle of radius a in the xy-plane that is oriented counterclockwise when viewed from the positive z-axis, then
$$\int_C \mathbf{F} \cdot \mathbf{T}\, ds = \underline{\qquad}$$
where **T** denotes the unit tangent vector to C.

3. (a) If σ_1 and σ_2 are two oriented surfaces that have the same positively oriented boundary curve C, and if the vector field $\mathbf{F}(x, y, z)$ has continuous first partial derivatives on some open set containing σ_1 and σ_2, then it follows from Stokes' Theorem that the surface integrals _____ and _____ are equal.

   (b) Let $\mathbf{F}(x, y, z) = 2z\mathbf{i} + 3x\mathbf{j} + 5y\mathbf{k}$, let a be a positive number, and let σ be the portion of the paraboloid $z = a^2 - x^2 - y^2$ for which $z \geq 0$ with upward orientation. Using part (a) and Quick Check Exercise 2, it follows that
$$\iint_\sigma (\operatorname{curl} \mathbf{F}) \cdot \mathbf{n}\, dS = \underline{\qquad}$$

4. For steady-state flow, the maximum circulation density occurs in the direction of the _____ of the velocity vector field for the flow.

EXERCISE SET 15.8   [C] CAS

1–4 Verify Formula (2) in Stokes' Theorem by evaluating the line integral and the surface integral. Assume that the surface has an upward orientation. ■

1. $\mathbf{F}(x, y, z) = (x - y)\mathbf{i} + (y - z)\mathbf{j} + (z - x)\mathbf{k}$; σ is the portion of the plane $x + y + z = 1$ in the first octant.

2. $\mathbf{F}(x, y, z) = x^2\mathbf{i} + y^2\mathbf{j} + z^2\mathbf{k}$; σ is the portion of the cone $z = \sqrt{x^2 + y^2}$ below the plane $z = 1$.

3. $\mathbf{F}(x, y, z) = x\mathbf{i} + y\mathbf{j} + z\mathbf{k}$; σ is the upper hemisphere $z = \sqrt{a^2 - x^2 - y^2}$.

4. $\mathbf{F}(x, y, z) = (z - y)\mathbf{i} + (z + x)\mathbf{j} - (x + y)\mathbf{k}$; σ is the portion of the paraboloid $z = 9 - x^2 - y^2$ above the xy-plane.

5–12 Use Stokes' Theorem to evaluate $\oint_C \mathbf{F} \cdot d\mathbf{r}$. ■

5. $\mathbf{F}(x, y, z) = z^2\mathbf{i} + 2x\mathbf{j} - y^3\mathbf{k}$; C is the circle $x^2 + y^2 = 1$ in the xy-plane with counterclockwise orientation looking down the positive z-axis.

6. $\mathbf{F}(x, y, z) = xz\mathbf{i} + 3x^2y^2\mathbf{j} + yx\mathbf{k}$; C is the rectangle in the plane $z = y$ shown in Figure 15.8.2.

7. $\mathbf{F}(x, y, z) = 3z\mathbf{i} + 4x\mathbf{j} + 2y\mathbf{k}$; C is the boundary of the paraboloid shown in Figure 15.8.3.

8. $\mathbf{F}(x, y, z) = -3y^2\mathbf{i} + 4z\mathbf{j} + 6x\mathbf{k}$; C is the triangle in the plane $z = \frac{1}{2}y$ with vertices $(2, 0, 0)$, $(0, 2, 1)$, and $(0, 0, 0)$ with a counterclockwise orientation looking down the positive z-axis.

9. $\mathbf{F}(x, y, z) = xy\mathbf{i} + x^2\mathbf{j} + z^2\mathbf{k}$; C is the intersection of the paraboloid $z = x^2 + y^2$ and the plane $z = y$ with a counterclockwise orientation looking down the positive z-axis.

10. $\mathbf{F}(x, y, z) = xy\mathbf{i} + yz\mathbf{j} + zx\mathbf{k}$; C is the triangle in the plane $x + y + z = 1$ with vertices $(1, 0, 0)$, $(0, 1, 0)$, and $(0, 0, 1)$ with a counterclockwise orientation looking from the first octant toward the origin.

11. $\mathbf{F}(x, y, z) = (x - y)\mathbf{i} + (y - z)\mathbf{j} + (z - x)\mathbf{k}$; C is the circle $x^2 + y^2 = a^2$ in the xy-plane with counterclockwise orientation looking down the positive z-axis.

12. $\mathbf{F}(x, y, z) = (z + \sin x)\mathbf{i} + (x + y^2)\mathbf{j} + (y + e^z)\mathbf{k}$; C is the intersection of the sphere $x^2 + y^2 + z^2 = 1$ and the cone $z = \sqrt{x^2 + y^2}$ with counterclockwise orientation looking down the positive z-axis.

13–16 True–False Determine whether the statement is true or false. Explain your answer. ■

13. Stokes' Theorem equates a line integral and a surface integral.

14. Stokes' Theorem is a special case of Green's Theorem.

15. The circulation of a vector field $\mathbf{F}$ around a closed curve C is defined to be
$$\int_C (\text{curl } \mathbf{F}) \cdot \mathbf{T}\, ds$$

16. If $\mathbf{F}(x, y, z)$ is defined everywhere in 3-space, and if curl $\mathbf{F}$ has no $\mathbf{k}$-component at any point in the xy-plane, then
$$\int_C \mathbf{F} \cdot \mathbf{T}\, ds = 0$$
for every smooth, simple, closed curve in the xy-plane.

17. Consider the vector field given by the formula
$$\mathbf{F}(x, y, z) = (x - z)\mathbf{i} + (y - x)\mathbf{j} + (z - xy)\mathbf{k}$$
(a) Use Stokes' Theorem to find the circulation around the triangle with vertices $A(1, 0, 0)$, $B(0, 2, 0)$, and $C(0, 0, 1)$ oriented counterclockwise looking from the origin toward the first octant.
(b) Find the circulation density of $\mathbf{F}$ at the origin in the direction of $\mathbf{k}$.
(c) Find the unit vector $\mathbf{n}$ such that the circulation density of $\mathbf{F}$ at the origin is maximum in the direction of $\mathbf{n}$.

FOCUS ON CONCEPTS

18. (a) Let σ denote the surface of a solid G with $\mathbf{n}$ the outward unit normal vector field to σ. Assume that $\mathbf{F}$ is a vector field with continuous first-order partial derivatives on σ. Prove that
$$\iint_\sigma (\text{curl } \mathbf{F}) \cdot \mathbf{n}\, dS = 0$$
[*Hint:* Let C denote a simple closed curve on σ that separates the surface into two subsurfaces σ_1 and σ_2 that share C as their common boundary. Apply Stokes' Theorem to σ_1 and to σ_2 and add the results.]
(b) The vector field curl$(\mathbf{F})$ is called the ***curl field*** of $\mathbf{F}$. In words, interpret the formula in part (a) as a statement about the flux of the curl field.

19–20 The figures in these exercises show a horizontal layer of the vector field of a fluid flow in which the flow is parallel to the xy-plane at every point and is identical in each layer (i.e., is independent of z). For each flow, state whether you believe that the curl is nonzero at the origin, and explain your reasoning. If you believe that it is nonzero, then state whether it points in the positive or negative z-direction. ■

19. (a)   (b)

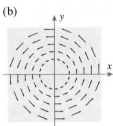

20. (a)   (b)

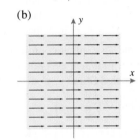

21. Let $\mathbf{F}(x, y, z)$ be a conservative vector field in 3-space whose component functions have continuous first partial derivatives. Explain how to use Formula (9) to prove that curl $\mathbf{F} = \mathbf{0}$.

22. In 1831 the physicist Michael Faraday discovered that an electric current can be produced by varying the magnetic flux through a conducting loop. His experiments showed that the electromotive force $\mathbf{E}$ is related to the magnetic induction $\mathbf{B}$ by the equation
$$\oint_C \mathbf{E} \cdot d\mathbf{r} = -\iint_\sigma \frac{\partial \mathbf{B}}{\partial t} \cdot \mathbf{n}\, dS$$
Use this result to make a conjecture about the relationship between curl $\mathbf{E}$ and $\mathbf{B}$, and explain your reasoning.

C 23. Let σ be the portion of the paraboloid $z = 1 - x^2 - y^2$ for which $z \geq 0$, and let C be the circle $x^2 + y^2 = 1$ that forms the boundary of σ in the xy-plane. Assuming that σ is oriented up, use a CAS to verify Formula (2) in Stokes' Theorem for the vector field
$$\mathbf{F} = (x^2y - z^2)\mathbf{i} + (y^3 - x)\mathbf{j} + (2x + 3z - 1)\mathbf{k}$$
by evaluating the line integral and the surface integral.

24. Writing Discuss what it means to say that the curl of a vector field is independent of a coordinate system. Explain how we know this to be true.

25. Writing Compare and contrast the Fundamental Theorem of Line Integrals, the Divergence Theorem, and Stokes' Theorem.

✔ QUICK CHECK ANSWERS 15.8

1. $\int_C \mathbf{F} \cdot \mathbf{T}\, ds$; $\iint_\sigma (\text{curl } \mathbf{F}) \cdot \mathbf{n}\, dS$ 2. $3\pi a^2$ 3. (a) $\iint_{\sigma_1} (\text{curl } \mathbf{F}) \cdot \mathbf{n}\, dS$; $\iint_{\sigma_2} (\text{curl } \mathbf{F}) \cdot \mathbf{n}\, dS$ (b) $3\pi a^2$ 4. curl

CHAPTER 15 REVIEW EXERCISES

1. In words, what is a vector field? Give some physical examples of vector fields.

2. (a) Give a physical example of an inverse-square field $\mathbf{F}(\mathbf{r})$ in 3-space.
   (b) Write a formula for a general inverse-square field $\mathbf{F}(\mathbf{r})$ in terms of the radius vector $\mathbf{r}$.
   (c) Write a formula for a general inverse-square field $\mathbf{F}(x, y, z)$ in 3-space using rectangular coordinates.

3. Find an explicit coordinate expression for the vector field $\mathbf{F}(x, y)$ that at every point $(x, y) \neq (1, 2)$ is the unit vector directed from (x, y) to $(1, 2)$.

4. Find $\nabla \left(\dfrac{x + y}{x - y} \right)$.

5. Find $\text{curl}(z\mathbf{i} + x\mathbf{j} + y\mathbf{k})$.

6. Let
$$\mathbf{F}(x, y, z) = \frac{x}{x^2 + y^2}\mathbf{i} + \frac{y}{x^2 + y^2}\mathbf{j} + \frac{z}{x^2 + y^2}\mathbf{k}$$
Sketch the level surface div $\mathbf{F} = 1$.

7. Assume that C is the parametric curve $x = x(t)$, $y = y(t)$, where t varies from a to b. In each part, express the line integral as a definite integral with variable of integration t.
   (a) $\displaystyle\int_C f(x, y)\, dx + g(x, y)\, dy$ (b) $\displaystyle\int_C f(x, y)\, ds$

8. (a) Express the mass M of a thin wire in 3-space as a line integral.
   (b) Express the length of a curve as a line integral.

9. Give a physical interpretation of $\int_C \mathbf{F} \cdot \mathbf{T}\, ds$.

10. State some alternative notations for $\int_C \mathbf{F} \cdot \mathbf{T}\, ds$.

11–13 Evaluate the line integral. ■

11. $\displaystyle\int_C (x - y)\, ds$; $C : x^2 + y^2 = 1$

12. $\displaystyle\int_C x\, dx + z\, dy - 2y^2\, dz$;
$C : x = \cos t,\ y = \sin t,\ z = t\quad (0 \le t \le 2\pi)$

13. $\displaystyle\int_C \mathbf{F} \cdot d\mathbf{r}$ where $\mathbf{F}(x, y) = (x/y)\mathbf{i} - (y/x)\mathbf{j}$;
$\mathbf{r}(t) = t\mathbf{i} + 2t\mathbf{j}\quad (1 \le t \le 2)$

14. Find the work done by the force field
$$\mathbf{F}(x, y) = y^2\mathbf{i} + xy\mathbf{j}$$

moving a particle from $(0, 0)$ to $(1, 1)$ along the parabola $y = x^2$.

15. State the Fundamental Theorem of Line Integrals, including all required hypotheses.

16. Evaluate $\int_C \nabla f \cdot d\mathbf{r}$ where $f(x, y, z) = xy^2z^3$ and
$$\mathbf{r}(t) = t\mathbf{i} + (t^2 + t)\mathbf{j} + \sin(3\pi t/2)\mathbf{k}\quad (0 \le t \le 1)$$

17. Let $\mathbf{F}(x, y) = y\mathbf{i} - 2x\mathbf{j}$.
   (a) Find a nonzero function $h(x)$ such that $h(x)\mathbf{F}(x, y)$ is a conservative vector field.
   (b) Find a nonzero function $g(y)$ such that $g(y)\mathbf{F}(x, y)$ is a conservative vector field.

18. Let $\mathbf{F}(x, y) = (ye^{xy} - 1)\mathbf{i} + xe^{xy}\mathbf{j}$.
   (a) Show that $\mathbf{F}$ is a conservative vector field.
   (b) Find a potential function for $\mathbf{F}$.
   (c) Find the work performed by the force field on a particle that moves along the sawtooth curve represented by the parametric equations
$$x = t + \sin^{-1}(\sin t)$$
$$y = (2/\pi)\sin^{-1}(\sin t)\qquad (0 \le t \le 8\pi)$$
   (see the accompanying figure).

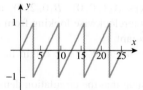

◀ Figure Ex-18

19. State Green's Theorem, including all of the required hypotheses.

20. Express the area of a plane region as a line integral.

21. Let α and β denote angles that satisfy $0 < \beta - \alpha \le 2\pi$ and assume that $r = f(\theta)$ is a smooth polar curve with $f(\theta) > 0$ on the interval $[\alpha, \beta]$. Use the formula
$$A = \frac{1}{2}\int_C -y\, dx + x\, dy$$
to find the area of the region R enclosed by the curve $r = f(\theta)$ and the rays $\theta = \alpha$ and $\theta = \beta$.

22. (a) Use Green's Theorem to prove that
$$\int_C f(x)\, dx + g(y)\, dy = 0$$

if f and g are differentiable functions and C is a simple, closed, piecewise smooth curve.

(b) What does this tell you about the vector field
$$\mathbf{F}(x, y) = f(x)\mathbf{i} + g(y)\mathbf{j}?$$

23. Assume that σ is the parametric surface
$$\mathbf{r} = x(u, v)\mathbf{i} + y(u, v)\mathbf{j} + z(u, v)\mathbf{k}$$

where (u, v) varies over a region R. Express the surface integral
$$\iint_\sigma f(x, y, z)\, dS$$

as a double integral with variables of integration u and v.

24. Evaluate $\iint_\sigma z\, dS$; $\sigma : x^2 + y^2 = 1\ (0 \le z \le 1)$.

25. Do you think that the surface in the accompanying figure is orientable? Explain your reasoning.

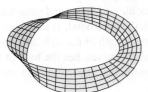

◀ Figure Ex-25

26. Give a physical interpretation of $\iint_\sigma \mathbf{F} \cdot \mathbf{n}\, dS$.

27. Find the flux of $\mathbf{F}(x, y, z) = x\mathbf{i} + y\mathbf{j} + 2z\mathbf{k}$ through the portion of the paraboloid $z = 1 - x^2 - y^2$ that is on or above the xy-plane, with upward orientation.

28. Find the flux of $\mathbf{F}(x, y, z) = x\mathbf{i} + 2y\mathbf{j} + 3z\mathbf{k}$ through the unit sphere centered at the origin with outward orientation.

29. State the Divergence Theorem and Stokes' Theorem, including all required hypotheses.

30. Let G be a solid with the surface σ oriented by outward unit normals, suppose that ϕ has continuous first and second partial derivatives in some open set containing G, and let $D_\mathbf{n}\phi$ be the directional derivative of ϕ, where $\mathbf{n}$ is an outward unit normal to σ. Show that
$$\iint_\sigma D_\mathbf{n}\phi\, dS = \iiint_G \left[\frac{\partial^2 \phi}{\partial x^2} + \frac{\partial^2 \phi}{\partial y^2} + \frac{\partial^2 \phi}{\partial z^2} \right] dV$$

31. Let σ be the sphere $x^2 + y^2 + z^2 = 1$, let $\mathbf{n}$ be an inward unit normal, and let $D_\mathbf{n} f$ be the directional derivative of $f(x, y, z) = x^2 + y^2 + z^2$. Use the result in Exercise 30 to evaluate the surface integral
$$\iint_\sigma D_\mathbf{n} f\, dS$$

32. Use Stokes' Theorem to evaluate $\iint_\sigma \text{curl } \mathbf{F} \cdot \mathbf{n}\, dS$ where $\mathbf{F}(x, y, z) = (z - y)\mathbf{i} + (x + z)\mathbf{j} - (x + y)\mathbf{k}$ and σ is the portion of the paraboloid $z = 2 - x^2 - y^2$ on or above the plane $z = 1$, with upward orientation.

33. Let $\mathbf{F}(x, y, z) = f(x, y, z)\mathbf{i} + g(x, y, z)\mathbf{j} + h(x, y, z)\mathbf{k}$ and suppose that f, g, and h are continuous and have continuous first partial derivatives in a region. It was shown in Exercise 31 of Section 15.3 that if $\mathbf{F}$ is conservative in the region, then
$$\frac{\partial f}{\partial y} = \frac{\partial g}{\partial x}, \quad \frac{\partial f}{\partial z} = \frac{\partial h}{\partial x}, \quad \frac{\partial g}{\partial z} = \frac{\partial h}{\partial y}$$

there. Use this result to show that if $\mathbf{F}$ is conservative in an open spherical region, then curl $\mathbf{F} = \mathbf{0}$ in that region.

34–35 With the aid of Exercise 33, determine whether $\mathbf{F}$ is conservative. ■

34. (a) $\mathbf{F}(x, y, z) = z^2\mathbf{i} + e^{-y}\mathbf{j} + 2xz\mathbf{k}$
    (b) $\mathbf{F}(x, y, z) = xy\mathbf{i} + x^2\mathbf{j} + \sin z\mathbf{k}$

35. (a) $\mathbf{F}(x, y, z) = \sin x\mathbf{i} + z\mathbf{j} + y\mathbf{k}$
    (b) $\mathbf{F}(x, y, z) = z\mathbf{i} + 2yz\mathbf{j} + y^2\mathbf{k}$

36. As discussed in Example 1 of Section 15.1, *Coulomb's law* states that the electrostatic force $\mathbf{F}(\mathbf{r})$ that a particle of charge Q exerts on a particle of charge q is given by the formula
$$\mathbf{F}(\mathbf{r}) = \frac{qQ}{4\pi\epsilon_0 \|\mathbf{r}\|^3}\mathbf{r}$$

where $\mathbf{r}$ is the radius vector from Q to q and ϵ_0 is the permittivity constant.

(a) Express the vector field $\mathbf{F}(\mathbf{r})$ in coordinate form $\mathbf{F}(x, y, z)$ with Q at the origin.

(b) Find the work performed by the force field $\mathbf{F}$ on a charge q that moves along a straight line from $(3, 0, 0)$ to $(3, 1, 5)$.

CHAPTER 15 MAKING CONNECTIONS

Assume that the motion of a particle of mass m is described by a smooth vector-valued function

$$\mathbf{r}(t) = x(t)\mathbf{i} + y(t)\mathbf{j} + z(t)\mathbf{k} \quad (a \le t \le b)$$

where t denotes time. Let C denote the graph of the vector-valued function and let $v(t)$ and $\mathbf{a}(t)$ denote the respective speed and acceleration of the particle at time t.

1. We will say that the particle is moving "freely" under the influence of a force field $\mathbf{F}(x, y, z)$, provided $\mathbf{F}$ is the *only* force acting on the particle. In this case Newton's Second Law of Motion becomes

$$\mathbf{F}(x(t), y(t), z(t)) = m\mathbf{a}(t)$$

Use Theorem 12.6.2 to prove that when the particle is moving freely

$$\int_C \mathbf{F} \cdot \mathbf{T}\, ds = \int_C m\left(\frac{dv}{dt}\right) ds = m \int_a^b v(t)\left(\frac{dv}{dt}\right) dt$$

$$= m \int_a^b \frac{d}{dt}\left(\frac{1}{2}[v(t)]^2\right) dt$$

$$= \frac{1}{2}m[v(b)]^2 - \frac{1}{2}m[v(a)]^2$$

This tells us that the work performed by $\mathbf{F}$ on the particle is equal to the change in kinetic energy of the particle.

2. Suppose that the particle moves along a *prescribed* curve C under the influence of a force field $\mathbf{F}(x, y, z)$. In addition to $\mathbf{F}$, the particle will experience a concurrent "support force" $\mathbf{S}(x(t), y(t), z(t))$ from the curve. (Imagine a roller-coaster car falling without friction under the influence of the gravitational force $\mathbf{F}$. The tracks of the coaster provide the support force $\mathbf{S}$.) In this case we will say that the particle has a "constrained" motion under the influence of $\mathbf{F}$. Prove that the work performed by $\mathbf{F}$ on a particle with constrained motion is also equal to the change in kinetic energy of the particle. [*Hint:* Apply the argument of Exercise 1 to the resultant force $\mathbf{F} + \mathbf{S}$ on the particle. Use the fact that at each point on C, $\mathbf{S}$ will be normal to the curve.]

3. Suppose that $\mathbf{F}$ is a conservative force field. Use Exercises 1 and 2, along with the discussion in Section 15.3, to develop the conservation of energy principle for both free and constrained motion under $\mathbf{F}$.

4. As shown in the accompanying figure, a girl with mass m is sliding down a smooth (frictionless) playground slide that is inclined at an angle of θ with the horizontal. If the acceleration due to gravity is g and the length of the slide is l, prove that the speed of the child when she reaches the base of the slide is $v = \sqrt{2gl \sin \theta}$. Assume that she starts from rest at the top of the slide.

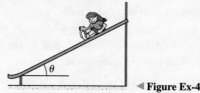

◀ **Figure Ex-4**

EXPANDING THE CALCULUS HORIZON

To learn how the topics in this chapter can be used to model hurricane behavior, see the module entitled **Hurricane Modeling** at:

www.wiley.com/college/anton

ANSWERS TO ODD-NUMBERED EXERCISES

1. **(a)** $(0, 0, 0)$, $(3, 0, 0)$, $(3, 5, 0)$, $(0, 5, 0)$, $(0, 0, 4)$, $(3, 0, 4)$, $(3, 5, 4)$, $(0, 5, 4)$
   (b) $(0, 1, 0)$, $(4, 1, 0)$, $(4, 6, 0)$, $(0, 6, 0)$, $(0, 1, -2)$, $(4, 1, -2)$, $(4, 6, -2)$, $(0, 6, -2)$
3. $(4, 2, -2)$, $(4, 2, 1)$, $(4, 1, 1)$, $(4, 1, -2)$, $(-6, 1, 1)$, $(-6, 2, 1)$, $(-6, 2, -2)$, $(-6, 1, -2)$

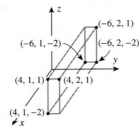

5. **(a)** point **(b)** line parallel to the y-axis
   (c) plane parallel to the yz-plane
9. radius $\sqrt{74}$, center $(2, 1, -4)$ 11. **(b)** $(2, 1, 6)$ **(c)** area 49
13. **(a)** $(x - 1)^2 + y^2 + (z + 1)^2 = 16$
    (b) $(x + 1)^2 + (y - 3)^2 + (z - 2)^2 = 14$
    (c) $\left(x + \frac{1}{2}\right)^2 + (y - 2)^2 + (z - 2)^2 = \frac{5}{4}$
15. $(x - 2)^2 + (y + 1)^2 + (z + 3)^2 = r^2$;
    (a) $r^2 = 9$ **(b)** $r^2 = 1$ **(c)** $r^2 = 4$

Responses to True–False questions may be abridged to save space.
19. False; see Figure 11.1.6.
21. True; see Figure 11.1.3.
23. sphere, center $(-5, -2, -1)$, radius 7
25. sphere; center $\left(\frac{1}{2}, \frac{3}{4}, -\frac{5}{4}\right)$, radius $\dfrac{3\sqrt{6}}{4}$
27. no graph
29. **(a)**   **(b)**   **(c)**

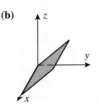 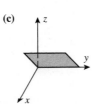

31. **(a)**   **(b)**   **(c)**

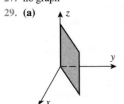
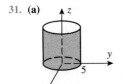

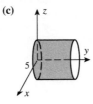

33. **(a)** $-2y + z = 0$ **(b)** $-2x + z = 0$ **(c)** $(x - 1)^2 + (y - 1)^2 = 1$
    (d) $(x - 1)^2 + (z - 1)^2 = 1$
35.   37.

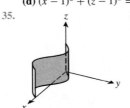
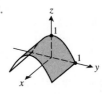

39.   41.

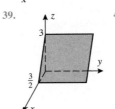
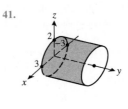

43.

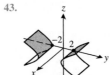

45.

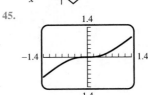
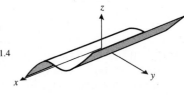

47. largest distance, $3 + \sqrt{6}$; smallest distance, $3 - \sqrt{6}$
49. all points outside the circular cylinder $(y + 3)^2 + (z - 2)^2 = 16$
51. $r = (2 - \sqrt{3})R$ 53. **(b)** $y^2 + z^2 = e^{2x}$

1. **(a-c)**   **(d-f)**

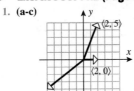
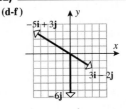

A1

3. **(a,b)** **(c,d)**

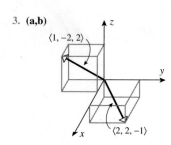 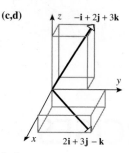

5. **(a)** $\langle 3, -4 \rangle$ **(b)** $\langle -2, -3, 4 \rangle$

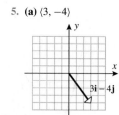 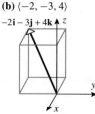

7. **(a)** $\langle -1, 3 \rangle$ **(b)** $\langle -7, 2 \rangle$ **(c)** $\langle -3, 6, 1 \rangle$

9. **(a)** $\langle 4, -4 \rangle$ **(b)** $\langle 8, -1, -3 \rangle$

11. **(a)** $-\mathbf{i} + 4\mathbf{j} - 2\mathbf{k}$ **(b)** $18\mathbf{i} + 12\mathbf{j} - 6\mathbf{k}$ **(c)** $-\mathbf{i} - 5\mathbf{j} - 2\mathbf{k}$
    (d) $40\mathbf{i} - 4\mathbf{j} - 4\mathbf{k}$ **(e)** $-2\mathbf{i} - 16\mathbf{j} - 18\mathbf{k}$ **(f)** $-\mathbf{i} + 13\mathbf{j} - 2\mathbf{k}$

13. **(a)** $\sqrt{2}$ **(b)** $5\sqrt{2}$ **(c)** $\sqrt{21}$ **(d)** $\sqrt{14}$

15. **(a)** $2\sqrt{3}$ **(b)** $\sqrt{14} + \sqrt{2}$ **(c)** $2\sqrt{14} + 2\sqrt{2}$ **(d)** $2\sqrt{37}$
    (e) $(1/\sqrt{6})\mathbf{i} + (1/\sqrt{6})\mathbf{j} - (2/\sqrt{6})\mathbf{k}$ **(f)** 1

Responses to True–False questions may be abridged to save space.

17. False; $\|\mathbf{i} + \mathbf{j}\| = \sqrt{2} \neq 1 + 1 = 2$

19. True; one in the same direction and one in the opposite direction.

21. **(a)** $(-1/\sqrt{17})\mathbf{i} + (4/\sqrt{17})\mathbf{j}$ **(b)** $(-3\mathbf{i} + 2\mathbf{j} - \mathbf{k})/\sqrt{14}$
    (c) $(4\mathbf{i} + \mathbf{j} - \mathbf{k})/(3\sqrt{2})$

23. **(a)** $\langle -\frac{3}{2}, 2 \rangle$ **(b)** $\dfrac{1}{\sqrt{5}} \langle 7, 0, -6 \rangle$

25. **(a)** $\langle 3\sqrt{2}/2, 3\sqrt{2}/2 \rangle$ **(b)** $\langle 0, 2 \rangle$ **(c)** $\langle -5/2, 5\sqrt{3}/2 \rangle$ **(d)** $\langle -1, 0 \rangle$

27. $\langle (\sqrt{3} - \sqrt{2})/2, (1 + \sqrt{2})/2 \rangle$

29. **(a)** $\langle -2, 5 \rangle$ **(b)** $\langle 3, -8 \rangle$

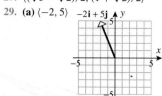 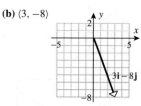

31. $\langle -\frac{2}{3}, 1 \rangle$ 33. $\mathbf{u} = \frac{5}{7}\mathbf{i} + \frac{2}{7}\mathbf{j} + \frac{1}{7}\mathbf{k}$, $\mathbf{v} = \frac{8}{7}\mathbf{i} - \frac{1}{7}\mathbf{j} - \frac{4}{7}\mathbf{k}$

35. $\sqrt{5}, 3$ 37. **(a)** $\pm\frac{5}{3}$ **(b)** 3

39. **(a)** $\langle 1/\sqrt{10}, 3/\sqrt{10} \rangle, \langle -1/\sqrt{10}, -3/\sqrt{10} \rangle$
    (b) $\langle 1/\sqrt{2}, -1/\sqrt{2} \rangle, \langle -1/\sqrt{2}, 1/\sqrt{2} \rangle$ **(c)** $\pm\dfrac{1}{\sqrt{26}} \langle 5, 1 \rangle$

41. **(a)** the circle of radius 1 about the origin
    (b) the closed disk of radius 1 about the origin
    (c) all points outside the closed disk of radius 1 about the origin

43. **(a)** the (hollow) sphere of radius 1 about the origin
    (b) the closed ball of radius 1 about the origin
    (c) all points outside the closed ball of radius 1 about the origin

45. magnitude $= 30\sqrt{5}$ lb, $\theta \approx 26.57°$

47. magnitude ≈ 207.06 N, $\theta = 45°$

49. magnitude ≈ 94.995 N, $\theta \approx 28.28°$

51. magnitude ≈ 9.165 lb, angle $\approx -70.890°$

53. ≈ 183.02 lb, 224.13 lb

55. **(a)** $c_1 = -2, c_2 = 1$

▶ **Exercise Set 11.3 (Page 792)** _____

1. **(a)** $-10; \cos\theta = -1/\sqrt{5}$ **(b)** $-3; \cos\theta = -3/\sqrt{58}$
   (c) $0; \cos\theta = 0$ **(d)** $-20; \cos\theta = -20/(3\sqrt{70})$

3. **(a)** obtuse   **(b)** acute   **(c)** obtuse   **(d)** orthogonal

5. $\sqrt{2}/2, 0, -\sqrt{2}/2, -1, -\sqrt{2}/2, 0, \sqrt{2}/2$

7. **(a)** vertex B **(b)** $82°, 60°, 38°$ 13. $r = 7/5$

15. **(a)** $\alpha = \beta \approx 55°, \gamma \approx 125°$ **(b)** $\alpha \approx 48°, \beta \approx 132°, \gamma \approx 71°$

19. **(a)** $\approx 35°$ **(b)** $90°$

21. $64°, 41°, 60°$ 23. $71°, 61°, 36°$

25. **(a)** $\left\langle \dfrac{2}{3}, \dfrac{4}{3}, \dfrac{4}{3} \right\rangle, \left\langle \dfrac{4}{3}, -\dfrac{7}{3}, \dfrac{5}{3} \right\rangle$
    (b) $\left\langle -\dfrac{74}{49}, -\dfrac{111}{49}, \dfrac{222}{49} \right\rangle, \left\langle \dfrac{270}{49}, \dfrac{62}{49}, \dfrac{121}{49} \right\rangle$

27. **(a)** $\langle 1, 1 \rangle + \langle -4, 4 \rangle$ **(b)** $\left\langle 0, -\dfrac{8}{5}, \dfrac{4}{5} \right\rangle + \left\langle -2, \dfrac{13}{5}, \dfrac{26}{5} \right\rangle$
    (c) $\mathbf{v} = \langle 1, 4, 1 \rangle$ is orthogonal to $\mathbf{b}$.

Responses to True–False questions may be abridged to save space.

29. True; $\mathbf{v} + \mathbf{w} = \mathbf{0}$ implies $0 = \mathbf{v} \cdot (\mathbf{v} + \mathbf{w}) = \|\mathbf{v}\|^2 \neq 0$,
    a contradiction.

31. True; see Equation (12).   33. $\sqrt{564/29}$ 35. 169.8 N

37. $-5\sqrt{3}$ J   45. **(a)** $40°$ **(b)** $x \approx -0.682328$

▶ **Exercise Set 11.4 (Page 803)** _____

1. **(a)** $-\mathbf{j} + \mathbf{k}$ 3. $\langle 7, 10, 9 \rangle$ 5. $\langle -4, -6, -3 \rangle$

7. **(a)** $\langle -20, -67, -9 \rangle$ **(b)** $\langle -78, 52, -26 \rangle$
   (c) $\langle 0, -56, -392 \rangle$ **(d)** $\langle 0, 56, 392 \rangle$

9. $\dfrac{1}{\sqrt{2}}, -\dfrac{1}{\sqrt{2}}, 0$ 11. $\pm\dfrac{1}{\sqrt{6}} \langle 2, 1, 1 \rangle$

Responses to True–False questions may be abridged to save space.

13. True; see Theorem 11.4.5(c).

15. False; let $\mathbf{v} = \mathbf{u} = \mathbf{i}$ and let $\mathbf{w} = 2\mathbf{i}$.

17. $\sqrt{59}$ 19. $\sqrt{374}/2$

21. 80 23. -3 25. 16 27. **(a)** yes   **(b)** yes   **(c)** no

29. **(a)** 9 **(b)** $\sqrt{122}$ **(c)** $\sin^{-1}\left(\dfrac{9}{14}\right)$

31. **(a)** $2\sqrt{141/29}$ **(b)** $6/\sqrt{5}$ 33. $\dfrac{2}{3}$ 37. $\theta = \pi/4$

39. **(a)** $10\sqrt{2}$ lb·ft, direction of rotation about P is counterclockwise
    looking along $\overrightarrow{PQ} \times \mathbf{F} = -10\mathbf{i} + 10\mathbf{k}$ toward its initial point
    (b) 10 lb·ft, direction of rotation about P is counterclockwise
    looking along $-10\mathbf{i}$ toward its initial point
    (c) 0 lb·ft, no rotation about P

41. ≈ 36.19 N·m   45. $-8\mathbf{i} - 20\mathbf{j} + 2\mathbf{k}, -8\mathbf{i} - 8\mathbf{k}$ 49. 1.887850

▶ **Exercise Set 11.5 (Page 810)** _____

1. **(a)** $L_1: x = 1, y = t, L_2: x = t, y = 1, L_3: x = t, y = t$
   (b) $L_1: x = 1, y = 1, z = t, L_2: x = t, y = 1, z = 1,$
   $L_3: x = 1, y = t, z = 1, L_4: x = t, y = t, z = t$

3. **(a)** $x = 3 + 2t, y = -2 + 3t$; line segment: $0 \leq t \leq 1$
   (b) $x = 5 - 3t, y = -2 + 6t, z = 1 + t$; line segment: $0 \leq t \leq 1$

5. **(a)** $x = 2 + t, y = -3 - 4t$ **(b)** $x = t, y = -t, z = 1 + t$

7. **(a)** $P(2, -1), \mathbf{v} = 4\mathbf{i} - \mathbf{j}$ **(b)** $P(-1, 2, 4), \mathbf{v} = 5\mathbf{i} + 7\mathbf{j} - 8\mathbf{k}$

9. **(a)** $\langle -3, 4 \rangle + t \langle 1, 5 \rangle; -3\mathbf{i} + 4\mathbf{j} + t(\mathbf{i} + 5\mathbf{j})$
   (b) $\langle 2, -3, 0 \rangle + t \langle -1, 5, 1 \rangle; 2\mathbf{i} - 3\mathbf{j} + t(-\mathbf{i} + 5\mathbf{j} + \mathbf{k})$

Responses to True–False questions may be abridged to save space.

11. False; the lines could be skew.

13. False; see part (b) of the solution to Example 3.

15. $x = -5 + 2t, y = 2 - 3t$ 17. $x = 3 + 4t, y = -4 + 3t$

19. $x = -1 + 3t, y = 2 - 4t, z = 4 + t$

21. $x = -2 + 2t, y = -t, z = 5 + 2t$

23. **(a)** $x = 7$ **(b)** $y = \dfrac{7}{3}$ **(c)** $x = \dfrac{-1 \pm \sqrt{85}}{6}, y = \dfrac{43 \mp \sqrt{85}}{18}$

25. $(-2, 10, 0)$; $(-2, 0, -5)$; The line does not intersect the yz-plane.

27. $(0, 4, -2)$, $(4, 0, 6)$ 29. $(1, -1, 2)$ 33. The lines are parallel.

35. The points do not lie on the same line.

39. $\langle x, y \rangle = \langle -1, 2 \rangle + t \langle 1, 1 \rangle$

41. the point $1/n$ of the way from $(-2, 0)$ to $(1, 3)$

43. the line segment joining the points $(1, 0)$ and $(-3, 6)$

45. $(5, 2)$ 47. $2\sqrt{5}$ 49. distance $= \sqrt{35/6}$

51. **(a)** $x = x_0 + (x_1 - x_0)t$, $y = y_0 + (y_1 - y_0)t$, $z = z_0 + (z_1 - z_0)t$

 (b) $x = x_1 + at$, $y = y_1 + bt$, $z = z_1 + ct$

53. **(b)** $\langle x, y, z \rangle = \langle 1 + 2t, -3 + 4t, 5 + t \rangle$

55. **(b)** $84°$ **(c)** $x = 7 + t$, $y = -1$, $z = -2 + t$

57. $x = t$, $y = 2 + t$, $z = 1 - t$

59. **(a)** $\sqrt{17}$ cm **(b)** 10 **(d)** $\sqrt{14}/2$ cm

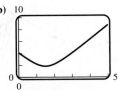

▶ Exercise Set 11.6 (Page 819)

1. $x = 3$, $y = 4$, $z = 5$ 3. $x + 4y + 2z = 28$ 5. $z = 0$

7. $x - y = 0$ 9. $y + z = 1$ 11. $2y - z = 1$

13. **(a)** parallel **(b)** perpendicular **(c)** neither

15. **(a)** parallel **(b)** neither **(c)** perpendicular

17. **(a)** point of intersection is $\left(\frac{5}{2}, \frac{5}{2}, \frac{5}{2}\right)$ **(b)** no intersection

19. $35°$

Responses to True–False questions may be abridged to save space.

21. True; each will be the negative of the other.

23. True; the direction vector of L must be orthogonal to both normal vectors.

25. $4x - 2y + 7z = 0$ 27. $4x - 13y + 21z = -14$

29. $x + y - 3z = 6$ 31. $x + 5y + 3z = -6$

33. $x + 2y + 4z = \frac{29}{2}$ 35. $x = 5 - 2t$, $y = 5t$, $z = -2 + 11t$

37. $7x + y + 9z = 25$ 39. yes

41. $x = -\frac{11}{7} - 23t$, $y = -\frac{12}{7} + t$, $z = -7t$

43. $\frac{5}{3}$ 45. $5/\sqrt{54}$ 47. $25/\sqrt{126}$

49. $(x - 2)^2 + (y - 1)^2 + (z + 3)^2 = \frac{121}{14}$ 51. $5/\sqrt{12}$

▶ Exercise Set 11.7 (Page 830)

1. **(a)** elliptic paraboloid, $a = 2$, $b = 3$

 (b) hyperbolic paraboloid, $a = 1$, $b = 5$

 (c) hyperboloid of one sheet, $a = b = c = 4$

 (d) circular cone, $a = b = 1$ **(e)** elliptic paraboloid, $a = 2$, $b = 1$

 (f) hyperboloid of two sheets, $a = b = c = 1$

3. **(a)** $-z = x^2 + y^2$, circular paraboloid opening down the negative z-axis

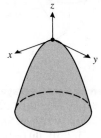

(b) $z = x^2 + y^2$, circular paraboloid, no change

(c) $z = x^2 + y^2$, circular paraboloid, no change

(d) $z = x^2 + y^2$, circular paraboloid, no change

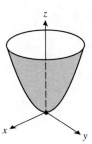

(e) $x = y^2 + z^2$, circular paraboloid opening along the positive x-axis

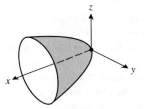

(f) $y = x^2 + z^2$, circular paraboloid opening along the positive y-axis

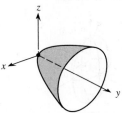

5. **(a)** hyperboloid of one sheet, axis is y-axis

 (b) hyperboloid of two sheets separated by yz-plane

 (c) elliptic paraboloid opening along the positive x-axis

 (d) elliptic cone with x-axis as axis

 (e) hyperbolic paraboloid straddling the x-axis

 (f) paraboloid opening along the negative y-axis

7. **(a)** $x = 0$: $\dfrac{y^2}{25} + \dfrac{z^2}{4} = 1$;

 $y = 0$: $\dfrac{x^2}{9} + \dfrac{z^2}{4} = 1$;

 $z = 0$: $\dfrac{x^2}{9} + \dfrac{y^2}{25} = 1$

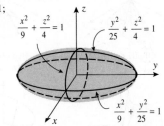

(b) $x = 0$: $z = 4y^2$;

 $y = 0$: $z = x^2$;

 $z = 0$: $x = y = 0$

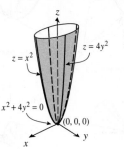

(c) $x = 0$: $\dfrac{y^2}{16} - \dfrac{z^2}{4} = 1$;

$y = 0$: $\dfrac{x^2}{9} - \dfrac{z^2}{4} = 1$;

$z = 0$: $\dfrac{x^2}{9} + \dfrac{y^2}{16} = 1$

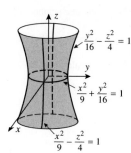

9. **(a)** $4x^2 + z^2 = 3$; ellipse   **(b)** $y^2 + z^2 = 3$; circle
(c) $y^2 + z^2 = 20$; circle   **(d)** $9x^2 - y^2 = 20$; hyperbola
(e) $z = 9x^2 + 16$; parabola   **(f)** $9x^2 + 4y^2 = 4$; ellipse

Responses to True–False questions may be abridged to save space.

11. False; "quadric" refers to second powers.

13. False; there need not exist a line such that all cross sections orthogonal to the line are circular.

15.

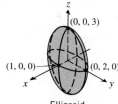

Ellipsoid

17.

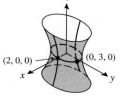

Hyperboloid
of one sheet

19.

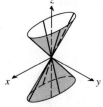

Elliptic cone

21.

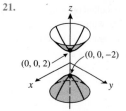

Hyperboloid
of two sheets

23.

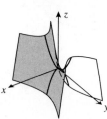

Hyperbolic paraboloid

25.

Elliptic paraboloid

27.

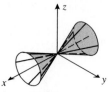

Circular cone

29.

Hyperboloid
of one sheet

31.

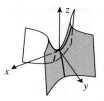

Hyperbolic
paraboloid

33.

35.

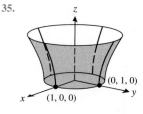

37.

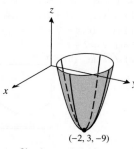

Circular paraboloid

39.

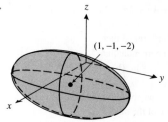

Ellipsoid

41. **(a)** $\dfrac{x^2}{9} + \dfrac{y^2}{4} = 1$ **(b)** $6, 4$ **(c)** $(\pm\sqrt{5}, 0, \sqrt{2})$
(d) The focal axis is parallel to the x-axis.

43. **(a)** $\dfrac{y^2}{4} - \dfrac{x^2}{4} = 1$ **(b)** $(0, \pm 2, 4)$ **(c)** $(0, \pm 2\sqrt{2}, 4)$
(d) The focal axis is parallel to the y-axis.

45. **(a)** $z + 4 = y^2$ **(b)** $(2, 0, -4)$ **(c)** $\left(2, 0, -\tfrac{15}{4}\right)$
(d) The focal axis is parallel to the z-axis.

47. circle of radius $\sqrt{2}$ in the plane $z = 2$, centered at $(0, 0, 2)$

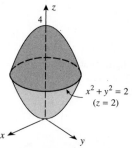

49. $y = 4(x^2 + z^2)$ **51.** $z = (x^2 + y^2)/4$ (circular paraboloid)

▶ **Exercise Set 11.8 (Page 837)**

1. **(a)** $(8, \pi/6, -4)$ **(b)** $(5\sqrt{2}, 3\pi/4, 6)$
(c) $(2, \pi/2, 0)$ **(d)** $(8, 5\pi/3, 6)$

3. **(a)** $(2\sqrt{3}, 2, 3)$ **(b)** $(-4\sqrt{2}, 4\sqrt{2}, -2)$
(c) $(5, 0, 4)$ **(d)** $(-7, 0, -9)$

5. **(a)** $(2\sqrt{2}, \pi/3, 3\pi/4)$ **(b)** $(2, 7\pi/4, \pi/4)$
(c) $(6, \pi/2, \pi/3)$ **(d)** $(10, 5\pi/6, \pi/2)$

7. **(a)** $(5\sqrt{6}/4, 5\sqrt{2}/4, 5\sqrt{2}/2)$ **(b)** $(7, 0, 0)$
    (c) $(0, 0, 1)$ **(d)** $(0, -2, 0)$
9. **(a)** $(2\sqrt{3}, \pi/6, \pi/6)$ **(b)** $(\sqrt{2}, \pi/4, 3\pi/4)$
    (c) $(2, 3\pi/4, \pi/2)$ **(d)** $(4\sqrt{3}, 1, 2\pi/3)$
11. **(a)** $(5\sqrt{3}/2, \pi/4, -5/2)$ **(b)** $(0, 7\pi/6, -1)$
    (c) $(0, 0, 3)$ **(d)** $(4, \pi/6, 0)$

Responses to True–False questions may be abridged to save space.
15. True; see Figure 11.8.1*b*.
17. True; see Figures 11.8.3 and 11.8.4.
19.

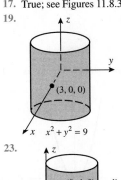

$x^2 + y^2 = 9$

21.

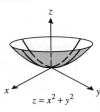

$z = x^2 + y^2$

23.

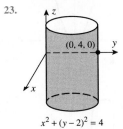

$x^2 + (y-2)^2 = 4$

25.

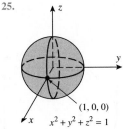

$x^2 + y^2 + z^2 = 1$

27.

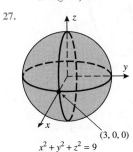

$x^2 + y^2 + z^2 = 9$

29.

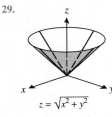

$z = \sqrt{x^2 + y^2}$

31.

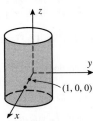

$x^2 + y^2 + (z-2)^2 = 4$

33.

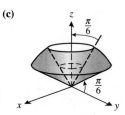

$(x-1)^2 + y^2 = 1$

35. **(a)** $z = 3$ **(b)** $\rho = 3 \sec \phi$ 37. **(a)** $z = 3r^2$ **(b)** $\rho = \frac{1}{3} \csc \phi \cot \phi$
39. **(a)** $r = 2$ **(b)** $\rho = 2 \csc \phi$ 41. **(a)** $r^2 + z^2 = 9$ **(b)** $\rho = 3$
43. **(a)** $2r \cos\theta + 3r \sin\theta + 4z = 1$
    (b) $2\rho \sin\phi \cos\theta + 3\rho \sin\phi \sin\theta + 4\rho \cos\phi = 1$
45. **(a)** $r^2 \cos^2 \theta = 16 - z^2$ **(b)** $\rho^2 (1 - \sin^2 \phi \sin^2 \theta) = 16$
47. all points on or above the paraboloid $z = x^2 + y^2$ that are also on or below the plane $z = 4$
49. all points on or between concentric spheres of radii 1 and 3 centered at the origin
51. spherical: $(4000, \pi/6, \pi/6)$; rectangular: $(1000\sqrt{3}, 1000, 2000\sqrt{3})$
53. **(a)** $(10, \pi/2, 1)$ **(b)** $(0, 10, 1)$ **(c)** $(\sqrt{101}, \pi/2, \tan^{-1} 10)$

▶ **Chapter 11 Review Exercises (Page 838)**

3. **(b)** $-1/2, \pm\sqrt{3}/2$ **(d)** true
5. **(a)** $r^2 = 16$ **(b)** $r^2 = 25$ **(c)** $r^2 = 9$
7. $(7, 5)$
9. **(a)** $-\frac{3}{4}$ **(b)** $\frac{1}{7}$ **(c)** $(48 \pm 25\sqrt{3})/11$ **(d)** $c = \frac{4}{3}$
13. 13 ft·lb   15. **(a)** $\sqrt{26}/2$ **(b)** $\sqrt{26}/3$
17. **(a)** 29   **(b)** $\dfrac{29}{\sqrt{65}}$ 19. $x = 4 + t, y = 1 - t, z = 2$
21. $x + 5y - z - 2 = 0$ 23. $a_1 a_2 + b_1 b_2 + c_1 c_2 = 0$
25. **(a)** hyperboloid of one sheet   **(b)** sphere   **(c)** circular cone
27. **(a)** $z = x^2 - y^2$ **(b)** $xz = 1$
29. **(a)**   **(b)**

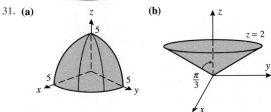

(c)

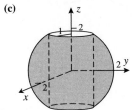

31. **(a)**   **(b)**

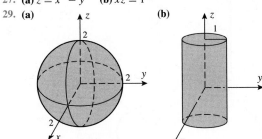

(c)

▶ **Chapter 11 Making Connections (Page 840)**

Answers are provided in the Student Solutions Manual.

▶ **Exercise Set 12.1 (Page 845)**

1. $(-\infty, +\infty)$; $\mathbf{r}(\pi) = -\mathbf{i} - 3\pi\mathbf{j}$ 3. $[2, +\infty)$; $\mathbf{r}(3) = -\mathbf{i} - \ln 3\mathbf{j} + \mathbf{k}$
5. $\mathbf{r} = 3\cos t\mathbf{i} + (t + \sin t)\mathbf{j}$ 7. $x = 3t^2, y = -2$
9. the line in 2-space through $(3, 0)$ with direction vector $\mathbf{a} = -2\mathbf{i} + 5\mathbf{j}$
11. the line in 3-space through the point $(0, -3, 1)$ and parallel to the vector $2\mathbf{i} + 3\mathbf{k}$
13. an ellipse centered at $(0, 0, 1)$ in the plane $z = 1$
15. **(a)** slope $-\frac{3}{2}$ **(b)** $\left(\frac{5}{2}, 0, \frac{3}{2}\right)$

17. (a) 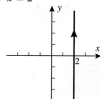 **(b)**

19. $\mathbf{r} = (1 - t)(3\mathbf{i} + 4\mathbf{j}), 0 \leq t \leq 1$

21. $x = 2$ **23.** $(x - 1)^2 + (y - 3)^2 = 1$

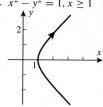

25. $x^2 - y^2 = 1, x \geq 1$ **27.**

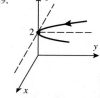 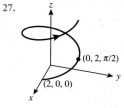

29.

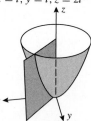

Responses to True–False questions may be abridged to save space.

31. False; the natural domain of a vector-valued function is the *intersection* of the domains of its component functions.

33. True; $\mathbf{r}(t) = (1 - t)\mathbf{r}_0 + t\mathbf{r}_1 (0 \leq t \leq 1)$ represents the line segment in 3-space that is traced from $\mathbf{r}_0$ to $\mathbf{r}_1$.

35. $x = t, y = t, z = 2t^2$

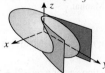

37. $\mathbf{r}(t) = t\mathbf{i} + t^2\mathbf{j} \pm \frac{1}{3}\sqrt{81 - 9t^2 - t^4}\mathbf{k}$ **43.** $c = 3/(2\pi)$

47. (a) III, since the curve is a subset of the plane $y = -x$
(b) IV, since only x is periodic in t and y, z increase without bound
(c) II, since all three components are periodic in t
(d) I, since the projection onto the yz-plane is a circle and the curve increases without bound in the x-direction

49. (a) $x = 3\cos t, y = 3\sin t, z = 9\cos^2 t$
(b)

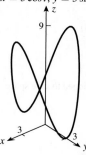

▶ **Exercise Set 12.2 (Page 856)**

1. $\langle \frac{1}{3}, 0 \rangle$ **3.** $2\mathbf{i} - 3\mathbf{j} + 4\mathbf{k}$ **5. (a)** continuous **(b)** not continuous

7. **9.** $(\sin t)\mathbf{j}$ **11.** $\mathbf{r}'(2) = \langle 1, 4 \rangle$

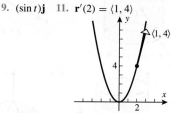

13. $\mathbf{r}'(0) = \mathbf{j}$ **15.** $\mathbf{r}'(\pi/2) = -2\mathbf{k}$

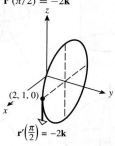

17.

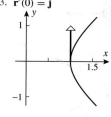

19. $x = 1 + 2t, y = 2 - t$
21. $x = 1 - \sqrt{3}\pi t, y = \sqrt{3} + \pi t, z = 1 + 3t$
23. $\mathbf{r} = (-\mathbf{i} + 2\mathbf{j}) + t(2\mathbf{i} + \frac{3}{4}\mathbf{j})$
25. $\mathbf{r} = (4\mathbf{i} + \mathbf{j}) + t(-4\mathbf{i} + \mathbf{j} + 4\mathbf{k})$
27. (a) $\mathbf{i} - \mathbf{j} + \mathbf{k}$ **(b)** $-\mathbf{i} + \mathbf{k}$ **(c)** 0
29. $7t^6; 18t^5\mathbf{i} - 10t^4\mathbf{j}$
31. $3t\mathbf{i} + 2t^2\mathbf{j} + \mathbf{C}$

33. $-(\cos t)\mathbf{i} - (\sin t)\mathbf{j} + \mathbf{C}$ **35.** $\mathbf{j}$ **37.** $(5\sqrt{5} - 1)/3$
39. $\frac{52}{3}\mathbf{i} + 4\mathbf{j}$

Responses to True–False questions may be abridged to save space.

41. False; for example, $\mathbf{r}(t) = \langle t, |t| \rangle$ is continuous at $t = 0$, but the specified limit doesn't exist at $t = 0$.

43. True; see the definition of $\int_a^b \mathbf{r}(t)\, dt$.

45. $(t^2 + 1)\mathbf{i} + (t^3 - 1)\mathbf{j}$
47. $y(t) = \left(\frac{1}{2}t^2 + 2\right)\mathbf{i} + (e^t - 1)\mathbf{j}$
49. (a) $(-2, 4, 6)$ and $(1, 1, -3)$ **(b)** $76°, 71°$ **51.** $68°$

▶ **Exercise Set 12.3 (Page 866)**

1. smooth **3.** not smooth, $\mathbf{r}'(1) = \mathbf{0}$ **5.** $L = \frac{3}{2}$ **7.** $L = e - e^{-1}$
9. $L = 28$ **11.** $L = 2\pi\sqrt{10}$ **13.** $\mathbf{r}'(\tau) = 4\mathbf{i} + 8(4\tau + 1)\mathbf{j}$
15. $\mathbf{r}'(\tau) = 2\tau e^{\tau^2}\mathbf{i} - 8\tau e^{-\tau^2}\mathbf{j}$

Responses to True–False questions may be abridged to save space.

17. False; $\int_a^b \|\mathbf{r}'(t)\|\, dt$ is a scalar that represents the arc length of the curve in 2-space traced by $\mathbf{r}(t)$ from $t = a$ to $t = b$ (Theorem 12.3.1).

19. False; $\mathbf{r}'$ isn't defined at the point corresponding to the origin.

21. (a) $x = \dfrac{s}{\sqrt{2}}, y = \dfrac{s}{\sqrt{2}}$ **(b)** $x = y = z = \dfrac{s}{\sqrt{3}}$

23. (a) $x = 1 + \dfrac{s}{3}, y = 3 - \dfrac{2s}{3}, z = 4 + \dfrac{2s}{3}$ **(b)** $\left(\dfrac{28}{3}, -\dfrac{41}{3}, \dfrac{62}{3}\right)$

25. $x = 3 + \cos s, y = 2 + \sin s, 0 \le s \le 2\pi$

27. $x = \frac{1}{3}[(3s + 1)^{2/3} - 1]^{3/2}, y = \frac{1}{2}[(3s + 1)^{2/3} - 1], s \ge 0$

29. $x = \left(\dfrac{s}{\sqrt{2}} + 1\right)\cos\left[\ln\left(\dfrac{s}{\sqrt{2}} + 1\right)\right],$
$y = \left(\dfrac{s}{\sqrt{2}} + 1\right)\sin\left[\ln\left(\dfrac{s}{\sqrt{2}} + 1\right)\right],$
$0 \le s \le \sqrt{2}(e^{\pi/2} - 1)$

33. $x = 2a\cos^{-1}[1 - s/(4a)]$
$\quad -2a(1 - [1 - s/(4a)]^2)^{1/2}(2[1 - s/(4a)]^2 - 1),$
$y = \dfrac{s(8a - s)}{8a}$ for $0 \le s \le 8a$

35. (a) $9/2$ **(b)** $9 - 2\sqrt{6}$ **37. (a)** $\sqrt{3}(1 - e^{-2})$ **(b)** $4\sqrt{5}$

39. (a) $g(\tau) = \pi(\tau)$ **(b)** $g(\tau) = \pi(1 - \tau)$ **41.** 44 in

43. (a) $2t + \dfrac{1}{t}$ **(b)** $2t + \dfrac{1}{t}$ **(c)** $8 + \ln 3$

▶ **Exercise Set 12.4 (Page 872)** _____

1. (a) 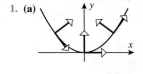 **(b)**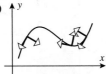

5. $\mathbf{T}(1) = \dfrac{2}{\sqrt{5}}\mathbf{i} + \dfrac{1}{\sqrt{5}}\mathbf{j}, \mathbf{N}(1) = \dfrac{1}{\sqrt{5}}\mathbf{i} - \dfrac{2}{\sqrt{5}}\mathbf{j}$

7. $\mathbf{T}\left(\dfrac{\pi}{3}\right) = -\dfrac{\sqrt{3}}{2}\mathbf{i} + \dfrac{1}{2}\mathbf{j}, \mathbf{N}\left(\dfrac{\pi}{3}\right) = -\dfrac{1}{2}\mathbf{i} - \dfrac{\sqrt{3}}{2}\mathbf{j}$

9. $\mathbf{T}\left(\dfrac{\pi}{2}\right) = -\dfrac{4}{\sqrt{17}}\mathbf{i} + \dfrac{1}{\sqrt{17}}\mathbf{k}, \mathbf{N}\left(\dfrac{\pi}{2}\right) = -\mathbf{j}$

11. $\mathbf{T}(0) = \dfrac{1}{\sqrt{3}}\mathbf{i} + \dfrac{1}{\sqrt{3}}\mathbf{j} + \dfrac{1}{\sqrt{3}}\mathbf{k}, \mathbf{N}(0) = -\dfrac{1}{\sqrt{2}}\mathbf{i} + \dfrac{1}{\sqrt{2}}\mathbf{j}$

13. $x = s, y = 1$ **15.** $\mathbf{B} = \frac{4}{5}\cos t\,\mathbf{i} - \frac{4}{5}\sin t\,\mathbf{j} - \frac{3}{5}\mathbf{k}$ **17.** $\mathbf{B} = -\mathbf{k}$

19. $\mathbf{T}\left(\dfrac{\pi}{4}\right) = \dfrac{\sqrt{2}}{2}(-\mathbf{i} + \mathbf{j}), \mathbf{N}\left(\dfrac{\pi}{4}\right) = -\dfrac{\sqrt{2}}{2}(\mathbf{i} + \mathbf{j}),$
$\mathbf{B}\left(\dfrac{\pi}{4}\right) = \mathbf{k}$; rectifying: $x + y = \sqrt{2}$; osculating: $z = 1$;
normal: $-x + y = 0$

Responses to True–False questions may be abridged to save space.

21. False; $\mathbf{T}(t)$ points in the direction of increasing parameter but may not be orthogonal to $\mathbf{r}(t)$. For example, if $\mathbf{r}(t) = \langle t, t\rangle$, then $\mathbf{T}(t) = \langle 1/\sqrt{2}, 1/\sqrt{2}\rangle$ is parallel to $\mathbf{r}(t)$.

23. True; $\mathbf{T}(s) = \mathbf{r}'(s)$, the unit tangent vector, and $\mathbf{N}(s) = \dfrac{\mathbf{r}''(s)}{\|\mathbf{r}''(s)\|}$, the unit normal vector, are orthogonal, so $\mathbf{r}'(s)$ and $\mathbf{r}''(s)$ are orthogonal.

▶ **Exercise Set 12.5 (Page 879)** _____

1. $\kappa \approx 2$ **3. (a)** I is the curvature of II. **(b)** I is the curvature of II.

5. $\dfrac{6}{|t|(4 + 9t^2)^{3/2}}$ **7.** $\dfrac{12e^{2t}}{(9e^{6t} + e^{-2t})^{3/2}}$ **9.** $\frac{4}{17}$ **11.** $\dfrac{1}{2\cosh^2 t}$

13. $\kappa = \frac{2}{5}, \rho = \frac{5}{2}$ **15.** $\kappa = \dfrac{\sqrt{2}}{3}, \rho = \dfrac{3\sqrt{2}}{2}$ **17.** $\kappa = \frac{1}{4}$

Responses to True–False questions may be abridged to save space.

19. True; see Example 1: a circle of radius a has constant curvature $1/a$.

21. False; see Definition 12.5.1: the curvature of the graph of $\mathbf{r}(s)$ is $\|\mathbf{r}''(s)\|$, the length of $\mathbf{r}''(s)$.

25. 1 **27.** $\dfrac{e^{-1}}{(1 + e^{-2})^{3/2}}$ **29.** $\frac{96}{125}$ **31.** $\dfrac{1}{\sqrt{2}}$

33. (a) 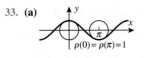 **(b)**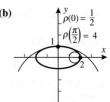

35.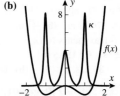

37. (a) $\kappa = \dfrac{|12x^2 - 4|}{[1 + (4x^3 - 4x)^2]^{3/2}}$ **(b)**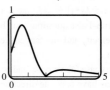
(c) $\rho = \frac{1}{4}$ for $x = 0$ and $\rho = \frac{1}{8}$ when $x = \pm 1$

41. $\dfrac{3}{2\sqrt{2}}$ **43.** $\frac{2}{3}$ **45.** $\rho = 2|p|$ **47.** $(3, 0), (-3, 0)$

51. (b) $\rho = \sqrt{2}$ **(c)**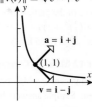

55. $a = \dfrac{1}{2r}$

63. $\tau = \dfrac{2}{(t^2 + 2)^2}$

65. $\tau = -\dfrac{\sqrt{2}}{(e^t + e^{-t})^2}$

▶ **Exercise Set 12.6 (Page 891)** _____

1. $\mathbf{v}(t) = -3\sin t\,\mathbf{i} + 3\cos t\,\mathbf{j}$
$\mathbf{a}(t) = -3\cos t\,\mathbf{i} - 3\sin t\,\mathbf{j}$
$\|\mathbf{v}(t)\| = 3$

3. $\mathbf{v}(t) = e^t\mathbf{i} - e^{-t}\mathbf{j}$
$\mathbf{a}(t) = e^t\mathbf{i} + e^{-t}\mathbf{j}$
$\|\mathbf{v}(t)\| = \sqrt{e^{2t} + e^{-2t}}$

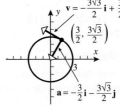 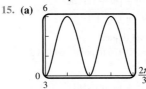

5. $\mathbf{v} = \mathbf{i} + \mathbf{j} + \mathbf{k}, \|\mathbf{v}\| = \sqrt{3}, \mathbf{a} = \mathbf{j} + 2\mathbf{k}$

7. $\mathbf{v} = -\sqrt{2}\mathbf{i} + \sqrt{2}\mathbf{j} + \mathbf{k}, \|\mathbf{v}\| = \sqrt{5}, \mathbf{a} = -\sqrt{2}\mathbf{i} - \sqrt{2}\mathbf{j}$

13. minimum speed $3\sqrt{2}$ when $\mathbf{r} = 24\mathbf{i} + 8\mathbf{j}$

15. (a) 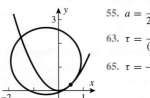 **(b)** maximum speed $= 6$, minimum speed $= 3$ **(d)** The maximum speed first occurs when $t = \pi/6$.

17. $\mathbf{v}(t) = (1 - \sin t)\mathbf{i} + (\cos t - 1)\mathbf{j};$
$\mathbf{r}(t) = (t + \cos t - 1)\mathbf{i} + (\sin t - t + 1)\mathbf{j}$

19. $\mathbf{v}(t) = (1 - \cos t)\mathbf{i} + \sin t\,\mathbf{j} + e^t\mathbf{k};$
$\mathbf{r}(t) = (t - \sin t - 1)\mathbf{i} + (1 - \cos t)\mathbf{j} + e^t\mathbf{k}$

21. $15°$ **23. (a)** $0.7\mathbf{i} + 2.7\mathbf{j} - 3.4\mathbf{k}$ **(b)** $\mathbf{r}_0 = -0.7\mathbf{i} - 2.9\mathbf{j} + 4.8\mathbf{k}$

25. $\Delta\mathbf{r} = 8\mathbf{i} + \frac{26}{3}\mathbf{j}, s = (13\sqrt{13} - 5\sqrt{5})/3$

27. $\Delta\mathbf{r} = 2\mathbf{i} - \frac{2}{3}\mathbf{j} + \sqrt{2}\ln 3\mathbf{k}; s = \frac{8}{3}$

31. (a) $a_T = 0, a_N = \sqrt{2}$ **(b)** $a_T\mathbf{T} = \mathbf{0}, a_N\mathbf{N} = \mathbf{i} + \mathbf{j}$ **(c)** $1/\sqrt{2}$

33. **(a)** $a_T = 2\sqrt{5}$, $a_N = 2\sqrt{5}$ **(b)** $a_T\mathbf{T} = 2\mathbf{i} + 4\mathbf{j}$, $a_N\mathbf{N} = 4\mathbf{i} - 2\mathbf{j}$
   (c) $2/\sqrt{5}$

35. **(a)** $a_T = -7/\sqrt{6}$, $a_N = \sqrt{53/6}$

   (b) $a_T\mathbf{T} = -\frac{7}{6}(\mathbf{i} - 2\mathbf{j} + \mathbf{k})$, $a_N\mathbf{N} = \frac{13}{6}\mathbf{i} + \frac{19}{3}\mathbf{j} + \frac{7}{6}\mathbf{k}$ **(c)** $\dfrac{\sqrt{53}}{6\sqrt{6}}$

37. $a_T = -3$, $a_N = 2$, $\mathbf{T} = -\mathbf{j}$, $\mathbf{N} = \mathbf{i}$ 39. $-3/2$

41. $a_N = 8.41 \times 10^{10}$ km/s^2

43. $a_N = 18/(1 + 4x^2)^{3/2}$ 45. $a_N = 0$

Responses to True–False questions may be abridged to save space.

47. True; the velocity and unit tangent vectors have the same direction, so are parallel.

49. False; in this case the velocity and acceleration vectors will be parallel, but they may have opposite direction.

53. ≈ 257.20 N

55. $40\sqrt{3}$ ft   57. 800 ft/s   59. $15°$ or $75°$ 61. **(c)** ≈ 14.942 ft

63. **(a)** $\rho \approx 176.78$ m   **(b)** $\frac{125}{4}$ m

65. **(b)** R is maximum when $\alpha = 45°$, maximum value v_0^2/g

67. **(a)** 2.62 s   **(b)** 181.5 ft

69. **(a)** $v_0 \approx 83$ ft/s, $\alpha \approx 8°$ **(b)** 268.76 ft

▶ **Exercise Set 12.7 (Page 901)**

7. 7.75 km/s   9. 10.88 km/s

11. **(a)** minimum distance $= 220{,}680$ mi,
   maximum distance $= 246{,}960$ mi   **(b)** 27.5 days

13. **(a)** 17,224 mi/h   **(b)** $e \approx 0.071$, apogee altitude $= 819$ mi

▶ **Chapter 12 Review Exercises (Page 902)**

3. the circle of radius 3 in the xy-plane, with center at the origin

5. a parabola in the plane $x = -2$, vertex at $(-2, 0, -1)$, opening upward

11. $x = 1 + t$, $y = -t$, $z = t$ 13. $(\sin t)\mathbf{i} - (\cos t)\mathbf{j} + \mathbf{C}$

15. $y(t) = \left(\frac{1}{3}t^3 + 1\right)\mathbf{i} + (t^2 + 1)\mathbf{j}$ 17. 15/4

19. $\mathbf{r}(s) = \dfrac{s-3}{3}\mathbf{i} + \dfrac{12-2s}{3}\mathbf{j} + \dfrac{9+2s}{3}\mathbf{k}$ 25. 3/5   27. 0

29. **(a)** speed   **(b)** distance traveled
   (c) distance of the particle from the origin

33. **(a)** $\mathbf{r}(t) = \left(\frac{1}{6}t^4 + t\right)\mathbf{i} + \left(\frac{1}{2}t^2 + 2t\right)\mathbf{j} - \left(\frac{1}{4}\cos 2t + t - \frac{1}{4}\right)\mathbf{k}$
   (b) 3.475   35. 10.65 km/s   37. 24.78 ft

▶ **Chapter 12 Making Connections (Page 904)**

Where correct answers to a Making Connections exercise may vary, no answer is listed. Sample answers for these questions are available on the Book Companion Site.

1. **(c)** (i) $\mathbf{N} = \frac{1}{\sqrt{5}}\mathbf{i} - \frac{2}{\sqrt{5}}\mathbf{j}$ (ii) $\mathbf{N} = -\mathbf{j}$

2. **(b)** (i) $\mathbf{N} = -\sin t\,\mathbf{i} - \cos t\,\mathbf{j}$

   (ii) $\mathbf{N} = \dfrac{-(4t + 18t^3)\mathbf{i} + (2 - 18t^4)\mathbf{j} + (6t + 12t^3)\mathbf{k}}{2\sqrt{81t^8 + 117t^6 + 54t^4 + 13t^2 + 1}}$

3. **(c)** $\kappa(s) \to +\infty$, so the spiral winds ever tighter.

4. semicircle: 53.479 ft; quarter-circle: 60.976 ft; point: 64.001 ft

▶ **Exercise Set 13.1 (Page 914)**

1. **(a)** 5   **(b)** 3   **(c)** 1   **(d)** -2 **(e)** $9a^3 + 1$ **(f)** $a^3b^2 - a^2b^3 + 1$

3. **(a)** $x^2 - y^2 + 3$ **(b)** $3x^3y^4 + 3$ 5. $x^3e^{x^3(3y+1)}$

7. **(a)** $t^2 + 3t^{10}$ **(b)** 0   **(c)** 3076

9. **(a)** WCI $= 17.8°$F   **(b)** WCI $= 22.6°$F

11. **(a)** 66%   **(b)** 73.5%   **(c)** 60.6%

13. **(a)** 19   **(b)** -9 **(c)** 3   **(d)** $a^6 + 3$ **(e)** $-t^8 + 3$
   (f) $(a + b)(a - b)^2b^3 + 3$

15. $(y + 1)e^{x^2(y+1)z^2}$ 17. **(a)** $80\sqrt{\pi}$ **(b)** $n(n + 1)/2$

19. 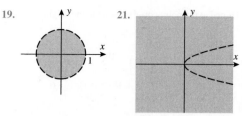   21.

23. **(a)** all points above or on the line $y = -2$ **(b)** all points on or within the sphere $x^2 + y^2 + z^2 = 25$ **(c)** all points in 3-space

Responses to True–False questions may be abridged to save space.

25. True; the interval $[0, 1]$ is the intersection of the domains of $\sin^{-1} t$ and $\sqrt{t}$.

27. False; the natural domain is an infinite solid cylinder.

29. 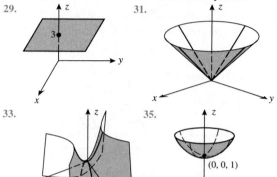   31.

33. 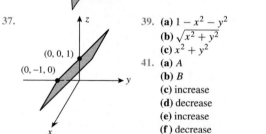   35.

(0, 0, 1)

37. 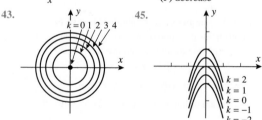   39. **(a)** $1 - x^2 - y^2$
   (b) $\sqrt{x^2 + y^2}$
   (c) $x^2 + y^2$

(0, 0, 1)
(0, −1, 0)

41. **(a)** A
   (b) B
   (c) increase
   (d) decrease
   (e) increase
   (f) decrease

43. $k = 0\ 1\ 2\ 3\ 4$ 45. $k = 2$, $k = 1$, $k = 0$, $k = -1$, $k = -2$

47.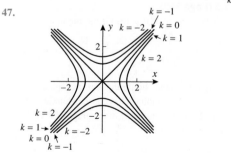

49.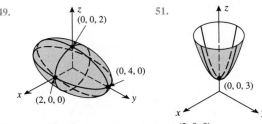

51.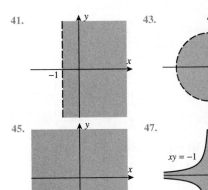

53. concentric spheres, common center at $(2, 0, 0)$

55. concentric cylinders, common axis the y-axis

57. (a) $x^2 - 2x^3 + 3xy = 0$ (b) $x^2 - 2x^3 + 3xy = 0$
  (c) $x^2 - 2x^3 + 3xy = -18$

59. (a) $x^2 + y^2 - z = 5$ (b) $x^2 + y^2 - z = -2$ (c) $x^2 + y^2 - z = 0$

61. (a) 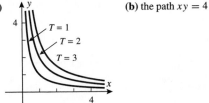   (b) the path $xy = 4$

63. (a) 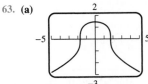   (b)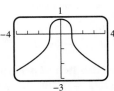

65. (a) 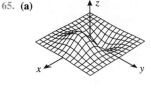   (b)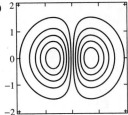

67. (a) The graph of g is the graph of f shifted one unit in the positive x-direction.
  (b) The graph of g is the graph of f shifted one unit up the z-axis.
  (c) The graph of g is the graph of f shifted one unit down the y-axis and then inverted with respect to the plane $z = 0$.

▶ **Exercise Set 13.2 (Page 925)**

1. 35 **3.** -8 **5.** 0

7. (a) along $x = 0$ limit does not exist
  (b) along $x = 0$ limit does not exist

9. 1 **11.** 0 **13.** 0 **15.** limit does not exist **17.** $\frac{8}{3}$ **19.** 0

21. limit does not exist **23.** 0 **25.** 0 **27.** 0

Responses to True–False questions may be abridged to save space.

29. True; by the definition of open set.

31. False; let $f(x, y) = \begin{cases} 1, & x \le 0 \\ -1, & x > 0 \end{cases}$ and let $g(x, y) = -f(x, y)$.

33. (a) no (d) no; yes **37.** $-\pi/2$ **39.** no

41.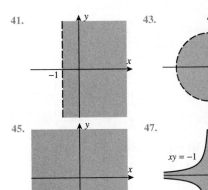

43.

45.

47.

49. all of 3-space

51. all points not on the cylinder $x^2 + z^2 = 1$

▶ **Exercise Set 13.3 (Page 936)**

1. (a) $9x^2 y^2$ (b) $6x^3 y$ (c) $9y^2$ (d) $9x^2$ (e) $6y$ (f) $6x^3$ (g) 36 (h) 12

3. (a) $\frac{3}{8}$ (b) $\frac{1}{4}$ **5.** (a) $-4\cos 7$ (b) $2\cos 7$

7. $\partial z/\partial x = -4$; $\partial z/\partial y = \frac{1}{2}$ **9.** (a) 4.9 (b) 1.2

11. $z = f(x, y)$ has II as its graph, f_x has I as its graph, and f_y has III as its graph.

Responses to True–False questions may be abridged to save space.

13. True; on $y = 2$, $f(x, 2) = c$ is a constant function of x.

15. True; z must be a linear function of x and y.

17. $8xy^3 e^{x^2 y^3}$, $12x^2 y^2 e^{x^2 y^3}$

19. $x^3/(y^{3/5} + x) + 3x^2 \ln(1 + xy^{-3/5})$, $-\frac{3}{5}x^4/(y^{8/5} + xy)$

21. $-\dfrac{y(x^2 - y^2)}{(x^2 + y^2)^2}$, $\dfrac{x(x^2 - y^2)}{(x^2 + y^2)^2}$

23. $(3/2)x^2 y(5x^2 - 7)(3x^5 y - 7x^3 y)^{-1/2}$
  $(1/2)x^3(3x^2 - 7)(3x^5 y - 7x^3 y)^{-1/2}$

25. $\dfrac{y^{-1/2}}{y^2 + x^2}$, $-\dfrac{xy^{-3/2}}{y^2 + x^2} - \dfrac{3}{2}y^{-5/2} \tan^{-1}\left(\dfrac{x}{y}\right)$

27. $-\frac{4}{3}y^2 \sec^2 x(y^2 \tan x)^{-7/3}$, $-\frac{8}{3}y \tan x(y^2 \tan x)^{-7/3}$

29. $-6, -21$ **31.** $1/\sqrt{17}, 8/\sqrt{17}$

33. (a) $2xy^4 z^3 + y$ (b) $4x^2 y^3 z^3 + x$ (c) $3x^2 y^4 z^2 + 2z$
  (d) $2y^4 z^3 + y$ (e) $32z^3 + 1$ (f) 438

35. $2z/x$, z/y, $\ln(x^2 y \cos z) - z \tan z$

37. $-y^2 z^3/(1 + x^2 y^4 z^6)$, $-2xyz^3/(1 + x^2 y^4 z^6)$,
  $-3xy^2 z^2/(1 + x^2 y^4 z^6)$

39. $yze^z \cos(xz)$, $e^z \sin(xz)$, $ye^z(\sin(xz) + x\cos(xz))$

41. $x/\sqrt{x^2 + y^2 + z^2}$, $y/\sqrt{x^2 + y^2 + z^2}$, $z/\sqrt{x^2 + y^2 + z^2}$

43. (a) e (b) $2e$ (c) e

45. (a) 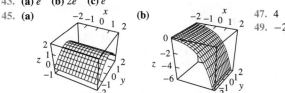 (b)   **47.** 4
        49. -2

51. (a) $\partial V/\partial r = 2\pi rh$ (b) $\partial V/\partial h = \pi r^2$ (c) 48π (d) 64π

53. (a) $\dfrac{1}{5}\dfrac{\text{lb}}{\text{in}^2 \cdot \text{K}}$ (b) $-\dfrac{25}{8}\dfrac{\text{in}^5}{\text{lb}}$

55. (a) $\dfrac{\partial V}{\partial l} = 6$ (b) $\dfrac{\partial V}{\partial w} = 15$ (c) $\dfrac{\partial V}{\partial h} = 10$

59. (a) $\pm\sqrt{6}/4$ **61.** $-x/z, -y/z$

63. $-\dfrac{2x + yz^2 \cos(xyz)}{xyz \cos(xyz) + \sin(xyz)}$; $-\dfrac{xz^2 \cos(xyz)}{xyz \cos(xyz) + \sin(xyz)}$

65. $-x/w, -y/w, -z/w$

67. $-\dfrac{yzw\cos(xyz)}{2w+\sin(xyz)}, -\dfrac{xzw\cos(xyz)}{2w+\sin(xyz)}, -\dfrac{xyw\cos(xyz)}{2w+\cos(xyz)}$

69. $e^{x^2}, -e^{y^2}$

71. $f_x(x,y)=2xy^3\sin(x^6y^9),\ f_y(x,y)=3x^2y^2\sin(x^6y^9)$

73. (a) $-\dfrac{\cos y}{4\sqrt{x^3}}$ (b) $-\sqrt{x}\cos y$ (c) $-\dfrac{1}{2\sqrt{x}}\sin y$ (d) $-\dfrac{1}{2\sqrt{x}}\sin y$

75. $-32y^3$ **77.** $-e^x\sin y$ **79.** $\dfrac{20}{(4x-5y)^2}$ **81.** $\dfrac{2(x-y)}{(x+y)^3}$

83. (a) $\dfrac{\partial^3 f}{\partial x^3}$ (b) $\dfrac{\partial^3 f}{\partial y^2\partial x}$ (c) $\dfrac{\partial^4 f}{\partial x^2\partial y^2}$ (d) $\dfrac{\partial^4 f}{\partial y^3\partial x}$

85. (a) $30xy^4-4$ (b) $60x^2y^3$ (c) $60x^3y^2$

87. (a) -30 (b) -125 (c) 150

89. (a) $15x^2y^4z^7+2y$ (b) $35x^3y^4z^6+3y^2$ (c) $21x^2y^5z^6$
(d) $42x^3y^5z^5$ (e) $140x^3y^3z^6+6y$ (f) $30xy^4z^7$ (g) $105x^2y^4z^6$
(h) $210xy^4z^6$

97. $\dfrac{\partial f}{\partial v}=8vw^3x^4y^5,\ \dfrac{\partial f}{\partial w}=12v^2w^2x^4y^5,\ \dfrac{\partial f}{\partial x}=16v^2w^3x^3y^5,$

$\dfrac{\partial f}{\partial y}=20v^2w^3x^4y^4$

99. $\dfrac{\partial f}{\partial v_1}=\dfrac{2v_1}{v_3^2+v_4^2},\ \dfrac{\partial f}{\partial v_2}=\dfrac{-2v_2}{v_3^2+v_4^2},\ \dfrac{\partial f}{\partial v_3}=\dfrac{-2v_3(v_1^2-v_2^2)}{(v_3^2+v_4^2)^2},$

$\dfrac{\partial f}{\partial v_4}=\dfrac{-2v_4(v_1^2-v_2^2)}{(v_3^2+v_4^2)^2}$

101. (a) 0 (b) 0 (c) 0 (d) 0 (e) $2(1+yw)e^{yw}\sin z\cos z$
(f) $2xw(2+yw)e^{yw}\sin z\cos z$

103. $-i\sin(x_1+2x_2+\cdots+nx_n)$

105. (a) xy-plane, $12x^2+6x$ (b) $y\ne 0, -3x^2/y^2$

107. $f_x(2,-1)=11,\ f_y(2,-1)=-8$

109. (b) does not exist if $y\ne 0$ and $x=-y$

▶ **Exercise Set 13.4 (Page 947)**

1. 5.04 **3.** 4.14 **9.** $dz=7\,dx-2\,dy$ **11.** $dz=3x^2y^2\,dx+2x^3y\,dy$

13. $dz=\dfrac{y}{1+x^2y^2}\,dx+\dfrac{x}{1+x^2y^2}\,dy$ **15.** $dw=8\,dx-3\,dy+4\,dz$

17. $dw=3x^2y^2z\,dx+2x^3yz\,dy+x^3y^2\,dz$

19. $dw=\dfrac{yz}{1+x^2y^2z^2}\,dx+\dfrac{xz}{1+x^2y^2z^2}\,dy+\dfrac{xy}{1+x^2y^2z^2}\,dz$

21. $df=0.10,\ \Delta f=0.1009$ **23.** $df=0.03,\ \Delta f\approx0.029412$

25. $df=0.96,\ \Delta f\approx0.97929$

Responses to True–False questions may be abridged to save space.

27. False; see the discussion at the beginning of this section.

29. True; see Theorems 13.4.3 and 13.4.4.

31. The increase in the area of the rectangle is given by the sum of the areas of the three small rectangles, and the total differential is given by the sum of the areas of the upper left and lower right rectangles.

33. (a) $L=\frac{1}{5}-\frac{4}{125}(x-4)-\frac{3}{125}(y-3)$ (b) 0.000176603

35. (a) $L=0$ (b) 0.0024

37. (a) $L=6+6(x-1)+3(y-2)+2(z-3)$ (b) -0.000481

39. (a) $L=e+e(x-1)-e(y+1)-e(z+1)$ (b) 0.01554

45. 0.5 **47.** $1,1,-1,2$ **49.** $(-1,1)$ **51.** $(1,0,1)$ **53.** 8%

55. $r\%$ **57.** 0.3%

59. (a) $(r+s)\%$ (b) $(r+s)\%$ (c) $(2r+3s)\%$ (d) $\left(3r+\frac{s}{2}\right)\%$

61. $\approx 39\ \text{ft}^2$

▶ **Exercise Set 13.5 (Page 956)**

1. $42t^{13}$ **3.** $3t^{-2}\sin(1/t)$ **5.** $-\frac{10}{3}t^{7/3}e^{1-t^{10/3}}$ **7.** $\dfrac{dw}{dt}=165t^{32}$

9. $-2t\cos t^2$ **11.** 3264 **13.** 0

17. $24u^2v^2-16uv^3-2v+3,\ 16u^3v-24u^2v^2-2u-3$

19. $-\dfrac{2\sin u}{3\sin v}, -\dfrac{2\cos u\cos v}{3\sin^2 v}$ **21.** $e^u, 0$

23. $3r^2\sin\theta\cos^2\theta-4r^3\sin^3\theta\cos\theta,$
$-2r^3\sin^2\theta\cos\theta+r^4\sin^4\theta+r^3\cos^3\theta-3r^4\sin^2\theta\cos^2\theta$

25. $\dfrac{x^2+y^2}{4x^2y^3}, \dfrac{y^2-3x^2}{4xy^4}$ **27.** $\dfrac{\partial z}{\partial r}=\dfrac{2r\cos^2\theta}{r^2\cos^2\theta+1}, \dfrac{\partial z}{\partial\theta}=\dfrac{-2r^2\cos\theta\sin\theta}{r^2\cos^2\theta+1}$

29. $\dfrac{dw}{d\rho}=2\rho(4\sin^2\phi+\cos^2\phi),\ \dfrac{\partial w}{\partial\phi}=6\rho^2\sin\phi\cos\phi,\ \dfrac{dw}{d\theta}=0$

31. $-\pi$ **33.** $\sqrt{3}e^{\sqrt{3}},(2-4\sqrt{3})e^{\sqrt{3}}$

Responses to True–False questions may be abridged to save space.

35. False; the symbols ∂z and ∂x have no individual meaning.

37. False; consider $z=xy, x=t, y=t$.

39. $-\dfrac{2xy^3}{3x^2y^2-\sin y}$

41. $-\dfrac{ye^{xy}}{xe^{xy}+ye^y+e^y}$ **43.** $\dfrac{2x+yz}{6yz-xy}, \dfrac{xz-3z^2}{6yz-xy}$

45. $\dfrac{ye^x}{15\cos 3z+3}, \dfrac{e^x}{15\cos 3z+3}$

59. $\dfrac{\partial w}{\partial\rho}=(\sin\phi\cos\theta)\dfrac{\partial w}{\partial x}+(\sin\phi\sin\theta)\dfrac{\partial w}{\partial y}+(\cos\phi)\dfrac{\partial w}{\partial z},$
$\dfrac{\partial w}{\partial\phi}=(\rho\cos\phi\cos\theta)\dfrac{\partial w}{\partial x}+(\rho\cos\phi\sin\theta)\dfrac{\partial w}{\partial y}-(\rho\sin\phi)\dfrac{\partial w}{\partial z},$
$\dfrac{\partial w}{\partial\theta}=-(\rho\sin\phi\sin\theta)\dfrac{\partial w}{\partial x}+(\rho\sin\phi\cos\theta)\dfrac{\partial w}{\partial y}$

63. (a) $\dfrac{dw}{dt}=\sum_{i=1}^{4}\dfrac{\partial w}{\partial x_i}\dfrac{dx_i}{dt}$ (b) $\dfrac{\partial w}{\partial v_j}=\sum_{i=1}^{4}\dfrac{\partial w}{\partial x_i}\dfrac{\partial x_i}{\partial v_j}, j=1,2,3$

▶ **Exercise Set 13.6 (Page 968)**

1. $6\sqrt{2}$ **3.** $-3/\sqrt{10}$ **5.** -320 **7.** $-314/741$ **9.** 0 **11.** $-8\sqrt{2}$

13. $\sqrt{2}/4$ **15.** $72/\sqrt{14}$ **17.** $-8/63$ **19.** $1/2+\sqrt{3}/8$ **21.** $2\sqrt{2}$

23. $1/\sqrt{5}$ **25.** $-\frac{3}{2}e$ **27.** $3/\sqrt{11}$ **29.** (a) 5 (b) 10 (c) $-5\sqrt{5}$

31. III **33.** $4i-8j$

35. $\nabla w=\dfrac{x}{x^2+y^2+z^2}i+\dfrac{y}{x^2+y^2+z^2}j+\dfrac{z}{x^2+y^2+z^2}k$

37. $-36i-12j$ **39.** $4(i+j+k)$

41.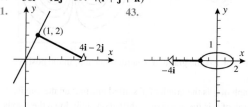

43.

45. $\pm(-4i+j)/\sqrt{17}$ **47.** $u=(3i-2j)/\sqrt{13}, \|\nabla f(-1,1)\|=4\sqrt{13}$

49. $u=(4i-3j)/5, \|\nabla f(4,-3)\|=1$ **51.** $\dfrac{1}{\sqrt{2}}(i-j), 3\sqrt{2}$

53. $\dfrac{1}{\sqrt{2}}(-i+j), \dfrac{1}{\sqrt{2}}$

55. $u=-(i+3j)/\sqrt{10}, -\|\nabla f(-1,-3)\|=-2\sqrt{10}$

57. $u=(3i-j)/\sqrt{10}, -\|\nabla f(\pi/6,\pi/4)\|=-\sqrt{5}$

59. $(i-11j+12k)/\sqrt{266}, -\sqrt{266}$

Responses to True–False questions may be abridged to save space.

61. False; they are equal. **63.** False; let $u=i$ and let $f(x,y)=y$.

65. $8/\sqrt{29}$

67. (a) $\approx 1/\sqrt{2}$
(b)

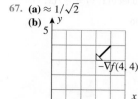

69. $9x^2+y^2=9$

71. $36/\sqrt{17}$

73. (a) $2e^{-\pi/2}i$

75. $-\frac{5}{3}(2i-j-2k)$

81. $x(t)=e^{-8t}, y(t)=4e^{-2t}$

83.

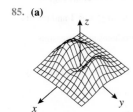

85. (a)

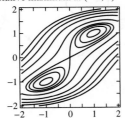

(c) $\nabla f = [2x - 2x(x^2 + 3y^2)]e^{-(x^2+y^2)}\mathbf{i}$
$+ [6y - 2y(x^2 + 3y^2)]e^{-(x^2+y^2)}\mathbf{j}$
(d) $x = y = 0$ or $x = 0, y = \pm 1$ or
$x = \pm 1, y = 0$

▶ **Exercise Set 13.7 (Page 975)**

1. (a) $x + y + 2z = 6$ **(b)** $x = 2 + t, y = 2 + t, z = 1 + 2t$
(c) $35.26°$
3. tangent plane: $3x - 4z = -25$;
normal line: $x = -3 + (3t/4), y = 0, z = 4 - t$
5. tangent plane: $48x - 14y - z = 64$;
normal line: $x = 1 + 48t, y = -2 - 14t, z = 12 - t$
7. tangent plane: $x - y - z = 0$;
normal line: $x = 1 + t, y = -t, z = 1 - t$
9. tangent plane: $3y - z = -1$;
normal line: $x = \pi/6, y = 3t, z = 1 - t$
11. (a) all points on the x-axis or y-axis   **(b)** $(0, -2, -4)$
13. $\left(\frac{1}{2}, -2, -\frac{3}{4}\right)$ **15. (a)** $(-2, 1, 5), (0, 3, 9)$ **(b)** $\frac{4}{3\sqrt{14}}, \frac{4}{\sqrt{222}}$
Responses to True–False questions may be abridged to save space.
17. False; they need only be parallel.
19. True; see Formula (15) of Section 13.4.
21. $\pm\dfrac{1}{\sqrt{365}}(\mathbf{i} - \mathbf{j} - 19\mathbf{k})$ **25.** $(1, 2/3, 2/3), (-1, -2/3, -2/3)$
27. $x = 1 + 8t, y = -1 + 5t, z = 2 + 6t$
29. $x = 3 + 4t, y = -3 - 4t, z = 4 - 3t$

▶ **Exercise Set 13.8 (Page 985)**

1. (a) minimum at $(2, -1)$, no maxima
(b) maximum at $(0, 0)$, no minima   **(c)** no maxima or minima
3. minimum at $(3, -2)$, no maxima   **5.** relative minimum at $(0, 0)$
7. relative minimum at $(0, 0)$; saddle points at $(\pm 2, 1)$
9. saddle point at $(1, -2)$ **11.** relative minimum at $(2, -1)$
13. relative minima at $(-1, -1)$ and $(1, 1)$ **15.** saddle point at $(0, 0)$
17. no critical points   **19.** relative maximum at $(-1, 0)$
21. saddle point at $(0, 0)$;
relative minima at $(1, 1)$
and $(-1, -1)$

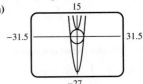

Responses to True–False questions may be abridged to save space.
23. False; let $f(x, y) = y$.
25. True; this follows from Theorem 13.8.6.
27. (b) relative minimum at $(0, 0)$
31. absolute maximum 0,
absolute minimum -12
33. absolute maximum 3,
absolute minimum -1
35. absolute maximum $\frac{33}{4}$,
absolute minimum $-\frac{1}{4}$
37. 16, 16, 16
39. maximum at $(1, 2, 2)$
41. $2a/\sqrt{3}, 2a/\sqrt{3}, 2a/\sqrt{3}$
43. length and width 2 ft, height 4 ft
45. (a) $x = 0$: minimum -3, maximum 0;
$x = 1$: minimum 3, maximum 13/3;
$y = 0$: minimum 0, maximum 4;
$y = 1$: minimum -3, maximum 3
(b) $y = x$: minimum 0, maximum 3;
$y = 1 - x$: maximum 4, minimum -3
(c) minimum -3, maximum 13/3
47. length and width $\sqrt[3]{2V}$, height $\sqrt[3]{2V}/2$ **51.** $y = \frac{3}{4}x + \frac{19}{12}$
53. $y = 0.5x + 0.8$
55. (a) $y = 63.73 + 0.2565t$ **(b)**
(c) about 84 years

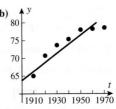

57. (a) $P = \dfrac{2798}{21} + \dfrac{171}{350}T$ **(b)** 190
(c) $T \approx -272.7096°C$

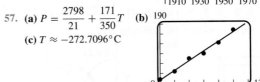

▶ **Exercise Set 13.9 (Page 996)**

1. (a) 4   **3. (a)**

(c) maximum $\frac{101}{4}$,
minimum -5

5. maximum $\sqrt{2}$ at $(-\sqrt{2}, -1)$ and $(\sqrt{2}, 1)$,
minimum $-\sqrt{2}$ at $(-\sqrt{2}, 1)$ and $(\sqrt{2}, -1)$
7. maximum $\sqrt{2}$ at $(1/\sqrt{2}, 0)$, minimum $-\sqrt{2}$ at $(-1/\sqrt{2}, 0)$
9. maximum 6 at $\left(\frac{4}{3}, \frac{2}{3}, -\frac{4}{3}\right)$, minimum -6 at $\left(-\frac{4}{3}, -\frac{2}{3}, \frac{4}{3}\right)$
11. maximum is $1/(3\sqrt{3})$ at $(1/\sqrt{3}, 1/\sqrt{3}, 1/\sqrt{3})$,
$(1/\sqrt{3}, -1/\sqrt{3}, -1/\sqrt{3}), (-1/\sqrt{3}, 1/\sqrt{3}, -1/\sqrt{3})$, and
$(-1/\sqrt{3}, -1/\sqrt{3}, 1/\sqrt{3})$; minimum is $-1/(3\sqrt{3})$ at
$(1/\sqrt{3}, 1/\sqrt{3}, -1/\sqrt{3}), (1/\sqrt{3}, -1/\sqrt{3}, 1/\sqrt{3})$,
$(-1/\sqrt{3}, 1/\sqrt{3}, 1/\sqrt{3})$, and $(-1/\sqrt{3}, -1/\sqrt{3}, -1/\sqrt{3})$
Responses to True–False questions may be abridged to save space.
13. False; a Lagrange multiplier is a scalar.
15. False; we must solve three equations in three unknowns.
17. $\left(\frac{3}{10}, -\frac{3}{5}\right)$ **19.** $\left(\frac{1}{6}, \frac{1}{3}, \frac{1}{6}\right)$
21. $(3, 6)$ is closest and $(-3, -6)$ is farthest   **23.** $5(\mathbf{i} + \mathbf{j} + \mathbf{k})/\sqrt{3}$

25. 9, 9, 9   27. $(\pm\sqrt{5}, 0, 0)$ 29. length and width 2 ft, height 4 ft
33. (a) $\alpha = \beta = \gamma = \pi/3$, maximum 1/8
    (b)

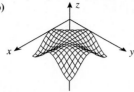

▶ **Chapter 13 Review Exercises (Page 997)**

1. (a) xy (b) $e^{r+s}\ln(rs)$
5. (a) not defined on line $y = x$ (b) not continuous
9. (a) 12 Pa/min   (b) 240 Pa/min
15. df (the differential of f) is an approximation for Δf (the change in f)
17. $dV = -0.06667$ m³; $\Delta V = -0.07267$ m³   19. 2
21. $\dfrac{-f_y^2 f_{xx} + 2f_x f_y f_{xy} - f_x^2 f_{yz}}{f_y^3}$ 25. $\dfrac{7}{2} + \dfrac{4}{5}\ln 2$ 27. $-7/\sqrt{5}$
29. $(0, 0, 2), (1, 1, 1), (-1, -1, 1)$ 31. $\left(-\frac{1}{3}, -\frac{1}{2}, 2\right)$
33. relative minimum at $(15, -8)$
35. saddle point at $(0, 0)$, relative minimum at $(3, 9)$
37. absolute maximum of 4 at $(\pm1, \pm2)$, absolute minimum of 0 at $(\pm\sqrt{2}, 0)$ and $(0, \pm2\sqrt{2})$
39. $I_1 : I_2 : I_3 = \dfrac{1}{R_1} : \dfrac{1}{R_2} : \dfrac{1}{R_3}$
41. (a) $\partial P/\partial L = c\alpha L^{\alpha-1} K^\beta$, $\partial P/\partial K = c\beta L^\alpha K^{\beta-1}$

▶ **Chapter 13 Making Connections (Page 999)**

Answers are provided in the Student Solutions Manual.

▶ **Exercise Set 14.1 (Page 1007)**

1. 7   3. 2   5. 2   7. 3   9. $1 - \ln 2$ 11. $\dfrac{1 - \ln 2}{2}$ 13. 0   15. $\frac{1}{3}$
17. (a) 37/4   (b) exact value $= 28/3$; differ by $1/12$
19.

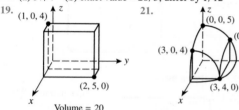

Volume = 20
Responses to True–False questions may be abridged to save space.
23. False; ΔA_k is the area of such a rectangular region.
25. False; $\displaystyle\iint\limits_R f(x, y)\, dA = \int_1^5 \int_2^4 f(x, y)\, dy\, dx.$
29. 19   31. 8   33. $\dfrac{1}{3\pi}$ 35. $1 - \dfrac{2}{\pi}$ 37. $\frac{14}{3}$ °C   39. 1.381737122
41. first integral equals $\frac{1}{2}$, second equals $-\frac{1}{2}$; no

▶ **Exercise Set 14.2 (Page 1015)**

1. $\frac{1}{40}$ 3. 9   5. $\dfrac{\pi}{2}$ 7. $\frac{1}{12}$
9. (a) $\displaystyle\int_0^2 \int_0^{x^2} f(x, y)\, dy\, dx$ (b) $\displaystyle\int_0^4 \int_{\sqrt{y}}^2 f(x, y)\, dx\, dy$
11. (a) $\displaystyle\int_1^2 \int_{-2x+5}^3 f(x, y)\, dy\, dx + \int_2^4 \int_1^3 f(x, y)\, dy\, dx + \int_4^5 \int_{2x-7}^3 f(x, y)\, dy\, dx$ (b) $\displaystyle\int_1^3 \int_{(5-y)/2}^{(y+7)/2} f(x, y)\, dx\, dy$
13. (a) $\frac{16}{3}$ (b) 38   15. 576   17. 0   19. $\dfrac{\sqrt{17} - 1}{2}$ 21. $\frac{50}{3}$

23. $-\frac{7}{60}$ 25. $\dfrac{1 - \cos 8}{3}$
27. (a)

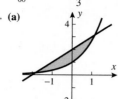

(b) $(-1.8414, 0.1586)$, $(1.1462, 3.1462)$
(c) -0.4044
(d) -0.4044

29. $\sqrt{2} - 1$ 31. 32
Responses to True–False questions may be abridged to save space.
33. False; $\displaystyle\int_0^1 \int_{x^2}^{2x} f(x, y)\, dy\, dx$ integrates $f(x, y)$ over the region between the graphs of $y = x^2$ and $y = 2x$ for $0 \le x \le 1$ and results in a number, but $\displaystyle\int_{x^2}^{2x} \int_0^1 f(x, y)\, dx\, dy$ produces an expression involving x.
35. False; although R is symmetric across the x-axis, the integrand may not be.
37. 12   39. 27π 41. 170   43. $\dfrac{27\pi}{2}$ 45. $\dfrac{\pi}{2}$
47. $\displaystyle\int_0^{\sqrt{2}} \int_{y^2}^2 f(x, y)\, dx\, dy$ 49. $\displaystyle\int_1^{e^2} \int_{\ln x}^2 f(x, y)\, dy\, dx$
51. $\displaystyle\int_0^{\pi/2} \int_0^{\sin x} f(x, y)\, dy\, dx$ 53. $\dfrac{1 - e^{-16}}{8}$ 55. $\dfrac{e^8 - 1}{3}$
57. (a) 0   (b) $\tan 1$ 59. 0   61. $\dfrac{\pi}{2} - \ln 2$ 63. $\frac{2}{3}$ °C   65. 0.676089

▶ **Exercise Set 14.3 (Page 1024)**

1. $\frac{1}{6}$ 3. $\frac{2}{9}a^3$ 5. 0   7. $\dfrac{3\pi}{2}$ 9. $\dfrac{\pi}{16}$ 11. $\displaystyle\int_{\pi/6}^{5\pi/6} \int_2^{4\sin\theta} f(r, \theta) r\, dr\, d\theta$
13. $8\displaystyle\int_0^{\pi/2} \int_1^3 r\sqrt{9 - r^2}\, dr\, d\theta$ 15. $2\displaystyle\int_0^{\pi/2} \int_0^{\cos\theta} (1 - r^2) r\, dr\, d\theta$
17. $\dfrac{64\sqrt{2}}{3}\pi$ 19. $\dfrac{5\pi}{32}$ 21. $\dfrac{27\pi}{16}$ 23. $(1 - e^{-1})\pi$ 25. $\dfrac{\pi}{8}\ln 5$ 27. $\dfrac{\pi}{8}$
29. $\frac{16}{9}$ 31. $\dfrac{\pi}{2}\left(1 - \dfrac{1}{\sqrt{1 + a^2}}\right)$ 33. $\dfrac{\pi}{4}(\sqrt{5} - 1)$
Responses to True–False questions may be abridged to save space.
35. True; the disk is given in polar coordinates by $0 \le r \le 2, 0 \le \theta \le 2\pi$.
37. False; the integrand is missing a factor of r:
$$\iint\limits_R f(r, \theta)\, dA = \int_0^{\pi/2} \int_1^2 f(r, \theta) r\, dr\, d\theta.$$
39. $\pi a^2 h$ 41. $\dfrac{1}{5} + \dfrac{\pi}{2}$
43. (a) $\dfrac{4}{3}\pi a^2 c$ (b) $\approx 1.0831682 \times 10^{21}$ m³   45. $2a^2$

▶ **Exercise Set 14.4 (Page 1036)**

1. 6π 3. $\dfrac{\sqrt{5}}{6}$ 5. $\sqrt{2}\pi$ 7. $\dfrac{(10\sqrt{10} - 1)\pi}{18}$ 9. 8π
11. (a)

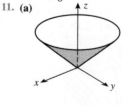

(b)

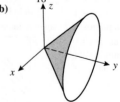

(c)

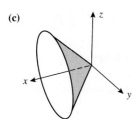

13. (a) $x = u, y = v, z = \frac{5}{2} + \frac{3}{2}u - 2v$ (b) $x = u, y = v, z = u^2$
15. (a) $x = \sqrt{5}\cos u, y = \sqrt{5}\sin u, z = v; 0 \le u \le 2\pi, 0 \le v \le 1$
    (b) $x = 2\cos u, y = v, z = 2\sin u; 0 \le u \le 2\pi, 1 \le v \le 3$
17. $x = u, y = \sin u \cos v, z = \sin u \sin v$
19. $x = r\cos\theta, y = r\sin\theta, z = \dfrac{1}{1+r^2}$
21. $x = r\cos\theta, y = r\sin\theta, z = 2r^2\cos\theta\sin\theta$
23. $x = r\cos\theta, y = r\sin\theta, z = \sqrt{9-r^2}; r \le \sqrt{5}$
25. $x = \dfrac{1}{2}\rho\cos\theta, y = \dfrac{1}{2}\rho\sin\theta, z = \dfrac{\sqrt{3}}{2}\rho$ 27. $z = x - 2y$; a plane
29. $(x/3)^2 + (y/2)^2 = 1; 2 \le z \le 4$; part of an elliptic cylinder
31. $(x/3)^2 + (y/4)^2 = z^2; 0 \le z \le 1$; part of an elliptic cone
33. (a) $x = r\cos\theta, y = r\sin\theta, z = r, 0 \le r \le 2$;
    $x = u, y = v, z = \sqrt{u^2+v^2}, 0 \le u^2 + v^2 \le 4$
35. (a) $0 \le u \le 3, 0 \le v \le \pi$ (b) $0 \le u \le 4, -\pi/2 \le v \le \pi/2$
37. (a) $0 \le \phi \le \pi/2, 0 \le \theta \le 2\pi$ (b) $0 \le \phi \le \pi, 0 \le \theta \le \pi$
39. $2x + 4y - z = 5$ 41. $z = 0$ 43. $x - y + \dfrac{\sqrt{2}}{2}z = \dfrac{\pi\sqrt{2}}{8}$
45. $\dfrac{(17\sqrt{17} - 5\sqrt{5})\pi}{6}$

Responses to True–False questions may be abridged to save space.
47. False; the surface area is $S = \displaystyle\iint_R \sqrt{[f_x(x, y)]^2 + [f_y(x, y)]^2 + 1}\, dA$.
49. True; see the discussion preceding Definition 14.4.1.
51. $4\pi a^2$ 55. $4\pi^2 ab$ 57. 9.099
59. $(x/a)^2 + (y/b)^2 + (z/c)^2 = 1$; ellipsoid
61. $(x/a)^2 + (y/b)^2 - (z/c)^2 = -1$; hyperboloid of two sheets

▶ **Exercise Set 14.5 (Page 1045)**
1. 8 3. $\frac{47}{3}$ 5. $\frac{81}{5}$ 7. $\frac{128}{15}$ 9. $\pi(\pi - 3)/2$ 11. $\frac{1}{6}$ 13. 9.425
15. 4 17. $\frac{256}{15}$
19. (a) $\displaystyle\int_{-1}^{1}\int_{-\sqrt{1-x^2}}^{\sqrt{1-x^2}}\int_{4x^2+y^2}^{4-3y^2} f(x, y, z)\, dz\, dy\, dx$
    (b) $\displaystyle\int_{-1}^{1}\int_{-\sqrt{1-y^2}}^{\sqrt{1-y^2}}\int_{4x^2+y^2}^{4-3y^2} f(x, y, z)\, dz\, dx\, dy$
21. $4\displaystyle\int_{0}^{1}\int_{0}^{\sqrt{1-x^2}}\int_{4x^2+y^2}^{4-3y^2} dz\, dy\, dx$
23. $2\displaystyle\int_{-3}^{3}\int_{\frac{1}{3}\sqrt{9-x^2}}^{} \int_{0}^{x+3} dz\, dy\, dx$
25. (a)

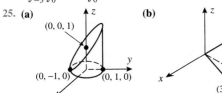

(b)

Responses to True–False questions may be abridged to save space.
27. True; apply Fubini's Theorem (Theorem 14.5.1).
29. False;

(c)

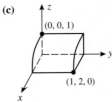

$$\iiint_G f(x, y, z)\, dV = \int_0^1 \int_0^{\sqrt{1-x^2}} \int_0^{\sqrt{1-x^2-y^2}} f(x, y, z)\, dz\, dy\, dx.$$

33. $\frac{3}{4}$ 35. 3.291
37. (a) $\displaystyle\int_0^a \int_0^{b(1-x/a)} \int_0^{c(1-x/a-y/z)} dz\, dy\, dx$ is one example.
39. (a) $\displaystyle\int_0^2 \int_0^{\sqrt{4-x^2}} \int_0^5 f(x, y, z)\, dz\, dy\, dx$
    (b) $\displaystyle\int_0^9 \int_0^{3-\sqrt{x}} \int_y^{3-\sqrt{x}} f(x, y, z)\, dz\, dy\, dx$
    (c) $\displaystyle\int_0^2 \int_0^{4-x^2} \int_y^{8-y} f(x, y, z)\, dz\, dy\, dx$

▶ **Exercise Set 14.6 (Page 1056)**
1. $\dfrac{\pi}{4}$ 3. $\dfrac{\pi}{16}$
5. The region is bounded by the xy-plane and the upper half of a sphere of radius 1 centered at the origin; $f(r, \theta, z) = z$.
7. The region is the portion of the first octant inside a sphere of radius 1 centered at the origin; $f(\rho, \theta, \phi) = \rho\cos\phi$.
9. $\dfrac{81\pi}{2}$ 11. $\dfrac{152}{3}\pi + \dfrac{80}{3}\pi\sqrt{5}$ 13. $\dfrac{64\pi}{3}$ 15. $\dfrac{11\pi a^3}{3}$ 17. $\dfrac{\pi a^6}{48}$
19. $\dfrac{32(2\sqrt{2} - 1)\pi}{15}$
Responses to True–False questions may be abridged to save space.
21. False; the factor r^2 should be r [Formula (6)]:
    $$\iiint_G f(x, y, z)\, dV = \iiint_{\substack{\text{appropriate}\\\text{limits}}} f(r\cos\theta, r\sin\theta, z)r\, dz\, dr\, d\theta.$$
23. True; G is the spherical wedge bounded by the spheres $\rho = 1$ and $\rho = 3$, the half-planes $\theta = 0$ and $\theta = 2\pi$, and above the cone $\phi = \pi/4$, so
    $$(\text{volume of } G) = \iiint_G dV = \int_0^{\pi/4}\int_0^{2\pi}\int_1^3 \rho^2\sin\phi\, d\rho\, d\theta\, d\phi.$$
25. (a) $\frac{5}{2}(-8 + 3\ln 3)\ln(\sqrt{5} - 2)$ (b) $f(x, y, z) = \dfrac{y^3}{x^3\sqrt{1+z^2}}$;
    G is the cylindrical wedge $1 \le r \le 4, \dfrac{\pi}{6} \le \theta \le \dfrac{\pi}{3}, -2 \le z \le 2$
27. $\dfrac{4\pi a^3}{3}$ 29. $\dfrac{2(\sqrt{3} - 1)\pi}{3}$

▶ **Exercise Set 14.7 (Page 1068)**
1. -17 3. $\cos(u - v)$ 5. $x = \frac{2}{9}u + \frac{5}{9}v, y = -\frac{1}{9}u + \frac{2}{9}v; \frac{1}{9}$
7. $x = \dfrac{\sqrt{u+v}}{\sqrt{2}}, y = \dfrac{\sqrt{v-u}}{\sqrt{2}}; \dfrac{1}{4\sqrt{v^2-u^2}}$ 9. 5 11. $\dfrac{1}{v}$
Responses to True–False questions may be abridged to save space.
13. False; $|\partial(x, y)/\partial(u, v)| = \|\partial\mathbf{r}/\partial u \times \partial\mathbf{r}/\partial v\|$; evaluating this at (u_0, v_0) gives the area of the indicated parallelogram.
15. False; $\partial(x, y)/\partial(r, \theta) = r$.

17.

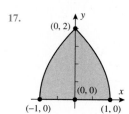

(0, 2)

(−1, 0) (0, 0) (1, 0)

19.

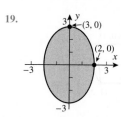

3 (3, 0)

(2, 0)

−3 3

−3

21. $\frac{3}{2}\ln 3$ **23.** $1 - \frac{1}{2}\sin 2$ **25.** 96π **27.** $\frac{\pi}{24}(1 - \cos 1)$ **29.** $\frac{192}{5}\pi$

31. $u = \begin{cases} \cot^{-1}(x/y), & y \neq 0 \\ 0, & y = 0 \text{ and } x > 0 \\ \pi, & y = 0 \text{ and } x < 0 \end{cases}$

$v = \sqrt{x^2 + y^2}$; other answers possible

33. $u = (3/7)x - (2/7)y$, $v = (-1/7)x + (3/7)y$; other answers possible

35. $\frac{1}{4}\ln\frac{5}{2}$

37. $\frac{1}{2}\left[\ln(\sqrt{2} + 1) - \frac{\pi}{4}\right]$ **39.** $\frac{35}{256}$ **41.** $2\ln 3$ **45.** $21/8$

▶ **Exercise Set 14.8 (Page 1077)**

1. $M = \frac{13}{20}$, center of gravity $\left(\frac{190}{273}, \frac{6}{13}\right)$

3. $M = a^4/8$, center of gravity $(8a/15, 8a/15)$

5. $\left(\frac{1}{2}, \frac{1}{2}\right)$ **7.** $\left(\frac{1}{2}, \frac{1}{2}, \frac{1}{2}\right)$

Responses to True–False questions may be abridged to save space.

9. True; recall this from Section 6.7.

11. False; the center of gravity of the lamina is $(\bar{x}, \bar{y}) = (M_y/M, M_x/M)$, where M_y and M_x are the lamina's first moments about the y- and x-axes, respectively, and M is the mass of the lamina.

15. $\left(\frac{128}{105\pi}, \frac{128}{105\pi}\right)$ **17.** $\left(\frac{1}{4}, \frac{1}{4}, \frac{1}{4}\right)$ **19.** $\left(\frac{1}{2}, 0, \frac{3}{5}\right)$

21. $(3a/8, 3a/8, 3a/8)$

23. $M = a^4/2$, center of gravity $(a/3, a/2, a/2)$

25. $M = \frac{1}{6}$, center of gravity $\left(0, \frac{16}{35}, \frac{1}{2}\right)$ **27.** (a) $\left(\frac{5}{8}, \frac{5}{8}\right)$ (b) $\left(\frac{2}{3}, \frac{1}{2}\right)$

29. $(1.177406, 0.353554, 0.231557)$

31. $\frac{27\pi}{4}$ **33.** $\pi k a^4$ **35.** $\left(0, 0, \frac{7}{16\sqrt{2} - 14}\right)$ **37.** $(3a/8, 3a/8, 3a/8)$

39. $(2 - \sqrt{2})\pi/4$ **41.** $(0, 0, 8/15)$ **43.** $(0, 195/152, 0)$

47. $\frac{1}{2}\delta\pi a^4 h$ **49.** $\frac{1}{2}\delta\pi h(a_1^4 - a_1^4)$ **53.** $2\pi^2 abk$ **55.** $(a/3, b/3)$

▶ **Chapter 14 Review Exercises (Page 1080)**

3. (a) $\displaystyle\iint\limits_R dA$ (b) $\displaystyle\iiint\limits_G dV$ (c) $\displaystyle\iint\limits_R \sqrt{1 + \left(\frac{\partial z}{\partial x}\right)^2 + \left(\frac{\partial z}{\partial y}\right)^2}\, dA$

5. $\displaystyle\int_0^1 \int_{1-\sqrt{1-y^2}}^{1+\sqrt{1-y^2}} f(x, y)\, dx\, dy$

7. (a) $a = 2, b = 1, c = 1, d = 2$ or $a = 1, b = 2, c = 2, d = 1$ (b) 3

9. $-\dfrac{1}{\sqrt{2}\pi}$ **13.**

1 $y = \sin x$

$y = \tan(x/2)$

$\frac{\pi}{2}$

11. $\displaystyle\int_0^1 \int_{2y}^2 e^x e^y\, dx\, dy$

15. $\frac{1}{3}(1 - \cos 64)$ **17.** a^2 **19.** $\frac{3}{2}$ **21.** 32π

23. (a) $\displaystyle\int_0^{2\pi} \int_0^{\pi/3} \int_0^a \rho^4 \sin^3\phi\, d\rho\, d\phi\, d\theta$

(b) $\displaystyle\int_0^{2\pi} \int_0^{\sqrt{3}a/2} \int_{r/\sqrt{3}}^{\sqrt{a^2-r^2}} r^3\, dz\, dr\, d\theta$

(c) $\displaystyle\int_{-\sqrt{3}a/2}^{\sqrt{3}a/2} \int_{-\sqrt{(3a^2/4)-x^2}}^{\sqrt{(3a^2/4)-x^2}} \int_{\sqrt{x^2+y^2}/\sqrt{3}}^{\sqrt{a^2-x^2-y^2}} (x^2 + y^2)\, dz\, dy\, dx$

25. $\frac{\pi a^3}{9}$ **27.** $\frac{1}{24}(26^{3/2} - 10^{3/2}) \approx 4.20632$ **29.** $2x + 4y - z = 5$

33. (a) $\dfrac{1}{2(u + w)}$ (b) $\frac{1}{2}(7\ln 7 - \ln 84, 375)$ **35.** $\left(\frac{8}{5}, 0\right)$

37. $(0, 0, h/4)$

▶ **Chapter 14 Making Connections (Page 1082)**

Where correct answers to a Making Connections exercise may vary, no answer is listed. Sample answers for these questions are available on the Book Companion Site.

1. (b) $\dfrac{\pi}{4}$ **3.** (a) 1.173108605 (b) 1.173108605

4. (a) the sphere $0 \leq x^2 + y^2 + z^2 \leq 1$ (b) 4.934802202 (c) $\pi^2/2$

5. (b) 4.4506 **6.** $\frac{4}{35}\pi a^3$

▶ **Exercise Set 15.1 (Page 1092)**

1. (a) III   (b) IV   **3.** (a) true   (b) true   (c) true

5.

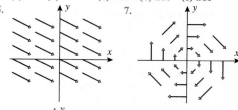

7.

9.

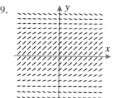

Responses to True–False questions may be abridged to save space.

11. False; the vector field has a nonzero **k**-component.

13. True; this is the curl of **F**.

15. (a) all x, y (b) all x, y **17.** div $\mathbf{F} = 2x + y$, curl $\mathbf{F} = z\mathbf{i}$

19. div $\mathbf{F} = 0$, curl $\mathbf{F} = (40x^2z^4 - 12xy^3)\mathbf{i} + (14y^3z + 3y^4)\mathbf{j} - (16xz^5 + 21y^2z^2)\mathbf{k}$

21. div $\mathbf{F} = \dfrac{2}{\sqrt{x^2 + y^2 + z^2}}$, curl $\mathbf{F} = 0$ **23.** $4x$ **25.** 0

27. $(1 + y)\mathbf{i} + x\mathbf{j}$

39. $\nabla \cdot (k\mathbf{F}) = k\nabla \cdot \mathbf{F}$, $\nabla \cdot (\mathbf{F} + \mathbf{G}) = \nabla \cdot \mathbf{F} + \nabla \cdot \mathbf{G}$, $\nabla \cdot (\phi\mathbf{F}) = \phi\nabla \cdot \mathbf{F} + \nabla\phi \cdot \mathbf{F}$, $\nabla \cdot (\nabla \times \mathbf{F}) = 0$ **47.** (b) $x^2 + y^2 = K$

49. $\dfrac{dy}{dx} = \dfrac{1}{x}$, $y = \ln x + K$

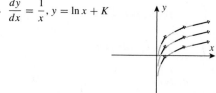

▶ **Exercise Set 15.2 (Page 1108)**

1. (a) 1   (b) 0   **3.** 16

7. (a) $-\frac{11}{108}\sqrt{10} - \frac{1}{36}\ln(\sqrt{10} - 3) - \frac{4}{27}$ (b) 0   (c) $-\frac{1}{2}$

9. (a) 3   (b) 3   (c) 3   (d) 3

Responses to True–False questions may be abridged to save space.

11. False; line integrals of functions are independent of the orientation of the curve.   **13.** True; this is Equation (26).

15. 2   **17.** $\frac{13}{20}$ **19.** $1 - \pi$ **21.** 3   **23.** $-1 - (\pi/4)$ **25.** $1 - e^3$

27. (a) $\dfrac{63\sqrt{17}}{64} + \dfrac{1}{4}\ln(4 + \sqrt{17}) - \dfrac{1}{8}\ln\dfrac{\sqrt{17} + 1}{\sqrt{17} - 1} - \dfrac{1}{4}\ln(\sqrt{2} + 1) +$

$\dfrac{1}{8}\ln\dfrac{\sqrt{2} + 1}{\sqrt{2} - 1}$ (b) $1/2 - \pi/4$

29. (a) -1 **(b)** -2 **31.** $\frac{5}{2}$ **33.** 0 **35.** $1-e^{-1}$ **37.** $6\sqrt{3}$

39. $5k\tan^{-1}3$ **41.** $\frac{3}{5}$ **43.** $\frac{27}{28}$ **45.** $\frac{3}{4}$ **47.** $\dfrac{17\sqrt{17}-1}{4}$

49. (b) $S = \displaystyle\int_C z(t)\,dt$ **(c)** 4π **51.** $\lambda = -12$

▶ **Exercise Set 15.3 (Page 1120)** ──────────────

1. conservative, $\phi = \dfrac{x^2}{2} + \dfrac{y^2}{2} + K$ **3.** not conservative

5. conservative, $\phi = x\cos y + y\sin x + K$

9. -6 **11.** $9e^2$ **13.** 32 **15.** $W = -\frac{1}{2}$ **17.** $W = 1 - e^{-1}$

Responses to True–False questions may be abridged to save space.

19. False; the integral must be 0 for *all* closed curves C.

21. True; if $\nabla\phi$ is constant, then ϕ must be a linear function.

23. $\ln 2 - 1$ **25.** ≈ -0.307 **27.** no   **33.** $h(x) = Ce^x$

35. (a) $W = -\dfrac{1}{\sqrt{14}} + \dfrac{1}{\sqrt{16}}$ **(b)** $W = -\dfrac{1}{\sqrt{14}} + \dfrac{1}{\sqrt{6}}$ **(c)** $W = 0$

▶ **Exercise Set 15.4 (Page 1127)** ──────────────

1. 0 **3.** 0 **5.** 0 **7.** 8π **9.** -4 **11.** -1 **13.** 0

Responses to True–False questions may be abridged to save space.

15. False; Green's Theorem applies to closed curves.

17. True; the integral is the area of the region bounded by C.

19. (a) ≈ -3.550999378 **(b)** ≈ -0.269616482 **21.** $\frac{3}{8}a^2\pi$ **23.** $\frac{1}{2}abt_0$

27. Formula (1) of Section 6.1   **29.** $\frac{250}{3}$ **31.** $-3\pi a^2$ **33.** $\left(\frac{8}{15}, \frac{8}{21}\right)$

35. $\left(0, \dfrac{4a}{3\pi}\right)$ **37.** the circle $x^2 + y^2 = 1$ **39.** 69

▶ **Exercise Set 15.5 (Page 1136)** ──────────────

1. $\dfrac{15}{2}\pi\sqrt{2}$ **3.** $\dfrac{\pi}{4}$ **5.** $-\dfrac{\sqrt{2}}{2}$ **7.** 9

Responses to True–False questions may be abridged to save space.

9. True; this follows from the definition.

11. False; the integral is the total mass of the lamina.

13. (b) $2\pi\left[1 - \sqrt{1-r^2} + \dfrac{r^2}{2}\right] \to 3\pi$ as $r \to 1^-$

   (c) $\mathbf{r}(\phi, \theta) = \sin\phi\cos\theta\mathbf{i} + \sin\phi\sin\theta\mathbf{j} + \cos\phi\mathbf{k}$,

   $0 \le \theta \le 2\pi, 0 \le \phi \le \pi/2$;

   $\displaystyle\iint (1+z)\,dS = \int_0^{2\pi}\int_0^{\pi/2}(1+\cos\phi)\sin\phi\,d\phi\,d\theta = 3\pi$

17. (c) $4\pi/3$

19. (a) $\dfrac{\sqrt{29}}{16}\displaystyle\int_0^6\int_0^{(12-2x)/3} xy(12 - 2x - 3y)\,dy\,dx$

   (b) $\dfrac{\sqrt{29}}{4}\displaystyle\int_0^3\int_0^{(12-4z)/3} yz(12 - 3y - 4z)\,dy\,dz$

   (c) $\dfrac{\sqrt{29}}{9}\displaystyle\int_0^3\int_0^{6-2z} xz(12 - 2x - 4z)\,dx\,dz$

21. $\dfrac{18\sqrt{29}}{5}$

23. $\displaystyle\int_0^4\int_1^2 y^3 z\sqrt{4y^2+1}\,dy\,dz$; $\dfrac{1}{2}\displaystyle\int_0^4\int_1^4 xz\sqrt{1+4x}\,dx\,dz$

25. $\dfrac{391\sqrt{17}}{15} - \dfrac{5\sqrt{5}}{3}$ **27.** $\frac{4}{3}\pi\delta_0$ **29.** $\frac{1}{4}(37\sqrt{37}-1)$ **31.** $M = \delta_0 S$

33. $(0, 0, 149/65)$ **35.** $\dfrac{93}{\sqrt{10}}$ **37.** $\dfrac{\pi}{4}$ **39.** 57.895751

▶ **Exercise Set 15.6 (Page 1146)** ──────────────

1. (a) zero   **(b)** zero   **(c)** positive   **(d)** negative   **(e)** zero   **(f)** zero

3. (a) positive   **(b)** zero   **(c)** positive   **(d)** zero   **(e)** positive   **(f)** zero

5. (a) $n = -\cos v\mathbf{i} - \sin v\mathbf{j}$ **(b)** inward   **7.** 2π **9.** $\dfrac{14\pi}{3}$ **11.** 0

13. 18π **15.** $\frac{4}{9}$ **17. (a)** 8 **(b)** 24 **(c)** 0

Responses to True–False questions may be abridged to save space.

19. False; the Möbius strip has no orientation.

21. False; the net volume can be zero because as much fluid passes through the surface in the negative direction as in the positive direction.

23. 3π **25. (a)** $0\,\mathrm{m}^3/\mathrm{s}$ **(b)** $0\,\mathrm{kg/s}$ **27. (b)** $32/3$

29. (a) $4\pi a^{k+3}$ **(b)** $k = -3$ **31.** $a = 2, 3$

▶ **Exercise Set 15.7 (Page 1157)** ──────────────

1. 3 **3.** $\dfrac{4\pi}{3}$

Responses to True–False questions may be abridged to save space.

5. False; it equates a surface integral and a triple integral.

7. True; see subsection entitled Sources and Sinks.

9. 12 **11.** $3\pi a^2$ **13.** 180π **15.** $\dfrac{192\pi}{5}$ **17.** $\dfrac{\pi}{2}$

19. $\dfrac{4608}{35}$ **21.** 135π **33.** no sources or sinks

35. sources at all points except the origin, no sinks   **37.** $\dfrac{7\pi}{4}$

▶ **Exercise Set 15.8 (Page 1164)** ──────────────

1. $\frac{3}{2}$ **3.** 0 **5.** 2π **7.** 16π **9.** 0 **11.** πa^2

Responses to True–False questions may be abridged to save space.

13. True; see Theorem 15.8.1.   **15.** False; the circulation is $\int_C \mathbf{F}\cdot\mathbf{T}\,ds$.

17. (a) $\frac{3}{2}$ **(b)** -1 **(c)** $-\dfrac{1}{\sqrt{2}}\mathbf{j} - \dfrac{1}{\sqrt{2}}\mathbf{k}$ **23.** $-\dfrac{5\pi}{4}$

▶ **Chapter 15 Review Exercises (Page 1166)** ──────────────

3. $\dfrac{1-x}{\sqrt{(1-x)^2 + (2-y)^2}}\mathbf{i} + \dfrac{2-y}{\sqrt{(1-x)^2+(2-y)^2}}\mathbf{j}$ **5.** $\mathbf{i}+\mathbf{j}+\mathbf{k}$

7. (a) $\displaystyle\int_a^b\left[f(x(t), y(t))\dfrac{dx}{dt} + g(x(t), y(t))\dfrac{dy}{dt}\right]dt$

   (b) $\displaystyle\int_a^b f(x(t), y(t))\sqrt{x'(t)^2 + y'(t)^2}\,dt$

11. 0 **13.** $-7/2$ **17. (a)** $h(x) = Cx^{-3/2}$ **(b)** $g(y) = C/y^3$

21. $A = \dfrac{1}{2}\displaystyle\int_\alpha^\beta r^2\,d\theta$

23. $\displaystyle\iint_R f(x(u,v), y(u,v), z(u,v))\|r_u \times r_v\|\,du\,dv$ **25.** yes   **27.** 2π

31. -8π **35. (a)** conservative   **(b)** not conservative

▶ **Chapter 15 Making Connections (Page 1168)** ──────────────

Answers are provided in the Student Solutions Manual.

INDEX